Here There Be Happy Readers . . .

"What a splendid, unusual and intriguing fantasy quest! You've got a winner here."
—Anne McCaffrey

"I think *The Unlikely Ones* is going to be a new classic for generations of young people to fall in love with. I already have."
—Marion Zimmer Bradley

"Beautiful . . . compelling; I got caught reading [*Pigs Don't Fly*] late at night, and lost sleep, because it did what fiction seldom does: held my attention beyond sleep."
—Piers Anthony

"Summer is a fully realized character . . . and there are generous dollops of humor to balance the tenser moments." —*Starlog*

"Delightful!" —*Kliatt*

"A captivating fantasy, with a lovable cast of characters." —*VOYA*

ABOUT THE AUTHOR

Best known for her popular quest fantasies, Mary Brown also wrote the historical romances *Playing the Jack* and *The Heart has Its Reasons*, the post-apocalyptic fantasy novel *Strange Deliverance*, and a fourth Unicorn Ring novel, *Dragonne's Eg*. Several of her fantasy novels were selected by the American Library Association for their Best Books for Young Adults list, by the New York Public Library for their annual list of Books for the Teen Age, and by the Young Adult Library Services Association for their Best Books for Young Adults list. Before becoming a full-time writer, she had been an artist's model, actress, caterer, and store clerk. She wrote her novels in a home located high in the scenic mountains of Spain, which she shared with her husband, cats, tortoises, and assorted fish and pigeons. Her death in 1999 was a loss to the many readers of her quirky and fascinating brand of fantasy.

BAEN BOOKS by MARY BROWN

Strange Deliverance

Here There Be Dragonnes (omnibus)
The Unlikely Ones
Pigs Don't Fly
Master of Many Treasures

Dragonne's Eg

Here There Be DRAGONNES

MARY BROWN

HERE THERE BE DRAGONNES

This is a work of fiction. All the characters and events portrayed in this book are fictional, and any resemblance to real people or incidents is purely coincidental.

A Baen Books Original Omnibus

Baen Publishing Enterprises
P.O. Box 1403
Riverdale, NY 10471
www.baen.com

ISBN: 0-7434-3596-6

Cover art by Carol Heyer

First omnibus printing, March 2003

Library of Congress Cataloging-in-Publication Data

Brown, Mary, 1929-
Here there be dragonnes / by Mary Brown.
p. cm.
Previously published as three separate novels: The unlikely ones, Pigs don't fly, Master of many treasures.
ISBN 0-7434-3596-6 (pbk.)
1. Young women—Fiction. 2. England—Fiction. 3. Rings—Fiction. I. Title.

PR6052.R6143 H47 2003
823'.914—dc21

2002038397

Distributed by Simon & Schuster
1230 Avenue of the Americas
New York, NY 10020

Produced by Windhaven Press, Auburn, NH
Printed in the United States of America

10 9 8 7 6 5 4 3 2 1

Contents

The Unlikely Ones

To the then of "C" and "Ly," my father and my mother and the now of Christopher, their great-grandson.

Acknowledgements

My thanks as usual to:

My husband, Peter;

My editor, Paul Sidey;

My typist, Anne Pitt.

Especial thanks to the author

A. C. H. (Anthony) Smith,

Without whose encouragement this book

would not have been written, and

Finally, last but not least,

Love and thanks to "Wellington,"

Once again my companion and also this time

Invaluable referee on the peculiarities of

animal behaviour . . .

The Beginning

The Thief in the Night

The cave itself was cosy enough as caves go: sandy floor, reasonably draught-proof, convenient ledges for storing treasure, a rain/dew pond just outside, a southerly aspect and an excellent landing strip adjacent, but the occupant was definitely not at his best and the central heating in his belly not functioning as it should. Granted he must have been all of two hundred and fifty years old but that was merely a youngling in dragon-years, measuring as he did a man-and-a-half (Western Hominid Standard) excluding tail, and at his age he should have been flowing with fiery, red health.

He was not. He was blue, and that was not good. Dragons may be red, scarlet, crimson, vermilion, rose-madder at a pinch, purple, gold, silver, orange, yellow, even certain shades of green—but not blue.

He lay in a muddled heap on the cave floor, not even bothering to arrange his tail into one of the regulation turns, hitches or knots, listlessly turning over and over the pile of pebbles that heaped the space before him. The dull, bluish-purple glow that emanated from his scales illuminated only dimly the confines of the cave but made mock-amethysts and sham-sapphires of the grey and white stones he sorted: a semiprecious illusion. Nothing could transform them into a ruby from a sacred temple of Ind, an emerald from the rainforests of Amazonia; a diamond from the Great Desert, a sapphire from the Southern Seas or a great, glowing pearl from the oyster-mouth of the grey Northern River. And that was the trouble: they were pebbles, nothing more, the insulting substitute left by The Thief . . .

For the three thousand two hundred and fifty-fifth time or so he went over in his mind that dreadful day, some seven years ago, when he had sallied forth all unsuspecting for the Year's-Turn Feast. Over the few years previously spent gold-and-silver-gathering in this retrospectively accursed, damp, boggy, sunless island, he had made the cave his principal headquarters and had twice-yearly, shortest day and longest, received his tribute of roast mutton, pork or beef from the village below (after he had explained that raw maidens were not in his line). He had good-humouredly tolerated the current yokel dragon-slayer brandishing home-made spear, sword or some-such who insisted on defending a symbolic maiden staked out in front of his feast; he even retreated the regulation ten paces in mock-submission before insisting on his roast. He had flown forth that day secure in the knowledge that he need only wait for the better weather of the equinox to return Home with the assorted extras of gold helm, breastplate, mail, dishes, brooches, bowl, buckles and coin (there was too much silver to carry) and the glory of the necessary jewels, and was urged on with a healthy hunger for his last tribute. The side of beef had, he remembered, been slightly underdone, and he had had to barbecue it a little himself to bring out that nice charred flavour that added scrunch to bones and singe to fat. He remembered, too, that he had obligingly restarted the damp, smoky fire on which his rather unflattering effigy was regularly cremated, and had even joined in the dancing and jollification that always succeeded his surrogate demise, and so it had been well after midnight when he had returned to the cave, replete, sticky and tired, to find—

The end of his world, and a heap of pebbles.

His quest had been specific: one each of ruby, emerald, diamond, sapphire and lastly, the pearl. And any incidentals by way of gold or silver, of course. The ruby had been an easy snatch-and-grab, but the emerald had required travel at the worst time of year over seas grey and wrinkled as an elephant's hide; the diamond had proved troublesome and the sapphire fiendishly difficult, but one expected a gradation of difficulty in all quests, and he had been well within the hundred-year limit when the fresh-water oyster had yielded the final treasure, his personal dragon-pearl beyond price, the largest and most perfect he had ever seen, mistletoe-moon-coloured and perfectly cylindrical.

And now? And now he remembered as vividly as ever his return to the furtive sweat-smell of excited theft in the night, an unidentified shadow that left only a silhouette of the sorcery that had accompanied it. He had roared out into the dark, his whole body twisting into an agonized coruscation of shining scales whose thunderous passage through the gaps between the mountain and the hills had left a rain of split rocks and splintering shale cascading in a black torrent to the valleys beneath. But there had been no sight, no sound of the thing he sought, only the taint of a thing that crawled, that flew, that walked, that ran; a shape intangible, a sniggering darkness that fled faster than he could pursue and left no trail to follow. And this—this Thief-without-a-name—had stolen his jewels, his quest, his very life, for he could not return Home without those precious things. The gold was still there, true, but it was merely incidental: every dragon collected gold as a child might gather shells from the shore, but the jewels were special. They were the confirmation of his maturity, the price of his transition from Novice to Master-Dragon, and without these proofs of his quest, the badges of his success, he was condemned to die. Oh, not a sudden execution, that perhaps he would have welcomed: rather an exile's slow withering, an embering and ashing of the once-bright fires, a shrivelling of scales from calcined bones, a fossil's hardening in the remorseless silt of the years. And if he attempted to return without his treasure there would be the turned shoulder, the stifled snigger, the, in itself, mortal loss of face that would be death in life. And he could not bear that: better to die a suicide of wasting, cold and hunger on this wretched Black Mountain far from home; better to suffer the slow pangs of winter and starvation than to return disgraced.

For a moment his tired brain flickered with pictures of his bright egg-brothers and sisters, a remembrance of sky-soaring flight, of play among the circumscribed cloudlets of his youth; once again he saw the heaven-turn of pagoda roof, heard the dissonant tonk of temple bells, felt the yellow sun of the yellow people gild his scales, tasted fire in his mouth, smelt sandalwood and cedar, and all at once he let out such a howl that for the first time in many, many moons the peasants in the village some two miles below heard him quite clearly; a cry of such piercing despair that it slunk under their ill-fitting doors like the keening of hound condemned to out-kennel in the worst of wolf-pelt winters. And those hearing crossed themselves, touched lucky charms, threw placatory offerings on the smoky fires, whichever pleased whatever God, gods or Fate to which their superstition turned. Then they cursed the dragon, near-forgotten in the years of silence, and at the same time were glad he still lived, for he was their very own living legend. They wished him gone and they wished him come, wished him dead and wished him living, all at one and the same time, like all disconcerting, uncomfortable, prestige-making myths-come-alive that they could neither control nor explain.

But this time the echoes of the dragon's despair went farther than the confines of the little village beneath the Black Mountain. Something of it travelled, thinner and more attenuated the farther it went, and eventually reached an ear just waking from sleep, an ear that had been seeking a diversion such as this. The owner of the ear thought about it for a moment, weighed the pros and cons, and then bestirred himself to look for a miracle.

And found it, in the unlikeliest septet imaginable . . .

The Gathering: One

The Unicorn and the Prince

He was bathing in a rainbow, the rainbow made by the long fall of waters, and the colours shone in bands of coloured light across the white screen of his hide. Long mane and tail rippled like silver seaweed in the clear waters and the golden, spiralled horn flashed and sparkled in the light. Tender pink of belly and gums assumed a rosy glow, the long white lashes were spiky with water and the cloven hooves stamped the spray with sheer enjoyment until it splintered into mist. He was a splendid creature, at the height of his powers, all white, pink and gold except for the dark, deep, beautiful eyes which held a colour all their own that none had been able to name, but that reminded some of the sky at night, others of dark, new-turned earth, a few of the tender greening spring slips of fir and pine.

The falls dropped hissing to foam about his hooves, the sun flickered and shone on the tumbling waters, a crowd of gnats danced in crazy circles above the ripples, a dragonfly, iridescent green and purple, darted away to the tall reeds on the left; a silver fish clooped a lazy arc downstream, not really caring that the mayfly were out of reach; kingfisher flashed blue to his nest in the bank and an otter drifted by on its back, paws tucked up on its chest, creamy belly-fur warmed by the sun, ruddered tail lazily steering. All was right with the world, all was beautiful, all was high summer and yet, suddenly, like the shadow of a bird across the sun, black and fleeting, an alien fear touched the unicorn and he knew that something unknown threatened his world.

Flinging up his head, the droplets scattering like diamonds from his thick, floss-silk mane, he snuffed the air through flaring nostrils, the long, pointed ears with their furred inners laid back against the small delicate head. There was no strange sound or scent, yet still a feeling lingered in the air. As he stepped from the stream, the waters flowed away from rounded shoulders and back to trickle into the plumed fetlocks above the bifurcated hooves. A green-white shadow, he slipped into the forest, bending in and out of the drowse-leafed trees, his hooves leaving no trace on the soft turf. Then, leaving the deciduous fringes for the quiet corridors of conifer, he heard it. A thin sound, a catch of music as plainly faery as himself, that stole like mist through the silent, bare trunks of the trees. Hurrying now, desperate at what he would find, he brushed heedlessly through the forest until he came to the clearing where he had left his prince, and the sudden sunlight shone upon a scene so unexpected, so bizarre, that he checked back violently on his haunches, hooves skidding on the grass.

In the middle of the open space between the dark avenues of trees a young man, no more than nineteen or twenty, was dancing. At first sight this was a beautiful thing to see: he moved so lightly, so gracefully, his whole being responding instinctively to the music—

The music? This appeared to come from a harp, played pleasantly by a pretty young girl seated on a hummock on the opposite side of the glade, but the unicorn had the eyes of faery and what he saw struck sudden fear to his heart. He saw the young maiden, assuredly, but she was merely an ephemeral outline, a deceiving frame for the evil thing that crouched within. A naked witch mouthed there, her wrinkled, sagging body twisting and turning within the illusionary young body that covered it like a second skin, her face alight with malice as she watched her prey dance himself to death. Already, even as the unicorn watched helplessly, the beautiful face of the prince aged some five years, and the lithe, lissom figure hesitated as it attempted a twisting leap into the air. But the music quickened, drove him on and on, and the movements of his dancing body grew more and more frenzied as his proud countenance tautened and paled.

The unicorn started forward, neighing his distress, and for a moment the music faltered and the young prince stumbled and slowed, but then the tune grew louder and more insistent and he danced on, his face now turned imploringly to the great white animal, his arms extended in entreaty while his body and legs turned and twisted to the infernal music. The unicorn reached his side by tremendous effort of will, it seemed, his body for the moment a shield from the witch, and the prince stopped dancing and laid his trembling hands on the curling mane, whimpering, "Help me, help me!" The great horned animal turned his head to gaze deeply into the distressed blue eyes so near his own, at the sweat pouring down the beautiful, ageing face, at the sweet mouth imploring his aid, felt the slim hand shaking as it clutched at his mane and the young/old heart racing close to his, and bent his head to nuzzle the damp tangled-gold curls.

"Trust me," he breathed. "I love you more than life, you know that . . ."

He turned to face the witch. And the birds of the forest fell silent, the small creatures were still, the wind held its breath and no cloud crossed the sun.

That very sun was declining behind the trees when at last the unicorn had to admit that he was beaten. The witch and her music now lay in an enchanted bubble that no hoof could break, no charging shoulder shift, no tooth pierce; he had blocked the tune effectively enough for a while by throwing a magic sound barrier round his beloved but the music had shifted, crept, sidled, turned about his shield and the prince was now lying exhausted on the grass of the shadow-lengthening glade and the unicorn dared not look into his face for fear lest all youth, all beauty had fled. Runnels of foam dripped from the animal's muzzle, flecking his neck and forelegs and the great head was lowered, the dark eyes full of pain. After a while the spiral horn on his forehead touched the ground in his exhaustion, sending a sharp pain through his body and jerking him fully upright once more. At once he knew what he must do. The magic horn, that which confers enchantment upon all unicorns, was irreplaceable; if it became damaged or broken he was no longer immortal. But he knew there was no choice—for the love he bore was greater than his fear of death and he lowered his head once more, giving himself no time to weigh the chances, and in that last moment before his magic horn pierced the bubble that encapsulated the witch and her killing music he at last saw fear in her eyes.

The bubble burst with the noise of a great crystal palace shattering around his ears, and the ringing and clattering echoed the great pain that suffused his head, his whole body. He knelt on the grass, his flanks heaving, a stink of singed flesh and horn in his nostrils, and knew without mirrored confirmation that his proud golden horn was no more. He was nothing now, a white horse with cloven hooves and no magic, but at least his beloved was safe and young again and beautiful, and would weep tears to heal the broken place where the horn had been, and together they would flee this horror, and find a kind of peace—

Not so. As he turned, he saw with dismay that the witch had escaped the destruction of her bubble and stood, tall, dark-cloaked and menacing over the senseless body of his prince. Even as the unicorn started forward to challenge her, the pain in his mutilated head receding to a dull, bearable ache, he heard her begin to chant a spell of such malevolence that he started back again, his great eyes wide with distress, realizing too late that without the magic horn he was impotent. The darkening forest seemed to close in against the reddening sky as between him and the witch there appeared a deep pool: not of water, but hard as diamonds and as clear, with the illusion of plants waving in invisible currents in its depths. And there, at the very heart of it, resting on a bed of pebbles, grey, blue and white, lay the prince, eyes closed, legs and arms flung carelessly as though he slept on some feather bed.

Vainly the unicorn stamped and pawed at the unyielding surface of the magic pond, neighing his distress. He turned once more to the witch and she answered his unspoken questions.

"Why? He refused me, that's why, even though I made myself young and beautiful as he: I was not to know he was a freak, a creature-lover, was I?" and she spat. "But no, he is not dead, he lies in spelled sleep. And the only thing that can save him—" and she laughed shrilly, confident in her revenge "—is a whole unicorn, who will sacrifice himself and his horn to pierce that sleep! And you—" she pointed derisively, "—you are hornless!"

And her shrieks of laughter pursued him like demons as he fled despairing into the forest.

The Gathering: Two

The Knight and a Lady

She was the fairest lady he had ever seen: eyes like sapphires, lips ruby-red, diamond-fair hair flowing down her emerald-green dress, skin translucent as pearl. Although the fire on which he had toasted the rye-bread of his supper had burned low this jewel-creature seemed to carry her own light and her voice was soft and caressing as she crossed the clearing towards him, her robes making the faintest susurration in the long, dry grass.

"All alone, fair knight?"

He rubbed his eyes, convinced he must be dreaming. Sure his eyes had been closed but a moment—too short a time for sleep—but what else in the world could this apparition be but a dream? This one must come from a towered castle somewhere in Germanica; she should live in pillared hall on the slopes of the Middle Sea; she would not have been out of place in a screened harem in the Great Desert; she could have come from anywhere beautiful, faraway, exotic: all he knew was that she did not belong here, on the scrubby edges of this shabby forest hundreds of miles from the nearest towers, halls or harems.

He pinched himself, half-hesitating even as he did so, for if this were indeed a dream, he would be fool to wake just as everything seemed to be going so nicely. The pinch hurt and she was still there so she must be real, and indeed now she was standing a mere foot or so away and her heady perfume flowed out round him like a bog mist, a miasma, near-palpable in its form. All at once he became conscious of the sleep in the corners of his eyes, his two-day stubble, untrimmed moustache and crumpled clothes. All else, sword, armour, purpose were instantly forgotten: she was all that mattered.

"I—I—" he stammered, for coherence was gone also.

"I—I—" she mocked, and laid her cool hand on his wrist, where it burnt like fire.

"L—Lady," he stuttered then recalled, by a tremendous effort of will it seemed, the courtesies and protocol demanded. Knights were always respectful and courtly; ladies, in return, gracious and yielding. The men were allowed a little flattery and boldness of the eye, plus a little twirl or two of the moustache and from the women one expected a fluttering and dimpling, a casting-down of eyes and an implied admiration. But of course at first one had to go through the preliminary ritual of polite verbal exchanges—How the hell did it go? Ah, yes . . .

"Lady, I am at your service, and with my sword will gladly defend you from all perils and dangers of this night." (When he had been a mere squire there had been the usual ribaldry with his fellows as to the true connotation of the "sword" and whether it was "night" or "knight.") "And if you will inform me of your desire, I—"

"Tu," she interrupted. "Tu es mon seul desir . . ."

Somehow her use of the Frankish tongue made this all much more difficult. Although he could not fault her courtly language, yet the words were in the wrong context: they were the words one would use to one's affianced or groom, and this one looked neither virginal nor a bride . . .

He found himself trembling, hot desire running like siege-fire into the pit of his loins. He gritted his teeth: this must be A Temptation, sent to test him; he had heard They sometimes took fleshly form, the better to ensnare and seduce. Sadly, Goodness usually came wrapped plain in everyday clothes and required effort of a different kind: a dragon slain (only nowadays there were none left), the routing of wolf or bear or somesuch. Anyway, This in front of him now, clad in shameless importunity and little else, was not Good, so therefore must be Bad, coming as It did in the middle of the night, that lonely vulnerable time when a man's strength is at an ebb and his resolve at its weakest. Still, if It were A Temptation, all one had to do was to summon up the required Formula, step smartly away, and deliver the words with clarity and feeling, and after a moment the temptation would disappear. Simple.

Pulling free of her hold he crossed himself.

"Begone, Foul Fiend!" he said, in capitals, and crossed himself once more, to be on the safe side. "For I Know You For What You Are . . ."

Initially he could not have wished for a more gratifying result. She hissed and drew back, her silken locks seeming to writhe like a nest of blond snakes, but before he could even draw breath for a sigh of relief that he had been right, everything was as it had been a moment since, only worse, for he found himself gazing, with a lust he found increasingly difficult to control, at a long, perfectly formed leg, bare to the thigh, and pointed, rosy-tipped breasts that spilled out like forbidden fruit, from a suddenly diabolically disarranged dress. These delights invited a more intimate examination than the eye alone could give, caressing hand or tongue or both, and he had to concentrate very hard on knightly vows, candled altars (priapic, phallic candles; bare naked, unclothed crosses—No! dear Lord, no . . .), hard, penancing stone floors, the weight of mail, the chill of steel at dawn (better . . .), chanting monks with tonsured heads, cold water and thin gruel, hair-shirts and such, before his rising excitement cooled sufficiently for him to be able to stand comfortably again. It did not help that instantly he wished to relieve himself.

Resolutely he drew his sword.

"Thou art an Evil Thing, a witch, and ere you suborn me further I shall set good Christian steel to your flesh . . ." It was all excellent stuff, learnt from *The Knight's Manual,* but unfortunately it seemed to have little effect on its intended victim. The manual had not provided for laughter, for disdain, for a flying-off of all clothes, for a moving forward until bare flesh was pressed skin-tight against his suddenly disarranged wear. Neither had it dealt with seeking hands that drew out a rebellious prick and caressed it unbearably sweetly.

If that had been all, then he would have been lost indeed, but even Evil makes mistakes.

"Swyve me, soldier-boy," she said.

Instantly his prick shrivelled like a salt-sprinkled slug and he felt as naked and cold as a fowl plucked living in a snowstorm. It was the words that did it. During his military service it had been an almost universal and convenient phrase that was accepted in all the stews and bordellos; it was used by the sluts on the quaysides, the wenches in the hedge, the girls (and boys) of the back streets all over the world, the preliminary to quick bargaining, the passing of coin, and even quicker release. It was a phrase become meaningless with time that nevertheless came trippingly off the tongue, alliteratively used as it usually was with other words than "soldier": sailor, sweetheart, sire, sugar, saucy, sheikh, sahib, sergeant, signor, senorita . . . But a lady would never say it, never, not even in extremis.

The court ladies he had known, in reality quite as randy as their stew-sisters, if not more so, were all brought up to use polite euphemisms. "Put the Devil in Hell" was a popular one, as was "Sheath the sword," and the less flattering "Pop the coney down its burrow." All these were perfectly acceptable, and the very words gave the actions a superficial respectability, so that the lady could ask whether the Devil found it warm enough yet, or the gentleman assure his partner that the scabbard was a perfect fit without blush staining either's cheek.

So, for the second time that night his proud prick took a tumble, for the words had dampened his ardour irretrievably. It was just like being asked to drink nectar from a piss-pot.

She sensed his withdrawal, and for an instant she seemed to him to flare and grow taller, then her face crumpled, her bosom sagged and she spat in his face from blackened, broken teeth.

"You will pay for this, my fine gentleman, you will pay!"

Considerably frightened, but more scared to show the fear, he recalled the torn edges of his dignity and neatly sewed them straight with the classic line: "Do your worst, foul hag: I am ready for you!" And perhaps he thought he was.

Stepping back, the once beautiful hair now a greasy grey thatch, she raised her left hand and pointed the index finger at him, the nail curved and blackened. She started to curse him, roundly and fluently. Shrinking back in spite of himself he forgot to cross himself: afterwards he wondered if it would have made any difference; on balance he thought not.

"I hereby curse you, and call the trees that stand and the stones that lie, the sun that rises and the moon that sets, the wind that blows and the rain that falls, the sky above and the earth below, and all creatures that walk, run, crawl, fly and swim betwixt and between to bear witness to the same . . ."

As if in answer there was a sympathetic growl of thunder: it had been a hot, sultry day.

"I curse you waking, I curse you sleeping; I curse you standing, sitting, lying; I curse you by day, I curse you by night; I curse you spring, summer, autumn and winter; hot or cold, wet or dry . . ."

So far, so good: it was the Standard Formula, nothing specific, and easy enough to be lifted by a bit extra to the priest and a few penances to the poor. The knight wondered if, after all, he was going to get away with it.

"And my special and irrevocable curse is this: may your armour remain rusty, your weapons blunted, your desires unfulfilled and your questions unanswered until you ask for the hand in marriage of the ugliest creature in the land!"

He started back, appalled, but before he could interrupt she went on: "May she not only be ugly, but poor, twisted and deformed as well! And may you be tied to her for life!" And she laughed, shrilly, exultantly. In a blind rage he snatched up his sword again from where it had fallen during the cursing and sprinted forward ready to run her through in his anger, female or no, but came bump! up against some invisible wall that snapped off his sword some three inches from the hilt and bloodied his nose. He went hurtling back as if he had been thrown in a wrestle, to lie on his back on the ground, his head ringing and the broken sword blade embedded in the turf an inch from his left ear.

When he finally rose to his feet, pale and winded, she had gone, leaving a foul, decaying stench that made him gag and pinch his nostrils. Gone, too, was his horse, probably miles away by now, to be appropriated by some grateful peasant in the morning, who would have great difficulty in persuading a fully trained warhorse to submit to the plough. He peered at his heaped armour; already small spots of rust, like dried blood, were speckling and spreading on the bright metal.

There was only one thing to do.

Falling to his knees he prayed: long, angrily and in vain.

The Gathering: Three, Four, Five, Six, Seven

The Slaves of the Pebbles

One moment our little world was predictable, safe, ordinary: the next we were nearly immolated in a welter of flame.

Predictable, safe, ordinary: I suppose those words could be misleading. Perhaps I should explain that "predictable" meant that we knew tomorrow would be as miserable as today; "safe" meant housed and tolerably fed without outside interference, and that "ordinary" meant just that. It meant an existence we had always known, as far back as faulty memory would take us; it meant a crouching, fearful, nothing-being, prisoned, chained and subject to the whims of our mistress. She should have a capital letter: Mistress. There. For that is what we called her, the only name we knew, slaves as we were, and woe betide any who even thought of her with a small "m" for she would know, or pretend she did, and punish us, and we were so accustomed to her domination that we believed she could read all our thoughts, sleeping and waking.

We? Us? There were five of her creatures in that small hut on the edge of the forest. Slaves, I should say. I was the only one ever let out of the hut, and that for necessaries alone—a sack of flour, tallow for dips, herbs from the hedgerow—and then I was spat upon, ridiculed, even pelted with stones upon occasion by the superstitious villagers who called me her "Thing," her Familiar. Even those intermittent forays were no freedom, for the stomach cramps hit me even worse when I was from her side, only easing when I returned, so it was no wonder that people only saw me as a humped, ugly, deformed thing. I could not even speak properly, for the only tongue I heard was an occasional command, spells and the words of my friends, the others who shared my thrall.

There was Corby, the great black crow, Puddy, the warty toad, Pisky the little golden fish and kitten-cat Moglet, and though we conversed quite freely amongst ourselves when the Mistress was out, it was a language of squawks, hisses, spits, bubbles, and more thought-communication than human speech. I told you I was held near my Mistress by stomach-cramps, and the others, in addition to cages, strings and bars were held in the same fashion, by a pain that increased by degrees of hurt the farther we were from our jailer. The origins of all these hurts were concrete enough; small pebbles or stones that clung to our bodies as though they were part of us. For me it was a sullen red stone that stuck to my navel like a crab; for Corby it was a blue chip that stopped the stretch of his right wing; for Puddy a green rock on his forehead that gave him headaches; for Moglet a crippling glass piece that was embedded in the soft part of her left front pad and for poor Pisky a great moon-coloured pebble that quite filled his starving, round mouth. Why not pull them out? We had tried and all we had got was an intensification of the pain, till it grew too excruciating to bear and we had to stop.

Perhaps the worst part was that we could not remember them being put there, nor coming to this place nor, even, who we were. Yet there were tantalizing remembrances for us all of another life of freedom without pain, in another place, another time: yet so fleeting was this recall to all of us, swift as the space between puff and candle-out, that it was only when the flame dipped and wavered and bent a little before expiring that one remembered a swoop of wings, a cool stone grotto, the rasp of another tongue on one's fur, a gnat at twilight and—another name, clash of swords, warm arms, crying . . . We all had these moments, yet even as we snatched at memory, like a snowflake on the tongue it dissolved and all form was lost. Some things we could remember, though: apparently Corby remembered us all coming, except himself; Puddy remembered me, Moglet and Pisky; I remembered the last two, but Moglet remembered only Pisky, and he not even himself. The interval between arrivals none could judge, so it could have been seven hours, days, weeks, months, years between first and last. Neither did we know why we were held thus, nor would She tell us, and all questions were answered by laughter, blows or the scorn of silence. Seasons meant little to us, cabined as we were, for we saw and felt little of sunshine or storm, light or dark, rain or warmth—the inside of the hut was always cold, a meagre fire kept burning and the one window shuttered fast, so that day or night, summer or winter were much the same to us. Sometimes birds whistled down the chimney or a hedgepig would pause on the doorstep when She was out, but always these encounters were reported to Her on her return by her Creature-in-the-corner, the broom that was her real familiar, and we were beaten for encouraging curiosity. Once, I remember, I asked a martin resting on the thatch whether it was spring or autumn, and when she heard of this from the sly, crackling spy, she had it beat me senseless.

Yet this Broom-Creature was not only violent towards us, for sometimes when the air, even inside, was sticky and hot, and it was difficult to sleep, She would take the thing into her arms and whisper to it and push the smooth, knobbed end under her skirt and it would jerk and throb until she cried out in what seemed pain and would thrust it from her, its tip swollen into the thickness of a man's fist and all glistening and wet with what looked like blood . . . But it was not real as she and we were. It was only a piece of wood bound with dried stems and twigs and she had to use words to bring it alive, the same sort of words she used to bring things into the hovel, things that were shadows so thin you could put your hand through them like smoke and yet which threw writhing coloured patterns on any surface they touched. These apparitions floated and gestured and whispered in an obscene language only she could understand and always after they had gone she became increasingly short-tempered and restless, and sooner or later would come the time when we would be caged and tied and she would begin the preparations for a Shape-Change.

In some ways I looked forward to this, for it meant that I was let out to gather plants and herbs for her spells: mugwort and valerian; comfrey and stinking hellebore; bryony and monkshood; oak galls and liverwort; fly agaric and pennyroyal. All the ingredients She used I did not know, for she had others in bottles and jars and boxes I was not allowed to see, locked away by magic words in cupboards and a chest. And of the mixing we saw little for She would go behind a curtained-off alcove at the other end of the hut when she was ready to begin. Then all we would know was the stink of dried, crushed and powdered ingredients in the smoke that rose from the blending of her concoctions, a stench that invaded every corner, lending foul odours to the dry bread we ate, the cold water we drank. We could hear a little of the muttered spells and incantations that accompanied all this and we were allowed to see all the transformation: I think having an audience for this somehow fed her overweening vanity, even of small account as we were.

She would come out from the alcove and stand in the middle of the hut, and gradually her whole appearance would change. First she would untwist her body and grow taller, then her greasy grey locks would untangle and grow lighter or darker, straighten or curl as she desired. Even as we watched she took breasts that rose firm and round, instead of flapping around her waist like empty goat-skins; her stomach flattened, her legs and arms grew shapely and hair-free; her skin whitened and discarded the liverish brown spots, the crooked, dirty nails on fingers and toes became pink and the dry, split pouch at her groin would rise, mounded with curling, moist hair. Lastly her face would take on the lineaments of a beautiful woman: gone the warts, the beard, the moustache and come rosy cheeks, sparkling eyes, white teeth and full, red lips. Then she would laugh and stretch her arms wide and her voice would come sweet and rich as she called from the air silks and fine linen to clothe her nakedness. Then she would beckon Broom, her creature, and sit astride, call on the roof to open and fly out into the dark.

But She would not forget us, oh no. The very last thing would be a spell to bind us faster than the rope, cage, chains and bars that already held us. But once She had gone we would breathe freer and stretch a little and talk, and that is when we practised conversing without the usual constraints of her presence, exchanged hopes and fears, ideas, what little we remembered of the past, and endless speculation on the immediate present. Talk of the future held small part in all this, for I found that my friends had very little conception of what it was, and I was afraid even to think about it.

Perhaps I should qualify "talk," for it was not the sort ordinary beings would recognize, let alone understand. When I had first arrived I had talked wildly in human speech to Corby and Puddy, and they had understood nothing except the terror and distress, but in their different ways they had tried to soothe and reassure and gradually I had come to understand a little of what they were trying to communicate, and had tried to copy. It had become easier when Moglet and Pisky arrived later. Communication of the simplest kind was usually by noise; more complicated ideas were expressed by bodily position, movement, odour—in this I was way behind the understanding, let alone the expressing—but the most refined, and to me eventually the easiest to understand and adopt, was thought. A simple dialogue between Moglet and myself would use all these processes:—

Moglet:—A loud, attention-seeking mew, on a particular pitch that meant "I'm hungry!"

Me:—"Mmmm?"

Moglet:—Body position tight, paws together: "And I've been waiting ages . . ."

Me:—"Have you?"

Moglet:—A thought, like a ray of light penetrating my mind, giving me a memory-picture of what happened, cat's eye level, of course: "Breakfast was the last meal and that was only gruel and it was a long time ago when that slant of sun was over in the corner and the fly buzzed up the wall and I caught it but Puddy ate it . . ."

Me:—"Mmmm . . ."

Moglet:—Left eye blinking twice. "You're not even listening straight!"

Me:—"You'll have to wait . . ."

Moglet:—Eyes glancing sideways, to the right. "Don't want to wait."

Me:— "Will a small piece of cheese rind do, for the moment?"

Moglet:—Blink with both eyes, lids returning to halfway. "Yes."

Me:—"Was that nice?"

Moglet:—Tail flat out behind, tip gently vibrating. "Very nice . . ."

Me:— "What do you want now, then?"

Moglet:—Tail gently swished from side to side, right, left, right. "More, please . . ."

Of course it was not all as easy as this. Abstract ideas like "fear," for instance, were most difficult to express, for they did not use words for these, rather a thought-impression of what frightened them most, and it was easy to get an actual picture of our Mistress approaching the hut mixed up with an impression of her doing so, which might approximate to, say, Corby's idea of fear. None of this came naturally to us: it was just that we were thrown together in such close proximity that we formed a sort of alliance of misery—and in some queer way I believe our burden of pebbles brought us and our understanding closer together. And so gradually I forgot my human speech and could barely mutter my requests in the marketplace: my mother tongue became almost a foreign language.

Instead I would listen while Corby would tell of the grasping of sliding air under the fingertips of his wings, or soaring heights and dizzy drops; then there was Puddy reminiscing of cool grottos, buzz of fly and crawl of worm; Moglet half-remembering a warm hearth and dishes of cream, a substance none had tasted save Her, which sounded rich, thick and delicious; Pisky recalling the silk-slide of summer waters, the bright shoaling of his kin. While I held a dream of an armoured warrior, a fair lady and someone singing—but who was to say that all these were not just imaginings, for none of us could recall a place, a time, nor indeed how or why.

These respites together were all too short and sometimes not worth Her absence, for twice latterly she had returned in daylight and a foul temper, screaming at the air, the times and us. The first time she had contented herself with kicking out at whoever had been nearest, joggling Corby's perch till he fell off and emptying most of Pisky's water till he gasped. But the second time was worse. Usually she returned in the garb and looks in which she had departed, losing them only gradually, but this time she dragged herself back with the dawn in her accustomed evil form and there was a slitting to her eyes and a slavering to her mouth that boded ill. At first she had laughed shrilly and pointed at me.

"I thought of you, you ugly thing, when I cursed him! Yes, I tried to think of the worst fate I could for the accursed fool, and then the thought came to burden him with the dirtiest, most hideous creature I could imagine and you came to mind, you filthy little obscenity! Twisted, monstrous, revolting—Thing—that you are . . ." And I had shrunk back, for the venom in her voice frightened me more than anything she had done before. "Yes!" she had howled, "I cursed him, for he refused—" but she suddenly snapped her mouth shut and seizing her Broom, proceeded to beat me so hard I could not help but cry, despite my determination never to let her see how much she hurt me either physically or mentally. Then she seized Moglet and tried to throw her on the fire, but I snatched her back and hid her, mewing pitifully, under my cloak. Thwarted, she kicked Puddy out of his crock and stamped down catching my hand instead, for he had jumped into my pocket for protection. Poor Pisky was next, for she threw his bowl against the wall where it smashed and he lay helpless and flapping on the mud floor till I stretched forth my uninjured hand and popped him into the leather water-bucket, drawing that also under my cloak. Then came Corby: she snapped the fine chain that kept him to his perch and pulled and twisted at his neck until he pecked her and spiralled down helpless to join the rest of the creatures huddled under my cloak. Then she seemed to go mad, and though she now made no attempt to touch us herself, she shrieked a curse that made all the pebbles we were burdened with hurt as they never had before. And then her Broom was beating and beating at my bowed head until the blood ran . . .

That seemed to calm her, the sight of my blood, for she called off her minion and I heard her whisper, as though to herself: "No, no not yet: They must have a living home, a living body, or He will seek them out . . . Hide, hide, my precious ones, till I find the formula . . ."

For a while after that She had stayed at home and life had resumed its monotonous sameness, but I never forgot that moment of utter terror when she had lost control and we had seemed to face extinction; nor had I forgotten how my friends, for that is what they were, had all sought refuge under my cloak, as though I were in some way responsible for them all. This action seemed to bind us all closer together in a way we all secretly acknowledged but never mentioned, which appeared to make our lives together easier and more hopeful in the days that followed.

And now came this day, the day that was going to change our lives irrevocably. The preceding night She had left the hut just before moon-high, and the whole of the two days preceding had been taken up with Shape-Changing. It was early autumn, for she had sent me out for a few heads of saffron which I had found easily enough and then lingered awhile at the edge of the forest gazing down at the village below. Two-wheeled carts laden with the last of the hay and straw creaked down the muddy street; children played with top and ball, their happy squeals and shouts loud in the still air; men trudged back from the fields, mattocks on their shoulders from breaking up the earth ready for the winter sowings; a woman beat out a rag rug and farther off they were burning off stubble, for the smoke curled up thin into my nostrils and stretched them wide with the acrid, sad smell that is the ending of the year. At last an extra-sharp twinge in my stomach reminded me of my Mistress and I hastened back in the blue twilight, snatching a handful of blackberries from a bush as I went and eating each bleb separately to make them last longer. I had been almost happy for a moment or two that afternoon, but there had been a cuff for my tardiness and another for my betraying, juice-stained mouth and I had gone into the corner by the fire and turned my face to the wall. And so, in a fit of the sulks, I missed that last change to beauty, with all its preenings and posturings, which to the others at least broke the monotony of their drab days. So once I heard her split the roof and disappear I was surprised as snow to find a beautiful lady return by the door some two minutes later, to fling Broom at my head with the remark to it: "No point in taking you, after all: it's not far. There'll be no point in the binding, either," and with a few words she loosened the invisible ties we were bound with, like a soaking in warm water softens dried meat. Broom hustled up next to me and rustled and chattered, so I moved away from my corner to join the others by the fire. Our Mistress paused once more before she left by the conventional door, swirling her long, purple gown: "I shall not be late," she warned. "So, quiet as mice and no tricks or I shall have you all with the cramps when I return . . ."

She looked very beautiful that night, with long brown hair the sheen of hazelnuts hanging down her back and eyes the colour of squirrel-fur. I wondered what it felt like to be beautiful.

It may seem strange that we never queried her Shape-Changing, nor questioned where she went in that guise, nor why, but it was so much a part of our lives that we just accepted it, I suppose: I do not remember puzzling over it—I was just glad that she was not there. Afterwards the reasons became clearer, but at the time we all took it as a sort of Holy Day, and relaxed. That night I rustled up some nice bone broth I had hidden away and ate it with freshish bread, sharing it with Corby and Moglet, and shaving a sliver of new-dead moth and slipping it with agonizing patience round the moon-pebble in Pisky's mouth, giving the rest, wings and all, to Puddy. I was comfortably dozing, back against the angle of the fireplace, when the door was flung open and she was back.

I could see that this time it was going to be different from any time before. She seemed to glow, to expand, to fill the whole room with a musky odour of femininity that scared me. Her eyes were sleep-puffed, satiated, and her lips full as a wasp sting and red as new-killed meat. There were scratches on her bare arms and legs as though she had run through bramble and her gown hung open on her breasts. But she seemed in a singular good humour and did not even ask whether we had behaved but whirled about the room in her ruined dress like the wind in a pile of new-fallen leaves.

"Now there was a man!" She sighed and yawned. "A village yokel maybe, but hard as iron and full of juices . . . This time there will be a child! And then you, my pets, will be superfluous . . ." We shrank back, for even in the unaccustomed mellowness of her tone there was an implied threat, even though the others could not clearly understand what she said. "I may decide however to keep you as you are for a while, slaves and servants, for Thing there at least is sometimes useful." She ran long, still-beautiful fingers through her hair, for the magic had not yet slipped away. "And of course the babe will need a nurse . . ." She mused. "I shall have to see . . ." and such was our awe of her that I believed in the immediate appearance of some infant witch, a smaller version of herself, and even peered into all the corners when one did not immediately materialize. I told the others what she had said and we huddled round the cheerless fire, trembling at this new threat, but she did not appear to notice and went into her alcove from whence we could hear her chinking glass and pouring liquid. She came out at last and drained a green, smoking mixture with every indication of enjoyment, but as she set down the drinking-flagon a couple of drops spilled on the oaken table and crackled and fizzed in the dark wood, leaving two shallow, smoking depressions.

She, however, looked more beautiful than ever, and as soon as she had drunk her fill she went over to her couch under the shuttered window. "I shall sleep long during the next few months, Thing, and you will have to keep the place tidy and provisioned. I want no disturbances, no undue noise, and I expect the stock-pot full if ever I wake and am hungry." She reached beneath her pillow for some copper coins and flung them to the floor, watching me scrabble in the dirt. "That should last till the turn of the year, if you are careful. Buy the cheapest you can find, remember: I am not made of money. Gruel and bones will do fine for you," and she yawned and lay down on the couch. "I shall want you to go out at first light in the morning: there is one more mixture I have to complete. Bring me ten drops of blood from a boar; three heads of feverfew and twelve seeds of honesty. Oh, and six fleas from a male hedgepig not more than six months old. You may wake me when you return," and with that, perfectly composed, she closed her eyes, her beautiful lips parted, and she started to snore as she usually did.

We looked at one another, afraid of being vocal, concentrating on thought, but were too frightened, too confused by the turn of events for the refinements we had so carefully practised. All I had from Corby was: "Oh Hell! Hell! Witch brat—that's all we need!" Puddy said "Shit!" and nothing more, but he was never a quick thinker. Moglet mewed that she was frightened and Pisky rushed round and round his bowl, talking to himself backwards, the thoughts and sounds bubbling up in little pops through the gaps between his stretched mouth and the moon-pebble. I tried calming thoughts for them all: grass, trees, lakes, rivers, wind, sky, stars, dark, sleep . . . And gradually they quietened and we settled into an uneasy doze.

As first light pinched through the edges of the shutters I blew the embers of the fire into a blaze and swung the gruel pot over the flames; it needed no salt, for as I mixed the oatmeal and water the miserable tears dripped from the end of my nose. I sensed change in the air and did not want it, for always change had been for the worse. My little friends stirred in their sleep; Corby creaked and hunched his feathers; Puddy glugged, his yellow throat moving up and down; Moglet stretched and mewed in the stretch as though her muscles hurt, but her eyes remained shut; Pisky's tail waved, once. In that quiet time, apart from my silent tears, I suppose we were at peace.

I went out while the dew was still on the grass and spiders' webs hung with diamonds. I found the pearl plates of honesty and harvested the black seeds, one from each pod; withering head of feverfew, with its pungent leaves, grew near the hut; an obliging hedgepig curled from his coat of leaves in the roots of an oak, only too glad to lose a few fleas at hibernation time. I tickled his coarse, ticked fur stomach and rolled him back into his hole with thanks, then set off for the village since wild pig were uncertain at the best of times, even though now was acorn-harvest, and I should have better luck with one of the domestic ones. A quick and relatively painless nick on the ear should do the trick and I had a pocketful of beechmast and acorns for sweeteners: in my experience one never took without giving, for that would upset the balance we all lived by. As I crept down the narrow path to the village I took care to keep well out of sight, for as I said before the peasants mistrusted me as a representative of my Mistress and would not hesitate to harm me if they could, especially if I was not buying anything. I found a convenient sty and struck a bargain with the boar, for my time with the others had given me a primitive understanding of all beast-talk and certainly enough to bribe a pig. I nicked his ear neatly enough and dripped the blood into the little glass phial I carried. The drops were slow in coming for it was a cold morning and I fed the pig a few more acorns to keep him still.

He whiffled contentedly. "Mmm . . . make a nice change, these do. What's your old woman been up to then? They say as she's gone too far this time . . ."

"How?" I questioned. Six drops; better make it seven.

"Seems as she rogered young Cerdic to death last night. Sprang on him and tuckered him out in five minutes . . . Mind you, these humans ain't got no stamina. Now I, I could tell you a thing or two about that . . ." and he rumbled away for a moment or two about servicing the sows they kept for him but I wasn't listening.

"He's dead?" I remembered the lad, bonny and brawny in the fields at haying, from my lonely spyings. Was that what my Mistress had meant, with all her talk of witch-babe? Had She taken man-seed into her body and now hoped—but she couldn't: she was too old. But then, her spells were strong. And was this what had happened on those other times, when she had returned angry and frustrated? Was this because her spells had not worked on those others, whoever they had been? My mind was in a whirl; why had she to kill that handsome young man, especially when he had obviously pleasured her so well? "Dead, you say?" I repeated.

"As firewood. Seems they're all cut up about it; say she's gone too far this time." His fanged mouth nudged me, none too gently. "Got any more?"

"Of course." To retreat safely from these razor-backed horrors, a precarious domestication a few generations back having done little for their manners, always required a diplomatic withdrawal. I threw down the rest of the mast and nuts and scuttled back over the fence.

"Where have they put him?"

"Huh? Oh, the dead 'un. Square. There's a meeting. All there. Come again . . ."

Stoppering and pocketing the phial, I crept cautiously round the back of the houses till I could see, between the washerwoman's and the whore's, that rectangle of trampled earth they called the Square. Sure enough the place was crowded, and there was talk I could not hear so, not daring to approach directly, I made a leap for the thatch of the washerwoman's house, luckily only a few feet from the ground at this point, and crept up among the straw till I could both hear and see without fear of discovery. Glancing sideways at the next roof I was glad I had chosen the one I was on, for the whore's roof was all rotten grey straw and loose with it; I could see an old nest or two and the roots of sear vervain: it would not have held me for two breaths.

Below me was a lake of people, heads bobbing like floats, and an angry hum of voices, a hive disturbed. In a space in the centre was a bier, roughly fashioned from larch poles and skins and the body of Cerdic lay disarranged upon it. His clothing was rough, homespun of course, but the young face held an unworldly look of disillusion and, strangely enough, an air of peaceful exultation too, at odds with the rough, uncomprehending features of the villagers surrounding him. The talk confused me, for I was not used to such a babble, but the gist was of witchcraft and revenge. They led forward a young woman, pretty enough, and she cast herself down weeping by the bier, clasping the careless dead hand of the young man and carrying it to her mouth, kissing it feverishly, and sobbing the while in an uncontrolled burst of emotion that made me hot all over.

I moved away, sliding back down the thatch till my feet found the ground, and crept back home, thoroughly bewildered and with a horrible feeling that something nasty was about to fall on my head or leap out and bite my ankles. The air was very still, as if everything was holding its breath, waiting, and I found myself glancing over my shoulder every few yards; I couldn't get back quick enough.

Back there, there where we all belonged, I tried to tell the others what I had seen and heard but it was only Corby and perhaps Puddy who understood. "Always like that when they turn the corner," said the former. "Turn a corner and see Death staring 'em in the face. Gets 'em all, one way and another. Know it's long past childbearing time but reckon a touch of magic might make the difference. Think they'll renew themselves. Seldom works, but I've heard tell of a deformed mippet born of an old witch. Nigh unkillable, too. Pity She couldn't keep it off'n her own doorstep, though; sounds as though she's stirred up a hornet's nest down there. Could mean trouble for us all . . ."

"Water," said Puddy. For a moment I thought he wanted a sprinkle from the water jar, but he continued his thought a space later, as was his wont. It was sometimes a little irritating waiting for a toad's thoughts, although they were usually worth having. "Don't like it. That and fire . . ." He appeared to meditate. "Best things for killing them off."

A hiss from Moglet alerted me as the Mistress yawned, stretched and rose from the bed in the corner. She still looked remarkably young and beautiful, so much so that I forgot to duck as her ringed hand slapped my cheek.

"Well, where are they? The things I sent you for?"

Humbly I offered my gatherings. She picked them over grudgingly, then took them over to the alcove, where we could hear her chopping and pounding and mixing during a long afternoon, while we huddled together, not sure what the next hours would bring. Twice I tried to tell her what I had heard and seen in the village and twice she stopped me, the second time with a jar hurled across the room and a threat that she would get Broom to beat me if I disturbed her further. "I am not interested in what those peasants do or think," she said, so I held my peace.

When it was dusk within and near enough outside I lighted a tallow and stirred the omnipresent stew; putting bowls by the fire to warm, I opened the earth-oven and took out the day's bread, standing it on end to cool and tapping it to make sure it was cooked through, for the oven was very slow. I fed the others surreptitiously, with an eye to the alcove and ear to the mixings and a nose pricked against the unpleasant aromas. When they were satisfied I gestured them back to their boxes, crocks and perches, for all day we had been uncharacteristically free to move and I did not want her reminded we were comparatively free.

"Supper is ready, Mistress," I said timidly, but as she came from the alcove I saw with horror that her beauty had faded by ten years while her smile showed that she had not consulted her mirror recently. What had happened to the magic she was convinced would keep her young forever now she was pregnant of a witch-child? And was she indeed? My eyes went to her swelling belly: she seemed some three or four months gone, and that in less than twenty-four hours.

"Nine days!" she said triumphantly, her eyes following my gaze. "Nine days, that is all! And then you will have a new Master, you miserable worm . . ." Her mood changed as she took the bowl and bread, well over half of what I had cooked. "What do you mean by giving me these slops? My baby needs good, red meat and fresh vegetables and fruit, and wine to strengthen his blood! Why did you not prepare such?"

"But Mistress," I faltered, "you told me to—"

I got no further for her free hand shot out and gave me a stinging slap. Holding my hand to my reddened cheek I backed away.

"Go now, and fetch me a rich pie from the village and a flagon of their best wine." She reached into one of her boxes and spilt coins, silver coins I had never seen, in a stream onto the floor. Scrabbling to obey I pocketed ten, twenty even. I knew my task would be difficult, or well-nigh impossible, at this time of the evening, for it was now dark and the villagers would equate me with the darkness and chase me from their doors—but which was worse, their vindictiveness or hers? And there was the dead man . . . I hesitated.

And even as I did so, everything began to happen at once.

There was a thump, as some large object struck the door and a crash as stones rattled against the shutters. Starting back I whimpered with shock and fright, my hand still tingling, for it had been on the latch when the door had vibrated under the blow. For a long moment my mewlings were the only sound in that confined space, then there was a voice outside; ragged, scared, but still truculent.

"Come out, Witch! Come out and meet your accusers!"

For a moment the stillness inside was intensified. Then my Mistress hissed like a snake behind me and, turning, I saw such a look of evil on her face that even I, inured as I was, cowered flat in terror. But her look was not for me, and her voice, when it came for those outside, was honey-sweet, though I could see her hair and fingers writhe like snakes.

"Who calls so late, and on what errand?"

"You know who's here, and why!" came the answer. "You knows what you've done, there were those that oversaw. Time's come to pay for it!"

She hissed again, but her voice was beguiling still. "I know not of what you speak . . . Has someone been hurt? Perhaps my medicines . . ." but even as she finished speaking she was muttering under her breath spells I had never heard even the echo of before. All at once the pretence of beauty was gone and her body resumed its usual hideosity—all except her belly. Her fine clothes dropped to the floor but her stomach seemed to swell visibly—a smooth, rounded mockery in that ancient frame. She caressed it with her fingers, still spell-making—the gnarled, dirty fingers were an obscenity against the youthful mound she touched.

"Grow, grow!" she muttered. "Grow, my manikin! I give you my strength, my lust for life—Make it not nine days, nor even nine hours . . . Not five, not four, not even one! Less, less!" and her voice became louder with the repeated rhythms of some incantation in a strange tongue. "Help me, help me, Master, and he shall be yours!"

Of a sudden it grew deathly cold and a foul stench filled the hut. I crawled back to the fireplace unregarded, to cower against the hearth where the fire now burned blue and heatless. Outside the clamour rose; more voices, more stones, and a flicker of flame blossomed behind the gaps in the shutters. They were firing the hut! Now there was a scrambling outside, another thump above our heads this time, and a tearing at the thatch on the roof and an ominous chanting.

"Burn the witch! Burn the witch!"

The smell of smoke filled my nostrils. There was a crackling, a flaming of tinder-dry straw roofing and the voices grew louder, a chant to rival my Mistress's mouthings.

"To the stake, to the stake! Burn the murderess, the witch!"

But my Mistress continued her spells, louder now and even louder till I covered my ears and shut my eyes, pressed back against the back wall of the hut as far as possible from threat and danger. It was cold; it was hot; flames shot up, smouldered down, till it all grew as regular as my pounding heartbeats and I was afraid as I had never been.

And there my life might have ended, choked by smoke and charred by fire, but for one thing—

The Gathering: Three, Four, Five, Six, Seven

Death of a Witch

A mew.

A small frightened mew from a small, helpless cat. All at once I stopped being so scared and gathered Moglet in my arms, soothing and caressing as I had done so often in the lesser bad times. At the same time I felt Puddy climb onto my lap and heard Pisky bubbling in distress and Corby thumped down from his perch, breaking his tie, to flap around my feet.

"Get us out, for goodness sake!" he croaked. "You'll have us all cinders!"

Get us out, but how? For a moment or two my brain would not work, then Puddy nudged my knee.

"Back wall. Weak. Corby's beak . . ."

Of course! Corby had heard too and we both remembered where the stones had fallen away from the side of the fireplace last winter with the cracking of the Great Frost, and how we had repaired it with a temporary amalgam of stones and mud. Tumbling the others from me I took out my sharp knife and tried to remember where our botched repairs had begun. There it was. I attacked it at once with the knife and beside me Corby pecked away with his strong, yellow beak—both unheeding everything else except the desperate need for clean air, for outside, for life. I knew the villagers would not be on this side, for out there the ground dropped steeply away to the stinking ditch where we emptied the slops. Desperately I chipped and scrabbled at the caked mud, my fingers tearing at stones, my nails breaking on flints, while behind me the clamour grew louder. Glancing round for one terrified moment I saw our Mistress outlined by the flames from the burning hut, her belly grown monstrous and huge, her screams rending the air and in the corner her familiar, Broom, with fire creeping towards the tangled heathers of its feet. Suddenly my bruised and torn hands jerked forward into open air and without thought I picked up Puddy and thrust him through the hole I had made, careless of where he fell.

"Escape, quickly!" I thought-shouted, then reached for little Moglet: "Run, my dear, run!" The hole was only just big enough for Pisky's bowl and I reached through the gap and balanced it carefully outside. But that was it: no way was the hole big enough for Corby, let alone me; the others would perhaps be all right—Oh Hell, however I hurt the bird must be given his chance, too! "Keep pecking, you great black gormless thing!" I hissed, and together we renewed our attack on the crumbling wall. A sudden blast of heat behind me redoubled my efforts and all at once the gap was large enough for me to push the crow through, scraping his feathers against the stone unmercifully. "Hop away, friend," I muttered, "and please push Pisky's crock down to the ditch; he may be able to find his way down to the stream. Help him, help the others . . ."

"Don't be so blasted silly!" came the hoarse croak from outside: "Come and do it yourself! Get scraping: I'm not nursemaiding this lot. We need you . . ." And there was a gurgle, a mew, a glug less than a foot away. They were waiting for me, they needed me to look after them! Perhaps without the incentive of their responsibility I might have succumbed, let the now-choking smoke take my last breath, but the knowledge that I was needed gave me the spur that fear and exhaustion had blunted.

With the last of my strength, from the crouching position in which I found myself, I charged that hole in the wall; my head was through, one shoulder. Breathing the fresh air outside aided my efforts; I twisted, scraped, shoved, tore and wriggled and with a final heave fell free of the inferno behind me, to lie gasping on the steep bank outside, my head lower than my heels, bruised, battered and exhausted, smoke pouring from the gap behind me.

"Come on then, Thing," they all cried. "Come on; we're not free of her yet . . ."

We crept stealthily to the edge of the wood, me carrying Pisky's crock, and hid behind a great bramble-patch. The hut was ringed by fire, except for the back part where we had escaped, and even now flames ran around the corner to eat the dry grass at that side. Not only ringed but crowned, for hungry tongues of fire leapt like bears licking for honey up among the thatch and all around was the choking smoke. The noise was indescribable: although we hid in comparative safety some hundred yards from the hut, yet the clamour, both of shouting villagers and their barking dogs, the crack and crackle of burning wood and the screaming of our Mistress seemed but a foot or two away. The men were gathered in a semicircle about the hut, most armed with clubs, billhooks or scythes, but even as we watched they were retreating step by step from the heat of the fire, hands before their faces. And what of my Mistress? Thoroughly sickened by the mad screaming we heard, I almost determined to go back and try to get her out through the hole in the back wall, but Corby grabbed my sleeve in his beak.

"Wait! She's not done for yet . . ."

True enough: as we watched there was a sudden change to the quality of the flames. One moment they were hot-tongued, roaring with insatiable desire, the next they were cool and pretty, green and blue, burning with a delicate flame that decorated rather than consumed. The hut now looked as if it were dressed for an autumn Maying, the scorched timbers and charred thatch hidden by the green leaves and blue flowers of the flames, and as we watched the whole place blossomed as the thatch burst asunder. The sudden flowering created a seed-pod burst as the witch, our Mistress, black and ripe and full, thrust from the roof, borne astride by her faithful Broom.

I picked up Pisky and with one accord we fled deeper into the forest as She swooped and shrieked among the villagers who cowered and ran from her as though she were a hornet, stinged and deadly. There was a path that twisted and turned away from the holocaust behind us, and at first the fluttering Corby was well ahead, with Moglet running behind, but before long they lagged back, crippled wing and foot hampering, so I stopped, gathered Moglet in my arms with Pisky's crock slopping water over all of us, perched Corby on my shoulder, pocketed the tired Puddy and scuttled as fast as I could, not even sure why I was except that somehow we all knew we had to get as far away as possible as quickly as we could. The trees grew denser and I halted, out of breath and lost, and in that moment they came again, those terrible pains near the seating of our pebbles so that I cried out and doubled up. I heard Puddy's moans and Moglet's mew, Corby's screech and Pisky's demented bubbles and realized that we were still in terrible danger.

"She wants us," breathed Moglet. "Wants us still . . ."

"Watch it," said Corby. "She's not going to let us escape if she can help it . . ."

"Help, help, help!" bubbled Pisky.

"What can we do?" I was screwed up in agony. "Oh, the pain . . ."

"Lake," said Puddy. "Head hurts . . . Left and down: hates water."

His words stuck in my fuddled, paining brain: "Lake . . . hates water . . ." Of course: clever toad. All witches avoid water like the plague and the stretch of lake lay to our left: I could see a glint of water in the direction Puddy had indicated. Gathering the others close once more, my stomach still contracting with pain, I crashed heedlessly through the bushes towards the stretch of water, tumbling at last down the steep bank to land us all splash! in the murky waters among the sear reeds and drowned twigs that littered its edge.

Not for nothing was this called the Dead Water, for nothing grew on or in it except the nastiest weeds. Even frogs, desperate for cool in the summer, eschewed its water, while in spring the shallowest puddle seemed preferable for their spawn. Long ago the lake had been fished-out and even restocking had failed, for the villagers said it was cursed by the drowned souls of a party of young men and women who had gone out on a raft for a dare on Beltane's Eve countless years ago and never returned. The raft had been found the following morning, caught in reeds at the edge, but of the dozen or so—the superstitious said thirteen—that had essayed the water there was no sign. Of course the villagers had gone out and dragged the depths with hastily made rope nets but these yielded nothing, and one intrepid fellow who had ventured the depths at the end of a line had burst to the surface with tales of huge snake-like leeches that had curled for him out of the watery dark and of a ring of dead bodies silently dancing among the tangled weeds of the deep, their white faces and open eyes full of the horrors of the drowned, and worms and bubbles rising from the open mouths that cried of devils and black magic. Certain it was now that no one would venture out on this black smoothness and I had seen none but the rash, unfearing wild pig ever drink from its waters when I had been out early for herbs.

Even now, stranded as we were among the shallows, me sitting in but two inches of water, Pisky bubbling up in his crock, which was bobbing up and down where I had dropped it, I had all the others clutched and clinging to my head and shoulders with beak, claw and damp feet rather than touch the waters.

"Pick me up, pick me up!" panicked Pisky.

"Help!" moaned Moglet.

"Let's up-an'-orf," croaked Corby.

"Not healthy," pondered Puddy.

All at once, of course.

I struggled to my feet, as much to escape their din as anything else, but then looked down with horror at the breeches I always wore, on our Mistress's instruction. I was damp from the waist down from sitting in the water and on the wet leather fat blue-grey worms crawled with open mouths, burrowing blindly for my naked skin. I struck out, brushing them back into the scummy water, only to feel them immediately fasten on my bare ankles. Stumbling to the bank I lay back against the sloping earth thrusting with panic at the evil things that still clung and sucked at my skin. Unexpectedly I was helped by Corby who fluttered from my shoulder and pecked at the slimy things with his beak, wiping them off into the sludge as a bird will clean his beak on a twig.

At last I was free and turned to struggle to the top of the bank when the pains struck us all again and we screeched and tumbled back towards the water. Desperately I clung to a gnarled tree root that jutted out above the water, my feet frantically scrabbling for a hold on the greasy earth, Pisky's bowl jammed under my chin, the others hanging on as best they could. Something made me look up and there a great bat-like shape blotted out the hazy light from a wisp-clouded harvest moon that rocked unsteadily through the trees, and with despair I realized that our Mistress had found us and was flying over our hiding place on Broom.

"She'll get us!" I screamed. "We'll never escape!"

This time I knew She would at last kill us and then throw our bodies into the black waters of the lake, and I could not think at all, only feel as the cramps clutched at me again and my terrified friends clawed and clung till I could feel the trickle of blood from torn shoulder-skin. I felt a sudden rush of stinking air as our Mistress swooped down on us and the smell of singed cloth overwhelmed even the stench of scummy water: a burning fragment from somewhere had landed on my arm and there was a smoulder of cloth which I beat at frantically as the witch misjudged her landing and soared away to approach from an easier angle.

I heard Puddy trying to say something, urgently for him, agonizingly slow for the rest of us in those few moments when everything—pain, fear, drowning, burning, death—was rushing upon us like a great, irresistible storm wind that will snap and crack even the most pliant tree in its fury.

"Can't get us surrounded by water . . ." but even as I understood and acknowledged what he was saying I knew I could not wade out into that lake of desolation and stand, helpless, while my flesh was sucked away from my bones by the unseen horrors that lurked beneath.

"Island somewhere," came Corby's hoarse voice, stirring into a sort of incredulous hope. "If you could wade out, Thing . . . Think it's over there to the left someways . . ."

I do not remember scrambling up the bank, scurrying through the thin belt of trees that lined the shore, searching ever for a darker shape on the waters, ducking automatically from the swooping thing that held off only because of the branches that hid us from full view. I do remember at last seeing a dark lump that rose from the water some hundred yards out and recall too the fear and pain that accompanied my wild splashings through the shadows; I remember that at one stage the water sucked greedily at my waist, at another my foot turned on a treacherous stone and slime rushed headlong into my open mouth, but that at last my feet found dry ground and I staggered free of the clutching waters to fall to my knees, shedding cat, bird, toad and fish's crock, and lie prone, crying my exhaustion.

The islet on which we found ourselves was only a scratch of ground barely ten feet long and half that wide with a stunted tree and a prickly bush for company: I looked back and the bank seemed an immeasurable distance away. Had I really crossed that stretch of water? I shivered with wet and cold and beside me Corby ruffled and rattled his feathers and Moglet tried to wipe herself dry against my ankles, mercifully leech-free: I supposed my wild splashings and the speed of our progress had hindered the creatures' blind seekings. For the time being, too, we were witch-free, but a massy heap of clouds raced up on the increasing wind that rattled the branches of the stunted tree above me and whispered in the bush to my right, fluttering the ivy that clung to the ground round our feet. I bent and straightened Pisky's bowl which was dangerously tilted and heard him mutter and cough as he rushed around backwards: "Horrid black stuff: chokes the lungs, black water does, not good for my gills. Oh, deary, deary me! If my great-grandfather could see me now . . ."

I put out my hand and stroked Moglet's damp fur. "Are we all right now?" she asked anxiously, purring a little to reassure us both.

Corby and Pisky were conversing in low tones. "Notice them trees?" I heard the bird mutter.

"And the ivy," said Puddy. "Should help."

"Wouldn't be a bad idea to form a ring, though," said Corby. "Can you remember any of that stuff? You know . . ."

"A little."

They turned to me.

"Best get into a circle and hold fast to each other: dip a finger in Pisky's bowl and touch his fin and toad here can do the same with a toe t'other side. Now, Thing dear, before it is too late . . ."

Hastily we arranged ourselves: me with Moglet and Pisky on either side, Corby and Puddy opposite. I did not question how or why for obviously these two knew something I did not.

"Now then, all close your eyes and empty your minds," said Corby urgently. "Let old Puddy and I do the thinking here, for this is what we knows. Go on, sharp about it! Listen to nothing save our words, our thoughts . . ."

"And don't let go," murmured Puddy. "Keep in touch . . ."

For a moment there was nothing as I knelt with closed eyes, listening to Corby muttering and Puddy coming in now and again with a single word, almost like the priest and congregation I had heard sometimes from outside the little church in the village. Then, as now, I did not understand what was being said, for it seemed to be in a language I had never heard, and yet in spite of this I felt a sort of strength flow back into my limbs and a string of hope seemed to circle between our points of contact; fingers, claws, paws and fins. I felt Pisky quieten under my touch and Moglet had ceased her trembling.

And then the pictures came into my mind.

A sunlit grove, whispering leaves, white berries, bearded faces with sad, dark eyes, a flashing knife and with all these an instinctive knowledge of great secrets, of ancient ways; between the mutterings something deeper and even more secret came from my left hand where Moglet's race-memory wandered back to an even earlier time where the dominant figure was female and the secrets were held only by women . . . On my right hand a golden sun, silk-embroidered cities, a great wall that wound like a snake; from somewhere else there was a rumble as the Sea-God stirred and cones of bright fire erupted on the hillsides bringing cliff and temple tumbling together; tall candles, a man kissing the cross-hilt of a sword—

"Hold fast, hold fast to that which is great, that which is good," came the message between us. "Keep your eyes closed, closed . . ."

Perhaps if I had not been reminded they were shut I should not have opened them just to see—

"She's coming again!" I screamed, jumping up and breaking the circle, and the others scattered as the great bat-like figure swooped down on us again, howling imprecations, only to veer at the last moment to avoid the tree, whose twisted branches defied a landing.

"A circle again, you dumb idiots!" yelled Corby, but the spell was broken and we were in disarray, all concentration gone, running hither and yon in the small space afforded us like rats terrier-struck in a pit. Again and again the figure dived down on us and in the end we stopped trying to escape and cowered between the prickly bush and the stunted tree clutching at anything to stop ourselves being scooped up off the island, up, up into her clutches.

Up? Or down? For suddenly it felt as though the island had turned upside down and we now hung by fingertip and claw from the strands of ivy as flies on a ceiling; I had Pisky's bowl under my chest and so great was the illusion of being topsyturvy that I remembered being amazed that the water from his crock did not pour all down my front.

But still She did not land, could not reach us, and I glanced up, or down, I was not sure which, and saw her hovering some twenty feet above, or below us, and I almost did not recognize her. She had grown incredibly old and ugly and was naked except for a few shreds and tatters that hung from her shoulders. And her belly—her belly was a huge, monstrous puffball of growth that rocked and swelled in front of her. Even as I watched in terrified fascination it seemed as though it were being struck like a great gong from within, a soundless blow that yet brought an answering scream from my Mistress.

"It is time!" she shrieked. "I give birth to my son, my monster, who shall rule you all! But I need blood, blood for him to suck, blood to bring him alive, and I will have it!" and she raised her arms and chanted a spell I remembered: the fire-bringing one, only this time much stronger and more vindictive than I had heard it when she had used it once or twice to relight our fire when the wood was too damp to do anything but smoulder. As we gazed up at her we saw her body redden with reflected flame and I glanced down to see flickers and sparks among the fallen leaves at my feet. Springing up I stamped frantically but all the time the ground was growing hotter and the stones started to glow like the embers of a fire, even as a tongue of flame licked the trunk of the twisted tree and ran up into the branches like a squirrel. Tearing off my cloak I flapped despairingly at the flames, and beside me Puddy and Moglet were leaping up and down squealing at the pain from singed paws; Corby had fallen on his back, feathers browning, and poor Pisky's bowl was steaming as he gasped away his life on the surface.

Then something inside me snapped, and I behaved like a mad thing, for the dreadful pains were twisting my guts again and I came outside myself with pain and stood like a creature of no substance and all substance and I was nothing and everything and had no power and all power. Stretching out my hands I gathered the flames into them and cooled them and rolled them into a living entity in my palms. Throwing back my head I stood as firm as a pillar of stone upon the ground beneath and opening my mouth I cursed the witch that hovered and swooped above us. Using no language and all language I cursed her into Hell and eternal fire, I cursed the monster she bore and wished it non-born; I cursed them living and dead and forbade earth, air or water to receive their bones. Then, gathering all my strength, I took the ball of fire that yet clung to my hands and flung it straight up into her face.

While I had been cursing her, she had dipped and wavered and I could see her shocked mouth and suddenly wary eyes. But as soon as the ball of fire left my hands she swerved away on Broom and then seemed to redouble her strength, as I collapsed like a pricked bubble on the stony ground, whimpering for the pain in my burnt hands. But at least the fire on the island was out, and the stones once more blessedly cool. The others clung to me and I felt Puddy spit into my burning palms and mutter something and at once they were soothed.

"Good try," croaked Corby, "but I'm afraid she's coming back . . ."

We all looked up at her then, waited for her to come down the inevitable last time, the time when we would have no strength, no reserves left. We were all brave now, I think, for there comes a time when death must be faced, and it is only the manner of the dying that matters. And as she rose to a greater height the better to gain momentum, then turned and bore down on us like a meteor, I felt strangely calm.

Like a meteor? With flames streaming out behind her? Even as I wondered, as I dared surmise, there was a sudden mew of excitement from Moglet, Pisky stopped going backwards and I do not think I heeded Corby's expletive or Puddy's awed croak. She had swerved her face and body from the ball of fire I had thrown but it had landed on the tail of Broom, where the bunched heather and twigs were already tinder-dry and needed only that final spark.

Down, down she came, either not knowing, or not caring in her madness that Broom was on fire, but then it added its scream to hers: "Mistress, Mistress, I burn, I burn! Put me out, put me out!" And it wavered in its course, bucked like an unbroken horse and twisted off course so that she passed us by yet again, missing the island by a hand's-breadth and soaring back into the blackness above. By now her bearer was truly on fire and I saw her lips move, one hand to belly, the other beating at the flames behind her. She must have been reciting the Flame-Cooler spell, for I saw the fire falter, turn for a moment blue and green and then steady, but at the same moment there was a rip of lightning to the east and a crack of thunder that momentarily deafened us, and I saw that her travail was beginning.

Desperately she tried to control her bearer, to quench the flames, to catch us, to give birth at one and the same time, but she could not do it and Broom in its insensate agony bore her away from us to the centre of the lake, to try and quench its tailing flames in the dark waters. Just as desperately she screamed imprecations and beat it with her fist, raising it by sheer willpower. By now she was afire also and the tattered remnants of clothing flamed and sparked. Even from where we stood, mesmerized by the drama that had suddenly made us spectators instead of victims, we could smell the sickening stench of burning flesh. In spite of my fear, my misery, my hatred of the evil tyrant who had kept us thralls to her pleasure for so long, I could not help a tremendous surge of pity: if then it had been within my power to quench the flames, to end her misery, I think I would have done so.

But the Power was now Another's, a greater force than mine, with perhaps a greater pity also, for at that moment there came a great fork of lightning that blinded us with its light and for a moment illuminated the whole world in which we stood. The same fork split our Mistress from breastbone to groin and a great gout of night-blackened blood ribboned into the air, and out from the gash emptied a twisting, tumbling manikin with mortal face and body and the claws and wings of a bat. It mewled and screeched and clawed at the air like a falling cat and its mother, our Mistress, stretched and grabbed at the hideous creature with hungry arms and it turned and bit her and scratched and sucked at the black blood that ran down her thighs and dripped, hissing, into the lake. It crawled up her legs and up to her breasts but, scorning the empty, flapping dugs, reached up for her throat and fastened there, sucking the last of the life-blood from scorched and blackened flesh. At last she realized just what she had spawned and beat at it with her fists: in vain, for it clung now like a lake-leech so that she, greasy hair now spitting and bubbling with the flames, her Broom and her manikin were one, sinking indivisible to destruction.

In a last effort she pointed Broom at the sky and they shot up like some huge, rocketing pheasant, but even as I thought they might escape another bolt of lightning struck them. For an instant time stood still, they hung in the air as though pinned to the night, and then—and then they plummeted slowly down, a dying, screeching, moaning, blackened bundle. And the waters of the lake rose to greet them, to eat them, to drown them, to exterminate them. There was a fearsome hiss as the burning mass hit the water which fountained into black fingers around them, fastened and drew them down, and then for a moment it seemed as though a ghostly ring of dancing figures ringed the yawning chasm that received them—

"Hang on lads," warned Corby. "And lasses. Here comes trouble . . ."

Huge waves, displaced by the falling bodies, were rearing and racing across the empty waters and instinctively I clung to the stunted tree, Corby and Moglet in the branches above me, Pisky's crock in my free hand, Pisky in my pocket. Then we were deluged with evil slime, weed and black water till I was sure we would drown; there was a moment's respite as the wall of liquid surged past us to beat against the banks and, frustrated, fall back so that we were subjected to the process in reverse. At last, choking and gasping, my mouth and eyes were free, but then came an immense pulling and we all clung for dear life as the waters rushed away from us to the centre of the lake, where it seemed a great whirlpool sucked all down into a vortex.

For a moment the last of the waters swirled about our feet, and then came a great rumble like thunder and I felt as though the soles of my feet had been struck a blow that drove them up into my hipbones, just like jumping off a roof in the dark, not knowing where the ground was. They stung with pain and instinctively I lifted them off the ground as a second jolt, slighter than the first, disturbed the island.

Then all was quiet.

We shook ourselves, moved all our legs, arms, wings, fins, joints and muscles to make sure they worked and felt hastily all over to make sure none of the leeches from the dark water were left behind. Just as we were reassured there came a great wind that thrashed the branches of the trees on the bank and buffeted us and tugged hair, fur and feathers the wrong way. On its heels came the rain: cold, hard, freezing us in a moment. But as we gasped and chattered with the chill the quality of the downpour changed and it was soft and warm. The rain came down like a torrent and we stood beneath a waterfall, and if we were wet before we were now drenched. But it was a cleansing, gentle rain, washing away all dirt, all grime, all fears and tears in its caress and even Moglet, who hated the wet, stood and steamed and licked and steamed again, and I emptied Pisky's crock three times, until the water felt like silk.

And then it stopped, as suddenly as it began, and the moon shone bright and sweet, a curved lantern high above us, and the stars pricked out one by one and, wet as we were, we collapsed where we stood and slept like dead things until dawn.

The Gathering: Three, Four, Five, Six, Seven

The Escape

We awoke to a beautiful morning, and a different world.

One by one we crept back to consciousness, stretched stiff joints, yawned, opened our eyes. And all, without exception, let out some exclamation of surprise: in fact my initial awakening was to an uncharacteristically unladylike screech from Moglet.

"Spiced mice! Marooned . . ."

Sitting up and surveying our position I was as inelegant as Corby: "Cripes!" while Puddy was puffing and panting and Pisky, who could see nothing at all except the sky, was rushing around in circles bubbling "Lemme see! Lemme see! Lemmelemmelemmesee . . ."

I lifted him up automatically, tilting his crock and murmuring soothing thought-sounds. Slowly I stood up and gazed at the scene around us. As I said before, it was a beautiful morning, the sun shining on the colouring of the leaves; the breeze, what there was of it, was from the south, birds sang their thin autumn songs and all in all the world seemed a promising place. The woods stood around us on the bank as though there had been no storm of the night before, no rain; the island was the same island, the stunted oak still holding its leaves, the prickly bush discovered as a holly with clusters of berries lightening to crimson, and the dark, secret ivy still clinging to the ground at our feet . . .

It was everything else that was different.

Before we had been surrounded on all sides by black, thick, scummy water, now the island on which we stood was still an island, but an island on dry land. We were about ten feet above the dried-up bed of a lake which had disappeared in the night. The ground beneath our perch was hummocky, pebbly, undulating, bare, but it was not a lake, not a pond, not even a puddle: it was dry, dry as a bone. Wildly I turned about. The bank was the same distance away, the bare expanse on which our islet stood was lake-size, but there was no water, no leeches, no nothing! I gazed down at the lake-bed: no scum, no mud; I looked out over the bare expanse to the lake-middle: stones, sandy soil, bones—bones?—bleached and bare, a heap of rocks in the middle like a sunken cairn, but still no lake, no water . . .

Slowly I sat down again. "What—What happened?"

There was a moment's silence, then Puddy delivered his opinion. "Earthquake."

I looked at Corby.

"The old lad may be right; summat happened, sure enough. Seems the land here rose and the lake drained away when old Mistress went to perdition."

I remembered the thump to the soles of my feet, the roaring noise, the vortex.

Pisky bubbled: "My great-great-great-grandmother told me of somesuch: when there is great evil the land and the sea conspire to destroy it. Earthquakes can happen undersea as well as on land and can swallow whole cities . . ."

Moglet said: "And you called out a spell, Thing; you said neither earth nor air nor water could receive Her body . . ."

"But my feeble curses couldn't have made any difference! Besides, I didn't realize what I was saying at the time."

"Doesn't really matter what did it," said Corby thoughtfully. "There was more'n one thing on our side. The oak, f'r instance: even has a sprig of mistletoe in the crook of that branch . . ."

"Holly and ivy," said Moglet.

"What do you mean?" I asked. "And where is the water?" But they did not answer. I persisted. "What do you mean, holly and ivy and oak and mistletoe? What's that got to do with it?"

Puddy tried to explain. "It's what one's used to: gods and suchlike. Forces. Good and evil."

I remembered him chanting with Corby and turned to Moglet. "Holly and ivy?"

"Older things in the world than we know, and sometimes they can be on your side. Sometimes . . ."

"She was a bad 'un, right enough," said Corby. "Bad through and through. And there was only one place for her." He nodded to the sunken place in the middle of the once-lake. "Down under there is fire like you never did see before, all running and boiling and bubbling like porridge, and that's where She belongs, her and her manikin. Down there all the bad things gets churned up and chewed-like, and then sometimes the old Earth gets indigestion, collywobbles, and burps or farts out the bad airs through them volcanoes and those hot mud-holes what travellers speak of."

"Geysers," said Puddy.

I looked at them with new respect: what a lot they knew! "You mean She won't ever come back? Not ever?"

"Not never," said Corby. "Just bits and pieces, she is now. 'Sides, plughole is blocked with them rocks, see?"

"Then . . . Then we're—we're free?"

"As air—an' twice as hungry . . ."

"Then why . . ." I suddenly felt terribly lonely. "Why does my stomach still hurt?"

We gazed at one another. Moglet tested her paw, and lifted it hastily. Corby stretched his wings: one side went the full distance, not the other.

"Still got heavy head," said Puddy.

I shook Pisky's crock but could see the pearly pebble firmly fixed in his mouth. "So we're not really free at all," I said slowly. "Her spell is still on us."

"Seems so," said Corby. "Yet I would have thought—"

We were interrupted by a wail from Moglet. "I'll never walk properly again! No mice, no birds . . ." and she spat at Corby.

"Now then, now then," he said, backing away. "You're not the only one, you know: Thing here has still got the cramps, and—"

"But not as badly," I said thoughtfully. "And at least we're free of her. There must be a way to break this last spell. Let me think . . ."

But it appeared I was not much good at this; besides, while the others were being quiet to let me concentrate they made a further discovery about themselves which was alien to me, who had spent at least part of my time out of doors when we lived with the witch. The first I knew of this new element in our lives was when Moglet crawled up on my knee and hid her head away from the nice, fresh air in the crook of my arm. A minute or two later she was joined by Puddy, who at least apologized as he crept into a fold of my tattered cloak. Next Corby shuffled up close to me, on the pretence of looking for woodlice under a stone, and Pisky started to swim backwards again.

"All right," I said. "What is it?"

"Outside," said Puddy after a considerable pause, which the others were unwilling, it seemed, to interrupt. "It's big. Bit overwhelming."

"Frightened of the open," supplemented Moglet, sniffling a little. "Not used to it, Thing dear—what happens when it gets dark?"

"Long time since I've been out in the wide-open spaces, as you might call 'em," said Corby. "Bit—well, different you know, if you've been used to a cage of sorts for as long as you can remember. There's rather a lot of it, too, if you follows my meaning: sky and trees and ground . . . Sun's a bit bright, too."

"Know where you are if there's a still crock or bowl," muttered Pisky. "All this moving about and rocking back and forth and jiggling up and down and not a bit of weed to soften the light—"

"Well, you miserable lot!" I cried, jumping to my feet and scattering them like discarded toys. "Here we all are, free from—from Her, and all you can do is grumble! As for all this talk of being afraid of the open air and not liking the sunshine and what happens when it gets dark and being jiggled back and forth—"

"Up and down," said Pisky. "Up and down for jiggles. Back and forth for rocking. I should know! Up and down gives you stomach-wobbles; back and forth makes you water-sick—"

"Oh shut up!" I was becoming exasperated, the more so because, at the moment, I could see no further than the next five minutes, knew they were looking to me for guidance and hadn't the faintest idea how to proceed. So I fell back on anger. "We're free, *free,* don't you realize that? Surely that means something to you after all those years we spent shut up in that hellhole? All you wanted then was to be free and look at you now! Whingeing and crying because you've got what you wanted, but it's going to take a little getting used to! The powers-that-be give me patience! Whatever did I do to be saddled with such a bunch of—of stupid animals!"

I had not meant to say that, and luckily for me they knew it, for even as the bright tears blurred my vision, making the trees on the bank dance up and down like unsteady puppets, I felt a rub of fur around my ankles and Pisky burped past his pebble.

"Don't blame you," said Corby. "Big responsibility, changing one's way of life."

"Insecurity breeds uncertainty," added Puddy.

"Oh, blast you all," I said unsteadily. "I love you all, you know that . . . Right! First thing to do is get off this island, then count up our assets and take a vote on what we do next. We'll go back to the hut and see if there is anything we can salvage, then we'll plan our next move. Any questions? No? Good." And as we climbed down from the islet, with difficulty, I added: "You're not alone in feeling a bit—afraid—of the open, but don't forget most people have managed it all their lives. It's just that we will take a little while to adjust to it, that's all."

I hoped that I was right.

Whatever I had thought to find at our former home I do not know—some food perhaps, clothes, useful things like cooking pots—but my hopes were doomed to disappointment, for as we neared the clearing where we had lived it was obvious that either the villagers had been up all night or they had risen at dawn, for they were there before us. As we crept down the track that led up to the lake we could hear them shouting to one another and banging and clanking, and as we came nearer we slid behind the big bramble bush, Corby hopping off my shoulder, Puddy out of my pocket and Moglet from my arms and Pisky's crock set with its mouth to the scene.

Through the thorned branches I could see our former home, or what was left of it, and that was not much. The hut had been mostly wattle and daub, built on the foundations of an earlier home, basically stone, and the roof had been thatched. I had expected that the roof would have gone and probably much of the upper walls, but what I had not expected was the total destruction that met my eyes. The peasants, some twenty or so of them, mostly men but I counted some women too, were tearing down what remained of the walls and scattering the stones about the clearing, stamping and chanting as they did so, words that, half-heard, appeared to relate to their relief at the disappearance of the witch. It was possible that they did not yet know of her death. What was certain was that they would ensure She would not return to her former home. I saw a large crock of precious salt standing ready: they were even ready to sow this on the ground which had held her, thus ensuring that no plant would grow there for the next ten years, to be infected with the evil she might have left behind.

"I wish I could hear what they are saying," I muttered. "Perhaps if we moved a little closer . . ."

"Not you!" said Corby sharply. "We don't know that they aren't still on the lookout for you, and if they catch you—" He made expressive gurgles in his throat. "Don't forget they will think you and She one and the same."

"I'll go," said Moglet. "I can creep through the grass, and even if I don't understand human speech I can tell by the tone of voice whether they mean us harm."

"Me too," supplemented Puddy. "Won't notice old toad. Perhaps we can hear them think, too."

"Well, just be careful," warned Corby. "Toads and cats are known witch-familiars . . ."

They were back within a half hour or so and the tale they had to tell was disturbing. Apparently some of the villagers had seen our Mistress soaring over the lake and then struck by lightning but were not sure of her fate. The manikin had also been spotted, although a few people thought it might be me, and that I had fallen to earth somewhere and was in hiding. They were going to finish making the hut and its environs unlivable-in, the priest was coming to pronounce a blessing or curse or somesuch, and then they were going to look for me, just to make sure.

"Said they would burn you," said Moglet. "All up, in a bonfire."

Frightened and bewildered, for I had never harmed any of the villagers that I knew of, I glanced round at the others. "What shall I—we—do?"

"Time for a strategic withdrawal," said Corby.

"What's that?"

"Beat a hasty retreat. Come on, where's a handy place to hide till they've cooled off a bit?"

We finally climbed to a convenient perch in the old oak tree that stood at the junction of the path from the lake to the remains of the hut, where it joined another that I used to use down to the village. From here we were hidden and could watch the comings and goings, and were an audience for the priest when he came, incense and all, to cleanse the witch's former abode from any lingering taint of evil. At noon he came back down the path, accompanied by most of the villagers, and I was just going to climb down after they passed for some nuts and berries at least, for we were all starving, when a shouting arose from the direction of the lake and a youngster dashed past down the road that led to the village and was stopped by two tardy peasants returning from the hut with the empty salt crock.

"Whoa there, lad," said one of the men, neatly stopping the boy by dint of tripping him full-length. "What be your hurry, now?"

"They've been up to the lake," he gasped, winded. "Found the bones of those drownded all that long time ago and ol' witch's burnt-out stick and no water left, none at all. I've to fetch the priest again and a cart for the bones so's they get decent burial . . ."

"Well, get along then," muttered the other and aimed a kick as the lad staggered to his feet again and set off running. "Come on, Matt: I've a mind to see all this for meself."

And the two left the crock where it was and set off at a fast pace for the lake.

Again I was about to climb down and seek sustenance when Moglet growled "Wait!" and a moment or two later it seemed the whole village streamed away below us in the direction of the lake; men and women, some still with tools or pots in hand; children and babes-in-arms, the latter carried by their siblings; the old and lame and fat on sticks and one in a litter. I even noted the village whore, dressing herself as she went, arguing with a sheepish fellow who was apparently unwilling to pay the full price for an obviously interrupted session. Bringing up the rear, jouncing and rattling on the uneven track, came a large cart driven by the miller and filled with his wife and the priest, once again hung all about with crosses and baubles and beads and robes and candles.

We waited for a moment or two longer when they had passed, until we heard shouts and exclamations from the lakeside, then I jumped down and extricated the others, arranging them on my person like a verderer's gibbet, for that seemed the quickest way to travel.

"Where now?" I panted, for together they were no light weight.

Corby spoke in my ear, claws firm on my shoulder. "Now, if'n they are looking for you, where's the last place they'd look?" And as I still did not understand he tweaked my hair. "Come on, Thing, where's your brains? Where's the one place they ain't at, right now?"

"Ow! The village?"

"Right! Best foot forward now, and see if we can't make summat of this yet!"

Ten minutes later we stood in an empty village square. Doors and windows swung open, piglets rootled, a tethered dog barked, chickens pecked at the dirt, but of people there was no sign. I had never had time to stand and admire the buildings before, for my visits to the market had been short, sharp, fear-filled: in and out as quickly as possible before someone threw a stone, or worse. But our Mistress's money had been good, and I was always charged over the odds for even the scraps she had me buy. Money! Suddenly I remembered: the money she had given me the night before—was it only a few hours past? It seemed like a year!—was it still in my pocket? Frantically I felt about. Yes! I drew them out into my hand: three small gold pieces, three large silver ones, six copper coins.

"We're rich!" I shouted. "Look, Corby, Moglet: I can buy stores to take with us . . ."

"Buy? Buy!" snorted Corby. "Why buy? There's no one about, things are here to take—and do keep your voice down, Thing, there might just be someone still here!"

"But I can't just take things: that would be stealing, and then they really would be after us!"

"They're after us anyway, by all accounts, and you might as well be hung for stealing as burnt for summat you ain't done! Come on, don't they owe us something for all the hard words you had and the shit they chucked after you? We'll only take what's necessary: it's for the sake of us all . . . Hurry, do!"

We needed food: a small sack of flour, a joint of fatty ham, a piece of cheese, half-a-pound of salt. All this went into a sack, together with a cooking pan, a large spoon and a couple of wooden dishes; I had my sharp knife, almost dagger-long, and flint and tinder, and I thought a length of fine rope and a small trowel would come in useful. Needle and thread were necessaries, filched from someone's workbasket. Anything else? Well, if I were to look tidily inconspicuous I would need a new cloak, preferably with a hood, my hose was a disgrace, and I had no shoes. I was tempted by yellow stockings and a red jacket, but in the end settled for brown wool hose, sensible short boots, and a splendid cloak that almost reached my ankles, with a deep hood, all in a mixture of dyed green, brown and black threads and thick as two pennies laid together. I think it belonged to the priest, for it lay just within the church porch. I also took a length of linen and a piece of leather, for I thought they might come in useful, too.

The only trouble with stealing was that you got used to it with alarming rapidity, and my greed nearly had us caught. Puddy had just found the most useful thing yet, a green glass bottle with a fat belly, a sensible corked top and threaded all about with a net of twine, ideal for carrying Pisky, and I entered the shop where he had found it. It was full of jars, boxes, containers, bottles, chests and other paraphernalia and I set down everything I had gathered just to admire and then covet an utterly useless bowl with decoration of interlacing gold snakes on its rim, when there was a squawk from Corby outside and Moglet came racing in, bad paw and all.

"Quick!" she mewed. "Some of them are coming back! Oh, Thing dear, please hurry!"

For a moment I panicked, then common sense reasserted itself. "How many?"

"Two—three. Old woman with stick, girl, young man."

"That'll be Gammer Thatcher: she lives at the far end with her daughter and son-in-law. Bad-tempered old soul: probably couldn't get to the lake fast enough to get a good view so pretended she was ill . . ."

I had a few moments to get myself ready. Rope round middle with knife; sack full on my right shoulder; Pisky transferred (only for a short while I hoped) to carrying-bottle—not without protest—and slung from my waist; Puddy in pocket, Corby on left shoulder, Moglet tucked in my jacket, new cloak over all.

"Ready?"

A muffled: "Yes . . . S'pose so . . . Just don't jiggle up and down . . .

Headache . . ." and I stuck my nose out of the doorway. All clear. Keeping to the sides of houses, scuttling behind the church, I soon left the village behind and found myself in unknown territory. Ahead was a track leading through fields of harvested grain, an orchard, a vegetable patch and ahead, low scrub melting into forest. A path led off to the left across the fields, another to the right, behind us the track back to the village.

"Which way?" It may sound stupid, but provisioning and unaccustomed freedom had taken up all my thoughts. Where and why were new.

"Away from the village," suggested Corby sensibly.

"Under cover," added Puddy.

A donkey, tethered on common ground to our right, trotted over as far as his tether would allow, and I more or less understood what he was trying to say.

"Want directions? Cut my rope, let me get at those thistles over yon, and I'll tell you which way is best."

Three minutes later we left him chewing ecstatically, safe in the knowledge that to the left was marsh and, eventually, sea; to the right the track led back to the lake; but straight ahead if we walked about two miles, we came to a great ditch that marked the boundary between the lord of this demesne and the next, and beyond that was forest for days. Once beyond the boundary none from this place could pursue . . .

We took the middle road.

The Gathering: Three, Four, Five, Six, Seven

The Fellowship of the Pebbles

Climbing up into a tree is normally fairly easy, climbing down the same. Sitting in a tree and just relaxing is a fine way to enjoy oneself, while the world passes by beneath. Using the vantage-point of a tree to spy out one's surroundings, or as an emergency escape route is useful too, but I had never tried sleeping in one. All night . . .

In theory it is a very good idea if you are travelling light with no fixed idea where you will find yourself at nightfall, and are too small a party to risk wolf, boar or robber by staying on the ground, and there are no convenient caves, ricks or ruins to provide shelter. Just find a nice, comfortable-looking tree with a fork in the main branches for a sleeping-place and lowest support not too far from the ground, hoist your belongings up with a rope and follow. Settle your bits and pieces in a convenient niche or crook, lean back in comfort against the main trunk of the tree and spread your legs along a branch or even let them dangle. Wrap your cloak about you and wriggle comfortable; tuck your hands around your body to keep them warm, close your eyes, listen to the pleasant little rustles and chirps of the nightlife around you and—

"Want to get down," said Moglet. "Must . . . You know."

"Oh dear . . . Can't you just do as Corby does? Over the edge?"

"Can't. It's . . . private. *You* wouldn't . . ."

"Maybe not, but I saw to all that before I came up here!"

Perhaps I should have said that all the necessary functions should be attended to before climbing the tree. So, now compose yourself for sleep, shut your eyes and—

Crash!!

"Bloody hell!"

Peering down from the branches: "What on earth are you doing, Corby?"

"What the bleedin' hell do you think I'm doing? Fell off, din't I? Trying to get me balance on that rotten branch, weren't I? Cracked, din't it? Well, what you waiting for? Not an effing squirrel am I?"

For the third time compose yourself for sleep, listen to the pleasant night-sounds—

Screech!!!

I should also add that if there is the slightest chance that a screech-owl might startle you out of your wits, it is perhaps a wise precaution to attach yourself securely to the trunk so that you do not fall out of it yourself.

One last word on trees as sleeping-places: they look much more comfortable than they really are, and in some of them, especially the more bendy and wavy ones, the actual motion when there is a wind blowing can make toads and fish sick—if, of course, you are idiot enough to take them up there in the first place.

We stood three nights of this, and could have made little more than six leagues progress during the days, when I called a conference.

"Now, listen!" I said. "We can't go on like this . . ." I was raggedy at the edges from lack of sleep and jumped and twitched at every sound, so had decided we would rest in the middle of the day and, leaving Corby as notional lookout, we had all settled under the shelter of a huge beech and slept for a couple of hours. Then I had lit a cautious fire—our first—and made thin pancakes to eat with a slice of the fatty ham. It tasted like the best food I had had for ages, and I had finished with a handful of late brambles and some just-ripe hazelnuts. Moglet had shared the ham and I had shovelled away at the earth under the nearest heap of leaves to provide a feast of insects and worms for Corby and Puddy, and had as usual coaxed a sliver round Pisky's pebble. We were fed, a little rested and warm and now, while daylight chased fears away, would be the best time to pool our ideas and decide where we were going, why and how. I knew animals found it difficult to concentrate, certainly on abstracts, for any length of time, so decided to keep it as simple as possible.

"We have been on the road—all right, Moglet, through the forest and in the trees—for nearly four days now; food is running short, we haven't had much sleep and we haven't made much progress, either. I reckon at this pace we might make a hundred miles by next new moon—if we survive that long. And we don't even know which way we're going, or why . . ." I glanced around at them, all attention, for the moment. "Now, let's think about this. Firstly: what was the most important thing we did four days ago?"

"Escaped from Her," suggested Moglet.

"Good! That was what was more important than anything else at the time. And we did it: we escaped! More by good luck and—" I glanced at Corby and Puddy, "—and a few charms than our own skill, perhaps. That was step number one. What was most important next?"

"Getting you—and us, probably—away from those nasty minded villagers, I reckon," said Corby.

"Right again. So we've managed two important things: we've gained our freedom, and we've kept it—so far. But what is most important to us now?"

"Food," said Corby.

"Water," said Pisky.

"Shelter," said Moglet.

"Safety," said Puddy.

"All short-time daily goals, yes," I said. "But what about the longer term? Why are we all together like this? What are we aiming for? What's stopping us, for instance, just splitting up and going our separate ways and finding different homes or colonies or ponds or what?"

And it was the usually feather-brained Puddy who got it right, rushing around his bowl in great excitement, making wavelets splash against the sides in his desire to get it out.

"We want to get rid of the nasty pebbles so we can eat and stretch and fly and walk and not be bad-tempered with headaches all the time," and he bumped his nose against the glass in the direction of Puddy. "We aren't any of us really free till we do that. Not until I have a pond of golden wives, Puddy has a lady toad and plenty of stones to hide under, Corby can go off and swim through the air again, the cat has cream and a fire and can go hunting at nights and you, dear Thing, can walk upright and not have cramps in your belly . . . So, can I have some sand and a nice plant in my bowl now 'cos I'm clever and it takes a golden king-carp like me to tell you what you ought to know anyway, and I want the plant now and how about another slice of that centipede or midge or whatever it was—"

I clapped my hands then, both to stop and applaud him. "What a clever king-carp! Yes, that is just what I meant. We are all here and belong together because we have a common aim: we want to get rid of these hurting, disfiguring pebbles! They have been with us ever since we can remember—and that's another thing: do any of you find you are recalling more about the time before?"

It was a regrettable digression for they all spent the next quarter hour telling me of brief flashes of memory they had experienced. I had had these too: I could remember now some time when I was without my burden; a pleasant villa in the country, a brown-faced nurse, music from a tinkling fountain—

"All right, all right!" I clapped my hands again. "So, for all of us, part of our Mistress's curse is wearing off. But not these burdens," and I touched my stomach, Corby's wing, Moglet's paw, Puddy's forehead and dipped my finger to Pisky's mouth. "So this is a stronger spell, but one we must be rid of if we are to lead normal lives, as Pisky suggests."

He stood on his tail and waved his fins but I interrupted quickly before he could remind us again about sand and plant.

"Now none of us can remember the stones being put in place, but that our Mistress set great store by them there is no doubt. There is another thing, too: She was so frightened lest they be discovered that she covered them all with a disguise of skin. Each of your pebbles, whether you can see them or not, is hidden under a covering like a blister: this is one of the things that makes me think they were stolen. What is more, I believe they were all stolen of a piece from the same person, for if you remember when we were apart from each other she would chastise us unmercifully, yet when you clustered under my cloak she would not dare touch us herself but would order Broom to beat me . . ."

"Brave Thing," murmured Puddy.

"Saved us all," said Moglet, and nuzzled against my hand.

"Nonsense," I said gruffly. "What I was trying to get at was that once the stones were together within us, near touching, they themselves gave us some sort of protection. A sort of power, if you like . . ."

"The Fellowship of the Pebbles?" suggested Corby caustically.

"Don't be silly! And yet . . . Yes, perhaps even that. This is why we must stay together for our own protection and seek the owner of these stones, for obviously they must be important to him. Or her. We must find this mysterious person and ask them to take the pebbles back. They will know how to remove them without hurting us." I hoped I was right. "But where do we look? That's our real problem."

They were all silent for a minute or two.

"Can't be from nearby," considered Puddy. "She'd never risk nearby."

"How do we know the owner won't kill us when he finds us, or we find him?" said Corby. "May think we pinched the bloody things!"

"It's a possibility," I admitted. "But we shall just have to explain. After all, only an idiot would burden themselves with these things voluntarily, and might be even bigger idiots to return them. I think that whoever it is will be so glad to have them back that he will reward rather than punish."

"Could be an ogre," said Moglet nervously. "Or another witch. Or a dragon . . ."

But at this Corby, Puddy and myself all jeered: there weren't any dragons. They were just a myth, a tale to frighten children.

"Now, concentrate: how do we go about looking for him, this pebble-owner?"

We were silent again for a while.

"Ask someone?" said Moglet.

"But who?" said Corby. "Use your chump, feline. Most people wouldn't have any idea what we were talking about."

"Magician might know the answer," said Puddy. "Or wise man. Or sage."

"A good idea," I said. "But how does one go about finding one? And how would we know we were going in the right direction? I don't even know whether there are any magicians or wise men any more, like Moglet's dragon—"

"My great-great-great-great-great-great-great-great-greatgrandfather used to live in a lake where dragon-shadows floated over like kites at noonday," said Pisky unexpectedly. "All colours they were, like jewels, and they sang songs like cymbals and temple-gongs . . ."

"But that must have been a long, long time ago," I said gently. "For each generation of king-carp lives for a great many years. No, I think we must try and find the owner of these stones. Somehow we must decide on a direction and it must be the right one, then when we have done that we can worry about food and transport and the quickest way of getting there.

"Now, can any of you remember anything the Mistress ever said or hinted or implied that might give us some idea where these came from?"

We all thought. I could recall little except that She had always seemed nervous that the pebbles would be found; not by the villagers certainly, for she was always contemptuous of them, and there were only certain times when she would not let me, who carried one of the stones in my navel for any to discover, out of the hut on errands. In winter I had been glad not to go when the easterly wind howled across the icy meadows, or when the wind veered northerly and flakes of snow or sleet stung one's cheeks; but sometimes when those same winds brought long, hot days, settled weather and even the far distant smell of the seas over which it had travelled—

But Corby was there before me. "There were times when she wouldn't let you out, Thing, even though we were down on provisions, times when it seemed she tested the wind to see if it blew too strong from one direction, or near it. Then she kept us all close, even in the hottest weather, when all within stank, as though she feared the scent would be carried downwind too far."

"The east wind," said Puddy, "and the northeast. So, who looks for these pebbles lives to the west, or southwest. That is the way we must go."

It was so simple, now we came to consider it! And the very next pond we came to Pisky was given his layer of sand, fresh water and a little green plant with two snails on it for company. He was so proud and happy that he was like a housewife in spring, moving that plant busily from one side of the bowl to the other, until Moglet remarked that perhaps we should fit wheels to it. The snails, too, though of somewhat limited intelligence, discovered something neither Pisky nor I had: the pebble would revolve in the fish's mouth and therefore, with some reminding, they would make a paste of whatever I offered Pisky, smear it on the pebble and revolve that segment into his mouth, which kept him going and was one less chore to worry about.

From then on, perhaps because we had a definite goal in view, however vast and faraway was the southwest, we made better progress and the weather held good for us. Now was the month of Leaf-Change, so we hastened as well as we could to beat the frosts of Leaf-Fall, splitting our sleeping into an hour or two at midday and pressing on well into dusk before seeking shelter and rising again at dawn. I had crept into a couple of villages we passed, usually at twilight when my appearance would cause less comment, for more flour, cheese and eggs, and supplemented this diet with berries, roots and nuts, and we were only hungry half the time.

Then with the new moon the weather changed and we ran into rain and wind, a roaring wind that swung crazily from south to northwest and back again, and we were chased from the shelter of barn by barking dogs, from warm rick by angry farmer. Corby was not too bad, Pisky of course couldn't care less and Puddy was more or less comfortable, but Moglet and I were thoroughly wet and miserable and shivered and growled and spat at ourselves and the others impartially. My cloak was reasonably weatherproof, but there came a time when it was so waterlogged and heavy that it would have been a pleasure to throw it away, and one night when it was too wet to light a fire and the flour and salt were damp and the cheese mouldy, I just threw myself on the ground scattering sack and animals anywhere, and sobbed my despair.

"Oh, I wish I were dead!"

The Gathering: Three, Four, Five, Six, Seven

Mushroom-Eaters

"Now then, that's no way for youngsters with all their life afore them to be speaking! Just a little rain it is and isn't the earth glad, her being so thirsty after the suns of ripening? And the wind running free like a 'prentice let out early . . . And can't you smell the salt of the sea and the pines and the black rocks and the heather and curving downs that he brings with him?" The voice was high, light and ran on like a stream over small stones.

At the first words I had sprung to my feet, knife at the ready, and of course all my friends were now clustered under my cloak, hampering any footwork I might need. But as the voice went on and on soothingly, a hand holding a flickering lantern appeared from beneath the stranger's cloak, was held steady for a moment and then moved slowly up and down so we could see who was speaking.

A tall, tall man, seeming almost as tall as a tree in that flickering, smoky light, and as thin as a shadow seen sideways. Clothes all browns and greens, like the earth and the grass and the leaves, and then a merry red cap atop an untidy cluster of black curls, all twisted and gnarled like the potbound roots of a youngling tree. A face round and guileless as a child's, full red lips and rosy cheeks, but skin tanned and seamed like leather; a pair of snapping black eyes, by turns bright and shy.

The figure bowed and set down a covered basket.

"Thomas Herrilees Trundleweed at your service, Missy. Commonly known as Mushroom Tom, by'r leave. On account of my tasting 'em and treasuring 'em, and gathering 'em and selling 'em, too. Out in all weathers I am, best to find my little darlings and talk to 'em and tickle 'em awake and pluck 'em and eat 'em raw, or cooked in a little butter, or added to a stew, or even dried at a pinch . . . And whom may I have the honour of addressing?"

His flow of talk was having its soothing effect on me, and apparently on the others as well: Moglet's fur flattened again. "Seems all right, Thing dear . . ." Corby rearranged his feathers. "Hmmm . . . Harmless enough, I reckon; still, keep a hand to that knife." Puddy snorted: "Mushrooms!" while Pisky rushed round and round, dislodging the disgusted snails: "My great-great-great-aunt on the paternal side told me of the efficacious properties of fungi . . ."

All this communication took but a moment, then I bowed in return.

"My name—my name is Thing, and these are my friends," and I introduced them.

"Thing? A Thing is a thing is a Thing—and there's more to you than a name, I'll be bound, you and your friends . . . Still, a merry meeting, masters and mistresses all!" He hesitated a moment then smiled, showing strong, long teeth rather like a horse. "None of my business why you are all out in the wet on a night like this, but Tom fancies company and has a pot bubbling and a fire burning just a little-ways ahead. Perhaps you travellers would do me the honour to share both, and perhaps a tale or two to brighten the evening?"

It would have been churlish to refuse, but anyway I had the feeling it would be all right, especially as Moglet needed no second invitation but was curling herself around his ankles, while Corby gave an approving "Caw!" So we followed him down an almost invisible trail to the right to find a ruined cottage with half its roof sagging to make the inside like a cave, and the aroma of a stew, that smelt like pigeon and hare and onions and turnip and mushroom, hit me like a blow to my empty stomach. A fire burned brightly in the old fireplace and a trickle of smoke rose from the hole in the turved roof.

We crowded in and Tom let down a flap of hide to make us enclosed and cosy.

"There, now! That's something like, isn't it?" Without waiting for an answer he had my wet cloak hanging over a rail near the fire, stoked the fire with more peat and wood till it blazed high, tasted the stew, brought forward a bundle of heather for me to sit on and with a wave of his hand invited us all to sit round the fire. "Now, who's hungry?"

Some half-hour later I leant back and licked my wooden platter clean. "Mmmm . . . That was the best meal I've ever tasted. Thanks!"

"Best till next time as you're starving and cold! That's one of the best things about food: every much-needed time is the best. Like love . . ." He stared at the fire. "All warm and cosy, now?"

I glanced round at the others: Puddy had earlier found some disgusting scuttling things in a corner and was nodding happily; Pisky burped round the remnants of the paste from the bread that had accompanied the meal; Corby was perched on a stack of logs, already half-asleep, and my little cat, her creamy black-barred stomach as tight as a barrel, was stretched out on the hearth, paws and eyes dream-twitching.

"Seems so," I said. "I don't know how to thank you. We—or I at least—had come to the end of my tether, I think. We all started out with such high hopes, but it's so slow, and winter's coming on and there is so far to go—" I shut my mouth with a snap, realizing I had said too much.

But Tom didn't seem to notice, stretching behind him for a flask. "Perhaps you'll join me in a little nightcap? Very thing to settle the stomach, soothe the nerves, dissipate the ill-humours that a soaking may bring and avert the chills: you don't want to be sneezing and coughing and shivering tomorrow, now do you?"

It was the last that decided me. I didn't want to catch cold, and the liquid looked innocuous enough. I had heard of drugs and suchlike, but if I were to watch him drink some first . . . I accepted the little horn cup he offered, and pretended to sip.

He laughed. "Nay, it's not poison, little Missy, and 'twill do you no harm. See, I'll drink some first," and he swallowed half his cup. I took a cautious sip: it tasted of honey, sunshine and herbs and ran down my throat like hot soup: unlike hot soup the warmth seemed to spread into my stomach, chest and limbs till I felt warm to my toes. I took another sip: definitely more-ish.

"Nice," I murmured.

He topped up my cup. "Drink up, then: plenty more where that came from." Leaning forward he appeared to throw some dust onto the fire: immediately it flared up then died down again and now appeared to shimmer like silk, all colours, red, blue, green, purple . . . In its depths I saw great trees as high as hills, hills as tall as mountains, and mountains touching the clouds . . . Little faces peeped out of the corners, cheeky mischievous faces which thumbed their noses at me and giggled. A fiery snake coiled itself into a knot and interlaced itself with another. Great molten rivers ran, earth shifted, winds blew, seas came and went, sun and moon and stars ran together in a mad dance . . .

"And where did you say you were going?" said someone.

"To find the owner of the pebbles, somewhere in the southwest. But maybe first a wise man, a sage, to show us the right path . . ."

"And where do you come from? And why? And how?" The voice seemed to come from the fire and dreamily I answered it, dreamily I told the fire the whole story.

"There now," said the fire. "There now . . . Finish your drink and lie down by me and rest till morning. There's nothing to fear and you are safe and your friends are safe and travelling will wait till later . . ."

I felt the spring of dried heather and bracken beneath me, a cloak over me, heard the rain pattering harmless on the roof, had Moglet curled up against my chest and I was warm and full and safe and so, so tired . . .

"You told him everything!" accused Moglet. "Every single thing!"

"All about the pebbles," added Corby. "And about the Mistress and Shape-Changing and her manikin."

"And about trying to find someone to take this great lump out of my mouth so I can eat again properly: I've never heard so much talk since my great-great-aunt on the maternal side came back from—"

"And about losing our memories and not knowing where we came from," added Puddy.

I had awoken some five minutes past. It was obviously well on into the morning, though no sun shone; it was not raining either, though the air was damp. Beside me the fire was damped down, a thin wisp of smoke curling up with its acrid, peaty smell. Swung over the fire was a small pot, contents simmering, and on a rack above my small sacks of flour and salt were drying.

"Did I?" I couldn't remember. I only knew that I felt rested as I had not in years, warm and comfortable, and extraordinarily well-disposed to the world in general.

"It was that drink that done it," said Corby. "Loosened your tongue something frightful!"

"My paternal grandfather's cousin twice removed—no, thrice times—told me sometimes men fell into the waters and drowned because of strong liquor," added Pisky, unhelpfully I thought, seeing there was nothing but his bowl for me to fall into.

I took refuge in indignation. "Well you lot didn't try and stop me! You were all flat out and snoring like pigs, as I remember . . . And, after all, what harm did it do?"

"Why, none at all, none at all," came a voice from the doorway. "Old Tom's got more than one secret tucked away in his noddle, and no one the wiser." And he came in, smelling of falling leaves and earth, in his hands a flat basket of mushrooms. "Mind you, there's not all of it I understood: 'tis a long time since you've used proper speech, aren't it, my flower?"

At his last words something flashed into my mind and was gone again, as swift as a blink. "Proper speech?" I said. "And why did you call me your flower?"

"Manner of speaking," he said easily, and bent over the pot to stir it. "As to speechifying: well, I understand a lot of what the birds and the trees and the creatures says, being as I've lived here and abouts many, many years, but though I reckon you can understand me well enough, some of your words come out like a man with the runs, all anyhow and in a hurry. Now then, 'tis breaking-fast time." And he held out his hand for my bowl. Thick gruel, nutty and sharp, with honey on mine, but none on Moglet's. Corby had a strip of dried meat, Puddy found something to his satisfaction in the hearth, and a small gobbet of the same, squashed, satisfied both Pisky and the snails. I had a second helping.

When we were all satisfied, Tom squatted down on his heels and tickled Moglet under her chin. "Like to come a-mushrooming, then? We've some six hours of daylight, and—"

"We really should get on," I interrupted, getting to my feet. "Thank you all the same."

"—of those perhaps two, two and a half will be fine," he went on, as though I had not spoken. "'Twill rain heavy again tonight, but clear by midnight and wind'll veer southeast for a day or two's fine weather. So, there's no point in you a-setting off till the morrow, to get wet again. 'Sides, then

I can put you on the road to another night's shelter and a lift partways, if'n I can get my baskets full. So, how do you say you help a man out for an hour or so?"

I learnt a lot in those two hours, about both mushrooms and fungi. I learnt to recognize the poisonous ones, especially the most dangerous of all, Death-Cap, deadly even to touch; I learnt that the prettiest—Red-Cap, Yellow-Belly, Blue-Legs, Blood-Hose and Magpie, the latter little white stars on black—were harmless but tasted foul, but that some that looked disgusting, like the tattered Horn of Plenty, the wavy-wild Chanterelle and the Oyster, the dull Cob and the Green-Nut, can all be cooked or eaten raw. Tom also gathered some he would not show me—"Later, Flower, later" —and with Corby's keen eyes and Puddy's ground-level view we had two baskets full before it started to spit with rain. We must have covered at least four or five miles, but had circled and were within easy distance of the ruined cottage, so did not get too wet. Moglet and Pisky, left behind at their own request, had obviously been idling away the day in sleep for they were both lively and hungry when we returned; I pointed Moglet to a rather large and hairy spider with short legs—the sort that go plop! when they drop off a shelf—and told her to cull it for Puddy and Pisky, but she pretended she couldn't see it: I think she was frightened of spiders. Tom set me to making oatcakes and getting a good blaze going, then fished around outside for a crock containing fat. He produced a large pan and some slices of smoked ham from a flank hung in the rafters and fried these up with a handful or two of mushrooms, including the raggedy Chanterelle we had picked and before long the insidious good smells were making us drool.

I fetched a jug of water from a stream some two hundred yards away and we feasted like kings, forcing me to say with a grin: "You were right: every much-needed time is best! I shall know how to find those mushrooms again and they will help our diet on—on the way . . ."

"Mind you, most of those we saw today you'll only see in woods: a tree-mixture, with some oak and some birch thrown in, is best."

"Well, I suppose we shall find plenty of woods: it's safer travel that way, rather than trying the roads . . ." I hesitated: I still couldn't remember, but the others had said—"I believe I told you all about us last night?"

He chuckled. "A goodly tale, and one to keep old Tom a-thinking on cold, dark nights!"

"It wasn't just a tale, it was true, all of it! At least, so the others say," I amended. "I don't really remember what I said . . ."

"Didn't say as how it wasn't true, just said it was the kind of tale to keep a man awake at night and wondering . . . You did say as you were a-looking for the party as those—pebbles, as you call 'em—belong to, and thinks your way might lie southwestish: well, I think as you are travelling in the right direction. As for finding a wise man or a magician to help you on your ways—well, there's plenty of magic still left in this old world and your direction is as good as any, especially as I heard tell a while back that a venerable sage lived near the sea thataways . . . But that, as I said, was a while ago, when the land was full of battle and surmise, and the beacons flared from down to hill—Why, what's the matter, Flower?"

"Beacons," I murmured, feeling strangely uncomfortable. "I seem to recall something about beacons . . ."

"Memory is a thing that can play strange tricks: it seems yours is buried deep and will only be dug up piece by piece. Don't try too hard, 'twill all come in good time."

I was silent for a while, staring into the fire: ordinary pictures now. "How can we ever thank you?" I said at last. "Not only have you housed and fed us, but taken us at our word and kept our confidence . . ."

"And who else would there be to tell, youngling? 'Sides, Tom's always kept his own counsel since—Never mind . . . You've all been good company, and worth your keep, for Tom gets lonely, sometimes."

"Do you live here all the time?"

"Here? Why, bless me, no! Tom has homes all over the place: he has another ruined cot like this, an abandoned charcoal burner's place, a hollow tree six feet across, a cavelet, even the corner of a derelict cell that once held an eremite—my home is everywhere and nowhere! Meadowland, ditch and hedgerow; pine forest, oak wood; heath, fen and bog, wherever my little darlings grow! And they may be found in the most unexpected places, too: halfway up a tree, under a turd, in among the ashes of last week's campfire . . . And they all have their uses, wet or dry, oh yes!"

And for a moment he looked sly and crafty and I did not like him so much—but then, like sun in and out of cloud, he was his normal, jolly self again.

"And does he live off his mushrooms, you ask yourselves, and the answer is yes: he gathers them and he eats them and he markets them, too. Tom's patch is a hundred miles all ways, give a league or two, and stretches north to where the hills begin and south to the great river; west to the farmlands and east—why, east as far as here, and lucky you are to find him this late, for winter comes and he should be working south now, to fetch up a moon or two hence in a snug little nest he knows."

"It sounds an interesting life," I ventured. "But don't you ever get . . . well, lonely?"

For a moment his face darkened, shadowed, then again he laughed. "No, for I see those I sell to when I have a need for company—and there, my friends, is where you can help me out. I have three baskets of mushrooms here, including those dried, which I would be obliged if you would deliver on your way tomorrow. Then I can stay here a further two-three days and look for some old Tough-Trunks: haven't seen any round here for a couple of years but they makes excellent eating, and if I try a couple of the larger clearings there might be a few left. They likes a bit of air and sun, see, but the shelter of the trees to run to if'n they wants. Left more'n a day or two 'twill be too late, for they're coming to the end of their season. Then, if I'm lucky, I can travel the way you go and pick up goods in pay to see me on my way. The folk I'll send you to will travel the next day to sell in the town, for mushrooms is best fresh, and so they'll carry you in comfort a mile or ten nearer your goal . . . How long is't since you laughed, Flower?"

It seemed such an odd question, coming after all that talk of mushrooms, that I gaped.

"Laughed?"

"Aye, laughed. Rolled around on your belly and held your ribs till they ached, and howled with merriment and joy? Laughed till tears ran from your eyes and your ears hurt?"

I could still only gape at him: I didn't know what he meant. The only laughter I had seen was the wild cackling of our Mistress when something pleased her, and sometimes I had seen young men and girls from the village laughing in the fields at harvest, as they chased each other in and out the stocks of corn, teasing with chaff, dried milkweed or poppy-heads . . .

I didn't know what it was to laugh.

I stretched my mouth as I had seen them do and gave an experimental "Ho-ho-ho, Ha-ha-ha" as I remembered the sound, but it didn't seem quite right and certainly felt very silly. It had an unexpected effect on Tom, too, for it sent him off into paroxysms of giggles that sounded strange coming from a grown man.

"I don't believe you know how!" he accused, and giggled again.

"Can't remember," I said crossly. "What does it matter, anyway? I'm not missing anything."

"Don't be too sure about that, then! All folks feels better after a good laugh: almost as good as a—Never mind: you're too young. Like to try some of Tom's magic?"

"You can do magic?" I gasped.

"Oh, not your old spells and suchlike, only the magic what's in my little friends here," and he opened his pouch and took out some more mushrooms, a large red one with white spots on it and some tiny brown ones with a little knob on top. "This one here, the big fellow, is what they call the Magic Mushroom. Why there are folks overseas who worship this one like a god on account of it gives them pleasant dreams if they take it in moderation, and kills their enemies for them taken in larger amounts: I reckon enough of 'em died finding the right doses . . . I ain't going to give you none of him 'cos you has to think of size and weight and age and tolerance to make the dose right for dreams and wrong for t'other, but these little fellows—Fairies Tits when they're fresh and Mouse-Dugs dried—these fellows I can measure out for you and give you nothing more'n a good laugh or two. Not that they ain't bad when taken too much, but I'll only give you a tickle.

"Well? You looks doubtful: then I'll take 'em too, like the drink last night, but I'll take twice as much . . ."

In the end he persuaded me, not so much from his words as from a mutter from Puddy: "Seen 'em before: not poison in small quantities. No more than the number of my toes, mind . . ."

And that is exactly the number he gave me, lightly cooked in the fat remaining in the pan-juices: fourteen tiny little mushrooms. I tasted one:

nothing special. I waited till he had eaten half his—double my quantity—before I started on the rest.

Then I waited for the laugh. Nothing.

He read my mind. "Oh, you has to linger awhile for them to work . . ."

"How did you come to know so much about mushrooms?" I asked curiously, while I waited.

That darkening of his face again. He seemed to hesitate, then shovelled the rest of his mushrooms into his mouth and drank the pan juices. When he looked at me he was smiling.

"A tale for a tale, then? 'Tain't much, when all's said and done, not really . . .

"Well, see, once Tom loved a fair lady and they lived in a fine house in a town many miles from here. Now Tom had a good living then and they were both happy, this beautiful lady and he, and their happiness was crowned when she told him there was a child on the way. And as is the way with ladies in that condition she came to have strange tastes, wanting things out of season and difficult to come by. But Tom, he kept her satisfied, going miles out of his way for strawberries in April and brambles in June. Then came a time, and she was near her lying-in, when of all things she wanted mushrooms, some of those wood mushrooms that grow best near pines. And Tom knew where he had seen some, near to a clump of fir trees, so off he went and picked them and rushed back and tossed them in a pan and carried them in to her on a silver platter, and she cried with joy when she saw them and kissed her Tom and turned to scoop them to her mouth . . ."

He stopped, and I knew, oh I knew, what was to come next and tried to stop him, but he shook his head.

"Better out than in, Flower . . .

"I should have known that smell: smelt of sleep, smelt of death." Now there was no third-person Tom, it was himself . . . "They was Destroying-Angel, all white in their purity, all black in their intent, and my lady died in agony and the child with her. After that I was a little mad, I think, for they shut me away . . .

"But I had time to think, there in the darkness of soul, and when they finally let me out and I found the business sold and all moneys gone I didn't care: it was the mushrooms that had taken from me all I held dear and by my own ignorance and I swore to spend the rest of my life learning about the little devils until I was always one jump ahead and could fair say I had beaten them at their own game. And so I have.

"So, old Tom's a mushroom expert, you might say . . ."

"I'm sorry," I said.

"No need to be, no need. 'Tis time past, and if there is one thing I did learn then it was to look to time present . . .

"And, talking of the present: how do you feel?"

Now he came to mention it, I was beginning to feel different, as if my stomach had a pleasant little fire chuckling away all warm inside it. The fire light seemed stronger too, making all colours brighter, but a little fuzzy round the edges.

Nice . . .

Then it happened. Tom got up to throw more wood on the fire, slipped, and for a moment, trying to regain his balance, stood on one leg like a heron, lanky and ungainly, arms flapping like wings, and such a comical look of surprise on his face that I felt a little tickle of amusement jerking my tummy, then another and another, till I was like a pot waiting to boil, bottom all covered with bubbles. I couldn't help it: I came to the boil, slowly but surely. Snorts, spasms, gasps all accompanied these completely new feelings till, with a painfulness that only those who laugh out loud but seldom could appreciate, merriment rose to the surface and, once there, wouldn't stop, and I was boiling away like a pot of forgotten water, salted by the tears of laughter that coursed down my cheeks. At first I thought I was dying, for I could not laugh and breathe and cry at the same time and got the hiccoughs, but in the end everything sorted itself out, except that by that time my ribs ached and so did the bones at the back of my ears.

The trouble was that once started, I couldn't stop: Moglet's studied aversion and turned back and Corby's offended stare only set me off worse than ever.

Tom poked me in the ribs: he too was laughing fit to burst, his arms hugging his ribs, knees up to his chin. "Tell—tell me: why—why do you wear that terribly tatty little flap of—of leather? Oh, dear me, what with a fringe of hair like a taggley pony and that flap of hide there's nothing but eyes like post-holes to be seen—oh, dear me!—all across your face."

I giggled helplessly. "'Cos—'cos I look like a fright without! I've worn it ever since—ever since I could remember! Our Mistress made me, so I didn't frighten the villagers to death! Got a face like a—like a cross between a pig and a snake without it . . . Oh, dear: how do you stop laughing? It hurts . . ." And I doubled up.

"How—how do you know what—what you look like, then?"

"Mistress showed me—in a mirror of polished metal . . . Ha! Ha! Ha! You should have seen me! Oh, dear, I shall die if I don't stop this . . . Said I was too ugly to go abroad without a mask, so I made—tee-hee!—this. Ho! Ho! And if any ask—He! He!—I say I am marked bad with the 'pox!"

"You don't mind looking like that, then?"

"Can't, can I? Always have, s'pose . . . Oh, mercy, mercy! Stop making me laugh!"

"What with that mask and walking around doubled up with that—stone—in your stomach, you look—you look much like a hobgoblin!"

"A hob—hobgoblin? Oh dear, yes, I must do! How—how hilarious! What a fright! Enough to scare the children, and the old folk from the chimney-corner . . . He-he-he . . ."

And thus was changed in my mind the hidden hurt of the day when our Mistress had found me trying to gaze at my reflection in a pail of water—just to see whether my fingers lied when they felt a straightish little nose, a wideish mouth and long lashes—and, muttering a few words, had shown me what a horror I really was, in that polished mirror of hers: jutting brow, little snake-like eyes downturned at the corners, a crooked nose, squashed like a pig's, uneven, jagged teeth, and a drooling, loose mouth. The whole face, from brow down, was covered in skin-blemishes: blue scars, pocks and a web of red like a spider's which had spread up from the red pebble in my navel like the plague . . . After that I had begged a piece of soft leather from her and hung it on a thong threaded through the top over my nose and across the rest of my face.

And she had laughed even more when she had seen it.

But now it was I who was laughing, and far harder than she had ever done.

After that I fell suddenly asleep, exhausted by the strange thing called laughter, but the others told me in the morning that even in my dreams I had been giggling happily, though when I awoke I could not recall a single thing.

The Gathering: One, Three, Four, Five, Six, Seven

The White Horse

The last sight we had of that extraordinary man, Thomas Herrilees Trundleweed, was of him bowing us exaggeratedly away, and then striking his head on a branch some seven feet up as he straightened, and being showered thus with last night's raindrops. I had smothered a giggle against the back of my hand, remembering the release of the night before, but he was, by then, too far away to have heard anyway. I was still not sure whether I really liked him, in spite of his kindnesses, for he was too mercurial and fey to understand completely, but I had to admit we had been very well treated and were now better off with a route to follow for the next few miles, full stomachs, dry clothes, fur and feathers, the promise of a lift partways, a grounding in the art of mushrooming—and in the case of the latter, a further present.

That morning Tom had handed me a small package of the dried Mouse-Dugs, as he called them, enough for two adult dosings.

"Though I doubt if you'll find any other that hasn't laughed for seven years . . ." But when I had queried the specific number seven he had just winked and tapped the side of his nose. "It's a number, just like any other, ain't it? 'Sides, old Tom listens to the trees and the birds, don't forget." And that was all I could get out of him, try as I would.

We made fair progress, although the village we were aiming for was a good ten miles away, and arrived soon after noon. Tom's contacts were an elderly couple, quiet and reserved, but ready enough with food and lodging once we had explained who we were; they said that it would be a waste of time to set out for the market till the following morning as it would take at least three hours at their donkey's sedate pace. So I had to curb my natural impatience to get on, and spent the afternoon learning to weave simple baskets and carriers, which was their trade. I grew quite proficient after an hour or so, and by the time the light faded and rushes were lit I had managed a creditable back-carrier, which they gave to me, pointing out that my sack was almost threadbare. The broad top of the carrier meant that there was somewhere for Moglet to perch, so that only one shoulder—Corby's—would be sore, and this I padded with a scrap of leather.

We suppered from fresh bread, goat's milk and cheese, and they parted with some eggs and a loaf for our journey, taking but one copper coin, so we bedded down in the lean-to shed at the side of the cottage with light hearts soon after eating, warned of an early start. They woke us before light as they had stock to feed and the little cart to load with their weavings and the mushrooms and me, and we eventually set off an hour before daybreak, to arrive at the market as early as possible. We slipped away before they came to the town proper, for though neither of them had made any comment about my friends, the woman especially had cast curious glances at my mask, and I judged it better not to risk us with the more open townsfolk.

So, considerably heartened, we set off again on our way south and west. Before long the broad road on which we found ourselves became too well populated, and we took to the byways and woods again, only using the main thoroughfare very early or very late and in this fashion, lucky with our nightly lodgings—ruined hut, upturned wagon, barn and, once, church porch—we made another fifty miles or so.

Then our luck changed. The road we were following took in another and turned to run due southeast/northwest for many miles, and though we followed the left hand for many miles it soon became evident that we were bearing ever more easterly, and when I assisted Corby with his keener eyes to the top of the tallest tree around he came fluttering to earth with the news that there was no change in direction "as far as a crow can see." I was disheartened, for that meant either a detour to find another road, or crossing the present one and plunging into forest that looked far less hospitable than the one we had so recently left. A detour was too risky, so for the next day or two it was scratched arms and legs from briars, whipped head and shoulders from tangled branches and snappy twigs and a rapidly dwindling store of food.

One thing I learnt: staying in one place and going round and about with an expert gathering mushrooms was one thing; gathering them without one on the march was another. You only saw them if they were right in front of you, or at least in eye-reach, and then one had to stop, dislodge Corby, wake up Moglet in the carrying-basket, set down Pisky, where he moaned that he couldn't see, and, if you were lucky, get away without disturbing Puddy in the side-pocket. Then, when you had examined the mushrooms they might turn out to be the wrong sort, or if they were the right kind there weren't enough of them to justify cooking or, more often, they were a species I had not come across before.

We were down to our last handful of flour and a rind of cheese when we came to a small village. Here, in the forest, were signs of cultivation: trees had been lopped and felled for building and fuel and the scrub thinned down in the direction of a navigable river, unluckily flowing the wrong way for us, otherwise I might have risked trying to hire a boat, but here the only transport available seemed to be large working rafts, and I did not have the strength to pole one of those against the current. Leaving the others on a knoll overlooking the river I slipped down to the village and paid the usual stranger's over-price for bread, cheese, apples and a hand of salt pork. This reduced our savings to two silver and two gold coins: these latter I was wary of changing, for the last time I had been short-changed and almost openly accused of being a thief, for obviously no one who looked as I did could possibly come by gold honestly.

I was anxious to rejoin the others as soon as I could because for the last few days, even as the trees had thinned and broadened into great stands of leaf-dropping beech and oak and the going had become easier, I had had the uneasy feeling that we were being followed. Not that there had been anything to see, merely a fleeting impression of something white through the trees to the left, the right; the half-heard sound of a footfall, muffled by leaves, ahead, behind; a soft breathing in the night-hours; a feeling of loneliness, of an empty heart . . . None of the others had seen anything, although they too were uneasy.

However, today the sun was shining full on the knoll, they were safe and sound, and we ate till we were comfortable. Stomach full I felt decidedly soporific: after all, if we had an hour or so's rest now, safe out of sight of the village, it would mean less time tonight in a possibly uncomfortable sleeping-place.

Unbuttoning my jacket to the pleasant rays of the sun, I laid aside my mask and stretched out, pillowing my head on my cloak.

"We'll stay here for a while," I told the others. "Moglet: you can keep half an eye open, can't you?" For I could see that Corby and Puddy fancied some leaf-turning.

Closing my eyes I slipped effortlessly into dreamless sleep.

"Pig, pigs, pig-person! Wake up, Thing—" Moglet's urgent mew in my right ear and I was struggling to open my eyes, to make some sense of what was happening. There was a rootling, grunting, scrunching noise, a strong, not unpleasant piggy smell and then Corby's raucous croak: "Geroff! That's mine, you big bastard! Find your own, you great vat of lard—" and then the sound of a stone striking the earth and a yelp from the crow. I leapt to my feet, the sun in my eyes, and squinted at a herd of swine grunting their way slowly along the fringes of the forest, and standing about six feet away the swineherd, another stone ready to follow the first.

Snatching up my mask with one hand and fumbling with the fastenings of my jacket with the other, I cursed Moglet for not waking me sooner.

"Fell asleep . . . wind in the wrong direction . . ." she whispered.

"Well-now-then," said the swineherd. "What-have-we-here?" Each word was slow, measured, calculating. He was a dirty-looking man, short and squat but powerful. He smelt of pig and frowsty nights of drink and even as I watched he took a flask from his pocket and offered it to me. I shook my head but he took a draught and replaced the stopper but not the flask. Instead he eyed me up and down and smiled. Not a nice smile: his mouth was too fat and he looked to have twice as many teeth as he should, yellow, sharp teeth with little pits in them. His skin, too, was pitted and the pits black; his nose was upturned, the nostrils sprouting black hairs like his ears, and his eyes were too small.

I backed away a step or two and Moglet backed with me, her fur anxious. Out of the corner of my eye I could see Corby hopping up and down, luckily undamaged, and the movement of grass as Puddy crawled closer.

"Keep back," I thought-ordered them. "I don't like the look of this fellow . . ."

"You'd like him even less if you'd had a ruddy great rock up your arse," was Corby's succinct reply. "And we're not abandoning you in a dangerous situation," he added. "Fellow like that means business. Where's your knife?"

"Words first," said Puddy. "Action second if necessary. You've never used that knife in anger . . ." No. It was the one I used for vegetables, peeling and slicing. But it was very sharp.

The swineherd had moved forward as I moved back, and now he was the same distance away as before. "No-harm-meant," he said ingratiatingly, and stretched out his free hand to my still half-covered chest. "Pretty-little-bubs-them. Shame-to-hide-them. Like-to-touch-them-I-would . . ."

I backed away again, looking away past him to where I had left our belongings, with Pisky's bowl in the shade of the wicker carrier. I received his anxiety and sent back a reassurance, but inside I was panicking. I did not know what this man intended: did he mean to kill us for our paltry belongings? He could not know I had our remaining coins hidden away in a pouch in my breeches. Perhaps if I offered them to him he would let us go . . . Frantically I dug down and his eyes followed my hand, his tongue passing slowly over his lips.

"Getting-them-off-for-me-then?" the voice was suggestive, nasty.

I held out the coins. "That's all I have. Please take them and leave us alone . . ."

His eyes lit up and he snatched the coins away from me and bit them. "Good-good . . ." He took another pull from the flask, pulling the cork with his teeth and spitting it to the grass. "Why-don't-you-speak-proper? Why-the-mask? And-what-you-got-over-there?" and he gestured in the direction of our belongings.

He wasn't going to leave us in peace, he wanted everything. "Take it all," I said despairingly. "Except my little fish. Then please let us alone . . ."

He put down the flask and placed the coins atop, where they winked in the sunshine. "Don't-hear-you-right-girl. Ain't-answered-my-questions. Let's-see-what-else-you-got-in-there—" and he made a grab for me but I jumped back, and this time my knife leapt to my hand, glinting to match the coins.

"Let us alone, or I'll—I'll kill you!"

He couldn't reach me but unfortunately Moglet had not moved fast enough and he grabbed her and held her high by the scruff of the neck, his other hand flashing to his own knife. He made as if to strike her and I screamed, a scream that was echoed by a strangled wail from Moglet.

"Help me, Thing dear, help me!"

"No, no!" I yelled. "Anything you want, anything!"

Apparently this time he understood, for he lowered my kitten, but his knife was still at the ready.

"Don't-want-me-to-harm-your-pet? All-right-put-your-knife-down-over-there-and-I'll-let-it-go. That's-right . . ." For a moment longer he held her, then opened his hand and she dropped, choking and gasping, to crawl back to my side. I bent to stroke her, but a moment later a hand was at my throat and I was forced backwards to the ground and his other hand tore at my belt. "Get-'em-down, get-'em-down," he muttered and pulled my trews past my knees. In hideous shame I tried to cover my red-pebbled belly with my hands and roll over, but he slapped my face till my head rang. "Lie-still-curse-you-or-it'll-be-the-worse-for-you—"

At that moment he broke off with a yell for all at once he was attacked by the spitting fury of Puddy, whose venom shot up into his face, the claws of an enraged Moglet, scratching blood from his hands, and the beak of an angry Corby, who tore at his rear.

"Run, Thing, run!" they yelled, but with a fist the swineherd punched Moglet from him, with a foot he kicked Puddy away and his knife flashed within an inch of Corby. I knew it was no use and called on them to stop.

"Go away, go away, my dear ones: you cannot help me now. Go into the forest where he cannot find you, and drag Pisky's bowl with you. I'll be all right, only please, please go!" But still they hesitated, crying and cursing, till I used the words of command. "Go, and do not disobey. I command you by all that holds the Earth, the Waters, the Sky in their accustomed places; the Now, the Then, the Hereafter . . ."

I heard them leave me, and the desolation of the abandoned tied my stomach in knots, spilt the tears from my eyes and cut at my heart as keen as any knife. The sun went behind cloud and the figure standing over me assumed the proportions of a giant. Why doesn't he kill me, I thought, and get it over with? And I sent a hope-call for my dear ones, to be left to fend for themselves. Let them be brave and resourceful, I prayed, let them find their own peace . . .

The swineherd unbuttoned his trousers. Staring upwards, all at once I realized what he intended: he meant to use me as Broom used to punish our Mistress, for the great thing that poked out from his groin was smooth-knobbed, and ridged and gnarled along its length like Broom, and it throbbed and pulsed and swelled like Broom, and like Broom it had a great bush of furze at its base the colour of dead heather, and it waved and nodded and beckoned just like Broom and any moment now it was going to thrust into my stomach where the pebble hurt and bring forth great gouts of blood and pain, and I began to whimper and cry.

"Oh, do not hurt me! Do not hurt me—I cannot stand more pain! Please, please!" I did not want to writhe and curse and bleed as she had done—

The sun came out from behind the clouds, there was a thudding noise on the turf, a wild neighing, and all at once the swineherd was gone, clear over the top of the knoll, and soft horse-breath was sweet on my face.

"Come up, youngling, come up! He is gone and you are safe, for the moment. Gather your things quickly, for he will be back . . ."

I stared up in bewilderment at the tattered, ragged-maned horse that stood over me.

"Gather your things quickly, before he returns," he repeated. "The others are safe: I will take you to them. Come!"

That night we had a fire, and ate at our leisure, and slept in the open. No looking for a tree to climb up, a hole to crawl into; that night we slept at peace for the first time since we had left on our great adventure. It is difficult to explain just why we all felt this sense of security—and we all felt it, not just me—except that the finding of the white horse, or rather his finding of us, was at the root of it all. Not then nor after did we ever question his unerring sense of direction, his knowledge, his warm benignity: we just accepted them, and him as something special.

Not that he was a splendid white stallion of some eighteen hands, like the great chargers I seemed to recall from some other time, some other place; he was small, perhaps a little larger than pony-size, with cloven hooves and tatty feathers, a long tail and mane, curly and tangled, and large, soft, brown eyes. It was probably those eyes that set the seal on it: they seemed brown most of the time, but in sunlight they were blue-green, in shade brown-green and they beamed—there is no other word for it. Reassurance, comfort and a strange other-worldliness shone from those eyes, and yet they were not happy . . .

He promised us nothing that first day, except that he would take us to a place of safety: he had carried us all smoothly and swiftly through the forest, stopping as twilight fell in a particularly pleasant glade to let us down. After gazing at us reassuringly for a moment or two he went to lie down a little distance away, leaving us, as I said, feeling so calm and confident that I had lighted a fire without further thought, and we slept in the open that night all wrapped under my cloak, for the nights were chill—all that is except Corby, who preferred to roost off the ground.

In the morning the white horse was still there, quietly cropping the sweet grass that still lingered in the hollows. He seemed shy of approaching us, so I went across with one of the small russets I had bought the day before.

"Please have one: they are nice and juicy."

Lipping the apple gently from my palm, he scrunched it with evident enjoyment. "Thank you."

"Talking of thanks, I quite forgot to offer mine—and ours—for the rescue and the ride and—and everything."

"I had been near you for some days: I thought sometimes you realized I was near."

"I thought someone, or something, was following us, but I wasn't sure. And if you hadn't, I don't know what would have happened to us. That—that man, with his—his—" I still wasn't sure what it had been.

"I followed you because you seemed a small and vulnerable party to be making your way in such a determined manner, and I was curious. Besides, you are a maiden, and even in my present state I have not forgotten my duties."

"Duties?"

"To defend all maidens and the pure and unsullied from Evil, in whatever form that may come . . ." The answer was confident as if it came from a much bigger animal, but my eyes must have mirrored my astonishment, for the white horse blew softly in my ear. "Things are not always what they seem," he said. "I was not always the wretched thing you see me now . . . No more of that. Now tell me, youngling—"

"My name is Thing," I interrupted. "And may I know just whom I have the honour of addressing?" I knew that was the correct way to ask someone's name because I had overheard two gentlemen meeting on the road one day, and they had addressed one another in just that way. I had crept away and practised it.

"You may, but not just now. Give me a name of your own: whatever you would call a white horse."

I thought of all the things that were white: clouds, linen, daisies, dough (sometimes); swan-feathers, chalk, marble, eggwhite; snow—Snow. "Would you mind if we called you 'Snowy'?"

"I would not mind being called Snowy at all," he said gravely. "I do not think I should have liked 'Doughy' or 'Eggwhitey' as much . . ." He had been reading my mind! That was another thing: all of us could understand him perfectly, but none of us considered this strange, although we had been used to our own methods of conversation for so long. And he seemed to sharpen our understanding of all the other creatures we met along the way, as if he were a catalyst through which all tongues became one. What surprises me now is that we accepted it without question at the time, but perhaps that was all part of his magic, too.

"And now," he said. "Would you like to trust me with your purpose in journeying so far and so poorly attended? I can see you have a tale to tell—but perhaps you would prefer it if we talked as we went? I am afraid I am not strong enough to carry you far in one go, but if you can manage to walk a league, say, and then travel on my back for the same distance, we could probably manage double your usual journeying."

"You go our way, then?" I said, delighted.

"For want of a better, my road lies with yours for a while, yes," replied the gentle creature.

It was a day of sun and shadow, wind and the falling of leaves. As we went I told our new companion our story, right from the beginning. He questioned me closely about our Mistress, then sighed. "You are sure She is indeed dead?"

I was sure, and he sighed again. "Then that is that: no hope that it may be changed." He seemed to make up his mind. "Then, if you will have me, I shall be with you till your journey's end.

"You wanted to find a magician, a wise man: I heard tell of a great sorcerer who lived once in the arm of the west. I had supposed him dead or fled, but you have such faith that it is possible he is still there. If he is, I think I know the way.

"Come, my friends: the sooner we are there the better. I have an idea the hour-glass has been turned for the last time . . ."

The Gathering: One, Two, Three, Four, Five, Six, Seven

The Rusty Knight

It had been a beautiful morning. For some days now we had been following the upstream course of a big river, which the white horse, Snowy, said was called the Tamesis. It was fordable, but he said the going was better on this side and we could make another seven leagues or so before crossing and striking more southward. We had woken that morning to the loud, sweet song of a little wren, and everything touched with frost fingers. It was near the end of the month of Leaf-Fall and soon we should be in the Moon of Mists, but the morning was sparkling and still and clear. We had spent the night cosily enough in an abandoned charcoal-burner's hut, but the sharpness of the morning turned my nose pink and snapped at my cheeks, or so Corby said. "You look just like a ripe apple, m'dear," which was a generous compliment to my maskless face, for I now only wore this disguise if there was a chance of meeting other folk on the way. Not that this was a frequent occurrence, for we left the road if we heard steps on the way, and hid till they were past.

Snowy had made no comment on my disfigured face, for which I was grateful: he just seemed to accept it as the others had. I always considered this a peculiarly delicate gesture on their part, until I overheard Moglet one day remark to Corby: "I don't know why Thing bothers with that silly piece of leather: she looks all right to me," to which the gracious bird replied: "She could be as beautiful as Heaven or ugly as Hell, as the saying goes, and it would be all the same to me: humans all look alike, don't they? I can't tell one from t'other 'cept by their height and the length of their beaks, and hers is nothing to beat the drum for. Now mine, mine you would call a patrician beak . . ."

So much for vanity.

The road swung away from the river for a while and lay between high banks where beards of traveller's joy draped the bushes and blackbirds feasted from the last brambles and watched the haws ripen. We had climbed a little and now stood on an escarpment. To the left, down by the river, a few houses hugged its curves, smoke rising straight and thin into a pale sky. Below us in a clearing was a winter barn full of hay; the southering sun shone on gleaming pebbles on its roof, and only when I saw their restless shift and heard the bubbling chatter carried up to us on the still air did I realize they were those tardy travellers, house martins, adorning like pearls the rough surcoat of the barn roof. Beside the barn someone had planted a line of fruit trees and these, for rapture of the morning, had shed their last leaves to lie, discarded red petticoats, around their feet, and stretched bare silver limbs to embrace the shafted sunlight. Beneath our feet, as we trod the rutted road, fallen leaves leapt away like frogs from our intrusion, and somewhere amidst the smells of cold stone, damp earth and the sweet sweat-smell of Snowy, was the evocative scent of burning apple logs—

"Listen!" It was Moglet, large pointed ears flickering back and forth.

We stopped and at first I could hear nothing, but as I watched the others their reactions told me what was afoot long before the faint sounds reached my ears. It was a stealth of ambush, a fight-back, a battle, and as we hurried towards the sound, half-afraid, half-curious, I found my heart beating with a rare excitement as if something special was about to happen. We rounded a corner, the road dropped away in a steep decline and there beneath us where the road banked high, river on one side, forest the other, a lone man in rusty chain mail was trying to fight off three sneak-thieves with his fists and a broken sword.

Even as we watched he was beaten to his knees then rose again, staggering, with scarce enough breath to call for help, and the next moment returned to the attack, in the name of one St. Patrick. He was a bonny fighter, but I could see he had no chance at all, and would be lucky to escape with a broken skull and the loss of his pack.

I turned impulsively to Snowy. "We must help him! We can't just stand by and let him be killed!"

"Are you sure you want to be involved? We could lie low till they have done . . ."

Somehow I knew this was no cowardice on his part, more a test of me, the biggest coward I knew. But—

"Of course we must help him! We must draw them off, distract them—"

"I can imitate a horn," said Corby, hopping up and down.

"Hear me shriek!" said Moglet.

"Poison in their eyes," muttered Puddy.

"You can borrow my water," bubbled Pisky. "But only borrow, mind . . ."

"Right," said Snowy. "I shall gallop round through the trees and try to sound like a troop of horses, dropping you off, crow, to make your horn-calls on the other side of the road, with cat doing her screeches. Toad, you shall be left nearer to aim your poison, and the maid here shall hide in the trees with the fish and bang against a pan and shout 'A rescue! A rescue!' in as deep a voice as she can. Ready?"

We had no time to think. Up on Snowy's back, then away like the wind down through the trees and into action. It was wildly improbable, highly dangerous, wholly exhilarating—and it worked. A perfect cacophony of horn and trumpets sounded from the river side of the road, accompanied by ear-splitting screeches. A cavalcade of horsemen thundered through the woods; one attacker was half-blinded by an evil jet of poison that shot from the bushes at his feet and my clattering sounded like at least three men in armour blundering through the trees. In a moment the three attackers were flying for their lives down the road away from us, leaving a huddled figure heaped in the ditch, pack still intact by its side. We approached warily from our various concealments, one eye on the dust of the attackers' retreat, the other on the victim. The only one making any noise was Pisky, furious at not being allowed to help in the attack, sulking vociferously at the bottom of his bowl.

The knight lay on his face in the muddy ditch.

"He's awfully still," I said doubtfully.

Puddy hopped closer. "He's breathing, though."

"All bloody," said Moglet. "Not nice . . ."

"I've seen worse get up and walk," said Corby. "But not much."

Pisky decided to ignore the whole thing.

"Well," said Snowy, "we should get him away from here in case they come back; we should be safer under cover. If you will pull him on to my back and walk beside to keep him steady we can make a mile or two to an abandoned anchorite's cell I know of in the forest. Can you manage his pack as well?"

Somehow we did manage, though we were all exhausted when at last we laid him on the floor of the cell, a gloomy place that smelt of old bones and cat-piss. I placed the knight's head on his pack, but carefully because the back of his head was sticky with blood, and covered him with my cloak. He moaned a little and moved his legs, so we knew they weren't broken; I flexed his arms: they were whole too, though his knuckles were broken and bruised with the fighting. He seemed to be whole in body, no holes or gashes, but I fancied from the bruising and his ragged breathing that a couple of ribs might be broken, but I dared not completely remove his rusty chainmail coat to confirm this. His head seemed worst hurt: it bled freely from a gash on his forehead, he had a black eye and a bloody nose, but these would heal; I was more worried about the injury at the back: a lump was already forming, though the blood oozed more slowly now.

I sat up from my examination. "Can we light a fire? He's very cold . . ."

"We're safe enough here," said Snowy.

Corby rattled off for some twigs for kindling, I found some larger pieces of branch and soon we had a fire blazing away in the corner. I remembered the so far unused piece of linen I had taken from our village, what seemed so long ago, and knew at last how to make my peace with Pisky as well. With dampened cloth, carefully dipped in his bowl, I wiped away the worst of the blood from the knight's head and bound up his wound as best I could; he moaned a little and grimaced but still remained unconscious, and I looked up anxiously at Snowy.

"Will he be all right?"

"Lift his head a little and give him half a cup of water from Pisky's bowl. Wait: put the cup on the ground," and I watched as he bent his head and covered it with his mane. I wondered for a moment whether he was checking for weed or snails, but when he nodded to me to take up the cup the liquid within was warm and cloudy and smelt of herbs. "Now, give him a drink."

I put the cup to his lips. "Drink, Sir Knight: you are in safe hands."

Obediently he swallowed the liquid and, as I held his head on my arm, a pair of autumn-brown eyes opened and gazed into mine. Too late I remembered I was maskless.

But he was whispering something. "Thank you, beautiful one . . ." His eyes closed and he was unconscious again, but he had looked at me, he had spoken, he would get better . . . He must, for at that look, those words, something in my middle had started galloping round like a colt in spring, ungainly and clumsy and untamed, and I knew I could not let him die, even if common sense told me that it was not me he had seen but some lady of dream.

"He'll do for the moment," said Snowy. "There's a spring down in the trees a small walk away. Make your suppers and put on some broth for when he wakens. I'll fetch herbs, and I think you'll find a flask of wine in his pack: put a cupful in the broth."

We kept watch all night, in turns, lest he should need us, and I put his broken sword in his right hand in case he woke and thought it lost. Dawn came in frost again and a chill wind, and I built up the fire and tucked my cloak more closely about him—though my teeth were chattering with cold and I could well have done with it myself. The broth I had prepared tasted strong and stimulating and I had a cupful myself and soon felt warmed through.

The sun spear-slanted among the trees as it rose and a shaft touched the Rusty Knight's face. His eyelids fluttered, he frowned, moved a little, and hastily I put away my dreams and donned my mask. The others crowded round: he opened his eyes once more, this time in puzzlement, put his hand to his head, shut his eyes again, groaned, winced, lay still. After a moment his eyes re-opened and this time he spoke, too.

"Wha—What happened? Where am I?"

I explained as best I could, introducing the others, lifting his head, offering the broth, but I was nervous and the words got tangled up and didn't sound right, so I tried again and that was worse.

The Rusty Knight raised himself on one elbow and opened his mouth again.

"By all that's holy! Would you credit it? I am attacked, I am wounded, I am rescued—and by what? A broken-down nag, a tatty black bird, a scraggy cat, a frog, something-in-a-bowl and—and a hobgoblin who talks scribble!"

The Gathering: One, Two, Three, Four, Five, Six, Seven

Peter and Paul

But by midday his breathing was worse and he had lapsed into unconsciousness again, muttering and moaning in delirium.

Snowy looked grave. "It would seem there is infection in the chest: I can do nothing about that, but if it is untreated he may succumb. Dangerous as it may be to move him, I think we should try."

"But where?" I cried, hearing the tiredness and tension in my voice. "There's just forest for miles!"

"Not quite: two leagues to the north there is a hump of folding hills where two brothers from an order of monks tend sheep from late autumn to lambing; they are experienced with animals of all kinds and would at least know what was best for the knight, of that I am sure. Come, we will have to start now, otherwise it will be night before we reach them."

It took over five hours, for Snowy could not carry his burden for long and had to rest as did I, burdened as I was with the others. Each time we had to move the poor knight he seemed worse, and I was in a right old state by the time we heard the distant blearing of sheep and emerged from the twilight of the forest to smoothly sweeping downs and the Evening Star pricked clear into the deepening blue of a frosty sky. The shieling was built of stones and mud and lay low to the ground, surrounded by wattle-fenced enclosures filled with restless sheep, just driven in for the night by a monk in brown habit and a couple of shaggy, point-nosed dogs. To the left was a barn, full of hay and housing a two-wheeled cart and a donkey, whose braying blotted out the baa-ing of sheep, calling of monk and barking of dogs.

We approached warily, my hands palm outwards to show we came in peace, and Snowy whispered a word of advice. "Play dumb, youngling: once they see he is injured you may leave the rest to them."

I took his words literally, and when the monk came running, a tall, thin figure with robe kilted up thin shanks to knobbly knees, I mouthed distress and pointed to our burden. Luckily he understood immediately.

"Tut-tut, whatever have we here? A poor wounded fellow and an assortment of animals . . . Deary, deary me! May the Good Lord preserve us!" and he crossed himself. "This person needs attention, yes indeed . . . An accident, perhaps?" He had a thin, high, fluting voice and his eyes were kind.

I mimed sword-play, an attack.

"Ah, yes; I see. How unfortunate: travelling has become so fraught these days . . . Well, well, well! Never mind, we must get him to shelter and comfortable as soon as possible. Brother Paul!" He had a surprisingly loud hail.

"Coming, Brother Peter!" and a fat, squat monk came running out of the shieling, his robe, even hitched as it was through his belt, trailing a little on the ground behind. "What is it, what is it?" His voice was as deep as the other's was high. "May His Holy Angels defend us! A wounded man, with servant and—and pets? Brother Peter, the place for him is inside, with a robe to cover, a posset to soothe and a fresh bandage for that head . . ." And, fussing and fretting, he led the way over to the barn. "Now then, now then: baggage and animals to remain here with Brother Donkey, and servant and master to the house . . ."

I thought-transmitted delay to the others, a later visit with food, but they were already abandoning themselves to sleep. Snowy was lying down, Corby had shuffled to the beam above the door, Moglet was curled up in the hay, weather eye open for the dogs, and Puddy, eyes shut, was sheltering under a convenient crock. I put a somnolent Pisky beside him, drawing hay round them both.

"I'll be back . . ."

I doubt if they heard for all had been made to walk, crawl and hop further than usual during the day. My eyes were closing too, as I followed the monks to their home. I looked round for the dogs, but they were obviously well-trained and were already kennelled, but unchained, ready, I supposed, to patrol the sheep pens against thief or even wolf, though the latter usually left their hunting so far south till winter really bit.

The room I was drawn into, in the wake of the monks and their burden of wounded man, was long and low, heat well-trapped in the rafters. To my right was a huge fire and simmering pot, a drying rack of herbs suspended from the ceiling; two stools, a table and hooks for cloaks and tools. Facing me were two pallets, straw-stuffed palliasses on a wood and rope frame; to my left sacks and bales of provisions, more tools and a barrel of apples. On shelves were arranged jars of ointment and pots of unguent and packets of dried leaves and there was also room around and about for shepherd's crooks, a large wooden tub, two leather buckets and a besom. My nose wrinkled as it was assailed by the assorted odours of plain stew, baking bread, leather, hay, sheep, dog, tallow, herbs, strong medicaments and rather smelly monks, and my eyes stung with tiredness.

Peter and Paul laid my knight carefully on one of the pallets and covered him with a woollen blanket, twittering and muttering to each other as they did so; then the taller one indicated the other pallet.

"Rest there, traveller, while we attend to your master and prepare supper."

I had meant to stay awake, to watch that they were careful of my knight, to return with food to the others, but as soon as my head touched the pillow, rustling with lavender, rosemary and thyme, I was asleep.

In the morning I woke guiltily, aware that I had overslept, vaguely remembering that I had woken briefly to drink a bowl of thick broth, then had fallen asleep again almost immediately. Aware, too, that I had neglected my friends in the barn shamefully, for I had not returned as promised.

Sunlight streamed in dusty bars through the open doorway beyond my bed, and the fat monk was sweeping out the dust into the yard, making the sunlight dance with motes that climbed and fell, twisted and turned like tiny peasants celebrating a miniature feast day. There was music too, for somewhere I heard the soft clucking of hens and the monk was humming through his nose, a little bass tune that repeated itself, then paused and was repeated in a higher key. It was soothing and yet somehow disturbing, as though it perhaps required a respect that lying lazing on a bed was not according it, so I jumped up. The broom fell with a clatter—a perfectly ordinary broom used for sweeping and nothing else, I was glad to see—and the little monk came fussing up, inquiring whether I had slept well and pouring me a mug of goat's milk and handing me a heel of bread.

Miming my thanks, I took these over to see the knight. It seemed he slept, though his breathing was ragged and he frowned a little. They had stripped him down to his shirt, and the discarded spotty mail lay to one side; his face had been cleaned up, to re-dress the head wound, and though now much of his head was covered with the bandage, over his brow a few springy curls escaped, russet as beech leaves, and looking curiously soft. Wondering a little, for lambs' coats look soft as down and are wiry instead, I stretched out a hand and lifted a strand, where it curled round my fingers like a living thing; soft, yes, but with a strength and hold I had not anticipated. It gave me a curious delight to touch, and next I laid a finger on one frowning brow and traced the curve to its outer edge. The skin beneath was burning hot, and under his high cheekbones the flesh was drawn in, hollowed, and a dark red stubble shadowed his chin.

I drew back as the monk approached, to take the empty mug from my hand.

"It is a pity you are dumb, poor creature, else could you tell us this knight's pedigree and destination. Brother Peter and I are most worried about his condition, indeed we are, and fear that he needs better care than we can provide in our humble quarters." He fussed round the patient, laying a hand on his forehead, shaking his own head, drawing the coverlets higher. "Not good, not good at all. We are used to sheep of course, sheep in a fever we can deal with, but this man needs Brother Infirmarar.

"Now, there is water to wash yourself; we prefer those who relieve themselves to go to the corner of the yard, where we have a trench. Waste products attract flies; flies lay maggots; maggots pester sheep. Simple enough if one uses logic . . ."

I washed my hands, wiped my mouth and escaped from his chatter to the yard. From thence, affecting an unconcern I did not feel, I sauntered over to the barn. The sheep were back in the fields, the pens were empty, save for one limping ewe, and there was no sign of Brother Peter or the dogs. I rounded the corner to the open front of the barn.

"Good morning," I said heartily. "Ready for some breakfast?"

"What happened to supper?" said Corby.

They let me suffer and apologize for fully two minutes before Snowy took pity and explained that "the thin one" had been over with a handful of oats for horse and donkey and some scraps for Moglet.

"And two eggs," said Corby, "for me. Broken eggs, and not of the freshest. Still, they were better than nothing." And he glared at me.

"Then this morning," said Moglet, "I had goat's milk. And more scraps."

I lifted the straw from Puddy and Pisky. The latter was languidly waving his tail and Puddy had a moth's wing sticking from the corner of his mouth.

"I see you two are all right," I said.

"Fair," said Puddy. "Fair."

"Likewise," bubbled Pisky. "A nice little sliver of moth . . . But you left me where I couldn't see, couldn't see, and you know how important it is to me to have a good view. A fish hasn't much choice, you know, shut up like a genie in a bottle—"

"A what?"

But he didn't reply, and went on grumbling till I explained that the straw was to keep his water temperate.

"And how is the knight?" asked Snowy. "Any better?"

I described his condition as best I could.

"I feared as much. I have seen that gasp of the breath in man before, and it can be grave."

"I just wish there were something I could do: I feel so helpless . . ."

"We could do," corrected Snowy, gently. "We are all in this together, for the present, anyway."

"Yes," I said. "Yes, of course." I must stop thinking of him as my knight, because he wasn't and never would be. And what would I, ugly, deformed Thing, want with a knight? And if I had one, what would I do with him? Tie him down to a bed or something forever, fasten his legs and arms down tight, just so I could get that strangely exciting feeling curling his hair around my grubby little fingers? The idea was ridiculous, and yet lying there he had seemed so vulnerable, so nice, so—

"Someone coming," warned Moglet.

I peered round the corner of the barn: Brother Peter was striding down the nearest field, his gown flapping vigorously against his thin shanks, the two sheepdogs slinking at his heels.

He saw me and waved. "How is our patient, the gallant knight? Such a well-set-up young man! Such strong shoulders, and a fine pair of . . . And his hair: my dear, such an unusual colour . . . Ah well."

I shook my head, remembering in time I was supposed to be dumb.

"No better? I feared not. And, much as I—as we—would like to keep him longer, I think it best if we take him up to the Priory."

I manifested alarm.

"Much better for him, much better. He will have a comfortable bed in the infirmary, where they have salves and ointments and infusions and draughts which will go a long way towards reducing the fever and healing his head.

"Come, now, we shall go and consult with Brother Paul: we always decide things together."

My—our—knight was worse, I could see that. The two monks consulted in a corner, a high mutter, a deep rumble, bobbing their heads up and down like ducks' tails, but at last they came to agreement.

"He must be taken to the Priory," said Brother Paul.

"So pack up his belongings," said Brother Peter. "We shall harness Brother Donkey to the cart, and perhaps you might ride your white nag—strange animal that: never seen hooves like that on a horse before—or perhaps you may prefer to walk: he does not look overly strong."

"It is not far," added Brother Paul. "You will be there before nightfall."

"Brother Paul will stay behind with the sheep," explained Brother Peter. "Sheep must be brought down before dark. Foxes; wolves; thieves after a nice piece of mutton, for all it is a hanging offence . . ."

"May the Lord forgive them." Brother Paul cast his eyes upwards. "And may we remember that He shared His last hours with such . . ."

"Amen, amen," intoned Brother Peter.

They were like two turtledoves, bowing and cooing to one another.

The two-wheeled cart was harnessed to the protesting donkey and a bed of bracken prepared. The two monks carried out the poor knight, bandaged head bobbing, and laid him carefully down, padding him round with blankets to stop him from rolling. I added Pisky's bowl, Moglet and Corby to the load, keeping Puddy in my pocket, and balanced Snowy on one side with our wicker carrier, the other the knight's pack, covering all with the knight's mail, now rustier than ever, for I thought it better if I tried to walk.

The day was fair enough, but a rising wind from the west scattered leaves about our feet and blew Moglet's fur the wrong way, and I was anxious lest it rain before we reached our destination. The way was uphill at the beginning and I found it hard going, but Brother Peter strode ahead, seeming almost to pull the cart himself plus the donkey, for the latter was mutinous at first, only cooperating when we reached flatter countryside and Brother Peter remembered the slices of raw turnip Brother Paul had put in his pocket, which was fed to the happier animal at appropriate intervals. The sky darkened early, and as we passed through the first of two small villages, large drops of rain plopped on my cloak. For a hopeful moment I thought we might stop and shelter but Brother Peter strode on, only stopping to cover the knight (who looked the worse for his jolting and bumping) with his cloak, under which crept Moglet and Corby as well.

Then it started to pour down in earnest: my cloak offered me some protection, but the poor monk was soaked in minutes and his sandals squelched and his robe dripped, and so did the end of his beaky nose. I pulled the end of the cloak over the knight's face, for he was getting rustier than ever, and I could see a stain of dark blood on his bandages. The donkey now stepped up his pace without bribery and we staggered and stumbled and rattled over tracks that were rapidly becoming impassable. At last, at long last, I saw through the drifting curtain of rain a lantern, a dim, twinkling light suspended over a pair of high, closed wooden gates. Away to either side stretched stone walls: Brother Peter lifted his staff and beat at the gates, the while hailing in his loud voice.

There was a shuffling, another voice raised in query, a drawing of bolts, a swinging back of one of the gates, and suddenly we were in a courtyard full of scurrying welcome . . .

The Gathering: One, Two, Three, Four, Five, Six, Seven

Illuminations

"Come along now," said a not unkindly voice, as Brother Matthew came into the stable carrying a large binding strap. "You and your animals will be eating us out of priory and refectory soon: how about taking your nag out to eat fresh grass instead of our precious hay, and bringing back some kindling in this strap to set against your keep?"

Brother Matthew was one of the younger brethren, lay brothers they were called, who were mainly concerned with the physical work of the Priory of St. Augustine. Shared with Brother Mark it was his concern to care for the stock and the provision of wood for the fires. They kept two heavy draught horses, five cows, three goats and a billy, two pigs for fattening and one for farrowing, and about three dozen hens, some of which, the poor layers, would be eaten during the winter. These two monks also kept the stables and courtyard clean, and the harness and tack oiled and mended, and this all between their numerous calls to prayer, signalled by the little bell in the chapel. I had been told that all the brothers, whatever their tasks, and all visitors, which included me, were expected to attend prayers three times a day—morning, noon and night, and the ordained monks those in between as well.

His request wasn't unreasonable and I got to my feet, yawning and shivering a little in the cold morning air that was rushing, unnecessarily fast, through the open door and dissipating the nice fug we had built up during the night. We were in a stable along the western side of the courtyard, a small one obviously for donkeys or ponies, for the stalls were not big enough for the larger horses. The mangers contained loose hay, more bales of it were stacked in a corner, and there was a comfortable layer of straw on the floor which I had not had to muck out, for I had asked Snowy and Moglet to please use the midden corner in the courtyard, and had persuaded Corby to turn his tail over one particular spot, which he usually remembered. If Puddy did anything I didn't find it, for he was eating less now and sleeping more, it being near winter-sleep for him, and of course the snails took care of Pisky.

I think it rather surprised Brother Mark the first time I escorted Snowy and Moglet over to evacuate themselves and empty out my bucket and wash it out, for he called Brother Matthew and they came over afterwards and asked me how I trained my animals. Of course I did not answer but merely shrugged my shoulders, for Brother Peter before he had returned to Brother Paul had told them all that I was dumb, as he truly believed of course.

Even had I not been the knight's servant, I believe they would still have treated me with kindness, for they believed, I think, that in strangers and the lost and afflicted they received their own God, who by all accounts was stern but kind. Sometimes, in the words they used in prayer, I thought I caught an echo of something I should remember, but was never quite sure. One thing I did find special was the chanting of the monks: a sort of extension of the humming of Brother Paul at the shieling, it had its own sort of magic. Sometimes in the night I would wake and hear them and the sound always made me comfortable and secure; when I was in the chapel, what with the dancing of the tallow dips and the question/answer of the chants, it made me feel as if I always wanted to be good and kind, and I usually managed to find something special for the others as a consequence: a bigger share of my supper for Moglet, some oats filched from the big horses for Snowy.

The knight was housed in the Infirmary, on the opposite side of the courtyard from the gateway, and one floor up. When we had arrived I had been allowed to carry up his pack and mail and see him safely bestowed on a raised pallet, and water and clean linen brought, before I was firmly shooed away to where I belonged: in the stable with the animals. I was allowed upstairs once daily to see my master, and I could see he was profiting from their care, for after a couple of anxious days when his bedside was always attended by a couple of the brothers praying, his fever abated slowly and—although the brothers had kept him largely unaware of what went on around him, aided I suspect by Brother Infirmarar's poppy-juice—he was nevertheless much better. On my brief visits, more to do me good than my master, I suspect, I was supposed to contribute to his recovery: at first I had not known what was expected of me and just watched as Brother Infirmarar sank to his knees by the unconscious man's bed, folded his hands, bowed his head and began to mutter in a foreign language. It was only after he had put out an impatient hand to tug me down beside him that I realized that I, too, must bow my head, fold my hands and pray. This last wasn't so difficult after all, for as I was supposed to be dumb I didn't have to say anything.

Once the knight was safely in the monks' care, why didn't we leave and continue our journey? One reason, I suppose, was that the brothers believed me his servant, the animals his pets. That would not have stopped us slipping away unnoticed while they were all in chapel, of course, but there was another, stronger reason why we did not leave him: it just never occurred to us that he was not part of the team. We would wait till he was better and go on together. It may not have been in any of their minds, of course, but they never said anything and I never asked: perhaps it was only that I was being selfish . . .

I think the monks all became a little wary of me, because of the way I could apparently manage my friends without words of command, and I even caught Brother Mark crossing himself one morning surreptitiously after I had forgotten to bring back the water bucket and asked Snowy to bring it back on his return. Because of this, perhaps, they tended to leave us alone, and this started me thinking of my curious position within our group, and the difficulties this posed in the world of man. I could communicate with my friends and some of the lesser beasts—the pigs and the donkey in our village, migrating birds—but though I understood human language I could only answer in what the knight had rightly called "scribble," on that awful day when he had called me a hobgoblin. And I didn't know how to correct this. I knew the words, understood the inflections, appreciated the intonations, but still my words came out like accidentally spilling a bag of dried peas: all over the place. To get any further—and especially to be able to explain things to the knight, I realized guiltily—I should need to practise words properly: everyone wasn't as clever as Mushroom Tom, who had lived so long away from people that the language of nature was more real to him.

One afternoon when, having collected a large bundle of wood in the morning and helped with mucking-out the other stables, I was free and bored and playing a game of tag in the courtyard with Moglet, who was bored too, I heard my name—or rather what the monks called me: "Boy!" —called from an upstairs window. That was another thing: the monks accepted my hunched back, my mask, my silence, but I would not have been allowed within the Priory if they had known I was female—or perhaps they guessed but were pretending not to know. After all, if I wished to relieve myself I had to squat, not having one of the useful pipes that men were equipped with, that allowed them to stand and spray all over the place for this most necessary of functions, and I couldn't be sure no one had seen me. I remember, when first I had noted this distinct advantage that males had, I felt envious; then I had thought perhaps it was more of a disadvantage, for one had to find somewhere to put it, to tuck it away, and I had finally come to the conclusion that being a female was probably tidier.

"Hist! Boy . . ." The voice came again, louder this time, and I looked up towards the library, which was on the upper floor to the left. The shutters were open at the end nearest the gateway and a youth leant out, his sandy hair catching the last gleams of the misty sun.

I nearly said "Hello!" back again because he had a nice, cheerful face, but I waved instead and Moglet came to wipe her dusty fur clean on my ankles.

"Doing anything special?" asked Cheerful Face.

I shook my head and picked up Moglet, wary of an extra chore.

He glanced around, saw the courtyard was empty but for us two. "Hang on a minute: I've a favour to ask." The head disappeared, but a moment later it reappeared, attached to a small wiry body clad in the usual brown, rope-girdled sack, at the bottom of a small stairway set in the wall at the corner of the courtyard. "Come up for a moment, if you can spare the time—please, that is?" It was the honest smile as well as the words that made me decide: I put Moglet down, but the young Brother held out his hand. "Please bring your little cat: I like them."

"It's all right," said Moglet. "He means it. He looks as if he has a comfortable lap. And perhaps milk . . ."

I followed the boy up the stairs, Moglet trotting just ahead of me.

She was disappointed about the milk, but there was a sliver of cheese. The room in which we found ourselves was obviously an annexe to the library proper, for an archway filled by a curtain separated it from the dusty main room, and here was a cheerful brazier burning, two candles, a large sloping desk, a table and two stools. On the table were quills, inks, brushes and tiny pots of different coloured liquids, tightly stoppered. On the desk was a partly written manuscript.

The boy followed my gaze. "That's Brother John's work: he has an ague at the moment so I'm on my own. I'm his apprentice and I have to finish the script on that page, but apart from the gilding I'm not yet allowed to make the illustrations. I'm to practise on these scraps of vellum—see?—and while I'm pretty good on leaves and flowers, I've had very little practice on animals. That's why I'd like to borrow your little cat—such splendid colours she is, all the bars and stripes and splotches of autumn woods—that is, if you could persuade her to sit still for a little while? I hear you're very good with animals," and he smiled ingenuously. "If you could manage to come two or three times—just before dusk is the best time, they leave me alone then—I could get some good sketches done. Please?"

I spoke to Moglet, who was agreeable so long as there was a tit-bit and she could pose near the fire.

"She says yes," I translated. "For a piece of cheese or somesuch and a share of the fire for each sitting," and it was only when I saw the boy's eyes round with shock that I realized I had broken my vow of silence.

"They told me you were dumb," he said after a moment, fiddling with a brush, but as he didn't rush away to tell on me or shout for help, I made up my mind to trust him and, speaking very slowly, carefully, weighing each word, I explained.

"I-am-not-dumb. I-have-been-with-my-friends-so-long-I-find-it . . . it . . ." I wavered.

"Difficult," he supplied.

"Dif-fi-cult-to-speak-man-talk." I stopped.

But he had understood. "You know the words: it's just practice, I suspect. You're not deaf, are you?" I shook my head. "Good. And you can understand what I say?" I nodded. "Fine! Tell you what: I'll draw little cat—what's her name? Such a pretty little thing . . ."

She bridled visibly, and the tip of her tail vibrated. "Nice man . . ."

"Moglet," I said.

"Moglet it is, then," and he bent to tickle her just behind her ears. "And if you can tell her what I would like her to do: stand, sit, lie down—you know—at the same time as I'm drawing her, I'll teach you to talk properly. How's that?"

I turned a somersault (easy with my humped back) and then had a sudden thought. "Keep-it-a-secret?"

"Of course! Half the fun!"

As it turned out, the fact that it took almost a month for our Rusty Knight to be anywhere near ready to continue the journey was a blessing in disguise, for in those four weeks Brother Jude-the-Less as he was called grew amazingly proficient at drawing cats, birds, toads and fish and my hands and feet (he was delicate enough not to ask me to remove my mask once I had explained) and I—I found I could speak human-talk. Not all at once, not every time, but day by day it grew easier to express myself so that others could understand. I suppose the most difficult was the radical switch from thought-pictures to word-symbols to describe the same thing. Apart from the more primitive sounds that normally expressed fear, pain, hate or desire, my animal friends usually presented most of their thoughts in visual gradations of fur, feathers, scales and so forth, in size and texture of touch, position of limbs and tail, attitude, flicker of eyes and movement of whiskers, ears or mouth. Apart from that, when it was less a matter of immediate communication than of thought, they sent vibrations in the form of pictures into one's mind, and I had become adept at receiving messages from their various eye levels, even through the distortion that Pisky's waterbound existence gave him.

At first I thought the human way of expressing oneself a clumsy and longwinded one, especially as people didn't always say what they really meant, but gradually I became used to it. I still sometimes got the order of words wrong, or missed out the, to me, unessential ones, but soon I found I could carry on a reasonable conversation with Brother Jude (the Less). We were undisturbed at our lessons because I would only creep back and forth by way of the side stair when the coast was clear, and at that time the monks were sitting down to break their daily fast before the first of the three evening prayer sessions. Brother Jude, being a lay brother, had a meal in the middle of the day and a snack in the evening.

I still performed my daily tasks of taking Snowy out to graze—although fresh grass was getting more difficult to find—fetching water, helping clean out the stables and sweep the courtyard, and I paid my daily visit to the Rusty Knight. By now the fever was gone, the gash on his forehead had healed and he was all cleaned up and presentable. They had bandaged his ribs as well and these, together with his ragged breathing, appeared to be mending. He was often awake now when I went to visit him, but there was a blank look in his eyes as though he were still dreaming and he obviously didn't recognize me, nor could he yet answer coherently the questions Brother Infirmarar or his assistant put to him.

But one day I had to face reality.

That day he was awake when I paid my visit, and not only awake but sensible and he recognized me.

"Sit down," he said. "There, on that stool. No, bring it nearer. I don't want the whole world to hear our conversation."

We were chaperoned, but only by old Brother Timothy, who was deaf as a blue-eyed cat and spent most of his days nodding away happily in a corner. Reluctantly I turned back to my inquisitor. Now that he was better and cleaned up and tidy I saw him properly for the first time, and I am afraid I ignored his first few words because I was listening to the lilt of them rather than the meaning.

" . . . remember it all. The monks have told me how I was brought here, but why did you give them the impression you were my servant?"

"I didn't: they just assumed it. They think I am dumb." Between the words I was studying his face. His hair curled as I remembered it, the colour almost that dull red of hedgerow hips.

"How could you possibly be dumb, when I remember that torrent of words with which you and—and your animals overwhelmed me? I do recall some animals?"

"Yes. They are my friends. We are travelling together." He has a broad, high brow, I thought, and his dark eyebrows are straight when he frowns and a lovely curve when he doesn't—

"And where do you travel?"

"To find the answers to our problems . . ." He is very pale still, and his cheeks hollow beneath the bones. He has a very firm chin—

Brother Timothy stirred from his stool and put a fresh piece of peat on the brazier, nodding and smiling over at us.

The knight lowered his voice. "Speak softly, now . . . What problems have you?"

"You see me: you called me hobgoblin, remember?" He had a firm mouth, too, under that curling moustache, but it looked as though it would curve upwards and transform his face if he smiled. "The others are deformed too. We seek release from this bondage."

"But surely if you are deformed there is no cure?"

"Not deformed by nature, by a spell." His eyes were brown like peaty water, yet clear and sparkling too.

"A spell! Then—" The curtain at the end of the Infirmary opened and another of the brothers entered, bearing a steaming bowl. "Quiet, now. I'll ask for you tomorrow, earlier maybe. Now, go!" I turned away but his hand shot out and caught my wrist. "Do you really talk with your animals, as the monks say? And what is your name?"

I nodded. "We do talk, and—and the only name I know is 'Thing' . . ."

Suddenly he grinned: it made him look five years younger.

"Perhaps you aren't so daft after all . . ."

I reported back to the others.

"We can go, then, now he's better?" said Corby.

"We could, I suppose," I said slowly. "But I had hoped . . ."

"That he would join us," said Snowy softly. "I think—I think we should give him the choice. You would be better with an escort, my little wandering ones. You will do well enough here for the time being . . ."

This left me wondering how long the white horse would remain with us if the knight joined us. We still had no firm destination, but that we were on the right path towards the owner of the pebbles I had no doubt. Since the witch's death our pains and cramps had been better, and once we had headed in the general direction of the southwest they had eased even more. Pisky was able to eat a little more, Corby's crippled wing stretched farther, Moglet's paw was less tender, Puddy complained less of headaches and I was standing at least an inch more upright, with only a stab now and again, as if I were pulling at stitched leather.

Out of, perhaps, a general feeling of optimism and inner gratefulness for the knight's recovery, I offered to comb out the tangles in Snowy's tail and mane. He was looking much sleeker and fatter since we came to the Priory, and he seemed calmer and less sad, so I thought it would be nice if he had to leave us sometime that he should do it looking tidy as well. When I offered he seemed to be surprised, and glanced round at his tail as if expecting it to be immaculate, then shook his head ruefully.

"You are reminding me that I have neglected myself . . . If you please, youngling; I would deem it a favour." He tended to talk like that, rather formally, but I supposed he had probably lived among courtly people at one time. A teasing thought about talking and speech touched my mind for a moment but was gone before I could identify it, so I started on Snowy's tail: burrs, tangles, mud, nasty bits and all. It took the rest of the evening, but by yawning-time it was sleek, curled and oiled like even the best horses in our village had been—though they had been beribboned as well—for the feasts of Beltane or Lugnosa.

"I'll do the rest tomorrow," I promised, as I blew out the lantern and settled to sleep, my head on his comforting flank, Moglet on my lap, Corby on his beam, Puddy and Pisky tucked up in their hay. My last thought was of the morrow, and seeing my—our—knight again . . .

But when I finally reached the Infirmary it was to disappointment. The knight was propped up in bed, but the Prior was there on a courtesy visit with his chaplain, and I was only allowed to join dumbly in the prayers before being dismissed. I did try to creep back later but Brother Matthew caught me and set me to replaiting and lashing some frayed rope-ends, which was a boring task that took till supper, which I always collected from the kitchen after six o'clock prayers. That evening, I remember, it was cold salt pork and black bread and, for once, a mug of ale, which I found sour but warming. Because of the pork, fatty from fingers, I had to go and rinse my hands at the well before starting on Snowy's mane with my rather battered comb. I made him lie down and leant against his warm flank, pulling all the mane over to my side. It had incredibly long, soft, silky hair and as I gradually worked from withers to ears it began to shine like a rippling curtain. I only had to cut out a couple of the really tangled bits, and he began to look beautiful.

"You should take more care," I said, as I reached his ears. "It was a shame to get it all tangled like that. Now, just your forelock—What's that?" For as I lifted the hair from his forehead my hand touched a knobbled lump in the centre and he started violently away, rising to his knees and giving a little whinny of pain. I patted his neck. "Poor old fellow! Did someone give you a bad knock, then? I'll be gentle, I promise . . ." But he pulled his head away. "Come on," I urged. "It won't hurt, I swear, and you look so—so beautiful now, almost like a faery horse—"

Snowy rose to his feet, and all at once he seemed to grow twice as large, and his hide shone like silver in the flickering lamplight.

"Oh wise young maid, wise for all your tattered clothes and crouched back—you have discovered what all others could not see . . ." He tossed back his forelock and stamped dainty cloven hooves on the straw. "See, maid; see, O wandering ones! See, and marvel, for this is probably the only time you will witness such again!"

I stared at the jagged coil of gold on his forehead, curled like a shell and rising perhaps an inch from the bone.

"Trotters and swill!" I breathed, my reverence in direct contrast to the words. "A unicorn!"

At these words the others, hitherto in disarray because of our jumping up and down, crept closer and gazed up at Snowy.

"A unicorn!" breathed Moglet. "Magic!"

"Should have known," muttered Corby. "Evening, Your Gracefulness . . ."

"A unicorn without a horn," mused Puddy. "Unusual . . . Cloven hooves: obvious when you think about it."

"Want-to-see, want-to-look; can't see a thing down here. Want-to-see, want-to-look!" So I lifted Pisky's bowl to a level with Snowy's head. "Hmm . . . My grandfather's cousin mentioned unicorns, but I don't see much more than a white horse here . . ."

"And that is all I am now," said Snowy quietly. "My precious horn is gone by the sorcery of a witch—your Mistress, little maid. You tell me she is dead and so there is no hope for me but to travel back to my once-kin and try to end my days, my now mortal days, in peace."

"But how?" I asked. "Why? And can't you grow another?"

"The how and the why I will tell you another time, perhaps. Suffice it for now to tell you that the spell is unbreakable, as far as I know. Once, a drop of dragon's blood, freely given, could reverse the spell, but there are no dragons any more that I know of. I had hoped . . ." He hesitated.

"Yes?" I encouraged.

"I thought maybe a wise man, a magician, could find a solution. There was one such, The Ancient, who lived the way we travel. But he must be dead a hundred years since . . . Then, when I heard your story, knew you had been cursed by the same witch, I had thought that some way we were bound together, might even find the answers—"

"Yes!" I almost shouted. "I am sure now there is someone, something that can help us all. Maybe not the immediate answer right away, but at least an indication of our next move . . . Don't give up on us, Snowy dear: we need you!

"Er . . . Should we call you something more formal now?"

"Snowy will do," and his voice was gentle. "My secret name is not for you, I'm afraid."

"Well, Snowy then: where do your kin live?"

"The last I heard, they too were in the southwest, in the forests of the Old Land."

"A double reason for coming our way! Please . . ." For a moment the unicorn-without-a-horn laid his cheek against mine.

"You are very convincing, little maid. Very well: I will stay with you all for as long as you need me . . ."

I realized afterwards that I should have been quicker to recognize our unicorn for something special, even if not for what he was, for of course there had been that question of words and language that had been nagging me. I had become so used to only communicating with my friends, and they with me, that we had all forgotten that talk across different species was unusual; of course most birds could speak with one another, gull, owl or sparrow, but they did not communicate, except in the most superficial way, with felines, reptiles and fish and the same applied to the others, and of course humans were special: it took a long time to work out what they meant, even if you were one yourself.

We five had almost evolved our own language and were so self-orientated that it had never occurred to us to question how easy it had been to understand, and be understood by, the white horse. Of course, coming across him in a moment of crisis had meant less formality, but now that we had been formally introduced, as it were, I understood why we had always felt so safe with him and why his manners and way of speaking sometimes sounded so old-fashioned: magic ones couldn't be expected to talk slang like we did.

Once again I was looking forward to my meeting with the knight, for there was now lots to tell him, but once again I was disappointed. For the second time it was other visitors, dumb attendance, lots of prayer, but on the next day we had the Infirmary to ourselves and he once more indicated that I should bring a stool close in case someone came in unexpectedly.

"Now," he said purposefully. He was propped up against high pillows, had on a clean linen shift open at the neck, and a little bulge-ended cross rested on a chain around his throat. "Now . . ." he began again, perhaps unnerved by my intent gaze. His skin was still pale but now there was a faint tinge of colour under the high cheekbones and his moustache was jauntier, the ends not drooping towards the corners of his mouth as it had before. No bandages now marred his head and a shaft of sun lit his russet curls.

"What are you staring at?" He glared at me.

"You," I said. "Very gratifying. Rather like picking up a stone and finding it an egg. Are you feeling better?" I had been practising my words, and they were coming out beautifully, though perhaps not exactly as planned: sometimes the thoughts better unsaid were coming out with the politenesses.

He had the sort of face that could scowl or smile, harden or become tender as if the expression had never been used before—

"I want an explanation," he said and folded his arms. "Begin."

"Where?"

"At the beginning of course, er . . . Thingummy jig."

I had a new name: I was delighted, and did not attempt to enlighten him.

"Right," I said. "Once upon a time there were five of us living with a witch . . ." It took some time to tell it properly, but when I finished he was staring at me as if he could not believe his ears.

"Take off that mask, Thingumabob," he commanded.

I wriggled: another name! "No," I said.

"Oh—please, then?"

"No," I said again, and explained why.

He gazed at me broodingly. "Shame," he said at last. "Shame . . ."

"I don't mind," I said, which wasn't exactly the truth. "But I think I would rather have known all along that I was ugly than have been surprised into it. Disconcerting, it was." That was a good word, and I said it again to make sure it came out right a second time, and then explained to him how Brother Jude (the Less) had been teaching me to speak properly. He was impressed, I could tell, because he stroked his moustache and under his hand I saw his lips twitch a little.

"And where do you go now?"

"To find the owner of the pebbles, of course: this is mine, see?" and I pulled up my jerkin.

"Put it away," he said hurriedly, and went quite red. "You shouldn't—never mind."

"You mean it's a secret?"

"Very. Don't do that again."

"But I just wanted to show—"

"All right! Enough . . . Just don't go—displaying—it like that again. Understand?"

I didn't, but I nodded wisely. "Are you coming with us, then?"

"With you . . . ?" He was plainly at a loss.

"Well, we came together, so we'd better leave the same way, I suppose, or the monks will think it rather funny."

"Oh. Yes. Of course."

"But I didn't mean just the leaving bit, I meant about coming with us to find a magician first. It's obvious you are also under some spell or other too, with that rusty armour and broken sword—"

"Nonsense!" he shouted. Really shouted, so that I fell off the stool in surprise and ended up on the floor. He glared at me again. "Nothing of the sort!"

The curtains at the end of the Infirmary parted and Brother Infirmarar came rushing in. "You called, Brother Knight, you called? You are worse?

Dearie, dearie me: too much excitement, I fear. Your servant must return to the stables, but before that we shall pray together, and then I will bleed you . . ."

I reported back despondently to the others, but Snowy comforted me.

"You did your best. Don't forget that we shall be leaving together and he may well change his mind once we are on the road . . ."

And so it was that, some five days later in the Moon of Frost, we seven were assembled at the gates of the Priory. Snowy was loaded with our gear and the knight's, the animals all in or on my wicker carrier. The knight and I were on foot. The Brothers came to wish us "God-speed," and Brother Jude (the Less) even gave me an affectionate hug, at which Brothers Matthew and Mark looked suitably scandalized. We were provisioned for three days and I saw the knight hand over a suitable "donation" to the Head Prior, for of course they would not charge for their charity to us. The size of the gift occasioned much bowing of heads, folding of hands and the beginning of what looked like another prayer session, but we didn't wait for the end because I nudged Snowy and we moved away, the knight following.

"Looks like snow," said Corby, and ruffled his feathers against the cold.

The Gathering: One, Two, Three, Four, Five, Six, Seven

Crossroads

We had our first confrontation that very evening.

We had walked due south from the Priory, because Snowy said there was a reasonable road some couple of leagues away that was heading in the right direction. At first the knight strode ahead, scornful of our slow pace, but after the third stop he made for us I could see he was still not as strong as he thought. He leant against a tree, ostensibly being very patient and forbearing of our tardiness, but I could see the beads of sweat on his forehead. Somehow I knew that his pride was a very big thing in him, and if necessary I should have to pretend sometimes to give him an excuse to indulge his weakness—

Another knight in another time, a woman feigning fatigue to hide his convalescent wound, an uncomprehending child who could run forever—

I shook my head, and the vision faded.

"I'm sorry we're so slow," I said. "But poor old Snowy is laden down and I've got much shorter legs than you. It was kind of you to wait."

He shrugged. "Doesn't matter. But the days grow shorter: perhaps we should look for a night's shelter soon."

I snatched at his suggestion. "Snowy says there is a ruined church some half-league away: most of the walls are standing and Puddy says it will be fine."

He scowled. "Which is Puddy, for God's sake? A toad! He says, the horse says . . . Never mind. Lead on then, but it had better be there!" and he gave Snowy a gentle slap on the rump. I hoped he didn't mind: I had forgotten to tell the knight he was magic.

The church had three walls left, but only a scrap of roofing, in the corner nearest where a desecrated altar still stood. The knight stood in the ruined nave and stared upwards to where a trefoil window, framed in still-green ivy, showed us the last of a reddening sun.

"Vandals," he muttered. "Barbarians."

Again my mind gave a sudden jump: soldiers in armour; horses, spears, swords; long hair, beards, distant shouting; a hiding place—Gone.

"What is there to eat?" demanded the knight, but did not wait for an answer, lifting his pack and my baggage from Snowy's back. "How about a fire, Thingummy, while I make this fellow more comfortable . . ." and I crept to the roofed corner and Corby brought me sticks. The knight rubbed Snowy down with a wisp or two of dried grasses, then gave him a handful of oats from the provisions sack. "There you are, old lad: there's still grass between the stones, and a dew-pond over there . . ."

We ate; cold lamb, rye bread and cheese, and shared a flagon of ale. The empty jar would be useful for water, in case we were away from a supply, so I packed it with our things: the knight had a proper one in his pack, but just in case he decided—But I would not think about things like that.

The fire burned brightly and we had no need of the lantern the Brothers had so thoughtfully provided.

"This is cosy," I said, throwing the rest of the crumbs to Corby and taking Moglet on my lap, where she continued to clean lamb-fat from her whiskers. "Find something to eat, Puddy?"

His throat moved up and down towards the roof of his mouth, which was a toad's way of toothless chewing. "Would you believe gnats? It's sheltered here: fine tomorrow, too."

I translated the last bit to the knight, and added that Snowy had said we were free from danger for the time being.

"I don't believe all that falderal about speaking with animals," said the knight, crossly. "None of you said a word just then: nobody even moved. I think you are just making it all up."

Patiently I explained about thought-messages, about the niceties of body-communication, but obviously my words were not enough.

"Prove it! Make them do things . . ."

"They're not performing animals!"

"I never said they were!" He was getting crosser by the minute: then he sighed and shook his head. "Sorry, Thingummybob—You must have some other name than that?"

I looked at the fire, and shrugged. "I've known no other, ever since I can remember." I didn't want to add that it was just "Thing," because I rather liked the way he added bits like "ummy" and "ummybob" at the end: it made it more personal between him and me. And nice.

There was a nudge on my chest. "If he wants some sort of proof," sighed Moglet plaintively, "I don't mind chasing my tail, or something like that . . ."

"Count me in," said Corby and Puddy and Pisky, one after the other, for I had been thinking to them what the knight had been saying, even while we were talking, and that hadn't been easy.

"All right, Sir Knight," I said. "My friends have volunteered to prove that we do communicate. First, here's Pisky. You remember I told you about the pebbles we were burdened with? Well, his is in his mouth so he can't eat properly. See?" And I held up his bowl.

The knight peered closely. "Won't it come out? No, you did say you'd tried. Poor fish: he won't get much bigger if he doesn't eat. Still, he's a handsome fellow, though, and with a bit more weight to him would be a real beauty. Very imposing fins . . ."

"Shall I ask him to wave them for you? First one, then the other and then his tail?" I took his silence for answer and relayed my request to Pisky, who performed his trick slowly and gracefully, ending with two extra large bubbles. "Thanks," I said. "Now, Puddy dear, forward. I shall ask him to turn around three times and then croak," I added to the knight. Puddy rather ponderously executed this, and I tickled him under his chin. "Puddy's pebble gives him headaches," I added. "It's in his forehead, as you can see. But we have all felt somewhat better since we started out on our quest. Now, Moglet: her pebble is in her paw—show him, darling—and she can't put much weight on it, but I will ask her to walk backwards three steps and then sit down. Will that do?" I glanced at the knight: his eyebrows were up somewhere near his hairline.

"My turn," said Corby, as Moglet returned to my lap. "I'll do the mating-dance if you like."

"Corby's pebble is in his wing," I explained, as the crow creaked his way through his ritual, ending with a couple of beak-scrapes on the knight's right boot. "That's his burden: he can't fly any more."

By now our audience was goggling. "All right," he said slowly. "I believe you have some hold over these creatures. But how do I know this isn't just something you've taught them, that they wouldn't do the same each time?"

I sighed: he really was a sceptic. "Well, then," I said. "How about you deciding what you want Snowy to do—if you don't mind, dear one? He's a unicorn, by the way, so he understands all speech, even yours. So, just ask him yourself what you want him to do."

"Unicorns, punycorns," said the knight. "Oh well, where's the harm? Here, horse: go over to the west window and find me that piece of wood that's lying underneath and bring it over here for the fire . . ." He obviously thought the whole thing was a joke, but his expression when Snowy laid the wood at his feet was a study. "All right," he said at last. "If you're a unicorn, where's your horn?"

Snowy tossed his head, exposing the golden stump.

"Don't touch it, please," I warned. "It still hurts him . . ."

Then the knight did a strange thing: he got to his feet and bowed to the white horse. Taking his broken sword from his pack, he offered it to Snowy, hilt first. "May my sword, broken or whole, never harm thee or thy kind, O Wondrous One. I offer you my friendship, my respect, my trust . . ."

Snowy bowed his head in return. "Peace, friend," he said. "If I could mend your sword, Knight, I would, but the spell under which you lie is stronger than I, no longer a unicorn, can break."

I started to translate to the knight, but saw he had understood the gist of Snowy's message.

"What spell?" I asked him.

He frowned and shook his head. (I wished he wouldn't frown so much: he would soon grow two little lines between his eyes if he went on like that.)

"No spell. Misfortune, perhaps. Nothing else . . . Time for bed."

But that night, and for a while afterwards, he talked in his sleep. During the next few days we made fair progress, thanks to clear days and cloudy nights, which made the weather unseasonably warm. Our Rusty Knight had obviously taken to heart our burdened plight, for he no longer strode ahead but suited his pace to ours and we made at least three leagues a day. He had money, a purse of silver coins, so we were never without food and several times sheltered in villages at night instead of the open. At those times I persuaded him I was happier in the stables with my friends, and everyone accepted me without question as his servant.

In this fashion we made fifty miles or so and it was near The Turn of the Year when we had another confrontation. Somehow, during all those miles together I had persuaded myself that we would continue to travel together, all seven of us, until we found someone to show us how to get rid of our burdens and spells, so I was utterly unprepared when we came to the crossroads.

The road we had been following had been well used, judging by the ruts, wheel-tracks and potholes, but on this particular day we came to another, much larger, going straight as a die north-south, and here the knight stopped.

"Well," he said. "It was fun while it lasted, but this is where we part company."

For a moment I did not understand. "Part company?" but even as I said the words I realized what he meant, and I felt as if someone had kicked me in the stomach and then pulled out the stuffing.

"Yes. Part company. Our ways lie in different directions henceforward." He tugged at his moustache. "I never said I would go all the way with you. Besides, I think your expedition is a waste of time. You're obviously hoping some miracle-man, like the fabled Arthur's Merlin, is sitting waiting for you, just longing to wave his magic wand and solve all your troubles." He snorted. "Me, I have more commonplace ideals. I'm going south to the nearest port to cross back to the Frankish lands, where I can easily find work as a mercenary. A few spots of rust on my mail mean nothing: I can afford more armour anytime I choose, and as for swords—"

"A few spots of rust!" I exploded, raging against his departure. "A few spots! Why, you are covered with it from shoulder to thigh like—like a beech-hedge! And any other armour you buy will be covered the same way in five minutes flat! You can't just get rid of a witch's curse by—by snapping your fingers—" I stopped.

"And how," he said, his voice nasty, and the scowl more ferocious than ever, "just how do you know about curses and spells and things? And your answer had better be good, or shall I believe you are in league with the Powers of Darkness yourself!"

I backed away. "You talked in your sleep . . ."

He flushed angrily. "And who says you should eavesdrop on a man in his most private moments? Besides, 'twas but dream, no foundation in fact—"

"We all heard you," I interrupted. "No help for it. You were shouting. All about a witch and a spurning, and the curses she laid upon you because of it. The rusty armour and the bit about asking the hand in marriage of the ugliest creature in the land. And how it was your father's sword, and—"

"I've heard enough!" he shouted, very red in the face now. "It's all a pack of lies, the lot of it, and I won't stay to listen to a word more on the subject. Goodbye!" And he snatched his pack from Snowy's back and flung it over his shoulder, before setting off at a determined pace southwards, towards where the smoke of a fair-sized village showed on the horizon.

I ran after him down the road, not thinking, just not wanting to lose him, hoppity-skip-jump down the rutted way till I fell flat on my face, out of breath and crying. With the last of my strength I yelled out: "And after we saved your life! And learnt to love you . . ." That last bit hadn't meant to come out at all, and I lay where I was and the rebellious tears seeped through my mask and dripped onto the road, where they dried in an instant on the hard-baked clay.

A moment later there was a snuffle and Snowy nudged my shoulder. "Don't worry, dear one: I am sure he will think better of it . . ."

"He won't!" I howled. "He's a pig, and an ungrateful wretch into the bargain!"

Moglet sat on my back and teased at my hair with her claws, but gently. "Come on, Thing dear, we love you . . ."

"And will go on with you whatever happens," added Corby.

"Of course. Goes without saying," said Puddy, from the now lopsided basket on Snowy's back.

"My great-great cousin twice removed said constancy was greatly to be admired," declared Pisky. "Don't make salt-drops, Thing dear: my very constitution shrinks from the thought of salt-drops . . . And can you come and straighten me up? I don't want to lose my snails."

I laughed through my tears. "Dear friends," I said, "you are idiots, and I love you! Who cares about Rusty Knights, anyway?" And we camped just across the road and I made an extra effort to give them a very special midday meal, even scrabbling under leaves to find insects Puddy could share with Pisky and letting Moglet and Corby have one of the pig's feet we had bought the day before. I drank the last of the goat's milk and even doled out a little fresh cheese to the others. By now it was darkening, and I gave Snowy an apple.

"Shall we move on a bit?"

He scrunched contentedly. "We can camp for the night right here. The night will be fine and we can build a fire without fear of passers-by: the road is empty of strangers."

I did not really care for the thought of a night in so exposed a position, even with the lattice-shelter of bare trees, but he had never been wrong, so I moved a bit further into the woods and soon had a fine blaze crackling up through the trees and spread my cloak among the fallen leaves, ready to dig a shallow pit if it grew too cold.

Perhaps because I was a little lonely, in spite of the nearness of my friends, perhaps because, although safe, I felt far from home, wherever that was, perhaps just because, I took off my mask and sang a small song, a lonely sort of song that came into my head from nowhere and ran down to my lips and tongue. I sat gazing into the fire, seeing ruined castles, great pits of flame, towering mountains and endless forest, and I sang the song of the traveller far from home. It had no words, just a rising and falling tune that could have rocked a babe to sleep, but in my mind's eye I was in a green and pleasant land; rolling meadows, gentle hills, smoke rising from a little cottage set in the angle between sea and down. In that home there were children, a woman waiting for—

I broke off suddenly as my tune was echoed by a voice from the road. Springing to my feet, my hand snatched at my dagger, but Snowy murmured "Steady, now!" and through the trees came the Rusty Knight.

Over his shoulder, besides his pack, was slung a sack of provisions, and these he slung to the ground, before remarking: "Trying to set the forest on fire? I could see your blaze for miles . . . Well, now: how are we all? Had something to eat? If not, I've got—"

"You've come back?" I interrupted, scarce believing, still poised dagger in hand.

"Well . . . Had a think about it, after I left you. Thought of what my mother might have said if she had known I was leaving you parcel of sillies to go forward on your own; thought about my duties as a knight to protect those weaker than myself; thought about my Christian conscience, too. Came to the conclusion I might as well see you to wherever you're going, before I set off on my own travels again. So, here I am again, for the time being at least—Whatever's the matter, Thingy?"

For I had leapt across the fire to embrace him in my enthusiasm, remembered in mid-leap I was still carrying my dagger but not wearing my mask, leapt straight back again to rectify both errors, and then jumped to his side once more, only to find that the idea of hugging him was ridiculous, so just stood there, feeling foolish.

"Welcome back," I said inadequately. "I say: how did you know my song?"

"Your song? I first heard that sung in some court or other abroad oh, years ago. It's a Frankish tune; I was going to ask you where you knew it from . . . I've forgotten most of the words, but it is something about a lady waiting in vain for her lover to come back from the wars. I remember the air, though: very pretty."

I couldn't tell him how I knew it, because I didn't know, but there were more important things to think about than a sad tune that teased at memory. He was back, he was coming with us, and the others shuffled closer, Moglet even going so far as to twine round his ankles. He bent to stroke her.

"They all say they're glad to see you back," I said. I didn't interpret exactly: would he have been as happy with Corby's "Well, I suppose he's better than nothing: at least he has silver for food," and Puddy's: "Tell him not to shout all the time: gives me a headache"?

"Have you eaten, Rust—er, Sir Knight?" I asked.

He glanced at me quizzically. "If we are to become fellow-adventurers 'tis as well for you to know my name, and where I come from . . ."

His name was Connor Cieran O'Connell of Hirland, and he was the younger son of a chief. When his father died, as was the custom, his lands and belongings had been divided equally among his kinsmen, and to Connor's lot had fallen a bag of gold and his father's sword, so, landless, he had set off to seek his fortune. He had travelled a great deal and had earned his knighthood in the Frankish lands, for some "trifling service" as he put it, to a Duke. Earlier this year he had travelled back to his homeland, found his brother dead, his mother remarried and an unwelcoming cousin the new chief. So he had decided to make his way back to the Duke's court and seek employment in the endless wars that part of the world produced.

"A man's life," he said, and scowled at me. "Still, there may have been something in what you were saying about swords and rust and—and spells and things. I'll tell you someday. But for the present we won't mention it again. Right?"

I nodded. "Don't worry," I said. "I know it will turn out all right; I feel it in my heart, Sir Connor."

He smiled then, and his smile was all I had known it would be.

"I wish I had your faith, little Thingummy, though I think it depends more on hope than experience. And never mind the 'Sir': call me Conn."

"Yes—Conn," I said shyly.

He glanced around at us all, his eyes sparkling, and pushed up the edges of his moustache with his finger. "A crippled cat, a creaky crow, a torpid toad, a miserable minnow, an unhorned unicorn and you and me, Thingy: did you ever see a more unlikely combination for high adventure? 'Twould make the angels themselves laugh fit to weep . . .

"Come, my friends: supper and bed, before I change my mind and regret the very day you rescued me!"

But he was smiling again . . .

The Gathering

The Turning-point

It may have been the sunlight that awoke him, low enough now at midday on the shortest day to shine momentarily on the neglected heap of pebbles; it may have been his dreams, too intolerable to be longer endured, concerned as they were with happier times, the search for his treasure—whatever it was, the dragon jerked in his sleep, coughed like one strangling, and opened his eyes to stare out over the snow-shrouded hills beyond his cave. He blinked once, twice, the narrow slits of pupil narrowing still further, then their gaze shifted to the piled stones before him, and a great sigh moved the scaly flanks that hung, mere skin upon bone now, behind the sharpened shoulders.

The sun prismed an icicle that hung from the mouth of the cave, and a single drip of water plopped onto the rock beneath. The dragon considered this for a moment, then his forked tongue flickered out of his mouth and he hissed. It took a long time for him to uncoil stiff joints and rise, and the sunlight had shifted away from the mouth of the cave by the time he reached it. Stretching up, his yellow fangs snapped off the icicle at its base and then scrunched the ice between his teeth, swallowing the pieces before they melted so that they rattled and chinked on their way down to his stomach.

He burped uneasily, then suddenly sniffed the air like a surprised hound that scents hare when he least expects it. For a moment his whole body tensed, straining after the elusive hint of something alien, then his brow wrinkled and he shook his head as if to clear it. Again he sniffed the clean, cold air, but the trail had gone stale, cold.

He went back and lay down again, this time not even glancing at his pebbles, but now his sleep was lighter, uneasier, and once or twice he rumbled and frowned and raised his head, as though the thing he thought he might have sensed had left the faintest trace of itself behind, to tease at the edge of consciousness with the merest shadow of hope . . .

Ki-ya the buzzard moved cramped pinions, one eye on the weather outside, the other warily watching the now sleeping dragon. He had sought shelter two days since during the blizzard, and had perched on the pinnacle of rock just inside the cave-mouth, stomach empty, one tail feather damaged. Now that feather, groomed, smoothed, oiled, would carry him on a favourable wind, but he would have to take care. A week ago he had strayed from his home territory, a bold yearling male, and the great southwesterly had caught him foraging on the edge of the moor. A more experienced bird would have sought shelter but he had thought, with his young defiance, that he was strong enough to ride out the storm, to slip the winds under his wings and rise above the worst of it, but the elements had decided to teach him a lesson and had lifted him high, high on a thermal, then tipped him sideways across the mouth of the Great Western River and flung him helter-skelter to the teeth of the Black Hills, where he had spun crazily from one down-draught to an up and vice-versa, until the wind had veered in a night, and dawn had found him disorientated and dispossessed on the ledge of the dragon's lair.

At first, with the northering wind fetching a blizzard, he had not noticed that the inner side of the cave was occupied, and when he had it seemed the heap of bones and scales was merely that: Now it was different: nest-tales had included Dragons, Fire-drakes and Wyrmes, but this was his first encounter with one. He was not even sure this was a dragon: parent tales had described him as such, but with fire in his belly and flying, higher and faster than even his own kin. But this thing looked near dead and its fires were out: still, a good enough tale to carry to The Ancient, if he were not off on his travels again. Fair exchange for a decent dinner . . . His stomach contracted and he spread his wings.

Five or so days later, living by rick and midden, tolerably full but defeated from straight flight by adverse winds, he followed a trail of footprints through the new snow some quarter mile below. The trail wound over the downs for half-a-league, going in his direction, and lazily he let it lead him, switching off the nagging pull and ignoring the pre-set markers for a while, till he saw the footprints halt in a huddle of creatures a mile or so from a village. Coasting down, for now he could feel a favourable veer in the wind was imminent and see the build-up of high, scattered cloud to the west, which would mean a good six hours' clear flight, he alighted silently in a tall pine some fifty yards from the party. Two humans, a unicorn if his guess was right, but in a sorry, hornless state, a crow, a . . . cat? something that looked amphibian in a basket and a bowl with a tiddler in it. The smaller human was holding the bowl and breathing on it to melt the thin coating of ice.

The crow glanced up. "Greetings, brother!" He had a crippled wing.

"Greetings: may the wind lift your wings and smooth your passing, your eyes never grow dim, nor your beak or talons less sharp." It was the standard predator's greeting. "Whither away?"

"Southwest, to seek a sorcerer they say still lives there."

"All of you?"

"All of us."

"A quest?"

"Something of the sort . . ."

"Travel well, brother: I shall be there before you," and he coasted up until he felt the familiar tickle of wind slide round to hug his body and then he spread the fingers of his wings to grasp at the air, joying in the buoyancy, the waves that met and passed him, the crests that he rode as easily as a gull on the estuary.

He screamed his name: "Ki-ya! Ki-ya!" that all should know him. Here was another tit-bit of news: he should reach the old man in a couple of days. He screamed again.

But *they* would have a longer journey . . .

The Gathering

Hedged by Magic

It was a long, hard journey and a long, hard winter.

At the turning of the year I had thought we were over the worst of it, but with the lightening of the days came a darkening of the weather. The Moon of Snows lived up to her name and by Inbolc, or Candlemas as Conn called it—a much prettier name—we were still up to our ears in the white stuff. Well, nearly. Well, Moglet was, and in the drifts Snowy was in to his belly. Twice we were forced to make long detours, once for unseasonable floods, and for two weeks we were holed up in one village, snow to the lintels. Conn's money ran low and mine was finished and by the Moon of Waters we were cold, hungry, tattered and snappy with each other. Puddy and Pisky fared better than the rest of us because they went into half-hibernation, stirring only on warm days and requiring little or nothing to eat. Corby and Moglet were reasonably sheltered and not unfed but Conn, Snowy and I fared worse. Conn, despite his long legs, found the going hard and his mail, which he wore all the time now to lighten Snowy's load, heavy and cumbersome, and he still did not have my belief in journey's end and the magician to lessen his burdens. Snowy, for all he was a unicorn, albeit no longer magic, could still feel hunger, cold, the weight of his burdens, and the frost struck cruelly at the poor, tender stump of his horn. And I? I felt I was colder, tireder, hungrier than all of them put together, and even the binding of my feet with rags, the wrapping of sacking around my shoulders and chest and Conn's purchase of a squirrel-fur hood did little to keep out the shivers that chattered my teeth and rattled my bones.

We almost quarrelled and parted company more than once, but now it was Snowy that kept us together. As the weather gradually changed for the better he declared he could smell spring on the softer winds from the south, and broke into a trot now and again, snuffling the breeze and discovering the new, tender mosses and thin slivers of fresh grass revealed by the thaw to persuade us. We crossed the downs and came to the high moors, and the last, bitter fling of a winter whose reign was nearly over. Below us to our left lay a grey-green expanse that Conn said was the sea, but all we were concerned with was struggling through bog, slough, bitter thicket and twisted, stunted wood. One night we spent crouched in the lee of some towered stones on the flank of the moor and even Snowy stamped his hooves and looked uneasy, and I dreamt of our Mistress and woke screaming till Conn clapped one hand over my mouth and with the other stroked my back until I calmed.

Then, suddenly, things changed.

We came off the moor after five days, slipping and sliding down a steep combe to a valley, and it was as if the Moon of Birth had arrived three weeks early and spent her first few days all out, day and night, to persuade us our sense of timing was all a-kilter and surprise us with her husbandry. On either side of the narrow track that led deep between bank and wood, bracken was uncoiling in shy green crooks, grass spiked in surprised clumps, colts-foot shocked with their bright heads, furred bramble leaves were gently unfolding and everywhere birds sang. Rounding a corner to where a stream chattered across stony hollows a willow was already greeny-yellowing with slim leaves, bending to the water to admire its reflection, and downs-pastured lambs ran wag-tailed to their dams with dirty knees and black faces as they heard us approach. Somewhere high above us a lark strove mightily with the heavens, and other birds darted busily across our path, twigs, dead leaves, sheep's wool and dried grass in their beaks, nest-building leaving them too busy to do anything but ignore our passing. A balmy breeze from the south kissed us in greeting and Corby shook up all his feathers.

"Not bad," he said. "Not bad at all. Feel like a dip in that puddle over there. Too much grease on your feathers and you can't fluff 'em up at night . . ."

"Think I'll try a walk," said Moglet. "Sun's warm. And a drink from the stream."

Puddy emerged, looking rather saggy and crinkled. "May we stop? Definitely need some water . . ."

Pisky swam to the top of his bowl. "I fancy a little dip, and perhaps a change of water. My grandmother always said . . ."

Conn and I watched them, and I kept an eye on Pisky in case the stream ran too strong, and re-filled his bowl with fresh water and set it in the sunshine to warm.

"D'you know," said Conn, stretching upwards till his fingertips burnt red in the sunlight, "I think they've the right idea. Mind if I wander off downstream and have a dip? The winter's sweat is sticky on my body like scum," and he ambled off down the road, whistling an experimental happiness.

I turned to Snowy. "A good idea: I could do with a wash. How about you, dear one?"

"If you could set down the packs for a while . . ." I unloaded him and he pranced like a yearling to the nearest patch of grass and rolled, his tummy pink and his hooves tucked up close to his body. I wandered down till I found a pool then undressed, hesitating for a delightful moment of anticipation before gasping into the water. It was freezing and exhilarating and glorious; putting on my old clothes while I was still damp was rather nasty, but I heard Conn returning and dared not shame him with my ugly nakedness.

He came striding down the road, jerkin and mail over his arm, his hair curled tight, dark red with the water, and it gleaming in drops on his shoulders and running to the darker hairs on his chest, and a smile on his face as he saw me. I felt a jolt in my insides like someone had kicked me, but without the pain and yet with it—

"Fish for dinner, Thingy dear!" and he held aloft two silver trout. "And I'd never have caught them but that the wash of my dive into the water threw them up onto the bank, and they surrendered without a fight . . . I had not realized how long your hair was; right down your back it is and black as Corby's wing," and he flicked the damp fringe on my forehead as he passed and I was absurdly pleased, almost as though he had told me I had turned pretty overnight, and I watched the muscles on his back and shoulders as he broke up some dead branches for our fire, and longed to touch their hard knots . . . Then laughed at my foolishness and went to gather up the others, fussing over them more than usual, stroking and holding them.

The fish were delicious and fed all of us, one way and another, although in truth they were but one man's dinner, but I made oatcakes to go with them for Conn and myself, and we had the snow-fed waters of the stream to wash them down. That night we found an old barn and slept warm and dry in the last of the winter hay and woke early, for though none of us said so, I think we all felt that the end of our search was near. And as we walked that day it seemed that spring walked with us, or ran a little ahead and turned and beckoned so that we had no need to ask the way, and all our aches and pains were smoothed away and we paced as if in a dream . . .

And so we came to the barrier.

"We can't get through there," said Conn, scratching his head. "Not without an axe or two," for our way was blocked by a tangle of briars and thorns well above man-height. "We shall have to go round," and indeed the track we had been following branched off to the left and right as though there had never been a way through, though the barrier seemed to stretch as far as the eye could see without a break.

"But that's the way," I said, pointing ahead, as sure as eggs, though I could not have explained why.

"It can't be," said Conn. "You must be wrong. There's nothing behind there, there can't be . . ."

"There is," I insisted. "I'm sure of it. Come on," and without thinking I walked forward straight into—and through—the thorny mass, just as if it hadn't been there. Snowy followed by my side, the others on his back, but when we found ourselves on the other side and I turned to look for Conn, I found he had not followed us.

"Bother!" I said. "Conn?" Faintly, very faintly, I heard him call back, as though he were on the other side of a house, for the thorn hedge had closed behind us as though there had never been a way through. "I shall have to go back for him," I said, and started forward, but this time I merely scratched my hands and arms, for the thorns would not give way. I shook the branches frantically, but try as I would they did not shift, and all the time I could hear Conn calling, calling . . . Bursting into tears I tore and pulled at the thicket till I was covered in scratches, but it was no good.

Rushing over to Snowy I clasped him round the neck. "Help me, dear one, help me!"

He breathed gently down my neck. "There is no way back, only forward. He can come to you, but you cannot return to him. You will have to use your mind, make him believe he can walk through, just as we did . . . Concentrate: call him to you."

"Call him?" But even as I questioned I knew what to do. Kneeling down I heeled my palms over my eyes till all was blackness and dug my fingers into my ears till all was silence and thought hard of Conn, conjuring him up in my mind from feet to crown of head and then walking towards him in my mind, back through the hedge, till I stood again by his side and held out my hand.

"Come," I said. "Come with me. Don't be afraid . . ."

But he looked at me as though I were someone different.

"I cannot go through there: it is solid. Must be five or six feet thick."

"It's not there," I said. "Not there. It's an illusion . . . Close your eyes, take my hand, and believe!"

And I took his hand and led him through the way I had come.

"What on earth—Are you all right, Thingy?"

I opened my eyes and they hurt with sunlight and I took my fingers from my ears and they rang, and there was Conn coming across the grass towards us. I stumbled to my feet and hobbled towards him.

"I'm fine . . . You all right?"

"Think so . . . Extraordinary thing: one moment I thought I'd lost you all, and then there was this gap—What is this place?"

We were standing in a glade, full of sun and sound and smell. To our left was the hedge we had come through, but already it seemed some distance away, and between it and us there were trees, some blossoming, some in full leaf, others with the tints of autumn and bearing scarlet and yellow fruit. Before us a meadow, full of daisies and buttercups and clover and blue, white and yellow butterflies. Beyond that was what I thought might be the sea, now sparkling and blue, with little white lines dancing towards the shore. To the right were more trees, a wood of conifer, all greens from black to yellow. Squirrels ran up and down the trunks and along the branches, nuts in their mouths, and tall ferns rustled as deer came out from the shadows and sniffed the air and gazed at us, their furred ears swinging back and forth, their tails wagging. Behind us a little spring gushed out of the rock and ran away, disappearing into a shallow pool. And by the spring was a cave, and at the mouth of the cave lines of strata where martlet and martin bubbled and chattered. And I could hear the sea and the trees and the birds and the bees and the wind in the grass and smell pine and ripe apples and clover and—

And on a rock-seat in front of the cave, apparently asleep, sat the largest owl I had ever seen.

"It's an illusion," I said, but I wasn't quite sure.

"Not all of it," said Conn, plucking and scrunching a rosy apple from a nearby tree.

Snowy was cropping the short, sweet grass and, reassured, I lifted down Puddy, who made for the stones by the pond; next I put Moglet down, and she was off batting at butterflies in a blink, but never quite catching them. I carried Pisky over to the pond and submerged his crock. "There," I said. "I think it's all right . . ." Corby had not waited: turning over a pile of leaves he had found some grubs, or what looked like grubs.

"Have an apple," said Conn, already on his second, but I shook my head. At my feet the runners of a strawberry were thick with tiny pointed, scarlet fruit which burst in my mouth in an explosion of delight.

But things were just not right: they looked as they should, felt as they should, tasted and sounded as they should, but where in the world would you find a place that held all seasons as one? The promise of spring blossom, the warmth of summer sunshine, the fulfilment of autumn's apples, the consolation of winter's conifers . . . But it didn't feel bad, not as though it were an enchantment to thrall us into evil: there must be an explanation.

I looked around me again for some sort of clue to these contradictions. My friends seemed to find nothing strange in the situation: they were peaceful and happy enough for the moment. I supposed I was meant to be too, but somehow I felt annoyed with whatever-it-was for presuming I could be so easily lulled into compliant acceptance of the situation. For something to do I picked and ate another strawberry, appreciating its tart sweetness, the gritting of pips in my mouth. One got stuck between my teeth, and I nudged it loose with my tongue; if anything were designed to convince one that life was normal a pip between one's teeth was the thing . . .

I felt a tickly feeling between my shoulder blades and whirled round: the owl was shutting his eyes again.

"All right," I said. "Explain!"

But the bird remained silent, eyes firmly shut, feathers fluffed, just as we had first seen him. I was sure now that I was right so I marched up to where he was sitting in the bright sunshine on that throne-like chair, and addressed him again. "I know you're foxing," I told him. "Tawnys don't sit out like that in the sunshine at midday. And all the rest of this," I waved my hand, "is just too perfect. So, bird, tell me what all this is about or I'll—I'll break your blasted neck!"

There was a little silence. The others left off eating or playing and came up behind me, Pisky swimming up the stream to where the spring gushed out, Corby wiping his feathers with his beak, Puddy damp, Moglet with pollen on her flanks, Conn with an applecore in his hand, Snowy smelling of new grass.

The owl opened one eye. "Just try it, that's all: just try it!"

He closed the eye again. He had spoken so Conn and I could understand, man-speech, but even as I registered this I realized he had also answered so the others could understand as well, the different sounds and attitudes echoing one behind the other with the fraction of a second between so that only I, and most probably Snowy, would know this was some kind of magic. I shook my head: only one way to deal with this. I did the same thing, talked so they could all understand, but whereas the owl had talked to each in their individual speech, I just used human speech and the special language my friends used. It was still like trying to do five things at once.

"I will, don't think I won't! We haven't travelled all this way to find a magician, a wise man, just to be put off by apples and strawberries and—and things! Now then, I know this is the right place, so please tell us where we may find your master?"

The owl opened his eyes again, and now they were full open, considering. "What business have you with The Ancient?"

"That's ours to say, to him. Tell your master we are here!" I sounded bold, but inside I was shaking. For the last few minutes—hours?—since we had arrived, ever since we had come across the thorny hedge in fact, I had seemed to assume charge, and now I realized how that was entirely against my nature; with Conn and Snowy so much better qualified than I, the strain began to tell. So I repeated what I had just said, but my voice was uncertain, to my ears anyway. "Tell him we're here . . ."

The owl shifted on his perch. "You're too late."

"Too late?"

"Too-hoo late. By about two-hoo hundred years . . ."

"What do you mean?" But even as I spoke I could feel the frustration, the despair of having walked so many, many miles for nothing, and my stomach contracted as it used to when we were with the witch, and it seemed the others were similarly affected, for I heard a curse from Corby, a wail from Moglet and sympathetic noises from the others, echoing my distress.

"Do you mean, by all the saints, that we've come all this way for nothing?" began Conn angrily, and it was only Snowy who said nothing, his large, dark eyes switching from me to the owl and back again. Somehow this gave me confidence, and I looked hard at the fluffy bird again. There was something cloudy, undefined about the area behind him, something not quite right . . .

"You say your master died—er, two hundred years ago? Can you prove this?" I spoke carefully, politely.

"Why, of course! Come this way," and he waved an inviting wing.

Conn had learnt enough about my friends by now to go back for Pisky's bowl without being asked, and we all followed the owl as he flew into the cave. Inside it was light, dry and airy, about twenty feet long by ten or twelve wide; torches burned quietly in sconces and there was no need for the owl to indicate a recess in the right-hand corner, for we could not have missed it.

Behind a kind of crystal curtain hung a suit of clothes, enclosing a skeleton. The clothes were ornate, jewel-encrusted, richly embroidered; the skeleton was—a skeleton, with a few wisps of greying hair still adhering to the skull. Though there can have been no wind behind that curtain, yet the whole thing swayed, very gently, back and forth.

The owl waved his wing again. "There you see the mortal remains of my dearly beloved master, trapped into a living death by a treacherous maiden," he intoned. "Here he wasted away, imprisoned by the webs you see fastening his legs and arms, enchanted by the power of a woman's wiles. For weeks he endured, railing against his fate, but at last he succumbed . . ." The owl wiped his eye, visibly affected. "With his last breath he forgave the errant maid who enslaved him, and now his remains are a reminder to mortal man that even the greatest may not be proof against female pulchritude and greed . . ."

It might have been a servant showing unexpected guests around a castle in the owner's absence, and I didn't believe a word of it. Conn, on our travels, had sometimes beguiled us with folk tales and legends, and among the latter I remembered various episodes in the life of one Artorius, a Romano-Saxon king of Wessex and his magician friend Myrddin of Cymri—but even Conn sometimes mixed these tales with others about an Arthur Pendragon of the Old Lands and a shaman of Scotia called Merlon—and although all these tales bore some similarity and indeed did have a treacherous maiden in them, sometimes it was the king who fell foul of her and other times the magician, so this hotch-potch of the owl's was obviously meant to beguile the superstitious into connecting a very-present enchantment with something that happened, or might have happened, two hundred years ago, and was obviously intended to deter us from further inquiries, pack ourselves up and go away.

But I had no intention of going away; here we were and here we stayed until we got some of the right answers, at least. I would have to be careful, though, and play it just right.

"Thank you, O Guardian of the late-lamented One," I said, bowing to the owl. "May we now go back outside? I find this sad atmosphere somewhat oppressive, and I am sure my companions do also," and I rushed back into the open, hoping for a glimpse of that shadowy something I thought I had detected behind the owl. Nothing. Still . . .

"What the hell are you doing?" queried Conn, but I turned my back to the cave and gave him a big wink.

"Trust me . . ." I turned to the owl, back once more on his perch on the stone. "May I question you a little further before we gather up our belongings and take our leave of this fair place?"

"But of course," said the owl, fluffing up his feathers and mollified, no doubt, by my obsequious tone. "Pray proceed."

"Your master (rest his soul) has been dead—or in this state in which we found him—for two hundred years, you said?"

"Alas yes, almost to the day. And many the pilgrims, like yourselves, who have passed this way to marvel and to mourn . . ."

"Alack-a-day," I said, and bowed my head. "It is the world's loss . . . Men say he could have been the greatest sorcerer and magician since the world began—"

"The greatest," asserted the owl, nodding his head wisely. "Indubitably."

"Yet I question this," I said. "Tell me—"

"Question it?" said the owl in a different voice. I looked again: yes, I was not mistaken. There was a sort of greyish, wavery background to the bird.

"Yes," I hurried on, for I was almost sure now: "for I have heard of other such who gave counsel and comfort to the great ones of the land who were accounted less great than this Ancient One we came to seek, and then lived their allotted span and passed away amid scenes of universal grief: they did not succumb to mortal wiles, they—"

"My master was greater far than these—these minor tricksters you speak of," said the owl, and he was definitely becoming more ruffled. "My master is—was—the greatest sorcerer the world has ever seen! Master of the Art of Illusion, Traveller in Time, Licentiate of Language, Far-Seer . . . Why, he was a man so great that the kings of the world came to him on bended knee asking him to solve their problems, work out their battle strategy, choose their companions, and would not rest until he had seen them and given them the benefit of his experience. It's not my fault if they didn't listen . . ."

I pretended not to hear this last. "Yet he succumbed to a bronze-coin's-worth of tawdry female," I said warmly. "Just like any other male. No magician worth his salt would even admit to—"

"Do you dare to question The Ancient?"

"Oh, I don't question his mortality, his frailty: I do question, yes, whether he ever was the great magician he claimed to be!"

"Not claimed to be: is! Er . . . was."

"No! For no magician as great as that could possibly behave as vulnerably as you say; no sorcerer with his reputation could be so reduced by a mere woman—" I moved closer. "And no Master of Illusion worth anything could resist the temptation to try and con ordinary people into believing he was dead and gone, if only because he was too lazy to—"

"Lazy!" came an indignant voice. "I've never been accused of being lazy all my life! And I am the greatest!"

"Then stop mucking about, Ancient or whatever you call yourself," I said.

"Right! You've asked for it," he said, and materialized behind the owl.

The Gathering

The Ancient

"You've asked for it!" repeated The Ancient crossly, swatting at the owl, who fluttered onto his shoulder and shut its eyes again. "I'm not used to visitors, don't want visitors! Anyway, you've come too soon—stop digging your claws in, Hoowi!—and I'm not ready . . ." and he went on grumbling and grousing to himself, a seamed old man with nut-brown wrinkles, bright blue eyes, long white hair and a longer tri-forked beard dyed yellow, red and blue. He wore a lopsided paper crown that kept slipping to one side, a mothy green velvet cloak edged with tarnished gold braid, and what looked like a rather lived-in yellow-woolly night robe. His feet were shoved in scuffed purple slippers; his fingernails looked chewed, although what teeth he had were decidedly rocky. His voice was high, nasal and singsong; not lilting like Conn's. His nose was rather large and definitely hooked; his ears stuck out, and behind the one that wasn't saving the paper crown was a quill pen; round his neck hung a rope of blue glass beads.

"Done weighing me up?" he snapped, but I fancied the snap was as harmless as an old dog threatening flies.

I bowed: time for politeness and diplomacy. I had tried him very hard and he had let me, but I thought that so far he was merely amusing himself, pretending wrath merely to see me crumple at his feet in awe. My bow extended so far I could almost bump my forehead with my knees, for this man was an unknown quantity.

"Dear Sir," I began. "Am I correct in supposing that we have reached journey's end? That I am, in fact, addressing The Ancient, a magician and sorcerer without parallel, whose reputation reaches far across the land?"

"That's not what you said two minutes ago . . ."

"Ah, but then you were playing games with us. I may have seemed presumptuous, but I assure you it was the presumption of desperation. We have come so far, and it has been such a hard journey, and we are so—so in need of your help . . ." My voice quavered: I couldn't help it.

"Indeed, sir, the little lassie speaks only the truth." Conn's hand was on my shoulder. "She can be a mite sharp-tongued perhaps, but this Thingummy has had one hell of a life and you have only to look at her to know she is really as guileless as a newborn lamb. She—"

"I know, I know," said The Ancient. "You all are. Lambs to the slaughter, all of you; except perhaps the White One, and even he has been foolish enough to forget the rules of faery and lose his heart along with his horn . . . Never mind, never mind. Come, all of you: you are all welcome. We shall eat, and then we shall talk." He looked at me. "Here you, Flora who brought the Fauna," and he wheezed at some joke only he could understand, although I felt a sudden jolt of recognition I could not account for. "Go back into the cave. On a shelf you will find oatcakes, butter, honey and a flagon of mead, a crock of goat's milk and some cheese . . ."

They were there as he said, and of course the silly skeleton had gone, as had the crystal curtain. Moglet had milk and cheese, Corby oatcakes and cheese, Puddy appeared to be devouring fireflies, though there were always as many again, but for Pisky there was something special: the old man scooped him up in his bowl, and sprinkled something into the water.

"Here, Emperor of the fishes: my de-luxe mixture."

This kept Pisky quiet for at least ten minutes, then I saw him glance down at his flanks, flirting his tail, standing on his head: "Emperor of the fishes, he called me. Did you ever! Emperor . . ."

At last I leant back, wiping my sticky mouth on the back of my hand: I was full. Any more and I should be uncomfortable. I looked round at the others. Snowy was lying down, legs tucked under. Puddy had his eyes shut, which meant he was still chewing; he burped. Pisky was still. Corby groomed his uninjured wing, oiling it evenly with his beak. Moglet was licking her stomach, with long, even strokes that left sticky runnels on it. Conn was lying full-length on the grass, chin in hand, his rusty armour a discarded heap in the shadows. It was a still, warm night, with just the faintest breath of a mint-smelling breeze to touch our faces, ruffle my hair. Somewhere a bird still sang, sweet and low, and fireflies danced among the trees. Perfect.

"Now then," said The Ancient. "We shall talk . . ."

I do not remember what tongue we spoke; I know we all understood. One by one we told The Ancient who we were, how we met and why we were travelling together. It was thus I learnt more fully of Conn's encounter with our Mistress and a little of what it had meant to Snowy, and less and less did it seem that our meetings were chance.

"So, you are bound together, all of you, by the unfortunate wiles of a powerful witch," mused The Ancient. His throne-like rock seat gave him an advantage, for sitting on it he was taller than any of us standing up, even Conn. "And so she is dead . . . I find it hard to believe she is gone, for she was an adversary worthy of even such as I, but she moved away to the east many, many years ago, so long that I have forgotten her name. Strange, for once I could recall her with ease . . . You are sure she is dead?"

We reassured him.

"One of the best Shape-Changers ever, too: I remember once . . . No matter." He stroked his beard. "Not at her best recently, I gather. However, good as she was, I fancy I could give her a run for her money. Watch this!"

And as we gazed his edges grew blurred, then he disappeared completely, leaving in his place a white rabbit washing its whiskers. Then it wasn't a rabbit but a hedgepig. Then a rather foolish-looking sheep. Then just a head, looking rather like Tom Trundleweed. Then a brightly spinning ball. Then nothing. Then The Ancient again.

He beamed at us. "How's that for Shape-Changing, then?"

Conn applauded, clapping his hands, but I frowned. "That's not Shape-Changing!"

"Then what is it, clever-sticks?" and he frowned, too.

"Illusion. Like your hedge. And a lot more here, I shouldn't be surprised."

"You're a fine one to talk of illusion!" He had half-risen from his seat, and Conn put a hand on my arm.

"Now then, Thingummy dear," he muttered. "You may be right and all that, but the laws of hospitality—"

I began to apologize, but The Ancient cut me short. "She's right, you know, right in her own way. Comes of spending her formative years with that old bitch of a witch What's-her-name . . . No, no apologies. I'm not a true Shape-Changer, but I am an Illusionist and, though I say it myself, the best!" He failed to look modest. "One can't do everything, and I concentrated on what I did best. Worth remembering that: forget what you want to do, find something you do better than anyone else, even if it's only turd-throwing, and become undisputed champion: better a champion shit-shoveller than a forty-second-rate turnip-carver . . . Where was I? Ah yes. Time-Traveller, too, and Master of Languages and the Crystal Ball. Not very good at the last: lost the old ball . . . Some are good at one thing, some at another. Never fancied the Resurrectionists, for example; there is always a price to pay for immortality, and sometimes it is far harder to render than the common coin of mortal clay. And who knows what one might have to bear? Watching those one has loved pass into decay and die; perhaps seeing all one believes in, had fought for, pass into disrepute . . .

"The enchanted may mourn, but they may not weep: that relief is the only compensation for mortal grief. My friend, the White One, knows that, do you not?" And he nodded at Snowy, who bowed his head until I could see the maimed stump where his horn had been.

Without thinking I rose and went to his side and knelt down and kissed him. "Never mind, dear one, The Ancient will help you find a new horn—you will, won't you?" I asked anxiously. "We've come all this way . . . Forgive my rudeness and help them. Please?"

"Depends on what you want, doesn't it? I can't work miracles!"

"Sure and we don't ask for the impossible, your Sagacity," said Conn earnestly, rising to his feet. "All we seek is your wisdom. As you said, it seems we are all enchanted by the same witch, and I, for one, will not believe that her spells cannot be broken."

"Broken, perhaps not: bent a little is what we seek. Never go at magic straight on, you'll only bruise your hopes. Sneak round the edges if you can. It's like Roman law: or," looking at Conn, "killing a boar, if you like. Get round to the flank." He blew his nose on an orange scarf he pulled from his cloak. "Now then, my White One, let's begin with you: what do you wish for? You know, of course, that it would take far stronger powers than mine to undo the ill to your enchanted prince? Only a life, freely given, may release him, and then only to a Between-World . . . So, if it is possible, you would wish your horn to be restored?"

Snowy bowed his head, and I thought I could see the gleam of a tear in his eye. "Yes, then if—if all else fails, I shall still have the right to rejoin my brethren in the west, and live out the rest of my life with them."

"Then I do have some hope for you; small hope, 'tis true, but one grain of salt on an egg is better than none at all. The witch's curse was powerful enough, but there was more concentration on the boy than on you, and I am fairly sure, from what you said, that she cut off the closing words that stifle all hope.

"Your horn, my friend, may be restored by one thing and one thing alone: a fresh drop of dragon's blood, freely given!"

"But that is not fair!" burst out Conn, coming over to Snowy's side. "There are no dragons! They all died out—oh, hundreds of years ago! You're just saying something to comfort the poor old thing that can't possibly come true, and that's the cruellest kind of hope—"

"Wait!!" thundered The Ancient, and for a moment, behind the doddery old man who rose unsteadily from his seat, I caught a glimpse of another, a tall stern-faced warrior wearing purple and blue and carrying a wand in his right hand . . . Then the vision faded, but it was my turn to catch at Conn's arm, anxious not to offend.

"Yes, wait, my dear . . ."

"For, if I mistake me not, all your problems resolve around the same end," said the old man, slowly resuming his seat, as if there had been no interruption. "Tell me now, Connor O'Connell, as you seem to like the sound of your own voice. What is your heart's desire?"

"My desire? Why sure and that's plain enough to see. My sword, my father's sword, is snapped in two and needs to be made whole; my armour is rusted past polishing and I want it once more bright!"

"And then?"

"Then? Oh, I see. Well, then I would go off to Frankish lands or Germanica and hire myself out as a mercenary, or maybe even seek adventure farther abroad. There is money to be made in service, you know, and perhaps more as free-sword."

"No settling-down, then?" The Ancient stroked his beard, the yellow bit on the right.

"Me? Not likely! There's all life to be lived out there. No, worthy Sir, I'm just not the settling-down kind!"

"Pity, pity," said The Ancient, "for part of the lifting of the witch's curse depended on your asking the hand in marriage of the ugliest female in the land, as I recall—and that part cannot be altered, not in essence, anyway."

Conn went bright red. "As to that—if I ever find this female, then 'tis to be hoped that for her sake she is rich; if she is, then might I ask for her hand, for then she'll be so grateful she'll give me her dowry, and I'll kiss her goodbye. And if she's not rich—why then she won't get asked. And any that question my right to travel this world in tarnished mail, then my sword—if I can get it reforged—will teach them a lesson they won't forget in a hurry!" He looked very fierce and pushed up the tips of his moustache, then spoilt the whole effect by apologizing to Moglet for nearly treading on her tail.

"You also wished your sword whole again: that curse cannot be lifted save by the same magic the White One seeks. In your case that sword, which bears magic runes not seen by mortal eye, can only be welded together by flame from dragon's tongue, again freely given."

Conn started up in protest, no doubt once again to point out that dragons were extinct, but The Ancient waved him to silence, and I felt a sudden surge of excitement, as if there was more to come.

He turned to me. "And you: do you believe in dragons?"

"I believe in them, yes of course, because everyone knows they existed once. My—the witch sometimes used powdered dragon-bones in her spells: the one to make different coloured flames, I think . . ."

The Ancient positively beamed. "Well, then?"

"But Sir . . ."

"Yes?"

"I must confess to believing, like Conn, that they—they . . ."

"Well?" He scowled.

"Well, that they—are extinct."

"Like witches and unicorns, I suppose. And magicians," he added maliciously.

"Well, no . . ." I trailed off.

"You see? Never take things like that for granted, youngster. You, of all people, with your upbringing, should know better! I daresay if you told the folk in—oh, say Sarum or Silchester of your life with the witch, they would pelt you with refuse for lying." He leant forward. "Now, leaving aside the question of dragon/no dragon for the moment, why have you come on this quest? What is your desire?"

"To get rid of my pebble," I said, on surer ground. "And so have the others," and I nodded at Corby, Puddy, Pisky and Moglet. "You see we all want to be whole and unencumbered and free of pain again. I want to be able to walk upright, Corby wants to fly, Puddy wants to be rid of his headaches, Pisky needs to eat properly and little Moglet wants to run fast enough to catch mice. And to do this we must find the person or thing who rightfully owns these pebbles and give them back; the witch stuck them fast but I expect the rightful owner might have a way to extract them. Oh, and we'd like our memories back, too," I added.

"Don't want much, do you?" but he was smiling. "Right: Let's have a look at these famous pebbles . . ."

One by one we showed him our encumbrances, and he himself picked up Pisky's bowl. Then, when he had inspected them all, he did a very strange thing.

He laughed.

He laughed till the rheumy tears ran down his cheeks, leaving rather dirty runnels; he laughed till he wheezed and coughed and, speechless, pointed to his back and Conn kindly went and gave him a couple of good thumps between his shoulder blades to stop him choking. At last he sat up, wiped his eyes on the orange scarf, blew his nose again, and took a swig from Pisky's bowl.

"Oh dear, oh dear," he said at last, still chuckling. "Oh dearie, dearie me . . ."

We looked at one another, feeling like idiots, and it was Corby who voiced our feelings. "What we done, then? Must be mighty foolish to make the Man o' Wisdom laugh as if we were the village idiot who saw his face reflected in the pond, thought it were the moon, an' tried to pluck it out to stop it from drowning—"

"No, no, my friend!" said The Ancient, trying to compose his features. "I'm not laughing at you: I'm laughing with you, and for you, for I think I have solved the mystery!"

We all began talking at once, but he raised his hand for silence.

"I'm going to tell you all a story," he said. "So settle down and listen . . ."

The Gathering

Dragon-Quest

So it was that the warm night closed around us like a cloak as we heard the tale of a young dragon sent out on his Master-Quest. We heard of the gold he collected, of the brilliant jewels he snatched, stole, retrieved, found; we heard how the last search, for his personal pearl, had led him to this land, and how he had stored his treasure high in a cave in the Black Mountains, and one night had left it unguarded to pay one last visit to the villagers nearby who had feasted him regularly during his years of search. How in that last feasting a black shadow, a greedy, grasping thing, crept to his cave and stole his hoard, fleeing into the forests of the night where he could not find her. And how the dragon could not return to his homeland without the jewels, and lay a-dying from grief and frustration in that same cave.

How the thief fled far, far away, as far as the winds would take her; how she had to hide the jewels, possession of which, given the correct spells and formulae, would give her a mastery of magic greater than any ever known. How she had not hidden them from the dragon by burying them deep, lest they be dug up; neither had she thrown them into the deeps, lest they be trawled to surface; nor had she hung them from a tree, lest they fall: rather had she fastened them safe into living creatures snatched at random from the highways and byways, as they came to hand. A netted crow, a toad pulled from under a stone, a kitten taken from its doorstep, a fish scooped from a rich man's pond, a child taken under promise of protection—

"It's us!" I shouted, bobbing up and down like some crazy creature. "It's us!"

"It's-us-is-us-is-us," bubbled Pisky. "Which have I got? What am I? Tell me quick!"

"My headache is a jewel?" pondered Puddy.

"Cripes!" squawked Corby, peering under his wing. "Bleeding 'ell! A sapphire for a splint . . ."

"Don't want it," mewed Moglet. "Take it away, Thing dear! Don't want a diamond . . ."

"I don't particularly want a ruby navel either, my pet," I said, after a quick peek to confirm, picking her up and cuddling her. "But at least we now know what they are. And just think how costly that paw of yours is now!"

Pisky was trying to squint at the bulge in his mouth. "What-is-it, what-colour, which-one? Quick! Quick!"

The Ancient took pity on him. "A moon-pearl, precious one. The dragon's special stone . . ."

"I-knew-it-I-knew-it!"

Puddy had got his by a process of elimination. "An emerald? Hmmm . . . could be worse, I suppose. Green *is* my favourite colour . . ."

"Ruby, emerald, sapphire, diamond, pearl," I said, musing. "Is that why we used to—still do—hurt? The spell she put on us to keep them hidden?"

"Yes," said The Ancient. "But the spell worked against her in the end. At first, individually, she could keep you in thrall but later, collectively, and without realizing it, you formed a bond between yourselves that was enforced by the holding of the jewels: if you like, the dragon's power was transformed into a shield against harm, as long as you kept together, and neither the witch, nor anyone else, could really hurt you. Especially if you kept in physical contact with each other."

I nodded. I could remember when she had had to set Broom to beating us because she dared not do so herself; those times when we huddled together under my cloak.

"And so she never really benefited from the jewels," said the old man. "You never gave her the chance: by the time her knowledge was sufficient to use them you lot had adopted them for yourselves. If you hadn't that last experiment would have worked, and powers that should lie hidden would have walked the Earth . . ."

I shivered: I could still remember with loathing that night on the island when our world had nearly come to an end . . .

Conn had remained silent until now. "But—does that mean that there really is a dragon still alive? That somewhere, in those Black Mountains you spoke of, he is waiting for Thingy and her friends to return his jewels?"

"I think he has given up all hope," said The Ancient, "but yes, he is still there." He glanced round at us all. "He is the only one who can rid you of your burdens, his jewels; he is the only one to mend your sword, Connor O'Connell, and grow your new horn, White One, with a blast of fire and a drop of blood. He is *your* only hope, my wandering ones . . ."

"I knew we all belonged together," I said. "I knew it!"

We talked far into the night—at least the others did, for all too soon the excitement, the warm night, my full stomach, the earlier travelling and, most of all, the knowledge that our quest had not been in vain, that there really was hope for us all, however far away, induced in me the most complete and utter weariness, and my eyes kept closing in spite of themselves. In the end I fashioned my cloak into a pillow and lay down, an equally soporific

Moglet tucked up to my chest. As we dropped off to sleep Conn was questioning the magician on Time-and-Space Travelling, and I heard him ask what the other side of the moon looked like.

"Very disappointing . . ."

And so I fell asleep to dream I travelled in a silver tube with windows open to the stars to where the moon grinned away like a yellow cheese; and then I spun round to her backside to find—

"But supposing you could," said Puddy. "Just how much would colour weigh?"

I drifted off again to find myself trying to scrape colours from a leaf, a stone, a jewel and weigh the differences in little pots and pans on my fingers . . . But before I knew where I was I had taken all colour from everything, and the whole world was white, white as snow; but white is a colour too, and I had to catch each snowflake and take away the white, and wash the white from every fleece of every sheep in the world, but Snowy was the only white thing that wouldn't play and ran off into the forest, but I could still see him for now everything else was without colour, clear as glass, transparent as crystal; and The Ancient was an icicle, and then he melted and dripped all over me—

"Come on children," he said. "It's starting to rain. You'll be better off inside."

And Conn picked me and Moglet up in one sleepy heap and carried us into the cave and plonked us down on a heap of bracken and heather, covered with some soft, silky material, and we snuggled down and I could smell thyme and rosemary. Someone covered me with my cloak, tucked it round snug, and then someone else was singing, a wordless song that ran and turned and curled back on itself like the golden ring Conn wore on his finger . . . And then I felt him lie down beside me, and his hand stroked my hair, and the trees and the rocks began to sing too, and the wind and the waters, a song so heart-catching and sad and beautiful that my eyes were full of tears, and yet I was smiling—

"Liebestod," said The Ancient, at least I think that is what he said. "But for you it will be Liebeslied . . ."

I didn't understand the words but I did understand my feelings, and I snuggled up to Conn's breathing, sleeping body and my heart sang with the music.

After breakfast the next morning—a helping of what looked like gruel but tasted of butter and nuts and honey and raspberries and milk—the magician led us outside into a morning sparkling with raindrops and clean as river-washed linen, but strangely the grass was dry when we seated ourselves in a semicircle in front of his throne. Hoowi, the owl, was again perched on his shoulder, eyes shut, and he took up Pisky's bowl into his lap. Although the birds sang, their songs were courtesy-muted, for The Ancient's voice was softer this morning as though he were tired, and indeed his first words confirmed this.

"I have been awake most of the night, my friends, pondering your problems. That is why I have convened this meeting. We agreed yesterday that you had all been called together for a special mission, a quest to find the dragon. You need him, but he also needs you." He paused, and glanced at each one of us in turn. "But perhaps last night you thought this would be easy. Find the Black Mountains, seek out the dragon's lair, return the jewels, ask for a drop of blood and a blast of fire and Hey Presto! your problems are all solved.

"But it is not as easy as that, my friends. Of your actual meeting with the dragon, if indeed you reach him, I will say nothing, for that is still in the realms of conjecture. What I can say is this: in order to reach the dragon you have a long and terrible journey ahead of you, one that will tax you all to the utmost, and may even find one or other of you tempted to give up, to leave the others and return; if that happens then you are all doomed, for I must impress upon you that as the seven you are now you have a chance, but even were there one less your chances of survival would be halved. There is no easy way to your dragon, understand that before you start. I can give you a map, signs to follow, but these will only be indications, at best. What perils and dangers you may meet upon the way I cannot tell you: all I know is that the success of your venture depends upon you staying together, and that you must all agree to go, or none.

"I can see by your expressions that you have no real idea of what I mean when I say 'perils and dangers': believe me, your imaginations cannot encompass the terrors you might have to face—"

"But if we do stay together?" I interrupted.

"Then you have a better chance: that is all I can say. It is up to you." He was serious, and for the first time I felt a qualm, a hesitation, and glancing at my friends I saw mirrored the same doubts.

"And if we don't go at all—if we decide to go back to—to wherever we came from?" I persisted.

"Then you will be crippled, all of you, in one way or another, for the rest of your lives."

"Then there is no choice," said Conn. "And so the sooner we all set off the better," and he half-rose to his feet.

"Wait!" thundered the magician, and Conn subsided, flushing. "That's better. I have not finished."

"Sit down, shurrup, be a good boy and listen to granpa," muttered Corby sarcastically, but The Ancient affected not to hear.

"There is another thing," said he. "If you succeed in your quest and find the dragon, and if he takes back the jewels, and if he yields a drop of blood and a blast of fire, if, I say . . . then what happens afterwards?"

The question was rhetorical, but Moglet did not understand this.

"I can catch mice again," she said brightly, happily.

But he was gentle with her. "Yes, kitten, you will be able to catch mice, and grow up properly to have kittens of your own—but at what cost? You may not realize it but your life, and the life of the others, has been in suspension while you have worn the jewels, but once you lose your diamond then time will catch up with you. You will be subject to your other eight lives and no longer immune, as you others have been also, to the diseases of mortality.

"Also, don't forget, your lives have been so closely woven together that you talk a language of your own making, you work together, live, eat, sleep, think together. Once the spell is broken you, cat, will want to catch birds, eat fish and kill toads; you, crow, will kill toads too, and try for kittens and fish; toad here will be frightened of you all, save the fish; and the fish will have none but enemies among you.

"And do not think that you either, Thing-as-they-call-you, will be immune from this; you may not have their killer instinct but, like them, you will forget how to talk their language and will gradually grow away from them, until even you cross your fingers when a toad crosses your path, shoo away crows and net fish for supper—"

"You are wrong!" I said, almost crying. "I shall always want them, and never hurt them! We shall always be together!"

"But will they want you," asked The Ancient quietly, "once they have their freedom and identity returned to them? If not, why is it that only dog, horse, cattle, goat and sheep have been domesticated and even these revert to the wild, given the chance? Do you not think that there must be some reason why humans and wild animals dwell apart? Is it perhaps that they value their freedom, their individuality, more than man's circumscribed domesticity? Is it not that they prefer the hazards of the wild, and only live with man when they are caught, then tamed and chained by food and warmth?"

"I shall never desert Thing!" declared Moglet stoutly. "I shan't care whether she has food and fire or not, my place is with her!"

"Of course . . . Indubitably . . . What would I do without her . . ." came from the others, and I turned to the magician.

"You see? They don't believe we shall change!"

"Not now," said The Ancient heavily. "Not now. But there will come a time . . . So, you are all determined to go?"

"Just a moment," said Conn. "You have told Thingmajig and her friends just what might be in store for them if we find the dragon: what of me and Snowy here? What unexpected changes in personality have you in store for us?" He was angry, sarcastic.

"You," said The Ancient, "you and my friend here, the White One, might just do the impossible: impossible, that is, for such a dedicated knight as yourself . . ."

"And what's that?"

"You might change your minds . . ."

"About what, pray?" And I saw Snowy shake his head.

"What Life is all about . . ."

"Never!"

"Never is a long time . . . Ah me, I'm getting old: another clitch."

"What's a clitch?" I asked, trying not to let the thought of losing Conn and Snowy at the end of it all, if ever we got to the beginning, upset me too much.

"A clitch?" He sniggered. "It's like 'It always rains before it pours' or 'Every cloud has a silver lining'—you know, the sort of hackneyed phrase everyone says over and over again until it becomes boring and predictable and—and a clitch. Cliché," he amended.

Although I had heard neither phrase before, I tried to look wise. "Comme: 'Toujours la politesse,' ou 'chacun à son goût,'" I suggested, then was shocked when I realized I didn't know where the words had come from, let alone what they meant.

"Exactly," he said, glancing at me sharply from under thatchy brows. "Exactement, p'tite . . . Couldn't have put it better myself . . ."

Conn looked as if he was going to say something, but didn't.

"Well," said The Ancient. "It's midday: supposing we meet again at supper, and you can tell me what you have all decided. Think about it carefully, mind, and don't forget what I told you." But he sighed: it must have been clear to him even then that none of us believed his dire predictions.

We all spent the intervening hours characteristically, I suppose.

Snowy disappeared into the wood and every now and again I saw his shadow flickering among the trees. Conn went to a little knoll, got out his broken sword and, holding it up before him hilt uppermost, prayed with his eyes open, face to the sky. Pisky spent the time rearranging his bowl to his liking, pulling the weed this way and that, nudging the poor snails all over the place. Corby went into a corner by himself, walking about in circles and muttering. Puddy found another corner and sat quiet, looking as though his head were aching. Moglet chased a butterfly or two, then washed herself from ears to toe and tail, then went and sharpened the claws on her good paw. And I? I, I regret to say, did none of these useful, constructive things. Instead, I crept closer till I could see Conn's profile, then lay back in the long grass and watched the clouds pass, then rolled over on my stomach to regard the busy ants scurrying to and fro. I listened to the ascending lark, smelt the cowslips, stroked Moglet and ate wild raspberries. And fell asleep and dreamt of nothing—

Conn shook my shoulder. "Suppertime, Thingumabob . . . Made up your mind?"

We all had, as I found out when we rejoined the others. We were determined to set out on this perilous venture, keep together and risk whatever came.

The Ancient heard us out, Conn the spokesman.

"Then all I can do, my friends, is to prepare you for your journey as best I can—and wish you luck. You'll need it . . ."

I was dreaming, a long, slow, wordless, placeless dream, and there were people I knew but could not know, and then someone was pulling me away and I was rushing faster and faster until the wind howled in my ears with the speed of my passing, and I was being pulled upwards to a hole in the ceiling, and then I bumped my head and fell back with a thud and—

"Wake up, child!" said The Ancient. "The others are almost ready, and you'll want a bite to eat before you set off."

I stumbled out into a mist that curled round my feet like an attenuated cat. Everything looked unreal, almost as though I were still dreaming, or had missed out on a day somewhere. I rubbed my eyes and Conn was busy loading up Snowy and the others were waiting, more or less patiently, for their turn. A hand appeared at my elbow: a hunk of bread with a slice of cheese tucked inside. A mug of goat's milk followed and I munched and drank, then moved forward to help the others.

Besides the meagre provisions we had brought with us there were flour and salt, apples, cheese and a large jar of honey, and the water-bottle was fresh-filled from the spring. Poor Snowy looked very laden, so I took Moglet in my arms and Puddy in my pocket and, to my surprise, Conn put Corby on his shoulder and strung Pisky's bowl round his waist.

Catching my look, he grinned. "We'll swap later! Besides, as we eat the provisions the old horse—sorry, unicorn—will find his burden that much lighter."

The Ancient was in his best today: a purple robe sewn with silver stars and his beard in three shades of blue, although his conical hat with a crescent moon on its tip was crooked and threatened to slip over his ears, protruding though they were. In his hand was a roll of soft leather.

"Your map," he announced. He unfolded it and we stared at squiggles, arrows, letters: it didn't look like a map at all.

I pointed to some humps and bumps. "What are those?"

"What do they look like?" snapped the magician. "Hills, mountains, that's what!"

"And the squiggles?"

"Rivers, streams . . ."

"The dotty places?" At least the forests were shown by recognizable trees.

"Waste land: moors, heaths, bogs . . ."

"The straightish lines?"

"Roads. Such as they are. Roman mostly: the straight ones are, anyway. Probably a bit out of date . . ."

Conn put his finger on the middle of the map, on a thing that looked like a cross between a star and a spider. "What's this?"

"A compass: north, south, east, west—"

"I've seen something like that before," said Conn. "Only they didn't call it a compass: a magic needle, I think. I was hitching a trip cross-channel on a Skandia galley—and damned uncomfortable it was too, full of great sweaty fellows splashing everyone with their oars—and they had this little sliver of metal suspended in a stone bowl of oil. They reckoned they could find their way in dark, fog, storm because the thin end of the metal pointed always north, whichever way they turned. The captain said he had it from a trader from the east, in exchange for a bale of furs. Swore he had the best of the bargain, too."

"There you are, then!"

"But we've no piece of metal," I said. "And if we are to go in any special direction . . . And what's that, round the edge?" I looked closer. "That says 'ENE,' or something: I've never heard of that word . . ."

"It's initials," said The Ancient impatiently. "East-north-east: those letters are your direction-finders. And you *have* got a magic needle, of sorts: the White One knows one way from t'other, and come to that so does the raggedy bird."

"Roughly," said Corby, looking slightly offended at the adjective. "As the crow flies, of course . . ."

"There are some tiny circles marked as well," said Conn, peering closely. "There is one on its own, and there's three together, and four—"

"Those are your markers," and the old man looked at each of us in turn. "And you have to go their way. One, then two, then three and so on up to seven. They are all standing stones, some higgledy-piggledy, some straight, some in circles. You go by the directions I have marked in the margin: there is the letter one, and a direction. Follow that and you come to the first stone, then letter number two and its direction et cetera."

"Sounds simple enough," said Conn, but he was frowning.

"It is simple: just follow your noses. And the directions, of course," he added hastily. "Now: are you all ready?"

"Thank you," I said, "from all of us. For the hospitality and the help and the food and—and everything."

He pinched my cheek, not hard, but I could feel it through my mask just the same. "Think nothing of it, Flower: it has been vastly amusing, so far. I was out of practice . . ."

I didn't quite understand what he meant. "Shall we see you again?"

"Very likely, if you follow the instructions and remember what I said about staying together. Don't look so gloomy: you will have your sunny days too, you know . . . Now, see that wood over there? Well that's a good enough marker for your first direction, east by south. That's your way. Goodbye, and good luck . . ."

The mist had thinned, and so had his voice: it sounded now like an echo.

We had all been straining our eyes to the wood, answered "Goodbye," and then turned to wave, but he had gone. So had the glade, the cave, the stream. We were standing on the highest point of a bleak moor in the burning-off of a summer mist that rolled away from our feet as rapidly as Brother Jude-the-Less's manuscripts rolled up across the table if they weren't weighted down. Nearby was what might once have been a ring of stones, but there was nothing else recognizable for miles: even the wood was a half-day's walk. It was as if something had picked us up from somewhere and dumped us down again nowhere.

"Well, I'll be . . . blest!" said Conn, scratching his head. "However did he manage that?"

But nobody had an answer. There was the illusion-bit, which I thought might help, but even I was uneasy about this. If I explored it too deep I should have to explain how it was we seemed to have only been with the magician a couple of days, reaching him in early spring, while now we were standing in countryside that was—

"High summer," said Moglet. "How nice. Didn't know we'd been there so long . . ."

There: where was there? What about all the anachronisms of season? The strange sleep that had fallen so easily on us all, a blanket of time-consuming dream so that one woke unsure whether one still slept? I should have pinched myself, but didn't, I don't know why.

We all felt the same, I could see that, but no one wanted to talk about it: a bit like suspecting there might be a wasp in the preserve, but hoping it will fly out of the window before you have to disturb it.

It was Snowy who pulled us together. "The wood is indeed east by south, and that is our first direction, is it not? Come, my friends, this quest is for all, and better to start at once than to question too much. We are together, that is what matters. Friend Corby, do you confirm the direction?"

Corby shuffled on Conn's shoulder. "As the crow flies, unicorn, as the crow flies. Not that crows allus fly straight, mind . . ."

The Binding: Unicorn

The Castle of Fair Delights

And so we went south by east and past the wood, and on to a different mark as we passed through it. The going was easy, the foods of the wayside plentiful, and both Conn and I found we had more money than we thought in our pockets, so it was easy to keep us all provisioned. It was almost dream-like, that progression, from the high heathlands to the downs, the plain to the valleys: everywhere they were bringing in the first cutting of hay, and the air was full of the sun-warmed smell of the drying grasses, the honey-heavy perfume of may, the bruise of wild garlic. Lambs, colts, calves, kids were younglings now, no longer babes, and the birds were feeding their second brood; sweet cicely pollen-powdered my knees, keck-parsley my hips, angelica my shoulders; corn-poppies, Demeter's bane, bled at my feet and elder laced my hair, and all day and every day the sun walked with us. There may have been days when it was cold or cloudy or it rained, but in truth I do not remember.

It was, therefore, something of a shock to all of us when we were brought abruptly back to the realization of our quest by finding the first standing stone. Bare, ragged as a sore tooth, twice man-height, it stood alone on the crest of a little hill and pointed with afternoon's shadow finger to the valley beneath, a valley ringed by forest and bearing in its midst a fair castle, towered and beflagged. The building lay in greensward; at the front a wide driveway led to the massive doors of the courtyard and at the back was what looked like a jousting-yard. From the four corners of the main building where little wooden towers rose like siege-toys, fluttered pennants, banners, flags in stripes of yellow and gold, seeming to beckon us down to this place that might have been painted onto the landscape one moment since, a scene from some legendary tale. Indeed I blinked twice, to make sure it was really there, and it was only on the second blink that I saw something I had missed before: the crescent-shaped lake that lay to the left of the castle. Even at this distance it was dark and deep and still, a black scar on the green.

"Ah!" exclaimed Conn. "And isn't that a sight to gladden the heart? There we shall surely find a warm welcome and hospitality of the finest if I'm not mistaken, Thingummy. And as the finger of the stone points that way and the direction on the map says the same . . . Well, then?"

I frowned. For no reason I felt shivery.

"If it's so fair . . ." said Puddy.

"And we're supposed to face great danger?" supplemented Moglet.

"What the hell's wrong with it?" added Corby. "Must be something we can't see from here."

"My great-great-great-grandfather was fond of remarking that the prettiest flies often hid the sharpest barb," contributed Pisky, helpfully.

"Oh, come on now! You're just a bunch of confirmed pessimists!" exploded Conn. "You see something nice and welcoming and all you want to do is run away from it, just because it *is* pleasant! That old magician did say that the sun would sometimes shine on our endeavours, didn't he? Well it is, and down there is a castle as fair as any I've seen, and I'm longing to sit at a table bearing venison pasties and beef and oyster pies and drink a decent Frankish burgundy. And when I've eaten and drunk I should like to be shown to a chamber containing a man-sized bed laid with real linen sheets and pull a bear-pelt over my toes—not lie out under the stars itching with hay-ticks and walked over by hedgepigs! Down there is civilization and that's where I'm going, and you can come or not, as you please!" He tugged at Snowy's bridle. "Well?"

"It is as The Ancient said," he replied cryptically. "This is the way we must go."

"Told you," exulted Conn. "Now, are you others coming or not?"

He knew we would, if only because we remembered what the old magician had said about the importance of keeping together, and indeed, as we descended the gentle path that led to the fringe of woods surrounding the castle, we all began to wonder—us pessimists, that is—what foundation, if any, our fears were grounded upon, for the day was fair and the sun indeed shone, and little fluffy clouds deliberately either missed it or else hid it for a moment only, just to remind us how beautiful it beamed uncovered; bees fed on deep trumpets of creaming honeysuckle, grasshoppers made a raspy music and above us larks climbed to their pinnacle of song—

Then we descended to the wood.

The trees closed in, the sun was a sullen greenish glow; there were no flowers for the bees, no grass for the grasshoppers and no bird sang. Silence, and only our footsteps on the loamy track that led, straight and true, through the heart of the trees. I felt as though I were in a bowl of silence, as confining as Pisky's crock; drowning, oppressed unbearably by the lack of sound. Conn had stopped whistling the merry tune he had had on his lips a moment since and even the echoes had fled without memory. We all trod softly, as if some terrible thing lurked asleep in the shadows, only waiting a snapped twig to waken to attack.

It was Moglet who voiced our fears: "Why no birds? Where are all the creatures who should be here? Are they all frightened of something?"

I could not have answered, but luckily there was no need for at that moment a half-dozen men-at-arms appeared on the path before us, clad in blue and yellow, spears at the slope, and at their head a knight, mounted on a black palfrey. He was elderly, moustached and bearded, and his hand was held up and open in the universal gesture of greeting.

"Peace, friends," he called, and we halted. At that moment I had Corby on my shoulder, Moglet in my arms, Puddy in my pocket, head out, and Pisky's bowl dangling from my elbow, and I could feel their united suspicion as they turned to the stranger.

Conn and I confirmed his gesture of greeting, and he dismounted, waving back the men-at-arms to stand easy.

"Greetings: name's Egerton de Ruys. Glad to welcome you, Sir Knight," and he strode forward to clasp arms with Conn. He had a nasal, pinched sort of voice and clipped his words off short; one eye socket was empty: a retired knight, if I was not mistaken. "You and y'r servant very welcome, by'r Lady! Saw you from the west tower, don't y'know, and m'niece, the Lady Adiora, sent me to beg you to take advantage of our hospitality in the Castle of Fair Delights and sojourn awhile. Be glad of y'r company."

"Well, and that's gracious enough," said Conn. "Hear that, you disbelievers?" But seeing that he was apparently talking to a broken-down pony, a hunched servant carrying a scrawny crow, a frightened kitten and a small fish, he pinched his lips together and stroked his moustache, trying to look nonchalant. It was evident that the time spent in our exclusive company had made him forget that, to anyone else, talking to animals and a mere servant like that would be considered eccentric, to say the least.

"Sir Egerton: your servant," he said formally, and introduced himself. "My—my servant and I would be glad to accept your hospitality . . ." and he turned and scowled at us, as if daring us to contradict.

So we came through that last fringe of wood, silent still save for the jingling of harness on Sir Egerton's horse, the plod-plod of the men-at-arms and the thudding of my heart.

The track broadened as we left the trees, and as we approached it I was better able to admire the grandeur of the castle. The bottom storey-and-a-half was built of stone, perhaps fifty or so years ago and, I guessed, founded on an earlier structure, Roman perhaps. The upper storey-and-a-half was completed in wood, as were the four towers, the whole gilded and pierced and painted in blue and gold and decorated with carved and sculpted figures of knights, ladies and mythical beasts with three heads or a dozen feet, and there were many little narrow windows, like surprised eyes. A bit draughty in winter, I thought. However, it was difficult to remember snow and ice on so pleasant a day, though paradoxically it certainly seemed cooler down here in the valley. Once more for no reason I shivered, and glanced sideways at the lake: it should have sparkled with sunshine and glinted in the breeze that cracked and snapped the pennons and flags atop the towers, but instead it lay dark and still, dead, and I felt the others shift and press closer as we passed through the heavy wooden gates into the courtyard. This was paved with white cobbles, and to left and right were stables and sheds, and servants in a scurry: one boy's task, I noticed, seemed to be solely that of picking up any stray leaf, straw, or other piece of rubbish that might mar the otherwise pristine approach. I hoped Snowy wouldn't disgrace us by relieving himself, because that would obviously have meant shovels, buckets and mops almost before he had finished.

The stable to which we were assigned was, again, almost too clean and, apart from two palfreys, clear of horses. Sir Egerton indicated the end stall, away from the other mounts.

"Can put your—er, nag, here, don't y'know. The other creatures—er, pets?"

"Er . . . yes," said Conn, his swift glance at us coloured by his suddenly luxurious surroundings to the extent that we obviously appeared to him suddenly exactly as we were: dirty and disreputable. "And my—my servant, er—Thingummy . . ."

"Well," said Sir Egerton, rubbing at the white whiskers on his chin. "Can see you have problems, yes indeed. Never can remember their names meself! Like to leave the animals here, and you and your er, servant can be housed within? M'niece don't care much for cats, or birds come to that, and that fish don't look big enough for eating."

I was frowning dreadfully at Conn, but he affected not to notice. "Why, of course, of course! Just leave the—the animals comfortable, Thingy, and follow me."

Making sure there was fresh fodder and water for Snowy and stowing the others in the manger, I wiped my grubby hands ineffectively on my jacket. "I'll be back," I said shortly. "Just spy out the land."

"Don't like this place," wailed Moglet.

"Neither do I," said Corby. "Summat wrong somewheres . . ."

Puddy hunched up. "Don't be long."

Pisky was at the very bottom of his bowl and said nothing.

I turned to Snowy. "Keep an eye on them, dear one."

He shook his head. "I agree with the crow. Listen hard when you are in that place, watch closely. All is too fair, too clean. And guard the Rusty One: we don't want to lose him."

"Lose him?"

"Are you coming?" said Conn, poking his head round the door. "For goodness sake! Leave those animals alone for a moment, can't you?"

So, it was just "animals" they were, was it? For a moment I almost hated him.

But only for a moment, for as soon as we entered the castle proper I was traitor too to my friends, and had eyes and thought only for the delights that surrounded us. We entered from the courtyard through a pillared portico raised, surprisingly, only a couple of feet from the white cobbles, unlike most castles in which the ground floor was used for stores and the main floor was reached by outside steps: this place was obviously not built for siege.

There were no windows in the great hall in which we found ourselves, but large oil lamps hung from the high ceiling in chains and a cheerful fire burned in a huge fireplace opposite the doors: another innovation, for most hearths were still in the centre. The walls were hung with fine fabrics and tapestries, and a long table stretched the length of the room, with the usual dais at the end for the gentry. The floor, again unusually, was not covered with rushes but laid bare a very fine and detailed mosaic of a hunting scene. It must have predated the present building by a couple of centuries at least and some pieces were missing, others trod pale of colour, but at one end a very convincing stag fled its pursuers, antlers laid back across its shoulders, one terrified eye glancing back at the pursuing hounds, while at the other end a huntsman wound his horn and another notched his bow.

"Ah, my weary travellers, you are welcome!" Down a marble staircase behind the pictured hunters floated a vision. Even to my inexperienced eyes she was a very lovely lady, clad in a clinging robe of blue, fair hair bound and twisted in bands of gold, slippers of the same colour on her feet. Her gown had a long train that whispered over the patterned floor as she moved towards us, hands outstretched to Conn, no eyes for me, and on her fingers and slim wrists more bands of gold. A Golden Lady with hair to match, and eyes as blue as her gown.

And now Sir Egerton was introducing them but to my eyes they needed none such, for her hands were in Conn's and his eyes locked to hers as if they would never let go. She was near as tall as he and slim as a wand, and as she talked and smiled and nodded her little pointed teeth shone and her pink tongue flickered over her lips and they had no eyes for any but each other.

I suddenly felt very small and mean and hunched and dirty and would have given anything not to have seen these two together, to be back with the others, outside, free . . . And even as I thought this I felt the ground beneath my feet groan and move and cry so that I almost stumbled, but even as I looked around, terrified, I saw that no one else had noticed anything out of the way. There it was again! A voiceless moaning, a wordless fear, an empty desolation that beat at the soles of my feet until I felt as though the whole floor moved, and in the flicker and sway of the oil-lamps the stag looked more terrified than ever; his eye shut and opened, his muzzle dripped foam and the hounds bayed their blood-lust—

I dropped to the ground, staggering at the shift in the floor, my eyes shut, my hands over my ears to stop that awful sound—

But Conn was shaking me. "Whatever's the matter, Thingy? Are you all right? Then for heaven's sake stand up and behave yourself! Whatever will the Lady Adiora think of you? Come now . . ." and he raised me and pushed me in the direction of the lady, but I would not look at her, and hung my head and shuffled my feet.

"But how clever of you, my dear Sir Connor!" she exclaimed, and I detected a slight lisp. "How amusing: a hunchie! Does it do tricks? Tumble? And it wears a mask—it must be perfectly hideous! Do let me see . . ." and she stretched out her hand, but with a curiously protective gesture Conn drew me against him.

"No creature for laughter or amusement, my Lady," he said quietly. "Merely a poor unfortunate that cannot help either the shape or the looks the dear

Lord saw fit to burden it with. And it is under my protection, as are the other creatures I travel with—"

But immediately she was all smiles, all contrition for her thoughtlessness, as she came to lay her hand on his arm.

She also trod on my foot, quite hard.

"But of course, Sir Connor! I did not mean to make fun of your servant or your playthings. 'Tis just that I, too, have an interest in finding—employment—for like unfortunates. You will see them tonight . . . And now, if you will follow me?" She gathered the train of her gown. "I declare! It is so good to see a fresh face! Sometimes I feel I shall *die* with boredom in this out-of-the-way prison . . ."

And she took his hand, as naturally as if they had known each other years, and led him towards the stairway and the first floor, me trailing miserably and awkwardly behind.

The room we were to share was octagon-shaped, in one of the towers overlooking the back of the castle. This part was built of wood, in the Moorish pattern, Conn told me, and the tall, leather-curtained windows looked out over the enclosed courtyard behind, curiously bare of ornamentation except for tubs of bay and myrtle, and with an open end enclosed by tall, pointed stakes of wood, with a gateway set in, firmly latched and bolted. Around the two sides were pavilions, set some ten feet from the ground, but there was no indication what it was used for: on closer acquaintance it was far too small for jousting or tourney. As I stared down at its emptiness, again I felt that desolation that I had experienced below, though all seemed fair on the surface.

"Did you ever see such a bed!" exulted Conn, and I turned back from the window to see him stretched out full length on a massive couch set on a platform, hung around with curtains and spread with clean linen and plump cushions and a great coverlet of wolf-skins. "Here's luxury, then!"

"Just what you wanted," I said. "Except it's wolf and not bear."

"One's as warm as the other, and there's only one thing wanting to make it perfect," and he winked at the ceiling, but did not elaborate. "Tell you what, Thingumajig: I reckon we've cat-fallen on our feet here, and no mistake! My nose tells me dinner's on the way, and did you see Milady? Have you ever seen anyone more beautiful?"

"No," I said truthfully, for though our Mistress had been more lovely still in some of her Shape-Changes, that had been magic and not painted prettiness like the Lady Adiora. "Conn . . ."

"Mmmm?"

"Did you notice anything—odd—downstairs? I mean a sort of feeling, a strangeness in the air, a sort of—well, unhappiness?"

"Not a thing, Thingy, not a thing!" He leant up on his elbow. "Was that why you came over all unnecessary?"

I nodded. "I just—felt something. Queer. Nasty . . ."

He leant back again, obviously bored with my imaginings. "Well, there's nothing nasty here, I assure you. Just good living, a beautiful lady, and—"

"And" was a servant, attired in the castle blue and yellow, scratching at the door with a flagon of wine and a Roman glass, green and fragile. One glass.

Conn filled and raised it. "Here's to adventure, Thingy: may all quests be as promising! Oh, look here, the servant must not have been told you were with me . . . A sip from mine: come now, no need to sulk!"

I wasn't sulking, far from it, but I suppose it must have looked that way. Obediently I sipped from the other side of the goblet: it was sweet and heady. I watched Conn help himself to another glass.

"You haven't eaten yet."

"No hurry, no hurry!"

But by the time other servants brought hot water and cloths and filled the tub in the corner, I had practically to undress him. A lot of water went on the floor while he splashed and sang, a mournful ditty of great emotion and little tune, and I had to help him into the clean linen, hose and embroidered surcoat that the Lady Adiora had thoughtfully provided, both to please her eye and put him more firmly in her debt, I had no doubt.

He spoilt the whole effect by falling asleep, fully clothed, on top of the bed, waking up crumpled and cross when a great dinner-gong sounded below some half-hour later. I had taken advantage of his unconsciousness to use the cooling water for a bath myself, and felt immensely better and enormously hungry when he woke, and trotted down to the hall quite happily at his heels, telling myself that my earlier unease was merely engendered by fatigue, an empty stomach and an overactive imagination.

This time there was noise enough to drown any half-imagined sounds from beneath my feet and food enough to ease the stomach-cramps—which strangely enough had re-occurred quite sharply since we came to the castle—and entertainment to feast the eye as well. Though I was seated well below the salt I had a good view of Conn and the Lady Adiora. She had him on her right hand, Sir Egerton on her left, and I could see they were all enjoying themselves. The food was excellent—there was even the venison Conn had craved—and I stuffed myself on pig and truffles and roast duck till I had no room left for the other dozen or so dishes. So I relaxed, pleasantly full of rich food, and listened to the conversation on either side.

My companions were inferior servants of the other gentlemen who attended the feast—there were no ladies save our hostess—and, although they ignored me except for a nod of courtesy and a look of disdain at my shabby wear, they chattered quite freely amongst themselves, and once I had done pigging I listened more carefully. What I heard disturbed me. There were six knights in attendance on the top table, four of whom were staying at the castle, the other two neighbours. They were all well attired, handsome, and of an age or younger than Conn, but once I realized what their servants were saying I observed them more closely.

The conversation I overheard went something like this:

Servant One: "Yours doesn't look too chuffed . . ."

Servant Two: "Yours neither." (Belch) "What do you expect? Stranger appears and knocks their noses together!"

Servant One: "Yours had had it anyway. Six weeks . . ."

Servant Two: "So what? Yours took longer, but look at his eyes! Doubt if he'll carry those saddle-bags round much longer."

Servant Three, from across the table, picking at his teeth: "What gets me is how she does it! Cool as the lake and twice as deep."

Servant Two: "Cool? By'r Lady, *she's* no more cool than this stew! Randiest whore I ever seen."

Servant Three: "Anyway, this one's no better than his stamina, and by the looks of him he's travelled hard already—"

Servant One: "Nothing to the road he has to ride!"

The others sniggered, then one of them glanced at me and winked his companions to silence, and after that I turned to their masters with more awareness. I saw pinched faces under the handsome exteriors: hollow eyes, nervous fingers crumbling unregarded bread, sidelong glances; tongues licking lips, but not of gravy; a hand too ready to stray to knife or dagger; damp palms, pallor, greed—and all directed to where Conn sat, blissfully ignorant, picking at a capon with idle fingers, his gaze always toward the sparkling Adiora, looking more beautiful than ever in a midnight-blue dress sewn with silver thread, her hair unbound save for a silver fillet round her brow. In spite of the look of bemused happiness on Conn's face, and the sight of his moustache once more elevated in eagerness, I felt uneasy: it seemed the lady's interest had antagonized just about everyone except Sir Egerton, who was dozing happily.

All at once I wanted to be back on the quest again together, in spite of my present ease and comfort; I wanted the sweet horsey smell of Snowy's flank to snuggle up to; I wanted Corby's caustic comments, Puddy's good sense, Moglet's soft fur, even Pisky's endless reminiscences, tangled as a nest of grass snakes . . . I wanted Conn back with us, dusty, irritable sometimes, gentle always—

Oh heavens! Hours ago I had promised to go back and report to the others, and by now they must be starving! Pretending I was still hungry I helped myself to a plate of the beef and oyster stew, then slipped away from the table unnoticed and found my way back to the stables. I expected the usual wails and moans about hunger and promises not kept, but they were remarkably quiet. It appeared Puddy had caught a couple of fat bluebottles and had shared shreds with Pisky, so it was only Moglet and Corby for stew. I thought of telling them about Conn's infatuation, about the strange sounds I thought I had heard, but decided it would be foolish: everything would probably be different in the morning, and after all we should be on our way again in a day or so. In the meanwhile, I was missing the promised entertainment at the feast, so after ten restless moments I announced I was going back inside.

Then in their eyes, all five pairs of them, I saw the knowledge of my neglect and guilt lent an angry and spiteful spark to my tongue.

"No reason why I shouldn't go and enjoy myself once in a while! Everyone but me seems to have fun, gets to eat at a table like the gentry, sometimes joins in pleasant conversation, exchanges gossip, has a change of company every now and again! Everyone but me, it seems, finds themselves among their own kind! And what have I got? The promise of a smelly stable and a load of helpless animals!" And, thoroughly frightened at my reaction, guilty at my outburst and lonely as hell without either my friends or Conn, I went back to the feast, to be faced by a thoroughly distasteful entertainment I would have done well to miss.

This consisted of "performances," if you could call them that, by dwarves, manikins, cripples and deformed animals. I found it very easy to imagine myself and the others in their place, and it seemed worse when I saw Conn, his flushed face and sparkling eyes telling only too well their story of too much food and wine, applaud and laugh as heartily as the rest at some poor creature with but one eye in the centre of its forehead and no arms, doing a wretchedly inept tumbling act which ended with it falling into the hearth and setting up a bewildered howl as its hair caught fire. I felt even sicker when they put an emaciated dog with only three legs into a sack with a giant rat: I did not wait for the outcome but ran out to the coolness of the courtyard and was sick on their nice, clean cobbles.

After that I was too ashamed to return either to the others or the feast, so crept away to the shadows of a side-stair and up to our chamber, and there lay down by the fire and sniffled myself to sleep.

I must have slept heavily, for when I awoke the bed in the shadows was already occupied. Still feeling slightly sick and with a nasty taste in my mouth, I blinked sleepily at the fire, which someone had replenished for it was now leaping and dancing like those wretched creatures downstairs, throwing shadows crooked enough to give one the frights. And it was not only the flames that made the shadows caper on the wall, for somehow there was a different shadow-play from the bed. The firelight shone ruddily on Conn's red hair, his eyes, shining bright, and over his thin, white body. But not only Conn: the Lady Adiora hung over him, and her hands and legs and teeth were busy on him, holding, twisting, biting, clutching, pulling, tearing until I heard him groan as if in pain and jumped to my feet despite my thumping head and scuttled over to the bedside.

"Stop it!" I cried shrilly to the lady, who was clad only in her golden hair. "You're hurting him!" And I drew my dagger, prepared to drive her away by force, for he now lay gasping as in a fever, with her sitting across his loins and raking his chest with her pointed fingernails till the blood darkened his skin like sloe-juice on a pigeon's breast. But he only gazed at me with unseeing eyes and groaned the more and she leant across and struck me on the cheek.

"Don't you dare interfere, you dirty little hunchie! You're—you're no better than those others in the dungeons: you should never have been allowed inside! Now, get out! Out, I say, or it will be the worse for you!" And she spat at me so hard that the gobbet stuck to my mask and I had to wipe it away with the back of my hand.

Slowly I sheathed my dagger and looked again at Conn, whose eyes and hands were on the lady's breasts.

"Er . . . it doesn't understand, my beautiful." He turned for a moment to give me an apologetic smile. "Do as she says, there's a good, er . . . Thingummy."

"And don't come back!" she hissed.

"But—but she's hurting you!" I faltered, but at that they both gave such a snigger that I started back, and then suddenly knew what they were doing.

I understood all at once about our Mistress and her Shape-Changes and the sticky head of Broom; about the swineherd who had threatened me with that great thing sticking out in front; all about what it meant to be a female; most of all what the parts of Conn's body were for, and hers—and mine, and it was as if someone had flung me naked from the warm into a bank of snow, so that I gasped with shock and disbelief and ran to the curtained doorway and fought my way through the thick folds and stumbled tear-blinded down the steep stairs, my shadow running hunched before me from the flaming cressets in the wall, until I fell down the last few steps to lie, stunned, on the patterned marble mosaic of the empty hall.

It was the cold that brought me to: I suppose I must have lain there no more than a few minutes, yet in that time it seemed everything had changed. The oil lamps still guttered in their chains, the dampened fire still stuttered and lisped in the fireplace, but the air was filled with an echo like a great gong and the mosaic beneath me sweated with fear. I managed to raise myself to my hands and knees, and from where I crouched I could see the glazed eye of the great stag, running away from me, hear the beat of his terrified heart, the thud of his hooves, the harsh rasp of his breathing and wiped a fleck of bloodstained foam from my hand. And then I was running with him, crashing heedless through the undergrowth, careless of stinging bramble and whipping branch, and the ground sprang away from beneath my feet and the knot of fear in my stomach grew into a physical pain that made me cry out, but still the pursuers came on and at last I turned to face them and an arrow hissed through the singing air and thudded into my breast and I was bleeding, dying, dead—

"Come back, come away, dear one!" All at once I heard my friends calling me, and with a great effort I dragged myself back to reality, staggered to my feet and hunched my way to the great oaken doors that led to the courtyard, struggled with bolts and latches strangely heavy and stiff, flung myself through the gap that offered and stumbled down the shallow steps and across the cobbled yard to the safety of the stable, where Snowy took my arms around his neck, Moglet caressed my ankles, Corby brushed his sound wing across my face, Puddy hummed gently and Pisky sang me a bubbly song.

"I'm sorry, so sorry!" I sobbed. "And so afraid!"

"We know," whispered Snowy, "but you are safe now . . ." and he let me cry out my tears and remorse and wipe my eyes on his silky mane. When I was comforted enough they asked me what had happened, and first I told them about Conn and the lady and then of the fear and sorrow that I had experienced in the hall.

They listened attentively, but it was Corby who summed up our problem, in his own inimitable way.

"So he's temporarily not one of us," he said slowly. "And there's something nasty under the floorboards . . ."

The Binding: Unicorn

The Terror under the Floor

After a good night's sleep we went over it all again, and I had to endure once more my memories of Conn and the lady, but my friends instinctively made it easy for me, and once again it was Corby's good sense that made it bearable.

"Time you grew up anyway, Thing dear, and my guess is that it was only a thing of the flesh and nothing to worry about in the long run. Sometimes with humans, I understand, it is a bit like eating: wasn't it the Rusty Knight himself that said he was tired of plain fare and craved venison? Fair enough, but a diet of venison day and night will make you liverish, and before long you're back to bread and cheese and ale, the stuff that keeps you going most of your life.

"So, let it be: he'll return to plain fare soon enough . . ."

After I was reconciled to all this—superficially at least—there was still the wonderment of realizing where men and women fitted into each other like mortice and tenon, their bodies tongued and grooved and dovetailed like fair furniture. But I had not thought that this coupling could be a thing of such violence, of cries and tearings, of hurt and passion. Still, it was interesting, just the same, and I thought about it at intervals for quite some time. The only sure thing in all this cogitating was that a body such as mine, all humps and crookedness, would need a very fine carpenter indeed to marry the parts to another.

Of the strange noises in the hall, the feelings of terror and despair, Snowy at least was positive something should be done. The trouble was, we did not know whether there was anything actually underneath the floor, as I suspected, though when I went back later and stamped, quietly, I reported back that there seemed to be an echo of sorts beneath my feet.

"Sounds like a cellar," said Puddy. "Or a dungeon."

Something tickled at the back of my mind: hadn't the Lady Adiora said something about a dungeon? But my thoughts were going back farther than that.

"The castle seems to have been built on the foundations of a large Roman villa," I said slowly. "And if I remember—if I recall—someone must have told me that those old villas had great storerooms underneath, and lots of pipes and channels for a hot-water warming system; sometimes these cellars extended even beyond the foundations of the house itself if there wasn't a ready supply of water adjacent—"

"The lake!" said Corby. "But they don't use it now: go a half-mile for fresh water from a river through on the other side of the woods. Heard one of the nags grumbling 'bout doing the journey three times a day or more when there's company."

"Water in that lake looks dead," said Puddy. "Can't have been alive for years."

"We must take a look," said Snowy. "All that you have said, Thing, makes me believe that there is something gravely amiss here. A larger amount of fodder than is necessary for the beasts here is collected daily, and some of it carried outside the castle walls. As far as I remember there are no outer stables, nor any cattle grazing . . . I think, friends, it is time we took some exercise."

So it was that I rode out of the stable, Moglet and Puddy inside my jacket, Pisky's bowl slung round my waist and Corby wobbling on my shoulder, to ask the soldiers on duty that the main gate be opened.

We were greeted by a shout of laughter. "Call that thing a horse?" guffawed one of the gate-guards. "And as for that tatty bird . . . Any more in the travelling circus?"

I frowned most dreadfully, and I could hear Corby grinding his beak, but Snowy behaved just like the clown they believed him: stumbled a little, flicked his ears back and forth, swished his tail and gave me some good advice in the midst of all this as well.

"Go easy, Thing dear: every human likes to laugh, and the more they despise us the more ready they will be to disregard us as a threat to whatever they are hiding. Play as silly as me, there's a good girl. And, wise crow, fall off your perch and try and look ridiculous, if you can . . ."

So we found ourselves outside the gate, with a good deal of chaffing on the guard's part, and a secret rage in my breast. I turned Snowy's head eagerly towards the side of the castle nearest the lake, but quite unexpectedly he stopped suddenly and lowered his head and I slid gracefully down his neck to land on the turf in a heap. I got to my feet, spilling cats and toads and fish all over the place.

"What on earth did you do that for?" I demanded furiously, but even as I asked I heard the sound of laughter carried from the gateway, and turned to see them all still watching us.

"That was the reason," said Snowy. "So, today we shall not go near the lake, but shall rather ride innocently through the forest for a while. Get up again, Thing: I promise none of this will be wasted."

So that day we rode the perimeter of the castle, but some hundred yards hidden in the forest. We found neither bird nor beast to disturb its stillness, but we did find another exit. We had originally approached the castle from the east, joining the woodland ride that approached it from the south; but running near north there was another ride that ended on a knoll looking over a swift-running river, which was obviously where the household water was collected each day. Beyond this was a wooden bridge, a small village on the other bank, and thick forest. We followed the ride back towards the castle, and found that we emerged some quarter mile from the strange enclosed space at the back of the building, and even as we watched from the shelter of the trees we could see that the pavilions inside were being enlarged and painted, and at one time someone opened the bolted wooden gates and we could see the gravel within being meticulously raked into formal patterns and the tubs of shrubs being moved to the sides.

Snowy sighed, and I could feel him shiver beneath me. "I think we are almost too late: tomorrow and the day after it will rain, and then I think they will leave it till the full moon . . . We have five days. Tomorrow we shall have to risk going by the lake. It is too soon, I fear, but it is a risk we shall have to take if we are to free them."

"Them?" I echoed, but he only shook his head, and carried us swiftly back through the rest of the semicircle of forest.

The next morning we were out again, but this time attracted far less attention from the guards, as Snowy had predicted. Again as he had promised the sky was overcast and a little warning wind rattled the flags on their poles, then died away.

I had attended supper again the previous night in the great hall, and had had to face once again the sight of Conn, utterly besotted, eyes only for the Lady Adiora. Upstairs there had been castle servants who shouldered me out of the way when the bathing-water was produced, and there were others to air his new clothes—russet and green, fine wool and silk—and make up the bed, so I was largely redundant as far as I could see. We had only exchanged a couple of words, when he had fallen over me in his hurry to bathe and change and then, as I had apologized for being in the way, he had looked at me with an air of puzzlement as if he did not recognize me, and had merely asked, after a moment, if my room were comfortable. I had said yes, of course I had, for it was obvious that he had forgotten about the rest of us, or at least put us to the back of his mind for the time being. So I had not reminded him I had been banished to the stables, had not told him our fear of what the dungeons held, and most of all had not let him know how I hated the Lady Adiora for stealing him away and despised him for letting her. In all this, of course, I was forgetting Corby's wise words, but solecisms and banalities, however true they may be to the objective eye, are no use at all to one who is subjectively green with jealousy all over like an unripe apple, even if that one has absolutely no right to be . . .

So, as I said, we went out that next morning to spy out the land on the lakeward side of the castle. I dismounted on the other side of a clump of sear and withered reeds and tipped Puddy and Pisky into the waters to see what life there was, if any, and Moglet was detailed to work her way around the edge, keeping as far as possible out of sight. Corby was set as lookout and Snowy was to crop aimlessly towards the castle and an interesting-looking dark, gullied gateway set in the castle wall. I was the distraction: if I thought anyone was watching I behaved like the village idiot, capering around and turning somersaults and picking daisies for a chain.

We agreed a sun-time, which I reckoned would be near enough an hour, and it must have been near midday when we met again, casually enough, behind the clump of reeds. Pisky and Puddy were last at the rendezvous and I had to haul them both out of the water, gasping and distressed, all too ready to blurt out their joint discoveries.

"It's all dark and lifeless and choking and black with slime and mud and there are no fish—"

"Water's stagnant, been like that a long time. Once connected to the castle. Long pipe, blocked up with mud. Tried to get down it but failed."

"Pipe is all choked up with clay and dead bones and gravel—"

"Could be cleared. Water level is above pipe-mouth."

"—and nasty, smelly, stinking water. A hand beneath the water and you can't see a fin in front of you. No water-bugs, no snails, no red bottom-worms even, no nothing . . ."

"There's something like a sluice gate above that pipe," said Moglet unexpectedly. "I've seen something like that before: the wood is sound, but it looks as though it hasn't been used for many years, and would need a good greasing before it would shift. The rest of the lakeside is barren, and there is very little cover."

"The Romans' water system worked something like that," I said, still wondering how I knew. "Water from an outside source ran through pipes that were heated in cavities under the house. A—a hypocaust . . ."

"Well," said Snowy. "I've been cropping grass till I'm swollen-bellied, but I still can't see a way into the dungeons, or whatever they are, to find what I know is there. There is nothing but that barred gate to see."

"That pipe runs right beneath the grass and through that gate," said Corby. "The grass is a different colour. Dug years ago, but you can always tell."

"But the water can't get through," I objected. "Moglet and Puddy and Pisky said so. It can't have anything to do with floods or things drowning—"

"'Ware strangers!" hissed Corby, and we all ducked down behind the reeds except Snowy, who was too big.

From the front of the castle came half-a-dozen or so stable-hands carrying sacks and fodder and as we watched they moved, bowed with the weights, to the dark gateway in the wall. One man took out a large key and unlocked it and they passed inside—and out from that unlocked gate flowed such a miasma of fear and despair that it crawled as palpable as a fog to where we lay hidden, and such overwhelming sorrow struck my heart that I beat my hands against invisible bars and sobbed out my prisonment.

"Shut up, Thing!" warned Corby. "They're coming out again."

And as we watched the stable-servants emerged with baskets of ordure and cast them into the cesspit beyond the lake and rapidly infilled with fresh earth, but as they did so Moglet and Snowy sniffed the wind.

"Deer, boar . . ."

"Hare, coney?"

"Bear? Wild pony, certainly."

"Badger."

"We must get in there somehow," said Snowy urgently. "My nose tells me that there are dozens of animals in there, and we still don't know why!"

The idea seemed ridiculous to me. Why keep animals imprisoned underground? If one wanted meat one either grazed cattle or hunted, that was part of life. Why keep them fed and watered underground, when it was so much cheaper to let them roam free? Deer and boar were plentiful, at least outside this forest, and so were the smaller game. Everywhere else but here: was that the answer? Was that why they stored them? But what of the absence of any kind of life: no birds, no hedgepigs, no mice, no rats? And the overwhelming fear that overlaid all? But why, *why?* There must be a simple explanation . . . A feast and a fair, that was it! They had some deer, boar and hare for the feast, ready for easy slaughter when the time was ripe. And the others were for the usual tainted entertainment this place seemed to afford. The smell of badger that Moglet had detected in the droppings must mean that one comer of that enclosed space they had been tidying and gravelling yesterday would be reserved for baiting, and the bear must be a tame one, trained for dancing. The wild ponies? Those I supposed would be for the lady's horsebreakers to show off their arts. If the general standards of entertainment in this place were anything to go by, this was an improvement: better than the stupid torturing pleasure they usually seemed to take with strange, twisted things like me . . .

"No," said Snowy, who had obviously been reading my thoughts. "No, there are too many, dear child, and their fear has infected all the land around. It is more than mere sport or entertainment."

"Then what?"

"I am not sure. Not yet . . . But one of us must get in there to find out."

It started to rain, quite heavily. One of the men carrying over more hay looked up and saw us.

"Hey you: Crookback! Yes, you . . . Bring that nag of yours over here and make him useful, otherwise we'll all get soaked."

I would have refused, but Snowy spoke urgently. "This is just the chance we have been waiting for! Take me over . . ."

"You're not a beast of burden at the beck of anyone!"

"Don't argue, for once. Just do as I say."

So I left the others sheltering as best they could and led Snowy over. "You want to borrow the pony?" I asked, sounding, and looking too, I suppose, like a halfwit.

The stable-hand grabbed Snowy's bridle and thwacked his rump. "C'mon, you bag-of-bones!"

I watched him load up, noted Snowy's meek head hanging down, saw him led down a slight incline to the mouth of a tunnel that revealed itself now I was nearer to the barred gate, then made my way back to the others.

Puddy and Pisky were fine, revelling in the warm summer rain, which was coming down faster now, but Moglet made a wild leap at me, burrowing under my jacket and proceeding to soak us both, and Corby, nothing loath, tried to huddle under my cloak. We made our way back to the castle, more or less together, and I stowed away the others, for I could not know how long Snowy would be. Then, as luck would have it, I ran straight into Conn and the Lady Adiora.

We had obviously missed their riding out, for they were now returning wet with rain, Conn mounted on a beautiful strawberry-roan Apparisoned with red velvet, both now dark with rain. I rushed over to clutch at his bridle but he looked down at me as though I were a stranger, all the while listening to the lady's prattle.

" . . . but because of the weather we had better postpone it. My weathermen say it should clear up by New Moon, so probably four days hence. You will have to practise your archery, meanwhile—What is that dirty creature doing?" In a different voice. I was frantically pulling at Conn's bridle to try to gain his attention. "Send it away! That part of your life is gone, my love, but if you still have a fondness for the creature I will find it work in the kitchens . . ."

Conn pulled away from me. "Not now, not now," he said. "Later, Thingy, later . . ."

I spat on the ground as they passed, but the angry tears were not far from my eyes, and when I went into the castle that night I was denied the table and pushed towards the kitchens, where a greasy scullion grabbed me and made me turn one of the spits while he dipped his fingers in the gravy and lay back at his ease, and every time I tried to escape he pulled me back by my ear, cackling with laughter at my discomfort.

I was worried, for Snowy had not returned by the time I went over to the castle, and each minute dragged interminably. When I finally escaped the rain had stopped and the summer stars were shining faintly, and low clouds obscured the moon. I had only had beans and bread for supper and water to wash them down, but managed to salvage a beef-rib bone from under the nose of a great hound and, dusted down, it would be more than adequate for Corby and Moglet. I hoped Puddy had managed to find one of his unmentionables during the day, and Pisky could have a sliver of the beef.

But when I reached the stable all this planning was forgotten, for there was Snowy, head drooping, flanks heaving, trembling as though in an icy blast. The bone went flying as I rushed forward, and I will give the others their due, that bone was not touched until we had heard Snowy's story.

At first I thought his distress was due to ill-treatment and abuse, and I ran my hands over his hide, his joints and tendons, looked to see he had water and fodder, but all was as it should be. And then, though he had volunteered nothing, I realized that the aura of near-palpable suffering that emanated from him was an exhaustion of the spirit that has had to suffer mental ill-treatment as real as if it had been beaten or starved, and I put my arms around his neck and leant my head against his jaw.

"Tell me—tell us—dear one, what has happened, what you saw that was so dreadful . . ." And as he told us it was as if we were there and could see through his eyes, hear through his ears, smell it and taste it and feel it.

As he had approached the open gate in the wall a great stench of animal came from it, and out of the dark, yawning mouth of the tunnel a belch of fear, raw and undigested, that had made him stop in his tracks, and the men had used a whip to urge him on, jesting that he could smell the wolves and was afraid he would be turned into their dinner.

And wolves there were, penned next to the great dusty bear and her yearling cub: three grey, slinking animals, eyes slitted sharp as their teeth. And next to the wolves two large badgers, almost as big as the half-dozen wild boar, both these pig-like animals full still of rage and lust for killing, wasting their strength on futile rushes against the bars as the men approached, the badgers' claws rattling impotently against the metal, the boars' tusks ringing as they clashed with their prison. And opposite these fierce creatures were the grass-eaters, the proud stag with his three terrified hinds, the wild ponies, mountain goats, hares, coneys—and their keepers rattled the bars and taunted them as they threw them their food, gave them their water, telling them how their days, hours, minutes were numbered.

"Four days from tomorrow you've got, my fine creatures, and then you'll be so much skin for the buzzards! Midsummer Night will be perpetual night for you all! And not from each other, oh no! 'Twill be the fine lords and ladies as will lead the massacre, and them getting points each for the ones they kill. Not so many for the bears, 'cos they're a bigger target, though more difficult to finish off, but big points for the hares, 'cos they're smaller and move faster. Roast venison all round from you, my fine fellow and your dames; only ones we can't eat are the pesky wolves and rancid badgers, but they'll do for bait for the next lot of meat-eaters. Ah yes, roll on the Midsummer-Night massacre!"

And so, Snowy told us, big-eyed with wonder and horror, he had had to calm all those beasts, tell them what they needed and hoped for.

"And what was that?" I asked, knowing what the answer would be even as I asked the question.

"Why, that we would rescue them all, of course," he said.

The Binding: Unicorn

Midsummer Madness

And, looking at the faith shining from those strange brown-grey-green eyes I almost believed we could, even as I asked the hopeless: "But—how?"

So he told us.

In essence the plan was to open the exit gates beyond the slaughter-yard and guide the animals away from the castle to the ride leading through the woods to the bridge across the river that marked the boundary between this petty tenure and another. The plan entailed opening well oiled gates, the control of panic among the animals and slowest ones to go first, and also a distraction at the castle end to divert those attending the Madness. Snowy promised to organize the animals and keep them from panic, if the rest of us could ensure the opening of the gates and the distraction.

"There," he said. "How about it?"

We all agreed enthusiastically, caught in the euphoria of the moment, but it was the common-sensical Puddy who brought us back to reality.

"A good idea," he said, with his sometimes maddening slowness, "but what would distract the lords and ladies enough not to send their servants chasing the beasts? And how would we escape afterwards? And what of the Rusty Knight? Remember, The Ancient insisted that we had all to keep together, and this is only the first of our trials. By all accounts he has eschewed his loyalties already."

Conn! Oh, dear Gods, I had forgotten him already!

No, I had not forgotten, that was not the right way to think of it. He was in my thoughts day and night, and I was made both fiercely jealous and desperately miserable by his defection to the beautiful Adiora, but he had assumed the proportion of a dream, not to be confused with the day-to-day realities of eating and drinking, sleep, discoveries, plans for the escape of the animals. I cursed myself for my forgetfulness of his place in the general scheme of things as I gazed blankly at the others.

"Thing-dear will think of something," said Snowy comfortably, and such was the assurance in his voice that at that moment I truly believed I would, and put the problem temporarily from my mind.

But there was still the question of a distraction, and it was Corby who suggested fire. "Top half of this place is all wood, and would make a merry blaze . . ." and so I volunteered the next day to scout around on the upper floors and try to find a convenient corner to set combustible material. For the escape afterwards Snowy promised that we would not be left behind. Pisky asked why the animals couldn't be let out now, please, but Snowy confirmed that there were guards on duty day and night around the castle, and escape before massacre-day would be impossible.

We settled down for the night, curiosity allayed by Snowy's story and a definite plan of action to follow, but perhaps because of this the stimulation of thought made us restless, bog-eyed sleepers when at last dawn broke on another grey, dripping day.

The stable-servants "borrowed" Snowy again, and I asked him specifically to look out for and question the prisoned animals as to the whereabouts of a particular item I thought might be in the dungeons; Conn and the lady went out riding again, accompanied only by two discreet grooms, and I shut my mind to reclaiming him for the time being. By dint of dodging servants on occasion and behaving as if I belonged on others, I managed to gain access to the upper floors of the castle. The first floor consisted of bedchamber after bedchamber, a magnificent solar and a small library, but the next floor with its jutting towers was more hopeful. Those rooms facing to the front of the castle were all occupied, but of the others overlooking the back Conn was in one and the last was full of empty chests, discarded pallets, hangings in need of repair and tattered tapestries: these were all dry, and would give off a good smoulder-smoke if lit.

All this reconnoitring took time, and I still had not had a chance to speak to Conn alone by the time the rest of us gathered in the stable after supper. I had managed a bowl of scraps for the others, having been relegated to the kitchens again, and also a useful pocketful of fat strips, ideal for starting a fire. I had also checked the gates out of the slaughter-yard: these had been opened again today, and while I noted the ease with which the bolts slid back, I also saw that it took two men to swing them open, largely because the ground sloped slightly upwards at this point. A careful removal of accumulated stones and debris was all that was needed, and I saw how I could play an idiot and build mudpies at this point, and also lay out a couple of arrow-pointers the way the animals were to go.

Snowy was able to confirm what I had suspected, that a pipe, now blocked with debris, led into the upper part of the dungeon and thence into a disused cistern, cracked and perforated.

"That must be the pipe that leads to the lake," I said eagerly. "Which animal is nearest?"

"Luckily for us it is the badgers; their cage holds both pipe and cistern. I have asked them to clear away what rubble they can and pile it under the pipe. Some of the smaller coneys are going to squeeze through their bars to help. Now it's up to you lot at the lake end. Have you spied out the escape route?"

"Tomorrow," I promised.

The next day was the penultimate one before the intended killings, and there was a lot to do. The most important thing, of course, was to investigate the escape route, but my idea about the underground pipe, which had started merely as a secondary diversion, now assumed greater importance in my mind, for if it succeeded it would mean no more "games" like these could be played at the castle ever again: fire from above, water from below . . .

But I was thinking ahead too fast: back to the first priority. That morning I begged a ride on one of the water-carts, Corby paying for our passage by playing counting tricks with stones, to my dictation: Pisky, Puddy and Moglet I kept hidden under my cloak. As soon as the cart stopped at the river and they started to fill the water-skins I excused myself, saying I would walk back. There was a wooden bridge across the river and I strolled across, to be accosted by a sleepy bridge-keeper on the other side, who demanded a copper coin before I could proceed to the village, five huts and a tavern.

"Lord Ric's demesne," yawned the bridge-keeper. "Naught to look at for miles. Forest clear through for five leagues at least, then the Hall. Looks of you, you wouldn't want to try it without a mount."

"Where does the river come from?" I ventured.

"Gawd knows! Somewheres to the west. Now, you coming or going?"

"Going," I said, and went.

So far, so good. A bridge guarded by one man, a forest north for miles, a river flowing east/west: the animals had a good chance if they got this far; it was to be hoped that there were meadows or clearings for the coneys and hares farther up the riverbank.

Now for the sluice in the lake. Luckily I got a lift back with a later water-cart because the pebble in my stomach was pulling again—no, not a pebble, the dragon's ruby: I kept forgetting. It was midday when we reached the scummy waterside, and I asked Pisky to swim down as far as he could to determine the construction of the sluice, and Puddy to hop down the pipe to see how far in it was blocked; I set Corby to find likely pieces of wood in case we had to lever up the sluice, and sat back on the bank for five minutes' rest, Moglet on my lap.

After a moment or two she became restless. "Why can't I do something?" she demanded. "Everyone else is being important . . ."

"I was just coming to that," I said carefully. "I couldn't manage without you, Moglet dear. We need a sentinel, a watcher, and I can't be in two places at once." I was improvising rapidly, my thoughts in careful man-speech so she wouldn't understand. "You were just what I had in mind; would you go behind that clump of dried grasses, keep an eye on the comings and goings at the castle, and watch the tunnel-gate as well?"

Pisky reported back, choking, that the nether end of the sluice was deep in mud, but that the mechanism seemed simple enough; the only bar to raising it seemed to be a block of iron placed crossways across the wheel that had to be turned north/south to engage a number of teeth that governed the height. Puddy said that, as far as he could judge, the tunnel, apart from silt, was clear up to within a foot of the walls of the castle: the echo of his splashes changed in quality with the weight of the walls above him. We called it a day after I had leant over as far as I dared to try turning the wheel, and had fallen in. The wheel needed greasing and I needed a bath.

That night I told an exhausted Snowy what we had found out. He nodded.

"The badgers have worked hard all day, and they say there is only a foot or so more of debris to move; they reckon they are right under the castle walls now. But the last bit will be the hardest: there are rocks and hard-packed earth in there."

"How deep is the water in the pipe?" I asked Puddy.

"Inches only. The silt piled up at the lakeward end is what holds the water back. Once the pipe is clear it will run straight down to the dungeon, provided the digging beasts get it clear. Pressure of water will take all before it—the last six inches, anyway."

I instructed Snowy to have the badgers excavate through as far as they dared, leaving an airway of about three inches at the top; the pipe's diameter was at least two feet, but we didn't want anyone excavating so far that they leaked the plot. On the other hand, if I could wind up the sluicegate just a little, at least we would know if our plan might work.

"Is it level, or does it slope down towards the castle—the pipe, I mean?" I asked Puddy.

"Slopes down. Only gradually. Exit is some foot or two lower than the lake end."

"Bother!" I said, thinking rapidly. "That means someone will have to come back for us, Snowy dear, after you have led the others out. Can you find someone else to lead them down to the river?"

"I am the only one who speaks all their languages. Perhaps I could send back a couple of the ponies . . ." he hesitated. "Is all this necessary, my dear?"

"Yes," I said. "Very necessary. The majority of the animals may well escape this time, but what about the next ones? And the next? We want to make certain, don't we, that it never happens again, and if we flood the dungeons it will take them a long time—a very long time—to dredge it out again. Perhaps never, as the lake is on a higher level than the castle. Then maybe they will give up this sort of thing forever. I hope so . . . Send us back whatever help you can, for there will be all five of us—"

"And what about the Rusty Knight?" asked Snowy.

What indeed about the Rusty Knight? About Conn, the redhaired wanderer who had captured my heart . . . I had not seen him, except fleetingly, since the night we arrived. And when I had tried to speak to him it would seem he had forgotten all about us, for his eyes were only for the Lady Adiora in all her seductive beauty. For a moment or two I felt sorry for myself, lying sleepless on the straw in the stable, while he—while he luxuriated in silks and linen, but then the straw pricked at my spine and with that discomfort came the realization that I hadn't done much, hadn't done anything in fact, to wrest him from his diversion. I had crept away like a whipped slave on the lady's bidding and had sobbed from the hurt his carelessness of me had engendered, but had I gone back upstairs and tried to win him back to us next morning? No. Had I fought for what I wanted, even though it might be impossible? No. Had I reasoned with him, bribed him, suborned him, warned him? No. Had I reminded him of the quest we were bound upon, of The Ancient's words, of the dragon? No. Had I rebelled, fought, poisoned, stabbed? No . . .

In fact I was a coward, that was the truth, as soft as Moglet who now lay across my chest, sides gently heaving, needing the reassurance of my body for her tentative purr. But then Moglet had me, and I had—? Them, of course, Snowy, Corby, Puddy, Pisky and my little cat. We were interdependent. Independent, too, by very virtue of our differences. But Conn? He and I should have been closer, for we were humans; but then he was a man, and men were different, it seemed. They had all sorts of privileges and greeds and lusts of their own, which they were allowed to indulge quite freely, it seemed, but didn't they too have such fundamental qualities as loyalty, for instance? Couldn't he, even for the short time the quest might take, leave his pleasures for another time?

I realized, of course, that he did not see the Lady Adiora quite as we did. To him she was a lovely body, a luxury, a dream to be indulged. To us she was a shallow, heartless queen who exploited the fears and vulnerabilities of helpless animals for her own pleasures and satiation, much as she was using Conn—

I sat up suddenly, disturbing a protesting Moglet. Of course! Just as she had to have this midsummer madness of a massacre to satiate her lust for cruelty, so also did she have to have this succession of men to satisfy her other lusts; not only Conn, but also those other knights with pale faces and jealous eyes who had stared at him on that first night. And Conn would become a cast-off, just like the rest of them, so soon as a fresh male appeared! Now I understood the mutterings of the servants, the angry looks of the desiccated knights. She was the spider, they the flies, to be seduced and devoured, sucked dry and discarded as and when she pleased.

And poor Conn believed she was the love of his life, true and tender and everlasting! But how could I possibly disillusion him, show him he was only one of many? And how, most important of all, persuade him to leave her the day after tomorrow? How make him understand what she was, his impermanence in her life? Make him realize about the massacre, her part in it? I didn't know, I just didn't know. And there was so little time . . .

There was less time than I had bargained for. That next morning there was more hustle and bustle than usual and I caught at a servant's sleeve.

"What goes on?"

"Her Ladyship's weathermen have been at it again, that's what! They say all's changing, and that if we leave the entertainment till tomorrow 'twill be wet. So, 'tis tonight, an hour after sundown, and there's lights and tapers and rushes to set—don't bother me, I've enough to do!"

I rushed back to Snowy. "It's today, tonight, at twilight! We'll never be ready!"

"The animals must be told," worried Snowy. "And if it is to be tonight they won't bother feeding them. I wondered why I had not been sent for . . ."

"But you must get in there, they won't know what to expect! If we ever manage it . . . There's Corby to stake out, the sluice to make operable, and—oh Gods! Conn . . ." And I ran my fingers through my tangled hair in desperation.

"Stop panicking," said Snowy gently. "All will be done. Just tell me when you expect everything to be ready . . ."

Hastily revising practically everything I set approximate times, my mind racing ahead with gates to clear, dried rushes and fat to add to fuel, Conn . . . oh dear! And the problem of everyone being prepared to escape.

"Just be ready at the end of the lake nearest where all will be moving," said Snowy. "Someone will pick you up. It may not be me, but you will be rescued, I promise. Now, your only real problem is to persuade the Rusty One to cooperate."

"But you—how will you get in to tell the other animals?"

"That is the easiest part! Go over now and tell the head-groom—that sharp-faced fellow in the striped yellow breeches—that your master has donated me to the entertainment. Go on: do as I say!"

"But—but that means . . ."

"That I shall be there to lead them to freedom, yes. Go, child: do as you are told. It's our only chance."

I wanted to say no, *no*! We can escape, we can leave the other animals to their fate, we seven can get away, but knew it would be no use, knew that our unicorn would never agree. To him those lost, frightened animals down there in the dark were just as important as we were and that was right, I knew, but the miserable cowardly bit of me would not admit it. I knew that those prisoners were just as important to the world as the king in his castle, the knights in their armour, the maidens in their towers, and I wished there was something, someone, who would look kindly on our enterprise just for the sake of all the lost and frightened and persecuted ones who could not help themselves. Conn prayed regularly: perhaps I should too. I shut my eyes and tried to think of a force, a power, a stream of goodness, pity, love.

"Please, please help us!" I prayed. "Help us to free those animals, help us to ensure it doesn't happen again. Help me to help poor Conn, help me to take care of them all; keep us together and safe . . ."

I should have liked to record that I felt an enormous force sweep through me in answer, making me feel ten feet tall, full of courage and capable of dealing with anything, but I regret to say that all I felt was Moglet's claws in my right ankle.

"Breakfast?"

❧ ❧ ❧

After that I was too busy to think of anything, except the searing compunction I felt as they led Snowy away.

They had laughed at my offer at first. "What, that decrepit old bag o' bones?" they had jeered. "Don't you know we don't take jades? Down there we have the pick of the fields and forests—what, an old hack like that?" Then: "But perhaps, being white and so slow an' all, he'd be an easier target for some of the less-practised ladies . . . All right, then, we'll take him."

And then, before I had time to think how desperately easily all this could go wrong, it was off to the kitchens to steal oil, tallow and fat-scraps, and racing upstairs to secrete it behind the other materials for Corby's fire. And back down again for some dried rushes . . . Then over to the lake. The waters had risen with the rain of the last couple of days and I had to grope for the lever that worked the sluice: it would still not budge further, but I had brought some tallow to grease it later. Then over to the wooden gates, and a frantic clearing of any dirt and stones that might impede their easy opening: no one took much notice. They were too busy with last-minute raking of the gravel, the fixing of tallow-dips, the hanging of silks and flags to the pavilions. Then I left the others in the stable while I attempted the task I had secretly been putting off till the last moment, the most difficult one of all . . .

Halfway up the steep, twisting stairs to Conn's room I hesitated. It was well into the morning: suppose he was due to go riding with Lady Adiora? Suppose he was with her now? Or perhaps with the other knights and newly arrived guests in the solar? Perhaps with Sir Egerton in the library? I realized I was trying to put more obstacles in my own way, and that maybe I could put it off till later: it was no use, procrastination would just make it worse. I should have to search until I found him and hope it would not be too long.

But I need not have worried. Pushing aside the curtain to his room, still not sure what to say, how to persuade him to leave with us, I found him stretched out on the bed, still apparently in the blue-and-silver garb he had worn to last night's banquet and certainly with the day before's stubble on his chin, and a stale, perfumed air about him. He lay flat on his back, his arms folded on his breast, his toes pointed down for all the world like a knight laid out for his burying. If it hadn't been for the frown and the open eyes I might well have believed him dead.

Going over to the bed I laid my hand hesitantly on his arm, still not sure of what I was going to say. "Conn? Are you all right?"

He didn't move, not even his eyes: it was as if he were in a trance. Then—"Thingy?"

"Yes."

"Haven't seen you for days—weeks." Slowly his eyes swivelled round to meet mine. "Yes, I'm all right. I think . . . Where have you been?"

I forebore to remind him how I had been thrown out. "Oh—around. You know . . ."

"Mmmm. What's been happening?"

"Nothing much. What about you?"

"The same." He sighed. "Er . . . I've been thinking . . ."

"Yes?"

"I had almost forgotten, in this—this Castle of Delights, that we were supposed to be on a quest. Came to me last night. Wasn't sleeping. You know . . ."

I nodded. "I know. Restless . . ." Keep up the pretence, especially as I knew how awkward he felt by the staccato sentences, just as he had been when he first met us, before he had become used to us and spoke with that lovely, running lilt I remembered so well.

Then, to my horror, my utter embarrassment, my downfall, he suddenly started to cry. Not noisy sobs, his head in his hands, but the slow, hopeless, unable-to-stop kind of tears that trickled from the corner of his eyes and ran down to his ears, leaving little snail-tracks glistening in the space between.

"Conn! Oh Conn, don't! My dear, don't cry!" and I reached forward, quite without thinking, and held his hands, my heart bursting. "What is it? Who has hurt you?"

He released one hand, but only to wipe away the emotion, then sniffed, blew his nose on the linen sheet, and drew me down to sit on the edge of the bed beside him. Propping himself on one elbow he regarded me steadily. "Thingummy, I've been a fool!"

I agreed wholeheartedly, but inside. "No," I said. "Of course you haven't! Whatever makes you think such a silly thing?"

"Don't deny it, you know I have!" Luckily he went straight on without expecting any more protests, because I am sure a second time around he might have noticed my insincerity. "I've been a complete idiot! I fancied myself a youth again and tried to behave like one, when I should have remembered I am nearly thir—"

I put my hand over his mouth. "Age doesn't matter," I told him firmly. "Just how you feel . . . Er, were you talking of the Lady Adiora?" I knew he was, but guessed it would be easier for him if I pretended I hadn't noticed his infatuation. I was right, for immediately he loosed a torrent of words, conveying his hopeless adoration, her surprising reciprocation, his forgetfulness of aught else—and then came the interesting bit. I think he had temporarily forgotten that I, the deformed, ugly little Thing, with potentially no knowledge of Life with a capital L, would, or should, be unable to understand what he was saying.

"—and I thought it was only because it was the first time for ages, you know, when one gets too keyed up and can't perform. Like drinking too much wine, when the intent is there but you can't raise a thing. But she seemed to be satisfied enough when I found myself in a permanent state of arousal, but getting nowhere. I tried, dear God! how I tried, but I just couldn't come off! It was all right for her, me with a permanent hard-on, but I got nothing from it except frustration and a sore prick . . ."

I understood enough now to anticipate his next remark.

"Then I remembered that old witch, cursing me in the forest, all that long time ago. She said—"

"That your desires would remain unfulfilled until you asked the ugliest woman in the world to marry you!"

He sat straight up on the bed and glared at me, his brow a thick, uncompromising and unbroken line across his forehead. "How the hell—!"

"You talked in your sleep. When you were sick after that ambush. And you told The Ancient too, remember?"

He subsided, but not for long. "Well, I'm damn well not going to ask any female to marry me, ugly or no! Sod that for a game . . . No, if I'm to get no satisfaction, I'll put the temptations out of the way from now onwards. Pity, never fancied celibacy. Still, could shave my head and become a monk, I suppose . . ." The grim lines were smoothing themselves out from his face.

"The Ancient said that some spells could be broken if one sneaked up on them, took them by surprise, went in by the side entrance," I reminded him, though how this would apply in his case I could not imagine. "He also said that if we completed this quest and returned the dragon's jewels our troubles would be solved. Remember?" Not *exactly* how he had put it, but still . . .

"Just what I was thinking first thing this morning," he said, more cheerfully. "I reckon we should be going back to the road in a day or two—"

"No!" I cried. "A day or two will be too late—" and for the next quarter hour, half hour, I tried to explain to him what was happening, what we had planned to do.

It was no use: he utterly refused to believe me.

"But that would be like—like the Slaughter of the Innocents! No hunter would trap animals like that and wipe them all out without a chance of escape. It's—it's just not done, that sort of thing!"

"But it will be done, just like that, unless we carry out our plan!"

"Rubbish, Thingumajig! Now you're letting your imagination run away with you—"

"Come with me!" and I half-pulled, half-dragged him from the bed. The lancet windows overlooked the yard at the back. "See? They have everything ready!"

"But for what? Lady Adiora said there was to be an outdoor entertainment, that was all . . ."

"Then why all those bows and spears stacked over there? And the carts outside the walls, waiting to carry off the dead animals? And the sand and sawdust in those leather buckets to cover up the blood, lest the ladies feel squeamish?

"Conn, wake up! *Believe* me . . ."

He still shook his head, but there were frown lines between his eyes. "No, you must be wrong . . ."

I could feel the tears of anger and frustration seeping through my mask. "Well, if you don't believe it, hard luck, that's all! We'll manage without you: you can stay with your—your precious Adiora and—and—and *never* 'come-off,' as far as I'm concerned!" and I turned and stumbled away towards the door. His bundle of clothes, the ones he had travelled in, were in a heap in the corner: we still had his mail in the stable. I glanced back. He was staring down from the window and his fingers were tapping restlessly on the sill. Gathering up the bundle of clothes I fled downstairs. Perhaps he would come. Perhaps . . .

The others were restless for action after being cooped up, and I hastily packed up all our gear and humped it and them over to the lakeside, then went back to beg some scraps for a meal, coming away with some bread and cheese, a ham-bone destined originally for the stockpot and a half-empty jar of honey. That would have to do, but I remembered to fill the water-bottle from one of the river-water buckets.

It may seem strange that no one grabbed me by the scruff of the neck and asked what the hell I was doing and where I was going, but everyone was, thankfully, far too busy preparing for the evening's festivities. In the kitchens the spits were turning with fowl and game and pork, bread and pies filled the ovens and the tables were already laden with sweetmeats and glazed confections, but I was too busy and apprehensive to feel hungry. Guests were still arriving, and already the wineskins were being broached, and more decorations were being carried through to the hall.

I crept back to the others, wondering what poor Snowy was feeling at this moment, far beneath us in the darkness. They could not help but hear some of the preparation and, perhaps because of this, my stomach began to stretch and pull in sympathy with the trapped ones. I would not have had our unicorn's courage, I knew that.

The others had sensibly hidden in the reeds with our gear, and we ate frugally, not knowing when food would come our way again, so I saved a little of everything and packed it with the rest. Then I stripped off, for as much as I hated the idea I knew I should have to climb down into that scummy water and clear away all the debris I could from round the sluicegate.

The water was cold as death and smelt of rotting corpses, and I was gagging as I came up for a breath of fresh air.

"It's impossible! I can't shift it!"

"Let me take a look," said Puddy, diving neatly into the stinking water. He came up filthy, and looking grave. "Gives me a worse headache than ever, down there," he said. "There's a great pile of silt on both sides of the gate. Goes down two or three feet at least. Have to be scooped away."

"What with?" I said despairingly, for looking round there was nothing to scoop with, no container of any sort except Pisky's bowl—

"No!" said the little fish. "Not never! Not my bowl . . ."

I was not even conscious of having transmitted the thought, but quickly reassured him. "No, no, my pet, not your bowl. I'll—I'll just have to dig it away with my hands and throw it up on the bank."

"There's the cooking-pot," said Corby slowly, "or, better still: this!" and he stalked over to Conn's pack and tapped sharply on the hidden shape of his conical helmet. I drew it out, rust-spotted and dented—it couldn't look worse. A little mud . . .

For two hours I struggled with the slimy muck that squelched between my toes, choked my nostrils and layered my body with its evil-smelling slime, and I was hot, dirty and exhausted when Puddy finally took another dive to see if it was clear. His report was optimistic.

"You've shifted all that was blocking it. Now try the lever—gently, mind. We don't want the water through yet."

I put my weight on the lever: nothing. I tried, again and again, and at last, to my gratification, felt the whole thing stir, quiver under my hand, and shift all of an inch to the next ratchet. Puddy went down again.

"It's moving. Jaws are locked and the wheel engaged with the teeth. Don't move it any more for a moment," and he disappeared again. Five minutes later he reappeared gasping for breath. "Water's trickling down the pipe. Three inches of debris only holding it back at the other end. Badgers did a good job. Can hear the animals."

"And Snowy?" I cried. "Is he all right?"

"Sorry. Forgot. Get my breath back and—"

"Oh, no! I can't let you go back!"

"My fault for not checking." And back he went, and this time he was so much longer that my nails were digging into my palms by the time his head emerged plop! from the water and he swam, very tired, to the bank.

I stroked his back and his belly and used some of the water from Pisky's bowl, eagerly offered, to wipe his eyes and mouth, then puffed a little of my air into his lungs. "Are you all right? You're a very brave toad . . ."

He perked up a little, but his skin was still pale and bloodless. I snapped my hand fast round a passing damselfly and stuffed it in his mouth. His throat worked up and down, an absurd wing sticking out of the corner of his jaw, but at last he swallowed, breathed more easily, and squatted down comfortably.

"I went right through, down the tunnel, over the barrier and into the dungeon. Snowy sensed I was coming and was there to meet me. Place stinks: haven't cleaned it out this morning, of course, but neither have they fed or watered them and they are all hungry and thirsty and it is stifling hot. But Snowy has kept them in stout heart, and he shines like a light in the darkness—"

"A light?" I questioned, momentarily distracted.

"Why, yes: the silver light, like star-glow, that shines from him all the time. You must have noticed it?"

"But I hadn't. The others had, of course, and it was strangely humbling to remember that I was merely a human being, and because of that missed so many things these animals took for granted, like a unicorn's light . . .

"I fear, though," added Puddy, "that his light grows dimmer, for he is near exhausted, I think. He says be sure to wait by the north side of the lake. Oh, and try your best to persuade the Rusty One. I think that was all," and he shut his eyes and went promptly to sleep, after the most sustained bout of communication I had ever heard him make, albeit the words had taken an agonizing ten minutes to emerge. It felt that long, anyway.

A horn sounded from the battlements behind us; it was about the sixth hour after noon, and a warning that the banquet was about to begin. I hid Moglet, Puddy and Pisky in the reeds as best I could and piled our belongings nearby where they would be readily accessible. Tucking Corby under my arm I scuttled back to the castle and was only just in time, for the gates were being shut as the last of the guests, a straggler knight, clattered into the courtyard.

I was pushed roughly out of the way for all the stables, including the one we had used, were full, and ostlers and grooms had no time for someone underfoot. So I made my way past them and into the Great Hall, where the noise and bustle were, if possible, worse. Creeping round the wall I went to the kitchens, and my only problem there was not to be grabbed to hold, baste, cut, drain, chop, pour, slice or wipe anything as the whole place was full of the reek of burning fat, people's feet and elbows, temperamental shouts and greasy tiles, but no one noticed as I slid past and made for a little-used staircase that wound up to the unused tower. Luckily the torches were already burning in their sconces, and there was one near enough to the room we had chosen for it to be easy enough for Corby to climb onto the stool I dragged out for him and pull it from its fastenings when the time came. I hid him behind a pile of heaped hangings, gave him a hug and my blessing.

"And mind, as soon as you see me wave . . ." The tall window gave an excellent view of the yard and the double gates. "Are you sure you will be all right coming down?"

He eyed the drop. "Nothing ventured, nothing gained," he said gloomily. "Just you take care, Thing dear: we couldn't manage without you."

Just for a moment I had a sickening realization of how inadequate I was; of how easily things could still go wrong; of how we seven were so separate, that should be together; how futile this venture really was—but luckily it was only a momentary pang, however sharp, for there was still so much to do, and doubts such as these had no place with action.

I went to see if Conn was in his room, but he had gone down with the others to the banquet. It was lucky, though, that I had checked his room for there, lying beside the bed, was his broken sword, so that meant a journey back to the lakeside, over the wall by the pigsties, where the others greeted me: nervous, on edge, and definitely scratchy. I reassured them, feeling far from confident myself, then made my way back to the castle, having to knock at the postern for admittance and receiving a cuff for bringing the porter out while he was relaxing with ale and a pie.

I aimed at the banquet, where the air made my eyes smart with its smoke of candles, tallow, fat and incense. Conn was at the top table but he was only picking at his food, and the Lady Adiora was fully engaged with a young knight on her left whom I had not seen before, though I noticed she kept a proprietary hand on Conn's wrist the while. Taking advantage of shadows and the distracting screech of pipes and the patter of drums from a troupe of musicians in the centre of the hall, I sidled up to the table nearest the main doors and scrabbled on hands and knees up on to the platform of the top table. Luckily distraction was provided by a juggler, in competition with the music, tossing brightly coloured wooden balls in the air, who lost his rhythm and his footing when he tripped over one of the bone-gnawing hounds.

I crept up to Conn's side in the ensuing merriment and plucked at his sleeve.

"What the devil—Oh, it's you, Thingy."

"Yes it's me," I said, unnecessarily. "We're all ready. Don't forget: Snowy is going to lead the animals out and across to the river. The rest of us will wait for you at the north end of the lake. I've got all your gear. Oh, and don't worry if the castle catches fire: it's all part of the plan," and I didn't give him time to question, but slid back the way I had come.

Now for the real business of the evening. Climbing out over the castle walls again, I made my way to the gates at the far end of the slaughter-yard. It was still light, although there were dark clouds massing to the west and the sun was glimmering through them like a lantern through strips of cloth, yellow light flashing intermittently. The air was heavy and close, and it was not only fear that made me sweat as I crawled round to my position. The bolts in the gates appeared well oiled, the gates themselves were free of obstruction, but I had not bargained for the two-wheeled carts that were already drawn up at one side, for the carcasses I supposed.

There were three drivers, playing five-stones in the lee of one of the carts, and I had to retreat swiftly in case they saw me. This was an added and unforeseen danger: would they stride forward and stop me opening the gates? I crouched behind the near wall, biting my nails, thinking furiously, but the more I thought the more my mind chased itself in circles, like a wasp in a jar. And as I thought, conjectured, despaired, the answer came from another source. A serving-man poked his head over the wall and waved his hand at the men cheerfully.

"There's ale at the side-gate. Cook's in a good mood. But you've to save a couple of hares and the smallest of the hinds—on the side, you understand. His cousin's brother will pick 'em up later . . ." And he tapped his nose and winked.

The drivers understood well enough; with a glance at each other they hobbled their horses and almost ran in the direction of the side-gate, one remarking to the other: "Well enough: there's coneys and to spare, so they said, and the wife fancies a badger-skin mantle. Pity they don't hold these do's more'n twice a year . . ."

Creeping forwards I went over to the carts: the grazing horses glanced at me incuriously and went on with their feeding, and I had not their language so could not explain that I wished them to pursue a policy of non-cooperation: instead, with my knife I cut through the leather strips that hobbled them and prayed that they would gallop their carts to the four winds once the animals were running.

And even as I moved back to the shelter of the gate, and the advantage of a knot-hole in the wood that afforded me all but a minimal viewpoint of what was going on, the fine lords and ladies came out from their feasting and took their places in the bright pavilions. The sky was more overcast than ever to the west and great clouds, castled and battlemented now, reared high and threatening, yet seeming not to move at all, and over everything was a sickly, greenish light, lurid and yet speaking of dark to come. The air was breathless and tasted of wet iron.

The audience, the murderers, were dressed in gay colours, the ladies in blues, yellows and reds, with fillets set with rough-cut stones on their brows; the gentlemen sported browns, purples and greens and all voices were high and shrill, light and laughing, and the liveliest and most beautiful of them all was the Lady Adiora. One could almost believe she had eaten magic mushroom to see her, all laughter and glinting teeth and tossing hair and swaying body. By her side, as she led him to the most resplendent pavilion, Conn looked dull and heavy and uneasy, and I could tell he had eaten little and drunk less for once, his eyes the only alive things about him, darting anxious glances from side to side.

I watched him carefully, for on him, on his reactions to what was about to happen, depended all our perilous venture. If he understood, soon enough, how depraved the Lady Adiora and her guests were, then he might be able to escape with us and the Seven would be together again; if, on the other hand he could not see how wrong it was to herd some fifty or sixty animals into an enclosure from which they could not possibly escape and proceed to make a sport of their slaughter, then he was lost to us indeed, as we were to him. No quest, no return of the jewels to the dragon . . .

A trumpet sounded. A herald, clad in the castle's colours of blue and yellow, advanced to the centre of the courtyard, and the knights and ladies settled themselves to listen with a great shushing of skirts and creak of leather, jangling of ornaments and clashing of ceremonial mail.

"My Lady Adiora, Sir Egerton, brave knights, fair ladies, esquires, gentlemen and franklins: this night will see the culmination of our pleasures, an entertainment especially designed by our hostess to determine the best archer amongst her guests. Shortly there will be released below you in the yard various ferocious beasts and creatures of the wild" (affected screams from the ladies) "some large and some small. The Lady wishes me to emphasize that in no way are you in any danger from these animals, ladies, for the pavilions have been placed too high for even the tallest to reach.

"You will each receive a bow and arrows—" the servants were distributing these as he spoke "—and each set of six arrows is notched or fletched in a different manner so as to be readily identifiable. After the—er, destruction of the game, scores will be added up for each hit. The highest number will win this jewelled casket, donated by the Lady Adiora. If several arrows hit the same animal, then that blow which would be deemed most fatal will be the winner.

"May the best marksman win!" and the herald stepped back and out of the way as four servants went to the wooden doors that led down to the dungeons, ready to fling them open on command.

This then was it. I glanced at Conn, and saw him expostulating with his hostess, his bow lax in his hand, and she ignoring him for the young knight I had seen earlier; but I could wait no longer. I was not aware of even breathing as I raised my hand clear and glanced up at the northwest tower; I had to strain my eyes for the night was now drawing in fast and my gaze had become accustomed to the glare of torchlight in the yard, but I managed to make out Corby perched on the lintel of the narrow window, and saw him flap his wing in answer to my gesture and disappear inside.

Then Lady Adiora must have given some signal, for at that moment, with a grinding of bolts and a creaking of hinges as cages were opened, the prisoning doors to the dungeons were thrown wide and I, like the rest of the audience, peered down into the blackness beyond, nose wrinkling against the stench. Already my hand was reaching for the bolts on the outside gates when something moved back there in the darkness, and two dozen arrows were notched to two dozen bows as we all waited for the prey to pour out, defenceless, into the brightly lighted arena—

But what did emerge was not at all what any of us had expected.

The Binding: Unicorn

The Running

Out of the darkness trotted a dainty white horse, trim and neat, mane curled, tail flowing, and on its back was a hare, an ordinary brown hare. Fingers relaxed on bowstrings, arrows drooped and were unnotched and a buzz of speculation ran round the audience. The white pony, in whom I scarcely recognized a transformed Snowy, knelt on one knee and bowed, his companion nodding on his back, paws stretched forward to prevent him sliding over the withers. Then Snowy executed a few light dancing steps, first to the left, then to the right, so that he zigzagged across the yard and in doing so approached the pavilion where the Lady Adiora was sitting, a bemused expression on her face. I distinctly saw him say something to Conn, who backed away with an unreadable expression on his face, then he was approaching the gate where I was hidden.

"All well, Thing dear? This nonsense will go on for a minute or two longer, but when I kick my heels against the gates, open them as fast as you can—" and he was gone, trotting like a white fire around and around the yard, faster and faster, now and again bucking and kicking up his heels, whilst the hare, descended from his back, was punching the air in the centre, turning somersaults, leaping in the air and twisting like a falls-riding salmon and now the audience were applauding and the bows and arrows were being laid aside, one by one. And now Snowy went faster still, until the wind of his passing streamed and extinguished the torch-light, and he seemed like a continuous incandescent circle. The hare bounded higher and higher and if one closed one's eyes the images spread right over the darkness and were still there when they opened again. All at once they stopped and with an almighty kick Snowy opened one of the gates, neighed shrilly, and called forward the other animals waiting at the entrance to the yard. Immediately I pulled back on the other gate and even as I did so a brown flood poured across the gravel. Coneys and hares, two badgers, a bear and her cub poured out of the gate and raced towards the woods and the river, led by the hare who had performed with Snowy.

The surprise lasted long enough among the audience for me to glance up at the northwestern tower in time to see a black, spiralling, flapping shape launch itself down the side of the building, bounce off the roof beneath and catapult out of sight to the ground. From the window it had left curled a lazy puff of smoke . . . Dear, good Corby! I hoped he had landed safely, then stopped thinking as the horses with the carrion carts at last took off across the gateway. I had to somersault out of the way and then was narrowly missed by a squealing of swine who rushed out at the same time, eyes red, teeth fearsome under curled lips. In their midst ran Snowy, and as he passed me he called: "The lake, the lake!" and I suddenly realized just what I should be doing. I risked one last, despairing look for Conn, but he seemed to have disappeared in a melee of shouting knights, screaming ladies, floundering servants and the tossing antlers of a great stag. One or two of the guests had drawn their bows and I heard a sudden cry as an animal was hit. Another arrow thudded into the open gate at my side, a couple of servants ran over to try and close the gates, a snarling wolf leapt and I fled.

Scuttling along as fast as I could I reached the lakeside to see a lick of flame and then another reflected from its black surface. I looked up at the tower: smoke was now thick and oily, fed well by the rancid fat I had poured over the rubbish earlier. A freshening wind from the west pushed the tongues of flame towards the roof between the northwest and northeast turrets. A cry of "Fire!" and I ran back towards the castle to the point where I had seen Corby fall. I found a still, black shape on the grass. Sobbing with fear I reached forward and gathered him into my arms, feeling with a sudden stab of relief the strong heart beating warm and fast beneath the draggled feathers.

He opened one eye. "Hullo, Thing: sorry to be a nuisance, but I still feel a bit groggy. Knocked myself out, I did, when I tried a glide—forgot all about the blasted old wing, didn't I? Sorry and all that . . ." and his eye closed. It opened again. "How's it going, then?"

I ran back to the lakeside, to find the others huddled expectantly beside the baggage, laid Corby on Conn's pack, with strict instructions to the others to look after him, then went round to the sluicegate. Grabbing the lever I heaved with all my strength: nothing. I heaved again, crying out with the pain in my stomach as the muscles of lifting fought with the cramps from the red stone, that contracted as the others expanded. At last there was movement beneath: a grudging, slurring sound, and the lever moved a little and I heard the rush of water seeking its lower level in the pipe. Eagerly, in spite of the pain, I strained at the lever again and with a crack! the handle broke off in my hand and I tumbled back onto the bank, the loose wooden lever sailing over my head to land on the grass behind me.

I crawled back to the sluice; the water was still running, but even as I listened I could hear the suck of mud and stones against the gate. Despairingly I shook the wooden structure, but the water had slowed to a trickle now, and there was the sound of running footsteps behind me. I turned to see three or four of the castle servants making for the near side of the lake, leather buckets in their hands.

There was only one thing for it: I dived into the stinking water, my hands scrabbling at the stones that choked the partially opened sluice. Lungs bursting I tugged and pulled upward at the gate, but it wouldn't shift. I rose to the surface gasping and blowing, to be greeted by a hand on the scruff of my neck hauling me out onto the bank to lie in a half-drowned heap.

"Out of the way, stupid child! This is man's work," said Conn, and he dived into the water just as the servants with the buckets arrived.

I was in a panic, and instead of realizing that three or four buckets of slopped-out water could not possibly halt the fire that was now almost enveloping the whole of the wooden upper structure of the castle I lost all reason, and flung myself at the servants, knocking the bucket out of one's hand and doubling another over with a butt to the stomach, then ran back to look anxiously at the turmoil of water that swirled where Conn had disappeared.

His head emerged, black with mud, his eyes like eggwhites in a dirty frying pan, his mouth opening briefly. "Bloody thing's well and truly stuck—" then he disappeared again. I felt a hand on my shoulder and turned to see one of the servants, dagger upraised, but even as I ducked beneath his arm a grey shape snapped at his heels. He swung with his knife and kicked out at the same time and the cabling wolf yelped as his shoulder was laid open and spun and collapsed as the boot caught his head. Instantly I straddled his inert body and snatched up Conn's broken sword, which lay where he must have dropped it.

"Don't dare touch him!"

The servant circled warily, dagger glinting in the lurid light that heralded storm; he feinted but I stood still, the hilt of Conn's sword to my stomach, both my hands to it, the jagged end of it about two feet from my body. Two of the other servants came running to his aid, the other went back to the castle presumably for more support, but help for me was at hand. Two other wolves, full adults, a dog and a bitch, hackles raised, had come to look for their cub and now snarled at my side. The young cubling struggled to his feet, shaking his head, obviously not too badly hurt. Even so, we were outmatched, for each of the servants was armed. I do not know how it would have ended but there was a sudden tremendous flash of lightning, a crack of thunder and then a roar that shook the ground as the sluicegate at last opened fully and a torrent of water plunged down the pipe towards the dungeons.

That was not all: a figure, back-lit by another flash of blue sheet-lightning, appeared to leap from the disappearing waters, as black in itself as the clouds now racing in from the west, its mouth and eyes white gashes in the dark, and it howled like a devil from hell. What it actually said was: "Thank Christ that's over! I thought I would choke . . ." but it came out like: "Worra-worra-worra!" To a man the servants flung down their weapons and fled convinced,

I am sure, that some black demon had drunk the lake dry and, appetite unslaked, had now risen to devour them. Watching them run I laughed weakly and collapsed, shouting: "We've done it! We've done it! Oh bravo, Conn!"

"Bravo, maybe," said my Rusty Knight, looking more like a tall, thin hobgoblin than a warrior, "but how the hell do we get out of here? And what in the name of goodness are you doing with a wolf in your arms?"

For I was soothing the young cub, afraid he was concussed still, and the two adults were anxiously nuzzling and licking his injured shoulder. But even as Conn spoke, the answer to his first question came in the form of two mountain ponies, who galloped up, manes tossing nervously at sight of the wolves. They patently offered themselves as mounts, though we had not their language: out of the corner of my eye I saw a further detachment of men appear beneath the castle walls, this time armed with swords and staves. With them was a knight, fighting to control a panic-stricken horse that screeched with fear as burning sparks from the building floated down on its quarters, singeing its tail.

"Up!" said Conn briefly, tossing me onto the back of the first pony and handing me a frightened Moglet, (inside-jacket-at-once), a pocketed Puddy and Pisky's bowl. Corby was recovered enough to ride on my shoulder and Conn snatched his sword from my hand and mounted the other curvetting pony, the packs set before him. "Right: go!" he shouted and dug his heels into his mount, which careered off in the direction of the wood, mine following, the wolves bringing up the rear, the youngster recovered enough to run, albeit with a limp.

We fled across the field to the white blur that was Snowy, guarding, encouraging and shepherding at the entrance to the ride in the woods that led to the river and safety. I glanced quickly back at the castle: all the upper part was well ablaze by now, and, as I watched, one of the towers, the south-eastern, swayed and collapsed into the cobbled courtyard behind. The slaughter-yard was still full of people milling around, and even now the stragglers among the animals were making their slow way to safety: a couple of bewildered coneys, a disorientated boar, a hind heavy with young, the last glancing anxiously behind her to where her stag, horns flailing, hooves striking out, was discouraging those few who essayed to follow the escaping animals, though few among the former audience could still believe that this flight and fire and flood was part of a planned entertainment.

My heart lurched for the stag when I saw his reason for lingering: an older hind lay twitching in her death throes, an arrow in her throat. I slipped from my pony's back and ran over to Snowy, indicating the stag. "Call him in, dear one! She is dead, his lady, but he has another in calf to care for and this one." I nodded at a younger hind who trembled indecisively just inside the wood.

Snowy nodded. "Just wait for the coneys—they are smaller, but just as precious," and a moment later he called out shrilly. Reluctantly the great stag, a twelve-pointer red, still angry and sad at the death of one of his wives, joined the other hind and the one in calf, snapping at two arrows sticking in his shoulder as if they were of no more consequence than buzzing flies. I slipped over and pulled them out as gently as I could.

"Come," said Snowy, "to the river. There is nothing left for us here . . ."

We were lucky that no humans followed until daybreak, for some of the animals, good for short runs, were paw-weary and fur-dulled by the time they reached the river. The swine had passed their lower brethren and crossed the bridge first, without a word of thanks; most of the hares, too, were over by the time we stragglers reached it. The five or six houses in the village on the other side were all barred tight shut—I should think the vision of all those animals charging across must have been too much for them. Even the bridge-keeper was missing.

The she-bear had waited with her cub to thank Snowy: she, too, had arrows in her hide but nothing serious for her coat was thick, and we removed the barbs before the animals slipped into the river, noses making arrowheads in the flowing water as they swam quietly upstream to a place they called Malbryn, bare hills to the northwest. The ponies who had carried Conn and me clattered across the bridge, all wild again; the shuffling badgers, tireder I should think than the rest of us put together, rattled their claws, snuffled and shuffled off bandy-legged into the undergrowth, and the great stag—so like the mosaic on the floor of the Great Hall we had left—bowed his head to us and led off his two surviving hinds.

It was the poor bewildered coneys who needed most help, and in the end we had to go back and find the last ones, weary and disorientated. I also ended up carrying one little doe in my arms across the bridge, but luckily on the other side we found a wise old buck who had come to investigate the commotion, and agreed to lead the survivors to a warren some two miles away, by easy stages.

As I watched them leave us it was sad to think that these animals, united in purpose so short a while ago, were reverting again to hunters and hunted, without more than a breath's pause. A cold nose touched my hand and I started back as three great grey shapes fawned at my feet, pushed at the back of my knees, nudged my thighs.

"They give you thanks for the cub," said Snowy. "They wish me to say that they and theirs are yours to command until the debt is paid."

"Ask them—ask them then not to hunt those who were their companions," I said, thinking of the tired coneys. I glanced down doubtfully at the pointed muzzles, the swelling cheeks, the slanting yellow eyes, and smelt the breath of meat-eater that curled up through the sharp teeth and the grinning, foam-flecked jaws. "That will repay, and more."

"They promise," said Snowy. "But they will travel a couple of leagues before they kill anyway, to lose the trail."

"Call it quits, then," I said, and knelt to embrace each of them. This time the words came plain to me.

"There is still a debt to pay," said the bitch softly. "One day, when your need is great, one will come . . ." and they melted into the trees like shadows.

Dawn was breaking. I looked at Conn. "You're *filthy*!"

"Seen yourself?"

"The river is clean and flows quiet on this side," said Snowy. "Go wash, children."

As I luxuriated in the clear, sharply cool water, washing the ooze and slime of the lake, the sweat of flight and the smuts of burning from my aching body, conscious of Conn, a shadow to my left, doing the same, I glanced up and saw a buzzard wheeling lazily against a sky the colour of daisy-petal tips.

"Ki-ya, ki-ya, ki-ya," he called.

Snowy on the bank above neighed once in answer. "He says the castle is in ruins: they are coming to seek for succour this side . . . Sir Rusty Knight, if you push quite hard on the bridge-piling to your left—"

The piling collapsed, its weakness no doubt exacerbated by the unusual amount of traffic it had had during the night, and the whole structure slid gracefully into the river, to drift away down the current even as the thud of hooves announced the arrival of the advance-guard from the castle. There were shouts, curses; Conn leant over to pull me from the water. Hurriedly I donned clothes and mask, grateful to realize that he had been too busy bridge-pushing to see I had been barefaced.

We set off along the riverbank towards the rising sun, but I don't remember much of the next half-hour or so; I was so tired that I could not even feel elation when Conn swung me up in his arms to carry me after I had stumbled and fallen for the second or third time.

Later, as he laid me down in the shelter of trees to sleep, my head on a mossy bank, and had assured me that, yes, the others were all right, I heard something that sounded strange after all those terrible days at the castle. Momentarily I forgot all about how tired I was and sat up, clutching at his arm.

"Listen, Conn, oh listen! All the birds in the world are singing!"

The Binding: Toad

The Trees that Walked

And after that all the birds in the world did indeed sing for us day and night, for a while at least. Although we found the stones we sought quite soon and followed the line of the second one, it was many recuperating days later before we happened on the next test. Meanwhile, I found we all seemed to be drifting into a dream-like state, not noticing the world about us. Towns and villages, feuds and dissensions, forests and rivers, all drifted past like a vision, and the most detached of all was myself, who probably should have been the most impressionable after my long years incarcerated with the witch. But now only our quest seemed real, the rest grey and apart . . .

When our next adventure came it was over almost before we realized, in a flash of fire: like paying one's penny in advance for the entertainment and then finding the performance over before one had had a chance to lay one's cloak upon the ground to appreciate the entertainment.

Only this was not entertaining . . .

The country we travelled turned upwards, and before long we were in the high down where wind twisted our clothes and pulled our hair and puffed from behind boulders and blew up our trews. Grey rock stuck up through ling and bracken like knees and elbows through tattered clothes and birds slid sideways in the wind. Villages were few and far between and the people startled and shy at our approach; not because they saw in us any threat, I think, it was just that visitors were rare.

Perhaps because of this the hospitality was greater when they granted it. One night, a week or so after we had escaped from the castle, we had been regarded at first with suspicion followed by tolerance, then given pallets and marrowbones, hare-stew, goat's milk cheese and bread, and were invited to sit round the host's fire for music with pipe and tabor. No one at any time thought it strange of us to be travelling with an assortment of animals, and all expected a story, a song, a tune to pay the way rather than the few coins we had to offer. That night Conn told a tale, I sang a lullaby I remembered from somewhere, Corby picked out a chosen stone or two and everyone was cosy and warm when one of the host's friends—for we were an entertainment in ourselves, and the whole village expected to be invited to meet us, that was clear—asked our destination.

But when we pointed north and east he crossed himself.

"Not the way of the Tree-People?"

"Tree-People?" questioned Conn.

"Yes. Those that walk the forests and devour travellers . . ."

"Walk the forests . . . ?"

"We never goes that way now. Time was there was safe passage through the heathland to the northeast. Time was trade came through the hills. But then *they* came . . ."

"Come, now, Tod," said our host uneasily. "That's talk, no more. None here's seen them—"

"Ever travellers come from that way?" said Tod. "No. Ever travellers go that way and come back to tell? No. Ever anyone from round here go that way? No . . ."

I took a nervous sip of my mead. "But we are bound that way . . ."

"Then more fool you," said Tod. "More fool you . . ." Around that fire others seemed to agree, for there were shaking heads, spittings into the embers, a furtive crossing of hands, pointing of two fingers, sighings, groans . . .

"Oh come now," said Conn. "What solid proof have you? Travellers do not return the same way if they quest as we do; visitors do not come that way for probably there is an easier route. And if you listen to old wives' tales here no wonder none of you ventures further!"

I looked at him with admiration. Since our time at the castle he seemed in some subtle way to have grown into his years. No more did he think of this as some careless expedition to be endured, now he was as dedicated as the rest of us; no longer was he just my dearest Rusty Knight, he was a thinking, caring man. But not once had I referred to the things he had confessed to me at the castle, nor had I ever mentioned the faithless Lady Adiora, much as my bitter tongue had wished it. For I knew, deep down in that submerged part of me that was totally female, that a man sets great store by his pride and that only a nagging wife or a fool would remind him of his fall from sense, and then be lucky not to have a slammed door and empty chair to remind them of their folly.

And I was neither wife nor nag—but would have wished for the choice.

The men round the fire stirred uneasily, glanced everywhere but at each other, then a short, stout man spoke up.

"We've been up there. Found a skellington. Flesh cleaned clear off . . ."

"Up where?" asked Conn sharply.

The man shrugged. "Anywheres. Near the trees. Doesn't matter: they can walk. Come out of the night . . ."

I shivered. "What come?"

"Knobby peoples. Root peoples. Tree peoples . . . Folks say as they *are* trees. Eating trees . . ."

"*Eating* trees?" I tried to keep the panic from my voice.

Conn put his hand on my arm, and his brown eyes were warm and kind.

"Folktales, Thingummy, folktales. Part of the night and the entertainment. Worry not, little one: they shan't touch you. Trust Conn . . ."

Oh, how I loved him! How that careless touch tingled my whole body, far stronger in that moment than the cramps that bound my stomach. Through the eyes and touch of imagination for one breathless instant I allowed myself the indulgence of my mouth touching his under the soft moustache, and flesh met flesh in a stab of loving—

"Doesn't sound all faery-tale to me," said Corby, considering.

"Don't want to go!" said Moglet, stirring uneasily on my lap.

"No smoke without fire," said Puddy gloomily from my pocket.

"My great-great-grandfather once said that some trees ate a village," offered Pisky, helpfully.

"Oh, shut up!" I said crossly, annoyed with myself for relaying both the conversation and my fears to them. "That's the way we have to go, so that's that! No, Pisky, not another word, or I'll—I'll move your snails!" This was a dire threat indeed, as Pisky felt threatened if any but he rearranged his bowl, which he did whenever he was bored. I felt mean as soon as I had said it, because in spite of the brave words I knew I was the most cowardly of them all.

No one in the room had understood our exchange of course, except possibly Conn, but the villagers looked tolerantly enough on someone who shook and twitched, breathed heavily, blinked, grunted and sniffed all of a sudden for no apparent reason. I saw one of them lean over and poke Conn in the ribs.

"That lad of yourn . . . ?" and he tapped his forehead. "Never mind: that sort's usually good with horses. Rubbed that old nag of yours down a treat earlier . . ."

Conn winked at me and rubbed the back of his hand over his mouth to hide the smile-twitch.

Two days later we had climbed even higher, into an area of twisting tracks, moorland turning purple and bracken browning; of startled flocks of plump brown birds who broke cover almost from beneath our feet; of keen winds that hissed through the dried grasses; of solitary trees leaning away from the blast; of hunting creatures that slipped sly and secret from our path; of the water tumbling icy from no source we could see; no people, no habitations, no woods . . .

Of that I think we were most glad, although no one was idiot enough to refer to the talk in the village. That would have been inviting Fate, or the gods, or whatever. No woods, that is, until the third day, when the land broke into deep combes where the north-flowing streams had bedded into the rock. Then there were trees: spindly rowans clinging for their lives to cracked rocks with only a pocketful of earth to offer; pines twisted beyond recognition, oaks leaf-shredded, ivy twisted and gnarled, ash already almost keyless in the Moon of Plenty . . .

We breathed easier. Nothing had come to threaten us, nothing had answered the description the villagers had given us of knobbly Tree-People, of devouring trees, and that night we camped in a convenient hollow, a riverlet to our left, heath and a few scattered pines on its banks, a small copse to our right. It had been wet all day, with that fine, penetrating rain that looks like mist and is as good as a bath you don't want. We lit no fire, for luckily the night was suddenly warm and we had oatcakes, cheese, a bottle of wine and honey. After our meal we drowsed in the hollow, unwilling to unpack and settle for the night and too lazy to move for the moment, while the few summer stars pricked into the deepening sky, a curlew called on its homeward flight and directly above us a buzzard swung his dreaming circles. He must have a wonderful view, I thought dozily. Miles and miles, from the village we had left to the edge of the uplands further north, and who knew what from side to side, and all the while he could even see a mouse bend the grasses, a hare's ear prick the bracken, a beetle on a rock, a fish in the stream . . .

Suddenly he called: high, weird, lonely, a warning perhaps: "Ki-ya, ki-ya, ki-ya . . ." and I saw Snowy fling up his dreaming head and warnings buzzed in my ears.

I sat up. Nothing had happened, nothing had changed. The others still lay where they were and Conn was chewing a blade of grass, his eyes closed. Dusk had crept down like an interloper to the bank of the stream, stretching towards the rocks, trying for entry. The trees to our right seemed to have moved in with the darkening to be nearer company, and the trees to our left *had their feet in the water and were already starting to cross—*

I could not put my fears into words. Instead, as I glanced behind me at the oaks, the ash, the ivy, then before me at the pines, the birch, the rowan—the hair on my head stirred.

"C—C—Conn," I whispered shakily. "S—S—Snowy . . . The trees. Oh, look at the trees . . . !"

Instantly all were awake and Snowy neighed once, shrilly, and started to circle us as fast as he could. It was no use; now I could actually see the trees moving, hear the rustle and squeak of leaf and branch, feel the earth tear beneath the protesting roots. Snowy's circle grew smaller as I rose to my feet, Conn at my side, and gathered the others into my arms. Now we could see gnarled roots stretch forth their questing feet, branches reach and curl, leaves glint and flash like eyes.

I was turned to stone. I could not move, could not speak, only whimper, seeing with despair the futile stump of Conn's sword waving and jabbing at the threat.

"Help us, dear Lord, help us . . ." It was my voice, but the words came from nowhere.

Then came another voice.

"Fire, Thing, fire! That is what they fear!"

With an astonishment quite separate from my terror I recognized the voice of Puddy, no longer slow and ponderous but sharp and decisive. Fire? Of course. Fire eats wood. With stiff fingers I fumbled for flint and tinder, but fear and a damp day would not produce even the tiniest spark. More urgently I chipped and struck: desperate, the tears ran down my cheeks and I prayed again and again: "Please, *help* us!"

The strong voice came again. "There is more than one kind of fire. Remember the words, remember what *She* used to say! Fire to set them back, to drive them away—the words, Thing, the words!"

I put my hands on Puddy and through my fingers I recalled the right spell as he put it on my tongue. The words, sharp and harsh, poured forth and instantly we were ringed by blue flame that licked and spat like a grass-fire. Immediately, or so it seemed, the crowding trees drew back and I saw clearly the evil, knotted, earthy brown faces, the squat bodies, the bulbous eyes, the yellow teeth, the pale tongues like the underside of slugs—

I seized a rotted branch and dipped it in the fire and ran with my torch at the nearest tree: there was a sigh, a hiss, a tearing sound and the ring melted, the trees dissolved into the night and we were alone once more—

Without another word we picked up our belongings and fled.

The Binding: Cat

Under the Mountain

Once more we were in the lowlands, in pleasant undulating countryside and heading due north. By unspoken consent the ordeal of the walking trees was forgotten, but once, in a quiet moment, I spoke of it to Conn.

"Did we see—what we thought we saw? Did those trees walk? Did they have grinning mouths and fingers like twigs? Or . . ."

"Or," said Conn. "Most probably. If we hadn't all been frightened out of our wits we would have seen an old army trick, I reckon."

"Trick?"

"Mmmm. I saw something like it once in Scotia, and again in the Low Lands—only then they used reeds." I wriggled impatiently and he ruffled my hair. "Patience, child! When I saw it in Scotia it was an ambush, sort of. There were these savage highlanders sitting round their campfires—oh, perhaps a hundred, two hundred—and the besieging force was less than half that, and their only advantage lay in surprise. So they cut down a rowan or two and some gorse bushes—have you ever tried to cut into a gorse bush in the daylight, let alone when it's pitch black? Bloody prickles everywhere . . . As I was saying, they had some dozen fellows move these, bit by bit, nearer to the enemy, and the others lined up behind in the shadows. They were into the camp before the defenders realized they were there."

"And the reeds?"

"Same idea, only this time the reeds were protection as well. A thick wall of reeds, green ones, the sort that arrows bounce off . . . There were more of them that time, so the odds were even. We lost. And ran."

"You were with the attackers the first time?" I said, remembering what he had said about gorse-prickles.

"And the defenders the second. I reckon that's what the Tree-People do. An outlaw band with perhaps an old campaigner like me among them, preying on unsuspecting travellers. Probably been watching us for days."

"You're not old," I said absently, trying to reconcile what I thought I had seen with what Conn had just said. But his reaction to my remark was entirely unexpected. His thin, warm, pale-freckled hand closed over my grubby paws.

"That's nice: no, I suppose I'm not really, not by actual years. It's just that time sometimes seems to be slipping by . . ." He released my hands with a sigh.

I looked at him compassionately. So my Rusty Knight was afraid of growing old. Men took a lot of understanding, I thought. One part of them is grown-up, brave, lustful, full of confidence, and the other, as I had also seen at the castle, is still little boy, needing encouragement and reassurance.

"You should try being me," I said, as cheerfully as I could. "I don't even know how old I am . . ."

"And ugly to boot," he said softly. "Never mind, Thingummybob, I love you . . ." He patted my head as kindly and absent-mindedly as a lord would pat one of his hounds. And he couldn't, even now, get my name right! If it was my name . . . I was glad, then, for the mask, for it hid and soaked up the stupid tears of frustration and disappointment his well-meant words engendered. But what right, I told myself furiously, did I have to be either? I had made the mistake of falling in love, and cripples should never make the error of doing that, especially if they are also ugly. If I had known how it would hurt, this love, then I should never have indulged in it.

And yet I didn't want to let it go, to deny it, for it made me alive in a way I had never known. I tingled from top to toe. I felt beautiful inside, as beautiful as the Lady Adiora. Love made me aware of Conn's frustrations and anxieties, made me willing to sacrifice all I was, anything I had, for his wellbeing. And, in an obscure way, it made me understand and love my animal friends even more.

I sensed now why Pisky talked like an ever-running stream, knew why Moglet was near as great a coward as I was myself, acknowledged the slowness of Puddy—except for the other night—and understood Corby's coarse carelessness. I was also starting to comprehend—but the fringes only, because he was magic—what our beloved Snowy had loved and lost, and how his love was different, somehow stronger than life itself. And as I realized this, a great calm and peace stole over me.

It rained, and it rained and it rained. Non-stop. For three nights and three days, and it was just our luck that we were between villages and had to seek shelter every night where we could. The first night it was in a deserted barn by a crumbling cottage, the second in the open and the third—

"A cave!" called Corby. "Just past the three stones—are those the ones we're looking for?"

For the last five miles or so we had encountered gently rising ground, and had begun to hear our own footsteps beneath us, each step with the faint echo of a drum. Snowy lowered each hoof with increasing suspicion.

"Underground caves," he said. "Deep ones, at that. With all this water about we shall have to be careful."

So when Corby hopped into the cave ahead of us, giving a hollow and thankful caw! as he arrived, Snowy was the only one to hesitate, but he could do little but follow when we all rushed in to celebrate our shelter. My flint and tinder was dry enough from the oiled pouch I now carried it in, and I soon had a lusty fire going where the floor fell steeply from the entrance towards a large passageway we had had no chance yet of exploring. The cave had obviously been used before. There were two piles of kindling, some logs and peat in a dry corner, although it was clear that the usage was not recent, for boulders had rolled down from the cave entrance, partially blocking the passageway, and the store of wood was almost rotted through.

It all made a fine blaze, however, and I soon had our last strips of pork fat spitting from skewers above, curling and browning with a smell that made my mouth water. I still carried cheese and some rather stale oatcakes and had picked wild raspberries earlier, so we made a fine supper and afterwards lay lazily around the fire, listening to the rain outside, while the smoke rose up in a wavering pillar and flattened itself against the roof of the cave.

"Funny," I said. "D'you think the bats don't like our smoke?"

"What bats?" said Conn lazily.

I sat up. "Well, the cave is a bit smelly, isn't it—"

"But dry—"

"But dry. And there are fresh bat-droppings around and bat-ledges up there, but no bats. And they wouldn't be flying in this weather. Perhaps they've gone off down the passage . . ."

"No bats," repeated Moglet, from my lap. "No bats; no rats, no bats but a cat . . ."

Of course Pisky took that up. "No bats, but a cat; no dish, but a fish with a wish . . ."

"A crow that can't go, and so full of woe . . ."

"A toad with a node, who bears a load on the road—"

"Quiet!" said Snowy sharply. I thought for an instant that he was annoyed with the game, that he didn't want one of them to come to the bit of the "unicorn with no horn"—I had already thought of rhyming "Knight" with "blight"—but as we stopped I could hear it too.

A queer, rumbly, shifting sound. A runnel of water slithered past my toe, and then another. I looked up at the mouth of the cave, some three or four feet higher than the place where we sat, and more muddy water was pouring over the lip. The sounds of movement intensified; small stones clattered over into the cave—but they were falling from *above*! I scrambled to my feet with Conn, even as a shape flitted past my ears, then another and another, flittering and piping, wide mouths agape on needle teeth, ears like open leather purses. I couldn't tell what they were trying to communicate, although the shrill sounds overrode the dull rumble that seemed all around us, but Snowy understood well enough. With a wild call he had us all gathering up our belongings in a scrambling haste. One moment Conn was loaded with everything, then I was, then Snowy and Moglet and Corby and Puddy and Pisky were passed from one to other of us like a first lesson in juggling but eventually—and this took but one bat-sweep round the cave—Conn had the baggage balanced on Snowy, Corby on one wrist and Pisky's bowl dangling from the other, and I had Moglet inside my jacket and Puddy in my pocket.

The bats' cries grew more urgent and the rumbling louder: I felt the floor shift and sway under my feet and clutched at Snowy's mane.

"What do we do? Where do we go?"

"The bats will show us. Take a brand from the fire—nay, better two, one to light from the other, and some kindling. But hurry, dear one, there is little time!"

I snatched a glowing branch, whereupon it snapped and sparked about my feet. I drew a deep breath; we were together, don't panic, nothing can harm us if we're together . . . I picked up a convenient bundle of kindling and thrust it into my jacket, where a protesting Moglet fought with the twigs. Selecting carefully I picked out a large gnarled branch and then another. Thrusting the tip of the first into the fire I soon had the tip ablaze and swung it round the cave: the bats were sweeping and squeaking round a jut of rock to the left. Ahead of us was the unexplored passage we had noticed earlier and Conn was scrambling towards that.

"No!" called Snowy. "Not that way, Rusty Knight: it's a dead end, they say!"

"But—"

There was a louder roar than before and by the light of my improvised torch we swung round to face the entrance of the cave. It was collapsing before our eyes. Where before there had been a clear, jagged outline with the fall of rain hanging like a curtain behind a stone arch, now the outlines were blurring before our eyes. The arch was changing shape, becoming rounder, lowering, cracking and the rain-curtain became a fall of stones that blotted out the last dim shapes we had seen before. But that was not all: the curtain now started to slide towards us, faster and faster, as if some wind had bellowed out behind an arras.

"Follow the bats: it's our only chance!" cried Snowy.

I thrust my burning branch into Conn's hand, grabbed his belt and he jinked behind the rock: so there was another passage. The bats flew ahead into the cold darkness and I followed Conn's first hesitating steps. I turned my head for Snowy but even as he followed I saw the river of slurry engulf our fire with a despairing hiss, and then all was black except for the flickering torch. The floor of the passage was painfully sharp with stones as we hobbled along. Of a sudden Conn's belt was jerked from my grasp. The torch went out and I could hear nothing but the great roar of stones behind, felt a great, stuffy blast of air buffet my ears and screamed as I fell helplessly into darkness—

The Binding: Cat

Stalagmites and Stalactites

It was cold. I was lying on bare rock, there was no light, my head hurt. The end of the world? Not quite. A raspy tongue was scraping my chin under the mask with anxious zeal. There was a terrible cursing in my right ear.

"Caw! Blind me—why can't someone strike a light? Black as a raven's armpit in here . . ."

But there was light, of a sort. A dim white shape stood where I thought my legs should be, if only I could think and see straight.

Snowy bent his head and snuffed gently. "All right, Thing dear? You will have a headache for a while—you bumped your head. But we're safe, for the time being . . ."

"No worse than *my* headache," said a muffled voice from my pocket, and I felt Puddy squeeze himself out. "How goes it, fish?"

"Well," said some extremely angry little bubbles. "I'm not broken, but a *lot* of water has slopped out, thanks to *nobody in particular*, and one of my snails is missing."

"Here's your snail," said Corby soothingly, "and a couple of nice new round pebbles." I heard three little plops. "And a—oh, no: it's a bone . . . Sorry."

"What sort of bone?" I sat up incautiously, to be rewarded with a pain that beat like a drum behind my eyes.

"Only a little 'un. Rat, mouse; bat perhaps . . ."

There was a shuffling behind me and Conn's groping hand closed on my shoulder. "Sorry about that, Thingy dear: there was a drop at the end of the passage. No bones broken?"

"I don't think so," I said crossly. "Where—where are we?"

Snowy shifted his hooves. "Under the mountain . . . Have you your flint and tinder safe?"

I felt in my pocket. "Yes, but—"

"What happened to the torch you carried?"

I groped. "Here . . ."

"Right. You have kindling somewhere about you, too; I saw you pick it up. Let's have some light, shall we?"

Given something to do, I felt better, and even more so when Snowy bent his head and touched the stub of his horn to my head. I heard his soft moan even as my pain lessened, and I reached forward to push him aside.

"Don't, oh don't! I can bear it. Don't hurt yourself . . ."

"We are one, child, all of us. All pain is to be shared, all troubles; all endeavour, all joys . . ." I felt an immense comfort, as though my mother had kissed me better, my nurse taken me on her lap, my father laid his hand upon my head. It was another of those elusive flashes of what I could not even call memory, and gone as swift as kingfisher-flash.

I lit the kindling—birch-bark, moss, twigs—and took from their friendliness a branch-tip of fire. As it flared I stood up, all aches and pains miraculously gone, and held it out to Conn.

"Hold it high—let's see where we are . . . Oh, oh!" I gasped in awe as Conn held up the torch. It flared and dipped and crackled and shone its flickering light upon towers, castles, trees, mountains, cliffs, frozen waterfalls, avalanches—all shimmering like ice and moon-glow. "What—what are they? So beautiful . . ."

"Stone castles," said Corby admiringly. "Cliffs; snow-slides . . . Caw . . ."

"Stalactites and stalagmites," said Conn, and he whistled through his teeth. "Magnificent! I've seen the like in Frankish lands, but nothing so grand . . ."

As we stood there, admiring, I heard a faint tinkling sound as first one great icicle and then another dripped into the silence. Moglet wrapped herself round my ankles.

"Too big," she said. I knew what she meant, and some of her unconscious, unspoken fear formed my next words.

"Which is—is the way out?" and even as I spoke the torch in Conn's hand flared and sputtered and I realized how little fuel we had left.

Then came Snowy's comfort. "There are several openings on the other side of the cavern. To save fuel we shall go without light, travelling around the perimeter and exploring each passageway as we come to it.

"I shall go first as, to some extent, I can see in the dark. Thing dear can come next, holding to my tail—but try not to pull it—and the knight shall bring up the rear. We shall not travel too fast, and if I come across any obstacles I shall try and warn you in plenty of time. Toad and cat with Thing, crow and fish with the knight . . . It will take some time, but we have that to spare. Now, get ready, and remember to bring what wood we have left and any kindling. Easy does it!"

I don't know about the others but I kept my eyes closed, pretending to myself that it was only a game and that if I opened them there would be light. Puddy was quiet in my pocket, but I could feel Moglet trembling against my chest. Snowy's tail was soft and silky and comforting to hold and Conn's hand warm on my shoulder. It seemed we stumbled, tripped, wandered for hours; sometimes we climbed over rocks, sometimes squeezed round or ducked under; sometimes there was open space and nothing tangible save the last step and the next. If we paused for even an instant, the silence clawed back into our consciousness as palpable as the ever-present dark. But there was always the tinkle-drip of water, sometimes nearby, sometimes seeming miles away, by its very randomness making the black silence all the more terrifying—the drip of melting snow in an immense and deserted forest, the crack of ice on a hollow lake, a child crying in a deserted house—

By now my mouth was dry, my brain in a vacuum, my senses like little sea-anemone tentacles, scared of touch or bruise. Some of the passages Snowy didn't even bother with, as if he knew at once they were dead ends; others we traversed for a hundred steps or so until they narrowed impossibly. I lost count: was this the fifth or twenty-fifth way we had gone? And all the while an uncooked lump as big as a cottage loaf, doughy and indigestible, was rising, ever so slowly, from my stomach to my throat, so that when the squeaking began all my tensions, all my fears, erupted in a small shrill scream.

"Quiet, child!" said Snowy sternly. The perspiration ran through my fingers into his tail and Conn's fingers gripped my shoulder so fiercely in answer to my terror that I could not help but cry out again. "Quiet: the bats are back!"

The bats! I had forgotten them, although it was they who had led us the right way after the deluge of water, mud and stones had destroyed our first refuge. I felt a sudden rush of air as myriad wings brushed my mask, stirred my hair, and a language I did not understand touched the high pitches of my hearing. Apparently Conn noticed nothing, neither did Puddy or Pisky, but Corby put his head on one side to listen and Moglet poked her head from under my jacket.

"What do they say?" I asked.

"That the way out is three openings to the right: we were nearly there," said Snowy comfortingly. "Best foot forward!"

We squeezed into a narrower passage than most we had tried, but even I beneath closed lids could feel the gradual difference in the quality of the light, and risked ungluing gummy lids. We found ourselves now in a smaller cave than the last. There was light but no magic castles of rock, no everlasting dripping. Ahead was a rift or chasm, and beyond it the cave mouth and the setting sun sending bars of rose-colour across the floor. We had been entombed for nearly twenty-four hours. No wonder I was suddenly ravenous!

Over the chasm stretched a natural bridge of stone, wide enough for two to cross abreast. I started towards it eagerly, only to be halted by a buffet of bat-wings and a hundred shrill voices, and Conn's voice, harsh and incredulous.

"Look! Sweet Jesus, Mary and Joseph! Look to the right, Thing!" He had got my name right at last but I did not heed it.

Across the chasm, stretched from side to side in eight equally spaced strands, was an enormous web. Even as we watched, a spider, as thick in body as a Lugnosa moon and as black and hairy as the Devil himself, legs jointed and hooked like some grotesque toy, ran across to the centre of the web and halted, multifaceted eyes glaring and mouth moving like the jaws of a wolf. I did not need Snowy's words to know we were beyond hope.

"The bats say that she stops all who would cross: see the corpses parcelled among the strands? They have tried to break through but fall helpless to the glue on the web. There is no way out for any of us, none, unless we can bring the spider to destruction . . ."

The Binding: Cat

Web of Despair

It was Conn's fighting Hirlandish temper that brought me to my senses. With a cry of rage he had charged the web, only to be repulsed by a twang! of impenetrable strands, a sticky front and a menacing clatter of joints from the spider. Conn collapsed on the ground by my side, such a comical look of frustrated fury on his face that I forgot my worries and patted his shoulder.

"You all right?"

"All right! All right? I'll kill the bastard, sure and I will! Just let me take my sword to its evil body and I'll—" but then he stopped and of course remembered that his weapon was in pieces. "Ah, wouldn't you believe it then! Just when I needed it . . ." He put his hands to his head and tugged at the unruly curls. All of a sudden he had shed ten years and was again an edgy, temperamental lad, the brogue tripping from his tongue like a slashed wineskin. "Ah, 'tis terrible, terrible! How in the world can we get past that—that black bag of air?" He sprang to his feet and began to pace the ten feet or so of rock in front of the chasm. "See, the bugger has stuck its net to the rock; there, there and there," and he pointed to thick suckers that anchored the strands. "And two at this side, one the other and two at the top—eight together, by the saints!"

Between the thick strands glistening with an evil, tarry glue that clung to whatever touched, were finer strands that glowed with a greyish light of their own. These were pearled with sticky droplets and clogged with pitiful little bat-parcels, some still feebly struggling in the last rays of the setting sun that slanted through the seemingly unattainable mouth of the cave. Freedom! So near, so frustratingly near! Were we, too, to end like those bats, waiting to be sucked to the bone, then discarded into the torrent of water we could hear echoing in the chasm far below the web? Or would we choose rather to drown in those depths, so far beneath the open sky, the woods, the fields we were used to? Or would we huddle here, cowards all, and slowly starve to death?

"Time for supper," said Snowy. "What have you got in the pack, Thing dear?"

Not much: half a flagon of water, some ends of ham, rinds of cheese, honey. We ate what we could, bunched close together and shivering now, for the sun had gone down. Conn doubled his cloak to sit upon, for the rock struck chill, and Snowy lay down behind us so that my cloak would do as a coverall. Beyond us and the web the cave mouth was pricked with stars and a near-full moon swung into view, her pale light too high to penetrate the gloom of the cave. A couple of desperately hungry bats dared the web; one pulled back at the last moment, the other, with a high-pitched scream, became entangled and a moment later a pair of pincer-like jaws fastened on the poor, furry body. Poisoned venom quickly did its work and the stunned bat was rolled and twisted into an obscene shroud. The dry rustling and shaking of the web ceased, and the only sign of the terror that lurked there was a hooked claw that crossed the rising moon, a bar sinister on the gold.

I leant back against Snowy. "What can we do? How . . ."

"We must think," he said. "Consider, assess. There must be a way . . . But now sleep, my friends, sleep. Often in dreams the answer comes. Sleep . . ."

And cold, still hungry, I dozed off, the comfort of a strangely silent Conn's shoulder my pillow.

"I'm thinking," said Moglet.

After breaking our fast—a bad joke, this, on what we had left—Moglet had washed her face and perched on an outcrop of rock some discreet ten yards from the web. With inscrutable eyes she had watched the loathsome spider take two bat-parcels and suck them dry, then spit the bones to the torrent below. She had watched the giant insect wipe its jaws with a rattle of forelegs and, satiated, settle back in the middle of the web, to watch us.

The rest of us, excluding Snowy who said nothing, had spent some two hours in fruitless argument and discussion, first one and then the other putting forward wild schemes that could come to nothing. The only idea that had seemed remotely feasible, that of Pisky's to dare the torrent below, had been dashed by one quick look, a wary eye on the spider the while. If we managed to miss the ledges and projections on the way down and avoided being dashed to pieces on the rocks that reared up like fangs, we should surely perish in the swirling black waters that disappeared into a gaping hole in the rock to heaven knew where.

Twice Conn had tried to get near the bridge of stone that spanned the chasm and twice had been threatened by an immediately alert spider who had run down the web to meet him, jaws clashing. It even pursued him on to the rock floor of the cave the second time, to be driven back by some stones I flung in desperation. After this we were exhausted, and it was only then I had noticed and questioned the non-participating Moglet.

A careless retort sprang to my lips on her reply, engendered perhaps by frustration, but Snowy blew softly down the back of my neck before I could say anything.

"It is perhaps her turn," he murmured softly, which I did not understand. "Gather close, all of you, and send your thoughts to her aid. Close your eyes and empty your minds of all except that which will help her thoughts. Concentrate on cunning, wisdom, energy and, above all, freedom. Now, my dears, now . . ."

So we did. Huddled together, hungry, thirsty, cold and in despair, we nevertheless freed our minds and sent them over to where Moglet sat, a little receiving statue.

At last she stirred. She had been sitting bolt upright, large ears forward, eyes apparently unblinking. But now she performed a long, slow stretch, arching her rump in the air, tail a relaxed loop, front legs stretched out, claws a-scrape against the rock, ears back, head sloped down between her front paws, jaws almost at right angles in an exaggerated yawn. The ritual done, she sidled over to us.

"Well?" I asked, aware that the sun outside was at its zenith, aware of time trickling away like water through carelessly cupped hands.

"Stones," said Moglet. "Lots of them. A big pile. As heavy as you can throw . . ." And, exasperating animal as she could sometimes be, she folded her front pads underneath her and promptly went to sleep.

Stones it was then, gathered in the half-gloom by Conn and myself, pecked from ledges by Corby, hoofed from their hiding places by Snowy, until there must have been two hundred of them of all shapes and sizes.

Moglet opened her eyes and considered. "That should be enough . . . Now then, Sir Rusty Knight, I want you to cut two strips from your cloak, about half a man-hand thick and a hand-and-a-half wide—"

"From my good leather cloak? You must be joking!" expostulated Conn.

"Do as she says," said Snowy quietly.

Surprised into compliance, Conn did as he was told and laid the tanned strips by the stones. "Now what?"

"Now," said my kitten, thoughtfully flexing her paws, "now I shall have to ask our white friend here to do some interpreting to the bats: don't speak their squeak myself, but I gather he does . . ."

Quickly she explained what she wanted, and while we were still exchanging glances wondering whether it would work, the bats had swarmed down and picked up, four to each strip, the pieces of leather. For a minute or two they practised flying in formation, a thing they were obviously not used to, the strips falling from their grasp twice, luckily onto the rocks close by. Then they were ready, hovering above us with strange clicks and twitters.

"Right!" said Moglet. "Thing dear and Conn, will you please throw stones as hard as you can at the web in the bottom right-hand corner, there where the web has been darned; the small strands, not the thick ones. As soon as you have made a hole, start to make another, still at the bottom, but this time on the left-hand side." She turned to Snowy. "Tell the bats to go as soon as I say 'Ready!' "

Conn and I started flinging the stones: his aim was much better than mine. Some of the missiles went through the fine meshes, clattering across to the cave mouth. Many of mine dropped soundlessly into the water-filled chasm, but before long we had a sizable hole in the right side of the web. As soon as the first stone struck, the spider was down to investigate, throwing out fast streamers to try and plug the holes we made. The stones themselves seemed to have little effect on it, bouncing off the tough carapace like pebbles off armour, but its anger at our attempted destruction of its trap was plain to see, for, even while knitting up the severed strands, it chattered and snapped its jaws.

I heard Moglet's "Ready!" to Snowy and would have stopped to watch the bats but for his hissed warning.

"Keep going: do not let your eyes stray!"

By now each stone was getting heavier and heavier, and as we switched to the left side of the web, Conn was throwing at least three to my one; in the end I was chucking them underarm, scarce able to see their direction for the sweat that ran down inside my mask and threatened to blind me. I thought I could do no more, but suddenly there was a loud twang! from above and the whole web dropped about six feet. With the speed of light the spider turned and ran up one of the central struts towards the roof. At last I could look up to see what the bats had been doing. The leather flaps had been wrapped round two of the central struts and, thus protected from the gluey stickiness, the bats had been able to bite completely through one strand so that the web hung now only from seven supports instead of eight. The other four bats had not fared so well: the second top main strut had not parted, and even as they tried to escape, one poor bat was caught in snapping jaws. No refinements this time: the spider crunched it with one bite and then spat it out to spiral down, back broken, into the torrent below.

Then the great insect went back to the repair of its web. Spreading itself on the surface of the rock above the break, it clung safe with the four back legs while holding the severed end in its front claws, dribbling some foul oozing mess on it and then drawing up the longer end to meet the shorter and binding all together with some kind of thread it teased from its belly.

"Now," said Moglet, her eyes green with concentration. "Take your sharp little knife, Thing dear, and a piece of leather to protect you from the stickiness, and saw through the left-hand bottom strut. You, Sir Conn, do the same for the upper right-hand one: you are the only one tall enough to reach, and your broken sword has a nice sawy edge. Don't worry: the spider cannot be in three places at once and I'll ask Snowy to get the bats to tackle the bottom strut on the right at the same time. That will account for four more struts; one is already through and the other nearly, I think. That leaves two, the extreme left one near the bridge and the one nearest us in the middle. Sir Conn, before you start please make a loop round that one—yes, more leather, please—and attach it by our rope in Thing's pack to Snowy. He may not be able to free it, but at least the shaking will give the creature pause." I marvelled at my incisive, logical, quick-thinking kitten; never would I have believed her capable of five minutes' sustained thought, let alone the drive and determination she had shown thus far. She gave a quick lick to each front paw. "I shall give each warning if the spider changes direction: off you go!"

An hour later we were totally exhausted, and the spider must have been too. The bats had gnawed through one more strand, Conn had cut through another and so had I, but all Snowy's weight had not shifted the bottom one. We had lost two more bats, but now the web was looking decidedly the worse for wear. Great holes marred it where the stones had gone through and the insect had only managed temporary repairs. Now, not counting the first strut the bats had failed to sever, four had been cut through and temporarily repaired, but did not look as though they would bear any weight until the tarry substance that anchored them had had time to set. And time was something none of us had to spare.

Moglet still burned with energy. Her eyes were huge in the early twilight, for the sun had sulked behind cloud since midday. None of us had had time to think of food but I would have given almost anything for a drink, and looking round at the others I knew they felt the same. For two pins I would have drunk Pisky dry and watched enviously as Moglet lapped a quick half-inch, with permission of course.

"Thirsty work," she remarked, fastidiously pawing the top clear of weed and snails. "Now: one last go! Conn, take the last right-hand strand and bats the left. Thing dear, sharpen that knife of yours once more, for the strand in the middle here is the strongest—"

The right-hand strand parted. Conn ran to my side and together we sawed away at the middle one. The last left-hand strand suddenly snapped loose from the wall above the bridge and the bats screeched above our heads as the maddened spider came rushing down towards us. The bats suddenly flew in a cluster at her eyes so that she could not see, and at last with a strange thrumming noise our strand broke. The others, the mended ones, sucked stickily away from their supports and now the whole web hung suspended by one single line.

The black creature retreated to the middle of her ruined web, hairy legs waving, jaws snapping, eyes darting from side to side judging which repair to make next. Then, crouching back, it gathered its legs to spring—

"A torch, Thing, a torch!" called Snowy urgently.

With a speed I had not thought my tired body possessed I grabbed what kindling we had left, bound it with the cord from Conn's cloak to a piece of wood and struck tinder and flint. In a moment I had a blazing torch that illuminated the whole cave even as the spider leapt from the web to the rock before me. Waving the torch I advanced.

"Back, back you thing of darkness and deceit! Back, I say—" and I flung the fiery brand straight at its eyes.

With a screaming hiss it leapt back for the web, which rocked crazily at the impact. There was a crack! like a whiplash and the last strand parted. For an instant web and spider seemed to hang suspended, then with a rush both fell down into the chasm. The torch followed, and as we rushed forward for a moment it lit up the shattered body of the monstrous creature—arms and legs broken and askew, all smothered by the broken web. Then the foaming waters closed over it and spun it away into the endless rivers below the mountain . . .

The Binding: Crow

The Great White Worm

Outside, in the clean, cool evening air, it was raining again. But now none of us would have exchanged the downpour for the deceptive shelter of those accursed caves. As for me, I opened my mouth and let the blessed water bounce off my tongue; I even sucked the ends of my hair for the precious drops. In spite of being drenched Moglet stood stiff-legged and tail-high as if she had just routed a pack of marauding toms from the backyard, revelling in our admiration and affection. As for the bats, they swarmed away in a great cloud, despite the rain, only to return in twos and threes to drop small fragments of food. I didn't fancy the idea myself but Corby, Pisky, Puddy and Moglet were delighted. It was the bats' way of saying thank you.

After a while common sense reasserted itself; I was pretty wet but Conn was in a worse plight. His cloak now, with all the pieces hacked from it and the cord missing, was more like a tatty head-cape, and he was drenched and shivering.

"Skin is supposed to be watertight," he grumbled, "but I'll swear this water is leaking through to my bones . . . There's a village of sorts down in the valley: I can see smoke. Shall we?"

Above our heads the last escort of bats swooped in farewell, and somewhere a buzzard called its lonely: "Ki-ya, ki-ya, ki-ya . . ."

An hour later I was dozy with heat, more-or-less dry and had a stomach full of a thick, meaty stew. The last piece of bread still firmly clasped to my chest, I fell asleep on the rushes.

We found the four stones the very next day, on the edge of the uplands north of the village, and consulted The Ancient's map.

"North from here, due north," said Conn. "That should be easy enough. Even I know north. Well, that's three adventures past us and we're still all in one piece. Allonz, mez enfants! Four to go . . ."

"What's that?" I asked. The words sounded familiar.

"What? Oh, allonz et cetera? The Frankish words for let's get going," he said condescendingly.

But I knew, even as he spoke I had heard them before—somewhere. Another of those tantalizing glimpses of another life.

"Don't you mean: 'En avant, mez braves?'" I suggested, and was rewarded by a startled look from those brown eyes, but he said nothing further.

The moors and forests through which our way led were bare, for the most part, of human life, but the cooler, crisp air did not deter an abundance of wild life. Hares, foxes, stoats, weasels; badger, deer, squirrel, marten; eagle, merlin, finch, tit; and the purple heath and heather, crisp, curling bracken and colourful butterflies, dingy moths and laden bees. Here I found, in the endless quest for berries and roots, two plants I had never come across before; one, with sticky-pad leaves, trapped small insects much as Puddy did with his tongue, and the other, looking deceptively like a large violet, had fleshy leaves which performed much the same function. Pisky declared the brownish water we replenished him with as "a nice change"; Moglet managed, even with her damaged paw, to find voles and mice. At times voles in particular were almost too easy to catch, running away from us like a brown wave in the long grasses. Indeed Moglet became rather blase about her new-found prowess, and shared her meals with Corby, so they both grew sleeker and better groomed. Snowy, too, enjoyed the change in diet. Now I only had to provide for Conn and myself and we relied mainly on what I could cull, for we had no bows, arrows or spears for hunting, and did not stay long enough in any one place to set snares.

We made good progress, only having to detour once when a stagnant bog barred our way, a question mark to safety with its green slime lying quiet on ominously inviting open stretches, midges dancing their one-day life above. The main impediment to any enjoyment was the rain that seemed to fall more plentifully on these bleak uplands, so perhaps it was with a sense of relief that we found the ground sloping away beneath our feet and that one day the rising sun showed us cliffs and the sea.

Again that nagging sense of a thing known and should-be-remembered tugged at my mind. The salty smell, the crash and roar of the waves, the endless shift of great waters, all these I had seen before, somewhere, sometime. Only the steep, black, boulder-shod cliffs were different; the ones I thought I remembered were—white? Cream? Gentler, with sandy beaches, not these pebble- and rock-encumbered stretches. A summer house by the sea, collected shells, sea-bright pebbles that faded without the lap of water, the grit of sand between teeth and toes, the salt-harsh cry of gulls—

The great gulls wheeled and broke before us, screamed a welcome, and for two days they accompanied us as we traversed the edge of those dark and frowning cliffs, unable to find a way down. On the third day we came to a small river, which afforded access to the beach below. It flowed gently between restraining banks to a large bay, some three miles across at the widest part but narrowing at its mouth to about fifty feet, enclosed by sharply rising cliffs. Here the sea frothed and seethed, eager to burst its bottleneck as the tide receded. The beach around the wishbone-shaped bay was broken with tumbled rocks and boulders but inland the terrain was smooth and low, until it rose behind to the moors we had left. In that fair and gentle valley lay a prosperous-looking village, more a small town, with houses on either side of the river and boats drawn up tidily on the shelving banks.

For a while as we descended to the beach, I became aware of a curious shifting movement among the rocks, and thought I could hear a strange mixture of sounds: keening, grunting, shuffling, splashing. The smell was less indistinct: a fishy, animal smell, but it was Corby's keen eyes, perched as he was on Conn's shoulder, that recognized all this for what it was.

"Caw! People of the Sea—ruddy millions of 'em!"

Almost at the same moment came Conn's voice. "Seals! A great colony of seals! But rather late, I should have thought . . ."

Even as we adjusted to the sight, a boy of ten or twelve, clad in rough homespun and barelegged, rose from behind a clump of gorse to our right and stood regarding us wide-eyed.

"Hullo," said Conn.

The boy's eyes opened wider than ever, as if he thought us incapable of ordinary speech. "Be you they travellers what are spoke of and expected?" It came out in a rush and in an accent strange to me and hard to follow. "If you be, then I bids you welcome, masters both, and ask that you follow me to't chief's house," and he set off forthwith down a narrow track leading to the village, with many a scared, backward look. I almost expected him to cross his fingers against the Evil Eye.

We looked at one another.

"We are travellers," said Conn. "But as to being expected—Or spoken of, come to that—"

"Strange tales travel with the wind," said Snowy. "And, like smoke, they change shape in passing."

"Well," I said, "we can only find out if they mean us by going down and asking."

" 'What am I?' as the worm said to the blackbird," contributed Corby, gloomily. "Oh, well, don't say as I didn't warn you . . ."

So we followed the boy, who kept pausing for us to catch up, as if afraid of losing us, but at the same time he kept his distance, as if afraid of what we might do if we came too close. We passed several huts and the people there also regarded us with a kind of wary fascination. The town was well laid out, with straight streets swept clear of rubbish, animals tethered or penned and folk decently dressed. Most of the people were tall and slim, many with fair hair, the men moustached and bearded, some with tattoos on their arms and fingers. As we walked I glanced over my shoulder: we were being followed. Men, women, children, all had put aside what they were doing and were pacing behind us. At another time this might have seemed menacing, but in spite of the numbers I was aware most of all of curiosity, and almost began to wonder whether we had all grown two heads, though the others looked normal enough to me.

After what seemed a very long walk, we reached a bluff overlooking the river and what I supposed to be the chief's house. It was a long, low building, the wooden supports curiously carved with serpentine figures picked out in red and blue, the shapes outlined with rows of white shells. We reached the entrance, preceded by a couple of townspeople obviously come to forewarn of our presence; no leather-hinged door, no curtained flap awaited us, instead two painted panels that fitted into well-grooved wood top and bottom and now slid apart to reveal a dark, smoky interior. I thought it a very good idea for a door and was busy examining the mechanics when someone nudged me forward and I found myself inside, adjusting my eyes to the gloom.

Wooden pillars down each side supported a steeply pitched thatched roof; behind these were stacked trestles and stools. In a central stone fireplace, raised some three feet from the ground, smouldered a peat fire, smoke wisping up through a square exit in the thatch. At the far end were curtained recesses, no doubt for sleeping and stores. Light was provided by stands holding small basins of strong-smelling oil with wicks floating inside, although iron sconces were set in the pillars should stronger illumination be needed.

Beside the fire stood a taller man than the rest, with white hair that curled to his shoulders, wearing blue woollen trews and a fine cloak to match, fastened by a cord drawn through ornamented bronze rings; on his right side hung a short, bright sword and his arms were braceleted above the elbow by golden snakes. By his side stood a tall, dark lady with plaited grey hair and the same strong features as her husband, and behind them lurked three tall boys and a girl, by the mark of their features their children.

"Welcome, travellers all," said the chief. He, too, used that strangely accented speech—they clipped the hard sounds short and drew out the soft ones—but he spoke, majestic and slow, so that it was easier to understand him than the boy earlier. "We have much to talk of, you and I. My name is Ragnar. My wife, Gunnhilde, and I welcome you to our house and our town of Skarrbrae. You must rest yourselves and eat. When the sun is low we shall speak again."

He clapped his hands and hot water and towels were brought. Conn and I retired to separate recesses, where I luxuriated in a clean body once again. When we emerged, stools and a wooden trestle were set in front of us with great wooden bowls of some fishy broth, strips of dried fish and a coarse bread. There were also bowls of goat's milk and a refreshing herbal brew, in which I thought I detected camomile and feverfew. Snowy and the others were not neglected either, and while I wondered at why (to them) a pony was allowed within doors, a great pile of hay was set in front of him; Corby was given fish-guts, Moglet the same with goat's milk, and I crumbled a paste of bread into Pisky's bowl. Puddy stayed quiet in my pocket after a snorted: "Fish!" I wasn't worried, as insects had been plentiful during our journey.

Stuffed full, we were led to a pile of rushes on which were spread fur rugs, and, perhaps because of the food, or the gloom, or simply because we were dry and warm and welcome, we all dozed off for a couple of hours. When I awoke, torches were being lit in the sconces along the pillars and

Puddy was sitting three inches away from my nose, a wing and a leg of some large insect sticking out of the corner of his mouth. His throat moved up and down decisively. As I watched the bits disappeared, and he burped.

"Disgusting!" I said.

"Each to his own," said Puddy. "Anyway, I didn't think you would like it marching down the back of your neck . . ." and he crawled back into my pocket, where I could feel him hiccoughing quietly.

"Serves you right," I said.

Corby came up and looked me in the eye—one of his to both mine. "Does one crap inside or out?"

I rose to my feet. "Those who wish to crap," I said carefully, "crap, to use your expression, outside." I looked down at my pocket. "And those who crap in my pockets, or sick-up because they're too greedy, get their mouths fastened together for a week!"

"Want to . . . the other," said Moglet. So did I, so we all went outside for five minutes.

When we returned, Ragnar and his wife were waiting for us and invited us to join them round the replenished fire. Everyone else had disappeared, and I judged the serious part of the business was about to start.

Ragnar nodded at us. "You may wonder," he began, "why it is that you are looked-for: but perhaps you know?"

I glanced at Conn, who shook his head. "No, we do not know how it is that you expected us," he said slowly, choosing his words carefully. "We are on a journey that means much to us but, I should have thought, little to others. Yet are we grateful for your welcome and hospitality, and if our appearance in your part of the country means that my friends and I can help you in any way, then I think I speak for us all when I say we will do our best." He glanced round at us all, receiving our agreement. "But may I ask why you need us particularly and how you knew that we should come—if, indeed, it is us you expected?" He sounded doubtful.

Gunnhilde took up some embroidery. "It is a combination of a need and a legend. The need I shall come to later, but I assure you it is very real." Her husband nodded gravely. "First, the legend. Our people have lived here for many generations. They say that folk from the northern lands were wrecked on this coast during a great storm; the survivors scrambled ashore and settled among the fisherfolk who already lived here, in a village much smaller than you see it now. The marriage of different peoples and variant skills brought both peace and prosperity to this part of the country; we had the sea for fishing, our friends who visited us every year—"

I looked at Snowy: the seals? He nodded.

"—sweet water from the river, good earth for crops and the uplands and forests for hunting and timber. For many years we prospered—I speak of a time before I was born, you understand—but a wise man, a shaman as we call them, who once lived and died here warned of a time when the sea should boil, the fish flee and our friends come no more to visit us. Then, it was a tale for children but even so his words were remembered, for who knows what the gods have in store? My mother's mother told me of the prophecies when I was a child and I remembered. But unlike some prophecy it was not all doom: there was a promise of deliverance also." She glanced at her husband. "You tell them, for you know the words as well as I."

"Indeed I do, for it was a tale to fright children into the dark imaginings of the night. We learnt it as it was told, in verse, so that no meaning should be lost by later mis-telling or exaggeration. It goes thus," and he straightened his back and delivered the lines in a deep, sonorous voice. I didn't think much of them as verse; they didn't even rhyme, but some of the words started with the same letters, so it had a kind of hypnotic beat to it, wrapped up as it was in symbolism and metaphor.

"And in that time: the token of the terror shall be thus:
The people of the sea shall come: and bring forth their young that year;
And the young that year shall be great: and their melody music the meadows.
But for jealousy of their joy: evil shall bring forth evil e'en greater
And the sea shall boil: and bring forth a beast to despoil.
Men shall starve and women too: and children cry from hunger,
And the sea-people and people of the sea: shall keen and cower,
While the great White Wyrme: shall devour the dead and despoil the sea . . ."

He paused. "If it were only that, then we should be lost indeed, for that which was prophesied has indeed come to pass—more of that later. But the prophecy speaks of a deliverance, and this is where I believe you were sent to help us." He cleared his throat.

"But this shall last only so long: then from the south shall come the seven;
A wight on a white horse: holding for help in his arms
The moon and stars for measure: and the stars shall be green as grass
Blue as a babe's eye: red as rust and clear as river running.
And the seven shall strive: and the White Wyrme shall wither.
And behold! all shall be: as before and better.
Then the people of the sea and the sea-people: shall gift and guard them,
For they go with the gods: and shall take the road west with weal . . .

"So, that is why we have looked for you, for now is the time of our greatest need, and in your company there would seem to be at least part of the promise of our deliverance. A man on a white horse, that is clear enough, but the prophecy foretold of seven. I count but six—"

"Seven," I said, and plonked Puddy on a free stool.

There was a moment's silence and then Gunnhilde laughed and put aside her sewing.

"Seven it is, seven. We are lucky husband, for in them the prophecy does come true!"

I wriggled on my seat. "But the bit about the moon and stars?"

Ragnar frowned. "That I cannot see, but there must be an answer . . ." He glanced at his wife but she was staring at Puddy and then picked up Pisky's bowl.

"Green as grass: the moon," and she threw back her head and laughed. "Under our noses, husband, other riddles to be read, I fancy . . . And you and you and you," she pointed to me, Corby, Moglet, "must hold the other 'stars?' "

I lifted Corby's wing and Moglet's paw and pointed to my stomach. "And there is another tale. But it hasn't been written yet, 'cos it isn't finished."

"The riddle is read," said Gunnhilde. "Husband, call them to prepare a feast!"

Amidst the bustle, the uproar, the feasting, the smiles, I caught a mutter from Corby. "First part's easy, all feasting and fal-lals and what-a-pretty-bird: I've an idea the second part will be more difficult . . ."

It was not until the morrow that we realized just what we had let ourselves in for, but that evening it was indeed all "feasting and fal-lals" for it was obvious the townsfolk were sure we were the answer to all their prayers. We ate and drank our fill and were entertained by their songs and dances until the small hours. It wasn't till all was quiet that I began to wonder what was in store for us. Then I remembered the verses and fell asleep uneasily wondering about boiling seas and great white worms which, together with the cheese I had eaten earlier, engendered weird and disturbing dreams. Twice I woke in a cold sweat, only to be soothed to sleep again by the gentle breathing of my companions and a sort of mournful lullaby that seemed to come in time with the distant rush and suck of the sea.

The next morning Ragnar, with about fifty interested townspeople in tow, took us down to the beach, and there, restlessly milling and turning, were about two to three hundred seals. They were of all ages and sizes, male, female and pups, and seemed to have little fear of humans, allowing us to walk amongst them on the rocks and the greyish-black sand. They became excited when they saw Snowy and gave soft hooting sounds and groans and I realized they were telling him something, recognizing that he was one who would understand. There were more of them bobbing about in the bay, seeming to stand on their back-flippers in the water eyeing us with curiosity. Some porpoised up and down, showing off, others with mouthfuls of seaweed were tossing their heads from side to side, threshing the water, exactly like a housewife beating clothes on stones in a river—another way of drawing attention to themselves, I supposed. All seemed jolly, a gathering of wild animals grown tame and choosing to live in close proximity with man, but there was an unease, a restlessness, a frustration that communicated itself as surely as the ever-moving sea.

Conn questioned Ragnar on their lameness. "Are they always like this?"

"Not always, but at the moment they have no choice; they are restless because they know the time has long passed this year when they should be at sea. Supplies of food are running low, both for them and us, though we have given them what we could." He paused. "You see, we have an arrangement with them; oh, nothing that has ever been written down by us nor agreed with them: one cannot speak with animals."

I opened my mouth, but Snowy nudged me, and I closed it again.

"The way it works is this: every year the seals are allowed to come to our beaches and have their pups, and then they mate again. During that time we leave them unmolested. Then, when autumn and winter comes we go forth to hunt them, mainly for their skins, for that is our only surplus for trading. By then they are out at sea, and it is an even battle between man and beast. Even then, we do not hunt indiscriminately; each spring the pups are counted. Of these a third will not survive their first year, from natural causes. We only cull a half of the number of adults of the number remaining, the population is kept more or less constant. There are enough pelts for us and enough fish for both man and beast."

I looked at Ragnar with new respect: a little different from Lady Adiora's method.

The tide was retreating now, making a noise on the pebbles like someone clearing their throat and then spitting. Ragnar waved to the townsfolk not to follow us further.

"We shall go on alone," he said. Alone? Where? Echoes of last night's dreams made my heart beat faster. "Of course there may be little to see: if the creature has eaten recently he may not show himself. But if we stay quiet and tempt him a little, then perhaps—" He beckoned to one of the men, who ran back to one of the huts and reappeared with some strips of dried goat's meat. "Ah, yes: this should do it."

With the chief leading we made our way round the bay to the southernmost tip, climbing steadily all the way and passing through a small flock of horned sheep, almost indistinguishable from their goat-brothers, so unlike the low-slung fatties Brothers Peter and Paul tended: still, I supposed the brothers' sheep would have been hard put to it to find sustenance on these harsher uplands, while Ragnar's sheep looked fit and well on their poor diet. More evidence of how careful husbandry had made this such a prosperous place. I supposed The Ancient would have a "clitch" for all this: "Difficult to tell sheep from goats when both wear horns"?

At last we stood on the edge of the cliff, the breeze from the sea ruffling Moglet's fur and snatching at my mask. The sea foamed and raced beneath us and some twenty feet away was the opposite cliff, crowned by an immense slab of rock that reared precariously over the edge with what looked to me like a dangerous tilt.

"The Look-Out Stone," said Ragnar. "The highest point around. We use it for spying out shoals of fish, for posting a beacon if anyone is overdue and, of course, for spotting the forerunners of the seal-cows in April. But there is a suggestion for building a tower on this side instead: that rock can sway dangerously in a high wind and we're not sure how firmly it's anchored." He sighed. "It seems we can have little use for either till the Wyrme is destroyed. When the seals whelped this year we had promise of good hunting, for there were more than usual and we only took the born-dead or injured as we always do. Then the Wyrme came, and they could not escape. They lost about twenty cows and pups, before the males arrived looking for them. They only got in by dint of numbers, a mad rush on a high tide. But now of course the beast knows where they are and also knows a mass exit will leave the pups behind. The cows will not risk the pups and the bulls will not leave the cows . . ." He sighed again. "And it is not only them, it is us also. We have tried to take to the boats and carry on our fishing but the Wyrme overturns them and anyone who swims is immediate prey. We are trapped and the seals are trapped! This is why we welcomed you, knowing that, through you, the second part of the prophecy would come to pass." And he began to recite.

"And the seven shall strive: and the White Wyrme shall wither.

And behold! all shall be: as before and better."

"Doesn't he know any nice cheerful little ditties?" muttered Corby. "Anyway, he's missed out that bit about the road west. And gifts . . . Fat chance! Looks as if we are trapped as tight as the rest. After all that mumbo jumbo can you see 'em saying 'Bye-bye, thanks for trying and all that?' No, we ain't going north, south or east, let alone west—"

"Well, then," said Snowy, "put your tongue back in its beak, where it belongs, and use your eyes and your cunning brain to see if you can come up with a solution! It could be your turn, you know."

There it was: "turns" again. Moglet's turn, Corby's turn—

"Watch," said Ragnar, who of course had heard none of this by-play. "Down there, in that wide cleft in the base of the opposite cliff where the water is calmer . . . That's where he rests and watches and waits." And with that he tossed a strip of goat's-flesh out as far as he could.

Nothing. We watched the meat sink slowly in the clear water beyond where the tide was racing out, until it touched bottom some twenty feet down. Ragnar took another strip of flesh; I was still gazing at the first and the water appeared to be cloudier, as though something had stirred the grey-black sand. Ragnar flung the second piece.

A gull, a yearling with less sense than it should have, flung itself seawards in a dive after the meat; they touched water together and for a moment I believed the bird had won, but there was a boiling beneath us, a great rearing and with the speed of my thought bright blood sprayed between great sharp teeth, teeth like a hundred bone needles, and the blood became the darker colour of the sea and there was a white, grey-tipped feather floating and nothing more . . .

The air was filled with the screaming of sea birds: gulls, guillemots, tern, as they rose from crevices in the cliff upwards from the sea, and the harsh cries of raven, crow and cormorant who banked and wheeled from their perches on the rearing rocks. Bird mingled with bird, and screamed with fright and mourned with despair and watched the feather as it slipped, alone and broken, away with the ebbing tide. Black and white, grey and grey, and the birds calling and Corby answering and trying to fly from my arms on one wing only, and me clasping him tight to save him from further harm, and the stone in my belly hurting—

And then Snowy called, loud and clear. What had been senseless flight settled into a pattern, rising and falling like the midsummer dance of gnats over a pond, and the voices softened and fell quiet. Corby ceased struggling and lay quiet too, except to say in a small voice: "Those are my brothers—if only I could fly!" I could do nothing save stroke his untidy feathers in sympathy.

Conn nudged me. "Did you ever see anything so fearsome, Thingumajig?"

Down there, some five feet below the surface, its body undulating with the unseen currents, was a great white worm-like creature. Despite the distortion of the water I could see quite clearly; I suppose it was not a true white, more a grey-tan colour but the green water gave it luminescence. At first, horror made it a hundred feet long and twenty wide at the least, but when sense reasserted itself I suppose it must have been about eighteen to twenty feet in length, including a flat, splayed, scooping tail. It was segmented, but the shell seemed to be soft, judging by the ease with which it arched and bent its spine; there were two vestigial suckers on the foremost segment behind the head, and double gills like fringed curtains. The head itself was the most frightening of all: it looked much as an eel's but the eyes were positioned much closer on the top of its head and the mouth was wider and set, as far as I could see, with a triple row of the fearsome, needle-sharp teeth.

I shivered. "Do you—" I said, "do you think it is the only one of its kind—or—or could there be others?"

"Well," said Conn. "The sight of that little monster does bring to mind a tale I heard once, told by one who had returned from seas on the other side of the world. He said it had been narrated to him (and I cannot vouch for its veracity, mind, though one of his longer tales about a great grey beast like a mountain with an extra arm in the middle of its head I do know to be true, for my friend Fitzalan had seen such) but, as I was saying, this traveller had been told that in a sea as warm as new milk, a seaman had fallen overboard and by chance bobbed up again where a lucky rope had saved him. But he had come aboard quite mad, babbling of a great forest of worms such as this one, waving beneath many fathoms like a field of sun-white grain. All thought him touched and suspected a knock on the head had addled his brains, but he insisted and it was all written down by the captain in his log."

Ragnar had been paying keen attention to this story and nodded his head. "The water you spoke of was warm; hereabouts, even in winter, there is a warm current that brings the fish in close to our bay. Maybe such a worm as you speak of could have lost its way and followed such?"

It all sounded highly unlikely to me, but here it was and here were we, and I was not looking forward to closer acquaintance. Neither were the others, to judge by the careful way they avoided looking at us and each other. There was not even a "Lemme see! Lemme see better . . ." from Pisky.

Ragnar brought us back sharply to the task in hand. "Well now, you have seen our monster: you can see our problem. I realize you will have to think about this, so I will leave you to confer."

"A conference was just what I had in mind," said Conn, as easy as if he were discussing the weather, and looking Ragnar straight in the eye. "Of course, you realize that deep magic such as we shall have to use takes a while to conjure . . ."

We watched the chief out of sight.

I turned to Conn admiringly. "You were great! Just what idea have you got?"

"Not a one, not a one in the world, Thingummy, but I thought we needed a breather. That fellow is not going to let us out of his sight until his little miracle-workers have got rid of that—that creature down there, and I thought we could talk more freely amongst ourselves. Now then, who's got an idea?"

No one, it seemed. I glanced desperately round our circle.

"We cannot dig it out," said Snowy. "Nor lead it away."

"Fire's no good," said Puddy gloomily.

"We can't spike it or claw it or carve it up," said Moglet.

"Can't starve it either," said Pisky, from the bottom of his bowl.

Which left little. I could think of nothing, save drinking the sea dry, and even I knew better than to make that sort of suggestion.

Eventually, aware of an uncharacteristic silence, we all looked at the culprit. We looked so hard that Corby started shifting from claw to claw and muttering to himself.

"Well?" I said.

"Well, nothing! Just don't expect me to come out pat with the solution. Still . . ."

I think we all shuffled forward a pace.

"Still . . ." he continued, musingly, "there's something a-tapping from the inside of the shell. Probably as addled as the rest of the eggs in the nest, but you never know . . . Tell you what: all right if we go into one of those huddles, like what we used to? You know, when we all held beaks and claws and things under Thing dear's cloak, in the good old days of Her Ladyship? Always felt it concentrated my mind wonderfully . . ."

It was stuffy and warm under my cloak and I was only too conscious of how silly we must have looked as we wriggled together, until I heard Snowy's thoughts through the thick folds and felt Conn's hand on my shoulder.

"Ideas, ideas," they seemed to say. "Think, think; concentrate, concentrate. Give Corby your minds, your help . . ."

Deliberately I tried to make my mind go blank, but still a series of pictures flashed across my mind, like the glint of sunlight on metal, seen a long way off. Cliffs; movement of green water; a rock; birds, flocks of birds; pecking beaks; the sky turning over—

"Got it!" cried Corby. "Leastways . . ."

I flung back the cloak and we all blinked in the midday sun.

"Gorrem-nidea," said Corby. "A possibility, anyways. Beaks out: can feel the sun. Now to chip away the rest of the shell . . ." I realized that what I had thought foreign language and complicated imagery merely meant that he had gone back to his nestling days. "Can't say for certain . . . Still covered with egg yolk at the moment. But, it might work . . ."

"What?" cried Conn in exasperation.

"Not in words. Not at the moment. Lot of thinking to do . . ."

"How can we help?" asked Snowy, practical as always.

Corby glanced up, but his gaze was abstracted. "Hmmm? Help? Oh—yes, you might at that. I need to get around this bay to the other side. Over by the big rock. Perhaps, if you wouldn't mind like, you could give me a lift . . ."

And so, for the rest of the afternoon, as the rest of us watched and wondered, Snowy or Conn carried him round the bay, back and forth the three miles or so that separated one headland from the other. Each time he reached the other side he was met by an increasing number of birds, many of them crows as ragged as himself. They all seemed to crowd and confer around the base of the great lookout rock that reared up across from us, but no one said anything specific, although Conn looked thoughtful when he came back with Corby the third time, and Snowy was obviously in on the secret too. For secret it was: Corby refused to discuss his idea with the rest of us, afraid, perhaps, that he might look a fool if it didn't work.

The only clue came from Moglet, who at one stage remarked frivolously that it might save time if we ran a cat's cradle between the two headlands, and Corby looked at her so sharply that I thought we were on to something. Unfortunately, I didn't know what.

His behaviour later that day when we returned to the town, also had us puzzled. He first asked Pisky if he could practise dropping pebbles in his bowl, and met an indignant refusal when the first one narrowly missed one of the snails. Then he asked Conn to fill him a leather bucket with seawater and by dusk was still picking stones from the beach and dropping them in the water until the container was full, then was asking Conn to empty them out and repeating the process until it was too dark to see.

If we were mystified, so were the townsfolk, and in the end Ragnar himself came down to watch.

"This is obviously powerful magic," he observed, but I could see one hand was stroking his beard and he was frowning.

"Yes," said Conn. "And it works better, it does, if the whole world is not breathing down our necks. Some things are meant to be secret, you know."

And, as everyone retreated precipitately, it was only I who caught his irreverent wink.

Later that night, Corby asleep before any by the smouldering fire, I tried Conn again.

"Can't you tell us?"

"Tell you what?"

"What's this business with the pebbles? Why did you ask Ragnar tonight about the weather and the times of the tides and so on?"

He pinched my cheek through the mask, but his eyes were dancing.

"'Tis Corby's secret, so it is, and it's for him to tell. Go to sleep, Thingy, and perhaps you'll learn all in the morning." And he ruffled my hair with an intimate caressing gesture that sufficiently banished sleep. If it had only been the puzzle over Corby's scheme for ridding the town of the White Wyrme I might have dropped off eventually, but what does one do when one tingles and throbs and glows from nose to toes? It wasn't as though he had meant it as something more than the pat he would give Snowy's flank, the tickle behind Moglet's ear or under Puddy's chin—My stupid, vulnerable inside made me want to make more of it, to kid myself that he had a special feeling for me, that he even looked beneath the hunched back, the mask, the hidden ugly face, and saw someone to love. I knew also that it was no good for me, for us, to think this way. Ever since we had rescued him from that ditch, so many moons away, I had loved him. And although the adventures we had undergone had bred an easy, superficial comradeship that sometimes helped me forget my hopeless love, it was at times like these when I lay unable to sleep; at dawn when we woke to a new day; at evening when the night cloaked our familiar forms; when we were nearest in joint endeavour and when we were farthest, like the time when he had conceived his passion for the Lady Adiora—it was at all these times that I held fast in my heart, knowing, hoping, despairing, realizing, the love I knew would never give me peace.

I looked over to where he lay, long and relaxed on the cushions, one hand flung over his head, the other curled close to his body, breathing gently in a deep sleep. If I had dared, I would have leant over and kissed his curving mouth—

"Do stop *fidgeting*!" said Moglet sleepily. "Got a tummy-ache?"

The Binding: Crow

The Sea-People and the People of the Sea

"What a marvellous idea!" I said, for Corby had at last outlined his plan. "But surely we can't manage it on our own? Can't we get the townsfolk to help?"

"That's the general idea," said Conn. "Corby thinks his friends, the other birds, can do a great deal, but we need some strong men or women, and we've got to get it all exactly right, the timing and everything."

"Then," said Snowy, "as we are supposed to be magic, it were surely best to see that all those details are worked out beforehand. If we ask for aid too early they may doubt our powers and perhaps realize that eventually ordinary brains such as theirs could have worked out such a solution—not to detract in any way from your achievement, Crow dear—so we shall give them a hint, but no more.

"Now," he continued, "there are the tides. At low on the slack, I think you said? Then there is the question of light: that from the sun is best. Dawn, or perhaps noon when the sun strikes sword-straight into the flesh of the water. The timings we shall leave to your discreet inquiries, Sir Knight. Corby will coordinate the birds so that they work from dawn till dusk, and the people shall be told that the headland is out of bounds—it would make sense to tell them that we are drawing a magic circle round the beast, or somesuch. I shall accompany the crow and also arrange for the decoy, which is most important, and keep the people of the sea from trying any more suicidal attempts to escape.

"Which leaves you, Thing dear, and Moglet, Puddy and Pisky. As you realize, we shall need two ropes, and at a pinch could manage by binding those available, but I should prefer entirely new ones, so I want you to explain that we need one rope one hundred feet long, with nine strands worked into nine twists—seven or eight would do, of course, but nine is a magic number and that they'll understand—and the other eighty feet long, twists and strands three and three (more magic), and a net the same, to measure three by nine. That should convince them they are being allowed on the fringes of our 'magic,' but just to add verisimilitude I want you to cast spells on the making, all of you, in full view of everyone. Not real ones, of course, any mumbo jumbo will do. And don't let them know what the ropes are for; let them believe, if you like, that they are to bind the beast when we have captured it. Anything: I'll leave it to you . . ."

It appeared the tides were approaching the midpoint between neap and flood, which meant we were in the Moon of Harvest, and the most favourable time—slack at midday and ideally a sunny day—would occur in seven days. Seven, a magic number, too . . . This made it easier to explain to Ragnar and Gunnhilde about the "magic" ropes. They fully appreciated the significance of numbers (this is why we made the ropes ninety-nine and eighty-one feet respectively, to fit in with the illusion), but it did not give Corby and his friends much time.

Moglet, Puddy, Pisky and I were so busy supervising and spelling the ropes, we saw little of what the others were doing, though of course we all compared progress at night. Corby said little, beyond moaning that his beak hurt, and indeed he looked more ragged and unkempt than ever. Conn said little either, but ate (and drank) more than he had for some time, declaring that "opportunity makes gluttons of us all"; Snowy was obviously tired, too, and we had little to report, for ropemaking is, even with "magic" rope, a very boring business. That is, until it gets snarled up . . .

Ever tried inventing convincing spell-words? Especially a different one for every foot of one-hundred-and-eighty feet of rope and a net? At first it's easy: you say things like "Shamma-damma-namma-a-do-ma" which doesn't mean anything, as far as I know—leastways it may in another language, but it didn't have any effect on the rope—and then you get bored and think you are clever to say things backwards (I was very proud of "Derobots-ra-et" and "Sra-etot-der-ob"). But eventually I became so "derob," both backwards and forwards, that I started to say anything. It was on the third day, after the net and the shorter rope were completed, I was half asleep and yawning and gabbled the first thing that came into my head—

"Er . . . Thing dear," said Moglet. "Did you mean to do that?"

I thought it had gone quiet. I opened my eyes. Everyone but us had fallen asleep where they were; standing, sitting; upright, leaning; working, idle. Fast asleep. Just like that.

"*What* did I say?"

"The instant turned-to-stone-where-they-stand one," said Pisky, rushing round excitedly. "*Isn't* it peaceful? None of that nasty dust flying around . . . When are you going to wake them up?"

I hadn't the faintest idea. I realized with horror that I had used, all unknowing, one of the Witch's spells. Not one I had ever heard her use, but one I must have read from her books when she was absent—and now, how on earth did I unsay something I hadn't known I'd said in the first place? I went cold all over.

"Puddy . . ."

His slow, quiet thinking reassured me. "Not to worry; no harm done. 'Tis a weak spell anyway, and needs but a break in the conjunction. Saw Her try to use it once, but She only had me and a bowl of water; need a cat or somesuch as well. You, me, Moglet and the fish's bowl make a filled triangle. Now, if we move a fraction . . ."

Of course the first time we all moved the same way so the conjunction stayed the same, with Pisky's bowl the central point, but we got it right the second time. I looked around fearfully, but all the folk were taking up their tasks as if there had been no break. My heart pounded sickeningly for a full five minutes and I was very careful after that. Not that it did us any harm in the long run, rather the reverse, for whilst the sleepers were not aware that anything untoward had happened, others too far away to hear the spell had seen what had occurred, and we were treated with an added respect and awe after that.

The seventh day dawned misty and damp. It must, it *must* be sunny at midday! The night before, Conn had told part of Corby's plan to Ragnar, who had promised to find the seven times seven volunteers to man the rope and do the pushing. And that was all of the plan he had outlined, on Snowy's advice. The headlands had been out-of-bounds for the last week, and although the increased activity of the birds, wheeling and crying, must have been some indication that something special was going on, no one questioned us—especially after my unfortunate slip—though I could see they were muttering amongst themselves. I had had awful stomach-cramps after the spelling, incidentally, almost as though by remembering the witch's spells in my unconscious I was also subconsciously calling up the pain associated with Her.

"The sun will show its face before midday," said Snowy, as if he had read our thoughts. "Come, you laggards: today is the day . . ." and so after a hurried breakfast of oatcakes, cheese and goat's milk we set off for the headland.

Conn and Snowy and Corby carried the beautifully coiled new ropes—well, the first two did, and Corby supervised—over to the far cliff. I left the others on the near clifftop and made my way to the narrow strip of beach below. From where I stood I could see Conn passing the longer rope around the base of the black slice of the lookout rock and tying it off in a complicated knot. Once he nearly slipped on the bird-droppings which whitened the surrounding stones, but eventually the rope was tied to Snowy's satisfaction. Then they made their way down to the beach opposite and I could see them bending over something else on the stones, but knew I must wait. There was a splash! the other end, then nothing for what seemed ages. As I was beginning to think everything had gone wrong, a round head with tearful brown eyes popped up in the shallows nearby and a large seal dragged itself up the beach to my feet.

Round its neck were the two ropes. Swiftly I stroked the seal's head, surprised to find how warm the skin over the skull was, then unlooped the ropes. It—I think it was a he—grunted, a soft moan, its eyes shining. I patted its head again. "Well done . . ."

I attached the shorter rope to the netting left on the beach with the tie Snowy had taught me, and helped the seal into his net-sling. "I think you are very brave," I said, and stroked him again.

Then it was up to my side of the clifftop again, hauling both ends of rope with me and paying it off as I went, puffing and panting with the effort. The longer piece, taut now across to the opposite headland, I tied to a pre-chosen rock, and the other I anchored under a stone nearer to the cliff-face.

I waved to Conn and Snowy. All set.

I gazed down into the dark, green sea, still half-hidden by wisps of morning mist that clung to the columns of the cliffs and wreathed the rocks. I was half-convinced I could see the shape of the White Wyrme, distorted by the water, lurking under the shelf of rock that was its favourite resting-place . . .

The sun brightened, the last wisps of mist blew away like smoke from a camp fire, the tide drew softer and softer away from the cliffs until the pebbles and rocks shone like jasper before catching the drying dullness of sun and breeze.

Behind me I heard the people who were to haul on the rope, twenty-eight of them; across on the other headland I watched Ragnar lead the other twenty-one behind the Look-Out Stone: I hoped someone had got their calculations right. There were onlookers too; I noticed the boy who had led us into the town on that first day sitting on his father's shoulder for a better look. Below us, in the bay, the people of the sea seethed like tadpoles in a drying rut, venturing ever nearer the mouth between the headlands.

Conn came up behind me, breathless. "Dear God, and isn't it a haul around that bay? Snowy says that when the sun strikes that submerged rock—there—it will be time. I'd better get the haulers briefed."

I watched the sun creep round, fascinated by the finger of light that probed—so slowly when watched, two inches at a time if you took your eyes away—deep into the waters below. About five minutes before time I glanced back at Conn who had his contingent holding the longer rope, just off the taut, ready between nervous fingers. Too late I wished we had had time to have a rehearsal, had a tug-of-war to test the ropes, had—

Conn was at my side again, this time taking the end of the second rope in his hand and thrusting it into mine. "Christ! I near forgot—You'll have to help me with this, Thing dear!" I was so astonished I grasped the rope without further thought. He had got my name right again . . . "Belay it now, round that rock, there's a good girl, and when I say 'Pull!' do it as though your life depended on it!"

Two inches of sunlight to go . . .

Below me one after another of the bull seals and a couple of the cows were venturing almost to the gap between the cliffs, and then seeming to think better of their effort were plunging back into the bay with a great slapping of the water with fins and tail.

"Oh, Conn!" I said despairingly. "It's too soon! Tell them—tell them to go back! They'll be killed . . ."

"Never worry," said a concentrating Conn. "Snowy has briefed them; they know what they are doing. Just stirring up a little interest . . ." As he spoke a greyish-white shape stirred under the ledge on the far side of the rocks and the White Wynne's monstrous head and six feet of his body came into view.

"A minute, a minute! Oh, dear Lord!" Conn muttered from beside me, his lean body coiled with tension. "Now, my friend, now!"

As if in answer to his fierce vehemence, a solitary seal swam into view beneath us, seeming to test the water, the tide, the creature itself. A foolish, young seal that behaved as though it had never heard of danger . . . Slow, hesitantly, it paddled right through the gap in the cliffs, and the very tide itself stood still . . .

And the sun, the sun, shining clear and true through the slack water, touched the special rock beneath us and the seal swam straight out into the sea, right into the sudden uprush of teeth from the monster below and Conn cried: "Pull! Pull, you bastards!" even as there was a shrill neigh from Snowy and all the birds in the world rose in the air screaming and Conn's hands closed over mine as we hauled desperately on the shorter rope and the weight below almost pulled my arms from their sockets and—

There was a crack! and groan from across the water and I watched almost unbelieving as the pinnacle of rock, the Look-Out Stone, shivered a little, leaned, hung for a moment at an impossible angle, and then toppled with at first maddening slowness and then faster and faster towards the water beneath.

"Leave go the rope!" yelled Conn to the haulers behind him. "Drop it, if you value your lives!" They let go just in time for the depth the rock had to plunge was far greater than its length of ninety-nine feet. I watched the end snake and whip over the edge of the cliff. There was an almighty great splash beneath us and then a high-pitched whistling sound. Conn belayed the taut rope we held around a rock and rushed forwards, grabbing my hand.

Through the mist of still-falling spray, the cloud of screaming birds, we peered into the waters beneath. The great black stone had fallen true, just as had been planned. The monster, the great White Wyrme, lay pinned beneath its biting edge, its back broken, a strange whistling noise coming from between its wicked teeth. A great cheer rose from the townsfolk and those with us ran back to join the others, all streaming back to the bay to launch anything seaworthy, mostly skin and wood boats for inshore and bank fishing. The people were armed with spears and short, stabbing swords, and these they waved in the air as they took to the water.

I went forward to check on our seal-lure, the animal we had hauled up with such desperate haste in his netting hammock. I saw him wriggle free, but as he dived the ten feet or so back into the sea I could see a gash on his shoulder, a torn flipper.

The people in their boats were racing across the bay, the bows throwing up steep little waves. The first boats were reckless, came too close, too soon, and one was overturned by a thrash of the dying beast's scooped tail and another's side was stove-in by the still-lethal jaws. But soon there were too many of them and the water oozed with a greenish-white murk as the spears and swords rose and fell; thrusting, tearing, gouging out great clumps of flesh until I had to turn away, sickened with the sight.

Snowy, a triumphant Corby on his back, nuzzled my shoulder. "The creature is dead: he can feel nothing . . ."

Conn nodded soberly, watching the carnage beneath. "'Tis often that way, after long fear and frustration; all a man's tensions build up, and unless one takes the lid off the pot—" He shivered, and a haunted look came into his eyes and was gone, so quickly I almost believed I had imagined it.

"Come on, now!" said the irrepressible Corby. "Where's all the feasting and fal-lals, then?"

The following morning we stood once more on the headland. The feasting was over, the songs sung, the thanks given, the gifts received. On Snowy's back, besides two panniers full of food and some herb wine, was a fresh-cured sealskin, soft and supple, ready to make into mitts, slippers, leggings, whatever we chose. Conn sported a new cloak, as like the old as made no difference, and our pockets were lined with silver. We were waiting for the great procession, the release of the seals—the people of the sea, and the townsfolk—the sea-people. It had been arranged that at midday, tide-slack, both animals and men would venture beyond the cliffs, past the mutilated body of the Wyrme, now fast disappearing down the throats of the constant sea birds, and out, out into the limitless sea. From then on, after this last day of amnesty, man and seal would revert to their natural roles, hunters and hunted. Until the spring, and the coming of the seal-cows . . .

I shivered a little as my hand crept to the soft hide on Snowy's back: perhaps this skin had come from some autumn killing like the ones that would start soon. I didn't want to think about it, for I had a secret, a secret only Snowy and I and one other shared. For last night . . .

Last night either the feasting had been too rich or my sleep had been too light, but suddenly, in the dark hour before dawn, I had awoken, all my senses keen, aware of far music in my ears. I sat up in the warm darkness of the hall. There it was again, quite unmistakable. Four notes in a descending scale, as though a child stepped down a great staircase, then an upward note as though he had gone back, up a missed step, and then down again to the ground on the last note, and all in a sadness of sound like innocence lost.

The melody was repeated, and I saw the shadow of our unicorn push aside the hangings from the shrouded doorway and disappear into the night. I tiptoed after him—none of the others, even Moglet of the bat-ears, had heard me go.

I followed Snowy down to the beach, his unshod hooves making no sound on the shingle, my stumbling progress plain enough to my ears and his, though he had not turned his head. There, beached on the pebbles, was the source of the song, our brave young seal-lure, his eyes swimming in the light of the half-moon, singing a song of loneliness and present pain. Snowy bent to the torn side, the injured flipper and I felt a shudder of power pass from him.

"There, my friend," he said. "It will heal. It is healed . . ."

I joined them, and in that dream, half-dream, I looked at the young, royal seal and thanked him again, and the scar on his side and the rip in his flippers shone white and healed. And it seemed to me that he asked whether I would like to try his world and that I agreed, and stripped off my clothes and mask and stepped into the waves and that they were as warm and smooth as new-drawn milk. And I put my arms about his neck, or so it seemed, and with Snowy's blessing we slid into the flooding bay, and the sea closed round us like the finest silk cloth, and there was the taste of salt in my mouth and the waves slid over my back with the gentlest of caresses.

The seal's body undulated like the weeds that waved in dark streamers from the rocks. When we reached the inlet, I felt the sudden great surge of the ocean and I held on tight, breathed deeply and then we were in his world, into the sudden cold beyond the cliffs, and the water sang and bubbled in my ears and lifted me from his back until only my arms held me to his curving, twisting body, and I knew what it was to fly in water and walk in water and live in water . . .

"You helped us," he said. "And because of that we shall sing to you when you come to your home by the water. Listen for us . . ."

Now, as we all watched from the headland, the tide from the bay started to flow out from the beach. First came the seals, the people of the sea; the males, the females, the younglings, surging out to meet their natural element, the sea; and after came the sea-people, the townsfolk and fishermen, singing and shouting and brandishing their spears, paddles flashing in the sun. And leading them *my* seal, breasting proudly the breakers that led to his freedom of the seas.

My eyes prickled with tears.

Over our heads the sea birds and the cliff birds screamed their victory, told of the long hours spent chipping away at the base of the great, lost Look-Out Rock and above them a lone buzzard spiralled, his call lost in the clamour.

"Shall we go?" said Conn. "They won't miss us now . . ."

The Binding: Knight

The Holy Terrier of Argamundness

The ruined fortified wall ran just the way we wanted to go, judging by our next marker: the five fingers of rock indicating northwest-by-north that we found on the edge of the moor above the town of the sea-people.

The shortening days were sunny and dry and bramble and hazel yielded a rich harvest. Brimstone (first and last in every year), tortoiseshell and peacock fluttered in ditch and hedge, some of the trees were goldening towards their fall and sheep fleeces were thickening. Folk were hospitable, for harvest was in, and for a time there would be an abundance of fruits and grain, and cattle- and pig-salting was still some way off while there was still stubble for the former and an abundance of acorns for the latter. Thatch was being replaced, wood chopped, peat stacked, preserves jarred, honey collected, grain threshed and stored; everywhere was bustle, harmony, plenty, and we ourselves were in fine fettle, exchanging shelter and food in the main just for a tale or two, a song, some of Corby's "tricks," but for the most part we just walked the wall, content with our own company and aware that we had in some way "turned a corner."

Conn had shown us The Ancient's map and with charcoal had traced the way we had come so far. "See, 'tis the four sides of a septagon we have done already: over halfway, and not a bone broken!"

"Yes," I objected, "but it has taken us at least three months to get this far: at this rate we will be into the Moon of Fogs at least before we finish. And who knows what else we have to face? Snowy got us and the animals out of that prison of a castle, Puddy reminded me of that fire-spell before we got eaten by tree-roots, Moglet thought of a way to get rid of that spider before we and the bats starved to death, and back there Corby and his friends chucked half a mountain at a sea-monster but—" I stopped. I had suddenly remembered what Snowy had said about it being someone's "turn," and thought flashed past thought; Snowy, Puddy, Moglet, Corby: they had all had their turns. Which left . . . ? Me, Conn and Pisky. "Oh dear!" I said.

Snowy gave me a sympathetic look. "They were not all as bad as each other."

"Bad enough!" I said gloomily, and spent the next couple of days in fruitless speculation on who would be the next one to save his comrades, and would it be difficult and long-drawn out or just plain scary? And would whoever-it-was prove equal to the task? (I meant me, of course.)

But the sun continued to shine by day, and when there were no hamlets we snugged down on colder nights in the remains of stables, dormitories and officers' quarters along the wall. We built fires against the ghosts that still marched those ramparts and stewed hare and wild fowl and vegetables, drank wine if we were lucky and water if we were not. Soon I forgot my cares and exulted in the peace and companionship and stared north up the steep decline from whence the blue-painted savages had challenged the ordered life and discipline of the Romans. I found a sandal, thongs broken, the haft of a sword, burnt grain scattered among broken shards, a pin without its set-stone, half a helmet . . .

"We turn here," said Conn. "Away from the wall, if we are to keep our direction." To the north the hills were starting to crowd down, though still blue with distance. We were on a plateau, but from now on the way was down, the slopes thickly wooded. It was a clear, pleasant day, but ahead lamb's-fleece cloud banked high on the horizon. "Leaf-Change will be with us soon, and the way lies through the woods. Corby, your eyes are best." He took him on his shoulder. "Is that the sea?"

I squinted through my lashes as he asked the question, but could only make out a haze, a deepening of colour, a glint of sun.

"Two rivers," said Corby slowly. "Small 'un and a bigger. Second one's got a wide estuary. Tide's out: plenty of sand."

"That's our way," said Snowy. "We could follow the river from its source, but it would be easier to cut down through the woods and join it nearer the mouth . . . What do you say?"

With the weather changing there was only one answer: we took our bearings and plunged into the forest. The way was difficult, for these woods were old as time and scarce of habitation, and fallen timber and thick undergrowth pestered our way, but I found plenty of mushroom and fungi to supplement our diet, though none of the Magic ones or the Fairies' Tits Tom Trundleweed had shown me. I remembered I still had a little packet of the dried ones in my pack, never used. I checked: they were still there, perhaps a bit squashed and crumbly, but better not to throw them away, just in case.

We descended to the river plain, and here the land had been cleared and farmers and smallholders raised sheep and a few cattle on the sparse, thin grass and fished the banks of the river for salmon and trout. Small, stunted trees bent their backs away from the westerly winds and the fleeced sky brought rain and an uneasy half-gale that gusted and died an instant before it was born. At last the river broadened into a wide estuary where the river Rippam, as it was called, ran fast and wide over great ribbed flats of sand, birds flocked and ran at low tide among the shrimped pools and worm-casts, and the heron flapped slow home with dab and eel in its craw.

We stayed in a fisherman's cottage the night of the Big Storm and lucky it was we found shelter, for the forest and fields of Argamundness, as it was called, were soon roaring with an equinoctial tide and a following gale that had waves leaping twenty feet high over the artificial barriers erected years ago in the little hamlet of Lethum in which we found ourselves.

We had crossed a precarious log roadway over the marsh; the earth and sand packed between the logs were seeping away, and more than once we found places where the logs themselves had disappeared. So it was with a sense of relief that we found the little hamlet tucked away on sand dunes, some twenty feet above the usual tide-level, and protected by an artificial barrier about ten feet high of smooth pebbles, glistening grey, pink and white under the onslaught of the waters. There were also the dunes of sand, bound by spiky marram grass, themselves a natural barrier to the west and north. The hamlet was a poor one, the only livelihood being the fishing that depended so much on wind and tide. Their sturdy boats, broad in the beam, could go out in all but the fiercest weather, and they had nets fine enough for shrimp and tough enough for plaice and dab, which hung pungently from the rafters of the cottages whose shuttered windows faced away from the prevailing westerlies.

Lethum was so poor, it did not even have an inn and the speech of its inhabitants reflected their isolation, being thick and sprinkled with a patois we could not understand. However, our coin they did recognize, and we fed well on fish stew, crabbed apples and goat's milk, and were provided with sacking pallets against the wall of one of the larger cottages. There was no problem with bringing Snowy inside either, for our host's few scrawny hens, a pig and a patient donkey were obviously used to sharing his space. It was warm, if fuggy, and I was more than accustomed to animal smells, so sleeping would have been no problem but for the violent wind.

Suddenly it was upon us, battering and hammering at doors and windows, skirling the rushes on the floor, puffing the smoke from the peat fire in our faces, and ripping great chunks of thatch from the roof, netted and weighted as it was. The mud-and-stone cottage seemed to crouch down upon itself, shrinking into the earth with ears back and eyes closed, a hare in the swirling, shifting dunes. Sand was everywhere; it gritted our teeth, rubbed the sore places in our skin, spun into little shifting castles on the floor. The whole world roared and bellowed and screamed and shouted outside like a huge army of barbarians come to pillage and destroy.

I found myself huddled in a heap on the floor, hands to my ears and eyes tight shut. I only realized I was moaning with fear when Conn took me by the shoulders and shook me.

"Pull yourself together: look at the others!"

I sat up, still shuddering. Snowy was fine, reassuring our host's animals with his mere presence, but poor Moglet was plastered like a dying spider against the far wall, eyes rolling in terror; Corby had his head under his wing in a corner and his feathers were twitching; Pisky had dived right to the bottom of his bowl and hidden his head under the weed; Puddy's throat was gulping up and down in distress and his eyes bulged more than ever. Our host crouched in a corner and was muttering, whether prayers, charms or incantations I could not tell.

I looked up at Conn; his eyes were troubled, and he moved as restlessly as a penned horse who has been used to the plain, but he showed none of the panic of the others. I took courage from his brown eyes, his firm chin, the challenge in his slim taut body.

"Well," I said, rising a trifle unsteadily to my feet. "It's going to be at least morning before this thing blows itself out, and I don't feel like sleep. Come, you lot, closer to me so I don't have to shout, and we'll think of a game to pass away the time." And I staggered over to Moglet and prised her claws from the mud wall, picked up Puddy and put him in my pocket, then made my way to Corby's side and indicated that he should join us by Pisky's bowl. Once there we went into our familiar huddle, all of them under the shelter of my cloak, and there we played "Going to Market" which Pisky won, having one of those retentive memories that remembers every detail, relevant or no; Corby was runner-up. Then we played it again, with the same result, for by now another sound had added itself to the din outside, and we were all trying our hardest to shut it out—

The sea.

The wind had been bad enough, but now there was the regular beat and fall of waves upon the barricade outside; on the mutable bank of pebbles, on the shifting sand dunes, and with every moment the thrusting, sucking roar came nearer and nearer. I glanced from under my cloak at our host: he was on his knees. I looked over at Snowy: he, too, was listening, poised on his hooves as if for flight. I opened my mouth to say something, I will never know what, and then Conn's arm was about my shoulders and his smile stopped my mouth.

"'Tis only the tide, Thingy dear. 'Twill soon be full, and then back it will go again . . . Can I join your game?"

Instantly everything was all right again, or very nearly. He must have been as anxious, if not actually as afraid, as we were, but all he was concerned with was our fear, our anxiety, and in so doing, in forgetting himself, he gave us all a courage we had not known we possessed. Suddenly all would be bearable, just so long as we were together. Even death, for surely the frightening part of that is not what comes after but the loneliness of dying, the actuality of leaving the world on one's own. But if we held one another tight and didn't let go, it would surely only be a little jump, like leaping down steps in one's dream and awaking with a sudden jolt into reality. And I supposed that Death must be as great a reality as Life. It must be, for everything, everyone, had once been alive, and would all be dead. So, if it happened to everyone, to everything, it could be no worse than Life, for everyone could manage that, one way or another. And, although Life could be difficult, at least it was never so bad that one wanted to leave it. And yet . . . ? Snowy? Had he not spoken of despair, of a longing so great it was a Death-Wish? If so, the Death was to be desired, for if Snowy knew it would bring him release from whatever tortured him, then surely—

"Tide's on the turn," said Conn. "And the wind has outrun itself. It's tiring . . ."

From the cracks in the shutters facing east came the first grey, sandy light of morning, and his words were true; the sound of the tide, once advancing so ferociously, was now retreating, but with a sullen roar that spoke of victory lost. The wind still buffeted the cottage but the impetus had gone.

I was suddenly tired, so tired, and I sank down upon the floor, the others huddled to me in like fashion, and now the sea became a lullaby. I felt Conn stretch out beside me, sensed Snowy's relaxation and I slept. We all slept.

It was well into daylight when we awoke, to a grudging bowl of oatmeal and milk, seasoned by sand, and a rind of cheese. The hamlet had suffered badly. Two roofs were blown clean away and the sand dunes, under the driving force of wind and sea, had changed their shape, creeping towards the huts, half-burying the one nearest the shore. Two boats were also lost; one, its sides smashed, had been flung high up the strand to lean crazily against a de-roofed cottage. And sand was in everything: gritty, pervasive, yielding like water and as impossible to shift, for it ran through one's hand and off shovels like liquid, only twice as heavy.

The pebble dyke was in most need of urgent repair; parts of it were entirely washed away where the sea had breached, and all in all it seemed some two or three feet lower. The villagers were working frantically for the tide was at the slack and they had barely six hours to patch things up before high. We offered to help, but even I could see that an inexperienced knight—a novice at building dykes, that is—however willing, and a small hunched female would be of more hindrance than help, so we left our host an overpayment of two silver pieces and set off again.

I could see Snowy becoming anxious, for we were running out of land. Ahead of us the deepening river channel was starting to curve across to the right, directly in our path, and ahead there was nothing but an uneasy ocean. Walking was difficult, for though the sand was firm enough the retreating water had ridged it into tight brown waves some two inches high and it was hillocked with sandworm casts so that I stumbled and stubbed my toes and cursed. The wind had shifted north and though it had lessened considerably it was strong enough still to skim the sand from the shifting dunes to our right and send it wraithing across the firmer beach to redden our legs and arms and grit our teeth. Above our heads tattered, yellow-eyed gulls screamed and slid, tip-winged, into the currents of air and beyond the river mouth we could still hear the sullen roar of surf. Our way was further hampered now by the detritus of the receded tide: uprooted trees and bushes, the carcases of drowned sheep, logs, bales of soaking straw and even a broken chair. One of the Lethum boats was also stranded, its stern shattered. Little brown crabs ran in and out of its broken ribs.

Moglet's ears pricked from the shelter of my jacket. "Listen! A dog barking . . ."

"Out here?" I said incredulously. "Don't be daft! There's nothing out here but sea and sand and wind and gulls—" But then I heard it too, a high yapping that seemed to come from our left. We peered through the clouds of sand that swirled round us and saw a sky-ring of gulls circling slowly about a sandbank.

"There's someone out there," said Conn. "Come on!"

We came upon an extraordinary sight. On a sand bar, some hundred feet long and half as wide, a tall, thin man was sitting on an upturned fishing boat, reading, his thin hair blowing in his eyes and as calm and unperturbed as if the tide was not already sneaking in behind him, fast and stealthy, scummy skirts brushing the sand to hide its hurrying feet. Between the man and us was a bubbling race of water, widening by inches every minute, and at the man's feet was the source of the barking: a small, dock-tailed mongrel terrier, white, brown and black. He was racing in circles, yelling his head off and now and again tugging at the voluminous skirts of the unheeding reader's habit.

We glanced at one another, then Conn hailed the stranded man. "Ahoy, there!"

The reaction was not what we had expected; the tall man merely looked up, regarded us, raised his hand in greeting, then fell to reading again, just as if all in the world was perfect and he were not threatened by imminent immersion, or worse.

But the little dog was different. Even as we stared in stupefaction at his master's apparently careless attitude to life, the animal had thrown himself into the channel that lay between us and was paddling valiantly in our direction. The race of the incoming tide inevitably carried him off to our left and he was struggling to reach our position, but Conn moved along the water's edge and, wading out, grabbed him by the scruff of the neck and bore him to safety, gasping and choking with the salt water.

Conn set him down. "Now then . . ." he said uncertainly. "Good doggie—"

"Bloody good doggie, nuffin!" hiccoughed the animal and, probably thanks to Snowy's mind-interpretation we could understand everything he said. "Bleeding salt-water—gets up yer nose, it does . . . Wait a bit, me hearties . . ." He sneezed and coughed and hacked and shook himself in a mist of droplets. "That's better!" He glanced at us all in turn, brown eyes keen and calculating. "Well, not exactly the Imperial Guard, are you then? Not even the rearguard . . . Still, *he* says you are the deliverers; more like the unlikely ones, you look to me, but you never can tell . . . What's the scheme, then? 'E can't swim, you know . . ."

"Scheme?" we echoed.

"Yus. How're you getting 'im orf, then?"

"Getting him off?" We must have sounded like the chorus to a play.

"Orf! Orf!! C'mon then, get the grey stuff workin'!" He really was worse than Corby, who could be difficult enough to understand sometimes. But then, I reminded myself, upbringing and privilege had a lot to do with it; he was obviously a Deprived Dog.

"I can't swim," said Conn. "Can you, Thingummybob?"

"I—I don't think so . . ."

"But I can," said Snowy. "Leastways, unicorns can and horses can—I've never tried it. But I guess now's the time . . . Conn, can you hang on to my tail and wave your legs up and down? Thing dear, you can ride on my back with the others as safe as possible. The water will be cold, but don't be frightened."

We got there, but it wasn't easy. Moglet screamed every time she got splashed, Pisky grumbled and choked on the odd drop of salt water and said it was making his snails curl up, Corby rattled his pinions and flapped a wet wing in my face and Puddy made a mistake and shot out a jet of evil-smelling liquid into my pocket, from the wrong end. And me? I was terrified, of course, cold and wet, and hung on to Snowy's mane as if it were a lifeline. It felt so strange to know there was no firm ground beneath his hooves, to know we were at the mercy of the tide, the waves, the water. And it was so cold, that tidal sea, the waters coming sweeping in from the deeps ready to freeze your legs, your arms, your stomach; pulling you gently, insistently, inexorably in the way it would go . . . I tried to remember my seal-friend, and how natural he had found it, and I felt a little better.

We landed on the edge of the sandbank, upriver where the tide had carried us in spite of Snowy's strong swimming legs, and walked back, shivering, to where the man in the long robe was still sitting. He raised his eyes from the page he was reading, still apparently oblivious of the encroaching waters that were creeping up behind his back.

"My friends: welcome!" He closed the book, leaving his finger as a marker. "I see you have met my companion." And he nodded at the dog, who was shaking himself again, wetting us even more. "Now, I am ready when you are. I do not, at this moment in time, see exactly how you will transport myself and my precious cargo—" He indicated with a wave of his fine, long-fingered hand a leather-wrapped bundle at his feet, "—across yon turbulent waste," (the ever-encroaching tide) "but as the Good Lord has sent you to my aid, I am confident in our safe passage." He drew the skirts of his habit absent-mindedly from an early wave, which retreated as if stung. "We have not long, I surmise . . ."

"I gather you need transport for yourself, the dog and—and those books, to dry land," said Conn, politely, but breathing hard. "It has proved a hard task to reach you; perhaps if you left behind those last—"

"And the books," said the other, firmly. I glanced up at his face; thin, ascetic, with deceptively mild, pale-blue eyes. A strong nose, thin-lipped mouth, long chin, large ears, almost nonexistent eyebrows; a large Adam's apple, unshaven chin whose hairs were whiter than the thin wisps that floated about his head. Pointy fingers, pale-skinned, the index finger of his left hand off at the second joint—not a recent injury—ridged fingernails, long elegant feet in much-mended sandals, with uncut toenails that either curved yellow round the toes or were broken off in jagged points. He smelt quite strongly, too.

"You will be doing the Lord's work, my son . . ." And he sketched a vague cross in the air, in Conn's direction.

I saw Conn bow and cross himself, and knew we were all now committed to getting this strange man and his cargo across to dry land, and Conn's next words confirmed this. "Any particular part you are bound for, Father?"

"The brothers at Whalley; my associates at Lindisfarne have lent their precious Gospels for the copying, and I have other relics, scrolls and records to convey to our order on the Holy Isle." He shifted his now decidedly wet feet again. "I should be obliged, Sir Knight, if we could proceed as soon as possible. The written word does not take kindly to immersion in salt water, and although I protected them as well as I could during the voyage across some two days since, and this morning on our trip from Martin's Mere, I fear that the Sea of Galilee and the Sea of Hirland have little in common. I did indeed try the Lord's commandment: 'Peace, be still!' but I fear I was presumptuous, and later said several 'Pater Nosters' to atone for this. However, the weather is now less inclement, and by this sign I see that He has graciously forgiven me . . ."

I hadn't a clue what to do next, but luckily that magic cross-in-the-air had worked a miracle on Conn. Motioning the tall monk to stand he upended the boat on which the man had been sitting and scratched his head. The craft was small, bluff-bowed, wooden, and two of the wooden planks in the bows were split. The rest was sound enough, but the mast was missing, snapped off some two feet from its stepping. Conn scratched his head.

It began to rain, quite hard.

"Right!" said the Rusty Knight. "The sealskin from the pack, Thingy, and the rope . . . Thanks." And in a moment it seemed he had slit the skin a third, two thirds, and the larger piece was wrapped round the bows of the boat, secured by twine, and the smaller effectually parcelled the books, including the one that was being read. The rope was attached to the stump of mast and a loop at the other end was placed round Snowy's neck. "Now, Father, if you will sit well back in the stern—the back of the boat—with the—er, books on your lap, my horse will tow you through the flood, letting the tide take us with it until we hit a sandbank or firmer ground. Right, Snowy?"

"What abaht me, then?" asked the dog. "Bloody swim again, is it? And how do we know our white friend can manage?" He jerked his head at Snowy. "Beggin' your pardon I'm sure, Your Worship, and appearances are deceptive, so they say, but you look fair knackered already, if you'll pardon the expression," and he sniggered to himself at the pun.

"Appearances," said Snowy mildly, "are, as you remarked, sometimes deceptive. As you should know," and he shot a glance full of such sharp intent at the dog that if it had had eyebrows to raise it would have done so.

"I see," said the mongrel softly. "I see . . ." and when Conn lifted him into the boat by his master's feet he made no further protest at the water slopping around his paws but settled down quietly. On his face, as he looked at Snowy, was much the same expression that Conn had worn when the monk had crossed himself.

With little ceremony Conn put Moglet and Puddy on the monk's lap, bade him hold Pisky's bowl safe and perched Corby high on the bows. By now water was sloshing round my calves, insidiously nudging at me like a dog, turning in little currents about my ankles, and any minute now it would rear up and butt me behind my knees. I dared not look at the increasing expanse of water that separated us from the nearest land. My breakfast rose to the back of my throat in sheer terror and I had to swallow back on the bitter bile.

"Ready?" asked Conn.

I nodded. "Any time," I squeaked, wishing I had kept it to the nod.

"Right, then—"

"It's raining," said the monk gently. "If you could just tuck the end of the wrapping more securely round the books . . ."

Grimly Conn re-wrapped the parcel. "All right now?"

The monk nodded, then rose to his feet in the now gently rocking boat and raised his right hand, upsetting practically everything in the process. "I think a blessing—"

"Sit *down*!" said Conn savagely. "And *stay* there . . ."

Luckily it was easier than I had expected, for the tide was stronger now and soon Snowy found the main current. We moved steadily upstream, Conn and I clinging to the sides, the better to tip up the suspect bows, gently kicking our legs up and down as Snowy directed. I felt better this time, partly because the exercise warmed me up; indeed I let go of the boat a couple of times, just to see what it felt like, and paddled with my hands. I even turned over on to my back and let the sea sing in my ears the way it had with my friend the seal, and my body unfolded in the water like seaweed and stretched itself, crooked back forgotten, and I floated, a log beneath the racing clouds—

"Thingy!" yelled Conn. "You're getting lost!" and in a frantic panic that forgot seal and swimming and turned my body awkward and deformed again I threshed my way back to the safety of the gunwhale, my throat and mouth full of choking, salty water.

We landed safely on a spit of land some miles upstream, where the river narrowed and curved to meet the opposite bank. Conn beached the boat, retrieved the rope and offloaded everything and everyone. I noticed how exhausted Snowy looked and slipped a comforting arm around his neck. "Another half-mile and it's shore and supper," I said. "You were great . . ." He nuzzled my neck, and I was aware in myself of an aching tiredness and the pain of cold limbs.

I looked round at the others: all present and correct, if as wet, cold and tired as me. All but our passenger; he seemed invigorated by the cold, revitalized by the water, and now flung his arms in the air and began invoking his Lord. Conn sank to his knees and bowed his head; I thought I had better do likewise, and let the foreign-sounding words flow over my head like a warm, drying wind.

Behind us, in the fervency of prayer, the boat slipped off the bank and rocked on its way upstream, with two thirds of the sealskin . . .

"I shall travel to my brothers at Friarsgate first," said our travelling monk.

"Will you not go with me part of the way?" He was addressing Conn, who shook his head.

"Thank you, but our way now lies—" he glanced at Snowy, "—southeast." There was the faintest interrogative lift to his voice.

"Six stones lie half a mile south," said Snowy.

"So we shall bid you farewell and safe journey," added Conn. He helped the monk arrange his pack of books—still wrapped in the other third of our sealskin—comfortably on his shoulders. "God speed you . . ."

"He will, He will," said the monk fervently. "He has my project in his care, for He sent you to my succour . . ."

I wished fervently at that moment that He, whoever He was, had thought to ask us first, for I could not remember ever having felt so damp and cold.

The monk hitched up his robe through his belt. "Goodbye, then, goodbye!" and he strode off towards the dunes behind us, wet robe flapping about his knees. "Ask for me if ever you come to Lindisfarne. Or the Holy Isle. Or . . . Name's Cuthbert."

The little dog still sat where he was; at last he stirred, had a good hoof of his left ear and shook out some salt water. "Oh, well," he sighed, and rose to his feet. "Better see the old boy doesn't turn left at Priorstown. Thanks, you lot . . . Still say you're unlikely."

"Why don't you travel with us?" I asked. "You're welcome, you know . . ."

"*He* knows," said the dog, nodding at Snowy. "He knows as how the old boy would be hopelessly lost without a guide. Sort of thing I've got to do, somehow. Sorry for the old bugger, really: head in the clouds, feet anywhere . . . Oh, well," and he sighed again.

I pulled out a piece of dried fish from the pack. "Here."

"Ta!" He swallowed it. "Can't live on fresh air like some people I could mention. Likes me nosh, I does." He burped fishily. "Don't worry; I'll get him where he wants to go. Keep him snug for the winter, then back to the bloody bogs come spring." He scratched again. "Gawd! Anyone'd think all that bleeding water would have drowned the perishers! Well, benny-bloody-dickerty, you lot!" And he was away, jaunty docked tail and ears erect, trotting off in the steps of his master.

"There are saints and saints," said Snowy cryptically.

"Will he be all right?" I asked, and didn't need to specify whom I meant.

"Of course," said Snowy. "They both serve the same Master, don't they? He is a good guide: he found us." He twitched his ears. "The unlikely ones: I rather like that . . ."

"Come on!" called Conn, by now well ahead. "I can see the stones, as you said. So we're on the right road . . . Got any dry wood, Thingummy? I fancy a hot drink of something-or-other . . ."

Slinging the others all over me as best I could I followed Snowy's sure steps, while above our heads a storm-driven buzzard or kite or whatever fled our path south.

The Binding: Fish

The Face in the Water

Pisky's adventure, when it came, was over in a flash of fins.

But there were many days of travel before he had his moment of glory, and all through the preceding misty mornings and sharp nights of Leaf-Fall I was wondering, on and off, whether it would be his turn or mine. Each day was so beautiful and smelt so of the poignancy of decay as the world wended its way to the long sleep of winter, that often I would forget and run to catch a falling leaf, or gather finger-staining dewberries for their sharp-sweet explosion of taste. The last flowers were a patchwork of butterflies and moths, and martlets gathered in soft twittering lines on bending sprays of hawthorn, their gaze south. Bees fed heavy and wasps found fallen fruit before I did, angry colours a warning. Squirrels raced the treetops, younglings not yet the russet of their parents, and chattered angrily as we plundered the nuts they would have hoarded and forgotten. We heard wild pig crashing in the undergrowth in their search for acorn and truffle, and at night their little prickly brothers wandered sharp-nosed and blind amidst our sleeping bodies, rootling for slugs and snails. At night, too, the dog-fox barked his territory and once, far away, we heard the howl of wolf. Rutting stags roared and clashed their antlers, owls ghosted through the twilight to screech threat to every tiny creature that cowered within range, and mushroom and fungi uncurled and swelled between dawn and dusk so that we trod a cushion of them, marvelling at the shelvings and bloatings that shawled and blanketed the trees with deep, livid colours in contrast with the other, more muted colours of autumn.

Then came storms that shook the trees, bent the brittling grass, drove the clouds so fast they seemed not to know whether to drop their rain or carry it on to another market. On such a day as this I found two martlets and three fledglings locked fast in a cot where the door had slammed shut and the latch fallen. We were seeking shelter ourselves and I was first to the hut—probably some charcoal-burner's—and wrenched open the door.

Immediately I was swathed with wings, and even without Snowy's interpreting presence I could understand what they said.

"Thank you, human, thank you: it is late, and we must fly. The children are fat, but little practised in flight. We had hoped . . ."

I listened to their soft trilling and stretched my arms wide so they might light on them. "Fear not, travellers; the wind is from the west and will carry you all high in its arms to safety. Fly now, and fear not . . ."

"We go, we go . . . And are grateful that you came. We and ours shall bring summer to your eaves when we return, and your home shall be blessed . . ."

And they were gone, the youngsters a little unsteady at first then, escorted tenderly by their parents, flying higher and higher till they were mere specks in the air and turning southeast—

"Gawd! Wish I could stretch my wings like that!" muttered Corby who had joined me, striding and hopping through the undergrowth.

"You will, you *will*!" I promised, bending down to stroke the ruffled feathers. "Not long now . . ."

But in spite of my optimism—had we not, after all, covered some hundreds of leagues in our quest and taken a whole summer and much of the autumn to do it?—the end of our travels, expected now in every turn of the road for there were only two adventures to go, still seemed as far away as growing up: the nearer, the farther. In the end even I grew impatient, feeling that if it were my "turn" next I should welcome it; anything would be better than this endless walking. Not that the way was unpleasant; rivers to follow, streams to cross, blue hills to our right, the vales to our left, woods full of the russet, yellow and browns of Leaf-Fall—but there was a sense of urgency in the air that sharpened and quickened with the first frosts and the great skeins of geese that passed swiftly overhead, the way we were going but so much faster!

We ate well enough from wood, river, coppice and field, for the earth gave forth in plenty that year. With our fast-dwindling stock of silver we paused at town and village as seldom as we could, but we exchanged a night or two for the nuts and mushrooms we gathered on the way and luckily did not fall foul of foresters or verderers, for great lords seemed few and far between. The robin began his song again and once more we heard the large voice of the wren and the twitter of sparrow, long silent over the summer.

Then we came to the meres, the pools, the lakes—and, in particular, one lake. We had managed, so far, to keep our direction by sidestepping, cornering, splashing straight through the shallower pools, but now we were faced by a lake whose ends, to right and left, seemed boundless. It was a misty, moist day and the sun shone faint as a moon through a veil of gauzy cloud. Ahead of us the water lay still, unnaturally still, its grey waters scarce rippling though all the while a cold steam rose from it and the reflected sun floated like a blob of yellow fat on its surface. Reeds stood up from the fringes some ten feet distant but they were winter-dying back to their roots and bent in dry hoops to their images, until the edges of the lake seemed looped with them. Ahead, perhaps some half-mile distant, hanging as though suspended above the surface, were trees, land; an island? The farther shore? There was no way of telling.

Conn chucked a stone into the water, as far out as it would go. There was a dull cloop! as though a lazy fish rose for sport instead of food, and a ripple or two ran in faint-hearted circles but disappeared before they reached the shore, as if the water were thick as oil.

"Hmmm . . ." he said. "A dead lake. Not very inspiring."

"Dead?" said Pisky's inquiring bubbles. "Lemme see, lemme see . . ."

I tilted his bowl nearer the water. "There . . ."

He said something surprising. "I want to try the water!" He had never said anything like this before, had never ventured willingly outside his bowl except at The Ancient's, and for a moment I hesitated, almost as though I was afraid that once in he would be lost.

"Don't be silly, Thing dear," he said, reading my thoughts. "I only want a quick look. Besides, my scales itch. My great-aunt on my mother's side always said that if one's scales felt itchy it was either a change in the weather or mites."

"Mites?"

"Tickly things that bite like the fleas you humans and animals have. Now, lemme *see*!"

Obediently I lowered his bowl to the still lake and tipped it until he had ingress and egress. He hesitated for a moment and I saw a convulsive shudder run through his little frame, then slowly he moved from the shelter of his weed and I saw what I had feared, a golden-orange shape dim and falter as he moved out into the deeper water. Almost, stretching out my hand, I betrayed his trust, distressfully trying to catch him back before I lost sight, but Snowy nudged me with his nose in time.

"He knows what he does, Thing dear: have faith! And patience . . ."

It nevertheless seemed an age before the orange blur moved back to his bowl again, very thoughtfully. "I don't know, I just don't know . . . Never seen or felt water like that before. Soft, soft as the robes of a courtesan, the robes they used to trail in the Great Pond at Chaykung . . . Misty on top, but there are clear pools. Bottom's thick mud and tangled roots. Difficult to swim in; slows you down, it does, but it's breathable, just. Nothing living that I can see, but I *feel* that there is *something*, or someone, down there . . . Curious. Whatever it is is not unwelcoming, there's just a kind of . . . nothingness. No feeling, nothing positive. Doesn't operate on any level that I recognize.

"Wouldn't do to fall in the deeper bits, Thingy . . ."

"As if I would!"

"There's a sort of boat here," called Conn and, sure enough, there was a broad-bottomed craft lying hidden under the bank some hundred yards further up. It was built of some tough, greyish wood and looked very old, but when I tried it with my dagger it seemed sound enough. The flat planking inside was almost covered by a drifting of last year's leaves. A long paddle lay amidships, obviously for steering and propelling the boat through a ring in the stern.

"Some sort of ferryboat?" I ventured. "Is it safe?"

"Seems so," said Conn, jumping down into the bows. He stamped around for a minute or two, but apart from the quiet ripples that spread in the water there was no other disturbance, hardly even a lowering of the boat's level from his weight. Jumping back on the bank he leant forward and pulled in the broad stern. "Well, the only way is across, and it seems there's land of sorts over there . . . Shall we risk it?"

"As you say, it's the only way," said Snowy. "However, I don't like the feel of this place and I shall be glad when we're across." He stepped delicately onto the boards and lay down, his hooves tucked close. Somewhere a bird cried mournfully, but there was no other sound save the sluggish lap of water. I went up to the bows carrying Pisky, and the others settled themselves beside Snowy. Conn pushed the boat away from the bank and leapt in after, stepping the steering-paddle.

It was an eerie passage, no sound save the creak and swish of the paddle, Conn's heavy breathing and the "sss" of the water past our bows. No one felt like talking: it was almost as though we held our breath for fear of waking something. I looked back at the bank we had left but already it was disappearing in mist. The land ahead looked no nearer, although the trees we could see held a dark and menacing aspect.

We were perhaps some three-quarters of the way across when, glancing down, I became aware of a difference in the quality of the water. Where before it had had a thickness, an opacity that made it look like liquid iron, now this seemed to be drifting away, like heavy clouds clearing a rainwashed sky. If it had been real sky then all one would have seen would be an infinite blue, but in the depths there seemed to be tantalizing glimpses of another world, a world in which there were trees, fields, mountains and valleys, an image so immediate and real that I glanced up, expecting to see it was merely a reflection. But no: the mist seemed thicker and, more disturbing, my companions appeared somehow different too; discontented, distorted, disturbingly alien, like the time when I had laughingly viewed them through a piece of broken green Roman glass on our journey. Suddenly they all seemed strangers and I turned from them in discomfort to look again at my prettier pictures in the water.

They had changed also. Where there had been vague landscapes, viewed from a distance, now I could see flowers in the fields, birds in the trees. I leant closer and someone spoke behind me; irritated, I turned back and saw Conn mouthing at me, but he was speaking as though he had a mouthful of rags, and his face and figure were as grey as the mist. Impatiently I turned back. There were other words, other voices still squeaking in my ears but I covered them and leant closer to the water, the better to appreciate the bright colours, the beautiful pictures that were such a contrast to the grim, grey reality above.

Now there were animals and people down there, too. Horses ran through the meadow, manes and tails flowing in the breeze; fair knights armed and helmed were practising swordplay; hounds were on the scent, their bright tongues lolling; birds, fishes, deer, all living in colours livelier than the day.

It was like some great new-woven tapestry, but a tapestry that moved and lived and breathed. And there, right in the middle of it all, was a lady, a beautiful dark-haired lady who stretched her arms out to me and smiled a smile that I remembered from times past. Surely my mother must have had a smile like that? I cried out to the pretty lady and she leant up to take my hand and I clasped hers in both of mine and was drawn down, down into the overwhelming brightness beneath.

The waters sang in my ears and I was warm as an infant enshawled. The lady, so like my mother must have been, drew me into her arms and rocked me back and forth and the knights smiled and nodded and clashed their weapons, the horses threw back their heads and neighed and the hounds bayed a welcome, their tails waving like weeds in a stream—

"Weeds in a stream! Weeds in a stream!" came a little voice in my ears, as insistent and annoying as the zinging of a gnat. "Rocks in a pool! Bones in a bog! Illusion, illusion and death! Come away, Thing dear, dearest dear, before you drown in a dream, before your lungs burst and the Creature nibbles your flesh from your bones in a kiss of death and arranges you in her gallery like the others . . . Look! Look, and *see* . . ."

And I looked, and I saw. As Pisky swam to and fro in front of my eyes I had to shift my focus and the lady's green gaze no longer held mine. Her arms were about me still, caressing and stroking and soothing and I was aware of her smiling, scarlet mouth and the questing teeth—

The knights were bones, the horses were bones, the hounds were bones. Their hair, their manes, their tails waved in the gentle current and they were prisoned by their feet, their hooves, their legs to the floor of the lake to dance and prance and bounce to the Creature's whim. And were long dead and Its playthings, as were the rocks and stones and weeds that made Its landscapes. I saw, too, that It had no heart, no evil intent even, just an overweening curiosity. And that curiosity drew me closer, closer, and I saw that It had drawn from me my own thoughts to create the illusions I had seen, and that It had no real form of Its own, just the locking arms and the open mouth and the teeth, that sought me and my blood and my breath and my being.

All at once I could not breathe and a little orange-gold fish with a pearl in his mouth swam between the teeth that threatened me and down the throat that waited and the Creature choked and gasped and convulsed and spat and loosed Its hold and I shot to the surface and was grabbed and hauled into the boat and all I could think about was a little fish and the sight of him disappearing down that gaping throat—

"Thing, darling, are you all right? Christ Almighty, she's near drowned!" came Conn's distracted, loving voice and even with my tortured lungs and rasping throat I recognized that he had used my right name for a third time while I lay on the bottom boards of the boat, heedless, soaking, abandoned to decency and decorum, and spewed up the foul, cloudy water, murmuring between the violent retchings that Pisky had saved me.

"No thanks to your abominable gullibility!" came a little bubbling voice in my ear, and there was my rescuer, leaping back into his bowl no worse for wear. "How anyone in their right mind could mistake an apparition like that for the real thing I do not know! My grandmother's cousin, twice removed, was once suborned by one such but her disgrace was never mentioned. By my fins and scales—"

"Pisky you're a darlin' and a hero, and if you weren't in that bowl I'd pick you up and kiss you, that I would!" declared Conn, and leaving the paddle he stepped forward to cradle my helpless, revolting body in his arms. "I shall never be able to thank you . . . But unless we get this child to dry land and the water pumped out of her—"

With a sudden jolt—just as I was warming to his utterly unexpected embrace and revelling in both my escape and the sweetness of breath in my lungs and wondering at the supreme courage of Pisky's rescue—the boat grounded on dry land and promptly broke up in pieces. I was shoved and trampled on as the others struggled with me and the baggage over rocks and boulders. Once there I was subjected to further indignity as Conn rolled me over on to my face and proceeded to press the air out of my lungs with the flat of his hand. I consequently threw up the contents of my stomach onto the ground, near choking with vomit and froth, my mask tangled in my mouth.

Just before I died from his ministrations Snowy luckily told him to stop and I was hauled round to sit upright, still gasping for air and shivering uncontrollably.

"Stay with her," ordered Conn to Moglet, Corby, Puddy and Pisky. "The unicorn and I will search for wood to make a fire before she perishes from cold."

"Wanna-come-with-you!" demanded Pisky, and, such was the aura of his recent success, Conn picked him up without demur and carried him off.

I staggered to my feet, I wanted to ask questions about the Creature in the water, about the bones and the hair and the pictures—but at that moment I looked up and saw the shadow of the seven stones and my adventure began . . .

The Binding: Thing

The Last Giants and Ogres

Except for the seat of my breeches which was still damp against the stone floor, at least now I was dry and warm for the fire was very hot. Not that I was exactly next to it: I lay bound and trussed like a recalcitrant chicken against the woven fence that formed the outer wall of the cave-house. The wind whistled past my ears and outside I could hear the gale that roared and tore at the last remains of the trees in the forest. It was night, for we—me, Moglet and Corby—had been carried here for many miles along twisting, curling paths after our capture.

Prisoners. I had never been physically tied up before and I didn't like it, not one bit. I closed my eyes, looked back on what had happened, wondered if it could have been different.

Conn, Snowy and Pisky had gone to find wood to build a fire and dry me out—so it had been my fault from the beginning. I had started to ask Moglet, Corby and Puddy a question—what question? It had all gone now, was not important any longer—and then had come that sudden crash, a cry from Conn, an unintelligible whinny from Snowy and the awful, hair-raising howl—

I had run, we had run, away from the lakeside, stumbling and cursing over the twisted tree-roots, tearing our way through the shoulder-high ferns, pushing through thicket and briar, and all the while the wild threshing and howling grew louder until—until we came to the clearing, the net and the pit.

At first I thought I had been carried away by the Night-Mare, and fought against the reality I saw, even shutting my eyes tight and throwing my arms wide in an effort to transport myself to another dream or even, please the gods! to awake sweating on some pallet, somewhere else . . .

But no; it was real, and it was horrible.

In front of me, almost at my feet, opened a pit, dark and deep, and the broken branches that had hidden it tipped, crazy and broken, laced with man-high ferns, to the bottom some ten or twelve feet below, where Conn and Snowy were milling about, pulling at the branches which slid down on top of them. Conn's anxious eyes lifted to mine, then I saw him glance over his shoulder towards the other side of the pit. I followed his gaze and recoiled in horror. There, illuminated by branch torches, sputtering with some oily foulness, stood half-a-dozen giants! Ogres. Trolls . . . ten feet high, more perhaps, covered with shaggy hair, their clothing a few skins. Barefooted, tangle-locked, with long yellow teeth, flat noses and great craggy brows overhanging small, dark, red-rimmed eyes. Legs bowed with the weight of their bodies, hands with hairy backs grasping clubs, a spear, a—

"Thing, look *out*!" yelled Conn, but even as I turned I was meshed in a creeper net, borne down by heavy bodies, smothered in the sharp tang of earth and leaves. I could not breathe, Moglet was nowhere, Puddy was missing, Corby was flapping on his back at my side; we were all panicking, panicking, and we shouldn't panic, we should—

I felt a thump on the side of my head, there were bright lights . . . then darkness.

I awoke to the realization that we were being carried in a kind of sling between two poles. My lungs were not fully recovered from the water, my head hurt, but even greater was the pain from creeper-fastened wrists and ankles. Worst of all was the terror of not knowing how or where, the disappearance of my friends, the awe-inspiring figures of my captors—Not knowing, not understanding what one is facing is far more terrible than facing the most tremendous calculable odds; the Tree-People had been worse than the Great Spider or the White Wyrme.

"Heart up, Thing!" came a hoarse croak above my head. "At least you're right-way up!" I glanced through tears at the ragged bundle trussed to the pole above me. Corby, poor dear Corby, was hanging by his bound legs, wing flapping, beak agape, eyes rolling. "Not as bad as it looks," he thought quietly at me. "Least I've got a better view . . ."

"Where are Puddy and Moglet?" I thought back urgently at him.

"Former jumped out of your pocket way back; latter is tied in a bundle at your feet."

"Thing! Corby! I can't see, I'm frightened—"

"Hush dear!" I tried to quiet her audible wails. "It'll be all right, I promise. Just lie still."

There were only three of us left. Somehow we had to escape, find out what had happened to the others. But supposing there were no others? Supposing the frightful creatures that captured us had killed them? Supposing, even now, that my beloved Conn was lying somewhere with his head smashed in by one of those vicious clubs, the bright blood shaming his russet hair, his fierce brown eyes staring up at a darkening sky he could not see? And dear, gentle Snowy? And silly, voluble last-minute courageous Pisky, and stolid, dependable Puddy? Had the one been gobbled in one bite, the other crushed in careless passing beneath some primeval foot? I sobbed again, but not for myself.

I suppose it must have been some half-hour later, and quite dark, when we arrived at the cave. We were untied from the carrying poles and carried roughly over stones, past a wicker fence, into the prison in which we now found ourselves. I had looked round it so many times during the last minutes—hours?—that I knew it by heart.

High-ceilinged with, as I have said, a wicker or wattle fence behind my back protecting about one half of the perimeter. The other half was the stone face of the cave, which extended back into the hillside about thirty feet, in a roughly semicircular shape. At the far end, in the shadows, was a deep ledge, about twelve feet wide and the same deep, and about two feet off the floor, on which was a pile of skins and three toothless and white-haired creatures with hanging dugs (though men or women I could not tell), who mumbled and waved and shrieked with laughter as the fire was replenished.

This same fire was built high in the middle of the cave, fed by large pieces of green wood which snapped and spat and twisted in sappy fury, belching great clouds of choking smoke up to the blackened roof. Every now and again a lurid flame leapt like a new-drawn sword to be as quickly spitting-sheathed in the scabbard of the dark logs, bejewelled by oozing black resin, before it had time to do more than stab twice, thrice at the darkness.

The torches had been extinguished as soon as we arrived, to conserve them I supposed, and were now stacked upright against the left-hand wall, together with clubs, spears and queerly shaped stone axes, wood-hafted and bound with twine. On the right-hand wall were hung more skins over a stack of roughly chopped wood. Behind this were heaped crudely fashioned pottery bowls and platters, and then a pen containing five or six skinny goats. These were nannies, all of them, who looked as if they had not seen a billy for years. There were no younglings. The floor of the cave was stony, dung-ridden, running with filth; no attempt had been made to sweep away the ordure, both human and animal, and the stench fought an even battle with the smoke.

And the giants, the ogres, the trolls, whatever they were? The flames threw their shadows flickering on the cave wall. They were the creatures of legend: threatening, huge, terrible—until one looked at the substance rather than the shadow. Six of them, that was all, not counting those elders on the ledge at the back. About four feet tall, perhaps a little more; covered with reddish hair and bandy-legged, with low foreheads, jutting chins and wide noses. The youngest I suppose was about fourteen, a boy; two women in their twenties; three men, ranging from early twenties to late thirties: and all of them weak, rickety, with missing teeth, sores on their bodies, arthritic joints. No children, either; where were their youngsters, their promise of a future?

The wood caught suddenly and flared its banners to the roof, and there, silent, vibrant, moving with the firelight, a whole host of creatures was revealed, chased by hunters wielding spears and clubs. A giant striped cat bared its fangs, incisors reaching beneath the chin; deer with mighty horns raced across the plains, hooves flying; a creature such as Conn had talked of, tail both ends, all coated in reddish hair like a shaggy goat, impaled a man with its yellow tusks as the spears in its hide maddened it past bearing. The man's mouth was open forever on a silent scream. Other men, defiant, puny, armed only with spears, managed to herd, pit, snare all these creatures in a magnificent display of primeval bravery and guile. Great fish opened their toothed mouths to engulf; huge lizards flicked their tongues; birds with strange, barbed wings, or ones hooked and spread like bats, flew shrieking from a rain of arrows, and still the hunters advanced, striking, stabbing, flaying, destroying—

They were sketches only, in browns, whites, blacks, greys, ochres, but the sudden firelight made them live and die in glorious movement on the walls of the cave. In a sudden pitying moment, quite divorced from my immediate terror, I could see how these few stunted survivors would spend their last years; drawing their pride, their comfort from the splendid, fierce deeds of their forefathers, those who dead a thousand years had yet ensured their present existence on earth.

My imagination when we were trapped in the pit had given our captors twice their height, three times their ferocity but they still outnumbered us, small, weak and diseased as they were; in this and in one other fact, lay their squalid strength. They had an overwhelming need that our combined strength could not overcome. They were hungry.

Not only hungry: starving.

I knew this because of their staring bones pushing at the skin as if mad to break out; I knew this because of the thin streams of saliva that ran between their bared and gappy teeth; I knew this because the fire had been built higher, higher; I knew this because of the water now boiling in the misshapen pot at the side of the fire. I knew it because I could see the skewers ready to be thrust into the heart of the flames; I knew it because of the animals they had prepared to thrust on those same bone skewers. I knew it because the first of those creatures was my darling Moglet, trussed up in a bundle on the end of a stick, paws together, jaws bared in agony, her pitiful wails half-drowned by the roaring of the flames. I knew it because my friend Corby was hanging by his legs, the next to go, his beak half-open, his eyes closed. I knew it because they had poked and pinched me, licked the salt from my face and hands with eager tongues, made to tear out my hair, pinched my legs until the blood ran . . .

Tears ran helplessly from my eyes and I could see nothing now between the swollen lids except a merciful blur. Then, oh then! something moved under my bound hands, something dry, warty, breathing fast.

"Puddy? Oh, Puddy!!"

"Courage," said the toad, puffing asthmatically. "I come from the others—"

"They are all right? Oh, dear one, say they are all right!"

"Yes, yes. They *will* be all right, given time . . ."

"Given time . . . ?"

"To get out of that pit."

"But how—?"

"It is not that deep. When I left them they were pulling down branches to raise the level. Then Sir Knight will climb out over the unicorn's back and throw down more foliage until *he* is able to scramble out. My feet . . . The webs are all stretchy."

I was filled with instant contrition. "Poor Puddy! Is it very far, then?"

He moved under my hands. "The way your captors took 'tis two, three miles, but straight up—toads can climb, you know—it's much less. But Snowy will find a way." His flanks were still heaving. "Let me see what's happening . . ." He moved out to get a better view. "Ye gods! 'Tis as well the fish is with the others, else would he boil!"

Someone picked up the stick on which Moglet's trussed figure swung and pointed it towards the crackling fire. I heard her anguished cry, saw the fire turn to lick at the fur, and then something suddenly clicked in my mind, like fivestones on a stone floor. I found myself remembering.

"Fire cold, flames die, heat go, no warmth . . ." but not in those words, in another language, an older one full of spits and clicks and grunts and as old as the earth. Words I had learnt long ago in another life, in another time than the feared one with our Mistress. Words older even than the creatures painted on the walls; words, not words, sounds only that came with the dawning of time when earth and air and fire and water were still one and four, and apart and together, divisible and indivisible, and Man crouched among the animals and was part of them and Woman was the God . . .

The fire burned blue and cold and died. The painted creatures on the walls faded and disappeared, and an ice crept into the cave. The giants, the ogres, the trolls became small and helpless and frightened and I stepped from my bonds and went to the middle of the cave and gathered the cat to me smoothing the charred fur until it was new, and took the plucked bird from his ties and the feathers grew again under my hand. And I stood in the ashes of the fire and the strength flowed up through the soles of my feet, until my fingertips tingled with the strength of it and I stood straight and tall and unblemished and nursed the creatures in my arms until they, too, were whole—

"Thing, darlin', oh, Thing! Are you all right, then?" And Conn was there, taking me and Moglet and Corby in his arms, while the creatures cowered in the farthest corner of the cave. Suddenly I was myself and glad of his human comfort, and fell in love again with the strength of his arms.

Snowy was holding the troll-men back, dancing on his hooves and neighing, striking out at their slowly recovering bodies.

"Come, my children, come: magic lasts only so long!"

Magic, I wondered, magic? For what I had been, what I had done, seemed of a sudden in another life, far away, and now there was only bewilderment as I glanced down at my chafed wrists. In my arms was a purring Moglet—the purr of relief rather than content—and a once-more sleek Corby. Puddy nudged my toe and Pisky was bubbling away in his bowl dangling from Conn's wrist, telling of dark pits and torches and spears, of great scrambles of wood and a swinging forest, of travel sickness and a lack of water. I looked up at Conn's smiling eyes, his shining white teeth and curling moustache, his sweat-dampened hair and thanked the gods, and his God too, for our preservation.

"Come!" called Snowy again. "I cannot hold them back any longer!" and indeed the troll-men from the corner were stealing forth again. The youngest seized a spear and hurled it in our direction, but luckily it missed. Conn tucked Moglet inside my jacket and Puddy in my pocket, picked up Corby and resettled Pisky, then grabbed my wrist and hurried us out of the cave, stumbling and swearing under his breath.

"Which way?"

"Follow your noses and then bear right . . ."

I heard scuffles behind me, howls of rage as Snowy carried on a rearguard action, then we were plunging helter-skelter through bush, thicket and wood, branches whipping our faces and shoulders, stones slipping under our feet and briars and nettles tearing and stinging. Pursuit was not far behind and the thump of feet mixed with the bearing of my heart. We had been running downhill but at last the ground levelled out and we were splashing amongst reeds, mud sucking at our feet. Now Snowy went ahead for we were in a quaking bog and heatless fires started at our steps, evil little voices sang in our ears and would have led us astray. All the while the stink of bubbling decay was in our nostrils, but Conn followed the white glimmer that was our unicorn and dragged me in his wake.

I stumbled and swayed from sheer exhaustion and did not even heed Moglet's panicky claws on my chest. At last the ground was firmer beneath our feet and the air smelt sweet and clean once more. We were on rising ground and the wind swung behind us, but it was chill, so that for all my exertions I shivered.

"Are we safe?"

"The men from the cave would not dare the bog," came Snowy's comforting voice. "Yes, we are nearly there. Just up this slope and you will see . . ."

I was not sure I could make it. My legs no longer seemed part of me, my feet were numb, my arms locked rigid around a protesting Moglet. There seemed to be a ring of stones—had I seen them before?—then some sort of prickly barrier, a hedge, I could hear a buzzard calling—

And firelight, gentle and warm, a familiar voice, hands taking Puddy and Moglet, a drink of fire and ice, a bed—

The Binding: Magician

Past, Present, Future

I opened my eyes to sun shining through the narrow opening to the cave. I was warm, I was refreshed with sleep, I was hungry. The cave! Which ca—

"Easy now, lambkin," said The Ancient, and pressed me back gently against the pillows. "Time enough to talk, to question. Here's oatmeal and cream and cheese. Break your fast at your ease. The others are taking the air."

"But—"

"Food first, buts later. Sufficient that you are safe, well, and finished with journeyings for the time being. Now, eat: there's a pitcher of spring water by your elbow, and if you want to wash there's a bowl of warm water by the fire and privacy and cloths behind that curtain. Oh, and the usual offices are where they were before . . ."

A wren was bursting his heart with sweet song when I at last hurried out to join the others. Conn was lying back in the sunshine, his jerkin unlaced and the dark red hairs on his chest glinting in the light; Corby was preening, Moglet chasing after a scarlet leaf on its breeze-helped progress across the grass, not really interested, but it was something to do; Puddy had his eyes shut, a revolting remnant of legs and wings sticking out of the left side of his mouth; Pisky's bowl was in the little pool nearby and he was housekeeping his weed and the snails, and making little flicking jumps in the air to rid himself of even the suspicion of parasites; Snowy, ungainly for once, pink belly in the air, tail and mane a'tangle, was rolling in the lush grass under the apple trees, where there was the usual bewildering mixture of blossom and ripe apple. I looked for The Ancient: he was walking some distance away on a rise in the ground.

"Better now, Thingummyjig?" asked Conn, stretching lazily.

"Come and play," said Moglet.

"Could you just pull my third tail-feather straight?" asked Corby. "No, from the left . . . *Your* left—"

"Nice morning," said Puddy, stickily.

"Just look how clear the water is," said Pisky. "I doubt if my grandfather, or even his, ever bathed in such as this. And some nice new pebbles, too . . ."

No answers here and it was answers I wanted, so after politely attending to the others I walked up to the hillock where The Ancient was standing, apparently lost in thought. He had one of his more absurd hats on this morning, green, with a white bobble that kept falling in his eyes, and yellow ribbons hanging from the back.

He greeted me effusively, perhaps too effusively, spreading an imaginary cloak on the ground and inviting me to sit down.

"A beautiful morning, is it not? You rested well, I hope?" Receiving no answer, he plucked at his beard, neatly plaited and tied off in a knot. "You are well, I suppose? No ill effects?" He looked at me again, then shuffled in his purple slippers, the ones with pointy toes. "No harm done, no harm done—and you completed the quest. Admirably, I might say—Go away!" he shouted, flapping his arms at a large buzzard importuning the air a few feet above his head. "Come back later . . . Pestiferous nuisance. Now, where were we?"

I shaded my eyes and looked up at the bird. "Perhaps you should give him his reward now," I suggested. "After all, he worked for it."

"Worked for it?" spluttered The Ancient, then turned the splutter into a fit of coughing.

"Well, he kept an eye on us all the way," I said, and plucking a stem of grass, pulled at the delicate inner core and nibbled it gently. "Go on: I can wait."

The Ancient flustered and puffed, but eventually called down the bird who alighted on his outstretched arm, wings a'tilt and yellow eyes wary at me.

Without concern I rose to my feet and stretched out my hand to the restless pinions and the surprisingly soft and warm breast-feathers. "Well done, Kiya." (I knew instinctively the bird's name.) "I'll vouch that you were there, all the time . . . What has he," and I nodded at The Ancient, "promised you?"

"Leave off!" said the old man, his beard coming untied as if it had a life of its own and curling up on either side of his face like lamb's fleece. "*I'll* deal with this . . . Now then bird, what was to be your reward?"

"You know well," said the handsome buzzard, fluffing his feathers, and I was surprised I could understand. "For a watching brief—a week only you said, and nothing of the distances, the time-shift, the abominable weather—you said you would find me—"

"Ah, yes," said The Ancient hastily. "Now I remember . . . Well, then: fly some seven leagues west-by-south—you'll have to correct with this wind—turn due south by the cross at Isca—now the new-fangled Escancastre, I believe—then another two leagues. Bear west again till you come to the old highway bearing roughly north-south. Two miles further on there is a sudden switch to east-west and there you will find a southerly track. Half a mile on there is a barton in a valley, a stream running east-west on its southern border: can't miss it, the place is full of sheep. In a wood just northeast of the barton—Totley, it's called—you will find a deeper wood, triangular in shape, and there you will find—what I promised you. She has," and he glanced at me to see if I was listening and, as I was, lowered his voice. I did not realize till afterwards that he was speaking bird-talk, but it didn't seem to make much difference: I still understood. "She has," he repeated to the bird, "been blown from oversea by that last southeasterly and is not used to us as yet. Wants to return to the mountains of Hispania . . . But doubtless you will be able to persuade her to stay. Tell her . . ." and he bent forward to whisper in Kiya's hidden ear. "That should do it!" And he tossed the buzzard in the air and it rode the wind, balancing delicately from wingtip to wingtip, before taking an updraught and sliding away out of sight above the conifers to my right.

"Now then," said The Ancient, flicking a lump of bird-dropping from his already liberally marked blue gown. "Now then—where were we? Ah, yes. You were about to thank me for my hospitality and ask about the next stage in—"

"Sit down," I interrupted, reseating myself and patting the turf beside me. "And explain. Please?"

But he remained standing, drawing the edges of his cloak together and becoming very tall all of a sudden.

"And don't," I said, "fly off into another dimension or something: we've had enough of that for the time being . . . Just think of me as your equal, for the moment, and, as such, wanting answers."

"To what?" But he did sit down, rather heavily it's true, and at a discreet distance. "What to?"

I crossed my legs, comfortably, and selected another blade of grass. "Lots of things . . . Firstly, how long has this quest taken us? The truth, mind!"

He regarded me under bushy eyebrows like the thatch of an ill-kept house. "Why—how long do you think it took?"

I recognized the ploy, but went along with it for the time being. "Well, the others obviously think it took at least six months—"

"So?"

"So why is my hair no longer? So why are my clothes no tattier? So why did we conveniently lose all those things on the way, like the sealskin, that could have proved we actually went anywhere? So why did Kiya still have the feathers of a yearling? So—"

"All right, all right, all *right*!" yelled The Ancient. "All right . . . I can see you have been talking to that blasted unicorn—"

"Not a word! So, you do admit—"

"I admit nothing! So there . . ." and he grabbed a stalk of grass, just like me, and stuck it in the corner of his mouth. "Just prove it, that's all! Prove it!"

"So there is something to prove, then?"

"I didn't say so—"

"You did!"

"Didn't!"

"Did!"

"Not!"

I lay back and laughed. "For an Ancient you are behaving more like a New—no, listen!" For he had half-risen and his face was all red. "I didn't mean to be rude, you know I didn't. But isn't it time we stopped being childish and started talking like—like adults?" Like human beings, I had been going to say, but I wasn't sure of his claim to this. I rolled over on to my stomach. "I admit I am being presumptuous, but there are certain questions I should like—more, I think I deserve—answers to. Straightforward answers. Agreed?"

"Agreed," came the rather sulky answer, but a sharp glance from under the bushy eyebrows accompanied it. "Shake on it?"

"Good!" I offered my hand, all unsuspecting. A moment later an almighty shock ran through my fingers and palm and up my arm into my shoulder and I was knocked sideways by a sudden strike of power that left me numb. I had not anticipated he would use anything like that: so far it had been a low-dice board game but now he had thrown a double and I was no match for this.

"Thanks," I said, rubbing my still-tingling arm. "All right, you're the boss. My strengths have been accidental, yours are calculated. Truce?"

For the first time he smiled, and nodded his head. "You are an endearing child, Flower . . . I must admit you have called upon powers that I would have thought impossible. Still, a flower may hold a thorn . . ." and he chuckled, shaking his head, and somewhere bells rang.

"You," I said, "have had ever so much more practice . . . Perhaps, then, because of what I did accidentally, you will accept that I have a right to some truthful answers? No more evasions? No more—" I rubbed my arm "—games?"

He nodded and his beard replaited itself, even to the knot. "No more games."

I studied him; at last we were on equal terms, but only perhaps because he had won earlier. "Right. Last things first: in that cave . . . The Power. Where did it come from? How did I manage to use it? And was it bad or good?"

"Backwards answer: neither good nor evil. Just there."

"Explain!"

He considered for a moment, chin in hands. "Under and over and about and through this old world of ours there flow sources of Power, as aimless as streams and rivers. As I said, they are neither good nor bad, they are just *there.* Clever magicians and wise men and shamans know where and when and sometimes how, but how *you* knew how to use it, I just don't know."

"But the gods—God—whatever; are they, It, good or bad, or just people like ourselves? Or forces and powers in their own right? And how many are there of them?" I was bewildered.

"I think—but I do not know, child, I do not know—that there must be a Supreme Being, above all others, who wishes for us, for the world as we know it, our good. There are also Forces, name them I cannot, who wish to take all Power for themselves: riches, domination, everlasting life. And they have forgotten the welfare of ordinary people. Just see you use whatever powers you find in the proper way. There is good, there is bad: make sure you choose aright!"

I wanted to ask whether it would make the slightest difference what I did, but then, stealing into my heart as soft as a mouse at dusk, came the answer; a tentative sureness that quietened my fears and gave me breath where before there had been none. It was a sureness outside of myself, borne on the gentle touch of breeze on my cheek, the feel of the crisscross of grass under my hand, the sad smell of autumn, the sweet call of the wren, the taste of doubt in my mouth—

"I will try," I said simply. It did not matter whether one used the prayer of the peasant or of the enlightened, the supplications of the Christian or the infidel, like smoke they would find their outlet, their goal. The only thing one had to remember was that one's reach had to be towards this goal, this good, and that prayer was the way—not for oneself, for all.

I smiled at The Ancient. "Thank you. I feel much better." I noticed him shuffle himself together, as if he had just got out of a tight corner and was now about to obliterate himself from further questions. "But there are other things . . ."

He glowered at me. "What things?"

"Time," I said. "Time . . . What is time?"

"Time? Time . . . is something man invented to table the night and the day. To explain the good times and the bad. To excuse the wrinkles in the skin. To count the falling of the leaves; to guard against the sudden sun—to know how long to boil an egg . . ."

"And our time?" I prompted. "*Our* time? The days, the weeks, the months we spent on our quest? Why did it take six months by our calculations and nothing by yours?"

"How did—? No, you have answered that question. All right. Time was invented by man: you understand that?"

I nodded. "Minutes, hours, days—yes. But not the concept in full." I hesitated. "We arrived with you in late winter, left on a summer's day when it seemed we had been with you but a week, and arrive back in late winter again apparently not one day older. Some of our travelling seemed to take weeks, some days. Some of the places we visited looked as if they existed now, others had a strangeness we could not account for—"

"You travelled," said The Ancient, "in time. As you know it."

"Explain!"

"Think of a tapestry. It perhaps shows a court scene, a country scene, a hunt; someone has embroidered part of it only. At the sides are the silks that wait to be sewn, the future. Those already in the picture are the past. The threads now on the needle are the present. All there, all at the same time, yet not all in the picture. Not yet. But the picture can be added to at any time without changing the essentials. It will still be a court scene, a hunt . . . And even if the tapestry is complete, or one thinks it is, as the hangings shift and sway in a draught and a candle brightens one fold and then another, one can imagine it is only the lighted corner that is important." He leant forward and cupped my masked face in his hands. "So, you found yourselves first in one part of time and then another." He wagged his beard. "And don't ask how I got you there and back, because a magician never gives away all his secrets. Suffice it to say that I had the power—" He laughed, and released me. "No, the knowledge to do it. And you didn't change anything: Time-Travellers are observers. Oh, you robbed the Tree-People of a meal, released some trapped animals, helped a traveller on his way, but you didn't change history; you can only do that in the now, when it is your hand guiding the needle."

I rose to my feet. I did not fully comprehend, but the image of the tapestry stayed in my mind. So time was a vast picture, never finished, that one could stitch oneself into at any point . . .

"I don't *really* understand," I said.

He laughed, and rose to his feet also. "Sometimes I feel I don't either, if that's any consolation!"

Together we walked back down the little hill towards the others, but slowly.

"Snowy? He understands all this?"

"Better than you or I, for he is immortal."

"Can the immortal never die?"

"No one can kill them, unless it is their choice to die."

We walked on in silence for a moment.

"Was it necessary for us to go the long way round?" I asked.

"The long way?"

"Yes. Making us suffer all that long journey, making us believe it took so long . . ."

"Maybe it was not necessary. But think how much you all would have missed, how much all those adventures and travelling together taught you of each other and of yourselves!"

"We might have been killed, any or all of us—"

"Not while you five held the jewels and the dragon was still alive in the Now. You were indestructible."

"And Snowy? And Conn?"

"As I said, unicorns are immortal, with or without their horns."

"And Conn?"

"Ah, well . . ." For the first time he looked guilty. "Well, I must admit that there I took a chance. But then . . ." He reached out and squeezed my hand, regaining his composure. "But then . . ." He winked and tapped his nose, "I knew you would look after him, you see . . ."

I frowned. "As far as I can recall he took care of himself, and all of us too, in the end. And it was rather presumptuous of you to suppose that I—"

"Loved him?"

I went all hot under my mask. "That has nothing—"

"Everything!"

"—to do with it! It was only in the beginning—"

"The Lady Adiora?"

"—that he faltered. In the end he was looking after everyone."

"Exactly!"

"Exactly what?"

"Your tests came when you were ready for them, not before. The first was Snowy, as you call him, to point the way."

"I notice I was last . . ."

"So? It was rather a grand finale, wasn't it?"

We stayed in that enchanted place for a week, allowing even for The Ancient's erratic sense of time, grew sleek and mended our gear and healed the last bruises the quest had engendered. And though it was winter away from this place, where we were the sun shone by day and the old man's owl too-whitted us to sleep at night, cosy in the cave. I was given a new comb by the magician and it did wonders for my tangles and for Snowy's mane and tail. I sharpened my little dagger on the honing-stone by the cave entrance till it was as sharp as a dragon's tooth. Conn looked over his spotty armour and pronounced it "no worse." Pisky's bowl was cleaned to his satisfaction, Corby's plumage once more lay straight, Puddy had a nice rest and declared his headaches much better, I played with Moglet with twine, leaf and nut till she grew tired, and The Ancient appeared in a different robe and headgear every day.

I didn't tell the others about the Time-Travel bit: it had confused me enough without my having to explain it to anyone else.

On the seventh day I found The Ancient on his hands and knees with a measuring stick at midday, frowning at the shadow it cast.

"One more day," he said.

"And?"

"Then it's on your travels again. The dragon still waits, or had you forgotten?"

No, I had not forgotten. I had just hoped against hope that perhaps we would have had a little longer . . .

The Binding: All

Journey to the Black Mountains

It was near the shortest day. Away from the shelter of The Ancient's hide away we found how much the weather had changed in the world outside. In spite of our thickest clothes we shivered in the chill wind that whined down from the northeast and huddled closer as he led us across moorland, past the stone circle where I now recognized we had started and ended our quest, and northwards towards the sea. Across the tumbled grey water of the straits one could see the farther shore, massed and woody on its lower slopes and soaring upward to bare scree and the distance-shrouded mountains, their tops capped like the magician himself with fanciful shapes, in their case of snow. It was both an awesome and an awe-inspiring sight and I was not the only one who drew back and trembled, for Moglet cuddled closer in my arms, Corby blinked and Conn whistled.

"Not easy, not easy at all! How do we get across, Sir Magician?"

For answer The Ancient leant among the reeds that bordered the little estuary in which we found ourselves and pulled on a rope. Slowly, silently, a narrow boat, half a man wide but the length of three and more, nosed its way to the bank. It was painted black but on the bows, on either side, were depicted great slanted eyes in some luminous, silvery substance, watching us from the beaked prow of the boat with a calculating stare.

Silently we boarded, silently The Ancient leant back to fend us off, and silently but for the slap of waves at the bow, we headed for the farther shore. There were no oars, no rudder, no sails and yet none of us thought to question our effortless progress. The Ancient stood in the prow, hatless for once, the wind blowing his white locks into strange patterns behind. It seemed that with his right hand he guided the passage of the boat and with the left gathered the waters behind to aid its progress. But still no one said anything and we moved as if in a dream on those dark waters, a great stillness all around us.

I do not know whether it was minutes or hours we were upon that ghostly passage, but it was with a sense of thankful awakening that I felt the bows of the craft ground upon the farther shore and my feet once more trod upon dry land. If all this had been magic, then I felt more comfortable without. I glanced back at the boat as we crunched up the shingle and the luminescent eyes stared back at me.

We found ourselves in a barren land. The trees were in their winter sleep, only showing they still breathed by the melted circles of frost beneath their branches; they were heavy with years and twisted by wind, and the moss and lichen that licked their roots and slithered down their northern sides only survived by grudging assent. There were no animals, no birds except a couple of gulls who came screaming down to see whether we had any scraps, but we had nothing to spare from our packs, for The Ancient had warned us that our journey would take over a week with no unnecessary stops. He was to come with us, partways as he said, to set us on the right path, and for the next few days, always cold, always hungry, we followed his tall and tireless figure ever higher among the folds of high hill that confronted us.

It was hard going, and even more so because of the hurt our burdens of the dragon's stones gave us. The nearer we came to him, still a mythical idea to me, the more we were reminded of the jewels we had carried so long, though of late they had seemed lighter and easier to bear. Now we were assailed by pains as strong as those that had hindered us while we were still prisoners of our Witch-Mistress. Puddy complained daylong, nightlong, of headaches and hid his eyes from the winter sun in my or Conn's pocket. Pisky was always hungry, in spite of the hibernation-cold and rushed around his bowl seemingly lightheaded and losing weight at an alarming rate. Corby dragged his injured wing, lost his cheery banter and grumbled all the time. Moglet could not even put her damaged paw to the ground and had to be carried inside my jacket. And me? The stomach-cramps became worse, I was more doubled-up than ever. Only Conn and Snowy—and, of course, The Ancient—seemed unaffected. Snowy had the restoration of his horn to think about and was impatient—as far as that most patient of creatures could be—of our necessarily slow progress; Conn was cheerful, for now it seemed he was nearing the end of his quest to mend his broken sword and go adventuring again. So, added to my burden of physical pain was an extra heartache. Seeing how optimistic Conn was becoming, I could not but realize that while his mended sword would mean escape for him once more to foreign lands, for me it would mean loss and an eternal worry as to his well-being; I cried a little, but under my mask, and any who saw reckoned it was the hurt of the stone I carried.

It grew colder, and the land became ever more barren save for the occasional green valley sheltering sheep and a few shepherds' houses, and they had little enough to spare for unexpected travellers. Our burdens became heavier even as our packs of food grew lighter, or so it seemed, and in the end Snowy, who alone seemed to thrive on the sparse herbage and icy streams, carried me as well as the remains of our food. The Ancient, too, another member of the Faery kingdom, or near-kin to it, seemed to stride faster, eat less and grow younger as the days passed and the hills grew taller.

We rested up at night, but although the days now gave but some seven hours of travelling light we made good progress. Ever nearer, glimpsed but fleetingly at first but now more menacing, loomed the cone-shaped Black Mountain. Tantalizingly far, ominously near, it was the first thing we looked for at dawning, the last thing at night. At first it had looked smooth, almost like a child's brick placed among the rougher stones of the other mountains, but as we drew nearer we could see the cliffs, gullies, crevasses that marred its surface. Corby swore that he, with his keen eyesight, could even see the cave, high up on the southern slopes, but I don't think any of us believed him. At last the mountain towered above all its fellows, dark, forbidding, looking virtually unclimbable, and that was the day that the magician led us through a high pass, chilly with the grey-sky threat of snow, into a bowl of green grass right by the mountain's root.

Here we were sheltered somewhat from the wind and here we found also a moderate-sized village, some twenty houses and huts, a meeting-house and even the ruin of a once-fortified manor. The priest that had occupied the little chapel—big enough to hold two dozen, no more—had died three years back and had not been replaced, but I noticed a ram's horn twisted with berries and fresh winter-ivy under the half-hidden shrine that held a rudely carved wooden figure that could have been either male or female, so religion of some sort still held their superstitions.

We were welcome in the village, albeit shyly, for travellers in this high valley were few and far between and we were more unusual than most; but over a supper of mutton broth, barley and rye-bread we learnt at first hand that our fabled dragon did indeed exist, and had last been seen in the valley some years back. He could be heard at certain times of the year when the wind was in the right direction, roaring in great desolation from his cave. No, no one had dared the mountain in pursuit but yes, they were sure he was still there, though it was six months back since last Michaelmas or Samain that any had heard him. Yes, once he had been a regular—and welcome—visitor, but since that last feasting some years ago—as far away in time as young Gruffydd here had years—he had not visited them. No, he never did them harm, but had entered pleasantly enough into the spirit of the jollifications they had held in his honour, and it was not many who could boast of a dragon on their doorstep. No, not large, but again not small. Yes, fire and smoke, but not too much damage. And were we really come to seek him out?

"So you see," said The Ancient, when we were at last alone, with the doubtful luxury of a smoky fire that seemed afraid of standing tall and puffing its smoke through the opening of the meeting-house in which we had been lodged, instead creeping along the floor and curling up among the smelly sheepskins we were to use for our bedding, "I wasn't telling stories. Your dragon is up there, on that mountain, waiting for the return of his jewels."

"But no one's seen or heard of him for an awful long time," said Conn.

"And if, as they say, he's not been down here to feast for some seven years or more, how do we know he's still alive?"

"We don't," said The Ancient, "but I think he is. Your stones still hurt, my children, don't they? Well, if he were dead, they would fall away from your bodies like dust, but you have all complained of greater hurt as we approached this mountain, have you not? And I can feel—and I think your unicorn can, too—a sense of latent power, a drawing-forward towards some central point . . ."

"He is still there," said Snowy. "But only just. The fires burn low . . ."

"Then the sooner you climb that mountain the better!"

"That sounds," I said, "as if you are not coming too."

"Right. I'm not. This is *your* quest. I am only your guide . . ."

We gazed at one another. Somehow this old man—older in years, but with the single-mindedness and determination of one much younger—had kept us all together without our giving much thought to what would happen next. We had all conveniently forgotten that he was only coming part of the way with us and now, faced with the reality of his departure, I think we all felt rather like that boat we had ridden in, rudderless, sailless, oarless, without the guiding force.

Conn cleared his throat. "And just how—er, hmmm, sorry; how will we know the right route?"

"You have guides: Corby's eyes and Snowy's good sense. They will show the way."

"And you? You will wait for us? Watch us go?" I thought perhaps he felt too tired to go further and didn't want to admit it.

But there was a flash of fire from those usually mild eyes. "And why should I? Think you that you are the only creatures on earth who have a task to fulfil? That you are the Only Ones because you are the Unlikely Ones?" He frowned, those thick eyebrows coming down over the windows of his eyes like snow-laden eaves. "You are not. But if you come through this—if, I say—I shall see you again. That is all!"

"But I thought—I thought it would be easy once we . . ." faltered poor Moglet.

His gaze softened. "Easier than your spider, my kitten, perhaps. But it will demand a great deal of physical effort. And you will be cold, very cold . . ."

"But it will be worth it, won't it?" she persisted. "For then we shall all lose our burdens and be whole again and able to run down the mountain and play!"

He smiled. "If that is what you choose . . ."

"Hang on," said Corby. "Of course that's what we choose. Isn't that what we came all this way for? To lose these wretched encumbrances!" And he flapped his burdened wing.

"Maybe that is what you wanted when you started. But perhaps you will not be of the same mind now—"

"Of course we are!" said Puddy. "Anything to rest this weary head of mine . . ."

"And I want to eat again," said Pisky. "Properly. A feast. Talk right, instead of with a mouthful of pebble. If my parents could see me now they would think I was last year's laying instead of . . . whenever it was," he finished lamely.

Conn glanced at us all. "I think you have your answer, Magician. I for one came on this journey for one reason, and one reason only: to mend my father's sword so that once again I can hold up my head and fight with the best!"

"And the armour?" said The Ancient, slyly.

"Oh, that! Well—I can buy fresh armour easy enough," but he scowled, obviously annoyed at being reminded of something he had patently forgotten.

"And before you ask it," added Snowy softly, "yes, I want my horn back, more than anything, and all that has happened will be worth just that. But I think, my friend, you were about to question our motives: and I confess mine are not as clear as I thought. I believed I had made up my mind—but I am not sure, not sure . . ."

I could not understand why The Ancient was sowing doubt in our minds, and making even the always-dependable Snowy have second thoughts!

"Look here!" I said, rising to my feet. "No one has asked me! I am determined to see this thing through to the finish as I want more than anything, whatever the cost, to rid myself of this accursed burden and walk straight!"

"Well done, Thingy!" applauded Conn. "We're all behind you—"

But The Ancient had caught at my words—and I suspect that he had chosen them for me even as I spoke. I sat down again sharply. "Whatever the cost? Whatever-the-cost? *Whatever*?" His voice, heavy and pregnant with meaning, filled the sudden silence until there was no room for further thought. "Think, oh think, my children of what I warned you, so long ago! You have forgotten, I believe, what I said . . ."

Yes, we had.

"I said then, and I repeat it most solemnly now: whatever we gain in this life must be paid for—"

"But we are about to give something back that we never asked for in the first place—"

He glared at me. "Did I say different? So—you offer back your burdens, in return for what?"

"Freedom from pain," I suggested. "A straight back, mended wing, whole paw, open mouth, clear head—"

"And do you not think that these also must be paid for?" he thundered, rising to his feet and towering above us, his robe drawn close about him. For a breathless instant I caught a glimpse once more of a younger, sterner warrior, helmed and dour-faced. "How can you have the presumption to imagine that life will then become a bed of mosses, free from trouble? The unicorn here has admitted that perhaps his motives have altered: can you be sure that you will not change also? All of you?"

"All right," I said, and stood up again. "Remind us. Tell us again of the cost we shall bear, that once before we said we could discount. Tell us what we have to lose, we who have nothing save pain and burden. What could possibly be worse than that?"

For a moment he glared at me, then slowly his hand came out to pat my head, very gently. "Why, nothing but the loosing. That is it. The loosing not only of the burdens but also of the bonds . . . Come, sit down. And listen."

He sat down by the fire and I followed suit, but immediately coughed at the crawling smoke. Almost abstractedly the old man waved his hand and the smoke gathered itself up from the floor, formed a wavery pillar and found the roof-exit.

"That's better . . . Listen well, my children, for I shall say this just once more." He turned to me. "You said just now 'We have nothing but burden and pain . . .' Now, is that entirely true?" I opened my mouth, but he waved me to silence. "None of your silly remarks now about being alive, food in your belly, clothes . . . Think, child, think! Look about you . . ."

"What I think he means, dear one," said Moglet, crawling onto my lap, "is that we have each other. That we all belong together, after our quest more than ever. That we love each other. That we have been through so much, shared so much, that we are more like one than five."

"O wise kitten," said The Ancient softly.

"And not just five," said Conn, smiling and leaning over to tickle Moglet's ears. "For have we not, the unicorn and I, shared your travels?"

"I like that," said Puddy ruminatively, a couple of sentences behind. "The seven who are one . . . Yes."

"Mmmm," said Corby. "Not bad; never thought of it that way meself. But now as you comes to mention it . . ."

"Comradeship," said Pisky, bubbling happily, "is one of the finest gifts one can ever expect, my great-great-grandmother used to say. When I was swimming around in shoals with my brothers and sisters and cousins and second cousins and half-brothers and half-sisters and—"

I dipped my little finger in his bowl. "Yes, dear one, it is." I was ashamed. When I had spoken so carelessly a few minutes ago, I had not really meant to sound callous and unthinking. I knew that I loved my companions and that they loved me, but I had been with the idea so long, took it so much for granted, that it was as much a part of me now as—as my mask. As night and day. As loving Conn, in a way that was not quite the same as loving the others . . .

"So you have all this," said the old man, no doubt reading my mind, "and you have your burdens. To you these burdens are your greatest handicap, the one thing you wish to be rid of—and once rid, you will be happy?"

"Of course!"

"And once Sir Knight has his sword and the unicorn his horn—then you will all be happy and all your problems will be solved?"

"Well, you know now that I shall be pitifully sorry to say goodbye to my friends, but I shall need to find my way to some indulgent duke or princeling who needs a mercenary—" Conn scowled suddenly. I reckoned he had remembered his armour again.

"And I can join my kindred again," said Snowy. "Or not . . . At least I shall have the choice . . ." There seemed to be more to this than I understood, but I could see The Ancient did.

"And we," I nodded at my friends, "must find somewhere to live, and the means of livelihood too . . ." I had not seriously considered this before. I supposed I could work at something to keep us all going, but what? Perhaps we could build a little cottage somewhere in the woods and grow our own produce and—and Moglet could catch mice and Puddy and Corby and Pisky would be all right, and I could gather mushrooms . . . No point in working it out in too much detail now. Getting rid of our burdens was the most important thing. It was! I could see the others were following my thought processes and agreeing, but—

The Ancient threw some powdery stuff on the fire and of a sudden it flared blue and a strange, sweet smell stole into—our noses, I was going to say, but it was more like our minds, and the perfume acted like a dousing of cold water, waking us up, sharpening what little wits we had, and I suddenly realized what he had been trying to say.

"The loosing? You are telling us that when—when we are whole again, we shall be so busy being ourselves again—real animals and people—that we shall not need each other anymore? That we shall be happy to split up, each to go his own way?" I knew we should lose Snowy and that I should never see my beloved Conn again, but the others? "Rubbish! We shall always want to be together, shan't we?"

They all agreed. Of course . . .

"And the forgotten years?" came the creaky, inexorable voice. "The years you have all forgotten? How long do you think you were with the witch? Now, you live in an enchantment of arrested and forgotten time: what happens when your memories return? And how old will you be? Were you with her five minutes, two days, six months, seven years? That time will have to be paid for, you know: soon, if all goes well, you will be as old as you really are. And those years will have gone and you will be left with what remains of your normal span—"

"Golden king-carp live for fifty years and more," said Pisky bravely, but his voice was smaller than usual. "My great-aunt on my father's side said her great-great-great-grandfather was over eighty . . ."

"Cats have nine lives—"

"Crows don't do so badly, neither!"

"And toads are noted for their longevity . . ."

"And I," I said slowly, "don't know how old I am, but I don't think it matters. And I don't think I have anything to go back to either. There *is* only forwards . . . Oh, why do you have to muddle us so!" I turned on The Ancient in a fury. "I'd never have thought about all this, but for you!"

"But you had to! You must not believe that just because your burdens are removed all your problems will be solved! You must not think that life will then be yours to do with as you will! I have to warn you—and not only you five jewel-bearers, but the knight and the unicorn too! You think that all your dreams will come true, just as you have planned, *and it may not be so*!"

"I don't care!" I turned to the others. "Just as we are so near our goal, just as we are about to realize our dearest wishes—don't listen to his gloomy forecasts! After all we have been through—" I turned back to our tormentor "—you don't think we will just give up, do you?"

"No. I did not expect it for one instant. I only wanted to remind you not to expect things to turn out exactly as you planned." He smiled brilliantly, and his face was transformed. "Thank the gods that you are all children of Earth! Yes, even you at times, my friend." He nodded at Snowy. "The world will never die when there are brave idiots such as you." He smiled. "Just remember that you always have a choice . . . And now, my children, my weary travellers, I will give you all one more thing to counter all that wearisome advice." He waved his hands and the lights in the wayward fire turned rose and green and violet and gold and we fell asleep in a moment, just where we were, and slept dreamlessly and deep.

And, in the morning when we awoke, he was gone.

The Binding: All

The Black Mountain

The first part was relatively easy, and the weather was with us. The lower slopes of the so-called Black Mountain—nearer to it was more dark grey, but littered with shiny black rocks that seemed to absorb the light, making it all look darker from a distance—were made up of hummocky ground bisected by small, cold streams that were no barrier to hurrying feet. Now that we were on the last lap, everyone was eager to finish the marathon endeavour as soon as possible. On the second day, however, it began to rain, rain that penetrated our furs and feathers and skins, and by nightfall we were grateful for the shelter of a cluster of pines that clung grimly, roots deep in crevices, to the inhospitable rock. We lit a fire, inadequate barrier to the cold stone beneath and the colder sky. By morning it had begun to snow; fine, thin snow as small as salt with none of the largesse of the patterned crystals that had delighted my eyes as a child—as a child! A sudden memory of stars on my window ledge . . . Gone. But this snow was different. It was hard as hail and ran away beneath our feet, only to circle back behind and around our ankles and paw up the backs of our legs. Before us we could see it form trickles, streams, rivers, sheets, whirlpools in the towering obsidian rocks above, pouring and falling and tumbling down to meet us.

The going became increasingly treacherous, for though Snowy's unerring hooves found a track of sorts that led up towards the top, yet it twisted and turned—one moment edging a crevasse, another stealing behind a buttress and yet again scaling in steps straight up the mountain. Gone were the sheltering trees. Only that morning we had seen our last, a twisted ash bent like an old woman, an incredible last bunch of skeleton keys clinging to the lowest branch, twig-fingers rattling them as if in an ague. Dark clouds raced overhead and no sun shone. Now there was only a lace-pattern of lichen, dank mosses, dead bracken, a few tufts of grass and once in this twilight world we saw five goats, their wild yellow eyes glaring, slanting in single file down the shoulder of the mountain towards the kinder shelter of the valleys beneath.

Only at night did the snow cease completely. Then the moon shone on a scene so desolate, so forlorn, that she would have been better to hide her face. We were halfway up the mountain by now but the climb, the lack of food and the thin air were all beginning to take their toll. That night we scarcely seemed to sleep at all in spite of our weariness, and used the last of our precious store of wood, our fire a brief and brave candle, and as near comfortless.

An inch of ice formed in Pisky's bowl, and in the morning Conn took his pack, unwrapped it and put on his rusty armour.

"'Tis only a further burden for poor Snowy here, and mayhap it will keep out a few of the draughts, rust and all . . ."

We continued our upward climb, clawing, slipping and stumbling, eyes half-closed from the bitter chill which rimed our eyelashes and made my teeth ache. The last of the food—oatmeal, apple and honey—we had eaten that morning, and the summit of the mountain seemed as far away as ever. My hands and feet ached with cold and the tears froze on my cheeks under the mask. Now Conn had rucked Corby within his cloak and looped a corner of it into his belt to hold Pisky's bowl. I had Moglet inside my jerkin and Puddy permanently in my pocket. Only Snowy seemed unaffected, but the breath from his nostrils came like plumed smoke.

At last we could go no further, although the sun was still a red ball in the southwestern sky. We crawled onto a wide shelf beneath an overhang of rock, too exhausted to speak. Moglet voiced what, I think, most of us felt.

"We're not going to get there! We're going to die . . ."

"Nonsense!" I said immediately, not because I believed what I was saying but because she was smaller and needed comforting. Conn echoed me at once, and much more convincingly.

"Blather and winderskite, kitten! Of course we'll get there!"

"Let me lie down—so," said Snowy, and positioned himself on the outer edge of the shelf so that he formed a retaining wall. "Now, if you put the creatures next to me and you, Thing dear, put your feet by me and Sir Knight sits behind you . . . That's better, isn't it?"

And indeed it was. Somehow that wonderful white creature threw out a warmth that thawed the fingers and toes and doubts of us all.

"And now," he said, "I think it is time for that little packet in your pack."

"Little packet?"

"Remember that evening in the forest with Tom Trundleweed, and the mushrooms?"

"Of course! The Mouse-Dugs . . ." I scrabbled frantically in the almost-empty haversack. At last I found the desiccated remains and held them up to Snowy. "How much?"

"Divide one between cat, crow and toad, and a sprinkle in the fish's bowl," he suggested. "I want none. Take two for yourself and three for Sir Knight. Let them lie first beneath your tongue to moisten, then chew them slowly . . ."

At first there was nothing, then gradually a warmth and fullness crept into my belly. The drug was quicker-acting on the animals. One by one they started talking. Pisky bubbled away of what he was going to eat when his pearl was gone, Puddy explained how much time he would have for constructive thought and philosophy once rid of the emerald, Corby described his anticipations of flight, and Moglet purred and licked her diamonded paw and thought of mice, until all at once they fell asleep. Moglet even snored a little.

I leant back and there was Conn's chest behind me, his mailed shoulder a pillow for my head. He didn't seem to mind, just shifted a little so that he was wedged more comfortably against the rock face, his knees on either side of me.

"They've got themselves all sorted out, haven't they?" he said.

"Mmmm. I hope it's all as instantaneous as they hope. Won't it leave a dent in Puddy's head? And, after all, if one hasn't flown for a while . . . ?"

"It'll all take time, I guess, but the loss of pain and inconvenience will be enough for a while, I suppose. Your stomach, fr'instance: that'll stop aching, but you won't be able to stand upright properly for a while. Your bones will have become used to being in a different position."

"Yours should be easier: one moment two halves of a sword, then suddenly—"

"If it works. If the dragon condescends to help. If he's in a good mood. If he's even there . . ."

"'Course he is! We'll give him our jewels first, then he'll be in a good mood for you . . . No, perhaps it would be better to give him one, then get your sword mended, give him one more, then ask for Snowy . . . Or perhaps two first, then Snowy, and once he had his horn back he could help to persuade the dragon with his magic and—"

"Stop whittering, child!" and Conn put his arms round me and squeezed. "God! you're as skinny as a starved rabbit!" And as I protested he shushed me. "Don't talk too loud, they're all asleep . . ." Glancing round, I saw that Snowy's white lashes, the last to close, were lying in a calm fringe on his cheeks. "Never mind about planning about dragons: let what will be happen . . ."

"That's not really the philosophy of a soldier, I shouldn't have thought." I snuggled closer.

He rested his chin on my head and I could imagine him staring out into the dark night, a frown of concentration between his brows. "No . . . Most military actions are planned, methodical—that's if we are hunting down an enemy, of course—but there is always a hell of a lot of waiting around just polishing up arms, tending the horses, mending gear . . . Of course in an ambush it's training plus instinct. And then there's the awful anticipation when two forces are drawn up opposite one another, each waiting for the other's attack; you spend the days with your stomach a'churn and the nights on your knees, praying, afraid to rest your head in case the other side takes advantage of the dark. You have to wait too for the high-ups to decide when and where: that's how planning comes into it. But it's never your decision.

For all you know you may be sacrificed as a diversion, a suicide troop, or may spend your time fuming in the rear as a reserve that never gets used at all—"

"Doesn't sound much fun to me," I observed.

"It's a way of life. Besides, what else is there for a youngest son with no skills but his sword and a touch, perhaps, of the old blarney?" I could hear the smile round the words.

"Blarney?"

"Aye, there's an old stone somewhere in Hirland, so they say, where they hang you by your heels to reach it and if you manage to touch it with your lips then you can charm the lassies into Kingdom-Come with just words. Me mother said as I had no need to seek it . . . Said it came as natural as a hen laying eggs . . ." The mushrooms made his voice more lilting. He shifted a little to make us both more comfortable. "And, believe you me, there were times when I found it useful." He laughed out loud. "Why, I could tell you such tales! When I attended my first court I had no idea at all what was expected of me . . .

"I had just been accepted in one of the courts of Brittanye on the recommendation of my father's name—for a grand warrior he was, and his name good as a password in all the lands across the water—and there was I, but a scrap of a lad from the bogs of Hirland with nothing to my name save the horse I rode, a second-hand suit of clothes and my father's sword, pitched of a sudden arse-over-noddle into the silks and jewels and soft hands of a parcel of women, the likes of whom I had never seen before! Plucked were their eyebrows and oiled their skins and painted their eyes and lips, and they walked small but tall in their pattens, like cripples, and swayed their hips and fluttered their scarves till I was as helpless as a newborn babe! And if it hadn't been that as a lad of fifteen I had already spent time with the lasses at home and learnt to give them pleasure, I would have had problems, I promise you.

"They all thought, you see, that it would be amusing to sport a little with me. Until I knew what it was all about, I played the innocent and listened to their soft words and pretended I did not know what lay behind them. It did not take me long to realize that they all suffered from the same thing: their lords were so often away at war, and worn out with battling when they returned, and had no time for the soft words, the strokes and caresses, that they were all like pullets without the cockerel. So, when one day they said I had to pass this test they had planned for me, and that six of the chosen ladies were to visit me one night to initiate me into the ways of the court, I knew what was coming.

"For three days I ate lamb's fries, bull's pizzle and herring roe and bathed in rose water till I was surfeited and stank in my own nostrils, but when they came I was ready for them and serviced them all, one after the other, with flattering words and pleasant courtesies between, till the eyeballs fair popped from their heads and they declared themselves worn out!" He chuckled again. "Took me a week to recover, so it did, but after that I could do no wrong. They declared I was a poet of the bedchamber, so they did!"

I think he had temporarily forgotten to whom he was talking, for he had never disclosed his past so freely before and the topic was not the most suitable for the youngster he obviously considered me. But I stayed quiet and did not remind him, for I was where I had always longed to be, in his arms, albeit as unregarded as a pup or a child's wooden doll. It was only gradually, I think, that I had fully realized my good fortune, for the drug we had chewed, while heightening our sensibilities in some ways, made stranger things as acceptable as they would be in dreams. So, it was only now that I realized the full implications of Conn's arms about me and I had to hide my jubilation, for it was in me to tremble and shake and behave as those women he had spoken of, perfumed and pretty and seductive in silks. Except that I was not like them and never could be, ugly and crooked and poor as I was!

But my love for him was beautiful, more beautiful even than they could ever be, for I loved him without subterfuge. I did not desire him from boredom, or the joy of conquest or in rivalry. I loved him firm and true and plain. Not unquestioningly, for we had travelled too long together for that, but acceptingly and thankfully, for he was a man who deserved to be loved and cherished, even if only in secret.

"I can see you cannot wait to get back to it all," I said wistfully, and with no hint of sarcasm. "I suppose the Castle of Fair Delights was a bit like that court?"

"Something like. But do you know, Thingy, the good life can pall after a while? A man can yearn for the simpler things, he can become tired of trailing across indifferent country through all the seasons to face an enemy he has never met, and would probably drink with instead of fighting if he had the chance. I was bored, for too long, and too often." He relaxed his arms about me. "That's why, I suppose, I began to spend so much time with the surgeons—"

"Surgeons?"

"Yes, the fellows who patch up the damage done by sword and axe, pike and spear, bolts, daggers, falling horses; the men who try to cure gangrene and chopped-off limbs, set bones, assuage fever, bandage boils on the bum, scalds from burning oil and give you a cure for the clap. The ones who give the same ointment for dog-bites and pox and saddle-blisters, who gave wine to all and unction to the dying if there was no priest about . . . Horse-doctors, most of them, used to galls and spavin, mange and sprains, but not to humans. But there was one—a little man, dark and pocked from some obscure town in Italia, I think, but married to an English wife, who had a gift with bones. He did not just bind and bandage and splint, he had a full set of human bones, of horse bones, of dog bones, and these he had cunningly strung together with wires so that they held like puppets on strings and he could study the way they moved and were dependent on each other. Also, when a man died of some blow to his head, back, hip, he would lay back the flesh when he could and study the injured bones, to see where and how they might have been mended." He sighed. "I learnt a lot from him, Thingummy. That's one of the reasons that makes me suspect that to straighten that back of yours will take more than a sudden dragon-spark. The spine is a marvellous thing, all locked and connected like a necklet of ivory shapes . . ." He settled back against the rock. "Got any more of those mushroomy things?"

"One."

"Let's split it. Thanks . . ." He chewed for a moment, then tucked the scrap under his tongue. "Mmmm, that's better . . . So, I might think twice before committing myself to anything too protracted this time; a short campaign, perhaps.

"And you—what will you do?"

I sighed. "Try to find somewhere to live, then make a home of it for the others. Scratch a living somehow, whether by trying to be self-sufficient with food, or by trading mushrooms, or—oh, something or other will turn up, I suppose. It must. It always has . . ."

"Optimist!"

"What else is there to be? Pessimists are always expecting the end of the world tomorrow, so don't bother doing anything in case it comes today instead. Optimists fall flat on their noses often, too often, but at least they don't believe the worst will happen till they've had time to get in the harvest, sow the winter wheat, spin the fleece, set the ram among his ewes, lay in wood, jar the honey—"

"Oh, darling Thingummyjig! You're a tonic for the footsore and heart-weary, truly you are!" And he threw back his head and laughed, quite forgetting I think that he had hushed me a moment since for the sake of the others. They stirred, but it was only to seek a more comfortable position. He hugged me. "I shall miss you, girl, sure and I will! You're more fun altogether than those fine court ladies with their fal-lals and insipid talk—and if it's more than that I seek, sure a willing trollop from the village is heartier and more honest by far!"

"I shall miss you too," I said, but I tried to keep my voice light. "We have had some good times together, have we not, even among the bad?"

"Sure we have!" He seemed to hesitate for a moment. "You know, I don't like to think of you and all those animals just going off into the wilderness after this is all over without making proper plans. Why, there's no telling what mischief you might get up to, and there's all those dangers along the road . . . 'Sides, you need someone to help build that house you spoke of . . ." He hesitated again, then seemed to make up his mind. "So—'tis in my mind to stay with you awhile, just until you're all set up. Then my mind would be at ease when I took to the road again."

I couldn't help the shiver of excitement that started in my stomach and ran out to fingertips and toes and shut my eyes on its way to burning my ears.

"You mean . . . ?"

"I mean that we'll be companions of the road that much longer."

I wriggled inside my clothes like an eel through grass. "Hurray! I mean—I mean thanks! I suppose I didn't really fancy being on my own, and then having to find somewhere and build a house with only the others to help.

A—" I was going to say "young woman" but changed my mind, "a person can have a hard time persuading villagers to accept them if they don't appear to have a—" oh dear, this was getting difficult; "—I mean, females do . . . If they don't . . . So you see it will help if they see you around at first: you can say I'm your—your servant . . ."

He didn't answer, so I twisted round in his arms anxiously for confirmation that he had understood, for by now I had a clear picture in my mind of myself, grown straight if not beautiful, dressed in a skirt instead of trews, spinning thread at the doorway of my little hut on the edge of the clearing near the village, and perhaps even leaving off my mask once Conn had gone, and of the villagers accepting me eventually and not even looking at my ugly face after a while, but glad to welcome me into their world because I had arrived with a great knight like Conn.

"I know it's a lot to ask, but if you just said—said to whoever is there that you would be back every now and again—you wouldn't really have to, of course—to see that I was comfortable, then I'm sure they would treat me as—as more normal. More like them . . ."

My voice trailed away, for I was suddenly aware how close we were, now I was facing him. His eyes glittered down into mine, our noses almost touched through my mask and his chainmail tunic rubbed my chin as he breathed. I quite forgot what I had been saying and when his next words came, for a moment they had no context.

"Servant? No, you deserve better than that." His breath came in little white puffs of vapour and for a moment he closed his eyes. "Dear Mother of God, she's such a helpless little Thing really . . . Let this be one unselfish thing I do." He opened his eyes. "So, Thing dear, as they all call you, before I go off on my travels again, if you're agreeable that is, we'll tie it up all nice and neat in a contract before the priest. I shall give you my name so you'll be the equal of all, and I'll have a home to come back to when I weary of my travels." He regarded me for a moment, then frowned. "Well?"

"I—I don't understand . . ." I didn't.

He gave me a little shake. "Thick, all of a sudden? Well, I'm telling you that my hand is yours, my name will be yours, and my sword to defend, if necessary, when I'm around. Damn it all, Thing—what is your real name, by the way? I can't marry 'Thing'—We'll have to find you a name; what would you fancy? How about Bridget? Or Freya? Claudia?"

"Marry?" I faltered, and it must have come out like the silliest bleat in the world.

"Of course. What did you think I had been trying to say?"

"You—you haven't seen my face, and I don't think I want—"

He misunderstood what I was trying to say, interrupting me so I should not get the wrong idea. "No, no, of course it won't be like that, silly girl! A marriage in name only, I promise you that. We'll be just as we are now, good companions, and you can keep your blasted mask on if you like, though I'm sure I could get used to what's underneath!"

"But supposing you find someone else, someone—well, er, more suitable you wished to marry? Marry properly, I mean. A pretty lady . . . With money?"

"I am nearly thirty years old and I have seen enough 'pretty ladies' to last me all my days! They are all alike, believe you me, and the prettier the worse! As for money—I can earn my keep, and if not, I've managed before and can again. And as for—the other—well, I can always find that when I need it, and I promise I would not disgrace you by seeking it while I was with you. No soiling your own front step and all that sort of thing . . . Well, what do you say?"

All sorts of thoughts were chasing through my brain. The first, illogical one: suppose I *had* been pretty? Would he by now have got so used to me that he would still have conferred his request for my hand like a royal order, assuming that I had no other choice—but that thought was so stupid, so illogical that I shocked it into oblivion. The second thought: the man I love above all others has asked me to marry him!! The stars should whirl from their courses, the rivers run backwards, hills grow flat, trees flower in winter and cattle bring forth in threes . . . Why, then, did they all stay as they were and why did I feel like crying? I knew the answer to that one in my rebellious heart, but frantically pushed it away. The third thought: I want to be sick . . . And the fourth? It suddenly burst like an overfull wineskin and I was drowned in intoxication for I loved him so, so, and here was my chance to really do something for my dearest knight at last—

I stumbled to my feet, pulling at his hands. "Stand up!"

"What?"

"Stand *up*! Now, quick: I have something for you—"

"An answer, I hope," he grumbled and unfolded himself so that we stood, precariously facing one another.

"Now what?"

"Now, say it over again. Formally. But before you do, just say that you realize just what I am—"

"What you are? Oh, come on, Thingy, no time for games—"

"No game. Promise! Listen . . ." I was trembling with excitement. "Am I or am I not poor and deformed?"

"At the moment, yes, but—"

"And am I not also the ugliest person in the world?"

He shifted his gaze. "Now, you know I would never say that . . ."

"You wouldn't say it, but do you not truly believe me to be so?"

"A man can get used—"

"Am I not?"

"Well, yes, I suppose you must be. You keep saying so, but remember I have never seen you unmasked."

"Still, you believe me to be?"

"I told you—"

"Never mind! In spite of all this," I spoke clearly, slowly, emphatically and could see out of the corner of my eye that Snowy was awake and the others stirring, and there was a hint of a lightening in the sky to the east, "in spite of all this, you have made me an offer?"

"Oh Thing, you know I have! Why all this rigmarole?"

"Then please ask me again."

"Ask what?"

"Ask me to marry you!"

"But why—"

"Ask!"

He looked at me impatiently for a moment, then his gaze softened and he smiled so that my heart turned over.

"All right, my dear, all right, have it your way . . . Hey, you lot!" He looked over at the others, all now awake and alert in the growing light. "Your Thingy doesn't seem to credit what I asked her a moment ago, and I need you as witnesses. So, we'll go over it once again, just so as we all get it right." Squaring his shoulders, he put his hand to the hilt of his broken sword. "In the full understanding that Thingy here is poor and deformed and I believe the ugliest person around—though I have told her that does not matter and I could get used to it—I hereby ask, in front of you all, for her hand in marriage. In name only," he added hastily, "on that we are agreed. But marriage, nonetheless . . ."

There was a gay, tinkling sound.

"And I refuse!" I said triumphantly, as the sun's first rays slanted full on my beautiful knight, glinting on his armour till it almost blinded us.

"Sir Conn," said the others, more or less in unison, "your armour isn't rusty any more . . ."

And indeed it wasn't, celebrated with all the "Begorras," "Hail Marys," holy shamrocks and all the saints in the calendar (especially St. Patrick), and a whooping and hollering that woke all the echoes in that previously God-forsaken spot.

He honestly hadn't remembered about the witch's curse when he had asked me to marry him and it had to be explained to him all over again.

"But you turned me down!" he expostulated.

"That didn't matter! You asked, that was all the curse said you had to do. Don't you remember how The Ancient said you can't face straight up to a curse like that, you had to go at it sideways? You could have broken it any time if you had bribed someone ugly enough to refuse you!"

"To the devil with anyone else! It was you I asked, and you refused. But I'm not taking no for an answer: I shall marry you whether you want to or no. As I told you, you need looking after—"

"Wait till all this is over then. Till we are all whole. You still have a broken sword—"

"And don't you think me still capable of defending you, even with my bare hands? Mother of God, you take some convincing! Very well, I shall ask you once again when all this is over, and you'll not refuse!"

It was a glorious morning. The snow sparkled on the mountain and all around us stretched a chain of hills white and shining, their shadows purple and blue and green. No longer were we hungry, no longer cold, and when Conn set off again up the steep slopes we followed with more enthusiasm than we had shown for many a day. When we were faced with what looked like a sheer wall of rock, Snowy took the lead, slipping and stumbling for all his surefootedness. I felt like a fly crawling up a wall, my hands grasping poor Snowy's tail like a lifeline, Conn panting behind, but at last we emerged on a ledge far bigger than we had seen before, wide and long enough to hold a wagon and two horses.

Even as we gazed out over the ridged carpet of hills below us we became aware of a sound, alien even to our harsh breathing.

There was somebody, something, up there with us—

Snoring.

The Binding: Dragon

The Dragon Awakes

Raised in natural steps some four or five feet above the ledge on which we stood, was the dark, triangular shape of a cave mouth, and it was from this direction that the sound came. Instantly we all retreated to the very edge of the ledge, clutching at one another in panic like children caught stealing apples. All, that is, except Snowy, who stood his ground, snuffing the air.

"He's asleep," he said. "Or in a coma."

"Is it . . . ?"

"Of course. We were bound to reach him sooner or later. Come, my children, you're not afraid?"

"No! . . . Certainly not . . . Afraid, us?"

But we were, of course we were. It was all right for Snowy, I reasoned, being of faery stock to begin with, but the rest of us were all mortal. Too late I began to recall all I had heard about dragons; immense scaly beings, with leathery wings and huge claws and mouths full of teeth and fire. They ate people, whole sometimes depending on size, and were capable of incinerating entire towns and villages with their flame. They guarded vast hordes of treasure with jealous attention and demanded a sacrifice of seven maidens every year. They hatched from golden eggs and took only a day to reach full size and after that a thousand years to die. They flew in swarms a hundred strong and mated once every nine years, laying nine eggs which took another nine years to hatch—

"Grumphhhh!!"

I jumped back as if I had been punched and fell over the edge of our precarious perch, luckily landing on soft snow only some five feet below, to be hauled back by an anxious Conn. Puddy and Moglet, in jerkin and pocket respectively, had of course accompanied my fall but as I had landed on my back they escaped with bumps but not bruises.

When we were all assembled back on the ledge I looked at Conn. "I'm not sure . . ."

"Neither am I, neither am I, dear girl, but this is what we all came for . . ."

"Bravo, Sir Knight!" said Snowy. "Now, shall we—?"

"I'm *frightened*!" said Moglet.

"So am I," I said. "But, dear one, Conn is right. This is what we came for. And we're together, so nothing can really hurt us—remember what The Ancient said?"

And so it was that, with Snowy ever so slightly in front, we climbed up the last steps of rock and found ourselves in the mouth of the dragon's cave.

The winter sun was at its highest, illuminating all but the farthest depths of the south-facing cave. Fearfully we peeped: a bare stone floor, stained with droppings; shelves running erratically across the back and sides, and on these humps and piles of metal: shields, helms, coins, a cup or two. In the middle of the cave a few discarded bones—bullock or sheep, perhaps—and a bluish leathery cloak or bag, flung aside from some foray probably, tattered and patched and torn.

But no dragon . . .

Perhaps there was an inner cave. Perhaps—my heart lifted, coward as I was—perhaps he had gone. Perhaps he had never been here. But there were the piles of metal, the bones . . .

"There's nothing here," I whispered. "Except rusty metal, old bones and rubbish."

"Rubbish is rubbish is rubbish," said Snowy cryptically, who alone of us did not seem disturbed, anxious or disappointed, the sun shining on the hairs on his chin and making his lips pink.

"Well there isn't," I said. "If—he—was here, then he's gone, long since. Look! These old bones were chewed years ago."

"And the noise we heard?"

"Oh—wind in the rocks, I expect . . ." I became bolder and advanced into the cave, while Conn stepped forward and examined the shelves.

"Darling girl, there's gold up here!" His voice was excited. "Lots of these shields and things are bronze or iron, but there's silver and gold coin and buckles and rings and brooches set with coloured stones . . ."

I put Moglet and Puddy down so they could explore. "So what? What good is gold on a mountain-top? We need broth and bread. And, besides, we came here to get rid of our burdens, not set up a second-hand armour stall in the market." I was disappointed now, angry with anticlimax. "The place is disgusting, that's what it is, and *this* heap of rubbish *smells*!" and I kicked the heap of leathery discard in the middle of the cave.

Upon which the bundle of rubbish stirred.

And opened one baleful eye.

Upon which we beat a fast retreat. I had heard of the phrase "one's hair standing up on one's head" and now I experienced it. It was horrid! I felt as though a hand had scooped its icy fingers up the back of my neck and yanked my hair by the roots.

Once again only Snowy seemed at ease.

"One doesn't kick dragons," he said mildly. "At least, not until one has struck up a friendly acquaintance."

Helplessly I stared at that yellow eye and, unbidden, a child's rhyme I had learnt—when? where?—popped suddenly into my mind.

"Let sleeping dragons lie;
Tread soft, child, pass him by.
Better not know the power and glory,
Learn it best by myth and story . . ."

Too late! I had awoken chaos, and ineptly too.

The bundle of rubbish stirred again, rearranged itself, snorted, sneezed, and opened the other eye, which was, if anything, more baleful and bleary than the first, and for a long—a very long—moment, we all stared at it, and it at us.

Then the bundle spoke, coughing out an ashy, cinderous breath. "*Who* disturbs my rest?"

Nobody moved, nobody even breathed, then suddenly an absolutely unstoppable sensation rose somewhere behind my eyes, gathered strength behind my cheekbones, ordered itself behind my tongue, pressing its advantage so firmly I had finally to snatch for breath and—

"A—*tish*—ooo!!" The best of it was that I hadn't sneezed for months.

"Bless you!" said the dragon, and suddenly everything was much better, so much so that almost without thinking I wiped my nose on my sleeve and advanced two paces.

"Good-day," I said, and bowed. "I regret that we disturbed your slumbers, O—O Magnificence, but I'm afraid it was necessary. Well, not *afraid* exactly: that's perhaps the wrong word." (It was the right word.) "But it *was* necessary . . ."

"Why?" Uncompromising. "And who are you, anyway? From the village, perhaps? Well, if you are, your climb was for nothing. I do not intend to play puppet for your silly games any longer." He yawned, and a furry yellow tongue curled up like a cat's around stained, yellow fangs. "Now, go away!"

"But—"

"At once!" He raised himself for a moment and his wings rustled as he half-opened them. A few dry, diamond-shaped scales fell to the floor in dusty disarray, and he sank back on his haunches.

I retreated one step but no further, for Snowy's nose nudged me forward again, none too gently.

"Please Sir, please Lord-of-the-Sky . . ."

The eyes, which had gone slitty, opened wide again. "What, still here?"

"Yes, if it please Your Eminence. I . . . I—We're not from the village; no, we're from much farther away. Much farther," I repeated firmly, for now I realized it was no good blurting everything out in one go. It would have to be told in stages, perhaps like a story, for I would have to wake this creature gradually to the reason we were here, lest he lose his temper and blow us over the edge. So, a tale for the fireside . . . "It all started this way: once upon a time . . ."

When I had got into my story and the dragon was clearly listening, his claws folded in front of him, I sat down cross-legged on the cave floor and made myself comfortable, giving him a condensed version of all that had happened, introducing us all by name at the appropriate moment, so he knew where we fitted in the story. When I spoke of the witch the dragon allowed a wisp of smoke to emerge from his right nostril, but otherwise there was little show of emotion. He glanced at Snowy once or twice and nodded when I spoke of The Ancient, as though they were acquainted, but otherwise he was a quiet and attentive audience. By the time I had finished, the sun's rays cast a fading light on the left wall of the cave.

I coughed heartily for my throat was now dry and parched, but Conn handed me Pisky's bowl and he sank warily to the bottom as I sipped.

"Is that it?" said the dragon, but it was not really a question. "So . . ."

Slowly he seemed to reassemble himself, taking deep breaths, scales rustling like a long-forgotten pile of dry leaves. Now I could see the shape of his ribs, the heave of his flanks and he seemed to swell to twice his original size before our eyes. Suddenly we all became less cold, as though we had stepped into a room where the ashes were still warm. Indeed little curls and wisps of smoke issued from the dragon's nostrils and when he opened his mouth I stepped back involuntarily, for a small flame licked momentarily between his teeth and then died back again.

"Fear not," he said. "I mean you no harm, but when a dragon wakes from as long a sleep as mine the fires take some time to get restarted. Come forward, nearer to me, you and your companions. Show me where the sorceress hid my treasure . . ."

Slowly the others joined me; I pointed to Puddy's head, lifted Corby's wing and Moglet's paw, held up Pisky's bowl and hefted my jerkin to expose my navel.

"It was true, then . . ." Somehow he was changing colour. At first he had been a dull, metallic grey-blue, but now the colour was deepening, brightening, and round the middle of his body assuming a purplish hue. I jumped back again as with a hissing, swishing sound his tail, which had so far been hidden, twitched and curled and unfolded itself, the tip, like a huge arrowhead, curling up against his left flank.

Now he addressed Snowy and Conn. "Come hither, let me look at you . . . Ah, I see. You both want restored that which you would not use . . ." They both looked puzzled, but he did not explain. "And what would you give, to restore a horn, to mend a sword?"

"What you would need of healing to set you free," said Snowy, stepping forward and nodding at the discarded scales.

"And I," said Conn, "will trim and sharpen your claws that you may take flight and return home without pain." And he indicated what I had not noted before, the bent and twisted claws on the right front paw.

The dragon nodded. "A fair bargain, from you both. Stand aside, Sir Knight, stand aside all save the unicorn!"

No need for second telling. We all pressed back against the cave wall as the dragon took several deep breaths and then shot a jet of flame that flared with a gassy roar, like those lumps of blackened wood that one sometimes finds in peat. A thick, acrid smoke curled in our nostrils and I put my hand over Pisky's bowl to save him from the smuts that floated down.

"Sorry," said the dragon. "Out of practice. Must concentrate." And now the flame quietened, burned steady, changed colour from yellow to orange to red to a sort of silvery pink and now we were all very warm indeed. The flame seemed to transmute into a shimmering glow.

Into that glow stepped Snowy, for all that I extended a last-minute hand to stop him and cried out: "No, no! You will be burnt . . ." and shut my eyes and put my hands over my ears. From her perch on my shoulder Moglet's cold nose nudged my cheek.

"Look! It's all right, really it is . . ."

The shabby little white horse, uncombed and uncared for, stood calmly in the silver fire. As the light streamed over his dumpy body and lifted his mane and tail with the breath of its passing, a curious change took place. The lumps and bumps and tangles were smoothed out and curried and combed and he stood taller, slimmer and shining with the light itself. And suddenly there were golden sparks and a ting! as of a golden bell and there, between his ears, on the sore little stump he had borne so long, there sprouted a beautiful, spiralling golden horn. The silver fire died down and he stepped forth, shining like the moon at Lugnosa, the harvest month; not gold, not silver, but a glorious mixture of both. For a moment he stood, a creature of pure faery, untouched and untouchable, the snow with the sun upon it, and I sank to my knees in awe as he reared and neighed his triumph. Then hooves found the floor of the cave again and he looked over at us.

"It's all right, you know," he said, and suddenly he was our beloved Snowy again. Going over to the dragon he bent on one knee, his horn touching the floor. "Thank you, O Master of the Clouds!" and, standing now, he circled the dragon on delicate hooves, bending to touch certain portions of the scaly hide with his golden horn. To my astonishment I saw the parts touched burn with a blue light which gradually faded to leave new scales growing in place of the old.

"Magic," I whispered. "Real magic . . ."

"Good magic," said Snowy, and came over to bend his head and nuzzle my hair, his rippling mane curtaining us both. "I am whole again . . ."

And now it was Conn's turn. He was told to place the broken halves of the sword upon the ground in front of the dragon. The latter carefully rearranged the pieces, muttering under his breath as Conn retreated to join us.

"Runes," murmured Snowy, "and a perfect alignment, north/south."

The dragon's tail lay straight behind him this time and the fire he breathed was red and hot, so hot that I began to perspire, and the sword itself glowed with a fire of its own. It seemed to me, through the shimmer of heat, that letters of fire appeared on the blade, but if so they were in symbols and words that I could not read. I could not have pinpointed the moment when the two pieces became one; suffice it to say that when the metal glowed as one piece the dragon suddenly roared for: "Snow! and plenty of it!" Conn and I ran outside, scooped up handfuls and placed them in heaps on the glowing metal. The snow hissed and melted as we watched, and then the blade of the sword gleamed blue and whole on the floor of the cave. Conn, in wonderment, bent to pick it up, but a claw fastened on his arm.

"Not yet, not yet: the metal still burns!"

"But the magic . . ." faltered Conn.

"No magic. Expert welding, that's all. Dragon-fire and snow."

It was many minutes before the hilt had cooled enough, even with more snow, but eventually Conn wrapped a piece of cloth around his right hand and raised the sword. Blue light still seemed to flow along the blade and it sang in the air as Conn swung, thrust, parried.

"Begorra, 'tis better than ever it was! A power in the hand with a mind of its own! Many thanks, Great Sky-Lizard, for giving me back my right arm!" and he bowed deeply to the beast, sword-point down, both hands folded over the hilt.

"Let's try the edge, then," said the dragon. "These pesky claws . . ."

The sun was much lower in the sky by the time his claws were trimmed to his satisfaction. I knew that it was now our turn and my heart seemed to bounce between my mouth and my boots as he beckoned us forwards. I had to carry Moglet, who by now was so terrified that I felt a warm trickle on my arm as I lifted her; Puddy and Corby shuffled forward slowly of their own volition, and the only one who seemed eager was Pisky, who was frisking about happily in his bowl.

"Going to see a dragon face to face, a thing even my revered great-grandparents never did; *their* parents, on the great-grandmother's side, had one drink from their pool, but they hid and were afraid. I'm not! This is a thing I am going to tell my great-great-grandchildren! Wish I could have something special to remember it by . . ."

So did I: instant oblivion.

"Now," said the dragon, as we arranged ourselves in a semicircle before him. "Now, did The Ancient, as you call him, tell you of the possible consequences of relinquishing these jewels?"

I nodded.

"You realize that you must give freely?"

"Yes."

"I cannot force you to give these jewels up—"

"We understand. But surely—"

"I could take them? No. You yourselves have bound them into a magic of your own, something never envisaged by the sorceress. She merely thought to hide them from me, knowing I should find them difficult to locate if she hid them within living flesh in five different locations. She did not reckon with the bond you forged between you, a bond so strong that, had she tried, she could not have taken them back."

"She—you—could kill us and rip them away . . ."

"No again. I could kill, she could have too, if you were separate, but even then the jewels would be worthless, dull and insignificant. You were given them to guard, whether you realized it or not, and a gift like that can only be returned freely, never forcibly taken."

"We—we have travelled many miles, not only to rid ourselves of our burdens, but to return that which is not ours to keep. We are not thieves: the jewels are yours, and we bring them to you through storm and fire, flood and cold, distance and dangers for precisely that reason. It was a joint decision," and I looked round at the others for confirmation.

"Agreed," said Puddy.

"Likewise," said Corby. "Mind you, I don't think I realized all that was entailed. Still . . ."

"I'm ready, ready, ready!" sang Pisky, happily. "Great privilege, meeting a dragon!"

"Don't want to," whispered Moglet. "Changed my mind . . . Frightened . . ."

"No, you're not!" I whispered back. "You want a nice painless paw, now don't you? So you can play and hunt properly? Surely my brave Moglet, who wasn't afraid of the wicked spider, won't balk at the last moment when all her friends are willing?"

"Are you?"

"Of course," I lied, more frightened than I could remember. "Of course!"

"That's all right then," said Moglet. "But you must hold me tight!"

The dragon had missed none of the exchange, I am sure, but he chose to ignore it. "You do realize, also, that you will regain your memories?" And he looked at me. "Not all at once, perhaps, but eventually you will remember where you were taken from, your past life, your home . . . And this may be more painful than anything else."

"We understand. But sometimes the torture of *not* knowing is worse. You should know that . . ." It was daring to speak thus to a dragon, but apart from a hiss and a wisp of smoke he did not respond.

I spoke again. "We are ready. How will you remove these stones?"

"Inspiration." I thought he meant one thing, but as it transpired he was being literal and physical rather then mental.

"Who will be first?"

We glanced at one another, then Puddy gamely dragged himself forward.

"I only hope it will not hurt too much," he said mildly. "Until now the headaches have been bad, but not unbearable. Will the hole in my head hurt worse?"

"I shall take care of that," said Snowy, stepping forward to stand beside the dragon. "My golden horn, now it has been restored, will heal your pain."

"Come," said the dragon, addressing Puddy. "Close your eyes and think of nothing save willing me back your burden, my treasure . . ."

The air grew soft, spring-like, and a greenish haze surrounded Puddy where he sat, feet planted firmly on the ground. The light grew brighter and it was now a sharp, metallic green and suddenly Puddy seemed impelled forwards towards the dragon's mouth. Without thinking I leapt forwards and grabbed him, found myself in the green haze and also in a visionless storm of wind sucking me forwards towards the dragon. Shutting my eyes I hung on grimly, my hands cupped round Puddy's frail body, and suddenly there was a pop! as if someone had squeezed a seaweed pod between finger and thumb, a tiny scream, and I was flat on my back still holding the toad, with Snowy bending over us both.

"There," he said. "It will soon be better . . ." and he touched Puddy with his horn.

"Sorry," said the dragon. "Took more breath than I thought. Been there near seven or eight years . . ."

I turned Puddy round anxiously, looking for the hole in his head, but there was only a shallow depression, through the thin, healing skin of which I could see a throbbing vein. "Are you all right, dear one?"

He considered, eyes shut. "Headache's gone. Head feels cold—sort of empty. Much lighter, though." He opened his eyes. "Bit like waking up out of hibernation: you feel stiff and cold for a while and have forgotten the taste of a meal. Get used to it. Much better, really; can't grumble . . ." He inclined his head to the dragon. "Thank you, Your Graciousness. My goodness! Was I carrying *that* around?"

Well might he express disbelief, for the greenish, muddy lump that I had grown so used to on his forehead now lay before the dragon, a shining, glittering clear green stone, sparkling like spring water at the edges, dark and deep as a forest in its depths. Lovingly the dragon curled his claws about it, turning it so that the low rays of the sun caught it with a sudden flash of green fire.

"You were," said the dragon. "An emerald from the cloudy heights of a rainforest on the other side of the world, where their gods demand a blood-sacrifice and the suns that shine from the gold they bear are as uncountable as the rays from this stone. Green it is as their forests, deep as their fears . . ."

I shivered, and looked at the jewel with new respect: it was not such as I would care to wear. No wonder it had given Puddy headaches.

"I'll go next," said Corby, after a doubtful look at Moglet, cowering again under my jacket. "Can't be so bad . . . 'Sides, I'm interested to see how long it takes before I'll remember how to fly."

"Well done, bird," said Snowy. "I'll be here to ease any hurt."

"I'd better hold you," I offered. "The pull is very strong, and we don't want you a dragon's dinner . . ."

I was only joking, but the dragon made a terrible frown and Snowy hastened to intervene. "The inhalation, the drawing of the burden, it worries them: the child but makes jest to lessen the fear . . ."

The dragon said nothing but settled down, elbow-joints protruding. I sat about six feet away, holding Corby's wing spread with one hand, the other binding him tight to my breast. "Close your eyes," I whispered. "Remember I've got you . . ."

The dragon intoned: "Concentrate, bird; will me your burden, my jewel . . ."

"Gawd knows I do," said Corby. "'Tain't no use to me, Your Worship . . ."

This time the drawing-power was greater, and I found the hair blowing forward round my mask as I hung on grimly to my friend, whose feathers were pulled forward as in a gale. His claws were fastened tight in my drawn-up knees and I had to clench my jaw to stop from flinching. Now the light was a burning, scorching blue, and before I closed my eyes from its intensity it seemed as though great waves were rearing their foaming crests and threatening to engulf us. Suddenly as we hung on there was a crack! as of a breaking branch and once again I was on my back on the cave floor, Corby by my side in a squawking, tangled heap.

Snowy stepped forward and stroked the injured wing with his horn, the bare featherless joint pathetically pink, and slowly the desperate fluttering stopped.

I lay eye to eye with the exhausted bird. "How does it feel, dear one?"

He considered, getting to his feet and bringing the injured wing gingerly to his side, then stretching it again. "No pain. Stiff, but it's getting easier every minute. Look!" and he flapped the wing—an awkward effort it was true, but still the first movement of the sort he had been able to make since I knew him. "Thanks again, Your Worship!" and he bowed to the dragon.

We looked over at the sapphire. Unlike the emerald it lay beside, rectangular and deep, the stone was oval and shallow, yet a blue more dense than I had ever seen. It was deeper than the deepest sea, yet on its edges was a lighter, sparkling fringe, like waves upon a shore. Now the great beast turned it in his claws, murmuring lovingly: "A fine journey I had for you, my friend: across the warm oceans, skimming the little islands that rose like pustules on the pocked sea; but I found you where others had hidden you, didn't I, left to rot as you were with the other jewels. But you were the prize, my beautiful one, as blue as the eyes of the dead who buried you . . ."

I gazed at the jewel with new respect: dead man's treasure, not such as I would wish to wear. No wonder it had twisted Corby's wing.

"And now," said the dragon. "The little cat and her diamond . . ."

"No, no, no, *no*!" howled Moglet, burying her head into my armpit, "I'm *afraid*! It's going to *hurt* . . ."

"Only a little, I promise," I said, comforting her trembling body. "Ask the others, ask Puddy and Corby: was it very bad, you two?"

"Not unbearable, I suppose," said Puddy. He looked very wrinkly and thin. "More unpleasant than anything."

"Felt for a moment as though my wing was coming out by the roots," admitted Corby, "but the feeling didn't last long." I noticed for the first time how grey the feathers were above his beak. Strange how fear sharpened the senses, for I was afraid, just like Moglet, yet for her sake hid it.

"There you are, you see?" I exhorted. "And Pisky's not afraid . . ."

"Then why can't he go first?" demanded Moglet. "I don't mind."

"But I do!" interrupted the dragon. "You are next, cat, but you must be willing."

"She is, she is!" I said. "You are really, you know, dear one: it's just that, like me, you don't like the unknown. I'm next, you know, and I can't get rid of this—this dreadful stomachache till you loose your burden."

"It's very deep," said Moglet, showing me her paw. "It'll hurt much more than the others . . ."

"Then it's very brave of you to agree," I said hastily, sensing her weaken. "You must show me how to be courageous."

"I wouldn't really mind keeping it," she said. "With you to carry me round. Still . . . If you say your stomach hurts most of the time?"

"Oh, it does!" I assured her, though at the moment it felt both numb and tingly at the same time.

"Right!" said Moglet and, shutting her eyes, she stretched out her burdened paw in the general direction of the dragon, while fastening the claws of the other three firmly in my sleeve.

"You are sure? You will me freely your burden, my stone?"

"Yes . . ."

The dragon gave her no time to reconsider. A roaring, sparkling wind surrounded us and my back bent further in its hunch as I tried to step no nearer the dragon. Stars wheeled and danced around us, there was a blinding flash as of a veritable avalanche of snow falling about our ears and, before I had to close my eyes against the unbearable aching of the light, I saw a rainbow that spanned the distance between Moglet's paw and the dragon's mouth. She howled, an awful sound, her claws tore trails of blood from the outer side of my wrist so that I nearly cried out too. There was a long ripping sound, the light died behind my clenched eyelids, I was on the floor again and Snowy was bending to Moglet's paw and my lacerated flesh.

"Better now?"

The dragon had three stones now and the latest, Moglet's burden, sparkled and spiked with a thousand coloured lights as he turned it in his claws. "A rare flight that was, the sands burning bright and the sun a molten dagger in one's back. They laboured to bring wealth out of the depths, they died in the darkness that this might have light . . ."

I shuddered: I would not willingly wear such. No wonder Moglet hadn't been able to put paw to ground.

But she was dabbing at my face. "Let go of me, I want to try it!" Already the healing hole was closing up, the blackberry pads drawing together. She seemed heavier, sleeker, pain now forgotten in the space of two breaths. I set her down, and gingerly at first but then with increasing confidence she set down the once-burdened paw on the ground. "Look! Look!" she cried with delight. "It's better! Soon be quite well . . ."

"Now you, little wanderer," said the dragon. "You are ready?"

No, I wasn't. Suddenly gripped by irrational fears I sank down again. It was not only the thought of more pain, sharp and quick-over though it might be, it was also the familiarity of the burden itself, like an aching tooth that, however irksome, is still an understood part of one till removed. Most of all, I think, it was the certainty that once I lost it and regained both health and memory, paradoxically this latter might prove a greater burden than the burden itself. I was afraid to be given a future so sudden, so different. Better the devil one knew—

"Come on, Thing darling," said Conn. "I've watched you bravely hold the others, now it's your turn to be held . . ." and the words—my name clear and "darling"—rang so loud in my ears that body was all unresisting as he reached down and lifted me to my feet, kneeling behind me on one knee, one arm across my thighs, one across my breast. He pressed me back against his chest and his breath was warm on my cheek. "Courage, girl, courage: 'twill soon be over and I'm here, your Conn is here . . ."

My Conn! I felt at least one joint of my backbone click as I tried to straighten. Without further hesitation I pulled my jerkin up with one hand, my trews down with the other and pre-empted the dragon's question.

"Yes, yes; I give freely my burden, your treasure. Take it, take it away quickly, please!"

I was staring straight at the dragon who seemed to grow immensely tall and then there was fire all about us and toppling towers and men and women crying out in fear. The fire blazed stronger and there was a tearing, twisting pain in my guts that I could not bear. I tried to bring down my hands to cover the agony but somehow Conn was preventing me, and I screamed. With a sound like tearing a snail from its shell, but horribly magnified, I felt my burden leave me and there was Snowy's horn to numb the pain and take away the sickness. Strangely the greatest discomfort was Conn's arm across my breasts, which suddenly felt full and tender. I straightened up one crick! more, drew together my clothes and turned, for an instant, to bury my head in Conn's shoulder. He patted my back and released me.

The ruby lay in the dragon's claw and burnt cool as he turned it lovingly. "The temple held it dear, but it was housed in a heathen idol that crumbled to the touch. The priests in their robes cried desecration and the temple dancers fled into the night as it was drawn from their grasp . . ."

I shuddered, and the stone seemed to wink back evilly at me; if I had known what I carried I would have cut it from my flesh like a canker. No wonder it had hurt . . .

"Are you ready, O King of Fish? You I have left till the last because the burden you bear is probably the greatest, my last and most beautiful gain . . ."

That muddy pebble?

"Of course, Lord of the Clouds, Master of the Skies; all my life I have wished to be acquainted with you and your brethren. It had been my ambition to mount the Dragon Falls that I might join you in the skies, but now that can never be. I shall be content to see you a little closer, perhaps to touch fin to scale. Pray, Thing dear, move my bowl nearer . . . so. It will do." In his exuberance bubbles broke from either side of the burden in his mouth. I knelt by his side, my finger in the water.

"You are sure?"

"Sure? Why, of course I am sure! I have been carrying this stone safe for a Dragon-Master and now I yield it with eagerness, with pride!"

The dragon bent closer and I flinched. But he did not notice.

"Here, little brother, take a closer look. Look your fill . . ."

For a moment dragon and fish touched, nose to nose as Pisky rose from the water. He looked so small, so defenceless, so like a gulp for breakfast that I leant forward, ready to snatch him away from danger, but he turned on me.

"No, Thing, no! This is *my* day, *my* moment that I have waited for so long and you must not spoil it!"

"I was only—"

"There is no need. We understand one another." It was the dragon who spoke, but the words might just as well have been Pisky's.

"He is so small . . . the wind of withdrawal . . ." I faltered.

"He is stronger than you think. Watch . . . It is given freely, and you are cognizant of the results?"

"It is," said Pisky. "I am. But spare my friends the snails; slow and unintelligent they may be, but excellent privy-servants. And prolific, I hope."

The air grew thick, like the mist that streams between the trees at shoulder-height on a late-autumn morning; then it was as if the moon rose on this same mist, silvering it until it glowed and shimmered with an unearthly light. I saw clear water running, waves tumbling, spray mounting the rocks, horses of sea-foam . . .

There was no sound when the pearl left Pisky's mouth: it rose like a little moon and hung between them like a sigh. Then the magic disappeared and Pisky sank back in his bowl, his mouth a pained O of surprise and hurt. Swiftly golden horn touched golden mouth and he sank to the bottom, the snails crowding close for comfort.

The dragon had a huge pearl between his claws—how its sheer size must have hurt poor Pisky!—but he was holding it with reverence, for it still glowed and shimmered and shone like a moon behind thin cloud.

"A hard struggle it was for you, my most precious of all; searching fjords and creeks, inlets and rivers; I glimpsed you beneath tossed waters and running streams; saw you in the reflection of the moon on swollen rivers and high tarns; you were the winter sun on ice, a wraith of summer stars; I tasted you on tumbling stones and in the thickness of reeds; sensed you in the flash of scales, the turn of fin; always you called to me and at last you came of your own free will when I had despaired . . ."

The pearl glowed, and it was a stone I, anyone, would have been glad to touch, admire, hold in one's hand, bear on one's breast . . .

"And now," said the dragon, "it is almost time for me to go. But, before I do, I would thank you all again for returning my jewels, my treasure. Because of you, because of your honesty and determination, I am now a Master-Dragon, as the little fish so truly observed." He bowed gravely to each one of us in turn. "Now, I must try my wings: if you will excuse me?" He went to the mouth of the cave and down the steps flexing his bony, leathery, creaky wings, which gusted a powdering of cinder-tasting snow back into the cave. I gazed at the ring of glowing jewels lying on the cave floor and wondered at their gathering, their binding, their loosing. Lying there like that, now that they were back with the dragon, they still seemed to have a magic of their own, a kinship; they seemed almost like a ring of animals who will turn into a tight circle to meet a common enemy, horns lowered and rear protected against wolf or bear . . . Like us, when we bore them—

There was a humph!! of flame from the dragon, a series of short, staccato bursts from his rear, as one who has dined too exclusively on pease-porridge, and then he turned to where we watched him, smuts on his face.

"A trial flight . . . I think the Lord of the Carp would like to see my world; after all, had he stayed in our country he might well have climbed the Dragon-Falls. This will only be a substitute, of course, but I think he would enjoy it. Would you be so kind as to accompany us and carry his bowl?"

He was looking at me, but I wasn't quite sure what he wanted. Pisky popped his head out of his bowl, speaking like someone who has had a tooth pulled.

"I should like it above all, Thing dear—please?"

"Yes, but I—" I suddenly realized what was expected. Oh, no! I couldn't, I couldn't! I looked at Snowy, and he nodded.

"It will be all right. You will be safe. I promise."

So, awkwardly, stiffly, still hunched, I clambered onto the dragon's back, Pisky's bowl clutched in my arms, and lay down, my face to the leathery scales, my heart thudding.

"Hold tight!" There was a slithering followed by a sudden sickening lurch. I opened my eyes and my mouth to yell as I saw the mountainside slipping away from me in a sideways slide. My breath was snatched away by the wind, my face froze and my cheeks blew inward with the sudden rush of air. There was another lurch that left my stomach behind somewhere and then we steadied and the mountain slid by.

"Sorry about that: trailing-edge muscles weren't working." I could only just hear the words, for the roar of wind and wings in my ears. My eyes were shut once more and would have stayed so but for a little bubbling voice beside my left ear.

"Isn't it beautiful? Just like being in a bigger, lighter bowl. Look, far down below are the weeds and the stony bottom, around us the waters rushing over our fins, and above the deep bowl of air beyond the rim of everything . . . Hold me up, Thing, that I may see and remember!"

"Let the King of the Carp see!" said the dragon, and such was the command in his voice that I obeyed at once, sitting up and holding Pisky's bowl high in my hands, though my fingers were half-frozen: I wound his string round my wrist to make sure he didn't fall. The rest of me was warm enough, for the huge reptile now exuded warmth, and the inside of my calves were, indeed, becoming uncomfortably hot. But all this was forgotten as I looked about and saw what Pisky saw, but with human understanding.

Below, so far as to take away fear, lay the village we had come from. It was dusk down there, for I could see the little twinkling lights of rush and candle; higher the sun still shone on snowy slopes, but to the west great purple shadows showed glen and canyon as they crept forward like a massed pack of wolves towards the lamb's-fleece snow of the nearer slopes. Black sticks of winter forest covered the lower slopes and iced streams lay like saliva among the black-fanged rocks: but it was all remote, like sand-houses made by children's hands and I was curious, but not fearful. Nearer, the mountains stood like sentinels and I saw great orange fires burst from the dying sun, so that it seemed that pustules of fever opened on a great sore.

No bird flew as high as we and all was silent save for the pumping of the dragon's fire-bellows, a gentle thrumming, and the whistle of the wind past my ears. I remembered my swim with the seal: as Pisky said, it was like, very like, an ocean of sky.

With a creak of wings we altered course, and once again I felt the cold air buffet my body and, too soon, we were again at the mouth of the cave. A sudden, jolting landing, a slurp of water from Pisky's bowl, and Conn's arms were lifting me, bowl and all, from the dragon's back.

"You all right, Thingummy?"

I nodded and clung to him, my legs strangely weak. As in a dream I watched the dragon pick up his jewels one by precious one and place them in a pouch of skin beneath his jaw, lastly his precious pearl, which he rolled around his forked tongue for a moment before placing it with the others. He was no longer a blue dragon, he was a pearl-pink dragon, and even the long whiskers on his jaw curled and vibrated as if fired with his new vitality. He gazed around the cave, and then at us, and in his eyes was a remoteness, as if we and the cave were discarded bones and his eyes were on another prey.

"That is all, then. Farewell to my imprisonment, and farewell to you, my deliverers."

With a scrabble of impatient claws upon stone he moved once more toward the opening of the cave.

"Wait!" called Conn. "The gold—the silver—you have left it!" He gestured to the shelves round the cave.

"Keep it: it is yours. You deserve it. The jewels were what mattered . . ." and he was gone, launching himself in a clatter of wings into the sunset.

The wind of his passing scuffled the dust in a spiral over the spot where his jewels had lain. When it settled there was no sign of their presence. It was as if they had never been.

Interlude
Dragon-Sky

In the country of his upbringing they would have recognized the special corkscrewing rocket-rise with the sideways twist, but all the watchers from the cave and the village below could say afterwards was that the dragon ascended like a reversed shooting star with a noise like twenty hungry bears.

A handful of rustic peasants and the seven weary travellers were the only witnesses of the most extraordinary and accomplished display of free—as opposed to compulsory—figures of dragon skyrobatics since the illustrious Master of the Chrysanthemum had given the Millennium Display for the Many-Titled Emperor-of-the-Thousand-Palaces five centuries past and three oceans away . . .

The dragon swam in the air as if it were water and he an otter, a shark, a seal, a fish. He used the air-currents and therms as an acrobat would use bars and trampolines and springboard, and all the while he played with his great pearl as though it were a ball, an essential part of his act, tossing it in the air so that it described milky arcs, letting it fall a thousand feet and diving like a thunderbolt beneath to catch it again.

For what seemed an hour, but might have been no longer than ten to fifteen minutes, the great beast played like a child in the nursery with its first toy, then as the sun dipped to touch the horizon with its burning belly and as the eastering shadows threw their arms across hill and valley alike, he snatched his pearl from the sky, a pearl now pink as an opened rose, stood on his spade-tail for a heart-stopping moment then clapped his wings together like a vengeful cormorant and dived the depth of the mountain towards the village below, the wind of his passing creating a down-draught like a thousand flocking geese at marshing-time. In a flash of fire he incinerated their alarm beacon and burnt the easterly copse.

The villagers cowered together, the men cursing and shaking impotent fists at the fast-retreating sky-climber, the women flapping useless aprons. Only the children cheered and waved. In their maturity, when visiting other villages, the story would crystallize into legend. They would tell of the thunder-crack of his passing, of a red dragon who soared over their impossibly green fields, until the telling became a symbol recognized by all who listened to a tale: an inspiration, a banner, under which princelings would rise to repel invaders, ordinary men would fight and fall, and a usurper unite and divide . . .

But the Master-Dragon's mind had turned from them all—the past imperfect, the passing present. Taking his bearings from the first stars that winked from the eastern sky, he wiped his memory free of time, of disappointment, of frustrations, tucked away his pearl with the other jewels in the pouch beneath his jaw, spun thrice on his spade-tail and then sang his farewell song.

To those watching and listening, dodging the mini-avalanches and fires set off by his rejuvenation, watching stone clatter down the slopes, regarding with dismay the collapsing huts that disintegrated like imploding puffballs, all they heard was an enormous clash and rattle as of giant metal plates tumbled together, a ringing of bells so huge their peals were as sound-sight, ripples of torturing light-noise in a stone-tossed lake—but to the dragon the cacophony was the best music he had ever made, a soaring passion of release from bondage, a paean of praise.

An ascending rocket-burst of flame, crackling in the still air, a rapid climb to five, ten, twenty thousand feet; a moment's hesitation when dying fires fell like shattered stars to the mountains beneath, and then the Master-Dragon shook free and headed east for Home.

The Loosing

Awakening

In spring the young shoots of corn struggle hesitantly from their blanket of earth and poke wary green heads up into the unfamiliar air; too soon, and the frosts nip them black; too late, and they are drowned in the shadows of their bigger brethren, starved of light and nourishment, and shrivel and die. Just as I, the new Thing, was not sure whether I had emerged from the darkness of forgetting to the lightness of an Inbolc or a Beltane. At first I was ill, tossing and turning in fever, waking briefly to moments of lucidity. But before I could reorientate myself, grab hold of life and become better, back I would slide into a haunted black vault of the mind where hope ran down the mazed tunnels of thought, knocking in vain on doors that would not open, with the hounds of Hell baying behind.

They said afterwards it was seven days I was unconscious, sent back into the earth to remember the seed from whence I sprang, but it could have been seven hours or seven years for all I knew. Conn was kept away from me for fear of contagion, for it seemed my skin sloughed away in great strips with the fever. They took away my clothes and burnt them.

When I woke up at last clear-headed, starving hungry, I felt the cold air touch my face with inquisitive fingers: when I put up my own I found my mask had gone, and panicked. Throwing the shift I was dressed in up over my head I screamed: "Where is it? Where is my mask?"

"There now, dearie, what a to-do!" Strong, warm hands pulled up the covers, covered my hands with hers. "No need to take on so! Come, take your hands from your face—"

"They'll see my ugliness! *He* will see . . ."

"Now, then! Ugliness is a state of mind, and there's none wrong with that face of yours that fresh air and sunlight and a little extra feeding-up wouldn't cure. Got eyes like piss-holes in snow, you have . . . Now, then: that's better! Let Old Nan (what has been chosen to care for you because she's born twenty and buried all but three, survived four husbands and the phlegm and the sores and the runs and vomits and scabs) let her comb out that nice, thick hair of yours and then Megan—she's the youngest, touched a mite some would say, but a grand girl with the sheep—she will fetch some broth and bread. Been told to make a fuss of you, I has, by that nice tall fellow with the sword. Soon as I lets him know you're better he's to come and see you, he says, and all those animals you brought . . ."

Unlike most chatterers her actions were suited to her words and she had me combed and tidied and fed in no time at all, all the while her strangely accented voice, hovering like a salmon in leap on the vowels until you sometimes wondered whether she would ever reach the smooth waters of the consonants, burbled on like a busy brook, soothing and stimulating at the same time. At my insistence she fashioned me another mask, from kidskin, although I could see she was bewildered by the need. In truth her face was so seamed and pocked that it was difficult to identify any features, except for toothless mouth and red nose, so perhaps my physical deficiencies were not so strange to her after all. I made up some tale about being handfasted to Conn, but having made a vow not to uncover my face until we were wed. This made sense to her, full of superstition like all country folk, who must explain away disaster and joy, gain or loss somehow. Their "little people," for instance, seemed to have a hand in everything, from birth to death; and they seemed to prefer these household gods to any other, although Conn found a deserted Christian shrine in the woods to say his prayers by.

Once my mask was on I couldn't wait to see the others again, and indeed the next time the door was left open Moglet was on the bed in a flash, and enthusiastically kneading my chest.

"Look! it's much better . . ." She turned over her damaged paw and now there was only the smallest hollow and increased width among the pink and black pads. "Are you better, too?"

"Been a bit worried about you," said Puddy, from under the bed. "Thought you were . . . Nice to see you. My head is much improved."

"Caw! Bleedin' cold out there!" said Corby, actually managing a flapping ascent to the rafters, and landing safely. "Best off where you are . . ."

"Look at me, look at me!" bubbled Pisky, borne in by Conn. "Twice the size I was already, they say, and eating better all the time. Sir Knight says that if I don't stop I shall have to have a bigger bowl, and the snails are complaining at the extra work—"

Conn sat down on the bed and took my hand. "How are you, Thingummy? We were all worried about you, but they said it was only a bad fever. Still, you've been away from us a whole week, and had it been but one day longer I should have insisted, infection or no, on taking a turn at minding you. How's the back?"

"The back?" I had genuinely forgotten my other deformity with the trauma of the mask. So much had happened in my feverish tossings and turnings, happened, that is, to memory and understanding, that I had had no recall of my twisted and bent spine. Now I sat up as best I could and eased back my shoulders. There was a little crick! as another knob in my spine straightened its alignment and I found that my eyes were on a level a good six inches higher. With Conn seated so near I could look almost straight into those kind, concerned brown eyes.

I saw him glance down in surprise at my front. "Why, you've—" He stopped, confused.

"Got a proper front," said Moglet happily, and pushed painfully against my budding breasts.

"Er—it's better, I think," I said, and I pulled away my hand, that had gone hot and sticky with embarrassment. I pulled up the covers to my chin. "Where's Snowy?"

"Here, dear one," and he stepped daintily through the doorway. A shaft of late sunlight followed him in and ran in admiration down the beautiful spirals of his golden horn and over the waves of his luxuriant mane and tail. "I only come in the village when there are few about, for I reckon a dragon-memory is enough for these simple folk, without having to get used to a unicorn as well. I can make them unsee me for a while, but it is more convenient to stay out of sight in the forest. Glad to see you are recovering . . ."

"But—isn't it awfully cold out there?"

He lifted his head in an unconsciously arrogant gesture. "Unicorns don't catch cold," he said.

I suppose we were there for about another three or four weeks. Gradually I grew stronger in body, although my mind was still full of darkness. When I got up they brought me woman's clothes, for another thing had happened that had sent me cowering to the floor in terror. Until Snowy explained. I had spent the day in bed, with intervals on the stool at the side, and had been feeling grumpy and unsettled all morning with a vague stomach-ache, then suddenly, as I stood up to practise walking a few steps, I was seized with one of the old pains I had thought gone forever. There was no one with me, as Old Nan was busy baking, Conn had gone hunting with Corby, and the others were holed up somewhere in the warm. The pain hit me again and of a sudden a bright scarlet plop! of blood hit the floor from beneath my shift and then another. In terror I flung open the door and rushed out into the snow, instinctively heading for the forest.

"Snowy, oh Snowy! The pain's come back, worse than ever, and there's *blood . . .*"

Another moment and he was there, his warm breath on my face, his mane sheltering us both as he bent and snuffed at me gently.

"No, dear girl, it hasn't, not in the way you think. Listen to me . . ." and he told me how I had become a woman, and that what was happening to me now was something I had been waiting for during the seven long years of the stone's captivity. "That is why it hurts so much: it means you are catching up on all those years in one go. Now you are girl-child no longer." He looked sad and I remembered—so many things to remember!—that unicorns appear only to young virgins, never to mature women, and I suddenly understood a whole lot more.

He bent his head and touched my stomach with his healing horn. "There: the pain is gone, and never will be so bad again."

I kissed him, suddenly shy. "I won't . . . I don't mean to . . ."

"I know. I shall be with you till you don't need me any more . . . Now, come: sit on my back and I will bear you to the hut, otherwise you will freeze to death!"

The pain disappeared, but when Snowy turned once more to return to his voluntary exile I noticed a small spot of blood on his otherwise flawless back, like the stain of a trodden berry . . .

At last the snow started to slide from roof and rick, the sun stayed longer with us, fingernails of ice fell with a tinkle from the swelling buds in the trees, and it was time to say goodbye to the village, for we all felt we should move on with the lightening days, though where we had no clear idea. Conn gave the headman three gold coins, a princely sum, for their care of us. He also told him that the dragon had left some treasure in the cave for them—silver and bronze armour, plates and cups (we had the gold coin)—as recompense for burnt thatch and general damage. I could see they could scarcely wait for the snows to melt. The coins and the anticipated treasure were celebrated in our farewell party, which included a roasted steer, mock dragon-fights and much mead, so that it was with a thick head that I turned for my last look at where our quest had ended. The villagers stood a quarter-mile away, still watching us go. I waved once more and then glanced up at the Black Mountain. I could not see the cave, and of a sudden clouds from a warmer air frothed and spilt over the top like scum from a mess of new-boiling bones until all was hidden from view.

The road ahead lay downhill. Once again we heard the tentative song of birds, buds were thick and sticky, and catkins hung like lamb's tails from the willow and everywhere there was promise and hope. Conn sang and the others grew strong and fat, but my heart still lay heavy and full of dread, for I had grown up.

Every day fresh memories arrived with the softening of the days. Sometimes I felt as though my heart would break, for I now knew who I was, where I had come from, some, not all yet, of what had happened in the twelve years before the witch abducted me. I remembered, too, what had befallen my parents and wept the inner tears of one who could only mourn too late. Conn kept glancing at me anxiously but I could not tell him, not yet. And there were the others: I began to appreciate fully what my "release" meant now for, as The Ancient had predicted, whole and free again, they spent far less time with me and I found my eyes and ears and touch and taste and smell not understanding them as before, as if a veil lay between us.

I think perhaps I realized more was to come, so I was not unduly surprised when one spring day we found ourselves in a countryside of rolling downs and there, sitting on a rock as coolly as if he had only wandered a little way ahead five minutes ago, was The Ancient.

Part of me wanted to run and embrace him, part to refute his very presence, to blame him in some obscure fashion for my private world of misery, so I stood and did nothing as the others crowded round him. Conn's sword, Snowy's horn, Puddy's forehead, Corby's wing, Moglet's paw, Pisky's mouth were all exhibited and admired: he did shoot one piercing glance at Conn's armour and then at me, but had the sense not to make any remark.

That night we spent round his campfire and ate better than we had for weeks. The only question he raised was, where were we bound? Had we thought of this? Yes. Come to any decision? No. It seemed everyone thought everyone else was leading the way . . .

At last Conn voiced all our thoughts. "We—we all thought there must be something else. What, we did not know. Perhaps it was you?"

"Not me," said The Ancient, taking off his red-and-white striped hat, decorated with shells, and scratching his head. "I'm merely here to see the fun . . ."

"The fun!" I exploded, exasperated at last into coherent speech. "What fun do you think it has been for us? Where have you been, that you think that cold and hunger and fear and illness constitute *fun*? What makes you think that the traumas, the tiredness, the soul-searchings, have been *fun*? You're just a stupid, uncaring, flippant old man who is concerned with nothing but his vicarious pleasures, and has merely learnt enough so-called 'magic' to think himself immune from us mortal creatures! You are complacent, narrow-minded, cold—" I ran out of words.

The others, except Snowy who merely looked amused, stared at me in varying degrees of horror.

"Magician," reminded Puddy.

"Bit strong," added Corby.

"Special case," remarked Moglet.

"I really don't think—" Puddy.

"Hang on, Thing dear, moderate it a bit," from Conn.

More or less all together.

"No," I said. "I won't moderate or anything! I meant it!" and burst into tears. Huffily pushing them all aside, I retired to a corner, wrapped myself in my cloak and pretended to go to sleep.

The next morning I arose very early and wandered off among the dunes to where the land sloped away into a haze of forest and fields. It had turned cold again, so the streams were marked by twisting snakes of mist that followed the waters and trees held a shadow-self of clear earth beneath their branches and the rest was tipped and branched and swathed with fingers of frost. I shivered.

"I'm sorry," said The Ancient. "Forgive me, Fleur?"

I remembered what he had called me before. "You knew . . . All the time?"

"Of course. And now you do, too?"

"Most of it. Some of it won't come yet."

"It has made you sad . . . And bitter."

Of course it had. To lose your parents, home, nurse, childhood all in one day, to lose your memory for seven years and then to remember everything at once, more or less, was like being forced to swallow huge doses of bitter herb-medicine. I felt disorientated and most of all, alone. Remembering nothing, I had had my friends: the comradeship, their love, and my passion for Conn. Now it was all coloured differently but, in spite of my new knowledge I was not sure who I was, what I felt, where I should be . . .

"I warned you."

"Yes, I know: but I didn't know it would hurt so much!"

"Don't forget that your friends are in exactly the same boat."

"The same?"

"Of course the same. As if it were yesterday. Your cat now remembers the home she was stolen from, the warm fire, the loving mother; the toad remembers his pond, the crow his treed brethren and the fish his capture and long travel from abroad while his kin died one by one in neglect . . . Don't you think that they, too, have regrets and memories? Are you unique in suffering just because you are a human being?"

"But they didn't say . . ."

"Of course not. You've been ill. You recover to look like a wet Lugnosa! What did you expect? You have always been something special to them, something that to them was better, more able to cope—of course they are uneasy when you appear to go to pieces."

"But we no longer talk as we used to . . ."

"I told you that would gradually go as well."

"But I don't *want* it to!"

"You said a lot of things last night that were true—about me being immune from reality, from mortality—well, I'll say the same to you, but in reverse. You *are* mortal, and being so must accept that mortality, with all it implies. You wished to escape from a painful and confining enchantment, but now you refuse to accept the responsibilities that go with the release!" His tone softened. "Being a human is hurtful at times but it can also be wonderful, more wonderful than the immortals can ever experience."

"How can that be? You have life everlasting, if you want it—"

"For that very reason! Quite apart from life itself becoming boring when one has lived it two, three, four times as long as anybody else, it is rather like always having enough money to buy whatever you desire. If you can always have what you want, on demand, it ceases to be desirable. In the end there is nothing left to experience." He frowned, and his look dared me to probe further.

"But do you—can you—never die?"

"Oh, yes. But only by our own choice, by our own hand. There is another way, but that involves the Powers I told you of once. They are stronger than all."

"The powers of good and evil, you mean?"

"I have told you, there are no such things. There *is* Power, there *are* so-called Forces. They are like—oh, like a team of strong horses, harnessed and ready for a driver. It is up to their user, whether he or she directs it to plough a field or ride down innocent bystanders." He nodded. "Mmm."

"I still don't quite see . . ." I hesitated. "This question of immortality: surely the promise of a life eternal, dependent on your own decision to terminate, must far outweigh our little lives, that are bound by the certainty of death?"

"That very thought of mortality adds spice to what you do, don't you see? A summer's day is all the more beautiful for the knowledge that storm could blight the blossoms and frost surely will; a child is all the more precious for the perils of growing-up and the winter of old age; love is all the more glorious for its very ephemerality, the pain of parting or disillusion." He frowned. "But perhaps worse than this is when immortal loves mortal . . ." His face darkened, and all at once in his place was a grim warrior standing: illusion, for the image passed and he was once again an untidy old man. "Ask Snowy . . ."

"Snowy?"

"He will tell you one day, perhaps."

"I don't understand . . ."

"You will, sooner or later."

My mind went off on another tack, perhaps inspired by all this talk of love. "And that's another thing: when I was—was hunched and miserable it didn't matter that I loved Conn, because he was so far out of reach. It seemed right. But now—" and I gestured to my nearly upright stance "—now I am nearly a respectable woman (except for my face, of course). I find I want more, desire more, *need* more. When it was impossible I could bear it: now, I can't!"

"So that's it . . ."

"No! Not *just* that—"

He grinned at me.

"It's *not*!"

"To me it's simple. Then, you loved like an idealistic twelve-year-old; now you are nineteen and a woman grown. At twelve one is allowed to worship from afar, because one's thoughts don't usually encompass anything physical, real . . . Now you are suddenly grown, the passions you feel are different. You have missed the years from twelve to now that would have made you someone's lover, wife, mistress, and now it is all coalescing into an unbearable desire that you think—"

"Know!"

"—cannot be satisfied, because under that mask of yours lies ugliness."

"Right."

"Wrong!"

I stared at him. "What do you mean—'wrong'?"

But he seemed to change his mind, became a grumpy old man again: even his hands started to dither and fuss among his brooches and fastenings till he seemed the very dotard I knew he was not.

I persisted. "What do you mean 'wrong'? My body may have changed, I can see and feel that, but my face hasn't. I know: I feel it all over every day when no one's looking, hoping against hope, but it feels exactly the same as it did when we lived with—Her."

He steepled his fingers and considered me under eyebrows like thatches. "What you need—what you all need—I reckon, is a bathe in the Waters of Truth."

"And where and what are they?"

"They are in the centre of the world that you know, and they have the gift of clearing your mind, making you see things as they really are."

I suppose I must have sounded wearily disbelieving. "And just how do we find these—these magical waters?"

He snorted crossly. "In order to get you lot off my back and out of my hair I shall lead you there myself. Right away!"

The Loosing

The Waters of Truth

We travelled by the Secret Ways, the paths known only to sage and faery. Under hedge, by forest path, through tunnels of ancient, gnarled wood, once through caves; and all that while we met none others save shadows, a disembodied greeting, a stirring of windless branches and a bending of grasses, laughter, the sound of dissonant harebells, and yet we knew They crowded us through our journeying, watching, guarding, guiding, enfolding us in their hands so soft we could not see . . . They? The spirits that man has driven from his world to hidden fastnesses among the rocks, the dells, the streams that wind through underground caverns. Listening to their laughter, feeling their mischievous hands I could understand and yet regret man with his earthy, clumsy honesty—but did not Time itself lay aside these Earlier Ones, for They were children of another world than ours, too delicate to survive in ours?

They loved Snowy, climbed on his back for rides, plaited his mane in the night, garlanded him with faery flowers none could see, but picture from their evocative scent. They tweaked The Ancient's beard unmercifully and rode unseen on his shoulders, and he was as indulgent as a father to his children. They pressed fruit I had never tasted and could not see against my lips till the juices ran down my chin, and yet when I opened my eager mouth they were gone, skin, flesh and seeds so that I stood there like a gaping idiot and their laughter tinkled in my ears and I could smell cowslips and rain.

We walked, rode, slept, talked, ate and drank like any other travellers, but of that time I remember less than any other. I do not even remember how long it took, faery time I suppose; all I know was that we left the dragon's village in early spring and it was near the summer of Beltane when we came to our destination. Like all things to do with The Ancient there was a certain dream-like quality about the whole thing, with none of the wear and tear associated with ordinary journeyings.

One evening we couched on soft moss in the forest, the next morning we burst through the thinning trees, breasted a soft green slope starred with day's-eye and lion's teeth, speed-you-well and bright-eyes, and there beneath us lay a secret valley. Behind us the deciduous forest, to the north steep crags, to the east a forest of pines, to the south downs melting misty blue with distance and cuddling a lazy river in their arms. Below us a thin cascade fell like a veil from the crags above onto dark rocks and down to a deep pool of water surrounded by banks stained with flowers. A rainbow arced the falls and from where we stood we could hear the birds sing.

As if in a dream we descended the steep sides of the valley almost as though we were floating, and dropped down by the water and drank deep. And fell asleep, fast asleep, all of us, without dream.

When we awoke the sun was still rising in the sky and we had no way of knowing whether we had slept five minutes or a whole day and night. We stretched, yawned and greeted each other with smiles as if this were one day when all was right with the world. A fire smoked lazily and there were thin pancakes and honey, a mess of vegetable, tiny strawberries and The Ancient in a sparkling robe of purple with golden glints, sleeves rolled up to the elbows, dishing out our breakfast. I moved in a daze, sticky and replete, my nostrils filled with strange, soft smells, my ears full of the rush and fall of water, the song of a blackbird—"veni, vidi, vici, Dubree, Dubree" (whoever he was)—my body warm, my eyes closed against the flicker of sunlight on water. I opened them to roll over on to my stomach and watched an ant climb a stalk of grass until it tilted with its weight against another, which it scaled, busy and full of purpose. My eyes closed again—

There was a slap on my rump that had me leaping to my feet with a yowl of indignation.

"What did you do that for?"

"You were asleep."

"Wasn't! I was just—resting my eyes."

"Sounded like snores to me," said The Ancient, nursing his right hand. "'Sides, that hurt me as much as it did you. What in the world have you got back there that is so hard?"

"My knife."

"You don't need that now."

"You never know . . . Anyway, why did you want me awake? To wash the pots? Can't you just wave a wand, or something?"

He ignored my flippancy. "We're here!"

"Where?"

"Here."

"Where's 'here'?" I was being naughty, for I saw all the others were seated around looking expectant and I knew we were about to have A Serious Talk, and I wanted to giggle instead and run away very fast and pick flowers. I did giggle, then clapped my hand to my mouth over my mask, remembering that I hadn't wanted even to smile for what seemed like months.

Conn patted the grass by his side. "Come and sit down by me, darling girl. Sure, and I haven't heard you laugh like that in an age!"

But I sat down cross-legged between Moglet and Corby, facing him. I could not trust myself nearer to Conn. Snowy blew down the back of my neck.

"Right," said The Ancient. "Now then . . . Well, this is it!"

"What?"

He glared at me. "Will you let me speak? Good. As I was saying—"

Puddy burped loudly and happily, his eyes closed, a wing or something worse sticking from the corner of his mouth.

"As I was saying—"

Corby bent his head under his left wing then rattled all over, ending with his tail, like a wet dog.

"As I was *saying*—" shouted The Ancient.

Moglet jumped, then scratched inside her right ear, contemplated the sticky mess on her claws, and licked them clean.

"Can't we go in the real water?" asked Pisky. "I've been waiting ever so long for real water and I am sure there are ever so many good things over there. My blood needs variety, you know, and when one is trying to regain weight after an enforced diet my aunt twice-removed on my mother's side used to say—or was it—"

"SHUT UP!" yelled The Ancient.

"No need to shout, now," said Conn peaceably. "We're all listening, you know, and—"

There was a sudden gesture from the old man and the fire jumped into a shower of blue and green sparks as if it had been booted across the grass. Then it died down into pale steady flame.

"Right! Now, can we get on without interruption? Good." The Ancient seated himself. "I have brought you here, as I promised, because I think you have all lost your purpose." He absent-mindedly plaited the wisp of hair above his right ear.

"My way is clear," said Snowy softly. "At least . . ."

"I think . . . I should . . . I ought . . . There are places I've never seen. Now my sword is mended . . ." said Conn vaguely, and trailed off into silence.

"Now these headaches are better," said Puddy slowly, "I suppose . . ."

"I could go and—" said Corby. "On the other hand . . ."

There was a protracted silence.

"I don't know!" wailed Moglet.

I hugged her. "Neither do I, dear one! Except . . ." I looked everywhere except at Conn.

"You see? I was right. This is why I brought you all here." The Ancient glanced round at us all. "Do you want to wander around for the next ten years or so wondering who, what, why and when? Or would you rather wash away the cobwebs, rattle your brains into some sort of order, discover again the ability to make decisions—your own this time, not everyone else's?"

There was another silence, all of ten heartbeats long. Then, faint and faraway, I thought I heard music. Not the flute and drum of village dances, nor the chant of monks, nor yet the harsh trumpet of battle, rather a gathering together of sounds from wind and sky and sea, rock and stream, trees and leaves . . . It was gone.

"What do we have to do?" I asked.

"That's my girl! Easy. Go bathe in the pool."

"Just that?" asked Conn. "Simple—too simple, methinks." He got to his feet and yawned. "Still, I could do with a dip. Wash off some of the grime. Coming, Thingy?"

I wanted to say that I wasn't Thing, Thingy, Thingummy, or Thingumajig, but held my tongue. "Perhaps. In a moment. You go."

"Wannagonow," said Pisky. "Carrymeover, carrymeover . . . !" Gently I tipped him into the water, so clear, so cold. His little body wriggled delightedly and sank like a stone to the bottom, where I could see him nosing among the plants—trouble was, that pearl had stretched his mouth so that he now ate twice as much as I was sure a fish should, even a starved one: still, I suppose he was making up for seven years—and sucking and spitting, standing on his head, flashing his sides against the sandy bottom as if to rid himself of mites.

"Oh, well," said Corby. "Nothing ventured . . ." and he splashed himself into the shallows, claws gripping at stones, wings flapping an arc of spray. "Corrr . . ."

Beside me Puddy slid into the water and paddled away, bubbling thoughtfully, then shooting off into the reeds with a stretch of legs and a flash of pale belly.

"Can't swim. Don't like water," said Moglet, but she dipped her paw in and shook off the droplets in a fine spray that diamonded her fur in a million droplets. "Still, water's warm. I'll soon dry off in the sun, I suppose," and she stepped delicately into a puddle and wriggled.

I looked around; Snowy had disappeared—strange, I should have thought he would be first into the water—and The Ancient was tending the fire, once more trying to go to sleep.

Conn? Ah, there was Conn. And I blushed and hid my eyes, then peered through my fingers. For Conn stood, naked, right where the cascade of water hit the pool and he was misted with water, his tall, slim body gleaming, the hair on his chest and under his raised arms darker than the hair on his head and the hair at his groin—

I hid my eyes and wished myself desperately somewhere, nearer, farther—

"Come on, Thingummy!" called Conn, splashing happily. "It's wonderful!"

"In a minute, a minute," I answered, but I crouched down and held my head in my hands. I did not want—

There was a tremendous shove in the small of my back and I was gasping, drowning, freezing, the water roaring in my ears, my dress floating up past my face, the hair on my head streaming like seaweed. I surfaced, spluttering, to see The Ancient grinning as he fished out my shift and dress with a stick and hauled it to the bank.

"You pushed me in!"

"If I'd waited for you to jump there'd be as much snow on your hair as mine." He picked up my clothing. "I'll dry these out by the fire. Enjoy your swim . . ."

For a moment I panicked and tried to climb out, only to slip on the wet grass and fall back in, struggling like a hooked trout, the water filling my eyes, my nose, my mouth once again; but suddenly I realized that the water was not cold, as my frantic mind had told my skin. It seemed now almost the same temperature as my own body. I relaxed, and it caressed me, tickling and stroking, hushing and soothing, a nurse calming her charge. I remembered again how the seal had borne me on his back out of the bay. I turned to embrace the water, and, sliding into the unseen depths, gave myself to the element as though we were indivisible so that I was almost resentful that I had to rise to the surface and take breath. Then, when I surfaced the sun struck me full upon the face. For a moment I did not recognize the significance, but when I did I dived straight back into the water searching frantically, but the mask had gone!

Borne away by the vagaries of the current maybe, tangled in the weed, trapped by a shifting stone: all I knew was that I could not leave the water without it. Why, I had rather stumble naked than bare my ugliness! At any moment now I might come face to face with Conn. Desperately I paddled away into the middle of the stream; perhaps I could ask Pisky and Puddy to look for me: but they seemed to have disappeared. If I gathered a handful of reeds, could I plait them into a square and hold that before my face? But the reeds bent away from my questing hands, slipping teasingly through my fingers, and all at once the water silvered with bubbles, like a pan of water just before it boils, and I forgot I needed to breathe, forgot everything except the shower of brightness that surrounded me.

It scoured my mind free of the stains of bitterness and despair, as it sloughed away all the remaining grime and dirt from my body, until I was as clean as a new-washed child, carefree at last. Now all the memories had returned, but tidied into their proper places; I knew how and where and why and what, and with this came a sort of peace, an acceptance of what I had been, what I was now, so that my face was my face and that was that; no moaning over lost looks, for I had been fair as a child, I had had my mother's silver mirror and my nurse's words for that. So, when the change? The day the raiders came? Had my nurse scarred me to be no longer desirable as a slave? Or had the witch disfigured me? There were no memories for this, but perhaps I had not known at the time. Useless to speculate: I was ugly now, would be ugly for the rest of my life, but at least now I was straight and slim, and unknotted in body as well as mind. Perhaps I could still be of use to Conn, keep house for him while he went off on his adventures. I recognized, too, that the paths of my other companions might take a different direction from mine.

I accepted all this, but it did not mean I wanted it so. No, what had been washed away in those waters was not desire or love or needing, but the worst of my selfishness. I was aware that I must show Conn my face before I lost courage, because this was the face he would have to accept if he were to ask me again to take his name. And if he changed his mind when he saw it, if he did not renew his offer, then I knew he would be gentleman enough at least to help me to find a place of my own. And with that I might have to be content . . .

I surfaced for breath and he was standing thigh-deep in the water, some dozen or so yards away, his back turned, the water running from his freckled shoulders down into the hollow of his back and dropping from his firm buttocks. I stood up and my hair streamed down my back and my face and body were naked to the sun.

Now! Now—or never. Oh, how I loved him, in that last moment before he turned. I should not be able to bear that look of revulsion, I knew that, but I had to, I had to, there must be truth between us. I held that last moment tight as a precious stone . . . I was aware that the water was quiet, the birds had hushed their song, that my friends were nowhere to be seen, except for the flicker of Snowy between the dark trees away to my right. I wished I knew how to pray . . .

"Conn!" I called softly. "Conn . . ."

And slowly, so slowly he turned and we stood face to face, and then the waters parted and he walked towards me and there was nothing except a loving astonishment in his eyes as he reached for my hands.

"And is it really you? Why, in the name of all the saints, did you hide that away and pretend to be ugly? Sure, and you're the most beautiful girl I've ever seen!"

And suddenly there was music, music that The Ancient had said was Love's Song rather than Love's Death, and all the earth sang until my whole body was filled with it and it spilt from my mouth, nostrils and ears and gushed from my eyes in astonished, grateful tears. For he told the truth. It was in his eyes, and to him, at least, I was beautiful. I freed my hands and put them to my face to discover the sudden difference but it was the same face. Then, how? Was he blinded by the waters? Had some spell diverted him from the truth? And how long would this illusion last?

"I'm not really. It's this place, I suppose. I'm ugly: I saw my face in the witch's mirror and felt it all over and the feel hasn't changed. It was scarred and twisted and blurred and askew, as though someone had ground their heel into the bones and turned it against the flesh. Truly, truly Conn . . ."

He smiled, and the tips of his moustache curled upwards and smiled also. His eyes held laughter-wrinkles at the corners and what I saw in their depths made me conscious that I stood breast to breast with a naked man, naked myself. I lowered my gaze and saw his body, which was more embarrassing still. I blushed, and would have turned away but he reached out and took my shoulders and held them fast. I was intensely aware of the rough callouses on his hands, the puckered scar that ran across his left palm. I raised my eyes to his again, surprised to see the reflection there in miniature of a face I did not recognize.

I had to know. "Tell me what—tell me what you see?"

"Vain is it now, and asking for compliments? Very well—" He saw me flinch, "—it's teasing I was. Now, let me see . . ." He stood back a pace. "Well, the hair is straight, and black as Corby's wings, that you'll agree. The skin is pale, as well it might be, hidden all that time behind that pestiferous mask! But I think it will always be milk rather than ale . . . Cheekbones that stretch the skin high and a chin that bodes ill for anyone that crosses you—No, no!" He leant forward and his hand caressed my cheek. "I did not mean ill, and if you scowl like that you'll turn the milk of your complexion sour, so you will . . . That's better!" He smiled again, a heart-turning smile, and I shut my eyes. "And if that's for me to admire your eyelashes, they're as long as grass-spider's legs . . . Look up. I'll tell you that your eyes are the colour of the violets under the hedge and big as an owl's, but twice as pretty. But your mouth . . ."

He frowned, and my heart stopped. Had I fangs like a wolf, a mouth like a fish? Or a beak like a bird? Was it puckered like a tight-drawn purse or sprouting with hairs? Was this last to spoil the whole?

He laughed, and the sun caught his eyes so that they screwed up. "Your mouth is different," he said. "It is the most kissable mouth I have ever seen!"

And he bent his head and placed his lips on mine.

The Loosing: Unicorn

The Sleeping Prince

"But then of course you always were pretty," said The Ancient.

In utter confusion I had fled Conn's embrace back to the fire, flinging on my still damp clothes with scant ceremony, and combing my hair furiously with my fingers. The Ancient had chuckled, obviously having overseen our dramatic meeting in the waters. Of course I had had to ask whether my new face would last, and he had told me it was my always-face. "The one you were born with," he had said, and somehow, even in all the confusion of remembering, the traumas of the quest, the half-forgotten pains, this little consolation was the most important thing of all.

"But it was different when I lived with the witch," I said, for he had reminded me that my nurse had called me her "pretty chick." My father told me that although I had my mother's colouring and eyes, I had his chin, cheekbones and hair. I could recall him well: tall, lean, fierce, with scowling brows yet with a mouth that could smile as easily as it would tighten in determination. And my mother; small, rounded, soft, with hair a little lighter than Conn's, skin like cream and a mouth to kiss and laugh—but remembering was still very painful. It was as though they had died a few days since, and I did not want to think of them as I had seen them last, not yet . . .

"Of course it was different with the witch," scoffed The Ancient. "Because you were told so."

I dragged my mind back to the present. "She showed me. She had a mirror . . ."

"A magic mirror. You saw what she wanted you to see. She told you you had a face like the arse-end of a pig with a curling snout, and that's what you saw in the mirror. You were conned, my flower, conned good and proper." He flung a couple more sticks on the fire and I leant forward to dry my hair the better. "Not surprising really."

"Why?"

"Why convince you you were ugly? She could see even then that you would grow into the beauty she could never be, save by sorcery. Number one: jealousy. Number two: even if you were unconscious of your attraction, those morons in the village would soon have sought you out as you grew. Notoriety of any kind she did *not* want. So, you became her hunched and ugly familiar, a Thing to be avoided by outsiders and ignored by her, for masked you were as anonymous as the furniture . . .

"Have you told him who you are?"

I blushed. "Not yet. We—we didn't have much chance . . ."

"Chance enough now." He dropped the stick he had been using to poke the fire as Conn came striding up towards us, his hair still darkened and wildly curling from the water. "Come, Sir Knight, and be properly introduced to your affianced!"

"I'm not—"

"She hasn't—" we said together, and then would not look at one another.

"Come, come now!" said The Ancient, absent-mindedly throwing a handful of some pungent powder on the fire so that we all started back, eyes smarting from the smoke. "Damnation and pestbags! Wrong one . . . Never mind. Chaudy-froidy then, you two?"

"Pardon?"

But apparently Conn understood his jargon. "Not exactly. Not as far as I'm concerned. But she—" he hesitated. "Her, Thingy I mean, er—She's different."

"Not at all! You agreed to give your name to a person, not a pretty face. You too, flower."

"That's another thing!" I said, glad to snatch at any excuse to change the course of this embarrassing conversation. "You knew my real name all along, didn't you? All that business of flowers and flora and fauna and things . . ."

"Flowers?" echoed poor Conn, the only one not in the know.

"Of course I did! What's the use of being unusually gifted—" He failed to look modest, "—if one doesn't use the gift? Come on now, tell him your real name . . ."

I remembered my manners and curtseyed formally in Conn's direction. "My name, Sir Knight, is Fleur de Malyon, only child of the late Sir Ranulf de Malyon of Cottiswode and his wife, Julia Flavia, second daughter of Claudius of Winkinworth . . . So my blood is just as good as yours!" I added childishly and glared at him.

"I never—"

"I know you didn't! But that's not the point . . ."

"Well what is? I still—"

"Not really! *Really,* really . . . It's just like buying a hen that lays one a month and then finding it performs every day instead. Or twinned lambs from a barren ewe . . . All of a sudden you develop a special affection for your liability—"

"I never said you—"

"I know you didn't! But that's not the point—"

"Well, in Heaven's name what is, then?"

"You thought it, even if you didn't say so!"

"I did not!"

"Anyway, I'm *not*, so there!" I left Conn standing with his mouth open and ran towards the river, angry tears rolling down my new-old face, not even sure why I was behaving this way. Was it because everything seemed to be going right, that now I had a reasonable face I also had bargaining power? Had I really wanted to be ugly, to make a martyr of Conn and a victim of myself? Wasn't I glad he would have a pretty face to look at? Did this mean that perhaps he would no longer want me, except as a plaything? Had my ugly security vanished? I didn't know, I didn't understand myself and, blinded by the futile tears, I ran straight into Snowy. "Sorry!"

"No bones broken, Fleur," he said mildly, and nuzzled my cheek. "Come now, no tears: life is for enjoying, my little one, and what seems an insurmountable mountain one day will be a molehill the next. No, don't try to explain—" for I had opened my mouth to sick-up my troubles, "—there is no need. Come, we shall pay a visit together . . ."

"A visit?"

"To a place I know nearby. I have a tryst to keep. Are you too ladylike to ride astride once more?"

"I'm no lady . . ."

"You will be some time, whether you wish it or no. We must all grow up."

So I vaulted to his back and clung to his mane as we splashed through the stream and moved into the dark forest on the other side. His coat was damp, so he, too, must have bathed in The Ancient's Pool of Truth. He carried me swiftly down a path that snaked among the cool, pale trunks of conifer that crowded in on either side, his hooves making no sound on the deep carpet of old needles. Although here it was dark, and the spring sun seemed far away, there was a sense of stealthy movement, of trees stretching and yawning from their sleep, and the slow stir of sap. Once or twice there was the russet flash of squirrel and roe deer, but for the most part only the soft beat of our passing. We emerged into a bare clearing, where the trees drew back into a circle—winter-blackened grass, a few scrubby bushes, a cloudy sky now visible above.

Snowy halted so smartly that I slid from his back.

"Are we here?" I said, struggling to my feet.

"We are . . . Come, I want to show you something." He paced slowly to the northernmost corner of the clearing and stopped. There was a bare patch, moss and lichen scraped away but recently, a space surrounded by rock and stone, about as wide and long as a man. Just like a grave—

"Look!" said Snowy. "Come and look close . . ."

I looked, and saw what seemed like a sheet of dirty ice, but as I knelt down the substance cleared when my breath touched it and it seemed as though I was staring down into a deep, transparent pool.

"Oh, dear Gods!" I cried. "There's a body down there! Snowy, Snowy, help me drag him out! He may not be quite drowned. See, there is colour still in his cheeks, and—"

"No, my dear one," said Snowy sadly. "There is no life there, not as we know it. Do not break your nails, child, it is useless . . ." For I was scrabbling vainly against what I first had taken to be ice, then water, and now knew to be neither. It seemed like some thick, diamond-clear glass, and yet the hair of the drowning boy waved with the weeds and if only I could— I looked wildly round for a rock, a stone.

"It is enchantment," said Snowy. "And one of her best."

"Her?" I questioned, but there was no need for the question. I knew at once who he meant. "You mean you fell foul of Her, too? But how?"

And then he told me of the dance of death his beloved prince had performed to her bidding, how he and the witch had battled and how the prince now lay in everlasting sleep, locked in the crystal pool. I gazed down at the long limbs, slim hips, broad chest, tapering fingers; at the cloud of fair hair that framed the handsome, perhaps too handsome face.

"But—but there must be *some* way of releasing him!" I said. "The spell she laid on us was dispelled by the dragon, that on Conn by a twist of words . . ."

"Oh yes, there is a way. But it means death, death to both of us. If I strike the crystal with my new golden horn, the one the dragon restored, then I cease to live in this world; I choose death, as mortals have to die. And my prince? Now, see, he dreams, and could be left forever in a kind of immortality. If I break the spell he dies also, for he is mortal like you. Do I choose that for him, or am I content to leave him to his dreams, and find my brethren in the west?"

"But how can you know what he dreams? See, he frowns, even now, and turns his head . . ."

Snowy reared up, and struck his front hooves hard on the crystal tomb. There was a hollow ringing, but no sign of a crack. "How do I know whether she locked away nightmares in that living death?" I put my arms around his neck, but what could I say? How could I, with my petty temper and uncertainties, console this faery creature whose agony was so much greater than mine had ever been? How could I reconcile the love of human being and immortal, when apparently I couldn't even manage a mortal affair myself?

When we reached the camp again it was dusk. I slipped down from Snowy's back and joined the others round The Ancient's fire, but no one asked where we had been, or what we had done.

There was a vegetable stew for supper and rye bread, and then a truffle cake, tasting sweet and warm and earthy all at once and we all, even Snowy and Moglet and Pisky, had generous helpings. It was strange, it seemed to answer all the needs for taste in the world. In a way it reminded me—

"Mouse-Dugs!" I accused, sitting bolt upright and glaring at The Ancient. "And something else . . ."

"Maybe. Maybe not," he answered mildly, tapping the side of his long nose. "And then again, perhaps."

"But you know it makes us all act funnily . . ." I giggled, remembering Tom Trundleweed and as suddenly sobered, recalling Conn's proposal.

"Does no harm. After all, it's our last meal together: you won't need me any more after tonight."

"Last meal?" said Conn. "Why, are you going away?"

"Away? Where's away? You knew I could not stay with you once the quest was completed. There *are* other little crises here and there, you know, and also with increasing age I need my sleep. A hundred years perhaps, and then something interesting might turn up . . ." His voice trailed away and he poked the fire until it burned blue.

I looked at him, it seemed for the first time. The trouble was, he kept shifting; like three or four people playing peep-and-hide all at the same time. One moment there was a very, very old man with cheeks wrinkled like a forgotten russet and wearing a silly hat, the next a young helmeted warrior sat there, dark and grim-faced; again, a merry-eyed child with inquisitive eyes and snapping fingers, or a mild-faced middle-aged man with receding hair and protruding teeth . . . I shut my eyes: it was too confusing. Which *was* The Ancient? Or was he all of them? Or they all part of him?

I must have dozed off. When I opened my eyes again the fire was pale green with crackling silver sparks. The Ancient was an old man again, answering some question of Conn's of which I caught the echo but not the sense.

" . . . a question of a different dimension," The Ancient was saying. "And only those who have been there could understand. They don't very often come back. It is, I suppose, very much like a vivid dream; you are real and there and experiencing everything as though it were here and now, but when you return you have to re-adjust to now as if *now* were the dream . . . It's confusing, especially if something momentous is involved: sometimes you wish to stay too long, and then you are trapped in that time forever . . ."

Time-Travel. I dozed again, and then someone else must have asked a question—Moglet?—for The Ancient was answering again.

"No, once they have gone, let them go. They have a journey to make and are only confused if you try and call them back, and might lose their way. You would not wake a smiling child from dream, nor yet a peaceful kitten, would you? No, let them go: in peace, and with your blessing."

Suddenly I did not like all this talk about "going"—was he talking about death? I sat up, rubbing the sleep from my eyes.

"You say we don't need you anymore, now we have completed our quest—but we haven't." I tucked my feet under me and glanced round at the others. Snowy's long mane hung down, hiding his eyes; Corby was preening, Puddy's throat moved up and down; Pisky's fins, beautiful now, waved gently from side to side; Moglet was purring with her eyes shut and Conn—Conn was looking across the fire at me, his eyes bright and soft at the same time: I took a deep breath and looked away. "What I mean is this: we have lost our burdens, thanks to you and the dragon, and you told us that once this was done we should be healed—which we are—" I stretched, feeling with pleasure the way my spine arched back, "—but you also said we should find our own destinies, or words to that effect, and you made us bathe in that pool over there to clear our minds. Well, has it? Cleared them, I mean?"

The fire was now a soft, rosy pink and the cinders gold and purple.

"Oh, I think they all know what they want," said The Ancient. "But let's ask them, just to make sure . . ."

"Well, now," said Puddy, "let me consider . . ." He made up his mind. "I have a picture in my mind of a low heath topped by a wood and dotted with broom, furze, gorse and thickets of bramble. There are two or three ponds—nothing too grand, you understand—and there is a jumble of rocks to hide amongst when the sun is too hot or the wind too cold. And there are others there of my kind, to exchange reminiscences with during the long days . . . A toad could grow old there, with pleasure."

"And I sees a bit of countryside, nothing too grand neither, with a bit of a village with fields and woods behind and cliffs in front," said Corby. "Something like that place of the White Wyrme. A place where the wind stretches your wings and there's food when you seek it and company in plenty and shelter if the going's tough. But the great thing is to have the fellers to natter to and the youngsters growing up to be taught to take your place . . ."

"A lake," said Pisky. "Full of bright shallows and deep crannies, so you may have the sun and the shadow when you wish it. People to come down and feed you and trail their fingers in the water, which warms at their touch; and they call you by name and there are other, lesser fish, who need a king, a consort. By and by the lake runs with your kind and your children and grandchildren and great-grandchildren come to you for your wisdom . . ."

"A fire and fish and milk and a cuddle," said Moglet. "Mice to catch, the run of the rooftops, a length of twine to chase, a basket full of milky kittens . . ."

And they lapsed into their dreams again, dreams that now had a purpose.

I thought, jealously, that I could find them their sandy heaths with pond, cliffs and woods, a small lake, a warm fire; they didn't have to sound as if it would all have nothing to do with me.

"And you, Flora?" said The Ancient. The fire was gold, all gold.

I leant back in the long grass and looked up at the stars, so near I could reach out and pluck them, then blow them away like thistledown . . . "I want a house, not a big one, but large enough to have separate rooms to sleep, to eat, to cook, to sew and just sit. It must be near enough to the sea for me to hear the seals sing, with a stream that wanders nearby. It would be nice if it were near a hump of hill that would shoulder away the north winds, and I should welcome the martlets in the eaves, come summer. I should grow herbs for the market and we should keep goats and chickens and have a big enough plot to keep us in vegetables . . ."

"We? Us?"

"Me and my husband and the children. Two boys and two girls. And cats. And a dog, something to guard us when my husband is away, but who will go hunting with him when he is home. Oh, and his horse, a mare so we can breed."

"And what is his name, this husband-to-be?"

I frowned; I had been able to see all this like a picture, a tapestry of bright colours, but somehow a draught had caught the weave and I could only catch glimpses, no faces, no names. "I don't know: he won't keep still. Perhaps if I close my eyes . . ." I did, and was drifting off into a dream where I was standing near a gate in the sunshine with a blue butterfly on my finger and the scent of honey in my nostrils, when I heard someone I knew talking nearby.

" . . . and I thought I would go back to travelling, to fighting, the only things I knew, but I have changed my mind. Once, I thought that all I wanted was a sword to be mended and armour to be clean, but now I know there are other, more important things in life than wandering. I, too, want a house, a home; I want a woman to love me and be loved in return, and I want children as well. The sword I was so proud of shall be used no more. I want to mend bones, not break them . . ."

I smiled in my dream: that was my husband talking. I knew who he was now and I turned to greet him and the butterfly flew out of my hands into the sun . . .

The Loosing: Unicorn

Snowy's Choice

I awoke with a start, clear in mind and very cold, for Corby and Moglet had appropriated my cloak. Puddy squatted on a stone nearby, Pisky was dreaming in his bowl, Conn and The Ancient were huddled under their cloaks, the latter snoring gently. We were complete still, in spite of all the talk earlier, all seven of us, eight with—I knew immediately what had woken me: Snowy was gone. Not just physically, for he often wandered off on his own; no, it was more than that. It was as though he had suddenly severed the ties that had bound us all, cut us from his heart, banished us from his thoughts, and with a growing sense of anxiety I knew what he was about to do. No wonder he had been silent earlier.

Springing to my feet I scanned the far bank of the stream . . . There was a ghostly shimmer of white among the dark trunks of the trees. I should not have seen him at all but that it was the still hour before dawn, when there is an almost imperceptible lightening, as though one veil at least has been drawn back from night's dark window. Without thought I followed him, splashing through the shallows of the stream and scrambling up the bank, running onto the silent pine carpet that aisled its way through the trees, always that pale glimmer tantalizingly far ahead. He was so much faster than I, too, and it was only my desperate desire to catch him before he abandoned us all that lent speed to my stumbling feet.

At last I reached the clearing and there he was, standing before the crystal pool. Stumbling over a fallen log I fell to my knees with a jolt that knocked the breath from me. But with the last of my ebbing strength I called out to him with my mind, my heart.

He raised his head and looked over at me. "I must," he said. "You know that, my little Fleur. Go back, child, to your love, and leave me to mine . . ."

"But my dear one, my dearest one, *we* need you too!" Crying helplessly now, I buried my face in my hands; only to feel his soft nose against my wet cheek, his mane brushing my hair.

"Peace, peace . . . I loved you, too. Remember us!" I listened to the soft thud of his hooves, dying away. Then there was silence. Opening my tear-blurred eyes, I started at a terrible crash and a scream of anguish I will always remember. Afterwards all that could be heard was the agonizingly slow tinkle as of thousands of glasses shattering.

I was almost afraid to look up. At the edge of the clearing, where the trees faded into darkness, stood my beloved unicorn, the first light of dawn catching the gleam of his golden horn. Standing by his side, one arm flung around his neck, stood the prince.

"You're all right," I whispered. "You're all right . . ."

They did not hear me, they could not hear me! Slowly they walked away from me into the forest, in a world of their own.

The tears were scalding my cheeks, as I watched them go, the most terrible thing of all was that I could see the trees beyond them right through their bodies, clearer and clearer, and the rising sun rose and dissolved them slowly, like mist, until they were merely a twist of smoke that rose into the air, hung for a moment like a frosty breath, and then were no more . . .

The Loosing: Toad + Crow

Six Feathers

Conn found me a little while later. He caught me close and hugged me, not entirely and unreservedly, but with a sort of courteous passion, as though he was not yet quite sure how I should welcome his embrace. "Don't cry, girl," he said. "It's what they wanted. And there are other worlds than this."

I looked up at last, wiping my swollen eyes. Everything had changed. Where there had been desolation, now the sun struck through the dim conifers, a diffused morning light that candled the wild anemones into pink and mauve and purple, touched late snowdrops into warm white, glowed among the violets, turned the coltsfoot into flame, uncurled the tiny daffy-down-dillies into open-faced wonder and crept like a hesitant visitor among the moss, lichens and first tender spears of grass. A squirrel raced down a tree and hesitated upside down, cocking his head, bright eyes gleaming, russet tail twitching as if timing the full-throated, sweet music of the wren on the branch above. A tiny round vole, furry, sat up and washed his whiskers in the dew.

I stood up. Where the crystal tomb had shattered a tiny spring rose and bubbled in the grass. With a breath that tore in my throat I stepped forward to pick up a scrap of gold that glistened in the clear water, and held it out to Conn.

"It's from his horn!" I said, marvelling at the three-spiralled gold ring.

Without a word, Conn took it from me, and gently slipped it on the middle finger of my right hand.

"Went at early light," said Puddy, back at the camp. "Packed up his things and just left."

"Without even saying goodbye?" said Conn.

"Not exactly," said Corby. "Sort of said it was time he made tracks. Said you two would understand."

"Well, I don't . . ."

"'Course you do," said Pisky briskly. "He said so last night. Not in so many words, I admit, but I understood him to say that we didn't need him any more now we knew what we were looking for . . ."

"He left you a message," said Moglet. "Well, all of us, really. 'A direction and some reminders' he said . . . Where's Snowy?"

So we told them.

"Glad for him," said Puddy.

"Brave thing to do," said Corby.

"Wish I had seen his prince," said Pisky. "Never seen a prince . . ."

"I wish I was brave," said Moglet. "When Snowy was here he made me braver."

Conn looked at me. "So, now what?"

"I suppose we pack up and go—wherever we belong," I said slowly. "Wherever that may be . . ." I would not look at Conn. "Where's this 'direction' you were talking about, Moglet?"

She led us over to a flat patch of ground. There, forming a rough arrow pointing southwestish, were six feathers. A rook's and a martlet's; a sparrow's and a cockerel's; an owl's and a dove's.

Conn took a sighting, then picked up the feathers one by one, scratching his head. "The direction's clear enough, but what's the reminder? What have any of us, apart from Corby here, got to do with feathers?"

" 'One each,' he said," said Moglet. " 'So as we wouldn't forget . . .' "

I looked at the feathers in Conn's hand. "Some of them do have meanings," I said. "Like flowers . . ."

"Of course! Cock feather for courage, owl for wisdom; martlet's traveller's luck; dove . . . Peace?"

"Or fidelity," said I. "Sparrow is for fecundity—Lots of babies," I explained to Moglet, because we had been talking human-speech.

"And a rook does nothing but chatter, so I suppose that one is for the power of speech," said Conn. "Well, who has what?"

I glanced at the others. "They could apply to us all, one way and another. Why don't you just pin them to your cloak until we discover which is which?" I said to Conn.

"Right," he said, twisting the feathers into a badge.

"Fleur, is everything packed up? Puddy, into my pocket! Corby, would you take a scan from the top of that tree and see if the path is clear: in line with the oak and the ash . . . Like a top-up before we go, Pisky? Moglet, you can run on a little until you get tired, then I'm sure Thingy—sorry, Fleur, won't mind carrying you for a while, I'll take the big pack, girl, if you can manage the other?"

I gazed at him in astonishment. Here was a new Conn, very definitely in command. He caught my gaze and winked. "Amazing what a few feathers will do, isn't it?"

We left that enchanted place in early summer, but when we left its shelter we found that the world outside was still in early spring and none too warm.

For the first few miles I missed both Snowy and The Ancient, maddening magician that he was. Sometimes I would look up, half-expecting to catch a glimpse of our unicorn. But I knew in my heart that he had gone for ever, and gradually his loss became less hard to bear. But Conn kept up a fast pace with Corby calling out the route from overhead. Moglet continually got lost in the bushes chasing inviting smells. Pisky demanded to stop every time we came to a likely pond. We also had to buy provisions in the first village we came to, and I had Conn's shirt and my shift to wash as well as a rip in his hose to mend.

We travelled the way The Ancient had indicated, and were happy in each other's company as every day the light grew stronger, the sun rose higher and the land burgeoned. Every day the animals grew stronger, braver, more capable of providing for themselves, and every night they slept nearby and every morning I found it easier to talk to Conn than to remember their speech, and forgot to remember why . . .

Until one day, just after Conn's Easter Feast. It had been cold at night and sharp during the day for a week. Spring had held back her buds, but that morning we awoke to a change of wind; a warm southerly breeze shook the pale catkins and ruffled my hair. We had been climbing a small escarpment under a hazy sun, and at midday I suggested we sit under the trees for bread and cheese.

"Can we go just a little further?" asked Puddy, restlessly shifting on webbed feet. "And a bit to the left?"

"What's 'a little further'?"

"I don't know; just a feeling. Can we?"

If only I had said no—but would it have been any different in the long run?

Instead I picked him up in my hands and followed his directions, the others trailing behind. The land dropped away into a sandy slope, rock-strewn and gorse-covered. Beyond lay scrub, marsh, two ponds—

"Oh, Puddy," I said. "Not yet, not yet!"

"But this is the place," he said simply. "My home."

"You can't! We belong . . ."

"Yes. We belong, and always will. But I had a picture in my mind, and this is it. Sorry, Thing dear, but this is where I want to live out the rest of my life." He looked up at me. "You wouldn't want to deny me this?"

I shook my head, not trusting any other form of communication.

"Glad for you," said Corby. "Hope it's as easy for the rest of us . . ."

"Nice ponds," said Pisky. "But too shallow for me, I suspect; a king-carp wants a larger territory. Still, I'm pleased you have found your destiny so soon. May luck go with you, my friend: cool summers and warm winters and food and company whenever you need it."

"Happiness!" said Moglet.

"Good place for toads, I should think," said Conn. "Shall I carry him down to the nearest pond?"

"Next one's best," said Puddy. "Doesn't dry up in a drought, as I remember . . ."

But I had to carry him, not anyone else. Making my way down between rocks and yellow gorse I trod upon the soft sand where all about me were the tracks of other creatures: water-birds, lizards, frogs, newts, grass snake, and I saw several toads bound on the same journey as Puddy. A brimstone butterfly brushed my cheek and joined another dancing towards the bright waters. Midges patterned rhythmically above our heads.

Gently I set Puddy down, looking for the last time at that warm, warty little body, the bright eyes, the tapered toes, the gulping throat, and the slight, light scar where the emerald had lived for so long. The wind was soft, the water ruffled with cat's-paws, and all around bird-song, the calling of frogs late, toads early.

"Oh, Puddy," I said. "I didn't realize how much it would hurt!"

Conn came over and tickled his finger under Puddy's chin. "Goodbye, old comrade: it was fun travelling together. Now, go and find a nice young lady toad . . ." I doubted if Puddy understood, for Conn was speaking human. "Come on, girl, he'll be just fine now."

But I knelt and cupped Puddy in my hands once more. "I love you," I said.

"Me too, human." He nodded at Conn. "I understood . . . Our ways are different now, but I shall not forget. It was good, was it not?" And he jumped from my hands and waded into the pond, turning at the last moment. "May your destiny be near," he said formally, "and me and mine will always live in peace with you."

"And I with you," I answered, equally formally. "And all creatures that share water and land shall be my concern and that of my children and theirs for ever more."

"Thanks. Can I have my feather? The rook's, I think: I have rather got out of the way of speech, of gossip . . ."

My fingers trembled as I unfastened the feather from Conn's jacket. "I'll stick it here, so you can see it when you come out of the pond . . ."

"Remember me!" he said, and I watched the gallant little form, moving a little stiffly, for he was well into middle-years, toad-time, swim down and down into the depths until he was hidden from view.

From then on it was as if I had forgotten how to speak to his kindred. I could never again, as long as I lived, converse with them as I had once done.

But Moglet snuggled up to me and whispered: "*I'll* never leave you . . ."

It was Corby's turn next.

After three days the wind changed yet again and came gusting in from the northeast, and farmers were looking anxiously at their orchards as the trees tossed and troubled, blossom falling too soon. One morning Corby declined breakfast, but stretched and flapped his wings, rising a few feet, then sinking down again, his eyes bright, his head restless.

"It's no use," he said at last. "I shall have to go; the winds are calling . . ."

"Oh, no, Corby! Not you, too!" I cried.

"Me too, lass. You knew it had to come."

"But so soon!"

"Human years are not crow years; I'm not a youngster any more, you know." It was true: around his bill, and under his wing where the sapphire had been, the feathers were greying. "The winds tell me of that village I was speaking of, remember? And I know my brethren are waiting: I can hear them call down the wind. You wouldn't deny me that, now would you?"

What could I say? But I tried to put him off, till tomorrow, next week—

"The winds are right and I can smell my way home. If I wait . . ."

"But—I shall never see you again!"

"Who knows, who knows . . . Better choose a feather, I s'pose . . . Give us the martlet's: traveller's luck, that's what I need." And he tucked it under his wing, where it blended with the rest of his feathers.

I wanted the others to help me to persuade him to stay, but once again they played me traitor.

"Fly the air like water," said Pisky. "And may you have food a-plenty, comradeship, and your choice of the ladies."

"Happiness!" said Moglet.

"Fare you well," said Conn. "Enjoyed your company, bird . . ."

I sank to the ground and held out my arms and he waddled to my lap, his beak nibbling my ear. "Now, come on then, human: your life lies ahead of you too, you know . . . We all knew this had to happen sooner or later, didn't we? Me and mine will always live in peace with you . . ."

"I love you," I said, and he walked from my lap and rose into the air, at first clumsily, then as a gust of wind caught him, riding the currents easily.

"Me too!" he cried. "It was fun, wasn't it? Remember me . . ." and he spiralled upwards and then headed northeast into the wind, and the sun hurt my eyes so I could not see for the tears.

"The winds be with you," I said unsteadily. "And all creatures that fly the air shall be my concern and that of my children and theirs for ever more . . ."

But from then on it was as if I had forgotten how to speak to his kindred and I could never again, as long as I lived, converse with them as I had once done.

For days after, whenever I saw an untidy bundle of crow on the ground, or heard their harsh cry or watched their erratic flight in the air, my heart beat faster, hoping against hope that it was Corby. But it never was.

There was no bright destiny waiting for me that I could see. But I had Pisky still, trapped in his bowl, and my beloved Moglet.

And every night now she snuggled up to me and whispered: "I'll *never* leave you . . ."

The Loosing: Fish

The Lake by the Castle

During the next six weeks I was lulled into a sense of false security, for the four of us travelled undisturbed and undivided. There seemed no change in anyone although there was, so subtle that I did not note it at the time. Every day, imperceptibly, Moglet's and Pisky's voices dimmed to me and more and more I heard Conn's. I grew stronger in body, more capable of walking the distances he demanded and, in secret, I bought a mirror at the first opportunity and it was as The Ancient had said: I was pretty, or at least not ugly. I begged silver from Conn for a new dress, sandals, a fillet for my hair and he indulged me without quibble, for we had plenty of dragon-gold to spare.

Once or twice I asked where we were bound, but he only answered that he followed The Ancient's directions. Still, it was pleasant travelling, for the weather was warm and I did not have to decide anything. There was one puzzling factor: Conn had never again referred to the contract between us; at first I was glad not to have to think of an answer, then I became a little uneasy, and at last I became downright anxious. Had he forgotten? Did he think, perhaps, that my metamorphosis from masked hunchie to presentable female absolved him? Was the new me—because less pitiable, less dependent—less attractive to him also? I longed to ask and almost succumbed once or twice but held my tongue. I had rather anything than be rejected, for my love, dimmed and almost forgotten sometimes in the trials we had endured, nevertheless had always burned true and clear.

Every day when I woke I checked first to see whether he was awake, perhaps to dwell on his sleeping, unprotected face, mouth calm under the curling red moustache; to watch the fluttering lids, so white against the lean brown cheeks; to touch, perhaps, the unruly curls that framed his head; and then, when he was awake before me, to note with delight the flash of those red-brown eyes, so clear, so positive; and all the while to watch the taut grace, the economy of movement, the sudden, fierce aggression. Had he some goal in mind that did not include me? I tried to remember what he had said that last night round the fire with The Ancient, when we had all eaten those tongue-loosening mushrooms, but could recall very little—something about healing instead of fighting? Memory teased at the fringes of consciousness, a cat's paw under the curtain.

The beginning of the Month of Maying, Beltane was warm, very warm, and it was with relief that we crested a hill and saw a castle off to our right, the town beneath us.

"Cool ale," said Conn. "And a fresh shirt. This one is in tatters."

"I need more needle and thread," I said. "And more provisions all round."

"Houses mean mice," said Moglet. "And things . . ." She did not specify what.

I looked at her. My kitten no longer, she was grown of a sudden to a full-size cat, small maybe, and dainty, but nevertheless mature.

"Did you say there was a castle?" asked Pisky. "A real one? Lemme see, lemme see . . ."

He was growing out of the bowl I obligingly raised, and he now had twelve snail retainers. His fins were bright red, not gold, and they waved like the pennons on the litter we saw being carried down from the castle towards us.

Pisky contemplated the castle and gave a bob of satisfaction, then his eyes slid sideways. "Is that gleam over there a lake by any chance?"

"Er . . . yes, I believe it is . . ."

"With trees all around, and a sunny bank covered with flowers?"

"Why, yes: but you can't possibly see—Oh, Pisky . . ."

"I only asked—"

"I know what you asked! And I won't let you! You can't walk over there, and I'm not going to take you, and besides the castle probably belongs to someone important and they will chase us away . . ."

I had been standing on the bank to let the litter go by. It swayed with white and gold curtains and was accompanied by six men-at-arms riding before and behind. Conn bowed courteously as it passed, the dust from flying hooves powdering his boots. I was so busy reprimanding Pisky that I shook his bowl, to emphasize my displeasure, and water splashed over my bare feet and I had to rescue a snail. There was an unseen command and the liner came to a lurching stop, and twelve unprepared horsemen reined in their skittish mounts with difficulty on the narrow path. The curtains of the litter parted and a dumpy little lady with her grey hair drawn back in an optimistic bun leant out. She spoke to one of the escort and he beckoned to us.

"The Lady Rowena wishes to speak with you!"

Conn held out his hand to me and slowly I descended the bank, Pisky's bowl in my hands, Moglet keeping pace safely from beneath my skirts. I curtseyed then looked up at the lady shyly. She had merry eyes, a round red face full of fine wrinkles, a generous mouth, and surprisingly looked all-over untidy. The gown she wore, though of stiffened silk, did not sit prettily on her overweight figure, the rings on her fingers were either too tight or too loose, hair wisped about her face because the pins in her bun had come out and she was eating sweetmeats out of a box and dropping the crumbs in her lap. But her voice was surprisingly young, clear and sweet.

"My dears . . . You did not mind me stopping you to have a word?" She didn't wait for a reply, but first dabbed at her sticky mouth with a linen cloth, then ineffectually flicked at the crumbs. "Oh dear, oh dear, I am so . . . Now, what was I saying? Ah, yes. Stopping you . . . You *did* say you didn't mind? But I thought it was—yes, it *is*!—just what I have been looking for all these years! I send my men far and wide, and seven years ago I was all but promised . . . He said it had been stolen: probably kept it for himself, if the truth were known . . . Inferior ones I have been offered from time to time, but this!" She tumbled out of the litter, all skirts and grey hair and crumbs, and clasped her hands round Pisky's bowl. "A king! A king Magnus golden carp! And in *such* condition! A youngster, not more than twenty years old—they take an unconscionable time a-growing, my dears—and this one has fifty—nay, seventy or more years to go and may end up as long—as long as my arm! And who would have thought . . . It's my birthday, you see, and I had meant to treat myself to some more . . . But no matter. Just to see *him* is sweetmeat enough! Here, my handsome fellow: a crumb of something special . . . There!" And she dropped a sliver of sweet stuff from her sleeve into his bowl.

"What does she say, what does she say?" said Pisky excitedly, between further offerings.

I translated the relevant bits, adding: "And she talks more than you do, even!" in human speech, but luckily she was casting about for the combs to fasten her hair at the time and didn't hear me. The combs and pins were all scattered in the dust, and she and Conn bumped heads companionably a couple of times before they were all retrieved.

I put my nose up against Pisky's: "And she's not having you," I added, but he was not listening either.

"There now, that's better!" said Lady Rowena, at last, patting a precarious pile. "And now—why, I don't even know your names! A handsome knight and a pretty young lady, a king among fish and—ah, yes! I thought so: a little cat, and so dainty, too . . . There must be a story to tell here . . . Now, come: I have quite lost interest in a trip to town; we must all go back to the castle and have some refreshment. My husband must see the fish! You, dear child, squeeze up beside me in the litter . . ."

And so, without going willingly at all, resisting her blandishments in my mind, I nevertheless found myself being carried back to the castle among the crumbs and scattered cushions, with a suspicious Moglet on my lap and Pisky's bowl cradled in hers. She chattered all the way to the keep, and although she asked questions she never quite waited for all the answers and by the time we were introduced to her husband, the lord of the manor of Warwek, she had twisted our names to Connie (me) and Flint.

Sir Ranulf was as tall, thin and cadaverous as his wife was short, plump and rosy, but his eyes were brown and kind. "Now then, Rosie dear, don't bewilder the young people . . ."

"Now, *would* I! But see here, Ranny darling, what the young lady has brought with her!" She exhibited Pisky, who was now beside himself, aware that all eyes were admiring. He pranced and danced, curved and pirouetted, rose and sank, fluted his fins and tail and pouted and gasped, till I muttered that he would run out of air.

"Shan't! But I want to see the water she talked about. Ask them, ask them, Thing dear! Please!"

I knew I had lost the battle as soon as they led us to the lake. It was large and calm, its northern side some hundred paces from the castle, shallow, reed-fringed waters dipping to a deep centre. On the eastern side were thick trees, to the south a smooth hillock and to the west the land sloped gently away. There were water lilies, a little artificial island, an arch of rocks, again artificial, and the water was warm and clear. A moorhen with her half-grown chicks swam away from the reeds at our approach and two black swans, younglings, curved to their high-winged reflections.

"Down in there," said the Lady Rowena, pointing down into the water, "there are twenty-five assorted fish, including three young golden carp princesses. My collection . . . It is mating-time now, and the water is the right temperature . . ." and she knelt down and pulled up her sleeve, testing the lake with her elbow, just like a nurse trying the water for a babe.

Sir Ranulf stood watching her, twirling the ends of his moustache. "Loves 'em, you know. Never had any children . . . Pity. Spends all her time caring for the fish. Feeds 'em every evening, rain or shine. Designed all this herself. Been looking for one like yours for years. Pride of her collection and all that. Still . . ."

"Now then," she said, "I should love him above all the others; I can't help thinking of those carp princesses waiting too . . . They are a little larger, being females, and they usually spend their time near the western bank, under the lily-leaves, just hoping . . . But I could never try to persuade these darlings to part with him against their will!"

"It's his decision," I said, knowing all the while what that decision would be, for he was leaping about now like something possessed. "Oh, Pisky, dear one, is this what you really want?"

"Lemme see first," he said, and gently I lowered his bowl to the waters and with a flash of silver belly he was gone. We waited for five minutes, for ten, for twenty . . . Oh, Pisky! I prayed for his return, I prayed for him not to like it, for disillusion to overcome the invitation of the lake. Conn looked at me, and in his expression I read that I was wrong.

"It's right, Fleur love," he said, and at that moment Pisky's head popped out of the water at my feet.

"Oh, Thing dear, you've no idea how beautiful it is! Everything laid on! There are waters deep and cool, waters shallow and warm and a veritable underwater garden to exclusive design, with tall spawning-trees just to fin! And I found them, the lady fish: they are a beginning, a beginning! Oh, dear one, my father, my grandfather, my uncles, my great-grandfather—they never had it so good! A fish could be happy here for a hundred years, he could found a generation that would last a thousand . . ."

I turned to Lady Rowena. "He wants to stay," I said, and my throat tightened on the words, thick with unshed tears. "A gift for your birthday."

Her face lightened with joy, and she bent to tickle Pisky's chin, very gently. "Bless you, King Carp!"

"Can I?"

"Pisky," I said. "You don't have to ask . . ."

"Good manners . . ."

"Yes," I said. "You always had those . . . Oh, Pisky, are you sure?"

"Sure as snails . . . Which reminds me: can I have them, please?"

I submerged his bowl in the water. "There; let them crawl out in their own good time."

"Now. I *am* king of the lake!" And, sure enough, the bowl was empty in double-quick time as I teased out the last of the weed.

"There, dear one . . ."

"Thanks . . ." He whirled away, but in a moment he was back, balancing on his tail. "It was a tremendous experience, wasn't it? I rode the winds with a *dragon* . . . Bless you both, and you, cat. I love you. Remember me!" and he was away, lost forever to me beneath the water of his lake. I plucked the sparrow feather from Conn's jacket and stuck it in the earth at the water's edge.

"I love you, too," I said unsteadily. "The waters give you peace . . . And all creatures that swim the waters shall be my concern and that of my children and theirs for evermore . . ."

But from then on it was as if I had forgotten how to speak to his kindred, and I could never again, as long as I lived, converse with them as once I had done.

They asked us to stay at the castle that night, and the Lady Rowena found me a gold pin and a pearl necklace she wanted me to have, but we pleaded urgent travel and refused both hospitality and gifts, and left them with her searching for ant's eggs for her "children" and spent the night in the nearest hostelry. I could not bear the thought of being so near to Pisky as to want to go and scoop him back into his bowl . . .

"Do you think he's all right?"

"The best of them all, so far." I didn't like the last two words. "He's found his kingdom. Be glad for him!"

"Oh, I am, I am!" I said, the stupid tears pressing hard behind my eyes, all the while cuddling my beloved Moglet, who had whispered earlier: "I'll never, *ever* leave you!"

"But I do miss him!"

"That's not what you said when you had to carry him all those miles without spilling!" said Conn.

"That was different." And it was. "He will—he will live for seventy years?"

"*And* found a dynasty. All of whom will be exactly like him, down to the smallest tiddler who, in hundreds of years to come, will bore *his* great-great-great-grandchildren with the tale of his great-great-great-grandfather who spoke to dragons and, for a little while, carried a Dragon-Pearl . . ."

"You're laughing at me!"

"Perhaps just a little . . . But think of it rationally, Thingy—sorry, I just can't get used to the 'Fleur' bit after all this time—if you can. Three creatures: a toad, happily basking in the sun in the company of his friends, and probably already having contributed to the increase of the toad population, is sitting with his eyes shut digesting some horrible insect, and remembering happily his moment of glory with the Walking Trees; he's home, and has no more headaches . . . Then there's that great crow, soaring happily over the cliffs somewhere, enjoying the feel of the wind under his once-crippled wing; remembering, too, his part in the White Wyrme adventure; beneath him, somewhere, his mate is on the eggs that will produce other Corbys. He is fulfilled. And Pisky: his own kingdom, able to eat what he wants, when he wants, a harem attendant on every wish, and memories of a dragon, and of rescuing you from that thing in the water—Dear Christ, girl, let them be! It's just selfishness to want them back!"

"I know," I said, cuddling Moglet tight. "I know . . ."

The Loosing: Cat

A Gain and a Loss

In the morning Conn declared his intention of going to buy a horse. "We're travelling too slowly."

"To where?"

"How should I know? The way The Ancient pointed us."

"But why the haste?"

"I don't know that, either. I just feel that something is waiting. And . . ." He hesitated again.

"Well?"

"Today I am going to buy a horse."

So we went to the market, held in the square. How he knew, I do not know, but it was the monthly horse-trading fair and we dodged hooves as they were trotted up and down, some still shaggy with winter. There was no other stock; on inquiry I found that apparently one week it was fowl and pigs, the second sheep and goats, the third cattle and the fourth horses. I left Conn watching the trading and wandered among the other stalls, Moglet under my cloak, buying eggs, salt, cheese, bread, honey and my needles and thread. I found some excellent cured pork and bought a small sack of oatmeal; it would hardly fit in my hard-pressed haversack, but I reckoned if Conn found a horse we should have saddlebags as well.

I reached the pens where the last of the horses were being held; there were a few left, the dregs by the look of it, but I glanced at them all, nevertheless. One never knew—Perhaps, that one in the corner . . . A pale mare, filthy dirty, with matted mane and tangled, soiled tail, her ribs sticking through her coat; unclipped, uncared for. I moved over, pushing the others aside, and pulled a tuft of grass from the stones outside the pen.

"Here, girl . . ." She did not raise her head. I coaxed. "Here my beauty . . ." The Roman nose lifted, dark brown eyes regarded me steadily, warm breath blew in my face. "So it's Beauty, is it? Here, take it . . ." Gently she lipped the grass, no snatching. I studied the collar marks that had seared the skin, the missing slashes of hair on the rump where the switches had bitten deep. "Here, Beauty, let's see . . ." I took the jaw and opened the mouth; six, seven years old, no more. She blew at me again, searching for response. "I can't talk your language, sorry . . ." But I blew back gently and brushed aside the ragged forelock, then slipped into the pen beside her, to run my hands down her legs, lift the hooves to look for rot, try the lameness test, legs held bent tight for a minute. She was basically sound, as far as I could see, but had been badly neglected, was weak with winter fasting and hard work. I had hooked my haversack over the nearest post, now I popped Moglet on top. "Keep an eye open; I'll be back in a minute."

Conn was watching a rangy chestnut being run up and down, all rolling eyes and flaring nostrils, ears laid back.

"Mettle, yes, but temper too. Did you find anything?"

He turned. "Was outbid on quite a nice grey, but I decided I would only pay twenty silver pieces top, and he went for twenty-two. You don't think this one . . . ?"

"No," I said firmly. "All fire and no heart; short-winded too, I shouldn't be surprised. Come on, I've found one to show you." I dragged him back to the pen and led him over to the corner. "See? There's a good horse lost under all that hair. She's been hard-used, but with a little feeding-up . . ."

"She wouldn't carry your kitten, let alone you or me! She's clapped-out!"

I leant forward and pulled at her halter. "You're not, are you, Beauty?"

"Beauty?" He managed to make it sound utterly ridiculous.

"Yes, Beauty." The mare gave a soft whinny and lipped at Conn's sleeve. He moved back, frowning, then suddenly leant forward and pulled aside her forelock.

"I don't believe it! I-just-don't-believe-it . . ."

I pulled at his sleeve. "Don't believe what?"

"Look here—there, on her forehead. Yes, there . . ."

There was a silvery patch arranged in a peculiar radiating whorl.

"Is that special?"

But Conn was dancing around like a mad thing. "Special? I'll say it is! And of course she's Beauty, you were right there. When I got her in the Low-Lands she was booty, and that's what I called her: 'Booty' or 'Beauty.' Seems she still knows her name. She ran off when—" He stopped abruptly.

"When the witch . . . ?" I prompted.

"Yes. Well—The horse got frightened by her fireworks and I never thought to see her again. Yet, here she is. I'm sure of it." He snatched a wizened apple from my pack and offered it to Beauty, who again took it gently and scrunched it happily, allowing him to pass his hands all over her. "Hmm . . . a bit of muscle strain in the right shoulder. No problem. Well, well, well . . ."

"You're sure it's her?"

"Quite. Here's the little knot in her shoulder where she was nicked by an arrow just before I got her. How's my old Booty, then?" and the beast nuzzled his shoulder only to start back nervously, flinging her head up, as a diminutive man came and perched himself on the pen rails.

"Thinking of buying 'er, then?" He had a cold. "Shouldn't. Not with 'er 'istory. Three owners already from 'ereabouts she's 'ad, and not a one satisfied. No good to none of them, she's been. Some feller east of here found 'er eighteen months back, tried 'er with the plough—"

"The plough!" snorted Conn.

"No good," continued the snuffly little man, nodding his head. "Got a good price for 'er though, none knowing 'er 'istory. Second feller, Wyngalf, tried putting her in shafts: no good. Still got a decent price, 'cos she were a looker, then. Peterkin's 'ad 'er overwinter—couldn't even put 'er to 'is stallion, she weren't 'aving none. No good for anything, if you asks me . . ."

"Perhaps not round here," said Conn, sarcastically. He ran his hand over the scarce-healed weals on her quarters. "Doesn't look to have been well-treated."

"That Peterkin's a violent man, 'e is. 'Eard 'im say as 'e'd carve 'er up for meat 'imself if she didn't fetch ten of silver . . ."

"Well," said Conn. "In spite of what you say, I've a mind to her."

The man jumped down from the rails. "Don't say as I didn't warn you, then." He shuffled off, then looked back. "'E'll ask fifteen, but'll take ten . . ."

Conn tossed him a coin. "Thanks for the advice. Get something for that cold of yours . . ."

We got her for the ten pieces of silver: no one else was interested beyond knacker's price. Afterwards Conn bought second-hand bridle, saddle and saddle-bags cheaply and led her to the nearest stables to give her a rub down, clean and file her hooves, curry her mane and tail and bed her down with oats and a bran-mash. "We'll spend another night here," he said cheerfully. "Give her time to get used to the saddle again tomorrow. See if the inn can put us up again, will you?"

"I'll leave the haversack with you, then," I said, setting it down. "And come back and let you know. Come on, Moglet . . . Moglet? Oh, Conn! I've lost Moglet!"

He stopped rubbing Beauty down, hearing the anxiety in my voice. "She was with us at the pens, because she hopped off the haversack when I gave Booty that apple. Don't worry, she can't have gone far. Just got lost in the bustle, I expect. She'll turn up."

Frantic, I ran back to where the horses had been corralled: no kitten-cat. I wasted time asking passers-by whether they had seen her; some were sympathetic, others just stared or tapped their foreheads significantly. I asked at every open doorway I could find, but still no cat. There were a couple of tabbies, a black and white, a ginger torn, but no multicoloured striped/brindled/spotted cat like Moglet. At last, almost crying, I went back to the stables, where I found that Conn had spread out some sacking in a corner and laid out bread, pies and ale.

"No inn tonight. Too late to get a decent lodging," he said, seeing from my face how miserable I felt. "We'll have a bite to eat and then I'll have a look with you for that wretched animal of yours." He was only teasing with the "wretched," I knew that, but I couldn't stop myself.

"You don't care about her!" I sobbed. "You don't care about me, either!

Now you've got that—that wretched horse of yours back again all you can think about is going off adventuring! You don't need us anymore . . ."

"Don't be silly!" He was quite sharp with me, a fact that set me wailing again. "Of course I care; but she'll be back—and, if not, don't you think she might have found something *she* wants to do, somewhere *she* wants to go? She's got the use of her paw back now and this town is full of nooks and crannies where mice hide out. She's probably out hunting her dinner—"

"She may have been stolen!"

"Why on earth would anyone want to steal a scrawny little scrap like that? Be sensible!"

But I didn't want to be sensible, all the more so because although he had been quick to assert that he did care about Moglet, he still hadn't mentioned me . . .

I ran out into the street, darkening now, with shadows deep in the alleyways. "Moglet! Moglet!"

A little figure, tail high in greeting, came running down the centre of the road. "I'm here: stop shouting!"

I scooped her up into my arms, my heart beating more wildly than hers, and now that I had her safe I scolded her like a mother who has snatched her child from under the hooves of a runaway horse, anger proportionate with relief. "You're naughty! Where on earth have you been? You had me worried sick—didn't you hear me calling?"

"I was hunting . . . Two mice! And I was invited into a house for supper. Such *nice* people! They fussed over me as though I belonged to them and had been lost, and in truth it *did* feel like some place I had been before. There is a girl there, younger than you perhaps, and she can't walk properly—like me when I had the stone in my paw. The back of their house leads down to the river and it's there, in their mill, that I caught the mice. And the miller's daughter, the one who is crippled, was watching him work and he saw me catch the mice and put me on her lap for a cuddle. And he has a little cart to wheel her in, because she can't walk, and I went back to their house in the cart with her, and they gave me a bowl of cream, real cream! Then they let me out, and the girl was sad. And then I heard you calling and I came . . ."

I had never heard Moglet talk so fast, so excitedly, nor had I been able to understand her so well for ages. At first I was so glad to get her back that the implications of what she was saying didn't register, but at last I understood: Moglet had found a family, a home—

She was the one of them all, perhaps, that I had loved the most, because she had been, then, like I was: small, crippled, female, frightened and tatty. Now she was a full-grown cat, quick, alert, loving and whole, and she wanted a fire to dream by, mice to catch, a bowl of cream and a basketful of kittens to croon over and tell how once she had been on a quest and had carried a dragon's diamond in her paw. And the kittens would not know what a dragon was, but would listen just the same. But she would be able to catch a spider for them and tell of the one that was as big as a house . . .

But I could give her all that! She could come with *me* and I would give her cream and shelter. She didn't need this—or the crippled girl who had to ride in a cart. I opened my mouth and my mind to say all this, to explain to Moglet that she mustn't be misled by the first family who fancied a mouse-catcher, to tell her that I needed her because I had no one else, but instead I listened to myself say: "Well, I'm glad you're back, 'cos I've saved some pie. Tell you what, we'll all go back and see these people tomorrow, shall we, and you can see that crippled girl again. I'm sure she'll be glad to see you." And Moglet purred, and lifted her face to my hand and showed her teeth and half-closed her eyes and opened her mouth to take in all my scent, the greatest show of affection a cat can give, and the back of my throat ached with the effort not to cry.

Magdalen was actually a very nice girl; small, pale, with a twisted and shortened leg, but eyes that were loving, and hands that gentled Moglet with a skill I had never achieved. Her parents had married late in life and obviously adored their only child. The home they lived in was one of the more prosperous in town with a large kitchen and eating room on the ground floor, with a solar and three bedrooms above.

I began by resenting the whole idea of the family and ended up by liking them, although I confess I was surprised by the way they had taken to Moglet, until the wife explained.

"It's like this, my dear; when that little cat appeared it was just like seeing a ghost! You see our mother cat, bless her, lived to fifteen years and only passed away last winter. She hadn't had kits for seven years and the last one she had was stolen off this very doorstep when our Mag was seven years old, and this one is as like as two peas, even to the one white whisker. My husband says she's a champion mouser, like our Sue that died, and Mag just fell straight in love with her! She cuddled her like she never did with dolls when that kitten was stolen. It were she, though, as knew that the cat belonged to someone else, and insisted we let her go, otherwise I'd have shut that door tight last night, bless me if I wouldn't! As it was, she cried fit to flood the meadows when the little thing slipped out and was away . . ."

I looked across the solar to where the sun shafted through the windows; Magdalen had rolled a scrap of leather into a fair imitation of a mouse, ears and tail and all, and had attached it to a length of her sewing silks, and now Moglet was playing catch-as-catch-can among the rushes, eyes intent, body totally involved. I realized with a pang that I had never played with her like that . . . At last the girl drew the toy up onto her lap and Moglet followed, to settle down in the sunshine with a yawn of delicious tiredness.

"Would you let her have kittens?" I asked.

"First thing," said the father (I never did find out their proper names). "I could do with a good mouser or two in the mill and there's plenty of the neighbours as could do with one too; been a shortage of good ones since our Sue died."

"There's a nice ginger tom down the road," said the mother. "He might do."

I glanced again at Moglet; she was purring. Yes, the ginger tom "might do" very well.

The girl glanced across at me, but her hands did not cease their caressing, I was glad to see. Her speech was slightly impaired, but I could understand her well enough. "But you love her too: we can't take her away. It wouldn't be right."

"She is not mine, nor yet Conn's," and I nodded in his direction. "She is her own creature, and as such is free to choose her own destiny. And if you will care . . . ?"

"Always," and she gently stroked Moglet's ears the right way so that she sighed happily and settled deeper.

I plucked the cock's feather, emblem of courage, from Conn's jacket and gave it to the girl. "Let her play with this sometimes . . ."

But we had not reached the turn in the street when there was a cry behind us and Moglet was in my arms.

"You are leaving me!"

For the last time I hugged her. "But you want to stay. So, we were only leaving you without saying goodbye because we thought it was best. Besides, I hate goodbyes . . ."

She looked up at me. "You don't mind? I thought . . . I thought . . ."

"Of course we mind! Don't be silly!"

"But I always said . . ." she hesitated.

"That you would never leave us," I supplied. "But—but *she* definitely needs you. She—she hasn't a dragon to cure her of that poor leg, and because you were crippled once you will be able to understand her better. And I am cured, and I—I have Conn."

"I still promised never to leave you . . ."

"And I said all sorts of things. And meant them, at the time. Circumstances change, my dearest one, and so do we."

"You won't cry, and call me back?"

"I can't promise not to cry, but I will try not to call you. But if I do, and you hear me, just ignore it . . . You may miss us too, you know."

"Oh, I will, I will!" and the little wet nose touched mine. "Always . . . But it was fun, wasn't it?"

I nodded, not trusting myself further.

"Even the bad times . . . I'll never forget!" She purred anxiously. "Are you *sure*?"

"Oh Moglet! You're grown-up now, so am I! Yes I'm sure. Go, and live your life, and kittens and mice and cream be yours always!" I spoke the formal words. "And all creatures that walk the earth shall be my concern and that of my children and theirs for evermore . . ."

She licked my right ear, briefly, rough-tongued, and then sprang down and away, back to where her new mistress waited hopefully by the open door.

"I love you!"

"Me, too," I whispered.

"Remember me . . ." and tail up, little pale dot-and-dash under her tail the last things I saw, she went happily to her new life.

"Oh, I will, I will!" and I turned to Conn and cried into his leather jacket until the front was all damp with my tears.

But from then on it was as if I had forgotten how to speak to her kindred, and I could never again, as long as I lived, converse with them as once I had done . . .

The Loosing: Dragon

The Journey Home

It was a long journey, that last one, the longest he had ever made in one haul. At first the very flush of enthusiasm, the knowledge of his quest ended, the eager thought of Home, carried him hundreds of miles with ease, helped by a fresh westerly. Initially, too, it was easy to forget the hunger, the thirst, the scorching heat as he flew nearer the sun by day, the searing cold of brittle nights, but he had forgotten how low his reserves had become over the bitter seven years of waiting. At first he had thought the sudden dizzy drop of a thousand feet or so, the giddy turns of a hundred-and-eighty degrees, the retching and nausea, were due to the weather and his inevitable weariness but at last, after an unplanned and disorientated plunge into the black cold of a northern fjord, which almost extinguished his fires forever, he realized that part of his trouble was lack of nourishment. Then, also, he remembered Precept No. 137 of Dragon-lore: never forage in a northern winter.

There was no food: berries, a pitiful few; nuts, a mere clawful; moss and cones a bland taste, no more, and the icy waters of the tarns and rivers gave him stomach-cramps and hiccoughs. Vainly he searched for frog, toad, newt, fish: they were all hibernating and sifted easily through claws grown desperate with famine as they scooped the silt of scummy, half-frozen ponds. And all the animals were crowded too deep in safe burrow or fled too fast to catch, and the domestic ones were close-byred or cottage-stabled for the winter.

Somehow he kept going, though his flights became shorter and lower, so that fanged mountains with glaciered saliva reached hungry jaws to scrape his belly. His tired eyes were forced to follow the slow, silver snake-wind of rivers instead of a higher scan for the headwaters and a shorter route, and all the while a north-falling dragon-shadow kept pace on the earth beneath, sometimes ahead, sometimes behind, depending on sun or moon. And then came the snow, borne in from the north in goose-feather flakes, striking across his path in cruel, blinding flurries that weighted his back and iced-up the trailing edge of his wings till he was forced to lie-up in a convenient pine forest for a few days, pondering his mistake in not taking the longer, southerly route home; but it was too late for him to change his mind for the detour would cost him precious weeks, and he doubted whether he would now have either the strength or the memory. His enforced stay in the forest brought him some sort of luck, however, for he found a cache of frozen meat left by some hunter, and managed enough heated breath to thaw out the chunks to an acceptable chewy stage, though he suffered from indigestion for days afterwards.

But there were many, many hundreds of miles still to go and the weather, if anything, grew worse. It was a mere shadow of a dragon that turned due south for the last few leagues and drifted down like a spent leaf into his own, welcoming valley. There was a cessation of singing wind in his ears, no more rattle of sleet on his stretched skin, no creak and flap of shedding wings. His breath no longer rasped painfully in his throat. It was suddenly warm in this sheltered valley, though the towering mountains that surrounded it seemed to touch the sky, their snow-covered tips tapering to the sun.

The sun! The golden sun that tinted the yellow skin of the villagers who crept out to look, to touch him, to wonder as he lay at last in the dusty square under the green Heaven-Trees that sheltered the temple. A tonk! tonk! of bells heralded more people still and there was the smell of cedar and sandalwood. A silken robe was slipped beneath his tired limbs. Warm, scented oils washed away the crusted tears of effort from his eyes and the dried saliva from jaws grown strangely slack. There was rice, too, in flat wicker baskets, but suddenly he was hungry no longer. Hunger and tiredness had no place here. All he wanted was the friendly scrape of scale against wing-tip, the intimate caress of spade-tail, the warm, ashy smell. He opened his eyes and there they were: gold upon silver upon red upon green upon yellow upon purple, breathing a fiery welcome from the steps, the walls, the doors of the temple. He lurched forwards crying his greeting, a clashing of cymbal and rattle of drum—

But there was no answering greeting, no surging forward to welcome him. The dragons were not real dragons, they were stone, they were wood, they were plaster, they were paint. He tore his claws reaching for them and swung round and round in his dismay until he was circled by his own disillusionment. The villagers fell to their knees at the sight of his distress, their pigtails bobbing in the dust. At last there was one brave, or wise enough, to come forward and explain: an old, old man with a moustache that hung like white string to his knees, and who lisped in the faded, once-familiar sing-song that the dragon remembered from his childhood. He told how the last of the dragons had left the valley in his father's father's time, taking their treasure back with them to the mountains from whence they came, but leaving gold to gild the temple and memory to make their likenesses.

And the tired dragon lifted his eyes to the distant peaks and he sighed.

After a little while he took out his pearl and looked at it for a long, long time. Then he took out the diamond, the ruby, the emerald and the sapphire and looked at them. He rolled the pearl on his tongue and then he put all the jewels back in the pouch under his jaw and sighed again and then seemed to fall asleep and all the people tiptoed away, shushing each other to let him sleep in peace.

But in the morning he was gone, leaving only the shallow depression where he had lain and several baskets of uneaten rice. So they painted his picture on the temple, in the one space above the doors that was left: a small blue dragon with a red belly and a pearl the size of the moon curled on his tongue. And they pointed out to visitors the high peaks where he must have gone and told of his last visit, until the paint faded from the temple in the time of their children's children and the dragon passed into legend.

The Gleaning: Dog

Wolf-fog

"Where the hell are we?" said Conn.

"How do I know? You're the one who's supposed to be guiding us."

The fog lay like a dense, muffling blanket all around. When we stopped all we could hear was our own breathing, the chink of Beauty's harness, the stamp of her hoof.

"I'm sure I heard . . ."

"What?"

"Something. It sounded like a dog howling. Yes, there it is again!"

"I can't—"

"Shut up, and listen!"

We were near to quarrelling. Over the past few days our relationship had worsened, and now, with the added uncertainty of direction, the baffling fog, the hint of something crying in the mist, I felt I hated everything and everybody, including Conn.

For nights I had lain awake mourning my lost ones and he had wearied of my sullenness and misery and told me so. And I had snapped back at him that he was unfeeling, uncaring, a man without sensitivity—and so it had gone on. Vanished was the comradeship, the warmth there had always been between us; instead there was a tension, a bitterness, a resentment on my part and irritation and arrogance on his. No longer did I wake early from sleep just to wonder at his resting form, nor watch his lithe movements during the day, nor tease a smile from those curving lips. No longer did he pay me little compliments, pick me a flower from the hedge, glance at me sometimes with an unfathomable look in his eyes that made me turn away, suddenly embarrassed. No, it had all gone as sour as yesterday's milk and every moment we spent together drove us farther and farther apart—

There it was again, a high, plaintive keening, a dog mourning. I shivered. Conn sighed with relief. "We must be near a farm, a village, some habitation. That dog is tethered, not roaming. Come on." He pulled at Beauty's bridle and started off in the direction of the sound, me trailing miserably behind, damp and cold. Who would have imagined weather like this in high summer?

The howl came again, but apparently from another direction, more to the left. We stopped.

"This damned fog," muttered Conn. "It distorts everything . . ." We listened, and again came the keening. "Left it is," said Conn.

We found the village, if you could call it that, after another half-hour of tripping and stumbling. The fog, if anything, was worse. There were some half-dozen hovels, single-roomed, and a somewhat larger farmhouse. Doors were closed, tallow-dips flared at midday through chinks in the shutters, but no one, not even dog or cat, was abroad. We groped our way towards the gate to the farmyard, for none but funerals or weddings went to the front door, and all the while we heard the keening of the dog grow louder.

"What the hell—!" I stopped behind Conn, fighting to control Beauty, who was doing her best to dislodge his hold, puffing and snorting and stamping her hooves, trying all the while to sidle away from whatever it was that hung threateningly from the tall farm gate. Peering past Conn's shoulder I saw snarling teeth, grey hair— "Thank the Lord!" said Conn. "It's only the skin . . . Still, one of the biggest I've ever seen."

It was a wolf-pelt, torn with rents as if from sword or spear, and those teeth were fighting even in death. "Poor thing," I said. The eyes had gone long since, probably pecked out by birds. I lifted one of the huge, bony feet and the dry claws rattled.

"Poor thing, my arse!" said Conn. "A great brute like that could even take a pony, let alone sheep or pig. Villagers were well rid of him. Shouldn't like to come up against such myself, without weapon."

But still I held the lifeless paw, remembering the wolves at the Castle of Fair Delights, so long, long ago . . . Had he forgotten so easily?

The gate was firmly bolted, and Conn rattled the latch. "Hola! Anyone at home?" For a long while it seemed as though the fog itself held breath, then a door opened and shut and we heard uncertain steps across the yard.

"Who's there?" It was a woman, the voice thin and quavery with a hint of fear beneath.

"Respectable travellers, Ma'am," said Conn in his most reassuring voice. "Me and—" he glanced at me, "—my wife, seeking shelter and a bite to eat. And with pence in their pocket." He jingled his purse.

"Go away!" came the uncompromising reply. "We want no strangers here!"

Conn glanced at me again, a quick frown on his face. "Strange: a poor village that needs no company and no copper . . ." He raised his voice again. "Bring your lantern nearer and see that we pose no threat to you and yours. We have but one sword and two daggers between us."

There was hesitation, the steps retreated then advanced again, and now I could hear clearly the click of dog's claws on the stones. I peered through a knot-hole in the thick wood of the gate and saw a middle-aged woman, some forty years old, advancing across the yard, lantern in one hand, a great bitch-hound on a leash in the other. She was an old dog, with thick curly hair, a long, lean body and small ears, obviously built for speed. I wondered if it were she we had heard howling earlier. They arrived at the gate and the woman thrust aside a looking-panel and gazed out at us.

Conn returned her gaze steadily. "We mean no harm, as you can see. Just shelter for the night, for 'tis miserable cold and dripping out here. And perhaps a bowl of broth and bread and a handful of hay for the horse?"

"There's no hay and no broth neither," said the woman, her eyes fearful in the wavering lantern-light. "And no letting-in of strangers. And hasn't been since that great devil came to the village at the turn of the year." And she indicated the great wolf pelt. The bitch hound reared up, as tall, taller, than the woman, and put her muzzle to the dried pelt. Gently she blew through her nostrils, stirring the skin, making a strange growl-snarl-wail in the back of her throat. Conn started and cursed. The dog turned her brown yellow-flecked eyes on him, considering.

"By the Saints! 'Tis one of the Great Ones!"

"Great Ones?"

"Aye, the Great Dogs of Hirland." As always when he was excited his voice held a singing lilt. "By all that's Holy! Here, girl . . ." and he placed his hands on either side of the great muzzle that poked out through the looking-panel. The woman gasped and dropped the wildly flickering lantern, as the dog growled softly in her throat but did not move her gaze from Conn's nor pull away from his hold.

The woman retrieved the still-burning lantern. "She's supposed to bite!" she whispered, her eyes large with distress. "She's supposed to kill!"

"Not this one," said Conn confidently. "Not with me. She's a princess, this one, and princesses know their own . . ."

The great dog still regarded him steadily, then whined softly and turned to look at me, her muzzle still in Conn's hold.

"She wants something," I said. "More than anything ever before . . . I don't know what it is."

"She's after that pup of hers," said the woman, and I could see by her guilty expression and the hand she clapped to her mouth that she had not intended to speak of it.

Conn released the dog. "What pup? Oh, come on now: you started to tell us."

She hesitated, then made up her mind. "You'd better come in." She unbolted and unlatched the gate. "He's away hunting . . ." She nodded back at the house, and I presumed she was speaking of her husband. She led the way into the yard and Conn looped Beauty's reins over a post, loosened her girths and offloaded the saddle-bags.

Inside the hall a cheerless fire burned fitfully, adding smoke to the fog that curled under the door and through the ill-fitting shutters. "You see? Even the fire won't burn true!"

"Insufficient draught," muttered Conn out of the side of his mouth, then he put some coin on the table, addressing the woman. "Some bread, perhaps?"

She put the coin back in his hand. "What I can give you will be a gift: we have tempted the Gods far enough." From a cupboard she brought stale bread, a rind of cheese, and from the barrel in the corner two horn mugs of sour ale. "'Tis all we have since—" She shivered.

"Since?" Conn prompted, making a face as the liquid touched his tongue.

"Since—What harm can the telling do now?" She was persuading herself. "None, I reckon . . . Well, it was like this . . ."

Like all tales it had grown in the telling and now was so twisted and twined with her own thoughts and local superstitions that it took two or three times as long as it should, but the bare facts were these. It had been a late, cold spring and just before lambing a number of wolves had pestered the village, setting the sheep and cattle to uneasiness and the dogs to singing the night long. This was not unusual, for many outlying villages were used to wintering packs like these, on the scavenge. What was unusual, apparently, was that their leader was a giant wolf, more cunning and ferocious than any seen before, who had led his inferiors in raids of such daring that the villagers had lost three tups and two swine before they had had time to organize themselves.

All efforts to drive the wolves away had failed, until the woman's husband had a bright idea. His hound, now old but still fertile, had come into season and he had staked her out one night and watched from the safety of a tree. It appeared that the giant wolf had not been able to resist this lure, and on the second night the husband had gathered all the able-bodied of the village together and when the wolf returned they had rushed in and slain him on the spot, though he had not given up without a fight. The pelt had been borne home in triumph and nailed to the gate. The village had celebrated, in anticipation of the routing of the wolves and a return to normality. Not so: from that moment the cattle had suffered from a murrain, the ewes had slipped their lambs, the hay crop had been blighted, blossom had not taken, milk went sour between udder and pail and the women had miscarried.

Apparently, the wolves had disappeared, but their presence was still felt. Paw-prints were spotted in the village street, chickens and a goat went missing, yet never was there clear evidence. No one ever *saw* anything . . . Added to this, the hound was now clearly in pup, and her behaviour so peculiar that it was suspected she was suffering from wolf-bite. She was short-tempered, skulked in corners, cried at night and would not hunt anymore. Eventually she whelped, one pup only. The husband and wife were not allowed near her nest in the barn, so it was only after the pup was able to crawl out into the open that they could see what had happened: the pup was part hound, part wolf, and the bitch was so intensely protective that she would still not let anyone near. Twice the husband, fearing the wolf blood, had tried to kill it and twice the bitch had forestalled him. But when the pup was some seven or eight weeks old, he had lured its dam with fresh-killed hare and had tied her up; he was about to hit the pup over the head when thick fog swirled in about them and they had heard the howling of a wolf at noonday. The wife had warned him against shedding the pup's blood in the face of these obvious signs and he had said: "Let his kinfolk have him then." Hurrying across the fields to the great pit where all the village rubbish was dumped, a deep gash in the earth with unscalable sides and a deep pool at the bottom, he had tossed the pup down. He had heard a yelp, a splash, then silence. He wasted no time in making for home, lantern swinging wildly, breaking into a run when he imagined he heard the padding of feet behind him.

This had happened only the night before last. Since then, the bitch had howled constantly, driving all distracted, and the unlifting fog was full of wolves, grey and vengeful.

It was a strange enough story. I looked over at Conn for his reaction, but he was frowning. The hound stood quietly by the door, now and again scratching at the lintel and whining softly. The wife jumped to her feet. "I shouldn't have let her loose! My husband said to hold her fast, lest she go after the pup!" She rose to her feet, but Conn forestalled her.

"Wait a moment . . . Fleur—Thingy dear—what's to do?"

For a moment I was so flummoxed with him calling me "dear" again that I could only stare, then I pulled myself together and went over to the hound. Lifting her chin in my hand I looked into her eyes aslant, avoiding the threat of out-staring, and although I could no longer receive her thoughts in my mind, nor give her mine, yet I could read puzzlement, hatred, yearning. I put my hand on top of her head and my fingers tingled, and all became clear.

I beckoned to Conn and he came to stand beside me, putting his hand over mine on the dog's head, then snatching it back and shaking his fingers. "Like touching iron in a thunderstorm! What is it?"

I kept my voice low, looking over my shoulder at the woman, who had backed away from us. "I don't want her to hear, otherwise they might destroy this one too . . . Somewhere near here is a Place of Power, where the lines cross—Oh, you know!" I said impatiently. "Don't you remember The Ancient saying that power sometimes lies beneath our feet, neither good nor evil, just waiting to be used?" He nodded, his eyes grave, his fingers fiddling with the little silver cross he wore about his neck. "Well, this one, without knowing it, has tapped the power. She grieves for her lost pup, she mourns the great wolf that was its father, and it is she that has cursed the village, albeit without conscious evil . . .

"You said she was a Great One?"

Conn nodded. "In Hirland her line is royal."

"Then would she have the greater power . . . Poor lass!" And I kissed the wide brow while the woman cowered behind us in terror. "You don't know what it's all about, do you?" I whispered softly to the dog. "What's her name?"

"He bought her from traders, ten year back. Deirdre, they called her . . ."

"Deidre of the Sorrows," said Conn. "I'll tell you the story sometime, Fleur."

My heart jumped and I reached for his hand and held it tight, for all the good was suddenly back between us. "Right now this princess is sorrowing for her pup. Coming?"

He nodded and turned back to the woman. "We are—we are going to lift the spell. But we shall need the bitch. All right?" Without waiting for an answer he lifted the latch and we slipped out into the fog, now denser than ever. "Which way?"

"Follow the dog . . ."

Out through the gate, down the narrow street, up on to the downs. I stumbled and fell once but dragged myself to my feet, for the great bitch was outrunning us. Instantly Conn whistled and she turned, ears pricked.

"Wait, girl, wait!"

After that we moved more easily, for she kept turning, to accommodate our slower speed. Behind us the fog closed in and I, too, could hear the pad of paws keeping pace to our right. I looked at Conn, but he had not heard it as clearly as I. "You are going to have to help me."

He misunderstood. "Not far now, I shouldn't think. Here, take my arm: I won't let you fall again, I promise."

I smiled to myself. Darling Conn, so eager to help even if he didn't understand . . . We were panting up a slope now and ahead of us the bitch had stopped and was whining softly. We reached the brink of the pit and gazed down together at the precipitous sides, the jagged boulders, the bushes dinging with precarious roots to the few pockets of earth.

Conn dropped a stone into the depths and counted under his breath before we heard the splash. "It's deep: we'll need a rope."

"You go back for one. I'll stay here."

The instant he had gone I felt the wolf-fog close in about me. "I'm going down," I said steadily into the mist. "He shall be brought up, never fear. Just wait, and do not harm my friends."

Hitching my now-cumbersome skirt into its waistband, longing for the once-despised trews and jacket, I lowered myself over the edge, clinging to a rowan tree as I did. I looked up at the bitch; she whined, and paced the edge of the pit. "It's all right, old girl; stay there. Conn will know where I've gone down. I'll bring your pup back if he's there, never fear." Slowly, cautiously, I lowered myself down, grabbing at whatever prominence or crevice I could for a finger- or toe-hold. It was nearer fifty feet than forty, and looking up, I realized I could never manage the ascent without help. By a miracle, I completed the descent without falling, and at last felt firm ground beneath my feet.

My arms and shoulders ached intolerably, my exposed legs were badly scratched and my nails broken, but at least I had made it. The fog was slightly less dense at the bottom. Piles of stinking rubbish, old bones, a broken wheel, shards of pottery, droppings, torn cloth lay around me. Behind me was a scummy pond, dancing with midges. Every now and again a plop! disturbed the surface, but there were no fish here. The borborygmi from decaying matter were eructating spontaneously from the foul depths. If the pup had fallen into that—! I moved forward and heard, just ahead, a whining snarl. So, he was here!

Forgetting caution, forgetting that I no longer held the power to communicate, I stumbled in the direction of the sound, to be brought up short by bared teeth and a definite growl. I peered through the murk; there, back against a rock, was one very hungry seven-week pup, stomach cramped, paws thrust hard against the earth to keep him upright, determined to fight to the last!

I crumpled to the ground, fighting a desire to laugh. I could have eaten him for breakfast! But still, the courage of the little thing! Recollecting myself, I feigned the surrender position, carefully avoiding looking him straight in the eye. "Come, little one, I mean you no harm . . ." I edged forward, my hands held for him to sniff. As if to help, I heard his dam's whine from up above and so did he; absurd ears cocked, he gave a little yelp, all the while keeping his eyes steady on mine. This time the teeth were not bared, although he shrank back as far as he could. I used all the powers I could remember to reassure, to comfort. At last I was near enough to reach out without the smell of fear on my fingers and stroke his muzzle.

"Come, little Great One: I am here to take you back. It's cold and lonely down here, and up there the world awaits you. Be brave, and let me take you back where you belong. I promise you no harm: my man and I will keep you safe, and you will grow into a great hound whose fame will travel far and wide. You are hungry, and your dam waits to feed you. Come to me, and show you are my friend, as I am yours . . ." I patted my lap. I do not know how much he understood but two seconds later I had a lapful of tired, desperate pup and a tongue sought my face and two very dirty paws were around my neck.

Luckily he appeared uninjured by his fall into the pit, so I wrapped us together tightly in my shawl, and when Conn's rope came snaking down I made a loop in it and he hauled us seemingly without effort to the top, using the rowan tree as a belayer. He embraced us both and I released the pup, who immediately rushed over to his dam, two days of deprivation emptying the two rows of teats in record time.

Conn watched him, still keeping his arms around me. "You all right?"

"Fine," I said. "Just fine!" I leaned against his shoulder, burning hands, scarred knees and aching shoulders forgotten for the moment.

Suddenly there was a low yipping from the other side of the pit. Peering through the fog, I thought I could see grey shapes and the glint of yellow eyes, a prowl of wolves reminding me that all was not yet well. I shivered for a moment then walked over to the pup: the concave stomach was now rounded and full and as I picked him up he once more smelt as any pup should, of fur and sunshine, warm milk and hay.

"Come on, you two," I said. "Time to get things sorted out . . ." And I led the way back to the village, the pup in my arms, Conn's hand round my waist, the bitch at our side. But keeping pace, just out of sight, something moved beside us in the fog.

Halting outside the gate of the farmhouse I hooked the pup's paws over the top bar and motioned to the bitch. "Up, girl!" She stretched to her full height so that now the pup was between the pelt of his father and the head of his mother, his body against my chest. I sensed rather than saw the woman on the other side of the gate and knew that eyes and ears in the village were pressed against gaps in the doors, chinks in the shutters. I took a deep breath and, summoning up memory and instinct, spoke clearly and slowly so that all who wished could hear and remember. Clasping the pup firmly with my right hand I raised my left, the sinister, the magic hand, to pass from pelt to pup to bitch.

"Father, son, mother; dog, pup, bitch; each of each and one of both; wild one, child, tame one: here I lay the spirit of the father to rest, nevermore to roam: may he give the little one his courage, his cunning, his hunting skills. I release the spirit of the bitch back to her owners. May she give the little one her speed, her wisdom, her devotion. I take this pup for me and mine. He shall be ours to take away, ours to keep, ours to cherish. He shall never come nigh this village again, and the curse that was laid upon this place shall vanish with his departure, never to return . . ."

I was exhausted: all this meant nothing in real terms, just reassurance for the villagers, the farmer's wife. Conn slipped an arm about me and the pup, his other hand through Beauty's bridle.

"Well done, dear one." What the others used to call me . . . "We've done all we can here. Give me the pup, and do you mount and ride for a while." He had no idea that this was only the beginning . . .

We progressed slowly down the main street, conscious that the skulking villagers spied our every movement. The great bitch trotted at our heels, her eyes fixed on the pup Conn was holding. I had a moment's unease; supposing . . . ?

We came to the edge of the village and I looked back; already the fog was thinning behind us. I slipped from Beauty's back and held out my arms for the pup. "Let me have him, Conn."

I put him to the ground and he gambolled over to his dam, nuzzling at the empty teats, and biting teasingly at her ears. Elbowing him aside I knelt to the bitch and used all the powers I had left to try to communicate, voicing the words to myself as I tried to remember the nuances of thought communication I had once so easily used with my friends, such a little while ago . . .

"He is old enough to leave you now, and if you take him back *they* will destroy him. Let us take him, Great One: we will care for him as one of our own and he will grow to be the greatest hound of his time and his children's children shall hunt with kings. Go back to your people, who have loved and cared for you over many years, and live out your life in peace . . ."

She was listening to me, but I could feel the power still rising through her, confusing thought.

"Give me your hatred, your bewilderment, your fear—Conn! Pick her up in your arms high above the ground, when I give the word—Now!" And as he did so, staggering under her weight, I flung myself directly beneath her and covered the Power, pressing it back to flow once more beneath the earth where it belonged. "Back, back!" I heard my tongue use words in a language I do not remember. Slowly, reluctantly it seemed, the tension eased. At last I nodded to Conn to put the bitch down; she whined, looked puzzled for a moment, shook herself all over from ears to tail, then turned towards the village.

"Back then, girl; but first say your goodbyes to the pup. He is in good hands: make him understand that he must not follow you."

I watched as she gently licked his head and under his tail. Then, as he jumped up, snapping playfully, she raised her head to us, eyes full of sorrow, then snapped back at him and growled. He shrank bewildered into an uncoordinated heap. I longed to pick him up and comfort him: not yet, not yet! The bitch turned and trotted off purposefully towards the village, and after a moment the pup gathered his feet together and stumbled after her. Conn started forward but I clutched his arm. "It's all right: wait . . ."

The pup reached his mother: she checked and turned. For a moment I feared, then as he attempted to nuzzle her she growled again and nipped him sharply in the flank. He yelped, and for a moment did not know where to turn, then came pelting back to us, ears back, tail between his legs, the whites of his eyes showing. I picked him up. "He has chosen . . . Conn, a rind of cheese from the pack!" I cuddled him, feeding him a scrap of cheese from my fingers, then deliberately walked on up the down, Conn following with Beauty. Once, I looked back. The bitch stood, just within misty vision, gazing at us. "Go on, girl," I willed. "Back home. And forget . . ."

She turned, and went her way.

We reached the top of the down and the fog was still with us. But now it had a different quality; before, it had blanketed all in still, grey anonymity, now it had shape. The pup shivered in my arms and Beauty flung up her head fretfully. Only Conn was steady as a rock at my side, asking no questions, trusting me.

I halted. "This is the place."

"The place?"

"The boundary between the village and *their* world. Listen!"

All around us the fog was advancing and retreating; paws rattling, tails swishing; whining, yapping; ears laid back, eyes yellow; teeth bared, tongues lolling—

"Dear God!" muttered Conn. "Are they real?"

"More or less. Take Beauty up to that small hawthorn and tether her tight, otherwise she will panic. They won't hurt either of you: they are only interested in the pup. I'll be all right . . ."

Brave words . . . Now I was alone with them. The pup lay quiet in my arms but now and again a shiver ran through him and a little trickle of warm wet ran down my arm. But he was trying hard to hide his terror and in that moment I accepted him as one of us.

The wolf-fog swirled closer and now I was truly alone, for no longer could I see either Conn or Beauty, some hundred yards away. The beasts were becoming braver, encroaching on the unwritten empty space that humans keep between themselves and other creatures, beyond which none may come unless invited. A tail brushed my leg, a muzzle snatched at my skirt, a paw struck my arm.

"Enough!" I said, and used a Word of Command, one that our Mistress had used.

The fog hesitated then steadied, and I had my space again. Remembering the witch's spells, The Ancient's commands, the bond that had existed between me and my friends, and now, most of all, the memory of Snowy, I summoned up all my strength. "I am not calling you back, dear one," I said in my mind, "for that I know is forbidden, but please give me what help you can . . ." Instantly, or so it seemed, the middle finger of my right hand itched intolerably. Absentmindedly I reached to scratch and touched the golden band around it. I felt a charge go through me. Touching the pup on the head with Snowy's ring, I boldly set him down at my feet.

"Once, long ago," I said to the fog, "you and yours said you were mine to command until a certain debt was repaid. The debt is still owing. I was also promised that when my need was great, one would come. I have him here: the answer to a need, the repayment of the debt." The words were only in my mind, but I felt their meaning ring round the circling mist. "This pup before you is not of yours; he is neither dog nor wolf, and as such is only acceptable to such as we. Let him go! His dam has released him: now it is your turn! This pup before you, sired by your dead leader, now belongs to me and the man who—"

The man who now strode urgently through the mist to my side, wading carelessly through tails and muzzles, to stand with sword drawn, his other arm encircling my waist.

"You're not tackling this on your own! We may be outnumbered, but my sword can bite as sharp as their teeth!" He never knew how near he came to upsetting everything, even while my heart sang with his "rescue," for as I let my attention turn to him the thread that kept the wolves at bay nearly snapped. In time I recalled myself.

"No need, I think, my dear Conn . . ." I touched Snowy's ring to my lips and concentrated again, willing a visual impression of that strange flight from the Castle of Fair Delights. I tried to project that last meeting with the three wolves, the bitch's last words . . . I felt the wolves about me grow still, then there was a pause, as though they were considering. The mist thinned a little and I could see a silent, watchful ring of animals. They sat or lay where they were as if waiting for something to happen. A young wolf, scarce six months, became tired of the delay and crawled towards the pup. Instantly an old bitch snapped it into submission.

We waited. And waited.

At length, trotting proudly through the pack, came the largest of the wolves. In its jaws were the dangling remains of a fresh-killed hare. He halted in front of me, eyes blazing. A pledge. I held out my hand and he laid the limp body of the hare in front of the pup, who immediately sniffed at the still-warm body. Kneeling, I took out my knife and, slitting open the body, brought out the liver, steaming in the cold mist. Quickly I sliced at the meat and handed a piece to the leader-wolf, who snapped it from my fingers. Quelling my nausea I stuffed a bit in my own mouth and handed a piece up to Conn.

"But—"

"Eat! and don't argue. It's important . . ."

The last piece I gave to the pup, who took it delicately and chewed likewise, his eyes never leaving the wolf. The body of the hare still lay before the leader: in one swift movement he snatched it up and tossed it over his shoulder, almost like a game, and immediately the whole pack fell on it, growling and snarling till there was not the smallest scrap of fur or bone left. The new wolf-leader looked at me, at Conn, then slowly, deliberately, he lifted his leg and urinated on the pup and then wheeled round into the thinning mist without looking back. One by one, in correct pack order, the other wolves got up and followed him until at last we were alone.

A fresh breeze blew from the west.

"Suppose," said Conn, "you tell me what all that was about?" I picked up the pup. "Pah! You smell, you poor little so-and-so! Let's find a stream and get you cleaned up . . . Yes, I'll tell you, Conn, but shall we get out of here? I'm hungry, and cold, and tired . . ."

Without a word he picked me up, pup and all, and carried me over to where Beauty was waiting.

The Gleaning: The Knight and His Lady

Journey's End

After that it was different. We were back to the easy, gentle relationship we had had when first setting out on our journey, when Conn had plucked me flowers from the hedge and I had gazed at him when I did not think he would notice.

But that was all: we were back where we started, but no further. It was just like going to all the trouble of preparing a meal, smelling the delicious aromas as it cooked, tasting to see that the juices blended right, preparing the table, sharpening the knives, wiping the bowls, even putting the serving spoon into the stew—and then, no food. Just the tantalizing smells, the salivating mouth, the stomach-turn of anticipation, the growing hunger. And surely, just like a meal that is kept too long, the meat would dry up, the bread go mouldy, the wine sour, and the chief guest disappear? I was hungry for love, real love, desperate to taste what I was sure would be the finest nourishment I had ever been offered, sure that it would fill me to satiation: but the guest at the meal was too polite to invite himself to dinner, and I was too proud to ask, lest I be refused.

That was the worst of all, I suppose, not knowing. When I had been ugly he had promised to take care of me; when I was pretty he had tried to renew his offer but I had sidestepped, and since then he had not referred to it again. I knew he had a journey's end in mind where everything would suddenly be right, why else had we hastened all these miles? But I was not so sanguine. Had I dreamt those moments round The Ancient's fire when he had talked about laying down his arms? Did I imagine in dreams that he had said he wanted to settle down with wife and children? Or had he some other person in mind? To me, love didn't wait on destinations—if, indeed, this were love, this funny, aching, irritating, lovely, despairing longing that I felt.

But thankfully I could not be introspective the whole time. We were travelling through countryside rich with late summer, through forests where the leaves hung heavy and the birds were almost too drowsy to sing, across streams and rivers where the trout lay in somnolent shoals, through villages where it was too hot to do anything but laze in the sun. Beauty grew sleek and plump, Conn and I became almost as tanned as the Dark People and the pup grew tall and strong. We had discussed what to call him. None of the names I tried—Misty, Silver, to do with his colour; Hero and Speedy (hopefully his attributes)—seemed to fit. Then Conn told me how, as a child, he had tumbled on the floor of the Great Hall of his father's home with all the hounds and dogs and terriers, and how he had had a chosen animal he had later hunted with and loved above the rest, one of the Great Ones named Bran. I looked at the pup. "Bran?" I said. He wagged his tail. So Bran it was.

He was already showing promise. Every day Conn, firm and dedicated, taught him obedience and exploited those skills in which he showed promise. For an hour at a time man and dog worked like teacher and pupil, both wearing frowns of concentration, both throwing all they had into the lessons. Then would come a break; Conn would relax, lie back with cheese and bread and the pup would come running to me, all smiles and wagging tail, and I laughed with him and we tussled on the ground together until we were both exhausted. He would roll onto his back, ears flopping in the dust and his hairless belly gleaming in the sunlight and I would kiss his nose and pick the burrs out of his coat . . .

"You spoil him," grumbled Conn. "He's a working dog."

"Not all the time. You weren't a soldier every minute of every day. He's only young: he's got to relax sometimes, just as you are doing now."

"I'm eating."

"And resting . . ."

"At least I'm not playing about!"

"Children must play sometimes; he's still only a youngster."

And then Conn would relent and come and join us, playing with the great paws and scratching him behind the ears. "He's going to be a beauty, just like his dam!"

But the pup would slide his slitted yellow eyes round to mine, eyes slanting back along his head that were pure wolf—

And so the promise they had made, all that long time ago when they escaped from their prison in the Castle of Fair Delights, was fulfilled . . .

And then we came to Encancastre, that the Romans before us had called Isca, through fields heavy with harvest and sickle Lugnosa moon at night. The town stretched away in front of us up narrow, winding streets, a roof-pattern of thatch and wood and tile—and the river ran away at our feet. A haze of smoke drifted down to our nostrils and somewhere was the merry sound of pipe and drum and all the usual hubbub of people living on top of one another: shouts, hails, laughter, complaint; a man singing, a cow bellowing, a dog barking, a child crying—

Civilization.

Part of me welcomed this, looked for the close intimacy of person to person, the comfortable proximity of my own kind; part rejected the whole idea and wished for the loneliness, the open spaces, the close communion that was possible between humans and nature—or was it that I was frightened of giving myself unreservedly to my own kind? Perhaps this had something to do with the gulf that still existed between Conn and myself? I knew, by that extra sense that all women have, that he was far from indifferent to me and even desired me, but I also knew that he was ignorant of the full extent to which his feelings were involved. I knew also that unless he was reminded fairly soon we should just drift farther and farther apart, until—

"—so I thought it would be fair if we split it two-thirds to you and one to myself," said Conn, arranging the gold pieces on a convenient tree-stump. "That means twenty for you and ten for me. I can earn my living easily enough now that I have Booty back and sword and armour. I'll leave Bran with you for the time being anyway, because you need some kind of protector and, although he's by no means full size yet, I'd not like to—"

"What are you *talking* about?"

He looked across at me, puzzled. "Weren't you listening? I said that now we had reached journey's end—"

"Journey's end?"

"I don't believe you heard a word I said!" He frowned. "A long time ago, or so it seems, I said I knew of an army surgeon and bonesetter from my Frankish days who had settled with his English wife in Isca and that I had a mind to learn his trade—"

"But you just said you were going back to fighting—"

"I said that now I had horse and armour I could earn my living, yes, but I intend to learn the trade of surgeon, to travel to where the battles are, fight if needs be, but to offer my services initially as mender rather than breaker."

I was silent. My insides had settled in a doughy lump and my head felt as if it were stuffed with uncombed fleece. He was really going, then: I was to be left on my own.

I tried to keep my voice steady. "I—I remember you saying you—you would see me settled . . ."

"Of course, of course!" He looked uncomfortable at the reminder, was speaking too heartily, would not look at me. "Well now, I've given the matter more than a little thought in the last few days—" (I'll bet! I thought bitterly) "—and the best idea is that I leave you with my friend's wife, who I am sure will prove an excellent chaperone until you get settled. You will have the gold as a nice little—dowry, or somesuch, and when you find someone—somewhere that you want to settle—What's the matter?"

He had said once that I had a stubborn chin: I stuck it out. "You said *you* would! I don't want just any old female looking after me, either! Besides—" I had a sudden, saving thought. "How do you know she'll agree? In fact, how do you even know they are still there?" I warmed to the theme.

"Hadn't you better make sure that this *is* journey's end before you start dividing up the dragon's gold?" And our lives, I added silently. "Why don't you take Beauty and go up into the town and find out? Bran and I will wait for you here." It sounded thoroughly reasonable, yet I thought he might detect the guile that had prompted my words.

He didn't. "Very well. You are sure you want to stay here?"

Oh yes, I was sure, very sure. Even if the animals conspired against our parting, Beauty turning her head twice to look back at me, and Bran whining to see them go.

"Traitor!" I murmured, and stroked his ears. "Now, it's long past noon already, and there is a lot to do . . ."

Further into the woods behind the town I found what I wanted and spent a very busy two or three hours. It was already blueing into twilight when I heard Beauty's hooves on the track. On one edge of the world a thin silver reaper's knife peeked over to counterbalance the gold-plated platter that was sliding away over the other side. Between them a star blinked and yawned, ready to blaze the night, and the air was very still: earth, sun, moon and stars in perfect conjunction and the paths of Power beneath my feet. All boded well and it must be near, or on, the actual feast of Lugnosa, when all good things ripened and fell to the knife and were gathered for harvest. Not the painful, cold birth of Inbolc, nor the frenzied coupling of Beltane, nor yet the haunted darkness of Samain, but still a time for magic . . .

"Did you find him?" I asked Conn as he tethered Beauty to the rowan where I had already tied Bran. Pretending to fuss I looped the garland I had prepared over her neck and turned for Conn's answer.

"After a fair bit of searching, yes. His name is Hieronymus, but he is called Jeremy here, so that complicated the search. But he is just the same, and his wife's as charming a lady as you could hope to meet: makes three of him but still handsome enough, and she's more than willing to take care of you—"

"And what does he say," I interrupted, "about you learning the trade?"

"He agreed at once! He wants us to set up in business together for a while, and says that after a year or so I shall be able to start up on my own if I wish, or buy him out, because he wants to return to his birthland and—"

"Well, isn't that nice!" I said. "Just what you had hoped for!"

"You'll like them too, darling girl. And now shall we—"

I was temporarily sidetracked by the "darling girl" but not so much as not to try and divert him as he moved back towards Beauty, obviously wanting us to go back to the town straightaway. "Let's just have a last, quiet supper on our own tonight and go and see them tomorrow first thing. I made a stew, just in case, and baked some bread, and I saved some of that mead you liked . . ."

The smoke from the fire drifted upwards in a careless spiral, the air was lazy and warm, and all the scents of the earth mingled and thrust at one's senses; great hawk-wings fluttered on teasel and late foxglove, bats swung low, and the ground was dry, the heath springy beneath one's feet. Such a perfect, sweet-smelling night meant unsettled weather for the next few days, especially as tabby-stripe clouds were rising slowly in the west, but now it was perfect.

As was the place I had chosen.

Once there had been a circle but now only the pestholes were left for those who cared to see. A minor place of power, else there would have been standing stones instead of rotted wood, but the rowan, ivy, holly and hawthorn were still there. There were paths of Power beneath our feet, and Conn had seated himself unknowingly on the old altar stone, a slab of rock half-overgrown by the ubiquitous ivy.

He stretched back, his arms behind his head. "What a perfect night! Just right for—" He stopped abruptly. "Er . . . Dinner ready, Thingy?"

Fine, it was going as I had planned.

"Nearly. Why don't you go over to the stream, down there in the hollow, and wash off the grime of the day? I have a clean shirt waiting for you. I'll just add a pinch or two of salt to the stew and cut the bread and then it'll all be ready."

If he thought it was a little odd having a dip at this time of day he made no sign and disappeared behind the bushes. Good. It was necessary to be cleansed.

I added the special touches to the stew, inhaling the pungent, earthy smell of the mushrooms before crumbling them into the bubbling pot, then laid the bowls and horn mugs ready, unstoppering the mead to let it breathe the night air. I had bathed earlier and now, in these few stolen moments, was the time to tune myself to the Power.

I was about to step into the circle to begin the incantations but suddenly there came the hoot of an owl, as out of season as The Ancient's Hoowi. Without thinking I looked across the clearing at Conn's discarded jacket, where the owl's feather and the dove's still blazoned the right breast. The owl's, wisdom; the dove's, peace and fidelity. The owl hooted again, urgently it seemed. Was that, then, my feather? Wisdom? And surely what I was about to do was the only wisdom: lulling Conn into an acceptance of what he really felt, make him declare that which was hidden—

My right hand spasmed as if it were cramped, but only for an instant. I opened the fingers again and stretched them: strange, for one's toes sometimes cramped, but not one's fingers . . . I stepped towards the circle, the owl hooted, my hand spasmed once more and this time the ring on my middle finger, Snowy's spiral of magic horn, bit into the palm of my hand. I pulled at it, tried to unwind the coil, but it was as firm as a fingernail yet still soft and malleable, and as like my own flesh as if it had grown into it, and it wouldn't shift.

Once again I stepped forward, once again my fingers clenched involuntarily. So, I was doing something wrong. Had I mispronounced one of the correct words, mispaced one of the steps, forgotten one of the essential herbs? Quickly I ran through them in my mind, but everything seemed as it should. Then through the soft night air came stealing a strange, alien odour, compounded of so many different things that were foreign to the time and place.

There was a warm, sweaty horse-smell, like but unlike Beauty; a scent of singed horn, fresh spring grass; water bubbling over rocks, summer hay; moss, trampled pine-needles—Snowy!

Forgetting, I turned to look for him, but the traitorous moon showed only emptiness. My eyes flooded with tears, aching for one more sighting of that beloved form, my hands reaching in vain for the soft curtain of his mane, my ears for that quaint, gentle speech. At this moment he was nearer to me than he had ever been since I had seen him pace away into oblivion with his prince, the prince he loved without subterfuge or dissembling or magic—

Oh, Snowy! Of course. Real love was either there or it wasn't. No need to conjure it with runes, bind it with ivy and hawthorn, induce it with mushrooms and mead! Love thus forced was as bad—worse!—than our Mistress's Shape-Changing that had seduced an innocent village-lad and near-trapped Conn also. What was I doing, what was I thinking of? If Conn loved me he would tell me: if he didn't then I had no right to drug him into believing he did!

Running over to Bran and Beauty I tore off their garlands, untied them from the rowan and tethered them again to an innocent oak sapling. Picking up the heavy cooking pot I attempted to heave away the contents into the bushes, but some of the scalding fluid tipped down my dress; panicking both from the heat of the liquid and from some imagined contamination I ripped it off and stood naked. Quickly I circled widdershins to counteract any lingering spells, then raced away to the stream to rinse my dress, without thinking further than that a great load was off my mind: I was free of power, spells and enchantments forever. Now I was me, myself, and never again would I be tempted to use a magic I was not entitled to!

Running through the bushes barefoot I stumbled more than once, but the knowledge that I must wash away all traces of my foolishness spurred me on. Splashing at last into the clear, cold water, I held my dress under and scrubbed away all traces of the magic between my ringers and looped it over a bush to dry, then turned to wash all fever from myself.

"Whatever in the world are you doing, Thingy dear?" There was a lilt to his voice like the turn of the water over the stones, and once more we stood face to face in running water, birth-naked the pair of us, but this time there was no shame on my part, no coyness, no hesitation. I had to know, I had to know right there and then, and convention and a few scraps of cloth, or rather the lack of them, were irrelevant.

"Oh, Conn! I had it all planned but it wasn't right, it was wicked and Snowy told me so and I think The Ancient's owl did too, but I spilt the supper down my dress and had to get myself clean and please say you don't mind, but I must know!"

"Darling girl, you're talking scribble again! Spilt the supper, have you? No bother: there's a tavern not a half-mile from here—"

"You don't understand!" I wailed. "I'm unclean, I—"

"Then that's soon remedied. Just stand still, girl dear, and I'll scoop some water over you . . . So." The water poured from his cupped hands over my shoulders, between my breasts and down my flat stomach to the cleft between my thighs. He lifted more, and this time the tips of his fingers accidentally brushed my breasts and I felt as though I had been kicked in the stomach. Looking down, I saw that my nipples were hard and firm like two wild cherries.

Looking down revealed something else, as well.

"Is that—is that because of me?" I asked wonderingly and put out my hand to touch, but he leapt back as though he had been stung, hands over his crotch, and all but lost his balance.

"Don't—don't!" he said. "You don't know, you don't realize . . ."

"I'm sorry," I said, but there was no consciousness of shame, only a lively curiosity. "I just wanted to touch. You see, that sort of thing has always frightened me before; there was Broom, and then the swineherd: they only wanted to attack, to hurt . . . But yours looks rather nice and friendly, not threatening at all. I have seen it before, you know," I added. "When you were ill, or bathing or getting dressed." I was going to say something about the Lady Adiora, but thought better of it.

"If you try and touch me," he said unsteadily, "knight or no, I won't answer for the consequences . . ."

"Do you mean—you would make love to me?"

"Just that!"

"Then—Oh Conn, I must ask! Does that mean you love me, just the littlest bit? Or is it only what they call lust? You see, I have to know. I've loved you so much all this time, ever since we found you in that ditch, in fact, and at one time I thought you might—Then you didn't ask again, and I thought you didn't . . . I know ladies aren't supposed to ask things like this, and it doesn't matter if you don't, I won't mind—well, not much anyway—but I must know—"

He stepped forward and kissed me then, quite hard, and I fitted nicely into his arms and everything was very interesting, because although my feet by now were cold from the stream and the skin was going all washerwoman-wrinkly, the rest of me was warm and smooth and tingly.

"Does that mean you do?" I asked, when I had got my breath back.

"Does it mean . . . ! Dear Christ, girl, I've worshipped you ever since I first saw you properly in those Waters of Truth! I loved you before, poor helpless little Thingummy that you were, but when I saw that beautiful face on you and the body to match and I knew you were born a lady it was just like your dull pebbles turning into the dragon's jewels: I felt you were way beyond my reach and would never consider an ageing, well-used adventurer!"

"But I *love* you—"

"But I wasn't to know, now was I? You never said . . ."

"Neither did you!" I thought back over the wasted miles. "You're not really well-used . . . Can I now?"

"What? Oh. Well . . ." He seemed a little disconcerted, but I looked down and saw that his body was still keen. Perhaps he was hungry. My mother had always made sure my father was fed and wined before she asked him something special, especially if she was afraid he might say no.

"Perhaps we could have supper first," I suggested. "There's bread left and a bit of cheese, and the mead—"

"Blow supper!" said Conn. "Hang supper! To perdition with supper!" And he picked me up in his arms and carried me all the way back to the fire.

On the way I tried to explain what I had intended to do and he kissed me in all the nicest places and told me he didn't need magic and moonlight and mushrooms to know that I belonged in his heart for always and then he laid me down and took me in his arms again and the earth stretched beneath us like a dreaming beast, and the sickle of the reaper took the last thread that bound me to my past and gathered me and tied me to my love and I heard the music again, the music The Ancient had called Love's Song, and the air sang with it the whole night through . . .

"How about breakfast?" said Conn.

"Breakfast?"

"Yes, breakfast: making love always leaves me with an appetite . . . Now you are to be my wife I shall expect all the comforts of home, you know: meals on demand, and all the rest of it . . ."

"Your wife? Am I really to be your wife?" I looked at him. He was laughing, his moustache curled upward, his eyes sparkled, and on his face was a look of love and contentment and on his jacket our two feathers: wisdom and fidelity. Yes, he meant it.

"Just as soon as we can say the right words in front of the right person." He reached over and spanked my rump. "Now, lazy one, get some clothes on and we'll go up to town." He followed the spank with a kiss on the offended portion. "And then if you'll bear with me learning the surgeon's trade for a while, we'll go on afterwards and find that home you dreamt of: sea, hills and a stream, wasn't it, with martlets in the eaves and seals to sing us to sleep? And we'll settle there and have children and love and quarrel and then kiss and make up. I'll cure the people and you will tend to the hurts of the animals, and we'll live happily ever after . . ."

And so we did.

And so the soldier: hung up his sword;
The hands that had hewn: turned to heal.
The loves she had lost: became different loves,
And the martlet made: his mansion in the eaves.
The wolf-cub waited: by the wall of the house
And the people of the sea: sang them to sleep.

Pigs Don't Fly

This one is for my little brother,
Micky-Michael, and my half-sister,
Anna, and their families.

Acknowledgments

Thanks, as always, to my husband Peter, for his care and patience.

Belated thanks—sorry, folks!—to Bobby Travers and his daughter Joanna for smoothing our way out here.

Thanks, too, to Margaret and Barry Shaw for their help with Christopher.

I am also grateful to our *alcalde,* Don Carlos Mateo Donet Donet, for his assistance and encouragement.

Last, but never ever least, thank you Samimi-Babaloo, my Sam—just for being yourself!

Part 1:
An End

Chapter One

My mother was the village whore and I loved her very much. Having regard to the nature of her calling, we lived a discreet distance away from her clients, in a cottage up the end of a winding lane that backed onto the forest. Once the dwelling had been a forester's hut, shielded by a stand of pines from the biting winter northerlies, but during the twenty years since she had come to the village it had been transformed into a pleasant one-roomed cottage with a lean-to at the side for wood and stores. Part of the ground outside had been cleared and fenced, and we had a vegetable patch, three apple trees, an enclosure for the hens, a tethering post for the goat and a skep for the bees.

Inside it was very cozy. Apart from the bed, which took, with its hangings, perhaps a third of the space, there was a table, two stools, hooks for our clothing, a chest for linen and a dresser for the pots and dishes. Above the fire was the rack for drying herbs or clothes, beside it a folding screen that Mama sometimes used when she was entertaining if it was too cold for me to stay outside—though as I grew older I preferred to sit among the pungent, resinous logs in the lean-to, wrapped in my father's cloak, thinking my own thoughts, dreaming my own dreams, where witches and dragons, princes and treasure could make me forget chilblains or a runny nose until it was time for Mama to call me back into the warmth and the comfort of honey-cakes and mulled wine in front of the fire.

Then Mama would sit in her great carved chair in front of the blaze—a chair so heavy with age and carving it couldn't be moved—a queen on her throne, me crouched on a cushion at her feet, my head against her knee, and if she were in a good mood she would talk about Life and all it held in store for me.

"You will be all I could never be," she would say. "For you I have worked and planned so that you may have a handsome husband, a home of your own, and a dress for every season. . . ."

That would be luxury indeed! Just imagine, for instance, a green dress for spring in a fine, soft wool, a saffron-yellow silk for summer, a brown worsted for autumn and a thick black serge for winter with fresh shifts for each. . . . A man who could afford those for his wife would have to be rich indeed, and live in a house with an upstairs as well as a downstairs. Even as I listened the dresses changed colour in my mind's eye as quick as the painted flight of the kingfisher.

Mama's planning for me had been thorough indeed. On a Monday she entertained the miller, who kept us regularly supplied with flour and meal for me to practice my pies, pastry and cakes; Tuesday brought the clerk with his scraps of vellum and inks for me to form my letters and show my skills with tally-sticks; on Wednesday Mama spent two hours with the butcher and once again I practiced my cooking. On Thursday the visit of the tailor-cum-shoemaker gave me pieces of cloth and leather to show off my stitching; Friday brought the Mayor, who was skilled with pipe and tabor so I could display my trills and taps and on a Saturday the old priest listened to me read, heard my catechism, and took our confessions.

Sunday was Mama's day off.

She had other visitors as well, of course, besides her regulars. The apothecary came once a month or so, sharing with us his wisdom of herbs and bone-setting, the carpenter usually at the same interval, teaching me to recognize the best woods and their various properties, and how to repair and polish furniture. The thatcher showed me how to choose and gather reeds for repairing the roof, the basketmaker, also an accomplished poacher, instructed me in both his crafts.

All in all, as Mama kept telling me, I must have been the best educated girl in the province, and she covered any gaps in my education with her own knowledge. It was she who taught me plain sewing, cooking and cleaning, leaving the refinements to the others. She insisted that as soon as I was big enough to wield a broom, lift a cooking-pot or heat water without scalding myself, that I kept us fed, clean and washed, and throughout the year my days were full and busy.

During the spring and summer I would be up before dawn—taking care not to wake Mama—and into the forest, cutting wood, fetching water, looking to my traps, gathering herbs and then home again to collect eggs, feed the hens, and weed the vegetables. Then I would milk the nanny and lay and light the fire, mix the dough for bread, sweep the floor and empty the piss-pot in the midden, so that when Mama finally woke there was fresh milk for her and a scramble of eggs while I made the great bed and heated water to wash us both; then I changed her linen, combed and dressed her hair and prepared her for her visitors. Once the ashes were good and hot they were raked aside for the bread, or if it was pies or patties I would set them on the hearthstone under their iron cover and rake back the ashes to cover them.

Once Mama was settled in her chair by the fire it was away again for more wood and water and once I was back there were the hives to check, a watch on the curdling goat's milk for cheese, digging or sowing or watering in the vegetable-patch and perhaps mixing straw and mud for any cracks in the fabric of the cottage. Then indoors for sewing, mending, washing pots and bowls, followed by any other tasks Mama thought necessary.

Once the gathering, storing and salting of autumn were over, my outside tasks during the winter were of a necessity curtailed, although there were still the wood- and water-chores, even with snow on the ground. There were the stores to check: jars of our honey, crocks of flour, trays of apples, salted ham, clamps of root vegetables, strings of onions and garlic, bunches of herbs, dried beans and pulses. That done, it was time for candle-dipping, spinning, carding wool, sharpening of knives, re-stuffing pillows and cushions, sewing and mending, mixing of pastes and potions and repairing of shoes.

Then came the time I liked best. While I dampened down the fire and made us a brew of camomile flowers, Mama would comb her hair and sing some of the old songs. We would climb into bed and snuggle down behind the drawn hangings for warmth, and if she felt like it my mother would either tell me a tale of wicked witches and beautiful princesses or else, which I like even better, would tell once more of how she had come to be here and of the men she had known. Especially my father.

I had heard her story many times before, but a good tale loses nothing in the retelling, and I would close my eyes and see pictures in my mind of the pretty young girl fleeing home to escape the vile attentions of her stepfather; I would shiver with sympathy as I followed the flight of the pregnant lass through the worst of winters and sigh with relief when she reached, by chance, the haven of our village, and my heart filled with relief when I re-heard how she had been taken in by the miller and his wife. Once her pregnancy was discovered, however, there was a meeting of the Council to decide what should be done with her, for now she was a Burden on the Parish and could be turned away to starve.

"But of course there was no question of that," said Mama complacently. "Once I had discovered who was what, I had distributed my favors enthusiastically to those who mattered, and all the important men of the village were well disposed to heed my suggestion for easing their . . . problems, shall we say? Of course much was tease and promise, for there is nothing more arousing to a man than the thought of undisclosed delights to come. . . . Remember that, daughter. You had better write it down some time. Of course I was far more beautiful and accomplished than the other girls in the village, though I say it myself, even though I was four months gone. I still had my figure and my soft, creamy skin, and of course every man likes a woman with hair as black and smooth as mine. . . .You would say, would you not, child, that my skin and hair are still incomparable?"

"Of course, Mama!" I would answer fervently, though if truth were told her hair had grey in it aplenty, and her skin was wrinkled like skin too long in water. But she had no mirror but me and her clients, and who were the latter to notice in the flattery of candles or behind drawn bed-curtains? Besides, those she entertained were mostly well into middle age themselves and in no position to criticize.

"So by the time the meeting of the Council came round it was a foregone conclusion that I would stay. It was decided to offer me this cottage and food and supplies in return for my services," continued Mama. "Of course I laid down certain conditions. This place was to be renovated, extended, re-roofed and furnished. I was also to entertain six days a week only: Sunday was to be my day of rest.

"At first, of course, I was at it morning, noon and night, but eventually the novelty-value wore off and my friends and I settled to a comfortable routine. Your elder half-brother, Erik, was born here and three years later your other half-brother, Luke. . . ."

Erik now was a man grown with a shrewish and complaining wife. Dark, long-faced, with tight lips, he had teased me unmercifully as a child. Luke I remembered more kindly. He was apprenticed to the miller and had the same sandy hair, snub nose and gap-toothed smile. It was obvious who his father was and he even resembled him in temperament: kind and a little dim.

And now came the part of Mama's story of which I never wearied.

"Some dozen or more years ago," she would begin, "your half-brothers were fast asleep and I was all alone, restless with the spirit of autumn that was sending the swallows one way, bringing the geese the other. It was twilight, and all at once there came a knocking at the door. It had to be a stranger, for there was fever in the village and I had forsworn my regulars until it had passed. . . ."

"And so there you were, Mama," I would prompt, "all alone in the growing dusk. . . ." Just in case she had forgotten, or didn't feel like going on. So vivid was my imagination that I felt the shivers of her long-ago apprehension, imagining myself alone and unprotected as she had been with the October mist curling around the cottage like a tangle of great grey eels, slither-slide, slither-creep. . . .

"And so there I was," continued Mama, "determined to ignore whoever, whatever it was. But again came that dreadful knocking! I grasped the poker tight in my hand, for I had forgotten to bolt the door—"

"And then?" I could scarcely breathe for excitement.

"And then—and then the door was pulled open and a man, a tall, thin man, stood in the shadows, the hood of his cloak pulled down so I could not see his face. You can imagine how terrified I felt! "What—what do you want?" I quavered, grasping the poker still tighter. He took one step forward, and now I could see his cloak was forest-green, and the hand that held it was brown and sinewy but still he said nothing. Then was I truly afraid, for specters do not speak, and of what use was a poker against the supernatural?"

I gasped in sympathy, crossing myself in superstitious fear.

"I think that my bowels would have turned to water had he stood there silent one moment longer," she said, "but of a sudden he thrust one hand against his side and held the other out towards me, saying in a low and throbbing tone: 'A vision of loveliness indeed! Do I wake or sleep? In very truth I believe the pain of my wound has conjured up a dream of angels.' "

How very romantic! No wonder Mama was impressed.

"The very next moment he crumpled in a heap on my doorstep, out like a snuffed candle! What else could I do but tend him?" and she spread her hands helplessly.

And that was how my father had come into her life. At once she had taken him into both her heart and her bed—what woman wouldn't with that introduction?—and nursed him back to health. For an idyllic month, while the village still lay under the curse of a low fever, my father and mother enjoyed their secret love.

"He was both a courtly and a fierce lover," said my mother. "A trifle unpolished, perhaps, but not beyond teaching. He was always eager to learn those little refinements that make all the difference to a woman's enjoyment. . . ." and my mother paused, a reminiscent smile on her face.

"And what did he look like, my father?"

But here always came the odd part. Perhaps the passage of years had played strange tricks with my mother's memory for my father never looked the same for two tellings. At first he was tall, then recollection had him shorter. Dark as Hades, fair as sunlight; eyes grey as storm clouds, blue as sky, brown as autumn leaf, green as duck-weed; he was loquacious, he was taciturn; he was happy, he was sad; shy, outgoing . . . I was sure that if ever I loved a man I would remember every detail forever, right down to the number of his teeth, the shape of his fingernails, the curl of his lashes. But then Mama had known as many men as there were leaves on a tree, so she said, and always tended to remember them by their physical endowments rather than their physiognomy. In this respect she assured me that my father was outstanding.

I hated the sad part of my father's story, but it had to be told. One frosty day, as my mother told it, the men from the village came and dragged him from the cottage and carried him away, never to be seen again. "They were jealous of our love," she said, and she had never ceased hoping that he would return, her wounded lover who came with the falling leaves and left with the first frosts.

He had left nothing behind save his tattered cloak, a purse full of strange coins, and a ring. Mama said the coins were for my dowry, but that the ring was special, a magic ring. She had shown it to me a couple of times, but it looked like nothing more than the shaving of a horn, a colorless spiral. It would not fit any of my mother's fingers, and she would not let me try it on.

"He wore it round his neck on a cord," she said, "for it would not fit him either. He said it was from the horn of a unicorn, passed down in his family for generations, but it did nothing for him. . . ."

She had tried to sell it a couple of times, but as it looked so ordinary and fit no one, she had tossed it into a box with the rest of her bits and pieces of jewelry—necklace, brooch, two bracelets—where it still lay, gathering dust.

My days were not all work and no play, though I mostly made my own free time by working that much harder. I had two special treats. If the weather was fine, summer or winter, I would escape into the woods or down by the river, lie under a tree and gaze up into the leaf-dappled sunshine and dream, or sit by the river and dangle my toes in the fast-running water. This would be summer, of course, but even in the cold and snow there were games to play. Skipping-stones, snowballs, imaginary chases, battles with trees and bushes . . . Away from the cottage I was anything I chose and could forget the confines of my cumbersome flesh and flew with the birds, swam with the fish, ran with the deer. Gaze up into the rocking trees in spring and I was a rook, swaying with the wind till I felt sick, my beak weaving the rough bundles they called nests. Dangle my fingers in the water and I was a fish, heading upstream into the current, the river sliding past my flanks like silk. Given the bright fall of leaves and I ran along the branches with the squirrels and hid my nuts in secret holes I would never remember. Winter and I sympathized with the striped badgers, leaving the fug of their sets on warmer days to search for the scrunch of beetle or a forgotten berry or two, blackened into a honey sweetness by the frost.

But the thing I loved most in the world to do was write in my book.

This had grown from my very first attempt at writing my letters, many years ago. Now it was thick as a kindling log and twice as heavy. At first the clerk had formed letters for me in the earth outside, or had taught me to mark a flat stone with another, scratchy one, but as I progressed he had shown me how to fashion a quill pen and mix inks, so it was but a short step to putting my first, tentative words on a scraped piece of vellum.

As parchment or skin was so expensive I sometimes had to wait for weeks for a fresh piece, but I practiced diligently with my finger on the table to ensure I should make no mistakes when the time came.

For the Ten Commandments, my first page, the old priest provided me with a fine, clear page, but by the time I finished it was as rough and scraped as a pig's bum. My next task was the days of the week, months and seasons of the year, followed by the principal saint's days and festivals of the Church calendar. Then came numbers from one to a hundred. This done, the elderly priest dead and another, less tolerant, in his place—he never visited Mama—I was free to write what I wished, whenever I could beg a scrap of vellum from the clerk. Down went recipes for cakes, horehound candy, poultices, dyes and charms.

I do not remember what occasioned my first essays into proverbs, saws and sayings. It may have been the mayor, once chiding me for hurrying my tasks. "Don't remove your shoes till you reach the stream," he had said, and this conjured up such a vivid picture of stumbling barefoot among stones, thorns and nettles that down it had to go. Not that it cured me of haste, mind, but it was an extremely sensible suggestion. Then there were my mother's frequent strictures on the behavior expected of a lady: "Do not put your chewed bones on the communal platter; reserve them to be thrown on the fire, returned to the stock pot, or given to the dogs." Or: "A lady does not wipe her mouth or nose on her sleeve; if there is no napkin available, use the inner hem of your shift."

She also gave me the benefit of her experience of sex; pet names for the private parts, methods of exciting passion, of restraining it; how to deal with the importunate or the reluctant, and various draughts to prevent conception or procure an abortion. Down these all went in my book, for I was sure they would one day prove useful, though she had explained that husbands didn't need the same titillation as clients. "After all, once you're married he's yours: you will need excuses more than encouragements."

When the pages of my book grew to a dozen, then twenty, I threaded them together and begged a piece of soft leather from the tanner for a cover and a piece of silk from Mama to wrap it in. A heated poker provided the singed title: *My Boke.* At first Mama had laughed at my scribblings, as she called them, for she could not read or write herself, but once she realized I was treasuring her little gems of wisdom and could read them back to her, she even gave me an occasional coin or two for more materials, and reminded me constantly of her forethought in providing me with such a good education.

"What with your father's dowry and my teachings, you will be able to choose any man in the kingdom," she said.

And that was perhaps the only cause of friction between us.

A secure, protected, industrious childhood slipped almost unnoticed into puberty, but I made the mistake one day of asking Mama how long it would be before she found me the promised husband, to be met with a coldness, a hurt withdrawal I had not anticipated. "Are you so ready to leave me alone after all I have done for you?" I kept quiet for two more years, but then asked, timidly, again. I was unprepared for the barrage of blows. Her rage was terrible. She beat me the colors of the rainbow, shrieking that I was the most ungrateful child in the world and didn't deserve the consideration I had been shown. How could I think of leaving her?

Of course I sobbed and cried and begged her on my knees to forgive me my thoughtlessness, and after a while she consented for me to cut out and sew a new robe for her, so I knew I was back in favor. Even so, as year slipped into year without change, I began to wonder just when my life would alter, when I would have a home and husband of my own, as she had promised.

And then, suddenly, everything changed in a single day.

Chapter Two

That morning Mama was uncharacteristically edgy and irritable. She complained of having eaten something that disagreed with her, and although I made an infusion of mint leaves and camomile, she still seemed restless and uneasy.

"I shall go back to bed," she announced. "And I don't want you clattering around. Have you finished all your outside jobs?" I had. "Then you can go down to the village and fetch some more salt. We're not without, but will need more before winter sets in. Wait outside and I'll find a coin or two. . . ."

This was always the ritual. Our store of coins, which Mama always took from passing trade, were hidden away, and only she knew the whereabouts. I didn't see the need for such secrecy, but she explained that I was such a silly, gullible child that I might give away the hiding place. I couldn't see how, as I scarcely spoke to anyone, but she insisted.

I picked up an empty crock and dawdled down the path towards the gate. It was a beautiful morning, and I was in no hurry to go. I hated these visits to the village, but luckily only made them when there were goods we could not barter for—salt, oil, tallow, wine, spices. I enjoyed the walk there, the walk back and would have also enjoyed gazing about me when I got there, but for the behavior of the villagers. When I was very young I did not understand why the men pretended I didn't exist, the women hissed and spat and made unkind remarks and the children threw stones and refuse. Now I was older I both understood and was better able to cope. When I complained, Mama always said she couldn't comprehend why the women weren't more grateful: after all, she took the heat from their men once a week. Like everyone else, she said, she provided a service. But that didn't stop the children calling after me: "Bastard daughter of a whore!" or worse.

"Here, daughter!" I turned back to where Mama stood on the threshold. She would never come outside. In summer it was "too hot," in winter "too cold." In autumn it was wasps and other insects, in spring the flowers made her sneeze, and through all the seasons it was a question of preserving her complexion. "I wouldn't want to be all brown and gypsyish; part of my attraction to my clients is my pale, creamy skin. You had better watch yours, too, girl: you're becoming as dark as your father. What's acceptable on a man won't do on a woman."

Now she handed me some coin. "Watch for the change: I don't want any counterfeit. And if I'm asleep when you return, don't wake me. I shall try and sleep off this indisposition."

"If you're really feeling ill I could fetch the apothecary—"

"Don't be stupid: I am never ill! Now, get along with you before you make me feel worse—and for goodness sake straighten your skirt and tie the strings on your shift: no prospective husband would look at you twice like that! Do you want to disgrace me?"

I kissed her cheek and curtseyed, as I had been taught, and walked away sedately till I was out of sight, then hung the crock over my shoulder by its strap, hitched up my skirts and scuffed my feet among the crunchy, crackly heaps of leaves along the lane, taking great delight in disordering the wind-arranged heaps and humming a catchy little tune the mayor had taught me for my pipe.

It seemed I was not the only one fetching winter stores. Above my head squirrels were squabbling over the last acorns. I could hear hedgepigs scuffling in a ditch searching for grubs, too impatient for their winter fat to wait till dusk, and thrushes and blackbirds were testing the hips and haws in the hedges and finishing off the last brambles, while tits and siskins were cheeping softly in search of insects. A rat, obviously with a late litter, ran across in front of me, a huge cockchafer in her mouth.

The sun shone directly in my eyes and shimmered off the ivy and hawthorn to either side, making their leaves all silver. I passed through a cloud of midges, dancing their up-and-down day dance—a fine day tomorrow—and on a patch of badger turd a meadow-brown butterfly basked, its long tongue delicately probing the stinking heap. My only annoyance was the flies, wanting the sweat on my face, and the wasps, seeking something sweet, so I pulled a handful of dried cow parsley and waved that freely round my head.

I purchased the salt without much notice being taken, for a peddler had found his way to the village, and the women and children were crowding round his wares. So engrossed were they that the miller passing by with his cart had time to give me a huge wink and toss me a copper coin. "Don't spend it all at once. . . ."

Money of my own! A whole coin to spend on whatever I wanted! At first I thought to buy a ribbon from the peddler, but that would need explanations when I returned home, and somehow I didn't think Mama would approve of her clients giving me money. Lessons and food were different. Food! I had just reminded myself I was hungry. I looked up at the sun: an hour before noon. Still, if I bought something now I needn't hurry home, and Mama could enjoy her sleep. I peered at the tray in the bakers. Ham pies, baked apples, cheese pasties . . . The pies looked a little tired and I had had an apple for breakfast, so I carried away two cheese pasties.

One had gone even before I reached the lane again, but I decided to find somewhere to sit in the sun and thoroughly enjoy the other. There was a bank full of sunshine a quarter mile from the cottage just where the lane kinked opposite one of the rides through the forest, and I seated myself comfortably and enjoyed the other pasty down to the last crumb, wiping my mouth thoroughly to leave no telltale grease or crumbs. I found a couple of desiccated mint leaves in the hedge behind and chewed those too, just in case Mama spotted the smell of onions, then burped comfortably and lay back in the sunshine, the scent of the mint an ephemeral accompaniment to the background of autumn smells: drying leaves, damp ground, wood smoke, fungi, a gentle decay.

I sniffed my fingers again, but the scent of mint had almost gone; strange how the pleasant smells didn't last as long as the stinks. I must put that thought down in my book. "Perfumes are nice while they last, but foul smells last longer"? Clumsy. What about: "Sweet smells are a welcome guest, but foul odors stay too long." Still clumsy; it needed to be shorter, more succinct, and could do with some alliteration. "Sweet smells stay but short: foul odors linger longer." Much better.

As soon as I had time to spare I would write that down. The trouble was that it took so long; not the actual writing, now that I was more used to it, but the preparation beforehand. First, I had to be sure I had at least a clear hour before me, then the weather had to be right: too hot and the ink dried too quickly; too wet and it wouldn't dry at all. It had to be mixed first of course to the right color and consistency, and the quills had to be sharpened and the vellum smoothed and weighted down and the light just right.

But then what joy! I scarcely breathed as I formed the letters: the full-bellied downward curve of the *l* the mysterious double arch of the *m,* the change of quill position for the *s,* the cozy cuddle of the *e*—each had its own individual pattern, separate symbols that together made plain the things I had only thought before.

Magic, for sure. First the letters themselves, precise in shape and order, then the interpretation into words and meaning and lastly the imagination engendered by the whole. The old priest had once given me a saying: "God created man from the clay of the ground: take care lest you crack in the firing of Life." I had dutifully copied this down, but once it was there it took on a new dimension. In my mind I could actually see little clay men running round with bits broken and chipped off them, crying out that the Almighty Potter had not shaped them right or had made the kiln too hot or too cold, and—

"Hey, there! Wake up, girl!"

Suddenly the sun had gone. I opened my eyes and there, towering over me, was the awesome bulk of a caparisoned horse, snorting and champing at the bit. Still half-asleep I scrambled to my feet and backed up the bank, wondering if I was still dreaming.

"Which way to the High Road?"

The horse swung round and now the sun was in my eyes again. I dropped down to the road, and was seemingly surrounded by a party of horsemen who had obviously just ridden along the ride out of the forest. Hooves stamped, harness jingled, men cursed and I was about to panic and run for home, when the face of the man on the caparisoned horse swam into view and I felt as though I had been struck by lightning.

He was the handsomest man I had ever seen in my life. It was the eyes I noticed first, so dark and deep a blue they seemed to shine with a light all their own. Dark brows drawn together over a slight frown, a high, broad forehead and crispy dark hair that curled down unfashionably to his collar. His skin was faintly tanned, his nose straight; there was a little cleft in his rounded chin and his mouth—ah, his mouth! Full and sensual, wide and mobile . . . I remembered afterwards broad shoulders, wide chest and long, well-muscled legs, but at the time I could only stare spellbound at his face.

Someone else spoke, a man who was probably one of his retainers, but the words didn't register. I couldn't take my eyes off his master.

The mouth opened on perfect teeth and the apparition spoke.

"I asked if you knew the way to the High Road."

"She's maybe a daftie, Sir Gilman. . . ."

I shook my head. No, I wasn't a daftie, I just couldn't speak for a moment. I nodded my head. Yes, I did know the way to the High Road. I was conscious of the sweat pouring from my face, an itch on my nose where a fly had alighted, could feel an ant run over my bare toe—

"If you follow the lane the way I have come"—I pointed—"you will come to the village. If you take the turning by the church you will have to follow a track through the forest, but it is quicker. Otherwise go across the bridge at the end of the village, past the miller's, and there is a fair road. Perhaps four miles in all." I didn't sound like me at all.

He smiled. "And that is the way to civilization?"

I stared. Civilization was here. Then I remembered my manners and curtsied. "As you please, sir. . . ."

He smiled again. "Thank you, pretty maid. . . ."

And in a trample of hooves, a flash of embroidered cloth, a half-glimpsed banner, he and his men were gone clattering down the lane.

I stood there with my mouth open, my mind in a daze. He had called me "pretty maid"! Never in my wildest imaginings had I conjured up a man like this! Oh, I was in love, no doubt of it, hopelessly, irrevocably in love. . . .

I must tell Mama at once.

I hugged his words to my heart like a heated stone in a winter bed as I raced home, near tripping and losing the salt. Flinging open the door and quite forgetting she might be sleeping, I rushed over to the bed where she sat up against the pillows.

I grabbed her hand. "Mama, Mama, I must tell you—Mama?"

Her hand was cold, and her cheek, when I bent to kiss it, was cold too. The cottage was dark after the bright outside and I could not see her face, but I didn't need to. She couldn't hear me, couldn't see me, would never know what I had longed to tell her.

My mother was dead.

Chapter Three

At first I panicked, backing away from the bed till I was brought up short by the wall and then sinking to my knees and covering my head with my arms, rocking back and forth and keening loudly. I felt as if I had been simultaneously kicked in the stomach and bashed over the head. She couldn't be dead, she couldn't! She couldn't leave me all alone like this! I didn't know what to do, I couldn't cope. . . . Oh, Mama, Mama, come back! I won't ever be naughty again, I promise! I'll work twice as hard, I'll never leave you, I didn't mean to upset you!

My eyes were near half-shut with tears, my nose was running, I was dribbling, but gradually it seemed as though a little voice was trying to be heard in my head, and my sobs subsided as I tried to listen. All at once the voice was quite plain, sharp and clear and scolding, like Mama's, but not in sentences, just odd words and phrases.

"Pull yourself together . . . Things to be done . . . Tell *them*."

Of course. Things couldn't just be left. I wiped my face, took one more look just to be sure, then ran as fast as I could back to the village. Luckily the first man I saw was the apothecary. As shocked as a man could be, he hurried back with me to confirm my fears. He examined Mama perfunctorily, asked if she had complained of pains in the chest and shook his head as I described her symptoms of this morning, as best I could for the stitch in my side from running.

"Mmm. Massive heart attack. Pains were a warning. Must have hit her all at once. Wouldn't have known a thing."

Indeed, now I had lit a candle for his examination I could see her face held a look of surprise, as though Death had walked in without knocking.

"Will tell the others. Expect us later." And he was gone.

Expect us later? What . . . ? But then the voice in my head took over again. "Decisions . . . Burial . . . Prepare . . . Food."

Of course. They would all come to view the body, decide how and when she should be buried, and would expect the courtesy of food and drink. What to do first?

"Cold . . . Water . . ."

The fire was nearly out and there was a chill in the room. For an absurd moment I almost apologized to Mama for the cold, then pulled myself together, and with an economy born of long familiarity rekindled the ashes, brought in the driest logs and set the largest cauldron on for hot water. With bright flames now illuminating the room, I checked the food. A large pie and a half should be enough, with some of the goat's-milk cheese and yesterday's loaf, set to crisp on the hearth. There were just enough bowls and platters to go round, but only two mugs; I could put milk into a flagon and what wine we had left into a jug and they could pass those round. Seating was a problem; the stools and Mama's chair would accommodate three, and perhaps two could perch on the table or the chest. The rest would have to stand.

The water was now finger-hot, and I turned to the most important task of all. Crossing to Mama's clothes chest I pulled out her best robe, the red one edged with coney fur, and her newest shift, the silk one with gold ribbons at neck and sleeve, and the fine linen sheet that would be her shroud.

The heat from the fire, which had me sweating like a pie, had relaxed her muscles, so it was an easy enough task to wash her, change the death-soiled sheets, pad all orifices and dress her in her best. That done, I combed and plaited her hair and arranged it in coils around her head, but was distressed to see that the grey streaks would show once I had the candles burning round the bed. She would never forgive me for that, I thought, then remembered my inks. A little smoothed across with my fingers and no one would notice. . . .

I crumbled dried rosemary and lavender between the folds of her dress for sweetness, then went outside and burned the soiled sheets and the dress she had been wearing when she died. Outside it was quite cool, the sun saying nearer four than three, and the smoke from the bonfire rising thin and straight: a slight frost tonight, I thought. On the way back in I gathered some late daisies and a few flowers of the yellow Mary's-gold, and placed them in Mama's folded hands, then set the best beeswax candles in the few holders we had around the bed, ready to light once it grew dark.

I looked at her once more, to see all was as she would have wished and to my amazement saw that Death had given her back her youth. Gone were the frown lines, the pinched mouth, the wrinkles at the corners of her eyes. She looked as though she were sleeping, her face calm and smooth, and the candle I held flickered as though she were smiling. She was so beautiful I wanted to cry again—

"Enough! Late . . . Tidy up. Wash and change . . ."

I heeded the voice, so like hers—but it couldn't be, could it?—and a half-hour later or so I had swept out and tidied, washed myself in the rest of the water, including my hair and my filthy clothes, hanging out the latter to dry over the hedge by the chicken run, and had changed into my other shift and my winter dress. Mama would be proud of my industriousness, I thought. But there was no time for further tears, for I could hear the tramp of feet down the lane. My mother's clients come to pay their last respects.

Suddenly the room, comfortably roomy for Mama and me, had shrunk to a hulk and shuffle of too many bodies, with scarce space to move. The only part they avoided was the bed.

They had all come: mayor, miller, clerk, butcher, tailor, forester, carpenter, thatcher, basket-maker, apothecary; all at one time my mother's regular customers. The new priest was the only odd one out. In spite of their common interest I noticed how they avoided looking at one another. At last, after much coughing, scratching and picking of noses, the mayor stepped forward and everything went as quiet as if someone had shut a door.

"Ah, hmmm, yes. This is a sad occasion, very sad." He shook his head solemnly, and the rest of them did likewise or nodded as they thought fit. "We meet here to mourn the sudden passing of someone who, er, someone who was . . ."

"With whom we shared a common interest?" suggested the clerk.

"Yes, yes of course. Very neatly put. . . . As I was saying, Mistress Margaret here—"

"Margaret? Isabella," said the miller.

"Not Isabella," said the butcher. "Susan."

"Elizabeth," said the clerk. "Or Bess for short."

"I thought she was Alice," said the tailor.

"Maude, for sure . . ."

"No, Ellen—"

"I'm sure she said Mary—"

"Katherine!"

"Sukey . . ."

I stared at them in bewilderment. It didn't seem as though they were talking about her at all: how could she possibly be ten different people? Then, like an echo, came my mother's voice: "In my position I have to be all things to all men, daughter. . . ."

The mayor turned to me. "What was your mother's real name?"

I shrugged my shoulders helplessly. "I never asked her. To me she was just—just Mama." I would *not* cry. . . .

"Well," said the priest snappily, "you will have to decide on something if I am to bury her tomorrow morning. At first light, you said?"

They had obviously been discussing it on the way here.

"It would be . . . more discreet," said the mayor, lamely. "Less fuss the better, I say."

"Aye," said the butcher. "What's over, is over."

"What I want to know is," said the priest, "who's paying?"

They all looked at me. I shook my head. I knew there were a few coins for essentials in Mama's box, but not near enough to pay for a burial and Mass.

"I don't think she ever thought about dying," I said. This was true. Death had never been part of our conversations. She had been so full of life and living there had been no room for death. I thought about it for a moment more, then I knew what she would have said. "I believe she would have trusted you, all of you, to share her dying as you shared her living."

I could see they didn't like it, but there were grudging nods of assent.

"What about a sin-eater?" said the priest suddenly. "She died unshriven. Masses for a year and a day might do it, but . . ."

More money. "There isn't one hereabouts," said the mayor worriedly. "I suppose if we could find someone willing we should have to find a few more coins, but—"

"I'll do it," I said. "She was my mother." I couldn't leave her in Purgatory for a year, even if I was scared to death of the burden. "What do I do?"

But no one seemed very sure, not even the priest. In the end he suggested I take a hunk of bread, place it on my mother's chest and pray for her sins to pass from one to the other. Then I had to eat the bread.

It near choked me, and once I had forced it down I was assailed by the most intolerable sense of burdening, as though I had been squashed head down in a small box after eating too much.

They watched me with interest.

"Is it working?" asked the priest.

"Yes," I gasped, and begged him for absolution.

"Excellent," said the priest, looking relieved. "We shall repair to the church, choose the burial site and you may confess your mother's sins and I shall absolve her."

It was cold inside the church for the sun was now gone and twilight shrouded the altar, mercifully hiding the mural of the Day of Judgment which, faded though it was, always gave me nightmares. To be sure, there were the righteous rising in their underwear to Heaven, but the unknown artist had had an inspired brush with the damned, their mouths open on silent screams as they tumbled towards the flames, poked and prodded by the demons of the Devil.

The priest led me through Mama's confession—it was very strange confessing unknown sins for someone else—and he told me to confess to absolutely everything, just in case. Some of those sins he prompted me with I had never even heard of.

"Now you may either say a thousand *Hail Marys* in expiation, or perhaps find it more convenient to make a small donation," he said hopefully.

As it happened I had the change from buying the salt still tied round my waist in my special purse-pocket, so he gave me a hurried full absolution to our mutual satisfaction. Immediately it seemed as though the dreadful heaviness left me, just like shucking off a heavy load of firewood after a long tramp home. Now Mama could ascend to Heaven happily with the rest of the righteous.

We came out into a dusky churchyard, and found the others grouped in the far corner against the wall.

"This'll do," said the mayor. Next to the rubbish dump. "It'll take less digging and is nicely screened from view. Why, you could even scratch the date of death on the wall behind. Pity she couldn't lie next to your father, girl, but of course his bones were tossed to the pigs long ago—"

"My *father*?" I could not believe what I was hearing. My father had been driven away by jealous villagers and dared not return; my mother had told me so.

"Of course. Led us a merry chase, but we caught him about two mile into the forest, and—"

"She doesn't know," interrupted the miller, glancing at my face. "Happen her Ma told her something different." He looked at the others. "No point in bringing it up now."

I could feel something crumbling inside me, just like the hopeful dams I had built as a child across the stream, only to see them crumble with the first rains. I had cherished for years the vision of a handsome soldier-father forced to leave his only love, my beautiful mother, and now they were trying to say—

"Tell me!" I shrieked, the anger and bewilderment escaping me like air from a pricked bladder, surprising them and myself so much that we all jumped apart as though someone had just tossed a snake into our midst.

So they told me, in fits and starts: apologetically, belligerently, defiantly. At first it was just as Mama had related it; there had been fever in the village, the stranger had sought refuge at our cottage and they had enjoyed their secret idyll. Then everything had gone wrong. Houses left empty by fever deaths had been looted, and as they reasoned no one in the village could have been responsible, they had searched farther afield, and had found some of the bulkier objects hidden in a sack at the rear of our dwelling. My father had run; they had pursued him into the forest where a lucky arrow had brought him down. Although he was dead they had had a ceremonial hanging in the village, then had chopped him in pieces and thrown the pieces to the pigs.

So the man whose memory I had cherished, the father who my imagination had made taller, handsomer and braver than anyone else in the world, was nothing more than a common thief!

"I don't believe you, any of you! You're all lying, and just because Mama isn't here you're—you're—" I burst into tears. But I knew they were telling the truth; they had no reason to lie, not after all this time. But the anger and frustration would out, and I switched to another hurt. "And I won't have Mama buried next to the midden! She must have a proper plot, a proper marker, a decent service and committal, just as she deserves—"

"Now look here, girl," interrupted the butcher angrily. "Don't you realize we have to pay for all this? Now your Ma's dead you have nothing, are nothing. Of all the ungrateful hussies—"

"Easy, Seth," said the clerk. "She's upset. None of this is her fault. It's up to us to do the best for—for . . . I'm sorry, girl, I don't think I remember your name."

"My name?"

"Yes," said the tailor. "Always just called you 'girl,' as your mother did."

There were nods, murmurs of confirmation from the others.

"Well?" said the priest.

I stared at them all aghast. I could feel myself falling. . . .

"I haven't the faintest idea. . . ." I croaked, then everything went black.

Chapter Four

They brought me round with hastily sprinkled font water.

I had never fainted before in my life and I felt stupid, embarrassed and slightly sick. Their faces swam above me like great moons, in the light from the miller's lantern. For a moment I could remember nothing, and then it came back like a knife-thrust: Mama was dead, my father a thief, and I had no name. In a way the last was the worst. Without an identity I was a blank piece of vellum, a discarded feather, the emptiness that is a hole in the ground. I felt that if I let go I should float up into the sky like smoke, and dissolve as easily. I was deathly frightened.

Then somebody had a good idea. "You must have been baptized." Of course, else would I not have been allowed to attend Mass.

They helped me to my feet and we all repaired to the vestry, where by the light of the lantern and the priest's candle, the fusty, dusty, mildewy parish records were dragged out of a chest.

"How old are you?"

But I couldn't be exact about that either, till the miller suggested the Year of the Great Fever, and there was much counting backwards on fingers and thumbs and at last the entry was found, in the old priest's fumbling, scratchy hand.

"Here we are. . . . Strange name to call anyone," said the present priest. Only the clerk, he and I could read, and I bent forward to follow his finger. There it was, between the death of one John Tyler and the marriage of Wat Wood and Megan Baker. The cramped letters danced in front of my eyes, but at last I spelled it out.

No date, but the previous entry was June, the latter July.

"Baptism of dorter to the Traveling woman: one Somerdai."

"Somerdai . . ." I tried it out on my tongue. "Summer-day." And Mama had called herself one of the Travelers. All right, she had given me an outlandish name, but at least I now existed officially. And, according to the records, I was seventeen years old, and knew something more of Mama's origins. All at once I felt a hundred times better, and was able to invite them all back for the funeral meats almost as graciously as she would have done.

It did not take them long to demolish everything. I closed the shutters, made up the fire and lighted the candles around Mama; they threw our shadows like grotesques on the whitewashed walls and made it look as though Mama sighed, smiled and twitched in a natural sleep.

The mayor accepted the dregs of the wine jug, drained them and brushed the crumbs from his front. Clearing his throat, he addressed us all.

"I now declare this special meeting open. . . ."

What meeting?

"Having determined to settle this little matter as soon as may be, I think it is now time for us to agree on our previously discussed course of action."

My! They had certainly been busy amongst themselves, either on the way here or in the churchyard. . . . But what "little matter"?

"Firstly, Summerhill, or whatever your name is—I should like to thank you on behalf of us all for the refreshments." Everyone murmured their approval. "We have already agreed to attend to the burial of the—the lady, your mother, and to defray all costs." He cleared his throat again. "Now we come to the distribution of the assets. . . ."

"My hens," said the butcher.

"My goat," said the tailor.

"My bees," said the clerk.

"The clothes chest—"

"The hangings—"

And suddenly they were all shouting against each other, pointing at our belongings, even gesturing towards the padded quilt on which Mama lay and touching the gown she wore.

I was horrified, but as they quietened down it became obvious that everything I had thought we owned, Mama and I, belonged in some way or other to her clients. They were just loans. If I had ever thought about it at all, which I hadn't, I should have guessed that the finely carved bed, the elaborate hangings, some of the fine clothes, could not have been gifts, like the flour, meat and pulses.

Now the butcher was on his feet. He was the man I had always liked least of Mama's clients, not only because he sometimes tried to put his hands down my front.

"Comrades . . . Quiet! I know what we all have at stake here, but we cannot leave the new whore entirely without."

Surely they couldn't mean that I—

But the mayor took over, with an uneasy glance in my direction.

"Normally, of course, we could have left all this for a day or two until everything settled down," he said. "But under the circumstances—"

"With her losing her job and all—" said the butcher.

"—we shall have to make a quick decision," continued the mayor.

My heart gave a sudden lurch of thankfulness. They hadn't been thinking of me as a replacement after all. But the mayor's next words hurt. "Normally we might have offered young Summer-Solstice here the job, as her mother's daughter, but under the circumstances I don't believe she would attract the same sort of custom. . . ."

"Oh, come on!" said the miller, always ready with a kind word. "She's not that bad! A nice smile, all her teeth, small hands and feet, a fine head of hair . . ." Even he couldn't think of anything else.

"Mama wished me to become a wife, not a whore," I said stiffly. Whores were special, but wives came in all shapes and sizes, so I had a better chance as the latter, especially with my learning and dowry—come to that, where was it? Mama had never said. And when I found the coins, how did I set about finding this elusive husband I had been promised? With winter coming on, it would be better to leave it until New Year. If what they had said about the furniture going to the next whore was true, the cottage would seem very bare. I had a few coins left of Mama's, and perhaps if they let me keep a couple of the hens and I could persuade the carpenter to knock me up a truckle bed, I could manage with what was laid aside. But I should have to buy some salted pork—

" . . . so, if it is convenient, shall we say noon tomorrow?" asked the mayor. "Although your brothers are not here now, they will attend the interment in the morning, and your eldest brother let it be known his wife would not be averse to the dresses. . . ."

I had lost something in his speechifying, but that pinched-nosed sister-in-law of mine was not going to wear my mother's dresses, and I told him so.

"Why not? They're of no use to you. Your ma was tall and thin."

"I still would not like to see another in her dresses—"

"Nonsense! Why waste them? The new whore, Agnes-from-the-Inn, would fit into them nicely, too. No point in wasting them."

So that sandy-haired, big-bosomed wench was to be the next village whore! "No," I said.

"As she's getting everything else," said the butcher, "including this cottage, why not chuck the dresses in as well? Not yours to dispose of, anyway."

"This place? But it's ours—mine, surely?"

The mayor shook his head. "Goes with the job. So, as I said a moment or two back, I can expect you out by midday tomorrow?"

"I can't! I've nowhere to go!" This just couldn't be happening. All in one day to lose my mother, the shreds of my father's reputation and also find I possessed a ridiculous name, then to be turned out into an unknown world with nothing to my name and nowhere to go—

I burst into tears; angry, snuffly, hurt, uncontrollable, ugly tears. Now Mama had always taught me that tears were a woman's finest weapon. She had also tried to teach me how to weep gently and affectingly, without reddening the eyes or screwing up the face, but all my tears produced were embarrassment, red faces and a rush for the door, just as if I had been found with plague spots.

"Back at dawn," called out the mayor. "We'll bring a hurdle for the body. . . ."

The priest was the last to leave. "Not even one coin for the Masses?" I shook my head.

I heard their footsteps retreating, then one set returning. The miller poked his head round the door.

"Just wanted to say—will miss your Ma. She was a lady. Sorry I can't take you in like your brother, but the wife wouldn't stand for it." He turned to go, then stopped. "Thought you might like to know; years after your dad—died—someone else confessed to planting those stolen goods. Said he was jealous. Dead and gone, now . . . Hey there: no more tears! Could never abide to see a lass cry. Here, there's a couple of coins for your journey. And don't worry, you'll do fine. I'll see the grave's kept nice," He sidled out through the door. "Sorry I can't do more, but you know how it is. . . ."

"Yes," I said. "I know how it is. . . ."

Alone, I sank to my knees beside the dying fire, my mind a muddle. Shock and grief had filled my mind to such an extent I was incapable of thinking clearly. All I wanted was for Mama to be back to tell me what to do, for I felt an itching between my shoulder blades that told me I had forgotten something, and could not rest till it was seen to.

A log crashed in the hearth and I started up. Mustn't let the fire die down, tonight of all nights—But why? Of course: tonight was All Hallows' Eve, the eve of Samhain. Tonight was the night when the unshriven dead rode the skies with the witches and warlocks and the Court of Faery roamed the earth. . . . Tonight was the night that, every year, Mama and I closed and locked the shutters and doors early, stoked up the fire and roasted chestnuts and melted cheese over toasted bread, thumbing our noses at those spirits who moaned and cursed outside, wanting to take our places and live again. But it was the fire that kept them away, so Mama said, that and the songs we sang: "There is a time for everything," or "After Winter cometh Spring," and "Curst be all who ride abroad this night."

I rushed outside and brought in all the wood I could gather. Why bother to save any for the new whore? Let her seek her own. And she had no daughter to fetch and carry as Mama had done: they would soon be sick of her. I even emptied the lean-to of our emergency supply, running back and forth under an uneasy moon, till the room was overflowing with faggots and logs. Tonight we would have the biggest blaze ever, Mama and I.

By the time I had finished I was quite light-headed, even addressing the still figure on the bed. "There you are, Mama! Enough to set the chimney alight!"

"And everything else . . ." came a voice in my head. "Everything must go with me. . . . Nothing left."

Was that what she wanted? Everything burned? But wasn't that what her people, the Travelers, did? Hadn't she told me once that when a chief died his van was piled with his belongings, his dogs and horses were sacrificed and all consumed in a great pyre? Then if that was what she wanted, that was what she should have.

I approached the bed again. "You shall have a bonfire fit for a queen,"

I told the silent figure. "They shall not have your bed, your dresses, your chair; I promise."

"Open . . . Fly . . ."

I frowned; what did that little voice mean: *Fly*? What was to fly? There was a moth doing a crazy dance round one of the guttering candles and I moved my hand to bat it away, upon which it swerved over my head and made for the shuttered window, beating frantically against the wood. Then I understood.

"Sorry, Mama . . ."

Ceremoniously I flung back the shutters onto the night, then wedged open the door. Coming back to the bed I blew out the candles, one by one, then knelt to pray. I prayed for a safe journey for my mother's soul, reminding God that her sins were all absolved. Then I leaned over for the last time and kissed her brow.

"All ready, Mama. Go with God." As I did so it seemed a little breeze stirred the hangings, and I distinctly felt a rap on my head—the sort Mama used to make with her knuckles when I had completed a task after a reminder. A moment later the door crashed shut. She had gone.

I refastened door and window, then bethought myself of my own arrangements. If I were to be away from here before they discovered what I had done, then I must pack up all I needed for my journey quickly. Clothes, food, utensils, blanket, money . . . Money. Where had Mama put my dowry? Frantically I searched all the places it could be and came up with nothing. It must be somewhere; Mama wouldn't have made it up. I wished it was light again, for the cottage was full of shadows and every corner looked like a potential hiding place. I must find it, I must! I couldn't face the wide world with the few coins left in Mama's box and the couple the miller had left me.

Opening Mama's box, however, discovered her bracelets, necklet and brooches, and the horn ring my father had left behind. I took them over to the bed, fastened the brooch and necklet, and then tried to force the ring onto her fingers, one after the other, but it wouldn't go: her fingers were too fat. Strange, she had long, slim fingers. I put on the bracelets, deciding I would take the ring with me, wearing it on a string round my neck. It might bring me luck, I thought, and without thinking slipped it onto the middle finger of my right hand, while I bent forward to adjust the bracelets on Mama's wrists to their best advantage.

As I placed her hands once more crossed upon her breast, I noticed something strange; although I was certain I had washed her thoroughly there was what looked like a sooty residue caught under the fingernails of her right hand—All at once I knew where the dowry would be. Rushing over to the fireplace I felt high up in the chimney, first to one side, then the other. At first all I got were scorched fingers and a fall of soot, but at last on the left-hand side my scrabblings found a ledge, and on the ledge a bag of sorts, which I snatched out to drop on the floor with a clink and chink of coin.

I fell to my knees on the hearth and gazed with excitement at the pile of coins that had burst from the split leather pouch that had contained them. I had never seen so much money in my life! And all the coins looked like either silver or gold. . . . All in all, a fortune. Hastily wiping my sooty fingers I began to examine them, one by one. All but two were strange to me, the inscriptions and symbols utterly alien. A scrap of singed paper fluttered to the floor. It was so brittle with age and heat it crumbled to pieces in my fingers even as I read it: "Thomas Fletcher, Mercernairy, his monnaies." There followed a list I could not follow, then "Ayti coyns in all."

So my father had been named, and could write, after a fashion! That surely was where I had got my learning skills. But eighty coins? There were less than half, surely, for even with the confirmation of my tally sticks there were forty-seven missing. I glanced over to the bed where my mother lay in all her finery, extra dresses and shifts spread around her, and my eyes filled with tears, remembering the silver coins and a couple of gold that had purchased them. At the time I had wondered where they had come from, and now I knew. But how was I to know that my father hadn't wished it so? After all, she had been his beloved, and I shouldn't grudge a single coin. Before me lay enough still for a fair dowry, even if the coins would have to be weighed for their metal content only, as they were foreign. But there were still a couple of our own coinage: I could manage for a while on those.

Before my eyes the piece of paper crumbled into ash, the pouch also, as if they had been just waiting for me to find them and were now dead like my mother. Carefully I packed the coins inside my waistband purse, determined as soon as possible to make them a separate hiding place.

As I tucked them away I noticed for the first time the ring upon my finger. I couldn't remember putting it there, and absent-mindedly tried to pull it off to tie round my neck, as I had originally intended. But it wouldn't come. There it was, settled snug on my finger as if it was part of the very skin. . . . Suddenly I tingled all over and everything became brighter and sharper, as if a veil had been pulled away.

As if a stranger I saw all the cracks in the wall, the shabbiness of the room; I heard the crackle of the fire, the creak of furniture as if it were talking to me; for the first time smelled the sweetish-sickly odor of decay coming from the bed so strongly I had to pinch my nostrils and swallow hard. There was a taste of soot and ashes in my mouth where I had licked my fingers and the hearth beneath my hands was rough with grit and dust.

But there was something else as well. Not exactly hope, that was too strong a word, but a sort of energy I had not known I possessed. Something enforced the knowledge that I was alone for the first time in my life, but also that I would manage somehow or other, that I wasn't a complete idiot, that life held more than I had expected.

I rose to my feet. There were things to be done and, as my inside time clock told it was near midnight, the sooner the better. Outside, when I went to check that the goat and chickens would be safe, the moon was riding clear of cloud, the stars were bright and a crispness to the air confirmed frost.

I loaded up the sledge I used for wood with what I thought necessary, did a last check, then piled wood around the bed, sprinkling it with oil the better to burn. I opened the shutters for a draught and left the door open. That done I made a last check, then gazed around the cottage that had been my home, expecting nostalgia.

Nothing. Nothing at all.

It was just a place that two people had lived in, an empty shell with now no personality left. A room, nothing more, as empty of life as the still figure on the bed, the living and memory seeping from it as surely as the body became cold in death. No, there was nothing for me here now.

"Goodbye, Mama," I said, and threw a lighted brand from the fire towards the bed.

Part 2:
Summer's Journey

Chapter Five

Someone had opened both shutters and door, and pulled back the bed clothes; the light was shining in my eyes and I was freezing—

I came to with a start. I was in a forest, so had I fallen asleep while collecting wood? Realization came as bitter as the early morning taste in my mouth, as I struggled out of the blanket I had wrapped myself in.

I was in the woods somewhere between the village and the High Road, I was alone, and I was hungry and needed to relieve myself. First things first, and as I squatted down I glanced around the little dell in which I had hidden myself the night before. Last night's frost still silvered the grasses and ferns, but the rising sun promised a warm day. Already a cloud of midges danced above my head and a breeze stirred the almost leafless trees. A pouch-cheeked squirrel darted across the glade ahead, and I could hear the warning chink of a blackbird as I scrambled to my feet. Otherwise everything was quiet, except for the tinkle of a stream away to my right.

So, I hadn't been followed. So far . . .

I cringed when I remembered my escape of the night before. Once I had been sure the cottage was blazing merrily, the flames lighting up the night sky until I feared the conflagration would be spotted in the village, I had set off down the path, dragging the loaded wood sledge behind me. Sighting the way had been easy, with the fire behind and the moon above, so I had not needed my lantern. But where had my caution, my fear of the night, gone? As I remembered it I had strode through the village as if it were a midsummer day, singing some crazy song I couldn't now remember, almost asking those within doors to come out and discover the suddenly-gone-mad girl who had made the cottage a funeral pyre for both her mama and all those goods that now belonged to someone else, and who was now disregarding the terror of All Hallows' night and marching down the road with the demons at her heels and the witches swooping around her head.

But no one had appeared. Doors remained bolted and barred, shutters firmly closed. Those who had heard my wild passage had probably hid beneath the bedclothes, crossed themselves and been convinced that at last all their fears walked abroad in ghastly form and that to look on such would snatch what little wits they had away forever. And in the morning, when they saw what remained of the cottage, with luck they might think it had all been a ghastly accident, and that I had been immolated with Mama. Of course, once the embers had cooled down and they could rake through the ashes they would probably realize what I had done and make some sort of search for me—but by that time I hoped to be well away beyond their reach.

My stomach gave a great growling lurch, reminding me it had had nothing since I couldn't remember when. I didn't remember eating a thing last night, so those cheese pasties must have been the last thing to comfort it. I scrabbled among the wreck of my belongings on the sledge—it had tipped over twice last night and scattered everything—and at last found twice-baked bread, cheese and a slice of cold bacon. Washing it down with water from my flask, I refilled the same from the stream nearby, determined next to sort out the things I had brought. But I was still hungry. I couldn't think straight without something else in my stomach. After all, to someone who was used to breaking her fast with gruel, goat's milk, bread and cheese, ham, an egg or two and honey cakes, this morning's scraps were more of an aggravation than a satisfaction.

Searching among the debris I found a heap of honey cakes I had forgotten about. I gobbled down one, two, three. . . . That was enough; I should have to go easy. I couldn't be sure when I would come upon the next village. Well, perhaps just one more: that would leave an even number—easier to count.

Feeling much better, the stiffness of the night nearly gone, I spread out my belongings on the grass. The sledge looked the worse for wear; too late I remembered it was due to be renewed as soon as possible: the carpenter had promised to make new runners. I should just have to hope it would carry my belongings as far as the High Road, then I would have to think again. Even now, there must be at least something I could leave behind to lighten the load.

An axe for chopping wood: I couldn't do without that. Tinder, flint and kindling, also necessary. Lantern, candles, couldn't do without those either. The smallest cooking pot, with a lid that would double as a griddle, a ladle, large knife and small one, spoon, two bowls and a mug. Essentials. Water flask, small jug, blanket, rope, couldn't do without those, either.

Clothes? I was wearing as much as I could, but surely I still needed the two spare shifts, ditto drawers and stockings? My father's comfortable green cloak, pattens for the wet, clothes for my monthly flow, comb, needles, thread and strips of leather for mending clothes and shoes. Packets of dried herbs and spices, seeds for planting when I finally reached my destination—onion, garlic, chive, rosemary, dill, bay, thyme, sage, turnip, marjoram—and a small pestle and mortar.

Which brought me to the food. A small sack of flour—bread to eat if nothing else—a crock of salt, bottle of oil, pot of honey, jar of fat, pack of oats. And for ready consumption two cheeses, a hunk of bacon, two slices of smoked ham, some dried fish, two loaves and twelve honey cakes.

Which left my writing materials, tally sticks and the Boke. Those came with me if nothing else did.

I surveyed the articles laid out on the grass with dismay. There was nothing, absolutely nothing, I could leave behind. Somehow or other I would have to pack them better, and trust the sledge would at least get me as far as the High Road. Then perhaps I could find a lift, or could repair the runners well enough to get me to a village.

The sun was already clear of the trees: I had better get moving. Setting to work I found the packing much easier and the result neater and better balanced, especially when I utilized one of the double panniers I had also dragged along for the eatables, salt and flour, and I reckoned I should get along much faster now.

Perhaps the pannier would be better balanced if I distributed the food more evenly: it must be ten o'clock, and I should travel better with a nibble of something in my stomach. That bread was already stale, so if I ate a crust and a slice of cheese—or two . . .

"Proper little piggy, ain't you?" said a voice.

I whirled around on my knees, sure I had been discovered. But there was no one in sight, the forest was in the same state of suspended alert and there was no sound of footsteps. I decided I must be light-headed and had imagined it. I took another bite of cheese, and—

"Some of us ain't eaten for two days," said the same voice. "Chuck us a bit of rind, and I'll go away. . . ."

Dear God! It must be one of the Little People, of which I had heard from Mama. I crossed myself hastily. What had she said about Them? Mischievous, usually only out at night, not to be crossed lightly. With shaking fingers I cut a piece of rind and threw it as far as I could, then hid my eyes, remembering that They don't like to be looked at either.

"Mmm, not bad at all," said the voice again. A very uneducated voice, I thought, then wondered if They could read minds. "How's about a bite of crust, while we're at it?"

Obediently I threw the crust, and this time there were distinct crunching noises, then silence. I decided I could risk a peep. Surely It had gone. . . .

At first I thought It was an Imp, a black Imp, then I saw that Whatever-it-was had taken the form of a dog. At least I think it was meant to be a dog. I shut my eyes again.

"Gam! I ain't that bad-lookin', surely?"

"Of course not," I said, still with my eyes shut tight. Heaven knows what would happen if I looked at it straight in the eye. "If—if there is nothing else, may I please go my way?"

"I ain't stoppin' you," said the Thing. "Though I thought as how you might like a bit of company, like."

"No thanks," I said hastily. "I'm fine, thanks."

"Pity," said the Thing. "Could be a lot of use to you, I could. Fetch and carry, spot out the way ahead, general guide, guard dog . . ."

"Guard dog?" I said, suddenly suspicious. "You did say 'dog'?"

"'Course. Don' look like a cat, do I?"

I scrambled to my feet and stared at the apparition. "I've seen you before somewhere. . . ."

"Course you have, in the village; seen you a coupla times, too."

I stared across the diplomatic space that still separated us. Of course he was a dog, how had I ever thought otherwise? But dogs don't talk. Especially this one. He resembled nothing so much as a scrap of rug you might leave outside the door to wipe your feet upon. He was like a furry sausage, a black and grey and brown sausage. One ear was up, one down; there was a tail of sorts and presumably mouth and eyes hidden under the tangle of hair at the front. The nose was there and underneath four paws, big ones like paddles, but set under the shortest set of legs imaginable. I remembered now where I had seen him before: chased down the village street by the butcher, those stumpy legs going like a demented centipede.

All right, he wasn't a figment of my imagination and he wasn't one of the Little People, but there was still something wrong. Dogs don't *talk*. . . .

"Where you goin' then?"

"To—to seek a new home. My mother died yesterday."

"Makes two of us—lookin' for somewhere, that is. Never had a place to set down me bum permanent-like. Folks is wary of strays."

Dogs don't talk. . . .

All right, if he wasn't the Devil himself—which was just possible—and he wasn't of Faery stock, then this must be magic. A very powerful magic, too. Surreptitiously I first crossed myself again, then made the secular anti-witch sign, the first two fingers of my hand forked. Nothing happened; he still sat there, but now he indulged in a fury of scratching and nipping, then hoofed out both ears with a dreadful, dry, rattling sound.

"Little buggers lively 's mornin'. . . . Tell you what: I'll just come with you as far as the road—that's where you're headed, ain't it? Keep each other company, like."

"No . . . Yes, I don't know. . . ." I said helplessly.

DOGS DON'T TALK!

"Aw, c'mon! What harm can it do? You and I will get along real well, I know we will. 'Tween us we'll make a good team—"

The scream would out. It had been sitting there at the bottom of my throat like a gigantic belch and I could hold it back no longer. It escaped like the tuning wail from a set of bagpipes, only ten times as loud.

"Go away, go away, go away! I can't stand it anymore! Dogs don't talk, *dogs don't talk,* DOGS DON'T TALK!"

And I ran away across the glade, screaming like a banshee, until there was a *thud!* in the middle of my back and I fell face down in a heap of leaves, all the wind knocked out of me.

"Shurrup a minute, will you? Want the whole world to hear? Got hold of the wrong end of the stick, you has. Just sit up nice and quiet-like, and I'll explain. . . ."

I did as I was told, emptying my mouth of leaves and pulling twigs from my hair. The dog sat about six feet away, his head on one side. Close to he was even tattier. I felt like a feather mattress that has been beaten into an entirely different shape.

"Now then you says as how dogs don't talk. Well o' course they does. All the time. Mostly to each other, 'cos you 'umans don't bother to listen. You expects us to learn how you speak, but when we tries you tells us to shut up. Ain't that so?"

I nodded. I had had nothing to do with animals, except the goat, hens and bees—Mama wouldn't have a dog or cat in the house: she said they were messy, full of disease, and took up too much space. Some of the dogs in the village were used for hunting, others as guards, a couple as children's pets, but I had never heard anything from their owners save a sharp word of command, though I had seen kicks and cuffs in plenty. Certainly no one talked to them.

"We don' only talk, we sings, too. P'raps you heard us sometimes o' nights, when the moon is full and the world smells of the chase and we can hear the 'Ounds o' Eaven at the 'eels of the 'Unter?"

Indeed I had. Some nights it seemed that the dogs of the village never slept, and even where we lived we could hear the howling and baying and yelping.

"Lovely songs they are too," he said. "'Anded down from sire to dam, from bitch to pup. . . ."

"But why," I said carefully, "can I now understand what you say?"

"Now, I could spin you a yarn as fine as silk and tell you as 'ow I was the magickest dog in the 'ole wide world, and you'd believe me. For a while, that is, till you found as you could talk with other animals, too. No, I won't tell you no lies, 'cos I believe we got business together, you and I—" He nipped so quickly at whatever was biting him that I jumped. "Got the little bugger. . . . Truth is, lady, that why I can talk to you and you to me is all on account of that there bit o' Unicorn you carries round with you." And he scratched at his left ear, the floppy one, till it rattled like dry beans in a near-empty jar.

I was lost. "Bit of a *Unicorn*?" Unicorns were gone, long ago.

"The ring you wear, you great puddin'! That what you got on that finger of yours. Bit of 'orn off'n a Unicorn, that is. Now you can understand what all the creatures say if'n you pays a bit of attention. Din' you know what you got?"

I sat looking at the curl of horn on my finger in bemusement. It still looked like nothing more than a large nail-paring, almost transparent. I tried to pull it off but it wouldn't budge. Indeed, it now felt like part of my skin. I tried again. "Ouch!"

"Once it's on, it's on," said the dog. "Only come off if'n you don' need it no more, or don' deserve it. Very rare, these days. . . . Come by it legal?"

I nodded, remembering my mother telling me how my father had worn it round his neck. So perhaps he hadn't needed it anymore—or hadn't deserved it. But I wouldn't think about that. Nor that it wouldn't fit my mother. But why me? Perhaps I needed it more than them, specially now

I was on my own. Indeed, it had a comforting feel, like something I had been looking for for a long time and had found at last.

"Well," said the dog. "We'd best be goin'. Day ain't gettin' any younger, and we've a ways to travel to the Road."

"I'm not sure I want . . . What I mean, is . . ." However I said it, it was going to sound ungracious, but I had no intention of sharing my dwindling rations with a smelly stray dog with an appetite even bigger than mine.

"Come on, now: you *needs* me. I can be your eyes and ears, I can. Best thief for fifty mile. Nab you a bit o' grub any time; never go 'ungry with me around. 'Sides, I'll be comp'ny, someone to talk to. Nighttimes I'll keep watch, so's you can sleep easy. No one creeps up on me, I can tell you!" He put his head on one side, in what I supposed he thought was an engaging manner. "What d'you say? Give us a trial. We can always part comp'ny if'n it don' work. . . ."

Some of what he said made sense, if he stuck to what he said. And I wouldn't really be any worse off, unless he decamped with all the food. He made it sound, too, as if all the advantages were on my side.

"And just what do you get out of it?"

He hung his head, and I could scarcely hear what he was saying. "P'raps I'm tired o' bein' on me own. P'raps, just for once, I should like to belong. Never had a 'ome, nor one I could call boss." He looked up, and there was a sort of defiant guilt in the one eye I could see. He shook his head as if to free it of water. "Got me whinging like a sentimental pup, you has. C'mon, let's get started; with all that fat you're carryin' it'll take us twice as long. . . . Now what's the matter?"

Just exactly what he had said: that was the matter. The words were carelessly cruel but none the less accurate. He had put into words a fact that everyone—me, my mother, her clients—all knew but never mentioned. The children in the village shouted it out often enough, one of the reasons I hated shopping there, but I could always pretend they were just being malicious. That was one of the reasons the mayor last night would not have accepted me as Mama's replacement; the reason the kind miller had run out of compliments past hair, smile, teeth and the size of my hands and feet.

The fact was I was fat. Not fat, obese. No, admit it: gross. I was a huge lump of grease, wobbling from foot to foot like ill-set aspic. I couldn't see my feet for my stomach, hadn't seen them for years; I had to roll myself in and out of bed, was unable to rise from the floor without first going on hands and knees and grabbing bedpost or chair. I couldn't climb the slightest rise without panting like a heat-hit dog; had lost count of my chins and got sores on my thighs with the flesh rubbing together.

And I had been unable to stop eating, which made it worse. Surprisingly Mama had made no attempt to stop me: she had even encouraged my consumption of honey cakes, fresh bread and cream after that time I had asked her about a prospective husband—

"Missin' your Ma, eh?" said the dog sympathetically. "Understand how you feels; felt the same myself once . . . Are you all right, then?"

❧ ❧ ❧

We had struggled on for perhaps another half mile when the dog stopped suddenly, his good ear cocked.

"Shurrup, and listen."

Gratefully I put down my burdens. I could hear nothing. Perhaps a kind of rustling and stamping far ahead, a sort of cry . . .

The dog was off through the undergrowth like a flash, his legs a blur of movement. He was gone what seemed like hours, but could only have been a matter of minutes, and arrived back literally dancing with impatience. "C'mon, c'mon! I got us transport!"

"A—a cart? Another sledge?"

"Nah! The real thin'! I got us a 'orse!"

Chapter Six

"That's—that's a horse? You're joking!"

A creature with four legs, sure, head and tail in the right place but the mess in between—was a mess. From what I could see, shading my eyes against the sun, it was swaybacked, gaunt, hollow-necked, filthy dirty and with a hopelessly matted mane and tail.

"Sure it's a 'orse. Got all the essentials. Needs a bit of a wash and brush-up, p'raps. . . ."

It would need more than that. As I walked cautiously forward, fearing it might run at sight of us, I saw that it wasn't going anywhere. It had got itself hopelessly entangled in the undergrowth by bridle, tail, hoof and the remains of a slashed girth and saddlebags that had ended up under its stomach. Its eyes widened with alarm as we approached and it made a token struggle against the bonds that held it, only to become more enmeshed than ever.

I halted a few feet away and spoke soothingly, using the words I had heard the villagers use to their workhorses, for I had never had cause to deal with one before and wasn't quite sure how to begin. The horse showed the whites of its eyes, as well as it could for the sticky tendrils of bindweed that clung to mane and ears.

"Speak to it nicely," said the dog. "Just like you would to me."

"You mean—it can understand me?"

"O-mi-Gawd!" he said. "Din' I tell you about the ring? 'Course it understands, but it's a bit scared right now and may not listen. Nice and easy, now." He walked nearer. "Now stand still, 'Orse, and 'er ladyship 'ere will see to you. . . ."

"Get away, get away! I'll kick you to death—"

"You an' 'oose army?"

I had understood this plainly enough, so I walked up to the horse more confidently and stretched out my hand. It made a halfhearted snap, but seemed quieter, though it still trembled till the branches and twigs which held it fast shook like wind-troubled water.

"Look," I said, "at my finger. I wear the ring of the Unicorn and that means we can understand each other. All I want to do is help. If I release you, will you promise not to run away till we have talked?"

It looked at the ring, at my face, and back at the ring. The shivering stopped, and I gathered it agreed, though I heard nothing definite.

It took a long time, and I was sweating as much as the horse by the time it was released and stood free. I picked away the last of the bramble and bindweed, and tried to comb out the worst tangles from mane and tail with my fingers. Standing free it didn't look much better. There was a long gash across its rump where someone had tried to slash the girths that held the now-empty saddlebags, but these had only loosened, not broken. I slid them up from under the belly and restrapped them.

"There, that's better. . . . Stand still a moment and I'll put some salve on the cut and the graze on your shoulder." In my belongings, dragged along behind as I followed the dog to his "'orse," was a pot of one of the apothecary's favorite healing balms, a mixture of spiderwebs, dock-leaf juice and boar's grease. I smeared some gently on the broken hide, and found another gash on one hock, which I treated the same way.

"There," I said, standing back. "Near as good as new. . . ."

"I thank you, bearer of the Ring," said the horse. It had a soft, gentle voice, quite unlike the dog's raucous voice. "I am in your debt—"

"Then you can help us carry 'er things," said the dog, who had been remarkably quiet during the last half hour or so, not surprising when I found he was chewing on the rest of the cheese I hadn't packed well enough.

"Thief!"

"There was ants on it . . . All right, all right! Won't do it again. Well, what about it, 'orse? Gonna 'elp?"

The horse glanced from one to the other of us. "I don't know. . . ."

"Of course I can't ask you to help if you belong to someone," I said. "That would be stealing. Is your master hereabouts?"

"All gone, all gone . . ." It started shivering again. "I ran away."

Obviously some disaster. "Calm down! Well, if you don't belong to anyone, what did you plan on doing, boy?"

I was interrupted by a loud snigger from the dog. "Blind as a bat, you is! 'E's a she. . . ."

I felt as though I had been caught in a thicket with my drawers down, and apologized profusely.

"My name is Mistral," said the horse, "and among my own people I am a princess. I wish to go back to where I came from, of course."

Anything less like a princess of anything I had yet to see, but I hadn't had much experience of horses. "And where was that?"

The horse hung her head. "That I do not know. They stole my mother when she had me at her side, and would not leave me to escape. She told me of our people, of how we lived, and of my inheritance. But she died, they killed her with overwork, and I was sold as a packhorse. That was a year, two, ago. All I want now is to find my way back to my people. . . ."

"And you have no idea where that is?"

"No, except that south and west feels right."

"Well," said the dog, "if'n you goes on your own you could be picked up by anyone; best you can get from that is 'eavier burdens or a knock on the 'ead for the glue in your bones and a tough stew or two. Then there's wolves if'n you're thinkin' o' goin' the long way round. Now we offers you a bit o' protection-like, a step or two in the right direction, reg'lar food and all in exchange for carryin' a light load for this lady. What d'you say?"

"And you go south, south and west?"

The dog must have seen my mouth open to say we had decided nothing like that, for he jumped in before I could say anything. "'Course we is! With winter comin' on, 'oo'd be idiot enough to go north? North there is snow, west there is storms, east there is icy winds, so south we goes. Right, lady?"

Weakly I nodded. Put like that it seemed like the only road to take.

"Right," I said. "And—and if you agree to come with us, then I will care for you as best I can and try and put you on the right road for your home. Is that fair?"

"Without you I should probably have starved to death, or worse," said Mistral. "I accept. And now, perhaps, we should load up. The sun starts to go down."

Indeed it was well past its zenith. Hastily I started to pack our belongings on the horse, only to be brought up short by her patient explanation of weight distribution, top-heavy loads, etc., so the light was already reddening as we set off. Even then she seemed curiously reluctant to go the way I wanted, the way the dog assured me led straight to the High Road.

"We'll have to go past *there,*" she said. "*There,* where it happened."

"Where what happened?"

"Yesterday . . . sun-downing. Men, horses, swords. Panic, fighting, blood . . . No, I can't go that way again!"

"Windy," muttered the dog.

"They came out of the trees, the sun behind them. Couldn't see . . . Noise and pain. I ran this way. . . ." Indeed I could see we were now following the road she must have taken: branches broken, shrubs torn by her wild progress, grass trampled and leaves scattered.

"Look," I said. "Whatever happened, happened yesterday. It sounds as though it was an ambush, but they will all have gone by now. It's perfectly safe, I promise. . . . Go forward, dog, and reconnoiter."

"You what?"

I explained, and he ran on ahead. The ground started to slope downwards towards a little dell and Mistral was breathing anxiously.

"Down there . . ." she whispered.

The dog came running back, his tail between his legs. "You ain't goin' to like this, lady: 'old your nose. . . ."

But I could already smell the stench of death, and hear a great buzzing of flies, the flap of carrion crow. There were four of them, lying sprawled in the random carelessness of sudden death, naked except for their braies. Their eyes had already gone, and the crows rose heavily gorged, the men's wounds torn still further by cruel beaks. I shouted and ran at the birds till they flapped to the nearest tree; they would be back, and there was nothing I could do about the clouds of flies, the ants, the beetles. I moved among the corpses, holding my nose, but there was nothing to say who they were, where they had come from, save a scrap of torn pennant under one twisted leg—

My heart gave a sudden, sickening lurch. Staring at the scrap of silk I suddenly recalled what I had completely forgotten until this moment: a tall, beautiful knight on a huge horse, who had smiled a heart-catching smile and called me "pretty." So much had happened since that encounter that he had not crossed my mind again—until this bitter moment. And I had sent him down this road. . . . No, no, it couldn't be! Life couldn't be that cruel!

Frantically I ran among the corpses in the dell, no longer squeamish, turning the lolling heads from side to side, seeking my knight. One head, already severed from the body, came easily to my hand, and I was left holding something that was shaped and heavy as a cabbage, but crawling with maggots. . . .

He wasn't there, he wasn't there! I ran up from the dell, farther into the forest, but there was no other stink of death, nor flies, nor carrion. I ran back to the horse, Mistral.

"What happened to him, where is he? Where is your master, Sir—Sir . . ." But I had forgotten his name.

"Who? What man?"

"He was a knight and rode a black horse—you must remember!"

"They killed the men and took the horses and the baggage. I ran away. That's all I know."

"All of them?"

"I don't know. I only saw my corner of it."

Maybe they had taken him for ransom. Perhaps they had ridden him away into the forest on his fine black horse, to bargain with his folks for far more than the horses and baggage they had stolen—I held the tattered piece of blue silk in my hand and prayed for his safety.

The dog nudged my knee. "Better find a place to kip for the night soon: near sundown."

I gestured towards the bodies. "We can't just leave them like this. . . ."

"You gotta spade and a coupla hours? No. Don't worry 'bout them. This track is used by those in the village; they'll deal with the remains. Bury them the way you 'umans do things. To my way o' thinkin', better leave bodies to the birds and the foxes to pick clean."

I muttered a prayer, crossed myself. "Right: lead on, dog."

About a half-mile farther along, as it grew too dark to see underfoot and my feet felt swollen to twice their usual size with the unaccustomed walking, the trees suddenly thinned and we found ourselves at the top of a steep bank. The moon rode out from behind some scummy clouds and there beneath us was a luminous strip of roadway, wide enough for six horsemen to ride abreast.

"Is that it?"

"Well, it's a road," said the dog. "Give or take . . ."

"It runs north/south," said Mistral.

"Come on, then," and in my eagerness I started to slide down the bank towards the shining expanse.

"Not so fast, lady," said the dog behind me. "You doesn't travel a road like this at night—"

"Scared?" and I slid down to the bottom, giving my right ankle a nasty jar, but determined to continue our journey now we had found what we were looking for.

"—'cos it's too dark to see," continued the dog, as the moon disappeared again.

"Neither do you travel alone," said Mistral. "There is safety in numbers. Look what happened to me."

A night-jar churred above my head and I lost one of my shoes in the scramble back. The dog retrieved it for me, all slathery from his mouth.

Scrabbling around in the dark, for I was now afraid of the risk of a lantern, I found the ham and the rest of the honey cakes, sharing a third, two-thirds with the dog. Afterwards, snugged down in my blanket, I listened to Mistral cropping the grass, sounding in the night like the tearing of strips of linen, and felt strangely comforted by the proximity of the two animals, even though the promised guard-dog, alert to every danger, the one who had promised to stay awake so I could sleep easy, was snoring heavily long before I closed my eyes.

I woke early and now that we had reached the road I was eager to be on my way. Not only impatience but also the knowledge that we were still within a half-day's travel of the village by foot, and those on horseback could travel much faster. I had no intention of being called to account for burning down the cottage and everything in it, and at mention of the villagers' possible vengeance the dog, too, looked thoughtful, then volunteered to scout out the road beneath us.

He was gone some twenty minutes, and arrived back to announce that all was clear as far as eyesight.

"Been a group of people past in the last twenty-four hours," he reported. "Mule turds, dried piss. Doubt if there'll be others on the road today."

I decided we'd risk it, and the sooner we were away the better. A quick snack of cheese for the dog and me and we all scrambled down the bank and onto the road.

My memory of the highway from the night before had been of a broad ghostly ribbon winding away smoothly into the distance, but the reality was far different. The surface was stony and uneven, marred by wheel-ruts and loose flints big enough to turn one's ankle, and it twisted and turned like a pig's tail, to follow the contours of the land. Nor was it the same width all the way. Sometimes it narrowed to pass through a gully or across a bridge, like the one that spanned the river that flowed away from our village; at other places it widened or split in two where the ground was obviously boggy after rain.

After an hour of this I felt I had had enough, even though Mistral matched her pace to my waddle—the dog scurried about like an agitated beetle, up and down, back and forth, till it made me dizzy to watch him—and I called a halt. The sun was shining in my eyes, sweat running into my eyes until they stung; my feet were swollen, my thighs sore with rubbing together and my stomach was howling-empty.

But unpacking the food gave me a shock. I hadn't realized how much I—we, I thought, scowling at the dog—had consumed. All that was left that didn't need cooking was a rind of cheese, a slice of cold bacon and one squashed honey cake. I threw the rind to the dog and ate what was left almost as quickly, while Mistral munched philosophically among the scrub at the side of the road, lipping at leaves I wouldn't have thought edible. Obviously her wasted look was partly due to starvation.

The dog, too, found something edible: he crawled out from under a bush crunching on an enormous stag beetle. I felt sick.

"Better get goin'," he said. "Only done a coupla miles . . ."

"Oh, do stop grouching!" I cried in exasperation, all the more annoyed because I knew he was right. "Grumble and grouch and eat, that's all you do all day! Matter of fact, that's what I'll call you from now on: 'Growch'! So there . . ."

He spat out stag-beetle bits, then hoofed his right ear and inspected the results. "Never had a name before," he said. "Thanks." He tried it out. "Growch, Growch, Growch . . . Not bad."

And I immediately felt mean: how would I have felt if I had been christened "Grumble"? Even though "Somerdai" was odd, it had nice connotations. But the dog seemed happy enough; I think he liked the subdued barking noise his name made.

We progressed better for the next hour or so, heartened by the various pieces of evidence that others had traversed this way earlier—a scrap of cloth, more droppings, a midday cooking fire. I began to feel much better, as if a great load had left my mind. I was no longer confined by routine, everything was new and exciting and different. All I encountered from now on would be fresh to my senses and would have to be dealt with by me alone, no one to tell me what to do. In a way daunting, in another exciting. I hoped I was equal to the challenge. But why not? With my education and God's help even I could have a stab at Life. True, not everything was on my side, and I now had the added responsibilities of the horse and the dog, but the former at least was more of a help than a hindrance.

So it was with a sense of lively anticipation that we topped a rise shortly after midday to see, spread beneath us, a huddle of roofs that meant safety and food. The air was still, and the northerly drift of house fires stained the deep blue sky like snarls of sheep's wool caught in a hedge.

I forgot my discomforts and hunger as we wound our way down into the valley beneath, and even though the journey was longer than I thought, due to the bafflement of distance in the clear air and the twists of the road, it was not much after two in the afternoon by the time we reached the outskirts of the sizable village. It must, I calculated, hold at least five times as many people as ours, if not more. Even without my tally-sticks that would mean well over a thousand: more people than I had ever seen in my life!

I stopped to enquire if a caravan of people had passed by of the first person I saw, an old crone catching the last of the sun outside her hovel.

"Went this way yesterday and on again this morning. Left the blind idiot behind."

My heart sank. The sun was now dipping away behind the hills to our right and there was no way we could hope to catch them up. That would mean we should have to shelter here for the night and think again in the morning. I asked if there was a traveler's rest place.

"Not as such. Ask at the inn down the road for stable space."

We trudged down the main street till we came to the tavern she had indicated, a mean-looking place with a tattered bunch of hops hanging over the doorway. I was not reassured by the surly landlord telling me he was short on both food and ale.

"Blame them as came through yesterday," he said brusquely. "More'n usual for this time o' year. Can do you a stew tonight and there's space in the stable out back."

"How much?"

He named an outrageous price, but Mama had taught me how to bargain and the matter was settled for a couple of coins. I begged a crust of bread in anticipation of the stew, which I shared with Growch, then bedded Mistral down in the dilapidated stable, collecting together some stray wisps of hay for her. Growch I left on guard, mindful of the packs I had stored away under the manger. I reckoned the threat of a horse's kick and a dog's bite would be enough to deter even the landlord or his wife, were they inquisitive enough to try and inspect my belongings.

I decided to take a walk through the village while it was still light. In the distance, from the direction of the church tower, came shouts of merriment and I made my way in that direction. Turning a corner I saw that the space in front of the church was crammed with people all apparently enjoying themselves heartily. Children were screaming and running about, playing tag, and over to my left folk were dancing to the strains of a bagpipe.

I caught the sleeve of a woman passing by with her friends. "Is it a festival? A Saint's Day?"

She stared at me and shrugged. "Not as I know. We just come to see the fun. Got a blind idiot in the stocks over there, been pelting 'im all day. Come night we drums 'im outa town, as the rules say."

I knew these "rules." Anyone liable to be a burden on the parish was got rid of, quick. I remembered what the old crone had said.

"Is this the man that was picked up on the road by the caravan yesterday?"

"The same. Now, if'n you'll 'scuse me . . ."

I peered over shoulders in the direction the woman went, but was too short. Might as well see what was going on. We had the small-brained in our village, more than one, but people were generally kind enough to them. After all they were part of the community, somebody's relatives.

Of course the worst ones got smothered at birth. This one must be something special.

Using my elbows I squirmed through for a better view. A few minutes later I was at the front, staring at the pathetic figure drooping over the stocks. He was naked except for a short pair of braies, and his hair and body were matted with filth.

Someone picked up a rotten apple, obviously used before for target practice, and chucked it, but it fell short.

I stared hard at the pilloried man. There was something familiar about that tall figure. But what did some disreputable blind idiot in the stocks of an out-of-the-way village have to do with me? I edged nearer: now I was only a couple of feet away. Look up, I begged him silently; let me see your face. . . .

I found I was twisting the horn ring on my finger, unreasonably agitated, as if something unexpected was about to happen.

And then it did.

Someone threw a stone which struck the man in the stocks a painful blow on the shoulder and he lifted his head and howled like a dog at his tormentors.

"Leave me alone! What have I done to you that you should torture me like this?"

My gasp of horror and recognition was lost in the jeers and catcalls of the crowd. How could I have been so blind? That filthy, disheveled, near-naked creature in the stocks had been wearing silks and riding a tall black horse the last time I had seen him.

It was my beautiful knight, Sir Gilman!

Chapter Seven

Horror, exultation, anxiety: all three emotions chased through my mind at the same time. Horror at his condition, exultation at his survival of the ambush, anxiety as to how I was to get him out of this terrible mess. Indulge in the other two later, I told myself: concentrate on the last. Come on, now: it's up to you. No one else can save him. You fell in love with him at first sight, remember? You never believed you would see him again, he was just someone to fantasize about. Well, here he is, just like all the stories you used to tell yourself. In those stories you got your hero out of the most impossible situations: what would your heroine do to save him?

I rushed to the foot of the platform on which stood the pillory and shouted up at him: "Sir Gilman! Sir Gilman? Can you hear me?"

But his face, bespattered with grime and with a two-day growth of beard, showed no recognition, his blue eyes staring past my right shoulder.

Behind me I heard ribald comments, requests to move myself, but my whole being was concentrated on the figure before me. I noticed a huge bruise on his right temple, extending from his hairline right down to his eyebrow; it was a livid, raised purplish-blue, and I recalled what they had said of him: "Blind idiot." Had the blow to his head robbed him both of his sight and his wits? I tried his name again, but there was no reaction.

"Move aht the way, yer silly cow!"

"Shift yer fat arse, and let's get a sight o' the action!"

A hand grasped my arm. A stout man with a colored sash round his waist frowned down at me. "Now then, lass . . ."

I twisted the ring on my finger in my agitation, opened my mouth to say something, but found I was speaking words out of the air instead!

"Are you in charge of—of this travesty, sir?"

"I'm the bailiff, yes, but—"

"Then kindly release my brother at once!" Now I knew what to say, what to do; it was just like my stories. I jingled the few coins in my purse. "I have been seeking him three days now. I am sorry if he has been a nuisance, but . . ." and I tapped my forehead significantly. "You know how it is."

He nodded. "And you come from . . . ?"

I mentioned the name of our village and even spoke the first deliberate lie of my life. "Of course, the mayor, our cousin, has been worried sick! He has always been very fond of—of er, Gill, and even lent me his horse to seek him out, and I have bespoke stabling for us all tonight at the 'Jumping Stag' down the road. . . . And now, if you would please release him, I promise to be responsible for the silly boy!" and I pressed a couple of coins into his hand.

He glanced at me keenly out of eyes like currants, pocketed the coins, and turned to address the restless crowd.

"Listen here, my friends . . ." and as he spoke I climbed up to the pillory and whispered in Sir Gilman's ear.

"Don't fret! I've got you out of this and we'll sort things out in the morning. . . ." I didn't want him disclaiming all knowledge of me.

He swung his confined head in my direction. "Who am I!"

"I know who you are, but you must be patient. Say nothing, just take my hand when you are free, and I will lead you to safety."

The bailiff took keys from his pocket and I led my knight down from the platform and through a clearly discontented crowd, already armed with sticks and stones to drive him out of town. These expulsions often meant the death of the victim, I knew that; I also knew that the bailiff believed little, if any, of my story. Still, he had the coins in his pockets and it was too late to send a horseman to the village to check tonight. Tomorrow I determined to be away at dawn.

I led Sir Gilman through darkening streets to the stables behind the inn, lucky to be unfollowed.

"What the 'ell's that?" said Growch.

But Mistral recognized him and crowded back in her stall. "He brings danger! He led the others—"

"Rubbish! He's in need of care and attention. He's no threat to anyone. Just stay quiet while I see to him."

I went to the inn and begged a bucket of washing water, but had to part with another small coin. I gave my knight a strip wash, even taking off his braies to rinse them out, and he stood quiet as a felled ox, even when I rinsed his private parts, which I noted were ample. But Mama had always said that the criterion was less in inches than in the performance.

Apart from his trousers he wore a pair of tattered boots, and that was all. I should have to make him something to wear, but in the interim I put my father's green cloak over his shivers and went to fetch the promised stew and a helping of bread. It was tasteless and stringy, but I added salt and a sprinkle of dried parsley and thyme to make it edible. I fed him with soaked bread until he pushed aside my hand and said: "Enough."

That was the first word he had spoken since his release, but as if a dam had been broken he now started with how's and why's and when's until I shushed him. "Enough for now. It's night and you should sleep. Rest easy. Does your head still hurt?"

"Very much. What happened to it?"

"I told you: in the morning. Lie still, and I'll put salve on it and give you a sleeping draught," remembering of a sudden the vial of poppy juice I had brought with me.

I led him out to piss against the wall, but two minutes later, after I had tucked him up in the straw, he was snoring happily. I fended off questions from the others, merely asking the more reliable of them to wake me at false dawn. That done, the rest of the stew shared between Growch and myself and a few strands more of hay scrounged for Mistral, I lit my lantern and settled down with scissors, needle and thread to turn the better of the two blankets into a tunic for my knight.

A round cut-out for the neck, plus a strip cut down the front for ease of donning; seams sewn down the sides, with plenty of room for arms; laces threaded through holes in the neckline and rope bound into an eye at one end, knotted and frayed at the other for a belt . . .

I opened my eyes, lantern guttered, stiff and sore, to find Mistral nudging me.

"An hour before dawning . . ."

We crept through the outskirts of the village till we found the road south and once out of sight of the village I cut an ash-plant stave from the roadside, thrust it into my knight's right hand, put his left on Mistral's crupper, and determined to put as many miles as I could between us and possible questions or pursuit.

We made about four miles before a growling stomach, the proximity of a nearby stream and the knight's questions decided me it was time to break our fast. As the thin flames flared beneath the cooking pot and the gruel thickened around my spoon, I answered Sir Gilman's questions as best I could. His name and station, the ambush, his blow on the head, that was all I really knew. And he knew no more. Even what I told him raised his eyebrows. "You are sure?"

I reassured him, but did not remind him of our meeting in the forest the day before, lest he remember a hideous fat girl he had courteously called "pretty." . . . Indeed, I was careful to avoid any physical contact except by hand or arm, so that he wouldn't guess at my bulk.

After I had explained twice all that I knew of his circumstances he was silent for a moment or two, spooning down his gruel which I had sweetened with a little honey.

"So I am a knight. But of what use is my knighthood without sight or memory? Where can I go? What can I do? How can I manage without my horse, my sword and armor, money? How do I even know which road to take?" He flung the bowl and spoon away and buried his face in his arms. I longed to put my arms about him, to thrill to the feel of his helplessness, but I knew better than to try. Instead I went over to Mistral and talked quietly to her.

"All I know is this," she said slowly in answer to my questions. "I was hired as a packhorse to carry his armor—and heavy it was. This was in a town many miles north of here. In winter it was very cold in that town, and the people's talk was heavy and thick, not like yours or his. When he set off he said farewell with much of your human embraces and tears with a young woman who seemed reluctant to let him go. Since then we have traveled south by west, and I gather there were many more miles to go. That is all I know."

"Who are you talking to?"

"No one, Sir Knight," I said hurriedly. "I was thinking aloud."

"And what conclusion have you come to?" he said sarcastically. "I for one am tired of walking in this stupid manner and eating food for pigs. I demand you take me to someone in authority and see that I am escorted—taken . . . That I am properly cared for till I regain my memory, and can return to my home. Wherever that is . . ."

He was being rather tiresome. After his experiences of the last few days, how on earth did he think that anyone would believe his story, even with my word as well? Folk would think we were trying it on. If he could have remembered where he came from, even, it would have been a simple matter of sending a messenger to his home, requesting assistance, and then waiting a week or so for grateful parents or family to rescue him. As it was, he was lucky to be still alive. Patiently I tried to explain this to him, but he was not in a receptive mood.

"Still," he said magnanimously, "I am grateful for your help, girl. You know my name: what's yours? And why are you here? Where is *your* home?"

What a wonderful tale I told! The only really true fact was my name. He learned of loving parents dying of fever, leaving their only child with a huge dowry, traveling south to find her betrothed—

"But why did you not wait till he could send for you?" he asked reasonably.

"Ah," I said, thinking rapidly. "The fact is, my parents did not entirely trust his family, although they paid over the dowry. They said, before they died—" I crossed myself for the lie: he could not see me. "—that it were better I arrive unannounced. Then they could not turn me away."

"Sounds chancy to me. Which way do you go?"

"I was just coming to that," thinking again as fast as light. "I am not in any hurry to reach my new home, so I thought we might try and find where you live first. You were traveling south, so why don't we both go that way and hope you recover your memory on the journey? I have very little money, but we'll manage—if you don't expect too many comforts. As for walking—it will do you good, help you recover. What do you say?"

"It seems I have little choice." He still sounded resentful. "But you will promise to speed my return when I regain my memory?" He sounded so sure.

"Of course! But in the meantime . . ." I could see so many problems ahead if we continued as we were. "It would seem strange if we travel together and I address you as a knight and no relation. We may have to share accommodation, so I think it best—until you regain your memory—if we pretended we were brother and sister, traveling south to seek a cure for your blindness. If you didn't mind I could call you Gill and you can call me Summer. . . . No disrespect intended, of course."

He sighed heavily. "Again I see no help for it. All right—Summer," and he suddenly smiled that heart-catching smile that had me emotionally groveling immediately. "Any more pig food? A drop more honey this time, please. . . ."

That night we were dry and cozy enough in a small copse off the road, with the slices of ham fried with an onion and oatcakes, but in the morning as I prepared gruel again, I had an argument with Growch. This precipitated another confrontation with Sir Gilman—Gill, as I must remember to call him. It still seemed disrespectful.

Growch:—"Is that all, then?"

Me:—"You've had as much as anyone else."

Growch:—"Gruel don't go far. . . ."

Me:—"We've all had the same."

Growch:—"'E's 'ad more'n me. . . ."

Me:—"He's a man. He needs more."

Growch:—"You gave 'im some o' yours; I saw you."

Me:—"So what? I wasn't very hungry."

Growch:—"Favoritism, that's what it is. Ever since 'e joined us you been 'anging round 'is neck like 'e was the Queen o' Sheba, 'stead o' a bloody hencumbrance. Don't know what you sees in 'im. Can't see a bloody thing; can't hunt, can't keep watch, all the time—"

Me:—"Shut up! Otherwise no dinner . . . Go and catch another beetle."

"You're doing it again," said Sir—said Gill, irritably.

"What?"

"Talking to yourself." I loved the way he spoke, with an imperious lilt to his voice—I must practice the way he pronounced things—but I wasn't too keen on some of the things he said, especially when I had to explain something awkward, like now.

I decided the truth was best. Some of it, anyway; he didn't look the sort of man to believe in magic rings, unicorns and such.

He wasn't. "What you're telling me, Winter—sorry, Summer—is that you possess a ring your father gave you that enables you to understand what the beasts of the field say?"

I nodded, then remembered he couldn't see. "Yes, more or less. It heightens my perceptions."

"What utter rubbish! There are no such things as magic rings, and as for conversing with animals . . . Does not religion teach that animals are lower creatures, fit only to fetch and carry, guard, or hunt and kill?"

I didn't think so. What did religion have to do with it anyway? I knew that Jesus had shown his friends where to fish, and had ridden on a donkey into Jerusalem but I didn't remember him talking about hunting and killing. And hadn't he somewhere rebuked one of his followers for holding his nose against the stink of a dead dog in the gutter, and said something like: "But pearls cannot equal the whiteness of its teeth?" It showed he noticed things, anyway.

But Gill hadn't finished. "I'm surprised you should try and deceive me in this way! I had thought you to be an intelligent girl, but now you're talking like a superstitious village chit!"

He was so persuasive that for a moment I began to doubt the ring, my own powers. Had I made up what Growch and Mistral said to me, a mere delusion bred of my loneliness and anxiety? I glanced down at the ring to make sure it still existed, and found it no longer a thin curl of horn but rather a sparkling bandeau, glittering like limestone after a shower of rain.

"What's 'e on about?" asked Growch. I opened my mouth, but daren't speak back. The dog cocked his head on one side. "Like that, is it? Don't 'eed 'im. 'E'll get used to the idea. You can think-talk, you know, long as you keeps it clear. Easier for us, too. Try it: tell me to do somethin' in your mind," and after I had successfully demonstrated that Growch would turn a circle and Mistral nod her head up and down, I felt much better.

I remembered something my mother had once said: "Don't expect them (men) to have any imagination, except what they carry between their legs. Don't forget, either, that they are always right; even if they swear black's white, just agree with them. No point in aggravation . . ."

This exchange had only taken a few moments—that was another thing: this communication by mind was much quicker than speech—and I was able to answer Gill almost immediately. "You are quite right, of course; and yet . . ."

"What?"

"Would you not call the commands you teach your dogs, horses and falcons a sort of magic?"

"Certainly not! Their response is limited to their intelligence. And they are our servants, not our friends and equals."

He really could be rather stuffy at times, but I had only to gaze across at him to renew my adulation. Torn and bruised he might be, my beautiful knight, with a three-day growth of beard and blind to boot, but he was all my dreams rolled into one. Nay, more: for what dreams could have prepared me for the reality! And the very best thing of all was that he was so helpless he needed me, fat, plain Summer, to tend him. And he couldn't see my blemishes; that was perhaps even better. To him I was just a voice, a pair of hands, and I could indulge my adoration unseen. It was just as if Heaven had fallen straight into my lap. All I could further hope was that it would be a long time before he regained his memory. In the meantime he was mine, mine, *mine*!

By midday we had made eight or ten miles and it started to cloud over. It had been gruel again for lunch, there was nothing else, and I was eager to press forward, especially as Growch's nose told him of smoke ahead, borne tantalizingly on the freshening breeze. Gill grumbled constantly and the weather worsened, so it was with a real sense of relief that we glimpsed the roofs of a village away on a side road to our right. I had given up hope of catching the caravan ahead of us, and was now resigned to spending the night in a stable. Money wasted, but at least we could stock up on provisions, even if it meant breaking into my dowry money. Needs must, and I thought I could recall at least two coins of our denominations.

We still had a couple of miles to go when it started to rain, hard. Leaning into the wind, my cloak soaked, my feet slipping and sliding in the mud, dragging behind me a reluctant knight and complaining animals, I had to think quite hard about my blessings. But then, in which of the stories I remembered did the heroine have it all her own way? On the other hand, reading and hearing of privations was quite different from enduring them.

Three quarters of an hour later the animals were rubbed down and fed, dry in a warm stable, and my "brother" and I were ensconced in front of a roaring fire, our cloaks steaming on hooks, our mouths full of lamb stew and mulled ale. I wanted nothing more than to nod off with the warmth and the food in my belly, but there were things to be done. Upon enquiry I found a cobbler and leather worker and a barber, and by suppertime Gill was washed, shaved, trimmed, and had mended boots, a leather jerkin and woolen hose, and we had paid for our food and lodging in the stable. That took care of the silver coin in my father's dowry, which left only the gold one of our coinage. The others were all strange to me, though mainly gold. These I would keep untouched, for unless I could find an honest money changer, as rare as bird's teeth, they would have to be handed over to my future husband intact. If I chose a sensible man, he would know what to do with them.

And when would I find this husband of mine, I wondered, as I lay quiet on my heap of straw, listening to the gentle snores of Gill and the snorting of Growch, who seemed to hunt fleas even in his sleep. When I had left home my plan had been to join a caravan, travel to the nearest large town, engage the services of a marriage broker and be wed by Christmas. Now I was promised to the service of a man who had lost his memory, had pledged assistance to a horse who had forgotten where she came from, and was lumbered with a dog nobody wanted—and they had preference over my plans, I realized. I was beginning to understand the meaning of the word "responsibility."

The weather had cleared by morning. By diligent enquiry I found that the larger caravans of travelers came past about once a week in either direction during the summer months, but far more rarely during autumn, scarcely ever in winter. The one we were pursuing hadn't stopped at the village, and I realized now that they had a two-day start and we should probably never catch them up. The nearest town, we were informed, was two days travel south—nearer three for us, I thought—but I wasn't going to waste money waiting for the next party of travelers or pilgrims. We had been safe from surprise on the road so far, and with Growch and Mistral as lookouts we could probably make it as far as the next town, where three roads met: a better chance to find traveling company.

But first I had to change my gold coin to buy provisions, and I knew it was a mistake as soon as I handed it over at the butcher's in exchange for bacon and bones for stew. He took the coin from me as though it were fairy gold, liable to disappear at any moment. He held it up to the light, turned it over and over, tested it on tongue and teeth, showed it to the other customers, then called his wife to a whispered conference.

Apparently satisfied it was real, he turned suspicious again and demanded to know where I had got it, implying with his look that no one as tatty-looking as I was could possibly have come by it honestly.

The real story was so preposterous—renegade father, a dowry of strange coins found stuffed up a chimney just before I sent my Mama's body up in flames and fled—that I realized I should have to make something up, and could have kicked myself for not thinking it out earlier. Embarrassed, unused to lying, I floundered.

"It's . . . it's . . ." In my distress I found I was twisting the ring on my finger and all at once, so it seemed, a story came out pat.

"It is a confidential matter," I said glibly, "but I am sure there is no good reason why I should not tell you." I looked around: the place was filling rapidly, and even the local priest had turned up. "My brother is blind, but he heard of the shrine of St. Eleutheria where it seems miracles have occurred, and there was nothing for it but that he must travel there. My father wished him to travel in comfort of course, with a proper escort, but my brother insisted that it must be a proper pilgrimage, every inch on foot, dressed poorly and eating the meanest viands on the way." I smiled at the priest. "You will agree, good Father, that this shows true religious intent?" The priest nodded, and I could see him trying the obscure saint's name on his tongue: I hoped it was right.

"As the youngest daughter," I continued, marveling at when I was ever going to find the time to confess all my duplicity, "it was decided I should accompany him to find the way. But my father was determined we should not want on the way, whatever my brother said, so he gave me a secret hoard of coin to smooth our passage. But no one must tell my brother," I said, gazing round at the assembled company in entreaty. "It would distress him to think we could not manage on the few copper coins he holds. . . ."

The priest gave us his seal of approval. "I shall pray for you both, my child," he said solemnly. "Take good care of the change: we are good, honest people here, but farther abroad . . ." and he shook his head.

After a deal of counting and re-counting I pocketed a great deal of coin, more than I had ever handled before, and made sure to give the priest a couple of small coins for prayers. On to the vegetable stall for onions, turnip, winter cabbage; the merchant for more oil, the millers for flour and oats and a small sack to carry everything in, and lastly the bakers for a loaf and two pies for the day's food. The cheese at the inn was of excellent quality so I bought a half there, then had to shuffle all round to get it packed tidily on Mistral's back.

Everywhere I went in the village I found my invented tale had preceded me, and folks nudged each other and nodded and smiled as I went past. It seemed everyone came to see us off, just as if we were a royal procession. Quite embarrassing, really, especially as I couldn't explain to Gill what all the fuss was about.

We made reasonable progress, stopping a little later than usual for our pies and bread and cheese. I had indulged in a couple of flasks of indifferent wine, but it was warming and stimulating, so that when we resumed I endured the discomfort of a blister long after it would have been prudent to stop, so that when it finally burst I found I could hardly walk. Cursing my stupidity I unpacked salve and was just applying it when both Growch and Mistral pricked up their ears.

"Someone coming," said Growch.

I was ready to pull off the road and hide, but Mistral reassured me. "Cart, single horse, coming fast so either empty or certainly holding only one man . . ."

By the time I had put on my shoe again I could hear it too, and after a minute or two a simple two-wheeled cart came into view, carrying a few hides. The driver pulled up beside us.

"Got problems?" he asked.

I recognized him as one of the men from the village. He had been in the butcher's when I was trying to change the gold coin, and afterwards I had seen him outside the inn just before we set off. He had a cheerful open face, a smile which revealed broken teeth and eyes as round and black as bilberries. I remembered what the priest had said about the villagers being honest, and smiled back.

"Not really," I said. "We're slowed down a bit because I've blistered my heel."

"Well now," he said, "seems as I came by just when needed! Couldn't ha' timed it better, now could I? We'll all get along fine if you an he"—he nodded at the knight—"just hops aboard the back o' the cart and you ties your horse to the tailgate. That way we'll reach my cousin's afore nightfall. He's got a small cottage on the edge of the woods a few miles on, and he'll welcome company overnight. By tomorrow you'll be in easy reach of the next town. That suit you?"

It suited me fine. The heavy horse he drove seemed more than capable of taking our extra weight—after all the cart was nearly empty—so I tied Mistral securely to the back and guided Gill to sit so that his long legs dangled free of the road, then pulled myself up beside him.

It was sheer bliss to be riding instead of walking, and the countryside seemed to slip by with satisfying speed. The only complaints came from Growch, and after I saw how fast those little legs of his were working, trying to keep up, I leaned down and hauled him up by the scruff of the neck and sat him beside us.

I relaxed for what seemed the first time in days. Soon, with the sun already dipping red towards the low hills to the west, we should be snug in some cottage for the night, with perhaps a spoonful or two of stew to warm our bellies.

The driver pulled to a halt, and skipped down to relieve himself. "Best do the same yourselves," he said cheerily. "Last stop before my cousin's. I'll help your brother, lass, and you disappear in them bushes."

I needed no encouragement: I had been really uncomfortable with the jolting of the cart over the last mile or so. I clambered down and looked about me. The road was deserted and the land lay flat and featureless, except for a dark mass of forest a couple of miles or so ahead. The nearest shrubs were a little way off, and as I trotted towards them the ring on my finger started to itch: I must have caught one of Growch's fleas or touched a nettle.

Squatting down in blissful privacy I looked up as a flock of starlings clattered away above my head, bound for roosts in the woods. It was suddenly cold as the sun disappeared: even my bum felt the difference as the night wind stirred the grasses around me and I stood up hastily and pulled up my drawers.

Suddenly there was a shout from the direction of the roadway, a clatter of hooves, frantic barking and the creak of wheels. Whatever had happened? Had we been attacked? Had the horse bolted? Had my beloved Gill been abducted? Hurrying as fast as I could, all caution forgotten in my anxiety, I tripped over a root and fell flat on my face. Struggling to rise I was immediately downed again by a hysterical dog.

"C'mon, c'mon, c'mon!"

"What's happened?"

"Come-'n'-see, come-'n'-see, come-'n'-see!" was all I could get out of him.

"I'm coming!" I yelled back at him, skirt torn, face all muddy, shaking like a leaf. "Get out of the *way*!"

The first thing I saw as I arrived at the roadside were the long legs of Gill waving from the ditch as he tried frantically to right himself. I rushed forwards and grabbed an arm, a hand, and by dint of pulling and tugging till I was breathless, managed to get him back on his feet again, spluttering and cursing.

"Are you all right?"

"No thanks to that cursed carter! Just wait till I see him again—till I get hold of him," he amended.

"The carter? Oh, my God! Where is he?"

"Gone," said Growch, back to normal, his voice full of gloom. "Gone and the horse and all our food with 'im. Waited till you went behind those bushes then tipped your fancy-boy into the ditch. Chucked a stone at me and was off down the road like rat up a drain. Got a nip at 'is ankle, though," he added more cheerfully. "Now what we goin' to do?"

Chapter Eight

What, indeed! As for this "we," it was down to me really, wasn't it? So, I could cry, scream, yell, kick the dog, run off down the road in vain pursuit. I could refuse to go any further, abandon both my knight and the dog, do my own thing. I could tear my hair out in handfuls, creep away into the wilderness and die; I could become a hermit or take the veil. . . .

I did none of these, of course. Instead I sat down by the roadside and considered, steadily and calmly, the options left to us. I was aware that despair was only just around the corner; I was also aware just how much I had changed. A few days ago, while Mama was still alive, I would have been totally incapable of coping. Then, if even the smallest thing went wrong, my fault or no, I had run to her skirts and asked for forgiveness, aid, advice, whatever; I had been whipped, scolded, but given my course of action. Now I was on my own.

No, not on my own. I had the others to consider. Without me they would probably perish, except perhaps for Growch. Had the unaccustomed responsibility brought this mood of somehow being able to deal with it all? Or had my "magic" ring wrought the change? It had certainly tried to warn me of danger when it prickled and itched on my finger. I glanced down at it wryly. In the stories I remembered one twist and straw would be spun into gold, a table spread with unimaginable delicacies—But of course! I still had all my money safe, so we wouldn't starve. We might have lost our transport, food, provisions, utensils and, saddest loss of all to me, my Boke and writing materials, but what was that against our lives and some money?

And my ring did give me the power to communicate with Growch and Mistral: why not send out a call to her to escape back to us if she could, however long it took? Given the choice, I would rather have her back than regain our goods. If the carter turned her loose perhaps she would find us. Shutting my eyes and praying that my thoughts had the power of travel I sent her a message, wondering at the same time if I wasn't being foolish to hope.

And while I was about it, an ordinary prayer wouldn't do any harm. So I made one, and Gill joined in with an "Amen."

Rising to my feet I dusted myself down, retrieved Gill's staff, put one end into his right hand and took the other in my left.

"Right! Hang on tight. I'll try and keep to the smoother part of the road, but it will soon be dark and we must seek shelter."

"Where?"

"There are woods a mile or so down the road."

"And what do we do for food?"

"I'll find something."

"Not more of your stupid 'magic,' I hope!"

"If you must know, yes, I have tried to reach Mis—the horse."

"What rubbish! She's miles away by now. You'll never see her again."

"Wait and see. . . ."

And in this way we set off down the road in the gathering gloom, a sneaky wind fingering my ankles and blowing up my skirts indecently. Then just as we reached the shelter of the first trees, it started to rain. It was now almost too dark to see, and we sheltered uneasily, unwilling to lose our footing venturing father into the forest. But the rain came down harder, and while the firs and pines provided some protection, the oaks and beech had lost most of their leaves by now and were useless as shelter.

From the distance came a growl of thunder, a gust of wind shook the branches above us, increasing our wet misery with a few hundred more drops, and we struggled on, Gill falling on every tenth step and Growch tripping me up on every twentieth. If we didn't find better shelter soon we could die of exposure—

A vivid flash of lightning flared through the trees, followed almost immediately by a tremendous clap of thunder and—

And something else.

A frightened cry. An owl? Something trapped? Someone in distress? It came again. The high-pitched whinny of a terrified horse. This time I recognised it at once.

"Mistral!" I shouted. "Mistral, where are you?"

An answer came, but from which direction? I plunged forward, forgetting Gill, and we near tumbled together.

"Mistral, Mistral! Here, we're here!"

But it took a few minutes more of stumbling around and calling before she found us. I flung my arms around her trembling neck, dropping my end of Gill's staff.

"What happened? Are you all right? How did you escape?" I had forgotten about thought-speech, forgotten that Gill would hear me.

She told me that when the carter had rattled off down the road she had resigned herself to her fate, but once she heard my thought-call—yes, she *had* heard it—she struggled to free herself, but alas! I had fastened her too securely to the tail of the cart. Then she had tried to bite through the rope, with little success until the cart had bumped over a particularly deep rut, when the chewed rope had at last parted, and she had galloped back to find us.

"Brought the food back with you?" asked Growch hopefully.

"Everything is just as it was. He didn't stop to investigate." She paused. "But now I am so tired and wet. . . ."

"Now you're back everything will be fine," I said. "I'll light the lantern and we'll find a snug spot in no time at all!"

"And eat," said Growch.

For once I was in full agreement with him. "And eat."

I held the lantern high to try and get our bearings and saw what seemed like a reflection of our light off to the right. I blinked my eyes free of moisture and looked again. As I watched, the lantern or whatever it was swung slowly from side to side. Yes, it wasn't my imagination.

I stumbled forward, never considering any danger I might be heading for. "Is there anyone there? Help, we need shelter. . . ." and grabbing Gill's hand I made off towards the other light.

The trees shuffled away into the shadows on either side and we found ourselves in a small clearing. A flickering lantern held by a small man threw dances of light onto a queer, humpbacked building, no taller than me, that crouched for all the world like a giant hedgehog beneath the trees. It must be a charcoal-burner's hut, I thought, and certainly not big enough to hold us all. A wisp of smoke trickled from the roof.

The small man bowed. "Welcome travelers. It is not often I have the pleasure of welcoming visitors so far into the forest. Pray take advantage of my humble dwelling, for methinks the weather can only worsen." He spoke in a creaky, old-fashioned way, as though speech came seldom to his tongue. He was elderly, and looked to be dressed in skins; the hand that clutched the lantern was gnarled like a bunch of twigs.

"Thank you, sir, for your kind offer," I said formally. I looked at the low doorway. "But there are four of us, and I fear . . ."

"Plenty of room: You will see."

One of us wasn't waiting; Growch pushed past and disappeared behind the hides that covered the entrance and I found myself pulling Gill in with me. Inside it wasn't a bit what I expected.

Somehow the roof seemed higher—perhaps we had come down a step or two—and the space far greater than I had imagined. It was quite roomy, in fact. The floor was clean sand, the walls wattle and daub; there were piled skins to sit on and a merry fire burned in the center, the smoke curling up tidily to a hole in the roof. To one side of the fire a cauldron simmered and on the other meat was skewered to a spit, browning nicely. A pile of oatcakes was warming on a flat stone, a flagon of wine stood by a jug and wooden bowls and mugs were piled ready. The tantalizing smell of the food was almost more than I could bear without drooling.

I guided Gill to a pile of skins and sat him down, hanging his sodden cloak on a hook in the wall. Growch was already steaming, as near to the fire as he could get, and biting at his reawakened fleas. I heard a munching sound and there was Mistral behind me, lipping at a bunch of winter grass.

It was all rather unexpected, but then I was still unused to much of the refinements of the world. Perhaps houses could, and did, stretch to accommodate extra guests; far more likely, I told myself, my eyes had deceived me outside and I had thought the place much smaller than it obviously was; if not, then we must be in some underground chamber.

Our host came forward, rubbing his hands together with a dry, whispery sound. "Help yourselves to refreshments, my friends. There should be more than enough for all."

Indeed there was. Gill and I spent the next half hour or so crunching into the delicious spicy meat, throwing the bones to Growch, and chasing the last of a thick, hearty broth with oat bread. Then with a mug or two of wine to follow I leaned back and relaxed. The fire still chuckled merrily, apparently without need of fuel, although our host threw a handful of what looked like powder into the flames and instantly the room was full of the scents of the forest.

He was much taller than I had thought, nearly as tall as Gill. How could I ever have thought him smaller than me, I thought muzzily. It was difficult to make out his features properly, too. He seemed to have greyish hair and bushy eyebrows, big ears like ladles and small, round eyes so deeply set I couldn't make out their color. I thought at first his nose was as round as an oak-apple, but in the firelight it suddenly seemed sharp as a thorn and twice as long. His mouth was hidden by an untrimmed beard, but one moment he seemed to have long, sawlike teeth, then none at all.

The food and the wine and the fire were getting to me, I thought: I must pull myself together. Glancing to one side I saw that Mistral's eyes were closed, her head drooping; Growch was staring vacantly at the fire and Gill had his head on his chest. I pinched myself on the hand, surreptitiously, to try and keep awake, catching at my ring as I did so. It seemed very cool to the touch.

I looked up at our host. "I thank you, from all of us, for your food and shelter."

"A pleasure, young traveler. As I said, it is rare for anyone to venture this far into my territory."

"*Your* territory?"

"Indeed. I said so. This forest is my domain."

Surely all land and the people thereon were owned by the lords of the manors? Even in our village we owed ours work in his fields and tithings.

"You are a lord?"

He chuckled, a sound like wind in the trees. "Lord of the Forest, yes. All around you are my trees, my shrubs, my brushes. My birds, my wild creatures. Every living thing . . ." He sounded quite fierce.

"It—it must be a big responsibility," I said weakly.

He shrugged. "Everything usually runs smoothly: I see to that. Besides, who is there to challenge my authority?"

Certainly not me, I thought, noting the scowl, the beetling brows.

"And now," he continued, "I should like to ascertain just how you come to invade my territory. You seem an ill-assorted company, if I may say so.

This young man . . ." Gill was fast asleep, too far gone even to snore. " . . . is a relative, perhaps?"

In the silence that awaited the answer to his question, short though it was, I suddenly became aware of all sorts of sights and sounds that had been hidden before. The uneasy prickle of the ring on my finger, the rush of wind and thunder of rain outside, the fire that needed no wood, the unnatural stillness of my companions. Even the shelter in which we found ourselves was seeming to change: the walls were closing in, the roof becoming lower. It's all a big illusion, I thought; he is trying his magic on me and if I tell him the wrong thing—

Before there had been a great compulsion to tell the truth, but now outside reality and I had erected a kind of barrier between the Lord of the Forest and us. So, I told him the story I had told everyone else, lying as though it were the truth.

At the end of it all he humphed! as if he knew it was untrue but couldn't fault the telling. I was beginning to relax again when he suddenly switched his attention to something else.

"That's an unusual ring you have on your finger. A pity it is so undistinguished. Not worth much, I should say."

"It is worth the love of my father, who gave it to me. Were it made only of thread, still would I treasure it. Of course, because it is part of the horn of a—" Horrified, I stopped myself, the ring itself now throbbing like a sore on my finger.

"The horn of a what? Some fabled creature who never existed, save in the imagination of man? I am surprised you believe in such a fable. Still," and now his face was all smiles, benign, kindly, "I am willing to exchange it for something far more valuable, just because I am grateful for your company. See here. . . ." and from his pocket he drew out a handful of jewels; gold, silver, green stones, red ones, blue, purple, yellow. "Rings, brooches, necklaces, bracelets: take your pick! Just slide that old piece from your finger and I will give you two for one! How's that?"

"It won't come off," I said flatly. "Not even if I wanted it to. Which I don't. It was my father's gift, and I shall keep it. Sorry."

Of a sudden I felt a great squeezing, as though the breath were being taken from my body by an unwelcome hug, and the walls were so close as to squash me up against the others. Instinctively I took hold of Gill's sleeping hand and cuddled Growch close. Above me Mistral's mane hung like a curtain before my face and I grabbed a handful with my free hand.

Then sleep came down with a rush like a collapsing tapestry.

A drop of rain plopped onto my nose, the aftermath of the storm. Opening my eyes, I blinked up at the trees above. I was cold and *very* hungry. I had been lying uncomfortably on a heap of twigs and stones and my hip and back ached. I sat up; where was the fire? A tiny charred ring in the grass. Walls had gone, roof disappeared. I let go Mistral's mane, Gill's hand, moved away from Growch. Whatever had happened? In a little heap beside the remains of the fire lay a pathetic heap of small, burnt bones: mouse, rat, vole? By them a small pile of desiccated skins crumbled to dust, and blew away on the morning breeze together with half a dozen acorn cups.

Gill stretched and yawned. "What time is it? I'm hungry."

"Hungry?" said Growch. "*Hungry*? I could eat an 'orse!"

"You can talk! I haven't eaten for twenty-four hours," said Mistral.

I gazed at them all. "But don't you remember last night? The food? The little man?" But none of them had the slightest idea what I was talking about.

Chapter Nine

After that, all I wanted was to get away back to normality, and I never thought I should be so glad to see a plain old ribbon of road again. We had no idea exactly where we were, but with the aid of a watery sun headed west by south; even so it must have been at least an hour of stumbling progress before we were free of the forest.

All the while I wondered about what had really happened during the night. As far as we four were concerned we shared the experience of seeing the flickering light between the trees, but after that the others remembered nothing but disturbed dreams. Only I recalled a gnarled old man first small then tall, a room that expanded then contracted, a fire that needed no fuel, food and drink. . . . And in the morning the Lord of the Forest had gone, if he had ever existed. So had his shelter. I might have believed myself the victim of hallucination, except for that tiny ring of charred ground, the little chewed vermin bones, the acorn cups. Magic of a kind, but not nice.

How many other travelers had succumbed, I wondered? If it hadn't been for my ring, the ring he had coveted, the ring that I realized had bound us all together as I gathered the others around me, we too might have been bones on the forest floor. I glanced down at the circle on my finger: it was the color of my skin and nestled quietly now. Whatever had threatened was behind us now, but I wouldn't rest easy till we were away from the forest completely. The trees still crowded the road on either side, dank and dripping, their rain-laden branches drooping down like disapproving faces, and no birds sang.

A half hour later we were out in the open. Standing once again in the blessed sunshine, I offered up a silent prayer for our deliverance. It was a chilly morning, last night's rain still lingering in pockets of mist that swirled about our feet and slithered down into the valley below. The countryside was spread out like a checkered quilt beneath us, and some five miles or so distant I could make out through the haze the snaking of a river that curled round the smoke of a fair-sized town. I even imagined that I could hear on the freshening breeze the faint ting-ting of a church bell.

There was little enough dry wood about, but with the aid of the kindling in my pack I soon had a fire going, and spread out cloaks on bushes as I hurried up the first solid food we had eaten for hours—bacon, fried stale bread, cheese and onions eaten raw. It seemed like a feast, but I still mentally gagged when I remembered the "food" of the night before and could swallow but little, busying myself instead finding choice bits of fodder for Mistral.

We reached the town by midday, and I managed to find an inn which provided both stable room and pallets in the attic. After hearing that a caravan from the east, heading south, was expected within the next couple of days—a rider coming through had reported passing it—I determined to stay until they arrived. Far better to travel in company after the misadventures of the last few days. It meant spending money, but at least we could tidy ourselves up and have the choice of provisions before the others arrived.

I took our washing to the river stones and beat it clean, bought hot water to cleanse ourselves and took Gill once more to the barber, investing in a razor which I thought he could use if careful. I also bought him a cloak with a hood, at horrible expense, and a silken scarf to tie around his eyes: although he could still see nothing, he complained of headaches and a cold prickling in the eyes themselves. The bump on his head was scarcely visible now, but I gave it more salve, just in case.

After decent food and a good night's rest I felt a hundred times better and much more optimistic. I sat Gill out in the sunshine while I caught up with the mending, and tried to jog his memory regarding his family, his home, anything relevant, but he still shook his head sadly.

"I don't remember, Summer: I'm sorry." I could not bear to see someone who should be so haughty and sure of himself brought so low. I tried to recall anything I could of that scene of carnage in the woods and suddenly bethought myself of the scrap of silk I had rescued. Digging it out from the baggage I showed it to Mistral, who sniffed at it, identified it as belonging to the knight's train, but knew nothing of color or shape, as I understood it. I took it to Gill, tried to describe the blue and yellow and what looked like a beak, but he still shook his head. I was sure I could recall a bird's head on the shield I had glimpsed that first day when he asked the way, and tried to combine it all in a drawing, but it was hopeless. Still, I asked about the town as best I could with the scrap of silk, but met with no success there either.

I was making my way back to the inn at dusk, after a wasted afternoon's questioning, when I came across a scuffle of small boys throwing stones up onto the roof of a deserted cottage, shouting and yelling with enjoyment. Looking up, I saw the feeble flapping of wings—obviously they were trying to finish off an injured bird. Even as I passed the bird fell off into the gutter, where it was scooped up by greedy hands and held on high by the tallest boy.

"Mine! Mine!" he chanted. "Pigeon pie for supper!" He was a thin, starved-looking child of about nine, and I couldn't blame him for capturing his supper, but as he put his hand around the bird's neck something made me put out a hand to stop him.

"Stop! Don't kill it. I—I'll buy it off you. . . ." I said impulsively, cursing myself for a soft-pate even as the words were out. What on earth did I want an injured pigeon for?

The boy hesitated, his hand still ready to wring the bird's neck.

"'Ow much you givin' us, fatty?"

I flushed with anger—but then I was fat, wasn't I, and he was as skinny as only starvation can make one.

"Twice as much as it's worth in the market. Only I want it alive—to fatten it up." I reckoned an alley-wise kid such as this would appreciate that argument. I pulled some coins from my pocket and jingled them invitingly. Immediately his eyes glowed fiercely, and I realized I had made a mistake: I should have only produced the two small coins I was willing to part with. I held out my other hand. "Give me the bird. Please."

He clutched the bird closer. "Four pennies, then."

"Rubbish! It's only worth one in that condition, and you know it." To my alarm I sensed the other children closing in around me. There were at least a half-dozen, and I knew I could never escape by running. The alley we were in was narrow and twisting, and if they made a concerted attack I would have no chance. They could crack my head open with a stone with as little compunction as they would wring the bird's neck and share the coins between them, and none the wiser.

If only I had thought to at least bring Growch with me! Nothing to look at, he still had a fearsome bark, a worse growl and very sharp teeth. I took a step back, which was a foolish thine to do. "I—I'll give you another half-penny on top, and that's my last offer."

But still they crept closer, so near that one child nudged my elbow. I took a further step back till I was up against the wall. My heart was beating like a tambour at a feast, and I felt like chucking the money in my hand away as far as I could and taking a chance on running. If only I could reach the end of the alley . . . I lifted my hand, but suddenly there was a small frightened voice in my ears.

"Help me!" The ring on my ringer tingled briefly. "Help me. . . ." It was the bird. Suddenly I felt a surge of anger and stepped away from the wall. "Give me the bird! At once! Or I'll . . ."

"You'll what?" But it was the boy who backed away.

"Just wait and see! Well?" I spoke from a confidence I did not feel but even as he shook his head my deliverance was at hand.

A black blur erupted at the far end of the alleyway and charged towards us, bringing its own cloud of dust, the little legs were working so fast. Then there was a nipping and a snarling and a yarling and a yelping and a barking and a biting and boys were scattering everywhere to escape. The pigeon's tormentor dropped the bird in his flight and I snatched it up and made for safety, closely followed by Growch.

We fetched up near the inn and I paused for breath. He spat a fragment of cloth from his mouth, tail wagging. His eyes were bright as blackberries and he smelt as high as hung venison. I made a mental note to dunk him in water whether he liked it or not.

"Lucky I was only dozin' when you called," he observed. "Saw that lot off pretty sharpish, din' I?"

"I called you?"

"Yeh, you yelled 'help!' in my ear. Took off like a flea on a griddle I did. What's that you got?"

Once again the ring had worked, and only a thought this time. . . .

"A . . . a pigeon," I said, and loosened my fingers a little, aware that I was holding the bird far too tight. "I think it has a broken wing."

"Supper?"

"Certainly not! Don't you ever think of anything except food?"

"Yes, but I ain't seen nor smelt any likely bitches recent. . . . Don' I get anything for helpin'? A reward, like . . ."

He was disgusting, but I bought a pie and gave him half, stuffing the rest into my mouth with relish. "Mmmm . . . Good."

"Might justa well been your bird. Pigeon pie, weren't it?"

"Of course not! Pork and sage," I said, before I realized he was teasing. The bird shivered in my hands.

Upstairs at the inn I examined it more closely. It was a handsome bird in an unusual coloring of soft pinky-brown and buff. On its leg was a tiny canister, locked tight. So, it was a homing pigeon. But from where? One wing lay splayed and crooked and I touched it gently, using slow thought for my question.

"Is this where it hurts?"

"Yes. Broken I think. Falcon strike, two days back. Hungry . . ." The voice in my head was faint but clear. A mug of water and some oats later and the voice was strong enough to guide me as I bound and strapped the wing with a splint of wattle and strips of cloth while he mind-guided my clumsy fingers into the most comfortable position.

"That'll take a while to heal," I said. "Where are you from?"

"South. A town tall with towers. I am a messenger."

"I can see that." I touched the canister on his leg. "How far have you come?"

"From north fifty miles or so. The same again three times to go."

"Well, you can't fly for a while. . . . South, you said?"

"Yes, and a little east."

"Is your message urgent?"

"It is a message of love from my mistress' betrothed."

Urgent enough to the one who waited. "We travel south," I said. "But not as fast as you could fly. I don't know how long you will take to heal, but you are welcome to travel with us if you choose. I can make a box for your transport."

Of course my dear Gill thought I was quite mad when he found out what I was doing sitting on the settle by the fire that night, weaving a little basket from withies I had gathered from the riverside by lantern light (with Growch for company this time). When I explained about the injured pigeon he snorted most unaristocratically and asked whether I was thinking of gathering any more encumbrances to hold up our journeying.

Of course I loved my knight most dearly, and could not now imagine the day when I could not refresh my heart by gazing at his beautiful face; marveling at the high forehead, straight nose, and those darkly fringed eyes, so blue in spite of their blindness—but I did wish sometimes that he would grumble a little less.

"Anything the matter?"

"Of course not. I'll just finish this, then perhaps I could ask the landlord for some mulled ale. You'd like that?"

"I should prefer a decent bottle of wine."

"Certainly." Wine was twice as dear. "I know how you must hate all this idleness, but perhaps the caravan will arrive tomorrow. . . ."

The travelers straggled in at midday the next day, some fifty of them. The inn and all the other lodging places in town were full that night and we had to share our pallets and those spare with a husband and wife and their three half-grown children. I doubled up with the wife and Gill with the largest boy. The latter grumbled that Gill took up too much room, while I found myself on the floor a couple of times, the wife having a thin body but a restless one, and the sharpest elbows this side of a skeleton.

The caravan did not waste time and was determined to set off again next day. I had had the forethought to stock up with provisions the previous day, so not for me the frantic buying of everything eatable. I already had flour, oats, cheese, salt pork, dried beans, honey, a small sack of onions and vegetables and a dozen apples, but I did remember to buy some barley for the pigeon and a truss of hay for Mistral in the morning.

I judged there would be room for barter on our travels, for I noticed a couple of goats and a crate of hens were traveling with us, part of a merchant's entourage. Milk and eggs would be a treat, although it was late in the year for laying.

Like all so-called "safe" caravans, this one was in charge of a captain and men-at-arms, six of the latter in this case. The captain's job was to determine our rate of progress, decide when and where to halt and to keep us safe from marauders. Our captain was a very large man called Adelbert; he looked quite outlandish, wearing skins and a huge helmet decorated with a pair of bull's horns sticking out on either side. He had a habit of hunching his broad shoulders and thrusting his head forward if anyone dared to question his decisions, that made him look more taurine than ever. His men were a surly bunch, too. They conversed with their captain in a guttural patois I didn't recognize and kept themselves well apart from the rest of us.

Before we set off the following morning "Captain" Adelbert explained his terms. In return for his guidance and protection he demanded a penny a day from each traveler, or sixpence a week in advance. Wagon and carts double, but no charge for horses, asses or mules. I was only too happy to relinquish my worries to someone else, so handed over money for Gill and myself. A week at a time would do.

That first day there were forty-seven of us. Besides the captain and his men, Gill and me, there were the merchant, his wife and four attendants, five lay monks returning south after pilgrimage to another monastery, our room companions of the night before, another family consisting of four generations and thirteen assorted people, a trader and his assistant, a clerk and a troupe of jugglers going south for winter pickings. Captain Adelbert himself led the caravan, two of his men brought up the rear, and the other four patrolled out on either side.

Our pace was of necessity that of the slowest amongst us. We were ruled by a rigid routine imposed by our leader, who became increasingly autocratic the farther south we traveled. We rose an hour before dawn, broke our fast and were on the road as the sun came up. We traveled for four hours, then broke for a meal—not longer than an hour: the captain had a very efficient sand-glass, which to me always traveled faster than the sun—then we were on the road again till dusk, another three hours, perhaps a little more. We camped where he stopped us, unless we were in reach of a town, then it was first in, best served. If we were camping out then we built fires for our evening meal, sometimes combining with others for a joint meal, which was a nice change: the merchant and his wife were too aloof, but the other families and the jugglers became good companions. If the weather was wet we supped cold and soon huddled beneath what shelter we could find.

Luckily we had few really cold days; farther north by now all would be huddled in front of roaring fires, waiting for the snow. I think this was the first thing that made me realize how far we had already come, for by the beginning of December I must have been at least a hundred and fifty miles south of my old home, if not more.

I began to enjoy my life outside, to look around me more. I started to notice weather signs, to see trees, rocks, stones, streams as separate entities. I delighted in the colors of the falling leaves—red, yellow, brown, purple, orange—was forever running off the road to supplement our diet with mushroom and fungi, and was the first of the humans to hear and see the skeins of geese winging south, though I must admit it had been our little pigeon who had alerted me.

He was healing slowly but well, and I didn't need to alter the splint of his wing. Seen at close quarters he was extremely handsome, his pinky-brown plumage set off by creamy beak and legs and bright eyes as red as rubies. He was in no doubt we were heading in the right direction for his home, though he found it difficult to explain why.

"Don't know for sure . . . Something inside my head pulls me the right way." He scratched behind his left ear, or where I supposed it to be, with a delicate claw, then followed the itch all around his neck. "You see, when I am taken away from home and then released to carry a message I climb slowly in spirals, looking all the while for familiar landmarks. If there are none, which means a long journey, I climb until the tug inside comes and I know which way to go." He settled down in his basket, fluffing out his breast feathers. "Of course if I am within ten miles or so of home, then I can see my way, and will be home, weather and hawks permitting, between strikes of the church of the tall tower, which is nearest my loft."

Three hours was the usual interval between strikes of the bell, if the priest was awake, to coincide with the church Offices.

"What does it look like, the earth, from so far above?" I asked hesitantly.

I had put his basket and our baggage on a rock while we took one of our halts, so that Mistral could graze unburdened, and now the bird looked up and then down and around. For a while he said nothing, then: "Stand you up and look down on this rock. This is a mountain. That clump of grass over there is a forest. Scratch a line on the ground and stick two or three twigs along it and you have a river with a town beside it. The ants you can see are the people . . ."

For an instant I could feel the currents of air beneath my wings, stroking my feathers, and glancing down watched the moving map beneath unfold, instinct pulling me farther and farther south—

"You all right?" asked Growch. "Got a funny look on your face, like you was goin' to be sick. If'n it's the bacon, I don' mind finishin' off that bit for you. . . ."

Gill had been remarkably silent about my exchanges with the animals ever since Mistral had found us in the forest; of course I now mostly used thought-communication, but sometimes forgot and used speech. I don't for a moment believe he thought I was really talking to them, or they to me, but he suspected there was something special between us and was no longer sure enough of himself to ridicule it.

The fresh air, plain food and walking miles every day did appear to be helping his memory a little; odd things, like: "I remember having my hair cut when I was a child, and the smell as the pieces burned on the fire," or: "My mother had a blue robe with a gold border," and: "I fell out of a tree when I was six and broke my arm." All endearing memories that made the child he was more real to me, but not really helpful as far as finding out where he lived. Still, it was a hopeful sign.

The caravan changed its character, size and shape as various travelers left or joined us. Among the former were the jugglers and the large family, but the farther south we went, the more our numbers swelled. There were more merchants, with or without wives and attendants, a merry band of students, a couple of pardoners, craftsmen and masons looking for work during the winter and even a dark-skinned man wearing a turban who had woven silk mats and hangings in his wagon.

Of course as the road became more traveled, the deeper the ruts and the more chance of being held up for repairs to wheels or axles. Then we would all stand round cursing the inaction while the Captain organized repairs and restless horses steamed in the chill of December mornings. In spite of this we still managed an average of some fifteen miles a day.

At this time we were traveling through broken countryside: small hills, stony heath, straggly old woods half-strangled with ivy, isolated coppices and turbulent streams. The road, from its usual width of twenty or thirty feet, had shrunk to a wagon's width. Earlier in the day we had come to a crossroads and Captain Adelbert had insisted on taking this narrower right-hand road, saying it was a short cut. I began to wonder if he had made a mistake. It had obviously rained heavily here in the last twenty-four hours, for in many places the horses were splashing through shallows and I had to lift my skirts to my knees and paddle. Once I actually had to carry the smelly Growch twenty yards when he pretended he couldn't swim—it was easier than arguing.

It was getting dark, with a lowering sky overhead, but there was no sight of a suitable camping site. The countryside looked even more inhospitable, outcrops of rock and tangled undergrowth crowding down towards the narrowing road. To make it worse Adelbert's men were harrying the train, trying to make us close ranks and we were soon almost treading on one another's heels. The wagon ahead of us snagged on an overhang and came to an abrupt halt. I was bursting to relieve myself, so dragged Gill and Mistral off the track and behind some rocks, just as the monks behind us closed up.

Our departure went unnoticed in the general hubbub, and I was able to squat down in peace. That was one of the only advantages of Gill's blindness: I had no need to hide myself. He took advantage of the break also, and I was just leading him back to Mistral when the ring on my finger started to itch and burn, and a moment later all hell broke loose in the direction of the road.

Shouts, screams, the thunder of hooves, the frantic barking of a dog, sickening thuds and crashes— Whatever in the world had happened? Making sure Gill had hold of Mistral's mane, I pulled at her bridle to lead her back to the road, but she dug in her hooves and refused to budge, wordless terror coming from her mind to mine. Well, if she wouldn't move I would have to come back for her, but I must see what was happening.

Just as I stumbled towards the rocks something thumped me hard in the stomach and down I went to my knees. Growch was tumbling all over me, stinking of fear.

"Get back, get back!" he barked over the increasing din. "Hide, quick! It's a massacre!"

Chapter Ten

I woke with a sudden jerk, as though I had plummeted down a steep stair, and gazed around wildly. Mistral blew soothingly through her nostrils. "All safe: sleep . . ."

I lay down again, chilled through to the core of my being, glad for once for the smelly warmth of Growch against my back. Gill was breathing heavily beside me and above the stars shone clear. I closed my eyes, tried to doze off again, but even if I managed a moment or two I soon jumped into wakefulness, fighting the hideous images that crowded sleep.

We had camped beneath an overhang of rock off the road—somewhere. It had been too dark to see, I had not dared light the lantern, and sheer luck and Growch had found this comparatively sheltered spot. We had eaten hastily of broken meats—some sort of pie, I judged—then had wrapped ourselves in the extra blankets and tried to sleep. Gill had dropped off first, but then he hadn't seen what I had. . . .

When Growch had cannoned into me crying "Massacre!" I had not at first believed him, despite the shouts and screams, the clash of weapons. At first I thought it was a minor ambush and that Captain Adelbert and his men were fighting off the attackers, glad that we were out of the way. I saw two monks flee past our hiding place, pursued by a man on horseback waving a sword. It was obviously not safe for us to emerge.

I crept back to Gill. "It looks as though the caravan has been ambushed. It's not safe to move until it's all over. . . ."

But the noise seemed to go on for ever. The screams of anguish and pain were the worst, and I held my hands over my ears; I saw Gill do the same. Perhaps through his dim memory he was reminded of the ambush in which he had been caught.

At last it grew quiet, as far as the screaming was concerned, but I could still hear the tramp of hooves, the crunch of wheels, men's voices, curiously exultant voices. The battle was over; someone had won. I crept forward for a better look. Nothing to be seen, just an empty road. I was about to step out for a better look when there was a fierce tugging at my skirt.

"No! Not yet," growled Growch. "Let me take a quick sken first."

"But—"

"No buts! You ain't got the sense of a newborn pup!" and he crawled forward on his belly and disappeared. I waited for what seemed an age, shivering a little from both fear and excitement, but he came back so stealthily that I heard and saw nothing until a wet nose was pressed into my hand, making me jump. He was shivering, too.

"What's happened? Is anyone hurt? Is it over?"

"S'over all right. They'll be movin' off soon, I reckon. Got what they wanted." He lay down, panting. "All dead."

"I can smell the blood," came the frightened thought from Mistral.

"Like a slaughterhouse," said Growch, still shivering. "Move back a bit: they'll be coming past in a minute or two."

"Who? Who will be coming past? You haven't explained anything! Who is dead? Who attacked us?"

"Never trust no one," was all he would say. "Never trust no one. . . ."

Impatiently I moved for a better view of the road, crouching down behind a rock, mindful through my curiosity of Growch's warnings. Two minutes later I nearly burst out of my hiding place with relief, for here rode our Captain on his stallion, leading behind him two pack horses laden with unwieldy packages. So we had beaten off our attackers! I opened my mouth to cry out, but then I saw the sword hanging from his hand, thick with congealing blood. Instinctively I shrank back; if I leapt out at him too suddenly he might use it without thinking. A moment later and his six men followed, one nursing a gash on his arm, but all chattering and laughing among themselves. Each one led two or three laden horses, and on one I saw the silken rugs from the dark merchant's cart. And surely those two piebalds were the ones who had pulled one of the other merchant's carts? And wasn't that mule the one belonging to one of the pardoners? Where were the others?

I craned forward; the horsemen passed, but there were no others behind. Their voices still carried clearly.

"Din' take too long. . . ."

"Pity about the younger woman—"

"Should'a thought o' that before you chopped her!"

"Whores aplenty where we're goin'."

"Why din' we take one o' the wagons?"

"Captain says as we're goin' cross-country."

"Three cheers for 'im, anyways! More this time than last!"

"'E says enough to lay up for the winter. No pickin's worth the candle till spring."

"What about those that ran?"

"Two-three at most. One o' the monks—"

"'Prentice—"

"Din' see the fat girl and 'er blind brother. . . ."

"Quite fancied 'er, I did. Like an armful, meself. . . ."

"Won't none of 'em get far. Not with the bogs all around."

"Shit! Dropped a bundle. . . ."

"Coupla blankets. Leave 'em. Got plenty. . . ."

Their voices faded as the road bent away, until there was only the dull clop of hooves and a tuneless whistling, and soon both were lost in distance and the growing dark.

I sat down heavily, my mind whirring like a cockchafer. Had I heard aright, or was it all some horrible nightmare? Had our captain, the man we all trusted, led us all astray and proceeded to massacre everyone for the goods we carried? And was it his living, something they did regularly?

Growch slipped past me. He was back in a couple of minutes, looking jauntier. "All clear. You can come out now. Not much to see, though. Or do . . ."

He was right, about the second part anyway. They were all dead, all our companions, strewn along the road for two or three hundred yards like broken dolls—

But dolls never looked like this. Gash a doll and you have splintered wood; wood does not bleed, and there was blood everywhere. My shoes stuck in it, clothes, faces, limbs were caked with it. Dark blood, pink, frothy blood, bright blood—my lantern showed it all. Who would have thought blood would have so many different shades?

And the flies—It was December: where had they all come from? Greedy, fat, blue-black flies crawling everywhere over the carrion that lay cooling in the dark. And in the morning would come the kites, the crows, the buzzards. . . .

Gill was at my side as we picked our way through the corpses, but of course he could see nothing. Growch sniffed his way from corpse to corpse, but there was no life left. We came to the end of death, and there, on the narrowest part of the roadway, a great tree blocked any further progress. At first I thought it had fallen, then I saw the axe marks. So, this had all been carefully planned, and by the look of the tree this way had been used before, this sudden death had come out of the dusk to other travelers.

I must leave word, warning, at the nearest town, I thought distractedly, but first we must get away from here ourselves. Mistral wouldn't come near, and the pigeon cowered in his basket. Taking Gill's hand once more I led him back through the obscenity of bodies, the bile rising in my throat and threatening to choke me. I found I was muttering: "Oh God! Oh God!" over and over as I turned from slashed limbs, contorted bodies, gaping wounds and from the faces that wore death masks of surprise, terror and pain.

Behind me Gill stumbled and cursed. "What the devil—?"

He jerked his hand from my grasp as he fell to one knee, groping in front of him.

"I kicked something: a flagon of wine, a bladder of lard?"

This time I was sick, though there was little save bitter water to spit out. The thing he had stumbled over was a severed head.

"Let's get outta here," said Growch. "Nothin' left but stink o' death."

True enough. The assassins had stripped the caravan of everything: clothes, goods, weapons, valuables, harness, horses and mules, even all food and drink. There was no reason to believe they would return, and they were probably miles away by now, but I still felt uneasy. They had said three others had run off, but if it were true about the bogs they were probably drowned by now.

As if to echo the dread and fear that still lingered among the corpses, a thick miasma of mist started to rise from the ground around us, curling round my ankles with cold fingers.

I took Gill's arm. "We must move. There is nothing we can do for these poor souls save give them our prayers." And we bowed our heads, the muttered prayers sounding loud in that unnatural stillness. There was only one way to go; that was down the road we had come by, for none of us wanted to linger near the slaughter longer than we could help. Even a mile or two would make a difference, for who knew what ghosts might not rise from those poor unshriven souls, to harry us through the night?

Growch slipped off ahead, and I extinguished the lantern: I could not risk the murderers seeing a light, though common sense told me we would never see them again. I knew the dog's and horse's ears were sharp enough to pick up any danger, but we walked forward cautiously, a step at a time. Growch came running back.

"No sign of anyone for miles, but there's a bundle what they musta dropped just ahead. Over to the right . . ."

Two new blankets, still smelling of sheep oil and practically waterproof. I strapped them on Mistral's back. They had been someone else's property, but that person was now dead: no point in leaving them there to rot. There was also a small sack of various broken foods: no point in wasting that either.

We stumbled forward for another mile or so, then Growch had found the rocks we were now sheltering beneath. I shared out the broken pies and bread and cheese and covered us with the new blankets, and then tried to sleep for a few hours.

And was still trying.

But the sights and sounds of the carnage we had left behind were still sharp and shrill in my imagination, too clamorous for sleep. Why did it have to end like that, the journey I was becoming so used to, was even beginning to enjoy? I had become accustomed to walking all day, to spending the occasional night huddled under the stars, to cleaning and mending and patching and gathering wood and cooking. I had met more people in the last few weeks than I had come across in the whole of my life before, seen more villages, towns, hills, rivers, forests and fields than any lord could own in one holding. Of course I had been bone-weary at times, hungry, cold and burdened with responsibility but, given the choice, I would not have retraced one step. Had not my father traveled the world, and Mama been one of the Travelers?

No, I would not have gone back—until now.

Right now I would give almost anything to be back in my own village, under any conditions—even working in the tavern, or as kitchen maid to the sharp-tongued miller's wife. I wanted desperately for life to be ordinary again, safe and predictable. I didn't want responsibility for anyone or anything but myself; I didn't want to think, to plan, to *lead.* I wanted to have all the decisions made for me. No more choices, please God! I couldn't cope, I couldn't, especially if they were going to turn out like this.

I snuggled into the scratchy, uncomfortable-because-new blanket, more awake than ever. Gill was now snoring loudly, Growch smelt like a dung heap and I was sure I was starting a miserable cold. . . .

I awoke with the sun full on my face.

"What time is it? Why didn't you wake me?"

"I thought you needed the sleep," said Gill gently, putting out a tentative hand till he found my shoulder, then patting it. "You do so much for us: you deserve a lie-in once in a while. We couldn't manage without you, you know. . . ."

And suddenly, somehow, it all seemed worth it.

Chapter Eleven

We regained the crossroads at midday. It was empty. The road north by which we had originally come stretched back into the distance, a straight arrow. The turnoff that had proved so disastrous, we left thankfully. There remained two ways: southeast and southwest. I sent the turd expert down first one then the other.

He came trotting back triumphantly. "Not thataway," he said, indicating southeast. "They went along some twelve hours back, then camped for the night and struck off 'cross the moor."

I turned to Mistral and the pigeon. "Does this southwest road seem all right to you?"

Unfortunately I had used human speech, and Gill stared towards me irritably. "Do we have to consult—pretend to consult—the impedimenta every time anything is to be decided? Or can't you make a decision on your own?"

"Animals have a much better sense of direction than we humans have," I said stiffly. "And I *do* communicate with them, whatever you may think!" And I explained about Growch's foray down the roads. "If you still aren't convinced, we can waste time going down the southeast road till we find the relevant horse droppings and you can feel and smell them for yourself!"

He shook his head and sighed. "No. I believe you somehow manage to tell them what you want, better than most. Now, can we go?"

I turned to Mistral and the pigeon once more. "What do you say?"

She snuffed the air. "We go the right way, for me."

"It will do," said the pigeon. "If only I could fly up and take a look . . ."

"Patience," I said. "You are healing nicely."

"I know . . . Not fast enough." He paused, and preened himself shyly. "They—the others—have names. I should like a name too. If you wouldn't mind. If it's not too much bother . . ."

"But of course!" I suddenly realized that the name had been there all the time. "I have been thinking of you as 'Traveler' all this while. Will that do?"

He crooned to himself. " 'Traveler' . . . Thank you."

We camped off the road that night, and made reasonable progress the next day, without seeing another soul. The same the day after, though by midday we were down to a handful of flour and two wrinkled apples, so it was with relief that I saw the outline of roofs and a church tower some distance ahead. The land around us became cultivated, there were sheep in a fold guarded by two dogs and I could hear wood being chopped in a wood to the west. Small tracks came to join the highway from left and right: it all pointed to a fair-sized town.

Indeed it was so prosperous that on the outskirts were two or three large houses standing in their own walled grounds, which must mean this was a peaceful area too. We were passing the last of these mansions when I stopped abruptly. My ring was tingling and I thought I heard something—no, not heard, rather felt.

"What was that?"

"Bells ringing for afternoon Mass," said Gill, as indeed they were.

"No. Something else. Listen. . . ." There it was again: a sad, cold, dying call.

"Came from over the wall," said Growch, ear pricked. "Somethin' shufflin' about."

"Anyone there?" I called and thought, "Answer me!"

There was a longish pause. "Help. . . ." The sound was faint, drawn out like a thread. "Sooo . . . cooold . . ."

I had to find out what It was, what It wanted. I looked about, but the pebble-dash walls surrounding the house were some ten feet high. No way could Gill lift me up—besides he'd discover just how fat I was—and there were no handy trees to climb. I followed the wall till I came to a small gate, but it was firmly bolted. Still—

I called Mistral and explained what I wanted. We managed it on the third attempt as she bucked me up high enough to grab the top of the gate, climb over and drop to the other side. The first thing I did was to draw back the bolts to ensure a swift exit, just in case. Then I looked about me.

I was in a small formal garden, with apple and pear trees, leafless now, graveled paths, boxed alleys, square and diamond-shaped plots edged with rosemary, a scummy pond and the remains of a camomile lawn. All winter-dead and desolate. The house beyond was shuttered and quiet too.

I peered around in the gathering gloom. Nothing moved. And yet—I started back. Over there, at the edge of the shriveled lawn a rock moved. Rocks don't move, I told myself firmly. But It did it again and I backed away:

"Heeelp . . ."

Talking, moving rocks? If it hadn't been for the positive feeling in the ring on my finger I think I would have fled, but instead I approached It cautiously, ready however to run if It jumped up and tried to bite. Seen closer It was a sort of rough oval, almost black, with orangey-brown patches. I stretched out my hands to pick It up and It suddenly sprouted a smooth head, four scrabbling claws and a stumpy tail. I sprang back: perhaps It did bite!

"Caaarefuuul," came the mournful, slow voice again. "Faairly fraaagile. Chiiip eaaasily . . ."

I squatted down to look more closely. "What are you?"

"*Reeeptillia-cheeelonia-testuuudo-maaarginaaata . . .*"

It was talking Latin, and that was not my best subject. I understood Church Latin and some market Latin—both understood wherever one went in a Christian country of course, whatever local language the native people spoke—but classical and scientific Latin were beyond me. "Er . . . How can I help you?"

"Cooold . . . Fooorgotten. Neeeeeed fooooood. Sleeeeeep . . ."

It was getting more and more difficult to understand. Obviously as the house was shut up It could expect no help from there. At least I could see It-whatever-it-was-in-Latin got some warmth. "You'd better come with me." I bent to lift It, my hands closing round a cool, horny shell. "Don't stick your claws in . . ." but I was brought up short by a sharp tug. I put It down again. "What's this?"

"Chaaain. Caan't escaaape. Caaan't buuurrow . . ."

Looking more carefully I could see that a thin chain was looped through a hole pierced in the rear of the shell and then went to an iron staple driven into the ground some eighteen inches away. It was an easy matter for me to lift the chain over the staple and release It, but I could see how constricting it had been, for the creature's walking round had worn a deep circular trench, the limit of the chain.

I looked around, but there was nowhere I could put It that wasn't just as exposed, and no food that I could see.

"What do you eat?"

"Greeeeeens. Fruuuit . . ."

I sighed. "And where do you come from originally?" but even as I asked I knew what the answer would be.

"Sooouth . . ."

Another one! Whatever would Gill say? I stooped to wrap the chain around Its shell and started to lift It, but was arrested by a hiss of pain. "Toooooo faaast . . . Huuurts heeead."

Slow and steady then. I wrapped him in my shawl and left by the side gate; I couldn't bar it again. There was nothing to steal in the garden, and anyone wanting to rob the house was perfectly capable of climbing the wall.

"What you got?" asked Growch. I showed him. "Hmmm. Smells like dried grass and shit."

Gill asked the same question and I placed It in his hands. He ran his hands over the shell and his face lit up. "Ah! A tortoise! Had one when I was a boy. . . . Laid eggs, but never came to anything. Ran off one August and we never found it again. . . ."

I was delighted. He had not only identified the strange creature, but it had also touched off another piece of memory, however irrelevant. And I had heard of tortoises, but never seen one before.

I hesitated. "Do you mind if we take it with us? I believe its kind live farther south. . . ."

"Of course. Tortoises can't stand winter here. Ours used to bury itself in cold weather. Where did you find it?"

I explained. "It feels as though . . . I think it's hungry. I believe they eat greens, but there aren't many to be found right now. . . ."

He was delighted to be consulted. "Some sops of bread in milk. Ours used to love that."

So that was one problem solved: bread and milk as soon as we reached a decent inn. I wrapped the tortoise in a piece of sacking and tucked him up on Mistral's saddle.

"Food soon. You may find your perch a bit rocky, but you'll get used to it. What do we call you?" I wasn't going to make the same mistake as I had with Traveler, the pigeon.

Now he was warmer his speech wasn't (quite) so slurred or slow. "Back at hooome," he said, shuffling around a little as if he were embarrassed, "the ladies called me Basher. Could hear me for miles," and he gave a little sound, which, if he had been human, I would have interpreted as nothing more or less than a snigger.

By the time we reached the town proper it was near dark and we were lucky to knock up an inn with reasonable stable accommodation, which we shared with the animals, snug enough on fresh hay. I was lucky also with chicken stew, bread and mugs of milk for Gill and myself, and Basher the tortoise had his first meal "for three or four mooonths," he said. He didn't eat much, but as he said: "Little and oooften. The shell is a bit cooonstricting on the stomach." Like armor must be, I thought.

"How did they come to forget you?" I asked.

"Neeews came. Somebooody ill. All left. Forgooot me."

I fingered the chain wrapped around him. "Shall I take this off?"

"Please. Dooon't want to be reeeminded."

I found there was a catch, easy enough to unfasten, and it now looked just like a gold necklet, something used as an expedient rather than something permanent.

"Who put this on you?"

"Maaan drilled hole. Huuurt. Lady put on chain. Laaaughed . . ."

"Do you want it? It looks as if it might be gold, enough to buy us more food and lodging."

"It's yours. Paaay for my travel . . ."

In the morning we found the town full of people, and the landlord told us many had come from roundabout for the feast day of the Eve of St. Martin, the last chance of fresh meat before the spring. There was a traditional fair to be held on a piece of common land and dancing on the green in front of the church. "Be glad when it's all over," he grumbled. "House is full of the wife's relations. We'll dine early tonight, if you don't mind. Everyone'll be at the fair later."

I didn't know whether to stay another night or no: it rather depended on whether the tortoise's necklet was indeed gold. I remembered Mama's strictures on trading and bargaining, and went to three different coin and metal traders. It was indeed gold and the middle one offered the best price but was too inquisitive: "Who gave it to you? Where are you from? Where are you bound for?" and in the end the last man, an elderly Jew, exchanged it for enough moneys to keep us in food and lodgings for many a day, and without too much haggling.

So much money, in fact, that I decided to sleep another night in the town and also visit the fair. I had never been to a fair before. I had been partly persuaded to find in my travels round the town that our acquaintances of a few weeks earlier, the jugglers, were to perform that night.

When told of the disaster that had overtaken us at the hands of Captain Adelbert and his men, the juggler's eyebrows rose into his thatch of fair hair, and his mouth made a great "O" of surprise. He crossed himself several times in thanks for his deliverance and promised us a free show that evening. I left him going into the church to give a donation for his lucky escape, for I was reminded to report the caravan master's perfidy to the authorities.

This took longer than I had expected, as everything had to be written down, and as it was a holiday the town clerk was nowhere to be found and I had to be content with his deputy, who was mighty slow with pen and ink. I could have done better myself. Then they had to have Gill's corroboration, for what it was worth, so we were only just in time for our midday meal—rabbit and mushroom stew, dumplings, bread, cheese and ale—and the fair was already in full swing by the time Gill and I arrived. I had wanted to leave Growch behind, but he had promised he would sneak out and follow us anyway.

"Like a couple of unweaned pups, you two! Not fit to let out on your own . . ." So he trailed a few yards behind us.

I took hold of Gill's hand, and because this was a leisure time, not leading him to relieve himself or across obstacles, the touch of his skin sent little shivers of excitement rolling up and down my spine. Routine flesh to flesh contact became, in my case, imbued with all sorts of undertones and overtones that had my palm sweaty in a minute, and I had to wipe it a couple of times and apologize.

It was difficult in any case to thread our way through the crowds that milled more or less aimlessly among the stalls, tents, platforms and stages that filled the common ground. Like me, I suppose, they wanted to see everything before making up their minds what to spend their money on. As it was afternoon, over half the crowd consisted of children: tonight husbands would bring their wives, young men their sweethearts and the singles would seek a partner.

We found our friends the jugglers easily enough and, as promised, had our free show, though I could tell Gill was bored, his blindness making a mockery of the tumbling balls, daggers and clubs. I found some musicians and we listened to those for a while, then I bought some bonbons which we shared. I described a couple of wrestling falls for him, as best I could, also the greasy pole contest, which to me was hilarious, but again irritated Gill because he could not watch the humor.

The further we went, the more I realized how much these entertainments relied on visual enjoyment—morris dancers, animal freaks, the strong man, a woman as hairy as a monkey, a "living corpse," and all the throwing, catching, running and contests of strength. The only real interest he showed was when I found a stall selling rabbit-skin mitts, and I treated him to the biggest pair I could find.

I was reluctantly leading him back, when I came across a treat I could not resist. Outside a tent hung a sign saying: THE WINGED PYGGE. To reinforce the words (for most could not read) there was a lurid poster depicting something that looked like a cross between a huge bat and a plum pudding with a curly tail. Perhaps I would have lingered for a moment, yearned for a while and then walked on, but at the very moment we stopped, the showman flung aside the flaps of his tent and strode forward, ready to capture the passing trade with his spiel.

"My friends, lads and lassies, youngsters: I invite you all to come in and see the marvel of the age!" His restless little eyes darted amongst us, noting those who had paused, those who would listen, those who were customers. "Here we have a magic such as I dare swear you never have seen! A horse may swim, an eel walk the land, but have you ever seen a pig fly? No, of course you have not! But here, fresh from the lands of the East—the fabled lands of myth and mystery—at great expense I have managed to purchase from the Great Sultan Abracadabra himself, the only, original, once-in-a-lifetime Flying Pig!"

The crowd around us was growing, their eyes and mouths round with speculation and awe. The showman knew when he was on to a good thing.

"Here is your chance to see something that you can tell your children, your grandchildren, your great-grandchildren, knowing they will never see the same! And how much is this marvel of the senses, this delectation of the eyes, this feast of the consciousness?" He had captured them as much with his long words as with his subject, I realized. "I am not asking the gold I have received from crowned heads, nor the silver showered on me by bishops and knights. . . . No, for you, my friends, I have brought down my price, out of my respect and fellow feeling, to the ridiculous, the paltry, the infinitesimal sum of two copper coins!"

The crowd hesitated, those at the fringe began to break away, but immediately the showman drew them back into his embrace with a dramatic reduction.

"Of course this ridiculous price includes all children in the family. And for the elderly, half price!" Some people who had been leaving turned back, but others remained irresolute. Down came the price again.

"All right, all right!" He spread his arms in supplication. "But this price is just for you: you must not tell your neighbor how little you paid, else will I starve. . . . My final offer: one copper coin, just one, for the treat of a lifetime! Come on, now: who will be first?"

Should we, shouldn't we? After all, I would have to pay for Gill and he would see nothing. I nudged Growch with my foot.

"There's supposed to be a pig with wings in there," I nodded towards the tent. "Be a dear and check up for me. I don't want to waste money if it's a con."

He slipped away towards the back, presumably to squeeze under the canvas unseen. A steady trickle of people were now paying their coin: soon the tent would be full. Growch nudged my ankle.

"Well?"

"Dunno. Honest I don'. There's summat in there. . . ."

"Is it a pig?"

"Could be . . ."

"What do you mean 'could be'? It either is or it isn't. Which?"

"Looks like one, but don' smell like one. Don' smell o' nuffin, really. Nuffin as I recognizes."

"Perhaps somebody washed him. Unlike some I could mention," I added sarcastically. "Does it have wings?"

He scratched. "Sort of. Bits o' leathery stuff comin' out o' its shoulders. Like bat wings . . ."

That decided me. I bargained for Gill's blindness but got a "takes-up-the-same-space-don't-he" answer. Inside it was dark and stuffy, lit only by tallow dips. Tiptoeing, I could see a small stage hung with almost transparent netting that stretched from floor to ceiling and was nailed to the floor. To stop the creature flying away, I thought.

There was a rustle of anticipation. The showman reappeared, on the stage this time. He was carrying a large cage which he set down before him, and then started another harangue.

"You've got your money," I thought. "Why prolong it?"

"Once in a lifetime . . . marvel of the age . . . far lands of the East . . ." It went on and on, and the thirty or so people in the tent started to grow restive, shuffle their feet, mutter to one another. A baby began to cry and was irritably hushed.

"Get on with it," somebody shouted from the back.

The showman changed his tack. "And now, here is the moment you have all been waiting for! Come close, my friends—not too close—and wonder at this miracle I have procured solely for your mystification and delight!" And with this he opened the cage, groped around in the interior and finally hauled forth, by one leathery wing, a small disreputable object that could have been almost anything.

It could have been a large rat, a mangy cat, a small, hairless dog or, I suppose, a pig. A very small, tatty pig. Pinkish, greyish, whitish, blackish, it certainly had four legs, two ears, a snout and a curly tail, but even from where I stood I could understand Growch's earlier confusion.

There was a murmur of astonishment from the audience, which quickly grew to ooh's and aah's of appreciation as the showman plucked at first one stubby little wing and then the other, extending them until the creature gave very pig-like squeals of protest.

"There now, what did I tell you? Never seen anything like this before, I'll be bound! Worth every penny, isn't it?" He brought the creature nearer to the front of the stage and the crowd pressed forward, making the tallow dips flare and the net curtains bulge inwards.

I held on tight to Gill, explaining what I had seen as best I could.

"Sounds like some sort of freak to me. . . . Are you sure those wings aren't sewn on?"

He wasn't the only one to express doubts. Once the first wonder had worn off there was muttering and whispering all about us, one man going so far as to suggest that there was a manikin sewn up inside a pig's skin.

"Let's see it fly, then," shouted one stalwart, encouraged by his wife. "You promised us a flying pig, so let's *see* a flying pig!"

His cry was taken up by the others, and for the first time I saw the showman discomfited.

"Well now, the creature does fly, I can certify to that, but it strained its wings last week, and—" but the rest of his words were drowned in a howl of protest.

"You promised . . . we paid good money . . . cash back . . ."

It was probably the last that decided him. Retreating to the back of the stage, he held the creature high above his head.

"Right, then!" He seemed to have recovered his equilibrium. "A flying pig you shall see! Stand back!" and he threw the creature as high as he could, as you would toss a pigeon into the air. For a moment it reached the top of the tent and seemed to hang there, desperately fluttering its vestigial wings. Then, abruptly, they folded and it spiraled to the floor, to land with a sickening thump and a heart-rending squeal.

Quite suddenly it was over. The creature was stuffed back in its cage and we found ourselves out in the sunshine. For no reason that I could think of I found my eyes were full of indignant tears. It was so *small*! I told Gill what had happened. He shrugged his shoulders.

"They would have done better to wire it up and suspend it in the air," was his comment. "I'm getting hungry: shall we go?"

I took Gill to Mass and then we ate a rather scrappy supper, everyone in the inn eager to be off to the evening's festivities. There was to be a bullock roasted in the churchyard, maybe two, and all you could eat for two pence. I was in two minds what to do. Part of me couldn't get the images of that pathetic little pig out of my mind and wanted to see him again, the other part knew that Gill would be bored and unhappy if I dragged him round the fair again.

My dilemma was solved in the most satisfactory way. One of the landlord's cronies came dashing into the inn for a quick ale before the festivities started, grumbling that their best tenor had dropped out of the part-singing with a sore throat.

"We'll just have to cut out 'Autumn leaves like a young girl's hair' and 'See the silver moon.' Pity: they're very popular. . . ."

From the corner by the fire came a soft humming, then a very pleasant tenor voice started to sing the descant from "Autumn Leaves." It was Gill;

I had never heard him sing before and my heart gave a sudden bump! of unalloyed pleasure.

Everyone turned to listen.

"Can you do 'Silver Moon'? 'The bells ring out'? 'Take my heart'?" and a half-dozen more I had never heard of. Gill reassured the landlord's friend he knew all but two.

"Then you've saved us all! You come alonga me, we'll slip into the church for a quick practice, then you're part of our singers for tonight. No arguments: there'll be plenty to drink and eat. Blind, are you? Pity, pity . . . Don't worry, we'll look after you!" and he took Gill's arm and whisked him away before one could say "knife." At first I was dubious, but one look at Gill's face reassured me. It was full of animation: at last he had found something he could do for himself, I realized, and wondered for a moment whether I was coddling him too much. No man likes to be smothered, Mama used to say. . . .

Which left me free for an hour or so. At first I pretended to myself that I was just going to have a general look around, perhaps buy a ribbon or two, arrive at the barbecue in time for some roast beef and then stay to listen to Gill sing, but my feet knew a different route. Before long I found myself once more outside the "Flying Pygge" tent listening to the showman's spiel. This time I pushed my way to the front, determined to be near the stage. And the silly thing was that I didn't know why, though there was a prickling in my ring that told me that somehow it was important.

I stopped the speech in mid-flow. "My penny, sir!"

He stopped and glared at me, and I realized he had not yet reached his "special reduction" bit. Blushing, I prepared to step back into the crowd, but he recognized me, and seized on his opportunity.

"See how eager this—this young lady is to see the show! Don't I remember you from this morning?"

I nodded.

"And you have come back because you marveled at the show, never having seen its like before? And you told all your friends about it, so I have had two more performances than usual?"

I nodded again. Anything, but let's get a move on!

He beamed. "There's your proof, then," he said to the rest. "Can't wait to see the performance again . . . The young lady perhaps forgets that the price is *two* copper coins, but I think that this time, as a special treat—and don't tell your neighbors—I shall do as she suggests and reduce the entrance to just one penny. . . ."

Once inside I rushed to the front as if blown by a gale and clutched at the curtains. The showman brought out the cage and far away in its depths I could see two sad little eyes staring out, and a great shudder shake the small frame. "It's not fair, it's not fair!" I thought angrily and, impelled by I knew not what, I bent down while the showman had his back turned and ripped up a section of the curtain nearest the bottom of the stage. Looking at the pig as he hung in the showman's hands I willed him to see what I had done. All the while the ring on my finger was pulsing like mad.

The pig was held on high, then hurled towards the ceiling. Once more it appeared to rise a little, then hover, but it was only an illusion, for down it came to land with a crash and a whimper right in front of me—

I ripped up the rest of the curtain, snatched the pig into my arms and, using surprise and my considerable weight, carved my way through the astonished crowd and out into the darkness. I could hear the howl of the showman behind and ran until there were a couple of stalls between us. Then I set down the pig and gave it a little shove.

"Now's your chance to escape! Run, run away as fast as you can!"

But the stupid creature wouldn't move. . . .

Chapter Twelve

I took a quick glance behind. The crowd were still pouring out of the tent, getting tangled up with the tent flaps, guy ropes and each other. I hesitated, then darted back and picked up the creature from under the noses of our nearest pursuers and set off once more. If the silly animal hadn't the sense it was born with—!

I ran in the direction of the town, dodging between strollers, around trees and bushes, tents, wagons and stalls until my heart was banging in my ears. I was wheezing like an old woman and could hardly draw a breath. My feet felt like balls of fire and the salty sweat was stinging my eyes till I could hardly see. Behind me I could hear the thud of pursuing feet and cries of "Thief! Stop thief!"

Twice I tried to rid myself of my burden but each time part of it became entangled with my clothing some way or another, and I was scared to pull too hard lest I damage its fragile wings. At one moment it felt as heavy as lead, at another as light as a farthing loaf; it seemed to change shape with every step I took: now long and thin, now short and fat; round, square, oblong—

"What the 'ell you *doin'*?" Growch was dancing alongside. "Got the 'ole town after you . . ."

"Don't—ask—questions," I panted. "Help me get away!"

He swerved off to one side and a moment later I heard a loud crash. Risking a backward glance I saw he had cannoned into a stall selling cooking pots; those that survived the fall were rolling about on the grass, bringing some of my pursuers down. But not the showman: he was in the van of about twelve yelling, shouting villagers. I then saw a blackish blur run between his legs and bring him crashing to the ground, also bringing down another who upturned a stall of fruit and vegetables in his wake. The rest of the pursuers lost interest in the chase and began to fill pockets and aprons with the spoils.

Slowing down I gained the outer streets of the town and sought the temporary refuge of a deserted doorway, panting, disheveled and exhausted, the pig-creature still clutched beneath my arm. Growch came trotting down the alley, tail jaunty.

"Well, that stirred 'em up! What was you doin' anyway?"

"Tell you later . . . Thanks, anyway. Let's get back to the inn."

I crept into the stable, looking fearfully behind, and deposited the creature in the manger.

There was a long moment of silence.

"W - e - l - l," said Growch. "Don't look any better close to. What you want to pinch that for?"

Mistral blew down her nostrils then sniffed, trying to catch its scent. "Strange . . ."

"Those supposed to be wings?" asked Traveler.

"Claaaws like mine . . ." mused Basher, awake for once.

Indeed, its cloven hooves did have tiny hooks embedded in the horn. Those must have been what caught in my clothes when I tried to put it down earlier.

"What *are* you?" I whispered, as if the whole world were asleep and the answer was a secret.

Was it a pig? The snout seemed too long, the bum too high, the skin hairless. The backbone was knobbed as though it hadn't eaten for ages and the tail had a little spade-like tip. The ears were small, and then there were the wings. . . . Scarcely stretching beyond the span of my hand, they were leathery like those of a bat, but without the claw-like tips. He was stretching them out tentatively right now—there was no doubt it was a he—but when folded they tucked away in a couple of pouches on either side of his shoulders. It was a freak—

"I am a pig. At least I think I am. . . . When I came out of the egg—"

He looked at me. "Yes. Does not everything come from an egg?"

I didn't mink so. As far as I knew horses, cows, sheep, dogs, cats, rats, mice, people and—yes—pigs were born bloody and whole from their dams. But on the other hand hens, ducks, birds, snakes, lizards, fish, frogs and toads laid eggs. But he wasn't one of the latter. It was all very puzzling. Perhaps he was a new species.

"Some creatures come from eggs," I said cautiously. "Are you absolutely sure you did?"

"I remember being in a tight place and fighting my way out with my nose. Then there was my mother and my brothers and sisters; they were all pigs. But they picked me out and sold me because of these things," and he nodded along his back to where his wings were folded away. "A man said pigs do not have wings. Said I was a freak. Called me not a pigling but a wimperling, because I cried so much when they tried to stretch my wings. So I suppose that is what I am."

"A Wimperling?" I shook my head. "I'm afraid I've never heard of one of those." It looked sadder than ever, its big brown eyes with the long lashes seeming ready to shed tears any minute. "But I'm sure you're not on your own," I added hastily.

"Thank you anyway for rescuing me. I hope I shall not get you into trouble?"

I hope not, too, I thought. Pig stealing was punishable by hanging. "Of course not. Er . . . Now you are here is there anywhere I can take you? Drop you off?" I waited for the dreaded word "south," like Mistral, Traveler, Basher and Gill, but it didn't come.

Instead: "I do not know where I belong. Nowhere I suppose. Perhaps I might travel with you a while? I shall be no bother. And I eat anything and take up but little space. . . ."

What could I say? After all, I had stolen him from his owner, and so I was now responsible for his well-being. But what about Gill? What would his reaction be when he learned I had burdened us with yet another responsibility? And another thought: how long would it be before they traced the stolen pig to me? After all, I was scarcely invisible and there were plenty of people to remember.

First things first. I must hide the little thing securely—from both the villagers and Gill. I made a space under the manger behind our baggage.

"Just for tonight. We'll be away early in the morning. Are you hungry?"

The Wimperling shook his head, but Growch muttered: "Starving, I am. What about all that roast beef?" and my stomach gave a growl of sympathy. I decided that my best cover was to go out again, in my hooded cloak this time instead of the shawl, and try and look as though I had been listening to Gill's singing all the time. Trying to be insignificant was easier than I thought; everyone was so busy enjoying themselves that no one gave me a second glance. Growch and I chewed the rather tough meat—the roasted ox was down to skin and bone by the time we got there—and I was able to listen to the last couple of songs, in which Gill comported himself very creditably.

Afterwards Gill's newfound friends escorted us back to the inn, roistering noisily. On the way I heard a strange tale of a long-haired witch who, accompanied by a pack of fierce hounds, had stolen a flying pig and rode up into the sky on him. . . .

"Wake me an hour before dawn," I said to Mistral.

In any event I was awake long before, spending most of the night tossing and turning, my snatched dreams full of visions of the hooded hangman. We were away long before anyone else was stirring. Gill, of course, had no idea it was still dark. Unfortunately it was a damp, misty morning, threatening rain. The dropleted air smelled of wood smoke, night soil, last night's bad ale and wet wool as we groped our way out of the town, but once on the road again it was wet leaves, damp earth, the complicated decay of December.

A fine, hazy rain started to fall, too light yet to do anything but lie on top of everything like an extra skin. Growch, as usual, grumbled like mad, but Mistral was easy, plodding forward at walking pace, her load balanced so the tortoise and pigeon were basketed on one side, the pig in a pannier on the other. I made sure Gill walked on the former side.

I had bethought myself the day before to renew our dry goods and buy more cheese, so we breakfasted by a quick, small fire on gruel, oatcakes and honey. I dowsed the fire as soon as the food was cooked, pleasant though it was, because I was still afeared of pursuit. I had made extra oatcakes for our midday meal, to be eaten with the cheese, and without thinking I handed them to Gill to tuck away under Mistral's blankets while I finished scouring the cooking pot. There was a sudden sharp squeal and a shout of anger.

"Summer! Come here. . . ."

Oh no! I had thought to get away with it a while longer. "Coming . . ."

"What is *this*?"

"What's what?"

"You know perfectly well what I'm talking about—"

"Oh, that . . ."

"Yes, that!"

"Um. It's a pig. Sort of. A very little pig. It'll be no trouble. . . ."

"And where did it come from?"

"Er . . . the town. Last night. It's come along for the ride."

"That's a ridiculous thing to say, and you know it!" He frowned in my direction.

"As you're determined on being flippant, I suppose you are now going to suggest to me that it's another of your talking animals and that it stood by the roadside and begged a lift? Tchaa!" he snorted. "Well, it can come right out of there and—What's *this*?"

Damnation, hell and perdition! He had been fumbling inside the pannier and he must have found—

"*Where did you get this animal?*"

"I told you—"

"You stole it! This is the creature we went to see yesterday afternoon, the one you told me had wings! You were the 'witch' they were all talking about last night!"

I wanted to giggle: he looked so—so *silly*, when he was angry, not at all like his usual handsome self. More like a cross little boy.

"I didn't exactly *steal* him; it was more of a rescue."

"Don't play with words! Don't you realize this could be a hanging matter?" Suddenly he looked scared. "And they might say I was aiding and abetting you—"

"Nonsense!" but my heart began to beat a little faster. I had never thought my deed might involve anyone else.

The pig's head popped out of the pannier like a puppet on cue. "I told you I don't want to be any bother. Let me out and I'll—I'll just disappear. No bother . . ."

"You just stay right where you are!" All this was beginning to make me quite angry. "I said you could come with us and I meant it." I turned to Gill. "This animal was being badly mistreated. If I had left it where it was it would have died. After that stupid story about a witch, no one is going to come after us. And as for anyone recognizing the animal, I'll—I'll make it a little leather coat so you can't see the wings. Satisfied?"

He looked dumbfounded. I had never shouted at him before. Growch sniggered. "All right, whatever you say. But don't blame me if we get caught."

"I won't." I shouldn't get the chance: everyone would be too busy blaming me.

We made damp progress during the rest of the morning and ate our midday meal on the move. Only a few weeks ago I hadn't been able to walk more than an hour without having to rest for another; strange how easily one became accustomed to a different life-style. Besides, it helped that I had lost at least a little weight; my clothes no longer fitted as tightly as before and I didn't have to lever myself up from the ground by hanging on to something. A small victory, perhaps, but it did me the world of good.

Around three in the afternoon it began to rain in earnest, the sort of rain that states its intention of continuing for some time. We pulled off the road to shelter while we donned our cloaks and I adjusted Mistral's load to give the animals maximum protection; it also gave Growch the opportunity to shake himself all over us.

It was lucky we were off the road, for Mistral pricked her ears and gave us warning of horsemen approaching. We crowded back farther into the trees as six horsemen rode by, looking neither to left nor right, mud splashing up from the horses' hooves to mire the fluttering cloaks of the riders. They went by too fast for me to recognize anyone and they were probably not seeking us at all, but their appearance gave us all a nasty jolt.

Besides, even innocent travelers were wary of sudden strangers, especially when they were as unprotected as we were. Bandits, brigands, mercenaries were none of them averse to slitting a quick throat and making off with the spoils and even opposing armies had been known to break off the conflict for long enough to plunder a caravan and share the spoils, then happily rejoin the conflict.

We waited for half an hour before rejoining the road, just in case, and the downpour grew steadily worse. We found we were plodding, head down, the freshening wind driving into our faces and under our clothes till we were all as blind as Gill and soaked through. There was little shelter to either side and I couldn't have lighted a fire, so we just struggled forward, hoping against hope for a deserted hut, a byre, anything at all we could use to get out of the wet.

To add to our misery there came an unseasonal thunderstorm, lightning crackling down the sky with a noise like ripped cloth and thunder bouncing along the road ahead of us. We even seemed to be walking through the fires of hell, for the road by now was a shallow lake with the rain, and the sheets and daggers of lightning were reflected off it like a burnished shield, till I was almost blinded.

A bolt of lightning split a tree off to our right and as I instinctively started back I thought I could see a building just beyond the smoldering tree. Another flash lit up the sky and yes! there was definitely something there. Grabbing Mistral's bridle with one hand and Gill with the other I started to follow a narrow path that seemed to lead in the right direction. As we drew nearer the building the storm revealed it as a small castle built of stone, but there was no sign of life.

We ended up in front of a massive oaken door studded with iron and with a huge ring set in one side. I thumped on the wood and shouted: "Anyone there?" two or three times, but there was no answer. I tried again with the same result, and at last, greatly daring, twisted the iron ring. At first it was so stiff it would not yield an inch, but when Gill lent a hand it slowly turned and the door, with our weights behind it, juddered open a fraction.

"Once more," I panted, and suddenly it swung wide with a loud groan. As I stepped forward into the stuffy darkness I became aware of two things: my ring was burning like fire and the pig was crying: "No, no, no! It's *bad*!"

Chapter Thirteen

Too late for any warnings: we were in. The relief was so great that any trepidation I might have had was canceled by the luxury of four walls and a roof. The place was dusty, fusty, stuffy, but it was sheer heaven contrasted with outside. Obviously old and untenanted, except probably by rats, mice and cockroaches, it nevertheless must have once been a place of some consequence.

It was fashioned on the old lines; a great hall on the ground floor with a fire in the center that would have found its way through a hole in the roof, a raised dais at one end for the lord and his guests to dine, and presumably outhouses for cooking and stabling. There were turret stairs leading to two round towers I had noticed from outside, but the stairs had collapsed and there was no way up. There was a stairway at the back, but this led only to the chaos of storm-ridden battlements.

Our priorities were warmth and food. There were plenty of crumbling sticks of furniture—tables, stools, benches—so I soon had a brisk fire burning in the central fireplace, unpacked Mistral and rubbed her down, plonked Gill down on a rickety stool near enough the fire for his clothes to steam and hung our sodden cloaks to dry. Deciding to feed the animals first, I gave the pigeon some grain and dashed out in the rain again to pull up some grass for Mistral and the tortoise. I set out some corn for the Wimperling, but he cowered under Mistral's belly, still moaning about things being "Bad, bad!"

Growch, stretched out beside the fire steaming gently and beginning to smell quite high in the warmth, told him quite rudely to shut his trap.

I rummaged in our packs for food, wishing I had had time to stock up better. There must be something. . . . In the end I decided on an experiment. I had plenty of beans and grain, but no time to soak the former. Perhaps the latter would yield to drastic treatment. I put some pork fat in the cooking pot, heated it till it smoked, then dropped in a handful of grain. The results were quite dramatic.

There was a moment's pause and then the pot crackled, spat, popped, and grain cascaded everywhere, all puffed up to three times its size or more. A lot sprang back into the fire, more over the floor and I caught some in my apron. Too late I slammed the lid on the pot. In the end I had a large bowlful of something crunchy and very tasty. I devoured a handful then gave the rest to Gill, under protest from Growch.

"Mmmm," said Gill. "Any more?"

The second and third lot was much better because I remembered the lid. Not entirely filling, but certainly better than nothing. I offered some to the Wimperling, hoping to tempt him out of his terrors, but he wasn't having any.

"No, no, not here! This place is bad. . . ."

"Suit yourself," I snapped, by now quite cross, more so because my ring was still tingling and yet my sight and common sense told me there was nothing wrong. The place was old, but it was empty of threat, I was convinced.

"Seems to be getting colder, Summer," said Gill. He was actually shivering. Suddenly it seemed also several degrees darker in the hall. Of course it would, I told myself: it must be well after the set of a sun we had never seen; time to make up the fire and settle down to a night's rest. I made up the fire, fetched out the blankets, luckily only slightly damp, and wrapped myself up tight. I fell into an uneasy sleep, waking every now and again almost choking with the smoke that no longer found its exit in the roof, but was wreathing the hall with bands and ribbons of greyish mist.

Growch and Gill were snoring, but Mistral was restless, twitching her tail; the pigeon was still awake, and so was the tortoise. There was no sign of the pig. I got up to replenish the fire yet again, but it was no longer throwing out any heat. It sulked and spat and burned yellow and blue around the wood, which smoldered but would not catch. I lay down again but sharp cold rose from the flagstones beneath me, making my bones ache. Flinging the blanket aside I grabbed Gill's stool and hunched as near as I could to the fire, till my toes were almost in the embers and the wool of my skirt smelled as though it were scorching, though it was cool to the touch.

"May I join you?"

I must be dreaming, I thought. I could have sworn somebody spoke. I glanced around: nothing but wreaths of smoke crowding the shadows. No one there except the animals, Gill and myself. I kicked the fire, hoping for flame, but there was none. It must be well after midnight—

"Greetings! May I join you?"

I whirled around, my heart beating like a drum. "Who—who's there?" It didn't sound like my voice, all high and squeaky. In spite of the cold I could feel myself beginning to sweat. Cautiously I slid my hand towards the bundles and luckily found a candle almost at once. Lighting it in a stubbornly flameless fire was more difficult, but the melting wax encouraged a quick flare. Holding the candle high I stood up.

"I said: 'Who's there?' "

"Only me. Sorry if I gave you a fright." Whoever it was gave a little laugh as though he was perfectly at home.

"Where are you?"

"Here . . ."

The voice came from the shadows on the other side of the fire, and now I thought I could see an indistinct shape among the clouds of smoke that made me cough and squint.

"Do I have your permission to join you?" From what I could make out the figure was small and slight, not much taller than I was. What a strange question though: presumably the place was as much his as ours; we were all trespassers.

"Are you alone?" I asked.

"Alone? I am always alone." Again that light, sneering laugh. "No one has visited this place for a very long time. You must be the first for . . . oh, I suppose at least fifteen years. Before that—Nice to see fresh faces. The last people here were a band of robbers. Not very nice people. No *culture* . . ." The figure came nearer, but the smoke made it seem blurred at the edges. "I ask again: may I join you?"

Why this insistence upon invitation? It was the fourth time. From the way he spoke—

"Is this your place? Do you live here?"

He paused for a moment, then laughed again. "This is my family home, yes. But I don't *live* here. Not exactly. More visitor's rights, you might say."

"Then we are the intruders. Please—" "make yourself at home" I was about to say, but there was an agonized squeal from the shadows.

"No, no, no!" cried the Wimperling. "Don't ask it in! Part of the spell! Bad, bad, bad!"

I felt him creep against my skirts, and nudged him with my foot. "What spell? You're being stupid. He has more right than us to be here. Just be quiet."

"Don't invite him to join you—"

But this time I kicked him quite hard, my irritation getting the better of me, and he scuttled away into the shadows again, with a pitiful cry like a child's. I was instantly sorry, of course, but turned my pity into a welcome for our visitor.

"You are most welcome. Please come and join us."

"Us?"

Couldn't he see? "My—my brother and our animals. They are all asleep. Except for the pig."

I could have sworn he hissed between his teeth. He moved forward, however, and now I could see him more clearly.

To my surprise our visitor was little more than a youth, perhaps a year younger than myself, with the beginnings of a fluff of beard. He was fair, with unfashionably long hair curling down to his thin shoulders, and likewise his clothes were unfamiliar. A long tabard reaching to below his knees, complemented with old-fashioned cross-gartered hose and set off with a short, dark cloak, fastened to one shoulder with a gold pin. In his left ear he sported a gold earring, and there were rings on his fingers and a twisted bracelet on his right arm. He carried, of all things, a tasseled fly-whisk, which he waved in one languid hand.

I vacated my stool. "Please . . ."

He smiled and sat down, showing small, pointed teeth. "I thank you, fair damsel."

Unaccountably flurried, I found a backless chair and joined him by the fire. We stared at one another across the cold flames. I was shivering, but he seemed perfectly comfortable.

"You said this was your family's home? Do you live nearby?"

"I regard this as my home. Do you know any stories?"

I blinked at the change of subject. "Why, yes, I suppose so. My mother was a great storyteller. But first—"

"Nothing like a good story to pass the time." He wriggled on the stool like an expectant child. "I hope you have a *great* story to tell me." He stroked his almost nonexistent beard. "A story is almost my favorite thing in the world. . . ." Close to he was very, very pale, almost chalk-like, the skin near transparent. Obviously he didn't get out much. Contrasted with him, Gill and I looked disgustingly tanned and healthy. So far he made me feel uneasy, uncomfortable: I couldn't say I liked him at all, but we were intruding in his home, and I thought I should try and make myself agreeable.

"Would you like something to eat? There isn't much, but—"

He turned on me a look of fury. "What makes you think I am hungry for your disgusting comestibles? Of what use are they save to make you better able to—Never mind. . . ." With a visible effort, it seemed, he settled back on the stool and gave another of those rather unpleasant sniggers. "Don't mind me; I am my own company much of the time, and it makes me forget the social niceties." He waved that absurd fly-whisk in front of his face. "Quite warm for the time of year isn't it?"

As I was practically freezing and it seemed to be getting colder and colder, I didn't know what to say to this. I changed the subject.

"You said this was your home?"

"I have lived here all my life." He leaned forward and quite deliberately passed his thin, white hands through the blue flicker of flame in the fireplace. I reached forward to snatch at him, but the fingers were white and unmarked as before. Suddenly I wanted to wake Gill, Growch, all of them. "Very fond of this place I am," he mused.

"I am sorry we intruded. I did call out. . . ."

"I heard you, but—but I was some way away at the time. Don't apologize. You are more welcome than you know. It is rare that I can welcome strangers these days. . . ." He stroked his beard once more, once more came that disconcerting giggle. "Of course in the old days this place was quite, quite, different. . . ."

A story was coming, I was sure of it. *His* story. I leaned forward on the chair, my chin in my hands, as I used to do when Mama had conjured up a fresh tale for my delight.

The stranger smiled, showing those pointy teeth again. "The story starts many years ago—I *am* enjoying this: it is many years also since I had the chance to tell it—when the country was wilder and less civilized than it is now. It all began when a great chief who had fought in many wars and gathered much plunder decided to build for himself and his new wife (part of his booty) a home in which to settle down and raise a family. He was now well into middle age and wearied of battle." The stranger almost absent-mindedly passed his hands through the flames again, and this time it seemed for a moment as though his thin, white fingers were lapped in fire. "He chose this site, near the highway, topping a small rise, surrounded by forest and near enough a stream for water. He annexed a thousand acres of the forest for his hunting and set those slaves he had captured to building this castle. By the time it was completed his eldest son was nineteen, the second seventeen, the youngest . . ." For a moment he hesitated. "The youngest near sixteen."

There was a movement at my side: Gill had woken and was propped on his elbow, listening. Quickly I explained what had happened. The stranger frowned petulantly: obviously he did not care for interruptions.

"To continue . . . The finished castle was furnished in the most exquisite way possible. The Lord had brought with him hangings, gold, silver, silk, wool, carved chests of sandalwood, pelts of wolf and bear, timber and pottery, all part of his conquests, and his wife, children—even his servants—were dressed in the finest of materials."

My eyes half-closed, I could see it all: the splendor, the comfort, the ease of living . . .

"It seemed nothing could ever mar this idyllic existence: a united family, devoted servants, a fine home, but all was not as it seemed." He shifted on his stool, stroked his wispy beard, flicked the fly-whisk, toyed with his earring. "From an outsider's point of view the three sons were all their father could have wished for. The eldest, tall and fair-haired like his father, was skilled at arms, a womanizer and a prodigious quaffer of ale; the second son was dark like his mother, merry and careless, with a fine singing voice. It was the third son who was different. Outwardly unlike either parent, except for his father's fairness and his mother's eyes, he was slighter, more refined in manner, a great reader and penman. His ideas were in advance of his time; he wanted his father to annex more land, build onto the castle, expand a common holding into a kingdom! But his parents were not interested." He frowned. "They should have known better. . . ."

I glanced around. All the animals were awake too.

"His father's hairs were grey now, and when he wasn't in the saddle with his falcons he was dozing by the fire. The mother died of a low fever and the two eldest boys ran wild, promising each other how they would enjoy life after their father's death, filling the castle with wine, women and song! They laughed at the youngest son, gibed at his bookish ways, his ineptitude at the hunt, his miserable showing with the two-handed sword, his distaste for wenching, his lack of prospects as the youngest. By law the estate should be divided between all three equally on their father's demise, but he knew he had little chance of a fair deal with two such brothers."

The stranger was still scowling, now biting at his nails between sentences. He really was absorbed in his story, I thought. The ring on my finger was now colder than I was. Biting cold . . .

"The youngest son smoldered with anger, with frustration, with contempt for his weak father, fear of what would happen when his brothers inherited. It was as he feared. His father was scarcely in his grave when the two eldest brothers filled the castle with whores and roisterers. Week-long, month-long, they caroused and capered till the air was thick with the stench of scorched meats, sour wine and stale sex!" He rose to his feet and paced back and forth, the smoke from the fire swirling round his fingers like an extra cloak. "Driven to near madness, the youngest son consulted a witch, then sought certain plants in the forest. Taking them up to the turret room where he spent his days he brewed and distilled them until he had a vial of liquid the color of blood and clear as wine. He tasted—Ach! Bitter! Too bitter to mix with anything. He added more water, cloves, honey; much better.

"Waiting for another night of feasting the youngest son crept down with the vial beneath his cloak to join the revelry. He watched until the servants had been dismissed and the eldest brothers were too drunk to notice his actions. He then proposed a toast to a long life and a happy one, taking care to open a new bottle and add his poison to the brew. It did not take long: within five minutes they were slumped at the table, no longer breathing. The young man then went out to the kitchens and stables and threw out the servants, not caring where they went. Coming back into the hall he gloated over the bodies at the table, then remembered his two young sisters, asleep in the other turret. Taking a knife he crept up the stairs and cut their throats as they slept. It was like slaughtering two suckling pigs. . . ."

I shivered, not from the cold this time. I saw out of the corner of my eye that Gill had made a grimace of distaste; he liked the story no better than I did. I liked even less the way it was being told—there was a sort of gloating about the stranger that I found scary.

"Coming back to the hall the young man noticed with horror that one of the brothers was groaning. Obviously diluting the poison had weakened it, so he took his brother by the hair, tilted back his head and slit his throat. Then he did the same to the other, just in case, and the bright blood spurted onto the linen cloth, quite ruining it." He sounded more regretful of the spoiled napery than the murders—I shivered again. I could swear that a fine mist was stealing through the high slit windows of the hall and under the door, to thicken the smoke that already seethed around us.

The young man reseated himself, rubbing his hands together with a dry, whispery sound like the shuffle of dead leaves. "A good story, don't you think?"

Gill sat up and rubbed the sleep from his eyes. "And all this happened right here? Then I am surprised it has not been pulled down long since! Such places are accursed! If we had known . . ."

"But we didn't and it has done us no harm," I said briskly, as much to convince myself as him. "I presume the young man was taken and hanged for his crimes?"

"No, it was not at all like that," said the stranger. "No one came near the place—the servants were all gone, if you remember, and this place is very isolated—so the young man's crimes went undiscovered. At first he delighted in the solitude, the peace, but after a while the silence began to oppress him and he found he was talking to himself, just to hear another voice. He even invented conversations with the corpses at the table. . . ."

"They were still there?" I queried, aghast. Something too terrible to name was nagging at the back of my mind, but as yet I couldn't put a name to it. But when I did—

"Oh, yes. He left them as they were, a reminder of his victory. As time went on and no one came to investigate, he loosed the horses, hounds and falcons and the corpses were chewed by rats till nothing but the lolling bones, strands of hair and scraps of clothing were left." He sighed. "After a while even talking to the dead began to pall, so the young man traveled to the nearest town, seeking company. He had not eaten for weeks and he thought perhaps the lack of food had made him transparent, for all passed him by as though he did not exist and none answered his pleas for help. In the end he went back to his dead family, for that was all he had left. After many years, at infrequent intervals, travelers—like yourselves—sought shelter. Then the young man was happy, for he persuaded them to tell him stories, tales to remember that he could hug to himself during the long years when no one visited." And he hugged his arms around his knees, much as that other young man must have done all those years ago.

"And the bodies?" I asked, glancing about me fearfully.

"Oh, they eventually crumbled into dust," said the stranger indifferently. "It all happened over two hundred years ago. Even the bodies of the last travelers are dust. . . ."

"The last travelers?" said Gill sharply, while a rising panic threatened to choke me. "Why did they not leave?"

"They didn't know any stories," said the stranger discontentedly. "The young man wove his spell about them, but still they didn't understand. He even offered to break the chain that held them, let them out one by one, but they still wouldn't play fair. So . . ." He fell silent.

"And so?" prompted Gill, and in his voice I heard an echo of all the horrors that were threatening to envelop me entirely.

"Eh? Oh, the usual thing happened. When they found they couldn't escape they went mad. Killed each other. The only exciting thing was betting on the survivor. Not that he ever lasted long on his own . . ."

Gill rose to his feet. "Then, with all these bloody murders, I'm surprised the place isn't haunted!"

"Oh, but it is," said the stranger. "It is haunted by the ghost of the youngest son. He still waits here for those who have a tale to tell."

I could feel the hair rising on my scalp. "Then—then why aren't you afraid?" I backed away, my chair overturning with a crash.

"Afraid? Why should I be afraid?" He smiled at us sweetly. "You see—I *am* the ghost!"

Chapter Fourteen

It is impossible to describe what happened in the next few moments. For one thing, I was too frightened to do anything except open my mouth and yell; for another, everything happened on top of itself.

I screamed, Gill fell over something and brought me down with him, the animals panicked and yelled as well and the stranger rushed round and round bleating trivialities like a demented sheep. That made it worse. My expectant terror had anticipated that he—It—would turn into something shrieking and gibbering, wearing a linen sheet, dragging Its chains and blowing like the east wind through a fleshless mouth—

Instead he—It—seemed to flow around us like the smoke from the fire, never touching us but making little patting, placatory gestures, tut-tutting in that high, mellifluous voice, soothing as if the terror I felt had an origin other than Itself. Apart from Its outlandish dress, It looked disturbingly normal, capering around us with Its senseless blandishments.

"No need to panic . . . didn't mean to alarm you . . . all a joke really. Want to be *friends* . . . you must stay awhile . . . don't run away . . ." It went on and on till the whisperings were as thick in my ears and nose and mouth as the air I breathed and I would have promised anything if it would just stop for a minute and let me *think*. . . .

So this—this creature—purported to be a two-hundred-year-old fratricide! This pale, frail youth walking and talking like anyone else . . . No, it just wasn't believable. It was a joke: in bad taste, to be sure, but still a joke. Well, I would call Its bluff.

"That's a—" My voice was coming out like a bat's squeak. I tried again. "That's a good act of yours. . . ." Better. "I congratulate you. But perhaps if you dressed differently, tried a few screams and howls, colored lights . . ."

It stopped rushing about and looked at me doubtfully. "What do you mean? I can't change myself. It's how I was—am! You don't like the story? I can't change that either." It seemed really put out. "You want special effects? Well, perhaps I can arrange some of those. Wait just a minute or two. . . ." and It turned and walked up to the other end of the hall.

There was a violent nudge at my ankle.

"Get away, quick!" whispered the Wimperling. "Now's our chance!"

"What for? I want to see what he's doing—"

"No, you don't!" and this time he gave me a sharp nip. "If he weaves a strong enough spell he can keep us here forever! Didn't you listen to his story?"

"Of course I did! But he's not a *real* ghost; ghosts don't look like that. He's just a storyteller, playing a game—"

"Game, my arse!" growled Growch, shivering so hard his teeth clattered. "You've lost yer senses of a sudden; let's go!"

I looked round at the others. Mistral had backed away into a corner and the pigeon and the tortoise had hidden their heads. I suddenly felt betrayed by them all. Even Gill looked disturbed, afraid, but I knew there was no harm in the youth: how could there be? All I wanted was to see what It would do next. Even my accursed ring was hurting so much I wanted to tear it off.

All right: if I couldn't have my fun, then I would teach them all a lesson! Striding over to the horse with the blankets over my arm, I rolled and stowed them, snapped shut the cages that held Basher and Traveler and fetched the cooking pot and slung it over the other goods. Lucky I hadn't unpacked all our gear. If I'd had to start at the beginning my temper would have gotten even worse.

Running over to the door I flung it open with a crash, letting in a howling gale and lashing rain.

"You are scared shitless? You want to go out in that? Then go, and good riddance! Me, I'm staying here."

They cowered away from me as though I had struck them, all save the Wimperling. He stood his ground.

"We're not going without you," he insisted. "But don't you *see* what danger you're in? There is no more substance to that—that *Thing* than the shadows which surround him!"

"Rubbish!" I snapped, and went back over to Gill, still standing by the cold fire, moving his blind head from side to side like a wounded animal.

"Summer? Is that you? What's going on?"

"I'm here. . . ." I took his hand, if possible even colder than mine and clammy with fear. "Don't worry; there's nothing to be scared of. The stranger has promised us some magic. Special effects, he said. Ah, it looks as though they are starting now."

Beyond us, on the dais where once the high table had stood, came a reddish glow. I moved down the room, dragging the reluctant knight with me, and out of the incandescence I could hear the high, mannered voice of the stranger.

"Come nearer, nearer! That's it, right at the front. No, you won't need that candle. . . . Now, watch!" It sounded just like a showman at a fair.

As I stared at the red light, which shifted and swayed like smoke, now brighter, now dimmer, I thought I could discern the outlines of a table, a bench, shadowy figures seated in front of dishes and goblets.

"Closer . . ." urged the voice, now almost in my ears. The smoky dimness swirled back like a curtain and everything became clearer. There was no sound and the outlines wavered now and again like wind on a tapestry, but I could see distinctly two men seated at the table, obviously enjoying the remnants of a feast. A silent carousal, I nevertheless added imagined sounds to myself. They chewed at lumps of meat, quaffed their wine, tossed back their heads and laughed, clapped one another on the shoulder. They both seemed to be dressed in the same quaint way as the stranger, but their outlines were so changeable it was difficult to be sure.

"Not perfect," said the languid voice in my ear, "but memory is not infallible. Watch this: enter the villain!"

Behind the two men I saw the stranger, a flagon of wine in one hand, a vial in the other. He was as insubstantial as the others but I saw part of the story he had told enacted before my credulous eyes. The vial was tipped into the flagon, the men drank a toast and then their heads sank to the table as though they were asleep, and the stranger tiptoed away with a silent giggle. The wavering picture remained thus for a minute or two and I explained to Gill what I had seen.

"It's very clever," I said. "I don't know how he does it!"

"I don't like it," muttered Gill. "Please can we go?"

"It's pitch-black, blowing a gale and raining torrents outside," I said. "Besides, I want to watch. . . ."

The men in the illusion were very still, but then one of them moved a little, choked, flung out an arm. The figure of the stranger appeared again, but this time he carried a knife, a knife that already dripped blood. A hand came out, plucked at the hair of the man who had moved, jerked back his head until the throat was stretched tight, and then slit it from ear to ear. At first a thin beaded seam where the knife had entered and then a great gush of blood that fountained across the table—The stranger turned to the second man—

"No, no!" I screamed. "I believe you, I believe you!"

I pulled at Gill's hand, my heart thumping, and turned to run, but now, between us and the open door at the other end of the hall, stood the grinning figure of the stranger, the murderous ghost, knife still in hand, and now he seemed of a sudden more substantial than anything else around us. Even the animals huddled by the door were assuming a dim and cloudy aspect, seeming to have lost their colors like well-leached cloth.

It smiled that sickly-sweet smile at us again. "Well, I gave you your special effects: did you like them? You must admit I have played *my* part: now it is *your* turn to entertain *me*." The last words were as sharp and threatening as the knife he carried.

"Let us go, we haven't harmed you. . . ." Why, oh why, hadn't I listened to the Wimperling?

"You haven't done me any good, either! That illusion-making takes it out of me." The tone was as sulky and whining as a child's. "Tell me a story, you promised me a story. Lots of stories! I'll let you go when you have told me a story—if I like it, that is. If I haven't heard it before." He moved closer, tossing the knife in the air and catching it. "Come on, we haven't got all night. . . ."

I backed away, still clutching Gill's arm, looking desperately for a way to escape, but the ghost was still between us and safety, and now he seemed to be taller, broader than before. I fetched up against the wall, sidestepped and seemed to find another I couldn't see, only feel—like cushioned stone. I moved the other way and there was another barrier. It seemed as though we were surrounded—was this what the Wimperling had warned me against? Was this the invisible "chain" that had trapped all others who visited the hellish place? There was only one thing for it.

"Just one story and you will let us go?"

"If I like it well enough."

"What—what kind of story?"

"Oh, knights and ladies, witches and dragons, giants and ogres, shipwrecks and sea monsters, spells and counter-spells—Heaven and Hell and the Four Winds!"

Up until that very moment I had known dozens of tales; ones my mother had told me, stories from the Bible the priest told us, tales we had heard on our travels, ones I made up for myself (the largest amount). I could have sworn that with a minute or two's thought I could spin a yarn to satisfy any critic, but all of a sudden my mind was completely empty. I couldn't even summon up the magic formula that started all stories, that first thread drawn from the spinning wheel that has all else following without thought.

"Well? Why haven't you begun?"

"I—I . . ."

"Get on with it! I warn you, I'm beginning to lose my patience! You're just like all the others: no fun. . . ." The voice managed at the same time to be both petulant and menacing. "'Once upon a time . . .'"

That was it! I looked once more at the ghost, who had stretched and expanded until his head nearly touched the beams overhead, a thin wraith like a plume of colored smoke, a genie escaping its lamp. I opened my mouth to start, hoping now that the rest would follow. My ring throbbed mercilessly.

"Once—"

"No!" It was another voice, a small voice but one made sharp and decisive by some sudden determination. It didn't sound like the Wimperling at all. "He'll have you if you do! Don't say another word. Just get ready to run. . . ." And with that I saw the most extraordinary sight.

A roundish object suddenly launched itself like a boulder from a catapult. As it reached a height of a couple of feet from the ground it seemed to waver for a moment, then there was a snap! and a crack! like a pennon flapping in a gale, and wings sprouted on either side, a nose pointed forward, a tail balanced back, and the pig rose to ten, twelve feet in the air and then, yelling like a banshee, swooped down and passed right *through* the ghost's body, just where its stomach would be!

The ghost-thing wavered and twisted and began to thicken and shrink back to its normal size, but where the Wimperling had flown through there was a great gaping hole, a sudden window through which everything once more looked clear and sharp. But the hole was beginning to close up again, to heal itself even as I dragged Gill forward. Then was a buzzing above our heads like a thousand bluebottles and the Wimperling zoomed above our heads, yelling: "I'm going to try it again, but my strength is failing. . . . As I go through, run for your lives!"

He arrowed down once more on the now normal-sized figure and as his flailing wings beat aside the trails and tatters of vapor that made up the creature, Gill and I ran hand-in-hand right through what remained. For one heart-stopping moment there was resistance, a sudden darkness, a frightful stench, then we were near the open door. Now the darkness was only that of night; the resistance, the wind; the smell that of rain. Never had I been so glad to face a storm before!

I grabbed Mistral's bridle with my free hand and we all ran down the path away from the castle, unheeding of dark and wind and rain. Some fifty yards away I stopped and counted heads.

"Oh, God! Where's the Wimperling? He must be . . . Wait there, the rest of you!" and I ran back to the castle door, my heart thumping with renewed terror. Growch, to do him credit, was right at my heels. I stepped into the hall and there was the ghost, still gathering pieces of itself together, gibbering and mouthing threats; there, too, was the little pig, trying vainly to drag its battered body towards the door. Growch hesitated only a moment then rushed forward, barking and snapping hysterically. Seizing my chance I dashed forwards, snatched up the pig, tucked him under my arm and, shouting to Growch to follow, escaped down the path once more.

As we moved off into the storm we could hear a wailing cry behind us, full of reproach and self-pity.

"Come back, come back! I wouldn't have hurt you. . . . all I wanted was a *story*!"

After that it was hard going, for all of us. The weather cleared for a while after that dreadful night, but the Wimperling lay for days in his pannier in a sort of coma, hardly eating anything. Tenderly I greased his sore wings and saved the choicest pieces of food, and gradually he started to pick up. Gill, however, caught a chill and could not shake it off; night after night I heard his cough get worse. Mistral, too, coughed and shivered; Basher the tortoise retreated into his shell and refused to eat, and Traveler's wing wouldn't heal. As for me, my stomach and bowels churned for days and I had to keep dashing off the road to find a convenient bush.

The weather grew steadily colder, with a biting east wind that snapped at our faces, bit at our heels, snatched at our clothes and blew a scud of leaves and grit into the food. The fires wouldn't light and if they did the hot embers scattered and threatened to set fire to everything. To add to our miseries, we seemed to have lost our way. All the roads were mere tracks between villages, and however much we asked for directions south and followed the road indicated, we still twisted and turned until, as often as not, we ended up facing north again.

The lodgings and food we found were poor and mean, and we were charged far too much: they knew, of course, that we had no choice but to pay what they asked. I began to think we were accursed, except that the ring on my finger was quiet—never again would I ignore its warning—and that of course Gill and I had made confession as soon as we could and been absolved. But the days themselves ceased to have individual meaning, apart from the labels of the Saint's days as we passed through various villages: Barbara, Nicholas, Andrew, Lucy, Thomas . . .

After a particularly hard day—we hadn't seen a village for forty-eight hours and were on short rations—and five hours, walking without rest, it started to snow. Just the odd flake floating prettily down, but the sky above held a grey cloak that was gradually spreading from the northeast and the air smelled of cold iron. I shuddered to think what might happen if we were caught without cover; we had escaped any heavy falls so far south, but that searing east wind canceled any advantage of distance.

But it seemed our luck had at last turned, for the next twist in the road revealed below us what seemed like a fair-sized town, with at least five or six streets, a large square and two churches. For the first time in days I could feel my cold face stretching into a smile.

"Warm lodgings and a fair supper tonight, for a change! Come on, it's downhill all the way. . . ."

By the time we reached the outskirts the snow was falling with that unhurrying steadiness that meant that, like an uninvited relation, it was here to stay. Because of the weather there were few folk around; those that were were engaged on last-minute precautions: putting up shutters, stabling beasts, hurrying home with a bundle of kindling or a couple of pies. We enquired for an inn, but the first we found was closed for the winter, as we were informed by the slatternly girl who answered my knock, slamming the door in my face before I could ask for further directions.

The snow was now so thick that we found the square by luck only; I caught at the sleeve of a man hurrying past with a capon under his arm and a sack over his head for protection.

"An inn, good sir?"

He paused for a moment, blinking the snow from his eyelashes, then pointed to the other side of the square, gave us a left and a right and a left. "Martlet and Swan," he said and was gone, swallowed by the swirling snow.

Now we were the only ones moving in a world of white. We found the first turning right enough, but I had a feeling we had missed the second. I could scarce see more than a few yards; the snow was clogging our footsteps and weighting our clothes. I took a last left turn, but it seemed as though we were right on the outskirts of town again. I was just about to turn and retrace our steps, knock at the first door that would open to us, when I caught sight of the inn sign swinging above my head. Snow had already obliterated most of the sign, but I could make out the "M-A" of the Martlet and the "S" of Swan, so I knew we were on the right road.

It was larger than the inns we had frequented so far. Double-fronted, the door was locked and barred and there were no lights to be seen. I knocked twice, but there was no answer. On the right, however, the gates were open onto a cobbled yard. We passed under the archway into lights, bustle, activity. On the far side a wagon had just been unloaded and was now being tipped against the snow, while its cargo of sacks was being hurried into shelter. Two steaming draft horses were being led into stables on the right, and buckets of water were sluicing down the cobbles. To our left the door was open onto firelight and the enticing smells of food.

Everyone was too busy to notice us, until I spied out the man who seemed to be directing operations, a well-fed man with a long, furred cloak and red hair, on which the snow melted as soon as it touched. I went over and tugged at his sleeve.

"Sir! Sir? You have lodgings and stabling for the night? For myself, my brother and the animals . . ."

The face he turned towards me had a pleasant, lived-in look, but he seemed to be puzzled.

"Lodgings?"

"Why, yes." Quickly I explained how I had been directed here. "And I saw the sign outside—only a couple of letters, but it was obviously the right place. You aren't full up, are you? I'm afraid my brother is not at all well, and we are cold and hungry. . . . If you are, perhaps you could direct us somewhere else, but . . ." Then I am afraid I started to cry. I couldn't help it. It had been a long, hard, frustrating time since we had fled the castle and the ghost.

He looked at me for a moment longer, then he smiled, a full, heartwarming smile. "Never let it be said . . . Come on, let's look at that sign of mine." Hurrying me out into the street, he gazed up at the nearly covered letters. "'Martlet and Swan' . . . Dear me: I must get that cleared. No matter, little lady: you found me." And he smiled again, and I knew we were home.

Before I knew what was happening, and with the minimum of direction from the landlord, Gill, his blindness noted, was being led away towards that enticing open door, and I, having insisted, was bedding down the animals with the help of the young stable boy. A rubdown and unloading for Mistral, followed by bran-mash; sleeping Basher tucked away in his box under the manger. Grain for Traveler and the run of the stall. Chopped vegetables and gruel for the Wimperling and a large bone for Growch: everything I asked for, diffidently enough, appeared as if by magic. But then the inn was obviously not full: Mistral had a commodious closed stall to herself, and there were only the draft horses and a brown palfrey to occupy the rest of the large stables.

The stable boy lighted me over to the side door, now closed, after fastening the yard gates and bolting them. He was obviously glad to be back in the inn, and after a dazzled look around the large kitchen in which I found myself I agreed with him wholeheartedly.

It was the largest kitchen I had ever seen, stretching the length of the stables which matched it across the yard. And there were *two* fires; one obviously incorporating some kind of oven, the other a large spit. Two long tables, one for preparation of food, the other for serving. Cupboards and shelves full of pots and crockery, long sinks for scouring and cleaning, wood stacked waist-high, clothes drying on racks, herbs, onions and garlic swinging gently from strings, hams and bacon hanging from hooks in the smoke-blackened ceiling, baskets of eggs and vegetables, jars of pickles, preserves and dried fruits . . .

And everyone merry and busy, not a long face or laggard step among them. And the nose-tickling smells . . . My mouth was watering as I followed a beckoning finger and found, behind a hastily slung screen, Gill immersed in a large tub of hot water.

"You all right?"

He couldn't answer, for at that moment one of the giggling maids who were scrubbing him put a cloth across his mouth, but he looked happy enough. The landlord poked his head behind the curtain.

"I thought it was the quickest way to warm him up. He'll feel better with the grime of the road away, too. You're next."

No arguments, I noticed. A moment later my clothes were taken away to be washed and I was relaxing in the hot, herb-scented water, my hair combed and rinsed. A brisk rubbing in warmed towels and someone handed me a clean shift and wrapped me in a blanket, shoving my feet into felt slippers a size too large.

I looked around for Gill, but he had evidently preceded me, for by the time one of the servants had ushered me into a parlor at the front of the house, he was already tucking into a bowl of thick vegetable soup. A small round table in front of a blazing fire was laid with linen, bread platters, spoons and knives. I sat down and was instantly served. As I supped I gazed around the comfortable room. Red tiles on the floor, shuttered window, tapestry, huge sideboard decked with pewter and silver, linen chest, a rack of wine . . . What a strange inn!

Hot baths, clothes washed, expensive surroundings—I hoped to God my purse would cover the cost! And where were the other guests? True, there was a third place laid at the table: we should have to wait and see. I must discuss terms with the cheerful landlord as soon as possible. I finished my broth and the bowl was whipped away, to be replaced by steaming venison-and-hare pasties, the juice soaking into the bread platter beneath. A pewter goblet of wine appeared at my elbow as I leaned over to cut Gill's pasty and guide his fingers.

"May I join you?" It was our host, changed into a crimson wool robe and a white undershirt, his feet in rabbit's-wool slippers. He should *never* wear that shade of red with his color hair, I thought abstractedly, even as I welcomed and thanked him for his excellent hospitality. I had better tackle him straightaway, I thought, even as fruit tarts and cheese were placed on the table. He gave me the opening I needed. "I trust everything is to your satisfaction?"

"Everything is just fine, sir, and we are most grateful, but I am afraid we cannot afford—"

He frowned, then smiled. "I had forgot. Perhaps I had better explain. That notice, so helpfully cloaked by the snow, does not read 'Martlet and Swan', but rather 'Matthew Spicer, Merchant.' The inn is two roads away, I'm afraid, but the natural mistake has given me the opportunity to enjoy your company. As my guests, naturally, so no more talk of money, little lady!"

Chapter Fifteen

Those weeks we spent in Matthew's house were like another world to me. Not only were we cosseted, fed, warm, entertained and cared for—we were *safe.* We had only been on the road some seven weeks or so, and yet it seemed to me that I had spent an eternity footsore, usually hungry and cold and always anxious. Not anxious for myself so much as the others. And to have that burden of responsibility taken, however temporarily, from my shoulders was like shucking off a load of wood I had carried, and immediately feeling I could bounce as high as the trees.

My mother had taught me a trick when I was little; lean hard against a wall, pressing one arm and shoulder as tight as I could. Count to a hundred then stand away from the wall. Your arm rises up of its own accord, like magic! I felt like that released arm.

Of course on that first evening there was a lot of explaining to do. At first I had felt like grabbing Gill's arm and rushing out into the night, so embarrassed was I at mistaking a rich merchant's house for an inn, but our host soon made us feel at home.

"A natural mistake, little lady, in all that confusing snow! And what would you have done in my place? Confronted by a damsel in distress, what could any Christian do but take her and her brother in?" He chuckled. "Besides, the servants tell me it is getting thicker by the moment out there. Six inches settled already, and by morning it will be two or three feet. No, it was Providence that brought you to my door, I'm convinced, and Preference will keep you here! But of course," he added hastily, "if after a while you tire of my hospitality, you are perfectly free to go elsewhere."

"But we cannot impose on you like this! You must allow me to—"

"Now you're not going to spoil our new acquaintanceship by talking about money, I hope! Money is one thing I don't need. Companionship I do. As a widower without family I find I do not make friends easily, and strangers such as yourselves will give me an interest to take me out of my usual dull routine. So, you will be doing *me* the favor by staying for a while. . . . Ah, mulled ale! Just what we need."

It was piping hot, redolent with cloves, cinnamon and ginger. I stretched out towards the fire, dazed with heat and food and drink. I hadn't felt as good as far back as I could remember—in fact since before my mother died, when we had stoked up the fire, told stories and eaten honey cakes, while the wolf wind of winter had howled down the chimney and keened under the door, making the sparks at the back of the chimney glow into patterns among the soot.

"Perhaps for a day or two, then . . ." I said weakly. He *had* sounded as though he meant it.

Gill was seized with a fit of coughing and clenched his fist against his chest with a look of pain. I leaned over and rubbed his back but the merchant went into action at once.

"Time we got your brother to bed. That cough sounds bad. Tomorrow we shall engage a doctor, snow or no snow."

He led us up a winding stair to the next floor and pointed to the left. "That is the solar. And here . . ." to the right: "the bedroom."

It was a lone, commodious chamber, strewn with rushes, hung with tapestries, dominated by a huge bed that would have slept six with ease. A huge fire burned in the hearth; candles were glimmering on a table by the fire and on two blanket chests against the walls. Two heavily carved chairs stood on either side of the fireplace and a series of hooks on one wall provided hanging space for clothes. Between the two shuttered windows was a small *prie-dieu.* A low archway at the far end was protected by a curtain.

"For washing and the usual offices," said the merchant, following my gaze. "I shall show your brother. Come, sir," and he led him away.

I moved over to the bed but let out a stifled gasp as I saw the covers move, and a moment or two afterwards a naked man and woman slipped from beneath the covers and unselfconsciously donned the clothes they had left on the floor. The woman bobbed a curtsy.

"I believe the chill is off the sheets now, mistress, but a maid will be up in a minute or two to renew the hot bricks. . . ." and with that the pair of them disappeared downstairs, leaving me open-mouthed. What luxury! Was this the way it was done among the rich? Come to think of it, many times at night my mother had insisted I retire first "to warm up the bed for my old bones. . . ." A maid scurried in with hot bricks wrapped with flannel, which she exchanged for those that must have already cooled. The bed looked very inviting, piled high as it was with furs.

The merchant came back with Gill, now shivering. "Into bed at once. Shall we put him on this side? No, I think it better if he is in the middle, then with you and me on either side he will keep warmer." He helped Gill under the covers and slipped into bed beside him. He nodded at the curtained recess. "Take a candle with you, little lady," and I headed for the *garderobe.*

When I returned another maid was handing Gill a posset; she waited till he drank it then snuffed all the candles but two slow burners, in case we needed to relieve ourselves during the night. She bobbed away, but I hesitated. I knew it was the custom for a host and his lady to share their bed with guests, but even in the ill-assorted places in which Gill and I had slept we had never shared a pallet. In the open we had slept with more intimacy, but the animals had been there too. . . .

Matthew Spicer propped himself on his elbow. "Something the matter?"

"Er . . . No. That is . . . I think I'll just stay here by the fire for a while. I—I'm really not tired—"

"Nonsense, young lady! You've been yawning and blinking for the past two hours!" He scrambled out of bed and came over to me, the long nightshift flapping round his ankles. "It's something I've done, isn't it? Or not done . . . Tell me." For a successful merchant, he had the least self-confidence I had ever seen. But perhaps women made him nervous. Mama had always said that men like that were a pain to begin with but sometimes made the best lovers. Eventually.

"No, no! You've been kindness itself. It's just that—" I glanced over to the bed: Gill was snoring softly. "You see, even at home I never shared a bed with my brother, and on our travels I slept separately also. I have never shared sleeping space with a man. Perhaps I'm being silly, but—"

He struck his forehead with the palm of his hand. "Of course, of course! Being a widower I don't have someone to remind me of the niceties. Come to think of it, if we had people staying overnight they were always married couples who shared. Since then all my guests have been men. Do forgive me! I shall have a pallet made up for you immediately. I—Whatever in the world is *that*?"

"That" was Growch.

He must have escaped from the stables and somehow infiltrated into the kitchen, for in his mouth was a large piece of pastry. He was soaking wet and smelled like a midden, but he rushed to my side and sat on my feet, growling softly through the pasty, his eyes swiveling from me to the merchant, the servants who were in pursuit, and back again.

He "spoke" through his full mouth. "Found you! What's goin' on then?"

"Nothing is 'going on'! You've no right up here! Why couldn't you stay where you were put?" To Master Spicer: "I'm sorry. It's my—our dog. I left him in the stables, but he's been spoiled, I'm afraid, and is not used to being on his own." To Growch I added furiously: "Just get back to the stables right now, and behave yourself!"

"No way! Needs lookin' after, you does. . . ." He belched, having swallowed the pastry whole. "My place is with you." I could see him eyeing the fire greedily. "Never tell what mischief you'll get into without me. No, here I am, and here I'll stay." He looked up at me through his tangle of hair. "Send me back down there again and I'll howl all night, full strength. Keep yer all awake . . . Promise!"

I turned to the merchant apologetically—my exchange with Growch had taken no more than a couple of silent seconds. "I'm sorry if he has been a nuisance. May he stay up here for tonight? I'll—I'll make some other arrangement tomorrow."

He considered. "I have no objection, though in the morning he might reconsider his decision. I happen to share the house with a rather large cat. . . ." He smiled. "Saffron will sort him out. In the meantime he could do with a bath. While they make up your bed."

No sooner said than done. Up came a large tub, in went Growch, and by the time his outraged grumbles had subsided, the bed was made up and he was clean and combed—probably for the first time in his short life. In the meanwhile Matthew Spicer sent for more wine and little spiced biscuits and we sat by the fire together. He didn't ask any questions, but I decided I had better tell him our names and our story. Not the real one of course: I used the one I had told everyone so far, but this time I killed off our parents and for some reason didn't mention my "affianced," or the dowry.

"You have had a hard time, Mistress Somerdai. That *is* a pretty name, by the way: most unusual. If I may say so, it suits you. . . . I see your bed is made up. We shall talk further in the morning."

Shyly I knelt before the *prie-dieu* to give hearty thanks for the temporary haven we had found, then cuddled down in the pallet by the fire. I lay awake for a while, tired though I was, listening to the gentle contrapuntal snores from the bed, and the occasional stifled cough from Gill. There was a soft *flumph!* from outside as a load of snow slid off the roof to the yard below. The fire crackled pleasantly but there was another, less endearing sound: Growch was scratching his ears, flap-flap-flap, and snorting into his coat as he chased fleas made lively by the heat. It seemed a bath wasn't enough.

I raised myself on one elbow, my head swimming with the need for sleep. By the light from the night-candle and the fire I could see that my scrawny little black dog was black no longer. He looked half as big again, now his cleaned coat had fluffed out—though nothing could lengthen those diminutive legs—and he was not only black, but tan and brown and grey and ginger and white also.

He sneezed six times.

"Can't you stop that?"

He glared at me from under a fuzzy fringe. "Sneeze or scratch?"

"Both."

"Listen 'ere . . . Never mind. All I can say is, if'n you 'ad these little buggers chasin' around, you'd scratch."

"You wanted to be beside the fire! And don't pretend it was all concern for my welfare, 'cos it wasn't! Anyway, why the sneezing? Caught a chill from the unexpected bath?"

"Nar . . . Stuff they washed me in: smell like an effin' whore, I do."

In the morning Gill was definitely worse, tossing and turning in a fever, his cough hard and painful. Matthew Spicer shook his head. "He needs treatment right away." He flung open the shutters: snow was still falling. He closed them again, and shook his head. "Don't worry; one of the servants will get through."

Up and dressed—my clothes returned clean, mended, pressed—I slipped across the cleared yard to the stables. The others were fine; Mistral had been given fresh hay, Basher was still asleep, and I found grain in the bins for

Traveler. The Wimperling's nose peeped out from a nest he had made for himself.

"Everything all right?"

I told him about Gill, and the merchant sending for treatment.

"Don't let him bleed the knight; he needs all his blood." I wondered what on earth he knew of doctoring, but let it pass. After all, he had been right before.

"Are you hungry?"

"A little grain will do. I've had a nibble of hay already."

The "apothecary" arrived an hour or so later, in a litter. I don't know what I had expected, but it was certainly not the small, scrunched-up man with the brown skin, hooked nose and black eyes whose candle-lit shadow on the stairs was the first I saw of him. The stooping silhouette with the grotesque reaping-hook nose at first made me cross myself in superstitious fear, but face to face there was nothing to alarm, quite the reverse. The black eyes sparkled with a keen intelligence, the mouth curved easily into a smile and the thin, hunched shoulders and long, clever fingers emphasised everything he said: a shrug of the body, a wave of the hands more expressive than mere words. These he spoke with a heavily accented touch, at first a little difficult to follow.

Matthew Spicer introduced him with pride. "My friend Suleiman, who comes from the East and specializes in many things, including medicine. We have worked together for many years. He has for a long time been my agent in Araby, but now he has been caught by the weather, providentially for us, I might add! I know of his healing powers and salves of old, and he has consented to treat your brother, Mistress Somerdai." He noted my expression of doubt—so did the visitor. "You couldn't do better, I assure you!"

This was soon evident, at least in Suleiman's meticulous examination of Gill. The Arab first questioned his patient thoroughly, asking for all the symptoms, their duration and severity, before he even touched his body. Then he felt his forehead, looked in his eyes and ears with a little glass, put a spatula in his mouth and peered down his throat, then counted the pulse at his wrist.

He glanced up at me. "Your brother has a high fever; to bring this down is our first priority, but first we must find the seat of it. I believe it is in the chest, and I shall now listen to this."

"How?" I was by now too interested for politeness.

"Watch." From the folds of his capacious red robes he brought forth a metal object shaped like a Madonna lily with a hollow, twisted stem. He held it out to me. "Copied from the horn of a rare antelope in the sands of the desert." He held a silver cup to Gill's mouth and asked him to cough, looking gravely at the sputum. "Too thick . . ." Then he placed the wide end of the metal object on Gill's chest, the thin end in his own ear, and listened intently. Repeating this on various parts of the knight's chest, he asked him to sit up and repeated the process on his back. He then beckoned to me. "Do as I did and listen; make sure the instrument is firmly against his chest."

At first all I could hear was a shush-beat, shush-beat which I realized must be the heart, then as Gill breathed in there was a gurgling wheezy noise, as he breathed out a whistling bubble. Incredible!

Master Suleiman took the instrument from me and held it to his own chest. "Listen to the difference. . . ." The steady heartbeat, somewhat slower, but no wheezing, no whistling. "You understand? Your brother has a deep infection in the lungs, hampering his breathing: it is almost as though he drowns in the ill humours that have gathered. So, we can only cure the fever by eradicating its cause: the lung infection. I shall return to my rooms and prepare certain medicines—"

"You're not going to bleed him, then?" I blurted out, remembering what the Wimperling had said.

He shot me a sharp glance from under dark brows. "Sounds as though you are no friend to leeches?"

"A—a friend of mine . . . He says it takes away your strength."

"Perfectly correct. I sometimes wish we had a method to pump blood *in* instead of taking it *out*." He looked over at Gill, manfully trying to stifle another bout of coughing. "We'll soon ease that. . . . Keep my patient warm, no solid food, plenty of drinks. I shall prepare herbs to be steamed over water on a low boil, to soften the air he breathes in here. Please see the fire does not smoke too much. I shall also prepare an expectorant, a potion to reduce the fever and a sleeping draught."

For once I didn't think of cost: whatever he needed, Gill must have. "Will . . . will he be all right?" I asked, hesitantly, fearfully.

Suleiman glanced at me sympathetically. "I tell the truth. He is very ill, your brother. I have seen men die in his condition and I have seen them live. His advantages are his youth and strength—and, I hope, my medicines. And a prayer or two wouldn't come amiss."

For three days my knight seemed to hover between life and death, but gradually the fever abated, his breathing grew easier and the coughing less painful. I did not leave his side save to tend the animals, relieve myself and wash. I even ate my meals by the bedside, though I have no memory of their content.

Suleiman called twice a day, Master Spicer fussed and cosseted, the maids washed and dried the patient, gave him fresh linen and night clothes daily. I dozed in fits and starts on a stool by the bed, trying always to be ready for the turn of the sand-glass for the regular dosings, to see the fire was kept topped up, to be ready with cooling drinks and a damp sponge to wipe away the sweat.

On the morning of the sixth day from our arrival Suleiman came in, examined his patient, then crossed the room and flung the shutters wide.

"The sun is shining, the wind has dropped, the temperature is rising and my patient is recovering! Some fresh air will do us all good." He glanced at me, dazed by sudden sun and ready to drop. "I have the very thing for you, Mistress Somerdai. . . ." and he handed me a vial of thick, greenish liquid. "Half of this in a glass of wine—now!—and I guarantee you will be a new young woman before you know where you are!"

I hadn't the strength to resist and downed the bitter-tasting liquid without a murmur. I don't know about feeling like a new woman, I thought, but if I just lie down for a moment or two and close my eyes I'm sure I will. . . .

"Time to wake up," said Matthew Spicer, gently pinching my earlobe. "I'll bet you are hungry. Hot milk and honey has been recommended. Sit up and take a sip."

I did as I was told, opening gummy eyelids, considering how I felt. Apart from an unpleasant taste in my mouth, soon dispelled by a sip or two of the milk, remarkably fit.

"What time is it?"

"A little after two in the afternoon."

"I must have slept over four hours! Sorry . . ."

"Four? More like twenty-eight. You took that draught yesterday morning."

"Yesterday? But I can't have. . . ."

"You did!" said another voice, and there, sitting in one of the large chairs by the fire, wrapped in blankets, sat Gill. A pale, thin Gill, but the hectic flush was gone from his cheeks. He smiled in my direction. "Sleepyhead Summer!"

My heart turned over with love and longing. It was a long time since I had had the chance to study him at leisure. Being on the road had been such a struggle just to survive, especially latterly, that I had grown accustomed to an unshaven, grumbling, blind man who needed all my spare attention. Now he was washed, shaved, fed and at ease, and I found once more I was seeing him as I had that first day, and all the old adoration rushed to the surface, so that I had to hide my face lest Matthew Spicer saw my confusion.

"And in case you are worrying about your menagerie," said the merchant, chuckling: "Don't! The horse and the pig—that one will never fatten—have been given mash, the pigeon grain and the reptile left to sleep. When we have some time you must tell me how you acquired such a motley collection! As for your dog—" he nudged a recumbent form lying in the hearth: "—he has been bathed again and near eaten his weight in leftovers. . . ."

Growch was stretched out in a nose-twitching, leg-paddling dream. His curly coat of black and tan, ginger and grey, his white chest and paws, all gleamed in the fire and candlelight, and his stomach was so full it was stretched as tight as the skin on a tabour, the thinner hair on his belly showing the pied skin underneath.

"He met Saffron, my ginger cat, on the stairs," continued the merchant. "And he retreated at once, as I knew he would: Saffron makes two of most dogs, especially in his winter coat. However, I think you will find they have come to some agreement. Your dog is allowed inside as long as he recognizes who is boss. . . . And now, Mistress Somerdai, when you are dressed and have broken your fast, perhaps I may show you something of my house?"

Through the archway at the top of the stairs was the solar, a pleasant room with a deep hearth, set with benches on either side. The floor was polished oak, partly covered with two large rugs the merchant told me had come from a place called Persher; these were pleasant underfoot and partially muffled the creak of the floorboards. Two carved chairs stood by the window, and leather-topped stools provided further seating. On one side of the curtained doorway were hooks for cloaks; there were two chests, one containing cushions for extra comfort, the other a set of games: chess, draughts, backgammon and dice.

In the center of the room was a table, the top inlaid in marble to represent a chess or draughts board; a hanging cupboard contained three precious books: a psalter, a breviary, and a delightful Boke of Beestes. Eventually I read this from cover to cover more than once, carefully examining the delightfully illustrated initials, head- and tail-pieces, marveling all the while at the strange creatures—spotted, dotted, patched, striped; furred, feathered, scaled; toothed, beaked, tusked, clawed—that curled, writhed, marched and snaked across the pages. There were creatures I had never heard of, others I couldn't believe in—gryphons, mermen, crocodiles, elephants—and yet, amongst them all were tortoises! Very strange . . .

The walls of the solar were part paneled, part painted, these latter in patterns of yellow suns, moons and stars on a pale blue background. Just as the bedroom windows overlooked the yard, the window in the solar looked out over the street in front, and it was this window that was the most curious item in the room. There were the usual shutters, of course, but now no one need freeze to death to look out on the busy street below, for the merchant had installed proper windows that opened outwards for summer and remained closed in winter—all of glass! Not just plain glass, either: he knew a man who restored stained-glass in churches, and the window was filled with a higgle-piggle of colors, all small pieces like a patched cloak—red, blue, yellow, green, purple and even some that had been part of trees, creatures, faces—so that one looked out on the street through colors that discolored the folk below, and yet when the sun shone these same pieces threw a rainbow of light onto the polished floor. Like a spring lawn sown with wildflowers . . .

Down the stairs and there were the long kitchens at the back where the staff lived, ate and slept. At the front was the room where we had dined on that first night: "Near the kitchens so the food doesn't get cold," my host explained, and, next to it, with a separate entrance and shuttered counter to the street, the shop where the merchant did his day-to-day business.

A long counter held weighing scales, paper, wax and string. Behind this were piles of small sacks, neatly tied and labeled and above them shelves reaching to the ceiling, filled with bottles, jars, pouches, boxes of all shapes and sizes and parcels. Behind the counter was the merchant's assistant, a small, pocked man called Jacob. But it was the smell of the place one remembered. All through Matthew Spicer's house little teasing scents met one on the stairs, hid in chests, fled down nooks and crannies, popped up in the linen, but here was the source, the heart of it all.

There were herbs in plenty—rosemary, thyme, dill, fennel, sage, rue, peppermint, balm, bay, basil, but it was the scent of the exotic spices that overlay all. Cloves, ginger, cinnamon, cardamom, nutmeg, mace, saffron, pepper, cumin, all combining to tickle the nose with their pungency and invite their flavors to match their aromas.

Matthew Spicer was a member of the Guild, and he explained that most of his goods came from the East to a place called Vennis, a magical town that floated on the sea like an anchored island. From there the goods traveled overland to the nearest western port and again took ship across the Mediterranean to a southern port. From there it came by road to the merchant's house, the bulk being stored in the large sheds at the back of the yard, to be packed into smaller containers ready for distribution to various large towns and cities throughout the country, and even farther north.

It sounded like a long and complicated business, and I said so.

"Certainly it is," he said. "Sometimes it can take up to three years between ordering something and its delivery."

"And what if one of the ships founders, or your wagons are attacked? Or the spices spoil in transit?"

"Luckily that doesn't happen very often. God is good." He crossed himself. "Also, there is a very good profit margin. I am not poor." He sighed. "But money isn't everything. I lost my wife seven years ago, God rest her soul, and I have no family to carry on the business."

"You could marry again. . . ."

"I could, yes, but if I found a woman who pleased me, who knows but that she might refuse me?" He attempted a smile. "I am not very good at understanding the fair sex, I'm afraid, and I am no longer a young man."

I presumed him to be in his early forties. Not stout, but not slim either; not handsome, but not ugly: he had a pleasant, lived-in sort of face. His reddish hair was thinning slightly but his teeth were still good. I spoke to him as I thought Mama would have done.

"I am sure any woman you chose would be only too pleased to accept your offer. Youth is only an attitude of mind, after all, and you are the kindest man I know."

His face brightened. "You really think so? You have cheered me more than I would have thought possible!"

What with Gill's illness we had missed any Christmas festivities, but with Suleiman as another guest we four celebrated the New Year in style: the rooms decorated with sprays of evergreen, sprinkled with rose water, alive with candles; Mass (except for Suleiman), then back to a veritable feast. Chicken stuffed with dates and olives—two fruits I had never tasted before—a baked ham stuck with cloves and glazed with honey, root vegetables in butter with a touch of ginger, small pastry cases full of meat and spices, the latter so hot they made you feel you breathed fire, roast chestnuts, rice with apple, apricot and other dried fruit and a soft, sheep's-milk cheese.

And to drink a toast to the rebirth of the year, an ice-cold sweet white wine that came, like the silken hangings, from a place called Sissilia . . .

I had anticipated taking our journey up again within days, but the visit to church had not done Gill any good—except spiritually, of course. He started to cough again, and Suleiman insisted that he stay quiet and within doors for a week or more at least. This meant that we fell into a certain routine. After breaking our fast we would, Gill and I, go into the solar, where I would take up sewing and mending, which our clothes sorely needed.

I was surprised to find just how much thinner I had become, and the chore of sewing was mixed with a secret delight in being able to take in my clothes as well as patch and repair them. I regretted that my things were so shabby and worn, but they still covered me well enough and I could not afford to indulge in non-necessities. Gill was a different matter. He had been used to so much better, whether he remembered it or not, and as I had taken to exercising Mistral and Growch if the weather was fine, I took the opportunity of buying some rough woolen cloth, burel, and fitting my knight for longer braies and a new surcoat. The town was a pleasant place and obviously Matthew Spicer was held in high regard, for once folk knew we were staying with him—and news travels faster than a grass fire in a place like that—we were welcomed with smiles and cheerful greetings. I suspect, too, that I was given a special price for my cloth, and for the repair of our shoes which was also essential.

One morning Matthew—he had asked us to dispense with the more formal address—came into the solar looking helpless, a length of fine green wool over his arm. He hesitated for a moment, then asked if I had much sewing in hand.

"Why, no. I have only to finish attaching the ties to these braies. Is there something you would like me to do?"

"Er . . . yes. There is, actually. If you're sure you don't mind? I have a sister, married to a Dutchman, and she writes in her letters that she finds it difficult to buy wool in this particular color." He held the soft wool against my shoulder. "Yes, the shade is just right! Her coloring is near yours, and I wonder . . ."

"Yes?" I encouraged, indulgent of this successful man who could yet be so diffident.

"If you could make her a surcoat," he said, all in a rush. "Something simple and serviceable, nothing fancy? You and she are much of a height and size, and if you make generous seams and hems . . . But perhaps I ask too much?"

"Of course not! I only hope I can do this beautiful material justice." I fingered it: strong and hard-wearing, it was still fine enough to hang practically creaseless. "A lovely color: like fresh mint."

He was obviously pleased. "Again, if it's not too much trouble, she would need two undercottes; I have some fine linen dyed a soft brown which would go nicely. . . ."

It was the least I could do. He had been so kind to us both: a man in a thousand.

During the time I sewed, Gill would be practicing on a small lute Matthew had found, or on my pipes, although he soon became bored and restless; sighing deeply, drumming his fingers on the furniture, yawning. Then I would coax him to sing: "Winter's weary winds," "Silk for my sweetheart," or, if Matthew joined us, tenor, baritone and soprano would essay a round: "The beggars now have come to town," or something similar.

Afternoons I would read while Gill rested, though if there were a hint of warmth and sunshine I would take a stroll with Growch—who had become so used to Matthew's majestic cat, Saffron, that they would now share the solar hearth together. In the evenings we played chess or draughts or backgammon, Matthew against Gill and me. Not surprisingly, Gill was familiar with all the games, and once recalled a chess set he had had, each piece carved in relief, birds for red, animals for white. If Suleiman joined us the men would swap rhymes and riddles while I stayed quiet and listened, for it was not proper for women to assume an equality with men in this sort of area.

If enough wine had been consumed after Suleiman went home, then Gill and Matthew would sing again, each trying to outdo the other. First Gill might chant the "Gaudeamus igitur," Matthew follow this with the drinking song: "Meum est propositum in taberna more" and both finish with the sentimental "My mistress she hath other loves."

We had further snow in mid-January, but by the end of the month Suleiman pronounced Gill fit enough to travel. He had been taking more exercise each day and almost looked as good as new. But Matthew was a puzzle: the nearer the time came for us to leave, the more restless he became. Then one night it all became clear. Gill had just retired and Matthew roamed around the solar, then abruptly followed Gill. I stretched and yawned, enjoying a few more moments before the fire, when suddenly the curtain was flung back and Matthew appeared, looking thoroughly upset. Had something happened to Gill? I rose to my feet in alarm.

"Whatever's the matter?"

He hesitated, then came towards me. His face was all red. "I'm not sure. . . . Perhaps you can explain?"

"I don't understand. . . ."

"I—I approached the man you call your brother upon—upon a certain matter, only to be told that you and he were not related at all." He really did look most upset. "I think I deserve an explanation!"

Chapter Sixteen

So I gave him one.

Not the real, entire, whole truth. He wouldn't have believed me. He heard about the knight passing through our village one day, being ambushed the next and wandering about blinded until I found him by chance and had promised to try and find his home, when it was obvious no one else either believed his story, such as it was, or was willing to help.

I told Matthew how Gill couldn't even remember his name, that all I could recall was an impression of his standard. I even brought out the scrap of cloth I had kept, but he shook his head. No help there. From there it was an easy progression to explaining away the "menagerie," as he called them. My dog, fair enough, a horse to carry our gear, no trouble there. The pigeon? Found wounded, a carrier, unusual color, might breed from him. Satisfactory. The tortoise? Abandoned, feed him up and sell him off. Fine.

The pig was more difficult. Runt of the litter, got him for next to nothing. Foraged off the land as we passed, always a useful standby for barter. He accepted that, too, and I breathed a sigh of relief. No need for him to know we "talked" among ourselves: animals didn't in Matthew's circle, in spite of all the folk tales of talking foxes, mice, bears and fish. People should pay more attention to stories: they didn't make themselves up.

I thought I had gotten away with it beautifully, but there was obviously something still bothering our host. He umm'd and aah'd and then came to the point.

"And you had no hesitation in—in helping this man, Sir Gilman?"

"Of course not! I had nothing to keep me in the village, I had some money put by, and thought I would like to see a little of the world before I settled down. Besides, if you had seen him that first time, all handsome and elegant, just like a prince in a fairy tale! He was so utterly unattainable, that when I saw him again, all threatened, maimed and desolate, it was like being given a present! Even beaten up and dirty as he was, he was still the handsomest man I had ever seen in my life! And with him being blind, it was like an extra bonus, because—" I stopped. I had given myself away well and truly this time.

He looked at me in a way I couldn't fathom. "Because what?"

So I told the truth. What did it matter, now? "Because he couldn't see me; he couldn't see how fat and ugly I was. And, please God, he never will. I don't ever want him to know what I look like: I couldn't bear it!" I paused: he was looking most odd. "There, now I've told you. I would be obliged if you don't disillusion him." I looked down at my feet—yes, I could just about see them now—feeling very uncomfortable; I hated remembering my ugliness, my obesity.

But he didn't give me time to feel sorry for myself. "Fat?" he said. "Ugly? Whatever in the world gave you that idea? A little on the plump side, perhaps, a comfortable armful for any man, but ugly? Not at all! You have lovely greeny-grey eyes, a straight nose and—"

"Please don't!" I cried. "You're only making it worse!" I lost all discretion: kindness and tact could go too far. I *knew* what I looked like: hadn't I seen my reflection in the river often enough? Piggy eyes, squabby nose, double chins and all? And Mama had sighed, but added that my superior education and dowry would "go a long way towards overcoming" my other deficiencies. "You know perfectly well that in a million million years I could never attract a man like Gill, that the only time I will ever be able to hold his hand, care for him, gaze unhindered on his beautiful face, is now, when he's blind!"

"You—you love him, then?"

"Of course I do! How could I not? He is the sort of man every woman dreams about, and I am lucky, *lucky,* that even part of that dream has come true! I don't *want* to find his home, I don't *want* him ever to see again, may God forgive me!" Suleiman had examined his eyes and could find no obvious cause for the sudden blindness and loss of memory, except the blow to the head. He had advised him that memory might return gradually and he could even regain his sight one day as quickly as it had gone, if the circumstances were right—what circumstances he wasn't prepared to say. "I shouldn't have said that, I know I shouldn't, but each day I have him as he is, is one day snatched from heaven!"

Matthew looked completely different: older, greyer, sort of crumpled. "I did not realize. . . ."

"And neither does he!" I said quickly. "He treats me like a sister since we decided on the story we told you earlier: it is easier to travel that way."

He gathered his robes tightly around him as if he were suddenly cold. "Don't worry: your secret is safe with me. . . ."

The next time we were on our own I asked Gill how he had come to betray our true relationship.

He laughed. "You won't believe this, Summer, but he actually came and asked me, as your brother and next of kin, if he had my permission to pay court to you! Of course I couldn't say yea or nay, could I? So I had to tell him we weren't related. Anyway, I gather you must have talked your way out of it. Pity: you could have done worse, I imagine, and he seemed very taken. . . ."

Just imagine what my mother would have said! She would have considered him the perfect catch. "You should have had more sense!" I could hear her scolding. "What future is there traipsing around the countryside with a blind and helpless knight, handsome though he may be, when there is absolutely no future in it? Here is a comfortable home, a good-natured husband who is bound to die before you and leave you with his wealth; you just haven't the sense you were born with!" and then she would have given me a good beating, and it would have been no use pointing out that I had no idea Matthew felt that way.

Too late now, and it wouldn't have made any difference if I had known: my heart, for however short the time, was given to Gill. I was truly sorry if I had hurt Matthew, but I hoped it wouldn't spoil our last few days with him.

I needn't have worried; he was quieter than usual perhaps, and spent more time at his work, but there were no sulks, no reproaches, although I sensed he was under strain and would be glad when we were gone. Suleiman was going to supervise a consignment of spices further north and it had been agreed we would accompany him as far as the crossroads on the main north-south highway, for we had indeed come much too far east for our purpose.

So we set off at Candlemas, in a fine drizzle, all save Mistral safe under cover of one of the wagons, with Matthew out to see us go. I watched him dwindle on the road and then vanish as we turned the corner towards the countryside. I said a short prayer for his future well-being: I felt sorry for him, but had no regrets as to my decision.

"Nice to be on the road again," said Gill. "Perhaps this time I can get nearer home. . . ."

I think the animals felt the same way. The rest and food had benefited them all: Mistral had filled out and her coat shone with regular brushing; Basher was eating a little and still sleeping a lot, but Traveler's wing was almost healed and he was taking short flights with increasing regularity. The biggest change of all was in the Wimperling. He had grown almost out of recognition; he was three times as big as before, easily, and tubby with it. No more lifts in the pannier for him: he would have to walk with the rest of us. There seemed to be changes in his shape as well. His nose was longer, the claws on his hooves were bigger, his rump was higher than his head and the vestigial wings were vestigial no longer, in fact they looked definitely uncomfortable. In fact he looked so odd that the first thing I did that first night on the road was to fashion him a sacking coat that at least hid the worst of his strangeness. Funnily enough, though, other people didn't seem to notice he was any different from a normal pig. Very strange . . .

Too soon our journey in comfort came to an end. At the crossroads, the third day after we had set out, I loaded up Mistral once more, checked and double-checked that everything was where it should be, then turned to say good-bye and thanks to Suleiman. He handed me a parcel.

"You'll have to find room for this," he said. "It's from Matthew."

Inside were the green woolen dress and undershifts I had made for Matthew's sister. "He must have made a mistake. . . ."

Suleiman smiled. "No mistake. He has no sister, never had." He handed me a small leather purse. "He said this was for the extra care of your knight." Inside were five gold coins. "He asked me to remind you that love cannot feed on thin air, and that the rain and wind are no discriminators. . . ."

Less than an hour later we were lucky enough to catch up with a small caravan of pilgrims and journeymen; the weather fined up, the road was easy, other travelers joined us. We became friendly with our companions of the road, swapping experiences and comparing dogs and horses: I even remember boasting that Growch was the cleverest dog for miles and that our pig could count to twenty—and this last idiocy got us into real trouble.

It all started about two weeks after we had left the crossroads. It was around midday, the sun was shining, a soft breeze came from the south, the grass was looking greener than it had for months, little shoots were pricking up through the earth, buds were starting to uncurl on bush and shrub, birds were becoming much more urgent in their courting and I was planning ahead for the next two days' meals. Someone ahead was singing a catchy little tune, behind us a baby was being hushed; Gill was whistling the same tune as the singer, the pigeon was giving his wings a tryout on Mistral's back and—

—and they came out of the woods on our left with a clatter of arms and thud of hooves. A dozen or so men, mounted and in half-armor, all in burgundy livery. They clattered to a halt and their leader drew his sword.

"Halt! Halt, I say! Stay right where you are, or it will be the worse for you!"

Panic does all sorts of strange things to people. Some freeze in their tracks, others run, it doesn't matter where; others scream and scream; some faint, others wet themselves. Remembering the last attack in which I was involved, I was about to run to the shelter of the tree—we were at the back, and I could probably have made it—but was brought up short remembering Gill and the others.

At least they weren't killing anybody yet, but a couple of the soldiers cantered down to our end and rounded up the stragglers.

"Move along there, now: not got all day . . ."

Now we were circled by restive, sweating horses, stamping their hooves, tossing their heads till the harness jingled. Behind me someone was moaning in terror. I reached for Gill's hand, whispered what was happening, conscious of Growch's unease, of the Wimperling rock-steady at my other side. My ring wasn't sending out signals, either.

The leader of the troupe stood in his stirrups and addressed us.

"Just shut up, the lot of you, and listen to me! I mean you, you miserable worms! I am Captain Portall from the Castle of the White Rock—look, if you aren't quiet I shall be forced to make you. . . ." and he raised his sword threateningly. "That's better. . . ." He gazed around us, his expression adequately conveying just what a sorry lot we were, how far below his normal consideration, and just how wearisome he found the whole business. "Now, as I said, I am from White Rock Castle, and my lady Aleinor is bored—

even more bored than I am in talking to you peasants." He brushed at his drooping mustache with a mailed fist. "And when the lady is bored we all suffer! And her husband and four sons being off on some crusade or other doesn't help; she wants cheering up, does the lady, and that's what I'm here for." He looked at us all once more, even more despondently. "Now, what I want to know is, which of you likely lot has the skills to entertain a lady? And you can drop that sort of thought," he said threateningly at a ribald snigger from somewhere at the back. "I mean singing, dancing, tumbling, juggling, minstrelsy, tricks, that sort of rubbish. Trifles to amuse, tales to entertain, ballads to hearten—something to make her *laugh,* dammit! Come now, half-a-dozen volunteers . . ."

Such was my relief at realizing that we were not about to be hacked to death, robbed or raped that I paid little attention to the captain's speech. Everyone else began to relax also, picking up whatever they had dropped, gathering their scattered belongings, chattering among themselves.

"Well, that's that!" I said to Gill confidently. "We should be on our way—"

"I meant what I said!" suddenly shouted the captain. "Unless I find volunteers to accompany me back to the castle to entertain the Lady Aleinor, there will be . . . trouble! And I mean trouble! I want half-a-dozen right now: if not, I shall start stringing you all up, one by one!" He leaned from his horse and grabbed a man by his ear. "And we'll start with this one!"

A woman and girl started wailing, and everyone seemed to shrink into little family and friends groups. The circle grew smaller as the horses closed in. Fear became something you could touch and smell.

"Well? I'm waiting. I shall count to ten. One, two, three . . ."

"I've done a bit of juggling in my time." A man pushed forward. "Nothing fancy, mind . . ."

"You'll do." Captain Portall released the ear he was holding and rose in his stirrups once more. "Who else? You'll get a meal and a handful of silver if you please the lady. Come on, now. . . ."

"Should have mentioned that earlier," muttered a man to my left. He raised his hand. "I know a ballad or two might suit her."

One by one we got a tumbler and his son, a teller of tales, a man who could twist himself into impossible positions.

"Is that all? I'm disappointed, very disappointed! Singers, tumblers, a juggler, contortionist, story-teller: can't any of you do something *different*?"

To my horror one of our fellow travelers piped up with: "That girl over there, the one with the blind brother, she's got a dog what does tricks and a pig that counts. . . ."

I could have sunk straight into the ground! What a fool, what an utter idiot I had been to boast in such a way the other night! And it was lies, all lies—

But the captain on his horse was towering over us. "A counting pig? Now that *is* different. Never come across one of those before. Right, that's enough! Get them all organized, men! This the pig? I'll take him, then." And before

I knew it he was down, had heaved up the Wimperling onto his saddle bow and remounted. "Heavy, isn't he?" and he turned and trotted off.

What could we do but follow? We couldn't desert the pig.

Our anxious way took us down a broad ride of the wood for perhaps a half mile, the fallen leaves of the autumn before muffling the thud of the escort's hooves, the chinking of the harness echoed by the chattering of a jay as it jinked away to the left. About twenty minutes later we came through thinning trees into the afternoon February sunshine and saw a picture that might have graced a Book of Hours.

Perhaps a couple of miles away, girdled by the neatest fields I had ever seen, rose the towers of faery. Perched on a grey-white outcrop of rock, from where we stood it looked insubstantial, a building from the edges of dream. There were four towers of unequal height, one much taller than the others. The castle itself was built from white stone, just whiter than the rock from which it rose; silhouetted against the clear, blue winter sky it looked like something one could cut from card.

As we drew nearer we could see the crenellations along the walls and even small figures patrolling the perimeters, and the road along which we traveled curving up towards a drawbridge and portcullis, over what looked like a moat of some kind. On our travels we had glimpsed other castles in the distance, most of them squat and frowning, with solid grey foundations and the hunched look of a sick animal, but this was quite different. Apart from its coloring, the way it seemed to spring upwards out of the rock, there were colored flags fluttering from the gateway, and the thin sound of a trumpet announcing our arrival.

We were traveling through fields plowed or already sown, through orchards of fruit trees beneath which not a single weed could be seen—unlike the unfamiliar orange groves outside the last town we had visited, the goat's-foot trefoil beneath their trunks a yellow so bright it seared the eye—and past the twisted, bare branches of dead-looking vines, that later would cluster with heavy grapes. There was also an avenue of pollarded oaks, their knobbed branches giving no hint of the summer lushness to come. Everything neat, everything tidy, not a wavy line in the plowing, not a weed in the fields, not a dead leaf on the paths. Perhaps I had an untidy mind, but I would have welcomed a little disarray, a hint that outside belonged to nature as well as man.

Small houses were clustered at the foot of the White Rock, all as spic and span as the rest, and these we passed, together with the huge communal bread ovens, as we trudged up the sudden steep ascent to the castle proper and clattered over the short drawbridge. I peered over the edge as I passed: as I thought, a dry moat, and judging by the stench and the brown streaks down the walls that had not been evident from a distance, showing that refuse from the kitchens and garde-robes was allowed to flow unchecked, it was evident that there was no constant source of water. The creaking of the portcullis preceded us, but it needed only to be drawn halfway for us all to squeeze beneath.

We found ourselves in a large, cobbled courtyard, full of noise and bustle.

Horses were being curried and exercised, wagons loaded and unloaded, soldiers were practicing with short swords, others examining armor and mail newly come from the sand barrels that were rolling up and down a short slope. A bowyer was stringing bows, a fletcher feathering arrows, an armorer busy at his anvil. Stable boys were shoveling ordure into an empty cart and a couple of cooks were gutting and jointing venison. The noise was indescribable.

Captain Portall dismounted his troop and started issuing orders as to our disposition. He lifted the Wimperling from his saddle with a look of distaste: the pig had just let loose a series of little popping farts.

Once down, the Wimperling nudged me. "We must be together. . . ."

"Right!" Captain Portall turned to me. "You and you—" he pointed to Gill: "—over there in one of those huts. Animals in the stables. Gerrout, you mangy hound!" and he aimed a kick at Growch, who was trying to christen his boots. "Whose is this?"

"Mine," I said firmly. "Just like the horse and the pig. All part of our act. And if you want a decent performance for your—your lady tonight, you'll see we are kept together. To rehearse," I added. "It is a couple of months since we have performed together. I presume you want us to be at our best?"

It worked. Ten minutes later we were snug in a stall at the end of the stables nearest the entrance, and a sullen stable boy was bringing hay, oats, mash and buckets of water.

"Two more buckets," I said firmly, twisting the ring on my finger to give courage. "This time of hot water. And towels. Hurry, boy."

Then I had to explain everything to Gill: where we were, what we were supposed to be doing.

"But we are performing nothing until we are clean and presentable: it's obvious the Lady Aleinor places great store on everything being just so. She also wants entertainment, so we've got to prepare something to please her. Besides, we could do with the silver she is offering."

"Have you ever done anything like this before?" asked poor, bewildered Gill.

"There's always a first time. . . ."

"And a last," muttered Growch. "Glad I'm not part of this farce."

"Oh, but you are," said the Wimperling unexpectedly. "We all are. That's why we couldn't be separated."

"Well, what we goin' to do, then? *She* said you could count, whatever that means: I heard her. What about me? The 'orse, the tortoise, the pigeon? Them," indicating Gill and me.

"Be patient," said the Wimperling. "And listen. . . ."

Chapter Seventeen

It was both hot and smoky in the hall. Although there was a huge modern hearth, tall and wide enough for half a dozen to stand upright, there seemed to be something amiss with the chimney, or perhaps the wind was in the wrong direction, for as much smoke came down and out as went up. The torches smoked in their holders on the walls, the candles on the tables smoked; an erratic wind would seem to have taken possession of the kitchens as well, for the bread was burned, the meat tasted half-cured, the fowls were charred on one side and nearly raw on the other and the underdone chickpeas, lentils and onions sulked in a sauce that reeked of too much garlic and was definitely full of smuts.

But we were too hungry to care much. The ale was good, the smoked herring and eels very tasty and the cheeses of excellent quality. We were seated at the very bottom of the left-hand table, and it was a good place from which to see everything. The edge off my hunger, and Gill well provided for, I had time to gaze around, and a word or two with our neighbors identified who was who.

There must have been upwards of a hundred and fifty people in the hall, counting servitors. The level of conversation was deafening, and this, coupled with the hysterical yelping and snarling of hounds fighting for bones and scraps in the rushes, the roar of flame from the fireplace, the clatter of knives, the thump of mugs impatient for refill and the intermittent screeching of a cageful of exotic multicolored birds, made hearing a sense to endure rather than enjoy.

So I used my eyes instead. At the top table, raised some two hands high from the rest of us, sat the Lady Aleinor with a neighbor, Sir Bevin, and his wife on her right, and on her left her sister and her husband on a visit. Also on the top table were her daughter, a pudding-faced girl of twelve or thirteen, her chaplain, steward and Captain Portall. Below the salt ran the two long tables, seating about thirty on each side, crammed elbow to elbow on benches with scarce room to lift hand to mouth. At the ends nearest the top table were accommodated the more important members of the household: reeve, almoner, chief usher, head falconer, armorer, apothecary, head groom and verdurers; between them and us were the middle to lower orders: smiths, farriers, bowyers, fletchers, coopers, dyers, gardeners, soldiers, hedgers, cobbler, tinder-maker, trumpeter, clerk, wine-storekeeper and all my Lady's maids, her housekeeper, tirewoman, sewing ladies and her daughter's nurse-companion.

The table manners of those nearest us left much to be desired. Those sharing two to a trencher were using their hands rather than their knives, and even those who had their own place were tearing at the bread and meat instead of cutting it neatly. There was much munching with open mouth and unseemly belching, and few were using cloths to wipe their fingers and mouths: it appeared sleeves were more convenient for the men, hems of skirt or shift for the women. Not that the manners on the top table were much better, though the Lady Aleinor did at least lick her fingers one by one before applying them and her mouth to the linen tablecloth.

We had not yet seen the lady close to and were bowing respectfully when she entered the hall, so I had only had a quick impression of a tall, slim woman in rich red robes and an elaborate headdress of linen, lawn and ribbons. Now I could see her more clearly I saw she was handsome enough, but her face was marred by a discontented expression—much as my mother used to wear if bad weather kept her customers away too long. The lady was obviously bored.

The hall grew hotter, noisier, smokier, but at last the tables were cleared, the hounds kicked into silence, a cover put over the squawking birds and water brought for finger-washing. The steward rose to his feet, banged on the top table for silence, and announced that the entertainment would begin. A young varlet, one of the two cadet-squires who had been serving at the top table—much more palatable food than we had been served with, I noticed—walked down the room and picked out the first of our "volunteers."

After a whispered conversation he walked back between the two lower tables, bowed to the lady, and announced that Master Peter Bowe would sing a couple of ballads: "Travel the Broad Highway" and "Lips Like Cherries." He had a pleasant enough voice, but it was suited to a smaller place than this vast hall, whose timbers reached up into a ribbed darkness like leafless trees. However the Lady spoke to her steward and he was rewarded with a couple of silver coins.

Next it was the turn of the juggler, who was reasonably dextrous. He was certainly good at improvisation, for he had only what lay around to toss and catch; eventually, one by one, he had two shriveled apples, a goblet, a large bone and a trencher all in the air at once. He, too, received two silver coins.

The teller of tales was found to be hopelessly drunk and was thrown out, so it was the turn of the tumbler and his boy. Once the man had obviously been very good, but he was well into middle age and I could tell by the grimaces that he suffered from rheumatism, and both his spring and balance were faulty. The boy did his best to cover for his father's deficiencies—one day he, too, would be very good—but in the end he was dropped heavily; judging by his resigned expression as he rose to his feet, rubbing his elbow, it wasn't the first time and wouldn't be the last. They were given three coins.

Now it was the turn of the contortionist, but I had to miss his performance to slip outside and collect Mistral and the others, for we were next—and last. I brought them in by the kitchen ramp, for the steps up to the main door would not have done: too steep. Leaving them just outside, I rejoined Gill for the applause and coin for the contortionist. The varlet walked up to us, I whispered to him, he went back and announced us.

"My lady . . ." a deep bow: "for your entertainment I present travelers from the north, the south, the east, the west: fresh from their successful performances all over the country, I crave your indulgence for brother and sister, Gill and Summer, and their troupe of performing animals!" Another deep bow, a ripple of interest.

Smoothing down the dress Matthew had given me with nervous fingers I led Mistral towards the top table, Gill on her other side, flanked on either side by a sedate dog and a sedater pig. Traveler was perched on Mistral's back. We all looked our best, I had seen to that, and the animals wore colored ribbons—a sad good-bye to my special ones, I thought. (We had had to leave Basher behind, for there isn't much lively capering to be got from a hibernating tortoise.)

Reaching the dais we performed the only trick we had rehearsed together: we all knelt—man, girl, horse, pig, dog. Traveler bowed his head.

Applause. Encouraged, I rose and addressed the lady. "First we shall show you a roundelay. . . ." and pulling my pipe from my pocket I gave Gill the note and he began singing the "Bluebell Hey." For a dreadful moment I thought it wasn't going to work, then my dear animals obeyed my unspoken instructions. Mistral and the pig revolved slowly, majestically, and Growch began to chase his tail. No matter they were not in time with the music: we were receiving applause already. Traveler rose into the air and gracefully circled the top table. . . . Then it happened.

It is well-nigh impossible to house-train birds, and Traveler was no exception. On his last circuit, obviously full of grain, he let loose and an enormous chunk of pigeon-dropping landed unerringly on the bald pate of the lady's chaplain. There was a long drawing in of breath and then total silence. I stopped playing, Gill stopped singing, Growch stopped chasing his tail. Mistral and the Wimperling stood like statues.

We all gazed at the Lady Aleinor. She rose to her feet, her face suffused with color. If she had said: "Off with their heads!" I would not have been surprised. I twisted the ring on my finger, still cool and calm. The lady's eyes seemed ready to pop out of her head, and the silence was something palpable, a thing you could touch and weigh. She opened her mouth—

And laughed.

And she went on laughing. Not a genteel titter behind her hand, as I had been taught, but a gut-wrenching belly laugh, the sort my mother had produced one day when the butcher had risen from her bed in a temper, tripped and landed bare-arsed and bum-high with his nose in the dirt.

What's more, she went on laughing. She laughed until the tears spurted from her eyes, she laughed till her ribs ached and she had to double up to stop the ache, till she had to cover her ears for the pain behind. And the more indignant the lugubrious chaplain became, trying to wipe the yellow mess from his bald head with the tablecloth, the more she laughed.

Her sycophantic household took its cue from her, and soon the whole place was rocking with guffaws and the very flames of the torches and candles were threatened by the shouts and table-thumpings. The most relieved face in the hall, apart from mine, was that of Captain Portall, who had promised amusement for his lady.

The noise, however, was upsetting Mistral, however I tried to calm her, and Traveler was no better. Growch, too, was starting to growl at the lymers, brachs and mastiffs who had started up again with their baying and yelping, so I grabbed the horse's bridle and led them back to the courtyard. Growch, of course, took advantage of this to snatch a rib bone from a distracted greyhound on his way out.

Picking up a leathern bucket I had appropriated earlier I rejoined Gill and the Wimperling, the latter of whom seemed totally unmoved by the hullabaloo around him. In fact his snout was working happily above exposed teeth, almost as though he were laughing too. As I re-entered the merriment was dying down, and the lady leaned forward and addressed us.

"I hope the rest of your act is as stimulating: I declare I have not been as diverted for months! Of course—" she waved her hand dismissively: "I realize it was but a fortuitous accident. Presumably the rest of your performance owes more to skill?"

I bowed. "My lady . . . First my brother will sing a ballad dedicated especially to yourself. An old tune, but new words." I gave Gill his note, and he began to sing:

"*When I hunger, there is meat;*
When I tire, there is sleep;
I am cold, there is fire;
I am thirsty, there is wine.
But when I love, unless you care,
I am poorer than the poor.
Hungry, thirsty, sleepless, cold.
But smile, lady, and I am full;
Touch me and I am warm;
Kiss me once and I
Need never sleep again. . . ."

It was a touching song, and Gill sang it as if he held a picture of a secret love tight behind his blind lids. So heartfelt was the throb in his voice that it gave me goose bumps. The lady seemed to like it too.

Now for the culmination of our act: I crossed my fingers and went down to the Wimperling.

"Ready?"

"If you are . . ."

I upended the bucket and lifted his front hooves onto the top, catching one of my fingers on the funny claws that circled them. "We will have to clip those. . . ."

"I think they are meant to be there . . ."

Gill finished his song to sentimental applause from Lady Aleinor, which everyone copied. So, the lady decided what amused and what did not. In that case, the Wimperling and I would play to her alone.

"And now, my lady, we present to you the wonder of this or any other age: a pig who counts. As good as any human, and better than most. Would you please give me two simple numbers for the pig to add together?" I saw her hesitate, and gathered that tallying was not her strong point. She would probably be furious if we exposed her weakness so I played it safe. "Perhaps we could start more simply: if you would place some manchets of bread in front of you in a line, so that your guests may see the number, then I will ask the pig to guess correctly. He cannot, of course, see what is on the table."

She looked more pleased and lined up five pieces of bread. I thought the number to the Wimperling, then made a great fuss and to-do with waving of arms and incantations.

Obediently the Wimperling tapped with his right hoof on the top of the bucket: one, two, three, four . . . There was a hesitation, a ghastly moment when I thought everything was going to go wrong, then I saw from the gleam in his eye that he was enjoying himself . . . five.

Applause, again, and from then on in it was easy. Shouts from those on the top table who could count: "Three and two . . . Six and one . . . two and four . . ." The lady was counting frantically on her fingers to keep up with her guests, then nodding and beaming as though she had known the answer all the time. Her daughter intervened in an affected lisp.

"Does the creature subtract as well?"

It could, if my mental counting was swift enough.

We finished, by prior agreement with the Wimperling, by me asking him a leading question: "You are a pig of perspicacity: tell me now, O Wise One, who is the fairest, the most generous, the most beloved lady in this castle?" I went along the tables, touching each woman on the shoulder as I passed, and each time the Wimperling shook his head—a pity, for some of the ladies were really far prettier than our hostess. At last, and last, I came to the Lady Aleinor. At once the pig drummed both hooves on the bucket, squealed enthusiastically and nodded his head.

Everyone clapped, as they knew that they had to, and the lady was so pleased she snatched the purse of silver from her steward and threw it to me. As I shepherded Gill back outside, the Wimperling trotting behind, I counted the coins: twelve!

"Told you it would be all right," said the Wimperling happily.

We had almost reached the stables when there were running footsteps behind us. It was the varlet who had introduced us earlier.

"You are invited to dine with the rest of the household at dawn," he panted, "and the lady requests that you and your brother—and the wondrous pig—attend her at noon in the solar. I am to come and fetch you at the appointed hour."

Back at the stables I requested more hay and made comfortable resting places for Gill and myself, then went to say goodnight and congratulate the animals.

"You were absolutely marvelous, all of you! The lady liked our performance, and we have a purseful of silver to prove it! She wants to see Gill and me and the Wimperling again tomorrow morning, but we shall be on the road again just after noon, I expect."

"Tonight was one thing," said the Wimperling, "but tomorrow might be different again. . . ."

"Oh, stop being such an old pessimist!" I cried. "You were the star of the show, remember?" and in my euphoria I raised his front hooves, bent down, and kissed him fair and square on his pink snout.

Bam! I felt as though I had been struck by a thunderbolt. Once when combing my hair at home by the fire, I had leaned forward to sip at a metal dipper of water and had the same sharp prickling, but this was a thousand times worse. I must have jumped, or been thrown, back about six feet, my lips numb and feeling twice their size, my hair standing up from my head. But this was as nothing to the effect it had on the pig. He leapt up at the same distance I had back, his wings creaked into action as well and bore him still further until he cracked his head against the rafters and came plummeting back down to the floor.

We stared at one another in horror. The feeling was coming back to my lips, but I still had to put up a hand to convince myself they weren't swollen. They tingled like pins and needles, only far worse.

"What *happened*?"

He shook his head as though his ears were full of ticks. "I don't know. . . . I feel as if all my insides have turned over. Most peculiar. I'm not the same as I was, I know that!"

"I won't do it again, I promise!"

"No, don't. It's just that . . . I don't know. Very strange. . . ."

I had never seen or heard him so confused. After a moment or two he slunk off into a corner under the manger and hunched up. I thought he would sleep, but when I settled down on my bed of hay he was still awake, his eyes bright and watchful in the light of the lantern that swung overhead.

When we entered the solar a little after noon, the Lady Aleinor was seated in a high-backed chair by a roaring fire; like all the chimneys in the castle, this one smoked. The lady's daughter was on a stool at her feet, the nurse and two tirewomen stood behind the chair.

Though the room was sumptuously furnished, it did not have the cozy, lived-in look of Matthew's solar: it was a room to be seen in, rather than used. Candles were lit because the shutters on the one window at the back were tight closed.

The lady received us graciously. We were invited to move into the center of the room—though not asked to sit down—and she started to question us: where we trained the animals, where we were bound, etc. From anyone except a fine lady like herself it might have seemed an impertinence, but we had been long enough together for the brother/sister story to come out like truth. It was more difficult to answer questions about the animals, but I did emphasize (in order that our performances were worthy of reward) the years of training, the bonds of familiarity that had to be forged, the difficulty of communication—and here I mentally crossed myself and touched my ring.

"But surely the whip speaks louder than words?"

I was shocked—would I have been before I wore the ring of the Unicorn? I wondered—but did my best to hide it. Her ways were obviously not ours.

"You may use a whip when breaking in a horse, my lady, or beat a dog, but how can you use punishment to train a pigeon? Our training is accomplished by treating the animals as if they were part of our family and rewarding their tricks, not punishing their mistakes. It has worked well, so far."

Her eyes flashed as though she would argue, then once more she was sweetness itself. "Would you let me see what else your pig can do? I am sure there were tricks you did not show us last night. . . ." I almost looked for the honey dripping from her tongue.

I was deceived, I admit it, even as a warning message came from the Wimperling. "Don't intrigue her too much. . . ."

"Hush!" I thought to him. And to the lady: "I am sure we can find something to divert you. . . ." Back to the Wimperling, quick as a flash: "Can you keep time to a song? Find hidden objects if I tell you where they are?"

He answered reluctantly that he thought he could: "But *don't* overdo it!" Why? More tricks, more money, and we should be away from here in an hour or two with enough to keep us going for weeks.

I asked Gill to sing "Come away to the woods today" which was a song with a regular, impelling beat, and my pig trod first one way and then the other in perfect time, to polite applause from the lady and her daughter.

"Now the pig on his own," demanded Lady Aleinor, dismissing Gill's song, which privately I thought wonderful, as a mere trifle. "Come on girl: show us what else he can do!"

"Very well. Perhaps, my lady, if you would hide some trifling object—yes, that needle case would do fine—while the pig's back is turned—so, then I will ask him to discover it."

And behind a cushion, under a chair, beneath the sideboard, in the wood-basket—he found it every time. After I had told him where to look, of course.

The lady watched him perform with a gleam in her eyes. "Very good, very good indeed! Anything else he can do?"

I was about to open my mouth and rashly volunteer his flying abilities, when his thoughts struck into my mind like a string of sharp pebbles to the head. "No, no, *no*! Don't tell her that! Tell her I am tired, anything! Let's get out of here!"

Confused, I stammered out an excuse. She looked at me coldly. "Very well, you may go now and rest. But I shall expect another performance tonight. I have sent out messengers to others of my neighbors and I look forward to an even better exposition of the pig's power." She saw my face. "What's the matter, girl? A few coins? Here you are, then. . . ." and she tossed a handful of silver at my feet.

Automatically I bent to retrieve it, then straightened my back. "It is not a matter of money, my lady, thank you all the same. Last night you were more than generous, and we had not planned to stay longer than midday today. We must be on our way as soon as possible."

Another flash of—what?—from those hooded eyes, then the pleasantness was back again, on her mouth at least. "Of course, of course, but I couldn't possibly let you go without one more of your marvelous performances! You can't let me down after I have invited extra guests! Please say you will do this last favor? One more treat for us all and then you may go on your way. . . ."

It would have been more than churlish of me to refuse, in spite of the warning signs I was getting from the Wimperling. Gill, poor dear, had no idea of the conflict that was going on and added his voice to the lady's plea.

"Of course we must oblige the Lady Aleinor, Summer: it will be no hardship to stay one more night, surely?"

I could hear the Wimperling almost screaming at him to stop, stop, stop! but of course he couldn't hear the pig's thoughts as I could, and he went on with a few more complimentary sentences until I could have screamed also. There was no doubt as to the outcome now, and I picked up the coins and we made our way down the winding stone stairs to the courtyard. Up had been much easier for all of us, and the Wimperling nearly ended by rolling down the last few twists. Once in the courtyard he started to say something, but I hushed him, using our midday meal in the hall as an excuse. Right at that moment I didn't want any prognostications of doom and disaster, so I saw him back to the stable before hurrying back for what was left of the meal.

I purposely lingered over the last night's leftovers, plus a thick broth, a blancmange of brawn and custards of potted meats, but I couldn't put off the reproaches forever. Even so, it was a little past two by the time Gill and I regained the stable, whereupon I immediately found a stool for him out in the sunshine, and returned alone to face the agitation I had sensed at once.

They all had something to say, but it was Growch who was noisiest. "What's all this, then? 'E tells me—" he nodded towards the pig: "—that we're all in danger! Danger from what, I'd like to know? Last night you was full of how well we done, and now 'e tells us the Lady-of-the-'Ouse is poison! In that case, why don't we all go, right now? O' course, if I was just to nip into the kitchens and fetch a bone first . . ."

"I think we should go," said Mistral restlessly. "But our companion tells us we must perform again tonight."

Traveler flapped his wings. "Listen to the pig: he is a wise one."

Thank the Lord the tortoise was still asleep! "What's all this, then?" I asked the Wimperling. "We have a purse full of money and will get more tonight. All we have to do is one more performance and we can leave in the morning. What's one more day? The more money the better."

"*If* it is only one more day . . . I do not trust her. I can read her heart a little way and it is full of wickedness, guile and greed. I cannot see what she intends, for I believe she does not yet know herself, but it is not good for any of us, of that I am sure."

"You have no proof—"

"No, Summer, but in this you must trust me. Tonight when the performance ends we must be ready to leave, all packed up. If we don't, tomorrow may bring disaster to us all."

I shook my head. I just couldn't believe she meant us harm. And yet—I recalled those flashes of spite from her eyes. Perhaps . . . "It would be too dark to see. Besides, the portcullis will be down."

"Stays up for them as was guests and isn't stayin' over," said Growch. "'Sides, we've traveled at night before. Moon's near full."

"I shall have to ask Gill," I said weakly.

"Consult 'im? When've you ever consulted 'im? You tells 'im what to do an' 'e does it! Couldn't 'ave got this far without you, an' 'e knows it!" Whenever he got particularly agitated Growch's speech went to pieces. "Consult 'im indeed!" And he emphasized his annoyance by kicking up a shower of hay with his back legs.

"You've all had your say: why shouldn't he?" I was angry, largely because I wasn't sure that they weren't right.

"Becoz-'e-don'-know-nuffin!" said Growch. "Not-nuffin!"

"That's only because he's blind," I said quickly. "You try going around for a while with your eyes tight shut and see how you get on! Anyway, I shall ask him just the same. We're all in this together."

And before I could change my mind I went outside and suggested to a dozy Gill that we leave that night. Of course I couldn't give the true reason, and, understandably, he couldn't see why we didn't postpone it till morning. I decided to wait and see what the evening brought, but packed everything ready, just in case.

We made a good job of our performance that night, repeating much of what we had done the evening before, but adding a couple more tricks to the Wimperling's repertoire. Led by the lady, we received prolonged applause, a purse from her and another from one of her guests. When we returned to the stable there was disappointment: none of the guests was leaving that night and the portcullis remained down.

Right, first thing in the morning then, when the first wagons came up with provisions. If we were ready in the shadow of the wall, we would sneak out as soon as the portcullis was raised. . . . I willed myself to wake up an hour before dawn.

I woke on time, loaded up our gear and we were ready in the darkest part of the courtyard a good quarter-hour before we heard the first wagon rumble across the drawbridge. The driver called out; two yawning soldiers ran across and started to wind up the portcullis with enough creaks and groans to awaken the dead. I shivered: my teeth were chattering both with the early morning chill and with dread.

Three wagons passed through, steam rising from the horses' and the drivers' mouths. I grabbed Gill's hand and Mistral's bridle, and we had almost reached the first plank of the drawbridge when two sentries I hadn't seen stepped out and barred our progress, their spears crossed in front of us.

"Sorry girl, sir," said one of them peremptorily. "None of you is to leave the castle. Orders of the Lady Aleinor . . ."

Chapter Eighteen

I stared at them in horror. "But why?"

They looked at one another and then the spokesman said: "We don't ask questions of the lady. All we know is, orders were sent down yesterday midday as you weren't to be let go."

"Doesn't pay to disobey," said the other soldier. "We just does as we're told. Sorry an' all that . . . Enjoyed your performance, by the way: that pig's a good 'un. Would he do a trick for me?"

"No, no," I said distractedly. "Only for me . . ." Which was the best answer I could have given, although I didn't realize it at the time. "Er . . . Under the circumstances, perhaps it would be better if—if the lady didn't think we were trying to leave." Scrabbling in my now full purse I handed out a couple of coins. "I think she might be annoyed if she thought we didn't appreciate her hospitality."

On our dispirited way back to the stables I noticed a boy from the village unloading his wagon and eyeing us speculatively: he had obviously seen the exchange of coin. I clutched my purse tighter and hurried past.

I was all for requesting an instant audience with Lady Aleinor, demanding to know the reason for our confinement and insisting on instant release, but Gill urged caution.

"I reckon that might make her more determined to keep us a while. She seems to be a very contrary lady. . . . After all, where's the harm of a few more days? Personally I'm growing a bit tired of singing love ballads to a woman I can't see, but at least it means more money, and we are fed and housed. Not that the food is all that good, but—"

"The most important thing is to be very, very careful," said the Wimperling. "We must find out what she has in mind. Don't force the issue: corner any vicious animal and you relinquish the initiative."

"I want to go," said Mistral impatiently. "This place is bad, and—"

There was a rustling noise from farther down the stable and silhouetted against the open door was the figure of the boy I had noticed earlier. "Hullo . . ." he called out tentatively.

I was in no mood to be polite. "What do you want?"

He hesitated for a moment then moved towards us, twisting a piece of straw between his fingers. He was dressed in a rough, patched jerkin, trousers tied beneath the knee with twine, and was barefoot. He was also filthy dirty—I could smell him from where I stood—and his thatch of hair could well have been fair if it had ever been washed. He could have been any age from twelve onwards.

"To see if I can help. I heard what was going on. Gather you want out of here?" His speech was country-thick but in the lantern light I could see a bright intelligence in those grey eyes.

I temporized: who knew where his real interest lay? "Maybe we do—but why should you help?"

"No love for the Lady 'Ell-an'-All," he muttered. "Killed my father she did," and he glanced over his shoulder as if he, too, was afraid of being overheard.

"Killed him?" and once he started telling us, I thought his story to the animals at the same time as he told it.

"We live in the hamlet beneath the castle. Two rooms, patch of ground behind. Lived there happy, father, mother, self and three young sisters. Father was a forester for the lady, mother helped in the fields with the girls, weeding and picking stones. I was a crow-scarer, then a shit-shoveler. Still am. Bad winter last year, after the lord and his sons went off. Not much food. Pa helped himself to a hare—"

"A poacher?"

"First time he ever done it. We needed the food, and there were a glut of 'em. Kept helping theirselves to our vegetable clumps. Pa caught this one with the dog, on our patch at the back. Someone saw him, told the Lady 'Ell-an'-All. No excuses, no trial. Hanged the dog, old Blackie, castrated my father—"

"Oh, my God!" It was Gill. "How barbaric! My father—My father . . ." He put his hands to his head. "I don't remember. . . ."

"And then she had his eyes put out," continued the boy, stony-faced. "My father stood it for six month. Last August we came in late, found he'd cut his throat. With the trimming knife. They let him keep that."

I put my hand on his arm, but he shook it off.

"Don't want no sympathy. Understand why he did it. Less than half a man . . . Anyway, if you means harm to the lady, then I'm your man."

I didn't know what to say. We still didn't know if our position was serious. It might just be that all the lady wanted was a couple more performances. Even as I tried to persuade myself that the situation didn't warrant any panic, I got a strong signal from the Wimperling to enlist this boy on our side.

"Thank you," I said formally. "We don't wish personal harm to the lady, but we do wish to leave here as soon as possible."

"If she's taken a fancy to you, here you stay."

"We've given her what she asked—"

"Obviously not."

"Look," I said. "First we have to find out exactly what is going on. I don't quite know how you can help, but—"

"You'd be surprised. Bet I can get you all out of here in twenty-four hours." He hesitated. "'Course, there'd be a price. . . ."

I thought rapidly of what we could afford. "Ten silver pieces. If we need you, that is . . ."

His eyes gleamed. "Done! I'm getting out myself, soon as I can, but can't leave Ma and the sisters without. See you later. . . ."

"But I don't understand," I said.

Gill and I were in the lady's solar again, having requested an audience after the midday meal. She had us standing in the center of the room as before while she reclined by the fire. There was more light in the room today, for the shutters at the window had been flung back on a sunny sky. The room must face south, for low bars of February sunshine slanted through the window and across the floor, specks of dust dancing like midges in the beams. Outside I could see a forest of leafless trees stretching to the horizon, while black specks rose and fell lazily above the branches, a soft breeze carrying the quarreling cries of nest-building rooks.

I had come straight to the point and asked why we had been refused permission to leave. She had gazed at us through half-closed lids.

"I should have thought that would be perfectly obvious."

But when I said I didn't understand, she seemed to come to life and sat up, arms gripping the sides of her chair: "You are not an idiot, girl. If I say you are not to leave, it is because I wish you to stay. And why? Because, for the moment, I find you and your animals—diverting. Life can be *so* boring. . . ." Leaning back in her chair she closed her eyes. "And now I shall rest for a while, I expect more entertainment this evening. Some new tricks, please. . . ." And she let her voice die away, as if indeed it was too tiring to try and explain further to peasants such as ourselves.

"But I don't want—*we* don't wish to stay," I said. "You told us we might leave if we gave an extra performance, which we did. We do have a life of our own to lead, you know, and—"

She rose to her feet in a sudden swirl of skirts, the cone-shaped headdress she wore wobbling dangerously.

"How dare you! How *dare* you! What matter *your* wishes, *your* little lives? All that matters here is what *I* want! This is *my* castle, *my* demesne! Within its bounds I have jurisdiction of life and death over everyone—*everyone*, do you hear?" She was almost hysterical, red blotches on her neck and face, her eyes snapping sparks like fresh pine bark on a fire. She rushed forward and struck first me and then Gill hard across the face. My eyes smarted with the sudden pain, for one of her thumb rings had caught my lip and I could taste the salt of blood. Gill swayed on his feet and would have fallen had I not caught at his arm and steadied him.

"God's teeth! What was that for, lady?"

"Impertinence, blind man! And there's more where that came from if you do not both watch your tongues. I will not be disagreed with, do you hear?"

I was so angry with the way she was treating us that given a pinch of pepper I would have sprung forward and given her a dose of her own treatment, but the presence of Gill gave me pause. That, plus the possible danger to the animals. God knew what she could do if further provoked.

"We have no wish to cross you," I said, as meekly as I could. "But we would like to know when we can leave. If you could let us know how many more performances you require? And if you have any special tricks in mind . . . Of course, it will take time to teach them all—"

"There is no need to teach them all fresh tricks: I am only interested in the pig! Any fool can make a horse turn, a dog obey, a bird fly in circles. You combine them cleverly, I agree, but it is only the pig that has real intelligence. Your brother has a pleasant enough voice, I dare say, but singers are a dozen a week, and you know it! No, the rest of you may leave as and when you wish, but the pig stays!"

"But—but he can't!"

"What do you mean 'can't'? If I say he stays, he stays." She looked at us for a moment, then changed her tactics. Sitting down once more, she smoothed her skirts, turned the rings on her fingers. "Of course you will be recompensed. I realize your pig is a means of livelihood and that you are seeking a cure for your brother's blindness, which will need special donations. I will give you what I reckon it will cost for a further three months' travel. Now, I cannot say fairer than that, can I?"

"You don't understand! It's not just—just what he could earn us, he is *part* of us: I couldn't leave him behind. Besides, he won't do tricks for anyone else, only me."

"Well, you can stay for a while, too. Just till you have taught me how he works."

The woman was mad! "But I can't teach you—"

"Can't? Or won't?" She rose from her chair again, as angry as before. She narrowed her eyes. "Everything can be taught—unless it's some form of magic. . . . Magic? Yes, I suppose that could be the answer. If so," and now her voice was full of menace: "I could have you denounced as a witch! And you know what that means: trial by fire, earth and water and lastly, being burned at the stake. . . ."

"I'm no witch!" I felt the ring of the unicorn cold, cold on my finger. Was that a form of witchcraft? It had never occurred to me, being as it was a gift from my dead father which helped me understand the speech of animals and also warned me of danger, gave me courage—yet perhaps to the lady, to the gullible majority, it would seem like a form of magic—

Suddenly I was terrified. Death came in many forms: illness, accident, war, pestilence, age, famine—but to be burned at the stake! God, please God, sweet Jesus, Mary, Mother of Sorrows, No! I was trembling; the lady saw it, and smiled gleefully.

"Then if it is not magic, it is trickery, and that can be taught. Right? And if you do not wish to teach me, and your—companions—are so precious to you, then perhaps *they* can be persuaded to persuade you. . . .

Pigeons' necks can be wrung, a horse can be hamstrung, a dog hung by its tail, a man—"

"Stop it, stop it!" I had my hands over my ears. "Leave them alone! They have no part in all this! You said they could all go. . . ."

I should not have been so vehement. I realized from the gleam in her eye that she now knew I was vulnerable to the threat of harm to the others.

"Certainly not! I have changed my mind. They can all be hostages to your good behavior. And just so as there will be no mistake, we can start the lessons right now! Go fetch the pig!"

There was nothing I could do but obey. As I led the Wimperling back I told him what had happened. "What are we going to do?"

He looked worried, as worried as I felt, the loose skin over his snout all wrinkled up in perplexity. "The only thing we can do is go along with what she wants for the moment and trust to luck. You had better make plans with that boy to escape if you can. In the meantime give me something simple to do—count to five, perhaps—give her some gibberish to learn, then say I can only adapt to a new mistress slowly and tomorrow she will learn more."

So it was decided, but unfortunately it didn't turn out quite as we had planned. . . .

At first it was all right. I gave the Lady Aleinor some rhyming words to repeat—taking great pleasure in correcting her twice—and obediently the Wimperling tapped his hoof five times. She practiced it half a dozen times, but in the middle of the nonsense the pig sent me an urgent message.

"Take a look out of that window. Remember everything you see."

I wandered over and did as I was bid. A sheer drop of some forty feet to the dry moat below; beyond that the forests, with a stretch of greensward in front of the trees.

"What are you doing, girl?"

I walked back. "Turning my back on the pig, lady, just to prove I am not influencing him. I just thought—"

"You do not think! You do as you are told. Come back here and teach me some more."

"The pig is tired, it will take time for him to get used to—"

"Rubbish! We have been at this less than an hour! Do as you are told!"

"He won't—"

"He *will*! You can make him." She paused, and her next words came honey-sweet and loaded with sting. "Unless, of course, you would rather I summoned my soldiers to give your brother here a painful lesson. They are experts, I assure you. . . ."

The Wimperling flashed me a warning. "Do as she says! Simple addition: two and one, two and two. She can't count."

And so it went on, until the Wimperling himself took a hand, sinking to the ground with a groan and puffing and panting, rolling his eyes round and around.

"There! I told you so!" For a heart-stopping moment I believed he was indeed ill, but as I rushed forward and knelt distractedly at his side, I saw him wink.

"Tell me, quickly, what you saw from the window. . . ."

So, as I fussed over him, I described the scene outside.

"Mmm . . . Doesn't sound too promising. Don't look so worried! We'll find a way out of this."

The Lady Aleinor at last seemed persuaded she could go no further today. She sank back in her chair, still repeating to herself the rubbish I had taught her.

"Very well," she said after a moment. "What does it eat?"

"*He* eats most things," I said. "When I get back to the stables I can ask for—"

"The stables? The creature stays here. It's mine now, and I shall look after it."

I was devastated. How in the world could we all escape together when we were down there and he was up here? Together we had a chance: apart, none.

"But—but he needs exercise, grooming, companionship, light. . . ."

"All of which he will get. My soldiers will escort him out twice a day—the exercise will do them good as well. A nice trot around the castle grounds . . . Now, you can go. Attend me tomorrow at the same hour."

"But—but I . . ."

"Do you want a beating? No? Then get out! The creature will soon adapt to its new surroundings. As soon as you have taught me all I need to know you may leave. But if there is any more argument or backsliding I shall have to reconsider. Just remember what I said about the expendability of your other animals. . . ."

Back in the stables I sobbed in despair, trying to explain to the others the mess we—I—had gotten us into. Gill patted me awkwardly on the shoulder, Growch whined in sympathy and Mistral and Traveler shifted from foot to foot in anxiety. I felt terribly alone. I had not realized before how much I had relied on the simple common sense of the Wimperling, his stoicism, his comfortable, fat, ugly little body. Not that he was so small anymore . . . Only a few weeks ago I had been able to tuck him under my arm, and now he seemed near full-grown. One of the nicest things about him was that he never grumbled, and now he had been taken from us I felt utterly helpless: I couldn't even think straight.

"There's the boy," said Gill. "He said he could get us out of here, remember?"

"But that was before she took the Wimperling," I wept.

"Let's see what he got to say, anyways," said Growch. "Ain't nuffin more than we can do today: gettin' dark already."

So it was, and we had missed the midday meal. I found, too, that no one was going to rush to feed the animals, and in the gathering gloom I had to find my own oats and hay, and fill the buckets with water from the well in the courtyard.

It was even more obvious that we didn't exist when we went into the hall for the evening meal. Word had obviously got around of the lady's displeasure, for we were elbowed away from the table, were not offered a trencher, nor any ale. In the end I snatched what I could for both of us and we ate standing; rye bread, stale cheese and a couple of bones with a little meat left on them.

Worse was to come. The Lady Aleinor brought in the Wimperling, an animal so bedecked with ribbons and bunting as to be practically unrecognizable. She made him go through what I had taught her in front of the whole assembly, mouthing the rubbish she had learned; she had a little whip in her hand with which she stroked his flanks: if she had actually struck him I don't know what I would have done.

The applause was loud and sycophantic, and as soon as she had done I rushed forward to give him a reassuring hug before they dragged me away. He managed some quick words: "See the boy! If the rest of you can get away, I think I can manage as well. . . ."

Slightly reassured, we all spent a better night, and in the morning, after feeding and watering the animals and snatching some bread and cheese from the hall for Gill and myself, we settled down to await the boy and his wagon. He brought winter cabbage, some turnips, a barrel of smoked fish and some firewood for the kitchens. Once he had unloaded he picked up a shovel and started to clear the far end of the stable.

"Down here as well, please!" I called out, as if I had never seen him before. He walked down the aisle, trailing a barrow behind him, and bent to shovel out Mistral's stall.

"Well? Thought about it, then?" All the while he spoke to us he never stopped his steady shoveling. "Still want out?"

"Yes, yes; we do. Are you willing to help us?"

"I said so, didn't I? Ten silver pieces you said? Good. How many are there of you?"

I pointed to the others. "And our packages." I mustn't forget the tortoise, either. "The—the pig has been taken into the castle."

He shook his head. "Can't help you there. There's no getting it out now. One of them out there—" he jerked his thumb over his shoulder: "—told me as how you had taught the lady some magic words?"

"Not really," I said hurriedly. "Just the words I always use to direct his act. She's a slow learner. . . . What about the rest of us, then?"

He carried on shoveling. "Dog can slip through the portcullis any time: bars are wide enough. Pigeon can fly over, right?"

"And my brother? He's blind."

"Him and your packages can go in the back of the wagon. I'll back it up to the door at the end of the stables tonight. He'll have to sit under a load o'shit, though, but I got a cover."

"And me?"

"Got a cloak? Right, then. Pin up your skirt and I'll bring a pair of my pa's braies. Be a tight fit, but . . . At dusk, won't matter as much. Get you a hat as well. Find a sack of something to put over your back, walk out t'other side from the soldiers. Dirty your face a bit, too."

"What about the horse?"

"Swap her for mine. Blanket over her, bit of muck on her quarters and head, sack on her back. I'll let on mine's lame and I'm borrowing."

"Tonight?"

"Quicker the better. We'll all meet behind the castle, in the forest. Follow the wood trail. Clearing about quarter-mile in."

"But . . . will it work?"

He stopped shoveling and grinned. "Got to. Else I don't get my money, do I?"

There was much to do. Everything, including the tortoise, to be parceled as small as possible, Traveler and Growch to be briefed as to our meeting place, Mistral to be dirtied up, Gill to be encouraged—

"Hidden in a manure cart? I couldn't possibly. . . ."

—and in between as much food as possible to be filched from the hall and kitchens.

Promptly at midday I was summoned once more to the Lady Hell-and-All (as I now thought of her). More instruction included the Wimperling "finding" lost objects. He was deliberately slow, earning one sharp reprimand and a slash with her jeweled girdle at me for not teaching her properly. In between I managed to convey to him what we had planned and where we were to meet.

"But what about you?"

"Have you forgotten? I can fly. . . ."

I thought he was joking, trying to make me feel better.

The afternoon seemed interminable, though there was only now some three hours till dusk. I checked and re-checked that all was packed and prepared; noted that the sky was clear and remembered there would be a helpful moon; worried lest we didn't get away quick enough, for the lady's soldiers and her scent-working lymers and brachs could pick up a trail easily enough if she discovered us missing too soon; I also prayed: hard.

In between I paced the courtyard restlessly, watching people come and go, all busy, all employed on some task or another. Soldiers drilling, squires practicing with wooden swords, wood being stacked, slops emptied, weapons being cleaned and sharpened, horses groomed and exercised, dogs fighting, chickens being plucked for the evening meal . . .

I felt terribly conspicuous, as if everyone could read my mind, knew what I was planning, but in fact no one took the slightest notice of me. Most were too busy, but as for the others, all knew I had incurred the lady's displeasure, so it was as if I didn't exist at all. If there had been any dungeons in the castle, I should have been shut away in those; being denied the gates, the courtyard was as good a prison as any.

At long last the sun started to sink behind the castle walls. The boy's was one of the last wagons to enter through the gate, and to my dismay he was directed, not to the stables, but to picking up empty water casks. This meant he was half-loaded. He then backed the wagon as near as he could to the stable door and muttered: "Can you get your dog to start a fight?"

Get Growch to fight? It had been with the greatest difficulty I had restrained him during the last few days, and now he needed no further bidding. He chose a pack of hounds near the gateway, slipped on his short legs beneath their bellies, and with a couple of sharp nips here and there and a heap of shouted insults had them in a trice snapping and barking and snarling and biting at one another, in an unavailing attempt to catch him. As soon as the pace got too hot, even for him, he careered through the open gates and across the drawbridge, yelling the dog equivalent of "can't-catch-me!" Half-a-dozen hounds tore off in immediate pursuit, which meant at least the same number of servitors went in pursuit, to ensure the lady's precious dogs came to no harm.

The chase was enlivening an otherwise boring afternoon, and more and more people were breaking off what they were doing to cheer, laugh or shake their heads disapprovingly. A couple of the horses who were being groomed chose that moment to display temper, snapping and kicking out at their handlers, scattering the rest of the dogs and some hens and ducks, whose squawks added to the commotion.

"Load up now!" hissed the boy, and in a fumblingly long moment I had Gill and our packages up and into the back of the wagon, and a tarpaulin hastily thrown over the whole. I threw Traveler up, and after a couple of abortive flutters he took wing and wheeled out of the gate, heading west. "Bring out the horse!" and in a moment he had exchanged her in the traces for his own animal, stooping to fiddle for a minute with his horse's off-hind hoof. He then thrust a bundle into my hand: "Change into these!" And a moment later was nonchalantly loading up a couple more casks and roping them down. All this had taken perhaps three minutes. "See you in the forest," he muttered, and led Mistral and the wagon towards the gateway, his own horse limping behind.

I watched them, my heart in my mouth, but no one took the slightest notice, and in a minute they were trundling across the drawbridge and away, just as the last of the protesting hounds were being led back to the courtyard. I heard a derisive bark from the far side of the moat and knew Growch was safe.

But I was wasting precious time. Ducking back into the stables I opened the package the boy had given me, tucked up my skirt as best I could and struggled into the braies, a very tight fit. I shoved my hair up under the broad-brimmed straw hat—why the hell hadn't I thought to braid it up!—and wrapped my cloak around me. Picking up the sack I had earlier filled with hay I flung it over my shoulder and stooped over as though I was carrying a much heavier burden.

It was perhaps twenty yards from the stable to the gateway, but it seemed like a million miles. I had to walk slowly, I had to hunch up to keep my face hidden, and with the broad brim of the hat I could only see a couple of paces in front of me. At last I could see the penultimate wagon ahead trundling through the gateway, and hurried a little to pass through in its wake. I had my hand out ready to hang on to the tailgate when everything went horribly wrong.

I had hurried too much in changing and hadn't fastened my skirt up securely. It started to drop down and, bending to retrieve it, I felt my hat fall off and my hair cascade down round my face. There was a shout off to my left and I dropped the sack and was panicked into running, my heart thumping like a drum. A soldier slipped from the shadows, stuck out a foot and I landed flat on my face in the dust, winded and bruised.

I was hauled to my feet, none too gently.

"What's all this, then? Trying it on again, are we? We'll just see what the lady has to say about all this. . . ."

Chapter Nineteen

The lady had a great deal to say, or rather scream, the words punctuated with slaps, punches and pinches which I was helpless to avoid, being held firmly by the two soldiers who had brought me upstairs. I was almost blinded by tears of rage and pain and at first I only half heard the little voice in my head. There it was again: "Courage; we'll soon be out of this. . . ." Then I realized the Wimperling must be in the solar as well.

The lady eventually ran out of breath and went back to her chair, her face crimson with rage and exertion. "After all I've done for you, you ungrateful little whore! Oh, I see I shall have to teach you a real lesson this time? Misbegotten little tart! You can't say I didn't warn you. . . ." She turned to the soldiers. "Go and wring the neck of that pigeon of hers, then take it to the kitchens and bid them make a little pie of it: I shall start my meal with it tonight. Then bring her brother here: we'll see how he likes losing his tongue as well as his eyes. . . ."

"Oh, no!" The words were out before I realized that the others had gone, were hopefully safe for a while, but she enjoyed my reaction, clapping as if she had just performed a clever trick and was applauding herself. Her tongue flickered back and forth between her teeth, a snake tasting the air for my terror.

"I'll show you just who is in charge here! If you don't want your brother to lose other parts as well—a hand, his ears, his balls perhaps—you will swear on God's Body not to dare cross me again!"

We were alone now—where *was* the Wimperling? The fire smoked abominably, my face hurt and the soft flesh on my upper arms throbbed where she had pinched and nipped with unmerciful nails. My loosened hair was plastered across my face, and I lifted my hands to braid it back, but she half-rose from her chair on an instant.

"No tricks, now, or I'll call the guard!" I let my hands drop again and she subsided. Just then the Wimperling appeared from behind her chair, festooned as before with ridiculous ribbons and bows. He gave me a reassuring wink; I could see his ears were cocked, listening to something I could not hear.

"Not on their way back yet," he said to me. "On my count of three run across to the window and open the shutters as wide as you can!" He started to take deep breaths. The lady's expression changed; she bent down to caress him.

"But you can't—"

"Don't argue!" he said. "Just go. Trust me. . . . One, two, three!"

I should perhaps have rushed to the window without risking a glance back. As it was I nearly knocked myself senseless on the corner of the ornate sideboard just to glimpse the lady rise from her chair and call out, the Wimperling circling her warily with exposed teeth—he had real tusks I noticed—all the while hissing gently.

I reached the window without further mishap and looked round wildly for the fastening. Of course! There was a heavy bar that dropped into slots on either side. I tried to lift it, but it wouldn't budge. Swearing under my breath, I heaved and heaved again. One side started to move, the other was stuck. Helplessly I shoved and pulled, then realized that one shutter hadn't been closed properly and was catching against the bar. I slammed it shut with the heel of my hand then hefted the bar once more. It came loose so easily it flew up in the air and narrowly missed my feet as it crashed onto the floor. I tugged the shutters open as hard as I could till they crashed back against the wall and suddenly the room was flooded with dusk-light and there was a great gust of welcome fresh air.

"Right!" I yelled, and turned back to an incredible sight. The Wimperling appeared to have grown to twice or three times his normal size: he was blowing himself up as one would inflate a bladder, and looked in imminent danger of bursting. I could hardly see his eyes, his tail stuck straight out like an arrow and his wings were unfolding away from his shoulders, because there was no room to tuck them away.

The lady's eyes were almost popping out of her head, but she was still making valiant attempts to reach me, thwarted by the pig's circling motions. I took a quick peep out of the window; we couldn't possibly escape that way. It was a sheer drop down to the dry moat and I didn't fancy suicide.

The Wimperling took a last, deep, deep breath, adding yet more inches all over, until his tightly stretched skin looked as if it were cracking all over onto tiny, fine lines like unoiled leather.

I could hear footsteps on the spiral stair.

"Bolt the door!" cried the Wimperling. "Then watch out!"

As I ran to the door I saw him charge the Lady Hell-and-All, knocking her flying into the hearth, shrieking and cursing. I threw both bolts and dashed back, the lady being occupied in trying to extinguish the smoldering sparks that had caught her purple woolen dress, doing less than well because the bright-edged specks were widening into holes and then crawling like maggots this way and that in the close weave.

Somehow the Wimperling had managed to heave himself up onto the windowsill, and was now balanced precariously on the edge. He was so fat he could barely squeeze his bulk through the frame.

"Hurry up, Summer!"

"What? Where?"

"On my back," he said impatiently. "Hurry!"

"You can't—"

"I *can*!"

I tried to scramble up, but whereas the windowsill had been on a level with my waist, with the pig's bulk on top his back was at chin-height and I kept slipping off. Now behind us we could hear a hammering on the door, the lady was still screeching and any minute she would rush over and snatch me back—

I grabbed a stool, climbed on that and found myself lying flat on the pig's back.

"Arms round my neck and hang on tight! Here we go-o-ooo!" and before I could take a breath there was a sudden sickening plunge and we were away. I felt a shriek of pure terror wind its way up from my stomach and escape through my mouth, the sound mingling with the screech of disturbed rooks and the rush of air past my ears. There was a sudden Whoosh! of sound and then a Crack! as of flags snapping in a sharp breeze, and we were flying!

A steady rush of air came from the Wimperling's backside and his wings spread out from his shoulders, balancing us on our downward path away from the castle. The moat slid away from beneath my frightened eyes; there were the trees of the forest, the patch of greensward rising gently to meet us. . . .

It was a terrifying, wonderful few moments. The wind blew my hair all over my face, I felt utterly insecure, my teeth were chattering with fear, yet there was enough in me left to appreciate just what I was experiencing. The world was spinning, I was a bird, I was going to the moon, I would live forever, I was immortal, omnipotent—

The hiss of escaping air behind us stopped suddenly, started again, then deteriorated into a series of popping little farts, and in an instant we were wobbling all over the sky. The world turned upside down and a moment later we landed on the strip of grass in front of the trees with an almighty crash that rattled my teeth and knocked all the breath from my body.

For a moment—a minute? longer?—I lay fighting to regain my breath, then sat up and felt myself all over. Plenty of bruises and bumps, but nothing broken. Where was I, what was I—?

The Wimperling! Oh, God, where was he?

I gazed around wildly, saw what looked like a shrunken sack lying a few yards away. "Wimperling? Are you all right?" I crawled over and poked the heap.

"Yes," said a muffled voice. "No thanks to you. I was underneath when we landed. . . ."

He sat up slowly, shook each leg in turn, then his tail and ears and took a deep breath. Immediately he looked less like a sack and more like a pig.

I shook my head admiringly. "How did you *do* it? The flying, I mean?"

"Improvisation. I don't think I'd try it again, though: not easy enough to control emission. Without it, though, I couldn't have managed you as well—my wings aren't strong enough yet."

There was a sudden shout from the direction of the castle. I looked back and could see the lady hanging out of the window we had just left, waving her arms and shouting, and around the corner of the castle came a party of foot soldiers, trotting purposefully our way. I scrambled to my feet.

"Quick! We've got to find the others. Something about a firewood trail . . ."

"I saw it on the way down, as well as I could for mouthfuls of your hair," said the pig tranquilly. "Off to the left." And he set out at a fast trot, with me stumbling behind. We swerved into the undergrowth and it was hard going, for the bushes were thick and overhead branches became tangled in my hair while roots tripped my feet. But the Wimperling kept going and soon we burst out into a twig-strewn ride.

Behind us we could hear shouts, the lady's fading screams, and we ran as fast as we could down the ride into the forest, me fearful lest we had missed the others. The trees swung away on either side and there were stacks of part-chopped wood, two charcoal-burner's huts and—yes, they were all there, Mistral already loaded.

Growch came bouncing to meet us. "Hullo! Got away all right, I see. Didn't I do well? Saw that lot off, I did."

Gill fumbled for my arm. "You all right? That cart . . . I smell terrible." He did.

I mind-checked the others: all well. Even Basher was awake, and grumbling. "A-a-all that bouncing . . . Chap ca-a-an't sleep. . . ."

The boy was dancing about impatiently. "Hurry! I must be away before they come. Wind's from the east—them to you, which'll help you with the dogs. I'll try and head 'em off. . . ." and he swung a smelly sack from his hand.

"Thanks!" I panted. I had a stitch in my side from running. "Why the extra help?"

"Catch you and they catch me," he answered succinctly. "If they screwed your arms out of their sockets you'd tell. Have to."

I pulled out my purse from under my skirt and poured coins into my hand. "Ten silver pieces: one, two— ey! What are you doing?" To my consternation a dirty brown hand had snatched the purse and scooped the coins from my hand.

The boy stepped back well out of reach. He pulled a knife from his belt, and I bent down to restrain a growling Growch.

"Why?"

"For my Mam and sisters, remember? Reckon they need the money more'n you. You got the pig: reckon he can earn for you. Better get going: the lady has a long arm. Take the path to your right, then first left to the stream. Walk in the water to confuse the hounds till you come to a grove of oaks. After that take the path either to the east or south. Lady's demesne finishes at the road you'll find either way. Twenty miles or so. Get going, will you?"

"Wait!" I called, as he made for the shelter of the trees. "What's your name?"

"Dickon. Why?"

I should have been furious with him, risked setting Growch on him, fought him myself for the money, but in a queer way I knew he needed it more. It was a shame, but I still had some of Matthew's money left: we'd manage. "When are you leaving?"

"Soon as the weather brings the first leaves on the beech. Go and get myself 'prenticed. Come back for the family once I'm earning."

"If you go north, seek out . . ." and I gave him Matthew's name and direction. "Say we sent you. He's a kind man but a canny merchant. He might fix you up with something. Treat him fair and he'll do the same."

"Thanks. I—" But there came a flurry of shouts and barking behind us and we fled one way, he the other.

At first it was easy, in spite of the deepening dusk. Behind us we could hear the hounds and then a sudden whooping, hollering sound and gathered they had picked up a scent. I only hoped it wasn't ours, but the sounds seemed to be away to our left, no nearer. We nearly missed the path to the stream, it was so overgrown, but at last we found ourselves splashing ankle-deep in freezing water, and by the time we managed to identify the grove of oaks the icy chill of my feet had crept up to my stomach and chest. It was near full dark; Mistral, the pigeon and the tortoise were fine, but Gill, Growch and I were so cold that all we wanted to do was light a fire and roast ourselves by it, forgetting bruised feet, turned ankles and scratched faces and hands.

But there was no way we could risk that. Far away I could still hear the mournful belling of the hounds, though the distance between us seemed to be increasing. I hoped Dickon was safe back home. Even if he had laid a trail, eventually when it came to an end they would cast back, though they would probably wait now until morning: the lady would not thank them for losing any of the hounds, even to catch us. And I knew she would be even keener to do that now she knew the pig could fly. . . .

We stumbled on as best we could through the long night, halting only for a quick snack of the bits and pieces I had managed to bring with me. We had the advantage of clear skies, a near-full moon and the prickle of stars, but it was still hard going. There were no rides here and the undergrowth hadn't been cleared for years. Fallen trees, hidden roots, sudden dips and hollows, the tangle of briars, an occasionally stagnant pond—all contrived to hinder our halting passage.

The noise of our progress effectively drove away most of the wildlife, though tawny owl hunted relentlessly. There was the intermittent scurrying in the undergrowth as some small animal was disturbed, and we almost fell over a grunting badger, turning the fallen leaves for early grubs. Towards dawn I called a halt under some pines and we hunkered down in an uneasy doze. There was nothing much to eat for break-fast but the rest of what I had brought from the castle, and that was little enough: the bread stale, the cheese hard, the pie so high only the Wimperling and Growch would touch it. Luckily there was grazing for Mistral, some seeds for Traveler; Basher had dozed off again.

It was a long day. Once or twice we heard the far-off sounds of men, dogs and even horses, but even these receded after a while. At the midday halt Mistral and the Wimperling foraged as best they could, the pigeon found some thistle heads, and Basher, thankfully, had decided to hibernate again. Gill and I just had to tighten our belts and trudge on. Luckily that afternoon I found some Judas' Ear growing on elder: it was a tough fungus with little taste, but after dusk I risked a small fire—during the light I reckoned smoke could be still seen from the turrets of the castle, but a tiny red glow in a hollow was more difficult to spot at night—and chopped the fungus into the pot with oil, salt, a pinch of herbs and a little flour and water and it made a filling enough mess. I also made some oatcakes to eat in the morning. Of course we were still hungry, but at least our stomachs didn't grumble all night.

And this was the pattern of the next two days. Luckily the sun shone and we took whatever promising trail we could, though very often these animal tracks started going east or south, and then wandered all over the place, sometimes even circling right back, and the undergrowth was too thick for us to wade through, unless we found bare ground beneath pine or fir. Twenty miles straight it might be, crooked it was not. I wondered how far we had really come: probably halfway only.

I looked for more fungi and found a few Scarlet Cups, better for color than taste, some Blisters, and a few Sandys. This time I boiled them up with a dozen or so chicory and dandelion leaves and the last of the flour. Growch dug up a couple of truffles and I added these and the result was quite tasty. Gill and I were down to one thin meal a day, though the animals fared better with their foraging, and the Wimperling it was who found us both some shriveled haws and the handful or so of hazelnuts the next day. But we were all weakened and weary by the evening of the fifth day when the trees started to thin out and at last we could walk straight with the setting sun to our right.

I don't think any of us quite believed it at first when we found ourselves actually stepping on a proper road, able to see in all directions and with no pushing and shoving along a trail. I looked back. Nothing save anonymous trees: it could have been anyone's demesne. I felt like putting up a great notice by the side of the road saying: "Beware! The Lady Aleinor is an evil Bitch!" But what good would it do? Most who passed here would not be able to read, and for those who did the castle was twenty miles away from this side.

I hadn't realized how tired I was: we were on a road, pointing in the right direction, but we had no food and no shelter: I didn't feel I could go a step further. Growch nuzzled my knee sympathetically, but it was Traveler who called to be let out of his cage.

"I'll fly a little way and see what I can see. . . ."

He was back in ten minutes, to report a hamlet some two miles ahead. I don't know how we made it but we did, just before dark. We had to knock them up, the food was poor, the shelter minimal, but at that stage we couldn't be choosers. We ate, we slept, and the next day we did the same. On the second day we were on our way again, wending from hamlet to hamlet. The weather remained dry, the village folk were hospitable, the food adequate, but I was worried at how far east we were veering, although there was no alternative except the occasional track. Even Traveler, who was a definite bonus, could see no alternative way, fly as high as he could.

The countryside was changing, too. It was becoming more rocky and the road more undulating, and we passed through scrub and pine as the land gradually rose. On either side mountains rose in sympathy, at first blue and distant, then nearer and sharper each day, till we could clearly see the tall escarpments, the towering crags, the black holes of faraway caves, the skirts of pine that clothed their waists. Above our heads we could hear the complaint of flocks of crows and sometimes see the mighty soar of eagles, their great wings fingering the winds we could not feel.

Understandably Traveler became wary of flying too far with so many predators about, but one day he came winging back to report a "town of sorts" off to our left. Three or four flights away, he said, but a pigeon's flight was variable, relying as it did day by day on weather conditions: wind, rain, cloud, sun and the type of flight needed to suit each variation.

"Can we reach it before nightfall?"

"Up the hill, down the hill, round the next hill, turn east, twisting road between high escarpments, down to the valley . . . Yes."

"And what's it like, this town?" A town meant proper shelter, a full replenishment of our stores, mending of shoes, a warm wash—everything we had sorely needed for the past two weeks.

"Difficult to say. Never seen anything like it. Lots of tents, few buildings. Many people and animals. No castle, no church. Big road leading on to the south."

And that is what decided me. This was the road we needed, and if it meant going through the "town" Traveler had described, then that was the way we had to go, although many times during that long day I cursed the pigeon's directions. Birds fly, they don't walk, and their "up" and "down" meant little to them, but a hell of a lot to those on foot. The narrow path we followed that crawled and looped what seemed a million miles towards the valley floor nearly finished us all off: it was so frustrating being able to see our goal one moment, and then having to turn away from it. That, plus the falling rocks, the blocked paths we had to climb around, the streams that poured on our heads or meandered across the track . . .

I had already lit the lantern and fixed it to Mistral's crupper by the time we reached the valley floor. Ahead was a short walk through well-trodden scrub to the perimeter of the "town," marked by a regular series of posts set into the ground, a very shallow artificial moat and a couple of temporary bridges. Beyond we could see a score of small stone buildings, a mass of tents, a half-ruined amphitheater and a slender temple, the broken columns throwing exquisite shadows in the moonlight. Obviously once this had been the site of an earlier civilization. And now?

We were stopped at the nearest bridge. Not by a soldier, but by a fussy little civilian with a mass of papers in his hand, a quill behind his ear and an ink pot in his pocket. His very officiousness calmed any fears I might have had, and before long I was trying not to smile at his earnestness. Here was normalcy: no shrinking houses, ghosts or wicked ladies.

"What have we here, then? There are only two weeks left, you know: you're late!" He consulted his lists. "Do you know just how many models we have had this year? Nearly two hundred! And of course now accommodation is at a premium. . . . Do you have a sponsor? No? Still, there is always Mordecai, the Jew, or Bartholomew. . . . I believe they are both short this year. Now, how many are there of you? A man, a lady and a horse . . . And what's this? A pig? and do I see a dog? Well, I don't think I've seen a pig, this year, but of course dogs are two a farthing. You have a pigeon? And a tortoise? Now that is a novelty! This might make all the difference. Quite a call for exotic creatures like that, especially for breviaries. Haven't by any chance got a coney or a hedge-pig, I suppose? Pity; both in short supply this year. Seven of you, then: lucky number, seven . . . Come far? Now, that will be nine of copper: two each for the humans, one for the animals."

I was completely confused. "Models," "sponsors," a tortoise to make all the difference? Instead of the expected normalcy, this place sounded like a madhouse. But the word "models" gave me a clue: perhaps this place contained artists who wanted various creatures to draw and paint, human and animal?

"How many artists here this year?" I asked diffidently, to make sure I was on the right track.

"Artists? A few more than last year . . ." So now I was right. "Now, let's have your names. . . ." He took them down.

"What—what are the rates?"

"Depends on your sponsor. You haven't been before? No, well if you follow me I will try and find someone to take you on."

He led us across the wooden bridge to a squalid huddle of temporary huts, a line of tethered horses, mules and donkeys. Small cooking fires burned in the deepening gloom and people scurried back and forth carrying washing, water, pots and pans, babes in arms.

"This is the poorer end," said our guide, wrinkling his nose. "Not organized at all, this lot . . . Farther in are the stores, stables, cooking and washing areas. Plus of course the hiring place, market and artists supplies . . . Stay here: I won't be long." And off he strode with a purposeful air, papers flapping.

"What *have* you got us into this time, Summer?" said poor Gill.

He might well ask!

Our guide, Master Fettiplace, returned, and led us a few hundred yards to a row of orderly tents. "Let me introduce you to Master Bumbo—" a small, bustling, bald-headed man, with a snub nose red from wine and a potbelly to match. "He is willing to take you on, providing terms can be agreed."

"No reason why not!" cried our new sponsor. He beamed at us all, but the smile did not reach a pair of small, black, calculating eyes. He would drive a hard bargain but we had no option. He had a large black mole on his left cheek, from which sprouted three bristly hairs: this should not have made him any less likable, but somehow it did.

"Come along, come along, all of you!" said Master Bumbo. "Let's get you settled in. You'll be hungry and tired, I have no doubt. . . . Er, you did say you had a tortoise . . . ?"

I sized up Master Bumbo, and decided it would be a battle. But we needed the money. . . .

"Of course," I said. "A trained one. As are the horse, the pigeon, the pig and the dog. Very expensive animals. They will do exactly as I say: stand, sit, walk, fly, or be perfectly still. But they only obey me. We do not come cheap, my brother and I. . . ."

"Of course, of course! My commission is small, very small—and in return you will have bountiful accommodation, free, and one good meal a day. And of course your fees for posing . . ." He walked along the row of tents, disappeared into one; there was the sound of an altercation and a moment or two later a tawdry female came flying out, followed by half a dozen cushions, a blanket and various pots and pans. Master Bumbo returned with an ingratiating smile and a bruised lip. "As soon as you like . . ." The tent smelled like a whorehouse, and showed signs of the hasty eviction of its former occupant: underwear, pots of perfume, a torn night dress. I handed these gravely to our sponsor.

"You mentioned a meal. . . . I think we will take today's now. And if I may accompany you to the cooking lines, I believe we shall have better service when we need it. Precooked meals, or will they cook our own?"

"Er . . . Either. They are not cheap, but who is these days?"

I decided to build our own fire. Hanging our lantern on a hook, I saw there was rush matting on the floor and a few rather tatty cushions. We had our own bedding, so that was all right. "Is there a bathhouse?"

"Over there." He pointed. "Again, not cheap . . ."

Right. We would pay for hot water once, and I would wash the clothes, myself; there must be a stream nearby.

He tried again. "Fodder for the animals a hundred yards to your right—"

"Not cheap," I said gravely.

"Er . . . No. Your horse can join the lines down—"

"My horse," I said, "stays here, behind the tent. She's trained, remember?"

And so the first small victory was mine, but it didn't remain that way for long. Every day it swung first one way then the other, as first Master Bumbo then I gained advantage. Of course he tried to cheat us, and I retorted by snatching the odd freelance for any of us I could.

The "town" was as I had suspected: a winter retreat for artists where they could paint, draw or sketch in peace with everything provided—from the latest tube or pot of Italian Brown to the row of whores' tents behind the temple. They had all the scenery they needed—a river, mountains, forests, romantic ruins—and all the models imaginable; black, white, brown; tall, short, wide, thin; dwarfs and giants, men, women and children; the beautiful, the ugly and those in between. They had animals of all shapes and sizes (but ours was the only tortoise), the flowers of the field carefully painted on wood and cut out to be placed where they wished and all the impedimenta of indoor life—pots, pans, candlesticks, stools, chairs, tables, hangings, goblets, knives etc. There were costumes and armor, swords and spears, in fact everything an artist could need. At a price.

Why in this hidden valley? I had thought we were miles from anywhere, but in fact the road Traveler had seen led straight to an important crossroads, and was only ten miles from the nearest town. The whole venture was run by an Italian, who had another such project in his own country, held in the autumn. Signor Cavalotti, whose brainchild this was, believed that exchanges of ideas and techniques were essential to the development of art; indeed, I was told there had been significant advances in perspective and the mixing of paints in the ten years the two "towns" had existed.

Well, Signer Cavalotti may have had high ideals and thought he was a philanthropist, but the consortium who ran this caper was very far from being either. Everything was very highly priced, but those who came off worst were probably the models like us. It went like this: the artist paid the model, who then relinquished some seventy percent to the sponsor; he in turn paid ten percent for food, five percent to pitch the tents, and then perhaps twenty percent to the consortium for the privilege of sponsorship. Probably the artists spent more than everyone else—space, canvas, paints, props, costumes, models, food, accommodation—but then they had the money to start with.

Most of them were sponsored by rich families or the church—I counted at least a dozen altar pieces and triptychs in various stages of completion—and many had private means. There was a handful of students and apprentices, but most of these were under the patronage of the artists themselves. Useful to be able to take credit for the important bits and have an unpaid lackey to fill in the background!

Master Bumbo had very little idea how to promote his models—he had ten others besides ourselves—but in spite of his laziness, incompetence and avariciousness Gill's good looks provided us with two St. Sebastians and a disciple; I got two crowd scenes, very background, and Basher was fully occupied with two young monks composing a bestiary and an artist creating a series of panels on popular legends. One artist was interested exclusively in birds and their plumage and anatomy and was very pleased with the (private) sittings with Traveler.

And what of the Wimperling in all this? All in all, he earned more than the rest of us put together. Master Bimbo gave up on him after the first day: he was, after all, a rather ugly pig—but I had better ideas. A German artist who had used poor Mistral in an allegory for famine recommended a Dutchman who was looking for "odd" creatures, and I saw why when I peeped round the corner of his screened off area. He was painting the pains of Hell on a large canvas, and very frightening they were, too. Fires, flames, smoke; imps, demons, devils, trolls, dragons: all delighting in torturing, beheading, raping and disemboweling the hapless sinners who cascaded down from the top of the canvas in a never-ending stream. And everywhere there was an inch or so of space capered creatures from a wildly demented imagination, gleefully cheering on the destruction.

These creatures could never have existed: birds with fish heads, lizards with horses' hooves, cats with six arms and two heads, mouths with thin spindly legs, spiders with human faces, torsos with heads in their stomachs, a pair of legs with wings—It was this last that gave me the idea. Withdrawing quietly before the artist noticed me, I returned later with a fully briefed Wimperling.

The artist was a thoroughly unpleasant little man, hunched and smelly, so much I had already heard, but I wasn't prepared for the brusque way he dismissed me before I had opened my mouth.

"Unless you've got an extra pair of tits or balls I don't want to know: bugger off!"

But I wasn't going to be thrown out just like that. Instead I dared his wrath and looked critically at the lizard-like thing with wings he was trying to draw.

"You've got the wings wrong," I said. "They should be more leathery and the tips less scooped. . . ."

"What? What do you mean? How do you know anything about Wyrmwings?"

"Look," I said, and the Wimperling carefully extended one wing. "And if it's claws and hooves you are after, just look at these. . . ." The pig lifted one hoof. "And as for fangs—" Obligingly the Wimperling bared his teeth. I hadn't realized just how sharp they were till now. The pig folded himself away again. "What do you say?"

"Christ-on-the-Cross!" breathed the artist. "Do that again!"

The Wimperling obliged.

"How much do you want for it?" snapped the artist, his eyes even piggier than the pig. "I'll give you what you want. Within reason . . . Ten gold pieces?" His ringers were crawling towards the pig with desire, his sleeve smudging the charcoal sketch I had criticized.

"He's not for sale," I replied firmly. "But I am offering him to you as a model: exclusive rights, of course. At a reasonable price."

"For the rest of the time here? Nine days? One gold coin."

"Two. He's worth far more, and you know it. *Exclusive* rights, remember: you'd better keep him hidden away." I was calculating on his artistic greed in this: I didn't want anyone else to know about the wings. I needn't have worried: the artist's "find" was far too precious to share, and at the end of our two weeks the artist had dozens of sketches of every part of the pig's anatomy, from the tip of his fanged snout to the end of his spade-tipped tail and everything in between.

I supposed this was the way to assure immortality, I thought, looking at the sketches, remembering the other drawings and paintings of all of us, even my crowd scenes. Some day, many years hence perhaps, people would look at a pigeon's wing, a horse's flanks, a scruffy dog, a tortoise in a bestiary, the wings on a creature from hell, a woman bending over a basket, a saint's agony, and maybe wonder at the originals they were created from. But only we would know, and we wouldn't be there to tell them. It was a shivery thought.

But once more on the road, with the warm wind lifting the hair from my forehead and the prickly-sweet perfume of the gorse on the hillsides tickling our noses, all such somber thoughts were chased away.

"I can smell spring," said Gill, lifting his blind eyes to the sun. "And after spring comes Summer!" and he smiled at his own little joke, a smile to lift my heart and renew my love.

Chapter Twenty

It was true, Spring had arrived, and with it came an uplifting of the spirit, a healthy optimism that had nothing to do with reality. I would wake in the mornings, stretch the creaks from my bones (for the nights were still cold), sniff the crisp dawn air and feel as though I had drunk a bucketful of chilled white wine.

As we traveled further and further south, I delighted in plants, trees and herbiage that were strange to my northern eyes. All seemed brighter, bigger, pricklier; citrus trees with evergreen leaves sprouted little dots of white bud; bushy grey-green cacti and succulents were tipped with barbs like daggers; a yellow cascade of mimosa poured over stone walls, and miniature iris and crocus speared up through the scrub under olive and carob. Of course I had to ask the names of all these, but there were plants I recognized, though their flowering was at least a month ahead of ours at home.

I found the pale tremble of pink-white-purple wood anemones, petals ready to fly on the slightest breeze; heart-shaped leaves of deepest green hiding the thick, soft scent of violets; the perfumed cream of wild jonquil; shaggy coltsfoot and tender celandine, days-eye, lions-tooth—the last two demanded daily by an awakening Basher, together with the tender young leaves of chicory and clover.

As we passed through villages and hamlets the pink smoke of almond blossom clothed the slopes of the hillsides, though the knobbed vines were still bare. I experimented with the new-grown herbs: wild mint (good with lamb and goat), young and bitter shoots of asparagus, pale among its prickly adult cage, the tasty tips of nettle, and thyme and rosemary (excellent with all meats and fish).

And the birds and animals echoed this burgeoning promise. Sparrows, thrushes, blackbirds, green- and gold-finch, tits, siskin, flycatchers, brambling, all were busy picking and pecking for insects, snails and young shoots, twigs, hair, moss and mud for nests. Wrens scuttled along old walls, tree-creepers sidled up the bark, and against the eaves of buildings the house martins were already building new nests or repairing last year's, dark mud against pale. In the trees the russet squirrels were dashing about with their usual indetermination, all mouth and ruffed tails; shy roe deer leapt among the ground elder and sweet cicely, the hinds already heavy with young; the jaunty scuts of coney were glimpsed flashing through the undergrowth, we could hear the crash and grunt of swine, the faraway howl of wolf and scream of vixen; the shepherds who walked their sheep and goats along the slope often carried new-dropped lambs, their wool still sticky with pale birth blood, the ewes reaching up anxiously to nuzzle their young, the dogs chewing at strings of afterbirth as they followed the flock. Above our heads came the first sweet babble of the ascending larks, and if you searched carefully you could find in nests soft with down and moss the incredible promise of eggs blue as the sky, or scrambled with speckles and blotches, like a child's scribbles.

The first flies came to torment us, yolk-yellow butterflies quivered on the scarcely less bright gorse and broom, mornings showed the sliver-slime trail of snails, clouds of midges danced about our heads, bees buzzed from flower to bush; from the groves of pines crept processions of striped caterpillars: I picked up a couple, disturbing the caravan of their passage, and was well rewarded with a crop of white blebs which itched intolerably till an old crone in one of the hamlets took pity on me and threw a jug of sour wine over me: I stank for days, but the irritation was gone.

In the ponds and ditches humps and strings of spawn showed where frog and toad had been: some had already hatched into flickering life and sun-warmed lizards ran along the stones. Fish began to spawn, a flurry among the stones of streams, three or four males to every female, or so it seemed.

The farther south we went, the more the countryside changed: arid, mountainous, yet conversely in the valleys, more fertile. The air was clearer, colors brighter, contours sharper; the people wore more colorful clothes, too: patterned skirt, red scarf, purple jacket although the elderly were still in a contrast of black, for mourning: who at their age had not lost a member of the family? We passed repainted shrines and gaily clad processions for St. Joseph's day, disregarding the rigors of Lent, and then the hearty celebrations for the new Year of Grace on March 25, a fiesta full of green branches, embroidered shawls and colored ribbons.

The going became easier the farther south we went, perhaps because our feet had become accustomed to the ruts, bumps, flints, pebbles and stones of the highways. More and more we traveled in company, too many for ambush or treachery. Many languages were distributed among the mighty campfires each evening; men spoke of ice, fog and snow in islands to the north and west, even in summer; of sand, sun and people black as ink to the southlands, of great temples of stone and creatures as tall as a house and with horns of ivory; when they spoke of the east they told of beasts of burden who never drank, yet carried houses upon their backs, of heathens who sang to their gods from tall towers, of men as yellow as a canary bird who fought like devils. The west was full of great grey seas, ships with bird's wings that skimmed the waves to deliver their cargoes of cloth and wine, spices and silk, of great sea monsters who devoured a ship in one mouthful, and of the sea maidens with long hair and fishes' tails who sang the mariners to destruction on the rocks.

All this talk was heady stuff: it whetted my appetite to see more of the world before I finally found a husband and settled down. If men could travel around the world, why not a woman?

Travel seemed to improve the health and well-being of us all. Gill became tan-skinned, his step was bolder, he lost his gauntness. Mistral grew rounder and sleeker, her tail and mane longer, her hide lightened to a creamy color. Basher ate till he filled his shell and developed an extra ridge on his carapace, demanding a short walk each day to exercise off the excess. Traveler declared himself fit and wing-whole again, taking longer and longer flights and dancing back in brightened browny-pink feathers to wheel and dive above our heads. The Wimperling grew stouter and stronger by the day, until he was fast becoming the largest pig I had ever seen, and I felt lighter and fitter every day.

But it was Growch who took full advantage of all spring had to offer. One day the caravan in which we currently traveled was joined by an abbess and her servants, bound to take healing waters. She rode in a litter with silk curtains and was too superior to mix with the rest of us. Not so, apparently, her dogs. With her in the litter, fed on a diet of chicken and milk and sleeping on silk cushions, were two small, long-haired bitches, silky hair trimmed, curled, plaited and beribboned; they were exercised four times a day by the lady's attendants, waddling around like small brown sausages, their long black claws clip-clipping on the road, their plumed tails cleaned every time they excreted, their hair combed free of tangles by their mistress herself, using the same comb she used on her own hair, it was rumored. Growch's inquisitive nose and eyes found them the first time they set paws to ground, although his first essay was beaten back by the lady's attendants.

"Stripe me like a badger! What little chunks of sweetness! Plump and petted and just ready for it! You've no idea—"

"Now just you keep away from them," I said severely. "We don't want any trouble. The lady's servants will chop you in half if you—"

"Gam! Got to catch me first! 'Sides, I can have 'em away any time I choose. They fancies me, I can tell. . . ."

And apparently they did, to my amazement, for first one and then the other managed to escape from the servants and disappear from sight in the undergrowth, hotly pursued by a dog I promptly disowned. The abbess was distraught and insisted on staying behind until her "darlings" turned up again. . . .

Growch rejoined us two days later, some fifteen miles further on, absolutely shattered, his belly dragging on the ground. He was even filthier than usual, and declared himself starved.

"You don't deserve a thing!" I said, giving him a hunk of cheese and some stale bread. "You're absolutely disgusting! Er—what happened to the bitches? Did their owner get them back?"

"'Ventually. Servants caught one, t'other went back when she was hungry. Not before we'd had a coupla nights of it . . . I can recommend a threesome. Never enjoyed one before," and he smacked his lips, whether from the cheese or fond memory I wasn't sure.

"I'd never seen dogs like them before," I said, remembering their snub noses, plumed tails and flouncy way of walking.

"Come from a place east, long-a-ways," said Growch, scratching furiously. He smelled like a midden, and I determined to dump him in the next stretch of water we came to and scrub him, hard. "Nice manners—none of this nonsense of equality between the sexes—just the right height with them little bow legs, and virgins as well . . . Not that that made much difference once they got goin'—"

"Shut up!" I said automatically. "I don't want to know!" I wondered whether the pups would look like him: probably a mixture. The abbess would have a shock. "They had nice faces. . . ."

"Faces? *Faces*?" He leered. "'Oo the 'ell was looking at their faces?"

We were holed up for five days by howling winds and driving rain, which Basher assured us were normal at this time of year. "Good for the young heather shoots," he said. Traveler took advantage of the downpour to sit in puddles and air his wing-pits to the rain.

"Gets rid of the ticks," he explained.

I decided to take the opportunity of tidying us all up. We had taken a large loft above the stable in a hospitable farmhouse and there were a couple of rain butts in the yard below, now overflowing, so we were allowed unlimited bucketfuls and paid for two cauldrons of water heated over the kitchen fires.

First I scrubbed Growch—who immediately went out and found something disgusting to roll in—then the Wimperling and Mistral, combing out the tangles in the latter's mane and tail. With fresh water I washed our winter clothes, hoping that now we could wear our lighter things. With the hot water I found an old tub and first submitted Gill and then myself to a thorough going over. I remembered thinking it was a good job he was blind, else he would have seen my blushes as I washed those parts difficult for him to reach. . . .

I felt wonderfully fresh myself after I had bathed and washed my hair, changing into a clean shift and my thinner bliaut, surprised to see how winter storage had stretched the material: it was far roomier than I remembered, and I had to take it in an inch or two down the side seams.

I finally caught Growch and washed him again, threatening permanent exile in the rain if he did it again.

Being a stock farm we were staying in, there was no lack of leather and I bought some and busied myself stitching fresh boots for Gill. I used my mother's simple recipe: triple leather soles turned up at the sides and hemmed for a lace that fastened at the front, the whole stuffed with discarded sheep's wool for comfort and warmth. While I was about it I also made us sandals for the warmer weather: thick soles, a single band across the instep, a toe thong to go between the big toe and its brother, and a loop at the back to thread with a lace that tied round the ankle.

When we took to the road again we found that the wind and rain had washed the world as clean and fresh and new as we were. The grass was greener and taller, all the trees were in leaf, the woods were full of birds shouting, singing, quarreling, wildflowers and weeds had sprung up overnight and the stones and rocks sparkled and glinted like jewels in the sun.

Now many roads joined the highway and wandered off again and the houses were whitewashed against the summer sun. People were smaller, darker and spoke with a harsher patois and used their shoulders, hands and their faces to express themselves, like actors in a play.

Our little group was just one of many traveling the roads, but I could see that while we were nothing out of the ordinary, the Wimperling did attract attention. He was so large that I could see by the speculation in many an eye that they were measuring him for chops, sausages, brawn, roasts and bones for soup. I was careful to keep him by my side at night, though I believe he was more than capable of taking care of himself.

By now I was content with our little group, used to all their idiosyncrasies and fond of them all, but I knew it couldn't last. One by one the animals would leave us when they found whatever haven they were seeking, and each departure would diminish me. Once I had been alone except for my beloved Mama; now it seemed I was friends with all the world via a dog, a horse, a pigeon, a tortoise and a pig. I couldn't bear the thought of losing any of them, and when the time suddenly came for the first of them to leave us, I was unprepared.

One fine morning Traveler ate a handful of grain, pecked digesting grit from the roadside, drank from a puddle and rose in the air to scan our road southward as usual. But this time he was gone longer than usual, so long in fact that I began to gaze anxiously up in the sky for eagles or falcons but could see none. I was beginning to get really fidgety when I saw him skimming back across the trees as he slowed his wings, starting to curve down at the tips, and waver a little as he gauged the wind. He skidded down in front of us, trembling from both excitement and exhaustion.

"I've found it! It's there! I had begun to think it wasn't—I hadn't—"

"Calm down!" He was so elated his beak was gaping and I was afraid his heart would stop. "Here, take a sip of this," and I poured some water from my flask into my horn mug. "That's better. . . . Now, tell us!"

It seemed he had flown higher than usual to surmount a range of hills to the southeast and had seen through the haze a large town and a ribbon of river, much like others on our journey, but as the mist cleared and he flew closer the sun touched the towers and pinnacles with gold, and he knew he had found his home town.

"I flew on and on, just to make sure, but there was no need. The knowing in my body, the thing that tells me where to go, it was pointing right at the city. . . ."

"What's going on?" asked Gill. "Why have we stopped? Don't tell me you are talking to your animals again. . . ."

"Hush! Let him finish. What then? You're sure it's the right place?"

"Sure as eggs become squabs . . ."

"Did you go near enough to find your home?"

"Not enough wing-time. Tomorrow, perhaps."

"Summer—"

I turned back to the pigeon. "Just a *minute,* Gill! Will you . . . Will you go on your own, then?" I was suddenly scared that the time had come to say goodbye, and I wasn't ready, not yet.

"No, of course not! I need you to tell the lady about the broken wing so she understands why I was so long."

"Very well . . . The message on your leg is for her, if I remember?"

"Yes, I told you. From her lover."

"Then she will forgive the delay, I'm sure. How far away is this town of yours?"

He considered. "For you, three, four days," and began to nibble at the tender shoots of grass by the roadside, tired of talking.

I knew Gill still didn't believe I had any real communication with the animals, but I reported exactly what the bird had said. There was a silence.

"I'd like to say I'll believe it when I see it," he said carefully. "But you know that's impossible. I'll say this, though; if we find this town, *and* his home, *and* the lady he speaks of, then I will ask your forgiveness for doubting you. If . . ." He suddenly grinned. "Ask him if the lady is pretty." And he grinned again, not really expecting an answer.

"He says he doesn't know the meaning of the word 'pretty' as applied to humans," I translated after a moment or two. "He says she is smaller than me and that her hair is straight and pale. He says she has a quiet voice and gentle hands."

He thought about it. "Well . . . Tell you what, as long as there's a town ahead, she can be tall or small, fat or thin, dark or fair, just so long as we have a day or two in comfort again. No reflections on your cooking, Summer, but it will feel good to have my feet under a table again, eat a great chunk of game pie and drink a quart of ale."

"Well in that case," I said stiffly, "the sooner we get going the better!"

We arrived at our destination mid-afternoon of the fourth day, guided all the way by an ever more excited pigeon. After a couple of his disastrous "shortcuts," we kept to the roads; the flight of a bird takes no account of hills, rivers, stones or forest.

Once we had entered the town by the west gate and paid our toll, Traveler disappeared. He had obviously flown straight on, but like all the towns we had been in, there was no straight way anywhere; side roads, crooked lanes, blind alleys, and everywhere choked with traffic: horses, mules, carts, wagons, litters, pedestrians laden and unladen, children, cattle, sheep, pigs, dogs and cats.

He eventually returned and tried to guide us, soaring above us one minute, on a ledge the next, but several times we lost sight of him altogether. I became more and more conscious of the curious glances we were attracting:

a blind man holding on to a horse's tail, and a scruffy dog, large pig and fat girl all scanning the rooftops like stargazers.

It seemed to take hours, but at last Traveler led us, fluttering just above our heads now, down a quiet street near the river, with high-walled houses on either side and a tall church at the end just striking the office for three hours after noon, echoed by others near and far.

Traveler came to rest atop a large double gate and fluffed his feathers. "It's here. . . ." I could feel his anticipation and anxiety as if it were my own and shivered in sympathy. Lifting my hand I knocked firmly: no answer. Somewhere down the road a dog, awakened from his siesta, barked for a moment. I knocked again, and there was a limping step, a creaking bolt and a face peered out at us, the chain still prudently fastened. Traveler hopped down to my shoulder.

"Yes?" said the door porter. He was almost bald and nearly toothless but had fierce, bushy eyebrows.

"I wish to—to see the lady of the house," I said, conscious that a name would have been better, but of course names meant nothing to a bird. "About a pigeon. This one," and I touched Traveler with my finger. "I believe he is one of hers. He has a message to deliver."

The porter stared out at us, at our travel-stained clothes, our generally tatty appearance, and I didn't blame him for his next remark.

"My mistress don't entertain rogues and vagabonds. Why, you don't even know her name, do you? Besides, how do I know it ain't all a trick to get in and rob us all? Could be anyone's pigeon you got."

"This color?" and I stroked Traveler's wing. "Pink pigeons don't come in dozens. Besides, only your mistress has the key to the message strapped to his leg. . . ."

He thought about it. Finally: "I'll go and see," and he shut the gate again.

We waited for what seemed an age. I urged Traveler to fly over the gate and find his mistress, but he refused.

"We go in together," he said firmly.

Once more the shuffling steps approached the gate, but this time one half was flung open. "Mistress Rowena is in the garden at the back. Leave the beasts here." I took Gill's hand and followed the way that was pointed out to me, across the cobbles and down a narrow alleyway at the side of the house to a garden full of sun and sleepy afternoon scents.

Square beds were planted centrally with bay or evergreen, fancifully trimmed, and edged with box or rosemary. In the beds themselves were the long runners and green tips of miniature strawberries, the soft faces of violet and pansy, the tight buds of clove carnations. Beside each bed ran a little canal of water, probably fed from the river I could see glinting at the foot of the garden, beyond a lawn starred with daisies, camomile and buttercups. Against one wall were trellises for the climbing roses, on the other were tall clumps of dark Bear's Braies and pale fennel, and behind was a thick hedge of oleander.

At the top end of the garden fat, lazy carp swam in a pond plated with water-lily pads and there, tossing pinches of manchet into their hungry mouths, was Traveler's owner, who turned to meet us with a smile. She was as the bird had described: small, slim, with icy blond hair hanging straight down her back with a blue and gold fillet binding her brow, to match her deep-sleeved dress. Her face was pale, as were her lashes, brows and blue eyes.

Her smile revealed white teeth as small as a child's, with tiny points. A cat's smile, I thought. She held out her hands and reached for Traveler, fluttering nervously on my shoulder, and pinioned him in her soft white hands.

"My servant, Pauncefoot, told me you had found one of my birds, but I never expected it to be my Beauty! Where did you find him?" and she put her cheek against his head, crooning softly.

I started to explain how I had rescued him, about the broken wing and how long it had taken to heal, but as soon as I mentioned the message on his leg I could see the rest didn't matter. Still nursing the bird she fumbled in her purse pocket and drew out a tiny key, as fine as a needle and in a moment the leg ring was open and she was unrolling a thin strip of paper between finger and thumb. For the first time I saw a tinge of color in her cheeks as she read the few words it contained. She looked at us, smiling that cat smile.

"He comes at the end of this month, as he promised. . . ." Her eyes were dreamy. "I knew he could not stay away. He was my father's apprentice. When he asked for my hand, my father stipulated that we spend a year apart and he sent Lorenzo north on business, with the added proviso that we should not communicate with each other. He still thinks Lorenzo is after my money. . . ." She cuddled Traveler closer. "I thought of a scheme to circumvent my father's dictum. Lorenzo took two of my pigeons with him: a grey, and Beauty here. The grey arrived back in October confirming his love, and he must have sent Beauty soon after. My father will know nothing of the message. He had bribed the servants to intercept any letters, but he never thought of the pigeons." She turned to me. "I cannot thank you enough: with my father ill I cannot ask you to stay overnight, but perhaps with these—" She handed me some coins, one gold, I noticed "—I can combine my thanks with assurance you may find good lodgings."

At first I was shy of accepting, but looking at the well-cared-for garden, her clothes, the tall house behind, I realized she could well afford it. "Thank you . . . The pigeon: his wing has healed, but he may not be able to manage such long flights as before. You will . . . ?"

"Still care for him?" she supplied. "Of course. Somehow he guided you here with my message—I can always breed from him. I have a couple of females the same shade. . . ."

I turned to go but suddenly Traveler—I couldn't think of him as "Beauty"—flew from her arms onto my shoulder. I turned my head to see his ruby eyes regarding me steadily. "Thanks," he crooned. "I shall always remember you, all of you. . . ." And he leaned forward and pretend-fed me, as an adult pigeon would a squab, then sprang from my shoulder and flew to the pigeon loft against the house wall.

I heard his owner draw her breath in sharply as she watched his flight, but my eyes were suddenly too blurred to see the expression on her face. She called out peremptorily to a gardener's boy raking the gravel between the flower beds. "Shut the loft door! Hurry . . ."

Out in the street again, the doors shut behind us, the coins jingling satisfactorily in my pocket, I should have felt satisfaction at a task well completed, a wanderer having found his home, but I didn't. I felt uneasy, depressed, somehow all *wrong*. I opened my mouth to say something and the ring on my finger, dormant so long, gave me such a sudden painful jolt that I cried out instead. At the same time a voice full of terror rang in my mind: "Help me! Help me. . . ." It was Traveler. What in the world had gone wrong?

Obeying an instinct stronger than thought or caution I turned and began to beat on the closed gate: "Let me in!" but there was no answer, and all the while I could sense the feather-flutter of Traveler's fear in my mind. I threw myself against the gate, but it wouldn't yield; by now the others, with the exception of course of Gill, had also "heard" the pigeon's panic. They needed no urging to help my assault on the gate. Growch barked hysterically, setting off other dogs down the road, the Wimperling added a shoulder-charge to my efforts and Basher even battered his head against his basket, but it was Mistral who got us in.

Turning, she aimed two vicious kicks at the gate panels, which gave on the second blow, allowing me to reach in and slip the bolts. As I reached the garden again at a run, I saw the gardener's boy hand a feebly fluttering bird to his mistress. Grabbing his wings cruelly with one hand she put the other hand around his neck, the tendons on her wrist already tightened to twist his head off. "Stop!" I cried. "In the name of God, stop!"

Chapter Twenty-One

She paused, her fingers still cruelly tight on Traveler's wings and neck. "Get out! What business is it of yours?"

"But you promised. . . ." I was bewildered. "You said you would care for him. . . . I don't understand!"

"It doesn't matter whether you understand or not!" she hissed. "It is *my* bird, to do with as I will! If I wish to wring the wretched thing's neck because it has betrayed me—"

"Betrayed you? How?"

She showed her small, pointed teeth in a grimace. "He is *my* bird, he does as *I* say, he owes *me* all his devotion! I saw what he did to you: he has never done that to me!"

She was jealous! Jealous of an affectionate gesture the poor bird had given me. . . . She must be mad. Feeling in my pocket I tossed her coins to the ground in front of her.

"Take your money: I don't want it! Instead, I'll take back a bird you obviously don't want either."

White lids came down over pale blue eyes, but not before I had seen the sudden gleam of cunning, so quickly veiled. "Very well," she said slowly, but her fingers were almost imperceptibly tightening round the bird's neck. At the same moment the ring on my finger gave me another sharp shock and my hand jerked forward, the ring now pointing at the Lady Rowena.

She screamed as though she had been stung and dropped Traveler, who lay at her feet, fluttering feebly, scrabbling round in the dirt in helpless circles. I picked him up gently and held him close. "It's all right now. . . ."

His owner backed away from me, crossing herself, her eyes wide with an emotion I couldn't fathom. "Witch! What have you done?" I moved towards her and she crossed herself again: I realized now the emotion she felt was fear. "All right, all right, take him! I wouldn't have kept him anyway: there is a knot in his wing, and I never keep anything that isn't perfect. . . ." And she spat at me, the phlegm landing in a yellow gobbet at my feet. "Now get out, before I call the servants to have you thrown out, or summon the soldiery and have you all arrested for theft and witchcraft!"

We went.

When I told Gill what had happened he actually put out a finger and stroked the still-trembling bird. "Poor little thing," he said. It was the first time I had seen him ever evince any interest in any of the animals: his usual stance was indifference. "What will you do with him now?"

"The first thing to do," said the Wimperling, "is to get out of this town right now, before she pulls herself together and does get us all thrown into jail. A woman like that cannot bear to be bested."

We took the southern gate from the city, not stopping even to eat. A trembling Traveler sat on my shoulder, looking back at the towers and pinnacles from which he had hoped so much, now bathed in the magical light of a yellow-orange sunset. I smoothed his feathers.

"Don't worry," I said. "We'll find you somewhere better. . . ."

"But that was my home," he said with sad, unassailable logic.

The Wimperling looked up. "A home is not one place," he said slowly. "A home can be a place where you are born and brought up, a place you like better than any other; it can be a dwelling where your loved one lives, a house in which your children are raised, or somewhere you have to live because there is no other. A home is made by you, it does not create itself. It can be large or small, beautiful or ugly, grand or mean. But in the end it is only one thing: the place where your heart is. And you don't have to be there in your bodily self; you can carry it with you in spirit wherever you go. . . . Like love," he added.

I thought about what he had said later that night when we had found a farmhouse and paid a couple of coins for well-water and a share of the undercroft with their other animals—goats and chickens. What did "home" mean to the bird, the tortoise, the horse, the knight? For them it was where they were born, where their own kind lived, simple as that. Growch and I were on the lookout for comfort and security, in my case a husband, and in his case I suspected he would settle wherever I did—and wherever it was, and with whom, there we would call "home."

But what about the Wimperling? He was the philosopher, but he had never indicated where he wanted to go, where his heart lay. Born from an egg (if his memory was to be believed), raised as the runt of a litter of piglets and sold into a life of performing slavery—where did *he* want to go? South, he had said, but I believed he had no clear direction. I must ask him. If he went on growing at his present rate he would have to go and live with the hellephunts, which I understood were as big as houses, or live by himself in a cave, for no sty would hold him.

We traveled south and west for six days and the terrain grew gradually wilder; the roads more tortuous. Now the hills were of limestone, striped by tumbling streams fed by the snow water that still lingered on the high peaks. Pockets of reddish earth were starred with the scalding yellow of gorse and broom, pink-plumed spears of valerian and blossom from wild cherry. The pines and fir were showing a new, tender green at their tips, and the air was full of the scribble-song of siskins; orioles swung above our heads, gold and blue; flycatchers, wagtails and bee-eaters chittered and bobbed ahead of us on the road, and from far away I could hear the strange call of the hoopoe. Bees droned on the bushes, all on the same soporific note, ants marched in lines across our path, wasps were after anything we ate and the dusk was full of the piping of pipistrelles—the airy-mouses of legend.

And above and beyond all this there was a teasing, ephemeral scent that came and went with the southern breeze: a smell that could have been wet rocks, a drying lake, salted fish, dried blood but was none of these.

"It is the ocean," said Traveler, soaring high above us.

"It's the Great Water," said Basher, now stuffing himself from dawn to dusk with heather shoots, clover and young grass till his scales shone and his voice no longer was drawn out, thin and feeble.

"It's the sea," said Mistral, her pink nostrils flaring as she snuffed the wind. "But not my sea. This is a little sea; mine is endless and comes crashing in from the far corners of the world and the foam is like the manes of my people as they outrun the waves. . . ."

"Can you see this Great Water from your home?" I asked Basher curiously.

"It is a glint in the sun, far, far away, but you can taste it in the breeze and the salt sometimes touches the air like seasoning." He scurried away among the undergrowth, his long black claws clicking on the stones. "Thirsty-making . . ."

Southward still we went, leaving the great snow-tipped mountains behind. The land was gentler, there were farms, orchards, tilled fields, small towns. The midday sun burned Gill's and my faces, arms and legs and we shed clothes till he only wore a pair of shortened braies and an open shirt, and I kilted my skirt between my legs, glad that he could not see my bare legs.

One night, when sudden warm rain and a gusting wind that chased up and down like a boisterous child made us seek shelter, we found a ruined chapel on a little hill. Once there had been a settlement of houses nearby, but these were deserted and had fallen into disrepair, like the chapel. There was no clue as to what had happened to the previous inhabitants, but beneath the chapel walls were more than the usual number of untended graves. Perhaps one of the sudden pestilences had decimated the villagers and they had abandoned their homes; perhaps marauders had carried off the women and children: who knows?

It was near dusk when we sought shelter under the crumbling tower of the chapel, and I found enough broken sticks of furniture in the deserted houses to build a good blaze. There were no church vessels to be seen, nor any crosses, and the once-colorful murals had faded to blisters of pale brown and yellow—an arm, a leg, part of a flowing robe—so the place had obviously been de-consecrated, and I had no hesitation in building a fire to cook our strips of dried meat and vegetables.

The smoke rose upwards and then wavered as the gusts of wind from the round-arched windows caught it and blew it like a rag. Soon enough the pot was bubbling and the seductive smell of herby stew set my—and

Growch's—stomach rumbling. I pulled the pot to one side and lidded it, to simmer till the ingredients were softer, and set about cutting up the two-day-old bread to warm through.

Suddenly there was a wild flutter and commotion above our heads and debris showered down amongst us. I was glad the lid was on the pot: I didn't fancy stewed pigeon shit.

"What in the world . . . ?"

Traveler took wing and circled our heads. "I'll go and see. . . ."

He was gone some time, and there were more flutterings, scrapings and dried excreta, which luckily burned well. The noise subsided, there were a couple of coos and soft hoots and he rejoined us, feathers ruffled and disheveled, but he looked brighter, less despairful, than he had since we left his hometown.

"There are couple of dozen of my kind up there—wild ones, with little civility, but they are thriving. They have been in the tower since any can remember, and manage well enough foraging off the land. I have promised we will douse the fire as soon as possible, for the smoke is choking the young squabs who cannot leave their nests. I shall talk to them again in the morning."

With the morning came the sun again, and I built a fire in the open for oatmeal porridge and cheese and toasted bread. At dawn Traveler had disappeared up into the chapel tower again, and I saw him perched on a ledge with some of the other grey pigeons, or flying around the tower in formation, his pinky-brown color the only dissonance in the otherwise perfect unison of their wheeling and turning.

I scrubbed out the cooking pot with grass and sand from the nearby stream, filled the water bottle, packed everything up, washed my hands, feet and face, and helped Gill to do the same, but Traveler still did not reappear. I went into the chapel again and called him, and eventually he came fluttering down to land on my shoulder, his feathers a little disarranged.

"Time to go," I said, stroking the soft feathers on his neck and scratching him under his chin. He shuffled about on my shoulder.

"Do you mind . . . Do you mind if I stay?"

I looked up at the tower above; little heads peeped down, there was a ruffling of neck feathers, a warning "hoof!" , a croon or two, the pleading cheep of a squab. "Are you sure? They don't look very friendly to me."

"They know I am different: it will take time. But there are more hens than cocks and rats got at the eggs last year. The ropes the rodents used to climb with have rotted and gone, but the flock needs building up. I think it will be all right. . . ." He sighed. "I hope so."

"But you don't know how to forage the countryside as they do," I objected. "You will go hungry."

He straightened up and preened himself. "Then I shall just have to learn, won't I? I have all the summer to learn, and by winter I will be no different from the others."

"This wasn't what I meant for you. . . ."

"I know that, but you cannot decide my life for me: only I have the right to do that, now that you have freed me. Do not worry, I shall be fine. It is better that I take this chance while I can for I may not find a better. Living is better than not-living, whatever it brings. . . ."

"Good-bye," I said and kissed the top of his head. He sprang away and flew up to the rafters.

We had not gone far down the road, however, when there was a rush of wings and he was circling above us. "May you all find what you seek. Remember me!" And he was gone, leaving me feeling as empty as though I had had no breakfast.

"We have a dovecote at home," said Gill unexpectedly. "Their cooing was the first thing I used to hear when . . ." He trailed off. "I don't remember any more."

But at least he was recalling more and more; inconsequential little fragments maybe, but one day they might all fit together like a tapestry. And if I was missing the pigeon so much, what would it be like when my beloved knight finally found his home?

It was about a week later that we came to a place on the road where the land sloped sharply down to the south and there, a glittering shield that stretched away as far as the eye could see, was Basher's Great Water. I sniffed the air and there it was again, that tantalizing salt smell that was like no other, even mixed as it was with pine, heather, wild garlic and gorse. I started to point it out to Gill, before I remembered he couldn't see.

Mistral was also snuffing the air, as was Growch, and Basher stopped chewing the chicory leaves I had put for him in his basket.

"It's here," he said. "Here, or hereabouts. We've found it. . . ."

"You're sure this is the place?"

"Smells right. There should be land sloping to the sea, way off in the distance. Lots of heather, sandy soil for the eggs and hibernation. Pools or a stream, trees for shade. Rocks to keep the claws strong. No people. Lots of lady tortoises."

"From what I can see—"

"Oh, let meee doooown," he said impatiently. "Let meee see . . ."

Holding him to my chest, I scrambled down the steep slope to level ground, Growch beside me. I stood and looked about me for Basher's specifications. The sea was about three miles distant and there was no sign of human habitation. The soil was sandyish, rocky, there was the sound of a stream off to the right and there were both pines and heather in abundance. Gorse, broom, wild garlic, oleander, fan palms, Creeping Jesus, the huge leaves of asphodel, thyme and rosemary—"Looks all right," I said cautiously. "But I can't see any other tortoises."

"I can!" helped Growch, who had christened every bush in sight and was now foraging farther down. "There's more movin' rocks down here: 'ow the 'ell do you tell if'n they're male or female? Looks all the effin' same to me. . . ."

"Females larger, flat shells underneath," said Basher succinctly. "Males undershells curved concave. Makes sense. Think about it . . ."

But I was about to get a demonstration. Growch came panting back. "Two females down there. Tell you what, don't like bein' up-ended! Cursin' like 'Ell, they is!"

By the time we got there they had righted themselves again, their pale brown patched shells disappearing into the undergrowth at speed. I put Basher down and immediately he was off, pausing only to eye the disappearing females with an experienced eye and turn in scurrying pursuit of the larger. A moment later there was a resonant tap-tapping noise, a pause, then a sort of triumphant mewing. Cats? No, just a tortoise enjoying himself; as I came nearer I could see him reared up at the back of the female, his mouth open on pointed pink tongue. "M-e-e-w! Oh, what bliss! How I've missed thiiiis! Hey—"

With several violent jerks from side to side, the female disengaged herself and charged off once again, Basher in pursuit. Then once again the tap-tapping, pause, and "M-e-w! Bliss . . ."

"Basher! Are you all right?"

"Couldn't be better! Thanks for eeeeverything . . ."

"Basher, wait . . ." There was something wrong, something about him, about the female . . . Oh, God! They were a different species! He was black and gold with a shell that frilled out at the back, they were pale brown shaped in a perfect hump. . . . I ran after him. "Wait! They're a different species! Come back, and we'll go on further. . . ."

"No fear!" His voice was rapidly diminishing. "This'll do me. Color isn't everything. . . . Their parts are in the right place!" Tap-tap. "This is far better than freezing to death! May you all find what you seeeeek. . . ."

When I rejoined the others, my heart heavy, Gill was listening, his ears cocked. "That tapping noise: reminds me of the cobbler mending my boots. . . . Is he all right?"

"Yes," I said. "He has—what he wants." What he thinks he wants, I added to myself. But there would be no eggs to hatch into little black and gold tortoises: his would be sterile couplings. Why couldn't he have waited till we found the right place? And yet, like Traveler, he seemed to be content with a substitute, and they had both said it was better than being dead. . . .

Were none of us to find what we really sought, I wondered?

"Half a loaf is better than none," said the Wimperling unexpectedly. "Especially when you're hungry."

"Talkin' of bein' hungry," said Growch: "Ain't we stoppin' for lunch today?"

Chapter Twenty-Two

We had come as far south as we could, without crossing into another country. As one accommodating monk explained when next we sought food and lodging (overnight stay in the guesthouse, sleeping on straw; stew and ale for supper, bread and ale for breakfast and please leave a donation, however small), our country was a rough square, bounded to the northeast by one kingdom, the southeast by another and the south by a third. The other boundaries were sea, but there was still a lot of the square to explore. He drew everything in the dirt with a stick so I could understand.

Because he was a monk I told him a bit more of the truth than I had anyone else, and once he understood I was looking for Gill's home he worked out roughly for me the way we had come, like the right-hand side of a tall triangle. He suggested that I travel along the ways that led from east to west till I came to the sea, then either complete the triangle by going northeast, or bisect it by going straight up the middle.

That seemed good advice, but there was not only Gill to consider. The Wimperling contemplated for a moment, then said he had felt no tuggings of place so far, and was content to continue as I suggested. Growch scratched a lot—warmer weather—and said that as long as there was food and company he wasn't bothered. But it was Mistral who was keenest on the idea. She said that the distance south seemed about right, and if there was a real sea to the west of us, that would be right too.

Not having told Gill about consulting the others, of course, he was happy enough to fall in with the idea, so we walked the many miles west during those spring days in a sort of dreamy vacuum. Mistral became more and more convinced we were heading in the right direction and I knew I wasn't about to lose Gill, for he had suddenly recalled that he couldn't see any mountains from his home—which was comforting to me, as we were leaving the highest ones I had ever seen to our left as we traveled. The range seemed endless, rearing purple, snow-fanged tips so high that the sun hid his face early behind them, the shadows stretching cold in our path.

But even the biggest mountains come to an end, and gradually they sank away the farther west we traveled. By now we looked like a band of gypsies, brown and weatherbeaten, our clothes comfortably ragged, although I tried to keep Gill as smart as possible by trimming his hair and beard regularly, and I kept my hair in its plaits. Mistral was shedding her winter coat, and I could have stuffed a mattress with the brown hair that came out in handfuls when I tried to brush her. Growch evaded all attempts to wash, brush or trim anything.

But it was the Wimperling that was changing faster than anyone else—so much so that his name seemed too childish to fit the long-as-me-and-growing-longer animal that trotted away the miles beside us. He was taller, too, near up to my waist, and his knobs and protuberances were growing more pronounced as well. The claws on his hooves were real claws, the tip of his tail more like a spade than ever and his wings were bigger as well.

He was shy of showing them off, preferring to flex them behind a tree or large rock or in a dell, but I saw them once or twice. They resembled bat's wings more than anything else, but they were proper wings, not extended hands and fingers like the night-flyers. I began to feel embarrassed in villages or with our fellow travelers, for fear they would think him some sort of monster and stone him to death, but for some peculiar reason they seemed to see him as just another rather largish pig: they even looked at him as if he were much smaller, their eyes seeming to span him from halfway down and halfway across. It was most peculiar, but the Wimperling merely said: "They see what they expect to see. . . ."

"But why don't I see you like that?"

"You wear the Ring." And quiet it was now, almost transparent, with tiny flecks of gold in its depths.

As he had no objection, every now and again the pig gave a simple performance in a village square, to augment our dwindling moneys—nothing fancy, just a bit of tapping out numbers, no flying, and Gill and I would sometimes literally sing for our suppers.

Growch disappeared a couple of times—I caught a glimpse of him once on the skyline at the very tail end of a procession of dogs (five hounds, two terriers, three other mongrels), following some bitch in season, but he had little success, I gathered, spending more time fighting for a place in the queue than actually performing. Being so small, he was a master of infighting, but he would have needed a pair of steps to most of the females he coveted. He remembered with nostalgia the two little bitches with plumed tails he had successfully seduced way back.

"Don't make them like that round here. Some day, p'raps . . ."

I hoped so. Fervently. Then perhaps we would all get some peace.

The terrain became flatter, more wooded, and every day I peered ahead to try for my first glimpse of the sea. Now and again I thought I caught a teasing reminder of that evocative sea smell, and Mistral was forever throwing up her head and snuffing the breeze. Now she had shed her winter coat she was a different creature. Her coat was creamy white, her mane and tail long and flowing, and the sharp bones of haunch and rib were now covered with flesh. Her step was jauntier, her chest deeper, her head held high and proud; she was no longer just a beast of burden, and sometimes in the mornings when I loaded her up I felt a little guilty, as though I were asking a lady to do the tasks of a servant.

At last one morning she sniffed the air for a full five minutes, and she was trembling. "It is here," she said. "Over the next ridge, you will see . . ."

And there, glittering in the morning light, some five miles or so distant across flat, marshy land, was her ocean.

"You are sure?"

"I am certain. This is the place. This is where I came from."

I looked more carefully and there, sure enough, some two miles away, were other horses, mostly white, some with half-grown brown colts, grazing almost belly-deep in grass. Perhaps because we were not as high as when we had seen Basher's Great Water, this sea seemed different: steely, clear, sharp against the horizon. And the smell was subtly different, too; colder and saltier.

"Right," I said, my heart strangely heavy. "Let's go and find your people, Princess." And taking Gill's hand I followed the sure-footed Mistral towards the shore. As we drew nearer the sands, I could see that the grassy stretches I had taken for meadows were in fact only wide strips of green, full also of daisies, dent-de-lions, buttercups and sedge, bisected by narrow channels of water, so that the ground was sometimes treacherous underfoot and we had to take a circuitous path.

Growch took a flying leap into the first channel we came to, after what looked like a bank vole, which disappeared long before we hit the water, and we had to spend the next five minutes or so fishing him out, as the banks were too high for a scramble. When he finally landed he was soaking wet and, choking and hawking and spitting, he managed to let us know that the water was: "salty as dried 'erring, and twice as nasty!"

Now we were in a marshy bit—it didn't seem to bother Mistral, and for the first time I noted that her hooves were wider than usual in a horse—and Gill and I took off our shoes and boots, squelching with every step. The Wimperling and Growch were even worse off, and when the horse noticed our difficulty she led us off to the right and firmer ground, through a thicket of bamboo twice as tall as Gill.

At last we emerged on a firm stretch of sand and there in front of us was the sea, stretching on right and left as far as the eye could see. From here I could see whitecapped waves that looked like the fancy smocking on a shirt, but moving towards us all the time, like never-ending sewing. A cool breeze lifted the hair from my hot forehead and flared Mistral's tail and mane.

I lifted the packs from her back, undid the straps and took off the bridle, laying them down on the sand. Strange: I had never thought how we were to manage our burdens when she was gone; share them out, I supposed now. I looked at the pile with growing dismay—we had taken her bearing of our goods so much for granted.

"There you are," I said. "You're free now. . . ."

In a moment she was flying across the ribbed sand away from us and towards the foam-fringed edges of the sea, then turning and galloping along the shoreline, her hooves sending up great gouts of water until she was soaked and streaming. Then she came thundering back and wheeled round us, her hooves whitening the sand as they drove out the water, the prints hesitating before they darkened again into hoof-shaped pools.

"This is wonderful," she neighed. "It's been so long, so long. . . . And now I'm free, free, free!" and away she galloped again, until she was only a speck on the horizon.

I sighed. Was that the last we would see of her?

"Let's walk down to the sea," I said to the others. "I have a fancy to paddle. And I want to taste it, too. I've never done either."

It was farther than I thought, nearer a mile than a half, but the long walk was worth it once I got there, for it entranced all my senses. The regular shush, shush, shush as the waves broke on the shore like a slow-beating heart, the faraway scream of a sea bird; the limitless horizon seeming to curve down at either side as if the world were round; the unutterably strange and pleasurable feeling of walking along the water's edge, the yielding sand spurting up between my toes, the sharp taste of salt on my tongue, the smell of water and mud and weed . . .

I stepped into the water and it lapped around my ankles like the warm tongue of a calf or pup. I had been so certain it would be cold that I threw away all caution and kilted up my skirt till my behind was bare and waded further in, until the water was round my knees, up to my thighs. I lifted my skirts higher, and now it was round my waist, but also noticeably colder, too.

Suddenly I began to feel the power of the sea. What at first had been a gentle push against my knees, my thighs, now became a more insistent thrust against the whole of my body. At first the sensation was pleasurable, then a stronger wave actually lifted me from my feet, knocked me off balance, and I tipped back into the water.

Help! I was drowning! There was a roaring in my ears, my hair was floating round my face, I swallowed a mouthful of water, I couldn't breathe, I didn't know which way was up. Desperately I flailed with my arms, paddled with my legs and, perhaps five seconds later, though it felt like forever, I was once more standing upright. I coughed and choked, dribble running from my mouth and nose, my eyes stinging, my ears still bubbling and popping.

As soon as I had pulled myself together I turned to wade back to the others—but they were miles away! Surely they had been nearer than that? Now I could see Gill waving, apparently calling my name, saw Growch shaking with barks, the Wimperling running up and down the shoreline anxiously, but I could hear nothing for the freshening breeze, which was whistling in my ears and making the waves angry, so that they swished past me with foam on their tips.

I set off towards the others as fast as I could, but I was now hampered with the drag of wet clothes, and fast as I tried to go the sea seemed to beat me, and I could see the others retreating even as I watched. The water was definitely pushing hard at me now, even when I was only thigh and knee deep, and twice I nearly stumbled and fell, but at last it was only round my calves, and I thought I was safe. But then came another hazard; as I reached the shoreline the waves no longer pushed, they pulled, scooping back from where they broke and drawing the sand with them so that I almost lost my feet again.

At last I stood on firm sand, chilled to the bone and shivering violently.

Gill groped towards the sound of my heavy breathing. "Are you all right? You were gone such a long time. . . ."

"Look just like a drowned rat," said Growch, with relish.

"I can't swim," said the Wimperling, "else I would have come in after you. Come on, we'd better get going: the tide's coming in fast."

"What's that?" I asked, wringing the water from my hair and skirt as best I could.

"The very thing that means you were on dry sand a moment ago and now are standing in water again," he said, retreating as the water washed over his hooves. "Twice a day the sea comes in, twice a day it goes out. That is a tide. Hurry, there's a way to go till we're safe."

We set off at a brisk walk, the sun and breeze soon drying my exposed skin, though my bodice was damp and my skirt flapped in dismal, wet folds, irritating skin already chapped by salt and sand. The latter had even got between my teeth, making them grind unpleasantly together.

The Wimperling was right: the tide was coming in very fast, and the haven of the fields ahead was still a long way away. We trudged on through sand that seemed to drag at our feet like mud, till my legs were aching and Growch was whimpering away to himself, lifting his feet more and more reluctantly. At last I picked him up and tucked him under my arm, only to have him grumble about my wet clothes.

"Shut up, or I'll put you down!" I threatened. Turning round I glanced back at the sea, to comfort myself that it was at least as far behind us as the fields were ahead, meaning we had come at least half way. To my horror the creeping water was only some twenty yards behind us, creaming forward inexorably like a brown flood. Surely we had not stood still? Even as I watched the next wave spread within a few yards of us. The tide . . .

"Run!" I yelled. "Run!" and I grabbed Gill with my free hand. As we stumbled along I saw we were at last keeping pace with the sea, it was no longer gaining on us, thank God! But now, on either side of us I could see arms of water creeping to surround us; with relief I realized the fields were much nearer, I could see the shrubs tossing in the wind, the heap of our belongings. . . . I slackened speed nearly there.

The Wimperling and Growch had galloped ahead as Gill and I caught our breath, but now I saw them come to a sudden stop, Growch running from side to side and barking hysterically. I pulled Gill forward again and my heart gave a sudden lurch of fear: ahead of us, cutting us off from safety, a swirling mass of water frothed and bubbled and roiled, growing wider and deeper by the second. To either side the arms of water encircled us and behind the tide raced to catch us up.

We were trapped!

Chapter Twenty-Three

I was riveted with fear and panic, terrified of coming into contact with that suffocating water again.

"Gill, we're cut off by the tide: can you swim?" I was unable to keep the panic from my voice.

He shook his head. "I don't think so. . . . Is it that bad?"

"Yes, and getting worse every minute!" I glanced back: the water was flooding towards us, and now we had to retreat a step or two from the flood in front as it bubbled and frothed. Without being asked Growch and the Wimperling dashed off in different directions to see if there was any escape to left or right, but returned within a few moments to report we were entirely cut off.

Now we were marooned on a strip of sand some hundred yards long and twenty wide, and it was getting smaller by the second.

"We shall have to try and wade across," I said firmly, twisting the ring on my finger to give me courage: strangely enough it was not emitting any warning signals; a little bit warmer than usual, with a light throbbing, that was all. We must be all right: we *would* be all right, please God! "The water can't be all that deep. Dogs can swim, Growch, so you'll be all right. Now's the time to find if you can paddle as well as you can fly, pig dear." I tried to smile, but it was difficult. "Right, Gill: keep tight hold. Off we go!"

The animals plunged in ahead of us gamely enough, Growch's legs going like a centipede, but the swirling currents were making a nonsense of him swimming in anything but circles, until I saw the Wimperling, who had floundered a couple of times, suddenly spread his wings and float like a raft. He came up alongside the dog, who grabbed his tail in its teeth and then they headed in the right direction.

I pulled Gill into the water, but as soon I did so I knew we had no chance. The water deepened after less than a couple of steps and the swirling water clutched at our legs, so that we had to lean sideways as if in a great subterranean wind. We couldn't swim and we couldn't float, and as soon as we took another step we were immersed up to our shoulders, our legs flailing helplessly in the water. I lost hold of Gill and we were swept apart, choking and gasping. I grasped his tunic and we were swept together again and somehow we managed to scramble back to our "island" again, now half its size.

I clutched the ring on my finger, shaking so hard it nearly slipped from my fingers. "Help us, please help us. . . ."

Across the widening stretch of water I saw the dog and the pig struggle out of the water and flop down on the sand, completely exhausted. Thank God, they at least were safe. Gill was muttering a prayer, but prayers were a last resort: surely there must be something we could *do*? If only there was something we could cling to and paddle across, if only the tide would suddenly turn—

I gazed around wildly, and suddenly saw what seemed like an apparition racing through the water towards us from our left, throwing up great clouds of spray as it came.

"Mistral! Gill, it's all right, it's all right! Mistral's coming!"

She arrived with a snort and a skid of hooves, her body flowing with water.

"I heard your call. . . ." The ring on my finger gave a sudden throb. "I should have warned you about the tides. Quick, follow me: it's shallower this way." She led us at a trot to a place where the water was wider, but I could see none of the eddies and swirls of deep currents. "It will only be a short swim this way; wade out as far as you can, one on either side of me, and then hold fast to my mane when I tell you." I told Gill what we were going to do, guided his hand to her neck, and after that it was easy, taking only a few minutes to cross what had once seemed impossible, her warmth and steadiness against me giving me back all my confidence, so that once we were safe I flung my arms about her neck and gave her a big hug.

"Thanks, Princess Mistral, thanks a million times!" Once the word "princess" applied to the tatty, broken-down horse I had first known was nothing more than a joke, but now it was nothing more or less than the truth. She was utterly changed from the swaybacked skinny creature who had trudged the roads with us, head down: now she was white as the foam of the sea, sleek as the waves; her eyes were bright, her neck arched, her long mane and tail like curtains of mist. "You are so beautiful now. . . ."

"Thanks to you."

"I did nothing. . . ."

"You rescued me, healed my hurts, fed me, talked to me and burdened me but lightly. I am grateful to you. And now . . ."

"And now you must go and join your kin. We shall miss you." I had seen out of the corner of my eye a mixed herd of horses, colts and foals, led by a great white stallion, moving across the fields to the reeds and shallows. She neighed once and the stallion flung up his head. She turned to me. "Make for that clump of trees; keep to the higher ground. You will be safe now. Remember me: and may you all find what you seek!" And she was gone, cantering up to the other horses and wheeling into the middle of the herd.

She was full-grown now, but I saw with a stab of pity how much smaller she was than the other mares. Her hard life had stunted her growth. Would the great stallion consider mating with one so undersized? Could she carry a foal to full term and deliver it successfully? To me she was the most beautiful of all those beautiful horses, but would they see it that way?

My eyes filled with tears. It was the tortoise and the pigeon repeated again. Why could not their lives be as perfect as they deserved? One robbed of his home and forced to fight a wilder existence, another living in the wrong place, and now one handicapped among her peers by the life she had been forced to lead. If these were to be the precedents, then what in the world would happen to Growch, the Wimperling, Gill and me?

"We keep thirty horses in the stables," said Gill suddenly. "My stallion is called Fleetfoot, but I take Dainty when I go falconing. My tiercel kills rooks and we . . ." He trailed off. "I forget. . . ."

I opened my mouth but was interrupted by Growch's salt-roughened bark. "Better get 'ere quick! The blankets is soaked and yer pots and pans is floating out to sea. . . ."

Midsummer's Day, and we were no nearer finding Gill's home. Yet there seemed no hurry. Deceived by a summer dreaminess we drifted down tiny lanes and dusty highways, the former further drowsing us with the honey-sweet scent of hawthorn and showering us in the pale petals of the hedge rose, the latter a patchwork of blinding white road and the black shadow of forest.

Everywhere color brightened the eye; scarlet poppies shaking out their crumpled petals, gold-hearted daisy and camomile, creamy elder and sweet cecily, sky-blue lungwort, vinca and chicory, pink mallow and bindweed, white asphodel, purple vetches. And all the greens in the world: willow, beech, oak, ash, pine, fir, reed, duckweed, grass, ground elder, horsetail, clover, moss, nettle, sorrel, ivy, bracken—grey-green, red-green, blue-green, yellow-green, shock-green and baby green: both a stimulus and a soothing to the eyes. There was color, too, in the myriads of butterflies, in the dragon- and damselflies and even in the barbaric stripes of wasp and hornet.

The spring shrillness of the birds had abated somewhat; at one end of their scales was the brisk morning chirping of sparrows scavenging hay and straw for seeds and the faraway bubble of ascending larks; in the middle, hot afternoons held the sleepy croon of wood pigeons and the evening sky rang with the high scream of swifts scything the sky. We passed lakes and ponds where frogs barked like terriers and sudden splashes marked the recklessness of mating fish; whirring grasshoppers sprang from beneath our feet, bees and hummingbird hawk moths droned like bagpipes, cicadas sawed away incessantly and great June Dugs racketed clumsily by.

We were surrounded, too, by the particular scents of summer; not just the dried dung and dust of the highways, the pungent smells of grass and leaves after rain, the thin, evocative perfume of wildflowers, but sudden surprises: a pinch of fresh mint, crush of thyme and rosemary underfoot, warm river water, salty smells of fresh sweat, the clean smell of drying linen, the oily smell of resin from fresh-cut logs stacked to dry for winter and the gentle, fading scent of drying hay.

Different tastes, too. Salads instead of stew, fresh meat instead of salted, plenty of eggs and milk, newly brewed ale. Fish and eel and shellfish from the rivers, butter and cheese so light they had practically no taste at all. A deal of vegetables I could collect myself from the fields and woods: hop tips, ground elder, duckweed, dent-de-lion, nettle, wood sorrel, broom buds, ash keys, young bracken fronds and the leaves of wild strawberry and violet. Chopped up with a little oil and salt and eaten with a hunk of cheese and fresh rye bread it made a feast.

Not that we were short of food. If there was a fair, a saint's day or a local fiesta, out would come my pipe and tabor and Gill would sing, Growch would "dance for the lady," answer yes or no and "die for his country." My instructions to him were simple enough; the "dance" consisted of him chasing his tail, yes and no barking once or twice, nodding or shaking his head—"bend your head down as if you had fleas under your chin, shake your head as if you had mites in your ears—you haven't, have you?"—and dying was merely lying down and pretending to go to sleep. But he had a short attention span, and if we really wanted to bring in more than a few coppers then the Wimperling would do some of his tricks.

He was still growing—which was just as well, for he was needed to share with Gill and me the carrying of our bundles—but still people saw him as smaller than he was: in fact one traveler accused us of overloading him! But he was looking at a pig he expected to see, as the Wimperling reminded me, not the giant he had become.

June became a warm, thundery July. Once I had decided that Gill's home must lie farther north—for he had not recognized many of the plants I had described to him, nor the terrain this far south—I led them first east northeast then west northwest as best my judgment and the countryside would allow, trying to cover both the left-hand side of the triangle the monk had described and the bisection of the whole at one and the same time.

Gill was recalling more and more as the days went by; little inconsequential things for the most part, like a favorite tapestry; the pool where they bred carp for the table, the time he was scraped by a boar's tusk—sure enough, there was a crescent scar on his thigh. Once or twice he did remember facts relevant to our search. I already knew there were no mountains, I realized that if he went falconing for rooks his home was probably surrounded by fields of grain crops and there must be woodland or forest for both the birds and wild boar; now he talked of the Great Forest half a day's ride across the plain where once the king had hunted. Which king? He shook his head. He also spoke of the wide and lazy river that curved round the estate, but again a name meant nothing.

So we were looking for a province of plains, rivers and forests, and as he never spoke of the sea we didn't travel too far west and kept the mountains to a distance. I continued to question people we met and showed them the sketch I had made of Gill's escutcheon, also the scrap of silk I had kept, but they all shrugged their shoulders and shook their heads.

The breakthrough, when it came, was entirely unexpected.

We had lodged on the outskirts of a largish town overnight, on the promise of celebrations for St. Swithin on the following day. There was to be a fair in the marketplace and dancing in the church yard, plus the usual roasts. I groomed both Growch and the Wimperling thoroughly, a ribbon round the neck of one, the tail of the other. The skies remained clear and as long as the prayers at Mass that morning were efficacious, it would remain that way until harvest, so the superstition went.

We did well in the marketplace, for folk were happy at the prospect of a good harvest, and wished to relax and enjoy themselves. There were other attractions of course, but a counting pig was still a novelty, and I collected enough coins that afternoon and early evening to keep us going for a week or two.

As it grew dusk, great torches were stuck in the ground and lanterns hung from the branches of the trees, and the people gathered to dance away an hour or so as the lamb carcasses turned slowly on the spits set in a corner of the square. A traveling band—bagpipes, two shawm, a fiddle, trumpet, pipe and tabor and a girl singer with a tambourine—performed for the dancers. Round followed reel and back again, until the dust was soon rising from the ground with the pounding and stamping of feet, jumps and twirls. When they paused for breath jugs of ale were brought out from the nearest tavern, and enterprising bakers sent their assistants round with trays of pies and sweetmeats.

As Gill couldn't see to dance I had not joined in, though my feet were tapping impatiently to the music. During one of the intervals I brought out the Wimperling again for a few more coins, then went and joined the line for slices of roast lamb and bread. Afterwards we sat for a while longer, watching and listening. As the evening wore on and it became quite dark, one by one the dancers dropped out, exhausted; couples snuggled up to one another in the shadows, children fell asleep in their parents' laps, babies were suckled, dogs snapped and snarled over the scraps, the church bells sounded for nine o'clock and some went in to pray. Somewhere a nightingale provided a soft background for the girl with the tambourine to sing simple, sad songs of love, of longing, of childhood.

She sang without other accompaniment than her tambourine, just an occasional tap or shake to emphasize a word, a phrase. She sang as if to herself and to listen seemed almost like eavesdropping. It was so soothing that I found myself nodding off, and was just about to gather us all together and find our lodgings, when Gill suddenly gave a great start as though he had been bitten.

"That song . . . !"

Song? A sentimental song of swallows, eternal summer, of home. One I had never heard before, with a plaintive descending refrain.

"What about it?"

But he wasn't listening to me, and when she started on the second verse, to my amazement he joined in, at first hesitantly, as though he had difficulty remembering the words, then more confidently. At first they sang in unison, then he took the harmony in the last verse.

> "*The sun is warm, the wind is soft,*
> *O'er wood and plain, house and croft;*
> *I long to wake again at dawn,*
> *In the land where I was born. . . .*"

Gill looked as though he had awakened from a dream and to my embarrassment I saw that tears were pouring down his cheeks. He rose to his feet.

"The singer . . . Take me to her!"

But she had come over to us. "Congratulations, stranger: you sing well. But where did you learn that song?" Close to she was no girl. The paint on her cheeks, eyes and mouth had disguised at a flattering torchlit distance that she must be at least thirty. "I had thought no one outside my own province knew it. Do you come from there?"

Gill stretched out his hand to her, and it was shaking. Quickly I explained his condition and that we sought his home, and this was the first real clue we had had.

"Tell me, are there great plains, a big river, forests, much grain growing?" I was trying to remember all Gill had recalled.

"Assuredly the land is flat. There are cattle, many fields of grain, great orchards—"

"Apples," said Gill. "And plum and cherry."

She glanced at him. "You are right. And there are wide rivers, and forests stretching as far as the eye can see. Can you not remember your name, now?"

He shook his head. "But I know that is where I come from," and his voice was strong with a confidence I had never heard in him before. "My nurse taught me that song when I was scarce out of the cradle." He turned to me. "That is the way we must go, don't you see? Oh, Summer, take me there, take me there!" And now his tears were spilling down onto the skin of my arm, warm as summer rain.

"Of course we will!" I turned to the singer. "Thank you so much, you don't know how much this means! We have been searching for nine months, so far. . . . Here, do you recognize this emblem?" and I pulled the scrap of silk from my purse.

She peered at it, listened to what else I could recall of it, but shook her head regretfully. "No, but it is a large country. I come from the southeast, but your—your friend may well live to the north and west. But you can ask again when you get there."

"How far away is it?" asked Gill eagerly. "How long will it take us?"

She shook her head again. "Straight, I do not know. Many days. You will have to ask my husband. We travel as the will and the weather take us, following as best we can fairs and feast days, the larger towns." She turned and beckoned, and the short, dark man who had been playing the fiddle joined us.

Once she had explained he, too, shook his head. "It lies to the northwest of here, but I can give you no direct route. If you head that way, and take the better roads, it might take a month, perhaps two. It depends on the roads, the weather, your pace, as you must know. If you are lucky, you will reach there in time for harvest—"

"The best time of the year," murmured Gill. "Great feasts, hunting songs, dancing . . . We must start at dawn."

"Yes, yes, of course," I said. "But now we must sleep. In this weather it's better to travel early and late and rest at midday—"

"But not for long! I could walk a hundred miles without rest if I knew home was at the end of it!" Gone was the often sad, sometimes complaining man I had known: here was an impatient young man with hope in his face, as eager for tomorrow as any eighteen-year-old.

The singer and her husband wished us luck, and I emptied the day's takings into her hand. "Pray that this time we were heading in the right direction. . . ."

Gill fell asleep as soon as he lay down in the straw of the stable we occupied that night; all the way back he had been humming the song that had awakened his memory, but I could not sleep. I tossed and turned restlessly. Outside a full moon shone through the gaps in the planking of the walls, its pale light seeming to touch my closed lids whichever way I turned on the rustling straw. I told myself I was relieved we knew the way at last, how happy I was for Gill; in a month, two at most, he would be restored to his family, and my responsibility towards him would end. Then I would be free to pursue my original objective and find a safe, respectable husband and a comfortable home.

And at that happy prospect, I cried myself to sleep.

Chapter Twenty-Four

It took us exactly six weeks.

We departed at dawn on the day after St. Swithin's and arrived on the feast day of Saints Cosmos and Damien. It was a long, hard trek, with a hotter August and early September than I could remember. At home with Mama, of course, I was not exposed to the merciless heat of an open road; I had been able to take my ease under the trees in the forest, once my chores were done, and perhaps cool my feet in the river. Even at night we sometimes slept with the door open, the goat tethered nearby to challenge any intruder and give us time to bolt the door.

But now I was walking all day—at least the hours between dawn and two in the afternoon, and then again for a couple of hours in the evenings. Often there were no trees to shade our path, no streams or rivers to cool our feet or to bathe in. In fact water became scarcer the farther we traveled, and often they had none to spare in the villages we passed through. I bought another flask and filled it when I could, sometimes walking a good way cross-country to find a river, after spying out the land to find the telltale signs of willow, shrub and reed which marked its course.

I think the flies were the biggest nuisance. Somehow they always managed to find us, great tickling, annoying things, alighting on any part of our exposed bodies to suck the salty moisture from our skins. They buzzed, they clustered, they crawled; other insects, midges, mosquitos, horseflies and wasps stung also, and unless one flailed ones arms like a windmill all day long, or waved a switch cut from the hedgerows, one was irritated to say the least and, more usually, infuriated and exhausted by nightfall, for they wouldn't even let us alone during the afternoon rest.

No food could be left uncovered for more than a moment because it was immediately attacked. I had never particularly disliked any insect before, except perhaps for the ugly black cockroaches that scuttled and tapped around fireplaces at night, but now I had a personal vendetta against any fly, wasp, hornet, midge, mosquito, horsefly or ant in the country. Gill was not as badly affected as I was—perhaps he didn't taste as good—and Growch's thick coat protected most of him, although he was regularly infested with sheep ticks, which were as difficult to dislodge as body lice.

Strangely enough, they all left the Wimperling well alone.

All around us the country was getting ready for harvest. In the south the grapes were swelling and coloring, often on land that looked too arid to support anything, and we passed olive and orange trees that looked ready for picking, but as we headed north it was the grain that caught the eye and the orchards of apple and espaliered pears that promised delights to come. It was a bounteous time in the woods and wayside, too, and many a skirt of raspberries and blackberries I gathered. Hips, haws and hazelnuts had a month or so to go, but the autumn mushrooms and fungi were coming to their best.

The drought dried many of the ponds and streams that would have provided fish, and sheep and cattle were being fattened for the winter salting, poultry were wilting in the heat and there was little milk, but we managed, though I could feel the lighter clothes I wore were hanging looser by the day, and Gill and Growch looked leaner and fitter. Not so the Wimperling.

He still appeared to eat anything and everything with gusto and to my eyes was bigger than a small pony and no longer as pig-like as before, though it was difficult to say exactly what he did resemble. One day I took a piece of the rope we used for tying our bundles and surreptitiously measured him as he lay snoozing. From stem to stern he was as long as Gill was tall, and, if my calculations were right, near as much around the middle.

"No, you're not imagining things," he said, opening one eye. "I'm growing. A lot of it is the wings, though."

I was so startled I dropped the piece of rope. "Wings?"

"Round the middle. Look." And he rose to his hooves and slowly, lazily, extended his left wing. What I had taken for fat was in fact a combination of the wing itself and the disguising pouch he hid it under, grown larger with its contents. The wing itself now extended some five feet away from his body, a warm, living extension of himself, lifting in the slight breeze of evening. "See?"

"I still don't understand how everyone else sees you as small," I said helplessly, more shocked by the revelation than I cared to say. "When—when will you stop growing?"

"I told you: people see what they expect, and to help that I think pig." He didn't answer the second question, I noticed. Perhaps he didn't know.

This was a silly conversation, and I decided to be silly, too. "So if I wanted people to believe me beautiful, all I would have to do was think it?"

"Matthew the merchant thought you were beautiful. . . ."

"But I didn't try and make him think so!"

"So perhaps you are anyway."

"Rubbish! My mother always said—"

"You shouldn't believe all she said. Many mothers tell their daughters they are plain in order to steal their beauty for themselves. Think yourself ugly and unattractive and you will be."

"My mother wouldn't have done a thing like that!" Would she? No, of course she wouldn't. That would have been cruel. Besides I must have been ugly: I was never considered as her replacement when she died. Then had I thought myself ugly, as he was suggesting? No, I remembered my reflection in the river: fat, double-treble-chinned, mouthless, eye-less, disgusting. "Anyway, I'm fat, gross, obese." These at least were true.

"Was."

"Was what?"

"Fat. Didn't you boast once to your knight about how well you were fed by your imaginary family?" How did he know I hadn't been telling the truth? "You said your mother fed you with all the greatest delicacies; it sounded more like force-feeding, and you were the Michaelmas goose. That was another way to make you less attractive than she was. No competition."

"Nonsense! She wouldn't have done a thing like that! It would be wicked!" Why, she had loved me so much she had had me educated for the best in the land, and could not then bear for me to leave her to seek a husband!

Apparently the Wimperling could read my mind. "Most men don't choose their spouses for their education. A pretty face goes further than being able to construe Latin. Child-bearing hips and a still tongue go even farther. And a dowry, of course . . ."

"I have that!" I said, stung with anger. "My father left it for me."

"All of it? Or was some of it gone? And did your mother show you it?"

"No, but—"

"Exactly. Another five years as her slave and there would have been no dowry left, only a grossly fat woman tied irrevocably to her mother's side, a useless human being who could hold a pen, add two and two, sew a seam, cook a meal—and eat most of it—and who would have had ideas far above her station. When your mother died you would have been released from your bondage only to starve, or become a kitchen slut. You would have been the pig, not I!"

"But she didn't know she was going to die!" I flung back at him. "She—she thought she would live a long, long time, and . . . and . . ."

"I know that, don't get angry. I don't suppose for a moment she realized how selfish she was: she just didn't want to lose you. But she went about it all the wrong way. There are people like that, so scared of losing the ones they love that they cling to them like ivy on a wall, not realizing that you have to let go to retain."

I thought about it: poor Mama, she should have realized I would never leave her. If she had found me a husband I would have been happy for her to live with us, or at least have a house nearby.

"But I'm not like that now," I said, subdued. "Life is very different on the road. . . ."

"Yes, and thank the gods for that! But mostly you have your father and the ring he left you to be grateful for."

"My father? The ring?"

"He bequeathed a ring to the child he would never see, a ring he knew he could no longer wear because he did not deserve it. It probably served him well in earlier years, but his life must have been such that the ring shed itself from his finger. The ring on your finger—diluted by age and wearing—is part of a Unicorn, and as such cannot be worn by anyone undeserving of its protection."

How did he know all this?

Again he seemed to read my mind. "Because your tumbled thoughts spill out into the wind sometimes, and before you have a chance to catch them back I can pattern them in my mind. Better than you, sometimes. Besides, I can sense the power. Unicorns—and witches and warlocks, wizards and dragons, fairies and elves, trolls and ogres—are become unfashionable in this modern world of ours. Yet all are still there, if you look for them or need them, although their power is greatly diminished by man's indifference and disbelief. One day they will disappear altogether, and the world will be a sadder place."

I looked down at the ring on the middle finger of my right hand. A sliver of horn, almost transparent, nearly indistinguishable from the flesh it clung to. And yet it had served me well. How else would I have been able to communicate with the others, the animals? I should have rejected Growch, probably misused Mistral, would not have been able to mend Traveler, never heard Basher in his cold misery. And what of the Wimperling himself? Would he not still be a showman's toy if the ring had not sharpened my pity when I heard his cry for help? Or dead?

One way or another, the ring had given them all another chance: me too.

The farther north we traveled, the more soldiery we came across. Not fighting, just minding their own business: wars were things that happened all the time. Some soldiers were quartered in the villages we went through, and there food was scarce: for whatever king, lord or seigneur they served made it a practice to utilize their subjects to supply their troops. Cheaper than having them loll around the castles idle, and out on the borders they were nearer the action, if and when it came.

Apparently no one had fought any battles for at least three years but rumors were rife of imminent attacks here, there and everywhere and hostilities were expected any time. I began to wonder if we should find Gill's home under siege or razed to the ground, but said nothing of my fears, for each day he grew more and more tense, fuller of longing to see his home again—for he was sure, too, that once back his sight would return also.

"It is a fine place, Summer: not a fortress, more a fortified manor house, as I recall. . . . I seem to remember my nurse's name was Brigitte. I think my mother was as tall as my father, but very thin. . . . We have lots of hounds. I seem to remember a friend called Pierre. I don't think I enjoyed my lessons. . . ." And so on.

I tried to keep him as clean, shaved and smart as I could, just in case we suddenly came across someone who recognized him, for I remembered only too well how magnificently he was dressed and accoutered that never-to-be-forgotten day when he had asked me the way to the High Road. Now I doubted even his mother would recognize him, in spite of my care. I bought a length of linen and made him a tunic that reached mid-calf, as befitted his station, but kept it hidden till the time was right. When the light lingered in the evenings I would take it out, to complete the key pattern I was edging the hem and side slits with, in a blue to match his beautiful, blind eyes. . . .

One August morning, around ten of the clock, we came to a confused halt, we and the dozen or so we were traveling with, for ahead of us the highway, which had broadened out considerably during the last few days, was now blocked by a formidable line of the military. A caravan ahead of us had also been halted, for beasts were already tethered for foraging by the side of the road, carts and wagons were drawn up in orderly rows, their occupants either resting or arguing with the captain of the troops, with much gesticulating and nodding and shaking of heads.

Whatever it was, it obviously meant delay. Seating Gill in the shade, I pushed my way forward, asking first one and then the other the reason for the delay, but got only confused replies. "It's the war. . . . Road ahead is blocked. . . . Plague . . . Robbers and brigands . . ." In the end I approached one of the ordinary soldiers, relieving himself in a ditch some way away from the others, a bored expression on his face. I remembered what the Wimperling had said about thinking oneself into what people expected to see, so I tried to project myself as pretty.

"Excuse me, captain. . . ." He turned, shook off the drops and tucked himself in again. I saw the boredom on his face replaced with interested speculation. Perhaps it was working!

"Yes, missy? How can I help you?" His gambeson was food- and sweat-stained, he hadn't shaved for days, his iron cap was missing and his hose full of holes. Most of his teeth were rotting or gone, and he spoke with a thick, clipped lisp.

I smiled sweetly. "I can make neither head nor tail of what is going on, sir, so bethought me to seek one out who surely would." Mama had taught me how to flatter. "One can tell at a glance those worth talking to." I smiled again. "A man of experience such as yourself must surely know *everything*. . . ."

It worked. He grinned self-consciously, then with a quick look over his shoulder to where his captain was still waving his arms about and shouting, he settled the dagger at his belt and took my arm, drawing me away behind a clump of elder bushes, strutting like the dung-heap cockerel he was.

"Well, look here, pretty missy, it's like this. . . ." The Wimperling had spoke true! He had called me "pretty"! "You knows of course we is at war, has been for as long as I can remember. . . ."

"But there haven't been any battles for years. . . ."

"That don't matter round here. 'Readiness is all,' as the captain says, and we can't afford to relax for a moment." He spat on the ground. "Arrogant bastard! Thinks he knows it all because he fought in a couple of campaigns abroad! Still, no use crossing him. Worth a flogging, that is." He peered at me. "What's a nice-spoken lass like you doing here, anyways?"

But I was ready for that. "Traveling north with my father, a spice merchant," I said quickly, conscious that he had moved closer. "He's over there," and I pointed in the direction of the still-arguing captain. "He's also trying to find out what is going on—but I think I am having a better success! Er . . . I heard somebody say something about a renewal of war?" And that was the last thing we needed, I thought.

"Not exactly, but there have been a couple of skirmishes on the border last few days. Still it puts us on alert, and means the border's closed for a while. Usually it's open twice a day for trade and barter: they likes the wine and fruits from the south, we likes their grain, cider and cheese. Everyone gets searched, 'cos that's enemy territory over there, there's a small toll, and everyone's happy. Not strictly official, mind . . ." He sucked his teeth. "Still, none o' that for a week or so." He looked disconsolate: I could imagine in whose pockets the "tolls" went.

Oh, no! Gill, I was sure, could not bear to be patient for so long now he was near his home. Our money was running out, there'd be little food nearby and as for entertaining, with only the soldier's pay to depend on, we should soon starve.

"Is there no other way across?"

He turned me round to face north, taking the opportunity to put his grimy hands round my waist. My mind shuddered at his touch, my nose wrinkled up at the stinking breath whistling past my left ear, but I kept my body still. He pointed over my shoulder.

"See there, that line o' trees? That's the border between *here,* what belongs to our king, and *there,* what belongs to the king over-water, Steady Eddie, they calls him. Got quite a bit o' land over here: that's what the battles are about. Road across goes through the trees. Left there's thick forest for miles, fifty or so, and their patrols go up and down there day and night." He swiveled me towards the right. "There's the village. T'other side o' that's the river what runs into enemy territory. They got their camp on the banks; we patrols this side, they patrols the other. No way through . . ."

But there had to be: somehow we must cross that border. From the other travelers I had confirmed that what lay ahead was indeed Gill's part of this divided country, so for his sake it was imperative we lingered no longer than was necessary. But how to evade the patrols? Alone, I might have tried to creep through their lines at night, especially with Growch to spy ahead, but a blind man was clumsy at the best of times and the Wimperling's bulk precluded any attempt for the four of us together.

Successfully evading the importunate soldier we ate what little we had left and lazed the day away, but in the evening, to quiet Gill's restlessness, I took him to the tavern in the village for an indifferent stew and a mug or two of thin ale, together with half-a-dozen or so other disconsolate travelers.

And there, in that stuffy, malodorous little ale house, came the answer to our prayers. . . .

Chapter Twenty-Five

"Hullo, Walter! How many this time? A dozen? Good. Welcome to our side, gents—and lady. . . ."

A trap, a stupid, miserable trap! All we had thought of was crossing the border, too eager to question the ease with which our "safe" passage had been procured. If I had had half the sense I credited myself with we should have been suspicious from the start and never joined this sorry enterprise.

Thinking back, Walter the ferryman had been a shifty-looking individual from the start, but his suggestion of slipping through enemy lines on his raft—at a price—had seemed like the answer to a prayer to all of us. He said that if we set off around three in the morning we could drift past the sentries on both sides, and assured us he had done it many times. Twelve of us had paid the silver coin demanded, and rushed back to gather up our belongings. The Wimperling said that nothing in the world would get him on a raft, he would spread his wings and float past, and Growch said that if he couldn't slip past a sentry or two we could chuck him in the river. Next time . . .

The raft nearly tipped twice, although the river was low and sluggish, for most of the other passengers were frightened of the water and didn't heed instructions to keep to the center and be still, but rushed from side to side, imperiling us all. The boatmen poled us out from the bank with a suck and a slurp and a pungent smell of mud, and once all was settled we drifted downstream through the oily water.

There was a quarter moon, few stars and an absence of sound: no wind, no birds. It was warm and still, the heat of the day still lingering in the heavy air. I trailed my fingers in the river: water warm as my skin. The banks on either side seemed deserted.

All at once the sneaky Walter started to pole us in towards the bank—surely we couldn't be beyond the enemy lines yet?—and I could see a makeshift landing stage through the gloom. The raft slapped against the pilings with a jolt that nearly had us all in the water, sudden torches flared, a dozen hands pulled us from the craft and hauled us up on the bank. By the flickering light I could see we were surrounded by soldiers. Different ones.

"Welcome," said their leader again, snickering. "Line 'em up, lads, and let's see what they got. . . ."

They relieved us of our packs and bundles, chuckling and commenting to themselves all the while. "Sorry-lookin' set o' buggers . . . Which pack belongs to the Jew? Pity they don' close the border more often. . . . Got a blind 'un here, with 'is girl. . . ." One of them gave a couple of coins to Walter, our betrayer.

"Bringin' more tomorrow?"

"If'n I can con 'em. Two lots if possible. Twenty-four hours'll make 'em keener. Don' let any o' these slip back to give a warnin'. . . ."

A moment or two later the Jew broke away from the rest of us and fled into the darkness and another of our companions jumped into the river, where he foundered and gasped and was twirled away on the current, flowing faster here, his mouth open on a yell drowned by a gurgle of water. A moment later he was swept out of sight.

They brought the Jew back five minutes later. He was unconscious and had obviously been beaten. He was thrown to the ground and disregarded, while the soldiery enjoyed themselves opening the packs and sharing out the contents, including our blankets, which they declared "a fine weave—good against the winter," and promptly confiscated. Luckily they could find no use for Gill's new tunic, and by the time they had emptied the other pack they were so surfeited with some golden spices, oils and unguents, jewelry, embroidered cloth, carved bone figures, some fine daggers and a silver crucifix that they tossed my pots and pans to one side. They were momentarily puzzled by my precious Boke, ripped off its cover looking for a hiding place, then tossed the loose pages into a bush.

Anyone who protested was beaten quiet. My pens and inks were scattered on the ground but they took what little food we had, chomping noisily on hastily divided cheese. The ten of us who could still stand were then searched. Rings were pulled from fingers (mine went suddenly invisible), brooches unfastened, earrings torn from ears, embroidered clothes ripped from the owner's back, leather boots pulled off. Ours were too tatty to bother with. Luckily Gill and I looked so poor that our search was perfunctory, and they didn't discover the dowry, or the few coins I had left of ordinary money.

Some of our compatriots were weeping and wringing their hands, but I held Gill's hand and preserved a stoical silence. What else could I do? I was worrying about Growch and the Wimperling, but at least we no longer had Mistral, Traveler and Basher with us: I could well imagine what would have happened to them if we did.

Searching and scavenging done, one of the soldiers ran off in the darkness to return a moment or two later with a man on a horse, obviously in command. There followed what was a well-rehearsed interchange between the captain and his troops. I don't think it fooled anyone.

Captain: "What have we here, then?"

Soldiers: (One, two, three or seven, it didn't matter which: sometimes they answered singly, sometimes together, like a ragged chorus. Suffice it to say they all knew their parts off pat.) "Infiltrators, sir! Crossing the border without permission, sir!"

Captain: "Have you examined them and their belongings?"

Soldiers: "Yes, sir!"

Captain: "And?"

Soldiers: "All guilty, sir! Carrying contraband, some of 'em . . ."

Captain: "Let me see the goods."

Here some of our fellow travelers tried to protest, but a stave round the legs, a buffet to the jaw soon silenced them. The captain dismounted and pawed through the heap of spoils, finally selecting the silver crucifix, one of the more ornamental daggers, a ring set with a ruby and the gold coins. "Mmmm . . ." He shook his head. "Obviously stolen goods. I shall have to confiscate these while further enquiries are made." He carried a big enough pouch to hold them all. "Now then, men: what is the punishment for spies and thieves?"

Chorus: "Death!"

I gripped Gill's hand so tightly I could feel my ring biting into flesh. One of the other travelers broke away and flung himself at the captain's knees, scrabbling at his ankles, sobbing pitifully.

"Mercy, kind sir, mercy! I have a wife, three children. . . ."

The captain kicked him away. "So have I, so have the rest of us! You should have thought of that before you entered a war zone." He rubbed his chin. "Mind you . . ."

I think we all took an anxious step forward, for the soldier's voice held a considering tone.

"Mind you . . ." he repeated: "If they were willing to pledge themselves against a little ransom, as an earnest of their repentance, men, I think we might reconsider, don't you?"

Immediately the man still on his knees was joined by three others, all well-dressed, pledging house, money, jewels, coin or livestock as bribes. The four were led aside into the darkness, their faces now expressing a hope none of the remainder could hope to match. The captain gestured at the unconscious Jew. "And him?"

"Caught trying to run off, sir . . ."

"His baggage?"

"Nothing of consequence. Papers mostly, sir." The soldier pointed to a scatter of vellum.

"Cunning bastard; not worth the investigation. Get rid of him!"

To my horror two of the soldiers came forward, picked him up and flung him into the river. A couple of large bubbles broke the surface and that was all.

The captain surveyed the rest of us. "Send the rest of them back: let their own side deal with them." My heart leapt, but I might have known it was just a cruel jest. "No, wait: they can either enlist with us or work as slaves: give them the choice." He turned away to remount but one of the soldiers who had been eyeing me with a leer went over and whispered in his ear.

The captain turned back, beckoned us nearer. "And what have you to say for yourselves?" He addressed himself to me.

I kept my gaze modestly lowered, my voice meek. "My blind brother and I are returning home, sir. We traveled south in a vain attempt to find a cure for him. We live in this province, we are not spies, and we have spent all our money in doctor's bills. We are only here because war does not take account of innocent travelers. . . ."

He stared at me in a calculating manner. "What was in their baggage?"

One of the soldiers indicated the scattered pots and pans, the flasks, odd bits of clothing. "Just these, sir."

"Whereabouts do you come from? What does your father do?"

I had dreaded such questioning. "Our—our father is a carpenter. We were sent—" I twisted the ring on my finger in my agitation and out of nowhere came a name I must have heard somewhere, sometime I could not recall. "We were sent south with the recommendation and blessing of Bishop Sigismund of the Abbey of St. Evroult," I said firmly, and raised my head to look at him straight.

He raised his eyebrows. "I see. . . . Let them continue their journey." He crossed himself. "I have no quarrel with the church." He turned away again, but once more the soldier whispered to him. He turned and looked at me again. "Very well: I am sure she will cooperate. But no rough stuff, mind." And with that he remounted and clattered off into the darkness.

The importunate soldier came over and took my arm, not unkindly. "You come along o' me, you and your brother."

"Our things . . ." I pointed to the pots and pans.

"Well, pack 'em up, then," he said impatiently. "Coupla minutes, no more . . ."

Well within that time I had retrieved everything, even my torn Boke, and tied it into two bundles. The pans were dented, one of the horn mugs was cracked and one of the flask stoppers had disappeared, but at least we were alive. The soldier plucked up one of the torches stuck in the ground and nodded to us to follow, winking at his fellows as he led us off.

"She'll keep till later!" one of them yelled, and suddenly I realized the implication of the captain's words: "I am sure she will cooperate. . . ." and a cold finger of fear and revulsion touched my spine.

He led us to a broken-down hut that must once have housed sheep or goats, for the earthen floor was covered with their coney-like droppings and the place smelled of fusty, damp wool. There was no place to sit so we huddled against a wall, and he took the torch with him so we were left in darkness. As we became more used to our surroundings, however, I could see, through the gaps in the wattle and daub walls and the rents in the reed thatch, a certain lightening outside: false dawn preceding the real one.

I tiptoed over to the flap of skin that served as a door and peeked out. To my right, about ten yards away, two soldiers sat cross-legged by a small fire, playing dice. No escape that way. Coming back into the darkness I felt my way round the wall seeking for a weakness, but apart from a few fist-sized holes there was nothing. If only we had been able to reach the roof, now, there was—

I nearly leapt out of my clothes as something damp and cold touched my bare ankle.

"For 'Eaven's sake! It's only me. . . ."

I knelt down and hugged him, tacky though he was. "Where've you been? Are you all right? Where's the Wimperling?"

"'Ush, now! We're all right. More'n I can say for you . . . Now, listen! I gotta message for you from the pig." And he told me what they planned to do, but when I started to question, he shut me up. "No time to argue: we gotta get goin'. Be light soon," and he slipped out of the door as I felt my way back to Gill and explained, slinging our packs ready as I spoke.

This time he didn't argue about talking to animals but shrugged his shoulders fatalistically. "Just carry on: we couldn't be in a worse position, I suppose."

I felt like saying that it was me, not him, that was liable to be raped, but thought better of it. "It'll be all right, I'm sure: just a couple of minutes more. . . ."

It felt like an eternity, and I kept wiping my hands nervously on my skirt because they were sweating so much, I pulled Gill over to the doorway with a fast-beating heart so that we were ready—ready for the shout that came moments later from over to our left. Peering through a gap in the hide covering I could see a tongue of flame shoot upwards at the fringes of the forest, some quarter-mile away, then heard the drumming of hooves from a couple of panicking horses. The two guards outside leapt to their feet, undecided what to do, but when a second tongue of flame started to run merrily towards the tents of the soldiery and there were more galloping hooves, ours abandoned fire and dice and started running towards the confusion.

Now was our chance. Grabbing Gill's hand I led him, stumbling, out of the hut and to our right, where the river should be. It was much closer than I thought and in fact we nearly fell in, because at the wrong moment I risked a glance behind us, to see a merry blaze had caught the summer-dry grasses at the fringe of the forest and, fanned by the dawn breeze, the flames were creeping towards the encampment. Luckily Gill fell full length as we reached the riverbank, just before we both plunged down the slope into the water, and a moment later Growch appeared to lead us further downstream to where a small rowing boat was tethered in the reeds. Untying the rope I helped Gill aboard, instructed Growch to jump in, and—

"Where's the Wimperling?"

"Right here," grunted a hoarse, cindery voice and he rolled up, panting and covered with smuts. "Don't wait: I'll float. Need to get rid of the smoke . . ."

"You're sure?"

"Just get going! Push off from the bank, keep your heads down and the boat trimmed."

"Trimmed?"

"Both of you in the middle. No looking over the side. The current will carry us away from all this."

It was as he said. I kicked off from the bank and collapsed in an ungraceful heap at Gill's feet, as the boat nudged out into the center and found the current. It seemed my knight had been in boats before, for he told me much the same as the pig: "Sit down in the middle, Summer, hands on both thwarts—" (thwarts? I presumed he meant the sides) "—and don't lean over the side, either. That's it. . . ."

Slowly and surely we gained speed to almost a walking pace. Over to our left fires were still burning, accompanied by shouts and curses, but everyone was too busy to have noticed our defection, and a moment later we swung round a bend in the river, shaded by trees, and the fire and commotion died away behind us. Gill seemed calm and content, but I was still terrified of rocking the boat, and desperately needed to relieve myself. The Wimperling was floating just behind us, so when I told him he gave the boat a nudge out of the current and I scrambled ashore, and thankfully ran behind some bushes, while Growch christened the nearest tree.

"Do we have to go back?" I asked the pig, gesturing towards the boat, where Gill was happily trailing his fingers in the water. "I—I feel safer on land."

"Not safe yet. Besides, we can travel faster by boat."

"We're not going very fast now," I objected.

"We will, just wait and see. Back you go. . . ."

We swung out into the channel again, and I gripped the sides as tight as I could, till my knuckles turned white with the strain. The Wimperling swam up behind us once more.

"Move towards the bow—the *front*—both of you." I told Gill and we both shuffled forward and it was just as well we did, for a moment later the rear of the boat tipped down as the pig hooked his useful claws into the broad bit. I thought for a moment he was going to try and clamber in, but a moment later there was a flapping noise and his wings lifted out of the water and spread until they caught the now freshening breeze behind us, and we were bowling along in a moment at twice the speed, and the banks of the river were fairly whizzing by.

We traveled this way for the rest of the day, with a couple of stops for me to forage for berries, for we had nothing to eat. We saw no one, and I became used to the rocking motion of the boat eventually. The only creatures we disturbed were water fowl, a couple of graceful swans with their grey cygnets and an occasional water vole. At dusk the Wimperling steered us to the bank again.

"There's a village ahead—you can see the smoke. You can find a buyer for the boat. It'll provide you with enough for some days' food."

"Thank the gods for that!" said Growch. "The sides of me stummick is stuck together like broken bellows. . . ."

And the thought of dry land, food, and perhaps a mug or so of ale, rather than the risk of river water, so filled my mind that I quite forgot the question that had been tickling at the back of my mind since our escape: how on earth had the Wimperling managed to light those fires?

No one questioned where we had come from, where we were going, and there were no soldiers. I got a reasonable price for the boat, even without oars, and that night we slept in comparative luxury in a barn attached to the alehouse. It was fish pie for supper with baked apple and cheese, but everything was fresh and tasty. There was no talk of war and battles, only of the approaching harvest. I tried once more to describe Gill's home and showed them the piece of silk, but they shook their heads.

"Further north's best place for grain and orchards. . . ."

My hopes were momentarily dashed, but Gill's enthusiasm was unabated. He declared he could hear in the villager's voices the echo of the patois they used near his home, and the more ale he drank the more details he seemed to remember. Wooden toys, servants, fishing, a boat, a blue silk surcoat, a flood . . . After he had downed his third flagon of ale I tried to dissuade him from more, but he declared petulantly that I was spoiling his evening and was worse than a nursemaid, so I mentally shrugged my shoulders and ordered a fourth.

Halfway through he fell asleep with his head on the trestle table, and I had to enlist the help of a couple of the locals to carry him back to the barn and lay him down on the straw, face down in case he vomited during his sleep. I stayed awake for a while, for sometimes when he had drunk too much he woke and the liquor excited that ache between the loins that all men have, so Mama used to say, and he would toss and turn and groan until his hands had accomplished relief; at times like that I couldn't bear to listen, and would tiptoe away till he had finished.

Tonight, however, everything was quiet and peaceful, so I wriggled myself about till I was comfortable and fell asleep at peace with the world—

To awake in the dark with a hand on my bosom and a voice in my ear.

"My dearest one . . . I've waited so long for this moment! I've been thinking of you night and day. Don't turn me away, I beg you, I implore you! I need you, oh, so much. . . ."

My heart was thumping, my breath caught in my throat with a hiccuping sob, and I reached up in wonderment to hold Gill's head with my hands, ruffling the familiar curly hair with my fingers. I had waited so long for a sign, anything to prove he cared for me, and now my whole body was filled with an aching, melting tenderness, a yielding that left me trembling and helpless. His hand left my breast and slipped beneath my skirt, his hand warm on my thigh, and his seeking mouth found mine in our first kiss. . . .

So that was what it was like to be kissed by the man you loved! A little, distracting voice from somewhere was whispering: "Not yet, not yet! He's drunk too much, you only lose your virginity once. . . ." But if he was drunk, then so was I: drunk with desire for this man I had secretly loved so long.

Already he was fumbling with the ties of his braies and I felt him gently part my thighs.

"My sweet Rosamund, my Rose of the World . . ."

Chapter Twenty-Six

I froze, like a rabbit faced by a stoat. Rosamund? Who the hell was Rosamund? Not me, anyway. But perhaps I had misheard. . . .

I hadn't.

He nuzzled my neck. "I have waited for this so long, my Rosamund of the white skin, the golden hair! At last you are mine. . . ." and he thrust up between my legs, still murmuring her name.

That did it. In a sudden spurt of anger, disappointment and frustration I kneed him as hard as I could then rolled away from beneath him, got to my feet and ran out into the night. He yelled with pain, then groaned, but I didn't look back: I couldn't. My fist stuffed into my mouth to stifle the sobs, I let the stupid tears run down my cheeks like a salty waterfall till my eyes were swollen and my throat felt all closed up.

I didn't know whether I hated him or myself the most.

Hating him was irrational, I knew that in my mind, but my heart and stomach couldn't forgive. He was drunk, and in his dreams had turned to a suddenly recalled love; he had found a female body and mistaken me for her.

But I was worse, I told myself. Without thought I had surrendered to my feelings and immediate emotions, forgetting all Mama had impressed upon me about staying chaste for one's husband, not succumbing to temptation, etc. All I wanted was to indulge myself with a man I had fantasized about for months—husband, future, possible pregnancy, all had been disregarded in the urgency of desire. And if I thought about it for even one moment, I would have realized that it could never lead to anything else once he returned home, for he was a knight and I was nothing. I cursed myself for my stupidity.

But at the back of my mind was something else, something worse: hurt pride. He had preferred his dreams, his memories, his vision, to me. In reality I hadn't even been there. Summer was a companion, his guide, his crutch, his eyes: if he had known it was me he wouldn't have bothered, drunk or no. The tears came so fast now they hadn't time to cool and ran down into my mouth as warm as when they left my eyes. They tasted like the sea.

There was a shuffling and a grunt behind me and the Wimperling lumbered out of the barn and looked up at the lightening sky, sniffing. "Another fine day . . . Did I ever tell you about the story of the pig with one wish?"

"Er . . . No." I couldn't see what he was getting at. Surreptitiously I wiped my eyes on the hem of my skirt. "What—what pig?"

"It was a tale my mother pig used to tell us when we were little. Once there was a pig who had done a magician some service, and in return he was granted one wish. He was a greedy thing, so immediately without thinking he wished that all food he touched would turn into truffles, because that was what he liked most. His wish was granted, and for days he stuffed himself so full he nearly burst. Then as he grew surfeited, he wished once more for plainer fare, and he cursed the day he had wished without thought. . . ."

"And then what happened?" I was interested in spite of my misery.

"Well, first he tried to punish himself by trying to starve to death, but that didn't work, so, because he was basically a kind and caring pig, he decided to turn his misfortune into a treat for others, going around touching other pigs' food so they had the treat of truffles. And it did his sad heart good to see them enjoying themselves. . . ." He stopped. "What's for breakfast?"

I smiled in spite of everything. "Not truffles, anyway! And then what?"

"Then what what?"

"The pig."

"Oh, the pig . . . I disremember."

"You can't just leave it like that! All stories have a proper ending. They start 'Once upon a time . . . ' and end ' . . . and so they lived happily ever after,' with an exciting story in between."

"Life's not like that."

"I don't see why it can't be. . . ."

"That is what man has been saying for thousands of years and look where it's got him! Without hope and a God the human race would have died out eons ago."

"You say that as if animals were superior!"

"So they are, in many ways. They don't think and puzzle and wonder and theorize, look back and look forward. What matters is only what they feel right now, this minute, and if they can fill their bellies and mate and keep clear of danger. And when they dream, and twitch and paddle in their sleep, then they are either the hunters or the hunted, nothing more. No grand visions, no romance—and no tears, either."

So he *had* noticed. I felt embarrassed and went back to his tale. "But the story was a story, so it must have an ending. . . ."

"Well, then, you give it one, just to satisfy your romantic leanings."

I thought. "Because the pig turned out to be so unselfish after all, helping his friends to enjoy the truffles when he could no longer, the wizard reconsidered his spell and then lifted it. And—and the pig was properly grateful to have been shown the error of his ways and never again yearned after something unsuitable. He married his sweetheart pig, who had stayed loyal to him through good times and bad, and they had lots of little piglets and lived happily ever afterwards. There!" I stopped, pleased with myself, then had another thought. "Oh, yes: The strange thing about it all was, that the piglets and their children and their children's children couldn't *stand* truffles!"

The Wimperling made polite applause noises with his tongue. "A predictable tale—redeemed, I think, by the last line. I liked that. And the moral of the story is?"

"Does it have to have one?"

"All the best ones have. Disguised sometimes, but still there."

"Er . . . Don't make hasty decisions; think before you open your mouth?"

"Or your legs," said the Wimperling. "Exactly!" And off he trotted.

Over a breakfast of oatcakes, fish baked in leaves and ale, Gill told me he had had a wonderful dream during the night. "And Summer, it seems my memory is really coming back!"

It was lucky for him he could not see my face, and did not sense the desolate churning in my stomach that made me push aside the fish with a sickness I could not disguise.

"In this dream I was wandering through a building that seemed familiar yet wasn't, if you know what I mean. Then I realized I was in the household where I had served my time as first page, then squire. But I was no longer a boy, I was as I am now, but without the blindness—you know how illogical dreams can be."

I nodded, then remembered. "Yes." In *my* dreams I was slim. And beautiful . . . How illogical could you get?

"Then suddenly I was in a barn—a barn in the middle of a castle, Summer!—and there, lying in the straw, was my affianced, my beloved, my Rosamund!"

"Rosamund?"

"Yes—I told you my memory was coming back. Any more ale?"

I handed him mine. "Tell me more about—about this Rosamund."

"Ah, what can I say? No mere words could do her adequate justice! I met her when I was a squire and with my parents' consent we became affianced. Her father was a rich merchant and his daughter Rosamund, the middle one of three, with a handsome dowry. She is two years older than I, but as sweet and chaste and demure as a nun. We plighted our troth five years ago, but I was determined to earn my knighthood before I claimed her as my bride. I journeyed north to bring her gifts from my parents and say we were ready to receive her, and on my way back I think I . . . That bit still isn't clear. I don't remember."

On that journey back he had been ambushed, and he wouldn't be here if I hadn't rescued him, I thought bitterly. "Is your bride-to-be as pretty as she is chaste?" I asked between my teeth.

"Pretty? Nay, beautiful! Tall, slim, perfectly proportioned. Her skin is white as milk, her cheeks like the wild rose, her hair like ripened corn—"

"And her teeth as white as a new-peeled withy," I muttered sulkily.

"How did you know? I was going to say pearls. . . . A straight nose, a small mouth—" He sighed. "Truly is she named the Rose of the World. . . ."

I rubbed my smallish nose and practiced pursing my not-so-small mouth.

He sighed again. "As I said, she is as chaste as a nun, and has never permitted me more than a kiss or two, a quick embrace. . . . But in this dream I had my impatience got the better of me and I threw aside her objections and embraced her long and heartily. It was just getting interesting when—when . . ."

"Yes?" I said sweetly.

"When all of a sudden I was in a tournament and my opponent unhorsed me, to the detriment of my manhood, if you will excuse the expression. . . ." He scowled. "Very painful."

"You got kicked in the balls," I said succinctly. "And woke up. Are you sure it wasn't the fair Rosamund defending her chastity?"

He looked shocked. "Really, Summer! Even in dreams she wouldn't be so—so unladylike! And she was never coarse in her language . . ."

Of course not. "Seeing how much your memory had improved, was there anything else you recalled that we might find useful in our search for your home and family? Such as a name, or a location?"

He looked surprised. "Oh, didn't I say? How remiss of me. I meant to. I remembered my father's name a few days ago, just before we came to the border. But then there was so much to think about, with escaping and all. . . ."

I could have throttled him. "Well?"

"My father's name is Sir Robert de Faucon and our nearest big town is Evreux; we live some thirty miles to the west. My mother's name is Jeanne, and—"

"Why in the world didn't you tell me before!" Of course: the bird on his pennant was a falcon; I remembered it now. And the name was the same. Simple.

"We were trying to cross the border—"

"But your name might have meant something—"

"Yes! A ransom. And we'd still be there."

Very reasonable, but I was sure it had never crossed his mind till now. I simmered down. We would make our way to Evreux, the place that had come so providentially to mind when we were questioned at the border, and from there on it should be easy.

Not as easy as I had hoped. There were fewer travelers on the road and fewer itinerants as well, for these latter were hoping for jobs with the imminent harvest. It was the wrong time and the wrong place for pilgrimages also, so we had to keep to the high roads in daylight and not chance evening walking. We also found these people of the north stingier with their money and their handouts, more suspicious of strangers: maybe it was the war that had been going on for so long, maybe their northern blood ran colder, I just do not know.

We took some money with a performance or two in the cathedral town of Evreux, and confirmed the westerly road towards Gill's home. Now we were so near our objective I would have expected him to be far more impatient to press on than he actually was. Instead he walked slower than usual, complained of blisters, said his back hurt, had an in-growing toenail. I pricked and dressed his blisters with salve, rubbed his back and examined a perfectly normal toe. Next day he felt dizzy, had stomach pains, nausea, vomiting and cramps. I treated all these, difficult to confirm or deny, but on the third day, when we were less than five miles from the turn-off that we had been told led straight to his estates, and he said his legs were too weak to hold him, I knew something was seriously wrong.

I sat him down under the shade of a large oak tree, dumped our parcels and asked him straight out what was the matter.

"For something is, of that I am sure. And it has nothing to do with bad backs, blisters or your belly!" I remembered how he had "forgotten" his father's name so conveniently, until I had jolted his memory. "For all your talk of your beautiful lady, you are behaving like a very reluctant bridegroom! One would almost think you didn't *want* to go home!" I was joking, trying to bring an air of ease to a puzzling situation, but to my amazement he took me seriously.

"Perhaps I don't."

"What do you mean? Ever since I first met you we have been trying to find out where you live, and no one has been more insistent than you! We have traveled hundreds of miles—never mind your blisters, you should see mine!—and have gone through great dangers, faced starvation, scraped and scrounged for every penny, crossed innumerable provinces, just so that we can bring you to the bosom of your family once more! You can't mean at this late stage that you don't want to go home, you just can't!"

His blind eyes were fixed unseeingly on his boots. He muttered something I couldn't catch, so I asked him to repeat it.

"I said: what use to anyone is a blind knight?"

Dear Christ, I had never thought of that. How terrible! When first I had rescued him I had thought of nothing but helping him to recover, largely, now I admitted, for my own gratification. His blindness had been an inconvenience for him, but a bonus for me. It had meant I could worship him unseen; feed him, clothe him, wash him, cut his hair and beard, touch him, hold his hand. . . . And all without him realizing how fat and ugly I was. Facing it now, I could see that all I had wanted was his dependence, in a false conviction that that would bring me love. And also boost my own self-importance: was that why I had also taken on a hungry tortoise, a broken pigeon, a decrepit horse? Just so that they would pander to my ego by being grateful to me? Dear God, I hoped not: I hoped it was the gentler emotion of compassion, but how could I be sure? I had had little choice with Growch, and the Wimperling was almost forced on me, but the others? It didn't bear thinking of.

And now my beloved Gill had faced me with an impossible question: what, indeed, was there for a blind knight? Knights fought in battles, competed in tourneys, hunted, went on Crusades—what did a knight know save of arms? Would his overlord, the king from oversea, want a man incapable of warring?

Quick, Summer, think of something. . . .

"There are plenty of things you can do," I said briskly. "People will still obey your commands, won't they? A blind man can still ride a horse, play an instrument, sing a song, run an estate, make wise judgments, and . . . and . . ." I had to think of something else. "Remember what that wise physician, Suleiman, said? He foretold you would regain your memory, as you have, and he also said there was nothing wrong with your eyes that time also couldn't cure. He said you could regain your sight suddenly, any day!"

I don't think he was listening. There was something even more pressing at the back of his mind. "Of what use is a blind husband?"

I was about to observe that most lovemaking took place in the dark anyway, but suddenly realized just how much he must be fearing rejection: some women wouldn't consider allying themselves to a blind man, never mind that to me it would be an advantage. But then, I wasn't beautiful. . . . I remembered that Mama had told me that a man's pride was his greatest emotion. Let's give him a boost and a get-out, however frivolous the latter.

I put my arms about him and hugged him. "Any woman would be crazy to look elsewhere!" I said comfortingly. "A handsome man such as you? Why, if she won't have you, I will!" I added in a lighthearted, teasing way. "We shall take to the road again, you and I, and have many more adventures, until your sight is returned. We'll go back and stay with Matthew the merchant for a start, and—" I stopped, because his hands had sought the source of my voice, and now they cupped my face.

"You know, you are the kindest and most warmhearted woman I have ever known," he said, then leaned forward and kissed me. "And I don't think I shall ever forget you. Tell me, Summer, are you as pretty as your voice? If so, I might even take you up on your offer," and now his voice was as light and teasing as mine had been.

I leapt to my feet, my stomach churning, my face red as a ripe apple, my mind all topsy-turvy. It was the first time he had ever offered me a gesture of affection. Why now? I screamed inside, why now when you are so near home and in a few hours I am going to lose you? If he had told me before of his fears, if he had once shown me any love, then I would have ensured it took twice as long to reach here. And now how I regretted refusing his love-making attempt: what would it have mattered if he had thought me someone else? What would have been simpler than to take what he offered and enjoy it, then perhaps confess to him afterwards?

But all I said was: "You can judge of that when you can see again. But the offer's open. . . ." in my gruffest voice, adding: "Enough of all this nonsense! Let's get you cleaned up, bathed and properly dressed, so you will not disgrace us all. And I must do the animals as well. . . ." and I grabbed Growch, who had gathered the main import of what I had been talking of in human speech, and was about to disappear down the road.

Luckily there was a meandering stream not far away through the trees, and though it was summer-low I managed to dunk the dog and comb out the worst of the fleas, and freshen up the pig. Then I gave Gill an all-over, my eyes and hands perhaps lingering too long on those special parts that would soon belong to another. I trimmed his beard and mustache as close as I could and cut his hair, then gave him a fresh shirt and the new blue-embroidered surcoat.

There was little I could do for myself except bathe, plaiting my hair, donning a fresh shift and the woolen dress Matthew had given me, but I felt clean and more comfortable. One bonus was to find some watercress to supplement our bread and cheese.

We still had several miles to walk before we reached Gill's home. Once we found the left-hand turning we were bounded by forest on both sides, and the road narrowed to a wheel-rutted track, but after a mile or so we came to a pair of gates that seemed to be permanently fastened back, and through them the road wound among orchard trees and harvested fields towards a fortified manor house some half-mile away. There were few people about, and no one challenged us as I led Gill slowly towards his home.

It was now late afternoon, but the sun had lost little of its heat and we finished off the water in the flask and I picked three apples from those near-ripe. Then another and another for the Wimperling, who had suddenly decided they were his favorite food. I picked them quite openly, for there were none to see, save a boy coaxing some swine back from acorns in the forest, and a gin with her geese picking at the stubble. Besides, I thought, these are Gill's orchards, or will be some day.

I started to describe our surroundings to him, but I had no need. Now his memory was nearly complete once more, he could smell, hear, taste and touch his own land; at first tentatively, then more assured as he described what lay on either side of us as we passed. Here a copse, there a stream, crabapples on one side, late pears on the other, and he even anticipated the flags flying from the gateway.

As he drew nearer I could see that his memory of the grandness of the manor house was a little exaggerated, like most fond memories. It was nothing special; we had passed much grander on our travels. The original structure was of wood, in two stories, but a high stone wall now surrounded it, embracing also the courtyard, stables, kitchens and stores; outside, small hovels housed the workers, though everything seemed empty and deserted.

"Entertainers?" said the porter at the side gate. "Everyone's welcome today, even your beasts. Round to your right you'll find the kitchens. Tonight's the Grain Supper: always held on this day, come rain or shine." And he went back to gnawing at what was left of a large mutton bone.

"This is ridiculous!" protested Gill, as we started off again across the courtyard, also deserted. "I belong here: this is my home! What in God's name are we doing creeping round like a couple of thieves? Just lead me over to the main door—no, I can find my own way!"

"Wait!" I said, catching hold of his arm. "Let's not rush it. You don't want to give them all heart failure! Let's surprise them gently. Listen a moment, and I'll tell you what we'll do. . . ."

Leaving Gill and the animals outside, I went to the kitchens and was given a large bowl of mutton stew and a loaf of the "poor-bread" I remembered as a child, before Mama could afford better: the grain was mixed with beans, peas and pulses, and this was fresh as an hour ago and very filling. We ate hungrily, sitting in the courtyard with our backs to a sunny wall, then I went back and asked to see the steward, asking permission to perform in the Great Hall later. As it happened there were a juggler and a minstrel already waiting, but we were added to the list.

All that remained was to keep out of the way of anyone who might recognize Gill, and a couple of hours later I was waiting nervously at the side door, Gill tucked away in the shadows with the hood of his cloak pulled well down over his face, Growch and the Wimperling at his side. As the minstrel sang the song of Roland, I peeped into the hall; so thick with smoke, I could barely see the top table, but obviously the thick-set, bearded man must be Gill's father, the thin woman with the tall headdress his mother. And there, sitting beside Gill's father, was a slim woman with long blond hair fastened back with a fillet: the fair Rosamund, if I wasn't mistaken. I wished I could see her more clearly.

Beside me the kitchen servants brushed past, ducking their heads automatically as they passed under the low lintel, laden with dishes and jugs, though this was the last course: fruits in aspic, nuts and cheese, so there was more clearing away than replenishing.

The juggler had passed back to the kitchens a half-hour ago, jingling coins in his hand, and now the minstrel was coming to the end of his recital. There was polite applause, the tinkle of thrown coins, and a hum of conversation as the singer made his way back to the kitchens. Our turn next: I don't think I had ever felt so nervous in my life.

One of the varlets announced us. "Entertainers from the south, with a song or two and some tricks to divert . . ."

Growch "danced" to my piping, somersaulted, rolled over and over, nodded or shook his head as required and "died" for his king, then the Wimperling did some very simple counting; a) because I was nervous to the point of nearly wetting myself and b) wanting to get it all over and done with, at the same time fearing the outcome—a little like having severe toothache and knowing the tooth-puller was just around the corner; it was the last few steps to his door that were the worst.

I finished the tricks to a good deal of applause and dismissed the animals, picking up the coins that were thrown and putting them in my pocket. "Thank you ladies, knights, and gentle-persons all. If I may crave your indulgence, my partner and I will conclude with a song," and taking a candle branch boldly from one of the side tables I walked back to the doorway where Gill was waiting, his hood hiding his face.

"When I come to the right words," I whispered, "throw back your hood, hold the candles high and march through the doorway, straight ahead. I'll come and meet you."

Walking back to the space in front of the high table I started to sing, beating a soft accompaniment on my tabor. It was an old favorite, the one where the knight rides away to seek his fortune.

A knight rode away.
In the month of May,
All on a summer's day;
"I shall not stray,
Nor lose my way,
But return this way,
On St. Valentine's Day. . . ."

It had several verses, with lots of to-ra-lays in between, and I had to sing quickly to turn "Valentine" to "Cosmos and Damien." The ballad tells of how news came to the knight's fiancee that he was dead; she visits a witch and sells her soul to the Devil in order that her beloved will return. And, of course, he returns, the rumor of his death having been exaggerated, right on the day he foretold. Just as she calls on the Devil to redeem his promise she hears the voice of the knight. This was Gill's cue, and his clear tenor rang out through the hall.

"I have returned as I said,
I am not dead,
But astray was led. . . ."

I answered his words with the words of the song:

"Knave, knight or pelf:
Come show yourself!"

Gill threw back the hood of his cloak, held the candles high and stepped firmly forward. There was a hush from the audience, then a muffled scream as his face was illuminated. He hesitated for a moment on the threshold, then threw back his head and marched briskly forward.

And then it happened.

There was a crack! that echoed all around as his head came into contact with the low lintel of the doorway. He teetered for a moment, rocking back and forth on his heels, then dropped like a stone to the rushes.

I ran forward with my heart full of terror and reached his side, kneeling to take his poor head in my arms, looking with horror at the red mark across his forehead where he had struck.

"Gill! Gill . . . Are you all right?"

He opened his eyes, thank God! and stared straight up at me.

"That bloody door was always too low. . . . And who the hell are you?"

Chapter Twenty-Seven

After that everything became confused.

I got up, was knocked down, rose again and tripped over the Wimperling and Growch, was overwhelmed by a great rush of bodies, flung this way and that, buffeted and elbowed. I saw Gill embraced, hugged, kissed, slapped on the back, borne off, brought back, cried over. Women fainted, men wept, dogs howled; trenchers, mugs, jugs, cups, food, drink littered the rushes. Trestles and small tables were overturned, candles burned dangerously and the clamor of voices threatened to bring down the roof.

Little by little the animals and I found ourselves, from being at the center of the fuss, to being on the fringes of the activity. Behind us was the door to the kitchens. I looked at them, they looked at me, and with one accord we marched off. The kitchens had been abandoned as the staff heard the commotion in the Great Hall, and we found ourselves alone, surrounded by the detritus of the Grain Supper in all its sordidness. Unwashed dishes, greasy pans, empty jugs; bread crusts, bones, fish heads, chicken wings littered the tables and floor, and half-eaten mutton and beef showed where kitchen supper had been left for the excitement elsewhere.

"Well . . ." I said, and sat down suddenly on a convenient stool. There didn't seem anything else to say.

Growch was sniffing round. "Pity to waste all this," he said, helping himself to a rib of beef almost as big as he was.

The Wimperling rested his chin on my lap. "Give it all time to settle down," he said. "He'll remember about us later. In the meantime, why not stock up on a bit of food and drink and find a stable or something to settle in for the night?"

I scratched his chin affectionately. "Why not?"

There were some boiling cloths drying on a rack, so I wrapped up a whole chicken, slightly charred, three black puddings, a cheese and onion pasty and a half-empty flagon of wine, and crept away guiltily to the courtyard. The stables were all full, but I found a small room that must have been used for stores, but was now empty except for a heap of sacks in one corner and a pile of rush baskets. The whole place smelled pleasantly of apples.

We could still hear sounds of revelry and carousing from the direction of the Great Hall, but it was full dark outside by now, so I closed the door and lit my lanthorn and we shared out the food. I had half the chicken and all the crispy skin, and the pasty, and I shared the rest of the chicken and the black puddings among the other two, though the Wimperling said the latter could be cannibalism.

"I thought you said you didn't know whether you were a pig or not," I said sleepily, for it had been a long day and the unaccustomed wine was making me feel soporific. I arranged the sacks to make a comfortable bed for us.

"True," said the Wimperling. "And I'm still not sure. . . ."

"Then pretend you're something else. A prince in disguise . . ."

Growch snorted.

We were wakened at dawn by an almighty hullabaloo. I was grabbed from the pile of sacks and held, struggling, between two surly men; another had hold of the Wimperling's tail and was hauling him towards the door and two others were trying to corner a snapping, snarling Growch. The storeroom seemed to be full of people all jabbering away, pointing at me, the animals. What had we done? Then I remembered the food I had filched from the kitchens the night before: was I about to lose a hand for thieving?

"Is this the one?" shouted one of the men who was holding me.

The steward stood in the doorway, consulting a piece of vellum. "A girl, named of Summer; a pig and a small dog. Seems we've got 'em. Well done, lads." And, addressing me: "Is your name Summer?"

What point in denying it? "Let the animals alone: they've done nothing!" I suddenly remembered. "I demand to see Gill—Sir Gilman, immediately! There's been some mistake. . . ."

He thrust the piece of vellum back in his pocket. "You're all wanted, girl, pig and dog. Do you realize just how long we've been looking for you?" He seemed in a very bad temper, and my heart sank. "Why, not a half-hour ago I sent mounted men out to chase you up. . . . Have to send more to recall them. All this fuss and pother, never a moment's peace. . . . Well, come on then! They're waiting. . . ." and without giving me time to tidy my hair or smooth down my dress I was hauled across the courtyard, in through the main doorway, across the Great Hall—still full of last night's somnolent revelers, the smoldering ashes of the fire and a stink of stale food and wine, dogs, guttered candles and torches, vomit and sweat—closely followed by a man carrying the Wimperling, who seemed to have shrunk of a sudden, and three others still trying to catch Growch.

Up a winding stone staircase hidden by an arras behind the top table and we were thrust, carried or chased into a large solar wherein were seated four people: the lord of the manor, Sir Robert, his wife, the golden-haired Rosamund and—and Gill. A Gill close-shaven, handsomer than ever, clad in fine linen and silks. He looked now just as he had when I first saw him: beautiful, haughty and unattainable.

As we were shoved into the room he rose from the settle where he had been holding hands with his affianced, a look of bewilderment on his face as he gazed first at me, then the animals, and back to me again.

"Can it be . . . ?"

The steward gave me a shove in the back that had me down on my knees and addressed Sir Robert. "Is this them, then?"

Sir Robert glanced at his son. "Gilman?" but Gill had started forward, a look of anger on his face as he helped me to my feet.

"Whether it is or no, you have no right to treat a girl like that! Leave us, I will deal with this!" The steward and his men bowed and retreated and Gill looked searchingly into my face. "Is it really you, Summer?"

Of course he had never seen me, except for that time he had asked the way, and he didn't know it was the same girl. I blushed to the roots of my hair that now he should see me in all my ugliness.

"Yes," admitted finally. "I am Summer. And this is the Wimperling and that is Growch," hoping he would stop staring at me.

"But I had no idea. . . ." He plucked a dried leaf from my hair abstractedly, then took my hands in his again. "I thought—I had thought you were quite different. . . ."

"Blind men have all sorts of strange fancies," I said, then forgot myself to ask anxiously: "You are all right, then? You can see properly again?"

"Apart from a slight headache, yes. You and Suleiman were right. I reckon it was the knock on the head that did it. It all happened so quickly I still feel confused—"

"And so you should!" came a cool voice from behind him and there stood the fair Rosamund, who pulled his hands from mine and tucked them round her arm, all so gently done that it seemed the initiative had come from him. She gazed at me, a faint sneer on her lips. "I'm not surprised you feel confused! Used as you are to the best, it must have been hell for you to traipse around the countryside with this tatterdemalion crew!" Her cold blue eyes raked me from head to foot. "Still, I suppose the girl needs some recompense, before she and her—menagerie—take to the road again." She paused. "I may well have a dress I need no more, though I doubt it would fit. . . ."

"Enough of this!" It was Gill's tall, thin mother Jeanne who spoke. I had the impression that nothing short of a catastrophe gave her the courage to speak normally, though now of course her beloved Gill's return must have sparked her into fresh resolution. "The girl brought our son back to us safe and sound, and she deserves the very best we can give her. As long as she wishes to stay, she is our honored guest. As—as are her pets! See that they are accommodated in the hall tonight: I myself will find a length of cloth so she is decently clad."

"The hall?" said Gill. "Father, Mother, nothing less than a good bed will do! Why, I am sure my betrothed would be only too glad to share her room with Mistress Summer?"

She looked at me as if I had the plague, then turned to Gill as sweet as honey. "My dearest, whatever you wish. But—" and she flashed me a glance that would have split stone as neatly as any mason's chisel and hammer: "—perhaps we should ask the young person herself? She may have other ideas. . . ."

Meaning I had better. She needn't have worried. The last person in the world I wished to share a bed with was her. Now, if it had been Gill . . . I pulled myself together and addressed Sir Robert and his wife.

"I thank you Sir, Lady, for your kind offer," I said, and curtsied. "The length of cloth would be most welcome, and I can make it up myself. As for accommodation, however, if I might be allowed to sleep in the storeroom where I spent last night, then I can be with our traveling companions, who are used to being with us and have been of great assistance in our travels, as no doubt Sir Gilman has told you." I curtsied again. "I should also be grateful for hot water for washing and some extra thread: I used the last to make Sir Gilman a surcoat."

There! I thought: that should give them something to *think* about. Polite, accommodating, clean, thrifty and yet independent, with a couple of reminders of the life we had led and how I had cared for Gill . . . I smiled at him. Never mind my ugliness: he still seemed to care about my welfare.

Sir Robert inclined his head. "As you wish. I shall see to it that the room you prefer is made more comfortable. And now, I think it is time to break our fast. . . ."

And while we ate—just below the top table this time: on it would have been too much to ask—the storeroom was transformed. Swept out, sacks and baskets removed, a table, stool and truckle bed installed, hooks for our packages knocked into the wall, two large lanthorns and a pile of straw for the animals—luxury indeed!

After breakfast servants brought hot water, soap, linen towels, and from Gill's mother came a length of fine woolen cloth in blue, needles and thread, a new comb and ribbons for my hair, and even a new shift: too long, of course, but surprisingly, none too tight. I took it up, cut out my new surcoat, mended my old one, washed and indulged recklessly in the bottle of rosemary oil that came with the soap and towels, washed my other two shifts and stitched my shoes where they were coming undone.

The midday meal was at noon, the evening meal at six, and by that evening I had my new surcoat finished, so for the first time I felt comfortable enough to survey my hosts at my leisure. My position just below the top table gave me ample opportunity to look at both Gill's parents and his affianced.

Sir Robert was stout rather than tall; he had fierce mustaches and a rather dictatorial manner, but he always treated me with kindness. His wife was normally silent, looked older than her husband, and her usually careworn expression only lightened when she talked to her beloved son. I scarcely recognized him that evening, for he had had his curly hair cropped short like his father's, to facilitate the wearing of the close-fitting helmet they affected in these parts. I liked him better with it long.

It was the fair Rosamund however who intrigued me most. "Fair" once I judged, but whatever she may have told Gill about her age, she must be at least four or five years older. Already fine lines radiated from the corners of her eyes when she smiled, which was seldom enough, and her mouth had a discontented droop. She was also missing two teeth; perhaps that was why she didn't smile much, that and the fear of deepening her lines.

She had pretty manners however, using her table napkin often to dab away grease from mouth or fingers. Her voice was pleasant enough, her figure good and her walk swaying and graceful and her hands were white and beautifully shaped. Her hair was rather thin—or mine was too thick—but it was her pale complexion I envied most of all; but, come to think of it, if she tramped the roads as we had, it would have reddened and blotched it a most unsightly way.

In all this I was fully aware that I was being over-critical, but I knew she didn't like me, and I hated the way she monopolized Gill, snatching his attention if ever he glanced over at me, and giving exaggerated little "oohs" and "aahs" as he told of our adventures. And it didn't do any good for me to remind myself she had a perfect right to do so.

Several times during the next few days he tried to speak to me alone, and each time he was foiled, usually by her, sometimes by other interruptions. Sometimes I would catch him gazing at me, and if I smiled at him he would smile back, but it was always an uncertain, puzzled smile. It got to the stage when I started worrying whether I had two noses or was covered in some disfiguring rash.

But life drifted by for a week in this lazy fashion, eating, sleeping, and I let it, for I was in no hurry to leave. A golden September would all too soon give way to October. The mornings even now held a hint of the chill to come, dew heavy on the millions of spiderwebs that carpeted the stubble till it glinted in the rising sun like diamonds; the swifts were long gone, but a few swallows still gathered on the tower tops, and martins on the slopes of the roofs like a scattering of pearls. The leaves of the willow were already yellowing, and across in the forest the trees were a patchwork of color.

Noons were still warm and heavy, the sparse birdsong drowsed by heat, only the robins still disputing their territory in fierce red breastplates. Nights were colder and it was nice to snuggle under a blanket once more and listen to the tawny owls practicing their "hoo-hoos" across the empty fields.

I thought of Mistral; at this time of year, she had told us, the tide sometimes raced in and overwhelmed the fields till even the horses ran from it, their coats flecked with foam from the waves that roared in over the ribbed sands from the other side of the world. I thought of Traveler, safe I hoped in the ruined chapel tower; at this time of year there were still seeds and fruits in plenty, but soon would come the harsh winter, when the weakest would die. I thought of Basher: about now he would be looking for a soft, sandy place to dig himself in for the winter, till that funny shelled body of his was safe for the long sleep. . . .

I thought of them all, I missed them all, I prayed for them all.

And what of the fourth of the travelers to find his "home"? The others had accepted less than they deserved: would Gill, too, be cruelly rewarded? I hoped not, but I sensed there was something amiss, in spite of the fact that he had regained his sight, his home, his beloved.

One night after supper he caught at my sleeve and murmured urgently, "At the back of the room you sleep in there is a stairway up to the walkway on the wall: meet me there in an hour. I need to talk to you."

My heart gave a great thump of apprehension: what was so important we couldn't discuss it openly?

I found the doorway he described, behind some stacked hurdles, but it was so small I could only just manage to squeeze my way up the dusty, cobwebbed spiral. Obviously it hadn't been used in years and there was a stout wooden door at the top, luckily bolted on my side, but it took all my strength to slide back the rusty iron.

Once out on the guarded walkway I felt a deal better; I had never liked confined spaces, and now I took deep breaths of the welcome fresh air. Not that it was all that invigorating: the night was cloudy, the atmosphere oppressive, as though we waited for a storm. Down in the courtyard the little chapel bell rang for nine of night and I could see one or two going for prayers. An owl hooted, far away in the forest; a dog barked from the cluster of huts beneath the wall. Somewhere a child wailed briefly, then all was quiet once more.

I leaned against the low parapet and rested my eyes on the darkness. I heard quick footsteps mounting the outside stair to my right but didn't turn; for a moment longer I felt I didn't want to know what Gill had to say, didn't want to become involved once more. Whatever it was, I had the feeling it would mean more heartache, one way or the other.

"Summer?"

"Here . . ." I turned and was immediately taken into an urgent, awkward embrace that had my nose squashed against his shoulder and the breath knocked out of me. I pushed him away as hard as I could.

"Are you mad—?"

He stepped back, but regained possession of my hands. "I'm sorry, I didn't mean . . . Look here, Summer, I can't stand this much longer, not being able to see you and speak to you! There is so much we must talk about, and I—"

"Hush!" I pulled my hands from his grasp. "If you yell like that you'll have everyone up here!" for his voice had risen with his anxiety. I looked down into the courtyard but all was quiet. "Now, just tell me—quietly—what on earth's the matter?"

"Everything."

"Don't be so dramatic! You are back home, safe and comfortable, you have your sight back, and are reunited with your betrothed—so what could possibly be wrong?"

He hesitated. "I don't know. . . . It's just that—that everything, everybody's changed. It's not what I expected. . . ."

My breathing slowed down a little. Silly fellow! "You've been away for over a year, you know! But they haven't done anything drastic like moving the house or burning down the forest, have they? Perhaps there are some new faces, old ones gone, different fields plowed, but—"

"It's not that. How can I explain it?" He ran his hand through his close-cropped hair. "Everything looks somehow smaller, shabbier, meaner!" he burst out.

"Shhh . . . That's easily explained. While you were away you'd built up a picture in your mind, that's all—like a dream. Things always look larger in dreams."

"But what about the people? My mother looks older, sort of—defeated. And I don't remember my father's beard having so much grey in it."

"But they are older: over a year older. So are you. . . . Life didn't just stand still, waiting for you to come home. They probably feel the same about you. You are thinner, browner, more restless, and have had enough adventures and mishaps to change anyone. You've got to have patience, time to settle in once again." I patted his arm. "There: lots of good advice! I'm afraid there's no other way I can help. . . ."

He turned away, gripped the parapet, stared out into the darkness. "Yes. Yes, there is."

"How? Do you want me to talk to them? I don't think they would take much notice of me."

"It's not that. . . . It's Rosamund." He exhaled heavily, as though he had been holding his breath, and turned back to me. "You see, I just don't love her anymore."

I was speechless. Of all the things I had expected him to say, this was the last.

"It happened as soon as I saw her again," he hurried on, as if now eager to tell everything as fast as possible. "Perhaps, as you say, I had built up an idealized picture of things in my mind, and especially her. It wasn't only that she looked—looked older, harder; it seemed she had changed in other ways, too. I hadn't remembered her as so overpowering and at the same time sickly-sweet. And I had forgotten her little mannerisms; things that I found once so enchanting now did nothing but irritate me. You must have noticed them, too."

Of course I had. But let him tell it in his own way.

"You know the sort of thing: the little cough to get attention, the way she keeps smoothing her throat to draw notice to its whiteness, how she holds her head to one side when she listens to you and opens her eyes wide like an owl's, the way she sucks her teeth. . . . She's stiff, unreal, mannered, like one of those jointed wooden puppets you can buy. . . . I can't explain it any better."

What could I say? I tried the same arguments I had used before, how it took everyone time to adjust, that he had changed too and there were probably things about him that annoyed her too, and all the while I had the horrible feeling that I knew just what he was going to say next, and I hadn't the slightest idea how to deal with it.

"But you are not like that, Summer! You are young, younger than I, and so full of life! If I had had the slightest idea what you were really like, if

I hadn't been blind in more ways than one, then—then I should never have come back! Not unless and until I could have brought you back with me as my wife!"

He couldn't mean it! Not now; it was too cruel a twist of fate! For how many months had I worshiped him in secret, never once letting him know how I felt? If only . . . He couldn't see the tears on my cheek but I tried to keep them from my voice.

"You know it wouldn't have worked. I'm not your kind, would never fit into this kind of life. No, wait!" For he had moved forward to embrace me. "Besides, you could never have broken your betrothal vows. They are sacred things, as sacred as marriage itself, and you know it. The dowry has been paid, she has been accepted into your family, there is no going back now. In the eyes of God you are already wed."

"God could not be so cruel, not now when I have found my one, my true and only love! To hell with the dowry, that can be paid back. . . ." He took me in his arms, and I could smell the acrid sweat of emotion and anxiety. "The contract can be canceled. Come away with me, Summer! We can go back on the road, we managed before. Now I can see again I can find work somewhere farther south where no one will follow us." He tipped up my chin with one hand. "And don't tell me you have no fondness for me: I know you have!" and he bent his head and kissed me, at first soft and then hard and hungry.

It was my first real kiss; I had always wondered where the noses went, how the faces would fit, what it felt like to taste someone else. Now I knew, but even as my whole body seemed to melt against him, part of me knew it was wrong, wrong!

"Stop it, Gill! Let me breathe, let me think. . . . Please!"

He released me and I had to cling to the parapet, I was shaking so much. He took my hand. "I know it's sudden, my dearest one, but don't you see? It's the only way. Please say you will at least consider it. I have some moneys, not a lot, but enough to find us a safe haven for the winter. I swear to you that I will make it worth your while. Why shouldn't we both be happy instead of both miserable?"

There were a hundred, a thousand reasons why, but I couldn't think straight. "Give me time to think. . . . I don't know, right now I don't know." And then the words that must have been spoken so many times in the past by women far less surprised than I: "This is all so sudden!"

He bent and kissed my hands, one after the other.

"Of course, my love, but not more than a couple of days. I am being pressed already by Rosamund to name the wedding date. Tonight is Tuesday; I'll meet you here for your answer the same time on Thursday. In the meantime," he added, "I shall find it extremely difficult to avoid grabbing you and kissing you in front of everyone! I love you, my dearest. . . ."

I staggered back to my room down the stone stairs in a complete daze. At the bottom, by the light of a candle I had left burning, I saw two pairs of eyes staring up at me accusingly. Too much to expect that, between them, they didn't know exactly what had happened.

"I'm going to bed," I said firmly. "Right now. We'll talk in the morning, if you have anything you want to say."

The truth was that for a few precious hours, just a few, I wanted to hug to myself everything he had said, everything he had done, without dissipating the secret joy a jot by sharing or discussing it. If you leave the stopper off a vial of perfume it soon evaporates, and this love potion I had received tonight was the sweetest perfume in the world, and I had every intention of staying awake all night to conserve and savor every drop. . . .

"Breakfast," said the Wimperling succinctly, "is outside the door. As we didn't turn up for breakfast, they brought it to you."

I opened bleary eyes, for a moment lost to the day and hour. Then I remembered. But surely I couldn't have fallen asleep—

"What time is it?"

"Getting on for two hours after dawn, I reckon."

So much for spending the night awake, relishing the declaration of Gill's love! I must have fallen asleep almost at once and been tireder than I thought, for now I was grouchy, headachy, scratchy-eyed. The storm that had threatened last night hadn't broken after all and, like most animals, I still felt the oppression in the air, like a hand pressing down on the top of my head. And there was so much to do, so much to think about. . . .

We ate, what I don't remember, but I know the others had most of whatever it was. All the while the thoughts in my head danced up and down, round and about, like a cloud of midges, and as patternless.

"I'm going for a walk," I said abruptly. "You can come or stay as you wish."

We left the courtyard and passed the cluster of huts below the wall. Ahead stretched the long, straight road that led through the fields and orchards, past the fringes of the forest, to the gates of the demesne. I walked, not even noticing the surrounding landscape, just thumping my feet down one after the other, my mind a hopeless blank. It was an unseasonably hot day and at last sheer discomfort made me turn off to the shade of one of the still-unpicked orchards. I sank down on the long grass, leaned back against one of the gnarled trunks and sank my teeth into one of the small, sweet, pink-fleshed apples they probably used for cider. The Wimperling wandered off in search of windfalls, and the breeze brought faint and faraway the sound of the chapel bell ringing for noon.

Even Growch knew what that meant. "We've missed the midday meal," he said plaintively, sucking in his stomach.

"I know," I said unsympathetically.

"Ain't you got nuffin with you? Bit o' crust, cheese rind?"

"No. You had most of my breakfast, remember? Go away and look for beetles or bugs or something and don't bother me. I need to think," and promptly fell asleep once more, to awake only when the lengthening shadows brought with them a chill that finally roused me from sleep. The Wimperling lay by my side, the freshening breeze lapping his hide with the dancing shadows of the leaves above; Growch was lying on his back, snoring, his disgraceful stomach, pink, brown and black-patched, exposed to a bar of sunshine.

I sat up, suddenly feeling rested, alert, alive once more. I stretched until my bones cracked and twanged, then bounced to my feet and snatched another apple, sucking at the juice thirstily, then another, not caring whether I got stomachache. Time to walk back, or we should miss another meal, and now I felt hungry.

I realized I was enjoying the leisurely walk back, and spoke without thinking. "It'd be nice to be back on the road again. . . ."

Then began the Great Campaign, as I called it later, though the first few words were innocuous enough.

"Nice enough when the weather is like this," said the Wimperling. "But it's autumn already. All right for those with stamina and guts."

"Remember how cold it was last winter?" said Growch. "His Lordship—beggin' your pardon, lady—caught a cold what turned to pew-money?"

"Certainly doesn't like cold weather," said the Wimperling. "His sort are used to riding: never liked walking far."

"Remember how he used to complain about his feet?" said Growch. "Used to whinge about the food, too. . . ."

"That's the trouble with knights," said the Wimperling. "Only trained for one life. Give them a sword, a charger, a battle, and they're happy. In civilian life they can loose a hawk, sing a ballad—"

"Or flatter a lady . . ." said Growch.

"Easy enough for them to get accustomed to being waited on, having the best of everything—"

"Soon enough blame anyone what robs 'em of it—"

At last I realized where all this was leading, refused to listen, stopped up my ears. How *dared* they try and influence what I was going to do! It had nothing to do with them, it was between me and Gill.

The trouble was, their words remained in my consciousness, as annoying and insidious as the last of the summer fleas and ticks. And what they had said, exaggerated as it was, still held a grain of truth. Gill *had* grumbled a lot—but then he had had a right to. But would choice make it any easier for him to bear a simple life? Yes, he did catch cold easily, yes he was a bit soft, but he hadn't been used to the traveling life. Would he be any better prepared now? A small voice inside me whispered that it had been a new way of life for me, too, though perhaps I had made a better job of it, but I brushed the thought aside impatiently: everyone was different.

It was true, too, that the only life he had known was that of a knight, and that in spite of his brave words he would find it difficult to turn his hand to anything else. And that bit about flattering ladies: were the words he had spoken to me merely the courtesies he thought I would like to hear, not meant to be taken seriously? If he found it so easy to be turned from his betrothed, would a week or so in bad weather have him feeling the same way about me?

I got through the rest of the day somehow or other, but at dinner that night I found myself studying Gill's face for signs of what he was really like. Was his chin just a little bit weak, compared with his father's? Had he always looked so petulant when something displeased him, as it did that night when a particular dish was empty before it reached him? And if he now disliked his fiancee so much, why was he paying her such great attention? His fine new clothes certainly suited him: that was the third new surcoat I had seen him in. Who would carry all his gear if we were on the road once more?

That night I couldn't sleep at all. Hoping a little fresh air would help, I crept up the spiral stair to the walls again, but just as I drew back the bolts, greased earlier in anticipation of my meeting with Gill on the following night, I saw that the walkway was already occupied, although it must be near midnight. A man and a woman stood close by, talking softly. I was about to descend again when something about her stance made me believe I recognized the woman, and curiosity kept me where I was.

". . . that makes it so important to risk being seen?" I couldn't identify his voice, and he had his back to me.

"I had to see you! As things are, I have to be with him all the time. . . ." Rosamund's face was as pale as the moon that rode clear of cloud as she turned fully towards the man before her. "Robert, what are we going to do? I'm at least two months pregnant!"

Chapter Twenty-Eight

I couldn't help a gasp of horror as I realized the implications of what she had just said, but they were so intent on each other that they didn't hear. Once again I knew I should retreat without further eavesdropping, but how could I? This concerned Gill's and my future so closely I *had* to listen.

"Two months, you say?" said Gill's father, after a pause. His voice never faltered: he might have been discussing the gestation period of a favorite horse.

"I have missed two monthly courses, yes. One could have been ignored perhaps, but I have always been as regular as an hourglass, and now there are further signs. . . ." A shrug of those cloaked shoulders. "It will start to show soon."

"Let me think. . . ." He started to pace up and down the walkway, up and back twice, his arms folded across his chest. How like Gill he walks, I thought. He came back to face her. "You were no virgin when I took you," he stated flatly. "How do I know . . . ?"

"Of course it's yours! You know it is. Whatever I did in the past has nothing to do with it."

He regarded her broodingly. "Maybe not, but you were already a practiced whore when you came here. You seduced me with sighs and words and gestures, and I believed you knew what you were doing, that there would be no harm in it. I am not in the habit of soiling my own midden."

"You were as eager as I," she said sulkily.

"Maybe . . . How come you never got caught before?"

"Medicines, herbs; they are not available here."

"Then it was either intentional, because you thought my son would never return, and you wished me to keep you as my mistress—"

"It was an accident. Do you think I wanted to spoil my figure on the chance you would accept the child? No: like you I gave way to something I could not help." She spoke with conviction, and apparently he accepted it.

"Then there are two ways to deal with this—three, if you count being sent home in disgrace. But I shall not do that. Your dowry has been paid, and some of it already spent. The second way is to seek out the witch in the wood, and try one of her potions—"

"I have already tried that. The maid you gave me was pregnant by one of the grooms, so I sent her for a double dose. It worked for her but not for me. Your child is lusty, Robert: it wants to live."

He thought for a moment. "Then it has to be the third way, and no delay. No one knows about this but us, so let's keep it that way, but I shall want your full cooperation. . . ."

She nodded. "You have it."

"Right. The first thing is to get my son to your bed now, tonight—no, listen to me! I will give you a potion that I have sometimes used when my wife has failed to excite me. Make sure he drinks it, and if you cannot tempt him to your bed, then visit his. He will be so befuddled he will not know whether he has or has not performed. He will sleep without memory, but make sure you are there beside him when he wakes. He is a simple man: he will believe whatever you say."

"And the child?"

"There are plenty of seven-month babes. And he could be away. . . . There are many errands I could send him on."

"But your wife . . . She would know."

"She will say nothing. Her only thought is of Gill, what would make him happy. She may suspect, but once the babe is born, she will accept it. And once he, and everyone else, is persuaded he has slept with you then the wedding can take place within the week."

"The sooner the better . . ." She moved forward and rested her hands on his shoulders. "You think of everything. I had rather it had been you, but I promise to make your son a good wife." She was smiling like a pig in muck. "And your son—*our* son—will be the next in line, after Gill. Quite something, don't you think?" She leaned forward and kissed him, and I noticed he didn't draw back, but rather folded his arms around her and returned her embrace. "And perhaps, another time?"

"Get away with you, hussy. . . ." but he didn't sound displeased. "Remember, my son mustn't suffer over this."

"Of course not! I am really quite fond of him. There will be no complaints from that quarter, I swear. I know some tricks that even that girl he traveled with would not know—which reminds me: I fancy he became quite close to her, and I would not wish her to distract him from what we have planned. I have caught him looking at her a couple of times as if he were quite ready to disappear with her again—and we can't have that, can we?"

Oh, Gill, you idiot! I thought, shrinking back into the shadows as far as I could go. She is much cleverer than you thought. . . .

"She shall be disposed of, if you play your part. By tomorrow morning I want to see everyone convinced that my son will be the father of your child."

"Disposed of?"

"An accident, a disappearance: what do you care? No problem. It will be in my interest as well as yours, remember? But first, you must do your part. Tomorrow I will take care of Winter, or Summer, whatever she calls herself. . . . Meet me in the chapel in ten minutes and I will give you the potion."

I started back down the stairs, carefully closing the door behind me, shocked and horrified by what I had just heard. First their arrant duplicity regarding Rosamund's pregnancy: what could I do? Rush and find Gill, tell him what I had heard? I didn't even know how to find him and if I did, would he believe me? I doubted it. Whatever happened, I realized that Gill's dream of running away with me was gone forever. If his father's plan succeeded, by tomorrow morning he would believe he had seduced a virgin, his betrothed, and would be honor bound to marry her as quickly as possible; in cases like these his knightly training would give him no choice, however much he fancied someone else. And had I the right to try and stop it, even if I could? That baby could not be born illegitimate; I was myself, and I knew how it felt, not to have a father and to be jeered at because my mother was a whore. It would be worse in the sort of household Gill's father ran, and I believed both he and the perfidious Rosamund would bring the child up as Gill's. He need never know, and I was sure he would make a good father.

So now the choice I had thought would be so difficult was taken from me. Why was it that with no decision to make, I now felt a great sense of relief? Did that mean that what had happened was for the best, that Gill was not, never had been meant for me? I should always remember his declaration of love, I thought, but now I need never discover he would change, or I would as we traveled the roads. It was as if he were dead to me already: I should just remember the best, and nurse a few sentimental regrets.

"Infatuation," said the Wimperling at my elbow. "Nothing like the real thing. You wait and see."

"What are you doing! You made me jump out of my skin!"

"Just wanted to remind you that we'd better not tarry—yes, I was listening to your thoughts—because I reckon they mean you harm. . . ."

Of course! How could I have forgotten. I had to be got out of the way, and that didn't mean a bag of gold and a lift to the nearest town, I knew that. Headfirst down the nearest well, a stab in the back, perhaps a deadly potion . . . It would have been better to leave right away but I wanted to be sure, quite sure, that there was no chance Rosamund had failed in her plan. I knew in my heart she would succeed, but something within me wanted to twist a knife in the wound already so sore in my heart. Besides, Sir Robert had said he would do nothing until the morning.

During that long night I packed everything securely into two bundles, one for the Wimperling, one for me. The only money we had left were the few coins tossed down for our performance before Gill's miraculous appearance on the first night, but I wasn't worried. The countryside was still full of apples, late blackberries, enough grain to glean to thicken a stew, fungi and mushrooms. Besides we could always give a performance or two.

The last thing I did was to write to Gill: I felt he deserved some explanation, even if not the true one, and it might also serve to put his father off trying to pursue us. I tore a blank page from the back of my Boke and thought carefully.

> "Gill:— I am sorry to leave without a farewell, but it is time I was on my way. Besides, I hate good-byes. Perhaps I should have confided my hopes to you earlier, but I have not had the chance to speak with you alone. . . ."

That should allay their suspicions, I thought.

> "I am going back to Matthew, and will now accept his proposal. It will be a good match for me."

I paused, flicking the end of the quill against my cheek. Yes . . .

> "Please thank your family for their hospitality. I wish you and your betrothed every happiness, and many sons."

I signed my name "Someradai" as it had been written in the church register at home. After some thought I scratched out "Gill" and substituted "Sir Gilman." There, that would do. I rolled it carefully and tied it with one of the ribbons Gill's mother had given me. I would leave it on the table.

Satisfied that I had done all I could until dawn, I snatched a couple of hours sleep, but was up and ready as soon as the kitchens opened. We might as well take something with us, so I made up some tale about spending the day out-of-doors, missing meals, etc., but everyone was only half-awake, so it wasn't difficult to help myself to a cold chicken, some sausages, a small bag of flour and a string of onions.

After taking these back and packing them, I slipped into the Great Hall for breakfast, as if everything was normal, the Wimperling and Growch with me as usual. We should have to eat as much as we could, for the other food would have to last some time.

I watched carefully as the family appeared, one by one, on the top table. First Sir Robert, yawning hugely, downing two mugs of ale before touching any food. He never even glanced in my direction. Next came Gill's mother, who picked listlessly at a manchet, dipping it in wine, her eyes downcast. Where, oh where was Gill?

At last he appeared, but I would not have recognized him. Even on our worst days on the road he had not looked so disheveled, haggard, outworn. Unshaven, tousled in spite of his cropped head, it seemed as though he had thrown his clothes together in a hurry, and as soon as he sat down next to his mother, he grabbed her arm and started whispering in her ear; no food, no drink, nothing. He didn't glance in my direction either.

Then came Rosamund, and as soon as she appeared she made the position quite clear. In an artfully disarranged dress, she yawned, rolled her eyes; her hair was unbound, her cheeks flushed, and as she made the obligatory curtsy to Sir Robert and his wife she pretended to stagger a little. She sat down next to Gill, and to everyone's fascinated gaze, proceeded to examine her arms and neck for imaginary bruises, smiling contentedly all the while. Above the neckline of her low-cut shift were strawberry bruises; love-marks. She could not have placed them there herself. She appeared to notice Gill for the first time, and her hands flew to her mouth and she gazed away as though she were ashamed.

It was a consummate performance, and it quite halted breakfast. Eating and drinking were temporarily suspended as elbow nudged elbow and nods and winks were exchanged. The message was quite clear, even to those on the bottom tables, and there was a sigh of envious relief as she suddenly swamped him in her arms, pouting, grinning, cuddling up, murmuring in his ear. He looked half-awake, bemused, bewildered, but she leaned across and spoke to his parents, then she nudged him and, prompting as she went, she made him say what she wanted.

I had seen enough, and even as Sir Robert rose to announce that his son's wedding would take place a week hence, the animals and I were making our way back across the courtyard. Now the plotting was confirmed, I had no intention of finding myself suffocated in the midden or letting the Wimperling crackle nicely on a spit; Growch would escape anyway, but what use was that to the pig and me?

I loaded up the Wimperling and myself as quickly as I could and made our way to the gate. We were in luck; two carts were about to go down to the cider-apple orchards, farthest away from the house, and we accepted a lift; no one questioned our right to leave, though all the talk was of the coming wedding and who would be invited. It had been less than a half-hour since Rosamund's performance, yet it seemed everyone had a topic of conversation to last for days. I tried not to listen.

We were only a quarter mile from the forest when the wagon halted. Getting down I thanked them for our lift, and at a nudge and thought from the Wimperling, asked for the quickest road to Evreux, making sure they remembered the direction I had asked for.

"Now, make for the gates as fast as possible," said the Wimperling and within a quarter hour, breathless, we were on the road again. A couple of foresters were at work clearing the undergrowth, and once again, on the Wimperling's prompting, I asked the road to Evreux. Once out of earshot I asked him why the insistence on that road.

"Because if they come after us, they will waste time looking along that way," he answered tranquilly. "We will take the other road west just to throw them off the scent."

"I see. . . . In the note I wrote to Gill I said we were going to Matthew's, so everything is consistent. Clever pig!"

"But your knight won't get the note."

"Why not?"

"If he had done, then he wouldn't bother any further, and the road would be clear for his father to pursue you uninterrupted. Without it he will worry, perhaps insist he goes out with a search-party. . . . Sir Robert won't have it all his own way, and it will give us a better chance."

I hadn't considered this: the Wimperling was cleverer than I thought. He must also know who I was writing to. How did pigs know things like that?

"But what did you do with the letter?"

"I ate it. Ribbon and all."

"Did it taste nice?" asked Growch interestedly.

"No."

"Oh."

"But why should anyone come after us now?" I questioned. "Sir Robert and Rosamund have everything as they want it, surely?"

He didn't answer for a moment, then he said: "Just suppose you had been bothered by a mosquito all night, but hadn't caught it? Then in the morning you saw it again, ready to swat? Would you leave it, on the off chance it would disappear, or would you annihilate it there and then, so there was no further chance of it biting?"

"I see. . . . At least, I think I do."

"All that matters to Sir Robert now is that his son is born legitimate, and no one to question it or deflect his son's interest. He is a very proud man, and to ensure this he would do almost anything, believe me."

The Wimperling wouldn't even let us stop to eat at midday; instead we had to march on, chewing at the chicken. I was getting crosser and crosser as we approached the fork in the road we had turned off before, the right-hand fork, leading to Evreux, the left to the west. I was about to demand a rest when we came across a swineherd grazing his half-dozen charges along the fringes of the forest.

By now I knew what question we were supposed to ask. He pointed the way to Evreux, but as soon as we left him at the turn in the road the Wimperling directed us into the trees to double back.

"Why? Can't we leave it a little longer? This is a good road, and so far no one has come after us. . . ."

"You've still got a lot to learn about human nature! Do as I say. . . ."

We crept back through the trees till we were almost opposite the fork in the road again, and skulked down behind some bushes. Ahead I could see the swineherd patiently prodding his pigs.

"Now what?"

"We wait."

Nothing happened for five, ten minutes, a quarter hour. Then I heard them: hooves thudding down the road from the de Faucon estate. A moment later two horsemen clattered by, wearing swords but no mail. They halted by the swineherd and one called out: "Seen a girl on the road with a couple of animals?"

The swineherd pointed in the direction we had supposedly gone, but when asked how long ago he looked blank; time obviously meant little to him.

The horsemen rode off in the direction of Evreux and in a moment were out of sight.

I stood up. "Gill might have sent them. Why should we hide?"

"They would hardly have come seeking you with an invitation to the wedding armed with swords and daggers! Be sensible. It's as I said; Sir Robert wants to be rid of you."

I had the sense to become frightened. "Then, what do we do?"

"Once they find you are not on the road they have taken, they will come back and take the western road. And if they don't find us, others will be sent out. So, we go back to the estate."

"You must be mad! That's straight back into danger!"

"Not at all. The last place they would look is on their own doorstep. Come on: there's a good five miles to go before sundown!"

Chapter Twenty-Nine

So, using the road, but dodging back into the forest when we thought we heard anything, we made our way back to the estate. We had one more narrow escape: Growch was fifty yards ahead, the Wimperling the same distance behind, and their danger signals came at the same moment. Luckily I had time to hide, only to find that the first couple of horsemen had ridden back, to meet up with a fresh contingent of four who had come straight from Sir Robert. They halted so near my hiding place I could smell both their sweat and that of their lathered animals.

"Find anything?" asked the leader of the second band.

"They took the road to Evreux, according to a peasant we met, but we went a good five miles down and no sign of them. Another fellow coming back from the town reported a wagon going the other way, but we saw no sign of it."

"Fresh instructions: Sir Robert found a door or something leading up to the walk-away, and has reason to believe the girl may be wise to the pursuit. Go back the way you came, search along the way for more clues. We are taking the western road. Orders are the same: lose 'em, permanently!"

"Jewels still missing?"

"So the lady says."

"How's the boy taking it?"

"State of shock. Can't believe it. I fancy he was sweet on her. Can't say as I blame him: know which one I'd've preferred."

And they rode off in the direction of the fork in the road, leaving me in a state of disbelief. So that was Sir Robert's excuse: I was supposed to have stolen some jewels! I realized that it would have made no difference what I had written; valuables would still have disappeared, and I should have been to blame. So now there was a price on my head, and death the reward. No turning back, however much I might have wanted to.

I wondered when the jewels would conveniently turn up again—or would Gill's father believe it worth the game to leave them buried or whatever, and buy Rosamund some more?

Once we reached the demesne, the Wimperling led us along deer tracks through the forest, at a convenient distance from the manor house. We described a great loop around the demesne, going short of food because I couldn't light fires, though the Wimperling and Growch were quite happy with raw sausages. On the third day the Wimperling declared us free of the de Faucon estate, and we found a road of sorts.

At the first village we came to, two days later, I threw caution to the winds, and spent far more than I intended on bought food, luxuriating on pies and roasted meat. In the next village and the next I recouped some of the results of my spendthrift ways with a performance, but villagers have little enough to spend at the best of times, and now the winter was fast approaching.

Which led to the question of where we were headed.

All I had thought about up to now had been escaping Sir Robert, but now was the time to consider our future. I knew Growch had said he wanted a warm fire, a family and plenty to eat, and I had set off on this whole enterprise with the thought of finding a complaisant and wealthy husband, but as far as I could see, neither of us were nearer our goal, once I had refused Matthew's offer. And what of the Wimperling? He had never asked for a destination, had seemed content to follow wherever we went. But we couldn't just go on wandering like this: if nothing else we had to find winter quarters, and soon.

The question of which way to go came up naturally enough. One morning we stood at a crossroads; all roads looked more or less the same, and I had no particular feeling about any of them, except that south would be warmer, and it might be easier to over-winter in or near some town.

"Which way?" I asked the others, not really expecting an answer, for Growch was a follower rather than a leader, and the Wimperling had never expressed a preference. Now, however, he did have something to say.

"Er . . . I'd rather like to discuss that," he said diffidently. "Perhaps we could sit down?"

"Lunchtime anyhow," said Growch, looking up at the weak sun. "Got any more o' that pie left?"

"We finished that yesterday. Cheese, apples, bean loaf, cold bacon—"

"Yes."

The Wimperling chose the apples and I munched on the cheese.

"Right, Wimperling, what did you have in mind?"

He still seemed reluctant to ask. "When—when you so kindly rescued me," he began, "I said I would like to tag along because there was nowhere special I wanted to go. . . ."

I nodded encouragingly. "And now there is?"

"There wasn't then, but there is now. Yes." He sat back on his haunches, looking relieved. "Let me explain. When I was little I was brought up as a pig and believed I was one—in spite of the wings and the other bits that didn't quite fit." He held up one foot, and looked at the claws, much bigger now. "See what I mean? Well, ever since then as I have been growing I have felt more and more that I wasn't a pig. What I was, I didn't quite know, though I had my suspicions. Then, that night when we crossed the border, I thought I knew. And the feeling has been growing stronger ever since."

"Can you tell us?"

He shuffled about a bit. "I'd rather not, just yet. In case I'm terribly wrong . . . But I should like you to come with me, to find out. You might find it quite interesting, I think."

I looked at Growch, who was practically standing on his head trying to get a piece of rind out of his back teeth. No help there.

"Of course we will come. Where do you want to go? How far away is it?"

"One hundred and twelve miles and a quarter west-southwest," he said precisely. "Give or take a yard or so."

I flung my arms about his neck, laughing, then planted a kiss on his snout. "How on earth can you be so—"

But before I had finished my sentence an extraordinary explosion took place. The Wimperling literally zoomed some twenty feet into the air vertically, then whizzed first right and then left and then in circles, almost faster than the eye could see. As he was now considerably larger than I was, I was tumbled head-over-heels and Growch disappeared into a bush, rind and all.

The whole thing can only have lasted some fifteen seconds or so, but it seemed forever. I curled up in a ball for protection, my fingers in my ears, my eyes tight shut, until an almighty thump on the ground in front of me announced the Wimperling's return to earth.

I opened my eyes, my ears and finally my mouth. "You nearly scared the skin off me! What in the world do you think you're *doing*?" I asked furiously. Then: "You're—you're *different*!"

He looked as if someone had just taken him apart and then reassembled him rather badly. Everything was in the right place, more or less, but the pieces looked as if they might have been borrowed from half a dozen other animals. His ears were smaller, his tail longer, his back scalier, his snout bigger, his chest deeper, his stomach flatter, his claws more curved, and the lumps on his side where he hid his wings looked like badly folded sacks. He looked less like a pig than ever, while still being one, and his expression was pure misery.

My anger and fright evaporated like morning mist. "Oh, Wimperling! I'm so sorry! You look dreadful—was it something I said? Or did?"

His voice had gone unexpectedly deep and gruff, as if his insides had been shaken up as well. "You kissed me. I told you once before never to do that again. . . . Remember?"

I did, now. "Sorry, sorry, sorry! It's just that—just that when one feels grateful or happy or loving it seems the right thing to do. For me, anyway." I thought. "It didn't have the same effect on Gill. And, come to that, I've never kissed Growch. . . ."

"Who wants kisses, anyway?" demanded the latter, who had crept out from his bush, minus rind, I was glad to see. "Kissin's soppy; kissin's for pups and babies an' all that rubbish!" Something told me that in spite of the words he was jealous, so I picked him up and planted three kisses on his nose.

"There! Now you're one ahead. . . ."

He rubbed his nose on his paws and then sneezed violently. "*Gerroff*! Shit: now you'll have me sneezin' all night. . . . Poof!" He nodded towards the Wimperling. "An' if that's what a kiss can do, then I don' wan' no more, never!"

I turned back to the Wimperling. "Better now?"

He nodded. "Think so . . ." His voice was still deep, and if I hoped he would regain his old shape gradually, I was to be disappointed. "As I was saying, before all—this—happened—" He looked down at his altered shape. "I should like to go to the place where it all started. The place where I was hatched, born, whatever . . . The Place of Stones."

This sounded interesting. "And is this the place that you said was a hundred miles or so to the west-something?"

He nodded.

I wasn't going to miss this, hundred miles or no. "Will you set up your home where you were born?" "Hatched" still sounded silly. Pigs aren't hatched.

"No. It will merely be the place from where I set out on a longer journey, to the place where my ancestors came from."

"A sentimental journey, then," I said.

"An essential one. Without going back to the beginnings I will not have my coordinates."

"Yer *what*?"

"Guidelines, dog. Itinerary to humans."

Growch scratched vigorously. "Me ancestors go back as far as me mum, and I doubt if even she knew who me dad was, and as for me guidelines . . . I follows me nose." And he accompanied the said object into the bushes, his tail waving happily.

"And how far is it to where your ancestors came from?"

"Many thousands of miles," said the Wimperling. "A journey only I can take. But I should be glad of your company as far as the Place of Stones. . . ."

"You have it," I said. We sat quiet for a moment, and I suddenly realized that my conversations had been, for a long time, on a different level with the Wimperling than with the others. He didn't just "talk" in short sentences about the food or the weather, he communicated with me as though we were two equal beings, talking about feelings and emotions, even philosophizing a little. He wasn't really like an animal at all—

"And then you will be free to seek that husband of yours," continued the Wimperling, as though I had just said something. "Will you tell him your real name?"

I gazed at him blankly. "My *real* name? What do you mean? My name is Summer—well, Somerdai."

"The name on the register, as you keep telling yourself. Your birth was recorded by the priest but he never knew the exact date. So he wrote 'Summer day,' only he ran the letters together and misspelled them because he was an old man. . . . But when you saw it written down you seized on the name, as a convenient way of burying deeper the hurt when you learned your real, given name. . . ."

I was stunned. How did he know about the register? But it was my name, it was, it was! If I'd had another, then my mother would have called me by it instead of "girl," or "daughter" as she always did.

"I know because the memory is still there inside you," he said, "hurting to get out. Thoughts like that escape sometimes when you are asleep because they want to be out in the open. I have become used to your thoughts in the time we have traveled together. You have tried to kill the memory because you are ashamed, but let it go and you will feel better. I know, because I am not what they called me, Wimperling, and when my new name comes I shall be a different person."

A nasty, horrid picture was forming in my mind, however hard I tried to stifle it, cry "Go away! I don't want to remember. It happened to someone else, not me!" A child, a girl of four or five, a fat little girl, was playing on the doorstep as one of her mother's clients came to the door. And the mother said to the child: "Go and play for a while, girl. . . ." And the man said: "Why don't you call her by her given name?"

" . . . and my mother said: 'How can I call that shapeless lump with the pudding-face *Talitha* when she is neither graceful nor beautiful, nor will ever be? I was pregnant when—when her father died, and he had made me promise to give her that name if it were a girl. Of course I agreed, never expecting she would be so plain and clumsy!'" I was crying now, hot tears of shame and remembered humiliation. "How could you remind me! I had forgotten, I didn't remember, it *hurts*!"

"And that is why you stuffed the memory away for so long, just because you were afraid of the hurt. But it was a long time ago, and things—and people—change. Now you have let it out, you will heal, believe me, and be whole." He hesitated. "I will not be with you much longer, so please forgive me. I did it for you."

"Yes, yes, I know you did. . . ." I tried the name on my tongue. Now I remembered my father had chosen it, it seemed right. "I feel better already. Thanks, Whimper . . . But you said you weren't. Aren't . . . you know what I mean! What is *your* real name?"

He shook his head. "That's the exciting thing. I don't know yet. It comes with the change, the rebirth if you like. All I know is that I took a form and a name that was convenient at the time, in order to survive. That's how I remember how far it is, counting the steps we traveled when they took me away. And that is how I can guide you there."

"Then what are we waiting for? Let's get going. Come on Growch, wherever you are: we are going to a place full of stones, and you can christen every one!"

"Oh, I don't think so," said the Wimperling. "These stones are—different."

We were now in the last couple of weeks of October, and the weather stayed fine. We made leisurely progress, ten or twelve miles a day, but the terrain changed dramatically with every turn of the road. Villages became smaller, more isolated, there were fewer farms and no great houses or castles. The land became rocky, wilder, less hospitable, and now, instead of dusty lanes, there were sheep tracks, moorland paths, great stretches of heather, thyme, gorse and broom. A barren land as far as crops went, but with a wild beauty of its own.

The winds blew with no hindrance, whirling my hair into great tangles and carrying in their arms gulls, buzzards, crows, peregrines and merlin. The undergrowth hid fox, hare, coney, stoat, weasel and an occasional marten; under our feet the ground was springy with mosses, lichen, heather, bilberry, juniper, cotton grass and bracken, the latter the color of Matthew's hair, Saffron's cat-coat. Away from the paths the going was tough; wet feet, scratched legs and turned ankles the penalty for trying a shortcut.

We came upon a small village, some seven days before the end of the month, and the Wimperling advised me to stock up. They had only had a small harvest, but were eager to have coin to buy in some grain, so I used what little I had left and was rewarded with cheese, salt pork, honey, turnip, onion and small apples, till I could hardly stagger away under the weight. Once away from the village however, the Wimperling insisted I load most of it on his back.

"My strength is much greater now I approach the end of my journey."

"So is your size," I said, for now he was truly enormous: over twice as big as me, length and breadth.

"Ah, but I have much to hide. . . ."

"If you hides it much longer you'll burst," said Growch. "If'n I had that load abroad I reckon me legs'ud be worn to stumps."

"Really? I was under the impression that is what had happened already. . . ."

The next day we topped a rise in the land and there were the Stones in the distance. Not just ordinary stones, but ones of great size and power, even from miles away. I could feel them now from where I stood, both repelling and attracting at the same time. We had already passed the odd standing stone and the stumps of plundered circles, but there for the first time was a veritable forest, a city of stones: circles, lanes, avenues, clumps; grey and forbidding, they pointed cold stone fingers at the sky, now whipped by a westerly into a roil of rearing clouds. Down here at ground level it was still relatively calm, but the heavens were racing faster than man could run.

The Wimperling heaved a great tremble of anticipation and satisfaction. "The Place of Stones starts here. Half a day's journey and we are there."

Briefly I wondered how we were going to find our way back to civilization without our guide, but I held my tongue, sure he would have a solution.

That night we sheltered in a dell, the freshening wind creaking the branches of the twisted pine and rowan above our heads, the latter's leaves near all gone, the few berries blackened. I fell asleep uneasily, with Growch tucked against my side, to wake half a dozen times. And each time it was to see the Wimperling standing still as the stones, his gaze fixed westward, the wind flapping his small ears, his snout questing from side to side and up and down, as though reading a message in the night only he could comprehend.

In the morning the wind had swung to the northwest and it was noticeably chillier. After breakfast, as I strapped the Wimperling's burdens to his back, I noticed how hot his skin felt, as if he was burning from some internal fever; I made some silly quip about burning my fingers, but I don't think he even heard. His gaze was fixed on the journey ahead, and he didn't seem ill in any way, only impatient to be off.

The further we went, the more stones; some upright, others broken, a few lying full length, yet more with a drunken lean like the few trees in this bare landscape, which all grew away from the prevailing westerlies, like little hunched people with their hoods up and their cloaks flapping in the breeze.

More and more stones, and yet we never seemed to get near enough to them to touch. There they were to left and right, ahead, behind, distinguishable apart by their different shapes, height, angle, markings and yet as soon as I headed towards one I found I had mysteriously left it behind, or it had grown more distant. I even felt as though I passed the same monolith a dozen times as if we were walking in circles through a gigantic maze, but the Wimperling still trotted forward confidently and the ring was quiet on my finger.

At last we came to a great avenue of stone, and there in the distance was a huddle of ruined buildings on a small rise. The Wimperling stopped and looked back at us. "There it is," he said simply. "Journey's end."

It didn't look like much to me, and looked less so the nearer we approached. It was the remains of what had obviously been a small farm—cottage, barn, stable and sty—and the buildings were rapidly crumbling. The thatch had gone, apart from some on one corner of the cottage, the broken-shuttered windows gaped like missing teeth and all walls and fencing had been broken down. The place was deserted, no people, no animals and, perhaps because it was the only sign of civilization we had seen in a couple of days, the desolation seemed worse than it probably was.

"And all this in less than a year," said the Wimperling, as if to himself. "They angered the Stones. . . ." Then he turned to us. "You must be hungry and tired. And cold, too. Come with me and don't be afraid. I promise you will feel better in a little while."

I hoped so. Just at that moment I felt I had had more than enough of the mysterious Stones: all I wanted was to find some cozy corner inside where I could curl up and forget outside.

He led us to that part of the cottage adjoining the barn where there was still a corner of roofing. The room itself was about twelve feet square, with a central hearth, but I dragged over enough stones to make another fireplace under the remaining thatch. There was plenty of wood lying about, and I soon had a cheerful blaze going, the smoke obliging by curling up and disappearing without hindrance. I found a stave in one corner and, binding some heather to the end, made a broom stout enough to sweep away the debris from our end of the room. Then I went out and gathered enough bracken to make a comfortable bed for later. The Wimperling showed me where a small spring trickled away past the house, and I filled the cooking pot and set about dinner.

I had the bone from the salt bacon, root vegetables and onion, and was just adding a pinch or two of herbs when the Wimperling strode in with a carefully wrapped leaf in his mouth. Inside were other leaves, some mushrooms and a powder I couldn't identify, but on his nod I added them all to the stew, and the aroma that immediately spread around the room had me salivating and Growch's stomach rumbling. I had a little flour left so I put some dough to cook on a hot hearthstone. I tasted the stew, added a little salt, then walked outside to join the Wimperling and Growch, who were variously gazing up at a waxing moon, some three or four days off full, riding uneasily at anchor among the tossing clouds, and searching the old midden for anything edible.

"Will it rain tonight?"

"Probably," said the Wimperling. "But we have shelter."

"Is it—time? Are you going tomorrow?"

"No, the time is not quite right. A day or two."

"We haven't got much food left. . . ."

"Don't worry. The food will last."

And that night it seemed he was right. However much we ate—and Growch and I stuffed ourselves silly on a stew that tasted like no other I had ever come across—the pot still seemed full. The Wimperling said he wasn't hungry, but he did have a nibble of bread.

As we sat round in the firelight, the fire damped down by some turves of peat I had found in the barn, I felt sleepier than I had for ages; not exhausted but happily tired, the sort of tiredness that looks forward to dream. Growch was yawning at my feet, stretching then relaxing, his eyes half-shut already.

"Gawdamighty! I could sleep fer days. . . ."

"Why not?" said the Wimperling.

"He'd die of starvation in his sleep," I said, laughing, and stifled a yawn.

"Not necessarily. What about those animals who sleep all winter?"

"Good idea," I said. "Wake me in March. . . ." And as I wrapped myself tight in my father's old cloak and lay down on the springy bracken bed, Growch at my feet, I gazed sleepily at the glowing embers of the fire, breaking into abortive little flames every now and again, or creeping like tiny snakes across the peat, till all merged into a pattern that repeated itself, changed a fraction, moved away, came back. Soothing patterns, familiar patterns, patterns in the mind, sleep-making patterns . . .

When I finally came to I found it was already mid-afternoon, and Growch was still snoring. The fire smoldered under a great heap of ash that seemed to have doubled overnight. I broke the bread, stale now, into the stew, and put it on to heat up. Then I went outside to relieve myself and look for the Wimperling, but he was nowhere about. I went down to the spring for a quick, cold wash, for I still felt sleepy, then combed out my tangled hair. Still no sign of the Wimperling. He couldn't have gone without saying good-bye, surely?

It had obviously rained overnight, for the ground was damp and the heather wetted my ankles as I lifted my skirts free from the moisture. After calling out three or four times I shrugged and went back to dish out the stew, leaving a good half for our companion. I cleaned out the bowls, banked up the fire and went outside again. The wind was still strong, but it seemed to be veering back towards the west and the biting chill had gone.

Something large trotted out of the shadows. "Were you looking for me?"

"Wimperling! Where have you been?"

"Around and about . . . Did you sleep well?"

"Like a babe! Your supper is waiting."

"I'm fine without, thanks." He gazed up at the sky, where the moon seemed to bounce back and forth between the clouds like a blown-up bladder. "Tonight I can sup off the stars and drink the clouds. . . ."

"And what about the moon? I teased, looking up at where she hung, free of cloud at last. "A bite or two of—Oh, my God!"

I felt as if I had been kicked in the stomach. "I don't understand!" Suddenly I was afraid. "Last night when I went to sleep the moon was three or four days short of full. And now . . ."

And now the moon was full.

Chapter Thirty

"Yes," said the Wimperling, following my gaze. "You have slept through four days. 'Like a babe' is what I think you said."

Just like that. Like saying I overslept. Or missed Mass.

There was still a clutch of fear in my stomach. "I don't understand! Magic? How? Why?"

"No magic, just a pinch of special herbs in your stew. They slowed down your mind and your body, therefore you needed less breath, less food, less drink. As to why . . . As you said, there was little food left, and I had some things to do while you slept."

I still felt scared that anyone's body could be so used without their knowledge and permission; suppose, for instance, the dose had been too strong? And did one age the same while in that sleep? Did one dream? I couldn't remember any.

As usual, he knew what I was thinking.

"I wouldn't hurt you for the world, you know that. The dose was carefully measured. All it meant was that you and the dog had a longer rest than usual, that's all. And saved on food. No, you haven't gained time and yes, you did dream. One has to. But you don't always remember."

"What—things—did you do?"

"I will show you. When—when I am gone, if you travel due west for two days, you will come to a road that leads either south or east. You will have enough food to last till you come to another village. As to coinage—Follow me!"

He led us back to the room we had slept in, and there, in a heap on the floor, were twenty gold coins.

"It takes time to make those," he said.

I ran the coins through my fingers. "Are they real?" They felt very cold to the touch.

"As real as I can make them. More solid than faery gold, which can disappear in a breath. But you must be careful how you use them. As long as they are used honestly for trade they will stay as they are, although each time they change hands they will lose a little of their value. A coating of gold, you might say. But if they are stolen or used dishonestly, then the perpetrator will die."

"How are they made?"

"White fire, black blood, green earth, yellow water."

None of which I had ever come across, but I supposed anything was possible with a flying pig-not-a-pig. A large flying pig. Very large. Now he almost reached my shoulder: those four days sleep of mine had made him almost twice as big again.

"You will soon be too big for your skin, you know," I said jokingly.

He looked at me gravely. "I hope so. . . . Come and see what else I have been doing. You'd better make up the fire, while you're at it."

"I've been letting it die down. I can light it again for breakfast. It's not cold."

"Don't you remember what your mother taught you? On no account let the house fires go out on the eve of Samhain, lest Evil gain entry. . . ."

"Samhain? All Hallows' Eve?"

He nodded, and I suddenly realized that it had been exactly a year ago that I had made a funeral pyre of our house for my mother and had set out on my adventures.

A year, a whole year . . . Somehow it seemed longer. That other life seemed a hundred years and a million miles away. I couldn't even clearly recall the girl I had been then: this Summer was a totally different person. For one thing she had a name—two names, in fact. For another, this person would not have been content to sit by the fire and dream, and eat honey cakes till she burst. In fact, I couldn't now remember when I had the last one. This girl now talked to animals, tramped the roads, thought less of her own bodily comforts and more of others, and had learned a great deal that was not taught in books. And hadn't used one single item of her expensive education that she could recall . .

I threw a couple more logs on the fire and then followed the Wimperling out and across the yard to where the pigsties had once been, an unusually subdued Growch tailing us. The Wimperling stepped over what had once been one of the walls of the sty, and now in the middle, rising some six feet high, was a newly built cairn of stones.

"Did you build this?"

"Takeoff point," he said.

I looked at him. He seemed so different from the little persecuted pig I had stolen from the fair and run off with tucked under my arm. Not just the size, which was phenomenal; he had also grown in confidence over the months I had known him. He was mature, patient, wise, and had saved us more than once with courage and good advice. I had lost my little piglet to an adult one, and wasn't sure whether to be glad or sorry.

"What are you going to do?"

"You will see. First let me tell you a little of what happened when I was young. . . ."

I sat down on part of the old wall and listened, Growch at my feet.

"This is where I was bom. The very spot I hatched." "Hatched" again, as though he truly believed he had come from an egg. "I was raised, as you know, among a litter of innumerable little piglets, although I didn't grow exactly the same and stayed the runt of the litter. As I told you, I would probably have made a fine dish of suckling pig if the farmer hadn't discovered my stubs of wings, and sold me. After weeks of torment you found me, and the rest you know."

"But if you were unhappy here, and pretending to be something you were not, why come back?"

"Because this place is a Place of Power. It was arranged that I start my breathing life here, and also meant that I eventually leave from here for the land of my ancestors. The fact that a farmer built a pigsty over my hatching place was an accident that couldn't have been foreseen. However, once I had been sold, the Stones made sure they left and destroyed what remained of the farm. The Stones are my Guardians, they have watched and waited for a hundred years for my birth and then the Change."

"What?" I couldn't believe what I was hearing. He was fantasizing. "You waited to be born—for a *hundred* years?"

"Legends have it as a thousand, but that is an exaggeration. A hundred is the minimum, though, but the warmth of the sty above me accelerated things somewhat and I only had ninety-nine years. This hadn't given my personality enough charge to resist the nearness of the other piglets, so I adapted their bodily conformation to give myself time to acclimatize before the Change. Exactly a year, in fact."

I was utterly bewildered. I had lost him somewhere. Hatching, a hundred years, Stones of Power, a "change," guardians . . . I seized on one question. "You say the stones around us are Stones of Power? What does that mean?"

"Listen. Listen and feel. Where we are now is the centre of it all, like the center of a spider's web. If you hung like a hawk from the sky you would see the pattern. This is not the only Center of Power, of course: they exist in other countries as well. Because of their special magic they have been used since understanding began for birth, breeding, death, religions, sacrifice, healing. I say again: listen and feel. . . ."

I tried. At first, although the night was still as an empty church, I could hear nothing special. Then there was a growl from Growch and I began to feel something. A low, very faint vibration, as though someone had plucked the lowest string of a bass viol, waited till the sound died away, then touched the silent string and still found it stirring under their finger. I put both hands flat on the ground and found I could hear it as well, though the sound was not on one note, it came from a hundred, a thousand different strings, all just on the edge of hearing. I felt the sound both through my body and in my ears at the same time, both repelling and attracting, till I felt as if I had been a rat shaken by a terrier. Beside me Growch was whimpering, lifting first one paw then the other from the ground—

"Understand now?" asked the Wimperling, and with his voice the noise and vibration faded and was still. "That is why I had to come back. Had my life been as it should, my hatching taken place at the right time, had

I not become part pig, I should have needed no one. But you were instrumental in saving my life, you have fed and tended me, and now I need you as the final instrument to cut me from my past. I cannot be rid of this constriction without you," and he flexed and stretched and twisted and strove as though he were indeed bound by bonds he could not loose.

"Anything," I said. "Anything, of course. How soon—how soon before you change?" I wanted to ask into what, but didn't dare. I didn't think I wanted to know, not just yet, anyway. In fact, just for a moment I wished I was anywhere but here, then affection and common sense returned: nothing he became could harm us.

He glanced up at the sky. The moon was calm and full and clear and among the stars there ran the Hare and Leveret, the Hunter, his Dog and the Cooking Pan. There were the Twins, the Ram, the Red Star, the Blue, the White. . . . No wind as yet, night a hushed breath, as if it, too, waited as we did.

Around us the ruins of the farm, all hummocks and heaps, farther away the Stones, seeming to catch from the moon and stars a ghostly radiance all their own, casting their shadows like fingers across the heath, so the land was all bars of silver and black like some strange tapestry bearing a pattern just out of reach of comprehension. And yet if one looked long enough . . .

"Five minutes," said the Wimperling. "When the shadow of the cairn touches the nearest Stone. Climb up with me and you will see. . . . That's right. See, there is room for us both at the top."

Growch yipped beneath us, and scrabbled with his claws at the stone but could get no further.

"This is not for you, dog," said the Wimperling. "Be patient." He turned to me. "Do you have your sharp little knife with you?"

"Of course." I touched the little pouch at my waist where it always lay, wondering why he wanted to know.

"Then it is farewell to you both, Girl and Dog. My thanks to you, and may you find what you seek soon." He took a deep breath. "I had not thought partings would be so hard. . . . Are you ready, Talitha?"

"Yes," I said, wondering what was to happen next. The shadow was creeping nearer and nearer to the Stone. . . . "At least I think I am."

"Then take out your knife, and when I count to ten, but not before, cut my throat. One . . ."

Chapter Thirty-One

"Two . . ."

"What are you *talking* about?"

"Three . . . Four . . ."

"I'm doing no such thing! How could I possibly hurt you?"

"Five—"

"Listen, *listen*! If I dig this knife into you—"

"Six—"

"—you will *die*! I thought you said you were going to—"

"Seven!"

"I won't, I can't!"

"Eight!"

"Wimperling, Wimperling, I can't kill you!"

"Nine! Do it! You *must*!"

"I love you too much to—"

"Do it *now,* before it's too late! Ten . . ."

And there was such a look of agonized entreaty on his face that I brought the knife out and drew it across his skin. The tiny gash started to bleed, a necklace of dark drops in the moonlight, and I couldn't do any more. I had rather cut my own throat.

"Talitha, Summer—there are only a few seconds left!" His voice was full of an imprisoned anguish. "*Please . . .*"

"I *can't*! Stay a pig: I'll care for you always, I promise!" and I flung away the knife, threw my arms around his neck and kissed him.

There was a tremendous bang! like a thunderbolt, a great blast of hot air, and I was toppled off the cairn. The moon and stars were blotted out and I lay stunned, conscious only of a huge tumult in the air, as if a storm had burst right over my head. I could hear Growch yelping with terror, but where was the Wimperling?

I sat up, my head spinning, and saw an extraordinary sight. The body of the flying pig was hurtling around the cairn like a burst bladder, every second getting smaller and smaller. Pony-size, man-size, hound-size, piglet-size, until at last it collapsed at my feet, a tiny bundle no bigger than my purse, and the moon appeared again.

Crawling forward I picked up the pathetic little bundle and held it to my breast, rocking back and forth and sobbing. Once again I had been asked to help, once again it had all gone wrong. At least I had never physically harmed any of the others, but there was my precious little flying pig burst into smithereens, and all I had left was a split piece of hide with the imprint of a face and a string of tail, four little hooves and two small pouches where his wings had been—

"Look up! Look up . . . !" The voice came from the air, from the clouds that were now massing to the west, from the Stones—

The Stones! They were alight, they burned like candles. One after the other their tips started to glow with a greenish light as if they were tracking another great shadow that glowed itself with the same unearthly light as it swooped, banked and turned, dived in great loops from sky to earth and back again. The sky was full of light and there was a smell like the firecrackers I had once seen, and a beating sound like dozens of sheets flapping in a gale.

Again came the voice: "Look up! Look up!" but I could only hug the remains of the Wimperling, little cold pieces of leather, and cry. Growch crept to my feet from wherever he had been hiding, whimpering softly.

"Great gods! What was it? Where's the pig? Are you all right? C'mon, let's get back inside. . . ."

But even as he whined there was a sudden rush of air that had me flat on my back again and there, balancing precariously on the cairn above us, wings flapping to maintain balance, clawed feet gripping the shifting stones was a—

Was a great dragon!

I think I fainted, for darkness rushed into my eyes and I felt my insides gurgling away in a spiral down some hole, like water draining away and out down a privy, and there was a peculiar ashy smell in my nostrils. Then everything steadied, I decided I had been seeing things because of the terror of the night, and cautiously opened one eye. . . .

It was still there.

The great wings were now quiet at its sides, and the scaly tail with the arrow-like tip was curled neatly around its clawed feet. The great nostrils were flared, as if questing my scent, the lips were slightly curved back above the pointed teeth, but the yellow eyes with the split pupils seemed to hold quite a benign gaze. I could see its hide rise and fall as it breathed.

I had never seen a dragon before, but it closely resembled the pictures I had seen, the descriptions I had read, so I knew what it was. Perhaps if I stayed perfectly still it would go away. It couldn't be hungry, for it had obviously eaten the Wimperling. So I waited, scarcely daring to breathe, conscious of Growch trembling at my side.

It cleared its throat, rather like emptying a sack of stones.

"Well?" it said, in a gritty voice. "How do I look?"

I swallowed, surprised it could speak or that I could understand. But of course the ring on my finger . . . Come to think of it, why wasn't it throbbing a warning? To my surprise it was still and warm. Perhaps after all, dragons didn't eat maidens, in spite of what the legends said.

"Er . . . Very smart," I said, my voice a squeak. "Very . . . grand."

It stretched its great wings, one after the other, till I could see the moon shine faintly through the thin skin, like a lamp through horn shutters. "Still a bit creaky, but they haven't dried properly yet," said the dragon. "Everything else seems to be stretching and adjusting quite nicely. Of course I shall have to take it in short bursts for a day or two, but—"

"What have you done with the Wimperling?" I blurted out. "He was my friend, and all he wanted was to return to his ancestors! He never harmed anyone, and—and . . . If you've swallowed him, could you possibly spit him out again? I have his skin here, and I could sew him up in it and give him a decent burial. And if you're still hungry, I have some salt pork and vegetables left. . . ."

He stared at me, and for a moment I thought if he hadn't been a dragon, he would have laughed.

"You want your little pig back?"

"Of course. I said he was my friend. Now I am alone, except for my dog. He—he's somewhere about. . . ." Hiding, I thought, as I should have been.

"You offered me salt pork. . . . Pork is pig."

"Not—not like the Wimperling. He was different. He wasn't a *real* pig. You want some? Wait a moment. . . ." and I dashed back inside and emerged with the cook pot and put it on the cairn. "I'm afraid it's only warm. . . ." But there was no sign of the dragon. "Don't go away! It's here," I called out.

"So am I," said a small voice. "But I can't reach it there," and a tiny slightly blurred piglet was at my feet, just the same size as the Wimperling when I first met him. I bent to scoop him into my arms, my heart beating joyously, but as my hands closed over him he was gone, only the scrap of hide I had earlier cuddled in my fingers. Then I was angry. I shook my fist at the sky.

"I don't care who or what you are!" I screamed. "You cheated me! Just eat your accursed stew, and I hope it chokes you. *Where's my Wimperling?*"

A man stepped from the shadows behind the cairn, a tall man wearing a hooded cloak that was all jags and points. I could not see his face and my heart missed a couple of beats. I snatched up my little sharp knife, the one I had thrown away only minutes ago, and held it in front of me.

"Keep away, or I'll set my dog on you!"

"That arrant coward? He couldn't—Ouch!"

Apparently Growch was less afraid of strangers than he was of dragons, for he darted from the shadows and gave the man's ankle a swift and accurate nip before dashing back, barking fiercely.

"Mmmm . . ." said the stranger. "I could blunt all your teeth for that, Dog!" He addressed me. "I mean you no harm, so put that knife away. You weren't so keen to use it five minutes ago, to help your friend."

So he had seen it all. I wondered where he had been hiding. I tried to peek under his hood, but he jerked his head away.

"Not yet. It takes time. . . ."

I didn't know what he was talking about. Just then the rising wind caught the edge of his jagged cloak and a hand came out to pull it back. I stared in horror: the hand was like a claw, the fingers scaled like a chicken's foot. What was this man? A monstrosity? A leper? He saw the look in my eyes.

"Sorry, Talitha-Summer. I had thought to spare you that. See . . ." and held out a hand, now a normal, everyday sort. "I told you it would take time. Better with a little more practice. And it's all your fault, you know. . . . If you hadn't kissed me—not once, but the magic three times—I would have appeared to you only in my dragon skin. As it is, I am now obliged to spend part of my life as a man." He sighed. "And yet it was that last kiss of yours that set me free. If you had but kissed me once there would have been a blurring at the edges every once in a while, human thoughts. Two kisses, a part-change now and again and a definite case of human conscience—which hampers a dragon, you know. But the magic three . . ."

"*Wimperling?*"

"The same. And different." He came forward and one hand reached out and clasped mine, warm and reassuring. The other threw back the concealing hood and there, smiling down at me, was at one and the same time the handsomest and most forbidding face I had ever seen.

Dark skin and hair, high cheekbones, a wide mouth, a hooked nose, frowning brows, a determined chin. And the eyes? Dragon-yellow with lashes like a spider's legs. Under the cloak he was naked; his hands, his feet, were manlike, but at elbow and knee, chest and belly, there was a creasing like the skin of a snake's belly. Even as I looked the scaly parts shifted and man-skin took their place.

"You see what you have done?"

"Does it hurt?" I asked wonderingly. Down there, at his groin, he was all man, I noted, with a funny little stirring in my insides.

"Changing? Not really. More uncomfortable, I suppose. Like struggling in the dark into an unfamiliar set of clothes that don't fit and are inside out."

"How long can you stay? When did you know what you were meant to be? When—when will you change back? Er . . . Do you want the stew?"

He laughed, a normal hearty man's laugh. "How long can I stay? A few minutes more, I suppose. Until I start changing back into my real self and my dragon-body. When did I know I was meant to be a dragon? Almost as soon as I was hatched, but the piglet bit fazed me a little. I was sure again that night when we crossed the border and I set the forest on fire with dragon's breath—" Of course! The question I had forgotten to ask at the time. "The stew? No, from now on my diet will be different. Here," and he lifted it down from the top of the cairn.

"Like what?" said Growch, already accepting the situation and sniffing around the stew pot. I tipped some out for him.

"Well, back east where my ancestors come from, there is a land called Cathay, and there—"

"And there they has those enticing little bitches wiv the short legs and the fluffy tails!" said Growch, the stew temporarily forgotten. "*That* was the name they used: Cathay!"

"And men with yellow skins and a civilization that goes back a thousand years! You have a one-track—no, two-track mind, Dog: food and sex. There are other things in life, you know. . . ."

"Not as important. Think about it, dragon-pig-man: reckon in some ways as I'm cleverer than you."

Sustenance and propagation, with the spice of fear to leaven it: he could be right.

But the Wimperling-dragon-man ignored him and took my hand. "Let's walk a way. I don't know how long I can stay like this. Trust me?" And we strolled towards the nearest Stones, an avenue shimmering softly in the moonlight, a soft green, nearly as bright as glowworms.

As we walked I became gradually aware of his hand still clasping mine, of the contact of skin to skin, and my whole body seemed to warm like a fire. There were tickly sensations on my groin, tingly ones in my breasts and I'm sure my face burned like fire. I had never realized that palm-to-palm contact could be so erotic, could engender such a feeling of intimacy.

He stopped and swung me round to face him. "Well, Talitha-Summer, this is journey's end for us. Where will you go?"

"Wait a minute!" I didn't want to say good-bye, and couldn't think straight. "You know my name, but what is yours? We called you the Wimperling, but that was a pet name, a piglet name."

He laughed. "In Cathay they will call me the One-who-beats-his-wings-against-the-clouds-and-lights-the-sky-with-fire, but that is a ceremonial name and you'd never be able to pronounce it in their tongue. My shorter name is 'Master-of-Many-Treasures,' and that does have a Western equivalent: Jasper."

"Like the stone," I said. "Black and brown and yellow . . . I don't want you to go!" Gauche, naive and true.

He didn't laugh, just took both my hands in his.

"If I were only a man, my beautiful Talitha-Summer, I would stay."

But that made me angry and embarrassed, and I pulled my hands away. "Now you are laughing at me! Don't mock; I am fat and ugly, not in the slightest bit beautiful. . . ." I was close to tears.

"Dear girl, would I lie to you? Look, my love, look!" And in front of us was a mirror of clarity I couldn't believe. I saw the reflection of the man-dragon beside a woman I didn't recognize. Slim, straight-backed with a mass of tangled hair, a pretty girl with eyes like a deer, a clear skin, a straight nose and an expressive mouth—a woman I had never seen before.

"You're lying! It's some fiendish magic! I'm not—not like *that*!" I gestured at the image and it gestured back at me. "I'm ugly, fat, spotty. . . ."

"You were. When you rescued me you were all you said, but a year of wandering has worn away the fat your mother disguised you with. She didn't want a pretty daughter to rival her, so she did the only thing she could, short of disfigurement: she fattened you up like a prize pig, so that only a pervert would prefer you. Now you are all you should be. Why do you think Matthew wanted to marry you? Gill leave all behind and run away with you? You're beautiful, Summer-Talitha, and don't ever forget it!"

I reached out my hand to touch the reflection and it vanished, but not before I had seen the Unicorn's ring on my finger reflected back at me. So, it was true.

"Look at me," said the dragon-man, the Wimperling, Jasper. "Look into my eyes. You will see the same picture."

It was so. Dark though it was, I could see myself in the pupils of his eyes, a different Summer. I shivered. Instantly he put his cloak around both of us and pulled me towards him, so I could feel the heat of his body.

"Too much to comprehend all in one day? Don't worry: tomorrow you will be used to being beautiful. And now I must go: it will take me many days and nights to—"

"Don't! Please don't leave me. . . ."

"I must, girl. From now on our paths lie in different directions. Go back to Matthew, who will love and care for you, take the dragon gold to a big city and find a man you fancy, travel to—"

"I want you," I said. "Just you. Kiss me, please. . . ." and I reached up and pulled his head down to mine, my hands cupped around his head. Suddenly he responded, he pulled me close, as close as a second skin, and his mouth came down on mine. It was a fierce, hot, possessive kiss that had my whole being fused into his and my body melting like sun-kissed ice into his warmth.

Then, oh then, we were no longer standing, we were lying and—and I don't know what happened. There was a pain like knives and a sharp joy that made me cry out—

And then I was pinned to the ground by a huge scaly beast and I cried out in horror and scrambled away, my revulsion as strong as the attraction I had felt only moments since.

"You see," said the dragon, in his different, gritty voice. "It didn't work. For a moment, perhaps, but you would not like my real self. Don't hurt yourself wishing it were any different."

I swallowed. "But for a moment, back there, you forgot the dragon bit completely. We were both human beings." I felt sore and bruised inside.

He was silent for a moment, shifting restlessly. "Perhaps," he said finally: "but it shouldn't have happened. It gave me a taste for . . . Never mind. Forget it. Forget me. Bury your remembrances with that scrap of hide you kept. Go and live the life you were meant to lead.

"And now: stand clear!"

He flapped his great wings once, twice, as a warning and I scrambled back to safety, watching from behind one of the Stones. He flapped his wings again, faster and faster, and it was like being caught in a gale. Bits of scrub and heather flew past my ears till I covered them with my hands and shut my eyes for safety. There came a roaring sound that I heard through my hands and a great whoosh!, a smell of cinders, my hair nearly parted from my scalp and I tumbled head over heels.

Once I righted myself and opened my eyes, my dragon was gone. A burned patch of ground showed where he had taken off and in the sky was a great shadow like a huge bat that circled and swooped and filled the air with the deep throb of wings. To my right—the east—the Stones had started to glow again, a long avenue of them, like a pointer.

The shadow swooped once more towards the earth then shot up like an arrow till it was almost out of sight, then it steadied and hovered for a moment before heading due east, following the direction the Stones indicated, head and tail out straight, wings flapping slowly. I watched until its silhouette crossed the moon, then went wearily back to the ruined farmhouse.

I wasn't even annoyed to see Growch with his head inside the now-empty cook pot. I was too tired. His voice sounded hollow.

"I saw you! Doing naughties, you was!"

"Naughties? What do you mean?" But even as I said it I realized what it must have looked like to an inquisitive dog. *Was* that what had happened?

"You know . . . you didn't do naughties with the knight or the merchant with the cat and the warm fires: why with *him*?" He pulled his head out of the pot a trifle guiltily and his ears were clogged with juice. "Sort of fell over it did; din' want to waste it. . . . Why don' we go to that nice place for a while? Likes you, he does, and it's too cold to stay outside all winter. Just for a coupla months . . ."

"Matthew?" I was deadly tired, confused, bereft, couldn't think straight. I must have time to sort myself out, and better the known than the unknown. "Yes, why not?"

Chapter Thirty-Two

Easier said than done. It was the beginning of November now, and we were all of three or four hundred miles from the town where Matthew lived, north and east. It took us two weeks to get anywhere near a decent, well-traveled road, and those people we met were usually traveling south as we had done the year before, so we were heading against the flow of traffic. Company and lifts were few and far between and I was burdened with all the baggage, now there was no Wimperling, and what I would have expected to travel before—ten or twelve miles a day—was now only five or six: less if we were delayed by rain.

For the weather had changed with the waning of the moon: cold, blustery, with frequent rain showers. We seldom saw the sun and then only fitfully, and too pale and far away to heat us. To ease my burdens I made a pole sleigh—two poles lashed together in a vee-shape, the tattered blanket acting as receptacle for the rest of the goods—but the majority of the roads were so rutted and stony that the sleigh either kept twisting out of my hands, or the ends wore away and the poles had to be renewed.

Thanks to a couple of good lifts, by the end of November we were over halfway, but every day now saw worsening weather, and at night sometimes, if the wind came from the hills, we could hear wolves on the high slopes howling their hunger. Mostly we slept in what shelter we could find by the way—an isolated farmhouse, a barn, a shepherd's croft—but sometimes I paid for the use of a village stable or a place beside a tavern fire. Careful as I was, the cost of food and lodgings was so high in winter that almost half the dragon gold had gone when disaster struck us.

One night in a tavern I had been paying in advance for a meal when my frozen fingers spilled the rest of the gold from my purse onto the earthen floor. I scooped it up as quickly as I could, but three unkempt men at a corner table were nodding and winking at one another slyly as I did so. That night I slept but little, although the men had long gone into the dark, and in the morning my fears were justified.

Growch and I had scarcely made a couple of miles out of the village when the three men leapt out from the bushes at the side of the road, kicked and punched me till I was dazed, snatched my purse, pulled my bundle apart and flung Growch into the undergrowth when he tried to bite them. They were just pulling up my skirts, determined to make the most of me, when there was the sound of a wagon approaching and they fled, taking with them my blanket, food, cooking things and my other dress.

The carter who came to my rescue was from the village I had just left, and he was kind enough to help me gather together what little I had left and give the dog and me a lift back. I was in a sorry state: my head and arms and face bruised and swollen and my clothes torn, but poor Growch was worse off, with a broken front leg. The tavern-keeper's wife gave me water to wash in, needle and thread to mend my torn skirt and sleeve and a crust of bread and rind of cheese for the journey and I made complaint to the village mayor, but as the thieves had not been local men there was nothing they could do, and I was hurried on my way with sympathy but little else, lest I became a burden on the parish.

Once out of the village I bound up Growch's leg, using hazel twigs wrapped with torn strips from my shift, and poulticing it with herbs from the wayside to keep down the swelling and aid the healing, using the knowledge I had and the feel of the ring of my finger to choose the best. Of course now I would have to carry him, so I discarded any nonessentials, leaving me a small parcel to strap to my back, and my hands free for Growch.

By nightfall, hungry and depressed, I reached a tumbledown hut just off the road. As I walked through the scrub towards it I saw various articles strewn by the way: a man's belt, a rusty knife, a tattered blanket—surely that last was mine? I shrank back into the undergrowth ready to run, but Growch sniffed, wrinkled his nose and demanded to be put down. My ring was quiet, but cold, so I let him hobble forward on three legs to investigate further.

He came back a few minutes later. "We're not dossin' down there tonight, that's for sure. They's all dead an' it stinks to high heaven."

I crept forward, but even before I reached the hut I was gagging, and had to hold my cloak across my face. There, huddled on the earth floor, were the men who had robbed us only this morning, dead and smelling as though they had been that way for weeks. The contorted bodies lay in postures of extreme agony, mouths agape on swollen tongues and bitten lips, arms and legs twisted in some private torture, a noisome liquid oozing from great suppurating blisters on their blackened skin. Surely even the plague could not strike so quickly and devastatingly?

Then I noticed a little pile that was smoking away in a corner, like the last wisps from a dying fire. It was from here also that the worst stench came. Carefully stepping over the bodies, I walked over to investigate. There, dissolving in a last sizzling bubble, were the remains of the coins of dragon gold the then-Wimperling had left for me. I remembered what he had told me: given or used for trade they were perfectly safe; stolen, they brought death and destruction. I shivered uncontrollably, but not from cold.

That night we spent in the open, the first of many. With no money but my dowry left, which coins the country people would not accept, not recognizing the denominations and being suspicious of strangers anyway, I was reduced to begging, to stealing from henhouses, a handful of grain from sacks, vegetables from clamps. It was a wonder I was never caught, but with a dog who could no longer dance for his supper what else could I do? I did find the occasional root or fungi and gather what I could of herbs and winter-blackened leaves, but every day I grew weaker. Growch's leg healed slowly, but he probably fared worse than I did, for I could no longer find even the beetles and grubs that he would eat if there was nothing else. I even tried to trap fish, as I had been taught as a child, but with the frosts the fish lay low in the water and it all came to nothing, even the frogs having burrowed down under the mud.

There were one or two remissions, like the time I came upon a late November village wedding—none too soon from the look of the bride's waistline—and I stuffed myself stupid in return for a handful of coins and a tune or two on my pipe and tabor which I had providentially kept. I took with me a sack of leftovers that lasted us for a week.

But that was the last of our good luck. The weather got even worse and our progress slowed to a crawl. Lifts, even for a couple of miles, were few, and the stripped hedgerows and empty fields mocked our hunger. A couple of times, dirty and disreputable though I now was, I could have bought us a meal or two by pandering to the needs of importunate sex-seekers, but somehow I just couldn't. I do not believe it had anything to do with morals, nor the off-putting stench of their bodies: it was something deeper than that. I had been infatuated with Gill—the Wimperling had been right about that—I had had an affection for Matthew, and—But I would think no further than that. The recent past I blotted out from memory. Sufficient that it stopped me from greater folly.

I have no clear recollection of those last few days. I know I was always hungry, always cold. My shoes had fallen to pieces but my numb feet no longer hurt on the sharp stones. I was conscious of a thin shadow that dogged my heels as a limping Growch tried to keep up, and I do recall him bringing me a stinking mess of raw meat he had stolen from somewhere and me cramming it into my mouth, trying to chew and swallow and then being violently sick. I also remember a compassionate woman at a cottage door, with half a dozen children clinging to her skirts, sparing me a mug of goat's milk and a few crusts, and finding rags to bind my feet, but the rest was forgotten.

It started to snow. At first thin and gritty, hurting my face and hands like needles, then softer, thicker, gentler, drifting down like feathers to cover my hair, burden my shoulders, drag at my skirt, but provide a soft carpet for my feet. I think it was then that I realized I wasn't going to make it, although some streak of perversity in my nature kept me putting one foot in front of the other. I remember falling more than once, stumbling to my knees many times, and on each occasion a small hoarse voice would bark: "Get up! Get up! Not far to go now . . . We ain't done yet. . . ."

But at the end even this failed to rouse me. The snow was up to my knees, above them, and I could go no further. Even Growch, plowing along in my dragging footsteps and then trying to tug at my skirt to pull me forward, failed to rouse me.

"Come on, come on, now! A little further, just two steps, and two more! Round this corner, that's right! You can't give up now. . . . Now, down here a step or two—don't fall down, don't!" Another tug at my skirt, and this time a nip to my ankle as well. I tried to thrust him away, but he was as persistent as a mosquito. I staggered a few steps, fell again. The snow was like a featherbed and no longer cold and forbidding. If I could just lie down for a few minutes, pull up the covers and sleep and sleep and sleep . . .

"Get up! Don't go to sleep! Up, up, up!" Nip, nip, nip . . .

"Go away! Leave me *alone*!" For the last time I got to my feet and stumbled down the road. "Leave me, go away, I don't want you anymore!" and I fell into a snowdrift that was larger, deeper, softer, warmer than any before. Shutting my eyes I burrowed deeper still and drifted away, the last thing I heard being Growch's hysterical barking: "Yip! Yip! Yip!" but soon that too faded and I heard no more. . . .

"I think she's coming round . . . How are you feeling?"

A strangely familiar face swam into focus, an anxious, rubicund face with a fringe of hair like the setting sun. I shut my eyes again, opened them. Did angels have red hair? Assuredly I must be in Heaven whether I deserved it or not, for I was warm, rested, lying I suppose on a cloud, and no longer hungry, thirsty or worried about anything. Except—

"Growch? Where's Growch? Is he here too?"

"She means the dog," said someone, and something walked up my feet, legs, stomach and chest, then thrust a cold wet nose against my cheek and I smelt the familiar, hacky breath.

"Been here all the time—'cept for breakfast 'n' lunch 'n' supper—thought at one time as how you wasn't goin' to make it. . . ."

I put up a strangely heavy and trembly hand to touch his head. *Did* they have dogs in Heaven, then? I'd think about it later. Just have a little sleep . . .

"Fever's down," said another voice I thought I recognized. "By the morning she'll be fine."

And by morning I was at least properly awake, conscious of my surroundings and hungry, though not exactly "fine" just yet, for all the damaged parts of me that had been exposed to the bitter weather started to smart and ache, and I was still very weak.

Of course I had ended up at Matthew's house, thanks to Growch. He had led us both over the last few miles, scenting food and warmth and comfort, and luckily my final collapse had taken place just outside the merchant's house, though it had taken Growch a long time to rouse them from sleep and he had ended up voiceless, for a few hours at least.

At first they were convinced I was dead, so pale and cold and lifeless I had become, but providentially for me Suleiman had been staying with Matthew once more and he found a thin pulse and proceeded to thaw me out.

"Not by putting you in hot water or roasting you by the fire, as my dear friend would have me do," he said. "That would have killed you of a certainty. Instead I used a method I learned when a boy, from the Tartars my father sometimes traded with in hides. A tepid bath, oil rubbed gently into the skin, a cotton wrapping, then the natural warmth of naked bodies enfolding you. The servants took it in turns. Then the water a little warmer, and so on again . . . It took many hours until you were breathing normally, though once I saw you could swallow, though still unconscious, I gave you warm sweet drinks.

"Unfortunately there was a fever there, waiting for your body to warm up, but with one of my special concoctions and poppy juice to keep the body asleep, we managed to pull you through, though it was a close thing. The bruises and cuts will heal soon, but you have two broken toes, and I have bound those together; you were lucky you did not get frostbite as well."

After I had done my best to thank him, I asked about Growch's broken leg.

"Ah, you did a good job there. He still limps a little, but I have removed the splints and renewed the healing herbs. He will be as good as new."

Once I started to eat again properly I made rapid progress and was soon allowed up to sit by the fire in the solar, with a fully mobile Growch at my feet, luxuriating in the idleness, and Saffron, the great ginger cat, actually venturing his weight on my lap, though he was singularly uncommunicative, even when he realized I could talk to him. Of course I was petted and pampered and cosseted by Matthew, who seemed delighted to have me back. Both he and Suleiman could hardly wait to hear of my travels and find out what had happened to "Sir Gilman," so I gave them an edited, but nevertheless entertaining, account of my wanderings.

I had had plenty of time while convalescing to think up a good story, for who would believe the real one? I told them about the ghost in the castle and about our sojourn in the artist's village, and they were suitably impressed, both believing in the supernatural and Suleiman having heard of the other artist's seminars in Italia. When I recounted our stay with the Lady Aleinor, I had a surprise, and further confirmation (to them) of the complete veracity of my story.

"I quite forgot to tell you!" exclaimed Matthew. "The lad who helped you escape, Dickon, came here eventually, he said on your recommendation. He seemed an enterprising sort of lad and brought news of you—though he did embroider the facts a little!"

"Something about you flying to safety on the back of that pig of yours," said Suleiman, but his eyes were speculative. "It was a good tale. . . ."

"Anyway, I decided to give him a chance, for your sake," said Matthew. "Sent him off on one of our caravans with a letter of introduction. He'll be away at least a year, and he may prove useful. We can always do with promising youngsters."

Of course I didn't tell them the whole truth about Gill. I made a great tale of our escape across the border and of the miraculous return of his eyesight, however, the latter gratifying Suleiman.

"A theory of mine proved. One blow to the head: blindness. Another knock, and whatever has been displaced in the brain is jarred back. I expect he will have recurrent headaches for a while, but all should be well."

Matthew looked uncomfortable, but after a while he asked: "And the young man's parents? They must have been glad of his return. . . . He—also had—others—who must have rejoiced?"

I nodded and said, my voice quite steady and unemotional, "His fiancee had almost given him up for dead. They celebrated their nuptials while I was there and Rosamund, a beautiful fair-haired lady, was already with child when I left, I believe. . . ." That at least was true.

"And the rest of your little menagerie?" asked Suleiman. "The horse, the pigeon, the tortoise and the—er, flying pig?"

"The pigeon flew away once his wing was healed and joined a flock of his brethren." Truish. "The tortoise I let loose in suitable surroundings." True, but short of the full facts. "The mare—she grew up into quite a fine specimen and went for breeding." Again, basically true, but not the full story.

But what is truth? I thought to myself. It is always open to interpretation. Even if I had told them everything it would have been colored by the telling, my subjectiveness, and they would have heard it with ears that would hear parts better than others, would remember some facts and forget others, so the story to each would be different. If someone asked you what you ate for breakfast and you answered truthfully: "eggs," that would be truth but still not tell the enquirer how many, how cooked and what they tasted like, though they would probably be quite satisfied with the answer.

"And the pig?" asked Suleiman. "The odd one out . . ."

"He—the pig, died." I said. Another sort of truth. "He just dwindled away. He doesn't exist anymore." I still had the little scrap of hide, shriveled still smaller now though still bearing the imprint of its owner's face and the remnants of his hooves. Stuffed, it would make a mini-pig, and child's plaything. My eyes were full as I remembered all that had happened.

"Well, it seems all turned out for the best," said Matthew comfortably. "Feel well enough for a game of chess, Mistress Summer?"

Through the colored glass of the window in the solar I watched the sun climb higher in the sky every day as the celebrations of Candlemas gave way to the rules of Lent. Matthew and Suleiman still insisted on convalescence, so I brought out my Boke, one of the few things I had managed to save, and wrote out my adventurings as best I could, but the version for my eyes only. When I had finished, the fine vellum Matthew had insisted on buying stood elbow to wrist high and my fingers ached. And even then the story wasn't complete.

It ended when the Wimperling "died," for there were still some things I couldn't bring myself to write down, or even think about.

Matthew and Suleiman brought out their maps, planning the year's trade and seeking a faster route to the spices of the East. I studied the maps too, fascinated by the lands and seas they portrayed, so far from everything I knew. At one stage Suleiman mentioned the difficulties of coinage barter and exchange between the different countries and I bethought myself of my father's dowry gift, bringing the coins to show him.

To my amazement and delight he recognized them all and spread out the largest map in the house, weighing it down at the four corners with candlesticks.

"See, these coins all belong to different countries: Sicilia, Italia and across the seas to Graecia. Then Persia, Armenia . . ." and he placed the coins one by one across the map so they looked like a silver and gold snake. South by east, east, east by north, northeast; all tending the same way. "Your father must almost have reached Cathay. . . . He did: look!" And he held out the last and tiniest coin of all, no bigger than a baby's fingernail and dull gold. "Either that, or he was friendly with the traders who went there. These coins follow our trade routes almost exactly. . . . Don't lose them: they might come in useful some day."

I offered the coins, my precious dowry, to dear, kind Matthew when he tentatively proposed marriage to me just before Easter, but he closed my hand over them. "No, I have no need of them; you are enough gift for any man. Keep them in memory of your father."

It was agreed we would be wed when he returned from a two-week journey to barter for the new season's wool in advance. He and Suleiman set off together one fine April morning and I waved them out of sight, clutching Matthew's parting gift, a purseful of coins, to buy "whatever fripperies you desire."

He had kissed me a fond good-bye, and as his lips pressed mine I remembered Gill's urgent mouth on mine. And another's . . .

"Well, then: that's settled," said Growch by my side, tail wagging furiously. "Home at last, for both of us. When's lunch?"

Part 3:
A Beginning

Chapter Thirty-Three

"Gotcha!"

I awoke with a start to find Growch trampling all over me, tail wagging furiously. Night had fallen early with lowering cloud, but I was snug in the last of the hay at the far end of the barn, wrapped in my father's old cloak, and had been sleeping dreamlessly.

"D'you know how long I been lookin' for you? Four days! Four bleedin' days . . . Fair ran me legs orf I did. You musta got a lift. . . ."

"I did. Yesterday." I sat up. "How did you know which way I'd gone?"

"Easy! Only way we ain't been. 'Sides, I gotta nose, and that there ring of yours got a pull, too."

I glanced down at it. Warm, but pulsing softly.

"Got anythin' to eat? Fair starvin' I am," and he pulled in his stomach and tried to look pathetic.

I gave him half the loaf I had been saving for breakfast. "And when you've finished that you can turn right round again and head back where you came from!"

He choked. "You're jokin'!"

"No, I am not. I left you behind deliberately. I even asked Matthew in my note to take care of you while I was away. . . ."

A note he wouldn't find yet, not for a couple of days at least, and by that time I should be aboard a ship for Italia, cross-country to Venezia and ship again for points east. And then to find Master Scipio and present myself to the caravan-master as Matthew's newest apprentice . . .

Once the merchant and Suleiman had disappeared I had had plenty of time to think.

Before, there had always been someone hovering, in the kindest possible way of course, making sure I wasn't hungry/cold/thirsty/tired/bored. I hadn't realized how constricted I had felt until they were both gone: the first action of mine had been to run from room to room, down the stairs, round the yard and then back again, flinging cushions in the air and the shutters wide open. Free, free, free! I sang, I danced, I felt pounds lighter, almost as if I could fly. Growch thought I was mad, so did the cat and surely the servants.

Once I had calmed down I asked myself why I had acted like that, and I didn't particularly like the answers I came up with. One of them was obviously that a year or more traveling the freedom of the roads had left me with a taste for elbow room; another that I was obviously not ready to settle down yet. The third answer was, in a way, the most hurtful: I obviously didn't care enough for Matthew to marry him—at least I didn't return his affection the way he would have wished.

And why should you expect to love him? I could hear my mother's voice like a dim echo. Marriage is a contract, nothing more. You are lucky in that you don't actively dislike him. Just look around you, see what you will have! A rich husband who will grant your every wish, a comfortable home, security at last . . . A little pretense on your part every now and again: is that so much to ask?

Yes, Mama, I answered her in my mind. You had my father, don't forget, you knew what real love felt like. You, too, had a choice. Didn't you ever regret not flinging everything aside and following him to the ends of the earth and beyond? A cruel and unjust death took him away from you, but at least you had your memories. And what have I got? A taste, just the tiniest taste, of what life could really be like, what love meant.

If I married Matthew now, feeling the way I did, I should be doing him a grave injustice and he was too nice, too kind a man for that. He would know I was pretending. Whereas if I tried to find what I was seeking and failed, then I could return and truly make the best of things. If he would still have me, of course. And if I succeeded . . . But I wouldn't even think of that, not yet. Besides, the odds were so great, maybe ten thousand to one, probably more. But I was damn well going to try!

That letter to dear Matthew had been difficult to write, for I knew how it would hurt him.

> I know you will be upset to find me gone, but I find I cannot yet settle down, much as I am fond of you and am grateful for your many kindnesses. I hope you can forgive me. I am not sure where I shall go, but I hope to return within a year and a day, all being well. By then, of course, you may well have changed your mind about me, but if not I hope I shall be ready to settle down with you.
>
> I have taken the bag of coins you gave me so I shall not be without funds, although I know you intended them for more frivolous purposes. Thank you again for everything. Please, of your goodness, take care of my dog till I return. . . .

There were two things—three—that I didn't tell him. I had spent a few coins in kitting myself out in boy's clothes: braies and tunic, stockings and boots. Also, I had cut my hair short. At first I had been horrified at the result, for now my hair sprang up round my head in a riot of curls, but I soon became used to the extra lightness, and it would be much more convenient. I had taken the discarded tresses with me, for there was always a call for hair to make false pieces and they might be worth a meal or two.

Another thing he wouldn't know was that I had copied his maps showing the trade routes, and the last way I had taken advantage was to use his seal and forge his signature to a letter of introduction to one of his caravan masters, the same one who had engaged young Dickon. Having memorized, unconsciously at the time, the schedules of the routes, I now knew I had a couple of days more to make the twenty miles or so to the first rendezvous. And now here came trouble on four legs just to complicate matters. . . .

"I locked you in deliberately to stop you following! You can't come with me! I'm not even sure where I'm going. . . ."

"Why can't I come? S'all very well tellin' the servants as you're goin' visitin', but I ain't stupid! They tried to keep me in, as you ordered, but I jumped out a window, I did. You ain't goin' nowheres without me. You knows you ain't fit to be let out on your own. Din' I get us to that fellow's house?"

I admitted he had.

"Well, then! There's gratitude for you. . . . I don' care where you're goin', I'm comin' too. Try an' stop me."

"I thought all you wanted was a comfortable home. Matthew would take good care of you. And all that lovely food . . ."

"I can change me mind, can't I? You have. Don' know what you wants do you? Well, then . . . Where we goin'?"

I gave up. "To sleep, right now. In the morning . . . east."

"Where the little fluffy-bum bitches come from? Cor, worth a walk of a hundred miles or so . . ."

Nearer thousands, I thought, as I lay down again. It was a daunting prospect, thought of like that. But otherwise how could my mind and body ever be rid of the ache, the questioning, the unknown, engendered on that never-to-be-forgotten night when my world had turned upside down?

Growch had been wrong there: I did know what I wanted.

Somewhere a dragon was waiting. . . .

Master of Many Treasures

Prologue

It was a difficult journey.

Once in the air he had thought the flight would be easy; after all, he would be flying higher than all but the largest raptors. The thermals, currents of air, clouds, and winds provided his highways, hills and vales, and the skyscape freed him from the pedestrian pace of those on the earth beneath. In that other skin he had once worn ten or fifteen miles a day had been enough, but now he could easily manage a hundred in one stint, though he usually cut this by half. After all, there was no hurry.

No problems with the route, either. Like all of his kind the ways of the air were etched into his brain as a birthright, a primitive race memory he shared with birds, fishes and some of the foraging mammals.

At first the wind aided him on his way and the sun shone kindly at dawning and dusk, for he preferred to return to land during the day for food and rest, ready for the guidance of the stars at night. The sleeping earth rolled away beneath his claws, and his reptilian hide adapted to the cold better than he had expected, not slowing him down with his reduced heartbeat as he had feared.

Rivers glinted in serpentine curves beneath the moon, hills reared jagged teeth, tiny pinpoints of light showed where those wealthy enough burned candles and tapers in castle or church, and he grew complacent, so much so that when the Change came, he wasn't ready for it.

It was that comfortable time between moondown and sunrise and he was cruising at about a thousand feet, ready to do a long glide down in search of breakfast, when he suddenly became aware that something was terribly wrong. Although his wings were beating at the same rate, he was losing height rapidly and feeling increasingly cold.

Glancing from side to side, he was horrified to see that his wings were almost transparent, were shrinking; his heartbeats were quickening, his legs stretching in an agony of tendons and muscles, his clawed forefeet turning into . . . hands?

Then he remembered.

She had kissed him, not once but three times, and so as part of those accepted Laws—Laws that until now he had dismissed as mere myth, though he had jokingly told her of them as truth—he would now have to spend part of his life as a human, earthbound as any mortal.

All right, all right, so he was going to be a man for a minute, two, five, but why no sort of warning? He was falling faster and faster, but all he could think about was there should be some way of delaying the Change, or of controlling it—

He landed plump in the middle of a village rubbish dump, all the breath knocked out of him but otherwise unhurt. For a moment he lay dazed and winded, then the stench was enough to make him stumble to his feet and stagger drunkenly down the main (and only) street, shedding leaves, stalks, bones and worse. Halfway down he realized he was not alone.

A small boy, perhaps five years old, clad only in a tattered shirt, was watching him with solemn brown eyes in the growing dawnlight. By his side was a smaller child, perhaps his two- or three-year-old sister, in a smock far too short for her, thumb stuck firmly in her mouth.

He thrust his hands out in a useless gesture of friendship. "Sorry, children: didn't mean to scare you. Just passing through. . . ."

Fiercely he concentrated on his real self—though what was real anymore?—and to his relief he began the awkward pain of changing back. In the midst of his discomfort he became aware of the children still watching him, their eyes growing rounder and rounder with amazement, and the humor of the situation struck him even as he took a running leap into the air, as clumsy as any heavy water fowl.

"Good-bye," he called, but it sounded just like the rumble of thunder, and he could see now the terrified children beneath him rush for the nearest hut and safety. Never mind, they would have a tale to tell that would keep the village buzzing for months.

After that the weather became more hostile, and not only was he battling against his "changes," which took time to recognize and regularize, but also strong easterlies, snow, and sleet, so it was well after the turn of the year before he saw in the distance his objective, four thousand miles from the Place of Stones of his transformation: a small conical hill set proud on a plain, a hill that shone softly blue against the encircling mountains. . . .

Part One

Chapter One

Venice stank. For the loveliest city in the world (so I had been told), center of Western trade, Queen of the Adriatic, she certainly needed a bath. One would have thought with all that water around the smells would have been washed away, but the reverse was true: it made it worse. The waters in the canals were moved only by the water traffic, which stirred but did not dissipate, and all the slops and garbage merely settled a few feet further on.

The city was certainly busy with trade and teeming with merchants and dripping with gold, but she was only beautiful at a discreet distance. Pinch one's nose and one could admire the tall towers, fine buildings, richly dressed gentry; one could feel the sun-warmed stone, listen to the sweet dissonance of bells and the calls of the gondoliers; watch the bustle at the quays as the laden barques and caravels were rowed in the last few yards . . . but keep one's nostrils closed.

I moved restlessly from bed to window and back again: three paces and then another three. It was hot and stuffy in this little attic room, but when I had opened the window some time back the stench had made me gag, so it stayed shuttered. Consequently it was not only stifling but also dark: I had trodden on my dog twice, but couldn't keep still.

Mind you, I was lucky to have a room to myself. Apart from Master Adolpho, the trading captain, all the others—horse master, interpreter, accountant, guards, cooks and servants—had to share. And why was I so privileged? Because I bore papers that proved I was under the personal protection of the wealthy merchant who had financed the expedition, Master Matthew Spicer.

And I was the only one who knew the papers were forged. By me.

I had a couple of other secrets, too, and secrets they must remain, else this whole journey would be jeopardized, and that mustn't happen. I had left too much behind, risked too much, hurt too many people to fail now. This was the most important journey of my life, and to justify what I had done, it must succeed.

A bad conscience and a real fear of pursuit had kept me glancing over my shoulder during our journeying the last couple of months, but at least then we had been moving, whereas for the last two weeks we had been stuck in this stinking city. No wonder I couldn't keep still. I—

Feet on the stairs, a thumping on the ill-fitting door.

"Hey, boy! Wake up there. . . . Cargo's in, we're going down to the quay. Coming?"

Action at last! Telling my dog, Growch, to "stay," I jammed my cap on my head, grabbed my tally sticks and clattered down three flights of wooden stairs to the street below. Outside it was scarcely less hot than my room, but at least there was shade and a faint breeze off the sea. Master Alphonso, the interpreter, and half a dozen others were milling around, but as soon as I appeared we set off for the quay, through the twists and turns of narrow streets, across the elegant curves of bridges, through the busy thoroughfares, all the while having to contend with the purposeful and the loiterers; carts, wagons, riders, pedestrians, children, dogs and cats impeded our progress. Watch out for the overhead slops—forbidden, but who was to see?—and be careful not to trip over that heap of rags, a sudden thin hand snatching at your sleeve for alms. Keep your hand on your purse and your feet from skidding in the ordure. . . .

Matthew's ship was already being unladen. Because of the press of the sea traffic she was anchored some way out, rowing boats busy ferrying the cargo ashore. A couple of our guards stood over the deepening piles of bales on the quayside, and our accountant started setting out paper, pens and ink on his portable writing desk, ready to itemize the cargo.

I tugged at Master Alphonso's sleeve. "How soon before it is all unladen? When can we go aboard? When do we sail?"

He twitched his sleeve away impatiently. "How many times do you have to be told, boy? When all the cargo is on dry land and checked by description against the captain's listings, then it is taken to a warehouse, opened and itemized, piece by piece. Then, and only then, will it be distributed as Master Spicer wishes. In the meantime the ship will take on a fresh crew and fresh supplies, the new cargo will be listed and loaded aboard. Then if the weather is fair, the ship sets sail. If not, it waits. Satisfied? I shan't tell you again."

I nodded, but inside I was in turmoil. Just how long would all this take? A week, at least . . . I turned away, but he stopped me.

"Just where do you think you're going? You may be Master Spicer's protegeé, but that doesn't mean you skip out every time there's work to be done. You're here to learn the business, that's what your papers say, so stop farting around and go help the accountant."

So I spent a long, hot afternoon working my tally sticks at top speed against the accountant's vastly superior abacus, then helped load the cargo for the warehouse. All my own fault; when I had forged Matthew's signature on the carefully prepared papers, I had represented myself as a privileged apprentice, to learn a merchant's trade from the bottom up. This was obviously the bottom. Up till now I had been a supernumerary; now it appeared I was about to earn my keep.

Snatching a meat pie and a mug of watered wine from a stall, I followed the cargo to a warehouse on the outskirts of the city. There the bales were off-loaded, recounted against the existing lists and at last opened to check the contents.

This was the exciting bit. Although Matthew was principally a spice merchant, and some eighty percent of the cargo was just this—mainly pepper, cloves, nutmeg, and mace—he also traded in whatever was out-of-the-way and unusual, sometimes to special order. Thus the rich, black furs would be auctioned off in Venice, the jewelry entrusted to another outlet; some rather phallic statues were a special order, as were certain seeds of exotic plants. This left drawings and sketches of strange animals, two curiously-shaped musical instruments, and several maps. These last were earmarked for Matthew himself, together with a couple of rolls of silk so fine it ran through one's fingers like water.

And who was in charge of these sortings and decisions? A tall thin man with a hawk nose, conservatively dressed, who Master Alphonso whispered to me was Matthew's agent in Venice, responsible not only for distribution and collection of cargo, but also for hiring and firing.

It happened that he and I were the only ones left later: he because he was arranging for warehouse guards, I because I was going back over one of my calculations which did not tally. By now I was almost cross-eyed with fatigue, so was only too grateful when the soft-spoken Signor Falcone came over and in a couple of minutes traced my mistake and amended it.

"Only one error: tenths are important, youngster. Still, well done." His fingers were long and well manicured. "You are Master Summer, I believe?"

I nodded. Relief at having finished without too much blame made my tongue careless and impudent. "Matthew must have great trust in you. I wouldn't—" and I stopped, blushing to the roots of my hair.

"Trust someone so greatly without supervision? Of course you should not, unless you know him well." He regarded me gravely. "But then, you see, I owe him and his friend not only my livelihood, but my education. And also my life."

"Your life?"

He hesitated.

"I'm sorry," I said. "I shouldn't be so inquisitive."

"No matter. At your age I was the same." He hesitated again. "It is not a tale I recount easily. Still . . ." His eyes were bright and dark as sloe berries. He took a bundle of keys from his belt and, beckoning me to follow, locked up the warehouse, nodded to a couple of armed men lounging nearby, and started back towards the center of the city. "Come, we shall walk together. . . ."

It was a strange enough tale, and I forgot my weariness as I listened.

"When I was eight years old I was sold into slavery by a parent burdened by too many children. It was in a country far from here, and I was pretty enough to be auctioned as a bum-boy—you understand what I mean?—

but I was lucky. A stranger stopped to watch the bidding and among those who fancied me was an old enemy of the stranger. So, to teach this man a lesson, the stranger bid for me too, and in the course of time he won himself a boy he had no use for. The stranger's name was Suleiman, on his way to visit his old friend Matthew Spicer—I see that first name means something to you?"

I wasn't conscious of having betrayed myself, but I nodded. "I met him while I was at Master Spicer's." I didn't add that it was the gifted Suleiman whose doctoring had saved the life of my blind knight, the man I had once fancied myself in love with.

"Then you will know that he is both wise and kind. He left me with his friend, to care for and educate, to learn to read, write and calculate. There I also learned French, Italian and Latin, for my own language was Arabic. At about the same age as yourself I was sent abroad to learn the ways of trade, and after some years Matthew appointed me his agent here. I have never regretted it, nor, I believe, has he. His is a generous and trusting nature, and such a man's trust is not easily abused. Nor should it be: remember that."

How could I not? For in my own way I had betrayed his trust in worse ways than Signor Falcone could imagine.

We had reached the end of the street where I lodged.

"Your journey starts in a day or two. I do not think you have the slightest idea how far it will take you, nor are you mentally prepared as you should be. About that I can do little, but at least I can see you are physically ready. Do not forget you will be representing Master Spicer, and you need a new outfit for that." He fished in his purse and brought out a handful of coin. He saw my eyes widen with surprise at the gold, and allowed himself a wry grimace. "Call this the Special Fund. For emergencies—and youngsters who need smartening up. Choose good materials, and something neat but not gaudy." He put a couple of coins in my hand. "You will also need travelling gear: leather breeches and jacket; a thick cloak; good, strong boots; riding gloves." Another couple of coins in my hand. "It can be cold at nights where you are going, so a woollen cap, underwear and hose." A last coin. "And a good, sharp dagger. Go to Signor Ermani in the Via Orsini and say I sent you." And he swung away across the square. "And get your hair cut! At the moment you look like a girl!"

It was so late by now that the pie shop around the corner was closing as I went past, but I managed to grab some leftovers and broken pieces for my dog, who was almost crossing his back legs in an effort not to relieve himself by the time I reached my room. So pressured was he that he forwent his supper until he had christened every post and arch within a considerable distance. I trailed after him without fear of marauders, for he had a piercing bark, an aggressive manner, and extremely sharp teeth.

And, after all, when one has bitten a dragon and got away with it, what else has a dog to fear?

That evening, what was left of it, I brought my journal up to date. This was Part Two of my life. Part One was already finished the day I left Matthew's for the second time. It was a bulky volume, bound with a wooden cover, and as I weighed it in my hands I realized how much of an extra burden it would be to carry it any further. It would be better to leave it with someone I could trust.

Part Two was far less bulky. I had already devised a form of shortened words and wrote smaller, so could justify taking it with me. Pen and inks would have to go with me as part of my job, and a couple of extra rolls or so of vellum were neither here nor there.

Next morning I went out in search of new clothes. Neat but not gaudy, Signor Falcone had said, but although hose, breeches and boots were easy enough in shades of brown, the jacket was an entirely different matter. Finding a good, plain one was practically impossible. They all seemed to be embroidered with vine leaves, pomegranates, artichokes, red and white flowers and even stars and moons, but then Venice catered mainly to the rich and fickle. The materials, too—silks and satins—were too fine for prolonged wear, but at least after a search I tracked down a fawn-colored jerkin with the minimum of decoration, and a green surcoat of fine wool, without the usual scallops, fringes and frills.

The afternoon I spent in mending my existing hose and underwear, a chore I detested, but just as I had decided it was candle time, there was a rush of feet on the stair and a hammering at the door.

"Master Summer? You there?"

"Yes . . ." I was practically naked, so the door stayed shut.

"Master Alphonso says you're to be ready at dawn."

"So soon?"

"Outbreak of plague reported in the south. Report to the quayside at first light." The feet stumbled back down the stairs.

Plague? Perhaps the greatest fear man had, far more threatening than battle or siege. Against a human enemy there were weapons, but the plague recognized no armies but—deadlier than sword, spear or arrowhead, unseen, unheard, unfelt—could decimate the largest army in the world within days. Either great pustules broke out on the skin and the victim died screaming, else it was the drowning sickness, when the chest filled with phlegm and a choking death came in less than a day—

I shivered in spite of the heat, fear closing my throat and opening my pores. No time to waste. I must call down for water to wash in, then collect my cloak from the laundry down the road. Once my father's, then my mother's, it was practically indestructible, being of a particularly fine and thick weave, though light and soft, with a deep hood. Much mended and much worn, it was nevertheless better than many new ones I had seen, but I had thought to have the mire and mud of the journey to Venice dispersed by a good soak.

So, that to collect, a good scrub for myself—and the dog, if possible—then everything to be packed as tight as could be. Something to eat, and lastly a safe place to leave Part One of my journal.

I hurried as well as I could, but the last streaks of gold and crimson were staining the skies to the west when I knocked at Signor Falcone's door, praying that he had not gone out to dine.

I was shown by a liveried servant to an upstairs room and gasped in wonder at the fine furniture, glowing tapestries, delicate glass and silken drapes. My host smiled at my expression.

"Without Suleiman and Matthew a mere slave could never have afforded all this. . . . What do you want of me, youngster?"

I started to explain about the plague and our early departure, but he cut me short.

"I know all this. We have worked throughout the day to get everything loaded and ready. What is that package under your arm?"

Straight to the point, Signor Falcone! I had rehearsed my story on the way.

"It contains a journal I have been keeping. Before I—before Master Spicer sponsored me I had some amusing adventures, which I have written down plain. If—if anything should happen to me on my travels I should wish Master Spicer to have it. A sort of thanks . . . It might also explain some of my actions more clearly." I was floundering, and I knew it. "Besides, it is too heavy to carry. Please?"

"So, if anything should happen to you on the way—Allah forbid!—this is to be forwarded to Matthew? Otherwise I hold it until your return; is that it? Very well. The package if you please." Going over to his ornate desk he extracted sealing wax and, rolling the stick in a candle flame, dropped the pungent-smelling stuff onto the knots in my package. He motioned to quill and ink. "Write Master Spicer's name there clearly. So. Now come with me."

Taking up a candle I followed him down a short passage into a small locked back room, windowless, full of shelves and nose-tickly with dust. Boxes, scrolls, books, small paintings and other packages lined the shelves, all neatly labelled. He placed my parcel high up on the nearest shelf.

"There, it will be safe till you return. And, should anything happen to me, my servants' orders are to forward everything in here to the name on the label. And now, if there is nothing else you wish to tell me, I think I shall take to my bed, and I would advise you to do the same." Ushering me downstairs, he opened the door on a night of stars, with a thin veil of mist creeping up from the east. "Hmmm. Don't like the look of the weather."

"There's no moon, no land breeze either, but the sky is clear enough."

"Exactly. Moon change and a sea mist. Still . . . off you go, sleep well." He turned to re-enter, then turned back. "I thought I told you to get your hair cut!"

Dear Lord, I had completely forgotten! Surely it would be too late at night now. Taverns, brothels, gaming houses, eating places would be open for business, but barbers . . . Collecting Growch from some odorous rubbish bin, I set out to look.

I was lucky, although it looked very expensive.

A gilded sign above the door hung motionless, announcing to those who could read that Signor Leporello was hairdresser and barber to the greatest in the land. On the door was tacked a list of prices; a trim didn't look too expensive. Telling Growch to wait, I lifted the latch and peered within. A little bell on a string gave a melodious tinkle.

"Hallo? Anyone there?" A couple of candles burned on a side table, otherwise the room was empty. I called again.

A moment's pause, then a bead curtain swung back and a creature teeter-tottered forward on those ghastly wooden-platformed shoes that the fashionable all seemed to be wearing these days. This man—if it was a man—had mismatched hose, red and blue, slashed sleeves and a surcoat flapping with pink and gold embroidery. Topping it all off was a huge green turban with a large purple stone set in the center. Probably real, which made it all worse. Gaudy, but not neat . . .

A waft of oil of violets, the glint of rings as he lit a couple more candles. "And what have we here? A late customer, I do believe. Come in dear boy, come in! A shave perhaps? No, not a shave, definitely not. A trim? Yes, a trim I think. A trim and a wash. Pretty hair like yours should always be clean and dust-free. . . ."

"Pretty hair?" I squeaked. This was obviously the sort of place and proprietor young boys were warned about. "I'm sorry, there is some mistake: I have no money, and—"

"Nonsense! You need a trim and I am in a good mood. Come, it shall be on the house," and before I knew what was happening he had plonked me down on a tall stool, and swiftly plucked a few hairs from my head, holding them to the candlelight. "See these? All different colors. Two shades of red, two of brown, blonde and black." It was true. "All together they are individually responsive to light and shade, like those clear eyes of yours. Now, bend over that basin and we'll begin!"

If there was to be a dangerous moment, this would be it, but my worries soon vanished as he washed, rinsed, rubbed, combed, brushed and clipped. At last he brought me a mirror, and even with its uncertain depths and the flicker of candles I was gazing at a different me. Gone was the tangle of jagged ends and unruly curls. The hair was layered and waved neatly to my head—

"Is he someone I would know? How long ago did you run away from your family—or the convent, perhaps? Come, I've seen all this before, many times. A young girl imprisoned against the unsuitability of her beloved, dresses as a boy, runs away to find him. . . ."

"A—girl!" I stammered, and I must have been as red as fire.

"Why, yes! Oh come!" and he leant forward and lightly brushed his fingers across my chest. "I have been leaning over you for near an hour . . . I happen to have some stretch webbing that will hide those breasts much more discreetly, young lady, and only a silver piece a yard. . . ."

Chapter Two

The morning was gray, dull, misty, chill. A sulky red sun lurked behind the mist and I was shivering, both from cold and anticipation. Strange to think the Shortest Day was but a week past: it felt more like November.

Dirty water slap-slapped against the piles of the Piazetta as the rowboats came and went, ferrying the last of the cargo aboard. Behind us the square was deserted, or so I thought, but at the last moment a figure came scurrying across carrying a tray of freshly baked rolls and pasties. They were delicious, the meat sending little pipes of steam into the air from the crumbling pastry. The baker was an enterprising fellow baking so early—but then his prices were enterprising too, as I discovered after Growch and I had burnt our tongues.

"Feel better?" asked a familiar voice. I turned to see Signor Falcone, well wrapped against the cold.

"Much!"

"Well try and keep it down. I still don't like the look of the weather; red sky at morning, sailor's warning . . . Still you're safer away from the plague, and the captain has done this run many times."

"Aren't you afraid of catching the sickness?"

He smiled. "It is as Allah wills. If it comes too close I have a small villa in the hills to the north. I usually spend August there anyway: it is pleasantly cool, and Matthew curtails his trade during the hottest months. In fact, the stuffs now in the warehouse are the last but one Master Alphonso will escort back till fall."

I glanced over to where the trade captain was talking to his accountant. "But—but I thought they were coming with us. . . . With me." I should be alone, no one to ask questions of, to depend on. A little fist of panic curled up in my stomach, and I could taste the pasties a second time around.

Falcone patted my shoulder. "Stop worrying. Master Scipio takes over on the other side, and he is a competent man, one of the best. You'll be safe enough with him. Matthew's papers and listings are on board, and mention has been made of you. . . . Have I said how much better you look with your hair cut?" He smiled. "Now, I must bid you farewell, but first I have a commission to execute." He pulled a small, tightly wrapped package from an inner pocket. "This arrived some time back, but I had to be sure it was going to the right person."

I took the package and turned it over. No name, no superscription. "Who's it from? How do you know it's for me?"

"The sender is a mutual friend. And how do I know it is for you? Just answer me one question: what is the name of your dog?"

"My *dog*? Why, Growch . . ."

"Exactly! That was the password, just in case I was not convinced by my own observations. You make a handsome enough lad, but I'm sure the woman underneath is even more attractive." He laughed a little at my stricken face. "Your secret is safe. Our—friend—believes he knows the purpose of your journey and its destination. You are a brave lass: may Allah be with you. Now go: you don't want to miss the boat."

As the rowers pulled away from the quay, my mind was in turmoil. Disguising myself as a boy had seemed a good idea at the time, but in less than twenty-four hours two men had discovered at least one of my secrets. Did anyone else suspect? I felt as though my face was burning as I tried to flatten my chest, pull my long legs in under my surcoat.

Of course even twelve months ago it would have been impossible to think of posing as a boy. At that time I had still been decidedly plump, decidedly female. It had been that last, impossible journey back to the haven of Matthew's home that had fined me down to the weight I now carried, that and the pain of losing the one love I could never replace, the love I had found too late by the Place of Stones. . . .

I had tried, of course I had, to be satisfied with a substitute, but even the kindest of men—and Matthew was certainly that—could not compensate for that searing moment when I discovered what true love really meant.

And that was why I was here, in this rackety little rowboat, heading for—for what? Even I wasn't sure. All I knew was that somehow I must find my love again, see him just once more, for the touch that had fired my blood with an indescribable hunger could never be satisfied by another.

Perhaps I would never find him, perhaps if I did he would spurn me, or be so changed I would matter less than a leaf on a tree but at least I had to *try*! Nothing else in the world mattered.

The rowboat bumped against the towering hull above, a rope ladder dangling just out of reach. Only the most agile of monkeys could have scaled that, what with the overhang and the sluggish dip and sway of the ship, but luckily there was one more bale to be hauled up by hand, and Growch and I went the undignified way, bumped and banged against the ship's sides on what felt like a bed of nails.

If I had expected a fanfare of trumpets to greet me once on board I was to be disappointed. In fact no one took the slightest notice of us at all. We were tipped unceremoniously off the bale, which was then lashed to others on the deck. The whole ship was boiling with activity, and gradually we were pushed into an obscure corner as sailors scurried around getting us ready for sea. Up came the anchor, down came the sails, two men unlashed the tiller and swung it across, and everyone seemed to be shouting commands and countercommands. What with that and the creak of chain, snap of sail, hiss of rope and scream of the gulls overhead, I doubt if anyone would have noticed if I had set fire to myself.

But all this frantic activity didn't seem to be getting us anywhere at all. The ship wallowed uneasily from side to side, the sails flapped listlessly, everything creaked, but we weren't moving. After half an hour or so, a flag was run up on the forward mast, and eventually a rowing barge came astern, took a line and ponderously towed us, tail first, outside of the shipping roads and into clear water.

Peering over the side, I could see how, even here, the contamination of the city behind us reached its dirty fingers into the main. The water was still brown and scummy and I could see flotsam from the sewers float past, plus a broken packing case and the bloated carcass of a goat. I glanced back at the city and now, at last, she resembled the lady I had heard about. She looked to float well above the water, the pale sun gilding her towers and cupolas till she seemed crowned like any queen.

The sails above me filled at last, the tiller was pushed over to starboard, and at first slowly, then with gathering speed, we headed northeast into the open sea. Immediately I had to grab at the side to keep myself from slipping: it was probably only a cant of a foot or so, but it was most disconcerting for me and worse for Growch, for his claws slipped and he slithered straight into the scuppers. We would have to find a place to call our own.

The ship was quieter now, although everyone seemed to have a job to do: trimming sails, coiling rope, swilling down the deck, and I could see an extremely large lady was shaking out bedding and punching energetically at what seemed to be a feather mattress. Probably the captain's wife: I had heard they often accompanied their husbands to sea. I had correctly identified the captain as the man who shouted the loudest and longest, and decided now was the time to introduce myself. He was a self-important looking man, stout and short, with a bristling beard and lots of hair in his ears. He stared at me as I approached.

"Who's this, then?"

I introduced myself, but had to explain who and what I was before his brow cleared and he nodded his head. Yes, yes, he'd heard I was coming aboard, but it had slipped his mind, and now he was too busy to deal with me personally. I would have to see the mate, find myself quarters, settle myself in. And keep that blasted dog from under everyone's feet. . . .

The mate, when I found him, had even less time for me. I was handed over to one of the crew, who showed me round in a desultory manner, and had me peering down the bilges—sick-making—and trying to climb in and out of a string bag he called a hammock; needless to say I fell out either one side or the other immediately. Apparently all the crew slept in these because a) they took up little space and b) they always stayed level, however the ship swayed. I went down into the hold, where everything was stacked away neatly, and into the galley, where it wasn't. Pots and pans, jugs, bottles, a side of ham, bags of flour, jars of oil, dried beans, strings of onions and garlic, sultanas and raisins, boxes of eggs, all hugger-mugger on shelves and floor. Outside, a couple of barrels rolled from side to side, and a couple of crates of scrawny chickens were stacked next to a bleating nanny goat. The cook was snoring it off in a corner.

But where was I to sleep? There were eighteen crew, split into three watches, so that at any one time there would be six on duty, six asleep and six relaxing, and I wasn't going to fall out of hammocks all day and night. Besides, there was no locker in which to stow my gear. I asked if there was any other space, but apparently not. The captain and his wife had quarters aft, the mate a tiny cubicle next to the rope locker and the cook slept in the galley.

The sailor had one useful suggestion. I could either doss down in the hold, although the hatchway was normally battened down, or find myself a niche topside, among the deck cargo.

I didn't fancy being shut away, so I inspected the bales on deck and, sure enough, they were so stacked that there was a cozy sort of cave to one side, which I thought would do. Even with my gear dragged in as well, there was room to lie down or sit up quite comfortably, and the smell of tarred string and sea salt was far pleasanter than bilge water.

I had about got myself settled down when bells rang for noon and food. I never quite got the hang of those bells; I knew they signalled change of watches, time passing, but the number of chimes never seemed to fit the hours, striking as they did in couples.

By the time I had unpacked my wooden bowl and horn mug I was almost too late; there was only a scrape of gristly stew left and a heel of yesterday's bread, plus some watered wine, but I wasn't particularly hungry so Growch benefitted. The bread and wine sloshed around uncomfortably in my stomach, for the ship was definitely rolling more heavily now. Before long, too, there came the pressing need to relieve myself. I had watched at first with embarrassment, then in increasing awareness of my own problems, as the crew relieved themselves when necessary over the side, and had seen the captain's wife empty a couple of chamber pots the same way. I couldn't do the first and hadn't got the second. Then I remembered there were some buckets and line in the rope locker. I pinched the smallest of the former and fastened it to a length of rope long enough to drop over the side and rinse in the seawater as I had seen the crew do when they needed water for swilling anything down.

Temporarily more comfortable, I slid my knife under the seals and string of the packet Signor Falcone had given me and drew out a letter. I might have known: it was from Suleiman.

"I believe this will reach you before you sail. Do not fear pursuit for there will be none. Matthew was most distressed to find you gone, and hopes for your return, but I know better, I think. Something changed you before you came back to us; I have seen that restless hunger in other eyes. So, go find your dragon-man—yes, you talked a great deal in your delirium, but I was the one who nursed you, so it is our secret. In case you did not copy all the right maps before you left, I enclose one that is the farthest east that I have.

"Use the gold wisely: you will need as much as you can, the way you go. May all the gods be with you, and may you find your dream."

There were tears in my eyes as I unfolded the map and found the gold coins he had enclosed. His understanding touched me deeply.

Sitting back I recalled the time Suleiman had taken the handful of coins my father had left me and arranged them across a map of the trade routes, showing how each one—copper, silver or gold—led inexorably towards the east and the unknown, the very way a certain dragon had gone, that night when he had left the Place of Stones—

And me.

Towards evening the weather steadily worsened. The wind blew in gusts, first from one quarter, then another, the lulls leaving the ship rolling uneasily on an increasingly oily swell. Dusk came down early, showing the thinnest crescent moon slicing in and out of the clouds; the cheese I had for supper was causing me great discomfort. At last it and I just had to part company, and I rushed for the rail, only to be jerked back at the last moment by the brawny arm of the mate.

"No puking into the wind!" he hissed. "Else you'll spend all night swilling down both the decks and yourself!"

I made it to leeward just in time, and spent the rest of that miserable night rushing back and forth to the rail. Sometime in the small hours all hands were called to shorten sail, and now I was pushed and cursed at and stumbled over, until in the end someone tied a rope around my waist and wrapped the other end round the after mast, leaving just enough room and no more for me to move between the rail and my improvised quarters.

In the end there was nothing more to come up and I curled up miserably in my cloak, dry-retching every now and again, a sympathetic Growch curled against my hip. In the morning I was no better; I staggered along the now alarmingly tilted deck to fetch food—cheese once more—but it was for my dog. I took a sip or two of wine, but up it came again, and as I was leaning over the rail a huge wave came aboard, near dragging me away back with it, and soaking me to the skin.

Somehow I just couldn't get dry again; rain came lashing down, and the ship was running bare-masted before a wind that had decided to blow us as far off course as possible. The whole vessel creaked and groaned under the onslaught of the waves, and it took three men to hold the ship steady, the tiller threatening to wrest itself from their grasp. I lay half in, half out of my shelter, too weak now to move either way, conscious of Growch's urgent bark in my ears, but lost in a lethargy of cold and darkness of soul and body. Soaked by the rain, tossed to and fro by the motion of the ship, stomach, ribs and shoulders sore and aching, I slipped into a sort of unconsciousness, aware only that I was probably dying. And the worst of it was, I didn't care, even though the ring on my finger was stabbing like a needle.

Suddenly an extra lurch of the ship rolled me right into the scuppers. This is it, I thought. Good-bye world. I'm sorry—

Someone grabbed me by the scruff of my neck, hauled me to my feet and shook me like the drowned rat I so nearly was. A couple of discarded chamber pots skittered past my feet and a voice boomed in my ears in a language I couldn't understand. I shook my head helplessly, muttered something in my own tongue and tried to be sick again.

"Ah, it is so? You come with me . . ." and I was tossed over a brawny shoulder and carried off in a crabwise slant across the deck. A foot shoved hard, a door crashed open and I was spilled onto the floor of a room full of fug, wildly dancing lantern light and blessed warmth.

Dimly I realized that the stout boots and swishing skirts that now stood over me were those of the captain's lady, and that it was her strong arms and broad shoulders that had brought me to the haven of their quarters. Squinting a little through the salt water that still stung my eyes, I saw the captain and mate seated at a center table screwed to the floor, studying what looked to be maps. They had obviously been discussing how far we had been blown off course, but the captain's wife wasn't interested.

I was hauled to my feet again.

"What is this poor boy doing out there? Who is he? Where he come from?" She was speaking my language, although with a strong guttural accent.

The captain rose to his feet. "Ah—an apprentice, my dear, to be delivered to Master Scipio—"

"Then what he do dying out there in storm? No good to deliver dead boy! What you thinking? Get out, both of you! I take charge now—"

"But my dear, we were just—"

"Out! This is now sick bay. Find elsewhere. I take care now. You go sail ship, storm slack soon."

There was a scuffle of feet, a door opened to let in a gust of tempest, shriek of wind. "And you find chamber pots and bring back clean. . . ." The door shut.

I was picked up again, more gently this time, and placed on a bunk in the corner. A large hand felt my forehead, brushed the salt-sticky hair from my brow.

"There, poor boy! You stay still and Helga will care for you, make you well again. Now, out of those wet things and we give wash . . ." and fingers were at the fastenings of my clothes.

I tried to sit up, to protest, but my voice was gone, my hands too feeble to pull my jacket tight across my chest.

"Now, boy, no modestness! I have born and raised six strong boys, and know what bodies is like! Lie still! Once I have . . . Ahhh!" There was a moment's pause. "What do we have here, then?" Rapidly the rest of my clothes were peeled off and I lay naked and exposed, in agonies of shame.

I think I expected almost anything but what I got: a great roar of laughter.

"This is what you call a joke, yes? I feel sorry for skinny lad, and what do I get? A young lady instead . . ." But the voice wasn't unkind, and even as I tried to explain in my cracked voice I was enveloped in a bone-breaking hug. "No talking, that come later. We get you warm and dry first."

A knock at the door. "You wait. . . ." Hastily she flung a blanket over me. "What is it?"

Apparently the return of the chamber pots. "Good. Now you fetch two buckets fresh water. Where are your things?" to me. I whispered. "And boy's things in bales on deck. He stay here. Hurry! What devil is *this*?"

"This" was Growch, a small, wet, filthy bundle that hurled itself across the cabin and onto my bunk, sitting on my chest and growling at everyone and everything, teeth bared.

I found my voice. "My dog. Very devoted. Please don't throw him out. He and I are alone in the world." Weak tears filled my eyes.

"Poor little orphans!" Another hug, for us both this time. "He can stay, but on the floor. Is *filthy*!"

As usual.

The water arrived plus my cloak and bundle. Ten minutes later I was in cold water, being scrubbed clean, my dirty clothes were handed out for washing, and then I was rubbed warm and dry, donned someone's clean shirt and drawers, and was thrust back into bed. A moment later and Growch was in the tub as well, too shocked to protest, and five minutes later he was shaking himself dry in a corner, thoroughly huffy.

Out went the dirty water, in came food, a sort of broth and some real bread. I went green at the thought of anything to eat, but the captain's wife insisted.

"If you going to be sick, better you be sick with something to be sick on. Dip bread into soup, suck juices, nibble bread. Count to ten tens—you can count?—then do again. And again. Try . . ."

I did, and it worked. After a few queasy moments I kept the first two pieces of bread down, and the rest was easy. The last few pieces of bread and broth I indicated were for Growch.

A hammering on the door again, and that loud-voiced martinet who strode the deck of his ship like a small but determined Colossus and ruled his crew with the threat of a rope's end, was heard asking his wife in the meekest way possible if he might have some more maps?

"Take them and be quick about it! Take also a blanket and your eating things. You will bunk with the mate. Now, be off with you! I have work to do. . . ."

I suppose my mouth must have been hanging open, because as he left she turned and winked at me. "Never let them get away with nothing, my chick," she said comfortably. "Out there—" she gestured to the sea, the storm, the tossing deck, "—he is boss. In here, I am, and he don't forget it."

I looked around the cabin. Comfortable, yes, but not luxurious. Not the sort of place one could call home.

"Do you sail with him all the time? I mean, haven't you got a place ashore? And aren't you ever afraid?"

She laughed. "No, yes, and yes. I sail when I want a change, go to new places. I have a home far from here, near youngest son, not yet married. Afraid? Of course. But this not bad storm, only little Levante who blow us off course forty-fifty mile. Rest of voyage routine. My man know this: he only want maps to make him look important." She bustled about, tidying the already tidy. "Now you get some rest. Tell me all about yourself when you wake up." She held up one of the chamber pots. "You or dog want pee-pee?"

I slept all through the rest of that day and the night, and when I awoke at last the storm was off away somewhere else, my sickness had gone, I was hungry for the first time in days and all I had to do was concoct a romantic enough story to satisfy my indulgent hostess. It wasn't too difficult: I remembered my beautiful blind knight, invented parents who didn't understand my love, relived parts of my earlier journeys, including a near rape, and finally sent my betrothed off on a pilgrimage from which he had not yet returned, thus my escapade.

Tears of sympathy poured from her eyes. She sighed, she sobbed as my tears—of hunger: where was my breakfast?—mingled with hers.

"My dearest chick! How often I wish for a daughter! Now my prayers will all be with you. . . ." She dried her eyes, glanced at me. "You are sure you are set on this knight of yours? My youngest son, he is not the brightest boy in the world, but . . ."

I was almost sorry to disappoint her.

One fine evening we sailed between two jaws of land into the mouth of a bay made bloodred by the setting sun. Climbing the hill behind was a beautiful city, with gold cupolas, pierced minarets, palaces and tree-lined streets. Even as we nudged in towards the quay, lights appeared in windows, along streets, moving with carriages or hand-held, until the whole city resembled a rosy hive alive with sparkling bees.

Matthew's ships had a permanently allotted landing stage, so we were rowed in and tied up right on the quayside. Immediately aboard was the Master Scipio I was waiting to meet. Of medium height, with a forked beard, he exuded authority. After a brief courtesy to myself, he took Falcone's papers from the captain and started the unloading with his own team, disregarding the swarm of itinerants who crowded the quay touting for work.

The cargo was checked by myself, now fully recovered, and Master Scipio's assistant, a dark man called Justus, then it was borne away to a warehouse for storage. It was well into the night by the time we finished and we ate where we stood, highly flavored meats on skewers with a sort of pancake bread. At last we went back to the ship for what remained of the night. It was strange to lie down and not be rocked from side to side, and it took a while, tired as I was, to get to sleep.

Added to the lack of motion there was the noise from ashore. Used as I was to the creaking of the ship, the noise of wind and sea, my ears were now assailed by the sounds of humanity at large, determined to wine and carouse the night away. The ship was moored right up against the "entertainment" part of the harbor, and the night was alive with singing, wailing and shouting, wheels, hooves, and musical instruments. I learned later that the captain's wife had stood guard for the rest of the night on the gangplank, armed with an ancient sword, turning back not only those members of the crew who wished to creep ashore, but also any enterprising whore who attempted to board.

Before we went ashore finally she drew me aside and pressed a small packet into my hand.

"Is a nothings," she said. "But pretty enough perhaps. You take it for present. My husband he bring it back as gift when he sail alone. Say it come from wise man down on his luck. . . ." She laughed. "Only truth is, I get gift means he has another woman somewhere. Guilty conscience. Better you have it for dowry," and she gave me another of her bear hugs, which almost had my eyes popping out. "Take care, chick; I so hope you find your man!"

On shore Master Scipio was waiting with his second-in-command, half a dozen guards and a horse master. After briefly introducing me, we went off for breakfast at a small tavern some half-mile from the port. We ate a thick fish stew, more of the pancakelike bread, olives, a bland cheese, and drank the local wine. A street and a half further on were our lodgings; a three-story house in a narrow twisting alley, that almost touched its neighbor across the street at roof level.

Our rooms were little more than cubicles, overlooking a central courtyard where a small fountain tinkled pleasantly amid vine-covered walls. I was lucky enough to have a small space to myself: a clean pallet and a stool, and it was relatively cool.

Master Scipio spoke to us from the stairs. "I have things to arrange. We shall meet again tonight at the same tavern. To those of you who are new to the city, a word or two of advice. Don't venture far and keep your hand on your purse. Don't get involved in arguments on religion or over women, because I won't bail you out. Watch both the food and the drink; if you are ill you are left behind. One last thing: do not discuss our cargo or our destination."

"How long are we here for?" asked one of the guards.

"We start out at dawn tomorrow. Anyone not packed and ready will be left behind," and off he clattered down the stairs. Not a gentle man, but at least one knew where one was with him.

Two of the guards set off almost immediately, to "see the sights," as they put it, but the others lingered. Eventually one, a local man, went off to visit some relative or other, and the others decided to go out sightseeing.

"You coming, youngster?"

I would dearly have loved to explore the city, but after last night's sleeplessness the pallet was more inviting. I took off my jacket and lay back, promising myself a good wash later. My eyes closed. . . .

At the foot of the pallet Growch made a great to-do of hoofing out his ears and nipping busily for fleas.

"Can't you do that on the floor?" I asked sleepily.

"More comfortable up 'ere." He was quiet for a moment or two, and I began to drift off. " 'Ow long you goin' to kip, then?"

"An hour or so. Why?"

"I'm 'ungry!"

"You're always hungry. . . ."

"Can you remember the last thing I ate? No, and neither can I."

"Just give me an hour," I said between my teeth. "One hour . . ."

Chapter Three

Actually he let me sleep for two and I woke gently and naturally, lying back in a luxury of lassitude. I could hear him out on the landing, snapping at flies. He was quite good at it, usually; having such short legs he tried to compensate in other ways, and quickness of paw, mouth, and eye were three of them.

And of course it was Growch who had alerted me to the other of my secrets: the power of the ring I wore on my right hand. One could hardly guess it was there, I thought, lifting my finger to gaze at it. As thin as a piece of skin it nestled on my middle finger as if it were a part of it. I couldn't remove it, either. According to what I had heard, the ring chose its wearer and stayed there, until either the wearer had no further use for it or grew unworthy to wear it.

This latter must have been what happened to my father, who had left the ring, some coins and his cloak as the only legacies to my mother and myself. He had been hunted down and killed on a false accusation before I had ever been born, but my mother—who was the village whore and no worse for it either—had kept the few pieces he left as mementos. She had worn the cloak I now possessed, had spent all the current moneys he had left, but was unable to change the curious coins I inherited, that had so fitted the maps Suleiman and I had studied. Coincidence perhaps, but intuition told me my father had once come this way, too. A good omen.

As to the ring I had slipped on my finger so thoughtlessly the night my mother died, it had been the most magical thing in my life. According to Growch, the first creature I had met after fleeing the village where I was born, it was a precious sliver of horn from the head of a fabulous Unicorn, and as such enabled me to communicate with other creatures and also, as I discovered later, warned of impending danger.

I wondered what sin my father had committed for it to leave his finger; my mother had not been able to fit it to hers either, whereas it had slipped onto mine like bear grease and stuck like glue.

I couldn't have managed without it. Nor, I thought with a wry smile, would I have once encumbered myself with not only a blind knight, but also a dog, Mistral the horse, Traveler the pigeon, Basher the tortoise, and my beloved little pig. . . . No, I mustn't think about the pig.

Be that as it may, the ring had completely changed my life. My mother had had ambitions for me. With the help of her "clients," I had been educated far beyond a village girl's station. I could read, write, figure, cook, sew, carpenter, cure, fish, hunt, brew, farm, spin and weave. She had plans for me to become the sort of woman who could choose her own husband and take a place in society, but the queer paradox had been that she couldn't bear to part with me, so had, knowingly or not, fed me with sweet cakes and honeyed fruits until I was the fattest, most unattractive girl in the province and no one would have me. I hadn't realized it until after she died, and it took a while to become reconciled to her duplicity, conscious or not.

But, as I said, the ring had changed all that. By the time I had learned to communicate properly with all the creatures I met and who needed my help, the original intent of seeking the first husband I could find had disappeared under other considerations.

Not that understanding the animals had been easy. Only one-tenth of animal speech is in sound—barks, neighs, bleats, etc.—and another three-tenths are in body movement, position of head, legs, ears, and feel of coat and fur. The other, and greater part, is thought-talk. This last was the most difficult for me, even with the help of the Unicorn's ring. Animals think in sorts of pictures, colored only by their own thoughts and seen from their own angles, so a bird didn't send back the same images as, say, a dog or a horse. Eventually, though, it became easier, and Growch and I spoke to each other almost entirely by thought.

Dear dog: all he had wanted in the beginning was a real home, a warm fire to curl up by in the winter, regular food and a pat or two, but he had left all that behind to follow me into an uncertain future. He had pretended that his real reason was to find more of those "fluffy bum" bitches he had fallen for in our earlier travels, pampered creatures from Cathay with legs as short as his and no morals whatsoever, but I knew better. He had decided that his real role in life was to keep an eye on me: he was convinced I couldn't manage on my own.

He trotted in now, one ear up, one down, as usual.

"Awake now, are we? 'Ow's about some food, then?"

We assembled in a small square behind our lodgings in shivering dawn. The sun would soon rise above the rearing mountains, but now the sky was a pale greenish-blue, and the mist lay knee-high in the streets. Breakfast was pancake bread and honey, and as the church bells called out six and a muezzin sang from his tower, the convoy got under way.

A string of heavily laden mules, two wagons, eight mounted guards and horses for Master Scipio, interpreter Justus, horse master Antonius and our guide, a skinny fellow called Ibrahim. Nothing for me: Master Scipio explained that I either walked or hitched a lift in one of the wagons.

"Do you good, boy," he said robustly. "Half day walk, half ride. And you can alternate the wagons. One driver doubles as the cook—you can give him a hand, he'll teach you what foods are best for travelling. T'other wagon is driven by the farrier: knows all there is to know about horses. Right?"

So we were off, all yawning, for we had none of us had much sleep at the lodgings. The guards had straggled back at all hours, full of the local wine and boasting of their winnings and/or conquests.

I reached up to pull at Master Scipio's sleeve.

"Where are we bound?"

"For the trading town of Küm."

"How long will it take?"

"Over the trails we follow, four or five days."

So long! Now that we were finally on our way proper I was eager to complete my journey east as fast as I could. It seemed I would have to be patient.

Our way lay to the northeast, and once we left the city behind the travelling was frustratingly slow. We twisted and turned along trails that followed the lowest contours of the land; the tracks had been there for time immemorial, the easiest for man and beast, and for the most part were within easy reach of water, but were also rutted and broken by the years of travel.

At first the surrounding countryside was relatively well wooded and we were hemmed by low hills, but the farther we travelled the wilder became the terrain. The hills grew higher and crowded closer, the trees gave way to low scrub and the sun burned us in the breezeless valleys. It was cooler at night, but we always built a fire, both to cook the evening meal and to deter any wild animal; every evening we heard mountain dogs howling at the moon, sometimes near, sometimes far.

We had brought our own provisions with us, to avoid paying high prices in the small villages we passed through, and this proved our undoing.

On the third night the cook prepared a stew, and in order to disguise the (by now) high smell and taste of the meat, threw some very pungent herbs and spices into the pot. I watched him take various packets from his pockets, but after asking the names of a few, all unknown to me, I lost interest; besides, he said my watching him made him feel nervous. He was a taciturn man at best, and poor company if I rode in his wagon. He wasn't a very good cook, either.

I took a portion of the stew over to Growch and sat down beside him to eat mine, but two very disconcerting things happened. One, my precious ring gave a little warning stab, and two, Growch took one sniff and flatly refused to eat any.

Now, my dog doesn't refuse food. Ever. He can devour stuff that turns my stomach even to look at.

"What's the matter? It smells all right. A little spicy, perhaps, but you've eaten worse." I lifted my spoon to my mouth but his tail got in the way, and at the same time my ring prickled again.

"Don' touch it! S'not good to eat. Don' know why, but somethin' in there ain't right."

"Are you suggesting it's poisoned?" I tried to laugh it off. I was hungry.

"Not poison. Told you, don' know what's wrong; all I know is, I'm not havin' any, and you shouldn' neither."

The ring stabbed again. "All right," I said crossly, as much to it as to Growch. "Cheese and dates."

"Skip the dates. . . ."

As I went to return our untouched food to the stew pot, I noticed others doing the same. Not all, by any means. About half the men were eating heartily, others were just picking. If I had needed any confirmation that it wasn't entirely palatable, I would have had it in the fact that the cook himself wasn't eating his own food: he had just handed the guide Ibrahim a plate of dried fruit and cut himself a heel of cheese, although he scowled when I asked for the same.

It wasn't until we had been on the road for a couple of hours the next day that the wisdom of avoiding the stew became apparent. One by one men groaned, clutched their stomachs and disappeared into the brush to be violently ill. By noon about half were incapacitated, unable to ride, and had to be hauled up onto the wagons, their horses tied behind.

Master Scipio called me over, his face gray and sweating.

"Here, boy: take my horse. I'm going to rest for a while," and off he disappeared into the bushes, to reemerge some moments later to help me up on the horse and then climb himself onto the nearest wagon.

At first it was just fine to be riding up so high, feeling well and fit while all around were groaning and moaning, but Growch was grumbling that he was wearing his legs down to their stumps trying to keep up with me as I rode from one end of the line to the other, as Master Scipio did, and after a while the high wooden saddle began to chafe and the bottom of my spine felt bruised. I checked up and down once more: half the mule drivers and half the guards were riding the wagons and the guide, Ibrahim, was driving the farrier's cart.

I brought the horse to an amble beside Master Scipio.

"Like to ride again? Or shall we halt and have a rest, water the horses?"

He looked better, but not much.

"Not yet. We won't stop, because if we do we'll never get going again. Keep riding; there's a good camping place a few miles further on. We'll stop there overnight."

The trouble was, we had had to travel so slowly with the overladen wagons that we had made very little progress by the time the sun slid behind the hills and the valley we travelled became gloomy and full of shadows. Once again I implored Master Scipio to take to his horse but once again he refused.

"A mile or so more, that's all, then we can rest, I promise. Ride up to the head of the line and see if you can hurry up those mules. . . ."

I was so sorry for myself and my saddle sores as I rode to the front, noting the weariness of the animals as they plodded on, heads hanging, puffing and blowing, that it wasn't for a moment or two that the growing noise behind me made any sense. It seemed that the hubbub and the prickling of my ring coincided, which meant danger, so I wheeled the horse as quickly as I could (not easy because the track had narrowed to a defile) and pushed him back towards the wagons and Master Scipio.

Our whole caravan stretched back now over a quarter-mile or thereabouts, because of the growing dusk, general weariness, lack of Scipio's incisive leadership and, most of all, the narrowness of the trail. As I kicked my reluctant jade to a faster pace, Growch panting at our heels, the noise—shouts, yells, neighing of horses, clash of swords—made no sense, until I rounded a curve and saw the horde of ragged men armed with spears, swords, clubs, and knives that were creeping out of the bush and attacking the wagons.

Ambush!

My heart gave a *thump* of terror, and the hand that fumbled at my belt for the dagger I kept there was slick with the sweat of fear. My horse had caught the scent of blood and reared suddenly, so that I lost the reins and had to hang on to his mane with both hands as he turned away from the battle. I tried my damnedest to pull his head round, find the reins again, but all of a sudden a figure leapt from the undergrowth, a knife between his teeth, a spear in his hand.

The ring was burning on my finger but I could do nothing but freeze in horror as the spear was lifted in my direction and the man's mouth opened in a howl of exultation. Death stared at me, and I couldn't even pray—

There was a growl, a yelp, a cry of pain, and the spear missed me by a fraction and struck my horse's rump. It reared with a scream of pain, its flailing hooves downed my would-be attacker, luckily missing Growch, then it plunged off again down the track and away from the fighting.

Once more it was all I could do to hang on as I was bounced and jounced like a sack of meal on that horrid hard saddle. I bumped both nose and chin on the high pommel, banged my leg on a rock as the horse swerved at the last moment, and scratched my arm on some branch or scrub that scraped our sides.

Tears of pain squeezed past my closed eyelids: would this never stop? We must have galloped at least—

The animal came to an abrupt halt, forelegs quivering, and the sudden lack of motion did what the flight couldn't. I fell off onto the ground and lay there with my head spinning and everything else hurting, while the wretched animal cropped the grass next to my ear with a sound like tearing linen.

I'm dead, I thought. I must be. No one could have survived that headlong gallop. I'll just lie here and wait for the golden trumpets. . . . Washed in the blood of the Lamb—

Nothing so sacred. I was being washed, but by a sloppy, anxious dog. I sat up gingerly.

"Go away, Growch! I'm all right. . . ."

"Then get up and tell 'em! 'Bout the ambush!"

I opened my eyes. We were in a clearing full of people running towards us. Over to one side a huge fire was flickering. For a desperate moment I thought I had stumbled into the ambushers' camp, but a closer look showed these were respectable travellers. In a moment I was surrounded and a babel of tongues was flinging questions at me till my head hurt worse than ever. I explained in my own tongue, market Latin, a little Italian and a couple of words of Arabic I had picked up (I think these last were profanities, remembering where I had heard them, but no one seemed to mind) and a moment or two later armed men were clattering away back the way I had come.

Someone led me over to the fire and smeared an evil-smelling grease on the more obvious bumps and bruises, and gave me a mug of spiced wine which I downed gratefully. I accepted another and a bowl of rice and chicken. Something nudged my arm, and half the contents of the bowl were on the ground.

"Ta!" said Growch pleasantly, licking up the last grains. "That was fun, wasn' it? That fella din' 'alf yell when I nipped 'im! Quite a battle . . ."

Of course! I remembered now. He had doubtless saved my life when he bit my attacker's ankle, though I didn't know whether he realized it. I tipped the rest of the rice out.

"Here: I'm not hungry. . . . Thanks."

"Nothing to it. 'Ere: why don't you ask for another bowlful?"

It appeared the ambush had been well planned. The stew had been dosed with a powerful emetic, and both the guide Ibrahim and the cook had made good their escape. We had lost two guards and a mule driver and there were several wounded, including Master Scipio, who finally rode in with his arm in a sling. But I was hailed as a hero for riding to seek help and feted with choice titbits and a handful of hastily gathered coin, a whip-round from the survivors.

I felt a trifle guilty as I accepted the coins and blushed when they called me a hero, but as Growch remarked, now was not the time to tell them my horse had bolted from a superficial spear wound and heroism had nothing to do with it.

Master Scipio accepted the offer of our new friends to travel under the protection of their bigger caravan—a friendship cemented in gold I noticed—as far as the trading city. Being a larger party, and with wounded to care for, our progress was of necessity slow, so it was on the third afternoon after our rescue that we topped the final ridge and I gazed down on the city of Küm.

Chapter Four

"But that's not a town," I said, bitterly disappointed. "It's just—just a collection of tents!"

Scipio drew his horse alongside the wagon I was riding in.

"Tents maybe, but still the largest trading center for hundreds of miles." He gestured below. "A plain some three miles wide, the same long, with a river to the east. Mountains all around, yes, but with age-old trails that lead in from Cathay, India, the Middle Sea, the Baltic, the Western Isles . . ." He leant back, let the reins lie slack, as we waited for the wagon ahead to start the narrow trail down. "Looks fine now, doesn't it? But in the autumn when the rains come the river down there is a raging torrent; in the winter the bitter winds blow in from the north, the river freezes over and the sands below are as sharp as hailstones as they whirl across the plain. In the spring the rain and the melting snows from the hills flood the plateau, but when the waters recede and the sun comes out, the grass and flowers grow thick and fast. Then the advance parties come, those who cut and dry the grasses for forage; after them come the men with tents for hire, the cooks, the laundrymen, the farriers, and the men who dig the cesspits. Local villagers bring in fresh fruit, vegetables, chickens, sheep, and goats, and there is a committee of those concerned who ensure everything runs smoothly for when the first of the traders arrive in mid-June. From then until mid-September the place is seething. I truly believe one can find anything in the world down there if needed. . . ." And off he spurred down the hill.

I turned to Nod, my driver. "Have you been this way before?"

"Oh, aye: wouldn't miss it for the world. Just as Master Scipio says: the world and his mate meet here. Nice rest for us too. We can just sit back and enjoy ourselves while the bosses natter and bicker and blather and dicker over every blessed piece of barter." He was chewing on a root of liquorice and spat a brown stream over the edge of the wagon as we began the descent. "I seen stuff there as you couldn't imagine: furs, silks, wools, dyes, carpets, rugs, 'broideries; copper pots, clay pots, glass, china; daggers, swords, spears; paintings and manuscripts, pens and brushes; all the spices you could think of and dried herbs; wines, dried fruits, rice, and tea. There's even bars of gold and silver, precious jewels, children's toys—Whoa, there!" He was silent for a moment or two as we negotiated a difficult turn. He spat out more juice. "Then there's the animals. . . ."

"Lions and tigers?"

"Sometimes. They're mostly to special order. I seen a panther and a spotted cat with jewelled collars, tame as you please, and even once, a helefant, with a nose longer than its tail. . . . No, mostly they's more portable. Monkeys, 'xotic birds, snakes as thick as your arm, queer little dogs . . ."

Oh, no! I thought. Not Growch's "fluffy bums"; keeping an eye on him in that place would be difficult.

"Then there's the slaves. Mostly men, 'cos women and children don't travel well, but you see the occasional two or three. All colors, too: mostly black or brown, but there's some yellows and near-whites. Dwarfs, sometimes, they fetch a good price." He spoke as indifferently as if they were bales of cloth.

We were on easier ground now, and the town beneath seemed to be taking on a pattern. The tents appeared to be arranged in rows rather than haphazardly, and although the number of people running around made it seem chaotic, there also seemed to be a purpose in all they did.

Nod pointed out the various vantage points with his whip.

"To the right there, by the river, is the laundries, below 'em the cesspits, above stables and forage. In the center the living accommodation, to the left the cooking areas. Below us are the money-changers. Top left the brothels. Clear space in the middle, the market, held daily. Doubles up for special entertainment at night."

"What sort of special entertainment?"

"Oh, dancing girls, snake charmers, acrobats—whatever's going. One year there were those belly dancers from Afriky: sight for sore eyes they were. . . ."

It seemed Master Scipio was right: everyone was catered for.

Rent-a-tent came first. We hired four. Scipio, interpreter Justus, horse master Antonius and I shared one, the remaining guards and mule drivers another, larger, and our goods took up the last two.

The sleeping tents were circular, those for the goods rectangular. The poles were bamboo, the canvas thin and light, for no rain was expected at this time of year. Other traders had brought their own, more luxurious, with hangings to divide the interiors into smaller sections for sleeping or entertaining. Some had oriental rugs and silken cushions to sit upon, small brass or inlaid wooden tables, oil lamps and fine crockery, but we had grass matting, stools and wood-frame beds strung with rope, which were highly uncomfortable. I stated my intention of sleeping on the floor, but Scipio pointed silently to a double column of ants, in one side of the tent, out of the other. He then handed me some small clay cups.

"Fill these with water, then put the feet of the beds in them, otherwise we'll have all sorts climbing up. Bad enough with the mosquitoes."

He wasn't joking; I spent a most uncomfortable night, listening with dread for the sudden silence which meant they had found their target. The next night I was given a jar of evil-smelling grease, which helped, but that first day I was as spotty as any adolescent lad.

Even without the mosquitoes, that first night would have kept me wakeful. I had not yet learnt how to fold my blanket so as to even out the rope sling I was suspended upon, the moon shone with relentless brightness through the thin walls of the tent, and the night was full of unaccustomed noise. There were snores from my companions, barking from scores of dogs—including Growch, who was absent without leave—the flap-flap of canvas as it responded to the night breeze, shouts and yells in the distance, and somewhere someone was singing what sounded like an endless dirge full of quarter tones that scraped at my sensibilities like the squeaks of an unoiled axle.

That first day—and many afterwards—was spent visiting tent after tent with the attendant interminable bargaining that seemed so much a part of any sort of trade out here. No price was ever fixed, not even for the food we ate, and even less so for the goods we bought and sold. A great deal of exchange and barter took the place of coin: we exchanged all our wool, for instance, for what seemed to me a minute quantity of saffron and some lily bulbs, but Scipio was more than satisfied.

I had to attend as it was part of my (supposed) training, and if it hadn't been for the endless hospitality—sherbet, yoghurt or mint tea, small sweet cakes or wafers—I should have dropped off long before the sun was high. Nearly everything had to be done through our interpreter, Justus, and one had to go through all the politenesses of enquiry about travel, friends, relatives, weather and health long before one revealed one's true objectives. It seemed such a waste of time, but Master Scipio was insistent that I realize it was the only way to get things done, and was less than sympathetic when I begged off the last visit with an ill-concealed yawn.

"I'm sorry: I didn't sleep very well last night. I'll be better tomorrow, I promise."

"And so you better had; you're here to work, to learn, to become a trader, and a night or two's lost sleep is neither here nor there. A young lad like you should party the night away and then be fresh as new milk in the morning. I don't know what the world is coming to: why at your age . . ." and so on.

They went off on their last visit, I smeared myself with grease, fell on the bed and must have slept for hours, for when I awoke, hungry and refreshed, they were all abed and snoring and it must have been around an hour past midnight. It was Growch's cold nose that had woken me: he was hungry too.

As he had been absent most of the day I wasn't sympathetic, would probably have turned over and tried to sleep again, except that my own stomach was grumbling likewise. I was also sweaty and sticky and needed a good wash. By the sounds outside, the food stalls would probably still be open, so I swung my legs off the bed and we crept out through the tent flap into the moony night.

It was as near light as day, and there was no problem in finding our way towards the cooking stalls. I found one of our guards seated on a long bench by a large barbecue and he invited me to join him in a dish of chicken, lentils and herbs. I sneaked some to Growch, then repaid the guard by buying the wine. While we travelled food and lodgings were paid for out of the travelling purse, so at a place like this we were given a food allowance every day, the same for all. The guards and drivers were either paid their wages at the end of the journey or re-engaged to be paid at the other end on their return, which was the case with our guards and drivers, so they would have little enough to spare. I left him a couple of coins for more wine, then strolled in the direction of the river, hoping it would be deserted enough for a wash.

It seemed, though, that some people worked throughout the night. The forage-and-horse lines were relatively quiet, but the launderers were hard at work, washing and rinsing, beating out the dirt on great flat stones and draping the clothes out on rocks to catch the early sun. Here the river was scummy with dirt, which flowed on down towards the cesspits, where I could hear the noise of digging.

I turned north, past the great tumps of hay and straw to where the land grew rockier and the river flowed faster, and was lucky enough to find a tiny sandy bay which curved round a pool where the water was quieter.

I gazed about me but could see no one, and all the activity seemed to be away south.

"Keep watch," I said to Growch. "I fancy a quick dip—"

"You're mad!" he snorted. "Wouldn' catch me bathin' in that! Un'ealthy, all this washin' . . ."

I stripped right down and plunged into the water, stifling a yell as the freezing mountain water all but numbed me. Summer it might be, but the water didn't know that. After the first shock, however, I luxuriated in the fast-flowing water as it washed away the stinks and grime of the last few days. Even my bruises from the bolting horse had started to fade, I noted. My underwear and shirt joined me in the water: they could dry out on my body, for the night seemed positively hot after the icy water.

My last act before getting clothed again was to pick up a furious, scratching, nipping Growch, and dump him in the deepest pool I could find. . . .

He cursed for a full fluid minute without repeating himself when he reached dry land, but I had a couple of raisin biscuits in my pouch which mollified him somewhat, though he did treat me to an exhibition of the hollow cough he had suddenly picked up, and shivered most convincingly.

"Don' ever do that again! 'Nough to give me my death, that was!"

I suggested a walk, to dry us both off.

"Quickest way to the food tents is straight across," he said, so that was the way we went, though I doubted they would still be serving. Luckily for him we found a couple of stalls still open and I bargained for some skewers of meat, which we chewed as we wandered back towards the sleeping tents.

Growch stopped in midstride. "Listen . . ."

At first I could hear nothing, then the wind picked up the sound. A soft whimpering, moaning, keening, like the sound a child will make when it has been punished and sent to bed, but dare not make too much noise unless it invites more punishment. The breeze changed direction and the noise died away, then I heard it again.

Growch's nose was working overtime. "Back there," he said tersely. His nose was pointing way beyond the rest of the encampment. "Not nice . . ."

My ring was warm on my finger, so there was no danger, and there was something in the sound that called out to me, like the despair of a trapped animal. Almost without conscious thought I started to walk towards the crying. At first, in spite of the moonlight, I could see nothing unusual, but as I rounded an outcrop of rock I saw what looked like a huge cage, or series of cages, like those in which they kept the exotic animals on offer.

But animals didn't sound like this, or smell like this either.

I wrinkled my nose with distaste and beside me Growch was growling, not in anger but rather in a mixture of bewilderment and disgust, as if this was a situation he did not know how to cope with. I moved closer till the moonlight threw the shadow of the bars across me like cold fingers, and I could see the full horror of what lay behind them.

The cages were crowded with human beings, men, women and children, all shackled, and all standing, sitting, or lying in their own foulnesses. Even in the stews of large towns I had smelt nothing like this, and it was not only the excrement but a sort of miasma of despair and fear that came from the unwashed captives that made me recoil in disgust.

Hands were stretched out between the bars towards me, the keening rose in volume and now there were words I could not understand, except that they were pleas for help. Against my will I moved closer and now the chains were clanking, the babble of words grew louder and fingers clutched at my sleeve with a strength I would not have thought possible.

"I can't do anything," I said urgently, although I knew they would not understand. "Let me go. . . ."

But their seeking hands found more and more of me, until there was a prickle from my ring and almost at once a shout and running feet. At once I was released and, looking back, I saw a couple of men with lanterns bobbing in their hands running towards the cages.

"C'mon," barked Growch urgently. "We don't want to be caught by that lot. They'll think we've been tryin' to help 'em escape. . . ."

Dodging in and out of whatever shadow I could find, I ran back to the safety of the lines of tents, my heart beating uncomfortably fast, my mind churning. It was not that I didn't know slavery existed—why, in the very village in which I had grown up, we were less than animals to the lord of the manor, who held the power of life and death, imprisonment or mutilation, as he chose. But there at least we had known the rules and abided by them, and life was comfortable enough if we paid our dues. Besides we knew no other existence; those poor captives back there had been snatched away from homes and families against their will—and what sort of future could they expect?

That they would be exploited there was no doubt. If you paid for something you expected your money's worth. Physical labor, prostitution, degradation, these were the least they could look forward to. Perhaps I should not have minded so much if I hadn't remembered Signor Falcone's far kinder fate—but where were the Suleimans of this world to rescue this batch? And the thousands of others, both now and in the future? How many of these would still be alive in, say, a year's time?

I was saddened and frustrated, and said extra prayers for those poor creatures before seeking what I thought would be a sleepless bed, but I must have been more exhausted than I thought, for I slept like a child.

The following days were spent in more trading. It seemed that you could exchange what you had for something of equal value, and the next day swap that for something you considered to be more valuable, sell half that, find a customer for the rest, use the money for another purchase and so on. In this way our tents of goods were emptied and filled at least three times to my knowledge. Master Scipio did not appear to lose by these deals for he went about with less than his usual degree of taciturnity, though whether this had anything to do with the nightly entertainments he went to, I do not know. Sufficient to note that he, Justus and Antonius seldom came to bed before the small hours.

The pattern of barter and trade soon became easier for me to follow, although I still found the whole process tedious and realized I would never have either the patience of Matthew nor the acumen of Suleiman. But this apprenticeship was the only way to my goal, so I tried my hardest to learn and even earned compliments from Scipio for my diligence. Of course there were still the language barriers, but I was picking up a word or phrase or two of Arabic every day and could refer to our interpreter, Justus, if I had need.

On the fifth day I asked Scipio how much longer we should be at Küm, to receive the answer that we awaited one particular trader to conclude our business.

"We shall do no more trading until he arrives," continued Scipio, "so why don't you take the afternoon off and see the sights? Here, go buy yourself a trinket or two," and he tossed me a couple of coins.

Glad enough not to be shut up in a stuffy tent for hours, Growch and I wandered off into the sunshine. For many this was the afternoon time, which meant we could roam at will without being trampled underfoot, so we stopped for sherbet and barbecued meat on sticks, then watched a basket weaver for a few minutes. Growch decided he was going to investigate what sounded like one of the interminable dogfights that went on day and night, so I just walked where my feet took me, refusing a sweet seller here, a rug seller there, until I found myself at the western end of the camp, beyond the tents.

Here on the edge of the encampment lived those too poor to hire tents, or nomads who preferred to wander the fringes with their flocks, sleeping under the stars. Among the former were the fearsome men from the far north who had brought their shaggy ponies laden with furs, carvings of wood and bone and metal ornaments in the shape of dragons and strange sea creatures. I had learned from the horse master, Antonius, that they found no trouble in disposing of their wares, exchanging them for salt, dried fruits, linen and presents for their women: combs, polished metal mirrors, needles and colored threads, but that as it was all strictly barter they were always short of cash for food and amusements, and often went to unorthodox methods to obtain it. Of course they could go straight home once the goods were exchanged, but it seemed they stayed as long as they could, loath to return to their cold and barren lands.

They were wild enough to look at, these northerners. Dressed in their outlandish gear of iron skullcaps (some with horns affixed), fur capes and short leather trews, their faces scarred with ritual knife cuts and adorned with straggling moustaches, they would have been fearsome enough even without the assortment of knives and axes they stuck in their belts.

If truth would have it though, they were probably no more fearsome than the adolescent town louts of any large town, swaggering the streets with boasts of their conquests on the field and in bed, swearing that they could drink anyone under the bench. All mouth and cock, as my mother used to say.

They appeared to have arranged some sort of wrestling match and had shouted up a reasonable audience for it, one man busy taking bets on the outcome. It was to be a no-holds-barred free-for-all, with kicking, gouging, biting, hair-pulling and balls-grabbing part of the fun, as a bystander explained to me; he seemed to think all the fights were fixed, but watching the first, in which the loser ended up with half an ear torn off and his face ground into the dirt till he lost consciousness, I wasn't convinced.

Someone came round with an upended skullcap and I tossed in the smallest coin I could find. Another bout was just starting—promising, from the look of the combatants, to be even bloodier than the first—but by now more people, siesta over, had arrived to watch, and being slighter and smaller than most I found myself elbowed out to the fringes, where I could see but little. I had just decided to look for amusement elsewhere when there was a nudge on the back of my leg and Growch, absent till now, said quietly: "Look at that feller over there; pickin' their purses, he is. . . ."

Nearby was a stack of bales, ready for loading onto the shaggy ponies when these warriors decided enough was enough and I moved behind it to watch the thief unobserved. He was younger than most—around seventeen I should guess—and slim, stealthy and quick. I could not help but admire the way he circled the back of the crowd, picking his next victim, then holding back till the people surged forward at a particularly vicious moment in the wrestling to yell encouragement to one or other contestant, then taking advantage of the press of bodies to lift a purse to his hand, weigh its possibilities—I saw him reject two in this way—and then use his sharp knife to detach pouch and contents from its owner. Judging from the bulge at the back of his trews he had been busy for quite a while.

I was so busy admiring his expertise that it wasn't until he had lifted three more purses that I realized that I should do something about it. But what? Shout "Stop thief!"? Thieving was a sin, but did I owe the gullible crowd anything? Besides he was an artist, in his own way, and nearly everyone would steal if the need was great—Stop it, Summer! I told myself severely. Never mind the ethics, just prevent him from further robbery.

I had a word with Growch, then stepped from behind my hiding place and tapped the young man on the shoulder. He jumped about a foot in the air and was about to bolt, but Growch's teeth were now fixed lovingly in his right ankle, and he had no alternative than to follow me to my hiding place behind the bales.

Perspiration was pouring off his forehead and I could smell the acrid sweat of fear. We knew not a word of each other's language but I mimed my disgust at his actions and threatened to trumpet his thefts to all within earshot.

He crumpled at my feet; purses and bags came tumbling from his trews. One by one he offered them to me, his hands shaking, but this was not what I had meant at all. He was obviously terrified, so the purpose of my intervention had worked: there would probably be no more stealing today.

I shook my head vigorously at the pile of purses at my feet and backed away, but he must have thought I wanted more, something special, for he offered me a blue amulet that hung round his neck, then an iron ring set with a red stone, and the more I shook my head, waved him away, the worse he got. I suddenly realized the reason for his fear; thieves could be hung, or at the least their hands cut off—

Something was thrust into my hands, a hard object wrapped in soft leather, and from the look of the thief's face it was his prize possession, the ultimate gift. I unwrapped it, curiously, but all it was was a piece of stone or rock or metal pointed at one end, about two fingers long and one wide. There was a small groove around the middle and wound round this was a piece of gut with a loop at the end so that it could be hung from one's finger. What was it? A weapon? A child's toy?

My puzzlement must have shown, for the thief took it from my hand, gestured to the north and held the stone so that it pointed in that direction. He looked at me, then turned the pointed end to the south, let it go—and it swung back to the north again. He handed it back to me and it worked once again. Sure that there was some trickery I twisted the gut round and round and let the stone twirl—still it ended up pointing north. Light dawned: this was a fabulous navigating instrument that would work even if the sun was hidden or the night without stars. Just think how wonderful it would be at sea, with no landmarks to steer by!

But apparently this stone had other properties, for he held out the iron ring on his finger and the stone swung towards it, then to his iron dagger and it did the same. He shook his head, indicating that it would only work away from iron.

As the sounds of the fight—which I had completely forgotten—rose to a real hubbub of yells and counteryells, I tried the stone myself on an iron spear, a discarded buckle, then back to the north again, thinking with wonderment as I did so that there must be the biggest mountain of iron in the whole world up there in the frozen wastes—

"'E's orf!" barked Growch. "Want me to chase 'im?"

I shook my head. The thief was gone with his gains, but he had left behind something far more precious to me: a magic stone!

When I returned to our tent and showed it to the others, I could not miss the look of envy on their faces.

"That there is a Waystone," said Antonius at last. "Heard of 'em but never seen one before."

"Look after it well, boy," said Scipio. "It could fetch a penny or two. Want to sell it?"

I shook my head.

"Where did you get it?" asked Justus.

I decided to tell them half the truth: the rest was too complicated. "I had it from one of the northerners. He wanted cash to spend before he left for home."

Luckily they didn't ask me how much I had spent, but apparently they, too, had a surprise for me. Sayid ben Hassan, the trader they had been expecting, had turned up at last, and we were to go to his tent at sundown for the usual courtesies.

"So, spruce yourself, boy; put on something more appropriate. And we don't take dogs."

Obeying Master Scipio's instructions I scared up a clean shirt and the clothes I had bought in Venice, sending the rest down to the laundry via one of the guards. Buying a bucket of water from one of the water sellers I made myself look as presentable as I could, and bribed Growch to be good in my absence with a pie from the stall nearest the tents.

Sayid ben Hassan's tent was at the end of a line. He had obviously brought his own, although the three next to it, full of goods, were hired. It was huge, to my eyes, easily rivalling any others I had seen. Fashioned of some dark-blue material, thicker than the usual canvas, it was layered like some extravagant fancy, the lowest being a sort of corridor, then the next, rising higher, compartmented into small rooms and the third and highest a spacious circle full of rugs, small tables and embroidered cushions.

Incense smoked on one of the tables—a sickly sort of smell, like powder—and water was bubbling in a little burner. A servant came in and made mint tea and remained to serve small dishes of nuts and raisins. Elaborate courtesies followed, meaning nothing but essential to Eastern hospitality. Then out came the cargo manifests from both sides and the haggling began. For once I didn't mind, for there was plenty to look at.

Sayid himself was a tall, slim Arab with a large hooked nose and piercing black eyes. He was dressed simply enough in white robes, but on his wrists were several gold bangles and the dagger at his belt had a jewelled hilt. The servant and the guards outside were all young, handsome men, dressed in short blue jackets and voluminous baggy trews; and the rugs, hangings, cushions, shawls, tables, lanterns and pottery were of the highest quality. I wouldn't mind living in such sybaritic luxury, I thought, but there was something perhaps a little too soft, too cloying, for it to be enjoyed forever.

I dragged my mind back to the haggling and Justus' whispered translations.

It seemed that we had raw ivory from Africa and cotton from the same source and he had a mix of spices and silk carpeting of an incredible lightness and color. I let my mind drift again, only to be brought up short by the mention of my name.

"Master Scipio just said that you will be travelling with Sayid to—"

"With him? Why not with you?" I interrupted. Surely I wasn't going to be shuffled off to someone strange yet again?

"I thought you understood that," said Scipio. "We all go only so far, you know. We each have our own territory and our own contacts. I go no further than this." He saw me open my mouth and snapped: "Don't argue! As an apprentice you do as you are told! If you don't wish to continue your journey now you may come back with me for the winter but you will have to start over again next year. Or, if you wish, you can surrender your papers right now and cancel your apprenticeship. It's up to you."

Out of the corner of my eye I could see Sayid listening to what was said, and from the expression on his face I believed he understood much more than people imagined. For some reason I began to blush, and I thought I saw a spark of amusement in the Arab's eyes. He murmured something to Scipio, who looked annoyed.

"What did he say?" I whispered to Justus.

"He said . . . He said he didn't know Master Scipio was in the habit of hiring children to do a man's job!"

All of a sudden I hated this supercilious Arab with his fine tent and expensive accoutrements and would have given anything not to be travelling with him. But what choice did I have? I had come this far in pursuit of a dream, far, far further than I had ever been before. How big was this world of ours, anyway? If I went back now I would be wasting all I had planned and saved for. And it would all be worth it in the end, it had to be!

"I shall be honored to travel with you," I said and bowed to Sayid.

"Good, good," said Scipio. "And now, if the business is concluded I believe Sayid wishes to visit the slave market?"

The Arab nodded.

"Then we shall join you. Come along, boy: it should be an interesting experience for you."

Chapter Five

We made our way to the open marketplace, cleared now of stalls and lit with flares and torches. A temporary platform had been erected in the middle and there, huddled together as if for mutual protection, were the captives I had seen in the cages.

They had all been washed down, for there was less smell, and now the shackles had been removed and they were roped loosely between the ankles. They looked reasonably well fed; most were dark-skinned, but one or two were lighter. An overseer stood on the platform with them, running the thongs of a whip through his fingers.

Many of those crowded round had merely come to watch, but there was a scattering of genuine traders like Sayid, who had their servants clear a way close to the platform.

The slave master, a fat Arab wearing rich robes, had a thin, drooping moustache and great dark pouches under his eyes. He waited until he reckoned all prospective buyers had arrived, then stepped up onto the platform and the sale began.

But first he had to extol the worth of his wares, the exotic locations they had come from, the distances travelled, the hardships he had had in transporting them, all to bump up the price as master Justus explained as he translated for me. "He doesn't say how many he lost on the way, though," he added.

I shivered, although it was a warm night.

One by one the slaves were paraded around the platform. Bids were called in a leisurely fashion, and betweentimes would-be buyers went up on the platform and examined the slaves as casually as they would choose fruit in a market. Mouths were wrenched open for teeth to be counted, heads inspected for ringworm or lice, joints tapped, eyelids lifted and—embarrassing to me at least—genitals were scrutinized for disease and, in the case of the men, testicles weighed in cupped hands.

"Estimating whether they will be good breeders," said Scipio. "Bit of a hit-and-miss way to do it, I should have thought. I remember . . ."

He turned to Antonius and I missed the rest.

The slave master could have earned his living on the stage. He had a rather high-pitched, whiny voice, but he wiggled and postured across the platform in spite of his bulk, all the while beseeching, cajoling, exhorting. He begged for bids, he pretended horror at their paucity and near wept with gratitude when his price was reached.

Sayid ben Hassan went up to examine four men of much the same height and age. He bid for three and settled for two, having them led off by four of his guards. Once again Justus explained to me.

"He had an order for two good-looking blacks for a widow in Persia. Got fancy tastes, apparently. Told to look for sweet breath and large, er, you-know-whats."

"Why didn't he bid for the fourth one?"

"Foul teeth and a leery left eye."

We were coming to the end; now there were only some four or five scrawny children left. These were going at much lower prices.

"Might survive, might not," said Scipio. "Not everyone wants to take a chance on a child. The next one, though, he's different: fetch the highest price of the night, I shouldn't wonder," and he pointed to a slight, exceptionally beautiful black boy of perhaps twelve or thirteen with huge, lustrous eyes.

"Why?"

He gave me a quick, almost contemptuous glance. "Where've you been, lad? Maybe you missed out on all that, but he's ripe for it. Bum-boys like that will be pampered pets for years, then go to train others. Wait for the bidding. . . ."

And indeed the boy fetched an astronomical sum, sold after brisk bidding to a thin Arab with long slim fingers that could not forbear from caressing his purchase even as he led him away. Another two children went for small sums, and now there was only one figure left. At first I thought it must be a dwarf, so much smaller and squatter he was than the rest. The other boys had been either brown or black, this one was a sort of yellowish color. His hair was as black as the others had been, but unlike theirs it was straight as a pony's tail, hanging over his eyes in a ragged fringe. His body was muscular enough, but his legs were slightly bandy and he scowled horribly.

For the first time the auctioneer seemed less than confident.

"What does he say?" I asked Justus.

"He says the boy is special. He comes from the east, was captured by brigands, nearly drowned trying to escape, was sold to someone or other who lost him in a game of chance. He speaks an unknown tongue, but is fit and healthy and good with horses." He yawned. "That's as may be, but the lad looks like trouble to me. Probably a pickpocket and thief—Ah!"

This exclamation was prompted by the said small boy suddenly bending down and freeing himself from the ropes around his ankles, butting the overseer in the stomach and jumping off the platform into the crowd. Although he seemed as slippery as an eel as he successfully eluded one pursuer after another, he really had no chance in that audience, and was finally hauled back onto the platform, kicking and biting. The overseer grabbed him by his hair, lifted him off the ground and hit him so hard across the face that he at last hung limp and shuddering.

My ring was suddenly warm on my finger, throbbing with my heartbeat.

The auctioneer stepped forward and spoke, but his words were lost in a howl of derision from the crowd.

"He says all the boy wants is a bit of correction and lot of understanding," translated Justus, without me asking. He snorted. "The only thing that child would understand is a rope's end. . . ."

The slavemaster made a last appeal; the overseer lowered the boy to his feet and gave him a shake. The boy turned his head and spat, accurately.

The audience clapped and jeered, but in a good-natured way, the overseer lifted his hand to administer another blow—and the ring on my finger throbbed harder than ever.

Without quite realizing what was happening, I found I was on my feet.

"I offer—ten silver pieces," I called out, astounded to hear my own voice. Now why on earth had I done that? I sat down again in confusion, conscious of the incredulous looks of those around me. Never mind: perhaps the auctioneer hadn't understood, for I was speaking in my own tongue.

But slave-trading auctioneers don't get rich without learning more than one language. He understood all right. He gesticulated, cupped his ear, pretended he had misheard my paltry bid. Then came the histrionics. The very idea that anyone could have the gall, the impertinence to offer a mere ten pieces of silver for this treasure of a boy! High spirited he might be, yes, but with a little judicious discipline . . .

He appealed to the audience: he would be generous. As a great favor he wouldn't ask for twenty-five silver pieces, though even that was a mockery: just this once he would settle for fifteen, although that in itself was sheer robbery . . . the bargain of the day! Now, what about it?

The audience laughed, they jeered, they clapped their hands together, they pointed at me.

"What are they saying?"

"That yours is the best offer he will get!"

As if to underline this the boy tried to kick the overseer where it would hurt the most and almost succeeded, to be rewarded by another blow to the head. My ring throbbed again and I leapt to my feet.

"Stop that! I said I offer ten silver pieces—"

Scipio reached up to pull me down. "Steady on, boy: if you're not careful you really will buy him, and you don't want . . ."

But I was pushing myself to the front. I stepped up on the platform, fumbled in my purse and took out the ten coins.

"My final offer! Take it or leave it!"

The slave trader stared at me. "Twelve?"

I knew enough Arabic to count and shook my head.

Behind us the audience were whistling and jeering. The auctioneer must have realized he was making an idiot of himself by trying to force up the price, because his face darkened and he snatched the coins from my hand, grabbed the boy and thrust him towards me.

"Take the son of Shaitan then," he hissed between his teeth in a sort of market-Latin. "And may Allah deliver me from such again. You deserve each other!"

The boy had sunk to the ground. I touched him on the shoulder and he flinched. Reaching for his hand, I pulled him to his feet.

"Come with me. There's nothing to fear."

I knew he would not understand, but hoped the tone of my voice was enough. The ring on my finger had quietened down, so I was obviously doing the right thing. Not according to Scipio, Justus and Antonius. They were loud in condemnation.

"Complete waste of time and money . . . be off as soon as you look away . . . watch your purse, etc. . . ."

Luckily Sayid ben Hassan had already left, so I didn't have to undergo his scorn as well. As it was I felt like a mother who has been left with her newborn for the first time: I hadn't a clue what to do next.

I needn't have worried. "What you goin' to do with that?"

Him as well! But that was the spur I needed. "We're going to feed him, wash him and clothe him, Growch: in that order. And you can come along to see he doesn't run off. Right?"

"Right!" If I hadn't named our chores in that particular order he probably wouldn't have been so cooperative.

Keeping a firm hold on the boy's hand we made our way over to the food. I let him choose. He pointed to rice, curd cheese, and yoghurt, mixing it together in the bowl and eating hungrily with his fingers, while Growch and I chose something more palatable. I let him have a second helping, then dragged him towards the river.

All at once he twisted away and was gone, running across the sand like a young deer.

"Growch . . ." But he was already in pursuit, his short legs a blur of determination. They both disappeared behind some rocks, there was a yell, a cry and then Growch's bark.

"Come and get 'im!"

When I reached them the boy was sitting on the ground rubbing his left ankle, where a neat row of dents, already turning blue, showed how my dog had floored him.

I knelt by his side and mimed a slap, upon which he immediately cowered, but I shook my head. "No," I said slowly. "But you must be good," and I made soothing gestures. "And now—" I mimed again "—down to the river to wash . . ."

Half an hour later we were all soaked, for it was obvious the boy and water were virtual strangers, but at least he didn't smell anymore. We found the tailors and menders next to the launderers, which should have been obvious. Now what clothes to fit him with? I looked at his naked body and could see faint marks which were paler than the rest. It seemed that once he had worn short trews of some sort and a sleeveless jacket. I asked the tailor in market-Latin and sign language for what I wanted, adding underdrawers and a short smock, remembering what Signor Falcone had said about the cold to come. We bargained, the tailor fetched a relative to help with the sewing, and the clothes were promised within the hour.

What next? I looked at the scowling little face: I could hardly see his eyes. At the barbers he panicked again once he saw the knives and shears, but this time I had a firmer grip. Patiently I mimed and he consented to sit on a stool, his eyes tight shut, shivering like a cold monkey as the barber snipped and cut his hair into a basin cut, so that at least his eyes, ears, and nape of the neck were free of the wild tangle that had obscured them before.

The barber brushed away the cut hair from the boy's face, neck, and shoulders, then proffered a polished silver mirror. The boy stared at his reflection, his narrow eyes slowly widening, until at last he flung the mirror away before bolting again.

"Probably never seen hisself afore," said Growch resignedly, before taking off in pursuit. This time he didn't get so far, and I led him back to the tailor's. The clothes were ready, and now, washed, barbered and decently dressed, he really looked quite presentable.

But how to keep him from running off? He looked quite capable of taking care of himself, but supposing another slave trader found him? Or if he was caught stealing and had his hands chopped off? Or starved to death because of not knowing the routes? No, I had bought him and he was my responsibility.

But how to convince him of that? How to explain that he would travel with us until he was near enough to his home and people to travel alone? How had things been explained to me as a child, when words were not enough?

Of course! I led him back out beyond the tents until I found a smooth stretch of sand. I motioned him to sit beside me, then pointed at myself, repeating my name slowly and clearly. Then I pointed at him and raised my eyebrows in enquiry. He just grinned as if it were some sort of entertainment, but at least it was the first time I had seen him smile. I tried again.

"Summer. Summer. Summer . . ."

A grunt, then "Umma . . ."

"Good, very good!" I clapped my hands. Did I have one of those salted nuts left in my pouch? I did, and popped it in his mouth.

"Summer. Summer . . ."

"Zumma. Summa . . ."

I clapped my hands again, gave him another nut, then pointed to him. He said nothing, so I cupped one ear as if I was listening and jabbed him in the chest.

A slow smile spread over his face, making his eyes crease up more than ever. He pointed to himself and out came a string of clicks and whines and grunts that sounded something like: "Xytilckhihijyckntug." I tried it out—hopeless! His black eyes crinkled up more than ever. He repeated the word more slowly and again I made a fool of myself, waving my hands in frustration. Again. And again. The only bit I could remember was the last syllable: tug.

I pointed to him. "Tug?"

He grinned again, then nodded. He pointed to me. "Summa" then to himself "Tug," clapped his hands as I had done and held his out for a nut.

So far so good, but now he had become withdrawn again, the scowl was back, and he kept glancing from side to side as if gauging his chances of escape.

Right, if words wouldn't do, it would have to be pictures. I smoothed out the sand, took out my dagger and drew a circle in the sand. The rising moon cast our images long across the ground, so I moved round until what I drew was clear of shadows. Inside the circle I drew a rudimentary tent, then pointed back at the encampment. Then came two little stick figures. I pointed to him and to me and the tent. He nodded his head. Now came the tricky bit. Moving a little way to the west I drew another circle, another tent, another stick figure, then pointed to myself. Then I "walked" my fingers slowly to the first circle. And stopped, pointing at him and then to the east. He took the dagger slowly from my hand, and I had a moment's panic, then he moved away to the path of the rising moon and drew a wavery circle. A tent inside the circle, a line with a little head atop, and his fingers walked back to the first circle the way mine had done. But had he understood so far? I hoped so, for the next bit was the important one.

Taking his hand, dagger safely back in my belt, I walked our fingers to the west, to my circle, then shook my head, making sure he was watching. Back in the center circle I pointed first to him then to me and used our fingers to reach his circle. I looked at him; his brow was creased in thought. At last he took my hand and we went through the same performance, only this time he did the finger-walking and it was he who shook his head at my circle. When we came to his he nodded his head vigorously, pointed at both of us and clapped his hands. I shared out the last of the nuts.

" 'E's got it," said Growch wearily. "The thickest pup in the world wouldn' 'ave taken that long. . . . Now do the bit about you 'avin' the cash an' buyin' the food and all that. . . ."

That night Tug slept at the foot of my bed, ants or no ants, with a watchful Growch stretched across the tent flap in case he did a runner.

The next morning Scipio and company were keen to be on their way. They were travelling back with another trader for extra safety, and I spent most of the day helping them load up, after making a careful inventory of the goods they carried. They set off midafternoon, with just enough time to make their first scheduled camp stop. Tug had stayed near my side all day, helping with the loading and carrying. He was even more anxious than I was to be on our way, and every now and again he would pull at my sleeve and point towards the east. I had no idea how much longer Sayid wished to stay, so I pointed at the sun, mimed it rising and setting twice, and luckily for Tug's faith in me, was exactly right.

That night I had presented myself at Sayid's tent, and one of the guards pointed me in the direction of the tents packed with goods, which suited us fine. It seemed we were not invited to eat with the rest of them, and I felt a little anxious about this, as food and lodging were normally included, but reasoned that once we were on the road things would be different. So we made pigs of ourselves on chicken and rice and slept comfortably on the bales of wool in the tent.

Tucked inside my jacket were my apprentice papers and a note from Master Scipio to the merchant at our next destination; they had been entrusted to me rather than to Sayid, and for this I was both apprehensive and grateful; apprehensive because it seemed that Scipio trusted Sayid about as much as I did, grateful because it meant that even if I was abandoned I had the means, and the money—for Scipio had given me an advance—to make my own way.

The next day, and the next, Sayid did more trading, we slept in the same tent and bought our own food. On the third morning, however, things were different. At dawn the tent was pulled down around our ears, a string of men carried the goods away and we found ourselves on the edge of the camp, shivering in the cool morning air, while a half-dozen grumbling, spitting camels and the same amount of mules were loaded up.

It was the first time I had been near one of these fabled camels, with the floppy humps, long legs and disagreeable manners. Growch had warned me about them: apparently he had been near enough to just escape being badly bitten. From what I had heard, however, they were the ideal beasts of burden over long journeys, being strong, swift, and needing little water: every three days was enough, Antonius had said.

Water: I had seen two or three large containers being loaded onto one camel. Did that mean we should bring our own? I turned tail and ran back to the water carriers, purchased two flasks and a fill from the yawning vendor. Why didn't anyone tell me? As I arrived back I saw my pack being loaded onto an already overloaded mule; hastily I strapped on my flasks.

It seemed we were ready. The camels were loaded, so were the mules, on two of which perched the cook and Sayid's personal servant. The two slaves the Arab had purchased were manacled in the space between camels and mules. The guards and Sayid were mounted on magnificent Arabs, but where was our transportation?

It seemed we were to walk. (Later it transpired that we were to share the mules, but it was an uneven swap: the servant and the cook were loath to set foot on the ground.)

Tug had given a moan of terror when he saw the chained slaves, but I quieted him. During the last couple of days I had spent an hour or two teaching him simple words and phrases, and he had responded remarkably well. Now was the time for another lesson.

I pointed to the manacled slaves. "Tug bad, chains. Tug good, no chains . . ."

"Tug good," he said perfectly clearly, and held out his hand for a reward.

Chapter Six

Thus began the most arduous part of my journey so far. Our destination, a town called Beleth, was some three hundred miles away, and it took four weeks to reach it. Of those three hundred miles, I reckon Tug, Growch and I must have walked two-thirds. Growch I carried when he was too exhausted to go further. Tug's feet were tough and horny, but after the first day my soft leather boots were the worse for wear and my feet were killing me.

At the first village we stopped at, Tug—yes, Tug of all people!—persuaded me with signs and a few words to buy a pair of the ubiquitous sandals worn there, and after that it became easier. It was Tug, too, who made the first contact with the rest of the caravan that eventually made our presence more welcome. Every night he helped with unloading the camels and mules, assisted with setting up Sayid's tent, brought wood for the cook and led the horses down to drink. He was a marvel with the horses, and before long the guards allowed him to ride their mounts for an hour or two each day. He was even allowed to groom Sayid's own mount, a magnificent white Arab, whose mane and tail nearly reached the ground.

Thus it was we found ourselves welcome in the big tent at night, albeit in the outer corridor with the slaves, and shared the somewhat monotonous food: couscous or rice with whatever meat or vegetables the cook had been able to buy.

We travelled a well-worn trail from village to village, though there were days when we camped out at night. A large fire was always built and the guards would spend the evenings in wrestling with each other or playing endless games of chance. I took these opportunities to teach Tug more of my language; in the meantime he was also picking up a good deal of Arabic. One day I noticed he wore a brand-new knife at his belt; I decided not to ask him where he got it, although I suspected he could gamble with the best.

For the most part the weather was fair, although it became progressively colder, not only because the nights were drawing in, but also because we were climbing, gradually but surely, into the foothills of the mountains that loomed ever nearer. Those nearest were green with thick vegetation; behind, some fifty miles farther away, they assumed a more jagged and unfriendly look, while those on the farthest horizon reared so high they seemed to touch the very sky, their sides white with snow.

Was it there, among those unimaginable heights, that my love, my dragon-man, had his home?

The terrain around us changed in character, too. From sun-baked earth, scrub, and tumbled rocks, with scant water trickling down deep canyons, we then travelled grass-covered slopes, with herdsmen tending their goats along the trail, and through deciduous woods and windswept valleys. As we trekked even higher we were among pines and spruce, seemingly brushed by the wings of great eagles soaring on the thermals that sometimes took them beneath us, to dive on some prey unseen. It seemed the less we saw other human beings, the more vigilant Sayid became, and the guards closed up every time we traversed any place likely for ambush, and were doubled at night.

As there were now four guards around the campfires at night, that meant Tug, Growch, and I moved into one of the smaller cubicles that led off the main room of the tent. It was so nippy after dark that I wished I had more blankets, and I envied Sayid the brazier that burned so warm in his inner sanctum. I envied, too, those guards he chose to share his luxury: a sort of reward, I supposed, for their devotion. Sometimes it was one, sometimes two or three. His method of choosing was always the same; he would tap the privileged one on the shoulder and offer him a sweetmeat, upon which they would disappear to the cosiness of cushions and warmth, and the silken drapes would be drawn to.

One night I, too, had my chance to sleep soft.

I had rolled myself up in my blanket and was drifting off to sleep when there was a touch on my head, more of a stroke really, and I opened my eyes to see Sayid squatting by my side. As I sat up, struggling free of the blanket, he popped a sugared fruit in my mouth and then another. Taking my hand he pulled me to my feet, nodding towards the inner tent as he did so.

I had taken no more than one step forward when there was a sudden commotion and somehow or other there was a fierce little Tug standing between us, knife in hand. Shoving me back he hissed: "No! No! Bad . . ." and then followed some words in Arabic I didn't understand.

But Sayid obviously did, for he backed away, a scowl on his face, after a moment choosing one of his guards to accompany him, who gave me a big grin and an obscene gesture before following his master.

"What in the world . . . ?" I turned furiously to Tug. "Why did you do that?"

"I shouldn't ask, I really shouldn't," said Growch.

But Tug was not inhibited, and after a minute or two of a few words and plenty of bodily gestures I realized what I had escaped.

"Yes, yes, thanks!" I said, to save further embarrassment. "Very good, Tug!"

I learned later that it was common practice among the Arabs to seek out their own sex for relaxation when away from women for any length of time and no one thought twice about it but, unprepared as I was at the time, I was both scared and disgusted. Luckily there was also a small bubble of amusement lurking around: whatever would have happened if Sayid had found out I was a girl? It would almost have been worth it to see his face. . . .

After that he was very cool towards me, and I also earned the derision of the guards, so it was perhaps just as well that we had our first sight of the city of Beleth less than a week later.

It lay like a child's toy extravaganza at the foot of a steep valley, probably some three thousand feet straight down from us. I could make out what looked like a large square with streets radiating from it, a palace, big and small buildings, twisty alleys and the smoke of a myriad house fires. I wanted to run down the track straightaway, but Sayid camped where we were for the night and I saw why in the daylight, for it took half a day to bring us all down safe, the precipitous trail winding like the coils of a snake in order to use the safest ground.

Everyone had spruced themselves up that morning, and there was a lot of combing, plucking and twisting of hair, oiling of skin and use of a blackened stick to enhance the eyes, but I decided to leave well alone, except for a clean shirt and the donning of my boots once again.

At noon, or a little past, we clattered across the wooden bridge that spanned the narrow river flowing to the west of the city. We had already passed through neat and obviously fertile fields, the soil dark and friable. At the town side of the bridge we passed under a splendid carved arch set in battlemented walls, and onto a broad street, paved with river cobbles, that led after a half-mile to the large square that dominated the center of the city. All the way along the route we were flanked by laughing children and saluted by well-dressed citizens. It seemed a well organized, wealthy city, and my spirits rose. A proper bed—

"A proper meal," said Growch.

And no more walking, at least for a while.

Everyone dismounted, and I was glad enough to squat down and rest in the sunshine as the unloading began and men rushed in all directions, presumably to herald our arrival. The square must have been a quarter-mile across; at the moment it was full of market stalls, but these looked about ready to pack up for the day. Tall houses, many set back in courtyards, ringed the perimeter, and facing us was the imposing facade of the palace, with—as I learned later—one hundred marble steps leading up to the columned portico, built in the Greek style. Some twenty or thirty soldiers lounged on the steps, and others were tossing a ball about in a corner of the square. All very relaxed and comforting: obviously they were more for show than use.

I glanced up at the houses. They were in different styles, although most were white with flat roofs, and the windows were either tightly shuttered or barred with a fancy fretwork. Smoke rose lazily into the air and there were tantalizing snatches of music, pipes and strings and a tabor. Growch's nose lifted.

"Food . . ." he said.

Just then one of Sayid's guards returned, accompanied by a fat, waddling creature in purple silks and a large turban. He was perspiring freely and mopping his brow with a long scarf, whose color matched his red leather shoes with curved toes. He and Sayid embraced conventionally and exchanged courtesies, then Sayid produced papers, the fat man did the same; another thin man in white started checking the bales and porters appeared from nowhere and started to carry off the items as soon as they were unloaded and checked on both manifests. In no time at all it seemed all that was left to be dealt with were two loaded mules, three loaded camels, the slaves, and ourselves.

Sayid signed to his guards and drivers and the animals were led away. He assigned two guards to the slaves and these also were led away, but in a different direction. Sayid remounted and swung his horse in a long curvette before bowing his farewells to the fat man.

"Hey! What about us?" I ran forward to clutch at his bridle.

He spat on the ground just in front of my boots.

"You go with him," and he nodded in the direction of the fat man, who had sat down on one of the bales, mopping his brow again. He shouted something which sounded nasty, indicated us, then reared his stallion so sharply the bridle was snatched from my hand and I tumbled back in the dirt, then rode away out of the square.

I got up, dusted myself down, and walked over to the fat man who had relinquished the last bale to one of his porters.

I looked at him, he looked at me.

I bowed, he did the same. We spoke together.

"My name is Master . . ."

"And whom do I have . . ."

He had a sense of humor, this fat man, because he grinned when I did. I handed him the sheaf of papers Master Scipio had given me and introduced myself. He read through the scrolls rapidly, then handed them back to me, and bowed again.

"Welcome, Master Summer. I am Karim Bey, accredited agent to Master Spicer, and have been these past fifteen years." He bowed again. "I am happy to welcome you to our city, and hope to make your stay as pleasant as possible."

He spoke my tongue very well, albeit in a slightly archaic manner.

"I am happy to be here," I said. "Tell me, what did Sayid say to you about us?"

"Something to the effect that I had inherited excess baggage . . . Do not mind him. He is a very proud man, he likes his own way. But he is trustworthy, and guards his goods well. And now, if you and—your friends—would please to follow me?"

He led us to a pleasant house down a side street, set in a courtyard draped with bougainvillea and with a fountain tinkling away in the center. He indicated a stone bench covered with a Persian rug. Tug and Growch perched themselves on either side of me. Karim Bey looked at me interrogatively.

"My friend Tug," I said, indicating the boy. "I rescued him from a slave market and am trying to find his people. The dog's name is Growch, and he has been with me on all my travels."

"Where does the boy come from?"

"I don't rightly know. He speaks a language no one seems to understand."

"From his looks he comes from farther north and east. Let me have a word. . . ." He tried various dialects, but Tug shook his head, speaking in his strange clicks and hisses. Karim shook his head, too. "No, the language is unfamiliar to me, and he does not appear to understand any Italian, French, Spanish, Arabic, Turkish, Hindi, or Persian, all languages familiar to me. I will make further enquiries." He clapped his hands. "And now I think we shall eat."

Five minutes later we were tucking into kebabs of meat and red peppers, boiled and fried rice, pastry cases full of beans, peas and bamboo shoots, with a dessert of stuffed dates, peaches, cheese, and yoghurt. There was a chilled red wine, sherbet or goat's milk to quench our thirst.

After dining we were invited to bathe and rest, while Karim Bey made arrangements for our lodgings. We were led to a room in which stood two tubs of warm, scented water, towels, and various oils. Tug needed persuading to the water, but not the ointments: he smelt like a bunch of mixed out-of-season flowers when he had finished. In the next room there were pallets for our siesta, and I persuaded him to take a nap so I could bathe in private, unafraid my true sex would be discovered. I luxuriated in the chance to have a proper soak and wash my hair, the first time since I couldn't remember when.

Around dusk Karim sent one of his servants to wake us up, and announced that we were to lodge with another of his "regulars"—whatever that meant—and that the servant would escort us. He added that he would be seeking my help the next day in the warehouses. More tallying, I thought dismally.

The servant shouldered my pack with ease and led us through a maze of streets and alleys until we arrived at a thick double gate. We found ourselves in a courtyard with a well in the center, stables to the left, living quarters to the right, and a low arch, on either side of which was a washhouse and a kitchen, leading through into what looked like a vegetable garden. Stone steps led up to a galleried upper floor, with half a dozen closed doors.

The servant put down my pack, saluted and left, just as a man emerged from the downstairs living quarters and hurried towards us. He was dark-skinned, black-haired, small and thin, clad in a white jacket, cap and a sort of skirt looped between his legs and tucked into his belt. On his fingers were many rings and a jewel dangled from one ear, though both metal and gems looked too large for real worth.

He was already gabbling as he came towards us, and his speech was the most amazing I had ever heard. He used words from every language I had ever heard, and some I hadn't, though when he found where I came from it settled into a mixture of Arabic, French, Italian, market-Latin, Greek and what I learned later was his native tongue, Hindi. Whatever it was, his sentences had a quaintness that kept me constantly amused.

"Velly welcome, isn't it? Chippi Patel at your service, young sir! Jolly damn glad see you. Room you are taking. Up this, pliss," and he led the way up to the verandah. Stopping at one of the doors he flung it open and ushered us into a small whitewashed room containing two pallets, two stools, two wooden chests, a grass mat, a row of hooks on the wall and a small, shuttered window at the back.

"Habitation of other young sir, Ricardus, happy to share. Boy sleep on mat. Dog too, yes?"

"You are most kind, Master Patel, but—"

"No, no, no! My name Chippi! Mix marriage, Daddy name Chippi, Mummy Patel. Many Patel, few Chippis."

"Very well, Master Chippi—"

"No mater-pater here! Just Chippi . . ."

"Well then, Chippi, my name is Summer, and—"

He took my arm and clasped it fervently, then clapped me on the back. "Happy you meet, Zuma! You happy here. Nice room, nice mate to share . . ."

"No, Chippi," I said firmly, disengaging myself from his clasp (he did smell awfully garlicky) and knowing that if I did not stop this garrulous little man right now I never should get my own way. "We need another. Just for us. For me, my friend Tug, my friend Growch." I indicated us in turn.

"Not friend with dirty pi-dog . . . ?"

"Not pi-dog . . ." I found to my exasperation that I was speaking just like him. "Dog is good friend for many miles. Long pedigree: much money. Not see another like him."

He looked askance at my filthy, tatty animal.

"You right there . . . Now, this room most commodious, and—"

"Karim Bey assured me we should have our own room," I said mendaciously.

That did it. At the mention of the agent's name Chippi scuttled away down the verandah and showed us into another room two doors down, the twin of the first. He had an injured air, but I learned later it was common practice to try to make newcomers share and collect for two separate rooms. Corruption became more rife the farther east we came, but it was all good-humored, played as a sort of game: you won some, you lost some, and within a minute or two Chippi was all smiles again, showing us the washhouse and taking away our dirty laundry, to be returned spotless within hours.

For the next few days I worked busily for Karim, first in the warehouses where I assisted his tally man as goods moved day by day; one morning we would exchange silks from Cathay for pottery from Greece, and in the afternoon check in rice or rugs or rich tapestries. Perishables were usually targeted to the market, but in the main office, full of scrolls, clerks and comings and goings, the rest of the goods were assigned to various caravans, north, south, east or west; orders were taken, part consignments made up, other traders contacted for out-of-the-way requirements. Karim also had an army of scouts distributed throughout the town and outlying villages, ready to report the unusual, and if he thought it worth his while he would send an expert to bargain for whatever it was. He also did his own trading, short journeys only, mainly in small goods and local pottery.

Besides the warehouses, and the office, I was also sent to the market to oversee the trading in the perishables, and by the end of that first week I earned a commendation for my hard work.

"And now we must concentrate on the language. Master Ricardus, he must be much of an age with you, and he was fluent in basic Arabic within weeks, could add and subtract faster than most and bargain with the best. An old head on young shoulders."

"And where is this young paragon now?" I asked, masking my irritation with a smile. I could just imagine this pompous, unbearable young man strutting around dispensing wisdom I didn't want at all hours of the day and night.

"He has accompanied a small caravan some seventy miles south, to act as my agent. It is the second such journey he has undertaken; he made me a good profit the last time. I expect him back within a couple of days."

But in fact he came back that very afternoon. When I returned to our room at sunset, after making a couple of deliveries of orders for ribbons and sewing materials to some small shops down the alleys, Chippi met me at the gate to the courtyard with a conspiratorial smile on his lips.

"Your new friend is back being with us. He has just had a big bath. . . ." He indicated the bathhouse. "At suppertime you will see."

I hurried up the steps, Tug and Growch close behind. I had better have a wash myself, find a clean shirt and comb my hair before I met Wonder Boy. But there was someone in my room already, bending over the wooden chest at the foot of my bed, just about to lift the lid.

"What the hell . . . !"

He straightened up guiltily, then just stared and stared.

"When I heard the name . . . You've come a long way, haven't you, *Mistress* Summer!"

The recognition was mutual.

"My God!" I said, "You . . ."

Chapter Seven

Instantly my mind was whirled back to a stretch of forest in a country hundreds of miles away. It must have been some eighteen months ago but it seemed like a hundred years. So much had happened in between that I didn't even feel like the same girl. Now the scene came back with sudden clarity, and I could see the dirty-faced stable lad who had helped me and my previous friends escape imprisonment and torture, been well paid for his trouble—and then robbed me of the rest of my moneys.

Even then I had somewhat admired his cheek and, remembering he was only stealing to help his widowed mother and sisters, I had told him to seek out Master Spicer, feeling sure that the kind man would give him a better-paid job in his own stables. I recalled Matthew had said the lad had been sent somewhere for "training," but until this moment had thought no more about it.

But the young man standing in front of me now, with his freshly coiffed hair, fine clothes and added inches of height—he must be at least as tall as I—bore little resemblance to the scruffy boy I had thought to be only about fourteen. Amazing what good food and an easier life could do; he must be about seventeen, I guessed, and the only familiar features were the thatch of fair hair—still untidy in spite of the fashionable basin cut with the curled fringe—the intensely blue eyes with their look of sharp intelligence, and the rather greedy mouth.

"What in the world are you doing here, Dickon?"

"Not Dickon anymore: Ricardus. I'm working for Matthew Spicer as a trainee trader and have done pretty well for myself—"

"So I've heard . . ."

"—and Dickon is a common, peasant name. Latinized it sounds far more impressive, don't you think?"

To me he was still Dickon. "How are your mother and sisters?"

A hint of a scowl. "Well enough. Master Spicer secretly sends them a part of my wages. My eldest sister has got married. . . . But what about you? Why are you here? And why dressed as a lad? What happened to the rest of the ragtag you carted round with you?"

"Part of it is still here," I said, pointing to Growch, who was growling softly. "Quiet, boy; you've met him before." I nodded at Tug. "He travels with us to find his people; he was stolen as a slave sometime back." Tug was scowling. "Friend, Tug. Ricardus. Say it . . ." But he wouldn't, and, still scowling, spat over his shoulder, which is neither easy nor a sign of approval.

"Looks a bit of a dimwit to me," commented Dickon. "What of the others?"

"The knight went back to his lady—"

"Thought you were sweet on him?"

"—and the mare, the tortoise and the pigeon found their own kind."

"What about the pig? The one I saw fly. What of him?"

"Nothing," I said defensively. I still didn't want to think about him. "He—went back to his beginnings." Which was true enough, but light on the full details.

"Thought you might have got some money out of it by selling him to a freak show. Pigs don't fly." His eyes were too sharp, too inquisitive.

"His wings were only temporary things. . . ."

"Oh, fell off did they? You should have sewed them on more firmly. . . . Still haven't told me why you're here, though. Must say you've got nice long legs, Mistress Summer!"

I pulled my jerkin down. "*Master* Summer, if you please!" I had had just about enough time to think. "I'm here for the same reason you are: to learn the business. Matthew—Master Spicer—thought I would be safer dressed this way." Why was I blushing?

He grinned, winked. "Way he talked about you, took me in without question on your word, thought he was keen on you. . . . Fact remains, dressed as a lad or not, this is no job for a female. Surprised he let you come."

"It wasn't a question of letting me—" I stopped. Better not tell him too much. Somehow I didn't feel I could trust him. Apart from that brief meeting a year and a half ago, what else did I know about him except that he was a thief, made the most of his opportunities and had become a bit of a snob?

His eyes were narrowed, considering me. "And no one knows of this change of sex, 'cept me?"

"Apart from Matthew, Suleiman—and Signor Falcone in Venice." Two of the three, anyway.

He seemed satisfied. "Must admit you don't look too bad. Bet you don't walk right, though; women walk from the hips, men from the knee."

"You haven't seen me walk," I objected.

"Not yet, but I'll bet you . . ."

"Just wait and see," I snapped. "At least I don't suppose you have ever been propositioned as a bum-boy!"

His eyes widened. "My, you have been living it up! How did you get out of that one?"

I shrugged. "A knife and a few words, carefully chosen . . ."

"I still can't believe Master Spicer sent you all the way out here just to learn the business." He narrowed his eyes again. "Are you sure you weren't sent out on a special mission? As a spy, perhaps?"

"Don't be ridiculous. I just wanted to see a bit of the world, that's all. I haven't the money to travel as a pampered female and I—we—thought this was a good way to do it." What had he been searching for in the wooden chest? Why was he afraid of someone spying? After all, he hadn't known I would turn up until he saw me.

Chippi came bustling up the stairs to announce that the evening meal was ready.

"Ah, the great friends they have met! Two such pretty young fellows, by damn! Much good pals will be. Wife has prepared special dish. Coming down for same, isn't it?"

Tables were set out in the courtyard as usual, but tonight Chippi deigned to sit with us at the table of honor nearest the kitchen. Mistress Chippi wouldn't join us, of course: women were generally of lower status than the menfolk out here. As dark as her husband, but much fatter, she bustled about setting out delicacies for starters: crisply fried savory biscuits, bean shoots, meat balls. Then came the special dish, a steaming heap of meat and vegetables on a bed of boiled rice. I watched how Dickon would cope; he took up one of the soft pancakes Chippi called chapatis, folded it round a mouthful of food, conveyed it to his mouth without so much as spilling a grain of rice and chewed appreciatively.

"Excellent!" He spoke with his mouth full: he hadn't learned everything yet.

It looked easy enough, and I managed quite nicely but, as I leant forward to scoop up another mouthful, a terrible delayed reaction set in.

My tongue, my mouth, my throat, my stomach—they were all on fire! I had been poisoned! My eyes were streaming, I couldn't breathe. . . . Struggling to my feet, choking and gasping, I signalled frantically for a drink—water, wine, sherbet, anything!

Slurping down whatever was offered—it could have been anything for all the effect it had on the terrible taste in my mouth—I could feel a gradual lessening of the burning heat. Perhaps I hadn't been poisoned after all.

At last I could breathe normally again. I mopped my streaming eyes and looked across at Dickon and Chippi—they were doubled over with laughter!

"It's not funny! What on earth was it?"

"Oh, dearie, dearie me!" Chippi blew his nose on his sleeve. "We are larks having, isn't it . . . First time you eat curry, yes?"

"What?"

"Curry. Very hot being. Wife cook it good, yes, Ricardus?"

"Very good," said the objectionable Dickon, tucking in heartily. "You'll soon get used to it, *Master* Summer."

"I will not!" And I kept my word.

For the next few days Dickon initiated me further into the mysteries of merchanting, and I took care not to show him how bored I became, trying to appear interested and attentive. He of course knew nothing of my true reason for taking on the guise of apprentice; my only worry was Tug, who was growing increasingly restless at being confined to the town.

I had a word with Karim Bey on the subject of moving on as soon as possible, pretending eagerness to travel further. He looked shocked.

"But it is entirely the wrong time of year to venture further, Master Summer; everything closes down shortly because the higher routes will soon become impassable. I had thought you would be content to over-winter here, and learn as much as possible for the spring journeys." He must have seen the disappointment on my face. "I myself shall not be sending out any more caravans. However, as you seem so keen, I will try and get you a place with an eastbound trader, if I can find one. You may well find that you end up at the back of beyond, forced to stay until the snow melts, and find it difficult to return. However, that is up to you."

And with that I had to be content. I told Tug we were waiting for a special trader to take us further east, and I think he believed me.

Our daily work had to finish sometime, and in the evenings after supper Dickon, Tug, Growch, and I took to wandering down the myriad side streets and alleys that radiated from the square right through to the edges of town, as haphazardly as the tiny veins on the inside of one's elbow.

Here lay the real life of the city, a place where the great and wealthy never came. During the day one might see town officials bustling about in the city proper, respectable citizens about their business, soldiers exercising, merchants fingering the goods on offer in the market, discreetly veiled ladies taking the air, either on foot or in gilded palanquins, and all around were the workers, those who catered to their whims: servants, both male and female, stall holders, farriers, cooks, children running errands, water carriers, weavers, tailors, hairdressers, beauticians, fortune-tellers, launderers, beggars, refuse gatherers, cleaners, night-soil collectors, rope makers, jewellers, wine sellers, oil vendors—in fact all those unregarded people without whom the city could not function at all.

At night, though, it was as if a soft blanket came down on all this bustle and the little side streets and alleys came into their own, for this was where the workers lived. Here they had their homes; here they were born, grew up, loved, hated, became ill, died. Here was all manner of meaner housing; tenements, small one-roomed hovels, stables, tents, holes in the ground or in the walls, shacks and even the bare ground.

Here also were the little family restaurants, minor businesses, brothels, stalls that sold items not available in the open market: strange drugs, stolen goods, information; here there was trade in quack medicines and human beings; much gossip and entertainment; and lastly were the stalls that sold those small, largely useless objects that might just fetch enough to buy the daily bowl of rice.

These alleyways were only dimly lit and the town guard generally gave them a wide berth. It was not wise for a stranger to walk there alone, but I had always felt safe with Tug and Growch, though we didn't go far. However when Dickon heard of our expeditions he insisted on accompanying us, ostensibly as guard, but I suspected he had never dared go alone before and we were merely an excuse. As it was he strutted and postured like a young lord, especially when there was a pretty girl about. He was trying to grow a moustache, none too successfully, and he fancied himself as a ladykiller. In fact on the third evening he thoroughly embarrased me, suggesting a visit to one of the many little brothels.

"I'm not going to one of those! How could I?"

"You're dressed as a lad. You don't have to—participate. You can just watch, can't you?"

"Certainly not! You can do what you like, but I'm staying outside."

"Suit yourself! Just don't get lost: I may be some time. . . ."

Which left the rest of us wandering up and down the street, pretending to examine the goods at one or another of the stalls, fending off too persistent vendors and generally feeling conspicuous. I had almost made up my mind to trust Growch's sense of direction to get us back to our lodgings, when Dickon reappeared with a smirk on his face and ostentatiously adjusting his clothing.

"I hope it was worth it," I said nastily.

"Of course. I always ensure that I get value for money. Pity in some ways you ain't a lad: I could show you a thing or two in this town."

"If I were, I doubt if I'd take advantage of your offer. I wouldn't want to risk catching something nasty."

"I know what I'm doing—"

"Good for you. Can we go now?"

He didn't repeat the experiment, if that was what it was. After all he certainly hadn't been in there more than a quarter hour, however long it had seemed outside. But perhaps that was the way they did things in those places. I wasn't going to ask.

Two nights later something very strange happened.

We had wandered farther than usual and came at last to a narrow street that twisted and turned like a snake almost under the tall battlements that protected the city. Here were more stalls than usual, some set out on the ground on scraps of cloth, others displayed on stools or tables, yet more in tiny cupboardlike niches in the walls. There was less noise than usual and those who passed by seemed to do so as if in a dream. Even the bargaining sounded muted, the examination of objects slow and unhurried. At one corner the street seemed as light as a fairground, at another full of shadows, much as a candleflame in a draught will flare one moment and be down to a mere flicker the next.

I found myself infected with the same strange lethargy, yet my mind seemed as sharp as a needle. I found I, too, was taking my time at each stall, examining everything minutely, yet no one was pressing me to buy. I looked at small prayer mats, embroidery silks, combs and brushes, painted scarves, brooches and bangles; I picked up a length of silk here, a phial of perfume there. I waved a fly whisk, tried on a pair of felt slippers, tapped a brass tray, turned over some table mats, flicked my finger at a tray of pearls that rolled about like a handful of dry white peas; I bought and ate a couple of sticky, green sweetmeats, passed by painting brushes, colored inks, charcoal, dyes, spices, pellets of opium. . . .

Between a hole in the wall occupied by a man selling sachets of sweet-smelling dried flowers and a conventional stall laden with pots and pans, an old man squatted behind a small folding table on which was displayed a heterogenous collection of what looked like secondhand curios. I bent down to see a small, blue brush jar with a chip, a dented brass bowl, a piece of dirty amber, a paperweight dull with use, some scraps of embroidery, a yellowed piece of carved ivory. . . .

I straightened up, ready to pass on, when the old man lifted his head and looked straight into my eyes. He was nearly bald, what was left of his hair hanging white on either side of his face to mingle with a wispy beard. There were laugh lines at the corners of his eyes, and his whole expression radiated a warmth and good humor, although if you asked me to describe him feature by feature I could not have done so.

He nodded at me as if we were old friends, said something I didn't understand, then indicated the tray in front of him. Obviously an invitation to look closer. I glanced around for the others. Tug was bargaining for some sweetmeats in sign language with some coins I had given him. Growch was flushing out imaginary rats from some rubbish heap, Dickon was chatting up the girl selling rice wine in tiny cups.

Why not indulge the old man while I waited for the others? He seemed pleasant enough, although I had seen nothing that attracted me on the tray, except perhaps that little ivory carving—

Strange. The goods looked different. A pearl, discolored; a chipped blue and white cup; a carved bamboo flute the worse for wear; an old inkpot—surely those had not been there before? Ah, there was something I recognized: the little ivory figure. I couldn't quite make out what it was meant to represent. The old man said something, and as I looked up he nodded, wreathed in smiles.

I smiled back and squatted down in front of the tray.

Now the tray was full, and every object, cracked, chipped, dented, worn or just old, all were carved or decorated with representations of living things. The blue brush jar had a lively dragon wrapped around its base, the brass bowl had raised figures of mice chasing each other's tails; inside the amber, carved as a fish's mouth, a tiny fly awaited its fate. Embroidery covered with lotus blossoms, a paperweight with a grasshopper for a handle, a carved bee on the side of the flute looking alive enough to fly away, a pearl etched with chrysanthemums, a blue and white cup painted with butterflies, and an inkpot decorated with a flock of small birds: broken they all might be, but these objects had an exquisite living grace. And around them all, lively as a kitten, cavorted the ivory carving.

Some part of me, the sensible part, told me there was something very amiss here. Half a dozen pieces, less than interesting, then others, and now both lots together, and all worth a second look. But the sensible side of Summer stayed quiet and the credulous Summer just accepted what she saw.

Or thought she saw . . .

The old man stretched out his right hand and took mine; in his left he held a green bowl of water that danced its reflections in the lamplight as the ring on my finger tingled, but not unpleasantly. He nodded at me again, indicating that I should look into the liquid. I leaned forward and found myself gazing into a swirl of colors. Figures passed through the water; I saw a white horse with a horn on its forehead, a frog or toad, a cat, a black bird, a fish. . . . Then something I thought I recognized: another horse galloping across the sands, a scrabbling tortoise, a pink pigeon, a small elongated dog with short legs, a pig . . . Ah, the pig!

A pig with wings. A pig I had kissed three times. A pig that turned into a dragon.

And the girl in the picture kissed the pig-that-was-a-dark-dragon for the third time, and he turned into a man. A dark man called Jasper, Master of Many Treasures, and my heart broke as he turned back into a dragon again and flew away from the Place of Stones—

Leaping to my feet, I dashed the bowl from the old man's hands. I could feel the stupid tears welling up.

"How could you know? Dickon?" I called over my shoulder. "Come and translate for me, please. I want to ask this old man a couple of questions."

He, too, had risen to his feet, although he still had hold of my hand. He was speaking again, but thanks to Dickon who must have been standing behind me, I now had a translation.

"I mean no harm, young traveller."

"The pictures in the bowl . . ." I stopped. I didn't want Dickon to know what I had seen.

"Before you there was another who wore a ring," said the old man, and now the translation was almost simultaneous. "Many, many years ago. She, too, adventured with animals she was wise enough to call her friends. The rest you saw was what you wanted to see."

"No! I never wanted . . ."

"Then the head denies the heart it would seem. You travel far, girl, to find what you do not want, then?" There was a gentle, teasing quality in his voice, which I now seemed to hear clearer than Dickon's. "It will be a long journey for the seven of you. . . ."

"Seven? Three, you mean." Me, Tug and Growch.

"Three is a lucky number, I agree, but seven is better. She who first wore the ring knew that."

"It's just three," I repeated firmly.

"Life does not always turn out the way you want it. I think you will need help with your journey, extra help."

"You—know where we are bound?"

"I know everything." He picked up the bowl again, and miraculously it was still full of colored water. "Look again. Closer . . ."

Forgetting Dickon, I gazed once more into the bowl. The colors paled, faded, and now there was just a milky haze. The haze steadied, snow was falling and I was in it, flying like a bird between high mountain peaks. But the snow started to drag at my wings, at the same time destroying my perspective of the land beneath, the familiar landscape I should know so well. Mountain after mountain, peak after peak, they all looked alike. The snow grew heavier and now I was weary, blinking away the flakes of snow that threatened to blind me. Each beat of my wings seemed to wrench them from their sockets; if I couldn't find what I was looking for soon I should have to land, but it was unlikely I would find shelter in unknown terrain.

Then, suddenly, I saw it.

A momentary lessening in the blur of snow, and the three fangs of the Mighty One, gateway to my goal, loomed up ahead. A turn to the left and I steered between the first two of the three rock teeth that were so steep that even now they gloomed blackly in the snow that could not rest against their sides.

Over at last and down, down, down into the valley beyond. There was the monastery on its hill, where the saffron-robed monks rang their gongs, sounded their queer, cracked bells and said their prayers to an endlessly smiling, fat god. Finally a switch to the right, away from the Hill of Constant Prayer and the village beneath, and a long slow glide to the Blue Mountain and the cave entrance hidden on the northern face.

Wearily I braked back, my leathern wings as clumsy as the landing gear of a youngling. Wobbling a little, I shoved forward my dragon claws and—

"Jasper!" I cried out, and smashed the green bowl into a thousand pieces. "Jasper! *I* was *him*!"

The old man stooped down and picked up one of the tiny shards of glass. One piece? No, for now all the others seemed to fly into his hand and the bowl was whole again. He tucked it away in his robe.

"And so you now know the way to go," he said. "It is always the last part of the journey that is the hardest."

My mind was in such turmoil that I could think of nothing to say—except thank him.

He bowed. "It is nothing; a breath of wind across a sleeping face, bringing with it a dream of the poppies over which it has travelled. . . . And now, young traveller, you were thinking of bearing something away from my tray."

I was? Yes, perhaps I was. That must be why I was bending over the tray again, and now all the creatures and flowers were real, alive. A butterfly perched on my finger, then flew to the old man's beard; a tiny fly cleaned its wings of the amber that had imprisoned it; a fish swam in the brass bowl that the old man tucked away in his robe; a string of mice disappeared up his sleeve; a tiny blue dragon flew to his shoulder then vanished down his collar; a grasshopper leapt to his head, a flock of tiny birds circled the stall and a bee, heavy with pollen, rested for a moment on my sleeve, before crawling up a fold of the old man's robe, whose lap now held a mass of flowers. . . .

Now all that was left on the tray was the little ivory figure. It was still difficult to make out exactly what it was meant to represent—he looked like a mixture of dog, horse, dragon, deer—but he did have a very intelligent expression.

"How much?"

"He is not for sale. He goes where he wishes." He spoke as though the creature had a will of its own, but then nothing would have surprised me now.

"May I pick him up?"

"If he will let you . . ."

What did he do then? Bite? Disappear in a puff of smoke?

Gingerly I bent forward, picked him up between finger and thumb and put him on my palm. Exquisitely carved, he had the body of a deer, hooves of a horse, a water buffalo's tail with a huge plume on the end, a stubby little face with a minihorn in his forehead and what looked like fine filaments or antennae sweeping back from his mouth. Funny that I hadn't been able to see him clearly before, especially as he was the only perfect piece. He sat quite comfortably on my hand.

"What is it—he?"

"That is for him to tell you. If he wishes."

I waited for something to happen, but nothing did, so with a strange reluctance I put him back on the tray. My ring was warm on my finger.

"Are you coming? The young lass over there says her dad has an eating house round the corner." Dickon spoke over my shoulder. "I'm hungry even if you're not."

All the lights were suddenly brighter, and I could smell sewers.

He nudged my arm impatiently. "You've been staring at that tray for hours. Looks like a lot of junk to me."

I looked down. An old man squatted in front of a tray of secondhand objects, none of which I had seen before. The ivory figure I thought I remembered seeing wasn't there.

I shook my head, as much to clear it as a form of negation. "I can't see anything I want," I said slowly. "Thanks for translating just the same." I bowed to the old man, and we moved away down the street. I felt all jangled inside as if someone had jumped me out of a dream too soon.

We were finishing off an indifferent dish of vegetables and rice when Dickon said suddenly: "What did you mean: 'thanks for translating'? I wasn't anywhere near you."

"Yes you were! I called you over because I couldn't understand what the old man was saying. You were just behind me."

"Was never!"

"You're kidding. . . ."

"I'm not!"

And the more I insisted, the more adamant he became. Had I imagined it all, then? The whole episode was becoming less clear by the minute, but still I clung to an image, a feeling: a dragon—me, him?—flying in the face of a storm to the Blue Mountain.

Jasper . . . lover-dragon, dragon-lover.

He was what this journey was all about, of course. Once upon a time I had rescued a little pig with vestigial wings from a cruel showman. The pig had grown and grown until one day when we found the place where he had hatched out, the pig's skin had been cast away and there was a beautiful, dark, fearsome dragon in the place of my pig.

But why fall in love with a dragon? Because I had loved the pig and the dragon wasn't a dragon all the time. And that was my fault. Three times I had kissed the pig, out of affection and gratitude, and because he was a dragon inside that pig skin I had broken a law of the equilibrium of the universe, and for each kiss the dragon was forced to spend a month a year in human form.

That's how he had explained it to me as he kissed me, made love to me as Jasper the man, just before he changed back into what he called his true self and flew away to the east, where all dragons come from, leaving me sick at heart beside the Place of Stones.

The blind knight had offered me love of a sort, Matthew Spicer had proposed marriage, but it had only been in the arms of Jasper, the Master of Many Treasures, that I had found that overwhelming joy that true love brings.

And that was why I was here, in this strange town many hundreds—nay, thousands—of miles from my home. I would find him, I had sworn I would. I would sacrifice anything for just one more embrace—

"Your turn."

"I beg your pardon?"

"Wake up, Summer!" said Dickon. "I said it was your turn to pay."

I fished among the small change I kept in my pouch (the greater coins I kept next to my skin) and all of a sudden I drew out an extraneous object and placed it on the table.

"What the hell's that?"

"The old man had it on his tray. . . . Quick, I must take it back," and I picked up the ivory figure and hurried out, leaving Dickon to settle up. Search as I would, however, there was no sign of the old man. Even the street seemed different, better lighted, less twisty, and when I found a stall holder I thought I recognized he said he had seen me standing in a corner talking to myself. Which was ridiculous!

In the end we returned to our lodgings, though I promised myself I would go back the next day and try and find the old man. In the meantime I put the figurine on the chest at the foot of my bed and curled up in bed seeking a sleep that seemed strangely elusive. I tossed and turned, flickered in and out of brightly colored dreams I could not recall, but was at last sinking into deeper slumber when all at once there was a voice in my ears, a tiny, shrill voice that snapped me back into consciousness at once.

"Stop thief! Stop thief!"

Chapter Eight

I sat up at once, my sleepy eyes just making out a shadowy form slipping through the open doorway into the near darkness outside. Stumbling off the bed I made my way over to the door, shut and bolted it. Normally I didn't bother with the bolt, as Dickon and I were the only occupants of the verandah at the moment. Feeling my way back to the chest, I discovered that the lid was open, meaning flint, tinder and candle stub must be on the floor somewhere. I found the first two and was fumbling for the third when that squeaky voice came again.

"To your right a little . . . That's it!"

Needless to say I nearly dropped the lot.

"Who's there?"

Nothing, save Tug's soft breathing and a snore from Growch. Fingers trembling, I at last managed a light and held the candle high. Plenty of shadows but no intruder. Tug rolled up on the floor in his blanket—he still wouldn't use the bed—and Growch curled up at the foot of mine. No one else—

"I'm here. On the floor by your feet. Please don't tread on me. . . ."

I stared down at the ivory figure. Surely not! I must be dreaming.

"Yes, it's me. You can pick me up, if you don't mind. Quite uncomfortable standing on one's head. Thanks."

I found I had picked it—him—up and put him on the chest, right way up. I stared down; no damage from his tumble as far as I could see. But the voice! Surely that would have woken the others, or one of them would have heard the intruder. If there was one. Suddenly I wasn't sure of anything anymore.

"If you could just touch me with your ring for a moment—that's it—then I shall find the transition much easier. . . ."

I did as he said: my ring thrummed with energy for a moment, but there was nothing but good here.

"Dearie, dearie me!" said the squeaky voice. "It's been such a long time! Ivory is pretty to look at but it hasn't the warmth of amber or the manipulation of wood. But with wood there's always the threat of woodworm of course. . . ."

I sank to my knees in front of the chest; this wasn't happening! That little figure wasn't talking to me, it wasn't, it couldn't!

"Oh, yes I am! I suppose it must be rather disconcerting for you, but if you will bear with me I'll try and make the change to living as quickly as I can. . . ." He thought for a moment. "If you could just hold me in your hands for a moment, warm me up. That's fine. Don't worry about your friends: they can't hear us."

I put him down on the chest again and sat back on my heels to watch one of the most amazing things I had ever seen. It was almost like a chicken breaking from an egg, a crumpled poppy unfurling its petals from the bud; you wondered how on earth it ever fitted inside. Of course this creature's task was different: it had to turn from inanimate to living, but the process seemed about the same.

First I saw the nostrils dilate as the first breaths of air were inhaled, then the nostrils became pinkish and the antennae at the side of his mouth flexed back and forth. Like a chick's feathers, dry little hairs released themselves from the ivory and fluffed up around his face; dark brown eyes blinked and moistened. Then came the ears and throat, the former twitching back and forth till they were set as he wanted. A forked tongue tested the air.

"A little rest: this is tougher than I thought. It's been a long time. Please excuse the delay. . . ."

He curled back his lips, panting a little, and I could see a tiny row of chewing teeth. Now the process speeded up; tiny hooves stamped, ribs expanded, a rump gave an experimental wiggle and lastly a short tail with an outsized plume gave an exultant wave.

"There! That's better. How do I look?"

"Er . . . very impressive." I didn't really know what to say. The whole process was mind-bending, but as I didn't know what he was supposed to look like, I couldn't really qualify my statement.

He seemed to be reading my mind. "You're quite right! I've forgotten the colors, haven't I? Just watch. . . ."

In a way this was the most impressive of all his tricks. From being a dullish creamy yellow, he rapidly developed a uniquely tinted body that glowed like a jewel on the lid of the chest. First came a bright yellow belly, then the fur on his back developed shades of blue, purple, violet, brown and rose, his legs and tail darkened to gray and lastly the plume on his tail fanned out into crimson, gold and green. For a brief moment it seemed that his whole body was lapped by flame, but then he was as before.

"Not bad, not bad at all. I'm particularly proud of the tail: not exactly conventional, but we are allowed a certain latitude. . . . Just a moment. I'd feel more comfortable with a bit more space."

And something that had been beetle-sized rapidly expanded to the dimensions of a mouse.

"Er . . . are you going to get any bigger?" I asked nervously, as the growth seemed to be accelerating.

"Sorry! Not for the moment. Would you like to see just how big I can grow?"

"Not at the moment," I said hastily. "Some other time."

"Very well. I suppose it has taken it out of me a little. . . . Let me introduce myself. My name is Ky-Lin." His voice was less squeaky.

"Ky-Lin," I repeated like a dummy. I found it difficult to cope with what was happening.

"Yes, and you?"

"My name is Summer. Pleased to make your acquaintance."

"A mutual honor."

A little silence, then I plucked up courage. "I'm sorry, but I'm afraid I'm not quite sure to what I owe the pleasure of your company? I found you in my pouch last night, and I was going to try and find the old man tomorrow to return you—"

"Didn't he say that I went where I wanted? Where I thought I was needed?"

"Yes, but—"

"So, I am here. You need me, I think. You have a long journey ahead of you and I believe I might prove useful. The trip sounds interesting and if I comport myself well I shall have earned myself more points."

"Points? For what?" This conversation was very confusing.

"For my Master."

"The old man?"

"No, no!" He looked scandalized. "He is one of the Old Ones, a Master of Illusion, but quite earthbound I assure you. No, I speak of my Lord." He settled back on his haunches. "A long, long time ago there lived a great and good man called Siddhartha, later known as the Buddha. He was so wise and so loving that he gave up all worldly distractions. He had to walk about the world in poverty, preaching of the Divine Way to Eternal Life. He saw life as a great wheel that eventually led to Paradise, which is a way of becoming part of the Eternal. But this way can only be realized by living a perfect life, and as man is not perfect he is given many chances. These take the form of various animal lives or incarnations, accompanied by rewards and punishments—points, if you like. You may be a good horse in one incarnation, and be rewarded by being a man in the next. Or you may be a bad man, and find yourself a lowly insect in another. Do you see?"

I thought so, though it was a novel idea, these many chances to be good. Like all people in my country I had been brought up a Catholic, but since then on my travels had come across many other religions: Judaism, Hinduism, Mohammedanism. It seemed there was more than one road to God. A clever God would understand that just as different countries, different climates, different cultures produced different ideas, so He could tailor these to men's beliefs so that their worship was comfortable to them.

"You are partly following my Lord's teachings," he continued, "because you care about animals. We are taught to go even further; we believe that we must not damage any living thing, because we might be hurting one of our fellows, temporarily on a lower path or incarnation."

"But you—you are not like any creature I have ever seen."

"Because I, and my many companions, were created especially by my Lord Himself to epitomize how many creatures may be one, a harmonious whole. We traveled with Him, as His guards and friends."

"Your Lord, whom you said lived many years ago, has presumably found His Eternal Life: why are you still here, and not with Him?"

There was a longer silence. "I hoped you wouldn't ask. . . ."

"Sorry, I didn't mean—"

"It's all right. You should know." Another silence. "The fact is, I should be perfect, and I'm not. Wasn't."

"Wasn't?"

The words came out in a rush. "I-was-careless-and-trod-on-the-grass. I-was-also-greedy-and-lazy-and-rebellious." He paused. "But the worst was—I-said-I-didn't-want-Eternity. . . . I thought it would be boring. There! Now you know. That's why I'm here. I can't change my shape, but I have to work off my badnesses by helping others, until my Lord Buddha decides I am fit to join Him."

It seemed so unfair to me. Poor little creature! How on earth could you remember not to tread on grass? I reached out a finger without thought and stroked his head, and there was a little grumbling purr, like a cat, but suddenly he twitched his head aside.

"You mustn't indulge me; that is pure pleasure, and I am forbidden anything like that. I've lost a point already, being proud of my plumed tail a moment ago."

"All right." I had made a mistake with my pig-dragon. "And how many points have you got now?"

"I don't know. The trouble is, my last choice was purely selfish, and my Lord recognized it as such. I came across an old man—he was nearly eighty—who wanted help translating Greek and Roman texts. I reckoned he might last another five years or so, but my Lord saw through my deception, and the old man lived to a hundred and ten. It was hard work, too," he added, and sighed.

I found myself trying not to smile. The idea of this vibrant little creature being tied to dusty scrolls for thirty years . . . I had another idea.

"You speak, or understand, other languages, too?"

"Most. My Lord arranged it so we have an inbuilt translator in our heads."

An extra bonus: perhaps he would be able to make sense of Tug's click-clicks, and find out where he came from.

Ky-Lin yawned, his forked tongue curling back on itself till I could see the ridged roof of his mouth. "And now, it is time for sleep. I shall, with your permission, curl up inside the chest, if you would open it up? Thanks."

A last wave of his tail and I found I couldn't keep my eyes open nor my brain fit to think over what I had just seen and heard. As I pulled the blanket up round my ears, I realized that I hadn't asked him who had been the potential thief he had disturbed.

And in the morning there wasn't time.

Karim Bey sent for both Dickon and I shortly after dawn. He had found a caravan that had come in the previous day and intended to leave at midday for points further east, with a special order of furs, perfume and German glass. When Karim told Dickon I had asked to accompany it, he at once volunteered to go too. "Just to keep an eye on a trainee," as he put it.

I was surprised: I thought the distractions of the town would have been more enticing. I wasn't sure whether to be glad or sorry; Dickon was a passable lad, a good linguist, knew far more than I did about merchandising and had always been helpful. But there was something, just something I couldn't put a name to, that made me uneasy in his company. It wasn't his womanizing, though that was annoying enough, nor was it his vanity—how many lads of seventeen or so wouldn't take advantage of good wages to dress well? If I were back in my girl's guise wouldn't I want ribbons and fal-lals? No, there was something else, something *sneaky* about him.

We were hurriedly introduced to the caravan owner, a small and undistinguished character called Ali Qased, then Karim paid out moneys for our food and lodgings and the hire of a couple of mules, making sure we realized that the latter would be deducted from our commissions.

I hurried back to our lodgings for a quick breakfast, an even quicker packing—a sleepy Ky-Lin tucked surreptitiously in the lining of my jacket—and a prolonged and formal farewell to Chippi and his wife, with much head bobbing and wringing of hands from them both.

The sun was high in the sky when we set off, winding away from the city and up again into the hills, this time to the east. Tug was beside himself with happiness that we were at last on the move, and sang tunelessly as he trotted along beside us, disdaining the offer of a ride.

I didn't find things so easy. For some reason I felt out of sorts, with a grumbling stomach, a sort of warning that things might get worse. I was snappy with the others, critical of the journey, couldn't sleep—in fact it reminded me of nothing so much as those times before my monthly loss. It was a shock to realize too that these had not manifested themselves for nearly a year, a fact I had initially put down to the terrible journey I undertook to return to Matthew, after my dragon had flown away and left me.

The lack of a monthly flow had been a boon in my travels as a boy, and I had completely forgotten about it until now. Perhaps I should be worried, I thought; perhaps there was something permanently wrong. Surreptitiously I felt my stomach: a little swollen, but nothing else. If it was pregnancy I was worried about, then there was nothing to fear, of course, for Jasper was the only man to touch me in that way and the nine months needed to make a baby had long gone. Just in case I checked my pack to make sure the cloths I had packed were still there if needed.

It grew rapidly much colder the farther east and north we travelled, with an intermittent icy wind sliding down the ever-nearing mountains, and it was with relief that we mostly found small villages in which to spend the lengthening nights; tents in the open were no substitute for four walls and a roof, however basic. Tug was the only one who didn't feel the cold, merely wrapping himself up tighter in his blanket.

I kept Ky-Lin hidden, as we mostly shared quarters with Dickon, and for some reason I was reluctant to share him. I fed him scraps of rice or dried fruit, because of his taboo on eating or killing anything live.

One night we were on our own, Dickon and Tug foraging for wood for the communal fire and Growch off on an expedition of his own. I set out some raisins and a few nuts in front of Ky-Lin, watching his pleasure as he nibbled at the latter.

"You like them?"

"Mmm. One of my favorites. You know what I like best of all?"

"No."

"Flaked almonds coated with honey, or a nice pod or two of carob. Very bad for the teeth, but quite delicious."

I made a mental note to seek out either or both as soon as I could.

As I watched him I suddenly remembered something I had meant to ask a long time ago.

"Ky-Lin, that first night you came to us . . ."

"Mmm?"

"You woke me up calling out 'Stop thief!' "

He nodded.

"Did you see him?"

He nodded again, mouth full of nut.

"Did you see who it was?"

Another nod.

"Who?"

It seemed ages before he answered. "Got sticky fingers that one."

"Who has?"

"Your friend Dickon, of course! Who did you think it would be?"

Chapter Nine

"I don't believe it!" I shook my head. "There's nothing there he would want."

"Have you anything in your baggage he desires?"

I thought through all my belongings: clothes, writing materials and journal, now written in a form of shortened hand and difficult to decipher; tally sticks, a few herbs and simples, my forged papers from Matthew, Suleiman's letter—had Dickon made something that wasn't out of that?—mug, bowl and spoon, plus the lump of glass the captain's wife had given me. This had proved rather disappointing: beautifully shaped and cut, it nevertheless had looked nothing other than dull when I had looked at it one gray evening when we had been on our way to the tent city of Küm. My other treasure from that city, the Waystone, I kept in a pouch about my neck, together with some little scraps of discarded skin that had come from a certain little pig; just a keepsake, I kept telling myself.

But there must be something. Think . . . I went through the list again in my mind. No, there was nothing else—nothing except the maps I had copied, and the one Suleiman had enclosed with his letter. Could it be these he had been looking for?

Ky-Lin was reading my mind. "Could be," he said. "Especially if he has the sort of suspicious mind that believes you are doing something other than just being an apprentice."

I remembered Dickon's accusations of being a spy, or on a secret mission for Matthew. "Let's take a look," I said. I peeked past the hanging leather that served as a door in this poor place; Tug was squatting by the fire, Dickon was talking to one of the village girls.

"All clear." I pulled out the two maps I had duplicated at Matthew's and spread them out on the dirt floor using elbows and knees to keep them flat. Ky-Lin trotted over to sit on the fourth corner.

I pointed to the first, larger map. "Here's where I come from, and that's the route, marked out, that we took to Venice. . . . Here's the sea we crossed to the Golden Horn, and this could be the way we took to Küm. But there are lots of trails leading from there, so we must have used the most easterly. I suppose we could be just about here, now. . . ."

Ky-Lin squinted horribly and shook his head from side to side which he explained helped him concentrate. "The trouble with maps is that they are never used by people who know the routes and know the terrain, so there is no one to update them. Most of them are hopelessly inaccurate, and at best are mostly guesswork. Distances, too, can be very misleading, for who counts his paces or even his days to mark his passage? Ask one caravan master how long it takes from this city to that and he will tell you ten, twenty days, depending on the weather. Another will take a different trail over easier ground and shorten the time by half, yet as the bird flies the mileage would be the same."

"It's marked with mountains and things," I said defensively. An erupting volcano graced part of Italia, a couple of small ships on the seas; there was what looked like a lion and a triangular temple on the coast of Africa, and Cathay was shown with snaky rivers and high mountains. In the corner where Ky-Lin was sitting was a great empty space and the legend: "Here be Dragons." That was one of the reasons I had been keen to have a copy.

"Pictures of them, yes, but are they where it shows them? I think you have a clue here," and he tapped his hoof right in front of where he was sitting. "To the ignorant layman, when you see the word 'dragons,' what would you immediately think of? Yes," he added, crossing my thoughts. "Treasure. Maybe your young friend believes you are on a treasure hunt, with or without Master Spicer's assistance or knowledge. Let me see the others. . . ."

The second of Matthew's maps he pronounced as better, but not much. I produced the one Suleiman had sent.

"Ah, this is more like it. The man who made this actually travelled these routes. I recognize this, and this, and this. . . ." He shook his head, crossed his eyes alarmingly, waved his plumed tail.

"But I can't read these squiggles. . . ."

"Those 'squiggles' are in Cantonese, but even without them I can see places I have visited. See, the Land of the Lotus, the Singing Gardens, the Desert of Death, the City of Golden Towers (not true, they are only gilded), and there are others I have heard of. The country of Snakes, the town of the Three-legged Men (named after an annual race they hold), the Blue Mountain, the—"

"Did you—did you say the Blue Mountain?"

"Yes. Here it is, just beyond the Three Fangs of the Mighty One. This means something special to you?"

All at once all I could think about was the vision the old man had shown me in that magical bowl of colored water, where I had been for a brief moment or two a dragon, steering my way through the Fangs and down to the valley beneath and the Blue Mountain with the hidden cave.

I jabbed my finger down on the map. "It's there, it's true, it's real! *That's* where I must go!" I was almost shouting with joy.

There was a sudden silence. The ivory figurine that had been holding down the map rolled off into the shadows. I looked up, and there was Dickon framed in the doorway.

I don't know how much he had heard or seen, but of course he pretended there was nothing amiss, merely saying that he had come to ask whether I would prefer rice or pancakes for our evening meal, but all the time he was speaking his eyes were darting suspiciously around the hut, glancing at the map I had immediately released so that it had scrolled itself and rolled into a corner.

Poor Ky-Lin, I thought: he will have to start all over again. Even while I was thinking this I was gathering up the maps and stuffing them back in my pack, and all the while chattering away like a demented monkey.

"Hello, Dickon, I didn't see you there! How nice of you to come and ask what I wanted. . . . Let me see, now. We had pancakes yesterday, didn't we? Or was it beans . . . On the other hand I'm a bit tired of rice. My stomach hasn't been all that good, as you know, so perhaps it had better be pancakes. Or do you think they will be too greasy? What do you suggest?"

I continued to rummage around for my writing things.

"I thought I would catch up with my diary of our travels, so I checked the maps to make sure I have the route all planned out correctly. They're not very accurate, though; what's this place called, do you know? Never mind, I'll just mark it as a village. . . ."

And so on, trying to cover my confusion and making it worse.

But he couldn't contain his curiosity for long. "I heard—I thought you were talking to someone . . . ?"

"Me? Now who could I be talking to: there's no one else here. The place is empty. . . ." *Think* of something quick, Summer! "Oh that! You heard me talking to myself, I suppose. Haven't you ever done that? It always helps if you're trying to work something out in your mind, makes it all much clearer. . . ."

I could see he wasn't satisfied, kept looking around the room, but there was nothing to see. "I'll order you rice then. It'll be ready soon."

As soon as he was gone, I rushed over to Ky-Lin and picked him up.

"I'm terribly sorry. I hope it isn't too difficult to come alive again?"

Almost at once out popped a living nose and mouth. "Easier each time. Give me a few minutes. Go and get your food; if you wouldn't mind bringing me a few grains of rice? I always get particularly hungry after a change. . . ."

The meal was an uneasy one. Dickon put himself out to be charming and entertaining, but I still worried about what he might have seen and overheard. Besides which, my stomach had started aching again and I definitely felt queasy. I couldn't finish all the rice and vegetables and excused myself before the others had finished, longing to just wrap myself in a blanket, lie down on my pallet and try to forget the pain in my guts in sleep. It wasn't particularly cold, but I was shivering.

"Did you remember . . . ? It doesn't matter. You look ill. . . ."

"Oh, hell! Sorry Ky-Lin. Yes. It does matter." I went to the door and called Tug over and explained what I wanted. He had been playing five-stones with the village boys, but he was always cheerful and willing these days. Two minutes later he was back with some rice and vegetables wrapped in a vine leaf.

"You still hungry, Summa?"

I made up my mind. "Tug come with me. New friend to meet."

Tug's eyes were as wide as I had ever seen them as Ky-Lin fluffed out his tail in welcome. But instead of dropping the rice or running off in horror, he instead gave a stiff little bow, then walked over to the creature and placed the food in front of him, standing back to watch him eat.

"Tug, this is a—"

"Ch'i-Lin," said Tug, and gave that jerky little bow again. "*Very* good. Go with Lord Buddha."

"He knows. . . ."

"My Lord's wisdom has travelled to many places, like the wind," said Ky-Lin, chasing the last pieces of rice with his forked tongue. "If I am not mistaken, this child comes from the Northern Plains."

"Can you speak his tongue?" Perhaps at last we should be better able to help him.

"I will try. . . ." And for the next few moments there was an incomprehensible (to me) series and exchange of clicks and hisses, at the end of which Ky-Lin's eyes were crossed and Tug had a broad grin on his face.

"I was right," said Ky-Lin. "The boy is one of the Plainsmen, the great Horsemen. They are nomadic herdsmen, live in tents, and travel many hundreds of miles in a year."

"And how far away is his homeland?" I asked, my heart already sinking in anticipation of his reply.

"Perhaps a thousand miles to the north, perhaps a little more."

It was as I had feared. I had promised Tug, in sign language if not in words, that I would take him back to his homeland, and I couldn't break a promise, even if it meant I went hundreds of miles out of my way. I looked at the hope in his face, and knew I couldn't let him down. How should I have felt if I had been snatched away from home and family at ten or eleven years old, transported hundreds of miles, only to be sold like an animal to the highest bidder? After all, my dragon would wait, wouldn't he?

"Do you know the way there, Ky-Lin?"

"I can guide you in the right direction, if that is what you wish; the way is quite clearly shown on that last map of yours. But I warn you that the country itself, besides being many miles away, is also far vaster than anything you have come across so far. Another thing; it will take many months to reach, and this caravan we travel with is taking us too far to the east."

Which meant we should have to abandon the safety of the caravan and strike out on our own. For a terrible moment I thought I hadn't got the courage; feeling as I did now, I would have been thankful to have just curled up for the winter and hibernated like the red-leaf squirrels near my old home. My ring gave a little throb, and I remembered we had Ky-Lin with us, and we hadn't failed up to now, had we? And we wouldn't: not with the help of God's good grace—and a little luck.

But we should have to be careful not to rouse Dickon's suspicions. He was the last person I wanted to accompany us, but if he got the slightest hint we were to be away on our own he would be sure to follow, especially if, as Ky-Lin had suggested, he believed we were after treasure. And, knowing Dickon, he would stick like a leech.

The following morning I made enquiries that all could hear as to when we would reach the next town, explaining that I needed the services of a competent purveyor of pills for my stomach pains. The answer was three days; once there I would plead indisposition and stay behind. Of course once I announced my indisposition, it miraculously cured itself, as an aching tooth will while queuing for the tooth puller, but I still pretended it was worsening, and this was aided by the fact that apparently I still looked pale and drawn.

In the meantime I introduced Growch to Ky-Lin, only to be informed that he had "known all the time, and just how many more spare parts was I going to invite along on what was, after all, supposed to be a special journey just for the two of us . . ." etc.

I realized that he was jealous, only had been too caught up in my own plans to recognize it, so from then on I made a special fuss over him, even going to the extreme of treating him to a bath and comb. He whined like hell, of course, but secretly I believe he thought any attention was better than none, and we were soon back to our old footing.

The journey that should have taken three days took five, due to torrential rains, but this worked to my advantage in the end, because Ali Qased, the caravan master, was eager to press on immediately before any more autumnal downpours held him up, and as far as he was concerned one sick apprentice more or less would only hold him up.

Using Dickon as my interpreter, he was quite willing I should stay behind until he returned—a guess of a month or more—but he also insisted that I consult the local apothecary, a shabby little man with an obsequious manner and a satchel full of phials of crushed insects, dried bats' wings, unidentified blood, powder of tiger claw, bitter herbs and pellets of opium. He prodded my stomach, shook his head, and went away to make up some pills.

To add color to my "illness," I took to my bed in the small attic room Dickon had found for me. He returned with powder in a twist of rice paper and half a dozen pills, insisting that I take them at once.

"You owe me two silver coins—"

"He's expensive!"

"Yes, but if you take these at once you may be better in the morning and ready to continue the journey. We don't leave till ten."

I fished out the money, then groaned. "I don't think I shall. . . . Now, leave me alone to get some rest."

"When you've taken your medicine. The powder is to be dissolved in water and the—"

"I haven't got any."

"What?"

"Water."

He nodded at Tug, who was arranging some stones on the floor in a complicated game. "Send your slave boy."

I was tired of his attitude towards Tug.

"Once and for all, he's not a slave. I bought him and gave him his freedom. And no, I'm not sending him: he couldn't make himself understood. Go yourself."

"He's a cretin. . . ."

"He's not that either. You just don't understand him."

I might add that Tug was perfectly well aware of Dickon's dislike and played up to it, acting like a village idiot when he was near, so Dickon's remark wasn't entirely unjustified. Now the boy stuck out his tongue and waggled his fingers in his ears.

"Tug . . ." I said reprovingly, wanting to giggle.

"Told you," said Dickon. "All right, I'll fetch you some water. Just stay here till I get back."

What did he think I was going to do? Fly out the window?

As soon as he had gone I scooped Ky-Lin out of my sleeve.

"Quick!" I said. "The medicines. Are they fit to take?"

He sniffed delicately at the twists of paper.

"Mmmm . . . the powder is harmless. Crushed pearl, a pinch of gentian for color, cinnamon for taste. The pills? Sweetener for coating, a little clay for setting; inside rat's blood, burnt feathers and a good dose of opium."

"Yeeuk!"

"You've eaten worse, certainly from my point of view! At least there is nothing to harm you permanently. Try and get away with just drinking the powder: the opium in a pill will make you sleep heavily, and if you want to be away tomorrow as soon as they leave . . . spit it out as soon as he's gone."

But the trouble was he wouldn't go. He watched me tip some of the powder into my mug and add water, stirring it with my finger till it was purple. I drank it down with an expression of disgust, though the taste was not unpleasant.

"I think I'll take a rest now. . . ."

"Pills first."

"In a minute! I'll just see if the drink will—"

"The pills are to be taken at the same time. Go on. Two."

"I am *not* taking two! Suppose they don't agree with me? Do you want to spend the night nursing me?"

"One, then. Now!"

I put it in my mouth, and tucked it quickly under my tongue, making exaggerated swallowing motions. "There! Now you can go and leave me alone."

He still wouldn't leave; instead he paced the floor, small though the room was: three steps one way, two back.

"How can I leave you on your own? Master Spicer would never forgive me if you worsened. . . . You said yourself that heathen boy can't make himself understood. No, my duty is to stay here with you. The caravan can manage without me."

The pill was gradually melting in my mouth. I could taste the bitterness through the coating.

"And Matthew would never forgive me if you broke your apprenticeship just to look after me! I'll be fine in a couple of days. I've enough money to stay here until you come back, and I can spend the time bringing my journal up to date and learning a bit more of the language. I wouldn't dream of you staying behind!"

"Don't tell me what I ought or ought not to do!" Then in a gentler tone: "I consider it my duty to look after you. Don't forget I am the only one who knows you are a girl . . ."

Was this an implied threat?

" . . . and you wouldn't want anyone else to find out, would you?"

Yes, it was.

"What harm can it do for me to stay and—you to go?" The pill must be taking effect. I mustn't go to sleep, I mustn't! "After all, I can't go anywhere, can I? Ali Qased said his was the last caravan expected this year. . . ." I yawned uncontrollably.

At last he left, promising to look in again, and the next thing was Ky-Lin hissing in my ear: "Spit it out! Spit it out!"

The pill, what little was left of it, dropped to the floor. I struggled up on my elbow. "Mustn't sleep . . . lots to do. Got to find out—find out—how to get away. Transport . . . food. Can't . . . can't sleep."

"Do-not-worry," said Ky-Lin, close to my ear. "We-will-see-to-it. Leave-it-to-us. Sleep-in-peace. . . ."

I didn't hear or see them leave, knew nothing else in fact until a bright light flashed across my eyelids. I tried to open my mouth, my eyes, but nothing happened. It was as if I was frozen to my bed. The light flashed again.

"Perhaps you were telling the truth after all, little witch," said a voice I should recognize. Then more sharply: "Wake up, Summer! Time to get up," and someone shook me, none too gently. I moaned and rolled over, but could respond no further, slipping back down into a velvety darkness.

Then something triggered a thought. Of course I recognized the voice: it had to be Dickon. With a supreme effort I opened my eyes. There was a lantern on the floor, and by its light I could see Dickon going through my papers, my pack open at his side. He held up first one map and then another, frowning and muttering to himself. "Can't see much there. . . . Possible, possible. We're way off track, though. . . ."

He rolled the maps, turned his attention to my journal but, as I had anticipated, he could make little of my scrawl, especially as it had been only recently that the former stable lad had learned to know his letters. "Still, I heard her say there was somewhere she had to go . . . but where, *where*?"

He glanced across at me, but luckily my face was in shadow and I closed my eyes quickly.

"Still, there's nowhere to go from here. Safe enough, I reckon."

At that moment there was a bark on the stone steps that led up to my room; the others were back.

With a speed that obviously owed much to practice, maps and papers were stuffed back in my pack and it was rapidly refastened. A moment later and he was standing over the bed, lantern held high.

Growch rushed in growling, closely followed by Tug. Dickon straightened up.

"Just checking on the patient, for the benefit of a cretin and a scruffy hound," said Dickon. "I know you can't understand, stupid bastards both, but I'll be back to check in the morning."

I heard his steps on the stair and tried to keep awake long enough to tell Ky-Lin, emerging from Tug's jacket, just what had happened, but he shushed me.

"Go to sleep. Don't worry about a thing. We have got it all organized. By this time tomorrow we shall be spending our first night afloat. . . ."

I could have sworn he said "afloat." But we weren't anywhere near the sea. I must have been dreaming.

And two minutes later I really was.

Interlude

He was bored. Restless. Unhappy.

He told himself not to be stupid, that he had everything he needed, that dragons did not admit to boredom, or restlessness. And, most of all, not to unhappiness. Yet how else could he explain why he felt as he did? Dragons usually were only affected by purely physical things: heat and cold, hunger and thirst; and by the pure pleasure, endless delight, of jewels and gems, and the retelling of tales of travel.

But then he wasn't a dragon all the time, was he? Like now. Now he was a man sitting on a deserted beach somewhere, chucking stones into the sea and suffering from indigestion.

And that was another thing: a man ate what a man ate, dragons were different. If one had a fire in one's belly, used regularly or not, one could digest anything, bones and all, but a man's stomach churned on the remains of a dragon dinner.

He gave a snort of disgust. This just shouldn't be happening to him. He had reported back, been welcomed and initiated into the proper rituals, then allowed the treat of inspecting the Hoard. He had been obliged, however, to disclose his Affliction, as he termed it, and been rewarded with consternation and disbelief. Spells had been cast, charms used, lore memory consulted, but all to no avail. Nothing like this had ever happened before; of course it was known that it could, but what mortal maid in her right mind had ever kissed a dragon?

At first, of course, they hadn't believed him, until he had done an involuntary change and back right there in front of them. It was the most exciting thing that had happened to the community since the Blue Dragon had returned hundreds of years back with his jewels and the tales of the witch who had stolen them, and the knight and the girl and the animals who had returned them.

His Affliction had had a mixed reception. Some of them thought it added to his powers, others that it must inevitably detract from the purity of line they had preserved.

Five minutes, ten, of thought, and he was still bored, restless and unhappy, and the sea a hundred stones fuller. He might as well admit it; he still hankered after that lass with the long legs who had rescued him from death in his first incarnation as a pig, cared for him, loved him and finally—irony of ironies!—given him the three kisses he would remember forever. That, and the moment of passion when he was caught between man and dragon—Aiyee! That experience had been enough to make anyone's toes curl!

Fire and ice! He must see her again—if only to convince himself that he didn't need to. . . .

It was late spring when he started his journey. Back first to the Place of Stones, where his transformation had taken place, then retracing her route back to that fat merchant she would probably marry. As a man he came down to earth to ask questions, see if she had passed that way, but to no avail. By midsummer he had even dared the servants at the merchant's house, only to find she had disappeared a few weeks before with her dog to parts unknown, and that the merchant, heartbroken, had gone on pilgrimage to Spain.

So, where was she, the girl whose memory still tormented him? North, south, east, west? He tried haphazardly: northern fjords, southern deserts, western isles, eastern mountains—but surely even she wouldn't travel that far. Why run away from a perfectly good marriage anyway? What was she looking for now? What worm was eating her brain this time, silly girl?

He grew crosser and crosser; what right had she to haunt him so? Time he pulled himself together; what he needed was a break, a few months, a year perhaps; time, anyway, that he sought some gifts for the Hoard, part of his dragon duty. Perhaps by then he would be free of what was rapidly becoming an obsession.

So, which way? Somewhere warm for the winter. Africa, India, the isles of the Southern Seas? It didn't really matter. . . .

Part Two

Chapter Ten

I had never thought it would be so wonderful to be one's own mistress again, to be free of caravans, merchants, warehouses, tally sticks, accounts, invoices, bales and bargaining. Most of all it was wonderful to be rid of Dickon. More and more he had constricted my every move and his suspicions had haunted me so much I found myself glancing over my shoulder even now to make sure he wasn't following.

Of course being free was a comparative term. I had the others to think about and care for, Tug to return to his people and my own journey to complete, but at least we could proceed at our own pace.

It was bliss to just lie back against the thwarts of the boat, even hemmed in as we were by peasants, farmers, children, sacks of grain, rolls of cloth, strings of dried fish and crates of chickens. Above us was a cloudless sky, rice fields and stands of bamboo slid past with a lazy regularity, and the smooth water of the Yellow Snake River gurgled and slapped against the hull, accompanied by the flap of sail and creak of rudder.

Ky-Lin, Tug and Growch had done well while I lay deadened by the opium. Ky-Lin had remembered from the map that the river looped briefly towards the town some five miles away and had ascertained that boats travelled regularly both north and south, and in fact we had picked up one this midafternoon. The river eventually turned to the east and Cathay, but by this way, though slower, we should be some two hundred miles farther towards our goal, with little effort on our part. Just as long as the money held out: we should have to be careful and economize where we could. Luckily nobody would charge for Growch, and Ky-Lin was tucked up in the hood of my cloak, both for safety and so he could whisper translations if necessary.

I patted Tug's knee. "Not bad, eh?" He shivered and snuggled nearer, his eyes rolling in fright. "It's all right," I said slowly, hoping he would understand. "Ky-Lin: tell him there's nothing to be afraid of."

But though the magic creature did his best Tug refused to be comforted, and I recalled my own experience with water. The first time I had been in a frail rowing boat carrying me away from marauding soldiers; the second

I had nearly been drowned when I was cut off by an incoming tide and the third had been that dreadful storm when we had left Venice, so perhaps Tug was to be pitied. I stretched out my hand but he had bolted to the side and heaved up into the river.

I moved over to rub his back, a thing my mother had done when I was a child in some sick situation, and I had always found it comforting. Remembering my ring had many powers, I drew that gently down his spine too, and wasn't surprised when he turned to me with a weak smile and announced he was: "Better with no tum!" He added: "Like ride horse. Fall off two three time. Learn quick." And after that he was all right.

We travelled from one stopover to another, at each one discharging cargo and passengers and taking on others. I had no word of the native tongue, even having to bargain for our fare with sign language and Ky-Lin's whispers, but the people were kind and cheerful, inviting us to share their meagre provisions. These were usually cooked on a brazier in the well of the boat, although occasionally we tied up for the night by some village or other and dined there in one of the tiny eating houses. In this way we travelled some seventy or eighty miles north, then the boat in which we were travelling turned back and we took another, smaller, which tied up every night. In order to eat I had to buy a small cooking pot, food on the way and have Tug forage for the wood for a fire. This took us another fifty miles, and then we swapped to a string of barges carrying cattle—not an experience to be repeated.

The weather gradually changed as autumn and the approaching north brought colder winds, rain, falling leaves, and cranes winging south. By now we were some hundred and fifty miles further on, but the river narrowed into a series of gorges through which water raced in a torrent, and only the hardiest and most reckless boatman would venture the rapids. It seemed this terrain was unchanged for fifty miles or so, and we decided to finally leave the river and start walking.

We hadn't gone more than a couple of miles or so when I, at least, was regretting it. I had gone soft, what with mule and river travel, and although Tug carried his fair share of the baggage, mine felt to weigh a ton, and we were all hot, sticky, and tired by the time we had walked ten miles that first day. A village gave us shelter for the night, we had a lift on a bullock cart the following day, which was a bit like travelling snail-back, but at least it gave my feet a rest. My stomach, too, had begun to play up again, but only intermittently. For the next three days it rained continuously and we were holed up in a miserable hovel with a dripping roof and I began to wonder if we had offended some local god.

On the fifth day our luck changed for the better. The sun shone warm, we dried out, and I reckoned we could risk a night in the open if we could find some bushes or convenient trees. During the day we had managed to gather some nuts and berries to supplement our diet, and as we were now in sight of a good-sized village, I decided to go in and buy rice or beans. Travelling on the river, the money had trickled away as fast as the water ran, and I had no idea how much farther we had to go.

We had just found a likely camping spot and set down our baggage, dusk was falling and Tug was about to forage for wood, when we heard the sound of pipes and firecrackers from the village. I never got used to the half and quarter tones of eastern music and firecrackers always made me jump, but Tug loved both, so we picked up our packs again and set off towards the celebrations. At the very worst there would be some scraps of food dropping from the tables for Growch to scrounge, and at best we might be invited to share with some hospitable villager.

Although the outer streets were deserted there had obviously been a procession of sorts earlier, for the ground was littered with scraps of colored paper and burned-out firecrackers, but the noise now came from the center of the village, as did a healthy smell of cooking meat and rice. We followed our ears and our noses and found ourselves in the village square.

In one corner a couple of spits were turning vigorously and large pans were simmering over a trench fire; while they waited for the food, the villagers were clapping an entertainment. As usual at these functions, like any other village in the world, certain unwritten rules for social behavior were observed. The elderly were comfortably seated around the perimeter, some with smaller children and babies on their laps, the young men congregated in one corner, the girls in the opposite, parents and middle-aged bustled from one group to another exchanging gossip, and the older children played tag and got under everyone's feet.

But for now all was relatively quiet as they watched the performers. A trio of children, some younger even than Tug, were working acrobatic tricks with a man who was obviously their father, while an older boy twisted himself into knots and did cartwheels round them; in another space a pair of jugglers tossed balls, rings and torches into the air and at each other, while on the fringes waited a great brown bear with a ring through its nose, shifting restlessly from paw to paw. Its owner, a thickset man with a pipe in his hand ready to play the music for the creature to dance to, suddenly jerked at the chain that ran through the ring in the bear's nose, which bit into the soft part of the nostril and made the poor thing squeal with pain. Simultaneously, it seemed, my heart jumped in sympathy and the ring on my finger gave a sudden stab.

The ring stabbed again, and all at once I had a brilliant idea. In what seemed another life my beautiful blind knight with his clear singing voice and the animals with me then had given performances such as these to pay our way. Why not try it again? True, the only original members of our troupe were Growch and myself, and all he had ever done was beg, turn somersaults, and lie down and "die," but surely we could concoct something between us. I asked Tug if he knew any tricks, through Ky-Lin.

"He says," translated the latter, "give him a horse and he is the best in the world. He also says he can turn cartwheels, do leaping somersaults and walk on his hands as well as the children over there. Oh, and he says he dances and plays the pipe also."

I had left my old pipe and tabor behind at Matthew's, but I supposed one could be bought somewhere here. In the meantime . . .

"Growch darling, come over here." But he had found some scraps under a table and was discussing their ownership vigorously with a couple of village curs. I dragged him away.

"What d'yer wanna do that for? Got 'em on the run, I 'ad—"

"Listen to me a moment! I'll buy you all the supper you want if you'll do me a small favor. Do you remember . . ." and I reminded him of our past performances, and tried to get him interested in some more immediate ones.

"Not on yer life! Right twit I used ter look, all ponced up in ribbons an' fings! Said then 'never again' I said. . . ."

"You never did!"

"Said it to meself. Never break a promise to yerself." And he scratched until the fur flew.

"Right. Have it your own way. But the only way we can buy supper—slices of juicy meat with lots of crackly skin, nice crunchy bones filled with marrow—is by earning some money performing here and now."

He hoofed out his left ear, looked at his paw and licked it. "Well, what you goin' ter do, then?"

What indeed. I didn't sing or play their music and couldn't stand on my head.

Ky-Lin spoke softly in my ear. "How about a little magic?"

"Real magic? How?"

"What they will believe is magic. How about a talking dog?"

"Growch?"

"Who else? Listen . . ." and he outlined a scheme so beautiful in its simplicity that I felt at once optimistic. We crept around a corner to rehearse.

I thought I foresaw a difficulty.

"How can I announce us and also name the objects when I don't speak a word of their language?"

"Simple!" said Ky-Lin. "Mime. I'll speak the words and you just open and shut your mouth and wave your arms about. Listen!" and all at once in my ear came my own voice, echoing my persuasions to Growch awhile back. This was followed by a rapid speech in the language of the country. As he was sitting on my shoulder it was like having an echo to the earlier part. "Convinced?"

With a little more practice it might just work. After all, they could only boo and jeer and turn us out of the village if they didn't like us, and we'd be no worse off. . . .

"Well," I said, patting my stomach, "I haven't eaten so well for weeks!"

"Very palatable," said Ky-Lin, licking the remains of the honey from his antennae.

"Good, good, good!" grinned a greasy-faced Tug, and belched—a habit which seemed to be the polite way to express appreciation in his country. "Do again, more money, more food . . ." He belched again.

"Growch? Are you satisfied?"

But a snore was the only answer. His stomach was so distended with rice, pork, beans and pancakes that it shone like a pink-gray bladder through the thinner hair of his belly. A couple of fleas scurried through the curls quite clearly. Oh, Growch! Still he had done a great job this evening: so had they all.

I curled up on my pallet in the small back room we had hired for the night and let the images of our performance dance behind my closed eyelids, secure in the comfortable discomfort of a just-too-full stomach and the consciousness of a pouch full of small coins . . .

"Illustrious villagers, fathers of industry, mothers of many, older folk with the wisdom of the years, youngsters who will grow strong and tall as their ancestors . . ."

"Move your mouth a bit more," whispered Ky-Lin. "It looks more authentic."

We should have to practice this more; still in the torchlight it probably didn't look too bad.

"Tonight we bring you, from the far corners of the world, an entertainment to delight and mystify. You will see marvels of agility from a prince of his people, feats of intelligence from a dog who learnt his wisdom from the Great Masters of the East, and finally an act so mind-bending that you will be telling your children's children of it for years to come. . . ."

It was strange to hear my voice ringing strong and confident, translating the words I gave Ky-Lin in a whisper into the local language. It was the showman's spiel, of course, used throughout the world with only local variations. Grab the attention of your audience, flatter them, then give them an inflated idea of the acts they were about to see, and provide the performers with exotic backgrounds for greater wonder and appreciation.

Puff the acts as they appear and keep the best till last, for that is how your audience will remember you when the bowl comes round for the coins. In this way Tug did his acrobatics, Growch his tricks. Then came the part I was dreading: if it failed we would be laughed out of town.

But it hadn't, the dear Lord be praised! In fact it had gone better than expected. After an introduction, explaining what we intended to do, Tug had moved among the audience borrowing an object here, another there. These he showed to Growch one by one, and the dog had then trotted over to where I sat with my back turned and "told" me what each object was with barks and yips, Ky-Lin, tucked up in my hood, correctly identifying the objects as Tug showed them to Growch. I then made a great thing of rising to my feet and pretending to consider what the dog had "told" me, Ky-Lin eventually announcing it in my voice. To add verisimilitude I had once or twice pretended that I hadn't understood, and made Growch repeat his noises with a little variation, till he had informed me he was giving himself a headache. . . .

Sleepily I began to plan ahead. If we could polish up the act a little, were sure of finding enough audiences, then we should not only not have to worry about money, but could afford some costumes: the more profitable you looked, the more likely you were to attract more money and greater respect.

It may have been the unaccustomed feast that lay uneasy on my stomach, but when I finally did fall asleep it wasn't of our better fortunes that I dreamt: it was of a poor tormented bear, dancing an eternal jig to a screech of pipes, his nose bleeding and his feet sore. . . .

From then on the travelling, though not perfect, became more tolerable. Our first "take" lasted until our next, more polished performance in a larger village. That one not only filled my pouch, but provided a bright costume for Tug (he wanted to wear it all the time) and ribbons for Growch (who never wanted them at all). Now we could afford a lift to the next villages and if, when we got there, they were too poor to pay us in anything except a bowl of rice and a room for the night, then that was all right too. We were moving in the right direction as Suleiman's map showed and my Waystone confirmed.

The only drawback was that the weather was worsening; it was now late fall and we were travelling towards the northerly cold as well. Every now and again a flurry of sleet bore down on the winds, and a chill breath lay over the early mornings. In the countryside the harvests of rice and grain were safely gathered, fodder for the wintering beasts stacked and fruits dried, cheeses stored. The peasants knew that their food had to last until spring so there was little enough to spare for travellers, even if they could pay. One could not eat coin, but two handfuls of rice saved meant another day's bellyful.

As we travelled farther, rumors began to trickle back about a great celebration to be held in one of the principal cities of the province. Ky-Lin (who listened to everything about him) reported that the second and favorite son of the ruler was to be married amid great pomp and ceremony.

"They say it will be a sight no man should miss. There will be enough food and drink to feed the whole city free for a week, and entertainments are to be held day and night. It is also said that those who have such entertainments to offer will be doubly welcome and paid accordingly."

"It might be just a rumor. You know how these things get exaggerated by hearsay."

He waved his plumed tail. "True, but judging by the consistency of the tales, I think we can safely say that there is to be a marriage, there will be celebrations and possibly entertainers would find it worth their while to attend."

"Is it far out of our way?"

"A little perhaps, but that should be outweighed by the fact that as we go towards the city more lifts will be available. The same after the celebrations, for everyone will disperse to their homes again, and that will include those who travel our way. It should bring us nearer Tug's people."

"Can we wait for a day or so more? Just in case . . ."

But it seemed that Ky-Lin was right. The roads became suddenly more crowded; not only with the usual traffic but with other entertainers and even a more prosperous traveller or two, able to afford his own transport, and they were all moving in the same direction. Now we were joined by caravans carrying goods and provisions, and it became more difficult to find food along the way, so we took to carrying and cooking our own, it having been tacitly decided that we would take our chances with the rest travelling to the celebrations.

Along the way we met other entertainers we had come across before—the father with his acrobatic children, two or three jugglers, a sword swallower. Also on the road were cages of exotic animals: I saw two lions, large apes, a striped horse and huge, comatose snakes. And then, in a largish village some seventy miles short of our destination, we came across the dancing bear again.

For once I had managed to secure a room for us in a ramshackle house on the edge of town, but at least it was shelter from the cold. The proprietor had also provided a reasonable meal of rice and vegetables, with even a bit of meat thrown in. It had been a miserably wet, windy day's travelling, but the rain let up in the evening, and we decided to take a stroll, having no intention of wasting a show on such an inclement night, but wanting to see if anyone else was desperate enough to try it.

As I thought, most houses were already tight-shuttered for the night, just a chink of light from their lamp wicks floating in saucers of oil to show they were occupied, and even these would soon be dowsed to save the precious fuel. It wasn't till we came to the ubiquitous square that we saw others had braved the weather. This village boasted the equivalent of a town hall, and on its steps lounged a couple of the village law enforcers, stout cudgels in their hands. In the square itself were half a dozen men, two women and about twenty children, watching the antics of a second-class juggler and a magician whose tricks were of the simplest. The juggler, a thin man with long, yellowed teeth, dropped his last few sticks, grimaced, and, picking up the single coin that had been dropped, disappeared down a side street. The magician continued to pull his colored scarves, open and shut his "magic" boxes, but now all eyes went to another attraction: the bear had emerged with his keeper, the latter obviously well away on rice wine.

The creature looked worse for wear than ever; he was shabbier and thinner than when I had seen him last, and his fur now stuck up in spikes from the soaking he must have got earlier that day. His owner was in a foul mood as well as being too drunk even to play his pipes properly. The worse he played, the more he jerked on the chain that ended at the bear's nose as it refused to respond, even kicking it with his heavy boots till it grunted in pain. A couple of the village curs decided to join in, nipping at the bear's heels till it roared in pain; the owner struck it on the nose with his pipe, the crowd jeered and the bewildered creature dropped to all fours.

The ring on my finger was throbbing, and I could bear the cruelty no longer. I started forward, but Ky-Lin hissed in my ear: "Wait! oh impatient one, wait a little longer."

"We must *do* something!"

"We will. Just be still. . . ."

Eventually the torture stopped. No coins were forthcoming, the dogs found something else to distract them and the bear owner gave a last cruel twist to the chain and led the beast off.

"Now we follow," said Ky-Lin, "if you still wish to help."

"Of course!" But how, I wondered.

We followed them at a discreet distance right to the outskirts of the village, where there was fifty yards or so of open land till thick wood crowded in. The bear and his keeper disappeared into the trees. With open ground to cover we were threatened with discovery.

"I'll go," said Growch. "See what 'e's up to. You wait 'ere."

Five minutes later he was back. "Anchored the bear to a rock in a clearin'," he reported. " 'E's on 'is way back. Better clear out."

We made our way back to our lodgings, but I couldn't settle.

"Can't we take him some food or something? The poor thing was starving." In a corner of our room, also used as a storeroom, there was a pile of root vegetables. I picked out two or three. "These'd do; I'll pay for them in the morning."

Ky-Lin thought for a moment. "We need a clear field," he said at last. "No interruptions. I think I can arrange that. Follow me. . . ."

At a little smoky eating house we found the bear keeper, seated on a stool, arguing with the two law keepers we had seen earlier. They were not inclined to argue back, I could see that, but Ky-Lin had a little magic at his disposal. I heard him chuntering away to himself, and a moment later the stool on which the bear keeper sat collapsed under him, he grabbed at one of the law keepers for support and the pair of them crashed to the floor, fists flying. In a moment the other man had joined in, and the upshot of it all was one rebellious bear keeper dragged away to the village's small lockup to spend the night.

"How did you do that?" I asked Ky-Lin, as we hurried off to feed the bear.

"All matter has its own composition; it just needed disarranging a little," he said, which I didn't understand at all.

Growch led us across the waste ground, littered with rubbish and odds and ends, and through the scrub to a path between the trees, now faintly illuminated by a quarter moon.

"Down 'ere a bit. You'll 'ear 'im afore you sees 'im, more'n like."

I had thought it was the moaning of the wind in the trees, but it was a voice, made clear and stark by the ring on my finger, throbbing once more in time with my heart.

"Oh me, oh my, how miserable I be! How I hurts, how I stings! How dark is the world, how drear . . . I be hungry, I be wet, I be cold! I long to be dead, dead or back in the land that gave me birth. My hills and forests, they call out to me. . . ."

" 'E's mad!" breathed Growch. "Stark, starin' . . . Don' go too near 'im, girl!"

In the clearing, chained to a rock, the bear was weaving his own kind of dance. Moonlight dappled his shabby fur as he swayed from front to back, his paws leaving the ground one after the other and back again, his head swinging from side to side, his eyes crazed and red.

Strangely I felt no fear, and my ring was comforting. I stepped forward and placed the roots on the ground in front of him, then stepped back again. "Food for you, Bear," I said slowly and clearly.

But the animal still swung back and forth, his eyes glazed, his jaw dripping spittle. I went forward again, and this time, in spite of an anguished squeal from Growch, I gripped the dripping muzzle firmly in my hands. "Stop it! We are friends. We have come to free you. . . ."

Gradually he stilled, and a pair of small black eyes looked straight up at me.

"Who are you?"

"A friend." I brought the ring close to his eyes. "We have come to help you."

"How? But how?" The head started swinging again. "I am chained, chained forever! Nose hurts, but keeps me chained . . ."

I hadn't thought about the chain. "Ky-Lin?"

A tiny sigh. "If I thought what I thought just then it would put me back another twenty points. . . . But I'm not going to think it. I am here to help. Now, listen: it is time for a little more magic. This time both yours and mine."

"How? I have no magic. . . ."

A patient sigh. "Of a sort. Just do as I say." He leaned over my shoulder and a tiny puff of smoke escaped his nostrils and drifted towards the bear. A moment later the beast's eyes closed, its head drooped. "He's asleep. Take out your Waystone and stroke it round and round the nose ring—no questions, just do as I ask. That's it: one hundred times, no more, no less. Are you counting?"

A minute, two, three. "Ninety-nine, one hundred. Now what?"

"Hold me close to the nose ring. . . ." There was a *ting* of metal and the ring snapped. "Twist it out of his nose." The chain fell to the ground, the bear opened his eyes and blinked. "Alteration of matter twice in one night: amazing! Just pass your Unicorn's ring across his nose: it'll ease the pain."

The bear was free: groggy, but free. I stepped back and breathed more easily. "Eat the food and then get yourself back to your hills or forests," I said. "Good luck, Bear!"

I was just going to ask Ky-Lin how on earth the Waystone had anything to do with snapping the ring in the animal's nose when I tripped over Growch who had stopped suddenly on the path back to the village. He growled menacingly.

I gazed ahead: nothing unusual. "One of these days you'll give me heart failure," I said. "Move over—"

It was then I screamed. Without any warning a heavy hand clamped down on my shoulder, a voice hissed in my ear.

"Got you! Thought you'd escaped me, didn't you? Well, you can think again. . . ."

Chapter Eleven

It was just as well I had no pressing need to relieve myself. I leapt away, Growch growling, Tug cursing, but it was a moment longer before I recognized the shabbily dressed figure.

"Dickon!"

"The same, my girl! I've had the devil's own job finding you, although at the end you left enough clues with your playacting—"

"But why? Why did you follow us? I told you—"

"A pack of lies! *I* know where you're bound, and why! I'm just not going to let you get away with it, that's all! I don't know whether you're in league with Matthew Spicer, or that darkie fellow Suleiman, or whether you're working on your own, but either way I'm going to be a part of it."

"Part of what? Oh Dickon! You're not thinking we're after treasure, are you? I tell you, there's no such thing!"

"You have maps. On it is the legend 'Here be Dragons.' And where there are dragons there is treasure. Everyone knows that!"

"Oh, you silly boy!" I said wearily. "If you could read a bit more you would know that all mapmakers put that when the terrain is unknown. It's their excuse, don't you see?"

"Then why are you headed that way? What's in it for you? What would drag you halfway round the world unless it was a fabulous treasure?"

"That's my business," I said. "Now why don't you leave us all alone and go back where you came from?" I was so utterly fed up with his sudden appearance that had I had a magic wand I would have waved him away to perdition. "I'm leaving, and I don't want to see you again."

His hand snapped down on my wrist. "Not so fast! I'm not letting you— Ow! Let go! Summer . . ."

"You want me to kill?" asked the bear, whom I had completely forgotten. On his hind legs he was taller than any man I knew, and he held Dickon against his chest as easily as I would hug a doll. I thought he had eaten his roots and disappeared, but it seemed he was trying to repay me for his freedom.

"No, no!" I said hastily. "You can let him go. Thank you just the same. He is no threat, just a bloody nuisance."

"You sure?" He sounded disappointed.

"I'm sure." I went forward to help Dickon to his feet, for the bear had dropped him pretty hard on his rear. "Get up, Dickon, and be on your way."

He scrambled to his feet. "You can communicate with that—that beast? I realized when I saw you all that time ago that you had some sort of rapport with the other animals, especially that flying pig of yours, but I thought it was just good training. But that—that Thing," and he nodded in the direction of the bear, now busy polishing off the roots I had brought him, "He's new to you, surely?"

"Best I've ever tasted," mumbled the bear. "Best I've ever tasted. My, oh my, oh my!"

I suppose I hadn't thought about it. My ring could give me access to animal communication, but this time I had just "talked" to the creature without prior reasoning. Well, it had worked.

"Yes," I said. "We can understand one another."

"Well, tell him to disappear," said Dickon, brushing himself down. "You've set him free, I saw you unlock his chain, but that's that, isn't it? Come on, let's get back to that room you've hired. I've got to talk to you. It's important."

To whom? I wondered. It meant that I couldn't get rid of him immediately, not if he had been following us so close he even knew where we lodged. I supposed the least I could do was explain once more and give him a few coins to speed him on his way. The trouble was, he had a very persuasive tongue. . . .

"Very well. You go ahead, you obviously know where it is. I'll just see this creature on his way. Growch, you go with him." I didn't want him searching my baggage again.

I turned to the bear, now cleaning his mouth with his paw of any residue of root.

"All better now? Good. Now you are free, free to go wherever you please. Your master is locked up for the night, but you had better get going so he doesn't catch you again. Why don't you go back home?"

The bear turned puzzled eyes towards me. "Home? Home many, many, many treks away. Not sure where to find. You help."

"Oh dear!" said Ky-Lin. "I should have guessed as much. Sorry, girl."

"What that?" said Bear, his scarred nose questing the air. "Demon?"

Ky-Lin showed himself and Bear seemed suitably impressed. "Good demon."

"I'm afraid he is of limited intelligence," said Ky-Lin for my ears only. "Probably taken too soon from his parents, and the treatment he has suffered would make it worse."

I felt that at any moment I should have a headache.

"Don't you have any idea which way is home?" I asked wearily.

He settled down on his haunches, closed his eyes and began to recite. "Long times ago, cub with sister. Hunters come, kill mother, take cubs."

He stopped, and his head began to sway from side to side again. "First treat good, feed well. Then hot stones to burn feet, make dance. Tie up with chain to stand high. Pipe make squeak, dance, dance . . ." and now his whole body was swaying, his paws leaving the ground rhythmically, one after the other. "Ring through nose, much pain. Sister lie down, not get up any more. Aieee, aieee!" and he lifted his muzzle and roared in pain and anger.

"Hush, now!" I was scared we were making too much noise. "No more pain. You'll find home soon. . . ."

"How? Bears not see good longways. Know from that way," and he nodded west. "Mountains. Trees. Streams. Caves. Honey, roots, grubs. Mother, warm, milk, play, sister, love . . ."

That did it. Love is so many things.

"If we show you the way to go?"

"Lose way without help. You help, Bear help. Show you where is honey, roots." He smacked his lips. "Bear find caves to sleep. Bear protect. Bear come with you."

I saw it was hopeless. "Very well. Bear come with us. First we find home for boy—" I nodded at Tug, who was keeping his distance, "—then we find your home. But we have little . . ." I hesitated, then drew some coins from my pocket. "We have little of these. They buy us food and lodging. You will have to forage for food."

"Is same as man get for dance—you want more? I dance for you. All eat well."

It was an idea, but we should have to move fast if we were to get away from his former master. If he wasn't chained we couldn't be accused of stealing him, I reckoned. I led the way back to our lodgings without meeting anyone. Perhaps the better for Dickon's peace of mind, Bear elected to sleep outside by the woodpile. I warned him to keep out of sight.

"If Bear want no see, no see."

Inside, Dickon had made up the fire in the brazier and was sitting on a stool nervously regarding Growch, who was perched like a hairy statue on top of the baggage. Part of his left lip was snagged back on a tooth, showing he had had occasion to snarl.

"Not very trusting, is he?" said Dickon, sucking the knuckles of his right hand.

"Depends. He takes his duties very seriously."

"I was just trying to be friendly. . . ." There were a couple of neat blue puncture marks on his hand.

"Friendly is as friendly does," said Growch. "Don' call it friendly when 'e puts 'is paw where 'e shouldn'."

I sat on the other stool, a sullen Tug crouched at my feet.

"Now, Dickon, what was it you wanted to say?"

He shifted uncomfortably. "It's a bit difficult. You see, when I left the caravan, I—I sort of resigned."

"You *what*?"

"Chucked it in, said I wasn't going back. You see, I thought that when I found you—"

"Not that stupid business of a treasure again! If I've told you once, I've—"

"I know you have! I just don't believe you. I thought it was worth the risk."

"Well it wasn't! It was just plain stupid of you to throw all that away. Just look at you: where are all your fine clothes, your fancy haircut?" There must be a way out of this. "If I give you some travelling money and a note to Matthew, I'm sure he'd take you back."

"Why? You two got something special going? He'll take me back just to keep my mouth shut? Is that it?"

"I assure you, once and for all," I said through gritted teeth, "what I'm doing here has absolutely nothing whatsoever to do with Matthew Spicer. Quite the reverse, in fact."

"Well, I can't afford to go back, not now. I used all the cash I had in tracing you." He gestured at his rags. "Even had to sell my clothes. Got anything to eat? I'm starving! I'm also broke, and cold. Didn't reckon you'd use the river: clever, that." He stood up. "Thanks for offering some travel money, but how far do you think I'd get before winter caught up?" His tone changed; now it held a wheedling note. "Look, I'll accept all you say about not going after treasure, but you must see that you need me. You're going somewhere, that's plain, and presumably also coming back. So why can't I go with you? If it's no secret, then how can you possibly object? After all, you're only a girl, and you need a man to look after you. . . ."

"I seem to have managed all right so far with Tug and Growch. And now the bear has volunteered to join us." I stood up. "Going somewhere? Yes. I'm taking Tug back to his people, then finding Bear his home; after that, who knows? So, there's nothing in it for you except a lot of travelling with companions you have already found—unfriendly. What's more, we just can't afford you. Back there you spoke the language, you had experience of the routes; here, you're less than we are. We have to work our passage and we have enough mouths to feed already."

"I can work!"

"Doing what? Standing on your head, walking on your hands, turning cartwheels? Or would you fancy a bit of mind reading? Oh, come on, Dickon!"

"No, no, no! Don't be silly, I've seen your act twice—just waiting a good moment to approach you—and I think you could do with someone more polished to choose the objects from the audience. We could establish a code, you and I; if I said 'what have we here?' it could mean a scarf; 'what is this?' a piece of jewelry—"

"Don't be silly! If you spoke in our language folk would believe you were telling me straight out what was in your hand, and you don't speak their tongue. Besides, I don't need your code; Growch manages quite well to tell me what Tug has in his hand. If you've seen us perform you'll know how it works."

"Stuff and nonsense! That cur wouldn't know how to describe—a spectacle case, for instance, or an embroidered purse, whatever primitive language you have going between you. I've seen you identify things like that, so, how do you do it? Mirrors? And where did you learn the language? They seem to understand you."

So he didn't know our secrets, didn't know about Ky-Lin.

"I don't need mirrors; I am told exactly what Tug holds up—by magic."

"Rubbish! No such thing. You can't kid me. It's all a trick, albeit a damned clever one."

I shrugged. "Think what you like. . . . So, what else could you do?"

"Manage the bear. With a bit more training, it'd—"

"He."

"He, then. I'm not in the business of sexing bears. *He* could learn a few more tricks, and we'd—"

"He doesn't like you."

"A bear on a chain doesn't have to like you. . . ."

"He's not on a chain, and he's never going to wear one again."

"Then how are you going to control him? He's vicious, you know."

"He's as gentle as—a lamb. Just a bit bigger, that's all."

"And the rest! That creature isn't safe! You can't control it with—"

"Him!"

"—a softly, softly approach. Now if you'd just let me have a go—"

"No!"

"Why not? We'd increase our profits, buy new clothes, even could hire a wagon to travel in; you'd like that, wouldn't you?"

All of a sudden he had become a part of the "we". . . .

"Of course I would," I said. "But I've freed Bear and in return for trying to find his homeland, he has already agreed to work with us. I don't know yet just what form this will take, but no way will I have a chain put back on him, or try and coerce him into something he doesn't want to do. He's suffered enough."

He looked at me for a long moment, but I couldn't read his expression. Then he looked away and shrugged his shoulders.

"Have it your way. I still think I could be an asset. Let me travel with you for, say, a couple of days: after that, if I don't prove my worth, we'll say farewell. Fair enough?"

"And if I don't agree?"

"I'd follow you anyway. And you wouldn't like any disruption to your plans, would you?"

That sounded like a veiled threat. Welcome me into the bosom of your little family, otherwise I'll throw firecrackers at the bear, interrupt your mind-reading sessions and tell everyone you're a girl. . . .

If I'd had more time to think, had considered how Ky-Lin could perhaps have come up with a better solution, I probably wouldn't have caved in so easily. As it was I was too tired to argue.

"Two days, then. We're off at dawn. Walking—until of course your grandiose schemes come to pass," I added nastily.

He had never been one to recognize sarcasm. Instead he beamed, giving me a glimpse of the handsome lad he had become, in spite of the rags.

"Thanks. I sort of thought you might see it my way eventually. We'll make a great team, you and I, Summer. You want to get ahead in the world, make some money, then I'm your man. You're really quite an attractive girl in your own fashion and if you let your hair grow and—"

"Have you eaten?" I was furious at his condescension. "Here you are!" I flung a couple of coins in his direction. "Don't disturb us when you come back. I'm sorry there isn't another blanket, but you could always go outside to the woodpile and curl up with Bear!"

But as it happened he did wake us, and that long before dawn.

I heard someone stumbling around, knocking over a stool, treading on my foot, groaning. It must have been around four in the morning, and I reckoned he must have spent most of his money on rice wine and was too drunk to keep quiet. Sitting up, I unwrapped myself and lit one of the oil lamps.

"Can't you keep quiet?" I hissed. "Some of us are—why, whatever's the matter? Are you sick?"

Even by the scanty light I could see his face had a greenish cast, and he was swaying from side to side, wringing his hands.

He shook his head, less in negation than in what seemed an effort to clear it of some awful memory.

"No, no, it's nothing like that. . . ." Even his voice was different: he sounded like a child afraid of the dark.

"Then, what? Here, sit down before you fall down. I've got some water—"

He waved it away. "No thanks. It's just that . . . I've never seen . . . Oh, Summer, it was terrible! You wouldn't believe—" and to my complete consternation he broke down and wept noisily. "We must get away, now!"

All animosity forgotten, I went over and laid a hand on his shoulder. "Tell me. Take your time, but I want to know. . . ."

I held my lantern high over the form of the sleeping bear, curled into a ball like any domestic cat, paws over his nose and snoring a little.

"Wake up, Bear," I said. "Time to go."

He opened his small black eyes, blinked, yawned and stretched. "Why go in dark? Wait till sun."

"No, Bear; we move now. Village not safe anymore. There are—there are men who seek to hurt you. Come, quick: we are ready."

"You say go, we go." He lumbered to his feet and had a good scratch, his loose skin moving up and down as if it were an extra coat. "Why men want to hurt Bear? Bear not do wrong. . . ."

No, Bear, I thought: you wouldn't think it wrong. To you it was the law by which you had been taught to live.

Dickon had told me how a man had come stumbling into the eating house where he had been sitting, yelling and shouting, pointing down the street towards the thatched hut where the bear owner had been imprisoned overnight. The clientele had all streamed out and followed the man to a terrible sight. The flimsy thatch on the low roof had been torn away, and inside lay the prisoner, the skin flayed from his back, his throat chewed open.

No, Bear, I said to myself again, you didn't do wrong. But I watched with a squeeze of horror in my heart as the animal completed his toilet by licking the last of the dried blood from his claws.

Chapter Twelve

We made the best speed we could that day and the next, but to my great relief no one seemed to have followed us. There was no reason why they should, of course; they would assume that the bear had killed his master and then fled into the wilderness. All the same, I didn't want anyone to see the animal until I had changed his appearance a little. To that end he had a thorough wash and brush and, at Ky-Lin's suggestion, I used some wood dye to darken his mask and paint a broad stripe down his back, like a badger's. In truth though, washing and brushing and good food made more alteration than anything else: after a few days I doubt anyone—even his old master—would have recognized him.

The thought of what he had done still gave me shivers, but once again it was Ky-Lin, the creature who could not even bend a blade of grass, who understood better than I.

"He is a child," he said. "In his last incarnation he was probably a neglected baby never taught right from wrong and died before he learnt. The Great-One-Who-Understands-All would not blame him. He has a chance now to learn from us that we all owe each other something and that includes living together in a social harmony. He was just removing something that had hurt him—like you humans think nothing of swatting a wasp."

I managed a weak smile. "Wasps don't sting you," I said. "They wouldn't dare!"

He fluffed out his plumed tail. "The colors put them off," he said, perfectly serious. "Besides," he added: "Like your Son-of-God, we are taught to turn the other cheek. One good thing has come out of this."

"What?"

"The bear's owner has been sent away before he can compound his crimes. Perhaps the Great One will bring him back as a bear, so that next time he will have learnt and will be redeemed to a higher plane."

I didn't feel I was competent to enter into a religious discussion with Ky-Lin; all I was grateful for was that Bear was gentle and sweet-tempered with us, and willingly cooperated in perfecting our act.

Tug did his acrobatics first, then Bear ambled in, wearing a soft red collar I had made for him, decorated with little bells. Tug coaxed a weird tune or two out of the pipe I had bought for him, the bear danced and when he had finished dropped to all fours. Tug climbed on his back with a shivering, eyes-tight-shut-all-the-time Growch in his arms. Bear rose to his hind legs as Tug climbed up his back and, having perfect balance, the boy stood on the bear's shoulders, holding Growch aloft as Bear slowly clapped his paws together. Needless to say, the only one who needed persuasion, bribes and petting, was Growch.

"S'not dignified," he said, "for the star performer, the talkin' dog, to be 'ung up in the air like so much washin'. 'Sides, makes me all dizzy!"

"But just listen to the applause," I said slyly. "How many of your kind do you know that could be as brave? And just look at all the fine meals we're having, and all because of you. . . ."

After that he didn't grumble as much, but he still kept his eyes tightly shut.

I kept Ky-Lin a secret from Dickon still, and although the latter now took over the job of selecting trinkets from the audience for me, dressed in a multicolored costume I had sewn from scraps of colored silks and cottons I had bargained for, he was still mystified at my "guesses," as he called them.

For the most part Ky-Lin lived either in the lining of my jacket or in the hood of my cloak, though if we had a room to ourselves at night, he would come out and prance around like a tiny pony, all fluffed up and full of energy. Separate rooms were becoming an increasing problem, though, as we neared the city. At most, with the increasing traffic, we were making only a few miles a day, and accommodation in the villages we rested at was becoming difficult to find, bespoke by those who came first. Sometimes we were lucky, sometimes not.

On one of the luckier occasions we were only twenty miles short of the city: we tried the houses on the edges of the village first and, just as it started to rain—a rain that would last for two, soaking days—we found a widow woman willing to rent us her house.

Through Ky-Lin I learned that her daughter-in-law was expecting her first and had taken to her bed, so the woman was going to keep house for her son till the baby appeared. It was less costly to hire than I thought, and I asked Ky-Lin (who had done the bargaining in my voice) just why.

"I told her that on the third day from now she would be nursing a fine, healthy grandson on her knee."

"Wasn't that chancing it a bit? Supposing it arrives tomorrow and it's a girl?"

"It won't and it won't be."

I opened my mouth and shut it again. By now I was learning not to question Ky-Lin: he was always right.

We spent a restful night. The house, if you could call it that, had a largish room, partitioned off by a screen to make a living and sleeping area. Outside was a woodshed, where Bear was comfortable enough. I lit the small brazier and cooked a meal I had sent Dickon out for: ubiquitous rice, beans, and some vegetables. Out of respect for Ky-Lin I kept our consumption of meat to a minimum (except for Growch). Him I kept content with a huge ham bone I had been saving, and Bear was perfectly happy with beans and some pancakes I made.

In the morning it was still raining, so I decided to do some sewing. I thought that my cloak, warm and comfortable as it was, needed tarting up a little for our performances, so had sketched a design of a blue dragon I had seen on a broken-down temple, bought a piece of sky-blue silk and now settled down to cut it out.

Suddenly I felt a cold breath touch my cheek, as though sleet had been chucked in my face. At the same time my ring stabbed like a pinprick and my stomach throbbed in sympathy. I had a vision of great mountains, like those that marched alongside our daily travels, but these were much nearer, rearing up until they filled the sky, the snow glittering on their sides, their tops clouded by the spinning of wind-driven flakes like a permanent veil. I saw a blue dragon, I saw a black dragon—

"Whassa matter?" said Growch. "Look like you seen a ghost. . . . Hey, you all right? That ol' stummick again? Too many of those black beans; been fartin' meself all mornin'."

"Nothing to do with the beans," I said, by now doubled over in pain, "I'll be better in a moment. . . ."

But I wasn't. It was worse by the minute, like I used to get with my monthly show, only sharper.

Ky-Lin whispered urgently in my ear. "Send Dickon out for a drink. Tell him you have woman's trouble and wish to be alone for a while. He'll go if you give him some coin: the rain's eased off a bit."

I gave him enough to get drunk twice over, and dragged myself off to my pallet in the partitioned part of the room. I heard Ky-Lin speak to Tug, and a moment later the boy had brought in both the little oil lamp and our own stronger lantern.

"Lie down," said Ky-Lin. "Take your clothes off and lie under the blanket—"

"Tug?"

"He has known all along you were a girl. You washed him once in a river, so he says, and you all got so wet your outline was unmistakable. He's never questioned it: I need him now to help me. Don't worry: it means nothing to him at his age."

"It hurts," I whimpered like a child.

"Not for long," and he spoke to Tug, and a moment or two later one of the opium pills I had kept in my pouch, just in case, was pushed into my mouth, followed by a draught of cool water.

I undressed with difficulty and lay on my back, as instructed by Ky-Lin. Then I was told to rub my ring in a circular movement round my navel, and whether it was the pill or that, or both, the pain diminished and I felt sleepy and relaxed. I began to fantasize. I saw again the cottage where I was born, the forest and river where I played as a child; I could taste the honey cakes my mother gave me, remembered the little church where the mural of the Last Judgment faded gently on either side of the altar. A knight rode by, a handsome knight; a white horse gambolled in surf no whiter than she; I heard a tortoise rustle away into the undergrowth and the clap of a pigeon's wings; I was flying, and then suddenly the dream changed. A castle whose stones were stained with the sins before committed, a thin, wheedling voice: "Tell me a story. . . ."

"Gently, gently," said a voice in my ear. "Nearly over . . ."

I dreamt again. A dog was barking, his voice ringing through woodland; I flew once more, then crashed to the ground, bruised and breathless; waves dragged at my clothes, I was so cold, so cold—

No, it was only my stomach that was cold, numbing the pain. . . .

"Rest, rest, lie still. Remember the Place of Stones and what happened there a year ago today?"

Yes, yes, of course I remembered! I was looking for a pig, a large pig, who had disappeared. It was All Hallows' Eve, exactly a year since I had left home, and the air about crackled with mystery and magic. And then I had found my pig, my dearest pig, and had kissed him and suddenly there was a stranger in his place, a dark stranger—but no! it was a dragon, a black dragon with claws that could rend me in twain—

"Just a minute more . . ."

And the dragon was the stranger, no stranger, again. And he had enfolded me in his arms. He had kissed me, lain with me, and a hot flood of feeling had filled me like an empty skin waiting to be filled and the pain had been so exquisite that I had cried out—

"Aaahhh . . ."

But when I opened my eyes he was a dragon again and had flown away into the east, his shadow passing across the moon, and I was alone. . . .

A warm tongue caressed my cheek and my nose was filled with the smell of warm, hacky breath. "Better, Summer dear?"

But I wasn't Summer: I was Talitha. *He* had called me Talitha, and he was . . . he was Jasper, Master of Many Treasures.

"Wake up!" barked Growch.

"All over," said Ky-Lin. "No more pain."

I tried to sit up, but there was a sort of stitchy feeling in my stomach. Tug's hands raised my head, propped something behind it and fed me some welcome, warming broth. Then I was lying down again, a blanket tucked under my chin.

"You can sleep now," said Ky-Lin. "No more pain."

"But I don't want—"

"Yes, you do. In the morning you will feel wonderful. Just breathe deeply and I will give you some Sleepy Dust. . . ."

My mouth and nose were filled with the scent and taste of fresh spring flowers, summer leaves, autumn fires, winter snow. . . . I breathed it all in greedily until I was floating way up, up, up till I could touch the damp edges of the clouds and twist and turn with the screaming swifts. Ghost-like, I flew on silent wings with the owls, hung on the tip of a crescent moon, fell back into a bed of thistledown, a nest lined with the bellyfur of rabbit, a bed with down pillows—a hard pallet with a couple of blankets and someone shaking me awake.

"Hey! You going to sleep all day as well?"

"Oh, piss off, Dickon!" I said irritably. "I was having a wonderful dream. . . ."

"Well, you can't sleep all day! We're all hungry, and you've got the money. . . ."

And will have to cook it too, I thought. "How long have I slept?"

"You were asleep when I came back yesterday, you've snored all night, and it's around noon now."

Nearly twenty-four hours! Still, it was as Ky-Lin had promised: I felt wonderful, relaxed, happy—and now I came to think about it: very hungry.

"Is it still raining?" A nod. "Well give me a few minutes to get dressed and we'll go to the eating house. My treat."

It was while I was dressing that I discovered something wrong.

"Ky-Lin," I hissed. "What's this around my waist?"

"Just something to keep you warm," came the small voice from under my pillow. "Leave it there for the time being, there's a good girl." He must have sensed my indecision. "Have I ever given you bad advice?"

So I left it where it was. It didn't discommode me at all, but I was a little disconcerted to find out I had started my monthly flow again, which was annoying after so long without.

It stopped raining on the afternoon of the third day, and with the weak sun came the widow woman, almost crying with joy, the rent money held out for me to take.

"It is as I said," whispered Ky-Lin. "Now, open and shut your mouth as you do in our performances. I have something to tell her. . . ."

And to the openmouthed astonishment of Dickon, out came a soft stream of words from my lips and, for a moment hidden from all but the woman, Ky-Lin showed himself.

She fell to the floor and gabbled, the tears of joy streaming down her face, then bowed her way out of the door. Dickon picked the coins up and tucked them in his pouch.

"What was all that gibberish about?"

Luckily Ky-Lin had briefed me.

"It was a prophesy; her grandson will become one of the great sages of the country."

"Still don't know how you do it," he muttered. "However, a nice way of conning her out of the rent."

I bit back an angry retort. Ky-Lin whispered in my ear.

"Right, everyone," I said. "Time to go. We'll steal a march on the rest who have stopped over. With the roads empty we can make good time. Oh, Dickon: leave that money on the stool. Call it a present for the baby. . . ."

We made reasonable progress during the next couple of days, and on the second night, Dickon having gone out scouting the prospects for a performance, Ky-Lin made me lie down on the bed.

"I want to take the bandage off." He seemed uncharacteristically nervous; he had gone a shaky sort of blue color all over. "Let's have a look. . . ."

He spoke to Tug, who slowly and carefully unwound the cloth.

"Mmmm . . ."

"What's the matter?" I tried to sit up; my stomach felt cold.

"Nothing. Nothing at all." His color had returned to normal. "Take a look. . . ."

Sitting up, I gazed down at my stomach; at first I could see nothing and then—

"Hey, Summer! We've got a performance!"

Damn and blast and perdition! Hastily pulling my shirt down and my breeches up, I staggered over to the bolted door. Dickon burst in.

"There's a rich caravan just pulled in and they were enquiring about entertainment; Arabs and Greeks mostly, so you'll have to 'Magic' some of their language. . . ." He sniggered. Little did he know Ky-Lin!

"But it's full dark; must be near nine at night."

"They're camping in the square, 'cos there's no other accommodation. Plenty of light, torches, lanterns. They're being fed now, so we'd better hurry before they decide to kip down for the night."

It was past midnight before we returned to our quarters, but my pouch was full of coins. It had been a treat to have a relatively sophisticated audience, for it was a rich caravan, and they had insisted on us performing twice over. They had travelled from the south, with a special order for the wedding: gold and silver platters, silver-handled daggers and filigree jewelry, and were near two weeks late. Tonight would be their last stop, for with horses and camels they could make the city easily by the next day.

So they were relaxed and generous, and Ky-Lin's Arabic, Greek and a little Persian was impeccable. When we packed up Dickon obviously had a yen to go farther afield, so I gave him a generous advance, knowing full well he had also gathered tips on the way from the audience, and he disappeared for a while in search of his own entertainment.

Growch was on a high; one of the objects held up for my "discovery" had been one of his "fluffy bum" pups, and he had nearly let us all down at this point, completely forgetting to concentrate, even running over to the puppy and investigating.

"Keep your mind on the job!" I hissed at him when at last he reached me.

"Thought I 'ad—*my* job. Why I came, an' all. Boy pup: pity."

I was so tired when we returned that all I wanted to do was flop down on my pallet and sleep, but there was one other thing to do: look once more at my stomach. I thought I had seen—but no, it couldn't be. I lay down, lifted my shirt and peered down, aware out of the corner of my eye that Ky-Lin was watching anxiously. At first nothing, then—

What looked like a pearl nestled in my belly button. I touched it gingerly: it gave a little to my touch. I tried to prize it out—

"No! Don't touch it yet; it hasn't quite hardened." Ky-Lin had gone quite pale again, and was peering anxiously over my shoulder. "Give it a day or two more. . . ."

"But what *is* it?" It resembled nothing so much as a jewel one might stick in a belly dancer's navel. "And how in heaven's name did it get there?"

"Er . . . I put it there. For safekeeping. Nicely insulated. Warm . . ."

"*What is it?*"

"Actually—well, it's quite simple really. It's a dragon's egg."

Chapter Thirteen

"A . . . what?" I was already asleep; I must be.

"Egg. Dragon's. Not yet set," said Growch succinctly. "Leastways, that's what I thought 'e said." He didn't seem the least surprised or alarmed—but then it wasn't happening to him.

I attempted to laugh it off, all the time nursing a horrible feeling it wasn't a laughing matter. "If this is all a joke, it's not in very good taste. Now be a good creature and take it away, Ky-Lin, and I'll forget all about it."

"I can't 'take it away,' just like that," said Ky-Lin unhappily. "It's yours. Yours and—*his*."

I knew immediately who he meant, but wasn't going to accept what he said. It was impossible! That sort of thing just didn't happen; it couldn't.

"That was what was hurting you, giving you the stomachache. It was ready to come out for the second stage of its development," said Ky-Lin. "Don't ask me how, or why; I'm no expert in this sort of thing, and indeed I doubt it has ever happened before just like this. Humans don't mate with dragons. Normally dragons are bisexual: they can reproduce themselves. Theoretically so can Ky-Lins; that's what my name means: male/female. We never have, though."

I remembered the pain of that embrace by the Place of Stones: the pain and the ecstasy. Had we bypassed the natural laws, my man-dragon and I? Was this, this tiny pearl, still semisoft and shining, a product of a love that had never been seen before, just because I had kissed a creature and made him man, however temporarily?

I gazed down at my navel and, gently, so gently touched the shining pearl. Just in case . . .

"But it's so tiny!"

"Oh, it grows. A fully developed egg, ready to hatch, will be at least as big as a human baby. But, I warn you, this one could take many, many years—longer than you have—to grow and mature. You will never see what it contains. You are just its guardian, for a little while. So, don't get fond of it. Your job is to keep it warm, give it its first few weeks of incubation." He sighed. "You are very privileged."

I didn't feel the least bit "privileged": quite the reverse, in fact. I felt confused, hurt, bewildered, used, somehow *dirty*.

Ky-Lin read part of what I was thinking. "You truly are privileged, dear girl. You may not realize it now but that egg, however it got there, has been a part of you for a year, you nourished it in your body, and whatever happens to it in the future, you will always be a part of it. Also remember, it was created in love."

I looked down again; right now it was tiny, soft, vulnerable. Anyone could squash it, crush it, snuff the little life that lay inside. . . . Without conscious thought my hands curled protectively over my navel, and emotion took over from instinct, realizing ruefully that once more I had conned myself into caring for yet one more burden. Once before they had all been maimed in their separate ways; this time they were all more or less normal, even if they still had their particular needs—except Ky-Lin, of course, though even he was trying to gain extra points towards his redemption.

"And so we are lucky seven," said Ky-Lin happily. "You and I, Growch and Tug, Dickon, Bear and the Egg. Just as the Old One foretold."

I shivered and crossed myself; the Good Lord protect us all and bring us to a safe haven. . . .

Two days later we topped a rise and there lay the Golden City beneath us. They called it golden because the stone used was a warm, yellow sandstone, quarried from goodness knew where, because the surrounding hills and mountains were dark and forbidding. Right now, at midday, the sun made the whole place glow, picking out the various towers and steeples that were gilded with real gold, till the whole scene shimmered with warmth and welcome.

We had a steep descent, but beneath us a wide river curled around the east of the city, a river so wide I could see the boats, like beetles at this distance, scurrying about on the water. To the south the plain widened out, and I could see a wide field, with men drilling and horses being exercised.

It looked like a place full of promise, but it took all of three hours to reach the city gates, the road ahead being crowded to suffocation with caravans, carts, wagons, cattle, horses and travellers on foot like ourselves. Past experience made us head for the side streets once we had passed through the west gate; the city would be crowded already, and the best chance of accommodation was out of the mainstream. We were lucky; entertainers were at a premium, and although I had to pay more than I had reckoned, we found two ground-floor rooms with accommodation in a shed for Bear, breakfast and midday meal included.

After a plain but satisfying meal of rice, chicken, and fruit, we left Bear behind and decided to explore the city. By now it was dusk, and evening fires hazed the rooftops. There was already a chill to the air but it made no difference to those who, like us, were determined to make the most of all the city had to offer. The main streets were paved and bordered with fine buildings, but the streets radiating from the main square were full of bustle, crowd, and character.

The stalls were crammed with all the goods in the world, or so it seemed. Over glowing braziers meat, fish, glazed chicken wings, and nuts sizzled and popped and every available space was filled with beggars, jugglers, fortune-tellers (bones, water, sand, and stones), and pretty ladies plying their charms, which is how we lost Dickon.

The rest of us found ourselves in the huge main square, deserted now except for a few gawpers like us. Ahead of us lay the palace, a heterogenous mass of gilded roofs, towers, tilted eaves, and balconies, approached by wide steps guarded by soldiers in green and gold. Flares, torches and lanterns kept the whole facade brightly lit, and through the screened and fretted windows could be glimpsed figures scurrying to and fro.

"This square is where the main celebrations for the wedding will take place," said Ky-Lin, who as usual had been listening to everything going on around him. "During the next few days, palace scouts will seek out the best entertainers and they will be invited to perform here in front of the prince and his prospective bride."

" 'Ow they goin' to choose us, then?" asked Growch.

"They go around the streets and smaller squares, list those they prefer, then send others for a second opinion."

We had already come across some half-dozen of these smaller squares. "Do we keep to one or try as many as we can?" I wondered.

"More the better," said Ky-Lin. "That way we reach a wider audience and have a better chance of being noticed. Even if we aren't picked, we can at least earn some money. There are many very good acts here already, so we need to polish up our performances, make some new costumes, and I will provide some powders to burn that will give you a better light, sprinkled on torches. Can you walk on your hind legs, dog?"

" 'Course I can! Well, sometimes. A bit. I could try. . . ."

His legs were so short and his body so long, I sometimes wondered how his messages got from one end to the other. "That would be very nice," I said enthusiastically. "Worth an extra bone or two."

And he tried, he really did; at the end of two days he could stagger at least two yards. . . .

We made—I made—new costumes, we played the small squares and larger side streets from one end of the city to the other, and at the end of four days both Dickon and Ky-Lin recognized the same nonpaying faces at our performances.

Ky-Lin nodded his head in satisfaction. "Definitely scouts," he said.

In the meantime we had been making more money than in all our journey so far and I was perplexed as to where to keep it—by now a small sackful—safe. I daren't leave it in our rooms: quite apart from thieves I couldn't trust Dickon's sticky fingers, and it was Growch who suggested the solution. " 'Oo's the one they're all scared of? That great bear. 'E can guard it day-times, and when we give performances, 'e can 'ave it tucked under 'is arm or sumfin'."

Which solved the problem.

With only twenty-four hours to go before the grand entertainment we were visited in our lodgings by two palace officials, smartly dressed in gold jackets and green trews, who informed me (through Ky-Lin) that we had been picked to perform in the Palace Square the following evening. It was a great honor, as the acts were limited to thirteen, the Moons of the Year. We were allowed a half-hour only, to give time for all the other acts, so we practiced curtailing Tug and Bear and it made for a crisper performance, which we took round the streets that night, able to boast that we were one of the chosen ones for the following night. Our purse was heavier than ever that day.

Our actual performance seemed to be over before it began. We had to wait through performing ponies, acrobats, contortionists, a magician, and a woman who climbed a ladder of swords and lay on a bed of nails with a man standing on her chest, but eventually the large hourglass was set down again in the sand and it was our turn. By now I had worked myself into such a lather of expectation that I was trembling in every limb, my mouth was as dry as the sands of the desert and I desperately needed to relieve myself.

Once we started, however, I was as cool as a draught of cold water, even remembering to direct our act towards the balcony where the prince had his seat. They said afterwards that the prince, a sophisticated man, was bored by much he saw, but that his prospective bride, an ingenuous girl, clapped enthusiastically the whole way through. Be that as it may, each performance was rewarded by a bag of silver coins, good, bad or indifferent, and was cheered impartially by the large crowd penned behind rope barriers at the perimeter of the square.

There were many acts after ours, but I fell asleep through exhaustion, tucked up against Bear, and only woke when Dickon nudged me. The square was emptying, torches guttering and a chill wind blew away the detritus of the evening.

"Bed," said Dickon. "There are three days till the wedding and after tonight the audiences will pay even better. . . ."

But the morning was to bring a further surprise. Before the first cock had even cleared his throat, another official from the palace, this one with gold braid and tassels, presented us with an invitation to perform that evening within the palace confines themselves. Apparently the prince and his bride-to-be wished a closer look at some of the acts they had enjoyed the night before.

"We've cracked it!" exulted Dickon. "Can't you just see it? We can advertise ourselves as by royal command!"

It was an attractive idea, but I could see it would only complicate matters. As far as I was concerned I had places to go, people and animals to answer to, and that was enough. I didn't want more than would carry us to our next destination, but Dickon wanted it all: gold, prestige, fame.

"Are you coming, then?" asked Dickon.

"Coming? Where?"

"I've just been telling you. Outside the city, on the parade ground, they're having races, entertainments, wild animals. It's a day out. It's a *free* day out. All you want is money for some food. Or, take our own. Hurry up, or all the best vantage points will be taken."

We left Bear in the shed; as the winter advanced, although he had never been allowed his natural hibernation since he was a cub, he nevertheless became more lethargic, and was quite happy to be left guarding the money and snoozing the day away. I hoped that when, and if, we ever found his homeland, he would find a convenient cave in which to sleep every winter till spring.

The races and entertainment were held in the amphitheater to the south I had noticed on first looking down on the city. Cordoned off and edged with a low wall of stones, it was an oval, sandy space perhaps three-quarters of a mile in length and half that distance wide. Roughly marked out were four staggered lanes for foot or horse racing, and in the center a raised circle for wrestling. Seats there were none, but plenty of boulders and banked sand, so we made ourselves comfortable behind the ropes, knotted with colored cloths, that kept us from the tracks.

Heats of the footraces had already been run, and the finalists rested while the children of the city had their turn. All kinds were represented, from the silk-kilted privileged to the half-naked urchins, and it was one of the latter I was glad to see that won the junior race, two laps of the track, to bear a purse back to his delighted parents.

I could see that Tug, too, would have liked to participate, but we didn't know the rules, so I consoled him with sticky sweetmeats from a peddler's tray. There was plenty to eat—if you could afford it—for behind the crowd there were braziers frying and roasting all sorts of delights, and trays of cheeses, cakes, boiled rice, and fruit. The poorer people had brought their own food, but we were in a festive mood and nibbled away all afternoon, fortified by drinks of water, wine, or goat's milk from the skins of the sellers.

The day wore on. We watched the wrestling—which seemed to be a near-killing exercise of arms, feet, hands, teeth and nails—and applauded the finals of the footraces. Then came the chariot races; light, wicker-framed two-wheeled carts with two horses. There were plenty of thrills and spills, and special applause when the prince's charioteer won the top prize. Next was an exhibition of kite flying, great monsters of birds, flowers, giants, and dragons, but there was little or no wind, so these were a disappointment. We were about to pack up and go back to our lodgings to ready ourselves for tonight's performance, when there was a clamor from far across the field.

A distant thunder of hooves, a murmur from the crowd: "The Riders of the Plains!" and into the arena galloped a troop of wild-looking horsemen, riding even wilder horses. They circled the arena at an even faster pace, churning the sand into swirls of smoke, manes and tails flying, the horsemen uttering wild yells of encouragement until suddenly, with no apparent signal, they crashed to a rearing halt in the center, shouting what sounded like a battle cry to my untrained ears.

There was an eruption at my side and Tug sprang to his feet, his face alight with joy, his fists raised over his head in salute.

"My people, my people! They come. . . ." and he was gone, scrambling over rocks and people with abandon, to disappear into the amphitheater amid the melee of men, horses, sand and dust.

I called after him, but it was no use: he couldn't, or wouldn't, hear.

"Leave him be," whispered Ky-Lin. "He will be back. Just watch."

And watch we did, an unparalleled exhibition of horsemanship. Horses raced, apparently riderless, till their riders twisted up from under their bellies; one horseman balanced on the backs of two, three, four mounts at a gallop; they threw spears at targets as they raced past, hitting them every time; they leapt to the ground first one side, then the other, rode with their heads towards the horse's tail; they fought mock battles; they jumped—one, two, three men—onto the back of a galloping horse until we were exhausted just watching.

The crowd was as stupified as we were, then on their feet yelling for more.

And Tug? He was in the midst of it all. Running, riding, vaulting, balancing; handstands, yells, two hands, one hand, no hands . . . On the ground he was a rather awkward boy with bandy legs and a usually sullen expression; put him on a horse and he was transformed. I could see now that those bandy legs had been used to riding from the time he could toddle and saw from his face how much being back with his own kind meant to him. I didn't need the confirmation of his words when he finally climbed back to us, tattered, sweaty, and utterly happy.

"Found them! They mine . . . Go home!" He started to speak in the few words of my tongue I had taught him, but soon lapsed into his own language, and I was glad to have Ky-Lin's whispered translation. Dickon stood by, his face a picture of bewilderment, but Growch's tail was wagging furiously: he at least understood what was going on.

"My people come for prince's wedding: special invitation. Prince rides with us, in disguise. . . ." He pointed to a taller man, dressed as the rest, who was sneaking off the field. "His treat . . ." He waved his hand at the rest of the horsemen. "They are of my people, but not of my tribe, although they know of my father. He is chieftain. They return to our lands tomorrow, next day, before snows come and I will travel with them."

"If your father is chieftain, then you . . . ?" I asked through Ky-Lin.

"I am my father's first son, and will be chieftain when he dies."

So, I had rescued a prince among his people, this shabby boy who now squatted before me, took one of my hands in his and pressed it to his forehead.

"I shall always be in your debt," he said simply. "You bought my freedom, fed me and clothed me, treated me with kindness. I shall never forget you. And you, Great One," and he bowed in the hidden direction of Ky-Lin.

"Rubbish!" I said gruffly, conscious that I had difficulty in speaking. I ruffled his hair, just as if he were the young boy who had already shared our adventures, and not a young prince.

Dickon had finally picked up the drift of what was happening. "He's not going, is he? Not before the performance tonight, surely! In the palace, by special request, remember? You don't turn up only with half your act!" He looked scandalized. "Out here they could cut your head off for a thing like that—or at least chuck you in a dungeon and throw away the key. . . . Besides, just think of the money!"

In the excitement I had completely forgotten; although I did not believe we should be punished for turning up without Tug, it would certainly mean a revision of our act. I asked Ky-Lin to explain as best he could.

As we had been talking, we had gradually become surrounded by Tug's fellow countrymen, smelling strongly of horses and sweat. Smaller in stature than most, they were still a fearsome-looking lot, with their yellowish faces, high cheekbones, long hair, fierce eyebrows and drooping moustaches. Like Tug, they had black eyes and bandy legs. They shuffled closer, and I had the distinct impression that they were quite ready to kidnap Tug and carry him away if we had any intention of trying to keep him.

But Tug listened to what Ky-Lin had to say, shrugged his shoulders and nodded. Turning to his people he made a little speech, indicating us, then bowed quite regally in dismissal. The men glanced at each other, then, thankfully, bowed also and moved away.

"I have told them," said Tug formally, "that I have an obligation to fulfill, but shall join them later tonight. All right, Summer-Lady-Boy?" And he grinned, once more the boy I would always remember.

Returning to our lodgings, we washed and dressed in our costumes and made our way as previously directed to the side door of the palace, giving onto the kitchens, armory, stores, laundries, etc. We crossed the large, cobblestoned courtyard and were shown into an anteroom. Like the largest houses I had seen, this part of the building was strictly utilitarian. No fancy clothes, no elaborate decoration, everything meant for use. In the anteroom the other three acts were already waiting, obviously as nervous as we were ourselves. They became positively agitated when they saw Bear, however, and that coupled with the thought of bear droppings on the carpets, made me ask through Ky-Lin if we might wait in the courtyard.

It was chilly out there, so I walked over to one of the braziers to warm myself up. There were some half-dozen of these, crowded by off-duty soldiers, kitchen porters, and itinerants waiting for the scraps of the feast now taking place. Obviously they were still eating, for enticing smells were coming from the kitchens: behind the bland scents of rice and vegetables came the aromas of fish and meat, sharpened to a fine edge by the pungency of spices such as ginger and coriander. My stomach started to rumble, although we had all eaten before we came out. A couple of trays of saffron-colored rice full of niblets of dried fish were thrust out into the courtyard; you ate, if you were lucky, with your fingers: the beggars had brought their own bowls.

I managed a handful for Bear and Growch; one of the better-dressed beggars shouted at me, gesticulating to his friends.

"What does he say?" I asked Ky-Lin, passing him a grain or two of rice.

"Not to waste good food on animals. Just ignore him."

"It's just that—I'm sure I've seen him somewhere before. . . ."

"Where?"

I racked my brains, but came up with nothing; here, there, somewhere, I was sure of it. "I don't know. . . ."

"Well, don't worry about it: it's our turn next."

It must have been near midnight when we came out into the courtyard again, still dazed by the lights, music, dancing, gold, embroideries, costumes, decorations, plate, jewelry, and sheer opulence of all we had seen, touched, heard, smelled, in the last couple of hours. The inner reality of the palace was like something from a legend; pointless to wonder where the money had come from to create such luxury: to marvel and enjoy was enough.

In the vast banqueting hall in which we had been called upon to perform there were patterned marble floors, thick colored rugs, gilded pillars, painted walls and ceilings, embroidered cushions, long carved tables, a silver throne, and men and women guests wearing robes of silk and fine wools, heavily sewn with gold and silver thread and studded with jewels. The whole area was lighted to brilliance with oil lamps, torches and flares, the light reflected from vast sheets of brass, placed the best for catching the flames.

Behind painted screens musicians sighed and wailed on strings and woodwind, with the insistent drubbing of a tabor; there was a heavy scent of incense, sweet oils, of opium and hashish, both cloying and exciting at the same time.

The prince, on a silver throne, had been gracious enough to lead the applause for our act, but as an audience the rich guests could not have been more different from our credulous village spectators. There was a background murmur of conversation all the while, the applause was polite and it seemed there was more attention paid to eating and drinking than to the performance. It was not just us though: all the other acts were received in the same way, a restrained appreciation for something far beneath such a sophisticated guest list.

Still, the coins we were paid with this time were of gold. . . .

As we came out into the courtyard we all breathed in the clean, cold night air with relief. All but a couple of the braziers had been extinguished and someone was unfastening the heavy gates for us, just as a shout came from away to our left, and a figure ran at us, followed by a half-dozen others. I stopped, bewildered; it was the man I thought I had seen somewhere before, but now he was yelling out something over and over again. Ky-Lin hissed urgently in my ear: "Run, girl, run! Tell them all to run and hide. . . ."

"But why? What's he saying?"

"That's the man you thought you recognized; he comes from the village where Bear's former master was found dead. They are going to arrest you and Dickon on a charge of murder!"

Chapter Fourteen

I opened my eyes: nothing.

I shut them tight again, screwed them up, rubbed them with my knuckles, opened them again.

Nothing. Black as pitch.

If I wasn't so cold and it didn't hurt when I pinched myself, I might have thought I was still asleep and dreaming, or in that muddled half-awake situation children find themselves in sometimes when nothing makes sense. Once—I think I was six or seven at the time—I found myself trying to pull up the earthen floor of the hut in which my mother and I lived, in the mistaken belief that it was a blanket. I had fallen out of bed but the fall had only half woken me, so I thought I was still there. I remembered crying with the cold and frustration, then Mama had leaned over and plucked me to her side again, scolding me heartily for waking her. . . .

I wanted my Mama again, right now, scolding or no. I wouldn't have cared if she had thrashed me—the physical blows wouldn't have counted against the warmth of contact with another human—but she was long dead and I was alone, totally alone, in a mind-numbing darkness that froze my mind and made icicles round my heart.

I hadn't even got the comforting presence of Ky-Lin: he had disappeared together with the others.

In the confusion of that sudden attack in the courtyard we had all become separated. The gate was half-open, I had shouted a warning, and a white-faced Dickon had been first away, followed by a bewildered Bear. I felt Ky-Lin leap from my shoulder, heard Growch growling and barking at my feet and was conscious of Tug trying to fend off my attackers. Somebody had grabbed the boy by his jacket, but he twisted free and punched someone else on the nose. Growch had another aggressor by the ankle and was being shaken like a rat, and a guard tried to catch me by the hair.

"Run, you idiots, run!" I yelled. "Watch the gate!" Which was already being closed again. I started off for the narrow gap that remained; ten feet, five, four. My hands touched the thick oak, I pushed with all my might, Growch squeezed through, then suddenly I tripped, fell flat on my face and was immediately pinned to the ground by half a dozen men. Fighting to keep my head clear, I saw the gate clang to, followed by a flying leap from Tug, who seemed to run up the ten feet or so like a cat scaling a wall, to disappear over the top.

So at least Tug, Growch, Bear and Dickon had a chance of escape, although I had no idea of Ky-Lin's whereabouts. Knowing how violence of any kind was anathema to him, I wondered if he had hidden himself away somewhere; wherever he was, I could certainly have done with his help during the next hour or so.

I had been hauled into the palace again, but this time to a small windowless antechamber, in which I was ruthlessly questioned, my accuser and his friends pointing the finger of guilt; a senior palace official tried to get a statement out of me. Impossible, of course: without a translator we couldn't understand each other at all. In any case I was so bruised, battered and confused by now, that I doubt I could have said anything sensible in any language.

My brain seemed to have gone to sleep, and after three hours we had gotten nowhere. For the moment it seemed it was one person's accusation against my silence, for my accuser was treated no better than I; finally we were both marched along endless corridors, down steps, across a winding walkway and finally into what could only be the dungeons. Then we were separated: my accuser went one way, I went the other, to end up in front of a low, barred door. The bolts were drawn, the door creaked open and I was flung headlong onto a pile of filthy straw; the door clanged shut and the bolts were drawn with a dull finality. Something was shouted from outside, and the footsteps marched away, their sound to be smothered all too soon in the darkness of the thick walls.

The stench of the cell was terrible. At first after I got to my feet I wasted my breath calling and shouting, but the air was so thick my voice lost itself in the gloom, and there was no answer. Next I felt my way all around the cell—with, strangely enough, my eyes shut: it seemed easier that way—only to find it was empty of all but a rusty ring on one wall with a chain dangling from it and a small drain in the floor, presumably for excreta. I must have spent an hour trying to find a way out, but in the end had sunk to my knees in the filth, as miserable as I had ever been in my life.

And what of the others? Dickon had got away and was capable of looking after himself, but Bear was too large and clumsy to hide. Tug and Growch would probably come looking for me, but what could a boy and a dog do on their own? And what had happened to Ky-Lin? I had not seen him at all and he was so small that someone might have trodden on him—But I could not bear to think of that.

I had no idea of time, for in that fetid darkness my inside body-clock seemed to have stopped; I found I could no more judge either time or distance.

My ears caught a sound: a tiny, scratching, rustling noise. My God—rats! No, I couldn't stand rats, I couldn't! There it was again. . . .

Rising to my feet I shuffled backwards until my trembling hands touched the damp wall. I listened: nothing, except a distant irregular drip of water. I must have imagined it. I took a deep breath, tried to relax. I counted to a hundred slowly under my breath. No sound—Scratch, scritch . . . thump!

I screamed: I couldn't help it. The sound bounced back off the walls in a dead, muffled tone. No one could hear me—I opened my mouth again—

"Steady there, girl," came a small voice. "It's only me. Quite a jump down—"

"Ky-Lin!"

"The same. Now, stand still, and I'll find you. . . ."

There were further rustlings and a moment later something touched my ankle. I bent down and found a plumed tail.

"You've grown!"

He was now puppy-sized.

"It seemed like a good idea. Better for getting around. There was a lot to do before we could get to you."

"We?"

"Tug, Growch, and myself. Bear was willing to help, but we left him guarding the money and baggage. All safe. Now, just listen; in another hour or so—"

"How did you get in?" I interrupted. The door was solid and I hadn't found the smallest space anything could crawl through. "How did you find the others? Where are they? Where's Dickon?"

"In what order am I supposed to answer these questions? Perhaps in reverse. The young man has disappeared: I smelled his fright as he ran—"

Typical Dickon, I thought. Keen for gold, coward for danger.

"The bear went back to your lodgings. I had climbed onto the boy's shoulder when I left you; we had to persuade the dog to follow us: he was all for staying by the gate."

Typical of Growch too: loyal and devoted, whatever the danger.

"We packed your belongings and moved them to a safe place. The boy went away to arrange certain matters and is less than two hundred yards away with the dog. As to how I got in? Through the window."

"What window?" I stared around once more. "I can't see any window!"

"Perhaps because you are not looking in the right place. Besides, there is no moon."

"Where?"

"Look to your right . . . no, much higher, to twice your height. Keep looking; let your eyes get accustomed to the dark. There now: do you see it?"

Yes, now I did. A grayish sort of oblong. Like all things, obvious once you knew where they were, I wondered how I could have missed it earlier. I stared and stared, with growing hope, until I got dancing specks in front of my eyes. Specks . . . and lines.

"But—there are bars across! You might be able to squeeze through those, but I couldn't. Besides, it's miles too high to reach!"

"Don't exaggerate! We've thought about all that."

"You're sure?"

"Sure." He hesitated. "At least . . ."

"At least—what?" Hope received a dent.

"If everything goes according to plan. Don't *worry*! If plan alpha doesn't work, we can always go to plan beta."

"If I don't get away from here before morning they'll probably haul me up for questioning again, and I'll need you to translate. And you can't hide in my cloak if you're as big as—"

"There is another hour until the false dawn, and now is the time when everyone sleeps deepest. That's why we chose it." He interrupted. "And now, if you will excuse me?"

"Don't go!" I was going to panic again, I knew it.

"Courage, girl! We have things to do. Firstly, put the Waystone in my mouth—that's it. Now lift me to your shoulders and bring me under the window. . . ."

He was much heavier now, and the spring he took from my shoulder nearly knocked me to the floor. I stared upwards, and could make out a darker shape against the outline of the window. He appeared to be doing the same he did with the bear's nose ring: stroking the iron bars in one direction. It seemed to take an age.

"Ky-Lin?"

"Shhh . . ."

I shushed, for what seemed a lifetime. At last the scraping noise stopped. "That should do it: catch!" The Waystone dropped into my cupped hands. "Can you climb a rope?"

"I don't know. . . ." I never had.

"Well, now's the time to find out!"

Something touched my face and reaching out a hand I found I was clutching a knotted rope. Looking up, I thought I detected movement, a muffled whisper, but still eight bars stood between me and freedom. It must be getting lighter, because now I could make them out quite clearly.

"Wait for a moment," breathed Ky-Lin. "But when I say 'move!' you move!"

A moment's pause, a straining noise, a muffled thud of hooves, and the first bar snapped cleanly away from the window. Two minutes later another, then a third. The fourth broke only at the top.

"Now!" said Ky-Lin urgently. I grabbed the rope tight, wrapped my legs around it and tried to pull myself up. The rope swung wildly, I made perhaps a couple of feet, banged hard against the wall, let go and dropped heavily to the floor of the cell. I didn't even manage a foot of climbing before banging my knuckles against the slime of the walls and falling down again.

"It won't work. . . ." I was desperate.

"Wait. . . ."

What seemed like a muttered conversation took place above, then Ky-Lin called down: "Wrap the rope around your waist, hold it tight in your hands, and hang on!"

I swung out and in against the wall, almost fainting at one stage from the pain of a bruised elbow, but gradually I was being hauled higher and higher. At last, when I thought the strain was too great and I would have to let go, a pair of hands gripped my wrists and pulled me up the last few inches till my shoulders were level with the window.

"Tug . . . !"

With his hands to help me I tried to wriggle through the space left by the missing bars. At first it was easy, and I was halfway through and could just make out, in the grayness that preceded the false dawn, a courtyard and a couple of the Plainsmen's small horses, ropes around their necks. At last I was breathing fresh air again, and Growch's eager tongue lapped at my cheek. Another pull, I was nearly there—and then I stuck.

That last bar, the one that had only broken halfway, was lodged against my hip, and I couldn't move. Tug tried to maneuver me past it, but it was hopeless. At last Ky-Lin slipped in beside me and pushed sideways as Tug pulled, and with a final jerk I was free, minus some trouser cloth and skin.

But there was no time to feel sorry for myself. I was shoved onto one of the horses. Tug led both out of the gates, then went back to bolt the gates on the inside, climbing back out when he had finished.

"That courtyard is where prisoners' friends are allowed to bring the food," explained Ky-Lin. "They are fed through the bars. For most that is all they get. The boy has bolted the gates so they will think you escaped by magic—or flew away with the dragons—and nothing will be traced back to his people."

The sky was lightening perceptibly as we moved silently through the deserted streets, the horses' hooves muffled with straw, to one of the smaller gates in the city wall. A few early fires smudged the clear, predawn air, a child whimpered somewhere, a dog howled, but that was all.

A smaller gate it might be, but it was still some twenty feet high, bolted, barred and with an enormous keyhole that could only encompass an equally enormous key. I knew these gates were not opened until the dawn call from the muezzin, and feared that if we lingered here my escape might be discovered. Besides which, we were a motley enough collection that any guards would remember, for at that moment two of Tug's people came to join us on horseback, Bear ambling amiably behind. Our packs were fastened on the horses.

I gazed fearfully at the gate house, expecting the guards to emerge any moment and tell us to be about our business; instead, Tug dismounted, went over, opened the door and a minute later reappeared with a key almost half his size. Over his shoulder I could see the two guards lying in a huddle on the floor.

"Sleepy Dust," said Ky-Lin, his tail fluffed out. "Good for another hour at least. . . ."

With a struggle Tug and his fellows managed to slide back the bolts and bars and manipulate the key; we slipped through the gate and there was a straight road leading north. Tug stayed behind to close up again and return the key, before scaling the gate and rejoining us on the road.

"Right!" said Tug, in my tongue. "Now ride. Slow first, then faster."

Once the city was out of sight behind a curve in the dusty road we quickened our pace; as we rode we shared rice cakes and a flask of water but there was no slackening until the sun was at its zenith, when Tug led us off the road into a stand of trees.

Behind the trees was a tumbledown, deserted hut, and Bear collapsed into the shade, closely followed by Growch. Tug dismounted and helped me down, bumped and bruised from the ride, my hip aching from the scrape against the broken bar in the cell. Tug's friends dismounted, took the muffles from all four horses' hooves and led them over to a nearby stream to drink. Our baggage they put in the shade. I drank deep of the clear, cold water then lay down in the winter sun, glad of the transient warmth. I felt I could sleep for a week. . . .

"Anyfin' to eat?"

I don't think I could have roused myself even for Growch's plaintive plea, but luckily Tug and his friends had lit a discreet fire and we were soon eating cheese, strips of dried meat and pancakes.

Tug pointed to the road ahead. "Bear's way," he said. "Keep to trail during day, not roads. Bear will soon sniff way. We go now." He bent and put his forehead to my hands. "My freedom—your freedom. It is right. When I man, I travel much. Good for learn better things my people."

I didn't kiss him good-bye, although I wanted to; I just ruffled his hair, waved, and listened to the sound of hooves as he and his followers rode away out of my life.

Just before I fell asleep, Growch already snoring at my side, Ky-Lin at my feet, I asked the latter a question that had been bothering me.

"Ky-Lin . . . if plan alpha had failed, what was plan beta?"

"Plan what?"

"Beta. You told me—"

"Oh that. I haven't the faintest idea, but we would have thought of something. Alpha, beta, gamma, delta . . . Now that really would have been a test. . . ."

Chapter Fifteen

As far as I knew, we were never followed. It would have been difficult for the townspeople to trace our route, even if they had bothered. Probably it was as Ky-Lin had surmised: they would think I had had magic to help me escape, and you can't chase magic.

I slept—we all slept—for the rest of the day and the ensuing night, waking cold, hungry, but thoroughly rested. Tug had left us provisions, so we broke our fast with gruel and honey, cheese and dried fruit.

Bear was eager to be away, declaring in his slow way that we were on the right road for his homeland. He sniffed the air, sneezed, then shook himself like a dog just out of water, his pelt rippling like a loose furry robe.

"Not far," he said, and sneezed again. "Air smells good. Woods, rivers, mountains."

Fine. The sooner the better as far as I was concerned, then we could take the more northern route to where I hoped I would find the Blue Mountain. Right at this moment, though, I couldn't see how we were going to move an inch further. I had repacked our baggage and rescued our money—including the gold from the palace performance—from Bear and tucked it away. I thought I could just about manage my pack, though how far I could carry it in one day was doubtful, but there was another problem. Tug had left us provisions, obviously believing we would find villages few and far between the farther we travelled, but now I looked with dismay at the sack of rice, the smaller ones of beans and oats, the pack of dried fruit, another of dried meat, a half of cheese and the three jars of salt, oil and honey.

Now there was no Tug or Dickon to share the burdens. I thought of Bear: he was big enough and strong enough to carry the burdens, but he was too unpredictable in his mode of travel. Sometimes he was content to lope along by my side, but he would often go off on his own for long periods of time, searching for grubs, roots, and honey. During one of these foragings he would be quite capable of forgetting his burdens, or dropping them, or just leaving them behind.

I scratched my nose; perhaps I could fashion a litter, or a form of sleigh, but they would have to be pretty tough to withstand the terrain. Perhaps Ky-Lin could think of something constructive.

But once again, he had read my mind and was now shaking his head from side to side in self-reproach. "Aieee! What a fool I am! If only we could all exist on fresh air . . ." He pulled himself together. "But we don't and can't, so there is the little matter of carrying the provisions is there not?"

"Not exactly a 'little' matter," I said. "There's enough there for a small pony!"

"Of course! Exactly what I had calculated. And I must now work twice as hard for not having anticipated all this, otherwise my Lord will be displeased. . . . You will excuse me for ten minutes, please?" and he disappeared into the undergrowth. Perhaps he had gone to look for some wood to build a litter, I thought; in any case, he had no need to reproach himself for anything; he had organized our escape, designed our performances and been a cheerful companion in all our journeying. And even now, running off like that, he had moved from stone to rock, in order not to even bend a blade of grass. His Lord was surely a hard taskmaster. On the other hand, the idea of not harming anything living if one could help it appealed to my soft heart. I should—

"'Elp! 'Elp! Go 'way! Geroff!" and Growch burst into the clearing, barking wildly, closely pursued by what looked like a running rainbow, about four times his size.

I leapt to my feet and snatched up the cooking pot, now fortunately attached to the other implements, but at least it made a satisfactory clanging noise. Both Growch and the apparition stopped dead. Pulling out my little knife and wondering where the hell Bear had disappeared to, I walked slowly nearer.

"Now then, what do you—my God! Ky-Lin!—but you've *grown* . . . ! Growch, it's all right: just turn around and look!"

Instead of the puppy-sized Ky-Lin, there stood a creature the size of a small pony, perhaps as high at the withers as my waist. He looked extremely diffident, in spite of his new size, for parts of him hadn't grown as quickly as the others. No longer neat and petite, he was now large and untidy. The only completely perfect part of him was his plumed tail, with a spread now like that of a peacock.

He looked down and around at himself.

"It's a long time since I did this," he said apologetically. "Unfortunately it would seem that not everything changes at the same rate. Perhaps a grain or two of rice, or a little dried fruit . . . Thank you."

Almost immediately the shortest leg at the back grew to the right size.

"A little more?" I asked.

Ten minutes later and he was more or less all of a piece, except for a smaller left ear, a bare patch on his chest and extremely small antennae.

"A couple of days and everything will be as it should," he said. "I hope. . . ." He glanced at the packs of food. "And now, if you would load me up please? If you would put the spare blanket on first, I would find it more comfortable, and I could manage the cooking things as well."

I tried to balance the load as evenly as I could.

"Have you . . . ? Can you . . . ? Do you do this often?"

"Bigger and smaller? Let me think. . . ." I could almost hear the sound of the mental tally sticks flying. "This will be the seventy-ninth time bigger. Three times with you: figurine to mouse-size, then puppy-size and now what you want, pony-size. Smaller? Fifty-three times. I think that's right."

"Try notchin' yer 'ooves," said Growch. He was still behaving in a surly way, just because he'd allowed himself to be panicked, and had let me see it.

"I couldn't do that," said Ky-Lin seriously. "They are living tissue and I mustn't harm anything living, you know that."

"Funny way o' thinkin' . . ."

"Well then, what is your philosophy of life, dog?"

"Filly—what? Oh, you means what life is? Life is livin' the best way you can for the longest time you can manage. Grab what you can while you can, is me motto. An' that includes nosh. Catch me eatin' rice an' leaves when there's rats and rabbits! Anyways, it don' make no difference when you're gone."

What a contrast! One striving for (to me) an impossible state of perfection, the other living only for the day. And I suppose I was somewhere in between. But even I was having rebellious thoughts about what I had been taught. After all I had experienced I couldn't imagine a happy Heaven without my animal friends somewhere around. And think how sterile it would be without trees and flowers, streams and lakes, sun and rain? Hold it, I told myself, crossing myself guiltily. God knows what He's doing. Would the Jesus who considered the beauty of the lilies, who knew where to cast a fisherman's net and admired the whiteness of a dog's teeth expect us to live without natural beauty in our final reward?

Bear made no comment when he saw Ky-Lin's change of size. As I said, he was a very phlegmatic bear.

We set off west by north, using the Waystone and a fixed point every morning. We used mostly trails, but also the occasional road, though these were few and far between, only existing between villages, which also became scarcer. Money meant little out here in the wilds, so if we came to a village Bear danced for our supper, Ky-Lin keeping well out of sight to save scaring the children.

It was Bear also who was adept at finding shelter for our nights in the open: a cave, an overhang of rock, a deserted hut—we usually stayed warm and dry. Without realizing it, the turning of the year passed us by, and it grew imperceptibly lighter each day.

Careful as I was with our food, our stores diminished rapidly, for the villagers had little to spare and had no use for our money, relying on the barter system. Hens don't lay in winter, and their stores of grain, beans, cheeses, and fruit were all calculated to a nicety for their own needs. Now of course, Ky-Lin was eating as befitted his size and work load, so I sent Bear foraging. He seemed to find a sufficiency for himself, so I hoped for something to supplement our diet. Nine times out of ten I was disappointed because he either hadn't found anything extra, or had eaten it or just plain forgotten, but occasionally he returned with a slice of old honeycomb, a pawful of withered berries or some succulent roots which I baked or boiled.

There was one thing he was excellent at, however, and which helped our diet considerably, but we only found that out by accident.

One morning we came to a small river swollen by melted snows. It wasn't deep, perhaps three or four feet at most, but it was wide, probably a hundred feet across, rushing busily over stones around rocks, forming swirling pools and mini-rapids. I turned downstream to find an easier place to cross; no point in getting the baggage wet.

" 'Ey-oop! Just look at that!" Growch's voice was full of genuine wonder. I turned, just in time to see Bear flipping a fat fish from the shallows and swallowing it whole. "That's the second one. . . ." He was salivating.

I ran back along the bank, just in time to see Bear miss number three. He growled with disappointment and turned away.

"Can you do that again?"

He stared at me, his little eyes bright as sloe berries. "If I want fish."

"Well, want!" I said. "Did it never occur to you that we should like some, too?"

He stared at me. "You not like grubs and beetles I bring. Should ask."

"You eat our gruel and rice: we like fish. I ask now, to try."

He caught two more and I cleaned and grilled them over a small fire for our midday meal. They were delicious. After that, whenever we came across a stretch of water we encouraged him to go fishing. All he caught didn't look edible to me, but he wasn't fussy and ate the rejections as well. A couple of times we even had enough to barter for salted meat or beans, and we ate tolerably well.

The mountains came nearer to the north and west of us, the terrain was rougher and the air colder. Growch and I tired more easily, though Ky-Lin seemed unaffected, and Bear was positively rejuvenated. He bounced ahead of us most days, sniffing, grubbing, rolling in the undergrowth, snatching at leaves like an errant cub, splashing noisily through any water we came across, eating like a pig and snoring like one at night, too.

I reckoned we must have covered near three hundred miles since we left the Golden City when we stood on a wide ridge and looked down on a limitless land of forests, rivers, lakes and crags. Not a village or hamlet to be seen, no sign of human habitation for miles.

Bear sniffed deep, then reared up on his hind legs, to tower over all of us.

"My land," he said. "Start here, go on forever."

I smiled at his enthusiastic certainty. "Then we can leave you here?"

He sank down on his haunches. "Be with me until I find cave to sleep for rest of the cold, and I find you food to take with you. My country; I find fish and honey."

Near though the woodland had seemed, it took us two days to reach the forest proper, and as we came to the more thickly carpeted ground it was a difficult time for poor Ky-Lin, sworn as he was not to tread on anything living. Once under the trees it was easier for him; they were mostly pine and fir, and the dead needles made a nice carpet for his hooves.

Three days later Bear found his cave. Entered through a narrow cleft that widened out into a cozy chamber behind, it had not been occupied for years, judging by the thick drift of leaves that had piled up. The cave was situated at the foot of a bluff; in front the land stretched down to a thick stand of conifers and a stream trickled away to the right. An ideal hibernation place for a winter-weary bear.

He grunted with satisfaction. "Stay here till spring. You need fish. Go get, you light fire. Stay here tonight."

And off he trotted. True to his earlier word he had found us honeycombs and half a sack of nuts. He had obviously spied or smelled some water, so we could stock up with fish as well, God willing.

I dithered over lighting a fire inside the cave or out, but decided on the latter, reckoning that lingering smoke might disturb our night's sleep. There was plenty of wood and I filled the cooking pot from the stream and set it on to boil with salt, herbs, and some wild garlic I found growing nearby. It all depended on what Bear brought back, but if the worst came to the worst I could chuck in some rice and dried meat.

Just as I sat back on my heels, enjoying the warmth of the fire, and Growch had come to lean against me, there came a noise, and simultaneously my ring gave a sharp stab. Growch stiffened, Ky-Lin's antennae shot out in the direction of the forest and I sprang to my feet. It wasn't Bear, it was men's voices I had heard.

There it was again: voices, crackle of twigs, a laugh.

"Quick! Back in the cave, Ky-Lin. Growch, stay with me." There was no point in us all retreating to the cave; the fire was sending up a thin plume of smoke and whoever was out there would soon be coming to investigate. I didn't fancy being trapped in a confined space, but they might miss Ky-Lin if we hid him away. If we were lucky it might just be a couple of hunters, but my ring was still sending out warning signs and the hair had risen on Growch's back.

He growled. "There they are. . . ."

There was a shout, another, and three figures stood at the edge of the pine trees and gazed up the short slope towards us. I ignored them, putting more kindling on the fire and stirring the pot, although my hands were trembling.

"They look bad 'uns to me," muttered Growch. "Rough. Got weapons, too. Better run . . ."

Where to? The bluff was too steep to climb, the cave a trap.

"Just don't get into trouble," I urged. "Low profile . . ."

The strangers moved up the slope towards us, and now I could see them more closely my heart sank. They were ragged, dirty and unshaven with straggling moustaches and their hair tied up in bandannas. As Growch had said, they were armed; a rusty, curved sword, a couple of daggers, a club spiked with nails. They were used to this: as they moved up the slope they spread out, so they were approaching me from three sides, their dark eyes darting from side to side in case of ambush.

They came to a halt some ten yards away and I could smell the rank stench of sweat, excitement and fear. The one in the middle stepped forward. He spoke, but my heart was hammering so hard I couldn't hear him, even if I had been able to understand. Perhaps Ky-Lin was sending a translation from his hiding place in the cave, but I couldn't hear that, either. I could feel my knees knocking together.

"What—what do you want?" I asked in my own tongue, but my voice came out high and very unladlike. They glanced at each other, and the one in the middle muttered out of the corner of his mouth. He addressed me again. This time I heard Ky-Lin's translation.

"They are asking if you are alone."

I nodded my head foolishly, then could have kicked myself. Why, oh why couldn't I have indicated four, five others in the forest?

They grinned, shuffled closer, their hands resting on their weapons. The middle one squatted down in front of the fire, warmed his hands, pointed at the pot and asked a question.

"He asks if there is enough for all, and where is the meat," translated Ky-Lin.

I tried to smile, but my face seemed frozen. I shrugged my shoulders and waved at the pot, then at them. If you want meat, then go get it yourselves.... The leader leered at me, plucked a dagger from his belt and made slicing motions in the direction of Growch, who was growling valiantly. The man's meaning was plain: no ready meat, then the dog would do.

I backed away, pushing Growch behind me, still trying to smile as though it was all some huge joke—but I knew it wasn't. I thought even I might not be safe if they were especially hungry; I knew that in certain parts of the world human flesh was considered a delicacy.

"No," I said. "Please no! Let us alone. . . ." and I could hear myself whimpering like a child as I retreated with Growch until my shoulders were hard against the bluff behind me.

The bandits were laughing as they closed in for the kill, but suddenly there was a call from the forest behind, then another and another, as if the forest were suddenly full of strangers. My attackers drew back uncertainly, and at that moment Ky-Lin leapt from the cave, his tail seeming aflame with color. I snatched my knife from my belt and Growch attacked the legs of the man on the right. For a moment I hoped we could scare them away, but then I realized that Ky-Lin couldn't attack any of them: he could only frighten. Growch's teeth were sharp but not killers, and I had never used a knife on anyone in my life.

I saw Ky-Lin dodge a sword thrust and then be clubbed over the head and crumple into a heap and lie still; Growch was still snarling and growling and snapping and had done some bloody damage to one of our attackers; then a boot caught him on the side of the jaw, he shrieked with pain and somersaulted through the air, to land with a sickening crack against one of the rocks. At the same time I was caught from behind, my arm was twisted behind my back and the knife clattered harmlessly from my grasp to the ground. I screamed, but the sound was choked off by the hand at my throat.

I could feel the blood thumping in my ears as the hand squeezed tighter. I couldn't draw breath, felt consciousness slipping away—

So this was what it was like to die, I thought: strange but it doesn't hurt that much, it's just uncomfortable. I was already rushing away down a dark tunnel, a long tube with a tiny light at the other end, when suddenly everything changed.

The pressure went from my throat, my breathing eased, but I could feel cold air on my body. As conscious thought returned I realized they must have been searching me for hidden moneys, but their rough handling had torn my clothes and revealed my true sex. Now their handling of me changed in character; they were eager for something other than my immediate death, they wanted to enjoy my body first.

I struggled now, really struggled, for the threat of rape seemed far more terrible than the certainty of death. I could feel the obscenity of their hands on my private parts, their hot breath on my face, something hard and thrusting against my thigh, and the more I fought them, the more they liked it. Despairingly I clenched my free hand, the right, and aimed for one of the faces above me. I missed, but felt another stab from my ring, my magic ring.

"Help me," I breathed, "please help me. . . ."

The hands still probed, my back was naked to the sharp stones on the ground, a mouth reached for mine, excited voices were laughing and urging each other on, then the whole world seemed to erupt in a world-shaking sound: an ear-splitting roar like a volcano.

Suddenly I was free. My attackers no longer threatened. The air was cold on my bruised flesh as I staggered to my feet, striving to cover my nakedness with the torn remnants of my clothes.

That dreadful roar came again, loud enough to make me cover my ears. I looked down towards the forest and there, coming up the slope towards us, was Bear!

But it was a Bear I had never seen before. . . .

Chapter Sixteen

Even I was frightened.

Bear stood on his hind legs, his great arms spread wide, the five oval pads set in a row on his front paws each sprouting a wickedly curved claw. The mane on his shoulders stood up like an extra fur cape, but the greatest change was in his head. Usually the fur framed his face rather like the feathers on an owl, his round ears pricked forward: now his ears were slicked back to his head, the ruff of fur was gone and instead there was a pointed snout with lips curled back in a snarl over a double row of pointed teeth. Saliva dripped down onto his chest and the little eyes were red with anger.

He roared again, and the sound seemed to reverberate from the rocks of the bluff behind me, then he dropped to all fours and bounded up the slope towards us.

Suddenly I was alone. The bandits were running helter-skelter towards the trees, their weapons scattered, the air full of their cries of terror. As one passed too close to the bear I saw a paw flash out and ribbons of cloth and skin flew from the gashed shoulder of one of my attackers. He shrieked and clasped his arm, blood dripping through his fingers, but he didn't stop running, though he stumbled now and again in his flight.

Bear reached me and reared up, his snakelike head twisting down till he nearly touched me. He sniffed, and almost too late I remembered how shortsighted he was.

"It's me, Bear. . . ."

He sniffed again. "So it is. Smell of them. Heard you call. All right? The others, then," and he whipped round and shambled off towards the forest, where the crashing sounds of the escaping bandits were growing fainter.

I pulled my clothes together as best I could, though needle and thread were urgently needed, found the pouch that had been ripped from my neck lying close by, then hurried over to where Growch lay, moaning a little. He wagged his tail however as I lifed his head to my lap.

"You all right?" As I spoke I was feeling him all over for breaks or wounds, but although he winced now and again there didn't seem to be anything broken, until—

"Ouch! Them's me ribs!"

"Do they hurt?"

"Reckon I cracked a couple." He struggled to his feet, shook himself, groaned, and spat out a couple of teeth, luckily not essential ones. "You all right? What about 'im?" He nodded towards the motionless figure of Ky-Lin.

He lay where he had fallen, utterly still. My heart kicked against my breastbone. No, not dear Ky-Lin! Not after all he had done for us. He had existed for so many hundreds of years, he couldn't suddenly end like this. I bent over him, the tears dripping off the end of my nose.

"You're wetting my fur," came a muffled voice.

"Ky-Lin! You're alive!"

"Of course I'm alive! Take more than a knock on the head to finish me off!" and a moment or two later he was up on his hooves again, shaking out his crumpled tail and straightening his twisted antennae.

"You all right? I heard your ring call the bear, and I presume he has chased them off. Oh dear . . ." and he sat down suddenly on his haunches, looking puzzled.

"What's the matter?" I asked anxiously, for his colors had also faded.

"Long years; lots of changes; body material not what it was . . . Would you be kind enough to examine the dent in my head? It feels quite deep."

It was, a cleft running from where his left eyebrow would have been to the opening of his right ear. The skin, or hide, didn't appear to be broken, but I wasn't happy about the bone beneath. Recalling the healing properties of the ring I drew it slowly and gently along the indentation.

"That's better; a Unicorn has great healing powers. Dog would benefit too, I believe."

And so he did. I found some Self-Heal growing nearby, mashed it into a paste, bound up Growch's ribs and Ky-Lin's head, and they both declared themselves much recovered, though Growch said the healing process would be accelerated by a spot of something to eat. . . .

I remade the fire, got the pot boiling again, and threw in rice and some rather dessicated vegetables in deference to Ky-Lin's tastes, Growch getting a strip of dried meat to chew.

Where was Bear? There was neither sight nor sound of him, and the sky was darkening into twilight.

"He'll be all right," said Ky-Lin. "Why not get out your needle and thread while you wait? Your clothes are falling to pieces!"

By the flicker of the flames I was able to cobble together my jerkin, rebind my breasts and renew the laces in my trews; my shirt was in ribbons, and I used it for binding up the animals, but I had one more in my pack. First, however, I scrubbed myself with cold water, determined to rid myself of any lingering taint from my attackers.

It was now full dark, and the dancing flames threw our shadows on the rocks behind, making them prance like demons. A larger shadow overtopped us all: Bear was back.

I hadn't heard him approach, but suddenly there he was, fur smooth once more, his face round and innocent, in his jaws a couple of trout.

He dropped them at my feet. "Took long time to catch."

I looked at him. He seemed as unconcerned as if he had been out for a stroll. Skewering the trout I laid them across the fire to broil.

"Have you eaten?"

"Trout. Roots. Full."

I turned the trout. "What happened?" I was dying to know how far he had chased them, but knew I would have to be patient.

"Long walk to lake. Take time to catch."

"No, not that! The men—the bad ones. Did they all go away?"

He looked puzzled, licked his paw.

"I called you: you chased them. . . ."

"Oh, them. Yes."

"They won't come back?"

"Not ever. Gone."

I breathed more easily. He seemed very sure.

"All dead. Lives for life. You help me, I help you. Will have some honey. . . ."

I carved him off a chunk, although I thought he had said he was full.

"But how . . . ?" I didn't know how to put it, was afraid of the answer.

"Men?" He thought for a moment. "In ravine. Long way down to rocks. All still." He turned to the pot. "Smells good. Small portion . . ."

And that was all I, or anyone else for that matter, ever got out of him, for the following morning he was so deep in his hibernating sleep that we couldn't rouse him even to say good-bye.

His deep, rumbling snores kept me awake that night—that and the various aches and bruises I nursed. I kept thinking about the complexity of the creature, if one could call one so simple complicated. The problem lay in me, I finally decided; I just couldn't comprehend a mind that thought in such straight lines. All that concerned him was food, sleep, and play. Like all simple souls he could only hold one thought at a time: once fixed, though, the idea was carried out ruthlessly, whether it was to catch a fish, scoop out grubs from a dead log, sniff out a honeycomb, chase a butterfly—or kill a man. And someone as simple as that would have no conscience, wouldn't know what one meant.

When we stepped out of the cave the following morning, we realized that Bear had the best of it, snoring away the winter in his drift of leaves, because the weather had changed for the worse. A nasty, nippy wind churned the ashes of last night's fire, whipping the tall grass into a frenzy and driving the tops of the distant pines into uneasy circles. The sky was gray, flat and oppressive, and looked as though it might hold snow.

We packed up quickly, then had to decide in which direction to go. I pulled out Suleiman's map and unscrolled it on a rock. Ky-Lin bent over it, doing his disconcerting bit of shaking his head from side to side with his eyes crossed.

"We are too far west," he said finally. "If we could all fly over the mountains for a thousand miles, it would be easy. But not even a dragon would go that way in this weather." His sensitive antennae traced a line to the northeast. "We need to turn east and find the Silk River, then follow it north to the headwaters. Then when the weather is better we find the Desert of Death, cross that, and we are within a few miles—say, a hundred—of our destination."

"Yes," I said. It sounded simple, and also rather daunting. I didn't like the sound of that desert, and a thousand miles in a straight line meant many more afoot.

Ky-Lin glanced at me. "Don't be disheartened; think how far we've come already! The next few days, till we reach the river, will be tough; but once we get there, there will be plenty of villages."

He was right: it was tough. It took over a week of hard slog to reach any sort of civilization, and by that time we had run out of provisions and were footsore and cold and weary to the bone. The snow held off, but the winds were fierce and biting, shelter hard to find and our faces burned from several sharp showers of sleet. It might be February, but the winter's hold was tightening rather than otherwise. Once we came to the river it was easier.

Apparently it connected farther south with another, larger, which in its turn coincided with the caravan routes, so the boatmen were used enough to taking paying passengers up to the headwaters, especially with the rivers being so low at this time of year.

The town at the head of the river was one that concerned itself with the weaving of plain silks, ready for transport in great flat barges to the caravan routes. During the winter months the river was too low for large-scale transport, so the townspeople used this time to spin the silks, dye some of the hanks and bale eveything up for the first barges to come through once the melting snows made the river navigable. We made our way to this town by leisurely stages from village to village, with a lift here, a boat trip there. Everywhere there were mulberry trees, the harsh winter making the icicles that hung from their branches tinkle like wind chimes.

The headwaters of the river were a disappointment. No waters gushing from a spring, rather a seeping from a huge bog that stretched for miles to the north. This was a smelly place, and I was not surprised to learn that it had been the custom, years back, to execute their criminals by tying them up with a hood over their faces and chucking them into the marsh. But the bog got its own back. Eventually the bodies were spewed forth again in the spring rains, to float away down the river, providing their own curiosity, for their long immersion in the bog had preserved their bodies like tanned leather. I saw one once; the clothes were stiff and shrunken, but the whole effect was rather that of an amateur wood carving. This practice of execution had been discontinued some fifty years back, but the odd corpse resurfaced now and again.

The town itself was a prosperous one with everyone, from children to grandparents, all engaged in work connected with the silk trade. At one end were the weaving sheds, at another the huge barns where the silkworms were reared, in artificial heat if necessary. In between were the huge vats for the dyes, the boiling rooms, and the sheds of drying racks. Nearer the docks were the baling sheds.

We rented one of the ubiquitous summer workers' houses; it was like a thatched clay beehive, one large room with shelves built into the walls for food and utensils, a sleeping platform, a central brazier and smoke hole, and niches in the walls for lamps. The floor was covered with rush matting and there were a couple of functional stools and a low table. Clothes were hung from a pole above the sleeping platform. No windows, and the door was like a heavy sheep hurdle, to be placed as one desired.

Once we reached civilization again Ky-Lin had decided to revert to a smaller size to avoid embarrassing questions, and now he travelled once more on my shoulder, ready to interpret if necessary. Coin was acceptable once more so there was no problem with food, nor with the warmer padded clothing I bought, the kind the locals wore. My hair had grown quite long, too, as it hadn't been trimmed since we were in the Golden City, and I adopted the local custom, used by men and women alike, of plaiting it into a pigtail.

For six weeks the weather pressed in on us; rain, sleet, snow, gales, frost and ice. The little house however was warm and dry, raised as they all were from the streets to prevent flooding, and there was plenty to keep me busy. Mending and repairing, bringing my journal up to date, going to the market, cooking and cleaning, buying off-cuts of silk for underwear—luxury!—and yet I yearned for action. To be so near and yet still so far from my objective kept me in a permanent fret for the better weather.

Growch, however, was in his element.

Fortunately for him, unfortunately for me, he had at last found his "fluffy bums." The town was full of them. It seemed that every family had one as a pet, and at the rate Growch was carrying on, there would soon be the same amount of half-breeds.

After the first complaint from an irate owner Ky-Lin and I put our heads together and decided Growch was one of the rarest dogs in the world: "He-whose-stomach-is-of-two-dogs-and-whose-legs-are-the-shortest-in-the-world." With a title like that, who could resist seeing what the puppies would be like? The bitches were soon literally queuing up and Growch was totally exhausted.

He came in one day, even filthier than usual, his fur matted and muddy, his stomach dragging on the ground, his tail and ears at half-mast, his eyes—what you could see of them—half-closed and his tongue hanging out like a forgotten piece of washing.

"Serves you right," I said unsympathetically. "It's what you wanted, isn't it? The reason you came all this way with me?" I jabbed my needle into the sandal I was finishing off, trying hard not to laugh. "Unlimited sex, that's what you wanted, isn't it? Well now you've got it, so don't complain!"

" 'Oose complainin'? I ain't. It's just—just I think I've gorra cold or somefin'. . . ."

"Dogs don't catch colds."

"Well, a chill, then. Think I'll stay in fer a coupla days. Have a rest."

"All right," I said placatingly. "I'll give you a dose of herbs, and if you have a fever we'll have to cut down on meat. Slops and gruel for you, my boy," and I bent over my sewing again and coughed to hide my giggles.

The transition from winter to spring, when it finally came, seemed to take place over a couple of days only. One moment a grim wind blew from the north and the ground was hard with frost, the next the sun shone, the ice melted and caged canaries were singing outside every door. It seemed thousands of little streams from the bog emptied into the river, which awoke from its sluggish sleep and ran merrily between its banks once more. Bales of silk were loaded onto flat-bottomed boats and set off southward, but the first trading boats didn't come upriver until the end of April, struggling against the swollen waters.

The whole town turned out to welcome the first string of barges, bearing long-needed supplies and the first of the seasonal workers, many of whom had relatives in the town. Ky-Lin and I had decided to start our journey north again within the week, so it was with holiday mood on me that I joined the rest of the town to watch the boats come in. I noted with satisfaction that the cargoes included dried fruits, grain, strips of meat and fish and cheeses, all goods that had been in short supply for the last month and that we would need for our journey.

Goods hauled ashore, passengers politely clapped and welcomed, bales of silk waiting to be loaded, we turned for our lodgings, content that the world had started awake again. In a few days we should be on our way.

"Got you!"

A hooded stranger, one of the passengers, had stepped from behind one of the warehouses and grabbed me by the wrist, so tightly I fancied I could hear the crunch of bone.

"Let me go! You're hurting me!" With my free hand I attempted to strike out at him, but he dodged the blow, holding me even tighter.

Growch growled warningly, and the stranger kicked out at him.

"You want to keep that cur of yours under control, Summer," came the voice again, but this time I recognized it, and my heart sank.

Dickon had found us again.

Chapter Seventeen

His explanation of what had happened to him since he ran away when I was arrested was very plausible; I think that after all the rehearsal it must have gone through he even believed it himself.

After I had fed him—and I admit he needed food; he looked half-starved—and had gone out for a jar of heady rice wine to loosen his tongue, he settled down on a stool by the brazier, a second mug of wine in his hand.

"I just didn't know what way to turn," he confessed. "I went chasing the bear, but he escaped me—where did he go, by the way? Never saw him again. Good riddance, I say. If it hadn't been for him murdering his master you would never have been arrested in the first place."

As I remember it, he had been running in a different direction from the animal; as for the reason for my arrest, how could I blame Bear? I had never had my feet scorched to make me dance. I didn't think it necessary to explain we had returned him to his own land.

"I couldn't find your dog, either, but I see you got him back. I saw that heathen boy and his friends carrying off your baggage, but there were too many for me to tackle. Once a thief always a thief, I say; I never trusted him."

He took another swig of the wine.

"After that I went back to the palace and demanded an interview, late though it was." Unlikely even a minor palace official would have bothered to get out of bed; besides, they were looking for him, too. "I begged, I pleaded to be allowed to see you; I even offered a bribe"—as far as I knew he had no money at all—"but they said I would have to wait until morning.

"I walked the streets all night, my mind in turmoil, turning over in my mind the options open to us. I had little money, no influence, and my command of the language was not as good as it should be. I thought of you, all alone and helpless in some underground dungeon—" he leant forward and patted my knee "—and I wept to think of your suffering."

I'll bet: he probably spent the night in a brothel. But now he was getting into his stride, aided by the wine.

"I went back to the palace at crack of dawn, to find everything in complete turmoil! I found that you had disappeared into thin air—'flown up into the clouds' was the way they put it—but of course I knew that was rubbish, even with your magic bits and pieces and talking animals, so I reckoned that you'd had some kind of help. I thought, too, that they might recognize me as having been with you, so I decided to lie low for a while till things settled down; found a nice young lady who let me stay rent free for a while. . . ." His face grew dreamy, and he finished the mug of wine. "That's why I didn't immediately come looking for you. How did you escape, by the way? Bribe the guards? Pick the lock?"

"As a matter of fact," I said stiffly, "that 'little thief' as you called him, and his friends, pulled the bars from my cell and saw me safe on the road, together with my baggage, money, and extra provisions. He called it an exchange for the slavery I rescued him from."

"Oh . . . well, you never can tell, I suppose. Any more of that wine?"

"It's quite strong," I said, refilling his mug for the third time.

"I've got a strong enough head to take piss water like this. . . . Now, where was I?"

"Hiding," I said.

"Not for long, my dear, not for long! I found it very difficult to pick up your trail, though; no one had seen you go, though I realized you must have used one of the gates. After having questioned everyone I knew, and some I didn't, I remembered those maps of yours. You know the ones: 'Here be Dragons'?" I wondered whether he realized he had given himself away by confirming he had seen them. "I recalled the direction was north, but where? Here I was lucky." He tapped his nose. "I came across a mapmaker and—for a consideration—was allowed to take a peek and managed to copy a couple. Here!" He reached into his tattered clothes and brought out a couple of pieces of rice paper, the folds marked with the sweat from his body.

Gingerly I unfolded the scraps, still warm from his body. The first one was very like the ones I had copied at Matthew's house although with more detail: a couple more rivers and towns, more routes. The other was far more precise and Ky-Lin, viewing them from his hiding place on my shoulder, gave a little hiss when he saw it. I looked more closely. The Silk River was marked quite clearly, although in the unintelligible (to me) picture scribble they used. Here was our town, mountains to the north and west, and what looked like a plateau to the northwest.

Dickon was now nodding, his eyes closed, his body swaying on the stool.

"Keep that one," whispered Ky-Lin. "That is one we could use. If he won't part with it, we'll copy it while he sleeps."

But even as I prepared to tuck it away in my jerkin the mug fell from his lax fingers, his eyes snapped open and he reached and took the map from my hand.

"Oh, no you don't! I'm not having you running off on your own again. I have the maps, and we go for the treasure together!"

"There isn't any treasure! There never was!"

"Rubbish! What kept you going all this long time? We've been all through this before, and I know you're lying."

There was no point in arguing.

"If you really believe that, then go and look for it on your own. As for me, I am on a private pilgrimage to find a friend and there is no, repeat no, money at the end of it." I rose to my feet. "There is a spare blanket over there but you'll have to sleep on the floor. If you wish to relieve yourself there is a communal latrine at the end of the street."

Later I peered down from the sleeping platform; he was muffled up in the blanket on one of the grass mats, snoring gently. Slipping to the floor I made up the brazier and brewed myself a mug of camomile tea, an excuse in case he woke, though I usually had one before I went to bed anyway.

"What's so special about the map?" I whispered to Ky-Lin.

He sipped at the tea. "Nice . . . The map shows that we are on the right track. It also indicates the way we must take once we cross the Desert of Death."

I shivered. "We must go that way?"

He nodded. "If you can study that map you will see it is the most direct route. The only other way lies through the mountains, which are notorious bandit country."

I had had enough of bandits.

"Then we had better pinch the map and copy it. Is he fast enough asleep, do you think?"

"I shall make sure. . . ." He trotted across the floor. I saw him touch Dickon's face with one of his hooves, there was a tiny puff of what looked like pinkish smoke, and he trotted back, nodding his head. "You can take it now; I gave him a little Sleepy Dust."

Together we studied the map. He pointed to where the town was marked: "We are here." With his delicate antennae he traced a way around the bog, shook his head and marked a path across the middle. "Quicker; as I remember there are markers."

I didn't ask how long it was since he had been this way. "What if they are no longer there?"

"We'll check first. After the bog the trail winds along that valley bottom to the desert. The Desert of Death," he repeated.

"Is it—is it that bad?"

He hesitated. "I have only been there once, and I was with my master and the others of my kind. Then it was not too bad, but you must realize that my brethren can manage on little water and food if necessary, and my Lord had reached such an exalted plane of consciousness that he could, I believe, have existed on air alone." He was perfectly serious. "Besides which, there was a town and temple halfway across."

"Isn't it very hot?"

"Yes, during the day. At night it can be equally cold. The terrain is difficult too. It is a bare, arid place, littered with small stones and rocks. It is necessary to carry all one's food and water; it is not called the Desert of Death for nothing. However if we take care and prepare ourselves properly it shouldn't be too difficult. I am sure I can find the temple again, and there we can stay for a while and stock up with fresh provisions; it is on the only oasis we shall come across."

He paused and his antennae flicked across the map.

"Once across the mountains we are in the foothills of the final range of mountains. Over them, just there, marked by a circle, is a Buddhist monastery. It looks over a deep valley, and in the center of that valley there is a conical hill—they say it could be the core of a long-extinct volcano—and because of the way the light falls and its distance, they call it the Blue Mountain. In the margin of the map is written: 'This is believed to be the home of Dragons.' This, by the way, and whatever your friend says, is an original map, not a copy."

"Then he must have stolen it. . . ." But I was not really concerned with that; all I could do was concentrate on that little hill on the map. It looked so near, but also, if the truth were told, so insignificant a thing to hold all my dreams.

"I saw it once in the distance," said Ky-Lin, "and it did look blue, but I did not know then that it was rumored a dragon lair. Come, you should make a copy before he wakes."

My hands were shaking so much both with anticipation and the discovery that my mountain did exist, that it took me longer than I had anticipated to complete the copy, but we managed to get the original back in Dickon's clothing without him waking.

"Ky-Lin," I whispered. "How soon can we go?"

He considered. "The weather is set fair, new provisions have come into the town, we have the confirmation of the map . . . two days, perhaps."

"Why not tomorrow?" I couldn't wait to leave.

"Provisions to buy and pack for a start; you need to make a proper list. Then we shall need a half-dozen water skins, more blankets, a length of rope and you could do with a new pair of strong boots. In order to carry all the baggage, I shall have to grow again, and you will have to alert your friend to my existence."

I glanced over at Dickon. "But he's not coming!"

"You don't want him to accompany us?"

"Certainly not! We've managed fine without him so far."

"He could be useful carrying the baggage. . . ."

"I—I just don't want him along, that's all." I couldn't explain it. It wasn't the sort of thing you could put into words. I could quote his cowardice, his obsession with the thought of treasure, his searching of my belongings, the way he literally seemed to haunt my every move, but it wasn't just that; it was something deeper and more frightening. Inside of me there was an unspoken dread of him: not what he was but what he might become. He posed a threat to my future happiness, of that I was sure, but how or why I had no idea. It was like waking to a day of brilliant sunshine and being convinced that it would rain before nightfall, but far more sinister than that. All I was sure of was that I couldn't explain it.

"Very well; if you can manage the purchasing tomorrow, and the packing, then we'll make it the day after. I'll tell you again what we need in the morning."

"Can you give him some more Sleepy Dust?"

Ky-Lin hesitated. "It is not good for humans to give them too much. Ideally there should be a twelve-month between each dose. But he did not take much tonight; perhaps a small dose will do no harm."

From the moment he awoke in the morning Dickon did his unintentional best to hamper all my attempts to organize our departure; he was a positive pain, following me round the town as I made my purchases.

"Why are you buying that? We've got a couple already. What do we need those for? When are we setting out? Where are you supposed to be going on your pilgrimage? How are we getting there? I hope you don't think I'm going to carry that. Are we going to hire some sort of transport? How much money have you left? Are we going to do another performance?" Etc., etc., etc., till I could have screamed.

But I knew I had to behave in a calm and rational manner, as if the last thought on my mind was to escape from him that very night, so I made up answers to those questions I couldn't answer truthfully, telling a heap of lies with a smile on my face and my fingers mentally crossed. Fifteen Hail Marys later . . .

By late afternoon I think I had persuaded him we would not be leaving for a few days' time, and I tried to make my frantic packing that evening look like routine tidying up. He eyed the sacks, packs and panniers with distrust.

"We'll never carry all that!"

"It's not more than we can manage; you carry your share, I'll carry mine."

"I shall just look like a donkey. . . ."

"No more than usual," I said briskly. "Now, what would you like for supper?"

We dined well, as Growch and I would be snacking until we had crossed the bog, and we didn't know how long that would take, so it was chicken soup with chopped hard-boiled eggs, fried pastry rolls filled with bean shoots and herbs, and chopped chicken livers in a bean and lentil pudding. I had camomile tea, Dickon had rice wine. I thought to allay further suspicion by begging for a further look at his maps, knowing what his reponse would be.

"Oh, no you don't! I'm not having you learn them by heart and then steal a march on me! Once we're on the road together you can take another look."

I yawned. "Have it your own way. There's no hurry. I'm for bed. The clearing-up can wait till the morning. Blow out the lamp before you go to bed, please. . . ."

I watched Ky-Lin scuttle out of the door to effect his "change," and lay down, convinced that I wouldn't sleep a wink, but my eyes kept closing in spite of it: must have been that heavy meal. Still, Ky-Lin would wake me as soon as he returned. . . .

I woke to broad daylight, Growch still snoring at my side and Dickon returning with a pitcher of water for washing.

"Wake up, sleepyheads!" he called out cheerily.

What in the world . . . Where was Ky-Lin?

The answer came from beneath my blanket. "I spend all evening changing to a suitable size, then find when I return that your ridiculous friend has so jammed the door tight shut that I can't gain entrance! So, I have to spend more time changing to be small enough to get back in again!" He wasn't at all happy.

"Sorry," I whispered. "We'll manage it better tonight, I promise."

But the matter was taken out of my hands by Dickon himself. That evening I left a stew of vegetables simmering on the brazier, and suggested we take a walk. I was hoping this would give Ky-Lin the chance for his change, since we had discovered that the house next door was empty, and he could hide in there while I ate less and didn't fall asleep before Dickon, so I could ensure the door was left open.

Dickon, however, had other ideas. We were wandering through the bazaar examining the goods without any intention of buying, when I straightened up in front of a stall selling slippers and found he had disappeared.

Not into thin air and not forever. On the other side of the road was a lighted doorway, screened by a beaded curtain still gently swaying as though someone had just entered. I crossed over and peeped inside. A waft of perfume, smoke from incense sticks, rustle of silks, a mutter of feminine voices. It was obvious what sort of place it was. I knew Dickon had no money, so wandered slowly off towards our lodgings, fairly sure he would seek me out. I was right; I had only gone a hundred yards when he caught me up.

"I say, Summer: got a bit of change on you?"

"No. It's suppertime. Come on, before it spoils."

"It's just that—that I saw there was to be an entertainment tonight and I thought I might take a look. . . . There's an entrance fee, of course, and I'd need a few coins for drinks. Come on, Summer! Life's short enough without missing out on all the fun! You're a real sobersides, you know: getting just like an old maid!"

Old maid, indeed! I should like to see anyone of that ilk who had travelled as far as I had, faced as many dangers, had two proposals of marriage and a dragon-lover! But I mustn't lose my temper.

I thought quickly. If he went to a brothel—place of entertainment as he preferred me to think of it—then he would roll home hungry at midnight and keep us all awake. On the other hand, if I could drag out supper till around nine, then give him extra moneys, he might well stay out all night, which would be perfect for our plans.

"Supper first," I said. "Then I'll see if I have a few coins to spare. Er . . . do you think it's the sort of entertainment I should enjoy?"

"Certainly not!" he said, and added hurriedly: "You might attract unwelcome attentions. It would be a shame if I had to escort you back just when it started to get interesting. . . ."

I made sure he had extra helpings of the meal, much to Growch's disgust, watched him finish off the rice wine and gave him more than enough coin to buy his choice for the night.

"Don't wake us when you return. . . ."

I waited until he had turned the corner, then went to the empty house next door to see how Ky-Lin was managing. Very well, he informed me, but was there a bowl of rice to spare? It helped the changeover.

I was too nervous to go to bed; I reckoned if Dickon was going to roll home before dawn it would be around two o'clock. At three he still hadn't arrived, so I went for Ky-Lin.

"Any reason why we can't leave right now?"

"We should wait for a little more light, but I expect we can manage. Light a lantern, and load me up."

Less than ten minutes later we were creeping through the deserted streets and, following Ky-Lin's lead, found ourselves in the poorer section of town. I kept the lantern as well shaded as I could, but in this part of town the streets were ill-kept, and we stumbled over rubbish and filth, so we needed the lantern on full beam. Ky-Lin was uneasy that someone would see us, but to me the streets were as quiet as the grave.

The ground beneath our feet became soft and spongy as we left the last straggle behind, and I was glad that my new boots had been thoroughly oiled.

"How much further?" We were splashing through pools of water now, and in the east the first graying of the sky announced the false dawn.

"Nearly at the causeway," said Ky-Lin, a large shadow ahead of me. "From there, about a mile to the first of the markers."

"Can't come too soon for me," grumbled Growch. "Me stummick is wet as a duck's arse and me paws full of gunge. When do we eat?"

Some time later we stood on a relatively dry pebbled causeway. Ahead of us lay a flat, steamy expanse of what looked like a vast, waterlogged plain, tinged pink by the just-rising sun. Tufts of grasses, the odd bush, a stunted tree or two, a couple of hummocks were all that interrupted the horizon, fringed in the distance by the ever-present and distant mountains.

Ky-Lin was concentrating: eyes crossed, head weaving from side to side. "Well, this is it. I can see the first marker. Shall we go?"

Chapter Eighteen

I was soaked to the skin. No, I hadn't fallen in the water, nor had it been raining; it was just the all-pervading miasma of damp that rose from the bog that drenched us all as thoroughly as if we had jumped in. Ky-Lin's coat shone with droplets of moisture, like a spider's web heavy with dew, and poor Growch's hair was plastered down to his body as if it had been soaked in oil. I was not only wet, I was cold. Although there was a sun of sorts, it had to fight its way through the steamy mists it sucked up from the stagnant pools all around us.

The ground beneath our feet was solid enough, thanks to Ky-Lin's instinct; how he did it I couldn't even guess, for I had seen nothing to guide us. Around us the bog bubbled, seethed, slurped, belched and burped, an ever-present reminder of the dangers we faced if we stepped off the invisible path we followed.

No animals, no birds. Plenty of insects, though; whining mosquitoes, huge flies, buzzing gnats, all of whom welcomed the chance to land on my face and hands, and Growch's nose, eyes and bum. Ky-Lin they left alone, as if he were composed of other than flesh and blood.

We seemed to have been walking all day but the sun was at less than its zenith when Ky-Lin called a halt. There was a small, knee-high cairn to our left, and we shed our loads, sat down and I unpacked some cheese and dried fruit. Growch had a knuckle of ham which he chewed on disconsolately, deliberately dropping it into the muck every now and again to emphasize how hardly used he was.

Ky-Lin insisted we continue our journey as soon as we had eaten.

"To the next marker, and then perhaps another rest," he explained.

I sighed as I packed up again. "I haven't *seen* a marker yet! How do you know where they are?"

"You're sitting on one," he said. "Or were. The last one we passed was that pile of peeled sticks, and the first was that moss-covered rock."

"And the next?"

"The skeleton of a bird with one wing missing."

"But how can you see from all that way off?"

"Because my antennae give me enhanced sensibilities—like extra eyes, noses and ears; two are arranged so they see further ahead; two tell me what goes on at the side; two what happens behind."

I was busy counting. "You've got four pairs. . . ."

"The last ones are for seeing beneath the ground for a few inches, so I don't damage anything growing out of sight; a germinating seed, a worm, an incubating chrysalis: my master thought of everything."

"Then you could see where a squirrel hoarded its nuts?"

"Or a dog a bone," said Growch, interested in spite of himself in what he had considered up to now to be a very boring conversation. "Or a burrow of nice, fat little rabbits?"

"If I could, I shouldn't tell you," said Ky-Lin. "The eating of flesh—"

"All right, you two," I said soothingly. There could never be true accord between one who believed all killing was wrong, and another whose greatest pleasure was eating red meat.

We had walked perhaps a half hour more when we came to a division of the ways. To our left the track had obviously been repaired, and was neatly outlined with stones; the track we had been following continued ahead, but was now rutted and pocked, with pools of standing water as far as one could see. Ky-Lin was plodding along the old path, head down, so I stepped onto the new one and called him back.

"Hey! You're going the wrong way!"

He turned his head. "No. I'm not. That way may look to be the right road but it is a deception. Especially constructed to trap the unwary. Go down that road and you step straight into a quagmire which will suck you down into an underground river that would carry you to a subterranean tomb."

But I was tired of him always being right, tired of the seemingly endless bog, tired of playing follow-my-leader! "I don't believe you! The road you are taking is the one that looks like it ends in disaster; why, even now you are nearly hock-deep in water!"

He splashed back to my side. "Very well, have it your own way. We will take this road. But I warn you, you are wasting our time."

I felt exuberant, glad that I had shown an obviously tiring creature the correct route, and for a while, as the ground beneath us remained firm and dry, my spirits rose still further, especially as it seemed a more direct route to the mountains ahead, and although my ring had started to itch intolerably, I ignored it, telling myself it was just another mosquito bite.

I turned to Ky-Lin who was some ten yards behind. "I told you this was the right—Ow!" Walking backwards, my feet suddenly found the path had disappeared and, scrabbling at the air for balance, I toppled back into the slimy, sucking mess, dragged down still further by the weight of my pack.

A moment later I felt Ky-Lin's teeth in my jerkin and I was dragged back onto the path, a sticky mess smelling like a midden.

I looked back: the open maw I had so nearly been sucked down into was closing up again, and in less than a minute the path gave the illusion of being as it was before.

"Better get cleaned up," said Ky-Lin. "There's a small spring a little way back. . . . You're not crying, are you? Anyone can make a mistake."

"But you *knew* I was wrong: why didn't you shout at me?"

"Ky-Lins don't shout."

"Well they should!" I sniffed and wiped my eyes with my filthy hand. "We're friends aren't we? Well then: don't be sweet and gentle and kind and forgiving all the time. Next time I do or say or suggest something stupid or silly, say so! Loudly . . ."

"You shouts at me—" grumbled Growch.

"If I shout at you, then you deserve it!"

"Not always! I remember—"

"All right, you two," said Ky-Lin, in such a perfect mimicry of my earlier attempts to soothe him and Growch, that I couldn't help laughing.

"Sorry, Ky-Lin! And thanks for pulling me out. From now on you lead the way." And next time I would heed the ring, I promised myself.

After that interruption it was a real slog to reach the spot Ky-Lin had decided would be our night stop. Several times, when we reached a comparatively dry spot, I begged him to stop, but he was adamant.

"There we will be safe. The ground is dry, but more important is our safety."

"But there's nothing to threaten us—except mosquitoes," I added, slapping at my face and neck. "You're not going to tell me there are monsters down there!"

"I do not know precisely what is down there. But I do know that the place I seek will keep us safe from whatever could threaten."

So we trudged on. The sun sank below the horizon, the mist thickened and it grew more chill. All at once the air above us was darkened by clouds of great bats, obviously seeking the insects who had so plagued us during the day. They weaved and ducked and swerved only inches above my head, and I found myself wrapping my hands about my head, uneasy at their proximity.

"They will neither touch you nor bite you," said Ky-Lin peaceably. "Those are not the bloodsuckers."

Then as quickly as they had come, they were gone.

Everything was quiet; now the whine of insects was gone there was nothing to break the silence except the sound of our steps and an occasional suck or blow from the bog itself. It was eerie.

"You'd better light the lantern," said Ky-Lin, his voice loud in the gloom. "It's getting dark, and we still have a couple of miles to go."

Easier said than done. The air was damp, so was I, and when I opened my tinderbox I couldn't raise a spark. More and more frantic, my fingers now bruised, my breath dampening the dried moss, I was ready to cry with frustration.

"Here," said Ky-Lin. "Let me try." He breathed over the box, and miraculously everything was suddenly dry, and my lantern lighted us over the last stretch.

When we reached the marker it was not in the least what I had expected, although it was a place that was recognizable. There was the skeleton of a bird, hanging upside down on a roughly fashioned wooden cross, and the whole area, a paved rough circle some eight feet across, was surrounded by a raised rim of stones a couple of inches high. Within the circle were a couple of stunted shrubs, one with sharp, prickly leaves like holly, the other bearing hairy leaves with a sharp, bitter smell. In the middle was a symbol picked out in white stones, but I couldn't make out exactly what it was meant to represent.

"Right," said Ky-Lin. "We can have a fire now, dry ourselves out. The dry kindling and charcoal are in the left-hand pannier."

In a few minutes the fire shut out the dark, creating a cozy circle like a room. I reheated some rice left over from the day before, adding herbs, and also ate some cheese and a couple of sweet cakes. The food, though dull, put new heart into me. I was warm for the first time that day, and we were drying out nicely. Even Growch had stopped grumbling.

"How much further?" I asked Ky-Lin.

"If we make good progress tomorrow, then we should be across by nightfall."

"Can't be soon enough," said Growch. "Never bin so cold or wet in me life, I ain't. 'Cept for now," he added, stretching his speckled stomach to the glow of the fire.

"Throw on the last of the charcoal," said Ky-Lin. "And sleep. If you wake, or think you do, pay no attention to what you see, or think you see."

"Why?" How could you see something that wasn't there?

"This is a Place of Power," he said. "And as such attracts both good and evil. But we are safe as long as we stay within the circle." Searching the ground he found a couple of discarded leaves from the bushes and threw them on the fire, where they blazed brightly for a moment then smoldered, giving off an unpleasant smell. "Lie down, close your eyes. . . ."

I scarcely had time to wrap myself in my blanket before I was asleep and slipping from one fragment of dream to another. I played in the dirt in front of my mother's house, drawing pictures on the ground with a stick; I struggled through a storm to reach shelter; once, for a startling moment I saw the father who was dead before I was born: I knew the tall smiling stranger was my father because I could see him from where I lay in my mother's womb. He had stretched out his hand to rest it on her belly and through his fingers I heard the resonance of the name he then gave me, that my mother later denied me: Talitha, the graceful one. My dragon had known that name. . . .

Another dream—no, this time a nightmare. I was shut in, enclosed, chained up in the dark, and something was there beside me, something with scrabbly sounding claws like a crab, something with fetid breath, something that was crawling nearer and nearer, something that had grabbed at my arm and was drawing me into its mouth—I screamed.

And woke.

And it was real, not a nightmare. Something had gripped my arm, something I couldn't see, and it was dragging me over the edge of the rim of stones, down into the stinking depths of the bog. I screamed again, Growch barked wildly and suddenly there was light, a flashing light, my jerkin was gripped in strong teeth and I was dragged back to safety beside a fire blazing up a shower of colored sparks, nursing a bruised arm.

"What—what happened?"

"You tossed about in your sleep and your arm went over the edge," said Ky-Lin. "Whatever you dreamt about awakened one of the creatures in the bog."

"But—what was it?"

"Look." And there, in the extended light thrown by the still-sparking fire, I saw the waters of the mere surrounding us stir and shift as strange creatures broke the surface. Just a claw, a spiny back, an evil eye, the glimpse of a whiplike tail, then they disappeared again in bubbles of foul-smelling gas.

"Some of these creatures are blind, some deaf, but all are hungry. They are not necessarily evil—evil needs an active determination—and that is a concept alien to them. They will eat you or their fellow creatures, even each other, but they lack discrimination. You should be afraid of them, but also feel pity. Human beings have choice, most animals too. They have none."

I shivered. They were foul, distorted creatures and they made me feel sick. If I had been dragged a little further I should now be beneath that slime with mud in my lungs, being chewed into fragments. How could I possibly show pity for such? I wasn't a saint like Ky-Lin, full of his Master's all-forgiveness, I was just a frightened human being.

The rest of the night Growch and I huddled together, both for warmth and for company. I slept but little, for the creature who had grabbed me seemed to have woken all the rest, and the waters around us seethed and gurgled, every now and again throwing up a great gout of water. I heard the wicked snapping of teeth, splash of tails, queer gruntings and groans. Even worse were the lights. Livid yellow, sickly green, lurid purple, they shone both above and below the surface. I couldn't tell whether they were animal or plant or some other manifestation, all I knew was some of them hovered, some zipped through the air, others hopped in and out of water like frogs, with a strange whistling sound.

I must have dozed off eventually, because when Ky-Lin woke me it was light again and, apart from the mist, insects and unhealthy-looking surroundings, all was as it had been the day before.

"Let's get going," I said. I couldn't stand the thought of another moment in that place. We ate breakfast as we walked, stale pancakes and dried fruit, and made good progress, although the path, if you could call it that, was almost covered with water most of the way. At noon we halted briefly at the last of the markers, so Ky-Lin told us, though to me it looked just like a bundle of dried rushes. There was little left that didn't need cooking, but even Growch didn't grumble at the rice cakes and cheese.

But Ky-Lin ate very sparingly, and kept glancing back the way he had come.

"What is it?"

"Not sure. We were followed earlier—men and horses, but they have gone back. But there is still someone back there, I am sure."

"Can't you see anything?"

"No. The land where we rested last night is on a sort of hummock, and that is between me and our pursuer, if there is one. No one from the village comes further than the circle, where they used to hold sacrifices and ritual executions—"

"You never told me that!"

"Would you have felt any easier?"

"Worse!"

"So all I can think is—"

He was interrupted by a scream, a howl of pure terror. In that misty desolation it was difficult to tell what direction it came from, but as it was repeated Ky-Lin's antennae got busy, swivelling this way and that and finally pointing firmly back the way he had come.

There was a further shriek: "Help me! Oh God, help me. . . ."

"It's Dickon!"

I felt a sudden violent jolt of revolt. If he were in trouble, then let him get out of it himself. I didn't want him with us, he had no right to follow, and more and more I felt he was a threat to us all. I wanted to run away, put my hands over my ears and escape as fast as I could, leave him to die, but even as I wished it my reluctant feet were carrying me back along the path we had come.

He was sinking fast. He had obviously stepped off the path, tried to cut a corner where the trail twisted back on itself after a half mile and had been caught in a morass. Already the green slime was bubbling up around his hips, and the more he struggled, the faster he sank.

He was crying, tears of pure terror, choking on my name.

I pulled the rope from Ky-Lin's pack, put one end between his teeth and threw the other towards Dickon; it fell short, and I drew it back, already slick with green slime. He started to flail his arms, and sank down further still.

"Stay still, you fool!"

This time he caught the end of the rope and Ky-Lin and I started to drag him out, but it was hard work, as at least half his body was now out of sight. We at last were making headway when the rope suddenly refused to move; we tugged again with all our strength and found we were not hauling at one body, but two: tangled up with Dickon was a corpse, one of the criminals executed ages ago. The face had been eaten away, and as Dickon caught sight of the grinning skeleton skull he gave another scream and let go the rope.

I threw it again and this time we managed to pull him free, the corpse releasing its hold and sinking back beneath the slime, throwing up its arms as it disappeared in an obscene gesture of farewell.

Dickon at last lay on the path, gasping and groaning, covered in stinking mud and slime. He staggered to his feet, attempted to thank me, but I had had enough.

I walked away from him and didn't look back.

Chapter Nineteen

And what is more I didn't even speak to him until we had finally crossed the bog by last light and reached firm ground. I let Ky-Lin lead the way and followed close behind with Growch, paying no attention to the plodding footsteps behind, the whimpers and groans.

The bog finally petered out into a series of dank pools, bulrushes, bog grass and squelchy mud. The land then rose sharply into a stand of conifers and we moved thankfully into the shelter of the trees and were immediately enclosed in an entirely different atmosphere. The needles underfoot cushioned our tread, the air was soft and full of the clean smell of resin, and the evening breeze soughed gently in the branches above.

I could hear a stream off to our right, so, after unloading Ky-Lin, I brushed aside the needles till I found some stones, then built a fire from pine cones and dead wood, before unpacking the cooking pot and going in search of the water.

The stream dropped into a series of little pools and, after filling the pot, I stripped off and stepped into the largest one, enjoying the shock of cold water, and scrubbed myself as best I could with my shirt and drawers, which I washed as well. Ky-Lin had followed me and drank deep, then stepped into the water and managed to surround himself with a fine cloud of spray, coming out as clean and fresh as ever.

I was about to don my clothes again, wet as they were, when he remarked: "The egg is ready to find another resting place: put it in your pouch for safety. Wrap it in a little moss."

I glanced down: it had certainly grown, and looked ready to pop out of my belly button any minute. I picked it up between finger and thumb expecting it to still give a little, but no. It was set hard and came away easily. I wrapped it in some dry moss, promising myself to make a proper purse for it as soon as I could. The pearly sheen had gone, and it now held a sort of stony sparkle, like granite in the sunshine.

A nose nudged my knee. "Where's the dinner then? Fire's goin' a treat, and all it wants is—"

"Clean diners," I said, picking him up and dropping him into the pool, leaving him scrabbling to get out and cursing me fluently.

Back at the fire, which I noticed had been replenished by a cowed Dickon, I put the pot on to boil, added dried vegetables, salt, herbs, dried fish and rice, and mixed some rice flour to make pancakes on a heated stone. A livid Growch came back in the midst of all this preparation and shook himself all over everything and everyone, so that the fire spat and sizzled and God knows what ended up in the cooking pot.

Dickon still cowered on the other side of the fire, a truly sorry sight, his clothes tattered and torn and covered with drying mud and slime, his face greenish under all the muck. I enjoyed my first words to him.

"You'd better go over to the stream and wash yourself. You stink! Wash your clothes out as well: you're not sitting down to eat like that. They'll soon dry out by the fire." Then, as he hesitated, glancing nervously at Ky-Lin, who was resting a little way away: "Go on; he won't bite you!"

"What . . . what is it?" he whispered.

" 'It' is a mythical creature called Ky-Lin. He and his brethren were guardians of the Lord Buddha. He is my friend."

His lip curled in a familiar sneer, obvious even through the layer of dirt on his face. "Oh, another of your only-talks-to-me creatures is he? Like the cur, the mad bear and the flying pig you once had—"

"Not at all!" I said sharply. "He understands you perfectly and talks as well as anyone. He's worth his weight in gold, and has been a perfect guide. If it hadn't been for him I could never have pulled you out of that morass, so mind your manners. Now, go wash!"

He told me later that the reason he had been able to find us was that someone from the seedy edge of town had seen us go, and he had persuaded a couple of horsemen to follow us as far as the Place of Power. But no further.

"I should have thought that by now you would have got the message," I said. "We don't need you; we can manage without your ceaseless suspicions and innuendos. The only reason you followed this time is because of your obsession with treasure, a treasure I have told you again and again doesn't exist. I am on a private pilgrimage to find a friend of mine and Growch has come along to keep me company."

"And—him?" He jerked his head in Ky-Lin's direction.

"I've told you that too. He is my guide and my friend, and I am his mission, if you like."

"Mission, suspicion . . . All a load of shit if you ask me. Anyway, who's this 'friend' you're looking for?"

"None of your business. And there is no place for you where I must go. I have a little money saved: I shan't need it where I am going, and I'm willing that you should have it if you will go back." I realized as soon as I opened my mouth that it was the wrong thing to say. By implying that I was unlikely to need money, it would only make him more convinced than ever that I was in expectation of finding more. I think my next remark made it worse, if possible. "I can give you ten gold pieces."

I still had the money Suleiman gave me, together with the coins my father had left me—but he wasn't having those.

I saw his eyebrows raise, but he was still staring into the fire, avoiding my eyes. The other two were already asleep, but I had stayed awake in order to have it out with him.

"If it is as you say," he said slowly, "then it matters little to either of us whether I go now or stay and see you safe. If I do the latter, then at least I can bear a message back to Matthew Spicer that I have left you safe and well. I can still be useful in fetching and carrying and I wouldn't feel I was doing my duty after all we've been through together if I didn't offer you my protection while I could."

Oh, very clever! I thought. Showing merely friendship and concern for my safety, but ensuring he kept his eye on me—and my money—right to the end. If I hadn't still had this indefinable feeling that only harm could come from his accompanying us, then I probably wouldn't have hesitated—but if I didn't know exactly what I was afraid of, how could I insist on leaving him behind?

"Very well," I said. "But I expect you to share all the chores and portage. And don't," I added, "grumble. Wherever you find yourself, or however tough it gets. I still think you're wasting your time."

"We'll see," he said, and by the next morning he was almost his usual cocky, arrogant self, just as if he had donned a new suit of clothes.

In fact more clothes were the first things we bought when we came across a decent-sized village. Our winter things had suffered badly in the bog, and besides the warmer weather was here and we needed thinner coverings. I bought us both loose cotton jackets and short breeches, reaching to the knees, and on Ky-Lin's recommendation, straw hats against the sun. I was going to buy sandals as well, but he advised me to keep my boots until we had crossed the desert.

As the villages we passed through were scattered, it didn't seem worthwhile Ky-Lin changing his shape or trying to hide, so we met a great deal of superstitious terror, but were better able to bargain: in many cases I believe they were only too glad to get rid of us!

As we worked our way through the foothills of the mountains towards our next objective, the Desert of Death, my spirits rose with each day that dawned, each mile we walked, each hour that passed. This was the last barrier to surmount, the last real test of our endurance. And with Ky-Lin to lead the way, what could possibly go wrong?

Suddenly, one day, there it was, stretching to the horizon as far as the eye could see. Even the mountains to the north seemed farther away than ever, misty blue in the haze that hung over the sand. There was no gradual approach; it seemed that one stepped off civilization into the wilderness like crossing a threshold. One pace and there you were.

We spent the night at the last village marked on the map, a tiny place squashed between two rearing crags, like a piece of stringy meat caught between two teeth. We were curiosities; very few travellers came their way, but even their awe at seeing Ky-Lin could not overcome their horror at the realization that we were intending to cross the desert.

At first Ky-Lin was reluctant to translate what they said, seated with us in the headman's hut that night, privileged guests, but I insisted, and he was honest enough to interpret literally.

Did we understand that it was called the Desert of Death?

Yes, we did.

Did we understand why it was called thus?

We thought so.

Did we know that no one returned from such a journey?

There was no call to, if they were travelling further on.

Then it was our turn to ask some questions.

Did the villagers ever venture out there?

Sometimes.

Why did they go?

To hunt desert foxes and hares.

Then there must be food for them, and water?

A shrug was the only answer.

How far did the hunters go into the desert?

Well provisioned they could last for a week, over a twenty-five-mile radius. After that there are no more animals to hunt.

What about other settlements?

Another shrug, then someone ventured that there were legends of a fabulous city, a great temple, but . . .

But what?

More shrugs. A long time ago, many lifetimes. No one came back to tell. Maybe it got lost under the Sand Mountains.

What are those?

Great hills of sand that march across the desert, eating everything they come across.

"Are you sure we're going in the right direction?" muttered Dickon.

"You can always turn around and go back," I whispered in return.

All the village turned out the next morning to see us off, and it didn't help one bit that they were burning incense, chanting prayers, and already looked at us as if we were ghosts.

"Don't worry too much," said Ky-Lin. "I assure you that out there, there is a huge temple and a thriving town: I've been there. It's situated on an underground river, but there is plenty of water. It was a while ago since I was there, but bricks and mortar and bronze and gold don't just disappear."

Comforted by his assurance we made our way to a line of scrub that, the villagers had informed us, marked the course of a now dried-up riverbed. Ky-Lin frowned a little as he gazed down at the river pebbles that lined the bottom.

"I remember a river running here. . . . Perhaps I was mistaken. Still it goes the way we want to, so let's follow it."

As the sun got higher in the sky the sweat started to trickle down my face, back and from under my arms. Five minutes later I saw Dickon drop behind and take a surreptitious swig from one of the water bottles he was carrying. He and I both carried four, and Ky-Lin another two, and these were meant to last us until we reached the temple: Ky-Lin's were for cooking and washing, ours for drinking. I was sorely tempted to copy him but decided to wait until Ky-Lin called a halt.

By my reckoning this must have been near noon, and we were now in a shimmering landscape, strewn with rocks under a baking sun. I blinked gritty eyes, but the shimmering persisted, like some curtain of gauze billowing out over a scene at best only guessed at.

"Right," said Ky-Lin. "Unload me, please, and then start digging."

I had wondered why we bought two mattocks some days past: now it seemed I was to find out.

"Digging?" Dickon and I queried in unison.

"Digging," said Ky-Lin firmly. "Every midmorning and every night you will dig a hole, or a trench, or whatever you prefer, to hide us from the worst heat of the day, and the extremes of cold at night. During the journey we will travel till noon, then rest until sunset. Then we shall march again till it gets too cold, and rest till dawn. That way we shall escape the worst extremes of temperature. First, a drink for everyone—only a mugful—and after the hole is dug we can eat."

Growch was so exhausted he just lay on his side, panting, his tongue flapping in and out like a snake tasting the air, so I served him first, letting him lap the lukewarm water from the cooking pot. He was so grateful that he showed us the best place to dig, and even helped for a while, the sand flying out between his hind legs far faster than we could dig. Once we had dug a reasonable trench we settled down in it and shared out the rice cakes, dried fruit, and cheese that was to be our midday meal from now on. At night we should have something cooked, and I would make enough rice cakes to eat cold at the next meal.

Propping a blanket across the trench, supported on the upended mattocks, I settled back to sleep for a while in sticky shade, but saw Dickon once again helping himself from one of his water skins, and was alarmed to see that he had almost finished one. Well, he'd get none of mine: I had to share with Growch.

I noticed that Ky-Lin had eaten but little and drank less; when the same thing happened that evening, I questioned him.

"I can manage for a few days; then I shall need rice, water, and salt in quantity."

"Salt? In this heat? It will only make you thirstier!"

"Not at all. Everyone needs salt, and you humans sweat it away in the hot sun. Without it you will become weak and dizzy, and your arms and legs will ache. That is why I insisted you bring salted meat with you: at least you will receive some that way."

We moved on again as the sun sank, a red ball, into the western sky, and kept the same routine day by night by day. It was very hard to reconcile the great extremes of temperature; at midday I would have given anything to be naked and blanketless, at night I could have welcomed two layers of everything. Once the shimmer of heat left the land at night, the stars were incredible; they seemed to be so much nearer, as if one could reach up and snatch them from the sky. It seemed some little compensation for the sting of sweat in one's eyes at midday, and the chattering of one's teeth twelve hours later.

Have you ever heard a dog's teeth chatter?

By the third day the mountains we had left had disappeared into haze, those we were moving towards seemed no nearer, those to the west invisible. The desert makes you feel very small: there is too much sky. There is nothing to mark your progress, no trees or bushes or other landmarks, so you might just as well be standing still, or be an ant endlessly circling a huge bowl.

When I woke on the fourth morning and reached for the last of my water flasks, I found it was missing. I had been careful to follow Ky-Lin's instructions; it would be on the fifth day that we would reach the temple, and the water must last that long. There was a full day to go, and there wasn't a drop left! Frantically I shook the other skins: all empty. I couldn't have dropped the full one, surely! No, I remembered clearly the night before shaking it to make sure none had evaporated.

Springing to my feet I was just in time to see Dickon emptying the last of the water down his throat and sprinkling a few drops over his head and face. He started guiltily as he saw me.

"Sorry! I was just so thirsty. . . . Anyway, it's not far now. We can manage for a day. . . ."

I struck him hard across the mouth. "You selfish bastard! You had four skins all to yourself, and Growch and I had to share! I wish you had never come, I wish you were dead!"

"Hush, child!" said Ky-Lin. "Bring Dog over to me and close your eyes. I will give you some of myself. . . ." and he breathed gently down his nostrils onto our faces. "There! You will not feel thirsty for a while."

And it was true. Both Growch and I managed that day without needing water; somehow Ky-Lin had transferred liquid, precious water from his body to ours: I only hoped that it would not hurt him. Magic only goes so far.

That day we travelled faster and further than any day before, and the following morning Ky-Lin woke us early.

"By midday we should be there," said Ky-Lin encouragingly. "Just over that little ridge ahead and you will see the temple. And then water, food, rest, shelter . . ."

The struggle up that ridge was a nightmare. The sweat near blinded me, I ached, my limbs wouldn't obey me, my throat hurt, I was too dry to swallow. At last we topped the incline and, full of anticipation, gazed down on Ky-Lin's fabled city.

Only it wasn't there.

Nothing, except a heap of tumbled stones.

Chapter Twenty

I gazed around wildly, thinking for one stupid moment that we were in the wrong place, but one look at Ky-Lin's stricken face told me the truth. It was Dickon who voiced all our thoughts.

"Well, where is it then? Where's your town, temple, water, food, shelter, and rest?"

I had never seen Ky-Lin look so dejected. For an eye-deceiving moment he lost all color and almost appeared transparent, his beautiful plumed tail dragging in the dust. But even as I blinked he regained his color, and his tail its optimism. The only sign of disquiet was a furrowing of his silky brow.

"Well?" Dickon was panicking, his voice hysterical. "What do we do now?"

"What happened, Ky-Lin? There was something here once. . . ."

He turned to me. "I don't know. I wish I did. I told you it was a long time since I was here. Let's go down and see. There must be something we can salvage from all this."

At my feet Growch was whimpering. "Sod me if I can go no further. Me bleedin' paws hurt, me legs is sawn off, me stummick tells me me throat's cut and I could murder a straight bowl of water. . . ."

I picked him up, though my body told me I ached as much and was twice as thirsty, and we all stumbled like drunkards down the slope to the first of the tumbled wrecks of stones. When we reached them we found they were not stones but mud bricks, and as I looked around I could see this was the remains of what had once been a street of shops or small dwelling places, and as they fell they had crumbled and broken.

Ky-Lin prowled down the street, looking here, there, everywhere. "No sign of war or pestilence. This place has been empty for many, many years, but it looks as if they went peaceably. Everything has been cleared away, no artifacts left about, no evidence of fire. . . . Let's take a look at the temple, or what's left of it."

Not much. We threaded our way through other deserted, tumbledown streets until we reached what must have been a courtyard. It surrounded a partly stone-walled temple, with now-roofless cells behind, which would have housed the monks. Sand had drifted deep on the temple floor, the roof had fallen in and the stone altar was empty. No idols, no incense, no prayer wheels, no bells. Only the wind, shush-shushing the sand back and forth across the stone floor in little patterns. On either side of the altar were a couple of stone lumps, now so eroded by sand, sun and wind that they were unrecognizable.

Unrecognizable to all but Ky-Lin, that was.

"Here, girl: come see what is left of my brothers. . . ."

Nearer I could see what must have once been their heads, their tails.

"Were they Ky-Lins too?"

He nuzzled the stones lovingly. "Once. But these two attained Paradise a long time ago, and the monks carved them to remind them of my Master's visit." He sighed. "At least it shows one thing, all this: the soul outlasts the strongest stone."

"How about getting your priorities right?" came Dickon's voice over my shoulder. "Souls belong to the dead: we're living. But we won't be much longer unless you find us something to eat and drink."

Without cooking I had a couple of rice cakes, some dried fruit, a little cheese.

"If you will unload me please," said Ky-Lin, "you will find one small water skin under the blankets. One mug of water each, no more; the rice cakes and cheese will be enough for now."

Strange: I had never noticed that particular water skin before, but then he was Magic. . . .

I shared my cheese and water with Growch, and although his share of the liquid was gone in half a dozen quick laps, I sipped mine as slowly as I could, running it over my parched tongue before swallowing, to get the maximum benefit; behind me I heard Dickon's water gone in a couple of quick gulps. I went over to Ky-Lin with some dried raisins and apricots.

"Come, you must eat something too; we depend on you to keep us going."

His forked tongue, ever so soft, lapped the fruit from my palm. "Now get some rest. Go into the shade of that wall. I am going to reconnoiter. I shall return as soon as I can."

I settled back with my back against the stone. Just five minutes' nap, and then . . .

And then it was dawn. Someone had tucked a blanket round Growch and me, and further away Dickon was snoring softly. I was neither hot nor cold, hungry nor thirsty, and I felt rested and refreshed. Beside me was a heap of wood, smooth, bleached wood that had obviously been around for a while. Beyond, Ky-Lin was curled around, fast asleep, only the rise and fall of his chest showing that he was still alive.

A surprisingly wet and cold nose was shoved in my face. "What's for breakfast, then?"

I used half the water that was left to boil up rice, beans, dried vegetables and herbs, on Ky-Lin's advice adding the rest of the salted meat, and some rather dessicated roots he had found. They smelt oniony, and looked like water lily suckers. The wood burned brightly and too fast, with a sort of bluish flame, and I kept it down as much as I could, for now the sun was high and extra heat was unwelcome. Just before it was cooked I took the pot off the fire and clamped on the lid tight, then buried it in the sand so it would retain heat and absorb the last of the liquid, as I had seen it done in this country to ensure both tenderness and conservation of fuel.

"And now," said Ky-Lin, "we must find somewhere to shelter. I can smell wind, and that here will mean a sandstorm." He led us through the remains of a small archway to the left of the altar. Behind was part of a wall and domed roof, and a set of steps leading down into the darkness. There was remarkably little of the ubiquitous drifted sand.

"The way the wind blows here," explained Ky-Lin, "the sand merely piles up on the other side of the wall. Now, we shall go down the steps to better shelter. Once at the bottom, if we spread out the blankets, we shall be snug enough."

Something scuttled past my feet and I gave a stifled scream.

"Scorpion," said Dickon. "I'm not going down there, and that's flat!"

He kicked out at the creature, who raised its stinging tail threateningly and disappeared through a crack in the wall.

"The ultimate survivors," said Ky-Lin. "When everything else has disappeared from the earth, the ants, the scorpions, and the cockroaches will have it all to themselves. Don't worry," he added. "There are no more down there. Follow me," and he disappeared down the flight of stone steps.

"You're on your own," said Dickon, as I prepared to follow. "I'm not going down."

I fumbled my way down steps worn smooth by generations of monks. Once at the bottom the air was pleasantly cool, with only a fine layer of sand underfoot. The light from above was enough for me to see that this was a little cul-de-sac, but large enough to hold us all comfortably.

"Come on down!"

"Not on your life," came Dickon's voice, oddly distorted by the turn in the stairs, although Growch had already joined me quite happily.

"In that case," I yelled back, "you can go out and fetch in all the baggage. And the cooking pot," I added.

I knew he wouldn't, and it took the three of us to transfer everything to safety, Dickon grumbling all the while. By the time all was stowed away safely the wind had risen enough for us to hear even at the bottom of the stairs, and when I went out to retrieve the cooking pot it was really nasty up top. The wind was whining like a caged dog, gusting every now and again into a shriek, and with it the sand was spiralling as tall as a man, blasting into any unprotected skin like the rasp of a file. The very heaps of sand in the courtyard had changed position so much that it took me several minutes to locate where I had buried the cooking pot; it was still hot, and I had to take off my shirt and wrap it in that to carry it safely, the driving sand stinging my bare skin unmercifully.

I served out half the contents of the pot; a bowl each, my meat ration for Growch, and half a mug of water, and as I scoured out the bowls with the ubiquitous sand I wondered which of us was still the hungriest and thirstiest. Settling down on my blanket, I asked the questions that would probably mean the difference between life and death to us. Somebody had to ask; I didn't want to, but it was obvious Dickon wanted to hear the answers even less than I did.

"What did you find out, Ky-Lin?"

"I searched the whole of the ruins while you were asleep. I gave you all a little Sleepy Dust to ensure you slept for a day and a half—" He raised his left front hoof as we protested. "Yes, yes, I know; but you needed the rest, and I wanted time without your worries burdening me. I needed to let my senses roam free.

"This place was abandoned some eighty years ago. What drove them out was probably the threat of famine. From what I could determine, the wells on which the town depended for its water started to dry up, due to the river deep beneath the desert floor changing course. There may still have been enough for drinking, but certainly not enough for irrigating their crops.

"Added to this, there was the unprecedented advance of the Sand Mountains, a phenomenon peculiar to this desert. The villagers mentioned them, remember? They are formed by a combination of wind and sand, and move to any place they are driven. They may not be seen for a hundred years, but given special conditions they can build up within days, and overwhelm anything in their path. Such a disaster overtook this town. They had enough notice to move out in an orderly fashion, so everything portable was taken with them. The monks were the last to leave."

"And where are the Sand Mountains now?"

He shrugged. "Who knows? They were not here long, but time enough to destroy the fabric of the buildings, as you saw."

"Where did the people go?"

He shrugged again. "Probably west and north. The way we go. . . ."

Here it was, the question I had so been dreading. "Any—any sign of water?"

He looked at me with compassion, then shook his head. "No, I found no trace of water. Not yet, anyway. That doesn't mean there isn't any."

Dickon leapt to his feet. "No water, no food—what the hell do we do now?"

"We would do well to pray. Now, together. Each to our own God or gods." He bowed his head. "In any case it will concentrate our minds if we are quiet for a few minutes. Prayer always helps. Focus on our predicament and ask for guidance. . . ."

I wanted to pray as my mother had taught me: speak to God direct, she had always said. But she had sent me to the priest to learn my letters and the Catechism, and it was these familiar formulas, as comforting as a child's rhymes, that I now found filled my mind; the priest had taught me that God could only be approached through His intermediaries, those like Himself. My mother, on the other hand, had never been afraid to speak her mind, and she told me God was there to be talked to, just like anyone else, person to person.

I don't know whether she believed in Him; I think she only believed in herself. I recited three rapid Ave's under my breath, not thinking of anything really, except the comfort of the formula. I glanced at the others; Ky-Lin was obviously in communication with his Lord, but Dickon's hands were twisting as if he was wringing out a cloth, his eyelids flickering. No point in looking at Growch; his god, Pan, was a heathen.

But it was Growch who saved us.

I was in the middle of my third Paternoster when a sacrilegious interruption destroyed all thought of prayer.

"Bloody 'ell! Effin' little bastards!"

"Growch!"

"Sor*ree*! But what d'you say if'n you'd just been bit on yer privates by a bunch o' ravenin' ants?"

"Ants? But—"

Ky-Lin and I had the same thought at the same time. Ants in a town deserted for many years and surrounded by an arid desert could mean only one thing: ants, to exist, need both food and water, however minimal. So, somewhere there was water!

"Move, dog!" said Ky-Lin. "Slowly and carefully. The lantern, girl!"

At first the flames flickered wildly all over the stone floor because my hand was shaking so much, but as it steadied we all saw what had so rudely interrupted whatever Growch had been thinking about. A double line of ants, both coming and going, the ones advancing towards us laden with what looked like grains, the others empty-legged. I swung the lantern to the left; the laden ants were disappearing into a large crack in the masonry, obviously behind which they had their nest. The outgoing ones, where did they go?

I swung the light the other way, but obviously too far: no ants.

"Gently does it," breathed Ky-Lin. "Back a little . . ."

And there it was. There was a long, straight crack in the floor, and down this the ants were appearing and disappearing without hindrance. I brushed away some of the sand, and there was another crack in the stone, this one at right angles to the first. Ky-Lin used his tail on the sand as well, and between us we uncovered a full square, some two and a half feet along each side. It was obviously an entrance of some sort to an underground storage area, but how did it work? I scraped away at the center: nothing! I blew at the sand, I scrabbled with my fingers, still nothing.

Ky-Lin's delicate antennae were probing the surface. "Try here," he said, indicating the corner farthest away. I brushed away the sand and there, recessed into the stone, was a rusty iron ring.

"That's it! That's it!" I was now in a fever of excitement. "There must be something down there, there must!" and bending down I tugged at the ring, but all I got was red, flaky dust on my fingers; the square had not budged.

Dickon had finally worked out what all the fuss was about, and exercised all his strength, again to no purpose except for rusty fingers.

"Let's try this scientifically," said Ky-Lin. "Neither of you is powerful enough to shift the trapdoor on your own and I cannot get a grip. Think, my children; how can we raise it?"

I knew he had something in mind, but Dickon and I could only gaze at each other in perplexity. It was Growch, puffed up with his success in finding the stone trapdoor, who provided us with the simple answer.

"Well, you are a coupla dummies! Rope, that's what you want: rope."

Of course! And while the increasing wind raged outside and the sand trickled its way in little drifts down the steps, we found the rope in the baggage, looped it through the ring in the floor and, one end tied round Ky-Lin's neck, the other held by Dickon and myself, we tried once more to heave the square of stone from its bed.

"One, two, three, heave! One, two, three, heave!" We heaved, we pulled, we jerked, we struggled, but the damned thing wouldn't shift. We tried again and again, and finally there was a faint grating noise and it seemed the trapdoor shifted just a fraction.

"We've got it!" yelled Dickon. "Just one more heave. All together now—heave!"

Another minuscule shift in the stone, then it settled back into its square with a little puff of dust. The ants had disappeared, not surprisingly.

"Once more," exhorted Dickon. "Pull up and back this time. Now!"

We heaved as hard as we could, there was a sudden snap and we all three landed in a tangled bruised heap in the corner, the rope coiling itself round our legs. I pulled the length through my fingers, conscious of a bruised shoulder. "But it hasn't broken. . . ."

"No," said Ky-Lin. "It was the ring that snapped; it had rusted right through."

I burst into tears: I couldn't help it. "It's not fair! I'm so thirsty. . . ."

Ky-Lin nuzzled my neck comfortingly. "Courage. We haven't lost yet." He inspected the broken ring. "It was weak at this one point. Perhaps it could be repaired. Remember the bars in your prison, girl? Well this time we shall have to try the process in reverse. Give me some space; I shall have to think about this."

Obediently we moved back, and one look at Dickon's stricken face told me what I must be looking like too. True, we didn't know what we would find down there, but hope had been rekindled, only to be dashed again by a few flakes of rust. I had never felt so thirsty in all my life, not even as a child in a high fever when I had cried and begged my mother for the cool spring water she had trickled down my throat from a wet cloth.

"Shut your eyes, children, you too, dog!"

Suddenly I felt the hair curl on my head, and even behind closed eyelids I was near blinded by a brilliant light. There was a smell of ozone, of snow, of wet iron. I opened my eyes to see Ky-Lin momentarily surrounded by a haze of colorless flame. I shut my eyes again, and when I opened them the ring was whole again, though considerably smaller.

I stretched forward to touch it, but Ky-Lin stopped me. "Not yet; it is not yet cool enough. . . ." He looked tired, diminished.

I put my arms about his neck. "Rest awhile; we can wait."

But it seemed an age before the ring cooled enough to try; up above it was full dark, and the wind still howled.

At last Ky-Lin nodded his head. "This time just keep pulling: no sudden jerks."

Once more I looped the rope around his neck, once more Dickon and I took up the slack at the other end. This was it.

"Now," said Ky-Lin softly. "Pull as hard as you can—and pray. . . ."

Chapter Twenty-One

This time I didn't pray; I swore.

It made me feel better as I once more took the strain of the rope, endured the aches in my shoulders and arms, the rasp in my throat, the grit between my teeth—oh yes, I really enjoyed that swear, and I used all the bad words I had ever heard, whether I knew their meaning or not, and included the sort of things one sees written on walls. In fact I was concentrating so hard on remembering all the words, with my eyes shut, that I didn't see the stone begin to shift.

The first I knew was Dickon's mutter: "It's coming, it's coming. . . ."

There was a sudden slither, a grinding of stone against sand, and the rope burnt through my fingers. I collided once again with the other two, but this time it didn't hurt, and I found I was staring down at a black hole in the floor, revealing a triangular gap and the glimpse of more stone steps leading downward.

With the opening came a sudden breath of stale air, thick with the stink of rancid oil, dust, decaying meal—

"I can smell water," said Growch. "There's some down there somewheres. Faint, but it's there. Shall we go?"

A gap that would admit a dog wasn't large enough for two adults and a pony-sized mythical creature, so we had to push the stone trapdoor right away to one side before we could descend, Ky-Lin in the lead and Dickon and I with the two lanterns. Growch in his eagerness near tripped me up. I sat down hurriedly on one of the steps, noticing that even here the sand had penetrated, the only clear spaces being the lines where the ants had trailed up and back over the years. I had a sudden idea, which got shoved to the back of my mind immediately I reached the chamber.

It was a huge cellar in which we found ourselves, the stone roof supported by a row of pillars marching away into dark corners our lanterns didn't reach. The floor was flagged, and on either side stone shelves lined the walls. Empty shelves, no sign of containers to hold the water Growch still insisted he could smell. Slowly we walked the full length of the cellar, the lantern light sending our shadows into black giants that climbed startled pillars, crept along stone walls, trailed our footsteps like devoted pets.

To the left and right of us there were only empty shelves, dust and ancient cobwebs like dirty, disintegrating lace. The atmosphere was dry and choking and I sneezed involuntarily, expecting the noise to echo and reverberate, but the cellar had a peculiar deadening effect and the sneeze seemed to die at my feet. It was like being stuck behind the heavy curtains of a four-poster.

We reached the far end and there, ranged against the walls, were several tall clay pots, seemingly sealed with wax stoppers. My heart gave a bound of anticipation and I rushed forward, lantern bobbing wildly, my knife cutting hastily through the seals. I stepped backward, covering my nostrils as a dreadful stench seeped out.

"It's fermenting grain," said Ky-Lin. "Not fit to touch. Except for the ants," he added. "This is what has kept them going over the years. With luck it will last for many years more. They are sensible creatures and will not overbreed, so perhaps—"

"But where is the water?" shouted Dickon, coughing and choking, all control gone. "Don't you realize, you stupid creature, that we will die without it? Who cares about bloody ants? Fuck the ants!"

"I care about them," said Ky-Lin severely. "And so should you. I care for all living creatures, and if you would just realize that those little creatures can point the way to your salvation—"

"Fuck salvation!" yelled Dickon. "And fuck you too!" and flung his lantern full into Ky-Lin's face.

There was a burst of colored light—red, green, purple, orange, blue, yellow—then nothing.

Darkness. Even my lantern had gone out.

A brief moment of panic, angry sobs from Dickon, then a comforting nudge at my ankle.

"You stay 'ere, nice an' quiet, an' I'll nip up top an' get your lightin' things. Don' move now," and Growch's claws click-clacked away over the stone floor. A faint light came from the opening above, and I saw him disappear over the last step. A moment or two later he was back, and thrust the box into my free hand with his muzzle.

"Nice bit o' light, an' things'll look different . . ."

My hands were shaking so much it took two or three goes before I could light my lantern. I swung it over my head and saw Dickon, his face all blubbery with angry tears, the other lantern shattered at his feet.

"I didn't mean to hurt him," he whined. "It wasn't my fault! He shouldn't have riled me! Where's he gone, anyway?"

Where indeed? I rushed from one end of the cellar to the other, my lantern swinging wildly, but there was no sign of Ky-Lin. Perhaps he had gone up the steps?

Growch shook his head. " 'E's not up there. 'E ain't nowhere as I can see. Can't smell 'im neither."

I stumbled and fell to my knees, the lantern nearly slipping from my fingers. I had fallen over something, a stone, a pebble—

No, not a stone, not a pebble. A tiny little image, looking as old as the stone from which it had been fashioned. Tears stung my eyes as I recognized the pudgy little features, the plumed tail.

"He's here," I said. "What's left of him."

The stone was cold in my hand. There was no life here, no flicker of movement. Just the small shell of what had been a vibrant, loving, colorful creature. Even my ring was cold and dead, like Ky-Lin.

I felt anger rising in me inescapably, like the sudden jet of blue flame from a burning, sappy log. I thrust the stone figure under Dickon's nose.

"You killed him! You destroyed him with your evil temper! I hate you! I hate you! I *hate* you!" I sobbed, and swung my lantern at his head as he ducked.

"Steady on there," said Growch mildly. " 'E wouldn't 'ave wanted no 'istrionics. What's done is done. Nuffin's ever truly lost. 'E may be just a bit of stone in yer 'and right now, but what 'e was is still 'ere. What 'e taught you. Well then, try and think like 'e would 'ave wanted you to. Pretend 'e's still 'ere. If you concentrate 'ard enough it'll be like 'e's still speakin' to us."

I could feel my ring warming up again; looking down it had a pearly glow. Growch was right, wherever his doggy wisdom had suddenly come from. My anger evaporated. I kissed the little stone figure and tucked it in my pouch, promising it a better resting place when I found one.

What would he have done now? I shut my eyes and concentrated. Looked for water, of course. Just before we came down here, when I was sitting on the step, I had had an idea, a good one, I was sure. But what was it? Something to do with . . . Stone? Tracks? Ants? Yes, that was it. But how could it help? Think, girl, think! Ants, sand-covered stone, tracks, Ky-Lin saying they had to have water—That was it!

Rushing back to the steps I held the lantern high, searching for ant trails, but our comings and goings had made a complete mess of anything I was looking for, and the ants themselves were milling around in aimless circles. Half-shuttering the lantern, I settled down to wait.

"What the hell are you doing?" asked Dickon irritably. "We're wasting time. We should be searching for water."

"I am."

"What? Sitting on your arse?"

"Just shut up, keep still, and be patient."

"I know, I know, I know!" said Growch triumphantly. "Clever lady."

Which left Dickon in the dark, especially as he couldn't understand Growch, but seeing us both concentrating he lapsed into silence. The ants settled down and began their marching from the nest above. Down the steps in a double line, then—yes, my theory was correct. The line split into two, one set of ants going off to the darkness at the rear end for food, the other half turning left, and—

"Under the steps!" I called out. "We never looked there!"

Behind the steps was a man-sized space and three shallow steps leading down to a small cistern and—a thousand candles to Saint Whoever when I could afford them!—it was still a third full.

The water was clear, but littered with unwary ant bodies and with a layer of silt beneath, but nothing had ever tasted so good. We scooped it with our mugs into the cooking pot, then all of us drank till we were full and I for one felt slightly sick.

Growch rolled over with a grunt and a distended belly. "Near as good as a beef bone . . ."

A drink seemed to bring Dickon back to sense once more and cooled his temper for days to come. "We mustn't stir up the water too much," he said. "We need to fill the water skins with clean."

Looking at the cistern more carefully, wondering how the water hadn't dried up long since, I noticed a darker patch at the back which felt damp to the touch, so there was obviously seepage from some long-forgotten spring or rivulet behind. Not enough to keep the temple in water, just enough for the ants—and us. Praise be!

By now it was full dark above and the wind still whined and shrieked unabated, so we moved everything down into the cellar and I used what fuel we had left to cook up enough rice to keep us going that night and the following morning.

We fell asleep over the meal, but I had had sense enough to remove everything eatable from the ants though, remembering Ky-Lin, I sprinkled a few grains on the floor near their trail. Ky-Lin would have done the same if he had been with us, of that I was sure, making some gentle remark about it being a "change of diet" for the insects. Anyway, they deserved it: they had shown the way to the water.

The following morning the wind was gone as though it had never been and the sun shone brilliantly from a clear sky. We all wanted to get going as soon as possible, but now there was no Ky-Lin to help with advice and porterage, we were faced with real problems. The mythical creature had told us that the temple was "halfway," which meant there were at least five more days of travel to endure. He had consulted the maps and shown me the route we should follow, and with my Waystone I thought I could manage that. Burdened as we were, though, we should probably have to expect at least one more day's travel, bringing it to six, which would be over the limit for even the stretching of what food we had.

Well, we could go hungry, but not thirsty. I spread out everything from our baggage, hoping we could leave at least half behind to lighten our load, while Dickon carefully filled the ten water skins. I knew how heavy these were from bitter experience, but they were essential. But what to leave behind? The remaining food, blankets against the cold, and mattocks, these must come as well. Money in a belt around my waist, personal possessions (and the egg) in a pouch at my neck. Cooking pot, spoons and mugs (I had dismissed the idea of boiling everything up before we went: in the desert heat it would be uneatable in twenty-four hours); honey and salt were heavy to carry, but both were necessary. Likewise my few packs of herbs, the maps, sewing kit and oil: all had their uses.

In the end all we could reasonably do without was everything we were not actually wearing, the broken lantern, one blanket out of three, my writing things and my journal. This last went with me, I was determined on that; at worst if our skeletons were found in the desert, it would explain everything. I hefted the bundle we could leave: I could lift it on one finger. Well, two. So that wasn't going to make much difference.

"Dickon," I called out. "We'll never carry all this!"

He emerged with the last two water skins. "I've been thinking about that. The water is covered with a small grid the monks must have stood on to bucket up the water, and if you recall, there was a metal cover lying to one side. We could use both as sledges; why carry if you can pull? Both are metal, so they shouldn't wear away. The grid is no problem, and the metal cover has holes where it fitted over the cistern, so if we cut the rope in half you can pull the grid as it's smaller, and I'll take the cover. Right?"

So it was decided. We then ate, packed up and waited for the worst of the day's heat to dissipate, deciding to keep to Ky-Lin's order of march: early evening and dawn. While we were waiting I soaked some beans and dried vegetables for the following day, ready to cook. Fuel was going to be a problem, but I persuaded Growch to pick up everything we could burn during the march. Before we left we drank as much as we could take from the cistern, and I even took the luxury of a quick wash, soaking my clothes as well for a cool start to the trek. The water was all cloudy by the time I had finished, but it would soon settle back for the ants and I left them a few more grains and a dollop of honey as compensation.

We left the trapdoor open, in case other travellers came that way, and I took a soft stone and drew the universally recognized symbol of an arrow on the cellar floor to indicate the position of the cistern.

And so we left the temple to the ants and set off across the desert towards the dying sun.

At first our progress was slow but steady. The management of the improvised sledges was difficult to master. The metal cover travelled easier, but was more unstable. As we travelled the sledges became lighter each day, and now we took turns with each. The weather stayed clear, my directions appeared to be correct, for each day we persuaded ourselves the mountains we were headed for came fractionally nearer.

Then on the fourth day we ran into trouble.

The night had been overcast, for once, and we had overslept after a hard day's trek the previous day. When we awoke the eastern sky was bright and we cast long shadows ahead of us. We ate a hurried breakfast—not as much as any of us wanted, but rations were short by now—and set off at a good pace for a steep rise just ahead. We hauled the sledges up the rise, looking forward to the incline beyond and—

"What the hell . . . !" If he hadn't said it, I would. Ahead of us, about a mile distant, reared a sudden and unexpected range of mountains.

Sand Mountains.

These were the ones Ky-Lin and the villagers had warned us about, the giants who could stay in one place for years and then, given the right conditions, move across the desert floor at a terrifying speed, destroying everything in their path. And here they were, straight across our path, barring our way to the mountains. At the moment they were quiet, a range of sandhills some fifty to a hundred feet high at their lowest. And they stretched for miles. As we moved close an errant wind agitated sand on the tops into whirls and curls like smoke, and every now and again miniavalanches of sand fell down the steeper slopes.

For the rest of the morning we tried to climb those restless, shifting mountains, but for every stride up, we tumbled back two. The sledges became bogged down in the sand and we sank to our knees in it, like falling into quicksand, and twice we nearly lost Growch. Eventually we tried to find a way between, but the sand blew in our faces and filled our footsteps within seconds.

There was only one thing for it: we should have to take the long trek round them; the worst of that was we had no idea whether the way east or west was shorter, as they stretched as far as the eye could see in both directions.

Three days later we struggled round the western end and tried to pick up our bearings. We had wasted three days to find ourselves in virtually the same spot we had started out from and the real mountains seemed as far away as ever. On we tramped, our travelling time curtailed by our increasing weariness from lack of proper nourishment. Two days later the last of our food and water was gone and we piled all our goods onto the smoother sledge, pulling it in tandem to conserve our strength.

I began to see things that weren't there—houses, lakes, trees, camels, people—shimmering in the distance some feet above the desert floor, and beside me Dickon was hallucinating too. On the tenth day we put Growch on the sledge because he could move no further and lay there with his tongue hanging out like one dead.

Dickon and I now fell every dozen yards or so and our throats were so parched we couldn't even curse each other. At last we both tripped and fell together and I just wanted to lie there forever and forget everything. I was conscious it was high noon already and I knew if we didn't get up and seek shelter we should surely be dead before nightfall.

I rose to my knees and peered ahead, but all I could see was one of those fevered images again: a train of camels seeming to stride six feet above the sand and some half mile away. I collapsed, without even the energy to rouse Dickon, to offer a last prayer, and drifted off into unconsciousness.

But somewhere, somehow, I could swear I heard a dog barking. . . .

Chapter Twenty-Two

. . . A dog barking. Cautiously I opened my eyes. Normally in the desert Dickon and I slept within feet of each other, but now all my hands encountered was a blanket. There was a dim light over to my right, it must be the moon. No stars. And where was Growch? I was sure I had heard him a moment ago. I struggled to sit up, and there was a cold, wet nose against my cheek.

"'Ad a nice kip, then? Thought we'd lost you at one stage. Feel a bit better?"

"I don't understand. . . . What's happened? I—" And then, suddenly, it all came back to me. The desert, the vast, terrible, unforgiving desert. Sun, heat, thirst, hunger, hallucinations, death already rattling in my throat, the last thing a dog barking . . .

I sat up slowly, stretched, wiggled my fingers and toes. I seemed to be all in one piece, but I was dreadfully stiff, my throat was sore and my head ached.

"Wanna drink? On yer right. On the table. That's it. Careful now, don' spill it."

Blessed, beautiful, clear cold water. The most wonderful liquid in the world. I drank it all, then burped luxuriously. I looked around me. I was obviously inside a house or hut, and the light I had thought the moon was a saucer oil lamp. I was on a pallet of sorts and it must be sometime at night. So, we had been rescued, but how and when? Where were we? And where was Dickon?

More than one question at a time flummoxed Growch. "I'll tell yer, I'll tell yer, but one at a time! Dickon? 'Is lordship is around and about in the town somewheres, and—"

"Which town? What's it called? Where is it?"

"'Ow the 'ell does I know? A town's a town ain't it? Same as all towns. 'Ouses, streets, people, dogs, food . . . We're still in the desert, but they got plenty o' water. Goats, chickens, camels. It was their camels as brought us in. I barked till I was 'oarse, managed to get over to the caravan, and they came back and picked you up."

"Oh, Growch! You saved our lives!" and I hugged him till he swore he couldn't breathe and why did I have to be so soppy? All the while his tail was wagging like mad, so I knew he was secretly as pleased as could be.

"An' afore you ask, all yer belongings is snug as well."

I felt for my money belt and neck pouch: all safe.

"Short and long of it is, they brought us in—gave you camel's milk out there, they did, an' you sicked it all up—" I was not surprised: the very thought of camel's milk made me ill again. "—then they gave you water an' things an' brought us 'ere. Got two rooms, an' I kep' 'is lordship away from all what is ours."

I stretched again, felt my headache lessening. "What time is it?"

"Middle evenin'. Sun down, moon not yet up."

"I must have been asleep for—nine or ten hours, then?"

"An' the rest! Four days ago it was when they brought us in. There's a woman been feedin' you slops an' things with a spoon."

"Four days!" I swung my legs over the edge of the bed, tried to stand up and fell back again. "By our Lady! I feel so weak!"

"Not surprised. Slops never did no one no good. Yer wants some good red meat inside of yer, like what I have." He smacked his chops. "Nuffin' like it. Treated me real well they 'as. Called me a 'ero . . ."

"And so you are," I said, giving him another hug. "Be a dear and go and find Dickon for me?"

Two days later I was up and about again, with an urge to get going as soon as we could. It was now well past Middle Year, we had been travelling for over fifteen months, and now I had recovered from my ordeal I felt a renewal of hope and energy. But it seemed we should have to wait a little longer. The nearest town, at the foothills of the mountains we were seeking, was a good four-day journey away by camel train—the same one that had rescued us—and they were not due to leave for another two and a half weeks, and strongly advised us not to try it on our own.

They were a hospitable people, and their town was clean and prosperous. Everywhere we went we were greeted with bows and smiles and clapping of hands, and though we couldn't speak a word of their language, we managed very well with sign language and the occasional drawing. As they existed solely on the barter system, our money meant nothing to them, and they insisted on treating us as honored guests. Which was lucky, seeing we had nothing to barter with.

Under the town was a river system that kept their cisterns full, with enough also for their crops of fruit and vegetables and the watering of their stock: goats, chickens, ducks, camels. They even kept ponds stocked with fish that looked rather like carp. The only goods they needed from outside were rice, clay for pots, and cotton cloth, and these they traded for with their own produce, which included pickled eggs, a special spiced pancake and other delicacies, desert fox furs, and exquisite carvings fashioned from the soft stone they found roundabouts. Once a month they journeyed to do their bargaining, and we agreed to await the next caravan.

There was plenty for us to do, however—for me at least, that is. Our clothes, what was left of them, were a disgrace, and I had spent four or five days doing the best I could with my sewing kit, when we had an unexpected bonus. Growch, investigating a tempting little bitch—what else?—had chased her into a store where cotton cloth awaited making up into the loose clothes the inhabitants preferred, and had been diverted by finding a huge nest of rats. He had set about them in true Growch fashion, and the grateful owner of the store had come to me, counting out at least twenty on his fingers, bearing also a roll of cloth sufficient to clothe both Dickon and myself.

Only when all my tasks were done, which included tedious things like washing blankets and mending panniers, did I keep a promise I had made to myself some weeks past. We had found out that the monks who had fled the destruction of the temple in the desert had found this town in time for survival, and had built a small temple to give thanks for their deliverance. This temple was now in the custody of one of the original monks, then a boy, now a blind old man of near a hundred. One of the village boys was his apprentice, and led him about the village with their begging bowls—always full—and assisted in leading the prayers.

One evening, when I knew the old monk and his acolyte would be dining, the sun tipping over the rim of the world had led to the lighting of the dried camel-dung fires for cooking and the last of the workers and herd's boys came tramping home, I made my way down the deserted streets towards the temple, the sad stone remnant of what had been Ky-Lin clutched in my hands.

It was only a small edifice, this temple, built from desert stone and mud bricks, but inside the floor was flagged, the air smelt of incense and oil saucers burned in front of the stone altar. Someone had left a garland of wildflowers by the crossed knees of the little smiling Buddha.

I had thought I would feel like an interloper, not knowing the language either, but it felt entirely natural to stand in front of the idol and speak in my own tongue.

I looked up at the statue, who stared above my head the while with empty, slanted eyes and an eternal smile, then I knelt down, as I would in one of my own churches, shut my eyes, and folded my hands around the remains of Ky-Lin.

"Please forgive me for not knowing your customs and language, Sir, but I have a special request. In my hands are the remains of a true friend, counsellor and guide, whom You lent to us to help us on our journey. He no longer has life, as You can see, but his death was a tragic accident, and he would have been the first to forgive.

"He was one of Yours, a Ky-Lin, who was left on earth to work off some trifling sins he had committed. Well *I* thought they were trifling. . . . Whatever they were, I assure You they must have been more than cancelled out by his care of us. So, will You please take him back? He spoke of a place where all was perfect and at peace: we would call it Heaven. Please allow him in Yours. Amen. Oh, and thanks for lending him to us. Amen again."

The Buddha had one gilded hand on his knee; the other was cupped on his chest. Reaching up as far as I could, I kissed the tiny stone that had been Ky-Lin and placed him gently in the cupped hand.

There: it was done. Ky-Lin could rest in peace.

I rose to my feet, bowed to the Buddha and backed out of the little temple. The idol seemed to be smiling more broadly than ever.

I had never ridden a camel before. It was extremely difficult to adjust to the rocking, swaying movement so far above the ground, and there was more than one moment when I definitely felt camel-sick. However, even the lap-held Growch agreed that it was better than walking, and in four days we were in a village in the foothills of the mountains where we said good-bye to our kind hosts, replenished our stores and set off in a direction of north by west.

At first we had an easy time of it; the tracks we followed led to other villages and small towns, where our money was accepted. We travelled easily into autumn, through reddening leaves, ripening fruit and the migration of small animals and birds: pint-size deer, foxes, squirrels; duck, swallows, swifts; the large butterflies flirting their just-before-hibernating wings on clumps of pink and purple fleshy-leaved plants. Peasants brought in the last of their harvest, stored their fruits, pickled and salted their meats, and the bats were coming out earlier and earlier to catch the last of the midges that stung us so heartily during the day. So, were the bats eating us, I wondered?

As we climbed higher the air became more exhilarating, and the streams were ice cold from the snowy heights above. All this, and the plain but adequate fare we ate satisfied me well enough, but Dickon was always grumbling, comparing our food with the comparative luxury he had enjoyed on the caravan routes.

"Nobody asked you to come," I said crossly one day, when he had been whining all day about not being allowed extra money to buy some more rice wine. "You're here because you wanted to be, remember?"

"And you're not being reasonable," he said, dodging the issue. "A man needs a bit of relaxation now and again, a sip or two of wine."

"You've already had a sip or four," I said. "And you said not yesterday that it was piss water, rotgut."

"Depends on the vintage . . ."

"This stuff doesn't have any vintage. They make it all the year round."

"I only want a nip. Set me up for the evening."

I flung him a coin. "Buy yourself a measure then. But only a small one, otherwise you won't be fit to go on."

I was right. That afternoon's trek was a complete waste of time. He swayed from side to side of the road, fell over twice, and when I went to help him up he made a grab at me.

"C'mon Summer: gi'e us a kiss!"

I kicked him where it hurt, and when he doubled up pushed him into a ditch and marched on for a half mile without him. By then, as I could see he wasn't following, I retrieved my steps, my temper near at boiling point, especially when I found him still in the ditch, snoring his head off. I was strongly tempted to leave him where he was and travel on alone, but common sense told me I couldn't manage the baggage on my own.

We climbed higher and higher, but the mountains we were aiming for, our last barrier, called on the maps Ky-Lin had explained to me the "Sleeping Giants," still seemed many miles away. Travelling during the day was still pleasant, but the nights were increasingly chill and we needed extra clothes plus the blankets to keep warm, especially if we spent nights in the open. A couple of times we slept under both blankets together, Dickon and I, but his behavior on these occasions worried and annoyed me. On both these times after I had dozed off, I awoke to find his hands where they shouldn't be.

At first I thought he was searching my person for money, but the intimate movement of his hands on my breasts and thighs persuaded me otherwise. I could not believe it was a personal thing, rather that he had been robbed of his usual visits to houses of pleasure, but in any case I found it highly embarrassing.

After all we had travelled together in enforced intimacy for many months, and in all that time, especially with all our differences, there had never been any hint of sexual familiarity. As it was, on both occasions I had turned away as if in my sleep, wrapping myself up tight so there was no way he could attempt anything further.

I tried to enlist Growch's help, but his views on sex being what they were—the more the merrier, whoever or whatever it was—I received little encouragement, until I slanted my argument towards the money I was carrying.

"I don't like him searching me like that when I'm asleep. Just think what would happen if he ran off with all our money!"

Growch knew what money meant: it meant food.

"Right, then. I'll see 'e don' touch you nowheres from now on. Sleep between you both, I will."

Which worked much better, especially as my dog by now smelt so high that Dickon and I slept back-to-back by choice. It was either that or holding our noses all night.

We came to the last village before the snow line of the mountains we planned to cross to our goal. I consulted the best of the maps. It showed a route that wandered away in the lee of the mountains to the east for what looked like a week's journey, before finding a gap into the valley beyond. There was another trail, however. This led almost due north from where we were now and, looking up, I could see, or believed I could see, past a thick stand of coniferous forest, the gap I was seeking, the first in the three-peaked range. This reminded me of the illusion/dream the old man in the market had engendered in me, when I had imagined I was a dragon flying through that very gap.

But when the villagers realized our intent there was an indrawing of breath, a lowering of lids, a shaking of heads.

"What's the matter with them? There's a trail that starts off that way. I can see it leading up to the forest."

Dickon shook his head. "They seem to be afraid of something up there."

"What?"

"How the hell do I know? Look at that old fool in the corner: he's been jabbering away for five minutes now, but I can't understand a word he's saying. Can you?"

"N . . . no. Not exactly. But he's making signs as well." I felt uneasy, not least because the ring on my finger felt uncomfortable, as if it was too tight. I went over to the villager and squatted in front of him watching his dirt-ingrained hands expressing alarm and dismay. Making signs that I didn't understand—oh, what I wouldn't have done for Ky-Lin's comforting presence!—I motioned him to slow down, hoping this would make him more intelligible. It didn't, but one of the brighter of his friends understood what I wanted and came to join us.

It went something like this—all in sign language, whether with hands, eyes, expression, body language, or sheer acting and mime.

Why can't we go that way?

Huge men up there. Giants.

No giants now.

Yes. They also eat people.

Cannibals?

They eat anything. Prefer meat.

Have you seen them?

Heard them howling.

Wolves?

No. Human voice.

How do you know they are human?

When they howl we leave them food at the edge of the forest.

How do you know they aren't animals?

Footprints.

What sort of print?

In snow.

Show me.

And that was the most puzzling of all. They drew in the dirt the outline of a foot, but it was no ordinary one. In general it followed the shape of a human foot, but it was two or three times as large. I drew one smaller, but they rubbed that out and drew an even larger one. What was worse, this foot had eight toes, with sharp long nails, if their drawings were to be believed.

I looked at Dickon. "Superstition?"

"Could be. They've never seen one of these creatures."

"Exactly. And if they've seen some prints in the snow—well, when snow melts so do the prints. Outwards. So a small print would look bigger after an hour or so. Right?"

"Could well be wolves, as you suggested."

"Wrong time of the year for them to be hungry. Shall we chance it? It'd save three or four days' travel. . . ."

"Why not? I'm game if you are."

"Of course!" At least I would have if my ring hadn't kept on insisting that somewhere ahead lay the possibility of danger. But this way would save so many days, and if we were careful . . .

In order to try and reach the gap before nightfall, we set off before dawn. None of the villagers came to see us off. At first it was easy, a clear track leading up towards the forest, which we hoped to skirt to the east. On the fringes we could see where the villagers below had started to clear the wood for fuel, for we came across chippings, a discarded and broken axe, a couple of sleds they used for transporting the wood.

Dickon pointed to one of these. "Why shouldn't we borrow one? It would make carrying all this stuff much easier. Quicker, too. The runners on the underside are obviously meant for snow."

Growch cocked his leg, then thought better of it. "Good for a lift, too, for those poor critturs as 'as short legs . . ."

"We can't just steal it. . . ."

"I said 'borrow,'" said Dickon quickly. "Once we get to the top we can send it back down. The slope'll carry it back."

"All right, we'll haul it unladen till we get to the snow line, to preserve the runners, then we'll load it up."

When we stopped to eat the sun was already high in the sky, and I reckoned we were nearly halfway to the summit. For some reason, although nothing stirred except a couple of eagles taking advantage of the thermals high above, we all felt irritable and uneasy. Dickon kept glancing over his shoulder in the direction of the forest we were skirting, my ring was getting more uncomfortable by the minute, although I reckoned any threat would come from the trees and we were giving them a wide berth. Growch said his mind felt "itchy." I knew exactly what he meant.

We carried on climbing. The forest thinned out to the left of us, and we came across the first patches of snow as the air grew colder. To our left the sun began its western descent and I realized it would be a race for the gap between us and the dark. We stopped briefly for food again, and this time we loaded the sled with everything portable, including Growch.

I looked up. Another couple of hours should do it, and there would be the valley I had dreamed of for so long, the valley that cushioned the fabled Blue Mountain. "Here be Dragons. . . ."

"Let's go," I said. "Let's go!"

Now we were crunching our way through real snow, unmelted all the way through summer, not the slush we had encountered on the lower slopes. The sled slid easily in our wake; we had attached the rope so that we could both pull it. The slope however grew steeper, and now we were bending forward, me at least wishing I had stouter boots: the cold was already striking through the soles and I had hardly any grip, but at least we were nearly there. The thinning forest was behind us and the gap was only some half mile away. The last bit looked the worst; the incline became so steep that it looked as though we should have to crawl on hands and knees.

We took a final breather; less than a half hour should do it. The breath plumed from our nostrils like smoke. Growch's eyebrows, such as they were, were rimed with frost. The sun was near gone, a red ball waiting to slide down the western mountains.

"Right," I said. "One more push should do it. . . . What's the matter?" Dickon was staring at something in the snow just ahead of us. With a sudden look of horror he backed away, his hands held out in front as though he was pushing the sight away from him.

"Look, Summer," he said. "Look there! It was true what they said!"

And there, clear as crystal in hitherto untrodden snow, was the print of an enormous eight-toed foot.

Chapter Twenty-Three

I clapped my hands to my mouth and stepped back in unconscious repudiation, but there was no denying what I had seen. It was as clear as the ice that lined it, reflecting the last of the red sun so it looked as though the giant that made the print had bled into the snow. Dickon pointed out another print, another and another. They came from just above us and then went away down towards the forest.

I swallowed, hard. Those footprints were just as large and terrifying as the villagers had indicated, and I couldn't begin to imagine the height and breadth of a creature who boasted feet that big. And eight toes . . .

Suddenly the sun was gone, like blowing out half the candles in a room at once, and a cold chill of terror gripped us all. Without realizing it Dickon and I were holding hands and a trembling Growch was actually sitting on my feet, his hackles raised, moaning softly.

"We—we'd better get going." I found I was whispering, although there seemed to be nothing moving in the snow. "It's clear straight up to the gap, and if we . . ."

My voice died away as a hideous ululating howl split the quiet around us, followed by another and another. With one accord we ran, sled forgotten, scrambling on all fours to find a grip. I could feel the hairs rising at the back of my neck and my heart was bounding like a March hare.

The howl came again, and this time it was answered by another—from ahead of us.

We came to a sudden, skidding halt.

"What the devil—!"

And Dickon's prophetic exclamation was answered by a horrific apparition that rose from behind a huge rock to our right. Nearly twice the size of a man, it was covered in fur—brown, black, gray—and its face was a twisted mask of hate, with huge fangs sprouting from its jaw. Slowly, lumberingly, it left the shelter of the rock and, with arms raised, came down the slope towards us, uttering that hideous howl we had heard before.

As one we fled down the slope towards the shelter of the forest, slipping, stumbling, falling, rolling, all thought gone save the urgency of escape, although something deep inside seemed to tell me to stop, not to run, but it was such a tiny voice that my fear drowned it.

Not looking where I was going I crashed into the trunk of a tree, knocking all the breath from my body, and I whooped and coughed with the effort to draw air into my lungs. I was aware of Growch gasping and panting beside me, and the inert form of Dickon a few yards away.

I struggled to my feet to see what had happened to him.

"Come on, Growch, we must get—"

"Too late!" he whimpered. "Look behind you!"

I turned, and found we were surrounded. Not by giants, but by strange, hairy humans holding stone axes and primitive spears. They were no taller than I, slightly hunched, and the hair on their bodies, thick on back and arms, was a reddish-black. Prominent brows and jaws, small eyes and noses, wide mouths with yellow teeth and long, tangled hair were common to all and they were mostly naked, though some of the women had bound their babies to their backs with strips of fur.

These creatures looked at us and chattered to themselves in a series of grunts, sibilants and clicks, and a moment later a couple of them dragged the half-conscious body of Dickon forward and dumped him without ceremony at my feet. He had a bruise the size of an egg on his temple. As I looked down he stirred, put his hand to his head and sat up, opening his eyes.

"Holy Mary, Mother of God!"

But he wasn't looking at the strange creatures who now crowded closer till I could smell the rank odor of their bodies; he was staring back up the hill the way we had come. I followed his pointing finger and gasped. Down the hill came striding the giant we had fled from, swaying from side to side, arms spread—Arms? What beast had four arms? I sank to my knees despairingly, clutching Growch for comfort, for surely the hairy people would have no defense against this hideous apparition.

From the giant came that dreadful wolflike howl again, and to my amazement it was answered with like from the hairy people around us, waving their weapons in the air in greeting with what could only be described as grins on their faces.

I scrambled to my feet, pulled Dickon to his. What the hell was happening? Surely the giant and the hairy people weren't in league with one another? Why didn't they—

Dickon and I gasped together. The giant careening down the hill towards us had been gathering speed in a more and more wild manner and now, suddenly, it broke in two! No, no, all in bits. Two pieces came rolling towards us, another sheared off to the left, one slithered to a stop against a tree—

And the hairy people were laughing, dancing, waving their spears!

"Laugh too," came a tiny voice from somewhere. "It's all a big joke to them. You've been had."

And I only realized just how much when two of the "pieces" came to a stop, unrolled, and became two more of the hairy people, one of them still wearing the misshapen boots that had made such a convincing giant's footstep. The other man went back and retrieved the mask that had so horrified us, plus the long cloak that had so convincingly covered one man riding on another's shoulders.

My heart sank even further as our captors, as they must be thought of now, closed in, pointing at the boots, the mask, the cloak, laughing and jeering and miming our terror, confusion and fear when faced with the "giant."

"Laugh with them," came that tiny voice again. "It's your only chance to get away. . . ."

But I couldn't. I tried; I forced the muscles of my face into what I knew was a hideous rictus, but I knew it only looked threatening, like that of a chattering monkey. I nudged Dickon, tried to make him smile, laugh, speak, do anything, but it was hopeless: he was almost rigid with fear.

One by one our captors fell silent, glanced at each other, at us, scowled: we weren't enjoying their joke. They muttered again, then gestured that we should follow them into the forest. Dickon fell to his knees again. Growch whimpered in my arms, and my ring felt as cold as ice.

"Do as they want," said the little voice in my head. "Don't despair!"

So on top of everything else, I was hearing voices. It must be all my terrified imagination, but the voice sounded so much like my dead-and-gone Ky-Lin that I could have cried. Perhaps it *was* his voice, perhaps his ghost had come back to comfort me. I could feel the tears, warm on my frozen cheeks.

"Help us," I whispered. "Wherever you are . . ."

Our captors hauled Dickon roughly to his feet and jostled us both along a narrow track through the trees. Too soon the last of the light was gone, forest gloom descended, and I had to hold one hand in front of my face to push aside the whippy branches I could hardly see. It was less cold under the trees, and the only sounds were the shush-shush of pine needles under our feet and an occasional grunt or snort from our captors, just like a sounder of swine.

After what seemed like hours, but can only have been minutes, we stumbled into a clearing. Other hairy people came out from the trees: the old ones and young children. About fifty or sixty surrounded us now, pointing, grimacing and, what was much worse, touching us; pulling at our clothes and hair, pinching our cheeks and arms, treating us as though we were strange animals instead of human beings.

I wanted so much to hear that ghosty voice of Ky-Lin's again, but, try as I could, the noise around us drowned all else. The sound of wood being dragged to the glowing pit in the center of the clearing, the hissing of the logs, the snorting grunts of those around us—I should have liked to cover my ears, but daren't put Growch down.

The women arranged a framework of sticks across the fire, and on these were spitted several small animals: squirrels, what looked like rats, a small snake. In baskets at the side were pine nuts, roots, wild herbs and a fungus of some sort. The smell of the cooking meat was hardly appetizing, nor was the sight of the filthy fingers that turned the sticks, poking the flesh now and again to see if it was cooked through.

Hands on our shoulders forced us down to sit a little away from the fire while the men went into a huddle, glancing over at us every now and again and then having some sort of discussion.

I poked Dickon, a rigid figure of fear. "It doesn't look too good, does it? Got any ideas?"

He shook his head, probably not trusting himself to speak, and I remembered what the villagers had intimated: these people were cannibals. I shivered, in spite of the heat from the fire, but the ring on my finger, though cold, didn't convey any threat of imminent danger; for the moment we were safe.

By my side lay one of the "giant's" boots; shifting Growch a little, I picked it up to have a closer look. It really was rather ingenious. The sole was made of two bear pads, sewn together, just four claws on each, making eight in all; the top was ordinary leather, the whole sewn over a wickerwork frame and padded, so there was just enough room for a human foot: it must have taken some practice to walk properly, especially with someone else perched on one's back.

One of the hairy ones saw me examining the boot, scowled for a moment, then nudged his fellows and brought over the other with a grin, miming their walk. He also brought over the mask for me to examine as well.

Near to it was quite crudely carved, I guessed from the hollowed stump of a tree, so that it fitted loosely over the head. The nose was a natural hooked beak of wood, stained red by some sort of dye, the eyes had been burnt out and were outlined in yellow. The top of the mask was covered with hair, real hair, and with a shock I realized it was human. Of course it could have been cut from someone's hair within the tribe but I had the terrible feeling that it came from some more reluctant source. They showed me the robe as well, and my suspicions were proved right: these were human scalps sewn together.

I pushed everything away with a sudden surge of revulsion, and they laughed as if it were the best joke in the world. Seeing them then one would have thought them a happy and harmless people, until one realized that their secrets would not have been shared if they had any intention of letting us go.

There was a diversion: apparently the meal was ready. Flat pieces of bark and large leaves were produced and filled with nuts, roots and fungi. Sticks were snatched from the fire and fought over, the meat on them charred on one side, raw on the other.

No one offered us anything.

They ate noisily, licking their fingers before wiping them on their stomachs, hair, each other, and the women spat out half-chewed bits to feed to the smallest of their scrawny brats. Too soon for us the meal was ended; they finished with the last of the unwashed pine nuts, crammed into their mouths so that the black, powdery stain covered their faces and hair, the grease on their skins spreading it still further.

Now they were looking for entertainment—or was it more food? Several of the women were rubbing their stomachs, looking at the men, looking at us. My ring was throbbing again, so cold it felt as though it would burn straight through my finger. I looked around desperately, but we were ringed in on all sides. Suddenly two of the men separated from the rest and came towards us; Dickon and I scrambled to our feet and backed away, a trembling Growch hugged close to my chest.

Dickon was pushed unceremoniously aside and they approached me, great grins on their faces; in the sudden clarity that terror can bring, I noticed how stained their teeth were: fangs for tearing at the front, grinding molars at the back—

One of the men leaned forward, jabbering excitedly—and tried to pluck the terrified Growch from my arms. I had thought they came for me, and was quite prepared to take out my knife and hurt them as much as I could before I was overpowered. But Growch? No, never! Not my little dog spitted over a fire till his hair singed and the blood and fat ran spattering into the fire! I had rather slit his throat myself to spare him the pain and betrayal.

"Get away! Get your filthy hands off!" I was shouting hysterically. "Dickon, for God's sake *do* something! Help me. . . ." Now my knife was in my right hand, Growch still held with my left, and as one man advanced still further I connected with a lucky slash across his arm and he retreated with a grunt, sucking at the blood.

Dickon's voice came to me. "Give them the wretched animal, for Christ's sake! It's him they want. Give us time to escape. . . ."

I couldn't believe my ears! Give up Growch! In sudden anger I turned on Dickon and slashed out at him also, and saw the bright beads of blood spring from a cut across his cheek. Turning, I hit out again at my two attackers, and had the satisfaction of seeing them spring back from the arc of my knife. But now the others behind were closing in and I couldn't deal with them all—

"Help me! Help me!" I didn't realize I was screaming, or to whom, but all of a sudden everything changed.

"Leave this to me!" boomed a voice, and with a burst of firecrackers that would have done justice to a town celebration, into the clearing came bounding a huge creature, an apparition surrounded with light and noise and color and fire.

The hairy tribe scattered in all directions, sparks from the unguarded fire catching at their hair and stinging their bodies. For a moment I thought we had exchanged one horror for another, then I suddenly recognized the creature for who he was, larger now than I had ever seen him—

"Ky-Lin! But how . . . What did—"

"Follow me! No questions, just hurry!"

I can't remember much of that frantic dash through the trees, out into the snow and up towards the gap. I do remember finding the sled, Ky-Lin taking the rope between his teeth and dragging us all as hard as he could towards safety. I remember, too, the chill of terror when we heard the howls of pursuit behind us, as the tribe realized Ky-Lin provided no threat and they were losing a source of easy food. Their noise came nearer and nearer, a couple of ill-thrown spears skimmed past our heads, and we were there!

A gap as wide as a door, no more, a glimpse of a valley, more hills and we were through. Ky-Lin loosed the rope and the sled careened faster and faster down a slope of snow towards the valley below.

Now the moon was up, and through the tears of cold in my eyes and the wind whipping my cheeks a scene of beauty spread itself beneath, and there in the midst of it all was a coldly blue shape on the horizon.

"Look, look!" I cried out to Ky-Lin who had been left behind. "It's there, we've found the Blue Mountain—"

The sled veered, skidded, struck something hard and I was lifted into the air. Suddenly everything was upside down, and then my head hit something, lights buzzed through my brain, and everything went black.

Part Three

Chapter Twenty-Four

The first thing I was conscious of was a pleasant smell: sandalwood, beeswax, pine, cedarwood. It reminded me of Ky-Lin. Then, what must have woken me, a dissonance, not unpleasant, of tinkling bells, and a far-away chanting, a deep resonance of a gong. For a moment longer I savored the light warmth of blankets tucked under my chin, then I became aware of a dull throbbing in my head and an unpleasant taste in my mouth.

I opened my eyes and sat up, immediately wishing I hadn't done either. I closed my eyes and lay down again, but must have groaned, because at once there was a rustle of clothing and a woman was chattering away quietly by my side. Her hands were cool on my forehead; my head was raised and a feeding cup pressed to my lips. The drink was warm and fragrant, tasted of mint and honey and camomile and took away the nasty taste in my mouth. I wasn't about to open my eyes or sit up again, but there was a sort of puzzle that wouldn't go away: where was I, and indeed *who* was I? I couldn't remember a thing, so decided to think about it later. . . .

When I opened my eyes again the room was full of soft lamplight and shadows and I remembered who and what I was, what had happened before, but I had no idea where I lay. My head still hurt, but the pain was lessening. Putting up a languid hand I found a cloth wound tight about my forehead, the rag cool and damp to my touch. The last thing I recalled was riding at a giddy speed on the sled down the mountain, of hitting some obstruction and flying through the air to hit my head on something—it must have been quite a bump for me to feel like this.

Something moved up from the foot of the bed, and a sloppy tongue and hacky breath announced the arrival of my dog.

"Feelin' better? Thought we'd lost you again we did; glad we didn'. Gawd, what a place this is! All corridors, steps, passages . . . 'Nuff to turn a dog dizzy! Don't think much of the nosh, neither. All pap, no gristle, nuffin' to get yer teeth into. Still, most 'portant thing is you're back with us. I said to meself yesterday, I said, if'n she don' wake up soon, I'm—"

"Growch!"

"Yes?"

"Can I speak? Can I ask you a couple of questions?"

" 'Course. Ain't stoppin' you am I? Now then, what d'you wanna know? Don' tell me, let me guess. . . . Where is we? Well, I ain't ezackly sure. It's a sort o' temple, high up in the mountains. Took us near a week to get 'ere, what with you bein' unconscious an' all, but that big beast, 'e pulled the sled wiv you on it all the way. 'Is lordship fancy pants weren't much use, 'e was all for stayin' in the first village we come to but Ky-Lin 'e said no, you needed special treatment and the best nursin'. Must say, though—"

"Growch?"

"Yes?"

"Where are Ky-Lin and Dickon?"

"Well, 'is lordship's next door, snorin' 'is 'ead orf, an' the lady what was tendin' you 'as gone fer a nap. Ain't seen much o' Ky-Lin, seein' 'e's special 'ere. 'E comes an' checks on you, then back 'e goes to them monks. They seem to think a lot o' 'im. 'E's the only one allowed inside their temple." He settled down on the pillow next to me, had a good scratch, licked my ear and continued.

"This place, bein' 'arfway up a 'ill, is sorta built in layers. The temple and the monks' part, they's at the top. This bit, the guests', is next down, then at the bottom is a 'uge courtyard, with goats 'n chickens 'n bees 'n things. All around is workshops—they weave these blankets down there; must say they're the softest I ever come acrost. Come from a goat wiv long hair what they combs. Cooking is done down there, too, an' the washin'. . . . Well, then: look 'oose 'ere!" and he jumped off the bed to greet Ky-Lin.

He seemed to have grown larger and more splendid than ever. His hide and hooves shone with health, his eyes were bright, his colors clear and vibrant. His plumed tail was truly magnificent and his antennae curled and waved like weeds in a stream. Bending over the bed he touched these latter to my head and immediately the dull ache lessened. I flung my arms about his neck in greeting.

"I thought it was you out there in the forest speaking to me—but then I believed I must have been hearing things! How did you come back to us? When I left you on that altar I was convinced you were—you were dead. Are you sure you are real?"

"Of course I'm real, silly one! I never really went away. I was hurt, yes, but we soon heal. A little rest, a word or two from my Master, and I was well enough to follow you. I was sitting in the lining of your jacket most of the time, staying quiet until you needed me."

I hugged him again. "Thank you a million, million times! Thank you for saving us, for bringing me here, for everything. Without you . . ." Words failed me. "But there is just one thing I don't understand."

"And that is?"

"When—when I thought you were dead . . ." I hesitated.

"Yes?" he prompted.

"I said a prayer for you. I said to the Buddha that I thought you had already done enough to go to your Heaven. Why didn't he listen?"

For the first time he looked embarrassed. He looked away, he looked back, his eyes crossed, he shook his head from side to side. Finally he mumbled something I couldn't catch.

"What did you say?"

"I said . . . said I was given a choice. My Lord was willing for me to go to rest with Him, or—go back and see it through. I'm afraid that for me there was little choice."

"How wonderful of you to choose the hard way!"

He raised a hoof, looked even more abashed. "No, no, no praise! It was partly selfish. I told you once before that I didn't think I would enjoy eternal peace and rest. Besides, I have grown used to this whole big, imperfect world. I actually enjoy being in it. I shouldn't, you know; it should be renounced, like anything imperfect." His head bobbed again. "My Lord said I was a child still, putting off the moment to go to bed."

The awkward silence was luckily broken by the entrance of Dickon, rubbing sleep from his eyes.

"What's all the noise about? Oh, you're awake at last, Summer. Feeling better? What's the matter? Why are you laughing?"

"What in the world are you wearing?"

"A nightshirt. What's so funny? You're wearing one too. . . ."

I had never seen him look so ridiculous. The high-necked gray garment had short sleeves and was slit down the sides, to end just below his knees, so that his thin, hairy shanks poked out below it, and if he moved incautiously, one caught a glimpse of dimpled backside.

Before I disgraced myself by laughing too much and gave myself a second headache the nursing woman bustled in, dismissing everyone except Growch—who retreated growling under the bed—gave me a bitter draught, blew out all the lamps bar one, tucked me up tight, and I had no alternative but to sink back again into a drugged sleep.

Three days later I was well on the road to recovery. My headache was gone, the cloth on my head had been removed, no more bitter draughts, and I was allowed out of bed to sit by the fire. There was a washroom down the corridor and at last I could have a tub of hot water to bathe in, although I had been sponged down while I was in bed.

Without asking, both Dickon and I had been provided with new clothes, the sort the peasants wore: padded jackets and trousers, with cotton drawers and undershirt and felt slippers.

The first thing I did, after a really good wash, was to check that all my belongings were safe, although Growch assured me that he had "guarded 'em with me life!" All was as he said, though I was surprised to see how much the egg had grown. One evening when Ky-Lin paid a visit, I asked about this.

"All the eggs I have ever seen stay their laying size: it's the chick inside that grows, not the shell. Why is this different?"

"The simple answer is that I don't know, but then I've never had to deal with a dragon's egg before. Obviously they don't behave like other eggs, but

I can assure you that there are live cells in there and I can hear them growing."

It was exciting, awesome, and although I knew I should never see what was inside, I desperately wanted to. "Can your antennae see inside?"

"If they could—and I'm not going to try it—I wouldn't tell you. Some things are best left alone." And with that answer I had to be content.

However he did reveal something to me I hadn't suspected, perhaps to take my mind off the question of the egg.

"Have you looked at that piece of crystal lately?"

"The one the captain's wife gave me? No, not recently."

"Then perhaps you should take another look."

"Now?"

"Why not?"

I unwrapped it carefully and laid it on the bed. "There's nothing special about it—oh!" Ky-Lin had rolled it to the end where it caught the light, and now it was as though a rainbow had entered the room. The lamps caught the glass in a hundred, a thousand bands, strips and rays; red, crimson, scarlet, orange, yellow, green, viridian, pine, cobalt, ultramarine, mauve, purple, violet—and colors in between one could only guess at.

"Hold it up," said Ky-Lin. "Let it find the light it has been denied so long. . . ."

I was blinded by color; it was the most wonderful jewel I had ever seen in my life. As I swung it between my fingers the light flashed around the room ever faster, creating a gem within a gem, and we were all patterned with color like strange animals—even Ky-Lin's tail was dimmed.

"What *is* it?"

"Whatever it is, turn it orf!" said Growch. "You talk about *your* 'ead achin'. . . ."

"It is only a crystal," said Ky-Lin. "But beautifully cut. I've never seen a better. Anyone would be delighted to own that."

I was reluctant to put it away, like a child with a toy. I must try it again tomorrow. . . . Tomorrow? Why was I wasting time like this?

"Ky-Lin . . . are we in the right place? Is the Blue Mountain near? Is that really the place of dragons?"

"Legend has it that this is one of the few places on earth where dragons can still be found. The Blue Mountain is a half-day's journey away."

"Then I must go there. Now. Tomorrow." But if this was the place where my dragon-man had headed for, why was it I had no sense of him being near? Surely my love was strong enough to sense his presence, even over a half-day's journey. I couldn't come this far to find I was wasting my time! "Tomorrow," I repeated firmly.

"You may go," said Ky-Lin, "when you are completely recovered. Not before. A week or so."

"But—but I want to go now!"

"At the moment you couldn't walk up a flight of steps, let alone climb a mountain. Come now, be sensible! It has taken months to get so far: surely a few days more won't change the world!"

"I shall be perfectly recovered in far less time than that," I said firmly, although I was fighting a rearguard action, and knew it.

"We shall see," was all he said, but three days later he came for me. Not to climb any mountains, but to speak to one of the monks, the Chief Historian and Keeper of the Scrolls.

I followed him down a narrow, twisting corridor, following the curve of the hill on which the monastery was situated, narrow slit windows giving hair-raising glimpses of the sheer drop below. Once I thought I caught sight of the Blue Mountain itself, but couldn't be sure. Down some steps, up a lot more and then we found ourselves in a small chamber, scarce six feet by six.

Facing us was an intricately carved grille, decorated with red enamel and gold paint. Beside the grille was a small brass gong and a shallow wooden bowl with a red leather handle. The silence lay as thick as last year's dust.

"Strike the gong once," whispered Ky-Lin. (It was a room for whispering). "Wait a count of five and strike it twice, then once again."

"What is this—some sort of secret society?"

"Each monk has his own call; if you do it any differently you may get the Chief Architect, the Cloth Master, the Master of Intercession or even the Reader of the Weather. Every monk is trained to be an expert in one thing or another."

I wondered if there was a Master of Sewers and Latrines. . . .

"Go on!"

I tiptoed to the gong—there was no need; the stone muffled even our whispers—struck it once, then stepped back hastily; it was far louder than I had expected.

"It won't bite," said Ky-Lin.

I struck the gong twice more, for a moment waited and struck it once again. As the last echoes died away, the silence seemed thicker than ever. Then came a faint creak, the distant sound of chanting, another creak, and the chant dying away. Another, more comforting sound; the flap, flap of sandals, a wheezy breath, a cough. Almost immediately a shadow formed behind the grille, a mere shift of light and shadow, and a thin high voice asked a question.

Ky-Lin answered, then turned to me. "If anyone knows of the dragons, he will. He has consented to speak to you through me. He is not allowed to speak to a woman directly. I will translate for you both. What is it you wish me to ask him?"

"Ask him how recently there were dragons here?"

Apparently the answer took some time, but eventually Ky-Lin translated. "He says it is unclear. There has been certain activity reported around the Blue Mountain during the last fifteen months, but these reports have not yet been substantiated."

"What sort of activity?"

"Strange lights, odd noises, a smell of cinders, an unexplained grass fire," he translated.

"And has it always been a tradition that dragons lived here?"

Apparently the records of the monastery only went back the three hundred years since its inception. At that time there was no direct mention of dragons, only a passing reference to the fact that the locals believed the Blue Mountain was "haunted." One hundred years later, when the monks had consolidated and had time on their hands, there were several references to a "Blue Monster," which had been reported many years back ravaging the crops in a particularly bad year for harvest. This particular monster apparently flew in the sky and breathed flame and smoke. There were no other sightings until another year of drought, when the creature was apparently spotted "drinking a river dry." Another time it was seen at night circling the valley, beating wings that "caused a great draught to blow the roofs off several houses, and the populace to take their children and hide them." Further sightings were reported over the years, but nothing recent.

"Is there nothing about dragons over the past two years?"

"He says not."

"Nothing at all out of the ordinary? However unlikely it might seem?"

"The Master has much patience, girl, but even I can see it is wearing a little thin. . . . However, I am sure he will give us a recital of every unusual or unexplained event that has come to his attention over the last couple of years, if I ask him."

Triplets, all of whom survived; a two-headed calf that didn't; a fish caught in the river with another fish in its belly; a plague of red ants; an albino child; another born with a full set of teeth; a rogue tiger carrying off villagers in the foothills to the north; rumors of a great battle to the east; the sudden appearance and disappearance of a stranger borne on a great wind; death of the oldest monk at the age of one hundred and twenty—

"Wait!" I said. "The stranger: does he know any more?"

Ky-Lin made his query, received his answer.

"Well?" I asked, for a tiny hope had started to flutter in my breast and Ky-Lin was looking puzzled.

"It seems . . ." He hesitated. "It seems all this happened in a village to the north of here, many miles away, and a report was brought in by visiting monks. There is doubt as to its authenticity as the only witnesses were children, yet there is no doubt that some unnatural phenomenon took place, for damage was done to buildings and many heard a strange noise. The children, a six-year-old boy and his three-year-old sister, went out early one morning to relieve themselves and suddenly there was a great wind and a man in a black cloak was standing by them. The children said he looked angry with himself, but then he laughed and spoke to them, but they don't remember what he said. They saw him run off down the street, then came the fierce wind again and they thought they saw a great bird in the sky."

I remembered a dark man in a black cloak, a man with a hawk nose, piercing yellow eyes and a mouth that could be either cruel or tender—

"That must have been Jasper!" I said excitedly. "He had to spend part of his life in human guise because I kissed him! Ask him—"

"Whoever—or whatever—it was, it won't be there now," said Ky-Lin firmly.

"And you may have one more question and that's it. You are here on sufferance, remember? Now, what do you want to ask?"

I thought for a moment. "Ask him how long ago this took place."

"Do you have the coins I asked you to bring?" I nodded. "Then when we receive our answer, bow once, place the coins in that bowl and push it under the grille. Then step back and bow again. The monks need the money, you needed the information, and the bows are common courtesy here."

"What did he say?" I pestered Ky-Lin as we walked back down the winding passage.

"He said that all this took place sometime during the winter before last, but the exact month is not known."

"But that means it could have been my dragon-man! He left me at the Place of Stones at the beginning of November and 'during the winter' could be anytime in the next four months!"

"Patience! There is absolutely nothing to indicate that he is here."

"But I've got to find out! And if you won't take me to the Blue Mountain, I'll go alone!"

Chapter Twenty-Five

"The one thing Ky-Lins can't do," said Ky-Lin firmly, "is fly. Ky-Lins can change their size, their substance, their colors. They can run like the wind, go without food and drink, speak any language. They can produce Sleepy Dust, firecrackers and colored smoke. They also possess certain healing properties, but fly they don't!"

We were standing at the foot of the so-called Blue Mountain. So-called because close to it didn't look blue at all. It was a sort of blackish cindery gray, rising steeply from the valley floor. Conical in shape, it was almost entirely bare of vegetation, and I was quite ready to believe it was the core of an extinct volcano. It smelled rather like the puff of air you sometimes get from a long-dead fireplace.

Ky-Lin had explained not once but twice why it looked blue at a distance, but I had become more than a little confused with the principles of distance, air, refraction (whatever that was), and vapor.

"Well," said Growch. "It's as plain as me nuts as we can't climb that. We ain't ruddy spiders."

Now Growch wasn't supposed to be here at all. Three days after Ky-Lin had questioned the monk, he had come to me suggesting we visit the Blue Mountain the very next day. "I can carry you," he had said, "but even with what speed I can make it will take several hours. I suggest, therefore, that we set off before light, in order to be back before nightfall. I shall wake you when I am ready, and shall ask one of the cooks to make you up a parcel of rice cakes and honey, and a skin of water."

"Don' eat 'unny," said Growch. "You knows I don'. Bit o' cheese'll do. An' a bone."

"You're not coming," I said firmly. "This is my journey. After all," I added placatingly, as his shaggy brows drew down in a dreadful frown, "this is only a reconnaissance. I just want to know what's there."

"Never!" he said. "Not never no-how. You ain't goin' nowhere without you take me. You'd never 'ave got this far without me, and you knows it. Why d'you think I left the comfort o' that merchant's 'ouse to go with you?

Not to be left behin', and that's flat! I bin with you since the day after yer Ma died an' you left 'ome, ain't I? An' if'n you even tries to go without me I'll bark the place down, that I will!"

Blackmail, that was what it had come down to, so he had come too, and to my secret satisfaction had hated every moment of Ky-Lin's erratic bounding from stone to rock to pebble, as he had borne us on his back across the valley.

So had I, if it came to that, but there's nothing like sharing one's woes, is there?

We had left well before dawn, Dickon unaware and asleep, and were let out through the gates of the courtyard by a half-awake porter. We had followed the twisting track down to the village below, and once on level ground I had climbed on Ky-Lin's back, taken Growch up in front of me and started the long journey across the valley floor.

At first, along the level bare tracks, it was easy, Ky-Lin skimming smooth and steady with scarce a jolt to disturb us, but when the trail petered out we had a much more adventurous journey. At first I couldn't understand why Ky-Lin was bounding about like an overgrown and demented grasshopper, but then I remembered his devotion to not even spoiling a blade of grass or errant ant. Obviously there must have been many such in our path, for we jigged and jagged our way across the plain till the breath was near knocked out of me.

"Sorry," said Ky-Lin at one point. "It's not all (bounce) that easy (leap) by the last light (swerve) of the (crunch) moon, but once the sun comes up (hop) it should be better." Bump.

I sure hoped so.

It was a relief to us all when we finally arrived at the foot of the mountain. Sliding off Ky-Lin's back I collapsed on the ground, dropping Growch as I did so, and we spent the next couple of minutes shaking ourselves together. We looked up at the mountain; smooth rock all the way to the top, no bushes, shrubs, trees, grass or foot- or hand-holds that I could see. Far, far above us was what could be a ledge of some sort and a hole in the rock, but it was too high up to see clearly.

"Now what?"

"Breakfast," said Ky-Lin, "and then I will scout around the base of the mountain."

He was gone about an hour, and appeared from the opposite direction.

"What did you find?"

"Better news, I think. Around the other side, to the south where the sun shines strong, there has been a certain amount of erosion over the years. The rocks are porous, and I think there is a way up, a narrow way that follows a crack in the rock. Up you get, and we'll take a look."

Perhaps because he had been this way before, our ride this time was easier, and the other side of the mountain provided a surprise. As Ky-Lin had said this side faced due south, and perhaps because of this the lower slopes were covered with vegetation—young pines and firs at the foot, and bushes, grass and scrub to about a third of the way up before it reverted back to bare rock. There were also numerous cracks, fissures and gullies worn away by rain, wind and sun.

I saw what I thought were several promising paths, but Ky-Lin ignored all these and led us about halfway round the southern side before stopping.

"Here we are: take a look."

I couldn't see anything, but Growch's eyes were sharper than mine.

"I sees it. Bit of a scramble, then there's a crack as goes roun' like a pig's tail an' outa sight roun' the other side."

"Does it go all the way up to that ledge we saw?"

"Seems to," said Ky-Lin. "We'll have to try it. It's the only way I can see to get us there."

After the first "scramble" as Growch had put it, which was a hands and knees job, the first part of the narrow path seemed easy enough. We were gradually working our way round to the westward, and when I looked down the first time the plain still looked only a jump away, but by the time we were facing northwest it looked a giddy mile away, although we could only have been a thousand feet up. Now the path became more difficult. It narrowed, and some of the footholds were crumbling away; at one point, when I paused for a moment's rest and gazed down again, I felt so dizzy I had to shut my eyes and cling to the rock, too paralyzed to move another step.

"C'mon, 'fraidy cat!" It was Growch's ultimate insult. "If'n I can do it, so can you!"

I chanced one open eye, and there he was, perched on a rock some three feet above me. As I watched he leapt down beside me and then up again.

"Up you comes!"

Then Ky-Lin was beside me. "I told you not to look down. Come on, I'll give you a lift up to the next bit. Don't let us down now, girl: there's only a short way to go."

And, incredibly, he was right. With a leap of anticipation I saw the ledge we were heading for not a hundred yards away, and five minutes later we were there.

It was obvious that the ledge was part natural, part engineered. The natural rock jutted out like a platform, perhaps six feet, but its inner side had been painstakingly excavated to a depth of about ten feet further and smoothed down, making a natural stage some fifteen feet deep and the same wide. Stage? What about a landing strip for a dragon? Especially as, at the back, leading into the heart of the mountain was a dark, yawning passage.

Suddenly the strange, cindery smell was much stronger and I wanted to gag, so much so that I turned away and looked across the plain to where the faraway mountains raised their snowcapped heads. And with the sight came a scent from the distance, a hint of snow, thyme, ice, pine, a perfume to dispel the one that had so disturbed me.

Ky-Lin lay down with a sigh, hooves tucked under. "Well, we're here. Are you going in?"

I stared at him. "Aren't you coming?"

He shook his head. "Dragons are not—not within my commitments. It's like . . ." He struggled for an explanation. "It's like two different elements. The difference between a fish and a bird. Our boundaries just don't cross. I have my magic, they have theirs."

I thought of flying fish, of sea-diving eagles; for a moment at least they tried different elements. But Ky-Lin was adamant.

"This is your adventure, girl. I brought you here, I can take you back, but in there I cannot help you."

For a moment I hesitated. The passage looked dark and forbidding. I wished I had had the forethought to bring some form of illumination. I looked at Growch.

"You coming?"

His ears were down, his tail between his legs. "'Course . . ." Not very convincing.

"Come on then: this is what I came for."

"What *you* came for! Orl right. Lead on. . . ."

But I didn't want to either. I closed my eyes, just to remind myself why I was here. The maps had shown a Blue Mountain, and I had no other lead to where my dragon-man had gone; he was the reason I had travelled so many miles, to try and find the one who had so roused my body and my heart to the realization that no one else but he would do. A dragon-kiss, that was why I was here.

I tried to recall the magic of that moment; the fear, the joy, the exhilaration of that moment nearly two years ago, when I had tasted what love really meant—but like all memories and the best dreams the edges were blunted by time, the sharpness rubbed off by recollection. However, this was why I was here, so how could I fail at the last moment, just because I was scared of a dark passage?

"You'll wait, Ky-Lin?"

"Of course. Just take it slow and easy. I don't believe there will be anything to fear except yourselves."

I peered down the tunnel. "It's very dark. . . ."

"You want a light? You should have reminded me humans cannot see in the dark like us. Here, pluck some hairs from the tip of my tail. Go on, it won't hurt you."

It might hurt him, though. I chose a small handful and gave a gentle tug; it stayed where it was.

"It won't hurt me either," said Ky-Lin. "As I say, I'm not a human."

I tugged harder and *pop*!—out they came, immediately fusing together into a minitorch that burned with a brilliant white light. I nearly dropped it.

"That won't hurt you either," said Ky-Lin. "You can even put your finger in the flame. It's really an illusion, like my firecrackers."

"How long will it last?"

"As long as you need it. Now, off you go: you're wasting time again."

Holding the torch high I stepped into the tunnel, Growch's wet nose nudging my ankles. Now that we had a light he didn't seem so reluctant. Step by step, my free hand against the tunnel wall to keep me steady, I stumbled along—stumbled because the way was littered with small stones, and even as we walked other stones and pebbles detached themselves from the roof and walls to complicate our passage.

At first the tunnel—some six feet wide—went straight, and if I glanced behind I could see the comforting daylight behind me. Then it kinked sharply to the left, to the right and to the left again, till the only light we had I held in my hand, except for a faint illumination I could not trace to its source. It was very still; the air smelled of rotten eggs and cinders, and it was strangely warm.

We seemed to have been travelling into the heart of the mountain for what seemed ages but could only have been a cautious five minutes, when suddenly the tunnel widened into a huge cavern. It was so wide and high that, even with the brilliance of Ky-Lin's torch, we couldn't see the roof or the far walls.

Two things I noticed at once: both the smell and the heat were suddenly increased, and as far as the latter was concerned it was like walking from winter into spring. The heat seemed to be coming from somewhere beneath our feet, as a hearthstone will keep the warmth long after the fire itself is out. It increased as we advanced further into the cavern, until we were halted by a great fissure that stretched from one side to the other, effectively blocking our way to the other side. It was from this great crack that the heat and the smell came.

Cautiously I peered over the edge, down into darkness so deep it was almost a color on its own. Up came a waft of hot air; Ky-Lin had said this was the cone of an extinct volcano, but there was certainly something down there still. No noise, however; no grumbling and bubbling, so perhaps I was mistaken.

I stepped back and held the torch as high as I could once more. It was like being in a huge cathedral, ribs and buttresses of rock rearing up into shadow. On the other side of the fissure, to add to the illusion, huge lumps of stone could well be mistaken for effigies of long-dead knights. But giant knights these, in fact the shadows thrown by the torch gave these effigies of stone less than human characteristics: heads and claws and scaly backs.

"There's a sorta bridge here," Growch grumbled. It wasn't the sort of place to be too audible.

A thin arch of stone spanned the chasm; perhaps a couple of feet wide, it looked both daunting and insubstantial, and the thought of what might lie below was more than enough to make me decide not to chance it. Besides, I persuaded myself, there was nothing over there to look at, only misshapen lumps of rock and, now I noticed for the first time, some irregularly spaced heaps of pebbles, the sort of heaps a child might make while playing.

I felt terribly let down. All that travelling, the building up of anticipation, the hard times, the dangerous ones: was it all to lead to an empty, hot cavern scattered with stones and smelling of cinders? And where, oh where was Jasper? Where was my wonderful man-dragon? How could the maps, the legends, my own intuition, all be so wrong?

In sudden frustration and anguish I called out his name. "Jasper! Jasper! Where are you?" but the echoes engendered by my voice magnified his name into a frightening "Boom! boom! boom!" that bounced off the rocks, hissing on the sibilant, popping on the plosive, till I felt as if I had been hurled headlong into a thunderstorm.

Terrified, I clapped my hands to my ears, dropping the torch, but to add to the din Growch started yelping in fear and the noise was so dreadful it almost seemed as if the stones themselves were adding to the clamor. To add to the confusion the fallen torch was now pointing directly across at the misshapen rocks and I definitely saw one move—

That did it. I snatched up the torch, and with one accord Growch and I headed for the tunnel and fled as if the Devil himself were after us, never mind stones and stumbles, emerging out onto the ledge again with a speed that nearly had us over the edge.

"Well," asked Ky-Lin, comfortingly matter-of-fact. "Was it worth the climb?"

Out it all came, my disappointment, the way we had almost scared ourselves to death, the sheer empty futility of it all.

"I had thought it would be so different," I finished miserably. "Just great big rocks and heaps of pebbles."

"What did you expect?" he asked mildly. "A welcoming committee? Besides, rocks are rocks are rocks, you know. . . ."

I could have done without his homespun philosophy right then, especially as I didn't understand what he was getting at, and nearly told him so. Instead we wended our way down the mountain again and endured another bumpy ride, and it was well past dark when we arrived back at the monastery.

And the last person in the world I wanted to face was Dickon, but there he was, near hysterical.

"Where the hell do you think you've been? You've been missing all day! What on earth time is this to return?"

"Oh shut up, Dickon," I said wearily. I was exhausted, bumped, bruised, fed up and near to tears. "I'm tired. I want a bath and I want to go to bed. I'll tell you all about it in the morning."

"I know what it is: you went off on your own to find the treasure!"

"How many times do I have to tell you?" I yelled back. "*There is no bloody treasure!* There never was!"

"Oh, yes?" he sneered. "That's what you keep on saying, isn't it? Well, let me tell you this; nothing you say will ever convince me that you dragged us all this way for nothing—"

"Us? You mean *you*! Who dragged *you*? *You* insisted on coming. Each time we tried to go on alone, *you* insisted on following. *You* left the caravan to follow us, *you* travelled up the Silk River to find us, *you* tracked us across the bog—"

He evaded that. "But where did you go today, then?"

"Look," I said. "If you will leave me in peace right now, I have already told you I'll explain it all in the morning."

"Promise?"

"I said so."

"I can trust you?"

"It's your only choice." I shrugged. "If you believe I am going to lie, I can do it as well now as tomorrow. Think about it. Goodnight."

But even after a welcome soak and a bowl of chicken and egg soup, and a bed that welcomed like coming home, I could not sleep. I nodded off for an hour or so, then woke to toss and turn. I was too hot, too cold, itchy, uncomfortable. The longer I tried to sleep, the worse it became. I dozed again, with dream-starts that melted one into another. One moment the once-fat Summer fled an imagined horror, the next a huge moon was shining too bright on my face; now great bats chased across the sky, their wings obscuring the same moon. I woke fretful and pushed a too-heavy Growch away. I rolled down a steep mountain to escape the pursuing flames, a sudden wind rattled the shutters and I opened my eyes to see the oil lamp guttering. It must have been about three in the morning.

Growch stretched and yawned. "You goin' ter tell 'im where we went?"

"What choice have I? And what does it matter anyway?"

And I burst into useless tears.

Chapter Twenty-Six

About two hours later I had had enough. Although it was still full dark I disturbed Growch again as I flung aside the blankets, donned my father's cloak and stepped outside onto the narrow balcony that served both my room and Dickon's.

Although it was October, the night was still comparatively warm and the stone of the balustrade under my fingers was no colder than the air. Below was a set of steps leading down to a small, ornamental garden, no bigger than ten feet by ten, facing south. I had sat there during the day a couple of times, on one of the two stone benches, amid pots of exotic plants, ivies, and those tiny stunted trees so beloved by the people of this land. Pines, firs, even cherry trees were bound and twisted into grotesque shapes no higher than my hand, yet it is said that they were as much as one hundred years old!

I wondered vaguely if it hurt them to be twisted so unnaturally, and whether it would be a kindness to dig them all up secretly and replant them in the freedom of unrestricted soil many miles away. Or were they so used to their pot-bound existence that they would perish without special nurturing?

The stars had nearly all gone to bed, those left pale with tiredness, but the waxing moon still held a sullen glow as it balanced on the tips of the faraway mountains. It was the color of watered blood, the warts and scars of its face showing up like plague spots. A faint breeze touched my cheek; false dawn would come with the going down of the moon. As I watched I could almost imagine it starting to slide down out of sight. My breathing slowed: I was in tune with the speed of the heavens.

Then, just as the jaws of the mountains gaped to swallow the moon, there came a lightening of the sky in the east. False dawn had turned everything dark gray, and somewhere a sleepy bird woke for an instant, tried a trill and fell silent once more.

And suddenly, like a stifling blanket being pulled off my head, came a lifting of both mind and spirit. I felt so different I could have cried out with the relief. But what had brought all this about? I gazed around at the fading stars, the sinking moon, a lightening in the sky to the east—no, it was none of these.

Then I looked back at the nearly gone moon and realized there was something different about the marks on its face. It was there, then it disappeared. I rubbed my eyes, but when I looked again the moon had slid away and so had the strange mark I thought—I imagined?—I had seen.

I wouldn't, couldn't allow hope to rise once more, only to be dashed. And yet . . .

I went back to bed and slept until midday.

And so, in the afternoon when Dickon again tried to question me about yesterday's activities I told him what we had done almost indifferently, as though it didn't really matter anymore. And at that moment it didn't.

"So you see we just went to look at the place the legends say the dragons live in, but after all that there was nothing there; nothing except an extinct volcano and heaps of rocks and stones, that is."

"Why didn't you let me come?"

"Ky-Lin carried us: he couldn't have managed you as well."

"I should like to have seen it. There might have been something you missed."

"Go see for yourself, then," I said recklessly, and described how he could climb up to the cavern. "But I tell you, it's a waste of time!"

"Then if there was nothing, and you didn't find this friend you told me about, why don't you just pack up now and go back to your tame merchant boyfriend?"

"Here's as good a place as any to overwinter."

"What about money?"

I shrugged. "I offered you some once. I still have it. I might even do a little trading myself. And you: what are you going to do with yourself now your journey is over?"

He looked aghast. "But—I understood we were together in this! I haven't come all this way just to be cast aside like an odd glove. I've got no capital! If you decide to trade, we trade together. What do you really know about buying and selling? Why, you can't even communicate with these people without that colored freak at your heels. . . ." He had always been jealous of Ky-Lin. "At least I have been learning the language in my spare time. You wouldn't last five minutes without me and you know it!"

"Well I shall have to try, shan't I? Don't worry, I shall manage. I shall stay around here for a while, and I shall stay alone. Apart from Growch, of course."

I felt mean, but somehow knew I had to shed him. I knew I had to be on my own, that whatever pass I had come to in my life, whatever awaited me, I had to meet it alone, free of the threat that someone like Dickon posed. No, not "someone like": it was the person himself I had to be free of. He had always made me feel uneasy, that was why I had tried so hard so many times to go ahead without him. And had failed. He was not evil, most people would just see him as a nuisance, and wonder why I had tried so hard to be rid of him. I couldn't explain it, even now: it was just something that was part of him that one day would do me great hurt, of that I was sure. It was nothing of which he was aware either, just as a straight man will not glance back to see he has a crooked shadow. . . .

I made one last try.

"My offer of the money still stands." I'd manage somehow.

"You can keep your ten pieces of gold—or were they thirty pieces of silver?" And he slammed out; as a parting shot it wasn't bad at all.

For the next hour I made a full inventory of my possessions. It was time I moved from the monastery, now I was fully recovered. I would try to rent a couple of rooms in the village below, rather than presume too much on the hospitality of the monks.

There wasn't much to take with me. A few well-worn clothes, sewing kit, leather for patching, monthly cloths, comb; my journal, writing materials and maps; a cooking pot, spoons, mug, and sharp knife; a bag or two of herbs. With a blanket to wrap it all in and my father's cloak, that was about it. Except, of course, for my money belt, in which I still had a little coinage from our performing days, Suleiman's gold, and the assorted coins from my father's dowry to me.

Lastly there were my special treasures: the Waystone, the beautiful crystal gem and, last but first as well, the dragon's egg. I took it out now and looked at it: even since the last time I had done this it seemed to have grown. I cradled it in my hands, marvelling at its perfect symmetry and the way the light caught the speckles that glinted like granite on its surface. I remembered what both my long-ago Wimperling and Ky-Lin had said about the hundred years or so of incubation it needed before hatching, and was sad I should never see what it contained; I should have to find a suitable place to leave it soon, for it needed quiet and rest, to develop as it should.

There were three or four hours to go until dark, so Growch and I hitched a ride taking woollen cloth from the monastery down to the village, but we hadn't gone far down the narrow, twisty track when Growch announced that we were being followed.

"Who is it?" I asked, peering back up the track. I could see nothing.

"'Is lordship. 'Oo else?"

"Hell and damnation! Why can't he leave us alone?"

"Wanna lose 'im?"

"Of course."

"Then when we gets to the first 'ouses, jump off quick an' follow me, sharpish."

Once on foot, I realized just how well Growch had used his time when he was off "exploring," as he put it. No doubt he had been in search of his "fluffy bums," but he had learnt the village like a cartographer.

He led me a swift left turn down a side alley, turned right into a courtyard and straight out again through someone's (luckily unoccupied) kitchen, across another street, into a laundry and out again, ducking under wet clothes;

two sharp lefts, three rights and then helter-skelter up some steps, down others and into a stuffy little room, greasy with the smell of frying pork and chicken.

Growch trotted up to the cook, who had obviously met him before, because he aimed a halfhearted blow with his skillet, then fished out a pig's foot.

"C'mon," said Growch through the gristle. "Out the back."

This led out onto a street where the unoccupied ladies of the town held their nightly "entertainments." Everything was now closed, shuttered and barred, and backed out onto some unattractive garbage heaps, but I could hear awakening chatter behind the closed doors. Growch went over to inspect the rubbish, but I called him sharply back.

"That's enough! You'll be sick. . . ."

"'Ow often you seen me sick?" It was a rhetorical question, and he knew it.

"Where now?" I asked, changing the subject.

"'E's a'ead o' us now. Let's see what 'e's up to. I'll scout, you follow close."

So we crept along the irregular streets, stepping in and out of afternoon-going-on-evening shadows, passing the elderly taking patches of sun, children playing primitive games with colored squares of baked clay, or chasing each other in the eternal game of tag. I ducked under lines of washing, stepped around rubbish, avoided the throwing out of slops. There seemed no system or plan to the village; it had just grown. Every now and then we passed through little squares, apparently there just because the houses had been built facing one another. Several lanes led nowhere.

Suddenly I heard Dickon's voice. He seemed to be involved in some sort of altercation and, rounding a corner, there he was, arguing with a couple of villagers over a tatty-looking horse. From the look of it he wanted to "borrow" the horse against future payment, but they were having none of it.

I ducked back into the shadows, but he had seen me. All that rushing around with Growch for nothing, but perhaps after all it had only been an excuse on the dog's part to pick up a snack or two. He wouldn't admit it if it was.

"Hey, Summer! Come here a minute. . . ." Dickon led me aside. "Look here. I've been thinking about what you said earlier: the parting of the ways and all that stuff. Well, I've decided to do something about it." He stood back and folded his arms. "I think it would be best if I took off for a few days, before the winter sets in. I could travel between the villages, see what opportunities there are for trade, check on what goods they are short of, that sort of thing. What do they import now? Rice, salt, oil, metals; those are taken care of, but there must be other commodities they could do with. Why, if I sat down and worked it all out I bet I could do substantial undercutting of the other traders."

"Very commendable," I said. Why was it I didn't believe him?

"Well, what do you say? I was just bargaining with these fellows for the loan of their horse for a few days, but they obviously want cash down. Now, if you want me to make a life of my own—if you still insist you don't want to come in with me, which is the most sensible thing to do, let's face it—then you can't deny me this chance. I just need a few coins to hire the horse and kit myself out—"

"How much?" At least it meant he would be out from under my feet for a few days.

He named a sum, but I shook my head. "Too much. I'll talk to them, or try to. . . ."

"No, no, no. No need. I'll do my own bargaining. Probably bring them down by half . . ."

Which meant he had been trying to con me out of some extra for himself. Apparently the men were satisfied with his revised offer, and I paid out a few coins from my money belt after they had shown us where the horse was stabled and included the hire of saddle and bridle.

We started back up the steep track to the monastery together, hoping for a lift on the way, but quite prepared to walk, though Growch would grumble long before the top.

"I suppose you were in the village looking for lodgings," said Dickon carelessly, when we had walked for about five minutes. "Any luck?"

"Not yet," I answered, equally carelessly. "Plenty of time."

"Oh. Yes, of course. Well you might as well wait now until I get back and I can give you a hand shifting your gear."

"There's not much to carry. Anyway, Ky-Lin can help me."

"How?"

"He can do the bargaining. Don't worry, just take your time. I'll be fine."

He hesitated. "In that case—I'll need a bit more money. For provisions."

I gave him a couple of coins. "That should be enough for some cooked rice and dried fruit."

He inspected the coins. "Not very generous, are you?"

"We've managed on less."

Just then we heard the rattle of the little wagon that carried goat milk down from the monastery twice a day coming up behind us, so we rode the rest of the way.

That he was determined on going somewhere there was no doubt; that night he was packed up well before bedtime, and had already arranged a lift down to the village before cockcrow.

Once again I couldn't sleep. Once again I went out onto the balcony, once again gazed out at the waxing moon. Had it been just my imagination that had showed me a fleeting shadow across that glowing surface? Was my sudden change of spirits due to no more than an illusion? And then, just as the moon touched the tip of the mountains I saw it again! No bigger than a distant leaf in autumn, it drifted across the face of the moon. I was almost certain now. Almost . . .

My heart thudding, not even bothering to throw a cloak over the nightshirt I wore, I ran down to the little garden below, my hands grasping the balustrade so hard they hurt. But there was nothing there, nothing.

Nothing other than the whisper of air across my cheek as though great wings were beating far above.

I waited and waited, but it seemed that was that. Despondently I trailed back to bed, and was just dozing off when there came a sudden rattling crash. It seemed to come from the direction of Dickon's room. He wasn't sleepwalking, was he? Or perhaps he had decided to get up extra early so as not to miss his lift to the village. Once again I hurried out onto the balcony; now the noise appeared to be coming from the little garden. The stupid boy hadn't fallen down the steps, had he?

"What the devil do you think you are doing, Dickon? Some of us are trying to sleep. . . ."

"Some of us can't sleep," came a voice from below. "And who the hell is Dickon? Not that stupid boy who stole your money all that long time ago, surely?"

Chapter Twenty-Seven

"Wimperling!" I called out joyously.

But no, it wasn't my little winged pig, the one who had flown me to safety all that long time ago, because he wasn't a pig at all, was he? He had almost broken my heart when he had burst to smithereens at my third kiss and left only a tiny piece of shrivelled hide that even now I wore in the pouch around my neck.

"Summer? Somerdai . . . my Talitha. Come here, my dear. Let me see you!"

A man, a tall man dressed in the colors of the night, was leaning on the balustrade in the little garden. I knew who it was although I couldn't see his face, of course I did, but was I still asleep and dreaming?

"Come on down! It's been a long time. . . ."

And many, many wearisome miles. Heat, cold, exhaustion, near starvation, danger; and my imaginings of it had not been at all like this, a hidden-faced stranger who lolled against a balustrade and called my name as though we had only parted yesterday. The memory that had sustained me had been of a snatched embrace, a burning kiss, a wrenching away. Quick, violent, fraught with emotion for both of us.

"Do I have to come up there and fetch you?" It wasn't a soft, warm voice like my blind knight had used in his seducing mood, nor the comfortable town-burr of the merchant, Matthew Spicer; it had a harsh, nasal quality, a sort of scraping reluctance for the words to form. A disturbing voice, a compelling one, but not necessarily a very nice one.

"No," I said. "I'm coming down."

And slowly, almost reluctantly, I moved down the steps till I stood on the bottom one, clutching the neck of my nightshirt as if it could be the one gesture that kept me from being stripped naked.

"You're thinner," said the voice. "And your hair is shorter. But your eyes are just the same; great big wondering eyes, mirrors of your soul. Why don't you come nearer? Are you afraid?"

"I—I don't know. I don't remember . . . I didn't think—"

"If you don't know, remember, think—then why are you here?" The voice was gentler now, as if it was getting more used to human speech, and there was even a hint of amused tenderness. "And why don't you use my human name?"

Jasper. Master of Many Treasures. The dragon-man, man-dragon I had travelled half the known world to find. And yet I couldn't even use his name. Why? I was frightened, shy, now uncertain of those feelings I had been so certain of before. Or thought I had. Even while I cursed myself for my stupidity I could feel the tears welling up in my eyes, spilling down my cheeks, blurring my vision, till the figure before me wavered and dissolved.

Something touched my face, and the corner of a cloak caught the tears as they fell, absorbed them as they coursed down my cheeks, wiped my nose.

"Blow . . . That's better! Am I so terrifying? Why you're trembling. . . . Here, wrap my cloak around you. There, isn't that better?"

As he was still wearing the cloak himself—yes, it was. Suddenly, very much better. But he didn't press it; he had one arm round my shoulders now and with the other hand he lifted my chin, but we were still inches away from a proper embrace. Physically, that is; emotionally, as far as he was concerned, I could see it was miles.

"Open your eyes: look at me! I don't bite."

"Dragons do," I said, still feebly resisting the temptations of his sudden nearness.

"I'm not a dragon all the time. I've learnt a lot in the time we've been apart, including how to keep my two selves separate—usually. I make mistakes, of course—and I still find it difficult to land on narrow balconies at night, as no doubt you heard. . . ."

"Have you been a dragon all the time till now?"

"Mostly, but not all. So now I am owed a little man-time."

"Three months in every year," I said, remembering.

"And all because you kissed a rather ugly little pig three times—"

"You weren't ugly! I mean the Wimperling wasn't! You—he—wasn't exactly beautiful, I suppose, but very endearing."

"More than me, I suppose! Perhaps I'd better reverse the process."

"You can't, can you?" Forgetting to be shy I opened my eyes properly and looked up at him.

It wasn't fair: I had forgotten just how handsome he was. The dim light threw half his face into darkness, but the dark, frowning brows, yellow eyes set slightly aslant, strong, hooked nose and the wide mouth that could express both harshness or humor, strength or tenderness, they were quite clear. Tentatively I raised my fingers to the hand that cradled my chin; two years ago it had been cold, with the traces of scales still evident, but now it was warm and smooth.

"Remember me?" He was teasing.

"Of course I do, but—" I lifted a finger to trace the thin line of moustache, the short hairs along his jawline. "You're not quite the same."

"Neither are you, my dear. You've grown up." He tipped my chin higher. "There are great shadows under your eyes, your mouth is firmer, you are much slimmer. . . . Was it bad, your journey? No, don't tell me now," and his mouth brushed mine so gently it was come and gone like the touch of a moth's wing. "We have plenty of time to talk." His lips met mine again, lingering there longer, exerted a stronger pressure. "I can't tell you how nice it is to see you again. And what a surprise!" The next kiss still teased, though it was more like a proper one. "You know something, my little Talitha? You are practically irresistible! Tell me something; how did you manage to end up here, of all places in the world to choose from?"

For a moment the meaning of what he had said didn't sink in, but when it did I pushed away from him and stood there, bewildered. His question meant that he didn't realize that I had come all this way just to seek him out; he didn't know how much I loved him. How could I now betray my foolish hopes, my enduring love, to someone who obviously thought of me just as a temporary plaything?

The hot blood rushed to my cheeks and I was about to cover my shame and confusion by muttering something utterly inane like "looking for treasure," when I was saved from making a fool of myself by glimpsing a sudden flash of white on the balcony above.

I tugged at Jasper's sleeve. "Quick, you must go! Dickon—yes, the same one—is up there on the balcony, and he mustn't see you!"

"Then I shall come again tomorrow night. Earlier."

"He's away this morning for a few days—"

"Good." He leapt up on the balustrade. "Tomorrow. Midnight . . ." He paused for a moment, then plunged over the edge.

My genuine cry of fright was echoed by a yell from Dickon above. I rushed over to the void, terror-stricken, my heart in my mouth, then I heard the *crack*! of opening wings and saw my man-dragon soar away into the darkness.

Dickon, who had seen nothing of this, joined me at the balustrade. "Who was it? What happened? Where did he go?"

I was still trembling, though he didn't notice this, and I tried to keep the shakes from my voice as I answered.

"I've no idea. A thief, a voyeur? I heard a noise, got up and came down here. I tried to talk to him, find out what he was doing—" how long had he been listening? "—but when he saw you he jumped down to the rocks below." I leant over the edge. "There's no sign of him now."

"You must be more careful! Are you sure that money of yours is safe? Bar your door and your windows. Get that lazy dog of yours to stand guard out here at night." He seemed genuinely worried, though whether it was me or my money he was more bothered about it was difficult to say. "Promise me you won't do anything—foolish—while I am away?"

No, I wouldn't do anything foolish. I had done enough of that already, including coming here in the first place, following an impossible dream.

"I promise," I said. "I shall be here when you return, safe and sound. And—" the thought coming to me unbidden and forcing itself into speech "—and I may change my mind about staying here after all."

"You mean . . . go back to the merchant?" He sounded incredulous. Then, suddenly, suspicious. "You have found what you seek, then?" I could almost see the picture of a heap of treasure in his mind, followed by the thought: where has she hidden it?

"Why not? There I was safe and secure. A good marriage . . ." I shrugged. "Or I could still go into trade somewhere else. It's not entirely a man's world, you know; there are women physicians, builders, painters, herbalists, farmers, metal workers, writers. . . . And now I'm going back to bed. Have a good journey."

It was a relief to be rid of him, but unfortunately this also gave me too much time to think. Over and over again I reviewed in my mind Jasper's visit, what he had looked like, what he said, and, more important, what he didn't. I had been stupid, shy, tearful, but he had been—different. I suppose it was ridiculous of me to suppose we could pick up just where we had left off over two years ago, for that had been a moment of such high intensity it could not be repeated, but I had expected him to understand why I had travelled all this way to see him again.

Instead he was treating me with an amused tenderness, just as you would a particular pet, indulging my tears and stupid behavior. But hadn't he said I was now grown-up, too? And did he truly not know why I was here? Long, long ago he had warned me against loving him: was this because he knew he was incapable of such emotion? Or was it that he no longer found me attractive?

Had my journey been in vain, then?

I'd be damned if it had! My pride wouldn't let me just creep away without a fight. I hadn't come all this way to be brushed aside. As for being attractive—well, just let him wait and see!

Off I went down to the village and when I returned spent the rest of the day with scissors, needle and thread, warm water, the opening of this jar, that bottle.

Ky-Lin visited me at around six. I hadn't seen him for days, but it seemed he knew, somehow, of Jasper's visit.

"Was it how you imagined it, girl? Was it worth all the journeying?" He looked around at my preparations. "You know, I remember something my Master used to say to his disciples: 'Be careful on what you set your heart, for it may just be you achieve your desire.' "

I didn't understand; surely to get what you wanted was the ultimate goal.

He looked at me steadily, his plumed tail swishing gently from side to side. "You will understand someday, I think." I had never seen him look so sad. "Do not forget I am still here to help you, if you need me."

At last I heard the monks chanting their evening prayers, the dissonance of their softly struck bells. Soon it would be midnight. I slipped the green silk gown I had made that afternoon over my head. There was no mirror of course, but it felt good, the dress swirling round me in soft, loose folds, as it did so catching the perfume of sandalwood oil I had used in my bathing water. On my feet were a pair of green felt slippers I had hastily cobbled once the dress was finished, and I had a green ribbon in my hair.

I had told Growch whom I was expecting and asked him to please not interrupt our meeting.

"Din' last night, did I? You goin' to do naughties tonight, like the first time you met?"

Ridiculously I felt myself blushing: fancy being embarrassed by a dog! "None of your business what I'm going to do!"

"You looks nice," he said unexpectedly. "Quite the lady . . ."

Probably I was now wearing the most beautiful dress I had ever possessed, and after what Growch had said, I wished, I wished I had a mirror. It would be nice to see a beautiful Summer, just for once, especially as I had spent so much of my life as a plain, fat girl nobody looked at twice.

I left a lamp burning in my room, took the lantern from Dickon's room and set it on the balcony. Tonight was overcast, the moon hidden behind a scud of cloud. There was a sudden sound behind me: only a moth, banging helplessly against the oiled paper of the lantern. I brushed it aside, although the flame was well shielded.

Suddenly it was cold; a chill wind came rushing from the snowcapped mountains to the north and whirled around me: my skin shivered into goosebumps and the breeze lifted the hair on my head into tangles. Winter was giving its warning—or was it something else that made me think of a dying end?

The wind ceased as suddenly as it had risen, the clouds parted and the moon shone clear and bright. I twisted the ring on my finger—strange, it seemed much looser; perhaps I was losing too much weight—but it was warm and comforting, and I pushed any dark thoughts from my mind as a shadow flicked across the edge of my sight and swooped away beneath.

I ran down the steps to the little garden and there, just climbing over the edge, was my man-dragon, his cloak flapping behind him like wings. He stopped when he saw me, one foot still on the balustrade.

"My, what have we here, then? A strange fair lady!"

"Wha—what do you mean?"

"To what do I owe this honor, beauteous maid?" Stepping down, he gave me a bow, his hand on his heart. "I swear you are the very vision of loveliness. . . ."

For a moment I truly believed he didn't recognize me, then he laughed, came forward, and took my hands.

"You look absolutely wonderful, Talitha! I wouldn't have believed it possible!" Did it depend so much on the clothes I wore, I wondered? "Of course you are beautiful anyway, always were, but that dress frames your loveliness perfectly! Did you make it especially for me?"

"Of course not!" I lied too quickly. (Never let a man think you've tarted yourself up just for him, Mama used to say. They are big-headed enough as it is. A little disarray is perfectly acceptable.) "It's just something I had put by."

He turned over my right hand, brushing his thumb across my index finger. "With fresh needle marks? You're not a good liar, my dear—no, don't be angry. I am deeply honored, believe me," and he sang a little song I used to be familiar with in my own country.

"Silver ribbons in your hair, lady;
"Golden shoon upon your feet.
"Crimson silk to clothe you, lady:
"And a kiss your knight to greet!"

Only he changed all the colors to "green," and I got a kiss at the end of it, a proper one this time.

In an instant my arms went around his neck and my body curved into his, so you couldn't have passed a silken thread between us. I felt as though I was melting, fusing with him until we were metal of the same mold. I couldn't breathe or think, all I could do was feel.

Then at once everything changed. Suddenly I was standing alone, scarcely able to keep my feet for the trembling in my limbs, shaking with a frustration I had no words for, an ache that came from the deepest parts of my body.

All I could say was: "Why?" and I didn't even realize I had spoken out loud.

"No," he said. "No, my very dear one, no."

I didn't understand. "What's wrong? What have I done?"

"Done? Nothing, nothing at all. But we can't let this happen again. It was bad enough last time, against all the laws of nature, and I was the one who let it happen. No, now don't cry. . . ." He came forward and held my hands again. "Remember this: we are different, you and I. You are human, through and through, and nothing but. I am three-quarters, nay more, of a completely different creature. Normally I have a different form, different morals, different view of life, different future. There is no way, absolutely none, in which we could ever have a future together, even for a few days, and anything less wouldn't be fair to you. Don't you understand?"

"What about the quarter that isn't dragon? What about the times when you are 'He who Scrapes the Clouds' or whatever is your dragon name? What about the man who stands before me now? What happens to Jasper?"

"Jasper," he said, "may be the Master of Many Treasures, but not of his own soul—if he has one, that is. He is ruled by his larger part and that is dragon; he is subject to dragon rule and dragon law. He may make no important decisions contrary to those that are already laid down, unless it is first referred to the Council for consideration. And unless this Jasper is a Master Dragon, which he is not, then there is no hope of changing the laws or of making any appeal against them. . . ." He was speaking in a dull, monotonous way, like a priest bored with the service.

I tried to humor him. "What is the difference between an ordinary dragon and a master?"

"Treasure. The gathering of enough to satisfy the Council. The last master brought five great jewels, still much admired. An emerald from a rainforest on the other side of the world, a sapphire from an island in the warm seas, a diamond from the mines of the southern desert, a ruby from a temple of the infidel, and a priceless freshwater pearl from the Islands of Mist."

"How long ago was that?"

"Some five hundred years."

I gasped. So long ago! "Then how long can a dragon live? And what is the Council?"

"A fit dragon can live for a thousand years, perhaps more. Once there were hundreds, all over the world, together with other similar creatures of all sorts, shapes and sizes. Now their bones lie scattered, for our legends say that a disaster came from the sky, a great ball of fire that brought with it a breath of death that destroyed millions of creatures, the dragons among them. Some survived, but very few, and those only in the high mountains, where the contamination couldn't reach them. Other pockets of safety conserved other creatures, mainly small ones: lizards, tortoises, lemurs. Then the world gradually changed, mammals growing strong at the expense of the dragon." He glanced at my indignant face. "That is what our legends say; yours are probably rather different."

"God created the world," I said stiffly. "And Adam and Eve came before dragons. I think. If He ever created them; some say they come from the Devil."

"Who's he?"

He didn't know? "And in any case I don't think Noah would have been able to cope with a pair of dragons in his Ark. It must have been difficult enough putting lions and sheep with rats and camels. . . ."

He was laughing now. "Oh Summer-Talitha, you take things so seriously, so literally!"

I was so happy to see him back to normal, as it were, that I couldn't take offense. I knew what was right, so what the dragons believed in didn't matter. "And the Council?" I prompted.

"All the Master Dragons who survive, eleven in all."

"And where is the Council?"

"You've seen them."

"I have?"

"Of course!" He smiled again. "Let us say they saw you, and the dog. They told me so."

"The Blue Mountain?"

"Yes."

"But there was nothing there—except rocks and stones and pebbles and dust and a nasty smell."

"Rocks and pebbles? Are you sure?"

I remembered something Ky-Lin had said: "Rocks are rocks are rocks, you know. . . ."

"You mean—the cavern was full of dragons? The rocks . . ."

"Yes."

"And the pebbles?"

"Treasure. Heaps of it."

So Dickon had been right after all! There *had* been a fabulous treasure waiting at the end of our journey. . . .

I was silent for a moment. "How do they hide—look like rocks?"

"A mist of illusion. Easy stuff."

"But don't you think it's an awful waste having all that treasure just sitting there doing nothing?"

"It's very pretty. A delight to run between one's claws, to taste with one's tongue. Did you know all jewels taste different? Like bonbons do to humans . . . Myself, I prefer the tang of a fire opal."

I thought he might be joking, but a glance told me he wasn't.

"I still think it's a waste."

"Why? What about all those kings and princes, merchants and misers who do precisely the same thing? They have rooms full of treasure that never see the light of day. What about those who bury treasure so it is lost forever? What about those vandals that actually destroy what you would call treasure, just for the joy of it? Why should a few ageing dragons be denied their simple pleasures? Which is worse: to steal a jewel every now and again, or to take lives in the name of religion, or whatever?"

"But dragons eat people, too!" I remembered the tales of my childhood; beautiful damsels chained to rocks, children offered up, young men stripped naked to fight with a wooden sword a battle they could not hope to win.

"Perhaps some did, once. There were many more of us then. Now we eat seldom, and then only to fuel our fires, speed our wings. And there are not many of us left who undertake journeys of any distance."

"Why?"

"Most of them are too old, some well over the thousand-year norm. All they want is a little heat, a little sleep, and their memories. They are great tale-tellers. To them the puny adventures and battles and wars of humankind are like a breath, soon expended."

I wondered. Sometimes he spoke of "us," sometimes of "them." Was this because of the life he was forced to lead? A quarter man, three-quarters dragon? I must try and keep him thinking of dragons as "them," and concentrate on making him feel like a man.

"Well, waste or no, I didn't come all this way for treasure," I said, choosing my words carefully.

"Why, then?" He released my hands and slipped an arm about my waist. "Adventure? Curiosity?"

No, Love, you great idiot! I thought, but of course didn't say it. "A little of both, I suppose," I said. "All that travelling we did, while you were still the Wimperling, gave me a taste for it. Besides which, I have had a chance of earning my own living. Real money . . ."

"And where did you pick up that little thief, Dickon, again?"

I explained. "I kept trying to leave him behind, but he persisted in believing that I was after treasure, dragon treasure. Thank God he has given up that idea and gone off for a couple of days looking for trading opportunities."

"Oh, I don't think he has given up. Did you tell him about your visit to the Blue Mountain?"

"Yes, but—"

"I flew over his encampment earlier, frightened his horse off into the bush. Take him the best part of a day to catch up with it again."

"You don't mean . . ."

"I do mean. He's camped at the foot of the Blue Mountain, and tomorrow, if I'm not much mistaken, he'll be climbing the path you took, looking for the treasure!"

Chapter Twenty-Eight

The crafty devil! Telling me he was looking for new opportunities, and making me pay for yet another treasure hunt! I should never have told him about the Blue Mountain; it was obvious he hadn't believed me.

"He won't find anything, will he?"

"No more than you did."

"Well, I hope he falls off the path!" I said crossly. "He's been nothing but trouble ever since we met up again."

"Tell me . . ." and he spread out his cloak on the stone flags of the little garden, sat cross-legged and pulled me down beside him. "I want to hear everything that's happened to you since the Place of Stones."

I glossed over that dreadful journey back to Matthew's, for after all it wasn't his fault I had near starved to death; I told him of my decision to turn down Matthew's offer (but not the real reason), made him smile over my forgeries of the merchant's signature and running off dressed as a boy to seek my fortune. I made my adventures as amusing as I could: storm at sea, ambush, imprisonment, the bog, bandits, the Desert of Death and the hairy people.

When I had finished he ruffled my hair, leant forward and kissed my cheek.

"I reckon it was a good job you had your friend Ky-Lin with you. I have heard of them, but never seen one. You could have easily died a dozen times without him. . . ." He frowned. "But all this doesn't explain why you left the caravan trails and came this way."

Ah, Jasper, my love, this was the difficult part. . . .

"I wanted to see you again," I said lightly. "Man-dragons are a little out of my experience, you see. Added to that, the coins my father left me led me all the way across every country to this one. And on Matthew's maps this part was marked: 'Here be Dragons.' Simple as that."

"Was it? Was it really?" He slipped his arm about my waist again. "You know something? I went back to look for you after I made my initial journey here. I worried that you would find it difficult to find your merchant's house again. But you had vanished from the face of the earth! Nice to know you were all right." He cuddled me closer. "Well, now that you've found your man-dragon again, what do you want of him?"

"A couple of kisses," I said promptly. "Proper ones. Not no-commitment-it's-dangerous-you-mustn't-get-entangled-with-a-dragon-man. Neither should it be let's-have-a-laugh-and-a-kiss-and-say-good-bye! I want you to pretend," I snuggled up closer, "just for a moment, that I am the most desirable woman in the world. . . ." My hand stroked his cheek. "I am a princess under a spell, and only you can break the ice about her heart." Had I gone too far? "It's not a lot to ask, it can't threaten your life! You're not going to change back into a pig, or anything like that—"

"I should hope not!"

He was chuckling; that was encouraging. At least there was no outright rejection.

"Well, then?" Now for it; my heart was beating uncomfortably fast and loud. "Or can't you pretend?"

"I don't need to pretend," he said, and gathered me in his arms.

At first he just held me close, his hands stroking my hair, my cheeks, my hands. Every time he touched me my inside tangled itself up into knots and I feared he would hear my heart, but he hummed a gentle little droning song, as soothing as the sound of a hive or the turning of a spinning wheel. Gradually the tune and his gentle touch calmed my mind, but not my body.

I was aware of my skin, my blood, my bones. I could see his shadowy face bent over mine; I could hear his soft voice, with the slight grating tone in the lower notes; in the air was the pungency of the rough-headed autumn plants in pots in the garden, the night-wind smell of Jasper's clothes, and a certain slightly musky scent that seemed to come from his skin. My whole body was stimulated to a point I had not thought possible, and now came the taste of his lips.

I thought of the tang of burnt sugar, the bitter black heart of an opium poppy, the smoke from autumn bonfires, the cold, iron smell of ice and snow, newly washed linen sun-dried, the sharp bite of a juicy apple, a snuffed candle—then I didn't think at all.

At first he was experimenting with my lips and tongue, but gradually as he pulled me closer I knew that at last it was me, me, me! that he wanted. I didn't care if it was lust without love, desire without commitment, I just kissed him back with all my heart. His hands found my breasts, his body was full of a hard urgency that found a response in my yielding form.

"Summer Talitha," he murmured. "My little love . . ."

For answer I pulled him down so we rested together on his cloak, our bodies inhibited only by the clothes we wore. For a brief instant it seemed he might think better of it, but then I took over the caressing, my fingers moving on his chest and stomach, untying the laces of his trews, my mouth thrust up hungrily to his. . . .

And then it was too late for either of us.

I remember the rip of silk as my dress parted company with its stitches;

I remember the feel of his crisp, dark hair under my fingers, the rasp of his beard against my cheek; I remember stifling my cries in the soft skin where his neck met his shoulder; I remember, oh I remember the hard thrusts I welcomed with fierce ripostes of my own; I remember—but there are no words to describe the cascades of delight that followed, never will be. No words, no music, no painting: nothing can adequately portray raw emotion like that. Until you have felt it you will never know, and if you have you will realize it is beyond description.

Afterwards we lay in each other's arms. Only now did my cheeks sting where his beard had rubbed them; only now was I conscious of the uncomfortable rucks of the cloak beneath us; only now did my insides ache with an inward tension as though they pulled against a cat's cradle of tiny inside stitches. I was sticky and sweaty, but so was he, and it didn't matter.

He stirred, sighed, stroked my hair. "You are a witch, girl: you know that?" He leant up on one elbow and gazed down at me. "You realize I had no intention of that happening?"

"I know." I put up a finger and traced the line of his nose. "But I did." I sat up. "And you wanted it too."

"Maybe. But it was wrong, wrong! We shouldn't have done it."

"Why not? Who are we hurting?"

"Ourselves." His voice was bitter. "In time I could have forgotten you and, whatever you think now, you would have forgotten me too. But now I shall always want you. You will always want me. If we looked for love elsewhere, or tried to do without, we should both think only of each other. We have forged a link that can never be broken."

"But that was the way I wanted it—"

"You didn't understand what you were getting yourself into. We can never be together, don't you understand? And you will suffer more than I. In my dragon form I can forget you for three-quarters of the year, but you—you will never forget!"

"Then I shall wait for the quarter-year you are a man," I said obstinately. "Wherever it is. That will be enough for me. Three months with you is better than none at all."

He rose to his feet in one swift movement and crossed to the balustrade. His whole posture was stiff, his hands clenched on the stone, his shoulders raised, his head bent.

"It's impossible."

I went to stand at his side, clutching at my torn gown, aware all at once of a chill wind that blew from the north, making the stars shiver in sympathy. The moon was down, but a pale light had followed her descent, a trace of silver on the permanent snows.

"Why is it impossible? Don't you want to see me again?"

He glanced at me, but I couldn't see his expression. "Of course I want to be with you, as often as I can—but that is just the point. It's not possible!"

"But *why,* if you want to? What's to stop you?"

He turned, gripped my shoulders. "It's not as simple as you seem to think!

If I could know for sure, say to you: all right, my dear, my love, I am yours from November until January. Find us a house where we can be one for those three months of the year. . . . Or if I could say: I can be with you in March, May and September, find me that house etc."

He released me, leant over the balustrade again. "But it doesn't work that way: I wish it did. I just don't have those certainties. These—" he gestured at himself "—these remissions, if you can call them that, give me very little warning. At first, they gave me none at all and it was dangerous. Then I had no idea how long they would last either: five minutes, five hours, five days. . . ."

He traced the line of my jaw with his finger. "That was one of the reasons I gave up looking for you; it was too unpredictable, the time I could spend asking questions, and twice I nearly got killed." He sighed. "It has become easier, like changing to come and see you. I can control it for a couple of hours or so, and if it is going to be longer, a week or so, I get a warning beforehand, a sort of painless headache. But I still don't know how long it will last."

I was devastated. "But—"

"No," he said firmly. "I couldn't live with you all the time. My dragon side is too unpredictable. Nor could you keep me in a shed at the bottom of the garden betweenwhiles, just waiting for my nicer side to come out. I think the neighbors might object," he added, with a smile. "Oh, come on darling: we'll think of something!"

"But what?" I was close to tears.

He shrugged. "Right now I have no idea. I shall consult the Council, though I warn you they are finding it difficult to accept that I am not completely dragon. No precedent, you see. Plenty of legends, but no firm records. At the moment I am something of a celebrity, but there are those who wish to cast me out." He shook his head. "I should have a better case to argue if I could bring them the jewels they so desire—my permit to become a Master Dragon. But that, of course, will take time."

"So it is just some jewels they need?"

"To become a Master Dragon and not a mere Apprentice—as I am now—I have to be able to perform the usual flying tricks: spirals, hovering, steep dives, flying backwards, backspins, and I also have to contribute something of value to the Hoard. It can be of gold or silver, but they prefer the easier-to-handle glitter of jewels, cut or uncut."

"Do there have to be a certain number of these?"

He shook his head. "Recently—within the last thousand years or so that is—it has become traditional to bring in a selection, but the foremost criterion is that of color. Sometimes one stone is enough; we possess, I believe, the largest uncut emerald the world has yet seen. As big as your fist, Talitha, but too fragile to cut."

An idea was forming in my mind. "Do they have light in that cave of theirs?"

"Of course. There are a number of small openings that let in both sun- and moonlight, and with a blast or two of fire they can light semipermanent torches. Why?"

"Just wait a moment. . . ." Running up the steps I found what I wanted in my room, disturbing a sleepy Growch, then went back out again, picking up the lantern as I rejoined Jasper in the garden. Setting the light on one of the benches I opened my fist and slowly twisted the crystal the captain's wife had given me in front of the flame. Even with that relatively dim illumination the crystal threw a thousand rainbow lights across the garden, the balcony, our faces and clothes, the wall above, the rocks beneath, and we were almost blinded by reds and greens, yellows and purples, blues and oranges.

Jasper took it from my fingers. "By the stars! This is the most beautiful . . . Where did you get it?"

I explained.

"Do you know what it is?" He sounded excited.

"A crystal. Nicely cut, but—"

"But nothing! This has been cut by a master! In fact—" He looked at it more closely. "In fact I believe this may be one of the thirteen lost many hundreds of years ago when pagan hordes overran the city of the Hundred Towers. . . . So far six have been traced of the thirteen that were made by the Master of Cut Glass—one for each lunar month, you see—and this might well be the seventh." He was handling it as reverently as I would a splinter of the True Cross. "We—the Council that is—already possess one of these, but to have a pair . . . Do you realize what this means? If you let me take it to them, that will mean automatic Dragon Mastership!" He wrapped his arms about me. "And that would mean I would be equal to any, and they would be bound to consider any request I made!"

"They could agree to—regularize your changes?"

"Yes! I can also ask to spend my man-time with you."

He was fairly dancing around the small space of the garden, holding me up high against his chest. "We can find somewhere. . . . Why, I've just remembered the very place! There is an island set in the bluest of seas, miles away from the trade routes, where the sun shines warm year round and the land is peopled by the gentlest of natives, who would welcome us both. Everything you planted would grow, and there are fish in the sea—"

"It sounds like Paradise," I said wistfully. I could see it now. Yellow sands running up to the greenery of a forest, cool streams running between moss-covered stones, hills blue in the distance, huge butterflies feeding from the trumpets of exotic lilies, trees alive with the chatter of multicolored birds. A little hut set in a clearing, not too far from the sea, lines set out for fish, a net for the collection of shellfish; a patch of ground for the vegetables, another for a few chickens and a goat; a hammock slung between the trees, and Growch for company when Jasper had to be away . . .

His kiss prevented any further daydreaming.

"And now I must go, and quickly; I can feel a change coming over me already. Forgive me, my dear: I shall hope to see you tomorrow." He kissed me again. "And I shall keep an eye on your Dickon. . . ."

"Not *my* Dickon!" I protested, but Jasper had disappeared. Instead a black dragon hung on to the balustrade: scaly body, gaping jaws, huge leathery wings outspread, yellow eyes burning in a bony skull. I was afraid, but not so frightened as I would have been two hours or so earlier if Jasper had suddenly appeared in his dragon shape without warning.

The intelligence in those yellow eyes was benign, I was sure of that, so I had no hesitation in picking up the crystal and placing it in one outstretched claw.

"Godspeed, my love," I said, then stepped back hurriedly as the wind of his wings blew hair, dress, leaves, petals around me like a whirlwind.

All that long day I was in a fever of impatience. I mended my green silk dress, sorted out my belongings for the umpteenth time, brought my journal up to date, couldn't eat; snapped at Growch, then hugged him; washed my hair and set it; didn't like the result and washed it again to hang loose, and sun-dried it.

Ky-Lin paid a visit around midmorning, looked at all my preparations, fluffed the tip of his tail up like a peacock and retired, remarking: "I hope you know what you are doing. . . ."

Of course I did! I was getting ready for my love, shedding what I did not need, preparing for the time when we would both be together forever, even if only for part of each year. Nothing was more important than this, yet the day seemed to crawl by, the sun standing still in the sky on purpose, the hours marked only by gongs, dissonant bells, and the soft, monotonous chant of the monks.

Several times I went out onto the balcony and looked in the direction of the Blue Mountain, wondering how Jasper was presenting his case to the Council; I wondered, too, if Dickon, that handsome treacherous boy, had reached the cave, only to be as disappointed as I had been.

At last the sun really did start to slide down the sky to the west. I supped some broth and bread, tasting nothing in my impatience, took a warm bath, slid into my mended dress, combed my hair until it sparked out from my head like a halo, then sat down by the door to the balcony to wait.

And wait.

The moon came up, near full now, and flooded the countryside with light, the stars pricked through their cover; at midnight a small wind blew up; at one it died down again, and I was yawning; by two I was half-asleep and must have drifted into a dream, because I thought I was talking to my old friends Basher, Traveler, Mistral, and the Wimperling, when suddenly the latter took wing, swung around in the sky and came back to land at my side, only this time he was a man.

"Jasper!" I started up, suddenly wide awake once more. "What did they say?"

"I am now a Master Dragon, thanks to your gift!" Glints like raindrops or tiny diamonds seemed to surround him. "But . . ."

"But what? Will they let you go?" I ran into his arms.

He kissed me, but there was a constraint in his manner. "They are considering it, yes. But they want to see you: face-to-face."

Chapter Twenty-Nine

I drew back, shocked and horrified. "B—but I can't! They might eat me!"

He drew me close again. "Nonsense! They are so pleased with the Dragon Stone that a whole village full of desirable maidens could parade in front of them and they would never notice! They were so euphoric they gave me the accolade of Master Dragon at once, without asking to assess my flying skills. Just as well: I think I would have failed on the backspins. . . ." He kissed my brow. "Then I asked for leave of absence from my dragon form for a fixed term each year. They wanted to know why, of course." He frowned. "It was very difficult for them to understand. To them, fair maidens were for dining on, not living with—in the legends, of course," he amended hastily.

"There must be lady dragons," I said. "Couldn't you have explained it that way?"

"There are no 'lady dragons' as you call them. There may have been once, I suppose, but now many of those left are hermaphroditic. There are others, like myself, who are totally male, who can fertilize the hermaphrodites, though most of them manage on their own. It's a bit difficult to explain, because it just—just happens. You don't think about it."

He was right: I didn't understand at all. Except the bit about him being totally male. I wouldn't like to think I had been making love with a hermaphrodite. Then I suddenly remembered something so important I couldn't get the words out straight.

"Supposing . . . if it's as you say . . . the dragon's eggs . . . your being a male . . . it isn't possible, is it? I mean you and me . . . Ky-Lin was so sure!"

"What in the world are you talking about?"

But I had second thoughts; my ring had given a warning tingle. Don't tell him yet: wait and see.

"Nothing. When were you thinking of taking me to see them?"

"When? Right now."

"*Now?* But I'm not ready, I've nothing suitable to wear, how do we get there, I don't want to—"

"Now!" he said firmly. "The sooner the better. Trust me—you do trust me, don't you? You would have trusted the Wimperling, as you called him, with your life, wouldn't you? Good. Go get your cloak and wrap yourself up tight: you're going to be dragon-borne tonight!"

And it all happened so quickly I had no chance to argue. One moment I was standing there in my silken dress, terrified at the whole idea, the next I was back on the same spot, swathed and hooded in my father's cloak.

Jasper held me close.

"You are not used to riding on the back of a dragon, and now is not the time to teach you properly." I could feel him laughing a little. "So we'll do it the easy way. I shall carry you—no, don't panic! You won't know much about it. Close your eyes and relax. I am going to make you go to sleep for a little while, long enough to get you safe to the mountain. I don't want you struggling at the wrong moment."

His lips came down on mine and I surrendered to his embrace as his fingers came up to my neck. A little pressure—in my mind or my body I wasn't sure—and I slipped into a sort of waking unconsciousness. I didn't dream, or anything like that, but the sensation of flying was curiously dimmed, though I could sense wind, the clapping of wings, a cindery smell. . . .

My stomach gave a sudden jolt, like the leap of a stranded fish.

"Sorry about that: I came down a bit sharply and changed early. You can open your eyes now, my love."

It was lucky his arm was around my waist, otherwise I might have tumbled to the ground. I was shaking and cold and my hair, in spite of the hood of my cloak, felt as though it had been attacked by a flying thornbush. I thought my eyes were open, but everything seemed as black as pitch. I blinked rapidly a couple of times and tried again. Looking up now I could see the stars and the moon illuminating the ledge on which we stood, but I had been staring straight at the entrance to the passageway that led to the cavern, and this still remained ominously dark. How could we possibly negotiate that without a light?

"Come," said Jasper. "Take my hand."

I pulled back. "It's so dark. . . ."

"I know the way, just as easily as you would in the dark of your own home without a candle. Besides, there is some light. Wait and see."

I allowed him to draw me into the passage, but closed my eyes like a child, only to be told to open them once we had passed the first turning.

"If you don't I shall let go your hand!"

Promptly they were open, to be faced with a faint silver glow from the rocks around us, like a seam of precious metal running through the stones. It was not so much a light as an emanation, and only extended a few feet in front and, glancing back, the same behind. As we paced it kept step with us.

"What is it? Dragon-magic?" I whispered.

He pressed my fingers. "No, it's a natural phenomenon; a kind of phosphorescence that is activated by the heat of our bodies as we pass."

The ring on my finger was tingling gently; no immediate harm, but a warning to go carefully; I wondered for the second or third time why it seemed to be getting so much looser.

The last time I had been in this passage I had cursed at the twists and turns, eager to reach the end; now I wished it would go on forever.

It didn't, of course. In less time than it takes to tell we had rounded the last corner and there was the cavern, lighted now by a broad spear of moonlight that shafted down from an opening in the roof of the cave and lit a pile of rocks—or were they? I gripped Jasper's hand more tightly.

Gently he loosed himself and stepped forward. "You are speaking with animals, so your ring will translate," he said to me. "Pay careful attention to what is said, and remember your manners. These are creatures as old and venerable as any in the land."

Then he spoke again, but this time it was in a series of creaks, groans, hisses, sighs, and rumbles.

"I have brought her. . . ."

I could understand what he said, the ring translating in my mind as he spoke. I had been staring straight ahead at the rocks, expecting some movement, but as he spoke I glanced to my side, and was horrified to see it was no man who stood at my side but a full-grown dragon! My heart gave a great jerk, then steadied. Didn't I say I would trust him? In spite of this I had backed away a little, but my ring, though still throbbing, had not increased its warnings.

The dragon at my side—black, with tiny pinpoints of light illuminating his wing tips—turned his bony face towards me, the yellow eyes still surprisingly kind. The rumble of dragon talk started again, but thanks to my ring, Jasper's own voice came through, warm and comforting.

"Don't be afraid: it's better that I appear to them this way. Come, stand by my side. And toss aside that cloak. I want them to see you as you really are."

I was quite glad to throw the cloak aside. It was very warm in the cavern. The fissure that divided us from the other side was throwing out a summer's night heat, and I found I was perspiring. I stepped to Jasper-dragon's side, aware once again of the cindery smell and the roughness of the stones beneath my feet. And now came a sound, a sort of stirring, slithery scrape—

"What is it?"

"Watch. . . ."

Across the chasm something stirred, a general sort of shifting; rocks altered their shape—round, square, oblong, irregular, jagged—and also changed their position relative to each other. A few pebbles rattled against each other. I could feel the hair rising at the back of my neck, although Jasper-dragon stood calm and quiet beside me. My ring gave a warning twinge, but no more.

I thought I saw a claw, a bony head, a wing, decided I must be mistaken, then all at once everything seemed to shimmer, like the sun on a long road on a hot day. No, not quite like that; perhaps more like glancing down into a swift-flowing stream, trying to make out what lay on the bottom through the uncontrollable shift of the water.

"Here be Dragons," I thought stupidly, and suddenly they were there.

Still half-veiled, distorted, shimmery, around a dozen of the huge creatures bestirred themselves, yawning, stretching, unwinding long sinewy tails, opening dark eyes, extending claws and wings. With them came color and light; it seemed they emanated their own illumination, for now I saw gleams and sparkles at their feet. The piles of pebbles, so dull and uninteresting before, now started to glow and sparkle with an unquiet riot of colors as the dragons stirred them with their claws. Ruby, beryl, garnet, fire opal, coral, rose quartz, topaz, peridot, emerald, sapphire, amethyst, aquamarine, agate, jet, bloodstone, jasper, opal, pearl, diamond—they were all there, plus gold and silver. Then I saw that the light that shone over all did not come from the heaps of gems, nor from the dragons, but rather from the shaft of moonlight catching the facets of a jewel that hung in the air above all: the crystal I had given Jasper.

He stepped forward and then came that confusing rumble of speech again that my ring sorted out for me.

"I have brought the girl, the giver of this gift that now shines above us all." A soft hiss from across the chasm.

"Bring her forward."

I was nudged forward by one of his wings. "Don't be afraid. . . ."

I went forward hesitatingly till I stood at the lip of the chasm and felt as well as saw the flickers of light that flashed across from the moonlit crystal; now everything I looked at had a strange unreality.

"I'm here," I said unsteadily. "What do you want of me?"

For a moment there was silence and I thought perhaps they had not understood my human speech, although the ring should be translating to them as well, but then came a low, grumbling growl, like Growch magnified ten times. I thought about turning and running, right away back and out to safety, but in spite of an involuntary step backwards, I otherwise stood firm.

The ring on my finger was still throbbing, but it was an encouraging feeling rather than a warning. I repeated my question.

"What do you want of me?"

When the answer came, it was not what I had expected. "You gave this Dragon Stone as a gift to our colleague. He-whose-wings-scrape-the-clouds?"

They must mean Jasper. "I did."

"And what do you hope for in exchange, daughter of man?"

I squared my shoulders; all or nothing. "When your new Master Dragon was in his first incarnation, I saved his life; I ask you now for the price of that life. Let him spend his man-life time with me, a quarter of each year that we may have together."

Another growling roar, louder this time. "You are impertinent!"

"I do not mean to be. If I had not been in that place, at that time, assuredly the growing creature that was to become your splendid He-whose-wings-scrape-the-clouds would never be standing here in front of you, an addition to your—your . . ." (what on earth was a collection of dragons? A flock? A gathering? The ring gave me the answer) " . . . your doom of dragons.

I admit that I kissed the creature he was then three times, causing this—this, to you, malfunction in his makeup, but that was a human manifestation of what you would recognize as kinship. . . ." Where were the words coming from? This wasn't me talking! Thank you, ring! "As it is, if you agree to my proposal, for nine months of the year you will have his company and his services, those of a Master Dragon. Can you afford to lose these? If you refuse our request—and it is his as well as mine—he will merely be sulky and uncooperative and absent himself from your meetings.

"There are few enough of you left: your distinguished race has been declining noticeably during the last thousand years. Do you want this to go on happening? I rescued one for you: surely you can grant me a quarter of his time?"

There was silence. And silence. The air in front of me shimmered and the lights went out, one by one, as the moon passed beyond the opening high in the cavern. The dragons disappeared and so did their jewels till only the rocks and pebbles remained.

I blinked back the tears. "Why didn't they listen to me?"

"But they did." He looked across the chasm. "They just haven't made up their minds, that's all. You were magnificent, by the way. . . ." If he had been in his human form, I'm sure he would have been smiling. "What's a day or two to a dragon, who measures your years as ten to his one? Give them time, my love, give them time. . . . And now I must take you back. Put on your cloak and wrap it tight. Close your eyes. . . ."

Once again I felt the pressure on my neck, his breath on my face and then I was asleep with the wind on my face, the flap of wings in my ears, the smell of cinders in my nostrils, the dizzy descent—

I was lying in my own bed and a voice whispered in my ear: "See you tomorrow."

"You gonna sleep the 'ole day away?" said Growch peevishly. "S'long after my breakfast . . ."

I sat up, blinking, to find the sun fingering its way through the shutters and the sound of chanting.

"What time is it?"

"Dunno. Near enough noon, I reckons."

I looked down. I was still wearing my green silk dress, my father's cloak. I remembered what had happened during the night, and I sighed. There must be something I could do to persuade them. . . .

"Enjoy yer trip?"

So he had been watching. "What? Oh, yes. I suppose so . . . Sorry, Growch, I've been neglecting you, but I've got a lot on my mind."

"That wouldn' include food, would it?"

I sighed again, but I loved him, grotty foulmouth that he was, and his devotion deserved some reward.

"I think that would do us both good. Let's go down to the market in the village and see what they've got."

And over honeyed and spiced roast ribs, egg noodles and sweet-berry tart I made final plans for the strategy I had been planning for the last couple of days. As far as I could see there was only one sure way of granting that which I wished for both Jasper and myself.

Tonight I would tell him my plan.

First, though, there was plenty to do. Practical things like hanging my dress free of wrinkles, taking my sheets down to the laundry woman in the courtyard, washing my hair free of wind tangles, warm water for a bath, bringing my journal up to date with last night's happenings. Certain things to be specially packaged, two letters to write. The first, to Matthew Spicer, was finished quickly. The other, to his agent in Venice, Signor Falcone, took longer. And I must have a talk with Ky-Lin.

And what if it all went wrong? The letters were easily torn up, but the rest? I wouldn't think about that.

Something else had been niggling me for days: I had been neglecting my prayers. Of course there was no Christian church within a thousand miles but God was God, wherever worshipped, so at the next call to prayer in the monastery I knelt and closed my eyes, offering up my heartfelt thanks for all that had gone before, and my various deliverances from evil. I prayed for those dead, my mother and my father, and for those I hoped still lived: the no-longer blind knight, Matthew and Suleiman, Signor Falcone, the sea captain and his big wife, little prince Tug, even Dickon. Then there were the animals. Jesus had been a shepherd to his people, so surely He would understand the prayers to those creatures I had loved and lost to their new lives: Mistral, Traveler, Basher, Ky-lin, of course, even Bear, and my darling Growch. Last of all there was Jasper, my one and only love, Master of Many Treasures. Easy enough to pour out my prayers for the man, but how did one pray for a dragon? I suppose if one owned a lizard that grew out of all proportion, turned nasty, started to fly around all over the place and charred all it ate, then one could pray for a dragon.

I tried my best, but even the patience of God must have been tried by my ramblings.

I took out the egg. It had grown even larger. I placed it on the clothes chest against the wall and covered it with my shift. I looked around the room: all seemed ready. Bed freshly made with clean sheets, my dress free of creases, a skin of honeyed rice wine and two mugs on the side table—

"'Spectin' 'im in 'ere, then? Where does you want me to go?"

Oh, poor Growch! But I had thought about him earlier. A large bone awaited him in Dickon's empty room next door.

"You goin' to do naughties again?"

I nearly cancelled the bone.

Chapter Thirty

The rest of the day dragged by on leaden feet, and two or three times I found myself pacing restlessly around and around my room like a caged animal, chewing my nails, until Growch planted his tail under my foot and I had to spend a quarter-hour apologizing.

The sun went down and I tried to stay relaxed, knowing that Jasper would not come till moonrise, for dragons don't like flying in full dark, and the few stars were still lie-abeds, reluctant to leave their day's sleep.

The night was chill: no wind, no clouds. I took to twisting my ring about my finger; it was definitely looser today, and with a pang I thought I knew the reason why. This was one of my possessions I had not taken into account on settling my affairs. I must see Ky-Lin. There was also an addition I must make to Signor Falcone's letter.

I could leave it until tomorrow—no, I would do it right now. So it was with pen in hand, paper in front of me, legs curled up beneath, and my tongue between my teeth (normal position when I was writing) that Jasper found me. I had my back to the balcony door, which was open, in order to sit as near as I could to the candles, and the first I knew was when he dropped a light kiss on the nape of my neck.

I jumped up, scattering paper, pen and ink; there was a huge blot on the paper which no amount of sand would soak up.

"Jasper! How did you manage to be so quiet?"

"You were busy!" He kissed me again, this time properly. "Catching up on your correspondence?" He was only joking, but it was too near the mark for me. I gathered up the papers, turned them facedown.

"Something like that . . . oh, I am glad to see you! I thought the moon would never rise."

He drew me out onto the balcony. "Well there she is, near full. Whatever they call the days and months here, do you realize that tomorrow night it will be two years since we returned to the place where I was hatched at that farm by the Place of Stones? All Hallows' Eve . . . Remember?"

As if I could ever forget. That was the night when my beloved Wimperling had turned into an even more beloved man-dragon. Fiercer, more unpredictable, someone to fear as well as love, an unknown quantity in many ways, he had still captured both my imagination and my heart. I had watched him fly away that night knowing he had taken part of me with him.

And that feeling of loss had never grown less. This was why I had travelled so far to find him, knowing that no other man would do for me. My thoughts scurried back to another All Hallows' Eve: the night I had found my mother dead and had left my home forever to seek my fortune. That had been three years ago, but it seemed more like ten. So much had happened to that naïve, ingenuous, then-plump girl who had believed that all she had to do was travel to the nearest town to find a husband! So proud I was then, I remembered, of my book learning and housekeeping skills. The ability to read, write and figure had been useful, especially when travelling as Matthew's apprentice, but as for my skills in cheese making, embroidery, rose-hip syrup, possets, headache pills, smocking, elderflower wine, besom making, green poultices, patchwork, face packs, spinning and weaving—none of these had ever been exercised.

The fine sewing had descended to plain sewing and mending, the cookery to tossing whatever there was into the pot on an outside fire, and the fat girl had slimmed down dramatically and was lithe as a boy.

So here came another All Hallows. I felt a tiny prick of foreboding—whether it came from the ring or not I wasn't sure—but after all, the saints had seen me through so far, and there was no need for the superstitions of a hag-ridden night to disturb me now.

"Yes, I remember," I said, in answer to his question. "I reckon they are lucky for me, those dates."

"Me too!" He hugged me tight. "Don't you want to know what the Council said?"

No, I had been too frightened to ask. "Yes, of course I do! Tell me?"

"Well it's not bad, and it's not good. They are still deliberating, but although it seems they will probably agree to my spending my man-time with you, they are still divided on whether I can have three months at a time. Most of them would prefer one, I think."

I pretended to consider, all the while knowing that I had something priceless with which to negotiate. "Yes, I suppose that would be better than nothing. April, August, December? Then I would have you for late spring, full summer and the snows of winter."

"Good." He was kissing my throat and shoulders now, and it was difficult to concentrate. "They want to see you again, tomorrow night, to hear their decision. That's good, because I don't think they would waste their time seeing you once more if they intended to refuse."

"Perhaps they mean to serve me up for supper," I said lightly.

My dress fell to my ankles; those shoulder ribbons were too easy.

"I told you, sweetheart, they don't eat damsels anymore—if they ever did."

"I believe you," I said obediently. My hands went to his head, feeling with pleasure the strong bones under my fingers as he bent to my breasts, the exquisite reactions this engendered almost unbearable. The rest of my body was shivering with anticipation—that or the night wind, I had no idea, nor did I care, for a moment later he had swept me up in his arms and carried me to the bed. As I felt his weight press down on me, his mouth on mine, his hands busy elsewhere, the rapture I felt surpassed anything I had ever known. But even as I lost myself in his embrace I thought I felt a faint tingle in my ring, and somewhere a dog barking—

But a moment later all was forgotten with his body in me, with me, by me, part of me. . . .

Later, much later, we lay in each other's arms, at peace. It must have been near dawn, for the last, low bars of moonlight lay aslant the floor and the candles were burning low. I snuggled closer, feeling his body stir in sympathy.

"Jasper?"

"Mmmmm?"

"Do you—do you . . ." But no, I couldn't ask him. Women always wanted the answer to "that" question, if it hadn't been volunteered before: men always tried to avoid committing themselves. That much my mother had taught me.

"Do I—do I . . ." he mimicked gently. "Of course I do! Why do you think I am here? But you want to hear me say it, don't you my love?"

"It doesn't matter, truly it doesn't—" Liar!

"It matters to both of us," he said gently. "You see when I saw you again and realized just how far you had travelled to see me—I know you pretended otherwise but it didn't work—I felt guilty. Then my conscience took over; my man-conscience, because dragons don't have one you would recognize. That conscience told me you would be far better off without me, so I tried to play it casual. I wanted you to think I no longer cared for you, because I knew I could never give you the sort of life you deserve—"

"But you have! I—"

"Hush! Let me finish. This sort of life we hope to wrest from the Council isn't anywhere near perfect. You could do much better: go back to your merchant. At least there you will be safe, secure and loved for twelve months of the year."

"I don't love him, I never did!"

"I know, I know! As the Wimperling I knew; as myself I know. But my conscience—that damnable thing that a certain young woman encouraged in a pig once upon a time—won't let me capture and keep you without a struggle. Dragons are totally selfish: sometimes men are not. I love you so much I want what is best for you."

There. He had said it. "And I love you, as you know. All I want is to be with you, even if it's only for a day a year, so don't let's have any more trouble from your conscience. Go ahead: be selfish!"

He smiled wryly. "I knew it wouldn't work. . . ."

"But I have something that might. . . ." I slipped from his side and, naked, crossed to the clothes chest, peeled back my shift from the egg, picked it up as if it were the finest porcelain and carried it back to the bed. "There! What do you think of that?"

He sat up, slowly at first, then suddenly, as though he had sat on a pin. "What's this?" He answered his own question. "It's a dragon's egg, or I'm—I'm a pig again! Where did you find it? How long have you had it?"

"I've had it for about a year. But it was hidden for a year before that, and it has grown a good deal since it first saw the light. When I first saw it, it was about the size and color of a freshwater pearl, but it was quite soft to the touch. So I kept it safe and warm until it hardened. Since then, until now, I have kept it in a pouch round my neck. Pretty, isn't it? Somehow I never thought a dragon's egg would look like this. . . ."

"Where did it come from?"

"Guess!"

He scowled. "I don't want to guess: I want to *know*! This is important, don't you realize that?"

"Of course I do! It is our bargaining power: it's the most valuable thing we have!"

He leant forward, took it in his hands. "This is incredible! The Council can surely refuse us nothing now. But I must know where you found it."

"Oh, it has an impeccable pedigree." I was enjoying this. "Like a mug of rice wine?" He shook his head impatiently. "It is a Master Dragon's egg, no less."

"How do you know that? How could you know . . ."

"Because it's yours, that's why!"

"Mine!" I watched the various expressions chase their way across his face: amazement, disbelief, doubt, hope, puzzlement and, finally, a sort of bewildered joy. "But—how do you know? How can it be?"

"That time at the Place of Stones. Remember? You held me in your arms, you kissed me, you changed back and forth from dragon to man, man to dragon, and all the while you were—you were . . . You made love to me."

"But—it couldn't happen that way! It's impossible!"

"You told me dragons could self-procreate and that's difficult for me to believe. If that can happen why couldn't you have produced a life of your own for me to hold?" I leant forward and kissed him. "All I am sure about is that it is yours, and that I held it within me for a year. I had no usual monthly flow during that time, and it was Ky-Lin, the creature I told you about, who helped me with the pain of producing it. Since then I have been normal. So, I truly believe we share it."

"Mine—and yours," he said wonderingly. "They say there is nothing new under the skies. . . . What do we do with it?"

"It belongs to those who are left: the Council, to guard and nurture until it is time for the hatching. Many years too late for me, my love . . . But surely, with a gift such as this, you can persuade them to give me your lifetime as a man to spend with me? Not a week, a year, our time as man and woman together. When I am—gone—then you can be theirs again. In return for the egg, another dragon for them."

He rose from the bed and took me in his arms.

"My dearest dear, my little love, there is nothing would please me more! I'm sure they will agree—and that island I promised you still waits for us!"

He drew me tight and showed me just exactly what I had to look forward to.

It was nearly dawn; the first flush of light was graying the outlines of the shutters as I opened my sleepy eyes. Jasper had left me as the last rays of the moon slanted across the valley, promising to put our request to the Council. He had left the egg with me.

"Tomorrow night we shall go together with the egg, and exchange it for our freedoms—don't worry: they will want our egg more than any jewel in the world: it is their promise of continued life. After tomorrow night, the world is ours! We can be an ordinary couple—even go to one of your churches and become man and wife. Would you like that?"

So, there were—how many hours? Perhaps sixteen. And everything to do. And nothing. I stretched luxuriously and turned over on my back. I would have just five minutes more, then get up and go down to the market and buy something special for Growch, to make up for sequestering him in Dickon's room all night.

It can only have been a couple of minutes' doze when I heard the door to the balcony creak open and soft footfalls on the matting. A moment later a hand stroked my shoulder. Jasper must have come back. I turned over to face him, my eyes still closed, my arms outstretched in welcome, disregarding the sudden prickle of my ring.

"Forgotten something, my love?"

A breath on my cheek, a fumbling hand and then a weight, an alien weight on top of me, a strange mouth grinding down on mine and an insistent knee pushing my thighs apart. I struggled violently, but an arm was across my throat, a hand pinioning my hands above my head. His sweat was rank in my nostrils, his knee grinding my thighs, his mouth and tongue a-slobber all over my face. I jerked my head aside, took a gulp of air and yelled as loud as I could.

Instantly the arm across my throat pressed down harder and now I was choking. My ears were full of a roaring sound, my eyes felt as though they were popping out, I couldn't breathe, but I knew I couldn't resist much longer—

There was a yell of surprise, a frantic growling and all at once I was free, gasping for welcome breath, and my assailant was rolling in agony on the floor, flailing and kicking ineffectually at a small dog, whose sharp teeth were fastened firmly in his left buttock.

I couldn't believe my eyes. "Dickon!" I croaked. "How could you! What in the world were you thinking about?"

"Get the bugger off me, damn you, get him off!"

I took my time, pulling down my green dress, wiping my face with the hem, spitting his taste from my mouth. "All right, Growch, let him go. He doesn't deserve it, but thanks anyway. Where were you?"

"Shut me in 'is room. Came out through the winder. 'E's bin askin' for that 'e 'as! Pretty boy won' be able to sit down for a day or two. Let 'im try showin' that to the ladies! Now if'n I'd got 'im at the front—"

"That's enough, Growch," I said hastily. Standing up, hands on hips, I glared down at Dickon, who was trying to examine his bites, a near-impossible task without a mirror. I was glad to note that all other pretensions had withered into insignificance.

"Now then," I said. "Why? What have I ever said or done to make you think you would be welcome in my bed?"

Dickon rose to his feet, rather unsteadily, but his chin was jutting out dangerously. "It's rather what you haven't done! All the time we've been together you've been playing the little virgin, Mistress-Hard-to-Get, and at the same time you've been giving me those come-hither looks, little enticements, half-promises—"

I was astounded. After doing my utmost to discourage anything like that! "You must be mad," I said finally. "Utterly mad."

"Don't kid me! I've seen you—it's been all I could do to keep my hands off you! Touching me, making suggestive remarks, all but stripping off and asking for it . . ." He ranted on, while I tried desperately to remember if I had ever given him the slightest encouragement, knowing all the while I had not. But the more I heard him, the more I realized that he truly believed what he was saying. In some part of his twisted mind his sexual psyche had convinced him that he was irresistible, so if I didn't fling myself at him it was my fault, all my refusals merely stimulating his desire still further.

"Why do you think I kept on going to those brothels? Because if I hadn't I wouldn't have been able to keep my hands off you!" His voice was rising, he was on the verge of hysteria.

"Dickon, I never meant you to believe—"

But he was past listening to anything except his own twisted logic.

"I worshipped you! I believed that one day, if I waited long enough, you would come to me, say you loved me, ask me to be with you while we worked together. That's why I followed you! Not for any treasure that doesn't exist: *You* were my treasure, my unspoilt, virgin bride!" He was so far out of control by now that his hands were tearing at the loose robe he wore.

"And then I come back unexpectedly and what do I find? You in the arms of a stranger as soon as my back is turned, all decency and decorum forgot! What do you think I felt, seeing your abandoned behavior? You, whom I thought above reproach behaving like a strumpet! Why, you're nothing but a whore, a bloody whore!" Saliva was trickling from the right corner of his mouth, and his eyes were glazed.

It took only a couple of steps and I had slapped him hard on both cheeks. "Don't you *dare* speak to me like that! You don't deserve an explanation, but I think you'd better know that the man you saw is my betrothed. He is the one I have been seeking all this long time, the 'friend' I told you I sought. My journeyings have all been towards this end and have never, ever, had anything to do with treasure! And now we have found each other again, we are going to spend the rest of our lives together." I paused. He had reeled back when I struck him, and now he was regarding me with a bemused expression on his face. But at least now he looked sane. "Now, isn't it time you apologized?"

"I—I—I . . ."

"I—I—I!" I mocked. "And you are supposed to have the gift of tongues! You'll have to do better than that."

He tried to pull himself together; it was a visible effort. "Of course, I didn't realize . . . but now you've explained . . ." He seemed to draw into himself; his eyes hooded any expression, his lips drew back into a thin line. "I am sorry," he said formally. "I was obviously mistaken. What are your plans now?"

I was surprised by how quickly he was back to normal. "I was going to see you later today if you were back," I said. "Or leave a message with Ky-Lin. But if you like we can talk now."

"Let's get on with it. Tell me." He sat down on the stool, drawing his confidence around him again, like his tattered clothes.

So I told him I was leaving that night with Jasper for another life in another place, where no one could follow us. I explained that I had not forgotten him. He was to have all the moneys I had left (excluding my father's coins, which were to go to the monks) on condition he took a package of letters and my journal and delivered them to Signor Falcone in Venice. This gentleman, I explained, would reward him handsomely for his efforts, but only if the packet was delivered intact.

"You will do as I ask?"

He stood up. "I have no alternative."

"Then I will leave it on my bed, together with my blanket, the cooking things and anything else I don't need. Do with them what you will." I held out my hand. "Thanks for your help. No bad feelings?"

Ignoring my hand he suddenly embraced and kissed me, then as quickly stepped back, so abruptly I nearly fell.

"No bad feelings," he said. "But you can't blame me for trying."

And that was the last I saw of him.

Ky-Lin visited me at midday. He knew without the telling what I was planning to do. He looked at me gravely, asked me once more if I truly knew what I was doing. Of course I reassured him, told him of my happiness, our hopes for the future. He looked so down, not like his usual ebullient self, that I feared he might be ill.

"Ky-Lins are never ill."

"Then what is it, my dear? You don't look at all happy."

"I cannot answer that. Ky-Lins are always supposed to be happy."

"I know—it's because your task is finished, isn't it? You've seen me through, done all you had to do—"

"No. I have not. But I am not allowed to interfere."

"I don't understand. . . ."

He must have seen my distress for he came forward and laid his head against me. I bent and kissed him, stroked his sleek hide.

"I wish you could come with us."

He drew back. "I told you: we do not deal with dragons. There is a rule. It is like your Waystone; there are laws that repel, others that attract."

Although I didn't understand what he was saying, that reminded me to tell him what I had done with Dickon, and how I had enclosed the Waystone in my package to Signor Falcone, asking him to deliver it to the captain's wife, telling her that the crystal she had given me had been a gift to my betrothed's kin. "Rather neat that, don't you think? After all, it has gone to Jasper's dragon relatives!"

But he didn't smile.

Later he took the pouch into which I had placed my father's coins, promising to deliver the money to the monks. I asked him if he would give Growch a tiny pinch of Sleepy Dust later, to make his flight to the Blue Mountain easier, and this he promised to do around suppertime.

The cloak I shall leave behind. Its color, weave and texture are the same as the cloth of the monks' robes, and now I am sure that the father I never knew once lived here. He probably committed some sin and had to leave; this would explain why the Unicorn's ring would no longer fit him and also why the coins of my "dowry" led me across the world to this place. So it is fitting that it remain here with the coins.

This is the last I shall write. Half an hour ago Ky-Lin left me, having given Growch his "dose." My dear dog is fast asleep on the bed now, snoring gently. I have told him nothing except that we are going on a trip, but have fed him all the things he likes best, in case it is a long journey.

Myself, I cannot eat. Surprisingly, I feel depressed. Perhaps it is something to do with my ring. It had been a part of me for so long that I felt a real sense of loss when it just slipped from my finger when Ky-Lin was here.

At first I couldn't believe it. I just stared at it, then picked it up between finger and thumb. It was so light, so thin, just a sliver of horn so delicate I could crush it between my fingers. . . . I tried to put it on again, but somehow it had curled around itself so that now it was too small.

"You have no need of it anymore," said Ky-Lin gently. "It cannot go where you go. Let me take care of it. I shall keep it safe until there is another who needs it."

"But aren't you due to go to your heaven?"

"My task is not finished. You have your future, but others . . . There is another who will need me for a while. And afterwards?" He shrugged. "Time is a relative thing."

"Don't talk in riddles! So, where will you keep my—the ring?"

He bent his head. "It will have a home on the horn of my forehead. Like to like."

Again he was being abstruse, but I placed the ring as he had said, and it fitted at once as if it were a part of him.

"And now, good-bye. It has been an interesting time. I shall miss you, girl, but I shall pray for you. Now if you cry like that, you will get my hide all wet, and Ky-Lins don't like the damp. . . ."

⁂

It is All Hallows' Eve, not far from midnight, and the moon, a bloodred full moon, has just risen. The piece of paper on which I am writing this I will tuck away into the package at the last moment.

It is strange, writing like this in the present; I have been used for so long to write in the past, catching up on my journal, which I hope will explain to Signor Falcone—and Matthew if he passes it on—exactly what has happened to me. I hope they will understand how all my life for the past two years has led to this moment, how this is the culmination of all my dreams.

How do I feel? Frightened a little, yes, but once Jasper is here all fear will go. The egg is by my side; I have sewn it into the scrap of skin that was once the Wimperling, the outer self of Jasper. Two years ago, to the day, we created this egg; a year earlier I started on this travelling, and now that I was about to lose it I had a sudden flood of maternal feeling for the egg and had to tell myself it was only a stone, even though within it lay hidden a tiny creature that was certainly a part of Jasper and perhaps of me too. But even if I kept it I would never see it hatch . . .

It has been a long, long journey. God keep all those I have loved.

Moonlight floods the room: out with the candle. The light that is the love of Jasper and myself will illuminate the rest of my life.

A last prayer . . .

Away with this. He is here!

Epilogue

To the illustrious Signor Falcone: greetings. This by the hand of Brother Boniface of the Abbey of the same name in Normandy.

Sir, I introduce myself as the Infirmar of the Abbey. Recently I took under my care a traveller by the name of Ricardus. When he was admitted to the Infirmary it was obvious he suffered from a low fever, with much coughing and spitting of blood. We kept him close, administered plasters to his chest, doses for the ill humors and bled him, but a practiced eye could see that the Good Lord was the only one who could intervene in a terminal illness.

Alas, this was not to be, our prayers being unavailing, and the Lord moving in mysterious ways.

Two days before the patient died, fortified by the rites of Holy Church, confessed and given the Last Rites, he asked to make a deposition that was to be forwarded to yourself. He had given us the last of his silver for Holy Church and was currently in a State of Grace, so I placed a young novice who writes in the shortened form by his bedside. He took down the words of Ricardus, later transcribing them into proper form, the result of which is here to your hand.

A great deal of what the patient said was not understood, and towards the end he rambled a great deal, but the words are his and will doubtless mean more to yourself, illustrious Signor.

I am dying: they told me so. They don't mince words, these monks. All that chanting; reminds me of a monastery where—

To be fair, I asked them, but then I think I knew, anyway.

I am accursed. . . .

At first, after I delivered Summer's package to you, and went on with the letter to Master Spicer, everything was fine. With the moneys you both gave me I set up in business for myself. For the first ten years I travelled the Western World and had ample compensation for my outlay. And yet . . .

Some years ago I caught a disease in a brothel in Genoa—God curse it!—which no medicines, poultices or prayers could assuage. Another infection caused my hair to fall out and great boils appeared on my body. Then, to add to all this, I contracted the Great Itch on my arms and legs and great sores in my groin that caused me much discomfort. Because of these afflictions I remain covered at all times, and have had to confine my business to the colder northern clime where such garb is accepted all year round.

Yet still did I prosper, enough to buy me those pleasures not readily available to those in my unfortunate condition, but during the last couple of years, due to unwise investment in cargoes that foundered, all my fortune has dwindled away, and now I only possess the silver in my pocket and a certain object which I shall ask to be forwarded to you. Of that, more later.

I lied to you, you know. When I brought Summer's journal, fifteen years ago, I made it sound so romantic, didn't I? And you have probably believed all these years that she flew off into the sunset with her man-dragon and lived happily ever after.

But it wasn't like that. That night didn't go as any of us expected, least of all her. Why didn't I tell you the truth? Because I thought you and Master Spicer would pay more for good news than for bad, that's why.

I fancied her myself, did you know that? When she turned up in that boy's gear, with those long legs and all . . . Respected her, too. All that reading and writing, the way she trained those animals of hers, the ladylike way she spoke. She never paid any attention to the men, either; always kept herself to herself, never flirted. She behaved like a virgin and I treated her like one. I mean, I never really tried it on. Not really. Not until the end, that is, when I saw her with that fellow of hers—

No more now, I'm tired. Leave me a candle. It'll be full dark ere long.

The patient worsened overnight, with much coughing up of blood and loss of breath, and was not well enough to dictate in the forenoon. In the afternoon we were afflicted with sudden gales, which stripped the last of the fruits in the orchard and loosened the roof on the guest house. These strong winds seemed to stimulate the patient, who indicated he wished to continue his deposition, albeit in a more disjointed and rambling way. . . .

Where was I? Oh, yes.

I fancied her, yes, but I doubt I would have left the caravans to follow her unless I was sure she was after treasure. There were the maps, you see—and who was right in the end?

She told me there was nothing, and I know now she believed that, but I thought she was trying to con me, wanted it all for herself. The thought of treasure can do strange things to your mind. . . . *Radix malorum est cupiditas . . .*

She talked your monk tongue, learnt it from an old priest. . . . But you met her, you know what she was like. No, not you, him . . .

God, I'm thirsty, give me wine! Gnat's piss . . .

Of course I didn't know about him then, her pig-man-dragon, did I? How could she prefer a man like that? All dark, with yellow eyes like a wolf! The girls have always said I was handsome, well endowed—still am, and know how to use it too—

Heard them that night, saw them as well. Disgusting, from one I had thought so pure! Tried it on after he'd gone, but she wasn't having any; set the dog on me, she did. Hated that dog!

But I knew what I knew then, didn't I? Knew that what I'd seen wasn't what it seemed. Heard enough to know where to go that night—

Moon was red as blood, bats flying like witches. Alone . . .

For Christ's sake, can't you stop that wind? I'm fucking dying, and I want some peace! Ahhh . . .

The patient being in obvious distress he was dosed heavily with poppy juice till he quieted and enjoyed an uneasy sleep. He continued late that night, when he awoke, although his testimony became increasingly disjointed.

I was there before them, knew where to hide, they didn't see my horse. They came down on the ledge and she had that blasted dog in her arms. One moment he was a dragon—near shit myself—then just the fellow she slept with. Followed 'em down the passage, not too close . . .

Got to the cavern. Hid in the entrance. They walked to the chasm, he said something and the whole place lighted up. Talk about fucking rainbows! There was this light. . . .

Thirsty: any more of that wine? God, how you drink it, I don't know! Now if you were me, travelled all over the world, tasted the wines of—What was that? Bells, bells, bells! Same in that monastery. Bloody monks . . .

The jewels! Never seen anything like those jewels! Piled up like mountains they were. Forgot to be afraid of the dragons. Gold, too. Enough to buy you and your trading empire out a thousand times. Dazzled . . .

There was a lot of growling and hissing and roaring and from what I had heard last night they were going to try and exchange that obscene thing she called a dragon's egg for him, her fellow, to stay human. Well, she brought it out from behind her back, held it up for them to see, then laid it on the ground together with her sleeping dog. It all went quiet, I tell you!

Then Summer and her boyfriend walked over a kind of bridge and there was a sort of ceremony, lots of spitting and hissing and roaring, and then they started to walk back, with smiles on their faces like they got what they wanted. It was their own fault, I tell you! They stopped in the middle of the bridge and started kissing and cuddling and I couldn't stand it no more!

Couldn't get near the jewels, but if that egg thing was that important, why shouldn't I have a piece of the action? Never meant no real harm, just a bit of a threat; hold it over the chasm, they'd give me enough of the loot to keep me going.

Crept forward, had my hands on the thing, when that bloody dog woke up and started barking—

How was I to know they thought it was a plot? How was I to know they thought she and him was in it too? I didn't mean no harm, honest! No one can say I haven't suffered for it neither. He was trying to shout something and she was clinging to him like ivy when it happened—

Oh, God, Jesu, I can see it, hear it, smell it, now!

I swear I didn't mean to. . . . The fires of Hell, I can feel them now! I'm burning, burning! Christ Jesus, I never meant to hurt her! I loved her, God curse it, I loved her. All right, so I was jealous; that too. But you don't hurt those you love, do you?

What time is it? Time for me to go. Creep into a dark corner, like an animal. Like the bloody dog . . . The rainbow creature came for him afterwards, all bloody and singed as he was, took him away and healed him. But you can't heal a mind, can you? She loved them both, more than she ever cared for me. . . . Hated them!

The fires, the fires! Have you ever smelled singeing flesh? She screamed, so loud it burst something in my heart. Couldn't feel anything for anyone after that.

It seemed the top of the world blew off. They were in the middle of the bridge when it collapsed, he had her in his arms and the flames came up and caught their hair. I saw him change man-dragon, dragon-man, so quick you couldn't blink and he wrapped his wings about her and then they were gone as though they'd never been!

That scream . . . she knew it was me. She looked at me. Just once. Oh, Summer, it wasn't my fault, it wasn't, I swear it!

Dark, it's dark; why don't you light the candles?

The patient became delirious, then relapsed into a coma; he awoke for the last time just before midnight. He was given wine, but was unable to drink it. He asked the time, day and date.

All Hallows' Eve? I might have known it. She had her revenge after all. Fifteen years . . . Oh, Lord: was it worth it all?

Ricardus lapsed again into a coma, the storm returned to harass us, and then, just before midnight, he woke once more, sat bolt upright in bed and uttered his last words.

But I did get something out of it! And now those dragons can search till Doomsday, God curse them and curse you all! Do with it what you will—

This is the testimony the man Ricardus asked us to forward to you. If you feel so disposed, our messenger will willingly bring moneys back to us for Masses to be said for the deceased's soul, for I fear he did not die in a State of Grace.

In fact any donation towards the upkeep of the Abbey would be most welcome. . . .

I also send with Brother Benedict whatever poor possessions Ricardus carried with him: his few clothes were distributed to the poor, as was his staff and mug and plate. There was, however, a certain object he referred to in his disposition and kept in a pouch around his neck; a round pebble wrapped in hide, and a scrap of paper. Although the object appears to be worthless, no doubt it will prove of sentimental interest to yourself. As you can see, the piece of paper bears the misspelt legend: "This be Dragonnes Eg."

Postscript

In the Indian Ocean there is a small island, situated well off the trade routes. It was charted in the eighteen thirties by the Portuguese, who mapped it as Discovery Isle. Many years later the missionaries arrived and, once they understood the native language, found that the inhabitants had always called it "Dragon Isle." When questioned, the islanders related the legend that accompanied the name.

There were two points of consistency, otherwise the tale had obviously changed with the years and recollection. The points of agreement were that one day in the distant past a great black dragon, sore wounded, had arrived in the skies from the northeast bearing a burden. It had circled the island three times before alighting somewhere in the hills to the north. The other point of agreement was that the creature eventually left in the same direction, after circling the island in the same fashion.

Between these two "facts," there were two different versions of events. The first had it that the dragon laid waste to the forests of the island till the air was black with the fires, then he buried whatever he carried in a cave high in the mountains before flying away again.

The other version had the dragon again alighting in the mountains with his burden and three days later a man and a woman, both badly injured, coming down to dwell among the islanders. This story would have it that the pair recovered and lived for many years at peace, the woman communing with the beasts of the field, the man a master of weather. In the fullness of time the woman died, and the man bore her body up into the hills and buried it, then the great dragon appeared again and flew away, sorrowing. . . .